George MacDonald

THE PARISH TRILOGY: Annals of a Quiet Neighbourhood, The Seaboard Parish & The Vicar's Daughter
(Complete Edition)

e-artnow 2018

Reading suggestions (available from e-artnow as Print & eBook)

Charlotte Brontë
Jane Eyre

Louisa May Alcott
LOUISA MAY ALCOTT Ultimate Collection: 16 Novels & 150+ Short Stories, Plays and Poems (Illustrated)

Walter Scott
Ivanhoe

Alexandre Dumas
QUEEN MARGOT (Unabridged)

Alexandre Dumas
THE VALOIS TRILOGY: Queen Margot, Chicot de Jester & The Forty-Five Guardsmen

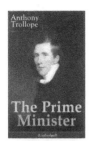
Anthony Trollope
The Prime Minister (Unabridged)

George MacDonald
MALCOLM & THE MARQUIS'S SECRET: Complete Marquise of Lossie Collection (Adventure Classic)

George MacDonald
THOMAS WINGFOLD, CURATE + PAUL FABER, SURGEON + THERE AND BACK - The Complete Series: The Curate's Awakening, The Lady's Confession & The Baron's Apprenticeship

George MacDonald
SIR GIBBIE & DONAL GRANT: The Baronet's Song and The Shepherd's Castle (Adventure Classic)

Kate Chopin
THE AWAKENING - A Solitary Soul (Feminist Classics Series)

George MacDonald

THE PARISH TRILOGY: Annals of a Quiet Neighbourhood, The Seaboard Parish & The Vicar's Daughter
(Complete Edition)

e-artnow, 2018
Contact: info@e-artnow.org

ISBN 978-80-268-9171-0

Contents

ANNALS OF A QUIET NEIGHBOURHOOD	15
CHAPTER I. DESPONDENCY AND CONSOLATION.	16
CHAPTER II. MY FIRST SUNDAY AT MARSHMALLOWS.	22
CHAPTER III. MY FIRST MONDAY AT MARSHMALLOWS.	25
CHAPTER IV. THE COFFIN.	31
CHAPTER V. VISITORS FROM THE HALL.	36
CHAPTER VI. OLDCASTLE HALL.	41
CHAPTER VII. THE BISHOP'S BASIN.	49
CHAPTER VIII. WHAT I PREACHED.	62
CHAPTER IX. THE ORGANIST.	65
CHAPTER X. MY CHRISTMAS PARTY.	77
CHAPTER XI. SERMON ON GOD AND MAMMON.	87
CHAPTER XII. THE AVENUE.	102
CHAPTER XIII. YOUNG WEIR.	106
CHAPTER XIV. MY PUPIL.	121
CHAPTER XV. DR DUNCAN'S STORY.	127
CHAPTER XVI. THE ORGAN.	136
CHAPTER XVII. THE CHURCH-RATE.	138
CHAPTER XVIII. JUDY'S NEWS.	144
CHAPTER XIX. THE INVALID.	147
CHAPTER XX. MOOD AND WILL.	153
CHAPTER XXI. THE DEVIL IN THOMAS WEIR.	158
CHAPTER XXII. THE DEVIL IN CATHERINE WEIR.	161
CHAPTER XXIII. THE DEVIL IN THE VICAR.	167
CHAPTER XXIV. AN ANGEL UNAWARES.	172
CHAPTER XXV. TWO PARISHIONERS.	175
CHAPTER XXVI. SATAN CAST OUT.	180
CHAPTER XXVII. THE MAN AND THE CHILD.	186
CHAPTER XXVIII. OLD MRS TOMKINS.	191
CHAPTER XXIX. CALM AND STORM.	198
CHAPTER XXX. A SERMON TO MYSELF.	203
CHAPTER XXXI. A COUNCIL OF FRIENDS.	210
CHAPTER XXXII. THE NEXT THING.	215
CHAPTER XXXIII. OLD ROGERS'S THANKSGIVING.	220
CHAPTER XXXIV. TOM'S STORY.	224
THE SEABOARD PARISH	233
VOLUME I.	235
CHAPTER I. HOMILETIC.	236

CHAPTER II. CONSTANCE'S BIRTHDAY.	238
CHAPTER III. THE SICK CHAMBER.	245
CHAPTER IV. A SUNDAY EVENING.	251
CHAPTER V. MY DREAM.	256
CHAPTER VI. THE NEW BABY.	258
CHAPTER VII. ANOTHER SUNDAY EVENING.	260
CHAPTER VIII. THEODORA'S DOOM.	264
CHAPTER IX. A SPRING CHAPTER.	269
CHAPTER X. AN IMPORTANT LETTER.	274
CHAPTER XI. CONNIE'S DREAM.	278
CHAPTER XII. THE JOURNEY.	282
CHAPTER XIII. WHAT WE DID WHEN WE ARRIVED.	287
CHAPTER XIV. MORE ABOUT KILKHAVEN.	292
CHAPTER XV. THE OLD CHURCH.	295
CHAPTER XVI. CONNIE'S WATCH-TOWER.	302
CHAPTER XVII. MY FIRST SERMON IN THE SEABOARD PARISH.	309
VOLUME II.	315
CHAPTER I. ANOTHER SUNDAY EVENING.	316
CHAPTER II. NICEBOOTS.	321
CHAPTER III. THE BLACKSMITH.	328
CHAPTER IV. THE LIFE-BOAT.	330
CHAPTER V. MR. PERCIVALE.	335
CHAPTER VI. THE SHADOW OP DEATH.	340
CHAPTER VII. AT THE FARM.	348
CHAPTER VIII. THE KEEVE.	351
CHAPTER IX. THE WALK TO CHURCH.	356
CHAPTER X. THE OLD CASTLE.	360
CHAPTER XI. JOE AND HIS TROUBLE.	370
CHAPTER XII. A SMALL ADVENTURE.	377
CHAPTER XIII. THE HARVEST.	384
VOLUME III.	391
CHAPTER I. A WALK WITH MY WIFE.	392
CHAPTER II. OUR LAST SHORE-DINNER.	397
CHAPTER III. A PASTORAL VISIT.	408
CHAPTER IV. THE ART OF NATURE.	412
CHAPTER V. THE SORE SPOT.	416
CHAPTER VI. THE GATHERING STORM.	422
CHAPTER VII. THE GATHERED STORM.	427
CHAPTER VIII. THE SHIPWRECK.	434
CHAPTER IX. THE FUNERAL.	443

CHAPTER X. THE SERMON.	450
CHAPTER XI. CHANGED PLANS.	455
CHAPTER XII. THE STUDIO.	459
CHAPTER XIII. HOME AGAIN.	465
THE VICAR'S DAUGHTER	467
CHAPTER I. INTRODUCTORY.	468
CHAPTER II. I TRY.	472
CHAPTER III. MY WEDDING.	477
CHAPTER IV. JUDY'S VISIT.	482
CHAPTER V. "GOOD SOCIETY."	485
CHAPTER VI. A REFUGE FROM THE HEAT.	488
CHAPTER VII. CONNIE.	491
CHAPTER VIII. CONNIE'S BABY.	493
CHAPTER IX. THE FOUNDLING RE-FOUND.	497
CHAPTER X. WAGTAIL COMES TO HONOR.	500
CHAPTER XI. A STUPID CHAPTER.	503
CHAPTER XII. AN INTRODUCTION.	506
CHAPTER XIII. MY FIRST DINNER-PARTY. A NEGATIVED PROPOSAL.	509
CHAPTER XIV. A PICTURE.	516
CHAPTER XV. RUMORS.	519
CHAPTER XVI. A DISCOVERY.	524
CHAPTER XVII. MISS CLARE.	529
CHAPTER XVIII. MISS CLARE'S HOME.	532
CHAPTER XIX. HER STORY.	535
CHAPTER XX. A REMARKABLE FACT.	545
CHAPTER XXI. LADY BERNARD.	548
CHAPTER XXII. MY SECOND DINNER-PARTY.	551
CHAPTER XXIII. THE END OF THE EVENING.	559
CHAPTER XXIV. MY FIRST TERROR.	562
CHAPTER XXV. ITS SEQUEL.	571
CHAPTER XXVI. TROUBLES.	577
CHAPTER XXVII. MISS CLARE AMONGST HER FRIENDS.	582
CHAPTER XXVIII. MR. MORLEY.	586
CHAPTER XXIX. A STRANGE TEXT.	592
CHAPTER XXX. ABOUT SERVANTS.	604
CHAPTER XXXI. ABOUT PERCIVALE.	607
CHAPTER XXXII. MY SECOND TERROR.	610
CHAPTER XXXIII. THE CLOUDS AFTER THE RAIN.	613
CHAPTER XXXIV. THE SUNSHINE.	618
CHAPTER XXXV. WHAT LADY BERNARD THOUGHT OF IT.	621

CHAPTER XXXVI. RETROSPECTIVE.	623
CHAPTER XXXVII. MRS. CROMWELL COMES.	625
CHAPTER XXXVIII. MRS. CROMWELL GOES.	636
CHAPTER XXXIX. ANCESTRAL WISDOM.	643
CHAPTER XL. CHILD NONSENSE.	647
CHAPTER XLI. "DOUBLE, DOUBLE, TOIL AND TROUBLE."	651
CHAPTER XLII. ROGER AND MARION.	655
CHAPTER XLIII. A LITTLE MORE ABOUT ROGER, AND ABOUT MR. BLACKSTONE.	659
CHAPTER XLIV. THE DEA EX.	661

ANNALS OF A QUIET NEIGHBOURHOOD

CHAPTER I
DESPONDENCY AND CONSOLATION.

Before I begin to tell you some of the things I have seen and heard, in both of which I have had to take a share, now from the compulsion of my office, now from the leading of my own heart, and now from that destiny which, including both, so often throws the man who supposed himself a mere on-looker, into the very vortex of events-that destiny which took form to the old pagans as a gray mist high beyond the heads of their gods, but to us is known as an infinite love, revealed in the mystery of man —I say before I begin, it is fitting that, in the absence of a common friend to do that office for me, I should introduce myself to your acquaintance, and I hope coming friendship. Nor can there be any impropriety in my telling you about myself, seeing I remain concealed behind my own words. You can never look me in the eyes, though you may look me in the soul. You may find me out, find my faults, my vanities, my sins, but you will not SEE me, at least in this world. To you I am but a voice of revealing, not a form of vision; therefore I am bold behind the mask, to speak to you heart to heart; bold, I say, just so much the more that I do not speak to you face to face. And when we meet in heaven-well, there I know there is no hiding; there, there is no reason for hiding anything; there, the whole desire will be alternate revelation and vision.

I am now getting old-faster and faster. I cannot help my gray hairs, nor the wrinkles that gather so slowly yet ruthlessly; no, nor the quaver that will come in my voice, not the sense of being feeble in the knees, even when I walk only across the floor of my study. But I have not got used to age yet. I do not FEEL one atom older than I did at three-and-twenty. Nay, to tell all the truth, I feel a good deal younger. —For then I only felt that a man had to take up his cross; whereas now I feel that a man has to follow Him; and that makes an unspeakable difference. —When my voice quavers, I feel that it is mine and not mine; that it just belongs to me like my watch, which does not go well-now, though it went well thirty years ago-not more than a minute out in a month. And when I feel my knees shake, I think of them with a kind of pity, as I used to think of an old mare of my father's of which I was very fond when I was a lad, and which bore me across many a field and over many a fence, but which at last came to have the same weakness in her knees that I have in mine; and she knew it too, and took care of them, and so of herself, in a wise equine fashion. These things are not me-or *I*, if the grammarians like it better, (I always feel a strife between doing as the scholar does and doing as other people do;) they are not me, I say; I HAVE them-and, please God, shall soon have better. For it is not a pleasant thing for a young man, or a young woman either, I venture to say, to have an old voice, and a wrinkled face, and weak knees, and gray hair, or no hair at all. And if any moral Philistine, as our queer German brothers over the Northern fish-pond would call him, say that this is all rubbish, for that we ARE old, I would answer: "Of all children how can the children of God be old?"

So little do I give in to calling this outside of me, ME, that I should not mind presenting a minute description of my own person such as would at once clear me from any suspicion of vanity in so introducing myself. Not that my honesty would result in the least from indifference to the external-but from comparative indifference to the transitional; not to the transitional in itself, which is of eternal significance and result, but to the particular form of imperfection which it may have reached at any individual moment of its infinite progression towards the complete. For no sooner have I spoken the word NOW, than that NOW is dead and another is dying; nay, in such a regard, there is no NOW-only a past of which we know a little, and a future of which we know far less and far more. But I will not speak at all of this body of my earthly tabernacle, for it is on the whole more pleasant to forget all about it. And besides, I do not want to set any of my readers to whom I would have the pleasure of speaking far more openly and cordially than if they were seated on the other side of my writing-table —I do not want to set them wondering whether the vicar be this vicar or that vicar; or indeed to run the risk of giving the offence I might give, if I were anything else than "a wandering voice."

I did not feel as I feel now when first I came to this parish. For, as I have said, I am now getting old very fast. True, I was thirty when I was made a vicar, an age at which a man might be expected to be beginning to grow wise; but even then I had much yet to learn.

I well remember the first evening on which I wandered out from the vicarage to take a look about me-to find out, in short, where I was, and what aspect the sky and earth here presented. Strangely enough, I had never been here before; for the presentation had been made me while I was abroad. —I was depressed. It was depressing weather. Grave doubts as to whether I was in my place in the church, would keep rising and floating about, like rain-clouds within me. Not that I doubted about the church; I only doubted about myself. "Were my motives pure?" "What were my motives?" And, to tell the truth, I did not know what my motives were, and therefore I could not answer about the purity of them. Perhaps seeing we are in this world in order to become pure, it would be expecting too much of any young man that he should be absolutely certain that he was pure in anything. But the question followed very naturally: "Had I then any right to be in the Church-to be eating her bread and drinking her wine without knowing whether I was fit to do her work?" To which the only answer I could find was, "The Church is part of God's world. He makes men to work; and work of some sort must be done by every honest man. Somehow or other, I hardly know how, I find myself in the Church. I do not know that I am fitter for any other work. I see no other work to do. There is work here which I can do after some fashion. With God's help I will try to do it well."

This resolution brought me some relief, but still I was depressed. It was depressing weather. —I may as well say that I was not married then, and that I firmly believed I never should be married-not from any ambition taking the form of self-denial; nor yet from any notion that God takes pleasure in being a hard master; but there was a lady-Well, I WILL be honest, as I would be. —I had been refused a few months before, which I think was the best thing ever happened to me except one. That one, of course, was when I was accepted. But this is not much to the purpose now. Only it was depressing weather.

For is it not depressing when the rain is falling, and the steam of it is rising? when the river is crawling along muddily, and the horses stand stock-still in the meadows with their spines in a straight line from the ears to where they fail utterly in the tails? I should only put on goloshes now, and think of the days when I despised damp. Ah! it was mental waterproof that I needed then; for let me despise damp as much as I would, I could neither keep it out of my mind, nor help suffering the spiritual rheumatism which it occasioned. Now, the damp never gets farther than my goloshes and my Macintosh. And for that worst kind of rheumatism —I never feel it now.

But I had begun to tell you about that first evening. —I had arrived at the vicarage the night before, and it had rained all day, and was still raining, though not so much. I took my umbrella and went out.

For as I wanted to do my work well (everything taking far more the shape of work to me, then, and duty, than it does now-though, even now, I must confess things have occasionally to be done by the clergyman because there is no one else to do them, and hardly from other motive than a sense of duty, —a man not being able to shirk work because it may happen to be dirty) —I say, as I wanted to do my work well, or rather, perhaps, because I dreaded drudgery as much as any poor fellow who comes to the treadmill in consequence —I wanted to interest myself in it; and therefore I would go and fall in love, first of all, if I could, with the country round about. And my first step beyond my own gate was up to the ankles, in mud.

Therewith, curiously enough, arose the distracting thought how I could possibly preach TWO good sermons a Sunday to the same people, when one of the sermons was in the afternoon instead of the evening, to which latter I had been accustomed in the large town in which I had formerly officiated as curate in a proprietary chapel. I, who had declaimed indignantly against excitement from without, who had been inclined to exalt the intellect at the expense even of the heart, began to fear that there must be something in the darkness, and the gas-lights, and the crowd of faces, to account for a man's being able to preach a better sermon, and for servant girls preferring to go out in the evening. Alas! I had now to preach, as I might judge with all probability beforehand, to a company of rustics, of thought yet slower than of speech, unaccustomed in fact to THINK at all, and that in the sleepiest, deadest part of the day, when I could hardly think myself, and when, if the weather should be at all warm, I could not expect many of them to be awake. And what good might I look for as the result of my labour? How could I hope in these men and women to kindle that fire which, in the old days of the outpouring of the Spirit, made men live with the sense of the kingdom of heaven about them, and the expectation of something glorious at hand just outside that invisible door which lay between the worlds?

I have learned since, that perhaps I overrated the spirituality of those times, and underrated, not being myself spiritual enough to see all about me, the spirituality of these times. I think I have learned since, that the parson of a parish must be content to keep the upper windows of his mind open to the holy winds and the pure lights of heaven; and the side windows of tone, of speech, of behaviour open to the earth, to let forth upon his fellow-men the tenderness and truth which those upper influences bring forth in any region exposed to their operation. Believing in his Master, such a servant shall not make haste; shall feel no feverous desire to behold the work of his hands; shall be content to be as his Master, who waiteth long for the fruits of His earth.

But surely I am getting older than I thought; for I keep wandering away from my subject, which is this, my first walk in my new cure. My excuse is, that I want my reader to understand something of the state of my mind, and the depression under which I was labouring. He will perceive that I desired to do some work worth calling by the name of work, and that I did not see how to get hold of a beginning.

I had not gone far from my own gate before the rain ceased, though it was still gloomy enough for any amount to follow. I drew down my umbrella, and began to look about me. The stream on my left was so swollen that I could see its brown in patches through the green of the meadows along its banks. A little in front of me, the road, rising quickly, took a sharp turn to pass along an old stone bridge that spanned the water with a single fine arch, somewhat pointed; and through the arch I could see the river stretching away up through the meadows, its banks bordered with pollards. Now, pollards always made me miserable. In the first place, they look ill-used; in the next place, they look tame; in the third place, they look very ugly. I had not learned then to honour them on the ground that they yield not a jot to the adversity of their circumstances; that, if they must be pollards, they still will be trees; and what they may not do with grace, they will yet do with bounty; that, in short, their life bursts forth, despite of all that is done to repress and destroy their individuality. When you have once learned to honour anything, love is not very far off; at least that has always been my experience. But, as I have said, I had not yet learned to honour pollards, and therefore they made me more miserable than I was already.

When, having followed the road, I stood at last on the bridge, and, looking up and down the river through the misty air, saw two long rows of these pollards diminishing till they vanished in both directions, the sight of them took from me all power of enjoying the water beneath me, the green fields around me, or even the old-world beauty of the little bridge upon which I stood, although all sorts of bridges have been from very infancy a delight to me. For I am one of those who never get rid of their infantile predilections, and to have once enjoyed making a mud bridge, was to enjoy all bridges for ever.

I saw a man in a white smock-frock coming along the road beyond, but I turned my back to the road, leaned my arms on the parapet of the bridge, and stood gazing where I saw no visions, namely, at those very poplars. I heard the man's footsteps coming up the crown of the arch, but I would not turn to greet him. I was in a selfish humour if ever I was; for surely if ever one man ought to greet another, it was upon such a comfortless afternoon. The footsteps stopped behind me, and I heard a voice: —

"I beg yer pardon, sir; but be you the new vicar?"

I turned instantly and answered, "I am. Do you want me?"

"I wanted to see yer face, sir, that was all, if ye'll not take it amiss."

Before me stood a tall old man with his hat in his hand, clothed as I have said, in a white smock-frock. He smoothed his short gray hair with his curved palm down over his forehead as he stood. His face was of a red brown, from much exposure to the weather. There was a certain look of roughness, without hardness, in it, which spoke of endurance rather than resistance, although he could evidently set his face as a flint. His features were large and a little coarse, but the smile that parted his lips when he spoke, shone in his gray eyes as well, and lighted up a countenance in which a man might trust.

"I wanted to see yer face, sir, if you'll not take it amiss."

"Certainly not," I answered, pleased with the man's address, as he stood square before me, looking as modest as fearless. "The sight of a man's face is what everybody has a right to; but, for all that, I should like to know why you want to see my face."

"Why, sir, you be the new vicar. You kindly told me so when I axed you."

"Well, then, you'll see my face on Sunday in church-that is, if you happen to be there."

For, although some might think it the more dignified way, I could not take it as a matter of course that he would be at church. A man might have better reasons for staying away from church than I had for going, even though I was the parson, and it was my business. Some clergymen separate between themselves and their office to a degree which I cannot understand. To assert the dignities of my office seems to me very like exalting myself; and when I have had a twinge of conscience about it, as has happened more than once, I have then found comfort in these two texts: "The Son of man came not to be ministered unto but to minister;" and "It is enough that the servant should be as his master." Neither have I ever been able to see the very great difference between right and wrong in a clergyman, and right and wrong in another man. All that I can pretend to have yet discovered comes to this: that what is right in another man is right in a clergyman; and what is wrong in another man is much worse in a clergyman. Here, however, is one more proof of approaching age. I do not mean the opinion, but the digression.

"Well, then," I said, "you'll see my face in church on Sunday, if you happen to be there."

"Yes, sir; but you see, sir, on the bridge here, the parson is the parson like, and I'm Old Rogers; and I looks in his face, and he looks in mine, and I says to myself, 'This is my parson.' But o' Sundays he's nobody's parson; he's got his work to do, and it mun be done, and there's an end on't."

That there was a real idea in the old man's mind was considerably clearer than the logic by which he tried to bring it out.

"Did you know parson that's gone, sir?" he went on.

"No," I answered.

"Oh, sir! he wur a good parson. Many's the time he come and sit at my son's bedside-him that's dead and gone, sir-for a long hour, on a Saturday night, too. And then when I see him up in the desk the next mornin', I'd say to myself, 'Old Rogers, that's the same man as sat by your son's bedside last night. Think o' that, Old Rogers!' But, somehow, I never did feel right sure o' that same. He didn't seem to have the same cut, somehow; and he didn't talk a bit the same. And when he spoke to me after sermon, in the church-yard, I was always of a mind to go into the church again and look up to the pulpit to see if he war really out ov it; for this warn't the same man, you see. But you'll know all about it better than I can tell you, sir. Only I always liked parson better out o' the pulpit, and that's how I come to want to make you look at me, sir, instead o' the water down there, afore I see you in the church to-morrow mornin'."

The old man laughed a kindly laugh; but he had set me thinking, and I did not know what to say to him all at once. So after a short pause, he resumed —

"You'll be thinking me a queer kind of a man, sir, to speak to my betters before my betters speaks to me. But mayhap you don't know what a parson is to us poor folk that has ne'er a friend more larned than theirselves but the parson. And besides, sir, I'm an old salt, —an old man-o'-war's man, —and I've been all round the world, sir; and I ha' been in all sorts o' company, pirates and all, sir; and I aint a bit frightened of a parson. No; I love a parson, sir.

And I'll tell you for why, sir. He's got a good telescope, and he gits to the masthead, and he looks out. And he sings out, 'Land ahead!' or 'Breakers ahead!' and gives directions accordin'. Only I can't always make out what he says. But when he shuts up his spyglass, and comes down the riggin', and talks to us like one man to another, then I don't know what I should do without the parson. Good evenin' to you, sir, and welcome to Marshmallows."

The pollards did not look half so dreary. The river began to glimmer a little; and the old bridge had become an interesting old bridge. The country altogether was rather nice than otherwise. I had found a friend already! —that is, a man to whom I might possibly be of some use; and that was the most precious friend I could think of in my present situation and mood. I had learned something from him too; and I resolved to try all I could to be the same man in the pulpit that I was out of it. Some may be inclined to say that I had better have formed the resolution to be the same man out of the pulpit that I was in it. But the one will go quite right with the other. Out of the pulpit I would be the same man I was in it-seeing and feeling the realities of the unseen; and in the pulpit I would be the same man I was out of it-taking facts as they are, and dealing with things as they show themselves in the world.

One other occurrence before I went home that evening, and I shall close the chapter. I hope I shall not write another so dull as this. I dare not promise, though; for this is a new kind of work to me.

Before I left the bridge, —while, in fact, I was contemplating the pollards with an eye, if not of favour, yet of diminished dismay, —the sun, which, for anything I knew of his whereabouts, either from knowledge of the country, aspect of the evening, or state of my own feelings, might have been down for an hour or two, burst his cloudy bands, and blazed out as if he had just risen from the dead, instead of being just about to sink into the grave. Do not tell me that my figure is untrue, for that the sun never sinks into the grave, else I will retort that it is just as true of the sun as of a man; for that no man sinks into the grave. He only disappears. Life IS a constant sunrise, which death cannot interrupt, any more than the night can swallow up the sun. "God is not the God of the dead, but of the living; for all live unto him."

Well, the sun shone out gloriously. The whole sweep of the gloomy river answered him in gladness; the wet leaves of the pollards quivered and glanced; the meadows offered up their perfect green, fresh and clear out of the trouble of the rain; and away in the distance, upon a rising ground covered with trees, glittered a weathercock. What if I found afterwards that it was only on the roof of a stable? It shone, and that was enough. And when the sun had gone below the horizon, and the fields and the river were dusky once more, there it glittered still over the darkening earth, a symbol of that faith which is "the evidence of things not seen," and it made my heart swell as at a chant from the prophet Isaiah. What matter then whether it hung over a stable-roof or a church-tower?

I stood up and wandered a little farther-off the bridge, and along the road. I had not gone far before I passed a house, out of which came a young woman leading a little boy. They came after me, the boy gazing at the red and gold and green of the sunset sky. As they passed me, the child said —

"Auntie, I think I should like to be a painter."

"Why?" returned his companion.

"Because, then," answered the child, "I could help God to paint the sky."

What his aunt replied I do not know; for they were presently beyond my hearing. But I went on answering him myself all the way home. Did God care to paint the sky of an evening, that a few of His children might see it, and get just a hope, just an aspiration, out of its passing green, and gold, and purple, and red? and should I think my day's labour lost, if it wrought no visible salvation in the earth?

But was the child's aspiration in vain? Could I tell him God did not want his help to paint the sky? True, he could mount no scaffold against the infinite of the glowing west. But might he not with his little palette and brush, when the time came, show his brothers and sisters what he had seen there, and make them see it too? Might he not thus come, after long trying, to help

God to paint this glory of vapour and light inside the minds of His children? Ah! if any man's work is not WITH God, its results shall be burned, ruthlessly burned, because poor and bad.

"So, for my part," I said to myself, as I walked home, "if I can put one touch of a rosy sunset into the life of any man or woman of my cure, I shall feel that I have worked with God. He is in no haste; and if I do what I may in earnest, I need not mourn if I work no great work on the earth. Let God make His sunsets: I will mottle my little fading cloud. To help the growth of a thought that struggles towards the light; to brush with gentle hand the earth-stain from the white of one snowdrop-such be my ambition! So shall I scale the rocks in front, not leave my name carved upon those behind me."

People talk about special providences. I believe in the providences, but not in the specialty. I do not believe that God lets the thread of my affairs go for six days, and on the seventh evening takes it up for a moment. The so-called special providences are no exception to the rule-they are common to all men at all moments. But it is a fact that God's care is more evident in some instances of it than in others to the dim and often bewildered vision of humanity. Upon such instances men seize and call them providences. It is well that they can; but it would be gloriously better if they could believe that the whole matter is one grand providence.

I was one of such men at the time, and could not fail to see what I called a special providence in this, that on my first attempt to find where I stood in the scheme of Providence, and while I was discouraged with regard to the work before me, I should fall in with these two-an old man whom I could help, and a child who could help me; the one opening an outlet for my labour and my love, and the other reminding me of the highest source of the most humbling comfort,—that in all my work I might be a fellow-worker with God.

CHAPTER II
MY FIRST SUNDAY AT MARSHMALLOWS.

These events fell on the Saturday night. On the Sunday morning, I read prayers and preached. Never before had I enjoyed so much the petitions of the Church, which Hooker calls "the sending of angels upward," or the reading of the lessons, which he calls "the receiving of angels descended from above." And whether from the newness of the parson, or the love of the service, certainly a congregation more intent, or more responsive, a clergyman will hardly find. But, as I had feared, it was different in the afternoon. The people had dined, and the usual somnolence had followed; nor could I find in my heart to blame men and women who worked hard all the week, for being drowsy on the day of rest. So I curtailed my sermon as much as I could, omitting page after page of my manuscript; and when I came to a close, was rewarded by perceiving an agreeable surprise upon many of the faces round me. I resolved that, in the afternoons at least, my sermons should be as short as heart could wish.

But that afternoon there was at least one man of the congregation who was neither drowsy nor inattentive. Repeatedly my eyes left the page off which I was reading and glanced towards him. Not once did I find his eyes turned away from me.

There was a small loft in the west end of the church, in which stood a little organ, whose voice, weakened by years of praising, and possibly of neglect, had yet, among a good many tones that were rough, wooden, and reedy, a few remaining that were as mellow as ever praiseful heart could wish to praise withal. And these came in amongst the rest like trusting thoughts amidst "eating cares;" like the faces of children borne in the arms of a crowd of anxious mothers; like hopes that are young prophecies amidst the downward sweep of events. For, though I do not understand music, I have a keen ear for the perfection of the single tone, or the completeness of the harmony. But of this organ more by and by.

Now this little gallery was something larger than was just necessary for the organ and its ministrants, and a few of the parishioners had chosen to sit in its fore-front. Upon this occasion there was no one there but the man to whom I have referred.

The space below this gallery was not included in the part of the church used for the service. It was claimed by the gardener of the place, that is the sexton, to hold his gardening tools. There were a few ancient carvings in wood lying in it, very brown in the dusky light that came through a small lancet window, opening, not to the outside, but into the tower, itself dusky with an enduring twilight. And there were some broken old headstones, and the kindly spade and pickaxe-but I have really nothing to do with these now, for I am, as it were, in the pulpit, whence one ought to look beyond such things as these.

Rising against the screen which separated this mouldy portion of the church from the rest, stood an old monument of carved wood, once brilliantly painted in the portions that bore the arms of the family over whose vault it stood, but now all bare and worn, itself gently flowing away into the dust it commemorated. It lifted its gablet, carved to look like a canopy, till its apex was on a level with the book-board on the front of the organ-loft; and over-in fact upon this apex appeared the face of the man whom I have mentioned. It was a very remarkable countenance-pale, and very thin, without any hair, except that of thick eyebrows that far over-hung keen, questioning eyes. Short bushy hair, gray, not white, covered a well formed head with a high narrow forehead. As I have said, those keen eyes kept looking at me from under their gray eyebrows all the time of the sermon-intelligently without doubt, but whether sympathetically or otherwise I could not determine. And indeed I hardly know yet. My vestry door opened upon a little group of graves, simple and green, without headstone or slab; poor graves, the memory of whose occupants no one had cared to preserve. Good men must have preceded me here, else the poor would not have lain so near the chancel and the vestry-door. All about and beyond were stones, with here and there a monument; for mine was a large parish, and there were old and rich families in it, more of which buried their dead here than assembled their living. But close by the vestry-door, there was this little billowy lake of grass. And at the end of the narrow path leading from the door, was the churchyard wall, with a few steps on each side of it, that the parson might pass at once from the churchyard into his own shrubbery, here tangled, almost matted, from luxuriance of growth. But I would not creep out the back way from among my people. That way might do very well to come in by; but to go out, I would use the door of the people. So I went along the church, a fine old place, such as I had never hoped to be presented to, and went out by the door in the north side into the middle of the churchyard. The door on the other side was chiefly used by the few gentry of the neighbourhood; and the Lych-gate, with its covered way, (for the main road had once passed on that side,) was shared between the coffins and the carriages, the dead who had no rank but one, that of the dead, and the living who had more money than their neighbours. For, let the old gentry disclaim it as they may, mere wealth, derived from whatever source, will sooner reach their level than poor antiquity, or the rarest refinement of personal worth; although, to be sure, the oldest of them will sooner give to the rich their sons or their daughters to wed, to love if they can, to have children by, than they will yield a jot of their ancestral preeminence, or acknowledge any equality in their sons or daughters-in-law. The carpenter's son is to them an old myth, not an everlasting fact. To Mammon alone will they yield a little of their rank-none of it to Christ. Let me glorify God that Jesus took not on. Him the nature of nobles, but the seed of Adam; for what could I do without my poor brothers and sisters?

I passed along the church to the northern door, and went out. The churchyard lay in bright sunshine. All the rain and gloom were gone. "If one could only bring this glory of sun and grass into one's hope for the future!" thought I; and looking down I saw the little boy who aspired to paint the sky, looking up in my face with mingled confidence and awe.

"Do you trust me, my little man?" thought I. "You shall trust me then. But I won't be a priest to you, I'll be a big brother."

For the priesthood passes away, the brotherhood endures. The priesthood passes away, swallowed up in the brotherhood. It is because men cannot learn simple things, cannot believe in the brotherhood, that they need a priesthood. But as Dr Arnold said of the Sunday, "They DO need it." And I, for one, am sure that the priesthood needs the people much more than the people needs the priesthood.

So I stooped and lifted the child and held him in my arms. And the little fellow looked at me one moment longer, and then put his arms gently round my neck. And so we were friends. When I had set him down, which I did presently, for I shuddered at the idea of the people thinking that I was showing off the CLERGYMAN, I looked at the boy. In his face was great sweetness mingled with great rusticity, and I could not tell whether he was the child of gentlefolk or of peasants. He did not say a word, but walked away to join his aunt, who was waiting for him at the gate of the churchyard. He kept his head turned towards me, however, as he went, so that, not seeing where he was going, he stumbled over the grave of a child, and fell in the hollow on the other side. I ran to pick him up. His aunt reached him at the same moment.

"Oh, thank you, sir!" she said, as I gave him to her, with an earnestness which seemed to me disproportionate to the deed, and carried him away with a deep blush over all her countenance.

At the churchyard-gate, the old man-of-war's man was waiting to have another look at me. His hat was in his hand, and he gave a pull to the short hair over his forehead, as if he would gladly take that off too, to show his respect for the new parson. I held out my hand gratefully. It could not close around the hard, unyielding mass of fingers which met it. He did not know how to shake hands, and left it all to me. But pleasure sparkled in his eyes.

"My old woman would like to shake hands with you, sir," he said.

Beside him stood his old woman, in a portentous bonnet, beneath whose gay yellow ribbons appeared a dusky old face, wrinkled like a ship's timbers, out of which looked a pair of keen black eyes, where the best beauty, that of loving-kindness, had not merely lingered, but triumphed.

"I shall be in to see you soon," I said, as I shook hands with her. "I shall find out where you live."

"Down by the mill," she said; "close by it, sir. There's one bed in our garden that always thrives, in the hottest summer, by the plash from the mill, sir."

"Ask for Old Rogers, sir," said the man. "Everybody knows Old Rogers. But if your reverence minds what my wife says, you won't go wrong. When you find the river, it takes you to the mill; and when you find the mill, you find the wheel; and when you find the wheel, you haven't far to look for the cottage, sir. It's a poor place, but you'll be welcome, sir."

CHAPTER III
MY FIRST MONDAY AT MARSHMALLOWS.

The next day I might expect some visitors. It is a fortunate thing that English society now regards the parson as a gentleman, else he would have little chance of being useful to the UPPER CLASSES. But I wanted to get a good start of them, and see some of my poor before my rich came to see me. So after breakfast, on as lovely a Monday in the beginning of autumn as ever came to comfort a clergyman in the reaction of his efforts to feed his flock on the Sunday, I walked out, and took my way to the village. I strove to dismiss from my mind every feeling of DOING DUTY, of PERFORMING MY PART, and all that. I had a horror of becoming a moral policeman as much as of "doing church." I would simply enjoy the privilege, more open to me in virtue of my office, of ministering. But as no servant has a right to force his service, so I would be the NEIGHBOUR only, until such time as the opportunity of being the servant should show itself.

The village was as irregular as a village should be, partly consisting of those white houses with intersecting parallelograms of black which still abound in some regions of our island. Just in the centre, however, grouping about an old house of red brick, which had once been a manorial residence, but was now subdivided in all modes that analytic ingenuity could devise, rose a portion of it which, from one point of view, might seem part of an old town. But you had only to pass round any one of three visible corners to see stacks of wheat and a farm-yard; while in another direction the houses went straggling away into a wood that looked very like the beginning of a forest, of which some of the village orchards appeared to form part. From the street the slow-winding, poplar-bordered stream was here and there just visible.

I did not quite like to have it between me and my village. I could not help preferring that homely relation in which the houses are built up like swallow-nests on to the very walls of the cathedrals themselves, to the arrangement here, where the river flowed, with what flow there was in it, between the church and the people.

A little way beyond the farther end of the village appeared an iron gate, of considerable size, dividing a lofty stone wall. And upon the top of that one of the stone pillars supporting the gate which I could see, stood a creature of stone, whether natant, volant, passant, couchant, or rampant, I could not tell, only it looked like something terrible enough for a quite antediluvian heraldry.

As I passed along the street, wondering with myself what relations between me and these houses were hidden in the future, my eye was caught by the window of a little shop, in which strings of beads and elephants of gingerbread formed the chief samples of the goods within. It was a window much broader than it was high, divided into lozenge-shaped panes. Wondering what kind of old woman presided over the treasures in this cave of Aladdin, I thought to make a first of my visits by going in and buying something. But I hesitated, because I could not think of anything I was in want of-at least that the old woman was likely to have. To be sure I wanted a copy of Bengel's "Gnomon;" but she was not likely to have that. I wanted the fourth plate in the third volume of Law's "Behmen;" she was not likely to have that either. I did not care for gingerbread; and I had no little girl to take home beads to.

But why should I not go in without an ostensible errand? For this reason: there are dissenters everywhere, and I could not tell but I might be going into the shop of a dissenter. Now, though, I confess, nothing would have pleased me better than that all the dissenters should return to their old home in the Church, I could not endure the suspicion of laying myself out to entice them back by canvassing or using any personal influence. Whether they returned or not, however, (and I did not expect many would,) I hoped still, some day, to stand towards every one of them in the relation of the parson of the parish, that is, one of whom each might feel certain that he was ready to serve him or her at any hour when he might be wanted to render a service. In the meantime, I could not help hesitating.

I had almost made up my mind to ask if she had a small pocket compass, for I had seen such things in little country shops —I am afraid only in France, though-when the door opened, and out came the little boy whom I had already seen twice, and who was therefore one of my oldest friends in the place. He came across the road to me, took me by the hand, and said —

"Come and see mother."

"Where, my dear?" I asked.

"In the shop there," he answered.

"Is it your mother's shop?"

"Yes."

I said no more, but accompanied him. Of course my expectation of seeing an old woman behind the counter had vanished, but I was not in the least prepared for the kind of woman I did see.

The place was half a shop and half a kitchen. A yard or so of counter stretched inwards from the door, just as a hint to those who might be intrusively inclined. Beyond this, by the chimney-corner, sat the mother, who rose as we entered. She was certainly one —I do not say of the most beautiful, but, until I have time to explain further-of the most remarkable women I had ever seen. Her face was absolutely white-no, pale cream-colour —except her lips and a spot upon each cheek, which glowed with a deep carmine. You would have said she had been painting, and painting very inartistically, so little was the red shaded into the surrounding white. Now this was certainly not beautiful. Indeed, it occasioned a strange feeling, almost of terror, at first, for she reminded one of the spectre woman in the "Rime of the Ancient Mariner." But when I got used to her complexion, I saw that the form of her features was quite beautiful. She might indeed have been LOVELY but for a certain hardness which showed through the beauty. This might have been the result of ill health, ill-endured; but I doubted it. For there was a certain modelling of the cheeks and lips which showed that the teeth within were firmly closed; and, taken with the look of the eyes and forehead, seemed the expression of a constant and bitter self-command. But there were indubitable marks of ill health upon her, notwithstanding; for not to mention her complexion, her large dark eye was burning as if the lamp of life had broken and the oil was blazing; and there was a slight expansion of the nostrils, which indicated physical unrest. But her manner was perfectly, almost dreadfully, quiet; her voice soft, low, and chiefly expressive of indifference. She spoke without looking me in the face, but did not seem either shy or ashamed. Her figure was remarkably graceful, though too worn to be beautiful. —Here was a strange parishioner for me! —in a country toy-shop, too!

As soon as the little fellow had brought me in, he shrunk away through a half-open door that revealed a stair behind.

"What can I do for you, sir?" said the mother, coldly, and with a kind of book-propriety of speech, as she stood on the other side of the little counter, prepared to open box or drawer at command.

"To tell the truth, I hardly know," I said. "I am the new vicar; but I do not think that I should have come in to see you just to-day, if it had not been that your little boy there-where is he gone to? He asked me to come in and see his mother."

"He is too ready to make advances to strangers, sir."

She said this in an incisive tone.

"Oh, but," I answered, "I am not a stranger to him. I have met him twice before. He is a little darling. I assure you he has quite gained my heart."

No reply for a moment. Then just "Indeed!" and nothing more.

I could not understand it.

But a jar on a shelf, marked TOBACCO, rescued me from the most pressing portion of the perplexity, namely, what to say next.

"Will you give me a quarter of a pound of tobacco?" I said.

The woman turned, took down the jar, arranged the scales, weighed out the quantity, wrapped it up, took the money,—and all without one other word than, "Thank you, sir;" which was all I could return, with the addition of, "Good morning."

For nothing was left me but to walk away with my parcel in my pocket.

The little boy did not show himself again. I had hoped to find him outside.

Pondering, speculating, I now set out for the mill, which, I had already learned, was on the village side of the river. Coming to a lane leading down to the river, I followed it, and then walked up a path outside the row of pollards, through a lovely meadow, where brown and white cows were eating and shining all over the thick deep grass. Beyond the meadow, a wood on the side of a rising ground went parallel with the river a long way. The river flowed on my right. That is, I knew that it was flowing, but I could not have told how I knew, it was so slow. Still swollen, it was of a clear brown, in which you could see the browner trouts darting to and fro with such a slippery gliding, that the motion seemed the result of will, without any such intermediate and complicate arrangement as brain and nerves and muscles. The water-beetles went spinning about over the surface; and one glorious dragon-fly made a mist about him with his long wings. And over all, the sun hung in the sky, pouring down life; shining on the roots of the willows at the bottom of the stream; lighting up the black head of the water-rat as he hurried across to the opposite bank; glorifying the rich green lake of the grass; and giving to the whole an utterance of love and hope and joy, which was, to him who could read it, a more certain and full revelation of God than any display of power in thunder, in avalanche, in stormy sea. Those with whom the feeling of religion is only occasional, have it most when the awful or grand breaks out of the common; the meek who inherit the earth, find the God of the whole earth more evidently present—I do not say more present, for there is no measuring of His presence-more evidently present in the commonest things. That which is best He gives most plentifully, as is reason with Him. Hence the quiet fulness of ordinary nature; hence the Spirit to them that ask it.

I soon came within sound of the mill; and presently, crossing the stream that flowed back to the river after having done its work on the corn, I came in front of the building, and looked over the half-door into the mill. The floor was clean and dusty. A few full sacks, tied tight at the mouth-they always look to me as if Joseph's silver cup were just inside-stood about. In the farther corner, the flour was trickling down out of two wooden spouts into a wooden receptacle below. The whole place was full of its own faint but pleasant odour. No man was visible. The spouts went on pouring the slow torrent of flour, as if everything could go on with perfect propriety of itself. I could not even see how a man could get at the stones that I heard grinding away above, except he went up the rope that hung from the ceiling. So I walked round the corner of the place, and found myself in the company of the water-wheel, mossy and green with ancient waterdrops, looking so furred and overgrown and lumpy, that one might have thought the wood of it had taken to growing again in its old days, and so the wheel was losing by slow degrees the shape of a wheel, to become some new awful monster of a pollard. As yet, however, it was going round; slowly, indeed, and with the gravity of age, but doing its work, and casting its loose drops in the alms-giving of a gentle rain upon a little plot of Master Rogers's garden, which was therefore full of moisture-loving flowers. This plot was divided from the mill-wheel by a small stream which carried away the surplus water, and was now full and running rapidly.

Beyond the stream, beside the flower bed, stood a dusty young man, talking to a young woman with a rosy face and clear honest eyes. The moment they saw me they parted. The young man came across the stream at a step, and the young woman went up the garden towards the cottage.

"That must be Old Rogers's cottage?" I said to the miller.

"Yes, sir," he answered, looking a little sheepish.

"Was that his daughter-that nice-looking young woman you were talking to?"

"Yes, sir, it was."

And he stole a shy pleased look at me out of the corners of his eyes.

"It's a good thing," I said, "to have an honest experienced old mill like yours, that can manage to go on of itself for a little while now and then."

This gave a great help to his budding confidence. He laughed.

"Well, sir, it's not very often it's left to itself. Jane isn't at her father's above once or twice a week at most."

"She doesn't live with them, then?"

"No, sir. You see they're both hearty, and they ain't over well to do, and Jane lives up at the Hall, sir. She's upper housemaid, and waits on one of the young ladies. —Old Rogers has seen a great deal of the world, sir."

"So I imagine. I am just going to see him. Good morning."

I jumped across the stream, and went up a little gravel-walk, which led me in a few yards to the cottage-door. It was a sweet place to live in, with honeysuckle growing over the house, and the sounds of the softly-labouring mill-wheel ever in its little porch and about its windows.

The door was open, and Dame Rogers came from within to meet me. She welcomed me, and led the way into her little kitchen. As I entered, Jane went out at the back-door. But it was only to call her father, who presently came in.

"I'm glad to see ye, sir. This pleasure comes of having no work to-day. After harvest there comes slack times for the likes of me. People don't care about a bag of old bones when they can get hold of young men. Well, well, never mind, old woman. The Lord'll take us through somehow. When the wind blows, the ship goes; when the wind drops, the ship stops; but the sea is His all the same, for He made it; and the wind is His all the same too."

He spoke in the most matter-of-fact tone, unaware of anything poetic in what he said. To him it was just common sense, and common sense only.

"I am sorry you are out of work," I said. "But my garden is sadly out of order, and I must have something done to it. You don't dislike gardening, do you?"

"Well, I beant a right good hand at garden-work," answered the old man, with some embarrassment, scratching his gray head with a troubled scratch.

There was more in this than met the ear; but what, I could not conjecture. I would press the point a little. So I took him at his own word.

"I won't ask you to do any of the more ornamental part," I said, —"only plain digging and hoeing."

"I would rather be excused, sir."

"I am afraid I made you think"—

"I thought nothing, sir. I thank you kindly, sir."

"I assure you I want the work done, and I must employ some one else if you don't undertake it."

"Well, sir, my back's bad now-no, sir, I won't tell a story about it. I would just rather not, sir."

"Now," his wife broke in, "now, Old Rogers, why won't 'ee tell the parson the truth, like a man, downright? If ye won't, I'll do it for 'ee. The fact is, sir," she went on, turning to me, with a plate in her hand, which she was wiping, "the fact is, that the old parson's man for that kind o' work was Simmons, t'other end of the village; and my man is so afeard o' hurtin' e'er another, that he'll turn the bread away from his own mouth and let it fall in the dirt."

"Now, now, old 'oman, don't 'ee belie me. I'm not so bad as that. You see, sir, I never was good at knowin' right from wrong like. I never was good, that is, at tellin' exactly what I ought to do. So when anything comes up, I just says to myself, 'Now, Old Rogers, what do you think the Lord would best like you to do?' And as soon as I ax myself that, I know directly what I've got to do; and then my old woman can't turn me no more than a bull. And she don't like my obstinate fits. But, you see, I daren't sir, once I axed myself that."

"Stick to that, Rogers," I said.

"Besides, sir," he went on, "Simmons wants it more than I do. He's got a sick wife; and my old woman, thank God, is hale and hearty. And there is another thing besides, sir: he might take it hard of you, sir, and think it was turning away an old servant like; and then, sir, he wouldn't be ready to hear what you had to tell him, and might, mayhap, lose a deal o' comfort. And that I would take worst of all, sir."

"Well, well, Rogers, Simmons shall have the job."

"Thank ye, sir," said the old man.

His wife, who could not see the thing quite from her husband's point of view, was too honest to say anything; but she was none the less cordial to me. The daughter stood looking from one to the other with attentive face, which took everything, but revealed nothing.

I rose to go. As I reached the door, I remembered the tobacco in my pocket. I had not bought it for myself. I never could smoke. Nor do I conceive that smoking is essential to a clergyman in the country; though I have occasionally envied one of my brethren in London, who will sit down by the fire, and, lighting his pipe, at the same time please his host and subdue the bad smells of the place. And I never could hit his way of talking to his parishioners either. He could put them at their ease in a moment. I think he must have got the trick out of his pipe. But in reality, I seldom think about how I ought to talk to anybody I am with.

That I didn't smoke myself was no reason why I should not help Old Rogers to smoke. So I pulled out the tobacco.

"You smoke, don't you, Rogers?" I said.

"Well, sir, I can't deny it. It's not much I spend on baccay, anyhow. Is it, dame?"

"No, that it bean't," answered his wife.

"You don't think there's any harm in smoking a pipe, sir?"

"Not the least," I answered, with emphasis.

"You see, sir," he went on, not giving me time to prove how far I was from thinking there was any harm in it; "You see, sir, sailors learns many ways they might be better without. I used to take my pan o' grog with the rest of them; but I give that up quite, 'cause as how I don't want it now."

"'Cause as how," interrupted his wife, "you spend the money on tea for me, instead. You wicked old man to tell stories!"

"Well, I takes my share of the tea, old woman, and I'm sure it's a deal better for me. But, to tell the truth, sir, I was a little troubled in my mind about the baccay, not knowing whether I ought to have it or not. For you see, the parson that's gone didn't more than half like it, as I could tell by the turn of his hawse-holes when he came in at the door and me a-smokin'. Not as he said anything; for, ye see, I was an old man, and I daresay that kep him quiet. But I did hear him blow up a young chap i' the village he come upon promiscus with a pipe in his mouth. He did give him a thunderin' broadside, to be sure! So I was in two minds whether I ought to go on with my pipe or not."

"And how did you settle the question, Rogers?"

"Why, I followed my own old chart, sir."

"Quite right. One mustn't mind too much what other people think."

"That's not exactly what I mean, sir."

"What do you mean then? I should like to know."

"Well, sir, I mean that I said to myself, 'Now, Old Rogers, what do you think the Lord would say about this here baccay business?'"

"And what did you think He would say?"

"Why, sir, I thought He would say, 'Old Rogers, have yer baccay; only mind ye don't grumble when you 'aint got none.'"

Something in this—I could not at the time have told what-touched me more than I can express. No doubt it was the simple reality of the relation in which the old man stood to his Father in heaven that made me feel as if the tears would come in spite of me.

"And this is the man," I said to myself, "whom I thought I should be able to teach! Well, the wisest learn most, and I may be useful to him after all."

As I said nothing, the old man resumed—

"For you see, sir, it is not always a body feels he has a right to spend his ha'pence on baccay; and sometimes, too, he 'aint got none to spend."

"In the meantime," I said, "here is some that I bought for you as I came along. I hope you will find it good. I am no judge."

The old sailor's eyes glistened with gratitude. "Well, who'd ha' thought it. You didn't think I was beggin' for it, sir, surely?"

"You see I had it for you in my pocket."

"Well, that IS good o' you, sir!"

"Why, Rogers, that'll last you a month!" exclaimed his wife, looking nearly as pleased as himself.

"Six weeks at least, wife," he answered. "And ye don't smoke yourself, sir, and yet ye bring baccay to me! Well, it's just like yer Master, sir."

I went away, resolved that Old Rogers should have no chance of "grumbling" for want of tobacco, if I could help it.

CHAPTER IV
THE COFFIN.

On the way back, my thoughts were still occupied with the woman I had seen in the little shop. The old man-of-war's man was probably the nobler being of the two; and if I had had to choose between them, I should no doubt have chosen him. But I had not to choose between them; I had only to think about them; and I thought a great deal more about the one I could not understand than the one I could understand. For Old Rogers wanted little help from me; whereas the other was evidently a soul in pain, and therefore belonged to me in peculiar right of my office; while the readiest way in which I could justify to myself the possession of that office was to make it a shepherding of the sheep. So I resolved to find out what I could about her, as one having a right to know, that I might see whether I could not help her. From herself it was evident that her secret, if she had one, was not to be easily gained; but even the common reports of the village would be some enlightenment to the darkness I was in about her.

As I went again through the village, I observed a narrow lane striking off to the left, and resolved to explore in that direction. It led up to one side of the large house of which I have already spoken. As I came near, I smelt what has been to me always a delightful smell-that of fresh deals under the hands of the carpenter. In the scent of those boards of pine is enclosed all the idea the tree could gather of the world of forest where it was reared. It speaks of many wild and bright but chiefly clean and rather cold things. If I were idling, it would draw me to it across many fields. —Turning a corner, I heard the sound of a saw. And this sound drew me yet more. For a carpenter's shop was the delight of my boyhood; and after I began to read the history of our Lord with something of that sense of reality with which we read other histories, and which, I am sorry to think, so much of the well-meant instruction we receive in our youth tends to destroy, my feeling about such a workshop grew stronger and stronger, till at last I never could go near enough to see the shavings lying on the floor of one, without a spiritual sensation such as I have in entering an old church; which sensation, ever since having been admitted on the usual conditions to a Mohammedan mosque, urges me to pull off, not only my hat, but my shoes likewise. And the feeling has grown upon me, till now it seems at times as if the only cure in the world for social pride would be to go for five silent minutes into a carpenter's shop. How one can think of himself as above his neighbours, within sight, sound, or smell of one, I fear I am getting almost unable to imagine, and one ought not to get out of sympathy with the wrong. Only as I am growing old now, it does not matter so much, for I daresay my time will not be very long.

So I drew near to the shop, feeling as if the Lord might be at work there at one of the benches. And when I reached the door, there was my pale-faced hearer of the Sunday afternoon, sawing a board for a coffin-lid.

As my shadow fell across and darkened his work, he lifted his head and saw me.

I could not altogether understand the expression of his countenance as he stood upright from his labour and touched his old hat with rather a proud than a courteous gesture. And I could not believe that he was glad to see me, although he laid down his saw and advanced to the door. It was the gentleman in him, not the man, that sought to make me welcome, hardly caring whether I saw through the ceremony or not. True, there was a smile on his lips, but the smile of a man who cherishes a secret grudge; of one who does not altogether dislike you, but who has a claim upon you-say, for an apology, of which claim he doubts whether you know the existence. So the smile seemed tightened, and stopped just when it got half-way to its width, and was about to become hearty and begin to shine.

"May I come in?" I said.

"Come in, sir," he answered.

"I am glad I have happened to come upon you by accident," I said.

He smiled as if he did not quite believe in the accident, and considered it a part of the play between us that I should pretend it. I hastened to add —

"I was wandering about the place, making some acquaintance with it, and with my friends in it, when I came upon you quite unexpectedly. You know I saw you in church on Sunday afternoon."

"I know you saw me, sir," he answered, with a motion as if to return to his work; "but, to tell the truth, I don't go to church very often."

I did not quite know whether to take this as proceeding from an honest fear of being misunderstood, or from a sense of being in general superior to all that sort of thing. But I felt that it would be of no good to pursue the inquiry directly. I looked therefore for something to say.

"Ah! your work is not always a pleasant one," I said, associating the feelings of which I have already spoken with the facts before me, and looking at the coffin, the lower part of which stood nearly finished upon trestles on the floor.

"Well, there are unpleasant things in all trades," he answered. "But it does not matter," he added, with an increase of bitterness in his smile.

"I didn't mean," I said, "that the work was unpleasant-only sad. It must always be painful to make a coffin."

"A joiner gets used to it, sir, as you do to the funeral service. But, for my part, I don't see why it should be considered so unhappy for a man to be buried. This isn't such a good job, after all, this world, sir, you must allow."

"Neither is that coffin," said I, as if by a sudden inspiration.

The man seemed taken aback, as Old Rogers might have said. He looked at the coffin and then looked at me.

"Well, sir," he said, after a short pause, which no doubt seemed longer both to him and to me than it would have seemed to any third person, "I don't see anything amiss with the coffin. I don't say it'll last till doomsday, as the gravedigger says to Hamlet, because I don't know so much about doomsday as some people pretend to; but you see, sir, it's not finished yet."

"Thank you," I said; "that's just what I meant. You thought I was hasty in my judgment of your coffin; whereas I only said of it knowingly what you said of the world thoughtlessly. How do you know that the world is finished anymore than your coffin? And how dare you then say that it is a bad job?"

The same respectfully scornful smile passed over his face, as much as to say, "Ah! it's your trade to talk that way, so I must not be too hard upon you."

"At any rate, sir," he said, "whoever made it has taken long enough about it, a person would think, to finish anything he ever meant to finish."

"One day is with the Lord as a thousand years, and a thousand years as one day," I said.

"That's supposing," he answered, "that the Lord did make the world. For my part, I am half of a mind that the Lord didn't make it at all."

"I am very glad to hear you say so," I answered.

Hereupon I found that we had changed places a little. He looked up at me. The smile of superiority was no longer there, and a puzzled questioning, which might indicate either "Who would have expected that from you?" or, "What can he mean?" or both at once, had taken its place. I, for my part, knew that on the scale of the man's judgment I had risen nearer to his own level. As he said nothing, however, and I was in danger of being misunderstood, I proceeded at once.

"Of course it seems to me better that you should not believe God had done a thing, than that you should believe He had not done it well!"

"Ah! I see, sir. Then you will allow there is some room for doubting whether He made the world at all?"

"Yes; for I do not think an honest man, as you seem to me to be, would be able to doubt without any room whatever. That would be only for a fool. But it is just possible, as we are not perfectly good ourselves-you'll allow that, won't you?"

"That I will, sir; God knows."

"Well, I say-as we're not quite good ourselves, it's just possible that things may be too good for us to do them the justice of believing in them."

"But there are things, you must allow, so plainly wrong!"

"So much so, both in the world and in myself, that it would be to me torturing despair to believe that God did not make the world; for then, how would it ever be put right? Therefore I prefer the theory that He has not done making it yet."

"But wouldn't you say, sir, that God might have managed it without so many slips in the making as your way would suppose? I should think myself a bad workman if I worked after that fashion."

"I do not believe that there are any slips. You know you are making a coffin; but are you sure you know what God is making of the world?"

"That I can't tell, of course, nor anybody else."

"Then you can't say that what looks like a slip is really a slip, either in the design or in the workmanship. You do not know what end He has in view; and you may find some day that those slips were just the straight road to that very end."

"Ah! maybe. But you can't be sure of it, you see."

"Perhaps not, in the way you mean; but sure enough, for all that, to try it upon life-to order my way by it, and so find that it works well. And I find that it explains everything that comes near it. You know that no engineer would be satisfied with his engine on paper, nor with any proof whatever except seeing how it will go."

He made no reply.

It is a principle of mine never to push anything over the edge. When I am successful, in any argument, my one dread is of humiliating my opponent. Indeed I cannot bear it. It humiliates me. And if you want him to think about anything, you must leave him room, and not give him such associations with the question that the very idea of it will be painful and irritating to him. Let him have a hand in the convincing of himself. I have been surprised sometimes to see my own arguments come up fresh and green, when I thought the fowls of the air had devoured them up. When a man reasons for victory and not for the truth in the other soul, he is sure of just one ally, the same that Faust had in fighting Gretchen's brother-that is, the Devil. But God and good men are against him. So I never follow up a victory of that kind, for, as I said, the defeat of the intellect is not the object in fighting with the sword of the Spirit, but the acceptance of the heart. In this case, therefore, I drew back.

"May I ask for whom you are making that coffin?"

"For a sister of my own, sir."

"I'm sorry to hear that."

"There's no occasion. I can't say I'm sorry, though she was one of the best women I ever knew."

"Why are you not sorry, then? Life's a good thing in the main, you will allow."

"Yes, when it's endurable at all. But to have a brute of a husband coming home at any hour of the night or morning, drunk upon the money she had earned by hard work, was enough to take more of the shine out of things than church-going on Sundays could put in again, regular as she was, poor woman! I'm as glad as her brute of a husband, that she's out of his way at last."

"How do you know he's glad of it?"

"He's been drunk every night since she died."

"Then he's the worse for losing her?"

"He may well be. Crying like a hypocrite, too, over his own work!"

"A fool he must be. A hypocrite, perhaps not. A hypocrite is a terrible name to give. Perhaps her death will do him good."

"He doesn't deserve to be done any good to. I would have made this coffin for him with a world of pleasure."

"I never found that I deserved anything, not even a coffin. The only claim that I could ever lay to anything was that I was very much in want of it."

The old smile returned-as much as to say, "That's your little game in the church." But I resolved to try nothing more with him at present; and indeed was sorry that I had started the new question at all, partly because thus I had again given him occasion to feel that he knew better than I did, which was not good either for him or for me in our relation to each other.

"This has been a fine old room once," I said, looking round the workshop.

"You can see it wasn't a workshop always, sir. Many a grand dinner-party has sat down in this room when it was in its glory. Look at the chimney-piece there."

"I have been looking at it," I said, going nearer.

"It represents the four quarters of the world, you see."

I saw strange figures of men and women, one on a kneeling camel, one on a crawling crocodile, and others differently mounted; with various besides of Nature's bizarre productions creeping and flying in stone-carving over the huge fire-place, in which, in place of a fire, stood several new and therefore brilliantly red cart-wheels. The sun shone through the upper part of a high window, of which many of the panes were broken, right in upon the cart-wheels, which, glowing thus in the chimney under the sombre chimney-piece, added to the grotesque look of the whole assemblage of contrasts. The coffin and the carpenter stood in the twilight occasioned by the sharp division of light made by a lofty wing of the house that rose flanking the other window. The room was still wainscotted in panels, which, I presume, for the sake of the more light required for handicraft, had been washed all over with white. At the level of labour they were broken in many places. Somehow or other, the whole reminded me of Albert Durer's "Melencholia."

Seeing I was interested in looking about his shop, my new friend-for I could not help feeling that we should be friends before all was over, and so began to count him one already-resumed the conversation. He had never taken up the dropped thread of it before.

"Yes, sir," he said; "the owners of the place little thought it would come to this-the deals growing into a coffin there on the spot where the grand dinner was laid for them and their guests! But there is another thing about it that is odder still; my son is the last male" —

Here he stopped suddenly, and his face grew very red. As suddenly he resumed —

"I'm not a gentleman, sir; but I will tell the truth. Curse it! —I beg your pardon, sir," —and here the old smile —"I don't think I got that from THEIR side of the house. —My son's NOT the last male descendant."

Here followed another pause.

As to the imprecation, I knew better than to take any notice of a mere expression of excitement under a sense of some injury with which I was not yet acquainted. If I could get his feelings right in regard to other and more important things, a reform in that matter would soon follow; whereas to make a mountain of a molehill would be to put that very mountain between him and me. Nor would I ask him any questions, lest I should just happen to ask him the wrong one; for this parishioner of mine evidently wanted careful handling, if I would do him any good. And it will not do any man good to fling even the Bible in his face. Nay, a roll of bank-notes, which would be more evidently a good to most men, would carry insult with it if presented in that manner. You cannot expect people to accept before they have had a chance of seeing what the offered gift really is.

After a pause, therefore, the carpenter had once more to recommence, or let the conversation lie. I stood in a waiting attitude. And while I looked at him, I was reminded of some one else whom I knew-with whom, too, I had pleasant associations-though I could not in the least determine who that one might be.

"It's very foolish of me to talk so to a stranger," he resumed.

"It is very kind and friendly of you," I said, still careful to make no advances. "And you yourself belong to the old family that once lived in this old house?"

"It would be no boast to tell the truth, sir, even if it were a credit to me, which it is not. That family has been nothing but a curse to ours."

I noted that he spoke of that family as different from his, and yet implied that he belonged to it. The explanation would come in time. But the man was again silent, planing away at half the lid of his sister's coffin. And I could not help thinking that the closed mouth meant to utter nothing more on this occasion.

"I am sure there must be many a story to tell about this old place, if only there were any one to tell them," I said at last, looking round the room once more. —"I think I see the remains of paintings on the ceiling."

"You are sharp-eyed, sir. My father says they were plain enough in his young days."

"Is your father alive, then?"

"That he is, sir, and hearty too, though he seldom goes out of doors now. Will you go up stairs and see him? He's past ninety, sir. He has plenty of stories to tell about the old place-before it began to fall to pieces like."

"I won't go to-day," I said, partly because I wanted to be at home to receive any one who might call, and partly to secure an excuse for calling again upon the carpenter sooner than I should otherwise have liked to do. "I expect visitors myself, and it is time I were at home. Good morning."

"Good morning, sir."

And away home I went with a new wonder in my brain. The man did not seem unknown to me. I mean, the state of his mind woke no feeling of perplexity in me. I was certain of understanding it thoroughly when I had learned something of his history; for that such a man must have a history of his own was rendered only the more probable from the fact that he knew something of the history of his forefathers, though, indeed, there are some men who seem to have no other. It was strange, however, to think of that man working away at a trade in the very house in which such ancestors had eaten and drunk, and married and given in marriage. The house and family had declined together-in outward appearance at least; for it was quite possible both might have risen in the moral and spiritual scale in proportion as they sank in the social one. And if any of my readers are at first inclined to think that this could hardly be, seeing that the man was little, if anything, better than an infidel, I would just like to hold one minute's conversation with them on that subject. A man may be on the way to the truth, just in virtue of his doubting. I will tell you what Lord Bacon says, and of all writers of English I delight in him: "So it is in contemplation: if a man will begin with certainties, he shall end in doubts; but if he will be content to begin with doubts, he shall end in certainties." Now I could not tell the kind or character of this man's doubt; but it was evidently real and not affected doubt; and that was much in his favour. And I couid see that he was a thinking man; just one of the sort I thought I should get on with in time, because he was honest-notwithstanding that unpleasant smile of his, which did irritate me a little, and partly piqued me into the determination to get the better of the man, if I possibly could, by making friends with him. At all events, here was another strange parishioner. And who could it be that he was like?

CHAPTER V
VISITORS FROM THE HALL.

When I came near my own gate, I saw that it was open; and when I came in sight of my own door, I found a carriage standing before it, and a footman ringing the bell. It was an old-fashioned carriage, with two white horses in it, yet whiter by age than by nature. They looked as if no coachman could get more than three miles an hour out of them, they were so fat and knuckle-kneed. But my attention could not rest long on the horses, and I reached the door just as my housekeeper was pronouncing me absent. There were two ladies in the carriage, one old and one young.

"Ah, here is Mr. Walton!" said the old lady, in a serene voice, with a clear hardness in its tone; and I held out my hand to aid her descent. She had pulled off her glove to get a card out of her card-case, and so put the tips of two old fingers, worn very smooth, as if polished with feeling what things were like, upon the palm of my hand. I then offered my hand to her companion, a girl apparently about fourteen, who took a hearty hold of it, and jumped down beside her with a smile. As I followed them into the house, I took their card from the housekeeper's hand, and read, Mrs Oldcastle and Miss Gladwyn.

I confess here to my reader, that these are not really the names I read on the card. I made these up this minute. But the names of the persons of humble position in my story are their real names. And my reason for making the difference will be plain enough. You can never find out my friend Old Rogers; you might find out the people who called on me in their carriage with the ancient white horses.

When they were seated in the drawing-room, I said to the old lady —

"I remember seeing you in church on Sunday morning. It is very kind of you to call so soon."

"You will always see me in church," she returned, with a stiff bow, and an expansion of deadness on her face, which I interpreted into an assertion of dignity, resulting from the implied possibility that I might have passed her over in my congregation, or might have forgotten her after not passing her over.

"Except when you have a headache, grannie," said Miss Gladwyn, with an arch look first at her grandmother, and then at me. "Grannie has bad headaches sometimes."

The deadness melted a little from Mrs Oldcastle's face, as she turned with half a smile to her grandchild, and said —

"Yes, Pet. But you know that cannot be an interesting fact to Mr. Walton."

"I beg your pardon, Mrs. Oldcastle," I said. "A clergyman ought to know something, and the more the better, of the troubles of his flock. Sympathy is one of the first demands he ought to be able to meet — I know what a headache is."

The former expression, or rather non-expression, returned; this time unaccompanied by a bow.

"I trust, Mr. Walton, I TRUST I am above any morbid necessity for sympathy. But, as you say, amongst the poor of your flock, — it IS very desirable that a clergyman should be able to sympathise."

"It's quite true what grannie says, Mr. Walton, though you mightn't think it. When she has a headache, she shuts herself up in her own room, and doesn't even let me come near her-nobody but Sarah; and how she can prefer her to me, I'm sure I don't know."

And here the girl pretended to pout, but with a sparkle in her bright gray eye.

"The subject is not interesting to me, Pet. Pray, Mr. Walton, is it a point of conscience with you to wear the surplice when you preach?"

"Not in the least," I answered. "I think I like it rather better on the whole. But that's not why I wear it."

"Never mind grannie, Mr. Walton. *I* think the surplice is lovely. I'm sure it's much liker the way we shall be dressed in heaven, though I don't think I shall ever get there, if I must read the good books grannie reads."

"I don't know that it is necessary to read any good books but the good book," I said.

"There, grannie!" exclaimed Miss Gladwyn, triumphantly. "I'm so glad I've got Mr Walton on my side!"

"Mr Walton is not so old as I am, my dear, and has much to learn yet."

I could not help feeling a little annoyed, (which was very foolish, I know,) and saying to myself, "If it's to make me like you, I had rather not learn any more;" but I said nothing aloud, of course.

"Have you got a headache to-day, grannie?"

"No, Pet. Be quiet. I wish to ask Mr Walton WHY he wears the surplice."

"Simply," I replied, "because I was told the people had been accustomed to it under my predecessor."

"But that can be no good reason for doing what is not right-that people have been accustomed to it."

"But I don't allow that it's not right. I think it is a matter of no consequence whatever. If I find that the people don't like it, I will give it up with pleasure."

"You ought to have principles of your own, Mr Walton."

"I hope I have. And one of them is, not to make mountains of molehills; for a molehill is not a mountain. A man ought to have too much to do in obeying his conscience and keeping his soul's garments clean, to mind whether he wears black or white when telling his flock that God loves them, and that they will never be happy till they believe it."

"They may believe that too soon."

"I don't think any one can believe the truth too soon."

A pause followed, during which it became evident to me that Miss Gladwyn saw fun in the whole affair, and was enjoying it thoroughly. Mrs Oldcastle's face, on the contrary, was illegible. She resumed in a measured still voice, which she meant to be meek, I daresay, but which was really authoritative —

"I am sorry, Mr Walton, that your principles are so loose and unsettled. You will see my honesty in saying so when you find that, objecting to the surplice, as I do, on Protestant grounds, I yet warn you against making any change because you may discover that your parishioners are against it. You have no idea, Mr Walton, what inroads Radicalism, as they call it, has been making in this neighbourhood. It is quite dreadful. Everybody, down to the poorest, claiming a right to think for himself, and set his betters right! There's one worse than any of the rest-but he's no better than an atheist —a carpenter of the name of Weir, always talking to his neighbours against the proprietors and the magistrates, and the clergy too, Mr Walton, and the game-laws; and what not? And if you once show them that you are afraid of them by going a step out of your way for THEIR opinion about anything, there will be no end to it; for, the beginning of strife is like the letting out of water, as you know. *I* should know nothing about it, but that, my daughter's maid —I came to hear of it through her —a decent girl of the name of Rogers, and born of decent parents, but unfortunately attached to the son of one of your churchwardens, who has put him into that mill on the river you can almost see from here."

"Who put him in the mill?"

"His own father, to whom it belongs."

"Well, it seems to me a very good match for her."

"Yes, indeed, and for him too. But his foolish father thinks the match below him, as if there was any difference between the positions of people in that rank of life! Every one seems striving to tread on the heels of every one else, instead of being content with the station to which God has called them. I am content with mine. I had nothing to do with putting myself there. Why should they not be content with theirs? They need to be taught Christian humility and respect for their superiors. That's the virtue most wanted at present. The poor have to look up to the rich" —

"That's right, grannie! And the rich have to look down on the poor."

"No, my dear. I did not say that. The rich have to be KIND to the poor."

"But, grannie, why did you marry Mr Oldcastle?"

"What does the child mean?"

"Uncle Stoddart says you refused ever so many offers when you were a girl."

"Uncle Stoddart has no business to be talking about such things to a chit like you," returned the grandmother smiling, however, at the charge, which so far certainly contained no reproach.

"And grandpapa was the ugliest and the richest of them all-wasn't he, grannie? and Colonel Markham the handsomest and the poorest?"

A flush of anger crimsoned the old lady's pale face. It looked dead no longer.

"Hold your tongue," she said. "You are rude."

And Miss Gladwyn did hold her tongue, but nothing else, for she was laughing all over.

The relation between these two was evidently a very odd one. It was clear that Miss Gladwyn was a spoiled child, though I could not help thinking her very nicely spoiled, as far as I saw; and that the old lady persisted in regarding her as a cub, although her claws had grown quite long enough to be dangerous. Certainly, if things went on thus, it was pretty clear which of them would soon have the upper hand, for grannie was vulnerable, and Pet was not.

It really began to look as if there were none but characters in my parish. I began to think it must be the strangest parish in England, and to wonder that I had never heard of it before. "Surely it must be in some story-book at least!" I said to myself.

But her grand-daughter's tiger-cat-play drove the old lady nearer to me. She rose and held out her hand, saying, with some kindness—

"Take my advice, my dear Mr Walton, and don't make too much of your poor, or they'll soon be too much for you to manage.—Come, Pet: it's time to go home to lunch.—And for the surplice, take your own way and wear it. *I* shan't say anything more about it."

"I will do what I can see to be right in the matter," I answered as gently as I could; for I did not want to quarrel with her, although I thought her both presumptuous and rude.

"I'm on your side, Mr Walton," said the girl, with a sweet comical smile, as she squeezed my hand once more.

I led them to the carriage, and it was with a feeling of relief that I saw it drive off.

The old lady certainly was not pleasant. She had a white smooth face over which the skin was drawn tight, gray hair, and rather lurid hazel eyes. I felt a repugnance to her that was hardly to be accounted for by her arrogance to me, or by her superciliousness to the poor; although either would have accounted for much of it. For I confess that I have not yet learned to bear presumption and rudeness with all the patience and forgiveness with which I ought by this time to be able to meet them. And as to the poor, I am afraid I was always in some danger of being a partizan of theirs against the rich; and that a clergyman ought never to be. And indeed the poor rich have more need of the care of the clergyman than the others, seeing it is hardly that the rich shall enter into the kingdom of heaven, and the poor have all the advantage over them in that respect.

"Still," I said to myself, "there must be some good in the woman-she cannot be altogether so hard as she looks, else how should that child dare to take the liberties of a kitten with her? She doesn't look to ME like one to make game of! However, I shall know a little more about her when I return her call, and I will do my best to keep on good terms with her."

I took down a volume of Plato to comfort me after the irritation which my nerves had undergone, and sat down in an easy-chair beside the open window of my study. And with Plato in my hand, and all that outside my window, I began to feel as if, after all, a man might be happy, even if a lady had refused him. And there I sat, without opening my favourite vellum-bound volume, gazing out on the happy world, whence a gentle wind came in, as if to bid me welcome with a kiss to all it had to give me. And then I thought of the wind that bloweth where it listeth, which is everywhere, and I quite forgot to open my Plato, and thanked God for the Life of life, whose story and whose words are in that best of books, and who explains everything to us, and makes us love Socrates and David and all good men ten times more; and who follows no law but the law of love, and no fashion but the will of God; for where did ever one read words less like moralising and more like simple earnestness of truth than all those of Jesus? And I prayed my God that He would make me able to speak good common heavenly sense to my people, and forgive me for feeling so cross and proud towards the unhappy old lady-for I was sure she was not happy-and make me into a rock which swallowed up the waves of wrong in its great caverns, and never threw them back to swell the commotion of the angry sea whence they came. Ah, what it would be actually to annihilate wrong in this way! —to be able to say, it shall not be wrong against me, so utterly do I forgive it! How much sooner, then, would the wrong-doer repent, and get rid of the wrong from his side also! But the painful fact will show itself, not less curious than painful, that it is more difficult to forgive small wrongs than great ones. Perhaps, however, the forgiveness of the great wrongs is not so true as it seems. For do we not think it is a fine thing to forgive such wrongs, and so do it rather for our own sakes than for the sake of the wrongdoer? It is dreadful not to be good, and to have bad ways inside one.

Such thoughts passed through my mind. And once more the great light went up on me with regard to my office, namely, that just because I was parson to the parish, I must not be THE PERSON to myself. And I prayed God to keep me from feeling STUNG and proud, however any one might behave to me; for all my value lay in being a sacrifice to Him and the people.

So when Mrs Pearson knocked at the door, and told me that a lady and gentleman had called, I shut my book which I had just opened, and kept down as well as I could the rising grumble of the inhospitable Englishman, who is apt to be forgetful to entertain strangers, at least in the parlour of his heart. And I cannot count it perfect hospitality to be friendly and plentiful towards those whom you have invited to your house-what thank has a man in that? —while you are cold and forbidding to those who have not that claim on your attention. That is not to be perfect as our Father in heaven is perfect. By all means tell people, when you are busy about something that must be done, that you cannot spare the time for them except they want you upon something of yet more pressing necessity; but TELL them, and do not get rid of them by the use of the instrument commonly called THE COLD SHOULDER. It is a wicked instrument that, and ought to have fallen out of use by this time.

I went and received Mr and Miss Boulderstone, and was at least thus far rewarded-that the EERIE feeling, as the Scotch would call it, which I had about my parish, as containing none but CHARACTERS, and therefore not being CANNIE, was entirely removed. At least there was a wholesome leaven in it of honest stupidity. Please, kind reader, do not fancy I am sneering. I declare to you I think a sneer the worst thing God has not made. A curse is nothing in wickedness to it, it seems to me. I do mean that honest stupidity I respect heartily, and do assert my conviction that I do not know how England at least would get on without it. But I do not mean the stupidity that sets up for teaching itself to its neighbour, thinking itself wisdom all the time. That I do not respect.

Mr and Miss Boulderstone left me a little fatigued, but in no way sore or grumbling. They only sent me back with additional zest to my Plato, of which I enjoyed a hearty page or two before any one else arrived. The only other visitors I had that day were an old surgeon in the navy, who since his retirement had practised for many years in the neighbourhood, and was still at the call of any one who did not think him too old-fashioned —for even here the fashions, though decidedly elderly young ladies by the time they arrived, held their sway none the less imperiously-and Mr Brownrigg, the churchwarden. More of Dr Duncan by and by.

Except Mr and Miss Boulderstone, I had not yet seen any common people. They were all decidedly uncommon, and, as regarded most of them, I could not think I should have any difficulty in preaching to them. For, whatever place a man may give to preaching in the ritual of the church-indeed it does not properly belong to the ritual at all-it is yet the part of the so-called service with which his personality has most to do. To the influences of the other parts he has to submit himself, ever turning the openings of his soul towards them, that he may not be a mere praying-machine; but with the sermon it is otherwise. That he produces. For that he is responsible. And therefore, I say, it was a great comfort to me to find myself amongst a people from which my spirit neither shrunk in the act of preaching, nor with regard to which it was likely to feel that it was beating itself against a stone wall. There was some good in preaching to a man like Weir or Old Rogers. Whether there was any good in preaching to a woman like Mrs Oldcastle I did not know.

The evening I thought I might give to my books, and thus end my first Monday in my parish; but, as I said, Mr Brownrigg, the churchwarden, called and stayed a whole weary hour, talking about matters quite uninteresting to any who may hereafter peruse what I am now writing. Really he was not an interesting man: short, broad, stout, red-faced, with an immense amount of mental inertia, discharging itself in constant lingual activity about little nothings. Indeed, when there was no new nothing to be had, the old nothing would do over again to make a fresh fuss about. But if you attempted to convey a thought into his mind which involved the moving round half a degree from where he stood, and looking at the matter from a point even so far new, you found him utterly, totally impenetrable, as pachydermatous as any rhinoceros or behemoth. One other corporeal fact I could not help observing, was, that his cheeks rose at once from the collar of his green coat, his neck being invisible, from the hollow between it and the jaw being filled up to a level. The conformation was just what he himself delighted to contemplate in his pigs, to which his resemblance was greatly increased by unwearied endeavours to keep himself close shaved. —I could not help feeling anxious about his son and Jane Rogers. —He gave a quantity of gossip about various people, evidently anxious that I should regard them as he regarded them; but in all he said concerning them I could scarcely detect one point of significance as to character or history. I was very glad indeed when the waddling of hands-for it was the perfect imbecility of hand-shaking —was over, and he was safely out of the gate. He had kept me standing on the steps for full five minutes, and I did not feel safe from him till I was once more in my study with the door shut.

I am not going to try my reader's patience with anything of a more detailed account of my introduction to my various parishioners. I shall mention them only as they come up in the course of my story. Before many days had passed I had found out my poor, who, I thought, must be somewhere, seeing the Lord had said we should have them with us always. There was a workhouse in the village, but there were not a great many in it; for the poor were kindly enough handled who belonged to the place, and were not too severely compelled to go into the house; though, I believe, in this house they would have been more comfortable than they were in their own houses.

I cannot imagine a much greater misfortune for a man, not to say a clergyman, than not to know, or knowing, not to minister to any of the poor. And I did not feel that I knew in the least where I was until I had found out and conversed with almost the whole of mine.

After I had done so, I began to think it better to return Mrs Oldcastle's visit, though I felt greatly disinclined to encounter that tight-skinned nose again, and that mouth whose smile had no light in it, except when it responded to some nonsense of her grand-daughter's.

CHAPTER VI
OLDCASTLE HALL.

About noon, on a lovely autumn day, I set out for Oldcastle Hall. The keenness of the air had melted away with the heat of the sun, yet still the air was fresh and invigorating. Can any one tell me why it is that, when the earth is renewing her youth in the spring, man should feel feeble and low-spirited, and gaze with bowed head, though pleased heart, on the crocuses; whereas, on the contrary, in the autumn, when nature is dying for the winter, he feels strong and hopeful, holds his head erect, and walks with a vigorous step, though the flaunting dahlias discourage him greatly? I do not ask for the physical causes: those I might be able to find out for myself; but I ask, Where is the rightness and fitness in the thing? Should not man and nature go together in this world which was made for man-not for science, but for man? Perhaps I have some glimmerings of where the answer lies. Perhaps "I see a cherub that sees it." And in many of our questions we have to be content with such an approximation to an answer as this. And for my part I am content with this. With less, I am not content.

Whatever that answer may be, I walked over the old Gothic bridge with a heart strong enough to meet Mrs Oldcastle without flinching. I might have to quarrel with her—I could not tell: she certainly was neither safe nor wholesome. But this I was sure of, that I would not quarrel with her without being quite certain that I ought. I wish it were NEVER one's duty to quarrel with anybody: I do so hate it. But not to do it sometimes is to smile in the devil's face, and that no one ought to do. However, I had not to quarrel this time.

The woods on the other side of the river from my house, towards which I was now walking, were of the most sombre rich colour-sombre and rich, like a life that has laid up treasure in heaven, locked in a casket of sorrow. I came nearer and nearer to them through the village, and approached the great iron gate with the antediluvian monsters on the top of its stone pillars. And awful monsters they were-are still! I see the tail of one of them at this very moment. But they let me through very quietly, notwithstanding their evil looks. I thought they were saying to each other across the top of the gate, "Never mind; he'll catch it soon enough." But, as I said, I did not catch it that day; and I could not have caught it that day; it was too lovely a day to catch any hurt even from that most hurtful of all beings under the sun, an unwomanly woman.

I wandered up the long winding road, through the woods which I had remarked flanking the meadow on my first walk up the river. These woods smelt so sweetly-their dead and dying leaves departing in sweet odours-that they quite made up for the absence of the flowers. And the wind-no, there was no wind-there was only a memory of wind that woke now and then in the bosom of the wood, shook down a few leaves, like the thoughts that flutter away in sighs, and then was still again.

I am getting old, as I told you, my friends. (See there, you seem my friends already. Do not despise an old man because he cannot help loving people he never saw or even heard of.) I say I am getting old—(is it BUT or THEREFORE? I do not know which)—but, therefore, I shall never forget that one autumn day in those grandly fading woods.

Up the slope of the hillside they rose like one great rainbow-billow of foliage-bright yellow, red-rusty and bright fading green, all kinds and shades of brown and purple. Multitudes of leaves lay on the sides of the path, so many that I betook myself to my old childish amusement of walking in them without lifting my feet, driving whole armies of them with ocean-like rustling before me. I did not do so as I came back. I walked in the middle of the way then, and I remember stepping over many single leaves, in a kind of mechanico-merciful way, as if they had been living creatures-as indeed who can tell but they are, only they must be pretty nearly dead when they are on the ground.

At length the road brought me up to the house. It did not look such a large house as I have since found it to be. And it certainly was not an interesting house from the outside, though its surroundings of green grass and trees would make any whole beautiful. Indeed the house itself tried hard to look ugly, not quite succeeding, only because of the kind foiling of its efforts by the Virginia creepers and ivy, which, as if ashamed of its staring countenance, did all they could to spread their hands over it and hide it. But there was one charming group of old chimneys, belonging to some portion behind, which indicated a very different, namely, a very much older, face upon the house once —a face that had passed away to give place to this. Once inside, I found there were more remains of the olden time than I had expected. I was led up one of those grand square oak staircases, which look like a portion of the house to be dwelt in, and not like a ladder for getting from one part of the habitable regions to another. On the top was a fine expanse of landing, another hall, in fact, from which I was led towards the back of the house by a narrow passage, and shown into a small dark drawing-room with a deep stone-mullioned window, wainscoted in oak simply carved and panelled. Several doors around indicated communication with other parts of the house. Here I found Mrs Oldcastle, reading what I judged to be one of the cheap and gaudy religious books of the present day. She rose and RECEIVED me, and having motioned me to a seat, began to talk about the parish. You would have perceived at once from her tone that she recognised no other bond of connexion between us but the parish.

"I hear you have been most kind in visiting the poor, Mr Walton. You must take care that they don't take advantage of your kindness, though. I assure you, you will find some of them very grasping indeed. And you need not expect that they will give you the least credit for good intentions."

"I have seen nothing yet to make me uneasy on that score. But certainly my testimony is of no weight yet."

"Mine is. I have proved them. The poor of this neighbourhood are very deficient in gratitude."

"Yes, grannie, — —"

I started. But there was no interruption, such as I have made to indicate my surprise; although, when I looked half round in the direction whence the voice came, the words that followed were all rippled with a sweet laugh of amusement.

"Yes, grannie, you are right. You remember how old dame Hope wouldn't take the money you offered her, and dropped such a disdainful courtesy. It was SO greedy of her, wasn't it?"

"I am sorry to hear of any disdainful reception of kindness," I said.

"Yes, and she had the coolness, within a fortnight, to send up to me and ask if I would be kind enough to lend her half-a-crown for a few weeks."

"And then it was your turn, grannie! You sent her five shillings, didn't you? —Oh no; I'm wrong. That was the other woman."

"Indeed, I did not send her anything but a rebuke. I told her that it would be a very wrong thing in me to contribute to the support of such an evil spirit of unthankfulness as she indulged in. When she came to see her conduct in its true light, and confessed that she had behaved very abominably, I would see what I could do for her."

"And meantime she was served out, wasn't she? With her sick boy at home, and nothing to give him?" said Miss Gladwyn.

"She made her own bed, and had to lie on it."

"Don't you think a little kindness might have had more effect in bringing her to see that she was wrong."

"Grannie doesn't believe in kindness, except to me-dear old grannie! She spoils me. I'm sure I shall be ungrateful some day; and then she'll begin to read me long lectures, and prick me with all manner of headless pins. But I won't stand it, I can tell you, grannie! I'm too much spoiled for that."

Mrs Oldcastle was silent-why, I could not tell, except it was that she knew she had no chance of quieting the girl in any other way.

I may mention here, lest I should have no opportunity afterwards, that I inquired of dame Hope as to her version of the story, and found that there had been a great misunderstanding, as I had suspected. She was really in no want at the time, and did not feel that it would be quite honourable to take the money when she did not need it—(some poor people ARE capable of such reasoning)—and so had refused it, not without a feeling at the same time that it was more pleasant to refuse than to accept from such a giver; some stray sparkle of which feeling, discovered by the keen eye of Miss Gladwyn, may have given that appearance of disdain to her courtesy to which the girl alluded. When, however, her boy in service was brought home ill, she had sent to ask for what she now required, on the very ground that it had been offered to her before. The misunderstanding had arisen from the total incapacity of Mrs Oldcastle to enter sympathetically into the feelings of one as superior to herself in character as she was inferior in worldly condition.

But to return to Oldcastle Hall.

I wished to change the subject, knowing that blind defence is of no use. One must have definite points for defence, if one has not a thorough understanding of the character in question; and I had neither.

"This is a beautiful old house," I said. "There must be strange places about it."

Mrs Oldcastle had not time to reply, or at least did not reply, before Miss Gladwyn said—

"Oh, Mr Walton, have you looked out of the window yet? You don't know what a lovely place this is, if you haven't."

And as she spoke she emerged from a recess in the room, a kind of dark alcove, where she had been amusing herself with what I took to be some sort of puzzle, but which I found afterwards to be the bit and curb-chain of her pony's bridle which she was polishing up to her own bright mind, because the stable-boy had not pleased her in the matter, and she wanted both to get them brilliant and to shame the lad for the future. I followed her to the window, where I was indeed as much surprised and pleased as she could have wished.

"There!" she said, holding back one of the dingy heavy curtains with her small childish hand.

And there, indeed, I saw an astonishment. It did not lie in the lovely sweeps of hill and hollow stretching away to the horizon, richly wooded, and-though I saw none of them-sprinkled, certainly with sweet villages full of human thoughts, loves, and hopes; the astonishment did not lie in this-though all this was really much more beautiful to the higher imagination-but in the fact that, at the first glance, I had a vision properly belonging to a rugged or mountainous country. For I had approached the house by a gentle slope, which certainly was long and winding, but had occasioned no feeling in my mind that I had reached any considerable height. And I had come up that one beautiful staircase; no more; and yet now, when I looked from this window, I found myself on the edge of a precipice-not a very deep one, certainly, yet with all the effect of many a deeper. For below the house on this side lay a great hollow, with steep sides, up which, as far as they could reach, the trees were climbing. The sides were not all so steep as the one on which the house stood, but they were all rocky and steep, with here and there slopes of green grass. And down in the bottom, in the centre of the hollow, lay a pool of water. I knew it only by its slaty shimmer through the fading green of the tree-tops between me and it.

"There!" again exclaimed Miss Gladwyn; "isn't that beautiful? But you haven't seen the most beautiful thing yet. Grannie, where's—ah! there she is! There's auntie! Don't you see her down there, by the side of the pond? That pond is a hundred feet deep. If auntie were to fall in she would be drowned before you could jump down to get her out. Can you swim?"

Before I had time to answer, she was off again.

"Don't you see auntie down there?"

"No, I don't see her. I have been trying very hard, but I can't."

"Well, I daresay you can't. Nobody, I think, has got eyes but myself. Do you see a big stone by the edge of the pond, with another stone on the top of it, like a big potato with a little one grown out of it?"

"No."

"Well, auntie is under the trees on the opposite side from that stone. Do you see her yet?"

"No."

"Then you must come down with me, and I will introduce you to her. She's much the prettiest thing here. Much prettier than grannie."

Here she looked over her shoulder at grannie, who, instead of being angry, as, from what I had seen on our former interview, I feared she would be, only said, without even looking up from the little blue-boarded book she was again reading—

"You are a saucy child."

Whereupon Miss Gladwyn laughed merrily.

"Come along," she said, and, seizing me by the hand, led me out of the room, down a back-staircase, across a piece of grass, and then down a stair in the face of the rock, towards the pond below. The stair went in zigzags, and, although rough, was protected by an iron balustrade, without which, indeed, it would have been very dangerous.

"Isn't your grandmamma afraid to let you run up and down here, Miss Gladwyn?" I said.

"Me!" she exclaimed, apparently in the utmost surprise. "That WOULD be fun! For, you know, if she tried to hinder me-but she knows it's no use; I taught her that long ago-let me see, how long: oh! I don't know—I should think it must be ten years at least. I ran away, and they thought I had drowned myself in the pond. And I saw them, all the time, poking with a long stick in the pond, which, if I had been drowned there, never could have brought me up, for it is a hundred feet deep, I am sure. How I hurt my sides trying to keep from screaming with laughter! I fancied I heard one say to the other, 'We must wait till she swells and floats?'"

"Dear me! what a peculiar child!" I said to myself.

And yet somehow, whatever she said-even when she was most rude to her grandmother-she was never offensive. No one could have helped feeling all the time that she was a little lady. —I thought I would venture a question with her. I stood still at a turn of the zigzag, and looked down into the hollow, still a good way below us, where I could now distinguish the form, on the opposite side of the pond, of a woman seated at the foot of a tree, and stooping forward over a book.

"May I ask you a question, Miss Gladwyn?"

"Yes, twenty, if you like; but I won't answer one of them till you give up calling me Miss Gladwyn. We can't be friends, you know, so long as you do that."

"What am I to call you, then? I never heard you called by any other name than Pet, and that would hardly do, would it?"

"Oh, just fancy if you called me Pet before grannie! That's grannie's name for me, and nobody dares to use it but grannie-not even auntie; for, between you and me, auntie is afraid of grannie; I can't think why. I never was afraid of anybody-except, yes, a little afraid of old Sarah. She used to be my nurse, you know; and grandmamma and everybody is afraid of her, and that's just why I never do one thing she wants me to do. It would never do to give in to being afraid of her, you know. —There's auntie, you see, down there, just where I told you before."

"Oh yes! I see her now. —What does your aunt call you, then?"

"Why, what you must call me-my own name, of course."

"What is that?"

"Judy."

She said it in a tone which seemed to indicate surprise that I should not know her name-perhaps read it off her face, as one ought to know a flower's name by looking at it. But she added instantly, glancing up in my face most comically—

"I wish yours was Punch."

"Why, Judy?"

"It would be such fun, you know."

"Well, it would be odd, I must confess. What is your aunt's name?"

"Oh, such a funny name! —much funnier than Judy: Ethelwyn. It sounds as if it ought to mean something, doesn't it?"

"Yes. It is an Anglo-Saxon word, without doubt."

"What does it mean?"

"I'm not sure about that. I will try to find out when I go home-if you would like to know."

"Yes, that I should. I should like to know everything about auntie Ethelwyn. Isn't it pretty?"

"So pretty that I should like to know something more about Aunt Ethelwyn. What is her other name?"

"Why, Ethelwyn Oldcastle, to be sure. What else could it be?"

"Why, you know, for anything I knew, Judy, it might have been Gladwyn. She might have been your father's sister."

"Might she? I never thought of that. Oh, I suppose that is because I never think about my father. And now I do think of it, I wonder why nobody ever mentions him to me, or my mother either. But I often think auntie must be thinking about my mother. Something in her eyes, when they are sadder than usual, seems to remind me of my mother."

"You remember your mother, then?"

"No, I don't think I ever saw her. But I've answered plenty of questions, haven't I? I assure you, if you want to get me on to the Catechism, I don't know a word of it. Come along."

I laughed.

"What!" she said, pulling me by the hand, "you a clergyman, and laugh at the Catechism! I didn't know that."

"I'm not laughing at the Catechism, Judy. I'm only laughing at the idea of putting Catechism questions to you."

"You KNOW I didn't mean it," she said, with some indignation.

"I know now," I answered. "But you haven't let me put the only question I wanted to put."

"What is it?"

"How old are you?"

"Twelve. Come along."

And away we went down the rest of the stair.

When we reached the bottom, a winding path led us through the trees to the side of the pond, along which we passed to get to the other side.

And then all at once the thought struck me-why was it that I had never seen this auntie, with the lovely name, at church? Was she going to turn out another strange parishioner?

There she sat, intent on her book. As we drew near she looked up and rose, but did not come forward.

"Aunt Winnie, here's Mr. Walton," said Judy.

I lifted my hat and held out my hand. Before our hands met, however, a tremendous splash reached my ears from the pond. I started round. Judy had vanished. I had my coat half off, and was rushing to the pool, when Miss Oldcastle stopped me, her face unmoved, except by a smile, saying, "It's only one of that frolicsome child's tricks, Mr Walton. It is well for you that I was here, though. Nothing would have delighted her more than to have you in the water too."

"But," I said, bewildered, and not half comprehending, "where is she?"

"There," returned Miss Oldcastle, pointing to the pool, in the middle of which arose a heaving and bubbling, presently yielding passage to the laughing face of Judy.

"Why don't you help me out, Mr Walton? You said you could swim."

"No, I did not," I answered coolly. "You talked so fast, you did not give me time to say so."

"It's very cold," she returned.

"Come out, Judy dear," said her aunt. "Run home and change your clothes. There's a dear."

Judy swam to the opposite side, scrambled out, and was off like a spaniel through the trees and up the stairs, dripping and raining as she went.

"You must be very much astonished at the little creature, Mr Walton."

"I find her very interesting. Quite a study."

"There never was a child so spoiled, and never a child on whom it took less effect to hurt her. I suppose such things do happen sometimes. She is really a good girl; though mamma, who has done all the spoiling, will not allow me to say she is good."

Here followed a pause, for, Judy disposed of, what should I say next? And the moment her mind turned from Judy, I saw a certain stillness-not a cloud, but the shadow of a cloud-come over Miss Oldcastle's face, as if she, too, found herself uncomfortable, and did not know what to say next. I tried to get a glance at the book in her hand, for I should know something about her at once if I could only see what she was reading. She never came to church, and I wanted to arrive at some notion of the source of her spiritual life; for that she had such, a single glance at her face was enough to convince me. This, I mean, made me even anxious to see what the book was. But I could only discover that it was an old book in very shabby binding, not in the least like the books that young ladies generally have in their hands.

And now my readers will possibly be thinking it odd that I have never yet said a word about what either Judy or Miss Oldcastle was like. If there is one thing I feel more inadequate to than another, in taking upon me to relate-it is to describe a lady. But I will try the girl first.

Judy was rosy, gray-eyed, auburn-haired, sweet-mouthed. She had confidence in her chin, assertion in her nose, defiance in her eyebrows, honesty and friendliness over all her face. No one, evidently, could have a warmer friend; and to an enemy she would be dangerous no longer than a fit of passion might last. There was nothing acrid in her; and the reason, I presume, was, that she had never yet hurt her conscience. That is a very different thing from saying she had never done wrong, you know. She was not tall, even for her age, and just a little too plump for the immediate suggestion of grace. Yet every motion of the child would have been graceful, except for the fact that impulse was always predominant, giving a certain jerkiness, like the hopping of a bird, instead of the gliding of one motion into another, such as you might see in the same bird on the wing.

There is one of the ladies.

But the other-how shall I attempt to describe her?

The first thing I felt was, that she was a lady-woman. And to feel that is almost to fall in love at first sight. And out of this whole, the first thing you distinguished would be the grace over all. She was rather slender, rather tall, rather dark-haired, and quite blue-eyed. But I assure you it was not upon that occasion that I found out the colour of her eyes. I was so taken with her whole that I knew nothing about her parts. Yet she was blue-eyed, indicating northern extraction-some centuries back perhaps. That blue was the blue of the sea that had sunk through the eyes of some sea-rover's wife and settled in those of her child, to be born when the voyage was over. It had been dyed so deep INGRAYNE, as Spenser would say, that it had never been worn from the souls of the race since, and so was every now and then shining like heaven out at some of its eyes. Her features were what is called regular. They were delicate and brave. —After the grace, the dignity was the next thing you came to discover. And the only thing you would not have liked, you would have discovered last. For when the shine of the courtesy with which she received me had faded away a certain look of negative haughtiness, of withdrawal, if not of repulsion, took its place, a look of consciousness of her own high breeding —a pride, not of life, but of circumstance of life, which disappointed me in the midst of so much that was very lovely. Her voice was sweet, and I could have fancied a tinge of sadness in it, to which impression her slowness of speech, without any drawl in it, contributed. But I am not doing well as an artist in describing her so fully before my reader has become in the least degree interested in her. I was seeing her, and no words can make him see her.

Fearing lest some such fancy as had possessed Judy should be moving in her mind, namely, that I was, if not exactly going to put her through her Catechism, yet going in some way or other to act the clergyman, I hastened to speak.

"This is a most romantic spot, Miss Oldcastle," I said; "and as surprising as it is romantic. I could hardly believe my eyes when I looked out of the window and saw it first."

"Your surprise was the more natural that the place itself is not properly natural, as you must have discovered."

This was rather a remarkable speech for a young lady to make. I answered —

"I only know that such a chasm is the last thing I should have expected to find in this gently undulating country. That it is artificial I was no more prepared to hear than I was to see the place itself."

"It looks pretty, but it has not a very poetic origin," she returned. "It is nothing but the quarry out of which the old house at the top of it was built."

"I must venture to differ from you entirely in the aspect such an origin assumes to me," I said. "It seems to me a more poetic origin than any convulsion of nature whatever would have been; for, look you," I said-being as a young man too much inclined to the didactic, "for, look you," I said-and she did look at me —"from that buried mass of rock has arisen this living house with its histories of ages and generations; and" —

Here I saw a change pass upon her face: it grew almost pallid. But her large blue eyes were still fixed on mine.

"And it seems to me," I went on, "that such a chasm made by the uplifting of a house therefrom, is therefore in itself more poetic than if it were even the mouth of an extinct volcano. For, grand as the motions and deeds of Nature are, terrible as is the idea of the fiery heart of the earth breaking out in convulsions, yet here is something greater; for human will, human thought, human hands in human labour and effort, have all been employed to build this house, making not only the house beautiful, but the place whence it came beautiful too. It stands on the edge of what Shelley would call its 'antenatal tomb' —now beautiful enough to be its mother-filled from generation to generation " —

Her face had grown still paler, and her lips moved as if she would speak; but no sound came from them. I had gone on, thinking it best to take no notice of her paleness; but now I could not help expressing concern.

"I am afraid you feel ill, Miss Oldcastle."

"Not at all," she answered, more quickly than she had yet spoken.

"This place must be damp," I said. "I fear you have taken cold."

She drew herself up a little haughtily, thinking, no doubt, that after her denial I was improperly pressing the point. So I drew back to the subject of our conversation.

"But I can hardly think," I said, "that all this mass of stone could be required to build the house, large as it is. A house is not solid, you know."

"No," she answered. "The original building was more of a castle, with walls and battlements. I can show you the foundations of them still; and the picture, too, of what the place used to be. We are not what we were then. Many a cottage, too, has been built out of this old quarry. Not a stone has been taken from it for the last fifty years, though. Just let me show you one thing, Mr. Walton, and then I must leave you."

"Do not let me detain you a moment. I will go at once," I said; "though, if you would allow me, I should be more at ease if I might see you safe at the top of the stair first."

She smiled.

"Indeed, I am not ill," she answered; "but I have duties to attend to. Just let me show you this, and then you shall go with me back to mamma."

She led the way to the edge of the pond and looked into it. I followed, and gazed down into its depths, till my sight was lost in them. I could see no bottom to the rocky shaft.

"There is a strong spring down there," she said. "Is it not a dreadful place? Such a depth!"

"Yes," I answered; "but it has not the horror of dirty water; it is as clear as crystal. How does the surplus escape?"

"On the opposite side of the hill you came up there is a well, with a strong stream from it into the river."

"I almost wonder at your choosing such a place to read in. I should hardly like to be so near this pond," said I, laughing.

"Judy has taken all that away. Nothing in nature, and everything out of it, is strange to Judy, poor child! But just look down a little way into the water on this side. Do you see anything?"

"Nothing," I answered.

"Look again, against the wall of the pond," she said.

"I see a kind of arch or opening in the side," I answered.

"That is what I wanted you to see. Now, do you see a little barred window, there, in the face of the rock, through the trees?"

"I cannot say I do," I replied.

"No. Except you know where it is-and even then-it is not so easy to find it. I find it by certain trees."

"What is it?"

"It is the window of a little room in the rock, from which a stair leads down through the rock to a sloping passage. That is the end of it you see under the water."

"Provided, no doubt," I said, "in case of siege, to procure water."

"Most likely; but not, therefore, confined to that purpose. There are more dreadful stories than I can bear to think of" —-

Here she paused abruptly, and began anew " —-As if that house had brought death and doom out of the earth with it. There was an old burial-ground here before the Hall was built."

"Have you ever been down the stair you speak of?" I asked.

"Only part of the way," she answered. "But Judy knows every step of it. If it were not that the door at the top is locked, she would have dived through that archway now, and been in her own room in half the time. The child does not know what fear means."

We now moved away from the pond, towards the side of the quarry and the open-air staircase, which I thought must be considerably more pleasant than the other. I confess I longed to see the gleam of that water at the bottom of the dark sloping passage, though.

Miss Oldcastle accompanied me to the room where I had left her mother, and took her leave with merely a bow of farewell. I saw the old lady glance sharply from her to me as if she were jealous of what we might have been talking about.

"Grannie, are you afraid Mr. Walton has been saying pretty things to Aunt Winnie? I assure you he is not of that sort. He doesn't understand that kind of thing. But he would have jumped into the pond after me and got his death of cold if auntie would have let him. It WAS cold. I think I see you dripping now, Mr Walton."

There she was in her dark corner, coiled up on a couch, and laughing heartily; but all as if she had done nothing extraordinary. And, indeed, estimated either by her own notions or practices, what she had done was not in the least extraordinary.

Disinclined to stay any longer, I shook hands with the grandmother, with a certain invincible sense of slime, and with the grandchild with a feeling of mischievous health, as if the girl might soon corrupt the clergyman into a partnership in pranks as well as in friendship. She fallowed me out of the room, and danced before me down the oak staircase, clearing the portion from the first landing at a bound. Then she turned and waited for me, who came very deliberately, feeling the unsure contact of sole and wax. As soon as I reached her, she said, in a half-whisper, reaching up towards me on tiptoe —

"Isn't she a beauty?"

"Who? your grandmamma?" I returned.

She gave me a little push, her face glowing with fun. But I did not expect she would take her revenge as she did. "Yes, of course," she answered, quite gravely. "Isn't she a beauty?"

And then, seeing that she had put me hors de combat, she burst into loud laughter, and, opening the hall-door for me, let me go without another word.

I went home very quietly, and, as I said, stepping with curious care-of which, of course, I did not think at the time-over the yellow and brown leaves that lay in the middle of the road.

CHAPTER VII
THE BISHOP'S BASIN.

I went home very quietly, as I say, thinking about the strange elements that not only combine to make life, but must be combined in our idea of life, before we can form a true theory about it. Now-a-days, the vulgar notion of what is life-like in any annals is to be realised by sternly excluding everything but the commonplace; and the means, at least, are often attained, with this much of the end as well-that the appearance life bears to vulgar minds is represented with a wonderful degree of success. But I believe that this is, at least, quite as unreal a mode of representing life as the other extreme, wherein the unlikely, the romantic, and the uncommon predominate. I doubt whether there is a single history-if one could only get at the whole of it-in which there is not a considerable admixture of the unlikely become fact, including a few strange coincidences; of the uncommon, which, although striking at first, has grown common from familiarity with its presence as our own; with even, at least, some one more or less rosy touch of what we call the romantic. My own conviction is, that the poetry is far the deepest in us, and that the prose is only broken-down poetry; and likewise that to this our lives correspond. The poetic region is the true one, and just, THEREFORE, the incredible one to the lower order of mind; for although every mind is capable of the truth, or rather capable of becoming capable of the truth, there may lie ages between its capacity and the truth. As you will hear some people read poetry so that no mortal could tell it was poetry, so do some people read their own lives and those of others.

I fell into these reflections from comparing in my own mind my former experiences in visiting my parishioners with those of that day. True, I had never sat down to talk with one of them without finding that that man or that woman had actually a HISTORY, the most marvellous and important fact to a human being; nay, I had found something more or less remarkable in every one of their histories, so that I was more than barely interested in each of them. And as I made more acquaintance with them, (for I had not been in the position, or the disposition either, before I came to Marshmallows, necessary to the gathering of such experiences,) I came to the conclusion-not that I had got into an extraordinary parish of characters-but that every parish must be more or less extraordinary from the same cause. Why did I not use to see such people about me before? Surely I had undergone a change of some sort. Could it be, that the trouble I had been going through of late, had opened the eyes of my mind to the understanding, or rather the simple SEEING, of my fellow-men?

But the people among whom I had been to-day belonged rather to such as might be put into a romantic story. Certainly I could not see much that was romantic in the old lady; and yet, those eyes and that tight-skinned face-what might they not be capable of in the working out of a story? And then the place they lived in! Why, it would hardly come into my ideas of a nineteenth-century country parish at all. I was tempted to try to persuade myself that all that had happened, since I rose to look out of the window in the old house, had been but a dream. For how could that wooded dell have come there after all? It was much too large for a quarry. And that madcap girl-she never flung herself into the pond! —it could not be. And what could the book have been that the lady with the sea-blue eyes was reading? Was that a real book at all? No. Yes. Of course it was. But what was it? What had that to do with the matter? It might turn out to be a very commonplace book after all. No; for commonplace books are generally new, or at least in fine bindings. And here was a shabby little old book, such as, if it had been commonplace, would not have been likely to be the companion of a young lady at the bottom of a quarry —

> "A savage place, as holy and enchanted
> As e'er beneath a waning moon was haunted
> By woman wailing for her demon lover."

I know all this will sound ridiculous, especially that quotation from Kubla Khan coming after the close of the preceding sentence; but it is only so much the more like the jumble of thoughts that made a chaos of my mind as I went home. And then for that terrible pool, and subterranean passage, and all that-what had it all to do with this broad daylight, and these dying autumn leaves? No doubt there had been such places. No doubt there were such places somewhere yet. No doubt this was one of them. But, somehow or other, it would not come in well. I had no intention of GOING IN FOR-that is the phrase now-going in for the romantic. I would take the impression off by going to see Weir the carpenter's old father. Whether my plan was successful or not, I shall leave my reader to judge.

I found Weir busy as usual, but not with a coffin this time. He was working at a window-sash. "Just like life," I thought-tritely perhaps. "The other day he was closing up in the outer darkness, and now he is letting in the light."

"It's a long time since you was here last, sir," he said, but without a smile.

Did he mean a reproach? If so, I was more glad of that reproach than I would have been of the warmest welcome, even from Old Rogers. The fact was that, having a good deal to attend to besides, and willing at the same time to let the man feel that he was in no danger of being bored by my visits, I had not made use even of my reserve in the shape of a visit to his father.

"Well," I answered, "I wanted to know something about all my people, before I paid a second visit to any of them."

"All right, sir. Don't suppose I meant to complain. Only to let you know you was welcome, sir."

"I've just come from my first visit to Oldcastle Hall. And, to tell the truth, for I don't like pretences, my visit to-day was not so much to you as to your father, whom, perhaps, I ought to have called upon before, only I was afraid of seeming to intrude upon you, seeing we don't exactly think the same way about some things," I added-with a smile, I know, which was none the less genuine that I remember it yet.

And what makes me remember it yet? It is the smile that lighted up his face in response to mine. For it was more than I looked for. And his answer helped to fix the smile in my memory.

"You made me think, sir, that perhaps, after all, we were much of the same way of thinking, only perhaps you was a long way ahead of me."

Now the man was not right in saying that we were much of the same way of THINKING; for our opinions could hardly do more than come within sight of each other; but what he meant was right enough. For I was certain, from the first, that the man had a regard for the downright, honest way of things, and I hoped that I too had such a regard. How much of selfishness and of pride in one's own judgment might be mixed up with it, both in his case and mine, I had been too often taken in-by myself, I mean-to be at all careful to discriminate, provided there was a proportion of real honesty along with it, which, I felt sure, would ultimately eliminate the other. For in the moral nest, it is not as with the sparrow and the cuckoo. The right, the original inhabitant is the stronger; and, however unlikely at any given point in the history it may be, the sparrow will grow strong enough to heave the intruding cuckoo overboard. So I was pleased that the man should do me the honour of thinking I was right as far as he could see, which is the greatest honour one man can do another; for it is setting him on his own steed, as the eastern tyrants used to do. And I was delighted to think that the road lay open for further and more real communion between us in time to come.

"Well," I answered, "I think we shall understand each other perfectly before long. But now I must see your father, if it is convenient and agreeable."

"My father will be delighted to see you, I know, sir. He can't get so far as the church on Sundays; but you'll find him much more to your mind than me. He's been putting ever so many questions to me about the new parson, wanting me to try whether I couldn't get more out of you than the old parson. That's the way we talk about you, you see, sir. You'll understand. And I've never told him that I'd been to church since you came —I suppose from a bit of pride, because I had so long refused to go; but I don't doubt some of the neighbours have told him, for he never speaks about it now. And I know he's been looking out for you; and I fancy he's begun to wonder that the parson was going to see everybody but him. It WILL be a pleasure to the old man, sir, for he don't see a great many to talk to; and he's fond of a bit of gossip, is the old man, sir."

So saying, Weir led the way through the shop into a lobby behind, and thence up what must have been a back-stair of the old house, into a large room over the workshop. There were bits of old carving about the walls of the room yet, but, as in the shop below, all had been whitewashed. At one end stood a bed with chintz curtains and a warm-looking counterpane of rich faded embroidery. There was a bit of carpet by the bedside, and another bit in front of the fire; and there the old man sat, on one side, in a high-backed not very easy-looking chair. With a great effort he managed to rise as I approached him, notwithstanding my entreaties that he would not move. He looked much older when on his feet, for he was bent nearly double, in which posture the marvel was how he could walk at all. For he did totter a few steps to meet me, without even the aid of a stick, and, holding out a thin, shaking hand, welcomed me with an air of breeding rarely to be met with in his station in society. But the chief part of this polish sprung from the inbred kindliness of his nature, which was manifest in the expression of his noble old countenance. Age is such a different thing in different natures! One man seems to grow more and more selfish as he grows older; and in another the slow fire of time seems only to consume, with fine, imperceptible gradations, the yet lingering selfishness in him, letting the light of the kingdom, which the Lord says is within, shine out more and more, as the husk grows thin and is ready to fall off, that the man, like the seed sown, may pierce the earth of this world, and rise into the pure air and wind and dew of the second life. The face of a loving old man is always to me like a morning moon, reflecting the yet unrisen sun of the other world, yet fading before its approaching light, until, when it does rise, it pales and withers away from our gaze, absorbed in the source of its own beauty. This old man, you may see, took my fancy wonderfully, for even at this distance of time, when I am old myself, the recollection of his beautiful old face makes me feel as if I could write poetry about him.

"I'm blithe to see ye, sir," said he. "Sit ye down, sir."

And, turning, he pointed to his own easy-chair; and I then saw his profile. It was delicate as that of Dante, which in form it marvellously resembled. But all the sternness which Dante's evil times had generated in his prophetic face was in this old man's replaced by a sweetness of hope that was lovely to behold.

"No, Mr Weir," I said, "I cannot take your chair. The Bible tells us to rise up before the aged, not to turn them out of their seats."

"It would do me good to see you sitting in my cheer, sir. The pains that my son Tom there takes to keep it up as long as the old man may want it! It's a good thing I bred him to the joiner's trade, sir. Sit ye down, sir. The cheer'll hold ye, though I warrant it won't last that long after I be gone home. Sit ye down, sir."

Thus entreated, I hesitated no longer, but took the old man's seat. His son brought another chair for him, and he sat down opposite the fire and close to me. Thomas then went back to his work, leaving us alone.

"Ye've had some speech wi' my son Tom," said the old man, the moment he was gone, leaning a little towards me. "It's main kind o' you, sir, to take up kindly wi' poor folks like us."

"You don't say it's kind of a person to do what he likes best," I answered. "Besides, it's my duty to know all my people."

"Oh yes, sir, I know that. But there's a thousand ways ov doin' the same thing. I ha' seen folks, parsons and others, 'at made a great show ov bein' friendly to the poor, ye know, sir; and all the time you could see, or if you couldn't see you could tell without seein', that they didn't much regard them in their hearts; but it was a sort of accomplishment to be able to talk to the poor, like, after their own fashion. But the minute an ould man sees you, sir, he believes that you MEAN it, sir, whatever it is. For an ould man somehow comes to know things like a child.

They call it a second childhood, don't they, sir? And there are some things worth growin' a child again to get a hould ov again."

"I only hope what you say may be true-about me, I mean."

"Take my word for it, sir. You have no idea how that boy of mine, Tom there, did hate all the clergy till you come. Not that he's anyway favourable to them yet, only he'll say nothin' again' you, sir. He's got an unfortunate gift o' seein' all the faults first, sir; and when a man is that way given, the faults always hides the other side, so that there's nothing but faults to be seen."

"But I find Thomas quite open to reason."

"That's because you understand him, sir, and know how to give him head. He tould me of the talk you had with him. You don't bait him. You don't say, 'You must come along wi' me,' but you turns and goes along wi' him. He's not a bad fellow at all, is Tom; but he will have the reason for everythink. Now I never did want the reason for everything. I was content to be tould a many things. But Tom, you see, he was born with a sore bit in him somewheres, I don't rightly know wheres; and I don't think he rightly knows what's the matter with him himself."

"I dare say you have a guess though, by this time, Mr. Weir," I said; "and I think I have a guess too."

"Well, sir, if he'd only give in, I think he would be far happier. But he can't see his way clear."

"You must give him time, you know. The fact is, he doesn't feel at home yet.' And how can he, so long as he doesn't know his own Father?"

"I'm not sure that I rightly understand you," said the old man, looking bewildered and curious.

"I mean," I answered, "that till a man knows that he is one of God's family, living in God's house, with God up-stairs, as it were, while he is at his work or his play in a nursery below-stairs, he can't feel comfortable. For a man could not be made that should stand alone, like some of the beasts. A man must feel a head over him, because he's not enough to satisfy himself, you know. Thomas just wants faith; that is, he wants to feel that there is a loving Father over him, who is doing things all well and right, if we could only understand them, though it really does not look like it sometimes."

"Ah, sir, I might have understood you well enough, if my poor old head hadn't been started on a wrong track. For I fancied for the moment that you were just putting your finger upon the sore place in Tom's mind. There's no use in keeping family misfortunes from a friend like you, sir. That boy has known his father all his life; but I was nearly half his age before I knew mine."

"Strange!" I said, involuntarily almost.

"Yes, sir; strange you may well say. A strange story it is. The Lord help my mother! I beg yer pardon, sir. I'm no Catholic. But that prayer will come of itself sometimes. As if it could be of any use now! God forgive me!"

"Don't you be afraid, Mr Weir, as if God was ready to take offence at what comes naturally, as you say. An ejaculation of love is not likely to offend Him who is so grand that He is always meek and lowly of heart, and whose love is such that ours is a mere faint light —'a little glooming light much like a shade'—as one of our own poets says, beside it."

"Thank you, Mr Walton. That's a real comfortable word, sir. And I am heart-sure it's true, sir. God be praised for evermore! He IS good, sir; as I have known in my poor time, sir. I don't believe there ever was one that just lifted his eyes and looked up'ards, instead of looking down to the ground, that didn't get some comfort, to go on with, as it were-the ready-money of comfort, as it were-though it might be none to put in the bank, sir."

"That's true enough," I said. "Then your father and mother—?"

And here I hesitated.

"Were never married, sir," said the old man promptly, as if he would relieve me from an embarrassing position. "*I* couldn't help it. And I'm no less the child of my Father in heaven for it. For if He hadn't made me, I couldn't ha' been their son, you know, sir. So that He had more to do wi' the makin' o' me than they had; though mayhap, if He had His way all out, I might ha' been the son o' somebody else. But, now that things be so, I wouldn't have liked that at all, sir; and bein' once born so, I would not have e'er another couple of parents in all England, sir, though I ne'er knew one o' them. And I do love my mother. And I'm so sorry for my father that I love him too, sir. And if I could only get my boy Tom to think as I do, I would die like a psalm-tune on an organ, sir."

"But it seems to me strange," I said, "that your son should think so much of what is so far gone by. Surely he would not want another father than you, now. He is used to his position in life. And there can be nothing cast up to him about his birth or descent."

"That's all very true, sir, and no doubt it would be as you say. But there has been other things to keep his mind upon the old affair. Indeed, sir, we have had the same misfortune all over again among the young people. And I mustn't say anything more about it; only my boy Tom has a sore heart."

I knew at once to what he alluded; for I could not have been about in my parish all this time without learning that the strange handsome woman in the little shop was the daughter of Thomas Weir, and that she was neither wife nor widow. And it now occurred to me for the first time that it was a likeness to her little boy that had affected me so pleasantly when I first saw Thomas, his grandfather. The likeness to his great-grandfather, which I saw plainly enough, was what made the other fact clear to me. And at the same moment I began to be haunted with a flickering sense of a third likeness which I could not in the least fix or identify.

"Perhaps," I said, "he may find some good come out of that too."

"Well, who knows, sir?"

"I think," I said, "that if we do evil that good may come, the good we looked for will never come thereby. But once evil is done, we may humbly look to Him who bringeth good out of evil, and wait. Is your granddaughter Catherine in bad health? She looks so delicate!"

"She always had an uncommon look. But what she looks like now, I don't know. I hear no complaints; but she has never crossed this door since we got her set up in that shop. She never conies near her father or her sister, though she lets them, leastways her sister, go and see her. I'm afraid Tom has been rayther unmerciful, with her. And if ever he put a bad name upon her in her hearing, I know, from what that lass used to be as a young one, that she wouldn't be likely to forget it, and as little likely to get over it herself, or pass it over to another, even her own father. I don't believe they do more nor nod to one another when they meet in the village. It's well even if they do that much. It's my belief there's some people made so hard that they never can forgive anythink."

"How did she get into the trouble? Who is the father of her child?"

"Nay, that no one knows for certain; though there be suspicions, and one of them, no doubt, correct. But, I believe, fire wouldn't drive his name out at her mouth. I know my lass. When she says a thing, she 'll stick to it."

I asked no more questions. But, after a short pause, the old man went on.

"I shan't soon forget the night I first heard about my father and mother. That was a night! The wind was roaring like a mad beast about the house; —not this house, sir, but the great house over the way."

"You don't mean Oldcastle Hall?" I said.

"'Deed I do, sir," returned the old man, "This house here belonged to the same family at one time; though when I was born it was another branch of the family, second cousins or something, that lived in it. But even then it was something on to the downhill road, I believe."

"But," I said, fearing my question might have turned the old man aside from a story worth hearing, "never mind all that now, if you please. I am anxious to hear all about that night. Do go on. You were saying the wind was blowing about the old house."

"Eh, sir, it was roaring!-roaring as if it was mad with rage! And every now and then it would come down the chimley like out of a gun, and blow the smoke and a'most the fire into the middle of the housekeeper's room. For the housekeeper had been giving me my supper. I called her auntie, then; and didn't know a bit that she wasn't my aunt really. I was at that time a kind of a under-gamekeeper upon the place, and slept over the stable. But I fared of the best, for I was a favourite with the old woman—I suppose because I had given her plenty of trouble in my time. That's always the way, sir.—Well, as I was a-saying, when the wind stopped for a moment, down came the rain with a noise that sounded like a regiment of cavalry on the turnpike road t'other side of the hill. And then up the wind got again, and swept the rain away, and took it all in its own hand again, and went on roaring worse than ever. 'You'll be wet afore you get across the yard, Samuel,' said auntie, looking very prim in her long white apron, as she sat on the other side of the little round table before the fire, sipping a drop of hot rum and water, which she always had before she went to bed. 'You'll be wet to the skin, Samuel,' she said. 'Never mind,' says I. 'I'm not salt, nor yet sugar; and I'll be going, auntie, for you'll be wanting your bed.'-'Sit ye still,' said she. 'I don't want my bed yet.' And there she sat, sipping at her rum and water; and there I sat, o' the other side, drinking the last of a pint of October, she had gotten me from the cellar-for I had been out in the wind all day. 'It was just such a night as this,' said she, and then stopped again.—But I'm wearying you, sir, with my long story."

"Not in the least," I answered. "Quite the contrary. Pray tell it out your own way. You won't tire me, I assure you."

So the old man went on.

"' It was just such a night as this,' she began again—'leastways it was snow and not rain that was coming down, as if the Almighty was a-going to spend all His winter-stock at oncet.'—'What happened such a night, auntie?' I said. 'Ah, my lad!' said she, 'ye may well ask what happened. None has a better right. You happened. That's all.'—'Oh, that's all, is it, auntie?' I said, and laughed. 'Nay, nay, Samuel,' said she, quite solemn, 'what is there to laugh at, then? I assure you, you was anything but welcome.'—'And why wasn't I welcome?' I said. 'I couldn't help it, you know. I'm very sorry to hear I intruded,' I said, still making game of it, you see; for I always did like a joke. 'Well,' she said, 'you certainly wasn't wanted. But I don't blame you, Samuel, and I hope you won't blame me.'—'What do you mean, auntie?' I mean this, that it's my fault, if so be that fault it is, that you're sitting there now, and not lying, in less bulk by a good deal, at the bottom of the Bishop's Basin.' That's what they call a deep pond at the foot of the old house, sir; though why or wherefore, I'm sure I don't know. 'Most extraordinary, auntie!' I said, feeling very queer, and as if I really had no business to be there. 'Never you mind, my dear,' says she; 'there you are, and you can take care of yourself now as well as anybody.'—'But who wanted to drown me?' 'Are you sure you can forgive him, if I tell you?'—'Sure enough, suppose he was sitting where you be now,' I answered. 'It was, I make no doubt, though I can't prove it,—I am morally certain it was your own father.' I felt the skin go creepin' together upon my head, and I couldn't speak. 'Yes, it was, child; and it's time you knew all about it. Why, you don't know who your own father was!'—'No more I do,' I said; 'and I never cared to ask, somehow. I thought it was all right, I suppose. But I wonder now that I never did.'—'Indeed you did many a time, when you was a mere boy, like; but I suppose, as you never was answered, you give it up for a bad job, and forgot all about it, like a wise man. You always was a wise child, Samuel.' So the old lady always said, sir. And I was willing to believe she was right, if I could. 'But now,' said she, 'it's time you knew all about it.—Poor Miss Wallis!—I'm no aunt of yours, my boy, though I love you nearly as well, I think, as if I was; for dearly did I love your mother. She was a beauty, and better than she was beautiful, whatever folks may say. The only wrong thing, I'm certain, that she ever did, was to trust your father too much. But I must see and give you the story right through from beginning to end.—Miss Wallis, as I came to know from her own lips, was the daughter of a country attorney, who had a good practice, and was likely to leave her well off. Her mother died when she was a little girl. It's not easy getting on without a mother, my boy. So she wasn't taught much of the best sort, I reckon. When her father died early, and she was left atone, the only thing she could do was to take a governess's place, and she came to us. She never got on well with the children, for they were young and self willed and rude, and would not learn to do as they were bid. I never knew one o' them shut the door when they went out of this room. And, from having had all her own way at home, with plenty of servants, and money to spend, it was a sore change to her. But she was a sweet creature, that she was. She did look sorely tried when Master Freddy would get on the back of her chair, and Miss Gusta would lie down on the rug, and never stir for all she could say to them, but only laugh at her. —To be sure!' And then auntie would take a sip at her rum and water, and sit considering old times like a static. And I sat as if all my head was one great ear, and I never spoke a word. And auntie began again. 'The way I came to know so much about her was this. Nobody, you see, took any notice or care of her. For the children were kept away with her in the old house, and my lady wasn't one to take trouble about anybody till once she stood in her way, and then she would just shove her aside or crush her like a spider, and ha' done with her.' —They have always been a proud and a fierce race, the Oldcastles, sir," said Weir, taking up the speech in his own person, "and there's been a deal o' breedin in-and-in amongst them, and that has kept up the worst of them. The men took to the women of their own sort somehow, you see. The lady up at the old Hall now is a Crowfoot. I'll just tell you one thing the gardener told me about her years ago, sir. She had a fancy for hyacinths in her rooms in the spring, and she Had some particular fine ones; and a lady of her acquaintance begged for some of them. And what do you think she did? She couldn't refuse them, and she couldn't bear any one to have them as good as she. And so she sent the hyacinth-roots —but she boiled 'em first. The gardener told me himself, sir. —'And so, when the poor thing,' said auntie, 'was taken with a dreadful cold, which was no wonder if you saw the state of the window in the room she had to sleep in, and which I got old Jones to set to rights and paid him for it out of my own pocket, else he wouldn't ha' done it at all, for the family wasn't too much in the way or the means either of paying their debts-well, there she was, and nobody minding her, and of course it fell to me to look after her. It would have made your heart bleed to see the poor thing flung all of a heap on her bed, blue with cold and coughing. "My dear!" I said; and she burst out crying, and from that moment there was confidence between us. I made her as warm and as comfortable as I could, but I had to nurse her for a fortnight before she was able to do anything again. She didn't shirk her work though, poor thing. It was a heartsore to me to see the poor young thing, with her sweet eyes and her pale face, talking away to those children, that were more like wild cats than human beings. She might as well have talked to wild cats, I'm sure. But I don't think she was ever so miserable again as she must have been before her illness; for she used often to come and see me of an evening, and she would sit there where you are sitting now for an hour at a time, without speaking, her thin white hands lying folded in her lap, and her eyes fixed on the fire. I used to wonder what she could be thinking about, and I had made up my mind she was not long for this world; when all at once it was announced that Miss Oldcastle, who had been to school for some time, was coming home; and then we began to see a great deal of company, and for month after month the house was more or less filled with visitors, so that my time was constantly taken up, and I saw much less of poor Miss Wallis than I had seen before. But when we did meet on some of the back stairs, or when she came to my room for a few minutes before going to bed, we were just as good friends as ever. And I used to say, "I wish this scurry was over, my dear, that we might have our old times again." And she would smile and say something sweet. But I was surprised to see that her health began to come back-at least so it seemed to me, for her eyes grew brighter and a flush came upon her pale face, and though the children were as tiresome as ever, she didn't seem to mind it so much. But indeed she had not very much to do with them out of school hours now; for when the spring came on, they would be out and about the place with their sister or one of their brothers; and indeed, out of doors it would have been impossible for Miss Wallis to do anything with them. Some of the visitors would take to them too, for they behaved so badly to nobody as to Miss Wallis, and indeed they were clever children, and could be engaging enough when they pleased. —But then I had a blow, Samuel. It was a lovely spring night, just after the sun was down, and I wanted a drop of milk fresh from the cow for something that I was making for dinner the next day; so I went through the kitchen-garden and through the belt of young larches to go to the shippen. But when I got among the trees, who should I see at the other end of the path that went along, but Miss Wallis walking arm-in-arm with

Captain Crowfoot, who was just home from India, where he had been with Lord Clive. The captain was a man about two or three and thirty, a relation of the family, and the son of Sir Giles Crowfoot'—who lived then in this old house, sir, and had but that one son, my father, you see, sir.—'And it did give me a turn,' said my aunt, 'to see her walking with him, for I felt as sure as judgment that no good could come of it. For the captain had not the best of characters-that is, when people talked about him in chimney corners, and such like, though he was a great favourite with everybody that knew nothing about him. He was a fine, manly, handsome fellow, with a smile that, as people said, no woman could resist, though I'm sure it would have given me no trouble to resist it, whatever they may mean by that, for I saw that that same smile was the falsest thing of all the false things about him. All the time he was smiling, you would have thought he was looking at himself in a glass. He was said to have gathered a power of money in India, somehow or other. But I don't know, only I don't think he would have been the favourite he was with my lady if he hadn't. And reports were about, too, of the ways and means by which he had made the money; some said by robbing the poor heathen creatures; and some said it was only that his brother officers didn't approve of his speculating as he did in horses and other things. I don't know whether officers are so particular. At all events, this was a fact, for it was one of his own servants that told me, not thinking any harm or any shame of it. He had quarrelled with a young ensign in the regiment. On which side the wrong was, I don't know. But he first thrashed him most unmercifully, and then called him out, as they say. And when the poor fellow appeared, he could scarcely see out of his eyes, and certainly couldn't take anything like an aim. And he shot him dead,—did Captain Crowfoot.'—Think of hearing that about one's own father, sir! But I never said a word, for I hadn't a word to say.—'Think of that, Samuel,' said my aunt, 'else you won't believe what I am going to tell you. And you won't even then, I dare say. But I must tell you, nevertheless and notwithstanding.—Well, I felt as if the earth was sinking away from under the feet of me, and I stood and stared at them. And they came on, never seeing me, and actually went close past me and never saw me; at least, if he saw me he took no notice, for I don't suppose that the angel with the flaming sword would have put him out. But for her, I know she didn't see me, for her face was down, burning and smiling at once.'—I'm an old man now, sir, and I never saw my mother; but I can't tell you the story without feeling as if my heart would break for the poor young lady.—'I went back to my room,' said my aunt, 'with my empty jug in my hand, and I sat down as if I had had a stroke, and I never moved till it was pitch dark and my fire out. It was a marvel to me afterwards that nobody came near me, for everybody was calling after me at that time. And it was days before I caught a glimpse of Miss Wallis again, at least to speak to her. At last, one night she came to my room; and without a moment of parley, I said to her, "Oh, my dear! what was that wretch saying to you?"—"What wretch?" says she, quite sharp like. "Why, Captain Crowfoot," says I, "to be sure."—"What have you to say against Captain Crowfoot?" says she, quite scornful like. So I tumbled out all I had against him in one breath. She turned awful pale, and she shook from head to foot, but she was able for all that to say, "Indian servants are known liars, Mrs Prendergast," says she, "and I don't believe one word of it all. But I'll ask him, the next time I see him."—"Do so, my dear," I said, not fearing for myself, for I knew he would not make any fuss that might bring the thing out into the air, and hoping that it might lead to a quarrel between them. And the next time I met her, Samuel-it was in the gallery that takes to the west turret-she passed me with a nod just, and a blush instead of a smile on her sweet face. And I didn't blame her, Samuel; but I knew that that villain had gotten a hold of her. And so I could only cry, and that I did. Things went on like this for some months. The captain came and went, stopping a week at a time. Then he stopped for a whole month, and this was in the first of the summer; and then he said he was ordered abroad again, and went away. But he didn't go abroad. He came again in the autumn for the shooting, and began to make up to Miss Oldcastle, who had grown a line young woman by that time. And then Miss Wallis began to pine. The captain went away again. Before long I was certain that if ever young creature was in a consumption, she was; but she never said a word to me. How ever the poor thing got on with her work, I can't think, but she grew weaker and weaker. I took the best care of her she would let me, and contrived that she should have her meals in her own room; but something was between her and me that she never spoke a word about herself, and never alluded to the captain. By and by came the news that the captain and Miss Oldcastle were to be married in the spring. And Miss Wallis took to her bed after that; and my lady said she had never been of much use, and wanted to send her away. But Miss Oldcastle, who was far superior to any of the rest in her disposition, spoke up for her. She had been to ask me about her, and I told her the poor thing must go to a hospital if she was sent away, for she had ne'er a home to go to. And then she went to see the governess, poor thing! and spoke very kindly to her; but never a word would Miss Wallis answer; she only stared at her with great, big, wild-like eyes. And Miss Oldcastle thought she was out of her mind, and spoke of an asylum. But I said she hadn't long to live, and if she would get my lady her mother to consent to take no notice, I would take all the care and trouble of her. And she promised, and the poor thing was left alone. I began to think myself her mind must be going, for not a word would she speak, even to me, though every moment I could spare I was up with her in her room. Only I was forced to be careful not to be out of the way when my lady wanted me, for that would have tied me more. At length one day, as I was settling her pillow for her, she all at once threw her arms about my neck, and burst into a terrible fit of crying. She sobbed and panted for breath so dreadfully, that I put my arms round her and lifted her up to give her relief; and when I laid her down again, I whispered in her ear, "I know now, my dear. I'll do all I can for you." She caught hold of my hand and held it to her lips, and then to her bosom, and cried again, but more quietly, and all was right between us once more. It was well for her, poor thing, that she could go to her bed. And I said to myself, "Nobody need ever know about it; and nobody ever shall if I can help it." To tell the truth, my hope was that she would die before there was any need for further concealment. "But people in that condition seldom die, they say, till all is over; and so she lived on and on, though plainly getting weaker and weaker. —At the captain's next visit, the wedding-day was fixed. And after that a circumstance came about that made me uneasy. A Hindoo servant-the captain called him his NIGGER always-had been constantly in attendance upon him. I never could abide the snake-look of the fellow, nor the noiseless way he went about the house. But this time the captain had a Hindoo woman with him as well. He said that his man had fallen in with her in London; that he had known her before; that she had come home as nurse with an English family, and it would be very nice for his wife to take her back with her to India, if she could only give her house room, and make her useful till after the wedding. This was easily arranged, and he went away to return in three weeks, when the wedding was to take place. Meantime poor Emily grew fast worse, and how she held out with that terrible cough of hers I never could understand-and spitting blood, too, every other hour or so, though not very much. And now, to my great trouble, with the preparations for the wedding, I could see yet less of her than before; and when Miss Oldcastle sent the Hindoo to ask me if she might not sit in the room with the poor girl, I did not know how to object, though I did not at all like her being there. I felt a great mistrust of the woman somehow or other. I never did like blacks, and I never shall. So she went, and sat by her, and waited on her very kindly-at least poor Emily said so. I called her Emily because she had begged me, that she might feel as if her mother were with her, and she was a child again. I had tried before to find out from her when greater care would be necessary, but she couldn't tell me anything. I doubted even if she understood me. I longed to have the wedding over that I might get rid of the black woman, and have time to take her place, and get everything prepared. The captain arrived, and his man with him. And twice I came upon the two blacks in close conversation. —Well, the wedding-day came. The people went to church; and while they were there a terrible storm of wind and snow came on, such that the horses would hardly face it. The captain was going to take his bride home to his father, Sir Giles's; but, short as the distance was, before the time came the storm got so dreadful that no one could think of leaving the house that night. The wind blew for all the world just as it blows this night, only it was snow in its mouth, and not rain. Carriage and horses and all would have been blown off the road for certain. It did blow, to be sure! After dinner was over and the ladies were gone to the drawing-room, and the gentlemen had been sitting over their wine for some time, the butler, William Weir-an honest man, whose wife lived at the lodge-came to my room looking scared. "Lawks, William!" says I,' said my aunt, sir, '"whatever is the matter with you?"—"Well, Mrs Prendergast!" says he, and said no more. "Lawks, William," says I, "speak out."—"Well," says he, "Mrs Prendergast, it's a strange wedding, it is! There's the ladies all alone in the withdrawing-room, and there's the gentlemen calling for more wine, and cursing and swearing that it's awful to hear. It's my belief that swords will be drawn afore long."—"Tut!" says I, "William, it will come the sooner if you don't give them what they want. Go and get it as fast as you can."—"I don't a'most like goin' down them stairs alone, in sich a night, ma'am," says he. "Would you mind coming with me?"—"Dear me, William," says I, "a pretty story to tell your wife"—she was my own half-sister, and younger than me—"a pretty story to tell your wife, that you wanted an old body like me to go and take care of you in your own cellar," says I. "But I'll go with you, if you like; for, to tell the truth, it's a terrible night." And so down we went, and brought up six bottles more of the best port. And I really didn't wonder, when I was down there, and heard the dull roar of the wind against the rock below, that William didn't much like to go alone.—When he went back with the wine, the captain said, "William, what kept you so long? Mr Centlivre says that you were afraid to go down into the cellar." Now, wasn't that odd, for it was a real fact? Before William could reply, Sir Giles said, "A man might well be afraid to go anywhere alone in a night like this." Whereupon the captain cried, with an oath, that he would go down the underground stair, and into every vault on the way, for the wager of a guinea. And there the matter, according to William, dropped, for the fresh wine was put on the table. But after they had drunk the most of it-the captain, according to William, drinking less than usual-it was brought up again, he couldn't tell by which of them. And in five minutes after, they were all at my door, demanding the key of the room at the top of the stair. I was just going up to see poor Emily when I heard the noise of their unsteady feet coming along the passage to my door; and I gave the captain the key at once, wishing with all my heart he might get a good fright for his pains. He took a jug with him, too, to bring some water up from the well, as a proof he had been down. The rest of the gentlemen went with him into the little cellar-room; but they wouldn't stop there till he came up again, they said it was so cold. They all came into my room, where they talked as gentlemen wouldn't do if the wine hadn't got uppermost. It was some time before the captain returned. It's a good way down and back. When he came in at last, he looked as if he had got the fright I wished him, he had such a scared look. The candle in his lantern was out, and there was no water in the jug. "There's your guinea, Centlivre," says he, throwing it on the table. "You needn't ask me any questions, for I won't answer one of them."—"Captain," says I, as he turned to leave the room, and the other gentlemen rose to follow him, "I'll just hang up the key again."—" By all means," says he. "Where is it, then?" says I. He started and made as if he searched his pockets all over for it. "I must have dropped it," says he; "but it's of no consequence; you can send William to look for it in the morning. It can't be lost, you know."—"Very well, captain," said I. But I didn't like being without the key, because of course he hadn't locked the door, and that part of the house has a bad name, and no wonder. It wasn't exactly pleasant to have the door left open. All this time I couldn't get to see how Emily was. As often as I looked from my window, I saw her light in the old west turret out there, Samuel. You know the room where the bed is still. The rain and the wind will be blowing right through it to-night. That's the bed you was born upon, Samuel.'—It's all gone now, sir, turret and all, like a good deal more about the old place; but there's a story about that turret afterwards, only I mustn't try to tell you two things at once. —'Now I had told the Indian woman that if anything happened, if she was worse, or wanted to see me, she must put the candle on the right side of the window, and I should always be looking out, and would come directly, whoever might wait. For I was expecting you some time soon, and nobody knew anything about when you might come. But there the blind continued drawn down as before.

So I thought all was going on right. And what with the storm keeping Sir Giles and so many more that would have gone home that night, there was no end of work, and some contrivance necessary, I can tell you, to get them all bedded for the night, for we were nothing too well provided with blankets and linen in the house. There was always more room than money in it. So it was past twelve o'clock before I had a minute to myself, and that was only after they had all gone to bed-the bride and bridegroom in the crimson chamber, of course. Well, at last I crept quietly into Emily's room. I ought to have told you that I had not let her know anything about the wedding being that day, and had enjoined the heathen woman not to say a word; for I thought she might as well die without hearing about it. But I believe the vile wretch did tell her. When I opened the room-door, there was no light there. I spoke, but no one answered. I had my own candle in my hand, but it had been blown out as I came up the stair. I turned and ran along the corridor to reach the main stair, which was the nearest way to my room, when all at once I heard such a shriek from the crimson chamber as I never heard in my life. It made me all creep like worms. And in a moment doors and doors were opened, and lights came out, everybody looking terrified; and what with drink, and horror, and sleep, some of the gentlemen were awful to look upon. And the door of the crimson chamber opened too, and the captain appeared in his dressing-gown, bawling out to know what was the matter; though I'm certain, to this day, the cry did come from that room, and that he knew more about it than any one else did. As soon as I got a light, however, which I did from Sir Giles's candle, I left them to settle it amongst them, and ran back to the west turret. When I entered the room, there was my dear girl lying white and motionless. There could be no doubt a baby had been born, but no baby was to be seen. I rushed to the bed; but though she was still warm, your poor mother was quite dead. There was no use in thinking about helping her; but what could have become of the child? As if by a light in my mind, I saw it all. I rushed down to my room, got my lantern, and, without waiting to be afraid, ran to the underground stairs, where I actually found the door standing open. I had not gone down more than three turnings, when I thought I heard a cry, and I sped faster still. And just about half-way down, there lay a bundle in a blanket. And how ever you got over the state I found you in, Samuel, I can't think. But I caught you up as you was, and ran to my own room with you; and I locked the door, and there being a kettle on the fire, and some conveniences in the place, I did the best for you I could. For the breath wasn't out of you, though it well might have been. And then I laid you before the fire, and by that time you had begun to cry a little, to my great pleasure, and then I got a blanket off my bed, and wrapt you up in it; and, the storm being abated by this time, made the best of my way with you through the snow to the lodge, where William's wife lived. It was not so far off then as it is now. But in the midst of my trouble the silly body did make me laugh when he opened the door to me, and saw the bundle in my arms. "Mrs Prendergast," says he, "I didn't expect it of you."—"Hold your tongue," I said. "You would never have talked such nonsense if you had had the grace to have any of your own," says I. And with that I into the bedroom and shut the door, and left him out there in his shirt. My sister and I soon got everything arranged, for there was no time to lose. And before morning I had all made tidy, and your poor mother lying as sweet a corpse as ever angel saw. And no one could say a word against her. And it's my belief that that villain made her believe somehow or other that she was as good as married to him. She was buried down there in the churchyard, close by the vestry-door,' said my aunt, sir; and all of our family have been buried there ever since, my son Tom's wife among them, sir."

"But what was that cry in the house?" I asked "And what became of the black woman?"

"The woman was never seen again in our quarter; and what the cry was my aunt never would say. She seemed to know though; notwithstanding, as she said, that Captain and Mrs Crowfoot denied all knowledge of it. But the lady looked dreadful, she said, and never was well again, and died at the birth of her first child. That was the present Mrs Oldcastle's father, sir."

"But why should the woman have left you on the stair, instead of drowning you in the well at the bottom?"

"My aunt evidently thought there was some mystery about that as well as the other, for she had no doubt about the woman's intention. But all she would ever say concerning it was, 'The key was never found, Samuel. You see I had to get a new one made.' And she pointed to where it hung on the wall. 'But that doesn't look new now,' she would say. 'The lock was very hard to fit again.' And so you see, sir, I was brought up as her nephew, though people were surprised, no doubt, that William Weir's wife should have a child, and nobody know she was expecting. —Well, with all the reports of the captain's money, none of it showed in this old place, which from that day began, as it were, to crumble away. There's been little repair done upon it since then. If it hadn't been a well-built place to begin with, it wouldn't be standing now, sir. But it's a very different place, I can tell you. Why, all behind was a garden with terraces, and fruit trees, and gay flowers, to no end. I remember it as well as yesterday; nay, a great deal better, for the matter of that. For I don't remember yesterday at all, sir."

I have tried a little to tell the story as he told it. But I am aware that I have succeeded very badly; for I am not like my friend in London, who, I verily believe, could give you an exact representation of any dialect he ever heard. I wish I had been able to give a little more of the form of the old man's speech; all I have been able to do is to show a difference from my own way of telling a story. But in the main, I think, I have reported it correctly. I believe if the old man was correct in representing his aunt's account, the story is very little altered between us.

But why should I tell such a story at all?

I am willing to allow, at once, that I have very likely given it more room than it deserves in these poor Annals of mine; but the reason why I tell it at all is simply this, that, as it came from the old man's lips, it interested me greatly. It certainly did not produce the effect I had hoped to gain from an interview with him, namely, A REDUCTION TO THE COMMON AND PRESENT. For all this ancient tale tended to keep up the sense of distance between my day's experience at the Hall and the work I had to do amongst my cottagers and trades-people. Indeed, it came very strangely upon that experience.

"But surely you did not believe such an extravagant tale? The old man was in his dotage, to begin with."

Had the old man been in his dotage, which he was not, my answer would have been a more triumphant one. For when was dotage consistently and imaginatively inventive? But why should I not believe the story? There are people who can never believe anything that is not (I do not say merely in accordance with their own character, but) in accordance with the particular mood they may happen to be in at the time it is presented to them. They know nothing of human nature beyond their own immediate preference at the moment for port or sherry, for vice or virtue. To tell me there could not be a man so lost to shame, if to rectitude, as Captain Crowfoot, is simply to talk nonsense. Nay, gentle reader, if you-and let me suppose I address a lady-if you will give yourself up for thirty years to doing just whatever your lowest self and not your best self may like, I will warrant you capable, by the end of that time, of child murder at least. I do not think the descent to Avernus is always easy; but it is always possible. Many and many such a story was fact in old times; and human nature being the same still, though under different restraints, equally horrible things are constantly in progress towards the windows of the newspapers.

"But the whole tale has such a melodramatic air!"

That argument simply amounts to this: that, because such subjects are capable of being employed with great dramatic effect, and of being at the same time very badly represented, therefore they cannot take place in real life. But ask any physician of your acquaintance, whether a story is unlikely simply because it involves terrible things such as do not occur every day. The fact is, that such things, occurring monthly or yearly only, are more easily hidden away out of sight. Indeed we can have no sense of security for ourselves except in the knowledge that we are striving up and away, and therefore cannot be sinking nearer to the region of such awful possibilities.

Yet, as I said before, I am afraid I have given it too large a space in my narrative. Only it so forcibly reminded me at the time of the expression I could not understand upon Miss Oldcastle's face, and since then has been so often recalled by circumstances and events, that I felt impelled to record it in full. And now I have done with it.

I left the old man with thanks for the kind reception he had given me, and walked home, revolving many things with which I shall not detain the attention of my reader. Indeed my thoughts were confused and troubled, and would ill bear analysis or record. I shut myself up in my study, and tried to read a sermon of Jeremy Taylor. But it would not do. I fell fast asleep over it at last, and woke refreshed.

CHAPTER VIII
WHAT I PREACHED.

During the suffering which accompanied the disappointment at which I have already hinted, I did not think it inconsistent with the manly spirit in which I was resolved to endure it, to seek consolation from such a source as the New Testament-if mayhap consolation for such a trouble was to be found there. Whereupon, a little to my surprise, I discovered that I could not read the Epistles at all. For I did not then care an atom for the theological discussions in which I had been interested before, and for the sake of which I had read those epistles. Now that I was in trouble, what to me was that philosophical theology staring me in the face from out the sacred page? Ah! reader, do not misunderstand me. All reading of the Book is not reading of the Word. And many that are first shall be last and the last first. I know NOW that it was Jesus Christ and not theology that filled the hearts of the men that wrote those epistles-Jesus Christ, the living, loving God-Man, whom I found-not in the Epistles, but in the Gospels. The Gospels contain what the apostles preached-the Epistles what they wrote after the preaching. And until we understand the Gospel, the good news of Jesus Christ our brother-king —until we understand Him, until we have His Spirit, promised so freely to them that ask it-all the Epistles, the words of men who were full of Him, and wrote out of that fulness, who loved Him so utterly that by that very love they were lifted into the air of pure reason and right, and would die for Him, and did die for Him, without two thoughts about it, in the very simplicity of NO CHOICE-the Letters, I say, of such men are to us a sealed book. Until we love the Lord so as to do what He tells us, we have no right to have an opinion about what one of those men meant; for all they wrote is about things beyond us. The simplest woman who tries not to judge her neighbour, or not to be anxious for the morrow, will better know what is best to know, than the best-read bishop without that one simple outgoing of his highest nature in the effort to do the will of Him who thus spoke.

But I have, as is too common with me, been led away by my feelings from the path to the object before me. What I wanted to say was this: that, although I could make nothing of the epistles, could see no possibility of consolation for my distress springing from them, I found it altogether different when I tried the Gospel once more. Indeed, it then took such a hold of me as it had never taken before. Only that is simply saying nothing. I found out that I had known nothing at all about it; that I had only a certain surface-knowledge, which tended rather to ignorance, because it fostered the delusion that I did know. Know that man, Christ Jesus! Ah! Lord, I would go through fire and water to sit the last at Thy table in Thy kingdom; but dare I say now I KNOW Thee! —But Thou art the Gospel, for Thou art the Way, the Truth, and the Life; and I have found Thee the Gospel. For I found, as I read, that Thy very presence in my thoughts, not as the theologians show Thee, but as Thou showedst Thyself to them who report Thee to us, smoothed the troubled waters of my spirit, so that, even while the storm lasted, I was able to walk upon them to go to Thee. And when those waters became clear, I most rejoiced in their clearness because they mirrored Thy form-because Thou wert there to my vision-the one Ideal, the perfect man, the God perfected as king of men by working out His Godhood in the work of man; revealing that God and man are one; that to serve God, a man must be partaker of the Divine nature; that for a man's work to be done thoroughly, God must come and do it first Himself; that to help men, He must be what He is-man in God, God in man-visibly before their eyes, or to the hearing of their ears. So much I saw.

And therefore, when I was once more in a position to help my fellows, what could I want to give them but that which was the very bread and water of life to me-the Saviour himself? And how was I to do this? —By trying to represent the man in all the simplicity of His life, of His sayings and doings, of His refusals to say or do. —I took the story from the beginning, and told them about the Baby; trying to make the fathers and mothers, and all whose love for children supplied the lack of fatherhood and motherhood, feel that it was a real baby-boy. And I followed the life on and on, trying to show them how He felt, as far as one might dare to touch such sacred things, when He did so and so, or said so and so; and what His relation to His father and mother and brothers and sisters was, and to the different kinds of people who came about Him. And I tried to show them what His sayings meant, as far as I understood them myself, and where I could not understand them I just told them so, and said I hoped for more light by and by to enable me to understand them; telling them that that hope was a sharp goad to my resolution, driving me on to do my duty, because I knew that only as I did my duty would light go up in my heart, making me wise to understand the precious words of my Lord. And I told them that if they would try to do their duty, they would find more understanding from that than from any explanation I could give them.

And so I went on from Sunday to Sunday. And the number of people that slept grew less and less, until, at last, it was reduced to the churchwarden, Mr Brownrigg, and an old washerwoman, who, poor thing, stood so much all the week, that sitting down with her was like going to bed, and she never could do it, as she told me, without going to sleep. I, therefore, called upon her every Monday morning, and had five minutes' chat with her as she stood at her wash-tub, wishing to make up to her for her drowsiness; and thinking that if I could once get her interested in anything, she might be able to keep awake a little while at the beginning of the sermon; for she gave me no chance of interesting her on Sundays-going fast asleep the moment I stood up to preach. I never got so far as that, however; and the only fact that showed me I had made any impression upon her, beyond the pleasure she always manifested when I appeared on the Monday, was, that, whereas all my linen had been very badly washed at first, a decided improvement took place after a while, beginning with my surplice and bands, and gradually extending itself to my shirts and handkerchiefs; till at last even Mrs Pearson was unable to find any fault with the poor old sleepy woman's work. For Mr Brownrigg, I am not sure that the sense of any one sentence I ever uttered, down to the day of his death, entered into his brain—I dare not say his mind or heart. With regard to him, and millions besides, I am more than happy to obey my Lord's command, and not judge.

But it was not long either before my congregations began to improve, whatever might be the cause. I could not help hoping that it was really because they liked to hear the Gospel, that is, the good news about Christ himself. And I always made use of the knowledge I had of my individual hearers, to say what I thought would do them good. Not that I ever preached AT anybody; I only sought to explain the principles of things in which I knew action of some sort was demanded from them. For I remembered how our Lord's sermon against covetousness, with the parable of the rich man with the little barn, had for its occasion the request of a man that our Lord would interfere to make his brother share with him; which He declining to do, yet gave both brothers a lesson such as, if they wished to do what was right, would help them to see clearly what was the right thing to do in this and every such matter. Clear the mind's eye, by washing away the covetousness, and the whole nature would be full of light, and the right walk would speedily follow.

Before long, likewise, I was as sure of seeing the pale face of Thomas Weir perched, like that of a man beheaded for treason, upon the apex of the gablet of the old tomb, as I was of hearing the wonderful playing of that husky old organ, of which I have spoken once before. I continued to pay him a visit every now and then; and I assure you, never was the attempt to be thoroughly honest towards a man better understood or more appreciated than my attempt was by the ATHEISTICAL carpenter. The man was no more an atheist than David was when he saw the wicked spreading like a green bay-tree, and was troubled at the sight. He only wanted to see a God in whom he could trust. And if I succeeded at all in making him hope that there might be such a God, it is to me one of the most precious seals of my ministry.

But it was now getting very near Christmas, and there was one person whom I had never yet seen at church: that was Catherine Weir. I thought, at first, it could hardly be that she shrunk from being seen; for how then could she have taken to keeping a shop, where she must be at the beck of every one? I had several times gone and bought tobacco of her since that first occasion; and I had told my housekeeper to buy whatever she could from her, instead of going to the larger shop in the place; at which Mrs Pearson had grumbled a good deal, saying how could the things be so good out of a poky shop like that? But I told her I did not care if the things were not quite as good; for it would be of more consequence to Catherine to have the custom, than it would be to me to have the one lump of sugar I put in my tea of a morning one shade or even two shades whiter. So I had contrived to keep up a kind of connexion with her, although I saw that any attempt at conversation was so distasteful to her, that it must do harm until something should have brought about a change in her feelings; though what feeling wanted changing, I could not at first tell. I came to the conclusion that she had been wronged grievously, and that this wrong operating on a nature similar to her father's, had drawn all her mind to brood over it. The world itself, the whole order of her life, everything about her, would seem then to have wronged her; and to speak to her of religion would only rouse her scorn, and make her feel as if God himself, if there were a God, had wronged her too. Evidently, likewise, she had that peculiarity of strong, undeveloped natures, of being unable, once possessed by one set of thoughts, to get rid of it again, or to see anything except in the shadow of those thoughts. I had no doubt, however, at last, that she was ashamed of her position in the eyes of society, although a hitherto indomitable pride had upheld her to face it so far as was necessary to secure her independence; both of which-pride and shame-prevented her from appearing where it was unnecessary, and especially in church. I could do nothing more than wait for a favourable opportunity. I could invent no way of reaching her yet; for I had soon found that kindness to her boy was regarded rather in the light of an insult to her. I should have been greatly puzzled to account for his being such a sweet little fellow, had I not known that he was a great deal with his aunt and grandfather. A more attentive and devout worshipper was not in the congregation than that little boy.

Before going on to speak of another of the most remarkable of my parishioners, whom I have just once mentioned I believe already, I should like to say that on three several occasions before Christmas I had seen Judy look grave. She was always quite well-behaved in church, though restless, as one might expect. But on these occasions she was not only attentive, but grave, as if she felt something or other. I will not mention what subjects I was upon at those times, because the mention of them would not, in the minds of my readers, at all harmonise with the only notion of Judy they can yet by possibility have.

For Mrs Oldcastle, I never saw her change countenance or even expression at anything—I mean in church.

CHAPTER IX
THE ORGANIST.

On the afternoon of my second Sunday at Marshmallows, I was standing in the churchyard, casting a long shadow in the light of the declining sun. I was reading the inscription upon an old headstone, for I thought everybody was gone; when I heard a door open, and shut again before I could turn. I saw at once that it must have been a little door in the tower, almost concealed from where I stood by a deep buttress. I had never seen the door open, and I had never inquired anything about it, supposing it led merely into the tower.

After a moment it opened again, and, to my surprise, out came, stooping his tall form to get his gray head clear of the low archway, a man whom no one could pass without looking after him. Tall, and strongly built, he had the carriage of a military man, without an atom of that sternness which one generally finds in the faces of those accustomed to command. He had a large face, with large regular features, and large clear gray eyes, all of which united to express an exceeding placidity or repose. It shone with intelligence —a mild intelligence-no way suggestive of profundity, although of geniality. Indeed, there was a little too much expression. The face seemed to express ALL that lay beneath it.

I was not satisfied with the countenance; and yet it looked quite good. It was somehow a too well-ordered face. It was quite Greek in its outline; and marvellously well kept and smooth, considering that the beard, to which razors were utterly strange, and which descended half-way down his breast, would have been as white as snow except for a slight yellowish tinge. His eyebrows were still very dark, only just touched with the frost of winter. His hair, too, as I saw when he lifted his hat, was still wonderfully dark for the condition of his beard. —It flashed into my mind, that this must be the organist who played so remarkably. Somehow I had not happened yet to inquire about him. But there was a stateliness in this man amounting almost to consciousness of dignity; and I was a little bewildered. His clothes were all of black, very neat and clean, but old-fashioned and threadbare. They bore signs of use, but more signs of time and careful keeping. I would have spoken to him, but something in the manner in which he bowed to me as he passed, prevented me, and I let him go unaccosted.

The sexton coming out directly after, and proceeding to lock the door, I was struck by the action. "What IS he locking the door for?" I said to myself. But I said nothing to him, because I had not answered the question myself yet.

"Who is that gentleman," I asked, "who came out just now?"

"That is Mr Stoddart, sir," he answered.

I thought I had heard the name in the neighbourhood before.

"Is it he who plays the organ?" I asked.

"That he do, sir. He's played our organ for the last ten year, ever since he come to live at the Hall."

"What Hall?"

"Why the Hall, to be sure, —Oldcastle Hall, you know."

And then it dawned on my recollection that I had heard Judy mention her uncle Stoddart. But how could he be her uncle?

"Is he a relation of the family?" I asked.

"He's a brother-in-law, I believe, of the old lady, sir, but how ever he come to live there I don't know. It's no such binding connexion, you know, sir. He's been in the milintairy line, I believe, sir, in the Ingies, or somewheres."

I do not think I shall have any more strange parishioners to present to my readers; at least I do not remember any more just at this moment. And this one, as the reader will see, I positively could not keep out.

A military man from India! a brother-in-law of Mrs Oldcastle, choosing to live with her! an entrancing performer upon an old, asthmatic, dry-throated church organ! taking no trouble to make the clergyman's acquaintance, and passing him in the churchyard with a courteous bow,

65

although his face was full of kindliness, if not of kindness! I could not help thinking all this strange. And yet-will the reader cease to accord me credit when I assert it? —although I had quite intended to inquire after him when I left the vicarage to go to the Hall, and had even thought of him when sitting with Mrs Oldcastle, I never thought of him again after going with Judy, and left the house without having made a single inquiry after him. Nor did I think of him again till just as I was passing under the outstretched neck of one of those serpivolants on the gate; and what made me think of him then, I cannot in the least imagine; but I resolved at once that I would call upon him the following week, lest he should think that the fact of his having omitted to call upon me had been the occasion of such an apparently pointed omission on my part. For I had long ago determined to be no further guided by the rules of society than as they might aid in bringing about true neighbourliness, and if possible friendliness and friendship. Wherever they might interfere with these, I would disregard them-as far on the other hand as the disregard of them might tend to bring about the results I desired.

When, carrying out this resolution, I rang the doorbell at the Hall, and inquired whether Mr Stoddart was at home, the butler stared; and, as I simply continued gazing in return, and waiting, he answered at length, with some hesitation, as if he were picking and choosing his words:

"Mr Stoddart never calls upon any one, sir."

"I am not complaining of Mr Stoddart," I answered, wishing to put the man at his ease.

"But nobody calls upon Mr Stoddart," he returned.

"That's very unkind of somebody, surely," I said.

"But he doesn't want anybody to call upon him, sir."

"Ah! that's another matter. I didn't know that. Of course, nobody has a right to intrude upon anybody. However, as I happen to have come without knowing his dislike to being visited, perhaps you will take him my card, and say that if it is not disagreeable to him, I should like exceedingly to thank him in person for his sermon on the organ last Sunday."

He had played an exquisite voluntary in the morning.

"Give my message exactly, if you please," I said, as I followed the man into the hall.

"I will try, sir," he answered. "But won't you come up-stairs to mistress's room, sir, while I take this to Mr Stoddart?"

"No, I thank you," I answered. "I came to call upon Mr Stoddart only, and I will wait the result of you mission here in the hall."

The man withdrew, and I sat down on a bench, and amused myself with looking at the portraits about me. I learned afterwards that they had hung, till some thirty years before, in a long gallery connecting the main part of the house with that portion to which the turret referred to so often in Old Weir's story was attached. One particularly pleased me. It was the portrait of a young woman-very lovely-but with an expression both sad and-scared, I think, would be the readiest word to communicate what I mean. It was indubitably, indeed remarkably, like Miss Oldcastle. And I learned afterwards that it was the portrait of Mrs Oldcastle's grandmother, that very Mrs Crowfoot mentioned in Weir's story. It had been taken about six months after her marriage, and about as many before her death.

The butler returned, with the request that I would follow him. He led me up the grand staircase, through a passage at right angles to that which led to the old lady's room, up a narrow circular staircase at the end of the passage, across a landing, then up a straight steep narrow stair, upon which two people could not pass without turning sideways and then squeezing. At the top of this I found myself in a small cylindrical lobby, papered in blocks of stone. There was no door to be seen. It was lighted by a conical skylight. My conductor gave a push against the wall. Certain blocks yielded, and others came forward. In fact a door revolved on central pivots, and we were admitted to a chamber crowded with books from floor to ceiling, arranged with wonderful neatness and solidity. From the centre of the ceiling, whence hung a globular lamp, radiated what I took to be a number of strong beams supporting a floor above; for our ancestors put the ceiling above the beams, instead of below them, as we do, and gained in space if they lost in quietness. But I soon found out my mistake. Those radiating beams were in reality book-shelves. For on each side of those I passed under I could see the gilded backs of books standing closely ranged together. I had never seen the connivance before, nor, I presume, was it to be seen anywhere else.

"How does Mr Stoddart reach those books?" I asked my conductor.

"I don't exactly know, sir," whispered the butler. "His own man could tell you, I dare say. But he has a holiday to-day; and I do not think he would explain it either; for he says his master allows no interference with his contrivances. I believe, however, he does not use a ladder."

There was no one in the room, and I saw no entrance but that by which we had entered. The next moment, however, a nest of shelves revolved in front of me, and there Mr Stoddart stood with outstretched hand.

"You have found me at last, Mr Walton, and I am glad to see you," he said.

He led me into an inner room, much larger than the one I had passed through.

"I am glad," I replied, "that I did not know, till the butler told me, your unwillingness to be intruded upon; for I fear, had I known it, I should have been yet longer a stranger to you."

"You are no stranger to me. I have heard you read prayers, and I have heard you preach."

"And I have heard you play; so you are no stranger to me either."

"Well, before we say another word," said Mr Stoddart, "I must just say one word about this report of my unsociable disposition. —I encourage it; but am very glad to see you, notwithstanding. —Do sit down."

I obeyed, and waited for the rest of his word.

"I was so bored with visits after I came, visits which were to me utterly uninteresting, that I was only too glad when the unusual nature of some of my pursuits gave rise to the rumour that I was mad. The more people say I am mad, the better pleased I am, so long as they are satisfied with my own mode of shutting myself up, and do not attempt to carry out any fancies of their own in regard to my personal freedom."

Upon this followed some desultory conversation, during which I took some observations of the room. Like the outer room, it was full of books from floor to ceiling. But the ceiling was divided into compartments, harmoniously coloured.

"What a number of books you have!" I observed.

"Not a great many," he answered. "But I think there is hardly one of them with which I have not some kind of personal acquaintance. I think I could almost find you any one you wanted in the dark, or in the twilight at least, which would allow me to distinguish whether the top edge was gilt, red, marbled, or uncut. I have bound a couple of hundred or so of them myself. I don't think you could tell the work from a tradesman's. I'll give you a guinea for the poor-box if you pick out three of my binding consecutively."

I accepted the challenge; for although I could not bind a book, I considered myself to have a keen eye for the outside finish. After looking over the backs of a great many, I took one down, examined a little further, and presented it.

"You are right. Now try again."

Again I was successful, although I doubted.

"And now for the last," he said.

Once more I was right.

"There is your guinea," said he, a little mortified.

"No," I answered. "I do not feel at liberty to take it, because, to tell the truth, the last was a mere guess, nothing more."

Mr Stoddart looked relieved.

"You are more honest than most of your profession," he said. "But I am far more pleased to offer you the guinea upon the smallest doubt of your having won it."

"I have no claim upon it."

"What! Couldn't you swallow a small scruple like that for the sake of the poor even? Well, I don't believe YOU could. —Oblige me by taking this guinea for some one or other of your poor people. But I AM glad you weren't sure of that last book. I am indeed."

I took the guinea, and put it in my purse.

"But," he resumed, "you won't do, Mr Walton. You're not fit for your profession. You won't tell a lie for God's sake. You won't dodge about a little to keep all right between Jove and his weary parishioners. You won't cheat a little for the sake of the poor! You wouldn't even bamboozle a little at a bazaar!"

"I should not like to boast of my principles," I answered; "for the moment one does so, they become as the apples of Sodom. But assuredly I would not favour a fiction to keep a world out of hell. The hell that a lie would keep any man out of is doubtless the very best place for him to go to. It is truth, yes, The Truth that saves the world."

"You are right, I daresay. You are more sure about it than I am though."

"Let us agree where we can," I said, "first of all; and that will make us able to disagree, where we must, without quarrelling."

"Good," he said—"Would you like to see my work shop?"

"Very much, indeed," I answered, heartily.

"Do you take any pleasure in applied mechanics?"

"I used to do so as a boy. But of course I have little time now for anything of the sort."

"Ah! of course."

He pushed a compartment of books. It yielded, and we entered a small closet. In another moment I found myself leaving the floor, and in yet a moment we were on the floor of an upper room.

"What a nice way of getting up-stairs!" I said.

"There is no other way of getting to this room," answered Mr Stoddart. "I built it myself; and there was no room for stairs. This is my shop. In my library I only read my favourite books. Here I read anything I want to read; write anything I want to write; bind my books; invent machines; and amuse myself generally. Take a chair."

I obeyed, and began to look about me.

The room had many books in detached book-cases. There were various benches against the walls between,—one a bookbinder's; another a carpenter's; a third had a turning-lathe; a fourth had an iron vice fixed on it, and was evidently used for working in metal. Besides these, for it was a large room, there were several tables with chemical apparatus upon them, Florence-flasks, retorts, sand-baths, and such like; while in a corner stood a furnace.

"What an accumulation of ways and means you have about you!" I said; "and all, apparently, to different ends."

"All to the same end, if my object were understood."

"I presume I must ask no questions as to that object?"

"It would take time to explain. I have theories of education. I think a man has to educate himself into harmony. Therefore he must open every possible window by which the influences of the All may come in upon him. I do not think any man complete without a perfect development of his mechanical faculties, for instance, and I encourage them to develop themselves into such windows."

"I do not object to your theory, provided you do not put it forward as a perfect scheme of human life. If you did, I should have some questions to ask you about it, lest I should misunderstand you."

He smiled what I took for a self-satisfied smile. There was nothing offensive in it, but it left me without anything to reply to. No embarrassment followed, however, for a rustling motion in the room the same instant attracted my attention, and I saw, to my surprise, and I must confess, a little to my confusion, Miss Oldcastle. She was seated in a corner, reading from a quarto lying upon her knees.

"Oh! you didn't know my niece was here? To tell the truth, I forgot her when I brought you up, else I would have introduced you."

"That is not necessary, uncle," said Miss Oldcastle, closing her book.

I was by her instantly. She slipped the quarto from her knee, and took my offered hand.

"Are you fond of old books?" I said, not having anything better to say.

"Some old books," she answered.

"May I ask what book you were reading?"

"I will answer you-under protest," she said, with a smile.

"I withdraw the question at once," I returned.

"I will answer it notwithstanding. It is a volume of Jacob Behmen."

"Do you understand him?"

"Yes. Don't you?"

"Well, I have made but little attempt," I answered. "Indeed, it was only as I passed through London last that I bought his works; and I am sorry to find that one of the plates is missing from my copy."

"Which plate is it? It is not very easy, I understand, to procure a perfect copy. One of my uncle's copies has no two volumes bound alike. Each must have belonged to a different set."

"I can't tell you what the plate is. But there are only three of those very curious unfolding ones in my third volume, and there should be four."

"I do not think so. Indeed, I am sure you are wrong."

"I am glad to hear it-though to be glad that the world does not possess what I thought I only was deprived of, is selfishness, cover it over as one may with the fiction of a perfect copy."

"I don't know," she returned, without any response to what I said. "I should always like things perfect myself."

"Doubtless," I answered; and thought it better to try another direction.

"How is Mrs Oldcastle?" I asked, feeling in its turn the reproach of hypocrisy; for though I could have suffered, I hope, in my person and goods and reputation, to make that woman other than she was, I could not say that I cared one atom whether she was in health or not. Possibly I should have preferred the latter member of the alternative; for the suffering of the lower nature is as a fire that drives the higher nature upwards. So I felt rather hypocritical when I asked Miss Oldcastle after her.

"Quite well, thank you," she answered, in a tone of indifference, which implied either that she saw through me, or shared in my indifference. I could not tell which.

"And how is Miss Judy?" I inquired.

"A little savage, as usual."

"Not the worse for her wetting, I hope."

"Oh! dear no. There never was health to equal that child's. It belongs to her savage nature."

"I wish some of us were more of savages, then," I returned; for I saw signs of exhaustion in her eyes which moved my sympathy.

"You don't mean me, Mr Walton, I hope. For if you do, I assure you your interest is quite thrown away. Uncle will tell you I am as strong as an elephant."

But here came a slight elevation of her person; and a shadow at the same moment passed over her face. I saw that she felt she ought not to have allowed herself to become the subject of conversation.

Meantime her uncle was busy at one of his benches filing away at a piece of brass fixed in the vice. He had thick gloves on. And, indeed, it had puzzled me before to think how he could have so many kinds of work, and yet keep his hands so smooth and white as they were. I could not help thinking the results could hardly be of the most useful description if they were all accomplished without some loss of whiteness and smoothness in the process. Even the feet that keep the garments clean must be washed themselves in the end.

When I glanced away from Miss Oldcastle in the embarrassment produced by the repulsion of her last manner, I saw Judy in the room. At the same moment Miss Oldcastle rose.

"What is the matter, Judy?" she said.

"Grannie wants you," said Judy.

Miss Oldcastle left the room, and Judy turned to me. "How do you do, Mr Walton?" she said.

"Quite well, thank you, Judy," I answered. "Your uncle admits you to his workshop, then?"

"Yes, indeed. He would feel rather dull, sometimes, without me. Wouldn't you, Uncle Stoddart?"

"Just as the horses in the field would feel dull without the gad-fly, Judy," said Mr Stoddart, laughing.

Judy, however, did not choose to receive the laugh as a scholium explanatory of the remark, and was gone in a moment, leaving Mr Stoddart and myself alone. I must say he looked a little troubled at the precipitate retreat of the damsel; but he recovered himself with a smile, and said to me,

"I wonder what speech I shall make next to drive you away, Mr Walton."

"I am not so easily got rid of, Mr Stoddart," I answered. "And as for taking offence, I don't like it, and therefore I never take it. But tell me what you are doing now."

"I have been working for some time at an attempt after a perpetual motion, but, I must confess, more from a metaphysical or logical point of view than a mechanical one."

Here he took a drawing from a shelf, explanatory of his plan.

"You see," he said, "here is a top made of platinum, the heaviest of metals, except iridium-which it would be impossible to procure enough of, and which would be difficult to work into the proper shape. It is surrounded you will observe, by an air-tight receiver, communicating by this tube with a powerful air-pump. The plate upon which the point of the top rests and revolves is a diamond; and I ought to have mentioned that the peg of the top is a diamond likewise. This is, of course, for the sake of reducing the friction. By this apparatus communicating with the top, through the receiver, I set the top in motion-after exhausting the air as far as possible. Still there is the difficulty of the friction of the diamond point upon the diamond plate, which must ultimately occasion repose. To obviate this, I have constructed here, underneath, a small steam-engine which shall cause the diamond plate to revolve at precisely the same rate of speed as the top itself. This, of course, will prevent all friction."

"Not that with the unavoidable remnant of air, however," I ventured to suggest.

"That is just my weak point," he answered. "But that will be so very small!"

"Yes; but enough to deprive the top of PERPETUAL motion."

"But suppose I could get over that difficulty, would the contrivance have a right to the name of a perpetual motion? For you observe that the steam-engine below would not be the cause of the motion. That comes from above, here, and is withdrawn, finally withdrawn."

"I understand perfectly," I answered. "At least, I think I do. But I return the question to you: Is a motion which, although not caused, is ENABLED by another motion, worthy of the name of a perpetual motion; seeing the perpetuity of motion has not to do merely with time, but with the indwelling of self-generative power-renewing itself constantly with the process of exhaustion?"

He threw down his file on the bench.

"I fear you are right," he said. "But you will allow it would have made a very pretty machine."

"Pretty, I will allow," I answered, "as distinguished from beautiful. For I can never dissociate beauty from use."

"You say that! with all the poetic things you say in your sermons! For I am a sharp listener, and none the less such that you do not see me. I have a loophole for seeing you. And I flatter myself, therefore, I am the only person in the congregation on a level with you in respect of balancing advantages. I cannot contradict you, and you cannot address me."

"Do you mean, then, that whatever is poetical is useless?" I asked.

"Do you assert that whatever is useful is beautiful?" he retorted.

"A full reply to your question would need a ream of paper and a quarter of quills," I answered; "but I think I may venture so far as to say that whatever subserves a noble end must in itself be beautiful."

"Then a gallows must be beautiful because it subserves the noble end of ridding the world of malefactors?" he returned, promptly.

I had to think for a moment before I could reply.

"I do not see anything noble in the end," I answered.

"If the machine got rid of malefaction, it would, indeed, have a noble end. But if it only compels it to move on, as a constable does-from this world into another —I do not, I say, see anything so noble in that end. The gallows cannot be beautiful."

"Ah, I see. You don't approve of capital punishments."

"I do not say that. An inevitable necessity is something very different from a noble end. To cure the diseased mind is the noblest of ends; to make the sinner forsake his ways, and the unrighteous man his thoughts, the loftiest of designs; but to punish him for being wrong, however necessary it may be for others, cannot, if dissociated from the object of bringing good out of evil, be called in any sense a NOBLE end. I think now, however, it would be but fair in you to give me some answer to my question. Do you think the poetic useless?"

"I think it is very like my machine. It may exercise the faculties without subserving any immediate progress."

"It is so difficult to get out of the region of the poetic, that I cannot think it other than useful: it is so widespread. The useless could hardly be so nearly universal. But I should like to ask you another question: What is the immediate effect of anything poetic upon your mind?"

"Pleasure," he answered.

"And is pleasure good or bad?"

"Sometimes the one, sometimes the other."

"In itself?"

"I should say so."

"I should not."

"Are you not, then, by your very profession, more or less an enemy of pleasure?"

"On the contrary, I believe that pleasure is good, and does good, and urges to good. CARE is the evil thing."

"Strange doctrine for a clergyman."

"Now, do not misunderstand me, Mr Stoddart. That might not hurt you, but it would distress me. Pleasure, obtained by wrong, is poison and horror. But it is not the pleasure that hurts, it is the wrong that is in it that hurts; the pleasure hurts only as it leads to more wrong. I almost think myself, that if you could make everybody happy, half the evil would vanish from the earth."

"But you believe in God?"

"I hope in God I do."

"How can you then think that He would not destroy evil at such a cheap and pleasant rate."

"Because He wants to destroy ALL the evil, not the half of it; and destroy it so that it shall not grow again; which it would be sure to do very soon if it had no antidote but happiness. As soon as men got used to happiness, they would begin to sin again, and so lose it all. But care is distrust. I wonder now if ever there was a man who did his duty, and TOOK NO THOUGHT. I wish I could get the testimony of such a man. Has anybody actually tried the plan?"

But here I saw that I was not taking Mr Stoddart with me (as the old phrase was). The reason I supposed to be, that he had never been troubled with much care. But there remained the question, whether he trusted in God or the Bank?

I went back to the original question.

"But I should be very sorry you should think, that to give pleasure was my object in saying poetic things in the pulpit. If I do so, it is because true things come to me in their natural garments of poetic forms. What you call the POETIC is only the outer beauty that belongs to all inner or spiritual beauty-just as a lovely face-mind, I say LOVELY, not PRETTY, not HANDSOME-is the outward and visible presence of a lovely mind. Therefore, saying I cannot dissociate beauty from use, I am free to say as many poetic things-though, mind, I don't claim them: you attribute them to me-as shall be of the highest use, namely, to embody and reveal the true. But a machine has material use for its end. The most grotesque machine I ever saw that DID something, I felt to be in its own kind beautiful; as God called many fierce and grotesque things good when He made the world-good for their good end. But your machine does nothing more than raise the metaphysical doubt and question, whether it can with propriety be called a perpetual motion or not?"

To this Mr Stoddart making no reply, I take the opportunity of the break in our conversation to say to my readers, that I know there was no satisfactory following out of an argument on either side in the passage of words I have just given. Even the closest reasoner finds it next to impossible to attend to all the suggestions in his own mind, not one of which he is willing to lose, to attend at the same time to everything his antagonist says or suggests, that he may do him justice, and to keep an even course towards his goal-each having the opposite goal in view. In fact, an argument, however simply conducted and honourable, must just resemble a game at football; the unfortunate question being the ball, and the numerous and sometimes conflicting thoughts which arise in each mind forming the two parties whose energies are spent in a succession of kicks. In fact, I don't like argument, and I don't care for the victory. If I had my way, I would never argue at all. I would spend my energy in setting forth what I believe-as like itself as I could represent it, and so leave it to work its own way, which, if it be the right way, it must work in the right mind,—for Wisdom is justified of her children; while no one who loves the truth can be other than anxious, that if he has spoken the evil thing it may return to him void: that is a defeat he may well pray for. To succeed in the wrong is the most dreadful punishment to a man who, in the main, is honest. But I beg to assure my reader I could write a long treatise on the matter between Mr Stoddart and myself; therefore, if he is not yet interested in such questions, let him be thankful to me for considering such a treatise out of place here. I will only say in brief, that I believe with all my heart that the true is the beautiful, and that nothing evil can be other than ugly. If it seems not so, it is in virtue of some good mingled with the evil, and not in the smallest degree in virtue of the evil.

I thought it was time for me to take my leave. But I could not bear to run away with the last word, as it were: so I said,

"You put plenty of poetry yourself into that voluntary you played last Sunday. I am so much obliged to you for it!"

"Oh! that fugue. You liked it, did you?"

"More than I can tell you."

"I am very glad."

"Do you know those two lines of Milton in which he describes such a performance on the organ?"

"No. Can you repeat them?"

"'His volant touch, Instinct through all proportions, low and high, Fled and pursued transverse the resonant fugue.'"

"That is wonderfully fine. Thank you. That is better than my fugue by a good deal. You have cancelled the obligation."

"Do you think doing a good turn again is cancelling an obligation? I don't think an obligation can ever be RETURNED in the sense of being got rid of. But I am being hypercritical."

"Not at all. —Shall I tell you what I was thinking of while playing that fugue?"

"I should like much to hear."

"I had been thinking, while you were preaching, of the many fancies men had worshipped for the truth; now following this, now following that; ever believing they were on the point of laying hold upon her, and going down to the grave empty-handed as they came."

"And empty-hearted, too?" I asked; but he went on without heeding me.

"And I saw a vision of multitudes following, following where nothing was to be seen, with arms outstretched in all directions, some clasping vacancy to their bosoms, some reaching on tiptoe over the heads of their neighbours, and some with hanging heads, and hands clasped behind their backs, retiring hopeless from the chase."

"Strange!" I said; "for I felt so full of hope while you played, that I never doubted it was hope you meant to express."

"So I do not doubt I did; for the multitude was full of hope, vain hope, to lay hold upon the truth. And you, being full of the main expression, and in sympathy with it, did not heed the undertones of disappointment, or the sighs of those who turned their backs on the chase. Just so it is in life."

"I am no musician," I returned, "to give you a musical counter to your picture. But I see a grave man tilling the ground in peace, and the form of Truth standing behind him, and folding her wings closer and closer over and around him as he works on at his day's labour."

"Very pretty," said Mr Stoddart, and said no more.

"Suppose," I went on, "that a person knows that he has not laid hold on the truth, is that sufficient ground for his making any further assertion than that he has not found it?"

"No. But if he has tried hard and has not found ANYTHING that he can say is true, he cannot help thinking that most likely there is no such thing."

"Suppose," I said, "that nobody has found the truth, is that sufficient ground for saying that nobody ever will find it? or that there is no such thing as truth to be found? Are the ages so nearly done that no chance yet remains? Surely if God has made us to desire the truth, He has got some truth to cast into the gulf of that desire. Shall God create hunger and no food? But possibly a man may be looking the wrong way for it. You may be using the microscope, when you ought to open both eyes and lift up your head. Or a man may be finding some truth which is feeding his soul, when he does not think he is finding any. You know the Fairy Queen. Think how long the Redcross Knight travelled with the Lady Truth-Una, you know-without learning to believe in her; and how much longer still without ever seeing her face. For my part, may God give me strength to follow till I die. Only I will venture to say this, that it is not by any agony of the intellect that I expect to discover her."

Mr Stoddart sat drumming silently with his fingers, a half-smile on his face, and his eyes raised at an angle of forty-five degrees. I felt that the enthusiasm with which I had spoken was thrown away upon him. But I was not going to be ashamed therefore. I would put some faith in his best nature.

"But does not," he said, gently lowering his eyes upon mine after a moment's pause —"does not your choice of a profession imply that you have not to give chase to a fleeting phantom? Do you not profess to have, and hold, and therefore teach the truth?"

"I profess only to have caught glimpses of her white garments, —those, I mean, of the abstract truth of which you speak. But I have seen that which is eternally beyond her: the ideal in the real, the living truth, not the truth that I can THINK, but the truth that thinks itself, that thinks me, that God has thought, yea, that God is, the truth BEING true to itself and to God and to man-Christ Jesus, my Lord, who knows, and feels, and does the truth. I have seen Him, and I am both content and unsatisfied. For in Him are hid all the treasures of wisdom and knowledge. Thomas a Kempis says: 'Cui aeternum Verbum loquitur, ille a multis opinionibus expeditur.'" (He to whom the eternal Word speaks, is set free from a press of opinions.)

I rose, and held out my hand to Mr Stoddart. He rose likewise, and took it kindly, conducted me to the room below, and ringing the bell, committed me to the care of the butler.

As I approached the gate, I met Jane Rogers coming back from the village. I stopped and spoke to her. Her eyes were very red.

"Nothing amiss at home, Jane?" I said.

"No, sir, thank you," answered Jane, and burst out crying.

"What is the matter, then? Is your——"

"Nothing's the matter with nobody, sir."

"Something is the matter with you."

"Yes, sir. But I'm quite well."

"I don't want to pry into your affairs; but if you think I can be of any use to you, mind you come to me."

"Thank you kindly, sir," said Jane; and, dropping a courtesy, walked on with her basket.

I went to her parents' cottage. As I came near the mill, the young miller was standing in the door with his eyes fixed on the ground, while the mill went on hopping behind him. But when he caught sight of me, he turned, and went in, as if he had not seen me.

"Has he been behaving ill to Jane?" thought I. As he evidently wished to avoid me, I passed the mill without looking in at the door, as I was in the habit of doing, and went on to the cottage, where I lifted the latch, and walked in. Both the old people were there, and both looked troubled, though they welcomed me none the less kindly.

"I met Jane," I said, "and she looked unhappy; so I came on to hear what was the matter."

"You oughtn't to be troubled with our small affairs," said Mrs. Rogers.

"If the parson wants to know, why, the parson must be told," said Old Rogers, smiling cheerily, as if he, at least, would be relieved by telling me.

"I don't want to know," I said, "if you don't want to tell me. But can I be of any use?"

"I don't think you can, sir,—leastways, I'm afraid not," said the old woman.

"I am sorry to say, sir, that Master Brownrigg and his son has come to words about our Jane; and it's not agreeable to have folk's daughter quarrelled over in that way," said Old Rogers. "What'll be the upshot on it, I don't know, but it looks bad now. For the father he tells the son that if ever he hear of him saying one word to our Jane, out of the mill he goes, as sure as his name's Dick. Now, it's rather a good chance, I think, to see what the young fellow's made of, sir. So I tells my old 'oman here; and so I told Jane. But neither on 'em seems to see the comfort of it somehow. But the New Testament do say a man shall leave father and mother, and cleave to his wife."

"But she ain't his wife yet," said Mrs Rogers to her husband, whose drift was not yet evident.

"No more she can be, 'cept he leaves his father for her."

"And what'll become of them then, without the mill?"

"You and me never had no mill, old 'oman," said Rogers; "yet here we be, very nearly ripe now,—ain't us, wife?"

"Medlar-like, Old Rogers, I doubt,—rotten before we're ripe," replied his wife, quoting a more humorous than refined proverb.

"Nay, nay, old 'oman. Don't 'e say so. The Lord won't let us rot before we're ripe, anyhow. That I be sure on."

"But, anyhow, it's all very well to talk. Thou knows how to talk, Rogers. But how will it be when the children comes, and no mill?"

"To grind 'em in, old 'oman?"

Mrs Rogers turned to me, who was listening with real interest, and much amusement.

"I wish you would speak a word to Old Rogers, sir. He never will speak as he's spoken to. He's always over merry, or over serious. He either takes me up short with a sermon, or he laughs me out of countenance that I don't know where to look."

Now I was pretty sure that Rogers's conduct was simple consistency, and that the difficulty arose from his always acting upon one or two of the plainest principles of truth and right; whereas his wife, good woman-for the bad, old leaven of the Pharisees could not rise much in her somehow-was always reminding him of certain precepts of behaviour to the oblivion of principles. "A bird in the hand," &c.—"Marry in haste," &c.—"When want comes in at the door love flies out at the window," were amongst her favourite sayings; although not one of them was supported by her own experience. For instance, she had married in haste herself, and never, I believe, had once thought of repenting of it, although she had had far more than the requisite leisure for doing so. And many was the time that want had come in at her door, and the first thing it always did was to clip the wings of Love, and make him less flighty, and more tender and serviceable. So I could not even pretend to read her husband a lecture.

"He's a curious man, Old Rogers," I said. "But as far as I can see, he's in the right, in the main. Isn't he now?"

"Oh, yes, I daresay. I think he's always right about the rights of the thing, you know. But a body may go too far that way. It won't do to starve, sir."

Strange confusion-or, ought I not rather to say? —ordinary and commonplace confusion of ideas!

"I don't think," I said, "any one can go too far in the right way."

"That's just what I want my old 'oman to see, and I can't get it into her, sir. If a thing's right, it's right, and if a thing's wrong, why, wrong it is. The helm must either be to starboard or port, sir."

"But why talk of starving?" I said. "Can't Dick work? Who could think of starting that nonsense?"

"Why, my old 'oman here. She wants 'em to give it up, and wait for better times. The fact is, she don't want to lose the girl."

"But she hasn't got her at home now."

"She can have her when she wants her, though—leastways after a bit of warning. Whereas, if she was married, and the consequences a follerin' at her heels, like a man-o'-war with her convoy, she would find she was chartered for another port, she would."

"Well, you see, sir, Rogers and me's not so young as we once was, and we're likely to be growing older every day. And if there's a difficulty in the way of Jane's marriage, why, I take it as a Godsend."

"How would you have liked such a Godsend, Mrs Rogers, when you were going to be married to your sailor here? What would you have done?"

"Why, whatever he liked to be sure. But then, you see, Dick's not my Rogers."

"But your daughter thinks about him much in the same way as you did about this dear old man here when he was young."

"Young people may be in the wrong, *I* see nothing in Dick Brownrigg."

"But young people may be right sometimes, and old people may be wrong sometimes."

"I can't be wrong about Rogers."

"No, but you may be wrong about Dick."

"Don't you trouble yourself about my old 'oman, sir. She allus was awk'ard in stays, but she never missed them yet. When she's said her say, round she comes in the wind like a bird, sir."

"There's a good old man to stick up for your old wife! Still, I say, they may as well wait a bit. It would be a pity to anger the old gentleman."

"What does the young man say to it?"

"Why, he says, like a man, he can work for her as well's the mill, and he's ready, if she is."

"I am very glad to hear such a good account of him. I shall look in, and have a little chat with him. I always liked the look of him. Good morning, Mrs. Rogers."

"I'll see you across the stream, sir," said the old man, following me out of the house.

"You see, sir," he resumed, as soon as we were outside, "I'm always afeard of taking things out of the Lord's hands. It's the right way, surely, that when a man loves a woman, and has told her so, he should act like a man, and do as is right. And isn't that the Lord's way? And can't He give them what's good for them. Mayhap they won't love each other the less in the end if Dick has a little bit of the hard work that many a man that the Lord loved none the less has had before him. I wouldn't like to anger the old gentleman, as my wife says; but if I was Dick, I know what I would do. But don't 'e think hard of my wife, sir, for I believe there's a bit of pride in it. She's afeard of bein' supposed to catch at Richard Brownrigg, because he's above us, you know, sir. And I can't altogether blame her, only we ain't got to do with the look o' things, but with the things themselves."

"I understand you quite, and I'm very much of your mind. You can trust me to have a little chat with him, can't you?"

"That I can, sir."

Here we had come to the boundary of his garden-the busy stream that ran away, as if it was scared at the labour it had been compelled to go through, and was now making the best of its speed back to its mother-ocean, to tell sad tales of a world where every little brook must do some work ere it gets back to its rest. I bade him good day, jumped across it, and went into the mill, where Richard was tying the mouth of a sack, as gloomily as the brothers of Joseph must have tied their sacks after his silver cup had been found.

"Why did you turn away from me, as I passed half-an-hour ago, Richard?" I said, cheerily.

"I beg your pardon, sir. I didn't think you saw me."

"But supposing I hadn't? —But I won't tease you. I know all about it. Can I do anything for you?"

"No, sir. You can't move my father. It's no use talking to him. He never hears a word anybody says. He never hears a word you say o' Sundays, sir. He won't even believe the Mark Lane Express about the price of corn. It's no use talking to him, sir."

"You wouldn't mind if I were to try?"

"No, sir. You can't make matters worse. No more can you make them any better, sir."

"I don't say I shall talk to him; but I may try it, if I find a fitting opportunity."

"He's always worse-more obstinate, that is, when he's in a good temper. So you may choose your opportunity wrong. But it's all the same. It can make no difference."

"What are you going to do, then?"

"I would let him do his worst. But Jane doesn't like to go against her mother. I'm sure I can't think how she should side with my father against both of us. He never laid her under any such obligation, I'm sure."

"There may be more ways than one of accounting for that. You must mind, however, and not be too hard upon your father. You're quite right in holding fast to the girl; but mind that vexation does not make you unjust."

"I wish my mother were alive. She was the only one that ever could manage him. How she contrived to do it nobody could think; but manage him she did, somehow or other. There's not a husk of use in talking to HIM."

"I daresay he prides himself on not being moved by talk. But has he ever had a chance of knowing Jane-of seeing what kind of a girl she is?"

"He's seen her over and over."

"But seeing isn't always believing."

"It certainly isn't with him."

"If he could only know her! But don't you be too hard upon him. And don't do anything in a hurry. Give him a little time, you know. Mrs Rogers won't interfere between you and Jane, I am pretty sure. But don't push matters till we see. Good-bye."

"Good-bye, and thank you kindly, sir. —Ain't I to see Jane in the meantime?"

"If I were you, I would make no difference. See her as often as you used, which I suppose was as often as you could. I don't think, I say, that her mother will interfere. Her father is all on your side."

I called on Mr Brownrigg; but, as his son had forewarned me, I could make nothing of him. He didn't see, when the mill was his property, and Dick was his son, why he shouldn't have his way with them. And he was going to have his way with them. His son might marry any lady in the land; and he wasn't going to throw himself away that way.

I will not weary my readers with the conversation we had together. All my missiles of argument were lost as it were in a bank of mud, the weight and resistance of which they only increased. My experience in the attempt, however, did a little to reconcile me to his going to sleep in church; for I saw that it could make little difference whether he was asleep or awake. He, and not Mr. Stoddart in his organ sentry-box, was the only person whom it was absolutely impossible to preach to. You might preach AT him; but TO him? —no.

CHAPTER X
MY CHRISTMAS PARTY.

As Christmas Day drew nearer and nearer, my heart glowed with the more gladness; and the question came more and more pressingly-Could I not do something to make it more really a holiday of the Church for my parishioners? That most of them would have a little more enjoyment on it than they had had all the year through, I had ground to hope; but I wanted to connect this gladness-in their minds, I mean, for who could dissever them in fact? —with its source, the love of God, that love manifested unto men in the birth of the Human Babe, the Son of Man. But I would not interfere with the Christmas Day at home. I resolved to invite as many of my parishioners as would come, to spend Christmas Eve at the Vicarage.

I therefore had a notice to that purport affixed to the church door; and resolved to send out no personal invitations whatever, so that I might not give offence by accidental omission. The only person thrown into perplexity by this mode of proceeding was Mrs. Pearson.

"How many am I to provide for, sir?" she said, with an injured air.

"For as many as you ever saw in church at one time," I said. "And if there should be too much, why so much the better. It can go to make Christmas Day the merrier at some of the poorer houses."

She looked discomposed, for she was not of an easy temper. But she never ACTED from her temper; she only LOOKED or SPOKE from it.

"I shall want help," she said, at length.

"As much as you like, Mrs. Pearson. I can trust you entirely."

Her face brightened; and the end showed that I had not trusted her amiss.

I was a little anxious about the result of the invitation-partly as indicating the amount of confidence my people placed in me. But although no one said a word to me about it beforehand except Old Rogers, as soon as the hour arrived, the people began to come. And the first I welcomed was Mr. Brownrigg.

I had had all the rooms on the ground-floor prepared for their reception. Tables of provision were set out in every one of them. My visitors had tea or coffee, with plenty of bread and butter, when they arrived; and the more solid supplies were reserved for a later part of the evening. I soon found myself with enough to do. But before long, I had a very efficient staff. For after having had occasion, once or twice, to mention something of my plans for the evening, I found my labours gradually diminish, and yet everything seemed to go right; the fact being that good Mr Boulderstone, in one part, had cast himself into the middle of the flood, and stood there immovable both in face and person, turning its waters into the right channel, namely, towards the barn, which I had fitted up for their reception in a body; while in another quarter, namely, in the barn, Dr Duncan was doing his best, and that was simply something first-rate, to entertain the people till all should be ready. From a kind of instinct these gentlemen had taken upon them to be my staff, almost without knowing it, and very grateful I was. I found, too, that they soon gathered some of the young and more active spirits about them, whom they employed in various ways for the good of the community.

When I came in and saw the goodly assemblage, for I had been busy receiving them in the house, I could not help rejoicing that my predecessor had been so fond of farming that he had rented land in the neighbourhood of the vicarage, and built this large barn, of which I could make a hall to entertain my friends. The night was frosty-the stars shining brilliantly overhead-so that, especially for country people, there was little danger in the short passage to be made to it from the house. But, if necessary, I resolved to have a covered-way built before next time. For how can a man be THE PERSON of a parish, if he never entertains his parishioners? And really, though it was lighted only with candles round the walls, and I had not been able to do much for the decoration of the place, I thought it looked very well, and my heart was glad that Christmas Eve-just as if the Babe had been coming again to us that same night. And is He not always coming to us afresh in every childlike feeling that awakes in the hearts of His people?

I walked about amongst them, greeting them, and greeted everywhere in turn with kind smiles and hearty shakes of the hand. As often as I paused in my communications for a moment, it was amusing to watch Mr. Boulderstone's honest, though awkward endeavours to be at ease with his inferiors; but Dr Duncan was just a sight worth seeing. Very tall and very stately, he was talking now to this old man, now to that young woman, and every face glistened towards which he turned. There was no condescension about him. He was as polite and courteous to one as to another, and the smile that every now and then lighted up his old face, was genuine and sympathetic. No one could have known by his behaviour that he was not at court. And I thought—Surely even the contact with such a man will do something to refine the taste of my people. I felt more certain than ever that a free mingling of all classes would do more than anything else towards binding us all into a wise patriotic nation; would tend to keep down that foolish emulation which makes one class ape another from afar, like Ben Jonson's Fungoso, "still lighting short a suit;" would refine the roughness of the rude, and enable the polished to see with what safety his just share in public matters might be committed into the hands of the honest workman. If we could once leave it to each other to give what honour is due; knowing that honour demanded is as worthless as insult undeserved is hurtless! What has one to do to honour himself? That is and can be no honour. When one has learned to seek the honour that cometh from God only, he will take the withholding of the honour that comes from men very quietly indeed.

The only thing that disappointed me was, that there was no one there to represent Oldcastle Hall. But how could I have everything a success at once!—And Catherine Weir was likewise absent.

After we had spent a while in pleasant talk, and when I thought nearly all were with us, I got up on a chair at the end of the barn, and said:—

"Kind friends,—I am very grateful to you for honouring my invitation as you have done. Permit me to hope that this meeting will be the first of many, and that from it may grow the yearly custom in this parish of gathering in love and friendship upon Christmas Eve. When God comes to man, man looks round for his neighbour. When man departed from God in the Garden of Eden, the only man in the world ceased to be the friend of the only woman in the world; and, instead of seeking to bear her burden, became her accuser to God, in whom he saw only the Judge, unable to perceive that the Infinite love of the Father had come to punish him in tenderness and grace. But when God in Jesus comes back to men, brothers and sisters spread forth their arms to embrace each other, and so to embrace Him. This is, when He is born again in our souls. For, dear friends, what we all need is just to become little children like Him; to cease to be careful about many things, and trust in Him, seeking only that He should rule, and that we should be made good like Him. What else is meant by 'Seek ye first the kingdom of God and his righteousness, and all these things shall be added unto you?' Instead of doing so, we seek the things God has promised to look after for us, and refuse to seek the thing He wants us to seek—a thing that cannot be given us, except we seek it. We profess to think Jesus the grandest and most glorious of men, and yet hardly care to be like Him; and so when we are offered His Spirit, that is, His very nature within us, for the asking, we will hardly take the trouble to ask for it. But to-night, at least, let all unkind thoughts, all hard judgments of one another, all selfish desires after our own way, be put from us, that we may welcome the Babe into our very bosoms; that when He comes amongst us—for is He not like a child still, meek and lowly of heart?—He may not be troubled to find that we are quarrelsome, and selfish, and unjust."

I came down from the chair, and Mr Brownrigg being the nearest of my guests, and wide awake, for he had been standing, and had indeed been listening to every word according to his ability, I shook hands with him. And positively there was some meaning in the grasp with which he returned mine.

I am not going to record all the proceedings of the evening; but I think it may be interesting to my readers to know something of how we spent it. First of all, we sang a hymn about the Nativity. And then I read an extract from a book of travels, describing the interior of an Eastern cottage, probably much resembling the inn in which our Lord was born, the stable being scarcely divided fron the rest of the house. For I felt that to open the inner eyes even of the brain, enabling people to SEE in some measure the reality of the old lovely story, to help them to have what the Scotch philosophers call a true CONCEPTION of the external conditions and circumstances of the events, might help to open the yet deeper spiritual eyes which alone can see the meaning and truth dwelling in and giving shape to the outward facts. And the extract was listened to with all the attention I could wish, except, at first, from some youngsters at the further end of the barn, who became, however, perfectly still as I proceeded.

After this followed conversation, during which I talked a good deal to Jane Rogers, paying her particular attention indeed, with the hope of a chance of bringing old Mr Brownrigg and her together in some way.

"How is your mistress, Jane?" I said.

"Quite well, sir, thank you. I only wish she was here."

"I wish she were. But perhaps she will come next year."

"I think she will. I am almost sure she would have liked to come to-night; for I heard her say" — —

"I beg your pardon, Jane, for interrupting you; but I would rather not be told anything you may have happened to overhear," I said, in a low voice.

"Oh, sir!" returned Jane, blushing a dark crimson; "it wasn't anything particular."

"Still, if it was anything on which a wrong conjecture might be built" — "I wanted to soften it to her —"it is better that one should not be told it. Thank you for your kind intention, though. And now, Jane," I said, "will you do me a favour?"

"That I will, sir, if I can."

"Sing that Christmas carol I heard you sing last night to your mother."

"I didn't know any one was listening, sir."

"I know you did not. I came to the door with your father, and we stood and listened."

She looked very frightened. But I would not have asked her had I not known that she could sing like a bird.

"I am afraid I shall make a fool of myself," she said.

"We should all be willing to run that risk for the sake of others," I answered.

"I will try then, sir."

So she sang, and her clear voice soon silenced the speech all round.

"Babe Jesus lay on Mary's lap;
    The sun shone in His hair:
And so it was she saw, mayhap,
    The crown already there.
"For she sang: 'Sleep on, my little King!

Bad Herod dares not come;
Before Thee, sleeping, holy thing,
    Wild winds would soon be dumb.
"'I kiss Thy hands, I kiss Thy feet,

My King, so long desired;
Thy hands shall never be soil'd, my sweet,
    Thy feet shall never be tired.
"'For Thou art the King of men, my son;

Thy crown I see it plain;
And men shall worship Thee, every one,
    And cry, Glory! Amen.'"

>"Babe Jesus open'd His eyes so wide!

>At Mary look'd her Lord.
>And Mary stinted her song and sigh'd.
>Babe Jesus said never a word."

When Jane had done singing, I asked her where she had learned the carol; and she answered, —
"My mistress gave it me. There was a picture to it of the Baby on his mother's knee."
"I never saw it," I said. "Where did you get the tune?"
"I thought it would go with a tune I knew; and I tried it, and it did. But I was not fit to sing to you, sir."
"You must have quite a gift of song, Jane!" I said.
"My father and mother can both sing."
Mr Brownrigg was seated on the other side of me, and had apparently listened with some interest. His face was ten degrees less stupid than it usually was. I fancied I saw even a glimmer of some satisfaction in it. I turned to Old Rogers.
"Sing us a song, Old Rogers," I said.
"I'm no canary at that, sir; and besides, my singing days be over. I advise you to ask Dr. Duncan there. He CAN sing."
I rose and said to the assembly:
"My friends, if I did not think God was pleased to see us enjoying ourselves, I should have no heart for it myself. I am going to ask our dear friend Dr. Duncan to give us a song. —If you please, Dr. Duncan."
"I am very nearly too old," said the doctor; "but I will try."
His voice was certainly a little feeble; but the song was not much the worse for it. And a more suitable one for all the company he could hardly have pitched upon.

>"There is a plough that has no share,
>But a coulter that parteth keen and fair.
>But the furrows they rise
>To a terrible size,
>Or ever the plough hath touch'd them there.
>'Gainst horses and plough in wrath they shake:
>The horses are fierce; but the plough will break.
>"And the seed that is dropt in those furrows of fear,

>Will lift to the sun neither blade nor ear.
>Down it drops plumb,
>Where no spring times come;
>And here there needeth no harrowing gear:
>Wheat nor poppy nor any leaf
>Will cover this naked ground of grief.
>"But a harvest-day will come at last

>When the watery winter all is past;
>The waves so gray
>Will be shorn away
>By the angels' sickles keen and fast;
>And the buried harvest of the sea
>Stored in the barns of eternity."

Genuine applause followed the good doctor's song. I turned to Miss Boulderstone, from whom I had borrowed a piano, and asked her to play a country dance for us. But first I said-not getting up on a chair this time: —

"Some people think it is not proper for a clergyman to dance. I mean to assert my freedom from any such law. If our Lord chose to represent, in His parable of the Prodigal Son, the joy in Heaven over a repentant sinner by the figure of 'music and dancing,' I will hearken to Him rather than to men, be they as good as they may."

For I had long thought that the way to make indifferent things bad, was for good people not to do them.

And so saying, I stepped up to Jane Rogers, and asked her to dance with me. She blushed so dreadfully that, for a moment, I was almost sorry I had asked her. But she put her hand in mine at once; and if she was a little clumsy, she yet danced very naturally, and I had the satisfaction of feeling that I had an honest girl near me, who I knew was friendly to me in her heart.

But to see the faces of the people! While I had been talking, Old Rogers had been drinking in every word. To him it was milk and strong meat in one. But now his face shone with a father's gratification besides. And Richard's face was glowing too. Even old Brownrigg looked with a curious interest upon us, I thought.

Meantime Dr Duncan was dancing with one of his own patients, old Mrs Trotter, to whose wants he ministered far more from his table than his surgery. I have known that man, hearing of a case of want from his servant, send the fowl he was about to dine upon, untouched, to those whose necessity was greater than his.

And Mr Boulderstone had taken out old Mrs Rogers; and young Brownrigg had taken Mary Weir. Thomas Weir did not dance at all, but looked on kindly.

"Why don't you dance, Old Rogers?" I said, as I placed his daughter in a seat beside him.

"Did your honour ever see an elephant go up the futtock-shrouds?"

"No. I never did."

"I thought you must, sir, to ask me why I don't dance. You won't take my fun ill, sir? I'm an old man-o'-war's man, you know, sir."

"I should have thought, Rogers, that you would have known better by this time, than make such an apology to ME."

"God bless you, sir. An old man's safe with you-or a young lass, either, sir," he added, turning with a smile to his daughter.

I turned, and addressed Mr Boulderstone.

"I am greatly obliged to you, Mr Boulderstone, for the help you have given me this evening. I've seen you talking to everybody, just as if you had to entertain them all."

"I hope I haven't taken too much upon me. But the fact is, somehow or other, I don't know how, I got into the spirit of it."

"You got into the spirit of it because you wanted to help me, and I thank you heartily."

"Well, I thought it wasn't a time to mind one's peas and cues exactly. And really it's wonderful how one gets on without them. I hate formality myself."

The dear fellow was the most formal man I had ever met.

"Why don't you dance, Mr Brownrigg?"

"Who'd care to dance with me, sir? I don't care to dance with an old woman; and a young woman won't care to dance with me."

"I'll find you a partner, if you will put yourself in my hands."

"I don't mind trusting myself to you, sir."

So I led him to Jane Rogers. She stood up in respectful awe before the master of her destiny. There were signs of calcitration in the churchwarden, when he perceived whither I was leading him. But when he saw the girl stand trembling before him, whether it was that he was flattered by the signs of his own power, accepting them as homage, or that his hard heart actually softened a little, I cannot tell, but, after just a perceptible hesitation, he said:

"Come along, my lass, and let's have a hop together."

She obeyed very sweetly.

"Don't be too shy," I whispered to her as she passed me.

And the churchwarden danced very heartily with the lady's-maid.

I then asked him to take her into the house, and give her something to eat in return for her song. He yielded somewhat awkwardly, and what passed between them I do not know. But when they returned, she seemed less frightened at him than when she heard me make the proposal. And when the company was parting, I heard him take leave of her with the words—

"Give us a kiss, my girl, and let bygones be bygones."

Which kiss I heard with delight. For had I not been a peacemaker in this matter? And had I not then a right to feel blessed? —But the understanding was brought about simply by making the people meet-compelling them, as it were, to know something of each other really. Hitherto this girl had been a mere name, or phantom at best, to her lover's father; and it was easy for him to treat her as such, that is, as a mere fancy of his son's. The idea of her had passed through his mind; but with what vividness any idea, notion, or conception could be present to him, my readers must judge from my description of him. So that obstinacy was a ridiculously easy accomplishment to him. For he never had any notion of the matter to which he was opposed-only of that which he favoured. It is very easy indeed for such people to stick to their point.

But I took care that we should have dancing in moderation. It would not do for people either to get weary with recreation, or excited with what was not worthy of producing such an effect. Indeed we had only six country dances during the evening. That was all. And between the dances I read two or three of Wordsworth's ballads to them, and they listened even with more interest than I had been able to hope for. The fact was, that the happy and free hearted mood they were in "enabled the judgment." I wish one knew always by what musical spell to produce the right mood for receiving and reflecting a matter as it really is. Every true poem carries this spell with it in its own music, which it sends out before it as a harbinger, or properly a HERBERGER, to prepare a harbour or lodging for it. But then it needs a quiet mood first of all, to let this music be listened to.

For I thought with myself, if I could get them to like poetry and beautiful things in words, it would not only do them good, but help them to see what is in the Bible, and therefore to love it more. For I never could believe that a man who did not find God in other places as well as in the Bible ever found Him there at all. And I always thought, that to find God in other books enabled us to see clearly that he was MORE in the Bible than in any other book, or all other books put together.

After supper we had a little more singing. And to my satisfaction nothing came to my eyes or ears, during the whole evening, that was undignified or ill-bred. Of course, I knew that many of them must have two behaviours, and that now they were on their good behaviour. But I thought the oftener such were put on their good behaviour, giving them the opportunity of finding out how nice it was, the better. It might make them ashamed of the other at last.

There were many little bits of conversation I overheard, which I should like to give my readers; but I cannot dwell longer upon this part of my Annals. Especially I should have enjoyed recording one piece of talk, in which Old Rogers was evidently trying to move a more directly religious feeling in the mind of Dr Duncan. I thought I could see that THE difficulty with the noble old gentleman was one of expression. But after all the old foremast-man was a seer of the Kingdom; and the other, with all his refinement, and education, and goodness too, was but a child in it.

Before we parted, I gave to each of my guests a sheet of Christmas Carols, gathered from the older portions of our literature. For most of the modern hymns are to my mind neither milk nor meat-mere wretched imitations. There were a few curious words and idioms in these, but I thought it better to leave them as they were; for they might set them inquiring, and give me an opportunity of interesting them further, some time or other, in the history of a word; for, in their ups and downs of fortune, words fare very much like human beings.

And here is my sheet of Carols: —

AN HYMNE OF HEAVENLY LOVE.
O blessed Well of Love! O Floure of Grace!

O glorious Morning-Starre! O Lampe of Light!
Most lively image of thy Father's face,
Eternal King of Glorie, Lord of Might,
Meeke Lambe of God, before all worlds behight,
How can we Thee requite for all this good?
Or what can prize that Thy most precious blood?
Yet nought Thou ask'st in lieu of all this love,

But love of us, for guerdon of Thy paine:
Ay me! what can us lesse than that behove?
Had He required life of us againe,
Had it beene wrong to ask His owne with gaine?
He gave us life, He it restored lost;
Then life were least, that us so little cost.
But He our life hath left unto us free,

Free that was thrall, and blessed that was bann'd;
Ne ought demaunds but that we loving bee,
As He himselfe hath lov'd us afore-hand,
And bound therto with an eternall band,
Him first to love that us so dearely bought,
And next our brethren, to His image wrought.
Him first to love great right and reason is,

Who first to us our life and being gave,
And after, when we fared had amisse,
Us wretches from the second death did save;
And last, the food of life, which now we have,
Even He Himselfe, in His dear sacrament,
To feede our hungry soules, unto us lent.
Then next, to love our brethren, that were made

Of that selfe mould, and that self Maker's hand,
That we, and to the same againe shall fade,
Where they shall have like heritage of land,
However here on higher steps we stand,
Which also were with self-same price redeemed
That we, however of us light esteemed.
Then rouze thy selfe, O Earth! out of thy soyle,

In which thou wallowest like to filthy swyne,
And doest thy mynd in durty pleasures moyle,
Unmindfull of that dearest Lord of thyne;
Lift up to Him thy heavie clouded eyne,
That thou this soveraine bountie mayst behold,
And read, through love, His mercies manifold.
Beginne from first, where He encradled was

In simple cratch, wrapt in a wad of hay,
Betweene the toylfull oxe and humble asse,
And in what rags, and in how base array,
The glory of our heavenly riches lay,
When Him the silly shepheards came to see,
Whom greatest princes sought on lowest knee.
From thence reade on the storie of His life,

His humble carriage, His unfaulty wayes,
His cancred foes, His fights, His toyle, His strife,
His paines, His povertie, His sharpe assayes,
Through which He past His miserable dayes,
Offending none, and doing good to all,
Yet being malist both by great and small.
With all thy hart, with all thy soule and mind,

Thou must Him love, and His beheasts embrace;
All other loves, with which the world doth blind
Weake fancies, and stirre up affections base,
Thou must renounce and utterly displace,
And give thy selfe unto Him full and free,
That full and freely gave Himselfe to thee.
Then shall thy ravisht soul inspired bee

With heavenly thoughts farre above humane skil,
And thy bright radiant eyes shall plainly see
Th' idee of His pure glorie present still
Before thy face, that all thy spirits shall fill
With sweet enragement of celestial love,
Kindled through sight of those faire things above.

Spencer

NEW PRINCE, NEW POMP.

Behold a silly tender Babe,

In freezing winter night,
In homely manger trembling lies;
Alas! a piteous sight.
The inns are full, no man will yield

This little Pilgrim bed;
But forced He is with silly beasts
In crib to shroud His head.
Despise Him not for lying there,

First what He is inquire;
An orient pearl is often found
In depth of dirty mire.
Weigh not His crib, His wooden dish,

Nor beast that by Him feed;

Weigh not his mother's poor attire,
  Nor Joseph's simple weed.
This stable is a Prince's court,

  The crib His chair of state;
  The beasts are parcel of His pomp,
  The wooden dish His plate.
The persons in that poor attire

  His royal liveries wear;
  The Prince himself is come from heaven —
  This pomp is praised there.
With joy approach, O Christian wight!

  Do homage to thy King;
  And highly praise this humble pomp
  Which He from heaven doth bring.
SOUTHWELL.

A DIALOGUE BETWEEN THREE SHEPHERDS.

1. Where is this blessed Babe

    That hath made
  All the world so full of joy
    And expectation;
  That glorious Boy
    That crowns each nation
  With a triumphant wreath of blessedness?
2. Where should He be but in the throng,

    And among
  His angel-ministers, that sing
    And take wing
  Just as may echo to His voice,
    And rejoice,
  When wing and tongue and all
    May so procure their happiness?
3. But He hath other waiters now.

    A poor cow,
  An ox and mule stand and behold,
    And wonder
  That a stable should enfold
    Him that can thunder.
Chorus. O what a gracious God have we!

  How good! How great! Even as our misery.
Jeremy Taylor.

A SONG OF PRAISE FOR THE BIRTH OF CHRIST.

Away, dark thoughts; awake, my joy;

    Awake, my glory; sing;
  Sing songs to celebrate the birth
    Of Jacob's God and King.
  O happy night, that brought forth light,
    Which makes the blind to see!
  The day spring from on high came down
    To cheer and visit thee.
The wakeful shepherds, near their flocks,

    Were watchful for the morn;
  But better news from heaven was brought,
    Your Saviour Christ is born.
  In Bethlem-town the infant lies,
    Within a place obscure,
  O little Bethlem, poor in walls,
    But rich in furniture!
Since heaven is now come down to earth,

    Hither the angels fly!
  Hark, how the heavenly choir doth sing
    Glory to God on High!
  The news is spread, the church is glad,
    SIMEON, o'ercome with joy,
  Sings with the infant in his arms,
    NOW LET THY SERVANT DIE.
Wise men from far beheld the star,

    Which was their faithful guide,
  Until it pointed forth the Babe,
    And Him they glorified.
  Do heaven and earth rejoice and sing —
    Shall we our Christ deny?
  He's born for us, and we for Him:
    GLORY TO GOD ON HIGH.
JOHN MASON.

CHAPTER XI
SERMON ON GOD AND MAMMON.

I never asked questions about the private affairs of any of my parishioners, except of themselves individually upon occasion of their asking me for advice, and some consequent necessity for knowing more than they told me. Hence, I believe, they became the more willing that I should know. But I heard a good many things from others, notwithstanding, for I could not be constantly closing the lips of the communicative as I had done those of Jane Rogers. And amongst other things, I learned that Miss Oldcastle went most Sundays to the neighbouring town of Addicehead to church. Now I had often heard of the ability of the rector, and although I had never met him, was prepared to find him a cultivated, if not an original man. Still, if I must be honest, which I hope I must, I confess that I heard the news with a pang, in analysing which I discovered the chief component to be jealousy. It was no use asking myself why I should be jealous: there the ugly thing was. So I went and told God I was ashamed, and begged Him to deliver me from the evil, because His was the kingdom and the power and the glory. And He took my part against myself, for He waits to be gracious. Perhaps the reader may, however, suspect a deeper cause for this feeling (to which I would rather not give the true name again) than a merely professional one.

But there was one stray sheep of my flock that appeared in church for the first time on the morning of Christmas Day-Catherine Weir. She did not sit beside her father, but in the most shadowy corner of the church-near the organ loft, however. She could have seen her father if she had looked up, but she kept her eyes down the whole time, and never even lifted them to me. The spot on one cheek was much brighter than that on the other, and made her look very ill.

I prayed to our God to grant me the honour of speaking a true word to them all; which honour I thought I was right in asking, because the Lord reproached the Pharisees for not seeking the honour that cometh from God. Perhaps I may have put a wrong interpretation on the passage. It is, however, a joy to think that He will not give you a stone, even if you should take it for a loaf, and ask for it as such. Nor is He, like the scribes, lying in wait to catch poor erring men in their words or their prayers, however mistaken they may be.

I took my text from the Sermon on the Mount. And as the magazine for which these Annals were first written was intended chiefly for Sunday reading, I wrote my sermon just as if I were preaching it to my unseen readers as I spoke it to my present parishioners. And here it is now:

The Gospel according to St Matthew, the sixth chapter, and part of the twenty-fourth and twenty-fifth verses: —

"YE CANNOT SERVE GOD AND MAMMON. THEREFORE I SAY TO YOU, TAKE NO THOUGHT FOR YOUR LIFE.'

"When the Child whose birth we celebrate with glad hearts this day, grew up to be a man, He said this. Did He mean it? —He never said what He did not mean. Did He mean it wholly? — He meant it far beyond what the words could convey. He meant it altogether and entirely. When people do not understand what the Lord says, when it seems to them that His advice is impracticable, instead of searching deeper for a meaning which will be evidently true and wise, they comfort themselves by thinking He could not have meant it altogether, and so leave it. Or they think that if He did mean it, He could not expect them to carry it out. And in the fact that they could not do it perfectly if they were to try, they take refuge from the duty of trying to do it at all; or, oftener, they do not think about it at all as anything that in the least concerns them. The Son of our Father in heaven may have become a child, may have led the one life which belongs to every man to lead, may have suffered because we are sinners, may have died for our sakes, doing the will of His Father in heaven, and yet we have nothing to do with the words He spoke out of the midst of His true, perfect knowledge, feeling, and action! Is it not strange that it should be so? Let it not be so with us this day. Let us seek to find out what our Lord means, that we may do it; trying and failing and trying again-verily to be victorious at last-what matter WHEN, so long as we are trying, and so coming nearer to our end!

"MAMMON, you know, means RICHES. Now, riches are meant to be the slave-not even the servant of man, and not to be the master. If a man serve his own servant, or, in a word, any one who has no just claim to be his master, he is a slave. But here he serves his own slave. On the other hand, to serve God, the source of our being, our own glorious Father, is freedom; in fact, is the only way to get rid of all bondage. So you see plainly enough that a man cannot serve God and Mammon. For how can a slave of his own slave be the servant of the God of freedom, of Him who can have no one to serve Him but a free man? His service is freedom. Do not, I pray you, make any confusion between service and slavery. To serve is the highest, noblest calling in creation. For even the Son of man came not to be ministered unto, but to minister, yea, with Himself.

"But how can a man SERVE riches? Why, when he says to riches, 'Ye are my good.' When he feels he cannot be happy without them. When he puts forth the energies of his nature to get them. When he schemes and dreams and lies awake about them. When he will not give to his neighbour for fear of becoming poor himself. When he wants to have more, and to know he has more, than he can need. When he wants to leave money behind him, not for the sake of his children or relatives, but for the name of the wealth. When he leaves his money, not to those who NEED it, even of his relations, but to those who are rich like himself, making them yet more of slaves to the overgrown monster they worship for his size. When he honours those who have money because they have money, irrespective of their character; or when he honours in a rich man what he would not honour in a poor man. Then is he the slave of Mammon. Still more is he Mammon's slave when his devotion to his god makes him oppressive to those over whom his wealth gives him power; or when he becomes unjust in order to add to his stores. —How will it be with such a man when on a sudden he finds that the world has vanished, and he is alone with God? There lies the body in which he used to live, whose poor necessities first made money of value to him, but with which itself and its fictitious value are both left behind. He cannot now even try to bribe God with a cheque. The angels will not bow down to him because his property, as set forth in his will, takes five or six figures to express its amount It makes no difference to them that he has lost it, though; for they never respected him. And the poor souls of Hades, who envied him the wealth they had lost before, rise up as one man to welcome him, not for love of him-no worshipper of Mammon loves another-but rejoicing in the mischief that has befallen him, and saying, 'Art thou also become one of us?' And Lazarus in Abraham's bosom, however sorry he may be for him, however grateful he may feel to him for the broken victuals and the penny, cannot with one drop of the water of Paradise cool that man's parched tongue.

"Alas, poor Dives! poor server of Mammon, whose vile god can pretend to deliver him no longer! Or rather, for the blockish god never pretended anything-it was the man's own doing-Alas for the Mammon-worshipper! he can no longer deceive himself in his riches. And so even in hell he is something nobler than he was on earth; for he worships his riches no longer. He cannot. He curses them.

"Terrible things to say on Christmas Day! But if Christmas Day teaches us anything, it teaches us to worship God and not Mammon; to worship spirit and not matter; to worship love and not power.

"Do I now hear any of my friends saying in their hearts: Let the rich take that! It does not apply to us. We are poor enough? Ah, my friends, I have known a light-hearted, liberal rich man lose his riches, and be liberal and light-hearted still. I knew a rich lady once, in giving a large gift of money to a poor man, say apologetically, 'I hope it is no disgrace in me to be rich, as it is none in you to be poor.' It is not the being rich that is wrong, but the serving of riches, instead of making them serve your neighbour and yourself-your neighbour for this life, yourself for the everlasting habitations. God knows it is hard for the rich man to enter into the kingdom of heaven; but the rich man does sometimes enter in; for God hath made it possible. And the greater the victory, when it is the rich man that overcometh the world. It is easier for the poor man to enter into the kingdom, yet many of the poor have failed to enter in, and the greater is the disgrace of their defeat. For the poor have more done for them, as far as outward things go, in the way of salvation than the rich, and have a beatitude all to themselves besides. For in the making of this world as a school of salvation, the poor, as the necessary majority, have been more regarded than the rich. Do not think, my poor friend, that God will let you off. He lets nobody off. You, too, must pay the uttermost farthing. He loves you too well to let you serve Mammon a whit more than your rich neighbour. 'Serve Mammon!' do you say? 'How can I serve Mammon? I have no Mammon to serve.' —Would you like to have riches a moment sooner than God gives them? Would you serve Mammon if you had him? —'Who can tell?' do you answer? 'Leave those questions till I am tried.' But is there no bitterness in the tone of that response? Does it not mean, 'It will be a long time before I have a chance of trying THAT?' —But I am not driven to such questions for the chance of convicting some of you of Mammon-worship. Let us look to the text. Read it again.

"'YE CANNOT SERVE GOD AND MAMMON. THEREFORE I SAY UNTO YOU, TAKE NO THOUGHT FOR YOUR LIFE.'

"Why are you to take no thought? Because you cannot serve God and Mammon. Is taking thought, then, a serving of Mammon? Clearly. —Where are you now, poor man? Brooding over the frost? Will it harden the ground, so that the God of the sparrows cannot find food for His sons? Where are you now, poor woman? Sleepless over the empty cupboard and to-morrow's dinner? 'It is because we have no bread?' do you answer? Have you forgotten the five loaves among the five thousand, and the fragments that were left? Or do you know nothing of your Father in heaven, who clothes the lilies and feeds the birds? O ye of little faith? O ye poor-spirited Mammon-worshippers! who worship him not even because he has given you anything, but in the hope that he may some future day benignantly regard you. But I may be too hard upon you. I know well that our Father sees a great difference between the man who is anxious about his children's dinner, or even about his own, and the man who is only anxious to add another ten thousand to his much goods laid up for many years. But you ought to find it easy to trust in God for such a matter as your daily bread, whereas no man can by any possibility trust in God for ten thousand pounds. The former need is a God-ordained necessity; the latter desire a man-devised appetite at best-possibly swinish greed. Tell me, do you long to be rich? Then you worship Mammon. Tell me, do you think you would feel safer if you had money in the bank? Then you are Mammon-worshippers; for you would trust the barn of the rich man rather than the God who makes the corn to grow. Do you say —'What shall we eat? and what shall we drink? and wherewithal shall we be clothedl?' Are ye thus of doubtful mind? —Then you are Mammon-worshippers. "But how is the work of the world to be done if we take no thought? —We are nowhere told not to take thought. We MUST take thought. The question is-What are we to take or not to take thought about? By some who do not know God, little work would be done if they were not driven by anxiety of some kind. But you, friends, are you content to go with the nations of the earth, or do you seek a better way-THE way that the Father of nations would have you walk in?

"WHAT then are we to take thought about? Why, about our work. What are we not to take thought about? Why, about our life. The one is our business: the other is God's. But you turn it the other way. You take no thought of earnestness about the doing of your duty; but you take thought of care lest God should not fulfil His part in the goings on of the world. A man's business is just to do his duty: God takes upon Himself the feeding and the clothing. Will the work of the world be neglected if a man thinks of his work, his duty, God's will to be done, instead of what he is to eat, what he is to drink, and wherewithal he is to be clothed? And remember all the needs of the world come back to these three. You will allow, I think, that the work of the world will be only so much the better done; that the very means of procuring the raiment or the food will be the more thoroughly used. What, then, is the only region on which the doubt can settle? Why, God. He alone remains to be doubted. Shall it be so with you? Shall the Son of man, the baby now born, and for ever with us, find no faith in you? Ah, my poor friend, who canst not trust in God —I was going to say you DESERVE-but what do

I know of you to condemn and judge you? —I was going to say, you deserve to be treated like the child who frets and complains because his mother holds him on her knee and feeds him mouthful by mouthful with her own loving hand. I meant-you deserve to have your own way for a while; to be set down, and told to help yourself, and see what it will come to; to have your mother open the cupboard door for you, and leave you alone to your pleasures. Alas! poor child! When the sweets begin to pall, and the twilight begins to come duskily into the chamber, and you look about all at once and see no mother, how will your cupboard comfort you then? Ask it for a smile, for a stroke of the gentle hand, for a word of love. All the full-fed Mammon can give you is what your mother would have given you without the consequent loathing, with the light of her countenance upon it all, and the arm of her love around you. —And this is what God does sometimes, I think, with the Mammon-worshippers amongst the poor. He says to them, Take your Mammon, and see what he is worth. Ah, friends, the children of God can never be happy serving other than Him. The prodigal might fill his belly with riotous living or with the husks that the swine ate. It was all one, so long as he was not with his father. His soul was wretched. So would you be if you had wealth, for I fear you would only be worse Mammon-worshippers than now, and might well have to thank God for the misery of any swine-trough that could bring you to your senses.

"But we do see people die of starvation sometimes, —Yes. But if you did your work in God's name, and left the rest to Him, that would not trouble you. You would say, If it be God's will that I should starve, I can starve as well as another. And your mind would be at ease. "Thou wilt keep him in perfect peace whose mind is stayed upon Thee, because he trusteth in Thee." Of that I am sure. It may be good for you to go hungry and bare-foot; but it must be utter death to have no faith in God. It is not, however, in God's way of things that the man who does his work shall not live by it. We do not know why here and there a man may be left to die of hunger, but I do believe that they who wait upon the Lord shall not lack any good. What it may be good to deprive a man of till he knows and acknowledges whence it comes, it may be still better to give him when he has learned that every good and every perfect gift is from above, and cometh down from the Father of lights.

"I SHOULD like to know a man who just minded his duty and troubled himself about nothing; who did his own work and did not interfere with God's. How nobly he would work-working not for reward, but because it was the will of God! How happily he would receive his food and clothing, receiving them as the gifts of God! What peace would be his! What a sober gaiety! How hearty and infectious his laughter! What a friend he would be! How sweet his sympathy! And his mind would be so clear he would understand everything His eye being single, his whole body would be full of light. No fear of his ever doing a mean thing. He would die in a ditch, rather. It is this fear of want that makes men do mean things. They are afraid to part with their precious lord-Mammon. He gives no safety against such a fear. One of the richest men in England is haunted with the dread of the workhouse. This man whom I should like to know, would be sure that God would have him liberal, and he would be what God would have him. Riches are not in the least necessary to that. Witness our Lord's admiration of the poor widow with her great farthing.

"But I think I hear my troubled friend who does not love money, and yet cannot trust in God out and out, though she fain would, —I think I hear her say, "I believe I could trust Him for myself, or at least I should be ready to dare the worst for His sake; but my children-it is the thought of my children that is too much for me." Ah, woman! she whom the Saviour praised so pleasedly, was one who trusted Him for her daughter. What an honour she had! "Be it unto thee even as thou wilt." Do you think you love your children better than He who made them? Is not your love what it is because He put it into your heart first? Have not you often been cross with them? Sometimes unjust to them? Whence came the returning love that rose from unknown depths in your being, and swept away the anger and the injustice! You did not create that love. Probably you were not good enough to send for it by prayer. But it came. God sent it. He makes you love your children; be sorry when you have been cross with them; ashamed when you have been unjust to them; and yet you won't trust Him to give them food and clothes! Depend upon it, if He ever refuses to give them food and clothes, and you knew all about it, the why and the wherefore, you would not dare to give them food or clothes either. He loves them a thousand times better than you do-be sure of that-and feels for their sufferings too, when He cannot give them just what He would like to give them-cannot for their good, I mean.

"But as your mistrust will go further, I can go further to meet it. You will say, 'Ah! yes'—in your feeling, I mean, not in words,—you will say, 'Ah! yes-food and clothing of a sort! Enough to keep life in and too much cold out! But I want my children to have plenty of GOOD food, and NICE clothes.'

"Faithless mother! Consider the birds of the air. They have so much that at least they can sing! Consider the lilies-they were red lilies, those. Would you not trust Him who delights in glorious colours-more at least than you, or He would never have created them and made us to delight in them? I do not say that your children shall be clothed in scarlet and fine linen; but if not, it is not because God despises scarlet and fine linen or does not love your children. He loves them, I say, too much to give them everything all at once. But He would make them such that they may have everything without being the worse, and with being the better for it. And if you cannot trust Him yet, it begins to be a shame, I think.

"It has been well said that no man ever sank under the burden of the day. It is when tomorrow's burden is added to the burden of to-day, that the weight is more than a man can bear. Never load yourselves so, my friends. If you find yourselves so loaded, at least remember this: it is your own doing, not God's. He begs you to leave the future to Him, and mind the present. What more or what else could He do to take the burden off you? Nothing else would do it. Money in the bank wouldn't do it. He cannot do to-morrow's business for you beforehand to save you from fear about it. That would derange everything. What else is there but to tell you to trust in Him, irrespective of the fact that nothing else but such trust can put our heart at peace, from the very nature of our relation to Him as well as the fact that we need these things. We think that we come nearer to God than the lower animals do by our foresight. But there is another side to it. We are like to Him with whom there is no past or future, with whom a day is as a thousand years, and a thousand years as one day, when we live with large bright spiritual eyes, doing our work in the great present, leaving both past and future to Him to whom they are ever present, and fearing nothing, because He is in our future, as much as He is in our past, as much as, and far more than, we can feel Him to be in our present. Partakers thus of the divine nature, resting in that perfect All-in-all in whom our nature is eternal too, we walk without fear, full of hope and courage and strength to do His will, waiting for the endless good which He is always giving as fast as He can get us able to take it in. Would not this be to be more of gods than Satan promised to Eve? To live carelessly-divine, duty-doing, fearless, loving, self-forgetting lives-is not that more than to know both good and evil-lives in which the good, like Aaron's rod, has swallowed up the evil, and turned it into good? For pain and hunger are evils, but if faith in God swallows them up, do they not so turn into good? I say they do. And I am glad to believe that I am not alone in my parish in this conviction. I have never been too hungry, but I have had trouble which I would gladly have exchanged for hunger and cold and weariness. Some of you have known hunger and cold and weariness. Do you not join with me to say: It is well, and better than well-whatever helps us to know the love of Him who is our God?

"But there HAS BEEN just one man who has acted thus. And it is His Spirit in our hearts that makes us desire to know or to be another such-who would do the will of God for God, and let God do God's will for Him. For His will is all. And this man is the baby whose birth we celebrate this day. Was this a condition to choose-that of a baby-by one who thought it part of a man's high calling to take care of the morrow? Did He not thus cast the whole matter at once upon the hands and heart of His Father? Sufficient unto the baby's day is the need thereof; he toils not, neither does he spin, and yet he if fed and clothed, and loved, and rejoiced in. Do you remind me that sometimes even his mother forgets him —a mother, most likely, to whose self-indulgence or weakness the child owes his birth as hers? Ah! but he is not therefore forgotten, however like things it may look to our half-seeing eyes, by his Father in heaven. One of the highest benefits we can reap from understanding the way of God with ourselves is, that we become able thus to trust Him for others with whom we do not understand His ways.

"But let us look at what will be more easily shown-how, namely, He did the will of His Father, and took no thought for the morrow after He became a man. Remember how He forsook His trade when the time came for Him to preach. Preaching was not a profession then. There were no monasteries, or vicarages, or stipends, then. Yet witness for the Father the garment woven throughout; the ministering of women; the purse in common! Hard-working men and rich ladies were ready to help Him, and did help Him with all that He needed. —Did He then never want? Yes; once at least-for a little while only.

"He was a-hungered in the wilderness. 'Make bread,' said Satan. 'No,' said our Lord. —He could starve; but He could not eat bread that His Father did not give Him, even though He could make it Himself. He had come hither to be tried. But when the victory was secure, lo! the angels brought Him food from His Father. —Which was better? To feed Himself, or be fed by His Father? Judge yourselves, anxious people. He sought the kingdom of God and His righteousness, and the bread was added unto Him.

"And this gives me occasion to remark that the same truth holds with regard to any portion of the future as well as the morrow. It is a principle, not a command, or an encouragement, or a promise merely. In respect of it there is no difference between next day and next year, next hour and next century. You will see at once the absurdity of taking no thought for the morrow, and taking thought for next year. But do you see likewise that it is equally reasonable to trust God for the next moment, and equally unreasonable not to trust Him? The Lord was hungry and needed food now, though He could still go without for a while. He left it to His Father. And so He told His disciples to do when they were called to answer before judges and rulers. 'Take no thought. It shall be given you what ye shall say.' You have a disagreeable duty to do at twelve o'clock. Do not blacken nine and ten and eleven, and all between, with the colour of twelve. Do the work of each, and reap your reward in peace. So when the dreaded moment in the future becomes the present, you shall meet it walking in the light, and that light will overcome its darkness. How often do men who have made up their minds what to say and do under certain expected circumstances, forget the words and reverse the actions! The best preparation is the present well seen to, the last duty done. For this will keep the eye so clear and the body so full of light that the right action will be perceived at once, the right words will rush from the heart to the lips, and the man, full of the Spirit of God because he cares for nothing but the will of God, will trample on the evil thing in love, and be sent, it may be, in a chariot of fire to the presence of his Father, or stand unmoved amid the cruel mockings of the men he loves.

"Do you feel inclined to say in your hearts: 'It was easy for Him to take no thought, for He had the matter in His own hands?' But observe, there is nothing very noble in a man's taking no thought except it be from faith. If there were no God to take thought for us, we should have no right to blame any one for taking thought. You may fancy the Lord had His own power to fall back upon. But that would have been to Him just the one dreadful thing. That His Father should forget Him! —no power in Himself could make up for that. He feared nothing for Himself; and never once employed His divine power to save Him from His human fate. Let God do that for Him if He saw fit. He did not come into the world to take care of Himself. That would not be in any way divine. To fall back on Himself, God failing Him-how could that make it easy for Him to avoid care? The very idea would be torture. That would be to declare heaven void, and the world without a God. He would not even pray to His Father for what He knew He should have if He did ask it. He would just wait His will.

"But see how the fact of His own power adds tenfold significance to the fact that He trusted in God. We see that this power would not serve His need-His need not being to be fed and clothed, but to be one with the Father, to be fed by His hand, clothed by His care. This was what the Lord wanted-and we need, alas! too often without wanting it. He never once, I repeat, used His power for Himself. That was not his business. He did not care about it. His life was of no value to Him but as His Father cared for it. God would mind all that was necessary for Him, and He would mind the work His Father had given Him to do. And, my friends, this is just the one secret of a blessed life, the one thing every man comes into this world to learn. With what authority it comes to us from the lips of Him who knew all about it, and ever did as He said!

"Now you see that He took no thought for the morrow. And, in the name of the holy child Jesus, I call upon you, this Christmas day, to cast care to the winds, and trust in God; to receive the message of peace and good-will to men; to yield yourselves to the Spirit of God, that you may be taught what He wants you to know; to remember that the one gift promised without reserve to those who ask it-the one gift worth having-the gift which makes all other gifts a thousand-fold in value, is the gift of the Holy Spirit, the spirit of the child Jesus, who will take of the things of Jesus, and show them to you-make you understand them, that is-so that you shall see them to be true, and love Him with all your heart and soul, and your neighbour as yourselves."

And here, having finished my sermon, I will give my reader some lines with which he may not be acquainted, from a writer of the Elizabethan time. I had meant to introduce them into my sermon, but I was so carried away with my subject that I forgot them. For I always preached extempore, which phrase I beg my reader will not misinterpret as meaning ON THE SPUR OF THE MOMENT, OF WITHOUT THE DUE PREPARATION OF MUCH THOUGHT.

>"O man! thou image of thy Maker's good,
>   What canst thou fear, when breathed into thy blood
>His Spirit is that built thee? What dull sense
>Makes thee suspect, in need, that Providence
>Who made the morning, and who placed the light
>Guide to thy labours; who called up the night,
>And bid her fall upon thee like sweet showers,
>In hollow murmurs, to lock up thy powers;
>Who gave thee knowledge; who so trusted thee
>To let thee grow so near Himself, the Tree?
>Must He then be distrusted? Shall His frame
>Discourse with Him why thus and thus I am?
>He made the Angels thine, thy fellows all;
>Nay even thy servants, when devotions call.
>Oh! canst thou be so stupid then, so dim,
>To seek a saving* influence, and lose Him?
>Can stars protect thee? Or can poverty,
>Which is the light to heaven, put out His eye!
>He is my star; in Him all truth I find,
>All influence, all fate. And when my mind
>Is furnished with His fulness, my poor story
>Shall outlive all their age, and all their glory.
>The hand of danger cannot fall amiss,
>When I know what, and in whose power, it is,
>Nor want, the curse of man, shall make me groan:
>   A holy hermit is a mind alone.
>* * * *

Affliction, when I know it, is but this,

>A deep alloy whereby man tougher is
>To bear the hammer; and the deeper still,
>We still arise more image of His will;

Sickness, an humorous cloud 'twixt us and light;
And death, at longest, but another night."

[Many, in those days, believed in astrology.]
I had more than ordinary attention during my discourse, at one point in which I saw the down-bent head of Catherine Weir sink yet lower upon her hands. After a moment, however, she sat more erect than before, though she never lifted her eyes to meet mine. I need not assure my reader that she was not present to my mind when I spoke the words that so far had moved her. Indeed, had I thought of her, I could not have spoken them.

As I came out of the church, my people crowded about me with outstretched hands and good wishes. One woman, the aged wife of a more aged labourer, who could not get near me, called from the outskirts of the little crowd—

"May the Lord come and see ye every day, sir. And may ye never know the hunger and cold as me and Tomkins has come through."

"Amen to the first of your blessing, Mrs Tomkins, and hearty thanks to you. But I daren't say AMEN to the other part of it, after what I've been preaching, you know."

"But there'll be no harm if I say it for ye, sir?"

"No, for God will give me what is good, even if your kind heart should pray against it."

"Ah, sir, ye don't know what it is to be hungry AND cold."

"Neither shall you any more, if I can help it."

"God bless ye, sir. But we're pretty tidy just in the meantime."

I walked home, as usual on Sunday mornings, by the road. It was a lovely day. The sun shone so warm that you could not help thinking of what he would be able to do before long—draw primroses and buttercups out of the earth by force of sweet persuasive influences. But in the shadows lay fine webs and laces of ice, so delicately lovely that one could not but be glad of the cold that made the water able to please itself by taking such graceful forms. And I wondered over again for the hundredth time what could be the principle which, in the wildest, most lawless, fantastically chaotic, apparently capricious work of nature, always kept it beautiful. The beauty of holiness must be at the heart of it somehow, I thought. Because our God is so free from stain, so loving, so unselfish, so good, so altogether what He wants us to be, so holy, therefore all His works declare Him in beauty; His fingers can touch nothing but to mould it into loveliness; and even the play of His elements is in grace and tenderness of form.

And then I thought how the sun, at the farthest point from us, had begun to come back towards us; looked upon us with a hopeful smile; was like the Lord when He visited His people as a little one of themselves, to grow upon the earth till it should blossom as the rose in the light of His presence. "Ah! Lord," I said, in my heart, "draw near unto Thy people. It is spring-time with Thy world, but yet we have cold winds and bitter hail, and pinched voices forbidding them that follow Thee and follow not with us. Draw nearer, Sun of Righteousness, and make the trees bourgeon, and the flowers blossom, and the voices grow mellow and glad, so that all shall join in praising Thee, and find thereby that harmony is better than unison. Let it be summer, O Lord, if it ever may be summer in this court of the Gentiles. But Thou hast told us that Thy kingdom cometh within us, and so Thy joy must come within us too. Draw nigh then, Lord, to those to whom Thou wilt draw nigh; and others beholding their welfare will seek to share therein too, and seeing their good works will glorify their Father in heaven."

So I walked home, hoping in my Saviour, and wondering to think how pleasant I had found it to be His poor servant to this people. Already the doubts which had filled my mind on that first evening of gloom, doubts as to whether I had any right to the priest's office, had utterly vanished, slain by the effort to perform the priest's duty. I never thought about the matter now. —And how can doubt ever be fully met but by action? Try your theory; try your hypothesis; or if it is not worth trying, give it up, pull it down. And I hoped that if ever a cloud should come over me again, however dark and dismal it might be, I might be able, notwithstanding, to rejoice that the sun was shining on others though not on me, and to say with all my heart to my Father in heaven, "Thy will be done."

When I reached my own study, I sat down by a blazing fire, and poured myself out a glass of wine; for I had to go out again to see some of my poor friends, and wanted some luncheon first. —It is a great thing to have the greetings of the universe presented in fire and food. Let me, if I may, be ever welcomed to my room in winter by a glowing hearth, in summer by a vase of flowers; if I may not, let me then think how nice they would be, and bury myself in my work. I do not think that the road to contentment lies in despising what we have not got. Let us acknowledge all good, all delight that the world holds, and be content without it. But this we can never be except by possessing the one thing, without which I do not merely say no man ought to be content, but no man CAN be content-the Spirit of the Father.

If any young people read my little chronicle, will they not be inclined to say, "The vicar has already given us in this chapter hardly anything but a long sermon; and it is too bad of him to go on preaching in his study after we saw him safe out of the pulpit"? Ah, well! just one word, and I drop the preaching for a while. My word is this: I may speak long-windedly, and even inconsiderately as regards my young readers; what I say may fail utterly to convey what I mean; I may be actually stupid sometimes, and not have a suspicion of it; but what I mean is true; and if you do not know it to be true yet, some of you at least suspect it to be true, and some of you hope it is true; and when you all see it as I mean it and as you can take it, you will rejoice with a gladness you know nothing about now There, I have done for a little while. I won't pledge myself for more, I assure you. For to speak about such things is the greatest delight of my age, as it was of my early manhood, next to that of loving God and my neighbour. For as these are THE two commandments of life, so they are in themselves THE pleasures of life. But there I am at it again. I beg your pardon now, for I have already inadvertently broken my promise.

I had allowed myself a half-hour before the fire with my glass of wine and piece of bread, and I soon fell into a dreamy state called REVERIE, which I fear not a few mistake for THINKING, because it is the nearest approach they ever make to it. And in this reverie I kept staring about my book-shelves. I am an old man now, and you do not know my name; and if you should ever find it out, I shall very soon hide it under some daisies, I hope, and so escape; and therefore, I am going to be egotistic in the most unpardonable manner. I am going to tell you one of my faults, for it continues, I fear, to be one of my faults still, as it certainly was at the period of which I am now writing. I am very fond of books. Do not mistake me. I do not mean that I love reading. I hope I do. That is no fault—a virtue rather than a fault. But, as the old meaning of the word FOND was FOOLISH, I use that word: I am foolishly fond of the bodies of books as distinguished from their souls, or thought-element. I do not say I love their bodies as DIVIDED from their souls; I do not say I should let a book stand upon my shelves for which I felt no respect, except indeed it happened to be useful to me in some inferior way. But I delight in seeing books about me, books even of which there seems to be no prospect that I shall have time to read a single chapter before I lay this old head down for the last time. Nay, more: I confess that if they are nicely bound, so as to glow and shine in such a fire-light as that by which I was then sitting, I like them ever so much the better. Nay, more yet-and this comes very near to showing myself worse than I thought I was when I began to tell you my fault: there are books upon my shelves which certainly at least would not occupy the place of honour they do occupy, had not some previous owner dressed them far beyond their worth, making modern apples of Sodom of them. Yet there I let them stay, because they are pleasant to the eye, although certainly not things to be desired to make one wise. I could say a great deal more about the matter, pro and con, but it would be worse than a sermon, I fear. For I suspect that by the time books, which ought to be loved for the truth that is in them, of one sort or another, come to be loved as articles of furniture, the mind has gone through a process more than analogous to that which the miser's mind goes through-namely, that of passing from the respect of money because of what it can do, to the love of money because it is money. I have not yet reached the furniture stage, and I do not think I ever shall. I would rather burn them all. Meantime, I think one safeguard is to encourage one's friends to borrow one's books-not to offer individual books, which is much the same as OFFERING advice. That will probably take some of the shine off them, and put a few thumb-marks in them, which both are very wholesome towards the arresting of the furniture declension. For my part, thumb-marks I find very obnoxious-far more so than the spoiling of the binding. —I know that some of my readers, who have had sad experience of the sort, will be saying in themselves, "He might have mentioned a surer antidote resulting from this measure, than either rubbed Russia or dirty GLOVE-marks even-that of utter disappearance and irreparable loss." But no; that has seldom happened to me-because I trust my pocketbook, and never my memory, with the names of those to whom the individual books are committed. —There, then, is a little bit of practical advice in both directions for young book-lovers.

Again I am reminded that I am getting old. What digressions!

Gazing about on my treasures, the thought suddenly struck me that I had never done as I had promised Judy; had never found out what her aunt's name meant in Anglo-Saxon. I would do so now. I got down my dictionary, and soon discovered that Ethelwyn meant Home-joy, or Inheritance.

"A lovely meaning," I said to myself.

And then I went off into another reverie, with the composition of which I shall not trouble my reader; and with the mention of which I had, perhaps, no right to occupy the fragment of his time spent in reading it, seeing I did not intend to tell him how it was made up. I will tell him something else instead.

Several families had asked me to take my Christmas dinner with them; but, not liking to be thus limited, I had answered each that I would not, if they would excuse me, but would look in some time or other in the course of the evening.

When my half-hour was out, I got up and filled my pockets with little presents for my poor people, and set out to find them in their own homes.

I was variously received, but unvaryingly with kindness; and my little presents were accepted, at least in most instances, with a gratitude which made me ashamed of them and of myself too for a few moments. Mrs. Tomkins looked as if she had never seen so much tea together before, though there was only a couple of pounds of it; and her husband received a pair of warm trousers none the less cordially that they were not quite new, the fact being that I found I did not myself need such warm clothing this winter as I had needed the last. I did not dare to offer Catherine Weir anything, but I gave her little boy a box of water-colours—in remembrance of the first time I saw him, though I said nothing about that. His mother did not thank me. She told little Gerard to do so, however, and that was something. And, indeed, the boy's sweetness would have been enough for both.

Gerard-an unusual name in England; specially not to be looked for in the class to which she belonged.

When I reached Old Rogers's cottage, whither I carried a few yards of ribbon, bought by myself, I assure my lady friends, with the special object that the colour should be bright enough for her taste, and pure enough of its kind for mine, as an offering to the good dame, and a small hymn-book, in which were some hymns of my own making, for the good man—

But do forgive me, friends, for actually describing my paltry presents. I can dare to assure you it comes from a talking old man's love of detail, and from no admiration of such small givings as those. You see I trust you, and I want to stand well with you. I never could be indifferent to what people thought of me; though I have had to fight hard to act as freely as if I were indifferent, especially when upon occasion I found myself approved of. It is more difficult to walk straight then, than when men are all against you. —As I have already broken a sentence, which will not be past setting for a while yet, I may as well go on to say here, lest any one should remark that a clergyman ought not to show off his virtues, nor yet teach his people bad habits by making them look out for presents-that my income not only seemed to me disproportioned to the amount of labour necessary in the parish, but certainly was larger than I required to spend upon myself; and the miserly passion for books I contrived to keep a good deal in check; for I had no fancy for gliding devil-wards for the sake of a few books after all. So there was no great virtue-was there? —in easing my heart by giving a few of the good things people give their children to my poor friends, whose kind reception of them gave me as much pleasure as the gifts gave them. They valued the kindness in the gift, and to look out for kindness will not make people greedy.

When I reached the cottage, I found not merely Jane there with her father and mother, which was natural on Christmas Day, seeing there seemed to be no company at the Hall, but my little Judy as well, sitting in the old woman's arm-chair, (not that she Used it much, but it was called hers,) and looking as much at home as-as she did in the pond.

"Why, Judy!" I exclaimed, "you here?"

"Yes. Why not, Mr Walton?" she returned, holding out her hand without rising, for the chair was such a large one, and she was set so far back in it that the easier way was not to rise, which, seeing she was not greatly overburdened with reverence, was not, I presume, a cause of much annoyance to the little damsel.

"I know no reason why I shouldn't see a Sandwich Islander here. Yet I might express surprise if I did find one, might I not?"

Judy pretended to pout, and muttered something about comparing her to a cannibal. But Jane took up the explanation.

"Mistress had to go off to London with her mother to-day, sir, quite unexpected, on some banking business, I fancy, from what I —I beg your pardon, sir. They're gone anyhow, whatever the reason may be; and so I came to see my father and mother, and Miss Judy would come with me."

"She's very welcome," said Mrs Rogers.

"How could I stay up there with nobody but Jacob, and that old wolf Sarah? I wouldn't be left alone with her for the world. She'd have me in the Bishop's Pool before you came back, Janey dear."

"That wouldn't matter much to you, would it, Judy?" I said.

"She's a white wolf, that old Sarah, I know?" was all her answer.

"But what will the old lady say when she finds you brought the young lady here?" asked Mrs Rogers.

"I didn't bring her, mother. She would come."

"Besides, she'll never know it," said Judy.

I did not see that it was my part to read Judy a lecture here, though perhaps I might have done so if I had had more influence over her than I had. I wanted to gain some influence over her, and knew that the way to render my desire impossible of fulfilment would be, to find fault with what in her was a very small affair, whatever it might be in one who had been properly brought up. Besides, a clergyman is not a moral policeman. So I took no notice of the impropriety.

"Had they actually to go away on the morning of Christmas Day?" I said.

"They went anyhow, whether they had to do it or not, sir," answered Jane.

"Aunt Ethelwyn didn't want to go till to-morrow," said Judy. "She said something about coming to church this morning. But grannie said they must go at once. It was very cross of old grannie. Think what a Christmas Day to me without auntie, and with Sarah! But I don't mean to go home till it's quite dark. I mean to stop here with dear Old Rogers-that I do." The latch was gently lifted, and in came young Brownrigg. So I thought it was time to leave my best Christmas wishes and take myself away. Old Rogers came with me to the mill-stream as usual.

"It 'mazes me, sir," he said, "a gentleman o' your age and bringin' up to know all that you tould us this mornin'. It 'ud be no wonder now for a man like me, come to be the shock o' corn fully ripe-leastways yallow and white enough outside if there bean't much more than milk inside it yet, —it 'ud be no mystery for a man like me who'd been brought up hard, and tossed about well-nigh all the world over-why, there's scarce a wave on the Atlantic but knows Old Rogers!"

He made the parenthesis with a laugh, and began anew.

"It 'ud be a shame of a man like me not to know all as you said this mornin', sir-leastways I don't mean able to say it right off as you do, sir; but not to know it, after the Almighty had been at such pains to beat it into my hard head just to trust in Him and fear nothing and nobody-captain, bosun, devil, sunk rock, or breakers ahead; but just to mind Him and stand by halliard, brace, or wheel, or hang on by the leeward earing for that matter. For, you see, what does it signify whether I go to the bottom or not, so long as I didn't skulk? or rather," and here the old man took off his hat and looked up, "so long as the Great Captain has His way, and things is done to His mind? But how ever a man like you, goin' to the college, and readin' books, and warm o' nights, and never, by your own confession this blessed mornin', sir, knowin' what it was to be downright hungry, how ever you come to know all those things, is just past my comprehension, except by a double portion o' the Spirit, sir. And that's the way I account for it, sir."

Although I knew enough about a ship to understand the old man, I am not sure that I have properly represented his sea-phrase. But that is of small consequence, so long as I give his meaning. And a meaning can occasionally be even better CONVEYED by less accurate words.

"I will try to tell you how I come to know about these things as I do," I returned. "How my knowledge may stand the test of further and severer trials remains to be seen. But if I should fail any time, old friend, and neither trust in God nor do my duty, what I have said to you remains true all the same."

"That it do, sir, whoever may come short."

"And more than that: failure does not necessarily prove any one to be a hypocrite of no faith. He may be still a man of little faith."

"Surely, surely, sir. I remember once that my faith broke down-just for one moment, sir. And then the Lord gave me my way lest I should blaspheme Him in thy wicked heart."

"How was that, Rogers?"

"A scream came from the quarter-deck, and then the cry: 'Child overboard!' There was but one child, the captain's, aboard. I was sitting just aft the foremast, herring-boning a split in a spare jib. I sprang to the bulwark, and there, sure enough, was the child, going fast astarn, but pretty high in the water. How it happened I can't think to this day, sir, but I suppose my needle, in the hurry, had got into my jacket, so as to skewer it to my jersey, for we were far south of the line at the time, sir, and it was cold. However that may be, as soon as I was overboard, which you may be sure didn't want the time I take tellin' of it, I found that I ought to ha' pulled my jacket off afore I gave the bulwark the last kick. So I rose on the water, and began to pull it over my head-for it was wide, and that was the easiest way, I thought, in the water. But when I had got it right over my head, there it stuck. And there was I, blind as a Dutchman in a fog, and in as strait a jacket as ever poor wretch in Bedlam, for I could only just wag my flippers. Mr Walton, I believe I swore-the Lord forgive me! —but it was trying. And what was far worse, for one moment I disbelieved in Him; and I do say that's worse than swearing-in a hurry I mean. And that moment something went, the jacket was off, and there was I feelin' as if every stroke I took was as wide as the mainyard. I had no time to repent, only to thank God. And wasn't it more than I deserved, sir? Ah! He can rebuke a man for unbelief by giving him the desire of his heart. And that's a better rebuke than tying him up to the gratings."

"And did you save the child?"

"Oh yes, sir."

"And wasn't the captain pleased?"

"I believe he was, sir. He gave me a glass o' grog, sir. But you was a sayin' of something, sir, when I interrupted of you."

"I am very glad you did interrupt me."

"I'm not though, sir. I Ve lost summat I 'll never hear more."

"No, you shan't lose it. I was going to tell you how I think I came to understand a little about the things I was talking of to-day."

"That's it, sir; that's it. Well, sir, if you please?"

"You've heard of Sir Philip Sidney, haven't you, Old Rogers?"

"He was a great joker, wasn't he, sir?"

"No, no; you're thinking of Sydney Smith, Rogers."

"It may be, sir. I am an ignorant man."

"You are no more ignorant than you ought to be. —But it is time you should know him, for he was just one of your sort. I will come down some evening and tell you about him."

I may as well mention here that this led to week-evening lectures in the barn, which, with the help of Weir the carpenter, was changed into a comfortable room, with fixed seats all round it, and plenty of cane-chairs besides-for I always disliked forms in the middle of a room. The object of these lectures was to make the people acquainted with the true heroes of their own country-men great in themselves. And the kind of choice I made may be seen by those who know about both, from the fact that, while my first two lectures were on Philip Sidney, I did not give one whole lecture even to Walter Raleigh, grand fellow as he was. I wanted chiefly to set forth the men that could rule themselves, first of all, after a noble fashion. But I have not finished these lectures yet, for I never wished to confine them to the English heroes; I am going on still, old man as I am-not however without retracing passed ground sometimes, for a new generation has come up since I came here, and there is a new one behind coming up now which I may be honoured to present in its turn to some of this grand company-this cloud of witnesses to the truth in our own and other lands, some of whom subdued kingdoms, and others were tortured to death, for the same cause and with the same result.

"Meantime," I went on, "I only want to tell you one little thing he says in a letter to a younger brother whom he wanted to turn out as fine a fellow as possible. It is about horses, or rather, riding-for Sir Philip was the best horseman in Europe in his day, as, indeed, all things taken together, he seems to have really been the most accomplished man generally of his time in the world. Writing to this brother he says—"

I could not repeat the words exactly to Old Rogers, but I think it better to copy them exactly, in writing this account of our talk:

"At horsemanship, when you exercise it, read Crison Claudio, and a book that is called La Gloria del Cavallo, withal that you may join the thorough contemplation of it with the exercise; and so shall you profit more in a month than others in a year."

"I think I see what you mean, sir. I had got to learn it all without book, as it were, though you know I had my old Bible, that my mother gave me, and without that I should not have learned it at all."

"I only mean it comparatively, you know. You have had more of the practice, and I more of the theory. But if we had not both had both, we should neither of us have known anything about the matter. I never was content without trying at least to understand things; and if they are practical things, and you try to practise them at the same time as far as you do understand them, there is no end to the way in which the one lights up the other. I suppose that is how, without your experience, I have more to say about such things than you could expect. You know besides that a small matter in which a principle is involved will reveal the principle, if attended to, just as well as a great one containing the same principle. The only difference, and that a most important one, is that, though I've got my clay and my straw together, and they stick pretty well as yet, my brick, after all, is not half so well baked as yours, old friend, and it may crumble away yet, though I hope not."

"I pray God to make both our bricks into stones of the New Jerusalem, sir. I think I understand you quite well. To know about a thing is of no use, except you do it. Besides, as I found out when I went to sea, you never can know a thing till you do do it, though I thought I had a tidy fancy about some things beforehand. It's better not to be quite sure that all your seams are caulked, and so to keep a look-out on the bilge-pump; isn't it, sir?"

During the most of this conversation, we were standing by the mill-water, half frozen over. The ice from both sides came towards the middle, leaving an empty space between, along which the dark water showed itself, hurrying away as if in fear of its life from the white death of the frost. The wheel stood motionless, and the drip from the thatch of the mill over it in the sun, had frozen in the shadow into icicles, which hung in long spikes from the spokes and the floats, making the wheel-soft green and mossy when it revolved in the gentle sun-mingled summer-water —look like its own gray skeleton now. The sun was getting low, and I should want all my time to see my other friends before dinner, for I would not willingly offend Mrs Pearson on Christmas Day by being late, especially as I guessed she was using extraordinary skill to prepare me a more than comfortable meal.

"I must go, Old Rogers," I said; "but I will leave you something to think about till we meet again. Find out why our Lord was so much displeased with the disciples, whom He knew to be ignorant men, for not knowing what He meant when He warned them against the leaven of the Pharisees. I want to know what you think about it. You'll find the story told both in the sixteenth chapter of St Matthew and the eighth of St Mark."

"Well, sir, I'll try; that is, if you will tell me what you think about it afterwards, so as to put me right, if I'm wrong."

"Of course I will, if I can find out an explanation to satisfy me. But it is not at all clear to me now. In fact, I do not see the connecting links of our Lord's logic in the rebuke He gives them."

"How am I to find out then, sir-knowing nothing of logic at all?" said the old man, his rough worn face summered over with his child-like smile.

"There are many things which a little learning, while it cannot really hide them, may make you less ready to see all at once," I answered, shaking hands with Old Rogers, and then springing across the brook with my carpet-bag in my hand.

By the time I had got through the rest of my calls, the fogs were rising from the streams and the meadows to close in upon my first Christmas Day in my own parish. How much happier I was than when I came such a few months before! The only pang I felt that day was as I passed the monsters on the gate leading to Oldcastle Hall. Should I be honoured to help only the poor of the flock? Was I to do nothing for the rich, for whom it is, and has been, and doubtless will be so hard to enter into the kingdom of heaven? And it seemed to me at the moment that the world must be made for the poor: they had so much more done for them to enable them to inherit it than the rich had. —To these people at the Hall, I did not seem acceptable. I might in time do something with Judy, but the old lady was still so dreadfully repulsive to me that it troubled my conscience to feel how I disliked her. Mr Stoddart seemed nothing more than a dilettante in religion, as well as in the arts and sciences-music always excepted; while for Miss Oldcastle, I simply did not understand her yet. And she was so beautiful! I thought her more, beautiful every time I saw her. But I never appeared to make the least progress towards any real acquaintance with her thoughts and feelings. —It seemed to me, I say, for a moment, coming from the houses of the warm-hearted poor, as if the rich had not quite fair play, as it were-as if they were sent into the world chiefly for the sake of the cultivation of the virtues of the poor, and without much chance for the cultivation of their own. I knew better than this you know, my reader; but the thought came, as thoughts will come sometimes. It vanished the moment I sought to lay hands upon it, as if it knew quite well it had no business there. But certainly I did believe that it was more like the truth to say the world was made for the poor than to say that it was made for the rich. And therefore I longed the more to do something for these whom I considered the rich of my flock; for it was dreadful to think of their being poor inside instead of outside.

Perhaps my reader will say, and say with justice, that I ought to have been as anxious about poor Farmer Brownrigg as about the beautiful lady. But the farmer liai given me good reason to hope some progress in him after the way he had given in about Jane Rogers. Positively I had caught his eye during the sermon that very day. And, besides-but I will not be a hypocrite; and seeing I did not certainly take the same interest in Mr Brownrigg, I will at least be honest and confess it. As far as regards the discharge of my duties, I trust I should have behaved impartially had the necessity for any choice arisen. But my feelings were not quite under my own control.

And we are nowhere, told to love everybody alike, only to love every one who comes within our reach as ourselves.

I wonder whether my old friend Dr Duncan was right. He had served on shore in Egypt under General Abercrombie, and had of course, after the fighting was over on each of the several occasions-the French being always repulsed-exercised his office amongst the wounded left on the field of battle. —"I do not know," he said, "whether I did right or not; but I always took the man I came to first-French or English."—I only know that my heart did not wait for the opinion of my head on the matter. I loved the old man the more that he did as he did. But as a question of casuistry, I am doubtful about its answer.

This digression is, I fear, unpardonable.

I made Mrs Pearson sit down with me to dinner, for Christmas Day was not one to dine alone upon. And I have ever since had my servants to dine with me on Christmas Day.

Then I went out again, and made another round of visits, coming in for a glass of wine at one table, an orange at another, and a hot chestnut at a third. Those whom I could not see that day, I saw on the following days between it and the new year. And so ended my Christmas holiday with my people.

But there is one little incident which I ought to relate before I close this chapter, and which I am ashamed of having so nearly forgotten.

When we had finished our dinner, and I was sitting alone drinking a class of claret before going out again, Mrs Pearson came in and told me that little Gerard Weir wanted to see me. I asked her to show him in; and the little fellow entered, looking very shy, and clinging first to the door and then to the wall.

"Come, my dear boy," I said, "and sit down by me."

He came directly and stood before me.

"Would you like a little wine and water?" I said; for unhappily there was no dessert, Mrs Pearson knowing that I never eat such things.

"No, thank you, sir; I never tasted wine."

"I did not press him to take it.

"Please, sir," he went on after a pause, putting his nand in his pocket, "mother gave me some goodies, and I kept them till I saw you come back, and here they are, sir."

Does any reader doubt what I did or said upon this?

I said, "Thank you, my darling," and I ate them up every one of them, that he might see me eat them before he left the house. And the dear child went off radiant.

If anybody cannot understand why I did so, I beg him to consider the matter. If then he cannot come to a conclusion concerning it, I doubt if any explanation of mine would greatly subserve his enlightenment. Meantime, I am forcibly restraining myself from yielding to the temptation to set forth my reasons, which would result in a half-hour's sermon on the Jewish dispensation, including the burnt offering, and the wave and heave offerings, with an application to the ignorant nurses and mothers of English babies, who do the best they can to make original sin an actual fact by training children down in the way they should not go.

CHAPTER XII
THE AVENUE.

It will not appear strange that I should linger so long upon the first few months of my association with a people who, now that I am an old man, look to me like my own children. For those who were then older than myself are now "old dwellers in those high countries" where there is no age, only wisdom; and I shall soon go to them. How glad I shall be to see my Old Rogers again, who, as he taught me upon earth, will teach me yet niore, I thank my God, in heaven! But I must not let the reverie which' always gathers about the feather-end of my pen the moment I take it up to write these recollections, interfere with the work before me.

After this Christmas-tide, I found myself in closer relationship to my parishioners. No doubt I was always in danger of giving unknown offence to those who were ready to fancy that I neglected them, and did not distribute my FAVOURS equally. But as I never took offence, the offence I gave was easily got rid of. A clergyman, of all men, should be slow to take offence, for if he does, he will never be free or strong to reprove sin. And it must sometimes be his duty to speak severely to those, especially the good, who are turning their faces the wrong way. It is of little use to reprove the sinner, but it is worth while sometimes to reprove those who have a regard for righteousness, however imperfect they may be. "Reprove not a scorner, lest he hate thee; rebuke a wise man, and he will love thee."

But I took great care about INTERFERING; though I would interfere upon request-not always, however, upon the side whence the request came, and more seldom still upon either side. The clergyman must never be a partisan. When our Lord was requested to act as umpire between two brothers, He refused. But He spoke and said, "Take heed, and beware of covetousness." Now, though the best of men is unworthy to loose the latchet of His shoe, yet the servant must be as his Master. Ah me! while I write it, I remember that the sinful woman might yet do as she would with His sacred feet. I bethink me: Desert may not touch His shoe-tie: Love may kiss His feet.

I visited, of course, at the Hall, as at the farmhouses in the country, and the cottages in the village. I did not come to like Mrs Oldcastle better. And there was one woman in the house whom I disliked still more: that Sarah whom Judy had called in my hearing a white wolf. Her face was yet whiter than that of her mistress, only it was not smooth like hers; for its whiteness came apparently from the small-pox, which had so thickened the skin that no blood, if she had any, could shine through. I seldom saw her-only, indeed, caught a glimpse of her now and then as I passed through the house.

Nor did I make much progress with Mr Stoddart. He had always something friendly to say, and often some theosophical theory to bring forward, which, I must add, never seemed to me to mean, or, at least, to reveal, anything. He was a great reader of mystical books, and yet the man's nature seemed cold. It was sunshiny, but not sunny. His intellect was rather a lambent flame than a genial warmth. He could make things, but he could not grow anything. And when I came to see that he had had more than any one else to do with the education of Miss Oldcastle, I understood her a little better, and saw that her so-called education had been in a great measure repression-of a negative sort, no doubt, but not therefore the less mischievous. For to teach speculation instead of devotion, mysticism instead of love, word instead of deed, is surely ruinously repressive to the nature that is meant for sunbright activity both of heart and hand. My chief perplexity continued to be how he could play the organ as he did.

My reader will think that I am always coming round to Miss Oldcastle; but if he does, I cannot help it. I began, I say, to understand her a little better. She seemed to me always like one walking in a "watery sunbeam," without knowing that it was but the wintry pledge of a summer sun at hand. She took it, or was trying to take it, for THE sunlight; trying to make herself feel all the glory people said was in the light, instead of making haste towards the perfect day. I found afterwards that several things had combined to bring about this condition; and

I know she will forgive me, should I, for the sake of others, endeavour to make it understood by and by.

I have not much more to tell my readers about this winter. As but of a whole changeful season only one day, or, it may be, but one moment in which the time seemed to burst into its own blossom, will cling to the memory; so of the various interviews with my friends, and the whole flow of the current of my life, during that winter, nothing more of nature or human nature occurs to me worth recording. I will pass on to the summer season as rapidly as I may, though the early spring will detain me with the relation of just a single incident.

I was on my way to the Hall to see Mr Stoddart. I wanted to ask him whether something could not be done beyond his exquisite playing to rouse the sense of music in my people. I believed that nothing helps you so much to feel as the taking of what share may, from the nature of the thing, be possible to you; because, for one reason, in order to feel, it is necessary that the mind should rest upon the matter, whatever it is. The poorest success, provided the attempt has been genuine, will enable one to enter into any art ten times better than before. Now I had, I confess, little hope of moving Mr Stoddart in the matter; but if I should succeed, I thought it would do himself more good to mingle with his humble fellows in the attempt to do them a trifle of good, than the opening of any number of intellectual windows towards the circumambient truth.

It was just beginning to grow dusk. The wind was blustering in gusts among the trees, swaying them suddenly and fiercely like a keen passion, now sweeping them all one way as if the multitude of tops would break loose and rush away like a wild river, and now subsiding as suddenly, and allowing them to recover themselves and stand upright, with tones and motions of indignant expostulation. There was just one cold bar of light in the west, and the east was one gray mass, while overhead the stars were twinkling. The grass and all the ground about the trees were very wet. The time seemed more dreary somehow than the winter. Rigour was past, and tenderness had not come. For the wind was cold without being keen, and bursting from the trees every now and then with a roar as of a sea breaking on distant sands, whirled about me as if it wanted me to go and join in its fierce play.

Suddenly I saw, to my amazement, in a walk that ran alongside of the avenue, Miss Oldcastle struggling against the wind, which blew straight down the path upon her. The cause of my amazement was twofold. First, I had supposed her with her mother in London, whither their journeys had been not infrequent since Christmas-tide; and next-why should she be fighting with the wind, so far from the house, with only a shawl drawn over her head?

The reader may wonder how I should know her in this attire in the dusk, and where there was not the smallest probability of finding her. Suffice it to say that I did recognise her at once; and passing between two great tree-trunks, and through an opening in some under-wood, was by her side in a moment. But the noise of the wind had prevented her from hearing my approach, and when I uttered her name, she started violently, and, turning, drew herself up very haughtily, in part, I presume, to hide her tremor. —She was always a little haughty with me, I must acknowledge. Could there have been anything in my address, however unconscious of it I was, that made her fear I was ready to become intrusive? Or might it not be that, hearing of my footing with my parishioners generally, she was prepared to resent any assumption of clerical familiarity with her; and so, in my behaviour, any poor innocent "bush was supposed a bear." For I need not tell my reader that nothing was farther from my intention, even with the lowliest of my flock, than to presume upon my position as clergyman. I think they all GAVE me the relation I occupied towards them personally. —But I had never seen her look so haughty as now. If I had been watching her very thoughts she could hardly have looked more indignant.

"I beg your pardon," I said, distressed; "I have startled you dreadfully."

"Not in the least," she replied, but without moving, and still with a curve in her form like the neck of a frayed horse.

I thought it better to leave apology, which was evidently disagreeable to her, and speak of indifferent things.

"I was on my way to call on Mr Stoddart," I said.

"You will find him at home, I believe."

"I fancied you and Mrs Oldcastle in London."

"We returned yesterday."

Still she stood as before. I made a movement in the direction of the house. She seemed as if she would walk in the opposite direction.

"May I not walk with you to the house?"

"I am not going in just yet."

"Are you protected enough for sucn a night?"

"I enjoy the wind."

I bowed and walked on; for what else could I do?

I cannot say that I enjoyed leaving her behind me in the gathering dark, the wind blowing her about with no more reverence than if she had been a bush of privet. Nor was it with a light heart that I bore her repulse as I slowly climbed the hill to the house. However, a little personal mortification is wholesome-though I cannot say either that I derived much consolation from the reflection.

Sarah opened the glass door, her black, glossy, restless eyes looking out of her white face from under gray eyebrows. I knew at once by her look beyond me that she had expected to find me accompanied by her young mistress. I did not volunteer any information, as my reader may suppose.

I found, as I had feared, that, although Mr. Stoddart seemed to listen with some interest to what I said, I could not bring him to the point of making any practical suggestion, or of responding to one made by me; and I left him with the conviction that he would do nothing to help me. Yet during the whole of our interview he had not opposed a single word I said. He was like clay too much softened with water to keep the form into which it has been modelled. He would take SOME kind of form easily, and lose it yet more easily. I did not show all my dissatisfaction, however, for that would only have estranged us; and it is not required, nay, it may be wrong, to show all you feel or think: what is required of us is, not to show what we do not feel or think; for that is to be false.

I left the house in a gloomy mood. I know I ought to have looked up to God and said: "These things do not reach to Thee, my Father. Thou art ever the same; and I rise above my small as well as my great troubles by remembering Thy peace, and Thy unchangeable Godhood to me and all Thy creatures." But I did not come to myself all at once. The thought of God had not come, though it was pretty sure to come before I got home. I was brooding over the littleness of all I could do; and feeling that sickness which sometimes will overtake a man in the midst of the work he likes best, when the unpleasant parts of it crowd upon him, and his own efforts, especially those made from the will without sustaining impulse, come back upon him with a feeling of unreality, decay, and bitterness, as if he had been unnatural and untrue, and putting himself in false relations by false efforts for good. I know this all came from selfishness-thinking about myself instead of about God and my neighbour. But so it was. —And so I was walking down the avenue, where it was now very dark, with my head bent to the ground, when I in my turn started at the sound of a woman's voice, and looking up, saw by the starlight the dim form of Miss Oldcastle standing before me.

She spoke first.

"Mr Walton, I was very rude to you. I beg your pardon."

"Indeed, I did not think so. I only thought what a blundering awkward fellow I was to startle you as I did. You have to forgive me."

"I fancy" —and here I know she smiled, though how I know I do not know —"I fancy I have made that even," she said, pleasantly; "for you must confess I startled you now."

"You did; but it was in a very different way. I annoyed you with my rudeness. You only scattered a swarm of bats that kept flapping their skinny wings in my face."

"What do you mean? There are no bats at this time of the year."

"Not outside. In 'winter and rough weather' they creep inside, you know."

"Ah! I ought to understand you. But I did not think you were ever like that. I thought you were too good."

"I wish I were. I hope to be some day. I am not yet, anyhow. And I thank you for driving the bats away in the meantime."

"You make me the more ashamed of myself to think that perhaps my rudeness had a share in bringing them. —Yours is no doubt thankless labour sometimes."

She seemed to make the last remark just to prevent the conversation from returning to her as its subject. And now all the bright portions of my work came up before me.

"You are quite mistaken in that, Miss Oldcastle. On the contrary, the thanks I get are far more than commensurate with the labour. Of course one meets with a disappointment sometimes, but that is only when they don't know what you mean. And how should they know what you mean till they are different themselves? —You remember what Wordsworth says on this very subject in his poem of Simon Lee?" —

"I do not know anything of Wordsworth."

"'I've heard of hearts unkind, kind deeds With coldness still returning; Alas! the gratitude of men Hath oftener left me mourning.'"

"I do not quite see what he means."

"May I recommend you to think about it? You will be sure to find it out for yourself, and that will be ten times more satisfactory than if I were to explain it to you. And, besides, you will never forget it, if you do."

"Will you repeat the lines again?"

I did so.

All this time the wind had been still. Now it rose with a slow gush in the trees. Was it fancy? Or, as the wind moved the shrubbery, did I see a white face? And could it be the White Wolf, as Judy called her?

I spoke aloud:

"But it is cruel to keep you standing here in such a night. You must be a real lover of nature to walk in the dark wind."

"I like it. Good night."

So we parted. I gazed into the darkness after her, though she disappeared at the distance of a yard or two; and would have stood longer had I not still suspected the proximity of Judy's Wolf, which made me turn and go home, regardless now of Mr Stoddart's DOUGHINESS.

I met Miss Oldcastle several times before the summer, but her old manner remained, or rather had returned, for there had been nothing of it in the tone of her voice in that interview, if INTERVIEW it could be called where neither could see more than the other's outline.

CHAPTER XIII
YOUNG WEIR.

By slow degrees the summer bloomed. Green came instead of white; rainbows instead of icicles. The grounds about the Hall seemed the incarnation of a summer which had taken years to ripen to its perfection. The very grass seemed to have aged into perfect youth in that "haunt of ancient peace;" for surely nowhere else was such thick, delicate-bladed, delicate-coloured grass to be seen. Gnarled old trees of may stood like altars of smoking perfume, or each like one million-petalled flower of upheaved whiteness-or of tender rosiness, as if the snow which had covered it in winter had sunk in and gathered warmth from the life of the tree, and now crept out again to adorn the summer. The long loops of the laburnum hung heavy with gold towards the sod below; and the air was full of the fragrance of the young leaves of the limes. Down in the valley below, the daisies shone in all the meadows, varied with the buttercup and the celandine; while in damp places grew large pimpernels, and along the sides of the river, the meadow-sweet stood amongst the reeds at the very edge of the water, breathing out the odours of dreamful sleep. The clumsy pollards were each one mass of undivided green. The mill wheel had regained its knotty look, with its moss and its dip and drip, as it yielded to the slow water, which would have let it alone, but that there was no other way out of the land to the sea.

I used now to wander about in the fields and woods, with a book in my hand, at which I often did not look the whole day, and which yet I liked to have with me. And I seemed somehow to come back with most upon those days in which I did not read. In this manner I prepared almost all my sermons that summer. But, although I prepared them thus in the open country, I had another custom, which perhaps may appear strange to some, before I preached them. This was, to spend the Saturday evening, not in my study, but in the church. This custom of mine was known to the sexton and his wife, and the church was always clean and ready for me after about mid-day, so that I could be alone there as soon as I pleased. It would take more space than my limits will afford to explain thoroughly why I liked to do this. But I will venture to attempt a partial explanation in a few words.

This fine old church in which I was honoured to lead the prayers of my people, was not the expression of the religious feeling of my time. There was a gloom about it—a sacred gloom, I know, and I loved it; but such gloom as was not in my feeling when I talked to my flock. I honoured the place; I rejoiced in its history; I delighted to think that even by the temples made with hands outlasting these bodies of ours, we were in a sense united to those who in them had before us lifted up holy hands without wrath or doubting; and with many more who, like us, had lifted up at least prayerful hands without hatred or despair. The place soothed me, tuned me to a solemn mood-one of self-denial, and gentle gladness in all sober things. But, had I been an architect, and had I had to build a church—I do not in the least know how I should have built it—I am certain it would have been very different from this. Else I should be a mere imitator, like all the church-architects I know anything about in the present day. For I always found the open air the most genial influence upon me for the production of religious feeling and thought. I had been led to try whether it might not be so with me by the fact that our Lord seemed so much to delight in the open air, and late in the day as well as early in the morning would climb the mountain to be alone with His Father. I found that it helped to give a reality to everything that I thought about, if I only contemplated it under the high untroubled blue, with the lowly green beneath my feet, and the wind blowing on me to remind me of the Spirit that once moved on the face of the waters, bringing order out of disorder and light out of darkness, and was now seeking every day a fuller entrance into my heart, that there He might work the one will of the Father in heaven.

My reader will see then that there was, as it were, not so much a discord, as a lack of harmony between the surroundings wherein my thoughts took form, or, to use a homelier phrase, my sermon was studied, and the surroundings wherein I had to put these forms into the garments of words, or preach that sermon. I therefore sought to bridge over this difference (if I understood music, I am sure I could find an expression exactly fitted to my meaning),—to find an easy passage between the open-air mood and the church mood, so as to be able to bring into the church as much of the fresh air, and the tree-music, and the colour-harmony, and the gladness over all, as might be possible; and, in order to this, I thought all my sermon over again in the afternoon sun as it shone slantingly through the stained window over Lord Eagleye's tomb, and in the failing light thereafter and the gathering dusk of the twilight, pacing up and down the solemn old place, hanging my thoughts here on a crocket, there on a corbel; now on the gable-point over which Weir's face would gaze next morning, and now on the aspiring peaks of the organ. I thus made the place a cell of thought and prayer. And when the next day came, I found the forms around me so interwoven with the forms of my thought, that I felt almost like one of the old monks who had built the place, so little did I find any check to my thought or utterance from its unfitness for the expression of my individual modernism. But not one atom the more did I incline to the evil fancy that God was more in the past than in the present; that He is more within the walls of the church, than in the unwalled sky and earth; or seek to turn backwards one step from a living Now to an entombed and consecrated Past.

One lovely Saturday, I had been out all the morning. I had not walked far, for I had sat in the various places longer than I had walked, my path lying through fields and copses, crossing a country road only now and then. I had my Greek Testament with me, and I read when I sat, and thought when I walked. I remember well enough that I was going to preach about the cloud of witnesses, and explain to my people that this did not mean persons looking at, witnessing our behaviour-not so could any addition be made to the awfulness of the fact that the eye of God was upon us-but witnesses to the truth, people who did what God wanted them to do, come of it what might, whether a crown or a rack, scoffs or applause; to behold whose witnessing might well rouse all that was human and divine in us to chose our part with them and their Lord.—When I came home, I had an early dinner, and then betook myself to my Saturday's resort.—I had never had a room large enough to satisfy me before. Now my study was to my mind.

All through the slowly-fading afternoon, the autumn of the day, when the colours are richest and the shadows long and lengthening, I paced my solemn old-thoughted church. Sometimes I went up into the pulpit and sat there, looking on the ancient walls which had grown up under men's hands that men might be helped to pray by the visible symbol of unity which the walls gave, and that the voice of the Spirit of God might be heard exhorting men to forsake the evil and choose the good. And I thought how many witnesses to the truth had knelt in those ancient pews. For as the great church is made up of numberless communities, so is the great shining orb of witness-bearers made up of millions of lesser orbs. All men and women of true heart bear individual testimony to the truth of God, saying, "I have trusted and found Him faithful." And the feeble light of the glowworm is yet light, pure, and good, and with a loveliness of its own. "So, O Lord," I said, "let my light shine before men." And I felt no fear of vanity in such a prayer, for I knew that the glory to come of it is to God only—"that men may glorify their Father in heaven." And I knew that when we seek glory for ourselves, the light goes out, and the Horror that dwells in darkness breathes cold upon our spirits. And I remember that just as I thought thus, my eye was caught first by a yellow light that gilded the apex of the font-cover, which had been wrought like a flame or a bursting blossom: it was so old and worn, I never could tell which; and then by a red light all over a white marble tablet in the wall-the red of life on the cold hue of the grave. And this red light did not come from any work of man's device, but from the great window of the west, which little Gerard Weir wanted to help God to paint. I must have been in a happy mood that Saturday afternoon, for everything pleased me and made me happier; and all the church-forms about me blended and harmonised graciously with the throne and footstool of God which I saw through the windows. And I lingered on till the night had come; till the church only gloomed about me, and had no shine; and then I found my spirit burning up the clearer, as a lamp which has been flaming all the day with light unseen becomes a glory in the room when the sun is gone down.

At length I felt tired, and would go home. Yet I lingered for a few moments in the vestry, thinking what hymns would harmonize best with the things I wanted to make my people think about. It was now almost quite dark out of doors-at least as dark as it would be.

Suddenly through the gloom I thought I heard a moan and a sob. I sat upright in my chair and listened. But I heard nothing more, and concluded I had deceived myself. After a few moments, I rose to go home and have some tea, and turn my mind rather away from than towards the subject of witness-bearing any more for that night, lest I should burn the fuel of it out before I came to warm the people with it, and should have to blow its embers instead of flashing its light and heat upon them in gladness. So I left the church by my vestry-door, which I closed behind me, and took my way along the path through the clustering group of graves.

Again I heard a sob. This time I was sure of it. And there lay something dark upon one of the grassy mounds. I approached it, but it did not move. I spoke.

"Can I be of any use to you?" I said.

"No," returned an almost inaudible voice.

Though I did not know whose was the grave, I knew that no one had been buried there very lately, and if the grief were for the loss of the dead, it was more than probably aroused to fresh vigour by recent misfortune.

I stooped, and taking the figure by the arm, said, "Come with me, and let us see what can be done for you."

I then saw that it was a youth-perhaps scarcely more than a boy. And as soon as I saw that, I knew that his grief could hardly be incurable. He returned no answer, but rose at once to his feet, and submitted to be led away. I took him the shortest road to my house through the shrubbery, brought him into the study, made him sit down in my easy-chair, and rang for lights and wine; for the dew had been falling heavily, and his clothes were quite dank. But when the wine came, he refused to take any.

"But you want it," I said.

"No, sir, I don't, indeed."

"Take some for my sake, then."

"I would rather not, sir."

"Why?"

"I promised my father a year ago, when I left home that I would not drink anything stronger than water.[sic] And I can't break my promise now."

"Where is your home?"

"In the village, sir."

"That wasn't your father's grave I found you upon, was it?"

"No, sir. It was my mother's."

"Then your father is still alive?"

"Yes, sir. You know him very well-Thomas Weir."

"Ah! He told me he had a son in London. Are you that son?"

"Yes, sir," answered the youth, swallowing a rising sob.

"Then what is the matter? Your father is a good friend of mine, and would tell you you might trust me."

"I don't doubt it, sir. But you won't believe me any more than my father."

By this time I had perused his person, his dress, and his countenance. He was of middle size, but evidently not full grown. His dress was very decent. His face was pale and thin, and revealed a likeness to his father. He had blue eyes that looked full at me, and, as far as I could judge, betokened, along with the whole of his expression, an honest and sensitive nature. I found him very attractive, and was therefore the more emboldened to press for the knowledge of his story.

"I cannot promise to believe whatever you say; but almost I could. And if you tell me the truth, I like you too much already to be in great danger of doubting you, for you know the truth has a force of its own."

"I thought so till to-night," he answered. "But if my father would not believe me, how can I expect you to do so, sir?"

"Your father may have been too much troubled by your story to be able to do it justice. It is not a bit like your father to be unfair."

"No, sir. And so much the less chance of your believing me."

Somehow his talk prepossessed me still more in his favour. There was a certain refinement in it, a quality of dialogue which indicated thought, as I judged; and I became more and more certain that, whatever I might have to think of it when told, he would yet tell me the truth.

"Come, try me," I said.

"I will, sir. But I must begin at the beginning."

"Begin where you like. I have nothing more to do to-night, and you may take what time you please. But I will ring for tea first; for I dare say you have not made any promise about that."

A faint smile flickered on his face. He was evidently beginning to feel a little more comfortable.

"When did you arrive from London?" I asked.

"About two hours ago, I suppose."

"Bring tea, Mrs Pearson, and that cold chicken and ham, and plenty of toast. We are both hungry."

Mrs Pearson gave a questioning look at the lad, and departed to do her duty.

When she returned with the tray, I saw by the unconsciously eager way in which he looked at the eatables, that he had had nothing for some time; and so, even after we were left alone, I would not let him say a word till he had made a good meal. It was delightful to see how he ate. Few troubles will destroy a growing lad's hunger; and indeed it has always been to me a marvel how the feelings and the appetites affect each other. I have known grief actually make people, and not sensual people at all, quite hungry. At last I thought I had better not offer him any more.

After the tea-things had been taken away, I put the candles out; and the moon, which had risen, nearly full, while we were at tea, shone into the room. I had thought that he might possibly find it easier to tell his story in the moonlight, which, if there were any shame in the recital, would not, by too much revelation, reduce him to the despair of Macbeth, when, feeling that he could contemplate his deed, but not his deed and himself together, he exclaimed,

"To know my deed, 'twere best not know myself."

So, sitting by the window in the moonlight, he told his tale. The moon lighted up his pale face as he told it, and gave rather a wild expression to his eyes, eager to find faith in me. —I have not much of the dramatic in me, I know; and I am rather a flat teller of stories on that account. I shall not, therefore, seeing there is no necessity for it, attempt to give the tale in his own words. But, indeed, when I think of it, they did not differ so much from the form of my own, for he had, I presume, lost his provincialisms, and being, as I found afterwards, a reader of the best books that came in his way, had not caught up many cockneyisms instead.

He had filled a place in the employment of Messrs ——— & Co., large silk-mercers, linen-drapers, etc., etc., in London; for all the trades are mingled now. His work at first was to accompany one of the carts which delivered the purchases of the day; but, I presume because he showed himself to be a smart lad, they took him at length into the shop to wait behind the counter. This he did not like so much, but, as it was considered a rise in life, made no objection to the change.

He seemed to himself to get on pretty well. He soon learned all the marks on the goods intended to be understood by the shopmen, and within a few months believed that he was found generally useful. He had as yet had no distinct department allotted to him, but was moved from place to place, according as the local pressure of business might demand.

"I confess," he said, "that I was not always satisfied with what was going on about me. I mean I could not help doubting if everything was done on the square, as they say. But nothing came plainly in my way, and so I could honestly say it did not concern me. I took care to be straightforward for my part, and, knowing only the prices marked for the sale of the goods, I had nothing to do with anything else. But one day, while I was showing a lady some handkerchiefs which were marked as mouchoirs de Paris—I don't know if I pronounce it right, sir-she said she did not believe they were French cambric; and I, knowing nothing about it, said nothing. But, happening to look up while we both stood silent, the lady examining the handkerchiefs, and I doing nothing till she should have made up her mind, I caught sight of the eyes of the shop-walker, as they call the man who shows customers where to go for what they want, and sees that they are attended to. He is a fat man, dressed in black, with a great gold chain, which they say in the shop is only copper gilt. But that doesn't matter, only it would be the liker himself. He was standing staring at me. I could not tell what to make of it; but from that day I often caught him watching me, as if I had been a customer suspected of shop-lifting. Still I only thought he was very disagreeable, and tried to forget him.

"One day-the day before yesterday-two ladies, an old lady and a young one, came into the shop, and wanted to look at some shawls. It was dinner-time, and most of the men were in the house at their dinner. The shop-walker sent me to them, and then, I do believe, though I did not see him, stood behind a pillar to watch me, as he had been in the way of doing more openly. I thought I had seen the ladies before, and though I could not then tell where, I am now almost sure they were Mrs and Miss Oldcastle, of the Hall. They wanted to buy a cashmere for the young lady. I showed them some. They wanted better. I brought the best we had, inquiring, that I might make no mistake. They asked the price. I told them. They said they were not good enough, and wanted to see some more. I told them they were the best we had. They looked at them again; said they were sorry, but the shawls were not good enough, and left the shop without buying anything. I proceeded to take the shawls up-stairs again, and, as I went, passed the shop walker, whom I had not observed while I was attending to the ladies. 'YOU're for no good, young man!' he said with a nasty sneer. 'What do you mean by that, Mr B.?' I asked, for his sneer made me angry. 'You'll know before to-morrow,' he answered, and walked away. That same evening, as we were shutting up shop, I was sent for to the principal's room. The moment I entered, he said, 'You won't suit us, young man, I find. You had better pack up your box to-night, and be off to-morrow. There's your quarter's salary.' 'What have I done?' I asked in astonishment, and yet with a vague suspicion of the matter. 'It's not what you've done, but what you don't do,' he answered. 'Do you think we can afford to keep you here and pay you wages to send people away from the shop without buying? If you do, you're mistaken, that's all. You may go.' 'But what could I do?' I said. 'I suppose that spy, B—-,' —I believe I said so, sir. 'Now, now, young man, none of your sauce!' said Mr—. 'Honest people don't think about spies.' 'I thought it was for honesty you were getting rid of me,' I said. Mr—-rose to his feet, his lips white, and pointed to the door. 'Take your money and be off. And mind you don't refer to me for a character. After such impudence I couldn't in conscience give you one.' Then, calming down a little when he saw I turned to go, 'You had better take to your hands again, for your head will never keep you. There, be off!' he said, pushing the money towards me, and turning his back to me. I could not touch it. 'Keep the money, Mr—-,' I said. 'It'll make up for what you've lost by me.' And I left the room at once without waiting for an answer.

"While I was packing my box, one of my chums came in, and I told him all about it. He is rather a good fellow that, sir; but he laughed, and said, 'What a fool you are, Weir! YOU'll never make your daily bread, and you needn't think it. If you knew what I know, you'd have known better. And it's very odd it was about shawls, too. I'll tell you. As you're going away, you won't let it out. Mr—-' (that was the same who had just turned me away) 'was serving some ladies himself, for he wasn't above being in the shop, like his partner. They wanted the best Indian shawl they could get. None of those he showed them were good enough, for the ladies really didn't know one from another. They always go by the price you ask, and Mr—-knew that well enough. He had sent me up-stairs for the shawls, and as I brought them he said, "These are the best imported, madam." There were three ladies; and one shook her head, and another shook her head, and they all shook their heads. And then Mr—-was sorry, I believe you, that he had said they were the best. But you won't catch him in a trap! He's too old a fox for that.' I'm telling you, sir, what Johnson told me. 'He looked close down at the shawls, as if he were short-sighted, though he could see as far as any man. "I beg your pardon, ladies," said he, "you're right. I am quite wrong. What a stupid blunder to make! And yet they did deceive me. Here, Johnson, take these shawls away. How could you be so stupid? I will fetch the thing you want myself, ladies." So I went with him. He chose out three or four shawls, of the nicest patterns, from the very same lot, marked in the very same way, folded them differently, and gave them to me to carry down. "Now, ladies, here they are!" he said. "These are quite a different thing, as you will see; and, indeed, they cost half as much again." In five minutes they had bought two of them, and paid just half as much more than he had asked for them the first time. That's Mr —-! and that's what you should have done if you had wanted to keep your place.' —But I assure you, sir, I could not help being glad to be out of it."

"But there is nothing in all this to be miserable about," I said. "You did your duty."

"It would be all right, sir, if father believed me. I don't want to be idle, I'm sure."

"Does your father think you do?"

"I don't know what he thinks. He won't speak to me. I told my story-as much of it as he would let me, at least-but he wouldn't listen to me. He only said he knew better than that. I couldn't bear it. He always was rather hard upon us. I'm sure if you hadn't been so kind to me, sir, I don't know what I should have done by this time. I haven't another friend in the world."

"Yes, you have. Your Father in heaven is your friend."

"I don't know that, sir. I'm not good enough."

"That's quite true. But you would never have done your duty if He had not been with you."

"DO you think so, sir?" he returned, eagerly.

"Indeed, I do. Everything good comes from the Father of lights. Every one that walks in any glimmering of light walks so far in HIS light. For there is no light-only darkness-comes from below. And man apart from God can generate no light. He's not meant to be separated from God, you see. And only think then what light He can give you if you will turn to Him and ask for it. What He has given you should make you long for more; for what you have is not enough-ah! far from it."

"I think I understand. But I didn't feel good at all in the matter. I didn't see any other way of doing."

"So much the better. We ought never to feel good. We are but unprofitable servants at best. There is no merit in doing your duty; only you would have been a poor wretched creature not to do as you did. And now, instead of making yourself miserable over the consequences of it, you ought to bear them like a man, with courage and hope, thanking God that He has made you suffer for righteousness' sake, and denied you the success and the praise of cheating. I will go to your father at once, and find out what he is thinking about it. For no doubt Mr —-has written to him with his version of the story. Perhaps he will be more inclined to believe you when he finds that I believe you."

"Oh, thank you, sir!" cried the lad, and jumped up from his seat to go with me.

"No," I said; "you had better stay where you are. I shall be able to speak more freely if you are not present. Here is a book to amuse yourself with. I do not think I shall be long gone."

But I was longer gone than I thought I should be.

When I reached the carpenter's house, I found, to my surprise, that he was still at work. By the light of a single tallow candle placed beside him on the bench, he was ploughing away at a groove. His pale face, of which the lines were unusually sharp, as I might have expected after what had occurred, was the sole object that reflected the light of the candle to my eyes as I entered the gloomy place. He looked up, but without even greeting me, dropped his face again and went on with his work.

"What!" I said, cheerily,—for I believed that, like Gideon's pitcher, I held dark within me the light that would discomfit his Midianites, which consciousness may well make the pitcher cheery inside, even while the light as yet is all its own-worthless, till it break out upon the world, and cease to illuminate only glazed pitcher-sides —"What!" I said, "working so late?"

"Yes, sir."

"It is not usual with you, I know."

"It's all a humbug!" he said fiercely, but coldly notwithstanding, as he stood erect from his work, and turned his white face full on me-of which, however, the eyes drooped —"It's all a humbug; and I don't mean to be humbugged any more."

"Am I a humbug?" I returned, not quite taken by surprise.

"I don't say that. Don't make a personal thing of it, sir. You're taken in, I believe, like the rest of us. Tell me that a God governs the world! What have I done, to be used like this?"

I thought with myself how I could retort for his young son: "What has he done to be used like this?" But that was not my way, though it might work well enough in some hands. Some men are called to be prophets. I could only "stand and wait."

"It would be wrong in me to pretend ignorance," I said, "of what you mean. I know all about it."

"Do you? He has been to you, has he? But you don't know all about it, sir. The impudence of the young rascal!"

He paused for a moment.

"A man like me!" he resumed, becoming eloquent in his indignation, and, as I thought afterwards, entirely justifying what Wordsworth says about the language of the so-called uneducated, —"A man like me, who was as proud of his honour as any aristocrat in the country-prouder than any of them would grant me the right to be!"

"Too proud of it, I think-not too careful of it," I said. But I was thankful he did not heed me, for the speech would only have irritated him. He went on.

"Me to be treated like this! One child a..."

Here came a terrible break in his speech. But he tried again.

"And the other a..."

Instead of finishing the sentence, however, he drove his plough fiercely through the groove, splitting off some inches of the wall of it at the end.

"If any one has treated you so," I said, "it must be the devil, not God."

"But if there was a God, he could have prevented it all."

"Mind what I said to you once before: He hasn't done yet. And there is another enemy in His way as bad as the devil—I mean our SELVES. When people want to walk their own way without God, God lets them try it. And then the devil gets a hold of them. But God won't let him keep them. As soon as they are 'wearied in the greatness of their way,' they begin to look about for a Saviour. And then they find God ready to pardon, ready to help, not breaking the bruised reed-leading them to his own self manifest-with whom no man can fear any longer, Jesus Christ, the righteous lover of men-their elder brother-what we call BIG BROTHER, you know-one to help them and take their part against the devil, the world, and the flesh, and all the rest of the wicked powers. So you see God is tender-just like the prodigal son's father-only with this difference, that God has millions of prodigals, and never gets tired of going out to meet them and welcome them back, every one as if he were the only prodigal son He had ever had. There's a father indeed! Have you been such a father to your son?"

"The prodigal didn't come with a pack of lies. He told his father the truth, bad as it was."

"How do you know that your son didn't tell you the truth? All the young men that go from home don't do as the prodigal did. Why should you not believe what he tells you?"

"I'm not one to reckon without my host. Here's my bill."

And so saying, he handed me a letter. I took it and read: —

"SIR, —It has become our painful duty to inform you that your son has this day been discharged from the employment of Messrs—-and Co., his conduct not being such as to justify the confidence hitherto reposed in him. It would have been contrary to the interests of the establishment to continue him longer behind the counter, although we are not prepared to urge anything against him beyond the fact that he has shown himself absolutely indifferent to the interests of his employers. We trust that the chief blame will be found to lie with certain connexions of a kind easy to be formed in large cities, and that the loss of his situation may be punishment sufficient, if not for justice, yet to make him consider his ways and be wise. We enclose his quarter's salary, which the young man rejected with insult, and,

"We remain, &c.,
"——-and Co."

"And," I exclaimed, "this is what you found your judgment of your own son upon! You reject him unheard, and take the word of a stranger! I don't wonder you cannot believe in your Father when you behave so to your son. I don't say your conclusion is false, though I don't believe it. But I do say the grounds you go upon are anything but sufficient."

"You don't mean to tell me that a man of Mr ——'s standing, who has one of the largest shops in London, and whose brother is Mayor of Addicehead, would slander a poor lad like that!"

"Oh you mammon-worshipper!" I cried. "Because a man has one of the largest shops in London, and his brother is Mayor of Addicehead, you take his testimony and refuse your son's! I did not know the boy till this evening; but I call upon you to bring back to your memory all that you have known of him from his childhood, and then ask yourself whether there is not, at least, as much probability of his having remained honest as of the master of a great London shop being infallible in his conclusions-at which conclusions, whatever they be, I confess no man can wonder, after seeing how readily his father listens to his defamation."

I spoke with warmth. Before I had done, the pale face of the carpenter was red as fire; for he had been acting contrary to all his own theories of human equality, and that in a shameful manner. Still, whether convinced or not, he would not give in. He only drove away at his work, which he was utterly destroying. His mouth was closed so tight, he looked as if he had his jaw locked; and his eyes gleamed over the ruined board with a light which seemed to me to have more of obstinacy in it than contrition.

"Ah, Thomas!" I said, taking up the speech once more, "if God had behaved to us as you have behaved to your boy-be he innocent, be he guilty-there's not a man or woman of all our lost race would have returned to Him from the time of Adam till now. I don't wonder that you find it difficult to believe in Him."

And with those words I left the shop, determined to overwhelm the unbeliever with proof, and put him to shame before his own soul, whence, I thought, would come even more good to him than to his son. For there was a great deal of self-satisfaction mixed up with the man's honesty, and the sooner that had a blow the better-it might prove a death-blow in the long run. It was pride that lay at the root of his hardness. He visited the daughter's fault upon the son. His daughter had disgraced him; and he was ready to flash into wrath with his son upon any imputation which recalled to him the torture he had undergone when his daughter's dishonour came first to the light. Her he had never forgiven, and now his pride flung his son out after her upon the first suspicion. His imagination had filled up all the blanks in the wicked insinuations of Mr ——. He concluded that he had taken money to spend in the worst company, and had so disgraced him beyond forgiveness. His pride paralysed his love. He thought more about himself than about his children. His own shame outweighed in his estimation the sadness of their guilt. It was a less matter that they should be guilty, than that he, their father, should be disgraced.

Thinking over all this, and forgetting how late it was, I found myself half-way up the avenue of the Hall. I wanted to find out whether young Weir's fancy that the ladies he had failed in serving, or rather whom he had really served with honesty, were Mrs and Miss Oldcastle, was correct. What a point it would be if it was! I should not then be satisfied except I could prevail on Miss Oldcastle to accompany me to Thomas Weir, and shame the faithlessness out of him. So eager was I after certainty, that it was not till I stood before the house that I saw clearly the impropriety of attempting anything further that night. One light only was burning in the whole front, and that was on the first floor.

Glancing up at it, I knew not why, as I turned to go down the hill again, I saw a corner of the blind drawn aside and a face peeping out-whose, I could not tell. This was uncomfortable-for what could be taking me there at such a time? But I walked steadily away, certain I could not escape recognition, and determining to refer to this ill-considered visit when I called the next day. I would not put it off till Monday, I was resolved.

I lingered on the bridge as I went home. Not a light was to be seen in the village, except one over Catherine Weir's shop. There were not many restless souls in my parish-not so many as there ought to be. Yet gladly would I see the troubled in peace-not a moment, though, before their troubles should have brought them where the weary and heavy-laden can alone find rest to their souls-finding the Father's peace in the Son-the Father himself reconciling them to Himself.

How still the night was! My soul hung, as it were, suspended in stillness; for the whole sphere of heaven seemed to be about me, the stars above shining as clear below in the mirror of the all but motionless water. It was a pure type of the "rest that remaineth"—rest, the one immovable centre wherein lie all the stores of might, whence issue all forces, all influences of making and moulding. "And, indeed," I said to myself, "after all the noise, uproar, and strife that there is on the earth, after all the tempests, earthquakes, and volcanic outbursts, there is yet more of peace than of tumult in the world. How many nights like this glide away in loveliness, when deep sleep hath fallen upon men, and they know neither how still their own repose, nor how beautiful the sleep of nature! Ah, what must the stillness of the kingdom be? When the heavenly day's work is done, with what a gentle wing will the night come down! But I bethink me, the rest there, as here, will be the presence of God; and if we have Him with us, the battle-field itself will be-if not quiet, yet as full of peace as this night of stars." So I spoke to myself, and went home.

I had little immediate comfort to give my young guest, but I had plenty of hope. I told him he must stay in the house to-morrow; for it would be better to have the reconciliation with his father over before he appeared in public. So the next day neither Weir was at church.

As soon as the afternoon service was over, I went once more to the Hall, and was shown into the drawing-room —a great faded room, in which the prevailing colour was a dingy gold, hence called the yellow drawing-room when the house had more than one. It looked down upon the lawn, which, although little expense was now laid out on any of the ornamental adjuncts of the Hall, was still kept very nice. There sat Mrs Oldcastle reading, with her face to the house. A little way farther on, Miss Oldcastle sat, with a book on her knee, but her gaze fixed on the wide-spread landscape before her, of which, however, she seemed to be as inobservant as of her book. I caught glimpses of Judy flitting hither and thither among the trees, never a moment in one place.

Fearful of having an interview with the old lady alone, which was not likely to lead to what I wanted, I stepped from a window which was open, out upon the terrace, and thence down the steps to the lawn below. The servant had just informed Mrs Oldcastle of my visit when I came near. She drew herself up in her chair, and evidently chose to regard my approach as an intrusion.

"I did not expect a visit from you to-day, Mr Walton, you will allow me to say."

"I am doing Sunday work," I answered. "Will you kindly tell me whether you were in London on Thursday last? But stay, allow me to ask Miss Oldcastle to join us."

Without waiting for answer, I went to Miss Oldcastle, and begged her to come and listen to something in which I wanted her help. She rose courteously though without cordiality, and accompanied me to her mother, who sat with perfect rigidity, watching us.

"Again let me ask," I said, "if you were in London on Thursday."

Though I addressed the old lady, the answer came from her daughter.

"Yes, we were."

"Were you in ——-& Co.'s, in ——-Street?"

But now before Miss Oldcastle could reply, her mother interposed.

"Are we charged with shoplifting, Mr Walton? Really, one is not accustomed to such cross-questioning—except from a lawyer."

"Have patience with me for a moment," I returned. "I am not going to be mysterious for more than two or three questions. Please tell me whether you were in that shop or not."

"I believe we were," said the mother.

"Yes, certainly," said the daughter.

"Did you buy anything?"

"No. We—" Miss Oldcastle began.

"Not a word more," I exclaimed eagerly. "Come with me at once."

"What DO you mean, Mr Walton?" said the mother, with a sort of cold indignation, while the daughter looked surprised, but said nothing.

"I beg your pardon for my impetuosity; but much is in your power at this moment. The son of one of my parishioners has come home in trouble. His father, Thomas Weir—"

"Ah!" said Mrs Oldcastle, in a tone considerably at strife with refinement. But I took no notice.

"His father will not believe his story. The lad thinks you were the ladies in serving whom he got into trouble. I am so confident he tells the truth, that I want Miss Oldcastle to be so kind as to accompany me to Weir's house—"

"Really, Mr Walton, I am astonished at your making such a request!" exclaimed Mrs Oldcastle, with suitable emphasis on every salient syllable, while her white face flushed with anger. "To ask Miss Oldcastle to accompany you to the dwelling of the ringleader of all the canaille of the neighbourhood!"

"It is for the sake of justice," I interposed.

"That is no concern of ours. Let them fight it out between them, I am sure any trouble that comes of it is no more than they all deserve. A low family-men and women of them."

"I assure you, I think very differently."

"I daresay you do."

"But neither your opinion nor mine has anything to do with the matter."

Here I turned to Miss Oldcastle and went on—

"It is a chance which seldom occurs in one's life, Miss Oldcastle—a chance of setting wrong right by a word; and as a minister of the gospel of truth and love, I beg you to assist me with your presence to that end."

I would have spoken more strongly, but I knew that her word given to me would be enough without her presence. At the same time, I felt not only that there would be a propriety in her taking a personal interest in the matter, but that it would do her good, and tend to create a favour towards each other in some of my flock between whom at present there seemed to be nothing in common.

But at my last words, Mrs Oldcastle rose to her feet no longer red-now whiter than her usual whiteness with passion.

"You dare to persist! You take advantage of your profession to persist in dragging my daughter into a vile dispute between mechanics of the lowest class-against the positive command of her only parent! Have you no respect for her position in society?—for her sex? MISTER WALTON, you act in a manner unworthy of your cloth."

I had stood looking in her eyes with as much self-possession as I could muster. And I believe I should have borne it all quietly, but for that last word.

If there is one epithet I hate more than another, it is that execrable word CLOTH-used for the office of a clergyman. I have no time to set forth its offence now. If my reader cannot feel it, I do not care to make him feel it. Only I am sorry to say it overcame my temper.

"Madam," I said, "I owe nothing to my tailor. But I owe God my whole being, and my neighbour all I can do for him. 'He that loveth not his brother is a murderer,' or murderess, as the case may be."

At that word MURDERESS, her face became livid, and she turned away without reply. By this time her daughter was half way to the house. She followed her. And here was I left to go home, with the full knowledge that, partly from trying to gain too much, and partly from losing my temper, I had at best but a mangled and unsatisfactory testimony to carry back to Thomas Weir. Of course I walked away-round the end of the house and down the avenue; and the farther I went the more mortified I grew. It was not merely the shame of losing my temper, though that was a shame-and with a woman too, merely because she used a common epithet! —but I saw that it must appear very strange to the carpenter that I was not able to give a more explicit account of some sort, what I had learned not being in the least decisive in the matter. It only amounted to this, that Mrs and Miss Oldcastle were in the shop on the very day on which Weir was dismissed. It proved that so much of what he had told me was correct-nothing more. And if I tried to better the matter by explaining how I had offended them, would it not deepen the very hatred I had hoped to overcome? In fact, I stood convicted before the tribunal of my own conscience of having lost all the certain good of my attempt, in part at least from the foolish desire to produce a conviction OF Weir rather than IN Weir, which should be triumphant after a melodramatic fashion, and-must I confess it? —should PUNISH him for not believing in his son when *I* did; forgetting in my miserable selfishness that not to believe in his son was an unspeakably worse punishment in itself than any conviction or consequent shame brought about by the most overwhelming of stage-effects. I assure my reader, I felt humiliated.

Now I think humiliation is a very different condition of mind from humility. Humiliation no man can desire: it is shame and torture. Humility is the true, right condition of humanity-peaceful, divine. And yet a man may gladly welcome humiliation when it comes, if he finds that with fierce shock and rude revulsion it has turned him right round, with his face away from pride, whither he was travelling, and towards humility, however far away upon the horizon's verge she may sit waiting for him. To me, however, there came a gentle and not therefore less effective dissolution of the bonds both of pride and humiliation; and before Weir and I met, I was nearly as anxious to heal his wounded spirit, as I was to work justice for his son.

I was walking slowly, with burning cheek and downcast eyes, the one of conflict, the other of shame and defeat, away from the great house, which seemed to be staring after me down the avenue with all its window-eyes, when suddenly my deliverance came. At a somewhat sharp turn, where the avenue changed into a winding road, Miss Oldcastle stood waiting for me, the glow of haste upon her cheek, and the firmness of resolution upon her lips. Once more I was startled by her sudden presence, but she did not smile.

"Mr Walton, what do you want me to do? I would not willing refuse, if it is, as you say, really my duty to go with you."

"I cannot be positive about that," I answered. "I think I put it too strongly. But it would be a considerable advantage, I think, if you WOULD go with me and let me ask you a few questions in the presence of Thomas Weir. It will have more effect if I am able to tell him that I have only learned as yet that you were in the shop on that day, and refer him to you for the rest."

"I will go."

"A thousand thanks. But how did you manage to —?"

Here I stopped, not knowing how to finish the question.

"You are surprised that I came, notwithstanding mamma's objection to my going?"

"I confess I am. I should not have been surprised at Judy's doing so, now."

She was silent for a moment.

"Do you think obedience to parents is to last for ever? The honour is, of course. But I am surely old enough to be right in following my conscience at least."

"You mistake me. That is not the difficulty at all. Of course you ought to do what is right against the highest authority on earth, which I take to be just the parental. What I am surprised at is your courage."

"Not because of its degree, only that it is mine!"

And she sighed. —She was quite right, and I did not know what to answer. But she resumed.

"I know I am cowardly. But if I cannot dare, I can bear. Is it not strange? —With my mother looking at me, I dare not say a word, dare hardly move against her will. And it is not always a good will. I cannot honour my mother as I would. But the moment her eyes are off me, I can do anything, knowing the consequences perfectly, and just as regardless of them; for, as I tell you, Mr Walton, I can endure; and you do not know what that might COME to mean with my mother. Once she kept me shut up in my room, and sent me only bread and water, for a whole week to the very hour. Not that I minded that much, but it will let you know a little of my position in my own home. That is why I walked away before her. I saw what was coming."

And Miss Oldcastle drew herself up with more expression of pride than I had yet seen in her, revealing to me that perhaps I had hitherto quite misunderstood the source of her apparent haughtiness. I could not reply for indignation. My silence must have been the cause of what she said next.

"Ah! you think I have no right to speak so about my own mother! Well! well! But indeed I would not have done so a month ago."

"If I am silent, Miss Oldcastle, it is that my sympathy is too strong for me. There are mothers and mothers. And for a mother not to be a mother is too dreadful."

She made no reply. I resumed.

"It will seem cruel, perhaps; —certainly in saying it, I lay myself open to the rejoinder that talk is SO easy; —still I shall feel more honest when I have said it: the only thing I feel should be altered in your conduct-forgive me-is that you should DARE your mother. Do not think, for it is an unfortunate phrase, that my meaning is a vulgar one. If it were, I should at least know better than to utter it to you. What I mean is, that you ought to be able to be and do the same before your mother's eyes, that you are and do when she is out of sight. I mean that you should look in your mother's eyes, and do what is RIGHT."

"I KNOW that-know it WELL." (She emphasized the words as I do.) "But you do not know what a spell she casts upon me; how impossible it is to do as you say."

"Difficult, I allow. Impossible, not. You will never be free till you do so."

"You are too hard upon me. Besides, though you will scarcely be able to believe it now, I DO honour her, and cannot help feeling that by doing as I do, I avoid irreverence, impertinence, rudeness-whichever is the right word for what I mean."

"I understand you perfectly. But the truth is more than propriety of behaviour, even to a parent; and indeed has in it a deeper reverence, or the germ of it at least, than any adherence to the mere code of respect. If you once did as I want you to do, you would find that in reality you both revered and loved your mother more than you do now."

"You may be right. But I am certain you speak without any real idea of the difficulty."

"That may be. And yet what I say remains just as true."

"How could I meet VIOLENCE, for instance?"

"Impossible!"

She returned no reply. We walked in silence for some minutes. At length she said,

"My mother's self-will amounts to madness, I do believe. I have yet to learn where she would stop of herself."

"All self-will is madness," I returned-stupidly enough For what is the use of making general remarks when you have a terrible concrete before you? "To want one's own way just and only because it is one's own way is the height of madness."

"Perhaps. But when madness has to be encountered as if it were sense, it makes it no easier to know that it is madness."

"Does your uncle give you no help?"

"He! Poor man! He is as frightened at her as I am. He dares not even go away. He did not know what he was coming to when he came to Oldcastle Hall. Dear uncle! I owe him a great deal. But for any help of that sort, he is of no more use than a child. I believe mamma looks upon him as half an idiot. He can do anything or everything but help one to live, to BE anything. Oh me! I AM so tired!"

And the PROUD lady, as I had thought her, perhaps not incorrectly, burst out crying.

What was I to do? I did not know in the least. What I said, I do not even now know. But by this time we were at the gate, and as soon as we had passed the guardian monstrosities, we found the open road an effectual antidote to tears. When we came within sight of the old house where Weir lived, Miss Oldcastle became again a little curious as to what I required of her.

"Trust me," I said. "There is nothing mysterious about it. Only I prefer the truth to come out fresh in the ears of the man most concerned."

"I do trust you," she answered. And we knocked at the house-door.

Thomas Weir himself opened the door, with a candle in his hand. He looked very much astonished to see his lady-visitor. He asked us, politely enough, to walk up-stairs, and ushered us into the large room I have already described. There sat the old man, as I had first seen him, by the side of the fire. He received us with more than politeness-with courtesy; and I could not help glancing at Miss Oldcastle to see what impression this family of "low, free-thinking republicans" made upon her. It was easy to discover that the impression was of favourable surprise. But I was as much surprised at her behaviour as she was at theirs. Not a haughty tone was to be heard in her voice; not a haughty movement to be seen in her form. She accepted the chair offered her, and sat down, perfectly at home, by the fireside, only that she turned towards me, waiting for what explanation I might think proper to give.

Before I had time to speak, however, old Mr Weir broke the silence.

"I've been telling Tom, sir, as I've told him many a time afore, as how he's a deal too hard with his children."

"Father!" interrupted Thomas, angrily.

"Have patience a bit, my boy," persisted the old man, turning again towards me. —"Now, sir, he won't even hear young Tom's side of the story; and I say that boy won't tell him no lie if he's the same boy he went away."

"I tell you, father," again began Thomas; but this time I interposed, to prevent useless talk beforehand.

"Thomas," I said, "listen to me. I have heard your son's side of the story. Because of something he said I went to Miss Oldcastle, and asked her whether she was in his late master's shop last Thursday. That is all I have asked her, and all she has told me is that she was. I know no more than you what she is going to reply to my questions now, but I have no doubt her answers will correspond to your son's story."

I then put my questions to Miss Oldcastle, whose answers amounted to this:—That they had wanted to buy a shawl; that they had seen none good enough; that they had left the shop without buying anything; and that they had been waited upon by a young man, who, while perfectly polite and attentive to their wants, did not seem to have the ways or manners of a London shop-lad.

I then told them the story as young Tom had related it to me, and asked if his sister was not in the house and might not go to fetch him. But she was with her sister Catherine.

"I think, Mr Walton, if you have done with me, I ought to go home now," said Miss Oldcastle.

"Certainly," I answered. "I will take you home at once. I am greatly obliged to you for coming."

"Indeed, sir," said the old man, rising with difficulty, "we're obliged both to you and the lady more than we can tell. To take such a deal of trouble for us! But you see, sir, you're one of them as thinks a man's got his duty to do one way or another, whether he be clergyman or carpenter. God bless you, Miss. You're of the right sort, which you'll excuse an old man, Miss, as'll never see ye again till ye've got the wings as ye ought to have."

Miss Oldcastle smiled very sweetly, and answered nothing, but shook hands with them both, and bade them good-night. Weir could not speak a word; he could hardly even lift his eyes. But a red spot glowed on each of his pale cheeks, making him look very like his daughter Catherine, and I could see Miss Oldcastle wince and grow red too with the gripe he gave her hand. But she smiled again none the less sweetly.

"I will see Miss Oldcastle home, and then go back to my house and bring the boy with me," I said, as we left.

It was some time before either of us spoke. The sun was setting, the sky the earth and the air lovely with rosy light, and the world full of that peculiar calm which belongs to the evening of the day of rest. Surely the world ought to wake better on the morrow.

"Not very dangerous people, those, Miss Oldcastle?" I said, at last.

"I thank you very much for taking me to see them," she returned, cordially.

"You won't believe all you may happen to hear against the working people now?"

"I never did."

"There are ill-conditioned, cross-grained, low-minded, selfish, unbelieving people amongst them. God knows it. But there are ladies and gentlemen amongst them too."

"That old man is a gentleman."

"He is. And the only way to teach them all to be such, is to be such to them. The man who does not show himself a gentleman to the working people-why should I call them the poor? some of them are better off than many of the rich, for they can pay their debts, and do it —"

I had forgot the beginning of my sentence.

"You were saying that the man who does not show himself a gentleman to the poor —"

"Is no gentleman at all-only a gentle without the man; and if you consult my namesake old Izaak, you will find what that is."

"I will look. I know your way now. You won't tell me anything I can find out for myself."

"Is it not the best way?"

"Yes. Because, for one thing, you find out so much more than you look for."

"Certainly that has been my own experience."

"Are you a descendant of Izaak Walton?"

"No. I believe there are none. But I hope I have so much of his spirit that I can do two things like him."

"Tell me."

"Live in the country, though I was not brought up in it; and know a good man when I see him."

"I am very glad you asked me to go to-night."

"If people only knew their own brothers and sisters, the kingdom of heaven would not be far off."

I do not think Miss Oldcastle quite liked this, for she was silent thereafter; though I allow that her silence was not conclusive. And we had now come close to the house.

"I wish I could help you," I said.

"In what?"

"To bear what I fear is waiting you."

"I told you I was equal to that. It is where we are unequal that we want help. You may have to give it me some day-who knows?"

I left her most unwillingly in the porch, just as Sarah (the white wolf) had her hand on the door, rejoicing in my heart, however, over her last words.

My reader will not be surprised, after all this, if, before I get very much further with my story, I have to confess that I loved Miss Oldcastle.

When young Tom and I entered the room, his grandfather rose and tottered to meet him. His father made one step towards him and then hesitated. Of all conditions of the human mind, that of being ashamed of himself must have been the strangest to Thomas Weir. The man had never in his life, I believe, done anything mean or dishonest, and therefore he had

had less frequent opportunities than most people of being ashamed of himself. Hence his fall had been from another pinnacle-that of pride. When a man thinks it such a fine thing to have done right, he might almost as well have done wrong, for it shows he considers right something EXTRA, not absolutely essential to human existence, not the life of a man. I call it Thomas Weir's fall; for surely to behave in an unfatherly manner to both daughter and son-the one sinful, and therefore needing the more tenderness-the other innocent, and therefore claiming justification-and to do so from pride, and hurt pride, was fall enough in one history, worse a great deal than many sins that go by harder names; for the world's judgment of wrong does not exactly correspond with the reality. And now if he was humbled in the one instance, there would be room to hope he might become humble in the other. But I had soon to see that, for a time, his pride, driven from its entrenchment against his son, only retreated, with all its forces, into the other against his daughter.

Before a moment had passed, justice overcame so far that he held out his hand and said: —

"Come, Tom, let by-gones be by-gones."

But I stepped between.

"Thomas Weir," I said, "I have too great a regard for you-and you know I dare not flatter you-to let you off this way, or rather leave you to think you have done your duty when you have not done the half of it. You have done your son a wrong, a great wrong. How can you claim to be a gentleman —I say nothing of being a Christian, for therein you make no claim-how, I say, can you claim to act like a gentleman, if, having done a man wrong-his being your own son has nothing to do with the matter one way or other, except that it ought to make you see your duty more easily-having done him wrong, why don't you beg his pardon, I say, like a man?"

He did not move a step. But young Tom stepped hurriedly forward, and catching his father's hand in both of his, cried out:

"My father shan't beg my pardon. I beg yours, father, for everything I ever did to displease you, but I WASN'T to blame in this. I wasn't, indeed."

"Tom, I beg your pardon," said the hard man, overcome at last. "And now, sir," he added, turning to me, "will you let by-gones be by-gones between my boy and me?"

There was just a touch of bitterness in his tone.

"With all my heart," I replied. "But I want just a word with you in the shop before I go."

"Certainly," he answered, stiffly; and I bade the old and the young man good night, and followed him down stairs.

"Thomas, my friend," I said, when we got into the shop, laying my hand on his shoulder, "will you after this say that God has dealt hardly with you? There's a son for any man God ever made to give thanks for on his knees! Thomas, you have a strong sense of fair play in your heart, and you GIVE fair play neither to your own son nor yet to God himself. You close your doors and brood over your own miseries, and the wrongs people have done you; whereas, if you would but open those doors, you might come out into the light of God's truth, and see that His heart is as clear as sunlight towards you. You won't believe this, and therefore naturally you can't quite believe that there is a God at all; for, indeed, a being that was not all light would be no God at all. If you would but let Him teach you, you would find your perplexities melt away like the snow in spring, till you could hardly believe you had ever felt them. No arguing will convince you of a God; but let Him once come in, and all argument will be tenfold useless to convince you that there is no God. Give God justice. Try Him as I have said. —Good night."

He did not return my farewell with a single word. But the grasp of his strong rough hand was more earnest and loving even than usual. I could not see his face, for it was almost dark; but, indeed, I felt that it was better I could not see it.

I went home as peaceful in my heart as the night whose curtains God had drawn about the earth that it might sleep till the morrow.

CHAPTER XIV
MY PUPIL.

Although I do happen to know how Miss Oldcastle fared that night after I left her, the painful record is not essential to my story. Besides, I have hitherto recorded only those things "quorum pars magna" —or minima, as the case may be —"fui." There is one exception, old Weir's story, for the introduction of which my reader cannot yet see the artistic reason. For whether a story be real in fact, or only real in meaning, there must always be an idea, or artistic model in the brain, after which it is fashioned: in the latter case one of invention, in the former case one of choice.

In the middle of the following week I was returning from a visit I had paid to Tomkins and his wife, when I met, in the only street of the village, my good and honoured friend Dr Duncan. Of course I saw him often-and I beg my reader to remember that this is no diary, but only a gathering together of some of the more remarkable facts of my history, admitting of being ideally grouped-but this time I recall distinctly because the interview bore upon many things.

"Well, Dr Duncan," I said, "busy as usual fighting the devil."

"Ah, my dear Mr Walton," returned the doctor-and a kind word from him went a long way into my heart —"I know what you mean. You fight the devil from the inside, and I fight him from the outside. My chance is a poor one."

"It would be, perhaps, if you were confined to outside remedies. But what an opportunity your profession gives you of attacking the enemy from the inside as well! And you have this advantage over us, that no man can say it belongs to your profession to say such things, and THEREFORE disregard them."

"Ah, Mr Walton, I have too great a respect for your profession to dare to interfere with it. The doctor in 'Macbeth,' you know, could

> 'not minister to a mind diseased,
> Pluck from the memory a rooted sorrow,
> Raze out the written troubles of the brain,
> And with some sweet oblivious antidote
> Cleanse the stuff'd bosom of that perilous stuff
> Which weighs upon the heart.'"

"What a memory you have! But you don't think I can do that any more than you?"

"You know the best medicine to give, anyhow. I wish I always did. But you see we have no theriaca now."

"Well, we have. For the Lord says, 'Come unto me, and I will give you rest.'"

"There! I told you! That will meet all diseases."

"Strangely now, there comes into my mind a line of Chaucer, with which I will make a small return for your quotation from Shakespeare; you have mentioned theriaca; and I, without thinking of this line, quoted our Lord's words. Chaucer brings the two together, for the word triacle is merely a corruption of theriaca, the unfailing cure for every thing.

> 'Crist, which that is to every harm triacle.'"

"That is delightful: I thank you. And that is in Chaucer?"

"Yes. In the Man-of-Law's Tale."

"Shall I tell you how I was able to quote so correctly from Shakespeare? I have just come from referring to the passage. And I mention that because I want to tell you what made me think of the passage. I had been to see poor Catherine Weir. I think she is not long for this world. She has a bad cough, and I fear her lungs are going."

"I am concerned to hear that. I considered her very delicate, and am not surprised. But I wish, I do wish, I had got a little hold of her before, that I might be of some use to her now. Is she in immediate danger, do you think?"

"No. I do not think so. But I have no expectation of her recovery. Very likely she will just live through the winter and die in the spring. Those patients so often go as the flowers come! All her coughing, poor woman, will not cleanse her stuffed bosom. The perilous stuff weighs on her heart, as Shakespeare says, as well as on her lungs."

"Ah, dear! What is it, doctor, that weighs upon her heart? Is it shame, or what is it? for she is so uncommunicative that I hardly know anything at all about her yet."

"I cannot tell. She has the faculty of silence."

"But do not think I complain that she has not made me her confessor. I only mean that if she would talk at all, one would have a chance of knowing something of the state of her mind, and so might give her some help."

"Perhaps she will break down all at once, and open her mind to you. I have not told her she is dying. I think a medical man ought at least to be quite sure before he dares to say such a thing. I have known a long life injured, to human view at least, by the medical verdict in youth of ever imminent death."

"Certainly one has no right to say what God is going to do with any one till he knows it beyond a doubt. Illness has its own peculiar mission, independent of any association with coming death, and may often work better when mingled with the hope of life. I mean we must take care of presumption when we measure God's plans by our theories. But could you not suggest something, Doctor Duncan, to guide me in trying to do my duty by her?"

"I cannot. You see you don't know what she is THINKING; and till you know that, I presume you will agree with me that all is an aim in the dark. How can I prescribe, without SOME diagnosis? It is just one of those few cases in which one would like to have the authority of the Catholic priests to urge confession with. I do not think anything will save her life, as we say, but you have taught some of us to think of the life that belongs to the spirit as THE life; and I do believe confession would do everything for that."

"Yes, if made to God. But I will grant that communication of one's sorrows or even sins to a wise brother of mankind may help to a deeper confession to the Father in heaven. But I have no wish for AUTHORITY in the matter. Let us see whether the Spirit of God working in her may not be quite as powerful for a final illumination of her being as the fiat confessio of a priest. I have no confidence in FORCING in the moral or spiritual garden. A hothouse development must necessarily be a sickly one, rendering the plant unfit for the normal life of the open air. Wait. We must not hurry things. She will perhaps come to me of herself before long. But I will call and inquire after her."

We parted; and I went at once to Catherine Weir's shop. She received me much as usual, which was hardly to be called receiving at all. Perhaps there was a doubtful shadow, not of more cordiality, but of less repulsion in it. Her eyes were full of a stony brilliance, and the flame of the fire that was consuming her glowed upon her cheeks more brightly, I thought, than ever; but that might be fancy, occasioned by what the doctor had said about her. Her hand trembled, but her demeanour was perfectly calm.

"I am sorry to hear you are complaining, Miss Weir," I said.

"I suppose Dr Duncan told you so, sir. But I am quite well. I did not send for him. He called of himself, and wanted to persuade me I was ill."

I understood that she felt injured by his interference.

"You should attend to his advice, though. He is a prudent man, and not in the least given to alarming people without cause."

She returned no answer. So I tried another subject.

"What a fine fellow your brother is!"

"Yes; he grows very much."

"Has your father found another place for him yet?"

"I don't know. My father never tells me about any of his doings."

"But don't you go and talk to him, sometimes?"

"No. He does not care to see me."

"I am going there now: will you come with me?"

"Thank you. I never go where I am not wanted."

"But it is not right that father and daughter should live as you do. Suppose he may not have been so kind to you as he ought, you should not cherish resentment against him for it. That only makes matters worse, you know."

"I never said to human being that he had been unkind to me."

"And yet you let every person in the village know it."

"How?"

Her eye had no longer the stony glitter. It flashed now.

"You are never seen together. You scarcely speak when you meet. Neither of you crosses the other's threshold."

"It is not my fault."

"It is not ALL your fault, I know. But do you think you can go to a heaven at last where you will be able to keep apart from each other, he in his house and you in your house, without any sign that it was through this father on earth that you were born into the world which the Father in heaven redeemed by the gift of His own Son?"

She was silent; and, after a pause, I went on.

"I believe, in my heart, that you love your father. I could not believe otherwise of you. And you will never be happy till you have made it up with him. Have you done him no wrong?"

At these words, her face turned white-with anger, I could see-all but those spots on her cheek-bones, which shone out in dreadful contrast to the deathly paleness of the rest of her face. Then the returning blood surged violently from her heart, and the red spots were lost in one crimson glow. She opened her lips to speak, but apparently changing her mind, turned and walked haughtily out of the shop and closed the door behind her.

I waited, hoping she would recover herself and return; but, after ten minutes had passed, I thought it better to go away.

As I had told her, I was going to her father's shop.

There I was received very differently. There was a certain softness in the manner of the carpenter which I had not observed before, with the same heartiness in the shake of his hand which had accompanied my last leave-taking. I had purposely allowed ten days to elapse before I called again, to give time for the unpleasant feelings associated with my interference to vanish. And now I had something in my mind about young Tom.

"Have you got anything for your boy yet, Thomas?"

"Not yet, sir. There's time enough. I don't want to part with him just yet. There he is, taking his turn at what's going. Tom!"

And from the farther end of the large shop, where I had not observed him, now approached young Tom, in a canvas jacket, looking quite like a workman.

"Well, Tom, I am glad to find you can turn your hand to anything."

"I must be a stupid, sir, if I couldn't handle my father's tools," returned the lad.

"I don't know that quite. I am not just prepared to admit it for my own sake. My father is a lawyer, and I never could read a chapter in one of his books-his tools, you know."

"Perhaps you never tried, sir."

"Indeed, I did; and no doubt I could have done it if I had made up my mind to it. But I never felt inclined to finish the page. And that reminds me why I called to-day. Thomas, I know that lad of yours is fond of reading. Can you spare him from his work for an hour or so before breakfast?"

"To-morrow, sir?"

"To-morrow, and to-morrow, and to-morrow," I answered; "and there's Shakespeare for you."

"Of course, sir, whatever you wish," said Thomas, with a perplexed look, in which pleasure seemed to long for confirmation, and to be, till that came, afraid to put its "native semblance on."

"I want to give him some direction in his reading. When a man is fond of any tools, and can use them, it is worth while showing him how to use them better."

"Oh, thank you, sir!" exclaimed Tom, his face beaming with delight.

"That IS kind of you, sir! Tom, you're a made man!" cried the father.

"So," I went on, "if you will let him come to me for an hour every morning, till he gets another place, say from eight to nine, I will see what I can do for him."

Tom's face was as red with delight as his sister's had been with anger. And I left the shop somewhat consoled for the pain I had given Catherine, which grieved me without making me sorry that I had occasioned it.

I had intended to try to do something from the father's side towards a reconciliation with his daughter. But no sooner had I made up my proposal for Tom than I saw I had blocked up my own way towards my more important end. For I could not bear to seem to offer to bribe him even to allow me to do him good. Nor would he see that it was for his good and his daughter's—not at first. The first impression would be that I had a PROFESSIONAL end to gain, that the reconciling of father and daughter was a sort of parish business of mine, and that I had smoothed the way to it by offering a gift-an intellectual one, true, but not, therefore, the less a gift in the eyes of Thomas, who had a great respect for books. This was just what would irritate such a man, and I resolved to say nothing about it, but bide my time.

When Tom came, I asked him if he had read any of Wordsworth. For I always give people what I like myself, because that must be wherein I can best help them. I was anxious, too, to find out what he was capable of. And for this, anything that has more than a surface meaning will do. I had no doubt about the lad's intellect, and now I wanted to see what there was deeper than the intellect in him.

He said he had not.

I therefore chose one of Wordsworth's sonnets, not one of his best by any means, but suitable for my purpose-the one entitled, "Composed during a Storm." This I gave him to read, telling him to let me know when he considered that he had mastered the meaning of it, and sat down to my own studies. I remember I was then reading the Anglo-Saxon Gospels. I think it was fully half-an-hour before Tom rose and gently approached my place. I had not been uneasy about the experiment after ten minutes had passed, and after that time was doubled, I felt certain of some measure of success. This may possibly puzzle my reader; but I will explain. It was clear that Tom did not understand the sonnet at first; and I was not in the least certain that he would come to understand it by any exertion of his intellect, without further experience. But what I was delighted to be made sure of was that Tom at least knew that he did not know. For that is the very next step to knowing. Indeed, it may be said to be a more valuable gift than the other, being of general application; for some quick people will understand many things very easily, but when they come to a thing that is beyond their present reach, will fancy they see a meaning in it, or invent one, or even-which is far worse-pronounce it nonsense; and, indeed, show themselves capable of any device for getting out of the difficulty, except seeing and confessing to themselves that they are not able to understand it. Possibly this sonnet might be beyond Tom now, but, at least, there was great hope that he saw, or believed, that there must be something beyond him in it. I only hoped that he would not fall upon some wrong interpretation, seeing he was brooding over it so long.

"Well, Tom," I said, "have you made it out?"

"I can't say I have, sir. I'm afraid I'm very stupid, for I've tried hard. I must just ask you to tell me what it means. But I must tell you one thing, sir: every time I read it over-twenty times, I daresay—I thought I was lying on my mother's grave, as I lay that terrible night; and then at the end there you were standing over me and saying, 'Can I do anything to help you?'"

I was struck with astonishment. For here, in a wonderful manner, I saw the imagination outrunning the intellect, and manifesting to the heart what the brain could not yet understand. It indicated undeveloped gifts of a far higher nature than those belonging to the mere power of understanding alone. For there was a hidden sympathy of the deepest kind between the life experience of the lad, and the embodiment of such life experience on the part of the poet. But he went on:

"I am sure, sir, I ought to have been at my prayers, then, but I wasn't; so I didn't deserve you to come. But don't you think God is sometimes better to us than we deserve?"

"He is just everything to us, Tom; and we don't and can't deserve anything. Now I will try to explain the sonnet to you."

I had always had an impulse to teach; not for the teaching's sake, for that, regarded as the attempt to fill skulls with knowledge, had always been to me a desolate dreariness; but the moment I saw a sign of hunger, an indication of readiness to receive, I was invariably seized with a kind of passion for giving. I now proceeded to explain the sonnet. Having done so, nearly as well as I could, Tom said:

"It is very strange, sir; but now that I have heard you say what the poem means, I feel as if I had known it all the time, though I could not say it."

Here at least was no common mind. The reader will not be surprised to hear that the hour before breakfast extended into two hours after breakfast as well. Nor did this take up too much of my time, for the lad was capable of doing a great deal for himself under the sense of help at hand. His father, so far from making any objection to the arrangement, was delighted with it. Nor do I believe that the lad did less work in the shop for it: I learned that he worked regularly till eight o'clock every night.

Now the good of the arrangement was this: I had the lad fresh in the morning, clear-headed, with no mists from the valley of labour to cloud the heights of understanding. From the exercise of the mind it was a pleasant and relieving change to turn to bodily exertion. I am certain that he both thought and worked better, because he both thought and worked. Every literary man ought to be MECHANICAL (to use a Shakespearean word) as well. But it would have been quite a different matter, if he had come to me after the labour of the day. He would not then have been able to think nearly so well. But LABOUR, SLEEP, THOUGHT, LABOUR AGAIN, seems to me to be the right order with those who, earning their bread by the sweat of the brow, would yet remember that man shall not live by bread alone. Were it possible that our mechanics could attend the institutions called by their name in the morning instead of the evening, perhaps we should not find them so ready to degenerate into places of mere amusement. I am not objecting to the amusement; only to cease to educate in order to amuse is to degenerate. Amusement is a good and sacred thing; but it is not on a par with education; and, indeed, if it does not in any way further the growth of the higher nature, it cannot be called good at all.

Having exercised him in the analysis of some of the best portions of our home literature, —I mean helped him to take them to pieces, that, putting them together again, he might see what kind of things they were-for who could understand a new machine, or find out what it was meant for, without either actually or in his mind taking it to pieces? (which pieces, however, let me remind my reader, are utterly useless, except in their relation to the whole) —I resolved to try something fresh with him.

At this point I had intended to give my readers a theory of mine about the teaching and learning of a language; and tell them how I had found the trial of it succeed in the case of Tom Weir. But I think this would be too much of a digression from the course of my narrative, and would, besides, be interesting to those only who had given a good deal of thought to subjects belonging to education. I will only say, therefore, that, by the end of three months, my pupil, without knowing any other Latin author, was able to read any part of the first book of the AEneid-to read it tolerably in measure, and to enjoy the poetry of it-and this not without a knowledge of the declensions and conjugations. As to the syntax, I made the sentences themselves teach him that. Now I know that, as an end, all this was of no great value; but as a beginning, it was invaluable, for it made and KEPT him hungry for more; whereas, in most modes of teaching, the beginnings are such that without the pressure of circumstances, no boy, especially after an interval of cessation, will return to them. Such is not Nature's mode, for the beginnings with her are as pleasant as the fruition, and that without being less thorough than they can be. The knowledge a child gains of the external world is the foundation upon which all his future philosophy is built. Every discovery he makes is fraught with pleasure-that is the secret of his progress, and the essence of my theory: that learning should, in each individual case, as in the first case, be DISCOVERY-bringing its own pleasure with it. Nor is this to be confounded with turning study into play. It is upon the moon itself that the infant speculates, after the moon itself-that he stretches out his eager hands-to find in after years that he still wants her, but that in science and poetry he has her a thousand-fold more than if she had been handed him down to suck.

So, after all, I have bored my reader with a shadow of my theory, instead of a description. After all, again, the description would have plagued him more, and that must be both his and my comfort.

So through the whole of that summer and the following winter, I went on teaching Tom Weir. He was a lad of uncommon ability, else he could not have effected what I say he had within his first three months of Latin, let my theory be not only perfect in itself, but true as well-true to human nature, I mean. And his father, though his own book-learning was but small, had enough of insight to perceive that his son was something out of the common, and that any possible advantage he might lose by remaining in Marshmallows was considerably more than counterbalanced by the instruction he got from the vicar. Hence, I believe, it was that not a word was said about another situation for Tom. And I was glad of it; for it seemed to me that the lad had abilities equal to any profession whatever.

CHAPTER XV
DR DUNCAN'S STORY.

On the next Sunday but one-which was surprising to me when I considered the manner of our last parting-Catherine Weir was in church, for the second time since I had come to the place. As it happened, only as Spenser says —

"It chanced-eternal God that chance did guide,"

—and why I say this, will appear afterwards —I had, in preaching upon, that is, in endeavouring to enforce the Lord's Prayer by making them think about the meaning of the words they were so familiar with, come to the petition, "Forgive us our debts, as we forgive our debtors;" with which I naturally connected the words of our Lord that follow: "For if ye forgive men their trespasses, your heavenly Father will also forgive you; but if ye forgive not men their trespasses, neither will your Father forgive your trespasses." I need not tell my reader more of what I said about this, than that I tried to show that even were it possible with God to forgive an unforgiving man, the man himself would not be able to believe for a moment that God did forgive him, and therefore could get no comfort or help or joy of any kind from the forgiveness; so essentially does hatred, or revenge, or contempt, or anything that separates us from man, separate us from God too. To the loving soul alone does the Father reveal Himself; for love alone can understand Him. It is the peace-makers who are His children.

This I said, thinking of no one more than another of my audience. But as I closed my sermon, I could not help fancying that Mrs Oldcastle looked at me with more than her usual fierceness. I forgot all about it, however, for I never seemed to myself to have any hold of, or relation to, that woman. I know I was wrong in being unable to feel my relation to her because I disliked her. But not till years after did I begin to understand how she felt, or recognize in myself a common humanity with her. A sin of my own made me understand her condition. I can hardly explain now; I will tell it when the time comes. When I called upon her next, after the interview last related, she behaved much as if she had forgotten all about it, which was not likely.

In the end of the week after the sermon to which I have alluded, I was passing the Hall-gate on my usual Saturday's walk, when Judy saw me from within, as she came out of the lodge. She was with me in a moment.

"Mr Walton," she said, "how could you preach at Grannie as you did last Sunday?"

"I did not preach at anybody, Judy."

"Oh, Mr Walton!"

"You know I didn't, Judy. You know that if I had, I would not say I had not."

"Yes, yes; I know that perfectly," she said, seriously. "But Grannie thinks you did."

"How do you know that?"

"By her face."

"That is all, is it?"

"You don't think Grannie would say so?"

"No. Nor yet that you could know by her face what she was thinking."

"Oh! can't I just? I can read her face-not so well as plain print; but, let me see, as well as what Uncle Stoddart calls black-letter, at least. I know she thought you were preaching at her; and her face said, 'I shan't forgive YOU, anyhow. I never forgive, and I won't for all your preaching.' That's what her face said."

"I am sure she would not say so, Judy," I said, really not knowing what to say.

"Oh, no; she would not say so. She would say, 'I always forgive, but I never forget.' That's a favourite saying of hers."

"But, Judy, don't you think it is rather hypocritical of you to say all this to me about your grandmother when she is so kind to you, and you seem such good friends with her?"

She looked up in my face with an expression of surprise.

"It is all TRUE, Mr Walton," she said.

"Perhaps. But you are saying it behind her back."

"I will go home and say it to her face directly."

She turned to go.

"No, no, Judy. I did not mean that," I said, taking her by the arm.

"I won't say you told me to do it. I thought there was no harm in telling you. Grannie is kind to me, and I am kind to her. But Grannie is afraid of my tongue, and I mean her to be afraid of it. It's the only way to keep her in order. Darling Aunt Winnie! it's all she's got to defend her. If you knew how she treats her sometimes, you would be cross with Grannie yourself, Mr Walton, for all your goodness and your white surplice."

And to my yet greater surprise, the wayward girl burst out crying, and, breaking away from me, ran through the gate, and out of sight amongst the trees, without once looking back.

I pursued my walk, my meditations somewhat discomposed by the recurring question:—Would she go home and tell her grandmother what she had said to me? And, if she did, would it not widen the breach upon the opposite side of which I seemed to see Ethelwyn stand, out of the reach of my help?

I walked quickly on to reach a stile by means of which I should soon leave the little world of Marshmallows quite behind me, and be alone with nature and my Greek Testament. Hearing the sound of horse-hoofs on the road from Addicehead, I glanced up from my pocket-book, in which I had been looking over the thoughts that had at various moments passed through my mind that week, in order to choose one (or more, if they would go together) to be brooded over to-day for my people's spiritual diet to-morrow—I say I glanced up from my pocket-book, and saw a young man, that is, if I could call myself young still, of distinguished appearance, approaching upon a good serviceable hack. He turned into my road and passed me. He was pale, with a dark moustache, and large dark eyes; sat his horse well and carelessly; had fine features of the type commonly considered Grecian, but thin, and expressive chiefly of conscious weariness. He wore a white hat with crape upon it, white gloves, and long, military-looking boots. All this I caught as he passed me; and I remember them, because, looking after him, I saw him stop at the lodge of the Hall, ring the bell, and then ride through the gate. I confess I did not quite like this; but I got over the feeling so far as to be able to turn to my Testament when I had reached and crossed the stile.

I came home another way, after one of the most delightful days I had ever spent. Having reached the river in the course of my wandering, I came down the side of it towards Old Rogers's cottage, loitering and looking, quiet in heart and soul and mind, because I had committed my cares to Him who careth for us. The earth was round me—I was rooted, as it were, in it, but the air of a higher life was about me. I was swayed to and fro by the motions of a spiritual power; feelings and desires and hopes passed through me, passed away, and returned; and still my head rose into the truth, and the will of God was the regnant sunlight upon it. I might change my place and condition; new feelings might come forth, and old feelings retire into the lonely corners of my being; but still my heart should be glad and strong in the one changeless thing, in the truth that maketh free; still my head should rise into the sunlight of God, and I should know that because He lived I should live also, and because He was true I should remain true also, nor should any change pass upon me that should make me mourn the decadence of humanity. And then I found that I was gazing over the stump of an old pollard, on which I was leaning, down on a great bed of white water-lilies, that lay in the broad slow river, here broader and slower than in most places. The slanting yellow sunlight shone through the water down to the very roots anchored in the soil, and the water swathed their stems with coolness and freshness, and a universal sense, I doubt not, of watery presence and nurture. And there on their lovely heads, as they lay on the pillow of the water, shone the life-giving light of the summer sun, filling all the spaces between their outspread petals of living silver with its sea of radiance, and making them gleam with the whiteness which was born of them and the sun. And then came a hand on my shoulder, and, turning, I saw the gray head and the white smock of my old friend Rogers, and I was glad that he loved me enough not to be afraid of the parson and the gentleman.

"I've found it, sir, I do think," he said, his brown furrowed old face shining with a yet lovelier light than that which shone from the blossoms of the water-lilies, though, after what I had been thinking about them, it was no wonder that they seemed both to mean the same thing, —both to shine in the light of His countenance.

"Found what, Old Rogers?" I returned, raising myself, and laying my hand in return on his shoulder.

"Why He was displeased with the disciples for not knowing —"

"What He meant about the leaven of the Pharisees," I interrupted. "Yes, yes, of course. Tell me then."

"I will try, sir. It was all dark to me for days. For it appeared to me very nat'ral that, seeing they had no bread in the locker, and hearing tell of leaven which they weren't to eat, they should think it had summat to do with their having none of any sort. But He didn't seem to think it was right of them to fall into the blunder. For why then? A man can't be always right. He may be like myself, a foremast-man with no schoolin' but what the winds and the waves puts into him, and I'm thinkin' those fishermen the Lord took to so much were something o' that sort. 'How could they help it?' I said to myself, sir. And from that I came to ask myself, 'Could they have helped it?' If they couldn't, He wouldn't have been vexed with them. Mayhap they ought to ha' been able to help it. And all at once, sir, this mornin', it came to me. I don't know how, but it was give to me, anyhow. And I flung down my rake, and I ran in to the old woman, but she wasn't in the way, and so I went back to my work again. But when I saw you, sir, a readin' upon the lilies o' the field, leastways, the lilies o' the water, I couldn't help runnin' out to tell you. Isn't it a satisfaction, sir, when yer dead reckonin' runs ye right in betwixt the cheeks of the harbour? I see it all now."

"Well, I want to know, old Rogers. I'm not so old as you, and so I MAY live longer; and every time I read that passage, I should like to be able to say to myself, 'Old Rogers gave me this.'"

"I only hope I'm right, sir. It was just this: their heads was full of their dinner because they didn't know where it was to come from. But they ought to ha' known where it always come from. If their hearts had been full of the dinner He gave the five thousand hungry men and women and children, they wouldn't have been uncomfortable about not having a loaf. And so they wouldn't have been set upon the wrong tack when He spoke about the leaven of the Pharisees and Sadducees; and they would have known in a moment what He meant. And if I hadn't been too much of the same sort, I wouldn't have started saying it was but reasonable to be in the doldrums because they were at sea with no biscuit in the locker."

"You're right; you must be right, old Rogers. It's as plain as possible," I cried, rejoiced at the old man's insight. "Thank you. I'll preach about it to-morrow. I thought I had got my sermon in Foxborough Wood, but I was mistaken: you had got it."

But I was mistaken again. I had not got my sermon yet.

I walked with him to his cottage and left him, after a greeting with the "old woman." Passing then through the village, and seeing by the light of her candle the form of Catherine Weir behind her counter, I went in. I thought old Rogers's tobacco must be nearly gone, and I might safely buy some more. Catherine's manner was much the same as usual. But as she was weighing my purchase, she broke out all at once:

"It's no use your preaching at me, Mr Walton. I cannot, I WILL not forgive. I will do anything BUT forgive. And it's no use."

"It is not I that say it, Catherine. It is the Lord himself."

I saw no great use in protesting my innocence, yet I thought it better to add —

"And I was not preaching AT you. I was preaching to you, as much as to any one there, and no more."

Of this she took no notice, and I resumed:

"Just think of what HE says; not what I say."

"I can't help it. If He won't forgive me, I must go without it. I can't forgive."

I saw that good and evil were fighting in her, and felt that no words of mine could be of further avail at the moment. The words of our Lord had laid hold of her; that was enough for this time. Nor dared I ask her any questions. I had the feeling that it would hurt, not help. All I could venture to say, was:

"I won't trouble you with talk, Catherine. Our Lord wants to talk to you. It is not for me to interfere. But please to remember, if ever you think I can serve you in any way, you have only to send for me."

She murmured a mechanical thanks, and handed me my parcel. I paid for it, bade her good night, and left the shop.

"O Lord," I said in my heart, as I walked away, "what a labour Thou hast with us all! Shall we ever, some day, be all, and quite, good like Thee? Help me. Fill me with Thy light, that my work may all go to bring about the gladness of Thy kingdom-the holy household of us brothers and sisters-all Thy children."

And now I found that I wanted very much to see my friend Dr Duncan. He received me with his stately cordiality, and a smile that went farther than all his words of greeting.

"Come now, Mr Walton, I am just going to sit down to my dinner, and you must join me. I think there will be enough for us both. There is, I believe, a chicken a-piece for us, and we can make up with cheese and a glass of-would you believe it?—my own father's port. He was fond of port-the old man-though I never saw him with one glass more aboard than the registered tonnage. He always sat light on the water. Ah, dear me! I'm old myself now."

"But what am I to do with Mrs Pearson?" I said. "There's some chef-d'oeuvre of hers waiting for me by this time. She always treats me particularly well on Saturdays and Sundays."

"Ah! then, you must not stop with me. You will fare better at home."

"But I should much prefer stopping with you. Couldn't you send a message for me?"

"To be sure. My boy will run with it at once."

Now, what is the use of writing all this? I do not know. Only that even a tete-a-tete dinner with an old friend, now that I am an old man myself, has such a pearly halo about it in the mists of the past, that every little circumstance connected with it becomes interesting, though it may be quite unworthy of record. So, kind reader, let it stand.

We sat down to our dinner, so simple and so well-cooked that it was just what I liked. I wanted very much to tell my friend what had occurred in Catherine's shop, but I would not begin till we were safe from interruption; and so we chatted away concerning many things, he telling me about his seafaring life, and I telling him some of the few remarkable things that had happened to me in the course of my life-voyage. There is no man but has met with some remarkable things that other people would like to know, and which would seem stranger to them than they did at the time to the person to whom they happened.

At length I brought our conversation round to my interview with Catherine Weir.

"Can you understand," I said, "a woman finding it so hard to forgive her own father?"

"Are you sure it is her father?" he returned.

"Surely she has not this feeling towards more than one. That she has it towards her father, I know."

"I don't know," he answered. "I have known resentment preponderate over every other feeling and passion-in the mind of a woman too. I once heard of a good woman who cherished this feeling against a good man because of some distrustful words he had once addressed to herself. She had lived to a great age, and was expressing to her clergyman her desire that God would take her away: she had been waiting a long time. The clergyman—a very shrewd as well as devout man, and not without a touch of humour, said: 'Perhaps God doesn't mean to let you die till you've forgiven Mr——.' She was as if struck with a flash of thought, sat silent during the rest of his visit, and when the clergyman called the next day, he found Mr —— and her talking together very quietly over a cup of tea. And she hadn't long to wait after that, I was told, but was gathered to her fathers-or went home to her children, whichever is the better phrase."

"I wish I had had your experience, Dr Duncan," I said.

"I have not had so much experience as a general practitioner, because I have been so long at sea. But I am satisfied that until a medical man knows a good deal more about his patient than most medical men give themselves the trouble to find out, his prescriptions will partake a good deal more than is necessary of haphazard. —As to this question of obstinate resentment, I know one case in which it is the ruling presence of a woman's life-the very light that is in her is resentment. I think her possessed myself."

"Tell me something about her."

"I will. But even to you I will mention no names. Not that I have her confidence in the least. But I think it is better not. I was called to attend a lady at a house where I had never yet been."

"Was it in —-?" I began, but checked myself. Dr Duncan smiled and went on without remark. I could see that he told his story with great care, lest, I thought, he should let anything slip that might give a clue to the place or people.

"I was led up into an old-fashioned, richly-furnished room. A great wood-fire burned on the hearth. The bed was surrounded with heavy dark curtains, in which the shadowy remains of bright colours were just visible. In the bed lay one of the loveliest young creatures I had ever seen. And, one on each side, stood two of the most dreadful-looking women I had ever beheld. Still as death, while I examined my patient, they stood, with moveless faces, one as white as the other. Only the eyes of both of them were alive. One was evidently mistress, and the other servant. The latter looked more self-contained than the former, but less determined and possibly more cruel. That both could be unkind at least, was plain enough. There was trouble and signs of inward conflict in the eyes of the mistress. The maid gave no sign of any inside to her at all, but stood watching her mistress. A child's toy was lying in a corner of the room."

I may here interrupt my friend's story to tell my reader that I may be mingling some of my own conclusions with what the good man told me of his. For he will see well enough already that I had in a moment attached his description to persons I knew, and, as it turned out, correctly, though I could not be certain about it till the story had advanced a little beyond this early stage of its progress.

"I found the lady very weak and very feverish —a quick feeble pulse, now bounding, and now intermitting-and a restlessness in her eye which I felt contained the secret of her disorder. She kept glancing, as if involuntarily, towards the door, which would not open for all her looking, and I heard her once murmur to herself-for I was still quick of hearing then —'He won't come!' Perhaps I only saw her lips move to those words —I cannot be sure, but I am certain she said them in her heart. I prescribed for her as far as I could venture, but begged a word with her mother. She went with me into an adjoining room.

"'The lady is longing for something,' I said, not wishing to be so definite as I could have been.

"The mother made no reply. I saw her lips shut yet closer than before.

"'She is your daughter, is she not?'

"'Yes,' —very decidedly.

"'Could you not find out what she wishes?'

"'Perhaps I could guess.'

"'I do not think I can do her any good till she has what she wants.'

"'Is that your mode of prescribing, doctor?' she said, tartly.

"'Yes, certainly,' I answered —'in the present case. Is she married?'

"'Yes.'

"'Has she any children?'

"'One daughter.'

"'Let her see her, then.'

"'She does not care to see her.'

"'Where is her husband?'

"'Excuse me, doctor; I did not send for you to ask questions, but to give advice.'

"'And I came to ask questions, in order that I might give advice. Do you think a human being is like a clock, that can be taken to pieces, cleaned, and put together again?'

"'My daughter's condition is not a fit subject for jesting.'

"'Certainly not. Send for her husband, or the undertaker, whichever you please,' I said, forgetting my manners and my temper together, for I was more irritable then than I am now, and there was something so repulsive about the woman, that I felt as if I was talking to an evil creature that for her own ends, though what I could not tell, was tormenting the dying lady.

"'I understood you were a GENTLEMAN-of experience and breeding.'

"'I am not in the question, madam. It is your daughter.'

"'She shall take your prescription.'

"'She must see her husband if it be possible.'

"'It is not possible.'

"'Why?'

"'I say it is not possible, and that is enough. Good morning.'

"I could say no more at that time. I called the next day. She was just the same, only that I knew she wanted to speak to me, and dared not, because of the presence of the two women. Her troubled eyes seemed searching mine for pity and help, and I could not tell what to do for her. There are, indeed, as some one says, strongholds of injustice and wrong into which no law can enter to help.

"One afternoon, about a week after my first visit, I was sitting by her bedside, wondering what could be done to get her out of the clutches of these tormentors, who were, evidently to me, consuming her in the slow fire of her own affections, when I heard a faint noise, a rapid foot in the house so quiet before; heard doors open and shut, then a dull sound of conflict of some sort. Presently a quick step came up the oak-stair. The face of my patient flushed, and her eyes gleamed as if her soul would come out of them. Weak as she was she sat up in bed, almost without an effort, and the two women darted from the room, one after the other.

"'My husband!' said the girl-for indeed she was little more in age, turning her face, almost distorted with eagerness, towards me.

"'Yes, my dear,' I said, 'I know. But you must be as still as you can, else you will be very ill. Do keep quiet.'

"'I will, I will,' she gasped, stuffing her pocket-handkerchief actually into her mouth to prevent herself from screaming, as if that was what would hurt her. 'But go to him. They will murder him.'

"That moment I heard a cry, and what sounded like an articulate imprecation, but both from a woman's voice; and the next, a young man-as fine a fellow as I ever saw-dressed like a game-keeper, but evidently a gentleman, walked into the room with a quietness that strangely contrasted with the dreadful paleness of his face and with his disordered hair; while the two women followed, as red as he was white, and evidently in fierce wrath from a fruitless struggle with the powerful youth. He walked gently up to his wife, whose outstretched arms and face followed his face as he came round the bed to where she was at the other side, till arms, and face, and head, fell into his embrace.

"I had gone to the mother.

"'Let us have no scene now,' I said, 'or her blood will be on your head.'

"She took no notice of what I said, but stood silently glaring, not gazing, at the pair. I feared an outburst, and had resolved, if it came, to carry her at once from the room, which I was quite able to do then, Mr Walton, though I don't look like it now. But in a moment more the young man, becoming uneasy at the motionlessness of his wife, lifted up her head, and glanced in her face. Seeing the look of terror in his, I hastened to him, and lifting her from him, laid her down-dead. Disease of the heart, I believe. The mother burst into a shriek-not of horror, or grief, or remorse, but of deadly hatred.

"'Look at your work!' she cried to him, as he stood gazing in stupor on the face of the girl. 'You said she was yours, not mine; take her. You may have her now you have killed her.'

"'He may have killed her; but you have MURDERED her, madam,' I said, as I took the man by the arm, and led him away, yielding like a child. But the moment I got him out of the house, he gave a groan, and, breaking away from me, rushed down a road leading from the back of the house towards the home-farm. I followed, but he had disappeared. I went on; but before I could reach the farm, I heard the gallop of a horse, and saw him tearing away at full speed along the London road. I never heard more of him, or of the story. Some women can be secret enough, I assure you."

I need not follow the rest of our conversation. I could hardly doubt whose was the story I had heard. It threw a light upon several things about which I had been perplexed. What a horror of darkness seemed to hang over that family! What deeds of wickedness! But the reason was clear: the horror came from within; selfishness, and fierceness of temper were its source-no unhappy DOOM. The worship of one's own will fumes out around the being an atmosphere of evil, an altogether abnormal condition of the moral firmament, out of which will break the very flames of hell. The consciousness of birth and of breeding, instead of stirring up to deeds of gentleness and "high emprise," becomes then but an incentive to violence and cruelty; and things which seem as if they could not happen in a civilized country and a polished age, are proved as possible as ever where the heart is unloving, the feelings unrefined, self the centre, and God nowhere in the man or woman's vision. The terrible things that one reads in old histories, or in modern newspapers, were done by human beings, not by demons.

I did not let my friend know that I knew all that he concealed; but I may as well tell my reader now, what I could not have told him then. I know all the story now, and, as no better place will come, as far as I can see, I will tell it at once, and briefly.

Dorothy—a wonderful name, THE GIFT OF GOD, to be so treated, faring in this, however, like many other of God's gifts-Dorothy Oldcastle was the eldest daughter of Jeremy and Sibyl Oldcastle, and the sister therefore of Ethelwyn. Her father, who was an easy-going man, entirely under the dominion of his wife, died when she was about fifteen, and her mother sent her to school, with especial recommendation to the care of a clergyman in the neighbourhood, whom Mrs Oldcastle knew; for, somehow-and the fact is not so unusual as to justify especial inquiry here-though she paid no attention to what our Lord or His apostles said, nor indeed seemed to care to ask herself if what she did was right, or what she accepted (I cannot say BELIEVED) was true, she had yet a certain (to me all but incomprehensible) leaning to the clergy. I think it belongs to the same kind of superstition which many of our own day are turning to. Offered the Spirit of God for the asking, offered it by the Lord himself, in the misery of their unbelief they betake themselves to necromancy instead, and raise the dead to ask their advice, AND FOLLOW IT, and will find some day that Satan had not forgotten how to dress like an angel of light. Nay, he can be more cunning with the demands of the time. We are clever: he will be cleverer. Why should he dress and not speak like an angel of light? Why should he not give good advice if that will help to withdraw people by degrees from regarding the source of all good? He knows well enough that good advice goes for little, but that what fills the heart and mind goes for much. What religion is there in being convinced of a future state? Is that to worship God? It is no more religion than the belief that the sun will rise to-morrow is religion. It may be a source of happiness to those who could not believe it before, but it is not religion. Where religion comes that will certainly be likewise, but the one is not the other. The devil can afford a kind of conviction of that. It costs him little. But to believe that the spirits of the departed are the mediators between God and us is essential paganism-to call it nothing worse; and a bad enough name too since Christ has come and we have heard and seen the only-begotten of the Father. Thus the instinctive desire for the wonderful, the need we have of a revelation from above us, denied its proper food and nourishment, turns in its hunger to feed upon garbage. As a devout German says—I do not quote him quite correctly—"Where God rules not, demons will." Let us once see with our spiritual eyes the Wonderful, the Counsellor, and surely we shall not turn from Him to seek elsewhere the treasures of wisdom and knowledge.

Those who sympathize with my feeling in regard to this form of the materialism of our day, will forgive this divergence. I submit to the artistic blame of such as do not, and return to my story.

Dorothy was there three or four years. I said I would be brief. She and the clergyman's son fell in love with each other. The mother heard of it, and sent for her home. She had other views for her. Of course, in such eyes, a daughter's FANCY was, irrespective of its object altogether, a thing to be sneered at. But she found, to her fierce disdain, that she had not been able to keep all her beloved obstinacy to herself: she had transmitted a portion of it to her daughter. But in her it was combined with noble qualities, and, ceasing to be the evil thing it was in her mother, became an honourable firmness, rendering her able to withstand her mother's stormy importunities. Thus Nature had begun to right herself–the right in the daughter turning to meet and defy the wrong in the mother, and that in the same strength of character which the mother had misused for evil and selfish ends. And thus the bad breed was broken. She was and would be true to her lover. The consequent SCENES were dreadful. The spirit but not the will of the girl was all but broken. She felt that she could not sustain the strife long. By some means, unknown to my informant, her lover contrived to communicate with her. He had, through means of relations who had great influence with Government, procured a good appointment in India, whither he must sail within a month. The end was that she left her mother's house. Mr Gladwyn was waiting for her near, and conducted her to his father's, who had constantly refused to aid Mrs Oldcastle by interfering in the matter. They were married next day by the clergyman of a neighbouring parish. But almost immediately she was taken so ill, that it was impossible for her to accompany her husband, and she was compelled to remain behind at the rectory, hoping to join him the following year.

Before the time arrived, she gave birth to my little friend Judy; and her departure was again delayed by a return of her old complaint, probably the early stages of the disease of which she died. Then, just as she was about to set sail for India, news arrived that Mr Gladwyn had had a sunstroke, and would have leave of absence and come home as soon as he was able to be moved; so that instead of going out to join him, she must wait for him where she was. His mother had been dead for some time. His father, an elderly man of indolent habits, was found dead in his chair one Sunday morning soon after the news had arrived of the illness of his son, to whom he was deeply attached. And so the poor young creature was left alone with her child, without money, and in weak health. The old man left nothing behind him but his furniture and books. And nothing could be done in arranging his affairs till the arrival of his son, of whom the last accounts had been that he was slowly recovering. In the meantime his wife was in want of money, without a friend to whom she could apply. I presume that one of the few parishioners who visited at the rectory had written to acquaint Mrs Oldcastle with the condition in which her daughter was left, for, influenced by motives of which I dare not take upon me to conjecture an analysis, she wrote, offering her daughter all that she required in her old home. Whether she fore-intended her following conduct, or old habit returned with the return of her daughter, I cannot tell; but she had not been more than a few days in the house before she began to tyrannise over her, as in old times, and although Mrs Gladwyn's health, now always weak, was evidently failing in consequence, she either did not see the cause, or could not restrain her evil impulses. At length the news arrived of Mr Gladwyn's departure for home. Perhaps then for the first time the temptation entered her mind to take her revenge upon him, by making her daughter's illness a pretext for refusing him admission to her presence. She told her she should not see him till she was better, for that it would make her worse; persisted in her resolution after his arrival; and effected, by the help of Sarah, that he should not gain admittance to the house, keeping all the doors locked except one. It was only by the connivance of Ethelwyn, then a girl about fifteen, that he was admitted by the underground way, of which she unlocked the upper door for his entrance. She had then guided him as far as she dared, and directed him the rest of the way to his wife's room.

My reader will now understand how it came about in the process of writing these my recollections, that I have given such a long chapter chiefly to that one evening spent with my good friend, Dr Duncan; for he will see, as I have said, that what he told me opened up a good deal to me.

I had very little time for the privacy of the church that night. Dark as it was, however, I went in before I went home: I had the key of the vestry-door always in my pocket. I groped my way into the pulpit, and sat down in the darkness, and thought. Nor did my personal interest in Dr Duncan's story make me forget poor Catherine Weir and the terrible sore in her heart, the sore of unforgivingness. And I saw that of herself she would not, could not, forgive to all eternity; that all the pains of hell could not make her forgive, for that it was a divine glory to forgive, and must come from God. And thinking of Mrs Oldcastle, I saw that in ourselves we could be sure of no safety, not from the worst and vilest sins; for who could tell how he might not stupify himself by degrees, and by one action after another, each a little worse than the former, till the very fires of Sinai would not flash into eyes blinded with the incense arising to the golden calf of his worship? A man may come to worship a devil without knowing it. Only by being filled with a higher spirit than our own, which, having caused our spirits, is one with our spirits, and is in them the present life principle, are we or can we be safe from this eternal death of our being. This spirit was fighting the evil spirit in Catherine Weir: how was I to urge her to give ear to the good? If will would but side with God, the forces of self, deserted by their leader, must soon quit the field; and the woman-the kingdom within her no longer torn by conflicting forces-would sit quiet at the feet of the Master, reposing in that rest which He offered to those who could come to Him. Might she not be roused to utter one feeble cry to God for help? That would be one step towards the forgiveness of others. To ask something for herself would be a great advance in such a proud nature as hers. And to ask good heartily is the very next step to giving good heartily.

Many thoughts such as these passed through my mind, chiefly associated with her. For I could not think how to think about Mrs Oldcastle yet. And the old church gloomed about me all the time. And I kept lifting up my heart to the God who had cared to make me, and then drew me to be a preacher to my fellows, and had surely something to give me to say to them; for did He not choose so to work by the foolishness of preaching? —Might not my humble ignorance work His will, though my wrath could not work His righteousness? And I descended from the pulpit thinking with myself, "Let Him do as He will. Here I am. I will say what I see: let Him make it good."

And the next morning, I spoke about the words of our Lord:

"If ye then, being evil, know how to give good gifts to your children, how much more shall your heavenly Father give the Holy Spirit to them that ask Him!"

And I looked to see. And there Catherine Weir sat, looking me in the face.

There likewise sat Mrs Oldcastle, looking me in the face too.

And Judy sat there, also looking me in the face, as serious as man could wish grown woman to look.

CHAPTER XVI
THE ORGAN.

One little matter I forgot to mention as having been talked about between Dr Duncan and myself that same evening. I happened to refer to Old Rogers.

"What a fine old fellow that is!" said Dr Duncan.

"Indeed he is," I answered. "He is a great comfort and help to me. I don't think anybody but myself has an idea what there is in that old man."

"The people in the village don't quite like him, though, I find. He is too ready to be down upon them when he sees things going amiss. The fact is, they are afraid of him."

"Something as the Jews were afraid of John the Baptist, because he was an honest man, and spoke not merely his own mind, but the mind of God in it."

"Just so. I believe you're quite right. Do you know, the other day, happening to go into Weir's shop to get him to do a job for me, I found him and Old Rogers at close quarters in an argument? I could not well understand the drift of it, not having been present at the beginning, but I soon saw that, keen as Weir was, and far surpassing Rogers in correctness of speech, and precision as well, the old sailor carried too heavy metal for the carpenter. It evidently annoyed Weir; but such was the good humour of Rogers, that he could not, for very shame, lose his temper, the old man's smile again and again compelling a response on the thin cheeks of ihe other."

"I know how he would talk exactly," I returned. "He has a kind of loving banter with him, if you will allow me the expression, that is irresistible to any man with a heart in his bosom. I am very glad to hear there is anything like communion begun between them. Weir will get good from him."

"My man-of-all-work is going to leave me. I wonder if the old man would take his place?"

"I do not know whether he is fit for it. But of one thing you may be sure-if Old Rogers does not honestly believe he is fit for it, he will not take it. And he will tell you why, too."

"Of that, however, I think I may be a better judge than he. There is nothing to which a good sailor cannot turn his hand, whatever he may think himself. You see, Mr Walton, it is not like a routine trade. Things are never twice the same at sea. The sailor has a thousand chances of using his judgment, if he has any to use; and that Old Rogers has in no common degree. So I should have no fear of him. If he won't let me steer him, you must put your hand to the tiller for me."

"I will do what I can," I answered; "for nothing would please me more than to see him in your service. It would be much better for him, and his wife too, than living by uncertain jobs as he does now."

The result of it all was, that Old Rogers consented to try for a month; but when the end of the month came, nothing was said on either side, and the old man remained. And I could see several little new comforts about the cottage, in consequence of the regularity of his wages.

Now I must report another occurrence in regular sequence.

To my surprise, and, I must confess, not a little to my discomposure, when I rose in the reading-desk on the day after this dinner with Dr Duncan, I saw that the Hall-pew was full. Miss Oldcastle was there for the first time, and, by her side, the gentleman whom the day before I had encountered on horseback. He sat carelessly, easily, contentedly-indifferently; for, although I never that morning looked up from my Prayer-book, except involuntarily in the changes of posture, I could not help seeing that he was always behind the rest of the congregation, as if he had no idea of what was coming next, or did not care to conform. Gladly would I, that day, have shunned the necessity of preaching that was laid upon me. "But," I said to myself, "shall the work given me to do fare ill because of the perturbation of my spirit? No harm is done, though I suffer; but much harm if one tone fails of its force because I suffer." I therefore prayed God to help me; and feeling the right, because I felt the need, of looking to Him for aid, I cast my care upon Him, kept my thoughts strenuously away from that which discomposed me, and never turned my eyes towards the Hall-pew from the moment I entered the pulpit.

And partly, I presume, from the freedom given by the sense of irresponsibility for the result, I being weak and God strong, I preached, I think, a better sermon than I had ever preached before. But when I got into the vestry I found that I could scarcely stand for trembling; and I must have looked ill, for when my attendant came in he got me a glass of wine without even asking me if I would have it, although it was not my custom to take any there. But there was one of my congregation that morning who suffered more than I did from the presence of one of those who filled the Hall-pew.

I recovered in a few moments from my weakness, but, altogether disinclined to face any of my congregation, went out at my vestry-door, and home through the shrubbery —a path I seldom used, because it had a separatist look about it. When I got to my study, I threw myself on a couch, and fell fast asleep. How often in trouble have I had to thank God for sleep as for one of His best gifts! And how often when I have awaked refreshed and calm, have I thought of poor Sir Philip Sidney, who, dying slowly and patiently in the prime of life and health, was sorely troubled in his mind to know how he had offended God, because, having prayed earnestly for sleep, no sleep came in answer to his cry!

I woke just in time for my afternoon service; and the inward peace in which I found my heart was to myself a marvel and a delight. I felt almost as if I was walking in a blessed dream come from a world of serener air than this of ours. I found, after I was already in the reading-desk, that I was a few minutes early; and while, with bowed head, I was simply living in the consciousness of the presence of a supreme quiet, the first low notes of the organ broke upon my stillness with the sense of a deeper delight. Never before had I felt, as I felt that afternoon, the triumph of contemplation in Handel's rendering of "I know that my Redeemer liveth." And I felt how through it all ran a cold silvery quiver of sadness, like the light in the east after the sun is gone down, which would have been pain, but for the golden glow of the west, which looks after the light of the world with a patient waiting. —Before the music ceased, it had crossed my mind that I had never before heard that organ utter itself in the language of Handel. But I had no time to think more about it just then, for I rose to read the words of our Lord, "I will arise and go to my Father."

There was no one in the Hall-pew; indeed it was a rare occurrence if any one was there in the afternoon.

But for all the quietness of my mind during that evening service, I felt ill before I went to bed, and awoke in the morning with a headache, which increased along with other signs of perturbation of the system, until I thought it better to send for Dr Duncan. I have not yet got so imbecile as to suppose that a history of the following six weeks would be interesting to my readers-for during so long did I suffer from low fever; and more weeks passed during which I was unable to meet my flock. Thanks to the care of Mr Brownrigg, a clever young man in priest's orders, who was living at Addicehead while waiting for a curacy, kindly undertook my duty for me, and thus relieved me from all anxiety about supplying my place.

CHAPTER XVII
THE CHURCH-RATE.

But I cannot express equal satisfaction in regard to everything that Mr Brownrigg took upon his own responsibility, as my reader will see. He, and another farmer, his neighbour, had been so often re-elected churchwardens, that at last they seemed to have gained a prescriptive right to the office, and the form of election fell into disuse; so much so, that after Mr Summer's death, which took place some year and a half before I became Vicar of Marshmallows, Mr Brownrigg continued to exercise the duty in his own single person, and nothing had as yet been said about the election of a colleague. So little seemed to fall to the duty of the churchwarden that I regarded the neglect as a trifle, and was remiss in setting it right. I had, therefore, to suffer, as was just. Indeed, Mr Brownrigg was not the man to have power in his hands unchecked.

I had so far recovered that I was able to rise about noon and go into my study, though I was very weak, and had not yet been out, when one morning Mrs Pearson came into the room and said, —

"Please, sir, here's young Thomas Weir in a great way about something, and insisting upon seeing you, if you possibly can."

I had as yet seen very few of my friends, except the Doctor, and those only for two or three minutes; but although I did not feel very fit for seeing anybody just then, I could not but yield to his desire, confident there must be a good reason for it, and so told Mrs Pearson to show him in.

"Oh, sir, I know you would be vexed if you hadn't been told," he exclaimed, "and I am sure you will not be angry with me for troubling you."

"What is the matter, Tom?" I said. "I assure you I shall not be angry with you."

"There's Farmer Brownrigg, at this very moment, taking away Mr Templeton's table because he won't pay the church-rate."

"What church-rate?" I cried, starting up from the sofa. "I never heard of a church-rate."

Now, before I go farther, it is necessary to explain some things. One day before I was taken ill, I had had a little talk with Mr Brownrigg about some repairs of the church which were necessary, and must be done before another winter. I confess I was rather pleased; for I wanted my people to feel that the church was their property, and that it was their privilege, if they could regard it as a blessing to have the church, to keep it in decent order and repair. So I said, in a by-the-by way, to my churchwarden, "We must call a vestry before long, and have this looked to." Now my predecessor had left everything of the kind to his churchwardens; and the inhabitants from their side had likewise left the whole affair to the churchwardens. But Mr Brownrigg, who, I must say, had taken more pains than might have been expected of him to make himself acquainted with the legalities of his office, did not fail to call a vestry, to which, as usual, no one had responded; whereupon he imposed a rate according to his own unaided judgment. This, I believe, he did during my illness, with the notion of pleasing me by the discovery that the repairs had been already effected according to my mind. Nor did any one of my congregation throw the least difficulty in the churchwarden's way. —And now I must refer to another circumstance in the history of my parish.

I think I have already alluded to the fact that there were Dissenters in Marshmallows. There was a little chapel down a lane leading from the main street of the village, in which there was service three times every Sunday. People came to it from many parts of the parish, amongst whom were the families of two or three farmers of substance, while the village and its neighbourhood contributed a portion of the poorest of the inhabitants. A year or two before I came, their minister died, and they had chosen another, a very worthy man, of considerable erudition, but of extreme views, as I heard, upon insignificant points, and moved by a great dislike to national churches and episcopacy. This, I say, is what I had made out about him from what I had heard; and my reader will very probably be inclined to ask, "But why, with principles such as yours, should you have only hearsay to go upon? Why did you not make the honest man's acquaintance? In such a small place, men should not keep each other at arm's length." And any reader who says so, will say right. All I have to suggest for myself is simply a certain shyness, for which I cannot entirely account, but which was partly made up of fear to intrude, or of being supposed to arrogate to myself the right of making advances, partly of a dread lest we should not be able to get on together, and so the attempt should result in something unpleasantly awkward. I daresay, likewise, that the natural SHELLINESS of the English had something to do with it. At all events, I had not made his acquaintance.

Mr Templeton, then, had refused, as a point of conscience, to pay the church-rate when the collector went round to demand it; had been summoned before a magistrate in consequence; had suffered a default; and, proceedings being pushed from the first in all the pride of Mr Brownrigg's legality, had on this very day been visited by the churchwarden, accompanied by a broker from the neighbouring town of Addicehead, and at the very time when I was hearing of the fact was suffering distraint of his goods. The porcine head of the churchwarden was not on his shoulders by accident, nor without significance.

But I did not wait to understand all this now. It was enough for me that Tom bore witness to the fact that at that moment proceedings were thus driven to extremity. I rang the bell for my boots, and, to the open-mouthed dismay of Mrs Pearson, left the vicarage leaning on Tom's arm. But such was the commotion in my mind, that I had become quite unconscious of illness or even feebleness. Hurrying on in more terror than I can well express lest I should be too late, I reached Mr Templeton's house just as a small mahogany table was being hoisted into a spring-cart which stood at the door. Breathless with haste, I was yet able to call out,—

"Put that table down directly."

At the same moment Mr Brownrigg appeared from within the door. He approached with the self-satisfied look of a man who has done his duty, and is proud of it. I think he had not heard me.

"You see I'm prompt, Mr Walton," he said. "But, bless my soul, how ill you look!"

Without answering him-for I was more angry with him than I ought to have been—I repeated—

"Put that table down, I tell you."

They did so.

"Now," I said, "carry it back into the house."

"Why, sir," interposed Mr Brownrigg, "it's all right."

"Yes," I said, "as right as the devil would have it."

"I assure you, sir, I have done everything according to law."

"I'm not so sure of that. I believe I had the right to be chairman at the vestry-meeting; but, instead of even letting me know, you took advantage of my illness to hurry on matters to this shameful and wicked excess."

I did the poor man wrong in this, for I believe he had hurried things really to please me. His face had lengthened considerably by this time, and its rubicund hue declined.

"I did not think you would stand upon ceremony about it, sir. You never seemed to care for business."

"If you talk about legality, so will I. Certainly YOU don't stand upon ceremony."

"I didn't expect you would turn against your own churchwarden in the execution of his duty, sir," he said in an offended tone. "It's bad enough to have a meetin'-house in the place, without one's own parson siding with t'other parson as won't pay a lawful church-rate."

"I would have paid the church-rate for the whole parish ten times over before such a thing should have happened. I feel so disgraced, I am ashamed to look Mr Templeton in the face. Carry that table into the house again, directly."

"It's my property, now," interposed the broker. "I've bought it of the churchwarden, and paid for it."

I turned to Mr Brownrigg.

"How much did he give you for it?" I asked.

"Twenty shillings," returned he, sulkily, "and it won't pay expenses."

139

"Twenty shillings!" I exclaimed; "for a table that cost three times as much at least! —What do you expect to sell it for?"

"That's my business," answered the broker.

I pulled out my purse, and threw a sovereign and a half on the table, saying —

"FIFTY PER CENT. will be, I think, profit enough even on such a transaction."

"I did not offer you the table," returned the broker. "I am not bound to sell except I please, and at my own price."

"Possibly. But I tell you the whole affair is illegal. And if you carry away that table, I shall see what the law will do for me. I assure you I will prosecute you myself. You take up that money, or I will. It will go to pay counsel, I give you my word, if you do not take it to quench strife."

I stretched out my hand. But the broker was before me. Without another word, he pocketed the money, jumped into his cart with his man, and drove off, leaving the churchwarden and the parson standing at the door of the dissenting minister with his mahogany table on the path between them.

"Now, Mr Brownrigg," I said, "lend me a hand to carry this table in again."

He yielded, not graciously, —that could not be expected, —but in silence.

"Oh! sir," interposed young Tom, who had stood by during the dispute, "let me take it. You're not able to lift it."

"Nonsense! Tom. Keep away," I said. "It is all the reparation I can make."

And so Mr Brownrigg and I blundered into the little parlour with our burden-not a great one, but I began to find myself failing.

Mr Templeton sat in a Windsor chair in the middle of the room. Evidently the table had been carried away from before him, leaving his position uncovered. The floor was strewed with the books which had lain upon it. He sat reading an old folio, as if nothing had happened. But when we entered he rose.

He was a man of middle size, about forty, with short black hair and overhanging bushy eyebrows. His mouth indicated great firmness, not unmingled with sweetness, and even with humour. He smiled as he rose, but looked embarrassed, glancing first at the table, then at me, and then at Mr Brownrigg, as if begging somebody to tell him what to say. But I did not leave him a moment in this perplexity.

"Mr Templeton," I said, quitting the table, and holding out my hand, "I beg your pardon for myself and my friend here, my churchwarden"—Mr Brownrigg gave a grunt —"that you should have been annoyed like this. I have —"

Mr Templeton interrupted me.

"I assure you it was a matter of conscience with me," he said. "On no other ground —"

"I know it, I know it," I said, interrupting him in my turn. "I beg your pardon; and I have done my best to make amends for it. Offences must come, you know, Mr Templeton; but I trust I have not incurred the woe that follows upon them by means of whom they come, for I knew nothing of it, and indeed was too ill —"

Here my strength left me altogether, and I sat down. The room began to whirl round me, and I remember nothing more till I knew that I was lying on a couch, with Mrs Templeton bathing my forehead, and Mr Templeton trying to get something into my mouth with a spoon.

Ashamed to find myself in such circumstances, I tried to rise; but Mr Templeton, laying his hand on mine, said —

"My dear sir, add to your kindness this day, by letting my wife and me minister to you."

Now, was not that a courteous speech? He went on —

"Mr Brownrigg has gone for Dr Duncan, and will be back in a few moments. I beg you will not exert yourself."

I yielded and lay still. Dr Duncan came. His carriage followed, and I was taken home. Before we started, I said to Mr Brownrigg-for I could not rest till I had said it —

"Mr Brownrigg, I spoke in heat when I came up to you, and I am sure I did you wrong. I am certain you had no improper motive in not making me acquainted with your proceedings.

You meant no harm to me. But you did very wrong towards Mr Templeton. I will try to show you that when I am well again; but —"

"But you mustn't talk more now," said Dr Duncan.

So I shook hands with Mr Brownrigg, and we parted. I fear, from what I know of my churchwarden, that he went home with the conviction that he had done perfectly right; and that the parson had made an apology for interfering with a churchwarden who was doing his best to uphold the dignity of Church and State. But perhaps I may be doing him wrong again.

I went home to a week more of bed, and a lengthened process of recovery, during which many were the kind inquiries made after me by my friends, and amongst them by Mr Templeton.

And here I may as well sketch the result of that strange introduction to the dissenting minister.

After I was tolerably well again, I received a friendly letter from him one day, expostulating with me on the inconsistency of my remaining within the pale of the ESTABLISHED CHURCH. The gist of the letter lay in these words: —

"I confess it perplexes me to understand how to reconcile your Christian and friendly behaviour to one whom most of your brethren would consider as much beneath their notice as inferior to them in social position, with your remaining the minister of a Church in which such enormities as you employed your private influence to counteract in my case, are not only possible, but certainly lawful, and recognized by most of its members as likewise expedient."

To this I replied: —

"MY DEAR SIR, —I do not like writing letters, especially on subjects of importance. There are a thousand chances of misunderstanding. Whereas, in a personal interview, there is a possibility of controversy being hallowed by communion. Come and dine with me to-morrow, at any hour convenient to you, and make my apologies to Mrs Templeton for not inviting her with you, on the ground that we want to have a long talk with each other without the distracting influence which even her presence would unavoidably occasion.

"I am," &c. &c.

He accepted my invitation at once. During dinner we talked away, not upon indifferent, but upon the most interesting subjects-connected with the poor, and parish work, and the influence of the higher upon the lower classes of society. At length we sat down on opposite sides of the fire; and as soon as Mrs Pearson had shut the door, I said, —

"You ask me, Mr Templeton, in your very kind letter —" and here I put my hand in my pocket to find it.

"I asked you," interposed Mr Templeton, "how you could belong to a Church which authorizes things of which you yourself so heartily disapprove."

"And I answer you," I returned, "that just to such a Church our Lord belonged."

"I do not quite understand you."

"Our Lord belonged to the Jewish Church."

"But ours is His Church."

"Yes. But principles remain the same. I speak of Him as belonging to a Church. His conduct would be the same in the same circumstances, whatever Church He belonged to, because He would always do right. I want, if you will allow me, to show you the principle upon which He acted with regard to church-rates."

"Certainly. I beg your pardon for interrupting you."

"The Pharisees demanded a tribute, which, it is allowed, was for the support of the temple and its worship. Our Lord did not refuse to acknowledge their authority, notwithstanding the many ways in which they had degraded the religious observances of the Jewish Church. He acknowledged himself a child of the Church, but said that, as a child, He ought to have been left to contribute as He pleased to the support of its ordinances, and not to be compelled after such a fashion."

"There I have you," exclaimed Mr Templeton. "He said they were wrong to make the tribute, or church-rate, if it really was such, compulsory."

"I grant it: it is entirely wrong—a very unchristian proceeding. But our Lord did not therefore desert the Church, as you would have me do. HE PAID THE MONEY, lest He should offend. And not having it of His own, He had to ask His Father for it; or, what came to the same thing, make a servant of His Father, namely, a fish in the sea of Galilee, bring Him the money. And there I have YOU, Mr Templeton. It is wrong to compel, and wrong to refuse, the payment of a church-rate. I do not say equally wrong: it is much worse to compel than to refuse."

"You are very generous," returned Mr Templeton. "May I hope that you will do me the credit to believe that if I saw clearly that they were the same thing, I would not hesitate a moment to follow our Lord's example."

"I believe it perfectly. Therefore, however we may differ, we are in reality at no strife."

"But is there not this difference, that our Lord was, as you say, a child of the Jewish Church, which was indubitably established by God? Now, if I cannot conscientiously belong to the so-called English Church, why should I have to pay church-rate or tribute?"

"Shall I tell you the argument the English Church might then use? The Church might say, 'Then you are a stranger, and no child; therefore, like the kings of the earth, we MAY take tribute of you.' So you see it would come to this, that Dissenters alone should be COMPELLED to pay church-rates."

We both laughed at this pushing of the argument to illegitimate conclusions. Then I resumed:

"But the real argument is that not for such faults should we separate from each other; not for such faults, or any faults, so long as it is the repository of the truth, should you separate from the Church."

"I will yield the point when you can show me the same ground for believing the Church of England THE NATIONAL CHURCH, appointed such by God, that I can show you, and you know already, for receiving the Jewish Church as the appointment of God."

"That would involve a long argument, upon which, though I have little doubt upon the matter myself, I cannot say I am prepared to enter at this moment. Meantime, I would just ask you whether you are not sufficiently a child of the Church of England, having received from it a thousand influences for good, if in no other way, yet through your fathers, to find it no great hardship, and not very unreasonable, to pay a trifle to keep in repair one of the tabernacles in which our forefathers worshipped together, if, as I hope you will allow, in some imperfect measure God is worshipped, and the truth is preached in it?"

"Most willingly would I pay the money. I object simply because the rate is compulsory."

"And therein you have our Lord's example to the contrary."

A silence followed; for I had to deal with an honest man, who was thinking. I resumed:—

"A thousand difficulties will no doubt come up to be considered in the matter. Do not suppose I am anxious to convince you. I believe that our Father, our Elder Brother, and the Spirit that proceedeth from them, is teaching you, as I believe I too am being taught by the same. Why, then, should I be anxious to convince you of anything? Will you not in His good time come to see what He would have you see? I am relieved to speak my mind, knowing He would have us speak our minds to each other; but I do not want to proselytize. If you change your mind, you will probably do so on different grounds from any I give you, on grounds which show themselves in the course of your own search after the foundations of truth in regard perhaps to some other question altogether."

Again a silence followed. Then Mr Templeton spoke:—

"Don't think I am satisfied," he said, "because I don't choose to say anything more till I have thought about it. I think you are wrong in your conclusions about the Church, though surely you are right in thinking we ought to have patience with each other. And now tell me true, Mr Walton,—I'm a blunt kind of man, descended from an old Puritan, one of Cromwell's Ironsides,

I believe, and I haven't been to a university like you, but I'm no fool either, I hope,—don't be offended at my question: wouldn't you be glad to see me out of your parish now?"

I began to speak, but he went on.

"Don't you regard me as an interloper now-one who has no right to speak because he does not belong to the Church?"

"God forbid!" I answered. "If a word of mine would make you leave my parish to-morrow, I dare not say it. I do not want to incur the rebuke of our Lord-for surely the words 'Forbid him not' involved some rebuke. Would it not be a fearful thing that one soul, because of a deed of mine, should receive a less portion of elevation or comfort in his journey towards his home? Are there not countless modes of saying the truth? You have some of them. I hope I have some. People will hear you who will not hear me. Preach to them in the name and love of God, Mr Templeton. Speak that you do know and testify that you have seen. You and I will help each other, in proportion as we serve the Master. I only say that in separating from us you are in effect, and by your conduct, saying to us, "Do not preach, for you follow not with us." I will not be guilty of the same towards you. Your fathers did the Church no end of good by leaving it. But it is time to unite now."

Once more followed a silence.

"If people could only meet, and look each other in the face," said Mr Templeton at length, "they might find there was not such a gulf between them as they had fancied."

And so we parted.

Now I do not write all this for the sake of the church-rate question. I write it to commemorate the spirit in which Mr Templeton met me. For it is of consequence that two men who love their Master should recognize each that the other does so, and thereupon, if not before, should cease to be estranged because of difference of opinion, which surely, inevitable as offence, does not involve the same denunciation of woe.

After this Mr Templeton and I found some opportunities of helping each other. And many a time ere his death we consulted together about things that befell. Once he came to me about a legal difficulty in connexion with the deed of trust of his chapel; and although I could not help him myself, I directed him to such help as was thorough and cost him nothing.

I need not say he never became a churchman, or that I never expected he would. All his memories of a religious childhood, all the sources of the influences which had refined and elevated him, were surrounded with other associations than those of the Church and her forms. The Church was his grandmother, not his mother, and he had not made any acquaintance with her till comparatively late in life.

But while I do not say that his intellectual objections to the Church were less strong than they had been, I am sure that his feelings were moderated, even changed towards her. And though this may seem of no consequence to one who loves the Church more than the brotherhood, it does not seem of little consequence to me who love the Church because of the brotherhood of which it is the type and the restorer.

It was long before another church-rate was levied in Marshmallows. And when the circumstance did take place, no one dreamed of calling on Mr Templeton for his share in it. But, having heard of it, he called himself upon the churchwarden-Mr Brownrigg still-and offered the money cheerfully. AND MR BROWRIGG REFUSED TO TAKE IT TILL HE HAD CONSULTED ME! I told him to call on Mr Templeton, and say he would be much obliged to him for his contribution, and give him a receipt for it.

CHAPTER XVIII
JUDY'S NEWS.

Perhaps my reader may be sufficiently interested in the person, who, having once begun to tell his story, may possibly have allowed his feelings, in concert with the comfortable confidence afforded by the mask of namelessness, to run away with his pen, and so have babbled of himself more than he ought-may be sufficiently interested, I say, in my mental condition, to cast a speculative thought upon the state of my mind, during my illness, with regard to Miss Oldcastle and the stranger who was her mother's guest at the Hall. Possibly, being by nature gifted, as I have certainly discovered, with more of hope than is usually mingled with the other elements composing the temperament of humanity, I did not suffer quite so much as some would have suffered during such an illness. But I have reason to fear that when I was light-headed from fever, which was a not uncommon occurrence, especially in the early mornings during the worst of my illness-when Mrs Pearson had to sit up with me, and sometimes an old woman of the village who was generally called in upon such occasions—I may have talked a good deal of nonsense about Miss Oldcastle. For I remember that I was haunted with visions of magnificent conventual ruins which I had discovered, and which, no one seeming to care about them but myself, I was left to wander through at my own lonely will. Would I could see with the waking eye such a grandeur of Gothic arches and "long-drawn aisles" as then arose upon my sick sense! Within was a labyrinth of passages in the walls, and "long-sounding corridors," and sudden galleries, whence I looked down into the great church aching with silence. Through these I was ever wandering, ever discovering new rooms, new galleries, new marvels of architecture; ever disappointed and ever dissatisfied, because I knew that in one room somewhere in the forgotten mysteries of the pile sat Ethelwyn reading, never lifting those sea-blue eyes of hers from the great volume on her knee, reading every word, slowly turning leaf after leaf; knew that she would sit there reading, till, one by one, every leaf in the huge volume was turned, and she came to the last and read it from top to bottom-down to the finis and the urn with a weeping willow over it; when she would close the book with a sigh, lay it down on the floor, rise and walk slowly away, and leave the glorious ruin dead to me as it had so long been to every one else; knew that if I did not find her before that terrible last page was read, I should never find her at all; but have to go wandering alone all my life through those dreary galleries and corridors, with one hope only left-that I might yet before I died find the "palace-chamber far apart," and see the read and forsaken volume lying on the floor where she had left it, and the chair beside it upon which she had sat so long waiting for some one in vain.

And perhaps to words spoken under these impressions may partly be attributed the fact, which I knew nothing of till long afterwards, that the people of the village began to couple my name with that of Miss Oldcastle.

When all this vanished from me in the returning wave of health that spread through my weary brain, I was yet left anxious and thoughtful. There was no one from whom I could ask any information about the family at the Hall, so that I was just driven to the best thing-to try to cast my care upon Him who cared for my care. How often do we look upon God as our last and feeblest resource! We go to Him because we have nowhere else to go. And then we learn that the storms of life have driven us, not upon the rocks, but into the desired haven; that we have been compelled, as to the last remaining, so to the best, the only, the central help, the causing cause of all the helps to which we had turned aside as nearer and better.

One day when, having considerably recovered from my second attack, I was sitting reading in my study, who should be announced but my friend Judy!

"Oh, dear Mr Walton, I am so sorry you have been so ill!" exclaimed the impulsive girl, taking my hand in both of hers, and sitting down beside me. "I haven't had a chance of coming to see you before; though we've always managed —I mean auntie and I—to hear about you. I would have come to nurse you, but it was no use thinking of it."

I smiled as I thanked her.

"Ah! you think because I'm such a tom-boy, that I couldn't nurse you. I only wish I had had a chance of letting you see. I am so sorry for you!"

"But I'm nearly well now, Judy, and I have been taken good care of."

"By that frumpy old thing, Mrs Pearson, and —"

"Mrs Pearson is a very kind woman, and an excellent nurse," I said; but she would not heed me.

"And that awful old witch, Mother Goose. She was enough to give you bad dreams all night she sat by you."

"I didn't dream about Mother Goose, as you call her, Judy. I assure you. But now I want to hear how everybody is at the Hall."

"What, grannie, and the white wolf, and all?"

"As many as you please to tell me about."

"Well, grannie is gracious to everybody but auntie."

"Why isn't she gracious to auntie?"

"I don't know. I only guess."

"Is your visitor gone?"

"Yes, long ago. Do you know, I think grannie wants auntie to marry him, and auntie doesn't quite like it? But he's very nice. He's so funny! He 'll be back again soon, I daresay. I don't QUITE like him-not so well as you by a whole half, Mr Walton. I wish you would marry auntie; but that would never do. It would drive grannie out of her wits."

To stop the strange girl, and hide some confusion, I said:

"Now tell me about the rest of them."

"Sarah comes next. She's as white and as wolfy as ever. Mr Walton, I hate that woman. She walks like a cat. I am sure she is bad."

"Did you ever think, Judy, what an awful thing it is to be bad? If you did, I think you would be so sorry for her, you could not hate her."

At the same time, knowing what I knew now, and remembering that impressions can date from farther back than the memory can reach, I was not surprised to hear that Judy hated Sarah, though I could not believe that in such a child the hatred was of the most deadly description.

"I am afraid I must go on hating in the meantime," said Judy. "I wish some one would marry auntie, and turn Sarah away. But that couldn't be, so long as grannie lives."

"How is Mr Stoddart?"

"There now! That's one of the things auntie said I was to be sure to tell you."

"Then your aunt knew you were coming to see me?"

"Oh, yes, I told her. Not grannie, you know. —You mustn't let it out."

"I shall be careful. How is Mr Stoddart, then?"

"Not well at all. He was taken ill before you, and has been in bed and by the fireside ever since. Auntie doesn't know what to do with him, he is so out of spirits."

"If to-morrow is fine, I shall go and see him."

"Thank you. I believe that's just what auntie wanted. He won't like it at first, I daresay. But he'll come to, and you'll do him good. You do everybody good you come near."

"I wish that were true, Judy. I fear it is not. What good did I ever do you, Judy?"

"Do me!" she exclaimed, apparently half angry at the question. "Don't you know I have been an altered character ever since I knew you?"

And here the odd creature laughed, leaving me in absolute ignorance of how to interpret her. But presently her eyes grew clearer, and I could see the slow film of a tear gathering.

"Mr Walton," she said, "I HAVE been trying not to be selfish. You have done me that much good."

"I am very glad, Judy. Don't forget who can do you ALL good. There is One who can not only show you what is right, but can make you able to do and be what is right. You don't know how much you have got to learn yet, Judy; but there is that one Teacher ever ready to teach if you will only ask Him."

Judy did not answer, but sat looking fixedly at the carpet. She was thinking, though, I saw.

"Who has played the organ, Judy, since your uncle was taken ill?" I asked, at length.

"Why, auntie, to be sure. Didn't you hear?"

"No," I answered, turning almost sick at the idea of having been away from church for so many Sundays while she was giving voice and expression to the dear asthmatic old pipes. And I did feel very ready to murmur, like a spoilt child that had not had his way. Think of HER there, and me here!

"Then," I said to myself at last, "it must have been she that played I know that my Redeemer liveth, that last time I was in church! And instead of thanking God for that, here I am murmuring that He did not give me more! And this child has just been telling me that I have taught her to try not to be selfish. Certainly I should be ashamed of myself."

"When was your uncle taken ill?"

"I don't exactly remember. But you will come and see him to-morrow? And then we shall see you too. For we are always out and in of his room just now."

"I will come if Dr Duncan will let me. Perhaps he will take me in his carriage."

"No, no. Don't you come with him. Uncle can't bear doctors. He never was ill in his life before, and he behaves to Dr Duncan just as if he had made him ill. I wish I could send the carriage for you. But I can't, you know."

"Never mind, Judy. I shall manage somehow.—What is the name of the gentleman who was staying with you?"

"Don't you know? Captain George Everard. He would change his name to Oldcastle, you know."

What a foolish pain, like a spear-thrust, they sent through me-those words spoken in such a taken-for-granted way!

"He's a relation-on grannie's side mostly, I believe. But I never could understand the explanation. What makes it harder is, that all the husbands and wives in our family, for a hundred and fifty years, have been more or less of cousins, or half-cousins, or second or third cousins. Captain Everard has what grandmamma calls a neat little property of his own from his mother, some where in Northumberland; for he IS only a third son, one of a class grannie does not in general feel very friendly to, I assure you, Mr Walton. But his second brother is dead, and the eldest something the worse for the wear, as grannie says; so that the captain comes just within sight of the coronet of an old uncle who ought to have been dead long ago. Just the match for auntie!"

"But you say auntie doesn't like him."

"Oh! but you know that doesn't matter," returned Judy, with bitterness. "What will grannie care for that? It's nothing to anybody but auntie, and she must get used to it. Nobody makes anything of her."

It was only after she had gone that I thought how astounding it would have been to me to hear a girl of her age show such an acquaintance with worldliness and scheming, had I not been personally so much concerned about one of the objects of her remarks. She certainly was a strange girl. But strange as she was it was a satisfaction to think that the aunt had such a friend and ally in her wild niece. Evidently she had inherited her father's fearlessness; and if only it should turn out that she had likewise inherited her mother's firmness, she might render the best possible service to her aunt against the oppression of her wilful mother.

"How were you able to get here to-day?" I asked, as she rose to go.

"Grannie is in London, and the wolf is with her. Auntie wouldn't leave uncle."

"They have been a good deal in London of late, have they not?"

"Yes. They say it's about money of auntie's. But I don't understand. *I* think it's that grannie wants to make the captain marry her; for they sometimes see him when they go to London."

CHAPTER XIX
THE INVALID.

The following day being very fine, I walked to Oldcastle Hall; but I remember well how much slower I was forced to walk than I was willing. I found to my relief that Mrs Oldcastle had not yet returned. I was shown at once to Mr Stoddart's library. There I found the two ladies in attendance upon him. He was seated by a splendid fire, for the autumn days were now chilly on the shady side, in the most luxurious of easy chairs, with his furred feet buried in the long hair of the hearth-rug. He looked worn and peevish. All the placidity of his countenance had vanished. The smooth expanse of his forehead was drawn into fifty wrinkles, like a sea over which the fretting wind has been blowing all night. Nor was it only suffering that his face expressed. He looked like a man who strongly suspected that he was ill-used.

After salutation, —

"You are well off, Mr Stoddart," I said, "to have two such nurses."

"They are very kind," sighed the patient

"You would recommend Mrs Pearson and Mother Goose instead, would you not, Mr Walton?" said Judy, her gray eyes sparkling with fun.

"Judy, be quiet," said the invalid, languidly and yet sharply.

Judy reddened and was silent.

"I am sorry to find you so unwell," I said.

"Yes; I am very ill," he returned.

Aunt and niece rose and left the room quietly.

"Do you suffer much, Mr Stoddart?"

"Much weariness, worse than pain. I could welcome death."

"I do not think, from what Dr Duncan says of you, that there is reason to apprehend more than a lingering illness," I said-to try him, I confess.

"I hope not indeed," he exclaimed angrily, sitting up in his chair. "What right has Dr Duncan to talk of me so?"

"To a friend, you know," I returned, apologetically, "who is much interested in your welfare."

"Yes, of course. So is the doctor. A sick man belongs to you both by prescription."

"For my part I would rather talk about religion to a whole man than a sick man. A sick man is not a WHOLE man. He is but part of a man, as it were, for the time, and it is not so easy to tell what he can take."

"Thank you. I am obliged to you for my new position in the social scale. Of the tailor species, I suppose."

I could not help wishing he were as far up as any man that does such needful honest work.

"My dear sir, I beg your pardon. I meant only a glance at the peculiar relation of the words WHOLE and HEAL."

"I do not find etymology interesting at present."

"Not seated in such a library as this?"

"No; I am ill."

Satisfied that, ill as he was, he might be better if he would, I resolved to make another trial.

"Do you remember how Ligarius, in Julius Caesar, discards his sickness? —

"'I am not sick, if Brutus have in hand Any exploit worthy the name of honour.'"

"I want to be well because I don't like to be ill. But what there is in this foggy, swampy world worth being well for, I'm sure I haven't found out yet."

"If you have not, it must be because you have never tried to find out. But I'm not going to attack you when you are not able to defend yourself. We shall find a better time for that. But can't I do something for you? Would you like me to read to you for half an hour?"

"No, thank you. The girls tire me out with reading to me. I hate the very sound of their voices."

"I have got to-day's Times in my pocket."

"I've heard all the news already."

"Then I think I shall only bore you if I stay."

He made me no answer. I rose. He just let me take his hand, and returned my good morning as if there was nothing good in the world, least of all this same morning.

I found the ladies in the outer room. Judy was on her knees on the floor occupied with a long row of books. How the books had got there I wondered; but soon learned the secret which I had in vain asked of the butler on my first visit-namely, how Mr Stoddart reached the volumes arranged immediately under the ceiling, in shelves, as my reader may remember, that looked like beams radiating from the centre. For Judy rose from the floor, and proceeded to put in motion a mechanical arrangement concealed in one of the divisions of the book-shelves along the wall; and I now saw that there were strong cords reaching from the ceiling, and attached to the shelf or rather long box sideways open which contained the books.

"Do take care, Judy," said Ethelwyn. "You know it is very venturous of you to let that shelf down, when uncle is as jealous of his books as a hen of her chickens. I oughtn't to have let you touch the cords."

"You couldn't help it, auntie, dear; for I had the shelf half-way down before you saw me," returned Judy, proceeding to raise the books to their usual position under the ceiling.

But in another moment, either from Judy's awkwardness, or from the gradual decay and final fracture of some cord, down came the whole shelf with a thundering noise, and the books were scattered hither and thither in confusion about the floor. Ethelwyn was gazing in dismay, and Judy had built up her face into a defiant look, when the door of the inner room opened and Mr Stoddart appeared. His brow was already flushed; but when he saw the condition of his idols, (for the lust of the eye had its full share in his regard for his books,) he broke out in a passion to which he could not have given way but for the weak state of his health.

"How DARE you?" he said, with terrible emphasis on the word DARE. "Judy, I beg you will not again show yourself in my apartment till I send for you."

"And then," said Judy, leaving the room, "I am not in the least likely to be otherwise engaged."

"I am very sorry, uncle," began Miss Oldcastle.

But Mr Stoddart had already retreated and banged the door behind him. So Miss Oldcastle and I were left standing together amid the ruins.

She glanced at me with a distressed look. I smiled. She smiled in return.

"I assure you," she said, "uncle is not a bit like himself."

"And I fear in trying to rouse him, I have done him no good, —only made him more irritable," I said. "But he will be sorry when he comes to himself, and so we must take the reversion of his repentance now, and think nothing more of the matter than if he had already said he was sorry. Besides, when books are in the case, I, for one, must not be too hard upon my unfortunate neighbour."

"Thank you, Mr Walton. I am so much obliged to you for taking my uncle's part. He has been very good to me; and that dear Judy is provoking sometimes. I am afraid I help to spoil her; but you would hardly believe how good she really is, and what a comfort she is to me-with all her waywardness."

"I think I understand Judy," I replied; "and I shall be more mistaken than I am willing to confess I have ever been before, if she does not turn out a very fine woman. The marvel to me is that with all the various influences amongst which she is placed here, she is not really, not seriously, spoiled after all. I assure you I have the greatest regard for, as well as confidence in, my friend Judy."

Ethelwyn-Miss Oldcastle, I should say-gave me such a pleased look that I was well recompensed-if justice should ever talk of recompense-for my defence of her niece.

"Will you come with me?" she said; "for I fear our talk may continue to annoy Mr Stoddart. His hearing is acute at all times, and has been excessively so since his illness."

"I am at your service," I returned, and followed her from the room.

"Are you still as fond of the old quarry as you used to be, Miss Oldcastle?" I said, as we caught a glimpse of it from the window of a long passage we were going through.

"I think I am. I go there most days. I have not been to-day, though. Would you like to go down?"

"Very much," I said.

"Ah! I forgot, though. You must not go; it is not a fit place for an invalid."

"I cannot call myself an invalid now."

"Your face, I am sorry to say, contradicts your words."

And she looked so kindly at me, that I almost broke out into thanks for the mere look.

"And indeed," she went on, "it is too damp down there, not to speak of the stairs."

By this time we had reached the little room in which I was received the first time I visited the Hall. There we found Judy.

"If you are not too tired already, I should like to show you my little study. It has, I think, a better view than any other room in the house," said Miss Oldcastle.

"I shall be delighted," I replied.

"Come, Judy," said her aunt.

"You don't want me, I am sure, auntie."

"I do, Judy, really. You mustn't be cross to us because uncle has been cross to you. Uncle is not well, you know, and isn't a bit like himself; and you know you should not have meddled with his machinery."

And Miss Oldcastle put her arm round Judy, and kissed her. Whereupon Judy jumped from her seat, threw her book down, and ran to one of the several doors that opened from the room. This disclosed a little staircase, almost like a ladder, only that it wound about, up which we climbed, and reached a charming little room, whose window looked down upon the Bishop's Basin, glimmering slaty through the tops of the trees between. It was panelled in small panels of dark oak, like the room below, but with more of carving. Consequently it was sombre, and its sombreness was unrelieved by any mirror. I gazed about me with a kind of awe. I would gladly have carried away the remembrance of everything and its shadow. —Just opposite the window was a small space of brightness formed by the backs of nicely-bound books. Seeing that these attracted my eye—

"Those are almost all gifts from my uncle," said Miss Oldcastle. "He is really very kind, and you will not think of him as you have seen him to-day?"

"Indeed I will not," I replied.

My eye fell upon a small pianoforte.

"Do sit down," said Miss Oldcastle. —"You have been very ill, and I could do nothing for you who have been so kind to me."

She spoke as if she had wanted to say this.

"I only wish I had a chance of doing anything for you," I said, as I took a chair in the window. "But if I had done all I ever could hope to do, you have repaid me long ago, I think."

"How? I do not know what you mean, Mr Walton. I have never done you the least service."

"Tell me first, did you play the organ in church that afternoon when-after-before I was taken ill—I mean the same day you had—a friend with you in the pew in the morning?"

I daresay my voice was as irregular as my construction. I ventured just one glance. Her face was flushed. But she answered me at once.

"I did."

"Then I am in your debt more than you know or I can tell you."

"Why, if that is all, I have played the organ every Sunday since uncle was taken ill," she said, smiling.

"I know that now. And I am very glad I did not know it till I was better able to bear the disappointment. But it is only for what I heard that I mean now to acknowledge my obligation. Tell me, Miss Oldcastle,—what is the most precious gift one person can give another?"

She hesitated; and I, fearing to embarrass her, answered for her.

"It must be something imperishable,—something which in its own nature IS. If instead of a gem, or even of a flower, we could cast the gift of a lovely thought into the heart of a friend, that would be giving, as the angels, I suppose, must give. But you did more and better for me than that. I had been troubled all the morning; and you made me know that my Redeemer liveth. I did not know you were playing, mind, though I felt a difference. You gave me more trust in God; and what other gift so great could one give? I think that last impression, just as I was taken ill, must have helped me through my illness. Often when I was most oppressed, 'I know that my Redeemer liveth' would rise up in the troubled air of my mind, and sung by a voice which, though I never heard you sing, I never questioned to be yours."

She turned her face towards me: those sea-blue eyes were full of tears.

"I was troubled myself," she said, with a faltering voice, "when I sang—I mean played-that. I am so glad it did somebody good! I fear it did not do me much.—I will sing it to you now, if you like."

And she rose to get the music. But that instant Judy, who, I then found, had left the room, bounded into it, with the exclamation,—

"Auntie, auntie! here's grannie!"

Miss Oldcastle turned pale. I confess I felt embarrassed, as if I had been caught in something underhand.

"Is she come in?" asked Miss Oldcastle, trying to speak with indifference.

"She is just at the door,—must be getting out of the fly now. What SHALL we do?"

"What DO you mean, Judy?" said her aunt.

"Well you know, auntie, as well as I do, that grannie will look as black as a thunder-cloud to find Mr Walton here; and if she doesn't speak as loud, it will only be because she can't. *I* don't care for myself, but you know on whose head the storm will fall. Do, dear Mr Walton, come down the back-stair. Then she won't be a bit the wiser. I'll manage it all."

Here was a dilemma for me; either to bring suffering on her, to save whom I would have borne any pain, or to creep out of the house as if I were and ought to be ashamed of myself. I believe that had I been in any other relation to my fellows, I would have resolved at once to lay myself open to the peculiarly unpleasant reproach of sneaking out of the house, rather than that she should innocently suffer for my being innocently there. But I was a clergyman; and I felt, more than I had ever felt before, that therefore I could not risk ever the appearance of what was mean. Miss Oldcastle, however, did not leave it to me to settle the matter. All that I have just written had but flashed through my mind when she said:—

"Judy, for shame to propose such a thing to Mr Walton! I am very sorry that he may chance to have an unpleasant meeting with mamma; but we can't help it. Come, Judy, we will show Mr Walton out together."

"It wasn't for Mr Walton's sake," returned Judy, pouting. "You are very troublesome, auntie dear. Mr Walton, she is so hard to take care of! and she's worse since you came. I shall have to give her up some day. Do be generous, Mr Walton, and take my side-that is, auntie's."

"I am afraid, Judy, I must thank your aunt for taking the part of my duty against my inclination. But this kindness, at least," I said to Miss Oldcastle, "I can never hope to return."

It was a stupid speech, but I could not be annoyed that I had made it.

"All obligations are not burdens to be got rid of, are they?" she replied, with a sweet smile on such a pale troubled face, that I was more moved for her, deliberately handing her over to the torture for the truth's sake, than I care definitely to confess.

Thereupon, Miss Oldcastle led the way down the stairs, I followed, and Judy brought up the rear. The affair was not so bad as it might have been, inasmuch as, meeting the mistress of the house in no penetralia of the same, I insisted on going out alone, and met Mrs Oldcastle in the hall only. She held out no hand to greet me. I bowed, and said I was sorry to find Mr Stoddart so far from well.

"I fear he is far from well," she returned; "certainly in my opinion too ill to receive visitors."

So saying, she bowed and passed on. I turned and walked out, not ill-pleased, as my readers will believe, with my visit.

From that day I recovered rapidly, and the next Sunday had the pleasure of preaching to my flock; Mr Aikin, the gentleman already mentioned as doing duty for me, reading prayers. I took for my subject one of our Lord's miracles of healing, I forget which now, and tried to show my people that all healing and all kinds of healing come as certainly and only from His hand as those instances in which He put forth His bodily hand and touched the diseased, and told them to be whole.

And as they left the church the organ played, "Comfort ye, comfort ye, my people, saith your God."

I tried hard to prevent my new feelings from so filling my mind as to make me fail of my duty towards my flock. I said to myself, "Let me be the more gentle, the more honourable, the more tender, towards these my brothers and sisters, forasmuch as they are her brothers and sisters too." I wanted to do my work the better that I loved her.

Thus week after week passed, with little that I can remember worthy of record. I seldom saw Miss Oldcastle, and during this period never alone. True, she played the organ still, for Mr Stoddart continued too unwell to resume his ministry of sound, but I never made any attempt to see her as she came to or went from the organ-loft. I felt that I ought not, or at least that it was better not, lest an interview should trouble my mind, and so interfere with my work, which, if my calling meant anything real, was a consideration of vital import. But one thing I could not help noting-that she seemed, by some intuition, to know the music I liked best; and great help she often gave me by so uplifting my heart upon the billows of the organ-harmony, that my thinking became free and harmonious, and I spoke, as far as my own feeling was concerned, like one upheld on the unseen wings of ministering cherubim. How it might be to those who heard me, or what the value of the utterance in itself might be, I cannot tell. I only speak of my own feelings, I say.

Does my reader wonder why I did not yet make any further attempt to gain favour in the lady's eyes? He will see, if he will think for a moment. First of all, I could not venture until she had seen more of me; and how to enjoy more of her society while her mother was so unfriendly, both from instinctive dislike to me, and because of the offence I had given her more than once, I did not know; for I feared that to call oftener might only occasion measures upon her part to prevent me from seeing her daughter at all; and I could not tell how far such measures might expedite the event I most dreaded, or add to the discomfort to which Miss Oldcastle was already so much exposed. Meantime I heard nothing of Captain Everard; and the comfort that flowed from such a negative source was yet of a very positive character. At the same time-will my reader understand me? —I was in some measure deterred from making further advances by the doubt whether her favour for Captain Everard might not be greater than Judy had represented it. For I had always shrunk, I can hardly say with invincible dislike, for I had never tried to conquer it, from rivalry of every kind: it was, somehow, contrary to my nature. Besides, Miss Oldcastle was likely to be rich some day-apparently had money of her own even now; and was it a weakness? was it not a weakness? —I cannot tell—I writhed at the thought of being supposed to marry for money, and being made the object of such remarks as, "Ah! you see! That's the way with the clergy! They talk about poverty and faith, pretending to despise riches and to trust in God; but just put money in their way, and what chance will a poor girl have beside a rich one! It's all very well in the pulpit. It's their business to talk so. But does one of them believe what he says? or, at least, act upon it?" I think I may be a little excused for the sense of creeping cold that passed over me at the thought of such remarks as these, accompanied by compressed lips and down-drawn corners of the mouth, and reiterated nods of the head of KNOWINGNESS. But I mention this only as a repressing influence, to which I certainly should not have been such a fool as to yield, had I seen the way otherwise clear. For a man by showing how to use money, or rather simply by using money aright, may do more good than by refusing to possess it, if it comes to him in an entirely honourable way, that is, in such a case as mine, merely as an accident of his history. But I was glad to feel pretty sure that if I should be so blessed as to marry Miss Oldcastle-which at the time whereof I now write, seemed far too gorgeous a castle in the clouds ever to descend to the earth for me to enter it-the POOR of my own people would be those most likely to understand my position and feelings, and least likely to impute to me worldly motives, as paltry as they are vulgar, and altogether unworthy of a true man.

So the time went on. I called once or twice on Mr Stoddart, and found him, as I thought, better. But he would not allow that he was. Dr Duncan said he was better, and would be better still, if he would only believe it and exert himself.

He continued in the same strangely irritable humour.

CHAPTER XX
MOOD AND WILL.

Winter came apace. When we look towards winter from the last borders of autumn, it seems as if we could not encounter it, and as if it never would go over. So does threatened trouble of any kind seem to us as we look forward upon its miry ways from the last borders of the pleasant greensward on which we have hitherto been walking. But not only do both run their course, but each has its own alleviations, its own pleasures; and very marvellously does the healthy mind fit itself to the new circumstances; while to those who will bravely take up their burden and bear it, asking no more questions than just, "Is this my burden?" a thousand ministrations of nature and life will come with gentle comfortings. Across a dark verdureless field will blow a wind through the heart of the winter which will wake in the patient mind not a memory merely, but a prophecy of the spring, with a glimmer of crocus, or snow-drop, or primrose; and across the waste of tired endeavour will a gentle hope, coming he knows not whence, breathe springlike upon the heart of the man around whom life looks desolate and dreary. Well do I remember a friend of mine telling me once-he was then a labourer in the field of literature, who had not yet begun to earn his penny a day, though he worked hard-telling me how once, when a hope that had kept him active for months was suddenly quenched —a book refused on which he had spent a passion of labour-the weight of money that must be paid and could not be had, pressing him down like the coffin-lid that had lately covered the ONLY friend to whom he could have applied confidently for aid-telling me, I say, how he stood at the corner of a London street, with the rain, dripping black from the brim of his hat, the dreariest of atmospheres about him in the closing afternoon of the City, when the rich men were going home, and the poor men who worked for them were longing to follow; and how across this waste came energy and hope into his bosom, swelling thenceforth with courage to fight, and yield no ear to suggested failure. And the story would not be complete-though it is for the fact of the arrival of unexpected and apparently unfounded HOPE that I tell it-if I did not add, that, in the morning, his wife gave him a letter which their common trouble of yesterday had made her forget, and which had lain with its black border all night in the darkness unopened, waiting to tell him how the vanished friend had not forgotten him on her death-bed, but had left him enough to take him out of all those difficulties, and give him strength and time to do far better work than the book which had failed of birth. —Some of my readers may doubt whether I am more than "a wandering voice," but whatever I am, or may be thought to be, my friend's story is true.

And all this has come out of the winter that I, in the retrospect of my history, am looking forward to. It came, with its fogs, and dripping boughs, and sodden paths, and rotting leaves, and rains, and skies of weary gray; but also with its fierce red suns, shining aslant upon sheets of manna-like hoarfrost, and delicate ice-films over prisoned waters, and those white falling chaoses of perfect forms-called snow-storms —those confusions confounded of infinite symmetries.

And when the hard frost came, it brought a friend to my door. It was Mr Stoddart.

He entered my room with something of the countenance Naaman must have borne, after his flesh had come again like unto the flesh of a little child. He did not look ashamed, but his pale face looked humble and distressed. Its somewhat self-satisfied placidity had vanished, and instead of the diffused geniality which was its usual expression, it now showed traces of feeling as well as plain signs of suffering. I gave him as warm a welcome as I could, and having seated him comfortably by the fire, and found that he would take no refreshment, began to chat about the day's news, for I had just been reading the newspaper. But he showed no interest beyond what the merest politeness required. I would try something else.

"The cold weather, which makes so many invalids creep into bed, seems to have brought you out into the air, Mr Stoddart," I said.

"It has revived me, certainly."

"Indeed, one must believe that winter and cold are as beneficent, though not so genial, as summer and its warmth. Winter kills many a disease and many a noxious influence. And what is it to have the fresh green leaves of spring instead of the everlasting brown of some countries which have no winter!"

I talked thus, hoping to rouse him to conversation, and I was successful.

"I feel just as if I were coming out of a winter. Don't you think illness is a kind of human winter?"

"Certainly-more or less stormy. With some a winter of snow and hail and piercing winds; with others of black frosts and creeping fogs, with now and then a glimmer of the sun."

"The last is more like mine. I feel as if I had been in a wet hole in the earth."

"And many a man," I went on, "the foliage of whose character had been turning brown and seared and dry, rattling rather than rustling in the faint hot wind of even fortunes, has come out of the winter of a weary illness with the fresh delicate buds of a new life bursting from the sun-dried bark."

"I wish it would be so with me. I know you mean me. But I don't feel my green leaves coming."

"Facts are not always indicated by feelings."

"Indeed, I hope not; nor yet feelings indicated by facts."

"I do not quite understand you."

"Well, Mr Walton, I will explain myself. I have come to tell you how sorry and ashamed I am that I behaved so badly to you every time you came to see me."

"Oh, nonsense!" I said. "It was your illness, not you."

"At least, my dear sir, the facts of my behaviour did not really represent my feelings towards you."

"I know that as well as you do. Don't say another word about it. You had the best excuse for being cross; I should have had none for being offended."

"It was only the outside of me."

"Yes, yes; I acknowledge it heartily."

"But that does not settle the matter between me and myself, Mr Walton; although, by your goodness, it settles it between me and you. It is humiliating to think that illness should so completely 'overcrow' me, that I am no more myself-lose my hold, in fact, of what I call ME-so that I am almost driven to doubt my personal identity."

"You are fond of theories, Mr Stoddart-perhaps a little too much so."

"Perhaps."

"Will you listen to one of mine?"

"With pleasure."

"It seems to me sometimes —I know it is a partial representation-as if life were a conflict between the inner force of the spirit, which lies in its faith in the unseen-and the outer force of the world, which lies in the pressure of everything it has to show us. The material, operating upon our senses, is always asserting its existence; and if our inner life is not equally vigorous, we shall be moved, urged, what is called actuated, from without, whereas all our activity ought to be from within. But sickness not only overwhelms the mind, but, vitiating all the channels of the senses, causes them to represent things as they are not, of which misrepresentations the presence, persistency, and iteration seduce the man to act from false suggestions instead of from what he knows and believes."

"Well, I understand all that. But what use am I to make of your theory?"

"I am delighted, Mr Stoddart, to hear you put the question. That is always the point. — The inward holy garrison, that of faith, which holds by the truth, by sacred facts, and not by appearances, must be strengthened and nourished and upheld, and so enabled to resist the onset of the powers without. A friend's remonstrance may appear an unkindness —a friend's jest an unfeelingness —a friend's visit an intrusion; nay, to come to higher things, during a mere headache it will appear as if there was no truth in the world, no reality but that of pain anywhere, and nothing to be desired but deliverance from it. But all such impressions caused from without-for, remember, the body and its innermost experiences are only OUTSIDE OF THE MAN-have to be met by the inner confidence of the spirit, resting in God and resisting every impulse to act according to that which APPEARS TO IT instead of that which IT BELIEVES. Hence, Faith is thus allegorically represented: but I had better give you Spenser's description of her-Here is the 'Fairy Queen': —

> 'She was arrayed all in lily white,
>   And in her right hand bore a cup of gold,
> With wine and water filled up to the height,
>   In which a serpent did himself enfold,
>   That horror made to all that did behold;
> But she no whit did change her constant mood.'

This serpent stands for the dire perplexity of things about us, at which yet Faith will not blench, acting according to what she believes, and not what shows itself to her by impression and appearance."

"I admit all that you say," returned Mr Stoddart. "But still the practical conclusion-which I understand to be, that the inward garrison must be fortified-is considerably incomplete unless we buttress it with the final HOW. How is it to be fortified? For,

> 'I have as much of this in art as you,
>   But yet my nature could not bear it so.'

(You see I read Shakespeare as well as you, Mr Walton.) I daresay, from a certain inclination to take the opposite side, and a certain dislike to the dogmatism of the clergy —I speak generally—I may have appeared to you indifferent, but I assure you that I have laboured much to withdraw my mind from the influence of money, and ambition, and pleasure, and to turn it to the contemplation of spiritual things. Yet on the first attack of a depressing illness I cease to be a gentleman, I am rude to ladies who do their best and kindest to serve me, and I talk to the friend who comes to cheer and comfort me as if he were an idle vagrant who wanted to sell me a worthless book with the recommendation of the pretence that he wrote it himself. Now that I am in my right mind, I am ashamed of myself, ashamed that it should be possible for me to behave so, and humiliated yet besides that I have no ground of assurance that, should my illness return to-morrow, I should not behave in the same manner the day after. I want to be ALWAYS in my right mind. When I am not, I know I am not, and yet yield to the appearance of being."

"I understand perfectly what you mean, for I fancy I know a little more of illness than you do. Shall I tell you where I think the fault of your self-training lies?"

"That is just what I want. The things which it pleased me to contemplate when I was well, gave me no pleasure when I was ill. Nothing seemed the same."

"If we were always in a right mood, there would be no room for the exercise of the will. We should go by our mood and inclination only. But that is by the by. —Where you have been wrong is-that you have sought to influence your feelings only by thought and argument with yourself-and not also by contact with your fellows. Besides the ladies of whom you have spoken, I think you have hardly a friend in this neighbourhood but myself. One friend cannot afford you half experience enough to teach you the relations of life and of human needs. At best, under such circumstances, you can only have right theories: practice for realising them in yourself is nowhere. It is no more possible for a man in the present day to retire from his fellows into the cave of his religion, and thereby leave the world of his own faults and follies behind, than it was possible for the eremites of old to get close to God in virtue of declining the duties which their very birth of human father and mother laid upon them. I do not deny that you and the eremite may both come NEARER to God, in virtue of whatever is true in your desires and your worship; 'but if a man love not his brother whom he hath seen, how can he love God whom he hath not seen?' —which surely means to imply at least that to love our neighbour is a great help towards loving God. How this love is to come about without intercourse, I do not see. And how without this love we are to bear up from within against the thousand irritations to which, especially in sickness, our unavoidable relations with humanity will expose us, I cannot tell either."

"But," returned Mr Stoddart, "I had had a true regard for you, and some friendly communication with you. If human intercourse were what is required in my case, how should I fail just with respect to the only man with whom I had held such intercourse?"

"Because the relations in which you stood with me were those of the individual, not of the race. You like me, because I am fortunate enough to please you-to be a gentleman, I hope-to be a man of some education, and capable of understanding, or at least docile enough to try to understand, what you tell me of your plans and pursuits. But you do not feel any relation to me on the ground of my humanity-that God made me, and therefore I am your brother. It is not because we grow out of the same stem, but merely because my leaf is a little like your own that you draw to me. Our Lord took on Him the nature of man: you will only regard your individual attractions. Disturb your liking and your love vanishes."

"You are severe."

"I don't mean really vanishes, but disappears for the time. Yet you will confess you have to wait till, somehow, you know not how, it comes back again-of itself, as it were."

"Yes, I confess. To my sorrow, I find it so."

"Let me tell you the truth, Mr Stoddart. You seem to me to have been hitherto only a dilettante or amateur in spiritual matters. Do not imagine I mean a hypocrite. Very far from it. The word amateur itself suggests a real interest, though it may be of a superficial nature. But in religion one must be all there. You seem to me to have taken much interest in unusual forms of theory, and in mystical speculations, to which in themselves I make no objection. But to be content with those, instead of knowing God himself, or to substitute a general amateur friendship towards the race for the love of your neighbour, is a mockery which will always manifest itself to an honest mind like yours in such failure and disappointment in your own character as you are now lamenting, if not indeed in some mode far more alarming, because gross and terrible."

"Am I to understand you, then, that intercourse with one's neighbours ought to take the place of meditation?"

"By no means: but ought to go side by side with it, if you would have at once a healthy mind to judge and the means of either verifying your speculations or discovering their falsehood."

"But where am I to find such friends besides yourself with whom to hold spiritual communion?"

"It is the communion of spiritual deeds, deeds of justice, of mercy, of humility-the kind word, the cup of cold water, the visitation in sickness, the lending of money-not spiritual conference or talk, that I mean: the latter will come of itself where it is natural. You would soon find that it is not only to those whose spiritual windows are of the same shape as your own that you are neighbour: there is one poor man in my congregation who knows more-practically, I mean, too-of spirituality of mind than any of us. Perhaps you could not teach him much, but he could teach you. At all events, our neighbours are just those round about us. And the most ignorant man in a little place like Marshmallows, one like you with leisure ought to know and understand, and have some good influence upon: he is your brother whom you are bound to care for and elevate —I do not mean socially, but really, in himself-if it be possible. You ought at least to get into some simple human relation with him, as you would with the youngest and most ignorant of your brothers and sisters born of the same father and mother; approaching him, not with pompous lecturing or fault-finding, still less with that abomination called condescension, but with the humble service of the elder to the younger, in whatever he may be helped by you without injury to him. Never was there a more injurious mistake than that it is the business of the clergy only to have the care of souls."

"But that would be endless. It would leave me no time for myself."

"Would that be no time for yourself spent in leading a noble, Christian life; in verifying the words of our Lord by doing them; in building your house on the rock of action instead of the sands of theory; in widening your own being by entering into the nature, thoughts, feelings, even fancies of those around you? In such intercourse you would find health radiating into your own bosom; healing sympathies springing up in the most barren acquaintance; channels opened for the in-rush of truth into your own mind; and opportunities afforded for the exercise of that self-discipline, the lack of which led to the failures which you now bemoan. Soon then would you have cause to wonder how much some of your speculations had fallen into the background, simply because the truth, showing itself grandly true, had so filled and occupied your mind that it left no room for anxiety about such questions as, while secured in the interest all reality gives, were yet dwarfed by the side of it. Nothing, I repeat, so much as humble ministration to your neighbours, will help you to that perfect love of God which casteth out fear; nothing but the love of God-that God revealed in Christ-will make you able to love your neighbour aright; and the Spirit of God, which alone gives might for any good, will by these loves, which are life, strengthen you at last to believe in the light even in the midst of darkness; to hold the resolution formed in health when sickness has altered the appearance of everything around you; and to feel tenderly towards your fellow, even when you yourself are plunged in dejection or racked with pain. —But," I said, "I fear I have transgressed the bounds of all propriety by enlarging upon this matter as I have done. I can only say I have spoken in proportion to my feeling of its weight and truth."

"I thank you, heartily," returned Mr Stoddart, rising. "And I promise you at least to think over what you have been saying —I hope to be in my old place in the organ-loft next Sunday."

So he was. And Miss Oldcastle was in the pew with her mother. Nor did she go any more to Addicehead to church.

CHAPTER XXI
THE DEVIL IN THOMAS WEIR.

As the winter went on, it was sad to look on the evident though slow decline of Catherine Weir. It seemed as if the dead season was dragging her to its bosom, to lay her among the leaves of past summers. She was still to be found in the shop, or appeared in it as often as the bell suspended over the door rang to announce the entrance of a customer; but she was terribly worn, and her step indicated much weakness. Nor had the signs of restless trouble diminished as these tide-marks indicated ebbing strength. There was the same dry fierce fire in her eyes; the same forceful compression of her lips; the same evidences of brooding over some one absorbing thought or feeling. She seemed to me, and to Dr Duncan as well, to be dying of resentment. Would nobody do anything for her? I thought. Would not her father help her? He had got more gentle now; whence I had reason to hope that Christian principles and feelings had begun to rise and operate in him; while surely the influence of his son must, by this time, have done something not only to soften his character generally, but to appease the anger he had cherished towards the one ewe-lamb, against which, having wandered away into the desert place, he had closed and barred the door of the sheep-fold. I would go and see him, and try what could be done for her.

I may be forgiven here if I make the remark that I cannot help thinking that what measure of success I had already had with my people, was partly owing to this, that when I thought of a thing and had concluded it might do, I very seldom put off the consequent action. I found I was wrong sometimes, and that the particular action did no good; but thus movement was kept up in my operative nature, preventing it from sinking towards the inactivity to which I was but too much inclined. Besides, to find out what will not do, is a step towards finding out what will do. Moreover, an attempt in itself unsuccessful may set something or other in motion that will help.

My present attempt turned out one of my failures, though I cannot think that it would have been better left unmade.

A red rayless sun, which one might have imagined sullen and disconsolate because he could not make the dead earth smile into flowers, was looking through the frosty fog of the winter morning as I walked across the bridge to find Thomas Weir in his workshop. The poplars stood like goblin sentinels, with black heads, upon which the long hair stood on end, all along the dark cold river. Nature looked like a life out of which the love has vanished. I turned from it and hastened on.

Thomas was busy working with a spoke-sheave at the spoke of a cart-wheel. How curiously the smallest visual fact will sometimes keep its place in the memory, when it cannot with all earnestness of endeavour recall a thought—a far more important fact! That will come again only when its time comes first.

"A cold morning, Thomas," I called from the door.

"I can always keep myself warm, sir," returned Thomas, cheerfully.

"What are you doing, Tom?" I said, going up to him first.

"A little job for myself, sir. I'm making a few bookshelves."

"I want to have a little talk with your father. Just step out in a minute or so, and let me have half-an-hour."

"Yes, sir, certainly."

I then went to the other end of the shop, for, curiously, as it seemed to me, although father and son were on the best of terms, they always worked as far from each other as the shop would permit, and it was a very large room.

"It is not easy always to keep warm through and through, Thomas," I said.

I suppose my tone revealed to his quick perceptions that "more was meant than met the ear." He looked up from his work, his tool filled with an uncompleted shaving.

"And when the heart gets cold," I went on, "it is not easily warmed again. The fire's hard to light there, Thomas."

Still he looked at me, stooping over his work, apparently with a presentiment of what was coming.

"I fear there is no way of lighting it again, except the blacksmith's way."

"Hammering the iron till it is red-hot, you mean, sir?"

"I do. When a man's heart has grown cold, the blows of affliction must fall thick and heavy before the fire can be got that will light it.—When did you see your daughter Catherine, Thomas?"

His head dropped, and he began to work as if for bare life. Not a word came from the form now bent over his tool as if he had never lifted himself up since he first began in the morning. I could just see that his face was deadly pale, and his lips compressed like those of one of the violent who take the kingdom of heaven by force. But it was for no such agony of effort that his were thus closed. He went on working till the silence became so lengthened that it seemed settled into the endless. I felt embarrassed. To break a silence is sometimes as hard as to break a spell. What Thomas would have done or said if he had not had this safety-valve of bodily exertion, I cannot even imagine.

"Thomas," I said, at length, laying my hand on his shoulder, "you are not going to part company with me, I hope?"

"You drive a man too far, sir. I've given in more to you than ever I did to man, sir; and I don't know that I oughtn't to be ashamed of it. But you don't know where to stop. If we lived a thousand years you would be driving a man on to the last. And there's no good in that, sir. A man must be at peace somewhen."

"The question is, Thomas, whether I would be driving you ON or BACK. You and I too MUST go on or back. I want to go on myself, and to make you go on too. I don't want to be parted from you now or then."

"That's all very well, sir, and very kind, I don't doubt; but, as I said afore, a man must be at peace SOMEWHEN."

"That's what I want so much that I want you to go on. Peace! I trust in God we shall both have it one day, SOMEWHEN, as you say. Have you got this peace so plentifully now that you are satisfied as you are? You will never get it but by going on."

"I do not think there is any good got in stirring a puddle. Let by-gones be by-gones. You make a mistake, sir, in rousing an anger which I would willingly let sleep."

"Better a wakeful anger, and a wakeful conscience with it, than an anger sunk into indifference, and a sleeping dog of a conscience that will not bark. To have ceased to be angry is not one step nearer to your daughter. Better strike her, abuse her, with the chance of a kiss to follow. Ah, Thomas, you are like Jonas with his gourd."

"I don't see what that has to do with it."

"I will tell you. You are fierce in wrath at the disgrace to your family. Your pride is up in arms. You don't care for the misery of your daughter, who, the more wrong she has done, is the more to be pitied by a father's heart. Your pride, I say, is all that you care about. The wrong your daughter has done, you care nothing about; or you would have taken her to your arms years ago, in the hope that the fervour of your love would drive the devil out of her and make her repent. I say it is not the wrong, but the disgrace you care for. The gourd of your pride is withered, and yet you will water it with your daughter's misery."

"Go out of my shop," he cried; "or I may say what I should be sorry for."

I turned at once and left him. I found young Tom round the corner, leaning against the wall, and reading his Virgil.

"Don't speak to your father, Tom," I said, "for a while. I've put him out of temper. He will be best left alone."

He looked frightened.

"There's no harm done, Tom, my boy. I've been talking to him about your sister. He must have time to think over what I have said to him."

"I see, sir; I see."

"Be as attentive to him as you can."

"I will, sir."

It was not alone resentment at my interference that had thus put the poor fellow beside himself, I was certain: I had called up all the old misery-set the wound bleeding again. Shame was once more wide awake and tearing at his heart. That HIS daughter should have done so! For she had been his pride. She had been the belle of the village, and very lovely; but having been apprenticed to a dressmaker in Addicehead, had, after being there about a year and a half, returned home, apparently in a decline. After the birth of her child, however, she had, to her own disappointment, and no doubt to that of her father as well, begun to recover. What a time of wretchedness it must have been to both of them until she left his house, one can imagine. Most likely the misery of the father vented itself in greater unkindness than he felt, which, sinking into the proud nature she had derived from him, roused such a resentment as rarely if ever can be thoroughly appeased until Death comes in to help the reconciliation. How often has an old love blazed up again under the blowing of his cold breath, and sent the spirit warm at heart into the regions of the unknown! She never would utter a word to reveal the name or condition of him by whom she had been wronged. To his child, as long as he drew his life from her, she behaved with strange alternations of dislike and passionate affection; after which season the latter began to diminish in violence, and the former to become more fixed, till at length, by the time I had made their acquaintance, her feelings seemed to have settled into what would have been indifference but for the constant reminder of her shame and her wrong together, which his very presence necessarily was.

They were not only the gossips of the village who judged that the fact of Addicehead's being a garrison town had something to do with the fate that had befallen her; a fate by which, in its very spring-time, when its flowers were loveliest, and hope was strongest for its summer, her life was changed into the dreary wind-swept, rain-sodden moor. The man who can ACCEPT such a sacrifice from a woman, —I say nothing of WILING it from her-is, in his meanness, selfishness, and dishonour, contemptible as the Pharisee who, with his long prayers, devours the widow's house. He leaves her desolate, while he walks off free. Would to God a man like the great-hearted, pure-bodied Milton, a man whom young men are compelled to respect, would in this our age, utter such a word as, making "mad the guilty," if such grace might be accorded them, would "appal the free," lest they too should fall into such a mire of selfish dishonour!

CHAPTER XXII
THE DEVIL IN CATHERINE WEIR.

About this time my father was taken ill, and several journeys to London followed. It is only as vicar that I am writing these memorials-for such they should be called, rather than ANNALS, though certainly the use of the latter word has of late become vague enough for all convenience-therefore I have said nothing about my home-relations; but I must just mention here that I had a half-sister, about half my own age, whose anxiety during my father's illness rendered my visits more frequent than perhaps they would have been from my own. But my sister was right in her anxiety. My father grew worse, and in December he died. I will not eulogize one so dear to me. That he was no common man will appear from the fact of his unconventionality and justice in leaving his property to my sister, saying in his will that he had done all I could require of him, in giving me a good education; and that, men having means in their power which women had not, it was unjust to the latter to make them, without a choice, dependent upon the former. After the funeral, my sister, feeling it impossible to remain in the house any longer, begged me to take her with me. So, after arranging affairs, we set out, and reached Marshmallows on New Year's Day.

My sister being so much younger than myself, her presence in my house made very little change in my habits. She came into my ways without any difficulty, so that I did not experience the least restraint from having to consider her. And I soon began to find her of considerable service among the poor and sick of my flock, the latter class being more numerous this winter on account of the greater severity of the weather.

I now began to note a change in the habits of Catherine Weir. As far as I remember, I had never up to this time seen her out of her own house, except in church, at which she had been a regular attendant for many weeks. Now, however, I began to meet her when and where I least expected—I do not say often, but so often as to make me believe she went wandering about frequently. It was always at night, however, and always in stormy weather. The marvel was, not that a sick woman could be there-for a sick woman may be able to do anything; but that she could do so more than once-that was the marvel. At the same time, I began to miss her from church.

Possibly my reader may wonder how I came to have the chance of meeting any one again and again at night and in stormy weather. I can relieve him from the difficulty. Odd as it will appear to some readers, I had naturally a predilection for rough weather. I think I enjoyed fighting with a storm in winter nearly as much as lying on the grass under a beech-tree in summer. Possibly this assertion may seem strange to one likewise who has remarked the ordinary peaceableness of my disposition. But he may have done me the justice to remark at the same time, that I have some considerable pleasure in fighting the devil, though none in fighting my fellow-man, even in the ordinary form of disputation in which it is not heart's blood, but soul's blood, that is so often shed. Indeed there are many controversies far more immoral, as to the manner in which they are conducted, than a brutal prize-fight. There is, however, a pleasure of its own in conflict; and I have always experienced a certain indescribable, though I believe not at all unusual exaltation, even in struggling with a well-set, thoroughly roused storm of wind and snow or rain. The sources of this by no means unusual delight, I will not stay to examine, indicating only that I believe the sources are deep. —I was now quite well, and had no reason to fear bad consequences from the indulgence of this surely innocent form of the love of strife.

But I find I must give another reason as well, if I would be thoroughly honest with my reader. The fact was, that as I had recovered strength, I had become more troubled and restless about Miss Oldcastle. I could not see how I was to make any progress towards her favour. There seemed a barrier as insurmountable as intangible between her and me. The will of one woman came between and parted us, and that will was as the magic line over which no effort of will or strength could enable the enchanted knight to make a single stride. And this consciousness of being fettered by insensible and infrangible bonds, this need of doing something with nothing tangible in the reach of the outstretched hand, so worked upon my mind, that it naturally sought relief, as often as the elemental strife arose, by mingling unconstrained with the tumult of the night. —Will my readers find it hard to believe that this disquietude of mind should gradually sink away as the hours of Saturday glided down into night, and the day of my best labour drew nigh? Or will they answer, "We believe it easily; for then you could at least see the lady, and that comforted you?" Whatever it was that quieted me, not the less have I to thank God for it.

All might have been so different. What a fearful thing would it have been for me to have found my mind so full of my own cares, that I was unable to do God's work and bear my neighbour's burden! But even then I would have cried to Him, and said, "I know Thee that Thou art NOT a hard master."

Now, however, that I have quite accounted, as I believe, by the peculiarity both of my disposition and circumstances, for unusual wanderings under conditions when most people consider themselves fortunate within doors, I must return to Catherine Weir, the eccentricity of whose late behaviour, being in the particulars discussed identical with that of mine, led to the necessity for the explanation of my habits given above.

One January afternoon, just as twilight was folding her gray cloak about her, and vanishing in the night, the wind blowing hard from the south-west, melting the snow under foot, and sorely disturbing the dignity of the one grand old cedar which stood before my study window, and now filled my room with the great sweeps of its moaning, I felt as if the elements were calling me, and rose to obey the summons. My sister was, by this time, so accustomed to my going out in all weathers, that she troubled me with no expostulation. My spirits began to rise the moment I was in the wind. Keen, and cold, and unsparing, it swept through the leafless branches around me, with a different hiss for every tree that bent, and swayed, and tossed in its torrent. I made my way to the gate and out upon the road, and then, turning to the right, away from the village, I sought a kind of common, open and treeless, the nearest approach to a moor that there was in the county, I believe, over which a wind like this would sweep unstayed by house, or shrub, or fence, the only shelter it afforded lying in the inequalities of its surface.

I had walked with my head bent low against the blast, for the better part of a mile, fighting for every step of the way, when, coming to a deep cut in the common, opening at right angles from the road, whence at some time or other a large quantity of sand had been carted, I turned into its defence to recover my breath, and listen to the noise of the wind in the fierce rush of its sea over the open channel of the common. And I remember I was thinking with myself: "If the air would only become faintly visible for a moment, what a sight it would be of waste grandeur with its thousands of billowing eddies, and self-involved, conflicting, and swallowing whirlpools from the sea-bottom of this common!" when, with my imagination resting on the fancied vision, I was startled by such a moan as seemed about to break into a storm of passionate cries, but was followed by the words:

"O God! I cannot bear it longer. Hast thou NO help for me?"

Instinctively almost I knew that Catherine Weir was beside me, though I could not see where she was. In a moment more, however, I thought I could distinguish through the darkness-imagination no doubt filling up the truth of its form —a figure crouching in such an attitude of abandoned despair as recalled one of Flaxman's outlines, the body bent forward over the drawn-up knees, and the face thus hidden even from the darkness. I could not help saying to myself, as I took a step or two towards her, "What is thy trouble to hers!"

I may here remark that I had come to the conclusion, from pondering over her case, that until a yet deeper and bitterer resentment than that which she bore to her father was removed, it would be of no use attacking the latter. For the former kept her in a state of hostility towards her whole race: with herself at war she had no gentle thoughts, no love for her kind; but ever

"She fed her wound with fresh-renewed bale"

from every hurt that she received from or imagined to be offered her by anything human. So I had resolved that the next time I had an opportunity of speaking to her, I would make an attempt to probe the evil to its root, though I had but little hope, I confess, of doing any good. And now when I heard her say, "Hast thou NO help for me?" I went near her with the words:

"God has, indeed, help for His own offspring. Has He not suffered that He might help? But you have not yet forgiven."

When I began to speak, she gave a slight start: she was far too miserable to be terrified at anything. Before I had finished, she stood erect on her feet, facing me with the whiteness of her face glimmering through the blackness of the night.

"I ask Him for peace," she said, "and He sends me more torment."

And I thought of Ahab when he said, "Hast thou found me, O mine enemy?"

"If we had what we asked for always, we should too often find it was not what we wanted, after all."

"You will not leave me alone," she said. "It is too bad."

Poor woman! It was well for her she could pray to God in her trouble; for she could scarcely endure a word from her fellow-man. She, despairing before God, was fierce as a tigress to her fellow-sinner who would stretch a hand to help her out of the mire, and set her beside him on the rock which he felt firm under his own feet.

"I will not leave you alone, Catherine," I said, feeling that I must at length assume another tone of speech with her who resisted gentleness. "Scorn my interference as you will," I said, "I have yet to give an account of you. And I have to fear lest my Master should require your blood at my hands. I did not follow you here, you may well believe me; but I have found you here, and I must speak."

All this time the wind was roaring overhead. But in the hollow was stillness, and I was so near her, that I could hear every word she said, although she spoke in a low compressed tone.

"Have you a right to persecute me," she said, "because I am unhappy?"

"I have a right, and, more than a right, I have a duty to aid your better self against your worse. You, I fear, are siding with your worse self."

"You judge me hard. I have had wrongs that—"

And here she stopped in a way that let me know she WOULD say no more.

"That you have had wrongs, and bitter wrongs, I do not for a moment doubt. And him who has done you most wrong, you will not forgive."

"No."

"No. Not even for the sake of Him who, hanging on the tree, after all the bitterness of blows and whipping, and derision, and rudest gestures and taunts, even when the faintness of death was upon Him, cried to His Father to forgive their cruelty. He asks you to forgive the man who wronged you, and you will not-not even for Him! Oh, Catherine, Catherine!"

"It is very easy to talk, Mr Walton," she returned with forced but cool scorn.

"Tell me, then," I said, "have YOU nothing to repent of? Have YOU done no wrong in this same miserable matter?"

"I do not understand you, sir," she said, freezingly, petulantly, not sure, perhaps, or unwilling to believe, that I meant what I did mean.

I was fully resolved to be plain with her now.

"Catherine Weir," I said, "did not God give you a house to keep fair and pure for Him? Did you keep it such?"

"He told me lies," she cried fiercely, with a cry that seemed to pierce through the storm over our heads, up towards the everlasting justice. "He lied, and I trusted. For his sake I sinned, and he threw me from him."

"You gave him what was not yours to give. What right had you to cast your pearl before a swine? But dare you say it was ALL FOR HIS SAKE you did it? Was it ALL self-denial? Was there no self-indulgence?"

She made a broken gesture of lifting her hands to her head, let them drop by her side, and said nothing.

"You knew you were doing wrong. You felt it even more than he did. For God made you with a more delicate sense of purity, with a shrinking from the temptation, with a womanly foreboding of disgrace, to help you to hold the cup of your honour steady, which yet you dropped on the ground. Do not seek refuge in the cant about a woman's weakness. The strength of the woman is as needful to her womanhood as the strength of the man is to his manhood; and a woman is just as strong as she will be. And now, instead of humbling yourself before your Father in heaven, whom you have wronged more even than your father on earth, you rage over your injuries and cherish hatred against him who wronged you. But I will go yet further, and show you, in God's name, that you wronged your seducer. For you were his keeper, as he was yours. What if he had found a noble-hearted girl who also trusted him entirely-just until she knew she ought not to listen to him a moment longer? who, when his love showed itself less than human, caring but for itself, rose in the royalty of her maidenhood, and looked him in the face? Would he not have been ashamed before her, and so before himself, seeing in the glass of her dignity his own contemptibleness? But instead of such a woman he found you, who let him do as he would. No redemption for him in you. And now he walks the earth the worse for you, defiled by your spoil, glorying in his poor victory over you, despising all women for your sake, unrepentant and proud, ruining others the easier that he has already ruined you."

"He does! he does!" she shrieked; "but I will have my revenge. I can and I will."

And, darting past me, she rushed out into the storm. I followed, and could just see that she took the way to the village. Her dim shape went down the wind before me into the darkness. I followed in the same direction, fast and faster, for the wind was behind me, and a vague fear which ever grew in my heart urged me to overtake her. What had I done? To what might I not have driven her? And although all I had said was true, and I had spoken from motives which, as far as I knew my own heart, I could not condemn, yet, as I sped after her, there came a reaction of feeling from the severity with which I had displayed her own case against her. "Ah! poor sister," I thought, "was it for me thus to reproach thee who had suffered already so fiercely? If the Spirit speaking in thy heart could not win thee, how should my words of hard accusation, true though they were, every one of them, rouse in thee anything but the wrath that springs from shame? Should I not have tried again, and yet again, to waken thy love; and then a sweet and healing shame, like that of her who bathed the Master's feet with her tears, would have bred fresh love, and no wrath."

But again I answered for myself, that my heart had not been the less tender towards her that I had tried to humble her, for it was that she might slip from under the net of her pride. Even when my tongue spoke the hardest things I could find, my heart was yearning over her. If I could but make her feel that she too had been wrong, would not the sense of common wrong between them help her to forgive? And with the first motion of willing pardon, would not a spring of tenderness, grief, and hope, burst from her poor old dried-up heart, and make it young and fresh once more! Thus I reasoned with myself as I followed her back through the darkness.

The wind fell a little as we came near the village, and the rain began to come down in torrents. There must have been a moon somewhere behind the clouds, for the darkness became less dense, and I began to fancy I could again see the dim shape which had rushed from me. I increased my speed, and became certain of it. Suddenly, her strength giving way, or her foot stumbling over something in the road, she fell to the earth with a cry.

I was beside her in a moment. She was insensible. I did what I could for her, and in a few minutes she began to come to herself.

"Where am I? Who is it?" she asked, listlessly.

When she found who I was, she made a great effort to rise, and succeeded.

"You must take my arm," I said, "and I will help you to the vicarage."

"I will go home," she answered.

"Lean on me now, at least; for you must get somewhere."

"What does it matter?" she said, in such a tone of despair, that it went to my very heart.

A wild half-cry, half-sob followed, and then she took my arm, and said nothing more. Nor did I trouble her with any words, except, when we readied the gate, to beg her to come into the vicarage instead of going home. But she would not listen to me, and so I took her home.

She pulled the key of the shop from her pocket. Her hand trembled so that I took it from her, and opened the door. A candle with a long snuff was flickering on the counter; and stretched out on the counter, with his head about a foot from the candle, lay little Gerard, fast asleep.

"Ah, little darling!" I said in my heart, "this is not much like painting the sky yet. But who knows?" And as I uttered the commonplace question in my mind, in my mind it was suddenly changed into the half of a great dim prophecy by the answer which arose to it there, for the answer was "God."

I lifted the little fellow in my arms. He had fallen asleep weeping, and his face was dirty, and streaked with the channels of his tears. Catherine had snuffed the candle, and now stood with it in her hand, waiting for me to go. But, without heeding her, I bore my child to the door that led to their dwelling. I had never been up those stairs before, and therefore knew nothing of the way. But without offering any opposition, his mother followed, and lighted me. What a sad face of suffering and strife it was upon which that dim light fell! She set the candle down upon the table of a small room at the top of the stairs, which might have been comfortable enough but that it was neglected and disordered; and now I saw that she did not even have her child to sleep with her, for his crib stood in a corner of this their sitting-room.

I sat down on a haircloth couch, and proceeded to undress little Gerard, trying as much as I could not to wake him. In this I was almost successful. Catherine stood staring at me without saying a word. She looked dazed, perhaps from the effects of her fall. But she brought me his nightgown notwithstanding. Just as I had finished putting it on, and was rising to lay him in his crib, he opened his eyes, and looked at me; then gave a hurried look round, as if for his mother; then threw his arms about my neck and kissed me. I laid him down and the same moment he was fast asleep. In the morning it would not be even a dream to him.

"Now," I thought, "you are safe for the night, poor fatherless child. Even your mother's hardness will not make you sad now. Perhaps the heavenly Father will send you loving dreams."

I turned to Catherine, and bade her good-night. She just put her hand in mine; but, instead of returning my leave-taking, said:

"Do not fancy you will get the better of me, Mr Walton, by being kind to that boy. I will have my revenge, and I know how. I am only waiting my time. When he is just going to drink, I will dash it from his hand. I will. At the altar I will."

Her eyes were flashing almost with madness, and she made fierce gestures with her arm. I saw that argument was useless.

"You loved him once, Catherine," I said. "Love him again. Love him better. Forgive him. Revenge is far worse than anything you have done yet."

"What do I care? Why should I care?"

And she laughed terribly.

I made haste to leave the room and the house; but I lingered for nearly an hour about the place before I could make up my mind to go home, so much was I afraid lest she should do something altogether insane.

But at length I saw the candle appear in the shop, which was some relief to my anxiety; and reflecting that her one consuming thought of revenge was some security for her conduct otherwise, I went home.

That night my own troubles seemed small to me, and I did not brood over them at all. My mind was filled with the idea of the sad misery which, rather than in which, that poor woman was; and I prayed for her as for a desolate human world whose sun had deserted the heavens, whose fair fields, rivers, and groves were hardening into the frost of death, and all their germs of hope becoming but portions of the lifeless mass. "If I am sorrowful," I said, "God lives none the less. And His will is better than mine, yea, is my hidden and perfected will. In Him is my life. His will be done. What, then, is my trouble compared to hers? I will not sink into it and be selfish."

In the morning my first business was to inquire after her. I found her in the shop, looking very ill, and obstinately reserved. Gerard sat in a corner, looking as far from happy as a child of his years could look. As I left the shop he crept out with me.

"Gerard, come back," cried his mother.

"I will not take him away," I said.

The boy looked up in my face, as if he wanted to whisper to me, and I stooped to listen.

"I dreamed last night," said the boy, "that a big angel with white wings came and took me out of my bed, and carried me high, high up-so high that I could not dream any more."

"We shall be carried up so high one day, Gerard, my boy, that we shall not want to dream any more. For we shall be carried up to God himself. Now go back to your mother."

He obeyed at once, and I went on through the village.

CHAPTER XXIII
THE DEVIL IN THE VICAR.

I wanted just to pass the gate, and look up the road towards Oldcastle Hall. I thought to see nothing but the empty road between the leafless trees, lying there like a dead stream that would not bear me on to the "sunny pleasure-dome with caves of ice" that lay beyond. But just as I reached the gate, Miss Oldcastle came out of the lodge, where I learned afterwards the woman that kept the gate was ill.

When she saw me she stopped, and I entered hurriedly, and addressed her. But I could say nothing better than the merest commonplaces. For her old manner, which I had almost forgotten, a certain coldness shadowed with haughtiness, whose influence I had strongly felt when I began to make her acquaintance, had returned. I cannot make my reader understand how this could be blended with the sweetness in her face and the gentleness of her manners; but there the opposites were, and I could feel them both. There was likewise a certain drawing of herself away from me, which checked the smallest advance on my part; so that —I wonder at it now, but so it was-after a few words of very ordinary conversation, I bade her good morning and went away, feeling like "a man forbid" —as if I had done her some wrong, and she had chidden me for it. What a stone lay in my breast! I could hardly breathe for it. What could have caused her to change her manner towards me? I had made no advance; I could not have offended her. Yet there she glided up the road, and here stood I, outside the gate. That road was now a flowing river that bore from me the treasure of the earth, while my boat was spell-bound, and could not follow. I would run after her, fall at her feet, and intreat to know wherein I had offended her. But there I stood enchanted, and there she floated away between the trees; till at length she turned the slow sweep, and I, breathing deep as she vanished from my sight, turned likewise, and walked back the dreary way to the village. And now I knew that I had never been miserable in my life before. And I knew, too, that I had never loved her as I loved her now.

But, as I had for the last ten years of my life been striving to be a right will, with a thousand failures and forgetfulnesses every one of those years, while yet the desire grew stronger as hope recovered from every failure, I would now try to do my work as if nothing had happened to incapacitate me for it. So I went on to fulfil the plan with which I had left home, including, as it did, a visit to Thomas Weir, whom I had not seen in his own shop since he had ordered me out of it. This, as far as I was concerned, was more accidental than intentional. I had, indeed, abstained from going to him for a while, in order to give him time TO COME ROUND; but then circumstances which I have recorded intervened to prevent me; so that as yet no advance had been made on my part any more than on his towards a reconciliation; which, however, could have been such only on one side, for I had not been in the least offended by the way he had behaved to me, and needed no reconciliation. To tell the truth, I was pleased to find that my words had had force enough with him to rouse his wrath. Anything rather than indifference! That the heart of the honest man would in the end right me, I could not doubt; in the meantime I would see whether a friendly call might not improve the state of affairs. Till he yielded to the voice within him, however, I could not expect that our relation to each other would be quite restored. As long as he resisted his conscience, and knew that I sided with his conscience, it was impossible he should regard me with peaceful eyes, however much he might desire to be friendly with me.

I found him busy, as usual, for he was one of the most diligent men I have ever known. But his face was gloomy, and I thought or fancied that the old scorn had begun once more to usurp the expression of it. Young Tom was not in the shop.

"It is a long time since I saw you, now, Thomas."

"I can hardly wonder at that," he returned, as if he were trying to do me justice; but his eyes dropped, and he resumed his work, and said no more. I thought it better to make no reference to the past even by assuring him that it was not from resentment that I had been a stranger.

"How is Tom?" I asked.

"Well enough," he returned. Then, with a smile of peevishness not unmingled with contempt, he added: "He's getting too uppish for me. I don't think the Latin agrees with him."

I could not help suspecting at once how the matter stood-namely, that the father, unhappy in his conduct to his daughter, and unable to make up his mind to do right with regard to her, had been behaving captiously and unjustly to his son, and so had rendered himself more miserable than ever.

"Perhaps he finds it too much for him without me," I said, evasively; "but I called to-day partly to inform him that I am quite ready now to recommence our readings together; after which I hope you will find the Latin agree with him better."

"I wish you would let him alone, sir—I mean, take no more trouble about him. You see I can't do as you want me; I wasn't made to go another man's way; and so it's very hard-more than I can bear-to be under so much obligation to you."

"But you mistake me altogether, Thomas. It is for the lad's own sake that I want to go on reading with him. And you won't interfere between him and any use I can be of to him. I assure you, to have you go my way instead of your own is the last thing I could wish, though I confess I do wish very much that you would choose the right way for your own way."

He made me no answer, but maintained a sullen silence.

"Thomas," I said at length, "I had thought you were breaking every bond of Satan that withheld you from entering into the kingdom of heaven; but I fear he has strengthened his bands and holds you now as much a captive as ever. So it is not even your own way you are walking in, but his."

"It's no use your trying to frighten me. I don't believe in the devil."

"It is God I want you to believe in. And I am not going to dispute with you now about whether there is a devil or not. In a matter of life and death we have no time for settling every disputed point."

"Life or death! What do you mean?"

"I mean that whether you believe there is a devil or not, you KNOW there is an evil power in your mind dragging you down. I am not speaking in generals; I mean NOW, and you know as to what I mean it. And if you yield to it, that evil power, whatever may be your theory about it, will drag you down to death. It is a matter of life or death, I repeat, not of theory about the devil."

"Well, I always did say, that if you once give a priest an inch he'll take an ell; and I am sorry I forgot it for once."

Having said this, he shut up his mouth in a manner that indicated plainly enough he would not open it again for some time. This, more than his speech, irritated me, and with a mere "good morning," I walked out of the shop.

No sooner was I in the open air than I knew that I too, I as well as poor Thomas Weir, was under a spell; knew that I had gone to him before I had recovered sufficiently from the mingled disappointment and mortification of my interview with Miss Oldcastle; that while I spoke to him I was not speaking with a whole heart; that I had been discharging a duty as if I had been discharging a musket; that, although I had spoken the truth, I had spoken it ungraciously and selfishly.

I could not bear it. I turned instantly and went back into the shop.

"Thomas, my friend," I said, holding out my hand, "I beg your pardon. I was wrong. I spoke to you as I ought not. I was troubled in my own mind, and that made me lose my temper and be rude to you, who are far more troubled than I am. Forgive me!"

He did not take my hand at first, but stared at me as if, not comprehending me, he supposed that I was backing up what I had said last with more of the same sort. But by the time I had finished he saw what I meant; his countenance altered and looked as if the evil spirit were about to depart from him; he held out his hand, gave mine a great grasp, dropped his head, went on with his work, and said never a word.

I went out of the shop once more, but in a greatly altered mood.

On the way home, I tried to find out how it was that I had that morning failed so signally. I had little virtue in keeping my temper, because it was naturally very even; therefore I had the more shame in losing it. I had borne all my uneasiness about Miss Oldcastle without, as far as I knew, transgressing in this fashion till this very morning. Were great sorrows less hurtful to the temper than small disappointments? Yes, surely. But Shakespeare represents Brutus, after hearing of the sudden death of his wife, as losing his temper with Cassius to a degree that bewildered the latter, who said he did not know that Brutus could have been so angry. Is this consistent with the character of the stately-minded Brutus, or with the dignity of sorrow? It is. For the loss of his wife alone would have made him only less irritable; but the whole weight of an army, with its distracting cares and conflicting interests, pressed upon him; and the battle of an empire was to be fought at daybreak, so that he could not be alone with his grief. Between the silence of death in his mind, and the roar of life in his brain, he became irritable.

Looking yet deeper into it, I found that till this morning I had experienced no personal mortification with respect to Miss Oldcastle. It was not the mere disappointment of having no more talk with her, for the sight of her was a blessing I had not in the least expected, that had worked upon me, but the fact that she had repelled or seemed to repel me. And thus I found that self was at the root of the wrong I had done to one over whose mental condition, especially while I was telling him the unwelcome truth, I ought to have been as tender as a mother over her wounded child. I could not say that it was wrong to feel disappointed or even mortified; but something was wrong when one whose especial business it was to serve his people in the name of Him who was full of grace and truth, made them suffer because of his own inward pain.

No sooner had I settled this in my mind than my trouble returned with a sudden pang. Had I actually seen her that morning, and spoken to her, and left her with a pain in my heart? What if that face of hers was doomed ever to bring with it such a pain-to be ever to me no more than a lovely vision radiating grief? If so, I would endure in silence and as patiently as I could, trying to make up for the lack of brightness in my own fate by causing more brightness in the fate of others. I would at least keep on trying to do my work.

That moment I felt a little hand poke itself into mine. I looked down, and there was Gerard Weir looking up in my face. I found myself in the midst of the children coming out of school, for it was Saturday, and a half-holiday. He smiled in my face, and I hope I smiled in his; and so, hand in hand, we went on to the vicarage, where I gave him up to my sister. But I cannot convey to my reader any notion of the quietness that entered my heart with the grasp of that childish hand. I think it was the faith of the boy in me that comforted me, but I could not help thinking of the words of our Lord about receiving a child in His name, and so receiving Him. By the time we reached the vicarage my heart was very quiet. As the little child held by my hand, so I seemed to be holding by God's hand. And a sense of heart-security, as well as soul-safety, awoke in me; and I said to myself,—Surely He will take care of my heart as well as of my mind and my conscience. For one blessed moment I seemed to be at the very centre of things, looking out quietly upon my own troubled emotions as upon something outside of me-apart from me, even as one from the firm rock may look abroad upon the vexed sea. And I thought I then knew something of what the apostle meant when he said, "Your life is hid with Christ in God." I knew that there was a deeper self than that which was thus troubled.

I had not had my usual ramble this morning, and was otherwise ill prepared for the Sunday. So I went early into the church; but finding that the sexton's wife had not yet finished lighting the stove, I sat down by my own fire in the vestry.

Suppose I am sitting there now while I say one word for our congregations in winter. I was very particular in having the church well warmed before Sunday. I think some parsons must neglect seeing after this matter on principle, because warmth may make a weary creature go to sleep here and there about the place: as if any healing doctrine could enter the soul while it is on the rack of the frost. The clergy should see-for it is their business-that their people have no occasion to think of their bodies at all while they are in church. They have enough ado to think of the truth. When our Lord was feeding even their bodies, He made them all sit down on the grass. It is worth noticing that there was much grass in the place—a rare thing I should think in those countries-and therefore, perhaps, it was chosen by Him for their comfort in feeding their souls and bodies both. If I may judge from experiences of my own, one of the reasons why some churches are of all places the least likely for anything good to be found in, is, that they are as wretchedly cold to the body as they are to the soul-too cold every way for anything to grow in them. Edelweiss, "Noble-white"—as they call a plant growing under the snow on some of the Alps-could not survive the winter in such churches. There is small welcome in a cold house. And the clergyman, who is the steward, should look to it. It is for him to give his Master's friends a welcome to his Master's house-for the welcome of a servant is precious, and now-a-days very rare.

And now Mrs Stone must have finished. I go into the old church which looks as if it were quietly waiting for its people. No. She has not done yet. Never mind. —How full of meaning the vaulted roof looks! as if, having gathered a soul of its own out of the generations that have worshipped here for so long, it had feeling enough to grow hungry for a psalm before the end of the week.

Some such half-foolish fancy was now passing through my tranquillized mind or rather heart-for the mind would have rejected it at once-when to my-what shall I call it? —not amazement, for the delight was too strong for amazement-the old organ woke up and began to think aloud. As if it had been brooding over it all the week in the wonderful convolutions of its wooden brain, it began to sigh out the Agnus Dei of Mozart's twelfth mass upon the air of the still church, which lay swept and garnished for the Sunday. —How could it be? I know now; and I guessed then; and my guess was right; and my reader must be content to guess too. I took no step to verify my conjecture, for I felt that I was upon my honour, but sat in one of the pews and listened, till the old organ sobbed itself into silence. Then I heard the steps of the sexton's wife vanish from the church, heard her lock the door, and knew that I was alone in the ancient pile, with the twilight growing thick about me, and felt like Sir Galahad, when, after the "rolling organ-harmony," he heard "wings flutter, voices hover clear." In a moment the mood changed; and I was sorry, not that the dear organ was dead for the night, but actually felt gently-mournful that the wonderful old thing never had and never could have a conscious life of its own. So strangely does the passion-which I had not invented, reader, whoever thou art that thinkest love and a church do not well harmonize-so strangely, I say, full to overflowing of its own vitality, does it radiate life, that it would even of its own superabundance quicken into blessed consciousness the inanimate objects around it, thinking what they would feel had they a consciousness correspondent to their form, were their faculties moved from within themselves instead of from the will and operation of humanity.

I lingered on long in the dark church, as my reader knows I had done often before. Nor did I move from the seat I had first taken till I left the sacred building. And there I made my sermon for the next morning. And herewith I impart it to my reader. But he need not be afraid of another such as I have already given him, for I impart it only in its original germ, its concentrated essence of sermon-these four verses:

> Had I the grace to win the grace
>   Of some old man complete in lore,
> My face would worship at his face,
>   Like childhood seated on the floor.
> Had I the grace to win the grace
>
>   Of childhood, loving shy, apart,
> The child should find a nearer place,
>   And teach me resting on my heart.
> Had I the grace to win the grace
>
>   Of maiden living all above,

>   My soul would trample down the base,
>   That she might have a man to love.
>   A grace I have no grace to win
>
>   Knocks now at my half-open door:
>   Ah, Lord of glory, come thou in,
>   Thy grace divine is all and more.

This was what I made for myself. I told my people that God had created all our worships, reverences, tendernesses, loves. That they had come out of His heart, and He had made them in us because they were in Him first. That otherwise He would not have cared to make them. That all that we could imagine of the wise, the lovely, the beautiful, was in Him, only infinitely more of them than we could not merely imagine, but understand, even if He did all He could to explain them to us, to make us understand them. That in Him was all the wise teaching of the best man ever known in the world and more; all the grace and gentleness and truth of the best child and more; all the tenderness and devotion of the truest type of womankind and more; for there is a love that passeth the love of woman, not the love of Jonathan to David, though David said so: but the love of God to the men and women whom He has made. Therefore, we must be all God's; and all our aspirations, all our worships, all our honours, all our loves, must centre in Him, the Best.

CHAPTER XXIV
AN ANGEL UNAWARES.

Feeling rather more than the usual reaction so well-known to clergymen after the concentrated duties of the Sunday, I resolved on Monday to have the long country walk I had been disappointed of on the Saturday previous. It was such a day as it seems impossible to describe except in negatives. It was not stormy, it was not rainy, it was not sunshiny, it was not snowy, it was not frosty, it was not foggy, it was not clear, it was nothing but cloudy and quiet and cold and generally ungenial, with just a puff of wind now and then to give an assertion to its ungeniality. I should not in the least have cared to tell what sort the day was, had it not been an exact representation of my own mind. It was not the day that made me such as itself. The weather could always easily influence the surface of my mind, my external mood, but it could never go much further. The smallest pleasure would break through the conditions that merely came of such a day. But this morning my whole mind and heart seemed like the day. The summer was thousands of miles off on the other side of the globe. Ethelwyn, up at the old house there across the river, seemed millions of miles away. The summer MIGHT come back; she never would come nearer: it was absurd to expect it. For in such moods stupidity constantly arrogates to itself the qualities and claims of insight. In fact, it passes itself off for common sense, making the most dreary ever appear the most reasonable. In such moods a man might almost be persuaded that it was ridiculous to expect any such poetic absurdity as the summer, with its diamond mornings and its opal evenings, ever to come again; nay, to think that it ever had had any existence except in the fancies of the human heart-one of its castles in the air. The whole of life seemed faint and foggy, with no red in it anywhere; and when I glanced at my present relations in Marshmallows, I could not help finding several circumstances to give some appearance of justice to this appearance of things. I seemed to myself to have done no good. I had driven Catherine Weir to the verge of suicide, while at the same time I could not restrain her from the contemplation of some dire revenge. I had lost the man upon whom I had most reckoned as a seal of my ministry, namely, Thomas Weir. True there was Old Rogers; but Old Rogers was just as good before I found him. I could not dream of having made him any better. And so I went on brooding over all the disappointing portions of my labour, all the time thinking about myself, instead of God and the work that lay for me to do in the days to come.

"Nobody," I said, "but Old Rogers understands me. Nobody would care, as far as my teaching goes, if another man took my place from next Sunday forward. And for Miss Oldcastle, her playing the Agnus Dei on Saturday afternoon, even if she intended that I should hear it, could only indicate at most that she knew how she had behaved to me in the morning, and thought she had gone too far and been unkind, or perhaps was afraid lest she should be accountable for any failure I might make in my Sunday duties, and therefore felt bound to do something to restore my equanimity."

Choosing, though without consciously intending to do so, the dreariest path to be found, I wandered up the side of the slow black river, with the sentinel pollards looking at themselves in its gloomy mirror, just as I was looking at myself in the mirror of my circumstances. They leaned in all directions, irregular as the headstones in an ancient churchyard. In the summer they looked like explosions of green leaves at the best; now they looked like the burnt-out cases of the summer's fireworks. How different, too, was the river from the time when a whole fleet of shining white lilies lay anchored among their own broad green leaves upon its clear waters, filled with sunlight in every pore, as they themselves would fill the pores of a million-caverned sponge! But I could not even recall the past summer as beautiful. I seemed to care for nothing. The first miserable afternoon at Marshmallows looked now as if it had been the whole of my coming relation to the place seen through a reversed telescope. And here I was IN it now.

The walk along the side was tolerably dry, although the river was bank-full. But when I came to the bridge I wanted to cross —a wooden one —I found that the approach to it had been partly undermined and carried away, for here the river had overflowed its banks in one of the late storms; and all about the place was still very wet and swampy. I could therefore get no farther in my gloomy walk, and so turned back upon my steps. Scarcely had I done so, when I saw a man coming hastily towards me from far upon the straight line of the river walk. I could not mistake him at any distance. It was Old Rogers. I felt both ashamed and comforted when I recognized him.

"Well, Old Rogers," I said, as soon as he came within hail, trying to speak cheerfully, "you cannot get much farther this way-without wading a bit, at least."

"I don't want to go no farther now, sir. I came to find you."

"Nothing amiss, I hope?"

"Nothing as I knows on, sir. I only wanted to have a little chat with you. I told master I wanted to leave for an hour or so. He allus lets me do just as I like."

"But how did you know where to find me?"

"I saw you come this way. You passed me right on the bridge, and didn't see me, sir. So says I to myself, 'Old Rogers, summat's amiss wi' parson to-day. He never went by me like that afore. This won't do. You just go and see.' So I went home and told master, and here I be, sir. And I hope you're noways offended with the liberty of me."

"Did I really pass you on the bridge?" I said, unable to understand it.

"That you did, sir. I knowed parson must be a goodish bit in his own in'ards afore he would do that."

"I needn't tell you I didn't see you, Old Rogers."

"I could tell you that, sir. I hope there's nothing gone main wrong, sir. Miss is well, sir, I hope?"

"Quite well, I thank you. No, my dear fellow, nothing's gone main wrong, as you say. Some of my running tackle got jammed a bit, that's all. I'm a little out of spirits, I believe."

"Well, sir, don't you be afeard I'm going to be troublesome. Don't think I want to get aboard your ship, except you fling me a rope. There's a many things you mun ha' to think about that an ignorant man like me couldn't take up if you was to let 'em drop. And being a gentleman, I do believe, makes the matter worse betuxt us. And there's many a thing that no man can go talkin' about to any but only the Lord himself. Still you can't help us poor folks seeing when there's summat amiss, and we can't help havin' our own thoughts any more than the sailor's jackdaw that couldn't speak. And sometimes we may be nearer the mark than you would suppose, for God has made us all of one blood, you know."

"What ARE you driving at, Old Rogers?" I said with a smile, which was none the less true that I suspected he had read some of the worst trouble of my heart. For why should I mind an honourable man like him knowing what oppressed me, though, as things went, I certainly should not, as he said, choose to tell it to any but one?

"I don't want to say what I was driving at, if it was anything but this-that I want to put to the clumsy hand of a rough old tar, with a heart as soft as the pitch that makes his hand hard-to trim your sails a bit, sir, and help you to lie a point closer to the wind. You're not just close-hauled, sir."

"Say on, Old Rogers. I understand you, and I will listen with all my heart, for you have a good right to speak."

And Old Rogers spoke thus: —

"Oncet upon a time, I made a voyage in a merchant barque. We were becalmed in the South Seas. And weary work it wur, a doin' of nothin' from day to day. But when the water began to come up thick from the bottom of the water-casks, it was wearier a deal. Then a thick fog came on, as white as snow a'most, and we couldn't see more than a few yards ahead or on any side of us. But the fog didn't keep the heat off; it only made it worse, and the water was fast going done. The short allowance grew shorter and shorter, and the men, some of them, were half-mad with thirst, and began to look bad at one another. I kept up my heart by looking ahead inside me. For days and days the fog hung about us as if the air had been made o' flocks o' wool. The captain took to his berth, and several of the crew to their hammocks, for it was just as hot on deck as anywhere else. The mate lay on a sparesail on the quarter-deck, groaning. I had a strong suspicion that the schooner was drifting, and hove the lead again and again, but could find no bottom. Some of the men got hold of the spirits, and THAT didn't quench their thirst. It drove them clean mad. I had to knock one of them down myself with a capstan bar, for he ran at the mate with his knife. At last I began to lose all hope. And still I was sure the schooner was slowly drifting. My head was like to burst, and my tongue was like a lump of holystone in my mouth. Well, one morning, I had just, as I thought, lain down on the deck to breathe my last, hoping I should die before I went quite mad with thirst, when all at once the fog lifted, like the foot of a sail. I sprung to my feet. There was the blue sky overhead; but the terrible burning sun was there. A moment more and a light air blew on my cheek, and, turning my face to it as if it had been the very breath of God, there was an island within half a mile, and I saw the shine of water on the face of a rock on the shore. I cried out, 'Land on the weather-quarter! Water in sight!' In a moment more a boat was lowered, and in a few minutes the boat's crew, of which I was one, were lying, clothes and all, in a little stream that came down from the hills above. —There, Mr Walton! that's what I wanted to say to you."

This is as near the story of my old friend as my limited knowledge of sea affairs allows me to report it.

"I understand you quite, Old Rogers, and I thank you heartily," I said.

"No doubt," resumed he, "King Solomon was quite right, as he always was, I suppose, in what he SAID, for his wisdom mun ha' laid mostly in the tongue-right, I say, when he said, 'Boast not thyself of to-morrow; for thou knowest not what a day may bring forth;' but I can't help thinking there's another side to it. I think it would be as good advice to a man on the other tack, whose boasting lay far to windward, and he close on a lee-shore wi' breakers-it wouldn't be amiss to say to him, 'Don't strike your colours to the morrow; for thou knowest not what a day may bring forth.' There's just as many good days as bad ones; as much fair weather as foul in the days to come. And if a man keeps up heart, he's all the better for that, and none the worse when the evil day does come. But, God forgive me! I'm talking like a heathen. As if there was any chance about what the days would bring forth. No, my lad," said the old sailor, assuming the dignity of his superior years under the inspiration of the truth, "boast nor trust nor hope in the morrow. Boast and trust and hope in God, for thou shalt yet praise Him, who is the health of thy countenance and thy God."

I could but hold out my hand. I had nothing to say. For he had spoken to me as an angel of God.

The old man was silent for some moments: his emotion needed time to still itself again. Nor did he return to the subject. He held out his hand once more, saying—

"Good day, sir. I must go back to my work."

"I will go back with you," I returned.

And so we walked back side by side to the village, but not a word did we speak the one to the other, till we shook hands and parted upon the bridge, where we had first met. Old Rogers went to his work, and I lingered upon the bridge. I leaned upon the low parapet, and looked up the stream as far as the mists creeping about the banks, and hovering in thinnest veils over the surface of the water, would permit. Then I turned and looked down the river crawling on to the sweep it made out of sight just where Mr Brownrigg's farm began to come down to its banks. Then I looked to the left, and there stood my old church, as quiet in the dreary day, though not so bright, as in the sunshine: even the graves themselves must look yet more "solemn sad" in a wintry day like this, than they look when the sunlight that infolds them proclaims that God is not the God of the dead but of the living. One of the great battles that we have to fight in this world-for twenty great battles have to be fought all at once and in one-is the battle with appearances. I turned me to the right, and there once more I saw, as on that first afternoon, the weathercock that watched the winds over the stables at Oldcastle Hall. It had caught just one glimpse of the sun through some rent in the vapours, and flung it across to me, ere it vanished again amid the general dinginess of the hour.

CHAPTER XXV
TWO PARISHIONERS.

I HAVE said, near the beginning of my story, that my parish was a large one: how is it that I have mentioned but one of the great families in it, and have indeed confined my recollections entirely to the village and its immediate neighbourhood? Will my reader have patience while I explain this to him a little? First, as he may have observed, my personal attraction is towards the poor rather than the rich. I was made so. I can generally get nearer the poor than the rich. But I say GENERALLY, for I have known a few rich people quite as much to my mind as the best of the poor. Thereupon, of course, their education would give them the advantage with me in the possibilities of communion. But when the heart is right, and there is a good stock of common sense as well,—a gift predominant, as far as I am aware, in no one class over another, education will turn the scale very gently with me. And then when I reflect that some of these poor people would have made nobler ladies and gentlemen than all but two or three I know, if they had only had the opportunity, there is a reaction towards the poor, something like a feeling of favour because they have not had fair play—a feeling soon modified, though not altered, by the reflection that they are such because God who loves them better than we do, has so ordered their lot, and by the recollection that not only was our Lord himself poor, but He said the poor were blessed. And let me just say in passing that I not only believe it because He said it, but I believe it because I see that it is so. I think sometimes that the world must have been especially created for the poor, and that particular allowances will be made for the rich because they are born into such disadvantages, and with their wickednesses and their miseries, their love of spiritual dirt and meanness, subserve the highest growth and emancipation of the poor, that they may inherit both the earth and the kingdom of heaven.

But I have been once more wandering from my subject.

Thus it was that the people in the village lying close to my door attracted most of my attention at first; of which attention those more immediately associated with the village, as, for instance, the inhabitants of the Hall, came in for a share, although they did not belong to the same class.

Again, the houses of most of the gentlefolk lay considerably apart from the church and from each other. Many of them went elsewhere to church, and I did not feel bound to visit those, for I had enough to occupy me without, and had little chance of getting a hold of them to do them good. Still there were one or two families which I would have visited oftener, I confess, had I been more interested in them, or had I had a horse. Therefore, I ought to have bought a horse sooner than I did. Before this winter was over, however, I did buy one, partly to please Dr Duncan, who urged me to it for the sake of my health, partly because I could then do my duty better, and partly, I confess, from having been very fond of an old mare of my father's, when I was a boy, living, after my mother's death, at a farm of his in B—shire. Happening to come across a gray mare very much like her, I bought her at once.

I think it was the very day after the events recorded in my last chapter that I mounted her to pay a visit to two rich maiden ladies, whose carriage stopped at the Lych-gate most Sundays when the weather was favourable, but whom I had called upon only once since I came to the parish. I should not have thought this visit worth mentioning, except for the conversation I had with them, during which a hint or two were dropped which had an influence in colouring my thoughts for some time after.

I was shown with much ceremony by a butler, as old apparently as his livery of yellow and green, into the presence of the two ladies, one of whom sat in state reading a volume of the Spectator. She was very tall, and as square as the straight long-backed chair upon which she sat. A fat asthmatic poodle lay at her feet upon the hearth-rug. The other, a little lively gray-haired creature, who looked like a most ancient girl whom no power of gathering years would ever make old, was standing upon a high chair, making love to a demoniacal-looking cockatoo in a gilded cage. As I entered the room, the latter all but jumped from her perch with a merry though wavering laugh, and advanced to meet me.

"Jonathan, bring the cake and wine," she cried to the retreating servant.

The former rose with a solemn stiff-backedness, which was more amusing than dignified, and extended her hand as I approached her, without moving from her place.

"We were afraid, Mr Walton," said the little lady, "that you had forgotten we were parishioners of yours."

"That I could hardly do," I answered, "seeing you are such regular attendants at church. But I confess I have given you ground for your rebuke, Miss Crowther. I bought a horse, however, the other day, and this is the first use I have put him to."

"We're charmed to see you. It is very good of you not to forget such uninteresting girls as we are."

"You forget, Jemima," interposed her sister, in a feminine bass, "that time is always on the wing. I should have thought we were both decidedly middle-aged, though you are the elder by I will not say how many years."

"All but ten years, Hester. I remember rocking you in your cradle scores of times. But somehow, Mr Walton, I can't help feeling as if she were my elder sister. She is so learned, you see; and I don't read anything but the newspapers."

"And your Bible, Jemima. Do yourself justice."

"That's a matter of course, sister. But this is not the way to entertain Mr Walton."

"The gentlemen used to entertain the ladies when I was young, Jemima. I do not know how it may have been when you were."

"Much the same, I believe, sister. But if you look at Mr Walton, I think you will see that he is pretty much entertained as it is."

"I agree with Miss Hester," I said. "It is the duty of gentlemen to entertain ladies. But it is so much the kinder of ladies when they surpass their duty, and condescend to entertain gentlemen."

"What can surpass duty, Mr Walton? I confess I do not agree with your doctrines upon that point."

"I do not quite understand you, Miss Hester," I returned.

"Why, Mr Walton—I hope you will not think me rude, but it always seems to me-and it has given me much pain, when I consider that your congregation is chiefly composed of the lower classes, who may be greatly injured by such a style of preaching. I must say I think so, Mr Walton. Only perhaps you are one of those who think a lady's opinion on such matters is worth nothing."

"On the contrary, I respect an opinion just as far as the lady or gentleman who holds it seems to me qualified to have formed it first. But you have not yet told me what you think so objectionable in my preaching."

"You always speak as if faith in Christ was something greater than duty. Now I think duty the first thing."

"I quite agree with you, Miss Crowther. For how can I, or any clergyman, urge a man to that which is not his duty? But tell me, is not faith in Christ a duty? Where you have mistaken me is, that you think I speak of faith as higher than duty, when indeed I speak of faith as higher than any OTHER duty. It is the highest duty of man. I do not say the duty he always sees clearest, or even sees at all. But the fact is, that when that which is a duty becomes the highest delight of a man, the joy of his very being, he no more thinks or needs to think about it as a duty. What would you think of the love of a son who, when an appeal was made to his affections, should say, 'Oh yes, I love my mother dearly: it is my duty, of course?'"

"That sounds very plausible, Mr Walton; but still I cannot help feeling that you preach faith and not works. I do not say that you are not to preach faith, of course; but you know faith without works is dead."

"Now, really, Hester," interposed Miss Jemima, "I cannot think how it is, but, for my part, I should have said that Mr Walton was constantly preaching works. He's always telling you to do something or other. I know I always come out of the church with something on my mind; and I've got to work it off somehow before I'm comfortable."

And here Miss Jemima got up on the chair again, and began to flirt with the cockatoo once more, but only in silent signs.

I cannot quite recall how this part of the conversation drew to a close. But I will tell a fact or two about the sisters which may possibly explain how it was that they took up such different notions of my preaching. The elder scarce left the house, but spent almost the whole of her time in reading small dingy books of eighteenth century literature. She believed in no other; thought Shakespeare sentimental where he was not low, and Bacon pompous; Addison thoroughly respectable and gentlemanly. Pope was the great English poet, incomparably before Milton. The "Essay on Man" contained the deepest wisdom; the "Rape of the Lock" the most graceful imagination to be found in the language. The "Vicar of Wakefield" was pretty, but foolish; while in philosophy, Paley was perfect, especially in his notion of happiness, which she had heard objected to, and therefore warmly defended. Somehow or other, respectability-in position, in morals, in religion, in conduct-was everything. The consequence was that her very nature was old-fashioned, and had nothing in it of that lasting youth which is the birthright-so often despised-of every immortal being. But I have already said more about her than her place in my story justifies.

Miss Crowther, on the contrary, whose eccentricities did not lie on the side of respectability, had gone on shocking the stiff proprieties of her younger sister till she could be shocked no more, and gave in as to the hopelessness of fate. She had had a severe disappointment in youth, had not only survived it, but saved her heart alive out of it, losing only, as far as appeared to the eyes of her neighbours at least, any remnant of selfish care about herself; and she now spent the love which had before been concentrated upon one object, upon every living thing that came near her, even to her sister's sole favourite, the wheezing poodle. She was very odd, it must be confessed, with her gray hair, her clear gray eye with wrinkled eyelids, her light step, her laugh at once girlish and cracked; darting in and out of the cottages, scolding this matron with a lurking smile in every tone, hugging that baby, boxing the ears of the other little tyrant, passing this one's rent, and threatening that other with awful vengeances, but it was a very lovely oddity. Their property was not large, and she knew every living thing on the place down to the dogs and pigs. And Miss Jemima, as the people always called her, transferring the MISS CROWTHER of primogeniture to the younger, who kept, like King Henry IV., —

> "Her presence, like a robe pontifical,
> Ne'er seen but wonder'd at,"

was the actual queen of the neighbourhood; for, though she was the very soul of kindness, she was determined to have her own way, and had it.

Although I did not know all this at the time, such were the two ladies who held these different opinions about my preaching; the one who did nothing but read Messrs Addison, Pope, Paley, and Co., considering that I neglected the doctrine of works as the seal of faith, and the one who was busy helping her neighbours from morning to night, finding little in my preaching, except incentive to benevolence.

The next point where my recollection can take up the conversation, is where Miss Hester made the following further criticism on my pulpit labours.

"You are too anxious to explain everything, Mr Walton."

I pause in my recording, to do my critic the justice of remarking that what she said looks worse on paper than it sounded from her lips; for she was a gentlewoman, and the tone has much to do with the impression made by the intellectual contents of all speech.

"Where can be the use of trying to make uneducated people see the grounds of everything?" she said. "It is enough that this or that is in the Bible."

"Yes; but there is just the point. What is in the Bible? Is it this or that?"

"You are their spiritual instructor: tell them what is in the Bible."

"But you have just been objecting to my mode of representing what is in the Bible."

"It will be so much the worse, if you add argument to convince them of what is incorrect."

"I doubt that. Falsehood will expose itself the sooner that honest argument is used to support it."

"You cannot expect them to judge of what you tell them."

"The Bible urges upon us to search and understand."

"I grant that for those whose business it is, like yourself."

"Do you think, then, that the Church consists of a few privileged to understand, and a great many who cannot understand, and therefore need not be taught?"

"I said you had to teach them."

"But to teach is to make people understand."

"I don't think so. If you come to that, how much can the wisest of us understand? You remember what Pope says,—

> 'Superior beings, when of late they saw
> A mortal man unfold all Nature's law,
> Admired such wisdom in an earthly shape,
> And show'd a Newton as we show an ape'?"

"I do not know the passage. Pope is not my Bible. I should call such superior beings very inferior beings indeed."

"Do you call the angels inferior beings?"

"Such angels, certainly."

"He means the good angels, of course."

"And I say the good angels could never behave like that, for contempt is one of the lowest spiritual conditions in which any being can place himself. Our Lord says, 'Take heed that ye despise not one of these little ones, for their angels do always behold the face of my Father, who is in heaven.'"

"Now will you even say that you understand that passage?"

"Practically, well enough; just as the poorest man of my congregation may understand it. I am not to despise one of the little ones. Pope represents the angels as despising a Newton even."

"And you despise Pope."

"I hope not. I say he was full of despising, and therefore, if for no other reason, a small man."

"Surely you do not jest at his bodily infirmities?"

"I had forgotten them quite."

"In every other sense he was a great man."

"I cannot allow it. He was intellectually a great man, but morally a small man."

"Such refinements are not easily followed."

"I will undertake to make the poorest woman in my congregation understand that."

"Why don't you try your friend Mrs Oldcastle, then? It might do her a little good," said Miss Hester, now becoming, I thought, a little spiteful at hearing her favourite treated so unceremoniously. I found afterwards that there was some kindness in it, however.

"I should have very little influence with Mrs Oldcastle if I were to make the attempt. But I am not called upon to address my flock individually upon every point of character."

"I thought she was an intimate friend of yours."

"Quite the contrary. We are scarcely friendly."

"I am very glad to hear it," said Miss Jemima, who had been silent during the little controversy that her sister and I had been carrying on. "We have been quite misinformed. The fact is, we thought we might have seen more of you if it had not been for her. And as very few people of her own position in society care to visit her, we thought it a pity she should be your principal friend in the parish."

"Why do they not visit her more?"

"There are strange stories about her, which it is as well to leave alone. They are getting out of date too. But she is not a fit woman to be regarded as the clergyman's friend. There!" said Miss Jemima, as if she had wanted to relieve her bosom of a burden, and had done it.

"I think, however, her religious opinions would correspond with your own, Mr Walton," said Miss Hester.

"Possibly," I answered, with indifference; "I don't care much about opinion."

"Her daughter would be a nice girl, I fancy, if she weren't kept down by her mother. She looks scared, poor thing! And they say she's not quite-the thing, you know," said Miss Jemima.

"What DO you mean, Miss Crowther?"

She gently tapped her forehead with a forefinger.

I laughed. I thought it was not worth my while to enter as the champion of Miss Oldcastle's sanity.

"They are, and have been, a strange family as far back as I can remember; and my mother used to say the same. I am glad she comes to our church now. You mustn't let her set her cap at you, though, Mr Walton. It wouldn't do at all. She's pretty enough, too!"

"Yes," I returned, "she is rather pretty. But I don't think she looks as if she had a cap to set at anybody."

I rose to go, for I did not relish any further pursuit of the conversation in the same direction.

I rode home slowly, brooding on the lovely marvel, that out of such a rough ungracious stem as the Oldcastle family, should have sprung such a delicate, pale, winter-braved flower, as Ethelwyn. And I prayed that I might be honoured to rescue her from the ungenial soil and atmosphere to which the machinations of her mother threatened to confine her for the rest of a suffering life.

CHAPTER XXVI
SATAN CAST OUT.

I was within a mile of the village, returning from my visit to the Misses Crowther, when my horse, which was walking slowly along the soft side of the road, lifted his head, and pricked up his ears at the sound, which he heard first, of approaching hoofs. The riders soon came in sight-Miss Oldcastle, Judy, and Captain Everard. Miss Oldcastle I had never seen on horseback before. Judy was on a little white pony she used to gallop about the fields near the Hall. The Captain was laughing and chatting gaily as they drew near, now to the one, now to the other. Being on my own side of the road I held straight on, not wishing to stop or to reveal the signs of a distress which had almost overwhelmed me. I felt as cold as death, or rather as if my whole being had been deprived of vitality by a sudden exhaustion around me of the ethereal element of life. I believe I did not alter my bearing, but remained with my head bent, for I had been thinking hard just before, till we were on the point of meeting, when I lifted my hat to Miss Oldcastle without drawing bridle, and went on. The Captain returned my salutation, and likewise rode on. I could just see, as they passed me, that Miss Oldcastle's pale face was flushed even to scarlet, but she only bowed and kept alongside of her companion. I thought I had escaped conversation, and had gone about twenty yards farther, when I heard the clatter of Judy's pony behind me, and up she came at full gallop.

"Why didn't you stop to speak to us, Mr Walton?" she said. "I pulled up, but you never looked at me. We shall be cross all the rest of the day, because you cut us so. What have we done?"

"Nothing, Judy, that I know of," I answered, trying to speak cheerfully. "But I do not know your companion, and I was not in the humour for an introduction."

She looked hard at me with her keen gray eyes; and I felt as if the child was seeing through me.

"I don't know what to make of it, Mr Walton. You're very different somehow from what you used to be. There's something wrong somewhere. But I suppose you would all tell me it's none of my business. So I won't ask questions. Only I wish I could do anything for you."

I felt the child's kindness, but could only say—

"Thank you, Judy. I am sure I should ask you if there were anything you could do for me. But you'll be left behind."

"No fear of that. My Dobbin can go much faster than their big horses. But I see you don't want me, so good-bye."

She turned her pony's head as she spoke, jumped the ditch at the side of the road, and flew after them along the grass like a swallow. I likewise roused my horse and went off at a hard trot, with the vain impulse so to shake off the tormenting thoughts that crowded on me like gadflies. But this day was to be one of more trial still.

As I turned a corner, almost into the street of the village, Tom Weir was at my side. He had evidently been watching for me. His face was so pale, that I saw in a moment something had happened.

"What is the matter, Tom?" I asked, in some alarm.

He did not reply for a moment, but kept unconsciously stroking my horse's neck, and staring at me "with wide blue eyes."

"Come, Tom," I repeated, "tell me what is the matter."

I could see his bare throat knot and relax, like the motion of a serpent, before he could utter the words.

"Kate has killed her little boy, sir."

He followed them with a stifled cry-almost a scream, and hid his face in his hands.

"God forbid!" I exclaimed, and struck my heels in my horse's sides, nearly overturning poor Tom in my haste.

"She's mad, sir; she's mad," he cried, as I rode off.

"Come after me," I said, "and take the mare home. I shan't be able to leave your sister."

Had I had a share, by my harsh words, in driving the woman beyond the bounds of human reason and endurance? The thought was dreadful. But I must not let my mind rest on it now, lest I should be unfitted for what might have to be done. Before I reached the door, I saw a little crowd of the villagers, mostly women and children, gathered about it. I got off my horse, and gave him to a woman to hold till Tom should come up. With a little difficulty, I prevailed on the rest to go home at once, and not add to the confusions and terrors of the unhappy affair by the excitement of their presence. As soon as they had yielded to my arguments, I entered the shop, which to my annoyance I found full of the neighbours. These likewise I got rid of as soon as possible, and locking the door behind them, went up to the room above.

To my surprise, I found no one there. On the hearth and in the fender lay two little pools of blood. All in the house was utterly still. It was very dreadful. I went to the only other door. It was not bolted as I had expected to find it. I opened it, peeped in, and entered. On the bed lay the mother, white as death, but with her black eyes wide open, staring at the ceiling: and on her arm lay little Gerard, as white, except where the blood had flowed from the bandage that could not confine it, down his sweet deathlike face. His eyes were fast closed, and he had no sign of life about him. I shut the door behind me, and approached the bed. When Catherine caught sight of me, she showed no surprise or emotion of any kind. Her lips, with automaton-like movement, uttered the words —

"I have done it at last. I am ready. Take me away. I shall be hanged. I don't care. I confess it. Only don't let the people stare at me."

Her lips went on moving, but I could hear no more till suddenly she broke out —

"Oh! my baby! my baby!" and gave a cry of such agony as I hope never to hear again while I live.

At this moment I heard a loud knocking at the shop-door, which was the only entrance to the house, and remembering that I had locked it, I went down to see who was there. I found Thomas Weir, the father, accompanied by Dr Duncan, whom, as it happened, he had had some difficulty in finding. Thomas had sped to his daughter the moment he heard the rumour of what had happened, and his fierceness in clearing the shop had at least prevented the neighbours, even in his absence, from intruding further.

We went up together to Catherine's room. Thomas said nothing to me about what had happened, and I found it difficult even to conjecture from his countenance what thoughts were passing through his mind.

Catherine looked from one to another of us, as if she did not know the one from the other. She made no motion to rise from her bed, nor did she utter a word, although her lips would now and then move as if moulding a sentence. When Dr Duncan, after looking at the child, proceeded to take him from her, she gave him one imploring look, and yielded with a moan; then began to stare hopelessly at the ceiling again. The doctor carried the child into the next room, and the grandfather followed.

"You see what you have driven me to!" cried Catherine, the moment I was left alone with her. "I hope you are satisfied."

The words went to my very soul. But when I looked at her, her eyes were wandering about over the ceiling, and I had and still have difficulty in believing that she spoke the words, and that they were not an illusion of my sense, occasioned by the commotion of my own feelings. I thought it better, however, to leave her, and join the others in the sitting-room. The first thing I saw there was Thomas on his knees, with a basin of water, washing away the blood of his grandson from his daughter's floor. The very sight of the child had hitherto been nauseous to him, and his daughter had been beyond the reach of his forgiveness. Here was the end of it-the blood of the one shed by the hand of the other, and the father of both, who had disdained both, on his knees, wiping it up. Dr Duncan was giving the child brandy; for he had found that he had been sick, and that the loss of blood was the chief cause of his condition. The blood flowed from a wound on the head, extending backwards from the temple, which had evidently been occasioned by a fall upon the fender, where the blood lay both inside and out;

and the doctor took the sickness as a sign that the brain had not been seriously injured by the blow. In a few minutes he said —

"I think he'll come round."

"Will it be safe to tell his mother so?" I asked.

"Yes: I think you may."

I hastened to her room.

"Your little darling is not dead, Catherine. He is coming to."

She THREW herself off the bed at my feet, caught them round with her arms, and cried —

"I will forgive him. I will do anything you like. I forgive George Everard. I will go and ask my father to forgive me."

I lifted her in my arms-how light she was! —and laid her again on the bed, where she burst into tears, and lay sobbing and weeping. I went to the other room. Little Gerard opened his eyes and closed them again, as I entered. The doctor had laid him in his own crib. He said his pulse was improving. I beckoned to Thomas. He followed me.

"She wants to ask you to forgive her," I said. "Do not, in God's name, wait till she asks you, but go and tell her that you forgive her."

"I dare not say I forgive her," he answered. "I have more need to ask her to forgive me."

I took him by the hand, and led him into her room. She feebly lifted her arms towards him. Not a word was said on either side. I left them in each other's embrace. The hard rocks had been struck with the rod, and the waters of life had flowed forth from each, and had met between.

I have more than once known this in the course of my experience-the ice and snow of a long estrangement suddenly give way, and the boiling geyser-floods of old affection rush from the hot deeps of the heart. I think myself that the very lastingness and strength of animosity have their origin sometimes in the reality of affection: the love lasts all the while, freshly indignant at every new load heaped upon it; till, at last, a word, a look, a sorrow, a gladness, sets it free; and, forgetting all its claims, it rushes irresistibly towards its ends. Thus was it with Thomas and Catherine Weir.

When I rejoined Dr Duncan, I found little Gerard asleep, and breathing quietly.

"What do you know of this sad business, Mr Walton?" said the doctor.

"I should like to ask the same question of you," I returned. "Young Tom told me that his sister had murdered the child. That is all I know."

"His father told me the same; and that is all I know. Do you believe it?"

"At least we have no evidence about it. It is tolerably certain neither of those two could have been present. They must have received it by report. We must wait till she is able to explain the thing herself."

"Meantime," said Dr Duncan, "all I believe is, that she struck the child, and that he fell upon the fender."

I may as well inform my reader that, as far as Catherine could give an account of the transaction, this conjecture was corroborated. But the smallest reminder of it evidently filled her with such horror of self-loathing, that I took care to avoid the subject entirely, after the attempt at explanation which she made at my request. She could not remember with any clearness what had happened. All she remembered was that she had been more miserable than ever in her life before; that the child had come to her, as he seldom did, with some childish request or other; that she felt herself seized with intense hatred of him; and the next thing she knew was that his blood was running in a long red finger towards her. Then it seemed as if that blood had been drawn from her own over-charged heart and brain; she knew what she had done, though she did not know how she had done it; and the tide of her ebbed affection flowed like the returning waters of the Solway. But beyond her restored love, she remembered nothing more that happened till she lay weeping with the hope that the child would yet live. Probably more particulars returned afterwards, but I took care to ask no more questions. In the increase of illness that followed, I more than once saw her shudder while she slept, and thought she was dreaming what her waking memory had forgotten; and once she started awake, crying, "I have murdered him again."

To return to that first evening:—When Thomas came from his daughter's room, he looked like a man from whom the bitterness of evil had passed away. To human eyes, at least, it seemed as if self had been utterly slain in him. His face had that child-like expression in its paleness, and the tearfulness without tears haunting his eyes, which reminds one of the feeling of an evening in summer between which and the sultry day preceding it has fallen the gauzy veil of a cooling shower, with a rainbow in the east.

"She is asleep," he said.

"How is it your daughter Mary is not here?" I asked.

"She was taken with a fit the moment she heard the bad news, sir. I left her with nobody but father. I think I must go and look after her now. It's not the first she's had neither, though I never told any one before. You won't mention it, sir. It makes people look shy at you, you know, sir."

"Indeed, I won't mention it.—Then she mustn't sit up, and two nurses will be wanted here. You and I must take it to-night, Thomas. You'll attend to your daughter, if she wants anything, and I know this little darling won't be frightened if he comes to himself, and sees me beside him."

"God bless you, sir," said Thomas, fervently.

And from that hour to this there has never been a coolness between us.

"A very good arrangement," said Dr Duncan; "only I feel as if I ought to have a share in it."

"No, no," I said. "We do not know who may want you. Besides, we are both younger than you."

"I will come over early in the morning then, and see how you are going on."

As soon as Thomas returned with good news of Mary's recovery, I left him, and went home to tell my sister, and arrange for the night. We carried back with us what things we could think of to make the two patients as comfortable as possible; for, as regarded Catherine, now that she would let her fellows help her, I was even anxious that she should feel something of that love about her which she had so long driven from her door. I felt towards her somewhat as towards a new-born child, for whom this life of mingled weft must be made as soft as its material will admit of; or rather, as if she had been my own sister, as indeed she was, returned from wandering in weary and miry ways, to taste once more the tenderness of home. I wanted her to read the love of God in the love that even I could show her. And, besides, I must confess that, although the result had been, in God's great grace, so good, my heart still smote me for the severity with which I had spoken the truth to her; and it was a relief to myself to endeavour to make some amends for having so spoken to her. But I had no intention of going near her that night, for I thought the less she saw of me the better, till she should be a little stronger, and have had time, with the help of her renewed feelings, to get over the painful associations so long accompanying the thought of me. So I took my place beside Gerard, and watched through the night. The little fellow repeatedly cried out in that terror which is so often the consequence of the loss of blood; but when I laid my hand on him, he smiled without waking, and lay quite still again for a while. Once or twice he woke up, and looked so bewildered that I feared delirium; but a little jelly composed him, and he fell fast asleep again. He did not seem even to have headache from the blow.

But when I was left alone with the child, seated in a chair by the fire, my only light, how my thoughts rushed upon the facts bearing on my own history which this day had brought before me! Horror it was to think of Miss Oldcastle even as only riding with the seducer of Catherine Weir. There was torture in the thought of his touching her hand; and to think that before the summer came once more, he might be her husband! I will not dwell on the sufferings of that night more than is needful; for even now, in my old age, I cannot recall without renewing them. But I must indicate one train of thought which kept passing through my mind with constant recurrence:—Was it fair to let her marry such a man in ignorance? Would she marry him if she knew what I knew of him? Could I speak against my rival? —blacken him even with the truth-the only defilement that can really cling? Could I for my own dignity do so? And was she therefore to be sacrificed in ignorance? Might not some one else do it instead of me? But if I set it agoing, was it not precisely the same thing as if I did it myself, only more cowardly? There was but one way of doing it, and that was-with the full and solemn consciousness that it was and must be a barrier between us for ever. If I could give her up fully and altogether, then I might tell her the truth which was to preserve her from marrying such a man as my rival. And I must do so, sooner than that she, my very dream of purity and gentle truth, should wed defilement. But how bitter to cast away my CHANCE! as I said, in the gathering despair of that black night. And although every time I said it-for the same words would come over and over as in a delirious dream—I repeated yet again to myself that wonderful line of Spenser, —

"It chanced-eternal God that chance did guide,"

yet the words never grew into spirit in me; they remained "words, words, words," and meant nothing to my feeling-hardly even to my judgment meant anything at all. Then came another bitter thought, the bitterness of which was wicked: it flashed upon me that my own earnestness with Catherine Weir, in urging her to the duty of forgiveness, would bear a main part in wrapping up in secrecy that evil thing which ought not to be hid. For had she not vowed-with the same facts before her which now threatened to crush my heart into a lump of clay-to denounce the man at the very altar? Had not the revenge which I had ignorantly combated been my best ally? And for one brief, black, wicked moment I repented that I had acted as I had acted. The next I was on my knees by the side of the sleeping child, and had repented back again in shame and sorrow. Then came the consolation that if I suffered hereby, I suffered from doing my duty. And that was well.

Scarcely had I seated myself again by the fire when the door of the room opened softly, and Thomas appeared.

"Kate is very strange, sir," he said, "and wants to see you."

I rose at once.

"Perhaps, then, you had better stay with Gerard."

"I will, sir; for I think she wants to speak to you alone."

I entered her chamber. A candle stood on a chest of drawers, and its light fell on her face, once more flushed in those two spots with the glow of the unseen fire of disease. Her eyes, too, glittered again, but the fierceness was gone, and only the suffering remained. I drew a chair beside her, and took her hand. She yielded it willingly, even returned the pressure of kindness which I offered to the thin trembling fingers.

"You are too good, sir," she said. "I want to tell you all. He promised to marry me, I believed him. But I did very wrong. And I have been a bad mother, for I could not keep from seeing his face in Gerard's. Gerard was the name he told me to call him when I had to write to him, and so I named the little darling Gerard. How is he, sir?"

"Doing nicely," I replied. "I do not think you need be at all uneasy about him now."

"Thank God. I forgive his father now with all my heart. I feel it easier since I saw how wicked I could be myself. And I feel it easier, too, that I have not long to live. I forgive him with all my heart, and I will take no revenge. I will not tell one who he is. I have never told any one yet. But I will tell you. His name is George Everard-Captain Everard. I came to know him when I was apprenticed at Addicehead. I would not tell you, sir, if I did not know that you will not tell any one. I know you so well that I will not ask you not. I saw him yesterday, and it drove me wild. But it is all over now. My heart feels so cool now. Do you think God will forgive me?"

Without one word of my own, I took out my pocket Testament and read these words: —

"For if ye forgive men their trespasses, your heavenly Father will also forgive you."

Then I read to her, from the seventh chapter of St Luke's Gospel, the story of the woman who was a sinner and came to Jesus in Simon's house, that she might see how the Lord himself thought and felt about such. When I had finished, I found that she was gently weeping, and so I left her, and resumed my place beside the boy. I told Thomas that he had better not go near her just yet. So we sat in silence together for a while, during which I felt so weary and benumbed, that I neither cared to resume my former train of thought, nor to enter upon the new one suggested by the confession of Catherine. I believe I must have fallen asleep in my chair, for I suddenly returned to consciousness at a cry from Gerard. I started up, and there was the child fast asleep, but standing on his feet in his crib, pushing with his hands from before him, as if resisting some one, and crying—

"Don't. Don't. Go away, man. Mammy! Mr Walton!"

I took him in my arms, and kissed him, and laid him down again; and he lay as still as if he had never moved. At the same moment, Thomas came again into the room.

"I am sorry to be so troublesome, sir," he said; "but my poor daughter says there is one thing more she wanted to say to you."

I returned at once. As soon as I entered the room, she said eagerly:—

"I forgive him—I forgive him with all my heart; but don't let him take Gerard."

I assured her I would do my best to prevent any such attempt on his part, and making her promise to try to go to sleep, left her once more. Nor was either of the patients disturbed again during the night. Both slept, as it appeared, refreshingly.

In the morning, that is, before eight o'clock, the old doctor made his welcome appearance, and pronounced both quite as well as he had expected to find them. In another hour, he had sent young Tom to take my place, and my sister to take his father's. I was determined that none of the gossips of the village should go near the invalid if I could help it; for, though such might be kind-hearted and estimable women, their place was not by such a couch as that of Catherine Weir. I enjoined my sister to be very gentle in her approaches to her, to be careful even not to seem anxious to serve her, and so to allow her to get gradually accustomed to her presence, not showing herself for the first day more than she could help, and yet taking good care she should have everything she wanted. Martha seemed to understand me perfectly; and I left her in charge with the more confidence that I knew Dr Duncan would call several times in the course of the day. As for Tom, I had equal assurance that he would attend to orders; and as Gerard was very fond of him, I dismissed all anxiety about both, and allowed my mind to return with fresh avidity to the contemplation of its own cares, and fears, and perplexities.

It was of no use trying to go to sleep, so I set out for a walk.

CHAPTER XXVII
THE MAN AND THE CHILD.

It was a fine frosty morning, the invigorating influences of which, acting along with the excitement following immediately upon a sleepless night, overcame in a great measure the depression occasioned by the contemplation of my circumstances. Disinclined notwithstanding for any more pleasant prospect, I sought the rugged common where I had so lately met Catherine Weir in the storm and darkness, and where I had stood without knowing it upon the very verge of the precipice down which my fate was now threatening to hurl me. I reached the same chasm in which I had sought a breathing space on that night, and turning into it, sat down upon a block of sand which the frost had detached from the wall above. And now the tumult began again in my mind, revolving around the vortex of a new centre of difficulty.

For, first of all, I found my mind relieved by the fact that, having urged Catherine to a line of conduct which had resulted in confession, —a confession which, leaving all other considerations of my office out of view, had the greater claim upon my secrecy that it was made in confidence in my uncovenanted honour, —I was not, could not be at liberty to disclose the secret she confided to me, which, disclosed by herself, would have been the revenge from which I had warned her, and at the same time my deliverance. I was relieved I say at first, by this view of the matter, because I might thus keep my own chance of some favourable turn; whereas, if I once told Miss Oldcastle, I must give her up for ever, as I had plainly seen in the watch of the preceding night. But my love did not long remain skulking thus behind the hedge of honour. Suddenly I woke and saw that I was unworthy of the honour of loving her, for that I was glad to be compelled to risk her well-being for the chance of my own happiness; a risk which involved infinitely more wretchedness to her than the loss of my dearest hopes to me; for it is one thing for a man not to marry the woman he loves, and quite another for a woman to marry a man she cannot ever respect. Had I not been withheld partly by my obligation to Catherine, partly by the feeling that I ought to wait and see what God would do, I should have risen that moment and gone straight to Oldcastle Hall, that I might plunge at once into the ocean of my loss, and encounter, with the full sense of honourable degradation, every misconstruction that might justly be devised of my conduct. For that I had given her up first could never be known even to her in this world. I could only save her by encountering and enduring and cherishing her scorn. At least so it seemed to me at the time; and, although I am certain the other higher motives had much to do in holding me back, I am equally certain that this awful vision of the irrevocable fate to follow upon the deed, had great influence, as well, in inclining me to suspend action.

I was still sitting in the hollow, when I heard the sound of horses' hoofs in the distance, and felt a foreboding of what would appear. I was only a few yards from the road upon which the sand-cleft opened, and could see a space of it sufficient to show the persons even of rapid riders. The sounds drew nearer. I could distinguish the step of a pony and the steps of two horses besides. Up they came and swept past-Miss Oldcastle upon Judy's pony, and Mr Stoddart upon her horse; with the captain upon his own. How grateful I felt to Mr Stoddart! And the hope arose in me that he had accompanied them at Miss Oldcastle's request.

I had had no fear of being seen, sitting as I was on the side from which they came. One of the three, however, caught a glimpse of me, and even in the moment ere she vanished I fancied I saw the lily-white grow rosy-red. But it must have been fancy, for she could hardly have been quite pale upon horseback on such a keen morning.

I could not sit any longer. As soon as I ceased to hear the sound of their progress, I rose and walked home-much quieter in heart and mind than when I set out.

As I entered by the nearer gate of the vicarage, I saw Old Rogers enter by the farther. He did not see me, but we met at the door. I greeted him.

"I'm in luck," he said, "to meet yer reverence just coming home. How's poor Miss Weir to-day, sir?"

"She was rather better, when I left her this morning, than she had been through the night. I have not heard since. I left my sister with her. I greatly doubt if she will ever get up again. That's between ourselves, you know. Come in."

"Thank you, sir. I wanted to have a little talk with you. —You don't believe what they say-that she tried to kill the poor little fellow?" he asked, as soon as the study door was closed behind us.

"If she did, she was out of her mind for the moment. But I don't believe it."

And thereupon I told him what both his master and I thought about it. But I did not tell him what she had said confirmatory of our conclusions.

"That's just what I came to myself, sir, turning the thing over in my old head. But there's dreadful things done in the world, sir. There's my daughter been a-telling of me —"

I was instantly breathless attention. What he chose to tell me I felt at liberty to hear, though I would not have listened to Jane herself. —I must here mention that she and Richard were not yet married, old Mr Brownrigg not having yet consented to any day his son wished to fix; and that she was, therefore, still in her place of attendance upon Miss Oldcastle.

"—There's been my daughter a-telling of me," said Rogers, "that the old lady up at the Hall there is tormenting the life out of that daughter of hers-she don't look much like hers, do she, sir? —wanting to make her marry a man of her choosing. I saw him go past o' horseback with her yesterday, and I didn't more than half like the looks on him. He's too like a fair-spoken captain I sailed with once, what was the hardest man I ever sailed with. His own way was everything, even after he saw it wouldn't do. Now, don't you think, sir, somebody or other ought to interfere? It's as bad as murder that, and anybody has a right to do summat to perwent it."

"I don't know what can be done, Rogers. I CAN'T interfere."

The old man was silent. Evidently he thought I might interfere if I pleased. I could see what he was thinking. Possibly his daughter had told him something more than he chose to communicate to me. I could not help suspecting the mode in which he judged I might interfere. But I could see no likelihood before me but that of confusion and precipitation. In a word, I had not a plain path to follow.

"Old Rogers," I said, "I can almost guess what you mean. But I am in more difficulty with regard to what you suggest than I can easily explain to you. I need not tell you, however, that I will turn the whole matter over in my mind."

"The prey ought to be taken from the lion somehow, if it please God," returned the old man solemnly. "The poor young lady keeps up as well as she can before her mother; but Jane do say there's a power o' crying done in her own room."

Partly to hide my emotion, partly with the sudden resolve to do something, if anything could be done, I said: —

"I will call on Mr Stoddart this evening. I may hear something from him to suggest a mode of action."

"I don't think you'll get anything worth while from Mr Stoddart. He takes things a deal too easy like. He'll be this man's man and that man's man both at oncet. I beg your pardon, sir. But HE won't help us."

"That's all I can think of at present, though," I said; whereupon the man-of-war's man, with true breeding, rose at once, and took a kindly leave.

I was in the storm again. She suffering, resisting, and I standing aloof! But what could I do? She had repelled me-she would repel me. Were I to dare to speak, and so be refused, the separation would be final. She had said that the day might come when she would ask help from me: she had made no movement towards the request. I would gladly die to serve her-yea, more gladly far than live, if that service was to separate us. But what to do I could not see. Still, just to do something, even if a useless something, I would go and see Mr Stoddart that evening. I was sure to find him alone, for he never dined with the family, and I might possibly catch a glimpse of Miss Oldcastle.

I found little Gerard so much better, though very weak, and his mother so quiet, notwithstanding great feverishness, that I might safely leave them to the care of Mary, who had quite recovered from her attack, and her brother Tom. So there was something off my mind for the present.

The heavens were glorious with stars,—Arcturus and his host, the Pleiades, Orion, and all those worlds that shine out when ours is dark; but I did not care for them. Let them shine: they could not shine into me. I tried with feeble effort to lift my eyes to Him who is above the stars, and yet holds the sea, yea, the sea of human thought and trouble, in the hollow of His hand. How much sustaining, although no conscious comforting, I got from that region

> "Where all men's prayers to Thee raised Return possessed of what
> they pray Thee."

I cannot tell. It was not a time favourable to the analysis of feeling-still less of religious feeling. But somehow things did seem a little more endurable before I reached the house.

I was passing across the hall, following the "white wolf" to Mr Stoddart's room, when the drawing-room door opened, and Miss Oldcastle came half out, but seeing me drew back instantly. A moment after, however, I heard the sound of her dress following us. Light as was her step, every footfall seemed to be upon my heart. I did not dare to look round, for dread of seeing her turn away from me. I felt like one under a spell, or in an endless dream; but gladly would I have walked on for ever in hope, with that silken vortex of sound following me. Soon, however, it ceased. She had turned aside in some other direction, and I passed on to Mr Stoddart's room.

He received me kindly, as he always did; but his smile flickered uneasily. He seemed in some trouble, and yet pleased to see me.

"I am glad you have taken to horseback," I said. "It gives me hope that you will be my companion sometimes when I make a round of my parish. I should like you to see some of our people. You would find more in them to interest you than perhaps you would expect."

I thus tried to seem at ease, as I was far from feeling.

"I am not so fond of riding as I used to be," returned Mr Stoddart.

"Did you like the Arab horses in India?"

"Yes, after I got used to their careless ways. That horse you must have seen me on the other day, is very nearly a pure Arab. He belongs to Captain Everard, and carries Miss Oldcastle beautifully. I was quite sorry to take him from her, but it was her own doing. She would have me go with her. I think I have lost much firmness since I was ill."

"If the loss of firmness means the increase of kindness, I do not think you will have to lament it," I answered. "Does Captain Everard make a long stay?"

"He stays from day to day. I wish he would go. I don't know what to do. Mrs Oldcastle and he form one party in the house; Miss Oldcastle and Judy another; and each is trying to gain me over. I don't want to belong to either. If they would only let me alone!"

"What do they want of you, Mr Stoddart?"

"Mrs Oldcastle wants me to use my influence with Ethelwyn, to persuade her to behave differently to Captain Everard. The old lady has set her heart on their marriage, and Ethelwyn, though she dares not break with him, she is so much afraid of her mother, yet keeps him somehow at arm's length. Then Judy is always begging me to stand up for her aunt. But what's the use of my standing up for her if she won't stand up for herself; she never says a word to me about it herself. It's all Judy's doing. How am I to know what she wants?"

"I thought you said just now she asked you to ride with her?"

"So she did, but nothing more. She did not even press it, only the tears came in her eyes when I refused, and I could not bear that; so I went against my will. I don't want to make enemies. I am sure I don't see why she should stand out. He's a very good match in point of property and family too."

"Perhaps she does not like him?" I forced myself to say.

"Oh! I suppose not, or she would not be so troublesome. But she could arrange all that if she were inclined to be agreeable to her friends. After all I have done for her! Well, one must not look to be repaid for anything one does for others. I used to be very fond of her: I am getting quite tired of her miserable looks."

And what had this man done for her, then? He had, for his own amusement, taught her Hindostanee; he had given her some insight into the principles of mechanics, and he had roused in her some taste for the writings of the Mystics. But for all that regarded the dignity of her humanity and her womanhood, if she had had no teaching but what he gave her, her mind would have been merely "an unweeded garden that grows to seed." And now he complained that in return for his pains she would not submit to the degradation of marrying a man she did not love, in order to leave him in the enjoyment of his own lazy and cowardly peace. Really he was a worse man than I had thought him. Clearly he would not help to keep her in the right path, not even interfere to prevent her from being pushed into the wrong one. But perhaps he was only expressing his own discomfort, not giving his real judgment, and I might be censuring him too hardly.

"What will be the result, do you suppose?" I asked.

"I can't tell. Sooner or later she will have to give in to her mother. Everybody does. She might as well yield with a good grace."

"She must do what she thinks right," I said. "And you, Mr Stoddart, ought to help her to do what is right. You surely would not urge her to marry a man she did not love."

"Well, no; not exactly urge her. And yet society does not object to it. It is an acknowledged arrangement, common enough."

"Society is scarcely an interpreter of the divine will. Society will honour vile things enough, so long as the doer has money sufficient to clothe them in a grace not their own. There is a God's-way of doing everything in the world, up to marrying, or down to paying a bill."

"Yes, yes, I know what you would say; and I suppose you are right. I will not urge any opinion of mine. Besides, we shall have a little respite soon, for he must join his regiment in a day or two."

It was some relief to hear this. But I could not with equanimity prosecute a conversation having Miss Oldcastle for the subject of it, and presently took my leave.

As I walked through one of the long passages, but dimly lighted, leading from Mr Stoddart's apartment to the great staircase, I started at a light touch on my arm. It was from Judy's hand.

"Dear Mr Walton ——" she said, and stopped.

For at the same moment appeared at the farther end of the passage towards which I had been advancing, a figure of which little more than a white face was visible; and the voice of Sarah, through whose softness always ran a harsh thread that made it unmistakable, said,

"Miss Judy, your grandmamma wants you."

Judy took her hand from my arm, and with an almost martial stride the little creature walked up to the speaker, and stood before her defiantly. I could see them quite well in the fuller light at the end of the passage, where there stood a lamp. I followed slowly that I might not interrupt the child's behaviour, which moved me strangely in contrast with the pusillanimity I had so lately witnessed in Mr Stoddart.

"Sarah," she said, "you know you are telling a lie Grannie does NOT want me. You have NOT been in the dining-room since I left it one moment ago. Do you think, you BAD woman, *I* am going to be afraid of you? I know you better than you think. Go away directly, or I will make you."

She stamped her little foot, and the "white wolf" turned and walked away without a word.

If the mothers among my readers are shocked at the want of decorum in my friend Judy, I would just say, that valuable as propriety of demeanour is, truth of conduct is infinitely more precious. Glad should I be to think that the even tenor of my children's good manners could never be interrupted, except by such righteous indignation as carried Judy beyond the strict bounds of good breeding. Nor could I find it in my heart to rebuke her wherein she had been wrong. In the face of her courage and uprightness, the fault was so insignificant that it would have been giving it an altogether undue importance to allude to it at all, and might weaken her confidence in my sympathy with her rectitude. When I joined her she put her hand in mine, and so walked with me down the stair and out at the front door.

"You will take cold, Judy, going out like that," I said.

"I am in too great a passion to take cold," she answered. "But I have no time to talk about that creeping creature. —Auntie DOESN'T like Captain Everard; and grannie keeps insisting on it that she shall have him whether she likes him or not. Now do tell me what you think."

"I do not quite understand you, my child."

"I know auntie would like to know what you think. But I know she will never ask you herself. So *I* am asking you whether a lady ought to marry a gentleman she does not like, to please her mother."

"Certainly not, Judy. It is often wicked, and at best a mistake."

"Thank you, Mr Walton. I will tell her. She will be glad to hear that you say so, I know."

"Mind you tell her you asked me, Judy. I should not like her to think I had been interfering, you know."

"Yes, yes; I know quite well. I will take care. Thank you. He's going to-morrow. Good night."

She bounded into the house again, and I walked away down the avenue. I saw and felt the stars now, for hope had come again in my heart, and I thanked the God of hope. "Our minds are small because they are faithless," I said to myself. "If we had faith in God, as our Lord tells us, our hearts would share in His greatness and peace. For we should not then be shut up in ourselves, but would walk abroad in Him." And with a light step and a light heart I went home.

CHAPTER XXVIII
OLD MRS TOMKINS.

Very severe weather came, and much sickness followed, chiefly amongst the poorer people, who can so ill keep out the cold. Yet some of my well-to-do parishioners were laid up likewise—amongst others Mr Boulderstone, who had an attack of pleurisy. I had grown quite attached to Mr Boulderstone by this time, not because he was what is called interesting, for he was not; not because he was clever, for he was not; not because he was well-read, for he was not; not because he was possessed of influence in the parish, though he had that influence; but simply because he was true; he was what he appeared, felt what he professed, did what he said; appearing kind, and feeling and acting kindly. Such a man is rare and precious, were he as stupid as the Welsh giant in "Jack the Giant-Killer." I could never see Mr Boulderstone a mile off, but my heart felt the warmer for the sight.

Even in his great pain he seemed to forget himself as he received me, and to gain comfort from my mere presence. I could not help regarding him as a child of heaven, to be treated with the more reverence that he had the less aid to his goodness from his slow understanding. It seemed to me that the angels might gather with reverence around such a man, to watch the gradual and tardy awakening of the intellect in one in whom the heart and the conscience had been awake from the first. The latter safe, they at least would see well that there was no fear for the former. Intelligence is a consequence of love; nor is there any true intelligence without it.

But I could not help feeling keenly the contrast when I went from his warm, comfortable, well-defended chamber, in which every appliance that could alleviate suffering or aid recovery was at hand, like a castle well appointed with arms and engines against the inroads of winter and his yet colder ally Death,—when, I say, I went from his chamber to the cottage of the Tomkinses, and found it, as it were, lying open and bare to the enemy. What holes and cracks there were about the door, through which the fierce wind rushed at once into the room to attack the aged feet and hands and throats! There were no defences of threefold draperies, and no soft carpet on the brick floor,—only a small rug which my sister had carried them laid down before a weak-eyed little fire, that seemed to despair of making anything of it against the huge cold that beleaguered and invaded the place. True, we had had the little cottage patched up. The two Thomas Weirs had been at work upon it for a whole day and a half in the first of the cold weather this winter; but it was like putting the new cloth on the old garment, for fresh places had broken out, and although Mrs Tomkins had fought the cold well with what rags she could spare, and an old knife, yet such razor-edged winds are hard to keep out, and here she was now, lying in bed, and breathing hard, like the sore-pressed garrison which had retreated to its last defence, the keep of the castle. Poor old Tomkins sat shivering over the little fire.

"Come, come, Tomkins! this won't do," I said, as I caught up a broken shovel that would have let a lump as big as one's fist through a hole in the middle of it. "Why don't you burn your coals in weather like this? Where do you keep them?"

It made my heart ache to see the little heap in a box hardly bigger than the chest of tea my sister brought from London with her. I threw half of it on the fire at once.

"Deary me, Mr Walton! you ARE wasteful, sir. The Lord never sent His good coals to be used that way."

"He did though, Tomkins," I answered. "And He'll send you a little more this evening, after I get home. Keep yourself warm, man. This world's cold in winter, you know."

"Indeed, sir, I know that. And I'm like to know it worse afore long. She's going," he said, pointing over his shoulder with his thumb towards the bed where his wife lay.

I went to her. I had seen her several times within the last few weeks, but had observed nothing to make me consider her seriously ill. I now saw at a glance that Tomkins was right. She had not long to live.

"I am sorry to see you suffering so much, Mrs Tomkins," I said.

"I don't suffer so wery much, sir; though to be sure it be hard to get the breath into my body, sir. And I do feel cold-like, sir."

"I'm going home directly, and I'll send you down another blanket. It's much colder to-day than it was yesterday."

"It's not weather-cold, sir, wi' me. It's grave-cold, sir. Blankets won't do me no good, sir. I can't get it out of my head how perishing cold I shall be when I'm under the mould, sir; though I oughtn't to mind it when it's the will o' God. It's only till the resurrection, sir."

"But it's not the will of God, Mrs Tomkins."

"Ain't it, sir? Sure I thought it was."

"You believe in Jesus Christ, don't you, Mrs Tomkins?"

"That I do, sir, with all my heart and soul."

"Well, He says that whosoever liveth and believeth in Him shall never die."

"But, you know, sir, everybody dies. I MUST die, and be laid in the churchyard, sir. And that's what I don't like."

"But I say that is all a mistake. YOU won't die. Your body will die, and be laid away out of sight; but you will be awake, alive, more alive than you are now, a great deal."

And here let me interrupt the conversation to remark upon the great mistake of teaching children that they have souls. The consequence is, that they think of their souls as of something which is not themselves. For what a man HAS cannot be himself. Hence, when they are told that their souls go to heaven, they think of their SELVES as lying in the grave. They ought to be taught that they have bodies; and that their bodies die; while they themselves live on. Then they will not think, as old Mrs Tomkins did, that THEY will be laid in the grave. It is making altogether too much of the body, and is indicative of an evil tendency to materialism, that we talk as if we POSSESSED souls, instead of BEING souls. We should teach our children to think no more of their bodies when dead than they do of their hair when it is cut off, or of their old clothes when they have done with them.

"Do you really think so, sir?"

"Indeed I do. I don't know anything about where you will be. But you will be with God-in your Father's house, you know. And that is enough, is it not?"

"Yes, surely, sir. But I wish you was to be there by the bedside of me when I was a-dyin'. I can't help bein' summat skeered at it. It don't come nat'ral to me, like. I ha' got used to this old bed here, cold as it has been-many's the night-wi' my good man there by the side of me."

"Send for me, Mrs Tomkins, any moment, day or night, and I'll be with you directly."

"I think, sir, if I had a hold ov you i' the one hand, and my man there, the Lord bless him, i' the other, I could go comfortable."

"I'll come the minute you send for me-just to keep you in mind that a better friend than I am is holding you all the time, though you mayn't feel His hands. If it is some comfort to have hold of a human friend, think that a friend who is more than man, a divine friend, has a hold of you, who knows all your fears and pains, and sees how natural they are, and can just with a word, or a touch, or a look into your soul, keep them from going one hair's-breadth too far. He loves us up to all out need, just because we need it, and He is all love to give."

"But I can't help thinking, sir, that I wouldn't be troublesome. He has such a deal to look after! And I don't see how He can think of everybody, at every minute, like. I don't mean that He will let anything go wrong. But He might forget an old body like me for a minute, like."

"You would need to be as wise as He is before you could see how He does it. But you must believe more than you can understand. It is only common sense to do so. Think how nonsensical it would be to suppose that one who could make everything, and keep the whole going as He does, shouldn't be able to help forgetting. It would be unreasonable to think that He must forget because you couldn't understand how He could remember. I think it is as hard for Him to forget anything as it is for us to remember everything; for forgetting comes of weakness, and from our not being finished yet, and He is all strength and all perfection."

"Then you think, sir, He never forgets anything?"

I knew by the trouble that gathered on the old woman's brow what kind of thought was passing through her mind. But I let her go on, thinking so to help her the better. She paused for one moment only, and then resumed-much interrupted by the shortness of her breathing.

"When I was brought to bed first," she said, "it was o' twins, sir. And oh! sir, it was VERY hard. As I said to my man after I got my head up a bit, 'Tomkins,' says I, 'you don't know what it is to have TWO on 'em cryin' and cryin', and you next to nothin' to give 'em; till their cryin' sticks to your brain, and ye hear 'em when they're fast asleep, one on each side o' you.' Well, sir, I'm ashamed to confess it even to you; and what the Lord can think of me, I don't know."

"I would rather confess to Him than to the best friend I ever had," I said; "I am so sure that He will make every excuse for me that ought to be made. And a friend can't always do that. He can't know all about it. And you can't tell him all, because you don't know all yourself. He does."

"But I would like to tell YOU, sir. Would you believe it, sir, I wished 'em dead? Just to get the wailin' of them out o' my head, I wished 'em dead. In the courtyard o' the squire's house, where my Tomkins worked on the home-farm, there was an old draw-well. It wasn't used, and there was a lid to it, with a hole in it, through which you could put a good big stone. And Tomkins once took me to it, and, without tellin' me what it was, he put a stone in, and told me to hearken. And I hearkened, but I heard nothing,—as I told him so. 'But,' says he, 'hearken, lass.' And in a little while there come a blast o' noise like from somewheres. 'What's that, Tomkins?' I said. 'That's the ston',' says he, 'a strikin' on the water down that there well.' And I turned sick at the thought of it. And it's down there that I wished the darlin's that God had sent me; for there they'd be quiet."

"Mothers are often a little out of their minds at such times, Mrs Tomkins. And so were you."

"I don't know, sir. But I must tell you another thing. The Sunday afore that, the parson had been preachin' about 'Suffer little children,' you know, sir, 'to come unto me.' I suppose that was what put it in my head; but I fell asleep wi' nothin' else in my head but the cries o' the infants and the sound o' the ston' in the draw-well. And I dreamed that I had one o' them under each arm, cryin' dreadful, and was walkin' across the court the way to the draw-well; when all at once a man come up to me and held out his two hands, and said, 'Gie me my childer.' And I was in a terrible fear. And I gave him first one and then the t'other, and he took them, and one laid its head on one shoulder of him, and t'other upon t'other, and they stopped their cryin', and fell fast asleep; and away he walked wi' them into the dark, and I saw him no more. And then I awoke cryin', I didn't know why. And I took my twins to me, and my breasts was full, if ye 'll excuse me, sir. And my heart was as full o' love to them. And they hardly cried worth mentionin' again. But afore they was two year old, they both died o' the brown chytis, sir. And I think that He took them."

"He did take them, Mrs Tomkins; and you'll see them again soon."

"But, if He never forgets anything——"

"I didn't say that. I think He can do what He pleases. And if He pleases to forget anything, then He can forget it. And I think that is what He does with our sins-that is, after He has got them away from us, once we are clean from them altogether. It would be a dreadful thing if He forgot them before that, and left them sticking fast to us and defiling us. How then should we ever be made clean? —What else does the prophet Isaiah mean when he says, 'Thou hast cast my sins behind Thy back?' Is not that where He does not choose to see them any more? They are not pleasant to Him to think of any more than to us. It is as if He said —'I will not think of that any more, for my sister will never do it again,' and so He throws it behind His back."

"They ARE good words, sir. I could not bear Him to think of me and my sins both at once."

I could not help thinking of the words of Macbeth, "To know my deed, 'twere best not know myself."

The old woman lay quiet after this, relieved in mind, though not in body, by the communication she had made with so much difficulty, and I hastened home to send some coals and other things, and then call upon Dr Duncan, lest he should not know that his patient was so much worse as I had found her.

From Dr Duncan's I went to see old Samuel Weir, who likewise was ailing. The bitter weather was telling chiefly upon the aged. I found him in bed, under the old embroidery. No one was in the room with him. He greeted me with a withered smile, sweet and true, although no flash of white teeth broke forth to light up the welcome of the aged head.

"Are you not lonely, Mr Weir?"

"No, sir. I don't know as ever I was less lonely. I've got my stick, you see, sir," he said, pointing to a thorn stick which lay beside him.

"I do not quite understand you," I returned, knowing that the old man's gently humorous sayings always meant something.

"You see, sir, when I want anything, I've only got to knock on the floor, and up comes my son out of the shop. And then again, when I knock at the door of the house up there, my Father opens it and looks out. So I have both my son on earth and my Father in heaven, and what can an old man want more?"

"What, indeed, could any one want more?"

"It's very strange," the old man resumed after a pause, "but as I lie here, after I've had my tea, and it is almost dark, I begin to feel as if I was a child again. —They say old age is a second childhood; but before I grew so old, I used to think that meant only that a man was helpless and silly again, as he used to be when he was a child: I never thought it meant that a man felt like a child again, as light-hearted and untroubled as I do now."

"Well, I suspect that is not what people do mean when they say so. But I am very glad-you don't know how pleased it makes me to hear that you feel so. I will hope to fare in the same way when my time comes."

"Indeed, I hope you will, sir; for I am main and happy. Just before you came in now, I had really forgotten that I was a toothless old man, and thought I was lying here waiting for my mother to come in and say good-night to me before I went to sleep. Wasn't that curious, when I never saw my mother, as I told you before, sir?"

"It was very curious."

"But I have no end of fancies. Only when I begin to think about it, I can always tell when they are fancies, and they never put me out. There's one I see often —a man down on his knees at that cupboard nigh the floor there, searching and searching for somewhat. And I wish he would just turn round his face once for a moment that I might see him. I have a notion always it's my own father."

"How do you account for that fancy, now, Mr Weir?"

"I've often thought about it, sir, but I never could account for it. I'm none willing to think it's a ghost; for what's the good of it? I've turned out that cupboard over and over, and there's nothing there I don't know."

"You're not afraid of it, are you?"

"No, sir. Why should I be? I never did it no harm. And God can surely take care of me from all sorts."

My readers must not think anything is going to come out of this strange illusion of the old man's brain. I questioned him a little more about it, and came simply to the conclusion, that when he was a child he had found the door open and had wandered into the house, at the time uninhabited, had peeped in at the door of the same room where he now lay, and had actually seen a man in the position he described, half in the cupboard, searching for something. His mind had kept the impression after the conscious memory had lost its hold of the circumstance, and now revived it under certain physical conditions. It was a glimpse out of one of the many stories which haunted the old mansion. But there he lay like a child, as he said, fearless even of such usurpations upon his senses.

I think instances of quiet unSELFconscious faith are more common than is generally supposed. Few have along with it the genial communicative impulse of old Samuel Weir, which gives the opportunity of seeing into their hidden world. He seemed to have been, and to have remained, a child, in the best sense of the word. He had never had much trouble with himself, for he was of a kindly, gentle, trusting nature; and his will had never been called upon to exercise any strong effort to enable him to walk in the straight path. Nor had his intellect, on the other hand, while capable enough, ever been so active as to suggest difficulties to his faith, leaving him, even theoretically, far nearer the truth than those who start objections for their own sakes, liking to feel themselves in a position of supposed antagonism to the generally acknowledged sources of illumination. For faith is in itself a light that lightens even the intellect, and hence the shield of the complete soldier of God, the shield of faith, is represented by Spenser as "framed all of diamond, perfect, pure, and clean," (the power of the diamond to absorb and again radiate light being no poetic fiction, but a well-known scientific fact,) whose light falling upon any enchantment or false appearance, destroys it utterly: for

"all that was not such as seemed in sight.
Before that shield did fade, and suddaine fall."

Old Rogers had passed through a very much larger experience. Many more difficulties had come to him, and he had met them in his own fashion and overcome them. For while there is such a thing as truth, the mind that can honestly beget a difficulty must at the same time be capable of receiving that light of the truth which annihilates the difficulty, or at least of receiving enough to enable it to foresee vaguely some solution, for a full perception of which the intellect may not be as yet competent. By every such victory Old Rogers had enlarged his being, ever becoming more childlike and faithful; so that, while the childlikeness of Weir was the childlikeness of a child, that of Old Rogers was the childlikeness of a man, in which submission to God is not only a gladness, but a conscious will and choice. But as the safety of neither depended on his own feelings, but on the love of God who was working in him, we may well leave all such differences of nature and education to the care of Him who first made the men different, and then brought different conditions out of them. The one thing is, whether we are letting God have His own way with us, following where He leads, learning the lessons He gives us.

I wished that Mr Stoddart had been with me during these two visits. Perhaps he might have seen that the education of life was a marvellous thing, and, even in the poorest intellectual results, far more full of poetry and wonder than the outcome of that constant watering with the watering-pot of self-education which, dissociated from the duties of life and the influences of his fellows, had made of him what he was. But I doubt if he would have seen it.

A week had elapsed from the night I had sat up with Gerard Weir, and his mother had not risen from her bed, nor did it seem likely she would ever rise again. On a Friday I went to see her, just as the darkness was beginning to gather. The fire of life was burning itself out fast. It glowed on her cheeks, it burned in her hands, it blazed in her eyes. But the fever had left her mind. That was cool, oh, so cool, now! Those fierce tropical storms of passion had passed away, and nothing of life was lost. Revenge had passed away, but revenge is of death, and deadly. Forgiveness had taken its place, and forgiveness is the giving, and so the receiving of life. Gerard, his dear little head starred with sticking-plaster, sat on her bed, looking as quietly happy as child could look, over a wooden horse with cylindrical body and jointless legs, covered with an eruption of red and black spots. —Is it the ignorance or the imagination of children that makes them so easily pleased with the merest hint at representation? I suspect the one helps the other towards that most desirable result, satisfaction. —But he dropped it when he saw me, in a way so abandoning that-comparing small things with great-it called to my mind those lines of Milton: —

"From his slack hand the garland wreathed for Eve,
Down dropt, and all the faded roses shed."

The quiet child FLUNG himself upon my neck, and the mother's face gleamed with pleasure.

"Dear boy!" I said, "I am very glad to see you so much better."

For this was the first time he had shown such a revival of energy. He had been quite sweet when he saw me, but, until this evening, listless.

"Yes," he said, "I am quite well now." And he put his hand up to his head.

"Does it ache?"

"Not much now. The doctor says I had a bad fall."

"So you had, my child. But you will soon be well again."

The mother's face was turned aside, yet I could see one tear forcing its way from under her closed eyelid.

"Oh, I don't mind it," he answered. "Mammy is so kind to me! She lets me sit on her bed as long as I like."

"That IS nice. But just run to auntie in the next room. I think your mammy would like to talk to me for a little while."

The child hurried off the bed, and ran with overflowing obedience.

"I can even think of HIM now," said the mother, "without going into a passion. I hope God will forgive him. *I* do. I think He will forgive me."

"Did you ever hear," I asked, "of Jesus refusing anybody that wanted kindness from Him? He wouldn't always do exactly what they asked Him, because that would sometimes be of no use, and sometimes would even be wrong; but He never pushed them away from Him, never repulsed their approach to Him. For the sake of His disciples, He made the Syrophenician woman suffer a little while, but only to give her such praise afterwards and such a granting of her prayer as is just wonderful."

She said nothing for a little while; then murmured,

"Shall I have to be ashamed to all eternity? I do not want not to be ashamed; but shall I never be able to be like other people-in heaven I mean?"

"If He is satisfied with you, you need not think anything more about yourself. If He lets you once kiss His feet, you won't care to think about other people's opinion of you even in heaven. But things will go very differently there from here. For everybody there will be more or less ashamed of himself, and will think worse of himself than he does of any one else. If trouble about your past life were to show itself on your face there, they would all run to comfort you, trying to make the best of it, and telling you that you must think about yourself as He thinks about you; for what He thinks is the rule, because it is the infallible right way. But perhaps rather, they would tell you to leave that to Him who has taken away our sins, and not trouble yourself any more about it. But to tell the truth, I don't think such thoughts will come to you at all when once you have seen the face of Jesus Christ. You will be so filled with His glory and goodness and grace, that you will just live in Him and not in yourself at all."

"Will He let us tell Him anything we please?"

"He lets you do that now: surely He will not be less our God, our friend there."

"Oh, I don't mind how soon He takes me now! Only there's that poor child that I've behaved so badly to! I wish I could take him with me. I have no time to make it up to him here."

"You must wait till he comes. He won't think hardly of you. There's no fear of that."

"What will become of him, though? I can't bear the idea of burdening my father with him."

"Your father will be glad to have him, I know. He will feel it a privilege to do something for your sake. But the boy will do him good. If he does not want him, I will take him myself."

"Oh! thank you, thank you, sir."

A burst of tears followed.

"He has often done me good," I said.

"Who, sir? My father?"

"No. Your son."

"I don't quite understand what you mean, sir."

"I mean just what I say. The words and behaviour of your lovely boy have both roused and comforted my heart again and again."

She burst again into tears.

"That is good to hear. To think of your saying that! The poor little innocent! Then it isn't all punishment?"

"If it were ALL punishment, we should perish utterly. He is your punishment; but look in what a lovely loving form your punishment has come, and say whether God has been good to you or not."

"If I had only received my punishment humbly, things would have been very different now. But I do take it-at least I want to take it-just as He would have me take it. I will bear anything He likes. I suppose I must die?"

"I think He means you to die now. You are ready for it now, I think. You have wanted to die for a long time; but you were not ready for it before."

"And now I want to live for my boy. But His will be done."

"Amen. There is no such prayer in the universe as that. It means everything best and most beautiful. Thy will, O God, evermore be done."

She lay silent. A tap came to the chamber-door. It was Mary, who nursed her sister and attended to the shop.

"If you please, sir, here's a little girl come to say that Mrs Tomkins is dying, and wants to see you."

"Then I must say good-night to you, Catherine. I will see you to-morrow morning. Think about old Mrs Tomkins; she's a good old soul; and when you find your heart drawn to her in the trouble of death, then lift it up to God for her, that He will please to comfort and support her, and make her happier than health-stronger than strength, taking off the old worn garment of her body, and putting upon her the garment of salvation, which will be a grand new body, like that the Saviour had when He rose again."

"I will try. I will think about her."

For I thought this would be a help to prepare her for her own death. In thinking lovingly about others, we think healthily about ourselves. And the things she thought of for the comfort of Mrs Tomkins, would return to comfort herself in the prospect of her own end, when perhaps she might not be able to think them out for herself.

CHAPTER XXIX
CALM AND STORM.

But of the two, Catherine had herself to go first. Again and again was I sent for to say farewell to Mrs Tomkins, and again and again I returned home leaving her asleep, and for the time better. But on a Saturday evening, as I sat by my vestry-fire, pondering on many things, and trying to make myself feel that they were as God saw them and not as they appeared to me, young Tom came to me with the news that his sister seemed much worse, and his father would be much obliged if I would go and see her. I sent Tom on before, because I wished to follow alone.

It was a brilliant starry night; no moon, no clouds, no wind, nothing but stars. They seemed to lean down towards the earth, as I have seen them since in more southern regions. It was, indeed, a glorious night. That is, I knew it was; I did not feel that it was. For the death which I went to be near, came, with a strange sense of separation, between me and the nature around me. I felt as if nature knew nothing, felt nothing, meant nothing, did not belong to humanity at all; for here was death, and there shone the stars. I was wrong, as I knew afterwards.

I had had very little knowledge of the external shows of death. Strange as it may appear, I had never yet seen a fellow-creature pass beyond the call of his fellow-mortals. I had not even seen my father die. And the thought was oppressive to me. "To think," I said to myself, as I walked over the bridge to the village-street —"to think that the one moment the person is here, and the next-who shall say WHERE? for we know nothing of the region beyond the grave! Not even our risen Lord thought fit to bring back from Hades any news for the human family standing straining their eyes after their brothers and sisters that have vanished in the dark. Surely it is well, all well, although we know nothing, save that our Lord has been there, knows all about it, and does not choose to tell us. Welcome ignorarance then! the ignorance in which he chooses to leave us. I would rather not know, if He gave me my choice, but preferred that I should not know." And so the oppression passed from me, and I was free.

But little as I knew of the signs of the approach of death, I was certain, the moment I saw Catherine, that the veil that hid the "silent land" had begun to lift slowly between her and it. And for a moment I almost envied her that she was so soon to see and know that after which our blindness and ignorance were wondering and hungering. She could hardly speak. She looked more patient than calm. There was no light in the room but that of the fire, which flickered flashing and fading, now lighting up the troubled eye, and now letting a shadow of the coming repose fall gently over it. Thomas sat by the fire with the child on his knee, both looking fixedly into the glow. Gerard's natural mood was so quiet and earnest, that the solemnity about him did not oppress him. He looked as if he were present at some religious observance of which he felt more than he understood, and his childish peace was in no wise inharmonious with the awful silence of the coming change. He was no more disquieted at the presence of death than the stars were.

And this was the end of the lovely girl-to leave the fair world still young, because a selfish man had seen that she was fair! No time can change the relation of cause and effect. The poison that operates ever so slowly is yet poison, and yet slays. And that man was now murdering her, with weapon long-reaching from out of the past. But no, thank God! this was not the end of her. Though there is woe for that man by whom the offence cometh, yet there is provision for the offence. There is One who bringeth light out of darkness, joy out of sorrow, humility out of wrong. Back to the Father's house we go with the sorrows and sins which, instead of inheriting the earth, we gathered and heaped upon our weary shoulders, and a different Elder Brother from that angry one who would not receive the poor swine-humbled prodigal, takes the burden from our shoulders, and leads us into the presence of the Good.

She put out her hand feebly, let it lie in mine, looked as if she wanted me to sit down by her bedside, and when I did so, closed her eyes. She said nothing. Her father was too much troubled to meet me without showing the signs of his distress, and his was a nature that ever sought concealment for its emotion; therefore he sat still. But Gerard crept down from his knee, came to me, clambered up on mine, and laid his little hand upon his mother's, which I was holding. She opened her eyes, looked at the child, shut them again, and tears came out from between the closed lids.

"Has Gerard ever been baptized?" I asked her.

Her lips indicated a NO.

"Then I will be his godfather. And that will be a pledge to you that I will never lose sight of him."

She pressed my hand, and the tears came faster.

Believing with all my heart that the dying should remember their dying Lord, and that the "Do this in remembrance of me" can never be better obeyed than when the partaker is about to pass, supported by the God of his faith, through the same darkness which lay before our Lord when He uttered the words and appointed the symbol, we kneeled, Thomas and I, and young Tom, who had by this time joined us with his sister Mary, around the bed, and partook with the dying woman of the signs of that death, wherein our Lord gave Himself entirely to us, to live by His death, and to the Father of us all in holiest sacrifice as the high-priest of us His people, leading us to the altar of a like self-abnegation. Upon what that bread and that wine mean, the sacrifice of our Lord, the whole world of humanity hangs. It is the redemption of men.

After she had received the holy sacrament, she lay still as before. I heard her murmur once, "Lord, I do not deserve it. But I do love Thee." And about two hours after, she quietly breathed her last. We all kneeled, and I thanked the Father of us aloud that He had taken her to Himself. Gerard had been fast asleep on his aunt's lap, and she had put him to bed a little before. Surely he slept a deeper sleep than his mother's; for had she not awaked even as she fell asleep?

When I came out once more, I knew better what the stars meant. They looked to me now as if they knew all about death, and therefore could not be sad to the eyes of men; as if that unsympathetic look they wore came from this, that they were made like the happy truth, and not like our fears.

But soon the solemn feeling of repose, the sense that the world and all its cares would thus pass into nothing, vanished in its turn. For a moment I had been, as it were, walking on the shore of the Eternal, where the tide of time had left me in its retreat. Far away across the level sands I heard it moaning, but I stood on the firm ground of truth, and heeded it not. In a few moments more it was raving around me; it had carried me away from my rest, and I was filled with the noise of its cares.

For when I returned home, my sister told me that Old Rogers had called, and seemed concerned not to find me at home. He would have gone to find me, my sister said, had I been anywhere but by a deathbed. He would not leave any message, however, saying he would call in the morning.

I thought it better to go to his house. The stars were still shining as brightly as before, but a strong foreboding of trouble filled my mind, and once more the stars were far away, and lifted me no nearer to "Him who made the seven stars and Orion." When I examined myself, I could give no reason for my sudden fearfulness, save this: that as I went to Catherine's house, I had passed Jane Rogers on her way to her father's, and having just greeted her, had gone on; but, as it now came back upon me, she had looked at me strangely-that is, with some significance in her face which conveyed nothing to me; and now her father had been to seek me: it must have something to do with Miss Oldcastle.

But when I came to the cottage, it was dark and still, and I could not bring myself to rouse the weary man from his bed. Indeed it was past eleven, as I found to my surprise on looking at my watch. So I turned and lingered by the old mill, and fell a pondering on the profusion of strength that rushed past the wheel away to the great sea, doing nothing. "Nature," I thought, "does not demand that power should always be force. Power itself must repose. He that believeth shall-not make haste, says the Bible. But it needs strength to be still. Is my faith not strong enough to be still?" I looked up to the heavens once more, and the quietness of the stars seemed to reproach me. "We are safe up here," they seemed to say: "we shine, fearless and confident, for the God who gave the primrose its rough leaves to hide it from the blast of uneven spring, hangs us in the awful hollows of space. We cannot fall out of His safety. Lift up your eyes on high, and behold! Who hath created these things-that bringeth out their host by number! He calleth them all by names. By the greatness of His might, for that He is strong in power, not one faileth. Why sayest thou, O Jacob! and speakest, O Israel! my way is hid from the Lord, and my judgment is passed over from my God?"

The night was very still; there was, I thought, no one awake within miles of me. The stars seemed to shine into me the divine reproach of those glorious words. "O my God!" I cried, and fell on my knees by the mill-door.

What I tried to say more I will not say here. I MAY say that I cried to God. What I said to Him ought not, cannot be repeated to another.

When I opened my eyes I saw the door of the mill was open too, and there in the door, his white head glimmering, stood Old Rogers, with a look on his face as if he had just come down from the mount. I started to my feet, with that strange feeling of something like shame that seizes one at the very thought of other eyes than those of the Father. The old man came forward, and bowed his head with an unconscious expression of humble dignity, but would have passed me without speech, leaving the mill-door open behind him. I could not bear to part with him thus.

"Won't you speak to me, Rogers?" I said.

He turned at once with evident pleasure.

"I beg your pardon, sir. I was ashamed of having intruded on you, and I thought you would rather be left alone. I thought —I thought —-" hesitated the old man, "that you might like to go into the mill, for the night's cold out o' doors."

"Thank you, Rogers. I won't now. I thought you had been in bed. How do you come to be out so late?"

"You see, sir, when I'm in any trouble, it's no use to go to bed. I can't sleep. I only keep the old 'oman wakin'. And the key o' the mill allus hangin' at the back o' my door, and knowin' it to be a good place to-to-shut the door in, I came out as soon as she was asleep; but I little thought to see you, sir."

"I came to find you, not thinking how the time went. Catherine Weir is gone home."

"I am right glad to hear it, poor woman. And perhaps something will come out now that will help us."

"I do not quite understand you," I said, with hesitation.

But Rogers made no reply.

"I am sorry to hear you are in trouble to-night. Can I help you?" I resumed.

"If you can help yourself, sir, you can help me. But I have no right to say so. Only, if a pair of old eyes be not blind, a man may pray to God about anything he sees. I was prayin' hard about you in there, sir, while you was on your knees o' the other side o' the door."

I could partly guess what the old man meant, and I could not ask him for further explanation.

"What did you want to see me about?" I inquired.

He hesitated for a moment.

"I daresay it was very foolish of me, sir. But I just wanted to tell you that-our Jane was down here from the Hall this arternoon — —"

"I passed her on the bridge. Is she quite well?"

"Yes, yes, sir. You know that's not the point."

The old man's tone seemed to reprove me for vain words, and I held my peace.

"The captain's there again."

An icy spear seemed to pass through my heart. I could make no reply. The same moment a cold wind blew on me from the open door of the mill.

Although Lear was of course right when he said,

> "The tempest in my mind
> Doth from my senses take all feeling else
> Save what beats there,"

yet it is also true, that sometimes, in the midst of its greatest pain, the mind takes marvellous notice of the smallest things that happen around it. This involves a law of which illustrations could be plentifully adduced from Shakespeare himself, namely, that the intellectual part of the mind can go on working with strange independence of the emotional.

From the door of the mill, as from a sepulchral tavern, blew a cold wind like the very breath of death upon me, just when that pang shot, in absolute pain, through my heart. For a wind had arisen from behind the mill, and we were in its shelter save where a window behind and the door beside me allowed free passage to the first of the coming storm.

I believed I turned away from the old man without a word. He made no attempt to detain me. Whether he went back into his closet, the old mill, sacred in the eyes of the Father who honours His children, even as the church wherein many prayers went up to Him, or turned homewards to his cottage and his sleeping wife, I cannot tell. The first I remember after that cold wind is, that I was fighting with that wind, gathered even to a storm, upon the common where I had dealt so severely with her who had this very night gone into that region into which, as into a waveless sea, all the rivers of life rush and are silent. Is it the sea of death? No. The sea of life—a life too keen, too refined, for our senses to know it, and therefore we call it death-because we cannot lay hold upon it.

I will not dwell upon my thoughts as I wandered about over that waste. The wind had risen to a storm charged with fierce showers of stinging hail, which gave a look of gray wrath to the invisible wind as it swept slanting by, and then danced and scudded along the levels. The next point in that night of pain is when I found myself standing at the iron gate of Oldcastle Hall. I had left the common, passed my own house and the church, crossed the river, walked through the village, and was restored to self-consciousness—that is, I knew that I was there-only when first I stood in the shelter of one of those great pillars and the monster on its top. Finding the gate open, for they were not precise about having it fastened, I pushed it and entered. The wind was roaring in the trees as I think I have never heard it roar since; for the hail clashed upon the bare branches and twigs, and mingled an unearthly hiss with the roar. In the midst of it the house stood like a tomb, dark, silent, without one dim light to show that sleep and not death ruled within. I could have fancied that there were no windows in it, that it stood, like an eyeless skull, in that gaunt forest of skeleton trees, empty and desolate, beaten by the ungenial hail, the dead rain of the country of death. I passed round to the other side, stepping gently lest some ear might be awake-as if any ear, even that of Judy's white wolf, could have heard the loudest step in such a storm. I heard the hailstones crush between my feet and the soft grass of the lawn, but I dared not stop to look up at the back of the house. I went on to the staircase in the rock, and by its rude steps, dangerous in the flapping of such storm-wings as swept about it that night, descended to the little grove below, around the deep-walled pool. Here the wind did not reach me. It roared overhead, but, save an occasional sigh, as if of sympathy with their suffering brethren abroad in the woild, the hermits of this cell stood upright and still around the sleeping water. But my heart was a well in which a storm boiled and raged; and all that "pother o'er my head" was peace itself compared to what I felt. I sat down on the seat at the foot of a tree, where I had first seen Miss Oldcastle reading. And then I looked up to the house. Yes, there was a light there! It must be in her window. She then could not rest any more than I. Sleep was driven from her eyes because she must wed the man she would not; while sleep was driven from mine because I could not marry the woman I would. Was that it? No. My heart acquitted me, in part at least, of thinking only of my own sorrow in the presence of her greater distress. Gladly would I have given her up for ever, without a hope, to redeem her from such a bondage. "But it would be to marry another some day," suggested the tormentor within.

And then the storm, which had a little abated, broke out afresh in my soul. But before I rose from her seat I was ready even for that-at least I thought so-if only I might deliver her from the all but destruction that seemed to be impending over her. The same moment in which my mind seemed to have arrived at the possibility of such a resolution, I rose almost involuntarily, and glancing once more at the dull light in her window-for I did not doubt that it was her window, though it was much too dark to discern, the shape of the house-almost felt my way to the stair, and climbed again into the storm.

But I was quieter now, and able to go home. It must have been nearly morning, though at this season of the year the morning is undefined, when I reached my own house. My sister had gone to bed, for I could always let myself in; nor, indeed, did any one in Marshmailows think the locking of the door at night an imperative duty.

When I fell asleep, I was again in the old quarry, staring into the deep well. I thought Mrs Oldcastle was murdering her daughter in the house above, while I was spell-bound to the spot, where, if I stood long enough, I should see her body float into the well from the subterranean passage, the opening of which was just below where I stood. I was thus confusing and reconstructing the two dreadful stories of the place-that told me by old Weir, about the circumstances of his birth; and that told me by Dr Duncan, about Mrs Oldcastle's treatment of her elder daughter. But as a white hand and arm appeared in the water below me, sorrow and pity more than horror broke the bonds of sleep, and I awoke to less trouble than that of my dreams, only because that which I feared had not yet come.

CHAPTER XXX
A SERMON TO MYSELF.

It was the Sabbath morn. But such a Sabbath! The day seemed all wan with weeping, and gray with care. The wind dashed itself against the casement, laden with soft heavy sleet. The ground, the bushes, the very outhouses seemed sodden with the rain. The trees, which looked stricken as if they could die of grief, were yet tormented with fear, for the bare branches went streaming out in the torrent of the wind, as cowering before the invisible foe. The first thing I knew when I awoke was the raving of that wind. I could lie in bed not a moment longer. I could not rest. But how was I to do the work of my office? When a man's duty looks like an enemy, dragging him into the dark mountains, he has no less to go with it than when, like a friend with loving face, it offers to lead him along green pastures by the river-side. I had little power over my feelings; I could not prevent my mind from mirroring itself in the nature around me; but I could address myself to the work I had to do. "My God!" was all the prayer I could pray ere I descended to join my sister at the breakfast-table. But He knew what lay behind the one word.

Martha could not help seeing that something was the matter. I saw by her looks that she could read so much in mine. But her eyes alone questioned me, and that only by glancing at me anxiously from, time to time. I was grateful to her for saying nothing. It is a fine thing in friendship to know when to be silent.

The prayers were before me, in the hands of all my friends, and in the hearts of some of them; and if I could not enter into them as I would, I could yet read them humbly before God as His servant to help the people to worship as one flock. But how was I to preach? I had been in difficulty before now, but never in so much. How was I to teach others, whose mind was one confusion? The subject on which I was pondering when young Weir came to tell me his sister was dying, had retreated as if into the far past; it seemed as if years had come between that time and this, though but one black night had rolled by. To attempt to speak upon that would have been vain, for I had nothing to say on the matter now. And if I could have recalled my former thoughts, I should have felt a hypocrite as I delivered them, so utterly dissociated would they have been from anything that I was thinking or feeling now. Here would have been my visible form and audible voice, uttering that as present to me now, as felt by me now, which I did think and feel yesterday, but which, although I believed it, was not present to my feeling or heart, and must wait the revolution of months, or it might be of years, before I should feel it again, before I should be able to exhort my people about it with the fervour of a present faith. But, indeed, I could not even recall what I had thought and felt. Should I then tell them that I could not speak to them that morning? —There would be nothing wrong in that. But I felt ashamed of yielding to personal trouble when the truths of God were all about me, although I could not feel them. Might not some hungry soul go away without being satisfied, because I was faint and down-hearted? I confess I had a desire likewise to avoid giving rise to speculation and talk about myself, a desire which, although not wrong, could neither have strengthened me to speak the truth, nor have justified me in making the attempt. —What was to be done?

All at once the remembrance crossed my mind of a sermon I had preached before upon the words of St Paul: "Thou therefore which teachest another, teachest thou not thyself?" a subject suggested by the fact that on the preceding Sunday I had especially felt, in preaching to my people, that I was exhorting myself whose necessity was greater than theirs-at least I felt it to be greater than I could know theirs to be. And now the converse of the thought came to me, and I said to myself, "Might I not try the other way now, and preach to myself? In teaching myself, might I not teach others? Would it not hold? I am very troubled and faithless now. If I knew that God was going to lay the full weight of this grief upon me, yet if I loved Him with all my heart, should I not at least be more quiet? There would not be a storm within me then, as if the Father had descended from the throne of the heavens, and 'chaos were come again.' Let me expostulate with myself in my heart, and the words of my expostulation will not be the less true with my people."

All this passed through my mind as I sat in my study after breakfast, with the great old cedar roaring before my window. It was within an hour of church-time. I took my Bible, read and thought, got even some comfort already, and found myself in my vestry not quite unwilling to read the prayers and speak to my people.

There were very few present. The day was one of the worst-violently stormy, which harmonized somewhat with my feelings; and, to my further relief, the Hall pew was empty. Instead of finding myself a mere minister to the prayers of others, I found, as I read, that my heart went out in crying to God for the divine presence of His Spirit. And if I thought more of myself in my prayers than was well, yet as soon as I was converted, would I not strengthen my brethren? And the sermon I preached to myself and through myself to my people, was that which the stars had preached to me, and thereby driven me to my knees by the mill-door. I took for my text, "The glory of the Lord shall be revealed;" and then I proceeded to show them how the glory of the Lord was to be revealed. I preached to myself that throughout this fortieth chapter of the prophecies of Isaiah, the power of God is put side by side with the weakness of men, not that He, the perfect, may glory over His feeble children; not that He may say to them —"Look how mighty I am, and go down upon your knees and worship"—for power alone was never yet worthy of prayer; but that he may say thus: "Look, my children, you will never be strong but with MY strength. I have no other to give you. And that you can get only by trusting in me. I cannot give it you any other way. There is no other way. But can you not trust in me? Look how strong I am. You wither like the grass. Do not fear. Let the grass wither. Lay hold of my word, that which I say to you out of my truth, and that will be life in you that the blowing of the wind that withers cannot reach. I am coming with my strong hand and my judging arm to do my work. And what is the work of my strong hand and ruling arm? To feed my flock like a shepherd, to gather the lambs with my arm, and carry them in my bosom, and gently lead those that are with young. I have measured the waters in the hollow of my hand, and held the mountains in my scales, to give each his due weight, and all the nations, so strong and fearful in your eyes, are as nothing beside my strength and what I can do. Do not think of me as of an image that your hands can make, a thing you can choose to serve, and for which you can do things to win its favour. I am before and above the earth, and over your life, and your oppressors I will wither with my breath. I come to you with help I need no worship from you. But I say love me, for love is life, and I love you. Look at the stars I have made. I know every one of them. Not one goes wrong, because I keep him right. Why sayest thou, O Jacob, and speakest, O Israel-my way is HID from the Lord, and my judgment is passed over from my God! I give POWER to the FAINT, and to them that have no might, plenty of strength."

"Thus," I went on to say, "God brings His strength to destroy our weakness by making us strong. This is a God indeed! Shall we not trust Him?"

I gave my people this paraphrase of the chapter, to help them to see the meanings which their familiarity with the words, and their non-familiarity with the modes of Eastern thought, and the forms of Eastern expression, would unite to prevent them from catching more than broken glimmerings of. And then I tried to show them that it was in the commonest troubles of life, as well as in the spiritual fears and perplexities that came upon them, that they were to trust in God; for God made the outside as well as the inside, and they altogether belonged to Him; and that when outside things, such as pain or loss of work, or difficulty in getting money, were referred to God and His will, they too straightway became spiritual affairs, for nothing in the world could any longer appear common or unclean to the man who saw God in everything. But I told them they must not be too anxious to be delivered from that which troubled them: but they ought to be anxious to have the presence of God with them to support them, and make them able in patience to possess their souls; and so the trouble would work its end-the purification of their minds, that the light and gladness of God and all His earth, which the pure in heart and the meek alone could inherit, might shine in upon them. And then I repeated to them this portion of a prayer out of one of Sir Philip Sidney's books: —

"O Lord, I yield unto Thy will, and joyfully embrace what sorrow Thou wilt have me suffer. Only thus much let me crave of Thee, (let my craving, O Lord, be accepted of Thee, since even that proceeds from Thee,) let me crave, even by the noblest title, which in my greatest affliction I may give myself, that I am Thy creature, and by Thy goodness (which is Thyself) that Thou wilt suffer some beam of Thy majesty so to shine into my mind, that it may still depend confidently on Thee."

All the time I was speaking, the rain, mingled with sleet, was dashing against the windows, and the wind was howling over the graves all about. But the dead were not troubled by the storm; and over my head, from beam to beam of the roof, now resting on one, now flitting to another, a sparrow kept flying, which had taken refuge in the church till the storm should cease and the sun shine out in the great temple. "This," I said aloud, "is what the church is for: as the sparrow finds there a house from the storm, so the human heart escapes thither to hear the still small voice of God when its faith is too weak to find Him in the storm, and in the sorrow, and in the pain." And while I spoke, a dim watery gleam fell on the chancel-floor, and the comfort of the sun awoke in my heart. Nor let any one call me superstitious for taking that pale sun-ray of hope as sent to me; for I received it as comfort for the race, and for me as one of the family, even as the bow that was set in the cloud, a promise to the eyes of light for them that sit in darkness. As I write, my eye falls upon the Bible on the table by my side, and I read the words, "For the Lord God is a sun and shield, the Lord will give grace and glory." And I lift my eyes from my paper and look abroad from my window, and the sun is shining in its strength. The leaves are dancing in the light wind that gives them each its share of the sun, and my trouble has passed away for ever, like the storm of that night and the unrest of that strange Sabbath.

Such comforts would come to us oftener from Nature, if we really believed that our God was the God of Nature; that when He made, or rather when He makes, He means; that not His hands only, but His heart too, is in the making of those things; that, therefore, the influences of Nature upon human minds and hearts are because He intended them. And if we believe that our God is everywhere, why should we not think Him present even in the coincidences that sometimes seem so strange? For, if He be in the things that coincide, He must be in the coincidence of those things.

Miss Oldcastle told me once that she could not take her eyes off a butterfly which was flitting about in the church all the time I was speaking of the resurrection of the dead. I told the people that in Greek there was one word for the soul and for a butterfly-Psyche; that I thought as the light on the rain made the natural symbol of mercy-the rainbow, so the butterfly was the type in nature, and made to the end, amongst other ends, of being such a type-of the resurrection of the human body; that its name certainly expressed the hope of the Greeks in immortality, while to us it speaks likewise of a glorified body, whereby we shall know and love each other with our eyes as well as our hearts. —My sister saw the butterfly too, but only remembered that she had seen it when it was mentioned in her hearing: on her the sight made no impression; she saw no coincidence.

I descended from the pulpit comforted by the sermon I had preached to myself. But I was glad to feel justified in telling my people that, in consequence of the continued storm, for there had been no more of sunshine than just that watery gleam, there would be no service in the afternoon, and that I would instead visit some of my sick poor, whom the weather might have discomposed in their worn dwellings.

The people were very slow in dispersing. There was so much putting on of clogs, gathering up of skirts over the head, and expanding of umbrellas, soon to be taken down again as worse than useless in the violence of the wind, that the porches were crowded, and the few left in the church detained till the others made way. I lingered with these. They were all poor people.

"I am sorry you will have such a wet walk home," I said to Mrs Baird, the wife of old Reginald Baird, the shoemaker, a little wizened creature, with more wrinkles than hairs, who the older and more withered she grew, seemed like the kernels of some nuts only to grow the sweeter.

"It's very good of you to let us off this afternoon, sir. Not as I minds the wet: it finds out the holes in people's shoes, and gets my husband into more work."

This was in fact the response of the shoemaker's wife to my sermon. If we look for responses after our fashion instead of after people's own fashion, we ought to be disappointed. Any recognition of truth, whatever form it may take, whether that of poetic delight, intellectual corroboration, practical commonplace; or even vulgar aphorism, must be welcomed by the husbandmen of the God of growth. A response which jars against the peculiar pitch of our mental instrument, must not therefore be turned away from with dislike. Our mood of the moment is not that by which the universe is tuned into its harmonies. We must drop our instrument and listen to the other, and if we find that the player upon it is breathing after a higher expression, is, after his fashion, striving to embody something he sees of the same truth the utterance of which called forth this his answer, let us thank God and take courage. God at least is pleased: and if our refinement and education take away from our pleasure, it is because of something low, false, and selfish, not divine in a word, that is mingled with that refinement and that education. If the shoemaker's wife's response to the prophet's grand poem about the care of God over His creatures, took the form of acknowledgment for the rain that found out the holes in the people's shoes, it was the more genuine and true, for in itself it afforded proof that it was not a mere reflex of the words of the prophet, but sprung from the experience and recognition of the shoemaker's wife. Nor was there anything necessarily selfish in it, for if there are holes in people's shoes, the sooner they are found out the better.

While I was talking to Mrs Baird, Mr Stoddart, whose love for the old organ had been stronger than his dislike to the storm, had come down into the church, and now approached me.

"I never saw you in the church before, Mr Stoddart," I said, "though I have heard you often enough. You use your own private door always."

"I thought to go that way now, but there came such a fierce burst of wind and rain in my face, that my courage failed me, and I turned back-like the sparrow-for refuge in the church."

"A thought strikes me," I said. "Come home with me, and have some lunch, and then we will go together to see some of my poor people. I have often wished to ask you."

His face fell.

"It is such a day!" he answered, remonstratingly, but not positively refusing. It was not his way ever to refuse anything positively.

"So it was when you set out this morning," I returned; "but you would not deprive us of the aid of your music for the sake of a charge of wind, and a rattle of rain-drops."

"But I shan't be of any use. You are going, and that is enough."

"I beg your pardon. Your very presence will be of use. Nothing yet given him or done for him by his fellow, ever did any man so much good as the recognition of the brotherhood by the common signs of friendship and sympathy. The best good of given money depends on the degree to which it is the sign of that friendship and sympathy. Our Lord did not make little of visiting: 'I was sick, and ye visited me.' 'Inasmuch as ye did it not to one of the least of these, ye did it not to me.' Of course, if the visitor goes professionally and not humanly, —as a mere religious policeman, that is-whether he only distributes tracts with condescending words, or gives money liberally because he thinks he ought, the more he does not go the better, for he only does harm to them and himself too."

"But I cannot pretend to feel any of the interest you consider essential: why then should I go?"

"To please me, your friend. That is a good human reason. You need not say a word-you must not pretend anything. Go as my companion, not as their visitor. Will you come?"

"I suppose I must."

"You must, then. Thank you. You will help me. I have seldom a companion."

So when the storm-fit had abated for the moment, we hurried to the vicarage, had a good though hasty lunch, (to which I was pleased to see Mr Stoddart do justice; for it is with man as with beast, if you want work out of him, he must eat well-and it is the one justification of eating well, that a man works well upon it,) and set out for the village. The rain was worse than ever. There was no sleet, and the wind was not cold, but the windows of heaven were opened, and if the fountains of the great deep were not broken up, it looked like it, at least, when we reached the bridge and saw how the river had spread out over all the low lands on its borders. We could not talk much as we went along.

"Don't you find some pleasure in fighting the wind?" I said.

"I have no doubt I should," answered Mr Stoddart, "if I thought I were going to do any good; but as it is, to tell the truth, I would rather be by my own fire with my folio Dante on the reading desk."

"Well, I would rather help the poorest woman in creation, than contemplate the sufferings of the greatest and wickedest," I said.

"There are two things you forget," returned Mr Stoddart. "First, that the poem of Dante is not nearly occupied with the sufferings of the wicked; and next, that what I have complained of in this expedition-which as far as I am concerned, I would call a wild goose chase, were it not that it is your doing and not mine-is that I am not going to help anybody."

"You would have the best of the argument entirely," I replied, "if your expectation was sure to turn out correct."

As I spoke, we had come within a few yards of the Tomkins's cottage, which lay low down from the village towards the river, and I saw that the water was at the threshold. I turned to Mr Stoddart, who, to do him justice, had not yet grumbled in the least.

"Perhaps you had better go home, after all," I said; "for you must wade into Tomkins's if you go at all. Poor old man! what can he be doing, with his wife dying, and the river in his house!"

"You have constituted yourself my superior officer, Mr Walton. I never turned my back on my leader yet. Though I confess I wish I could see the enemy a little clearer."

"There is the enemy," I said, pointing to the water, and walking into it.

Mr Stoddart followed me without a moment's hesitation.

When I opened the door, the first thing I saw was a small stream of water running straight from the door to the fire on the hearth, which it had already drowned. The old man was sitting by his wife's bedside. Life seemed rapidly going from the old woman. She lay breathing very hard.

"Oh, sir," said the old man, as he rose, almost crying, "you're come at last!"

"Did you send for me?" I asked.

"No, sir. I had nobody to send. Leastways, I asked the Lord if He wouldn't fetch you. I been prayin' hard for you for the last hour. I couldn't leave her to come for you. And I do believe the wind 'ud ha' blown me off my two old legs."

"Well, I am come, you see. I would have come sooner, but I had no idea you would be flooded."

"It's not that I mind, sir, though it IS cold sin' the fire went. But she IS goin' now, sir. She ha'n't spoken a word this two hours and more, and her breathin's worse and worse. She don't know me now, sir."

A moan of protestation came from the dying woman.

"She does know you, and loves you too, Tomkins," I said. "And you'll both know each other better by and by."

The old woman made a feeble motion with her hand. I took it in mine. It was cold and deathlike. The rain was falling in large slow drops from the roof upon the bedclothes. But she would be beyond the reach of all the region storms before long, and it did not matter much.

"Look if you can find a basin or plate, Mr Stoddart, and put it to catch the drop here," I said. For I wanted to give him the first chance of being useful.

"There's one in the press there," said the old man, rising feebly.

"Keep your seat," said Mr Stoddart. "I'll get it."

And he got a basin from the cupboard, and put it on the bed to catch the drop.

The old woman held my hand in hers; but by its motion I knew that she wanted something; and guessing what it was from what she had said before, I made her husband sit on the bed on the other side of her and take hold of her other hand, while I took his place on the chair by the bedside. This seemed to content her. So I went and whispered to Mr Stoddart, who had stood looking on disconsolately: —

"You heard me say I would visit some of my sick people this afternoon. Some will be expecting me with certainty. You must go instead of me, and tell them that I cannot come, because old Mrs Tomkins is dying; but I will see them soon."

He seemed rather relieved at the commission. I gave him the necessary directions to find the cottages, and he left me.

I may mention here that this was the beginning of a relation between Mr Stoddart and the poor of the parish —a very slight one indeed, at first, for it consisted only in his knowing two or three of them, so as to ask after their health when he met them, and give them an occasional half-crown. But it led to better things before many years had passed. It seems scarcely more than yesterday-though it is twenty years ago-that I came upon him in the avenue, standing in dismay over the fragments of a jug of soup which he had dropped, to the detriment of his trousers as well as the loss of his soup. "What am I to do?" he said. "Poor Jones expects his soup to-day." —"Why, go back and get some more." —"But what will cook say?" The poor man was more afraid of the cook than he would have been of a squadron of cavalry. "Never mind the cook. Tell her you must have some more as soon as it can be got ready." He stood uncertain for a moment. Then his face brightened. "I will tell her I want my luncheon. I always have soup. And I'll get out through the greenhouse, and carry it to Jones." —"Very well," I said; "that will do capitally." And I went on, without caring to disturb my satisfaction by determining whether the devotion of his own soup arose more from love to Jones, or fear of the cook. He was a great help to me in the latter part of his life, especially after I lost good Dr Duncan, and my beloved friend Old Rogers. He was just one of those men who make excellent front-rank men, but are quite unfit for officers. He could do what he was told without flinching, but he always required to be told.

I resumed my seat by the bedside, where the old woman was again moaning. As soon as I took her hand she ceased, and so I sat till it began to grow dark.

"Are you there, sir?" she would murmur.

"Yes, I am here. I have a hold of your hand."

"I can't feel you, sir."

"But you can hear me. And you can hear God's voice in your heart. I am here, though you can't feel me. And God is here, though you can't see Him."

She would be silent for a while, and then murmur again—

"Are you there, Tomkins?"

"Yes, my woman, I'm here," answered the old man to one of these questions; "but I wish I was there instead, wheresomever it be as you're goin', old girl."

And all that I could hear of her answer was, "Bym by; bym by."

Why should I linger over the death-bed of an illiterate woman, old and plain, dying away by inches? Is it only that she died with a hold of my hand, and that therefore I am interested in the story? I trust not. I was interested in HER. Why? Would my readers be more interested if I told them of the death of a young lovely creature, who said touching things, and died amidst a circle of friends, who felt that the very light of life was being taken away from them? It was enough for me that here was a woman with a heart like my own; who needed the same salvation I needed; to whom the love of God was the one blessed thing; who was passing through the same dark passage into the light that the Lord had passed through before her, that I had to pass through after her. She had no theories-at least, she gave utterance to none; she had few thoughts of her own-and gave still fewer of them expression; you might guess at a true notion in her mind, but an abstract idea she could scarcely lay hold of; her speech was very common; her manner rather brusque than gentle; but she could love; she could forget herself; she could be sorry for what she did or thought wrong; she could hope; she could wish to be better; she could admire good people; she could trust in God her Saviour. And now the loving God-made human heart in her was going into a new school that it might begin a fresh beautiful growth. She was old, I have said, and plain; but now her old age and plainness were about to vanish, and all that had made her youth attractive to young Tomkins was about to return to her, only rendered tenfold more beautiful by the growth of fifty years of learning according to her ability. God has such patience in working us into vessels of honour! in teaching us to be children! And shall we find the human heart in which the germs of all that is noblest and loveliest and likest to God have begun to grow and manifest themselves uninteresting, because its circumstances have been narrow, bare, and poverty-stricken, though neither sordid nor unclean; because the woman is old and wrinkled and brown, as if these were more than the transient accidents of humanity; because she has neither learned grammar nor philosophy; because her habits have neither been delicate nor self-indulgent? To help the mind of such a woman to unfold to the recognition of the endless delights of truth; to watch the dawn of the rising intelligence upon the too still face, and the transfiguration of the whole form, as the gentle rusticity vanishes in yet gentler grace, is a labour and a delight worth the time and mind of an archangel. Our best living poet says-but no; I will not quote. It is a distinct wrong that befalls the best books to have many of their best words quoted till in their own place and connexion they cease to have force and influence. The meaning of the passage is that the communication of truth is one of the greatest delights the human heart can experience. Surely this is true. Does not the teaching of men form a great part of the divine gladness?

Therefore even the dull approaches of death are full of deep significance and warm interest to one who loves his fellows, who desires not to be distinguished by any better fate than theirs; and shrinks from the pride of supposing that his own death, or that of the noblest of the good, is more precious in the sight of God than that of "one of the least of these little ones."

At length, after a long silence, the peculiar sounds of obstructed breathing indicated the end at hand. The jaw fell, and the eyes were fixed. The old man closed the mouth and the eyes of his old companion, weeping like a child, and I prayed aloud, giving thanks to God for taking her to Himself. It went to my heart to leave the old man alone with the dead; but it was better to let him be alone for a while, ere the women should come to do the last offices for the abandoned form.

I went to Old Rogers, told him the state in which I had left poor Tomkins, and asked him what was to be done.

"I'll go and bring him home, sir, directly. He can't be left there."

"But how can you bring him in such a night?"

"Let me see, sir. I must think. Would your mare go in a cart, do you think?"

"Quite quietly. She brought a load of gravel from the common a few days ago. But where's your cart? I haven't got one."

"There's one at Weir's to be repaired, sir. It wouldn't be stealing to borrow it."

How he managed with Tomkins I do not know. I thought it better to leave all the rest to him. He only said afterwards, that he could hardly get the old man away from the body. But when I went in next day, I found Tomkins sitting, disconsolate, but as comfortable as he could be, in the easy chair by the side of the fire. Mrs Rogers was bustling about cheerily. The storm had died in the night. The sun was shining. It was the first of the spring weather. The whole country was gleaming with water. But soon it would sink away, and the grass be the thicker for its rising.

CHAPTER XXXI
A COUNCIL OF FRIENDS.

My reader will easily believe that I returned home that Sunday evening somewhat jaded, nor will he be surprised if I say that next morning I felt disinclined to leave my bed. I was able, however, to rise and go, as I have said, to Old Rogers's cottage.

But when I came home, I could no longer conceal from myself that I was in danger of a return of my last attack. I had been sitting for hours in wet clothes, with my boots full of water, and now I had to suffer for it. But as I was not to blame in the matter, and had no choice offered me whether I should be wet or dry while I sat by the dying woman, I felt no depression at the prospect of the coming illness. Indeed, I was too much depressed from other causes, from mental strife and hopelessness, to care much whether I was well or ill. I could have welcomed death in the mood in which I sometimes felt myself during the next few days, when I was unable to leave my bed, and knew that Captain Everard was at the Hall, and knew nothing besides. For no voice reached me from that quarter any more than if Oldcastle Hall had been a region beyond the grave. Miss Oldcastle seemed to have vanished from my ken as much as Catherine Weir and Mrs Tomkins-yes, more-for there was only death between these and me; whereas, there was something far worse —I could not always tell what-that rose ever between Miss Oldcastle and myself, and paralysed any effort I might fancy myself on the point of making for her rescue.

One pleasant thing happened. On the Thursday, I think it was, I felt better. My sister came into my room and said that Miss Crowther had called, and wanted to see me.

"Which Miss Crowther is it?" I asked.

"The little lady that looks like a bird, and chirps when she talks."

Of course I was no longer in any doubt as to which of them it was.

"You told her I had a bad cold, did you not?"

"Oh, yes. But she says if it is only a cold, it will do you no harm to see her."

"But you told her I was in bed, didn't you?"

"Of course. But it makes no difference. She says she's used to seeing sick folk in bed; and if you don't mind seeing her, she doesn't mind seeing you."

"Well, I suppose I must see her," I said.

So my sister made me a little tidier, and introduced Miss Crowther.

"O dear Mr Walton, I am SO sorry! But you're not very ill, are you?"

"I hope not, Miss Jemima. Indeed, I begin to think this morning that I am going to get off easier than I expected."

"I am glad of that. Now listen to me. I won't keep you, and it is a matter of some importance. I hear that one of your people is dead, a young woman of the name of Weir, who has left a little boy behind her. Now, I have been wanting for a long time to adopt a child ——"

"But," I interrupted her, "What would Miss Hester say?"

"My sister is not so very dreadful as perhaps you think her, Mr Walton; and besides, when I do want my own way very particularly, which is not often, for there are not so many things that it's worth while insisting upon-but when I DO want my own way, I always have it. I then stand upon my right of-what do you call it? —primo-primogeniture-that's it! Well, I think I know something of this child's father. I am sorry to say I don't know much good of him, and that's the worse for the boy. Still ——"

"The boy is an uncommonly sweet and lovable child, whoever was his father," I interposed.

"I am very glad to hear it. I am the more determined to adopt him. What friends has he?"

"He has a grandfather, and an uncle and aunt, and will have a godfather-that's me-in a few days, I hope."

"I am very glad to hear it. There will be no opposition on the part of the relatives, I presume?"

"I am not so sure of that. I fear I shall object for one, Miss Jemima."

"You? I didn't expect that of you, Mr Walton, I must say."

And there was a tremor in the old lady's voice more of disappointment and hurt than of anger.

"I will think it over, though, and talk about it to his grandfather, and we shall find out what's best, I do hope. You must not think I should not like you to have him."

"Thank you, Mr Walton. Then I won't stay longer now. But I warn you I will call again very soon, if you don't come to see me. Good morning."

And the dear old lady shook hands with me and left me rather hurriedly, turning at the door, however, to add—

"Mind, I've set my heart upon having the boy, Mr Walton. I've seen him often."

What could have made Miss Crowther take such a fancy to the boy? I could not help associating it with what I had heard of her youthful disappointment, but never having had my conjectures confirmed, I will say no more about them. Of course I talked the matter over with Thomas Weir; but, as I had suspected, I found that he was now as unwilling to part with the boy as he had formerly disliked the sight of him. Nor did I press the matter at all, having a belief that the circumstances of one's natal position are not to be rudely handled or thoughtlessly altered, besides that I thought Thomas and his daughter ought to have all the comfort and good that were to be got from the presence of the boy whose advent had occasioned them so much trouble and sorrow, yea, and sin too. But I did not give a positive and final refusal to Miss Crowther. I only said "for the present;" for I did not feel at liberty to go further. I thought that such changes might take place as would render the trial of such a new relationship desirable; as, indeed, it turned out in the end, though I cannot tell the story now, but must keep it for a possible future.

I have, I think, entirely as yet, followed, in these memoirs, the plan of relating either those things only at which I was present, or, if other things, only in the same mode in which I heard them. I will now depart from this plan-for once. Years passed before some of the following facts were reported to me, but it is only here that they could be interesting to my readers.

At the very time Miss Crowther was with me, as nearly as I can guess, Old Rogers turned into Thomas Weir's workshop. The usual, on the present occasion somewhat melancholy, greetings having passed between them, Old Rogers said—

"Don't you think, Mr Weir, there's summat the matter wi' parson?"

"Overworked," returned Weir. "He's lost two, ye see, and had to see them both safe over, as I may say, within the same day. He's got a bad cold, I'm sorry to hear, besides. Have ye heard of him to-day?"

"Yes, yes; he's badly, and in bed. But that's not what I mean. There's summat on his mind," said Old Rogers.

"Well, I don't think it's for you or me to meddle with parson's mind," returned Weir.

"I'm not so sure o' that," persisted Rogers. "But if I had thought, Mr Weir, as how you would be ready to take me up short for mentionin' of the thing, I wouldn't ha' opened my mouth to you about parson-leastways, in that way, I mean."

"But what way DO you mean, Old Rogers?"

"Why, about his in'ards, you know."

"I'm no nearer your meanin' yet."

"Well, Mr Weir, you and me's two old fellows, now-leastways I'm a deal older than you. But that doesn't signify to what I want to say."

And here Old Rogers stuck fast-according to Weir's story.

"It don't seem easy to say no how, Old Rogers," said Weir.

"Well, it ain't. So I must just let it go by the run, and hope the parson, who'll never know, would forgive me if he did."

"Well, then, what is it?"

"It's my opinion that that parson o' ours-you see, we knows about it, Mr Weir, though we're not gentlefolks-leastways, I'm none."

"Now, what DO you mean, Old Rogers?"

"Well, I means this-as how parson's in love. There, that's paid out."

"Suppose he was, I don't see yet what business that is of yours or mine either."

"Well, I do. I'd go to Davie Jones for that man."

A heathenish expression, perhaps; but Weir assured me, with much amusement in his tone, that those were the very words Old Rogers used. Leaving the expression aside, will the reader think for a moment on the old man's reasoning? My condition WAS his business; for he was ready to die for me! Ah! love does indeed make us all each other's keeper, just as we were intended to be.

"But what CAN we do?" returned Weir.

Perhaps he was the less inclined to listen to the old man, that he was busy with a coffin for his daughter, who was lying dead down the street. And so my poor affairs were talked of over the coffin-planks. Well, well, it was no bad omen.

"I tell you what, Mr Weir, this here's a serious business. And it seems to me it's not shipshape o' you to go on with that plane o' yours, when we're talkin' about parson."

"Well, Old Rogers, I meant no offence. Here goes. NOW, what have you to say? Though if it's offence to parson you're speakin' of, I know, if I were parson, who I'd think was takin' the greatest liberty, me wi' my plane, or you wi' your fancies."

"Belay there, and hearken."

So Old Rogers went into as many particulars as he thought fit, to prove that his suspicion as to the state of my mind was correct; which particulars I do not care to lay in a collected form before my reader, he being in no need of such a summing up to give his verdict, seeing the parson has already pleaded guilty. When he had finished,

"Supposing all you say, Old Rogers," remarked Thomas, "I don't yet see what WE'VE got to do with it. Parson ought to know best what he's about."

"But my daughter tells me," said Rogers, "that Miss Oldcastle has no mind to marry Captain Everard. And she thinks if parson would only speak out he might have a chance."

Weir made no reply, and was silent so long, with his head bent, that Rogers grew impatient.

"Well, man, ha' you nothing to say now-not for your best friend-on earth, I mean-and that's parson? It may seem a small matter to you, but it's no small matter to parson."

"Small to me!" said Weir, and taking up his tool, a constant recourse with him when agitated, he began to plane furiously.

Old Rogers now saw that there was more in it than he had thought, and held his peace and waited. After a minute or two of fierce activity, Thomas lifted up a face more white than the deal board he was planing, and said,

"You should have come to the point a little sooner, Old Rogers."

He then laid down his plane, and went out of the workshop, leaving Rogers standing there in bewilderment. But he was not gone many minutes. He returned with a letter in his hand.

"There," he said, giving it to Rogers.

"I can't read hand o' write," returned Rogers. "I ha' enough ado with straight-foret print But I'll take it to parson."

"On no account," returned Thomas, emphatically "That's not what I gave it you for. Neither you nor parson has any right to read that letter; and I don't want either of you to read it. Can Jane read writing?"

"I don't know as she can, for, you see, what makes lasses take to writin' is when their young man's over the seas, leastways not in the mill over the brook."

"I'll be back in a minute," said Thomas, and taking the letter from Rogers's hand, he left the shop again.

He returned once more with the letter sealed up in an envelope, addressed to Miss Oldcastle.

"Now, you tell your Jane to give that to Miss Oldcastle from me-mind, from ME; and she must give it into her own hands, and let no one else see it. And I must have it again. Mind you tell her all that, Old Rogers."

"I will. It's for Miss Oldcastle, and no one else to know on't. And you're to have it again all safe when done with."

"Yes. Can you trust Jane not to go talking about it?"

"I think I can. I ought to, anyhow. But she can't know anythink in the letter now, Mr Weir."

"I know that; but Marshmallows is a talkin' place. And poor Kate ain't right out o' hearin' yet. —You'll come and see her buried to-morrow, won't ye, Old Rogers?"

"I will, Thomas. You've had a troubled life, but thank God the sun came out a bit before she died."

"That's true, Rogers. It's all right, I do think, though I grumbled long and sore. But Jane mustn't speak of that letter."

"No. That she shan't."

"I'll tell you some day what's in it. But I can't bear to talk about it yet."

And so they parted.

I was too unwell still either to be able to bury my dead out of my sight or to comfort my living the next Sunday. I got help from Addicehead, however, and the dead bodies were laid aside in the ancient wardrobe of the tomb. They were both buried by my vestry-door, Catherine where I had found young Tom lying, namely, in the grave of her mother, and old Mrs Tomkins on the other side of the path.

On Sunday, Rogers gave his daughter the letter, and she carried it to the Hall. It was not till she had to wait on her mistress before leaving her for the night that she found an opportunity of giving it into her own hands.

Then when her bell rang, Jane went up to her room, and found her so pale and haggard that she was frightened. She had thrown herself back on the couch, with her hands lying by her sides, as if she cared for nothing in this world or out of it. But when Jane entered, she started and sat up, and tried to look like herself. Her face, however, was so pitiful, that honest-hearted Jane could not help crying, upon which the responsive sisterhood overcame the proud lady, and she cried too. Jane had all but forgotten the letter, of the import of which she had no idea, for her father had taken care to rouse no suspicions in her mind. But when she saw her cry, the longing to give her something, which comes to us all when we witness trouble-for giving seems to mean everything-brought to her mind the letter she had undertaken to deliver to her. Now she had no notion, as I have said, that the letter had anything to do with her present perplexity, but she hoped it might divert her thoughts for a moment, which is all that love at a distance can look for sometimes.

"Here is a letter," said Jane, "that Mr Weir the carpenter gave to my father to give to me to bring to you, miss."

"What is it about, Jane?" she asked listlessly.

Then a sudden flash broke from her eyes, and she held out her hand eagerly to take it. She opened it and read it with changing colour, but when she had finished it, her cheeks were crimson, and her eyes glowing like fire.

"The wretch," she said, and threw the letter from her into the middle of the floor.

Jane, who remembered the injunctions of her father as to the safety and return of the letter, stooped to pick it up: but had hardly raised herself when the door opened, and in came Mrs Oldcastle. The moment she saw her mother, Ethelwyn rose, and advancing to meet her, said,

"Mother, I will NOT marry that man. You may do what you please with me, but I WILL NOT."

"Heigho!" exclaimed Mrs Oldcastle with spread nostrils, and turning suddenly upon Jane, snatched the letter out of her hand.

She opened and read it, her face getting more still and stony as she read. Miss Oldcastle stood and looked at her mother with cheeks now pale but with still flashing eyes. The moment her mother had finished the letter, she walked swiftly to the fire, tearing the letter as she went, and thrust it between the bars, pushing it in fiercely with the poker, and muttering—

"A vile forgery of those low Chartist wretches! As if he would ever have looked at one of THEIR women! A low conspiracy to get money from a gentleman in his honourable position!"

And for the first time since she went to the Hall, Jane said, there was colour in that dead white face.

She turned once more, fiercer than ever, upon Jane, and in a tone of rage under powerful repression, began: —

"You leave the house-THIS INSTANT."

The last two words, notwithstanding her self-command, rose to a scream. And she came from the fire towards Jane, who stood trembling near the door, with such an expression on her countenance that absolute fear drove her from the room before she knew what she was about. The locking of the door behind her let her know that she had abandoned her young mistress to the madness of her mother's evil temper and disposition. But it was too late. She lingered by the door and listened, but beyond an occasional hoarse tone of suppressed energy, she heard nothing. At length the lock-as suddenly turned, and she was surprised by Mrs Oldcastle, if not in a listening attitude, at least where she had no right to be after the dismissal she had received.

Opposite Miss Oldcastle's bedroom was another, seldom used, the door of which was now standing open. Instead of speaking to Jane, Mrs Oldcastle gave her a violent push, which drove her into this room. Thereupon she shut the door and locked it. Jane spent the whole of the night in that room, in no small degree of trepidation as to what might happen next. But she heard no noise all the rest of the night, part of which, however, was spent in sound sleep, for Jane's conscience was in no ways disturbed as to any part she had played in the current events.

It was not till the morning that she examined the door, to see if she could not manage to get out and escape from the house, for she shared with the rest of the family an indescribable fear of Mrs Oldcastle and her confidante, the White Wolf. But she found it was of no use: the lock was at least as strong as the door. Being a sensible girl and self-possessed, as her parents' child ought to be, she made no noise, but waited patiently for what might come. At length, hearing a step in the passage, she tapped gently at the door and called, "Who's there?" The cook's voice answered.

"Let me out," said Jane. "The door's locked." The cook tried, but found there was no key. Jane told her how she came there, and the cook promised to get her out as soon as she could. Meantime all she could do for her was to hand her a loaf of bread on a stick from the next window. It had been long dark before some one unlocked the door, and left her at liberty to go where she pleased, of which she did not fail to make immediate use.

Unable to find her young mistress, she packed her box, and, leaving it behind her, escaped to her father. As soon as she had told him the story, he came straight to me.

CHAPTER XXXII
THE NEXT THING.

As I sat in my study, in the twilight of that same day, the door was hurriedly opened, and Judy entered. She looked about the room with a quick glance to see that we were alone, then caught my hand in both of hers, and burst out crying.

"Why, Judy!" I said, "what IS the matter?" But the sobs would not allow her to answer. I was too frightened to put any more questions, and so stood silent-my chest feeling like an empty tomb that waited for death to fill it. At length with a strong effort she checked the succession of her sobs, and spoke.

"They are killing auntie. She looks like a ghost already," said the child, again bursting into tears.

"Tell me, Judy, what CAN I do for her?"

"You must find out, Mr Walton. If you loved her as much as I do, you would find out what to do."

"But she will not let me do anything for her."

"Yes, she will. She says you promised to help her some day."

"Did she send you, then?"

"No. She did not send me."

"Then how-what-what can I do!"

"Oh, you exact people! You must have everything square and in print before you move. If it had been me now, wouldn't I have been off like a shot! Do get your hat, Mr Walton."

"Come, then, Judy. I will go at once.—Shall I see her?"

And every vein throbbed at the thought of rescuing her from her persecutors, though I had not yet the smallest idea how it was to be effected.

"We will talk about that as we go," said Judy, authoritatively.

In a moment more we were in the open air. It was a still night, with an odour of damp earth, and a hint of green buds in it. A pale half-moon hung in the sky, now and then hidden by the clouds that swept across it, for there was wind in the heavens, though upon earth all was still. I offered Judy my arm, but she took my hand, and we walked on without a word till we had got through the village and out upon the road.

"Now, Judy," I said at last, "tell me what they are doing to your aunt?"

"I don't know what they are doing. But I am sure she will die."

"Is she ill?"

"She is as white as a sheet, and will not leave her room. Grannie must have frightened her dreadfully. Everybody is frightened at her but me, and I begin to be frightened too. And what will become of auntie then?"

"But what can her mother do to her?"

"I don't know. I think it is her determination to have her own way that makes auntie afraid she will get it somehow; and she says now she will rather die than marry Captain Everard. Then there is no one allowed to wait on her but Sarah, and I know the very sight of her is enough to turn auntie sick almost. What has become of Jane I don't know. I haven't seen her all day, and the servants are whispering together more than usual. Auntie can't eat what Sarah brings her, I am sure; else I should almost fancy she was starving herself to death to keep clear of that Captain Everard."

"Is he still at the Hall?"

"Yes. But I don't think it is altogether his fault. Grannie won't let him go. I don't believe he knows how determined auntie is not to marry him. Only, to be sure, though grannie never lets her have more than five shillings in her pocket at a time, she will be worth something when she is married."

"Nothing can make her worth more than she is, Judy," I said, perhaps with some discontent in my tone.

"That's as you and I think, Mr Walton; not as grannie and the captain think at all. I daresay he would not care much more than grannie whether she was willing or not, so long as she married him."

"But, Judy, we must have some plan laid before we reach the Hall; else my coming will be of no use."

"Of course. I know how much I can do, and you must arrange the rest with her. I will take you to the little room up-stairs—we call it the octagon. That you know is just under auntie's room. They will be at dinner-the captain and grannie. I will leave you there, and tell auntie that you want to see her."

"But, Judy,—-"

"Don't you want to see her, Mr Walton?"

"Yes, I do; more than you can think."

"Then I will tell her so."

"But will she come to me?"

"I don't know. We have to find that out."

"Very well. I leave myself in your hands."

I was now perfectly collected. All my dubitation and distress were gone, for I had something to do, although what I could not yet tell. That she did not love Captain Everard was plain, and that she had as yet resisted her mother was also plain, though it was not equally certain that she would, if left at her mercy, go on to resist her. This was what I hoped to strengthen her to do. I saw nothing more within my reach as yet. But from what I knew of Miss Oldcastle, I saw plainly enough that no greater good could be done for her than this enabling to resistance. Self-assertion was so foreign to her nature, that it needed a sense of duty to rouse her even to self-defence. As I have said before, she was clad in the mail of endurance, but was utterly without weapons. And there was a danger of her conduct and then of her mind giving way at last, from the gradual inroads of weakness upon the thews which she left unexercised. In respect of this, I prayed heartily that I might help her.

Judy and I scarcely spoke to each other from the moment we entered the gate till I found myself at a side door which I had never observed till now. It was fastened, and Judy told me to wait till she went in and opened it. The moon was now quite obscured, and I was under no apprehension of discovery. While I stood there I could not help thinking of Dr Duncan's story, and reflecting that the daughter was now returning the kindness shown to the mother.

I had not to wait long before the door opened behind me noiselessly, and I stepped into the dark house. Judy took me by the hand, and led me along a passage, and then up a stair into the little drawing-room. There was no light. She led me to a seat at the farther end, and opening a door close beside me, left me in the dark.

There I sat so long that I fell into a fit of musing, broken ever by startled expectation. Castle after castle I built up; castle after castle fell to pieces in my hands. Still she did not come. At length I got so restless and excited that only the darkness kept me from starting up and pacing the room. Still she did not come, and partly from weakness, partly from hope deferred, I found myself beginning to tremble all over. Nor could I control myself. As the trembling increased, I grew alarmed lest I should become unable to carry out all that might be necessary.

Suddenly from out of the dark a hand settled on my arm. I looked up and could just see the whiteness of a face. Before I could speak, a voice said brokenly, in a half-whisper: —

"WILL you save me, Mr Walton? But you're trembling; you are ill; you ought not to have come to me. I will get you something."

And she moved to go, but I held her. All my trembling was gone in a moment. Her words, so careful of me even in her deep misery, went to my heart and gave me strength. The suppressed feelings of many months rushed to my lips. What I said I do not know, but I know that I told her I loved her. And I know that she did not draw her hand from mine when I said so.

But ere I ceased came a revulsion of feeling.

"Forgive me," I said, "I am selfishness itself to speak to you thus now, to take advantage of your misery to make you listen to mine. But, at least, it will make you sure that if all I am, all I have will save you —"

"But I am saved already," she interposed, "if you love me-for I love you."

And for some moments there were no words to speak. I stood holding her hand, conscious only of God and her. At last I said:

"There is no time now but for action. Nor do I see anything but to go with me at once. Will you come home to my sister? Or I will take you wherever you please."

"I will go with you anywhere you think best. Only take me away."

"Put on your bonnet, then, and a warm cloak, and we will settle all about it as we go."

She had scarcely left the room when Mrs Oldcastle came to the door.

"No lights here!" she said. "Sarah, bring candles, and tell Captain Everard, when he will join us, to come to the octagon room. Where can that little Judy be? The child gets more and more troublesome, I do think. I must take her in hand."

I had been in great perplexity how to let her know that I was there; for to announce yourself to a lady by a voice out of the darkness of her boudoir, or to wait for candles to discover you where she thought she was quite alone-neither is a pleasant way of presenting yourself to her consciousness. But I was helped out of the beginning into the middle of my difficulties, once more by that blessed little Judy. I did not know she was in the room till I heard her voice. Nor do I yet know how much she had heard of the conversation between her aunt and myself; for although I sometimes see her look roguish even now that she is a middle-aged woman with many children, when anything is said which might be supposed to have a possible reference to that night, I have never cared to ask her.

"Here I am, grannie," said her voice. "But I won't be taken in hand by you or any one else. I tell you that. So mind. And Mr Walton is here, too, and Aunt Ethelwyn is going out with him for a long walk."

"What do you mean, you silly child?"

"I mean what I say," and "Miss Judy speaks the truth," fell together from her lips and mine.

"Mr Walton," began Mrs Oldcastle, indignantly, "it is scarcely like a gentleman to come where you are not wanted —-"

Here Judy interrupted her.

"I beg your pardon, grannie, Mr Walton WAS wanted-very much wanted. I went and fetched him."

But Mrs Oldcastle went on unheeding.

" —-and to be sitting in my room in the dark too!"

"That couldn't be helped, grannie. Here comes Sarah with candles."

"Sarah," said Mrs Oldcastle, "ask Captain Everard to be kind enough to step this way."

"Yes, ma'am," answered Sarah, with an untranslatable look at me as she set down the candles.

We could now see each other. Knowing words to be but idle breath, I would not complicate matters by speech, but stood silent, regarding Mrs Oldcastle. She on her part did not flinch, but returned my look with one both haughty and contemptuous. In a few moments, Captain Everard entered, bowed slightly, and looked to Mrs Oldcastle as if for an explanation. Whereupon she spoke, but to me.

"Mr Walton," she said, "will you explain to Captain Everard to what we owe the UNEXPECTED pleasure of a visit from you?"

"Captain Everard has no claim to any explanation from me. To you, Mrs Oldcastle, I would have answered, had you asked me, that I was waiting for Miss Oldcastle."

"Pray inform Miss Oldcastle, Judy, that Mr Walton insists upon seeing her at once."

"That is quite unnecessary. Miss Oldcastle will be here presently," I said.

Mrs Oldcastle turned slightly livid with wrath. She was always white, as I have said: the change I can describe only by the word I have used, indicating a bluish darkening of the whiteness. She walked towards the door beside me. I stepped between her and it.

"Pardon me, Mrs Oldcastle. That is the way to Miss Oldcastle's room. I am here to protect her."

Without saying a word she turned and looked at Captain Everard. He advanced with a long stride of determination. But ere he reached me, the door behind me opened, and Miss Oldcastle appeared in her bonnet and shawl, catrying a small bag in her hand. Seeing how things were, the moment she entered, she put her hand on my arm, and stood fronting the enemy with me. Judy was on my right, her eyes flashing, and her cheek as red as a peony, evidently prepared to do battle a toute outrance for her friends.

"Miss Oldcastle, go to your room instantly, I COMMAND you," said her mother; and she approached as if to remove her hand from my arm. I put my other arm between her and her daughter.

"No, Mrs Oldcastle," I said. "You have lost all a mother's rights by ceasing to behave like a mother, Miss Oldcastle will never more do anything in obedience to your commands, whatever she may do in compliance with your wishes."

"Allow me to remark," said Captain Everard, with attempted nonchalance, "that that is strange doctrine for your cloth."

"So much the worse for my cloth, then," I answered, "and the better for yours if it leads you to act more honourably."

Still keeping himself entrenched in the affectation of a supercilious indifference, he smiled haughtily, and gave a look of dramatic appeal to Mrs Oldcastle.

"At least," said that lady, "do not disgrace yourself, Ethelwyn, by leaving the house in this unaccountable manner at night and on foot. If you WILL leave the protection of your mother's roof, wait at least till tomorrow."

"I would rather spend the night in the open air than pass another under your roof, mother. You have been a strange mother to me-and Dorothy too!"

"At least do not put your character in question by going in this unmaidenly fashion. People will talk to your prejudice-and Mr Walton's too."

Ethelwyn smiled. —She was now as collected as I was, seeming to have cast off all her weakness. My heart was uplifted more than I can say. —She knew her mother too well to be caught by the change in her tone.

I had not hitherto interrupted her once when she took the answer upon herself, for she was not one to be checked when she chose to speak. But now she answered nothing, only looked at me, and I understood her, of course.

"They will hardly have time to do so, I trust, before it will be out of their power. It rests with Miss Oldcastle herself to say when that shall be."

As if she had never suspected that such was the result of her scheming, Mrs Oldcastle's demeanour changed utterly. The form of her visage was altered. She made a spring at her daughter, and seized her by the arm.

"Then I forbid it," she screamed; "and I WILL be obeyed. I stand on my rights. Go to your room, you minx."

"There is no law human or divine to prevent her from marrying whom she will. How old are you, Ethelwyn?"

I thought it better to seem even cooler than I was.

"Twenty-seven," answered Miss Oldcastle.

"Is it possible you can be so foolish, Mrs Oldcastle, as to think you have the slightest hold on your daughter's freedom? Let her arm go."

But she kept her grasp.

"You hurt me, mother," said Miss Oldcastle.

"Hurt you? you smooth-faced hypocrite! I will hurt you then!"

But I took Mrs Oldcastle's arm in my hand, and she let go her hold.

"How dare you touch a woman?" she said.

"Because she has so far ceased to be a woman as to torture her own daughter."

Here Captain Everard stepped forward, saying, —

"The riot-act ought to be read, I think. It is time for the military to interfere."

"Well put, Captain Everard," I said. "Our side will disperse if you will only leave room for us to go."

"Possibly *I* may have something to say in the matter."

"Say on."

"This lady has jilted me."

"Have you, Ethelwyn?"

"I have not."

"Then, Captain Everard, you lie."

"You dare to tell me so?"

And he strode a pace nearer.

"It needs no daring. I know you too well; and so does another who trusted you and found you false as hell."

"You presume on your cloth, but —" he said, lifting his hand.

"You may strike me, presuming on my cloth," I answered; "and I will not return your blow. Insult me as you will, and I will bear it. Call me coward, and I will say nothing. But lay one hand on me to prevent me from doing my duty, and I knock you down-or find you more of a man than I take you for."

It was either conscience or something not so good that made a coward of him. He turned on his heel.

"I really am not sufficiently interested in the affair to oppose you. You may take the girl for me. Both your cloth and the presence of ladies protect your insolence. I do not like brawling where one cannot fight. You shall hear from me before long, Mr Walton."

"No, Captain Everard, I shall not hear from you. You know you dare not write to me. I know that of you which, even on the code of the duellist, would justify any gentleman in refusing to meet you. Stand out of my way!"

I advanced with Miss Oldcastle on my arm. He drew back; and we left the room.

As we reached the door, Judy bounded after us, threw her arms round her aunt's neck, then round mine, kissing us both, and returned to her place on the sofa. Mrs Oldcastle gave a scream, and sunk fainting on a chair. It was a last effort to detain her daughter and gain time. Miss Oldcastle would have returned, but I would not permit her.

"No," I said; "she will be better without you. Judy, ring the bell for Sarah."

"How dare you give orders in my house?" exclaimed Mrs Oldcastle, sitting bolt upright in the chair, and shaking her fist at us. Then assuming the heroic, she added, "From this moment she is no daughter of mine. Nor can you touch one farthing of her money, sir. You have married a beggar after all, and that you'll both know before long."

"Thy money perish with thee!" I said, and repented the moment I had said it. It sounded like an imprecation, and I know I had no correspondent feeling; for, after all, she was the mother of my Ethelwyn. But the allusion to money made me so indignant, that the words burst from me ere I could consider their import.

The cool wind greeted us like the breath of God, as we left the house and closed the door behind us. The moon was shining from the edge of a vaporous mountain, which gradually drew away from her, leaving her alone in the midst of a lake of blue. But we had not gone many paces from the house when Miss Oldcastle began to tremble violently, and could scarcely get along with all the help I could give her. Nor, for the space of six weeks did one word pass between us about the painful occurrences of that evening. For all that time she was quite unable to bear it.

When we managed at last to reach the vicarage, I gave her in charge to my sister, with instructions to help her to bed at once, while I went for Dr Duncan.

CHAPTER XXXIII
OLD ROGERS'S THANKSGIVING.

I found the old man seated at his dinner, which he left immediately when he heard that Miss Oldcastle needed his help. In a few words I told him, as we went, the story of what had befallen at the Hall, to which he listened with the interest of a boy reading a romance, asking twenty questions about the particulars which I hurried over. Then he shook me warmly by the hand, saying —

"You have fairly won her, Walton, and I am as glad of it as I could be of anything I can think of. She is well worth all you must have suffered. This will at length remove the curse from that wretched family. You have saved her from perhaps even a worse fate than her sister's."

"I fear she will be ill, though," I said, "after all that she has gone through."

But I did not even suspect how ill she would be.

As soon as I heard Dr Duncan's opinion of her, which was not very definite, a great fear seized upon me that I was destined to lose her after all. This fear, however, terrible as it was, did not torture me like the fear that had preceded it. I could oftener feel able to say, "Thy will be done" than I could before.

Dr Duncan was hardly out of the house when Old Rogers arrived, and was shown into the study. He looked excited. I allowed him to tell out his story, which was his daughter's of course, without interruption. He ended by saying: —

"Now, sir, you really must do summat. This won't do in a Christian country. We ain't aboard ship here with a nor'-easter a-walkin' the quarter-deck."

"There's no occasion, my dear old fellow, to do anything."

He was taken aback.

"Well, I don't understand you, Mr Walton. You're the last man I'd have expected to hear argufy for faith without works. It's right to trust in God; but if you don't stand to your halliards, your craft 'll miss stays, and your faith 'll be blown out of the bolt-ropes in the turn of a marlinspike."

I suspect there was some confusion in the figure, but the old man's meaning was plain enough. Nor would I keep him in a moment more of suspense.

"Miss Oldcastle is in the house, Old Rogers," I said.

"What house, sir?" returned the old man, his gray eyes opening wider as he spoke.

"This house, to be sure."

I shall never forget the look the old man cast upwards, or the reality given to it by the ordinarily odd sailor-fashion of pulling his forelock, as he returned inward thanks to the Father of all for His kindness to his friend. And never in my now wide circle of readers shall I find one, the most educated and responsive, who will listen to my story with a more gracious interest than that old man showed as I recounted to him the adventures of the evening. There were few to whom I could have told them: to Old Rogers I felt that it was right and natural and dignified to tell the story even of my love's victory.

How then am I able to tell it to the world as now? I can easily explain the seeming inconsistency. It is not merely that I am speaking, as I have said before, from behind a screen, or as clothed in the coat of darkness of an anonymous writer; but I find that, as I come nearer and nearer to the invisible world, all my brothers and sisters grow dearer and dearer to me; I feel towards them more and more as the children of my Father in heaven; and although some of them are good children and some naughty children, some very lovable and some hard to love, yet I never feel that they are below me, or unfit to listen to the story even of my love, if they only care to listen; and if they do not care, there is no harm done, except they read it. Even should they, and then scoff at what seemed and seems to me the precious story, I have these defences: first, that it was not for them that I cast forth my precious pearls, for precious to me is the significance of every fact in my history-not that it is mine, for I have only been as clay in the hands of the potter, but that it is God's, who made my history as it seemed and was good to Him; and second, that even should they trample them under their feet, they cannot well get at me to rend me. And more, the nearer I come to the region beyond, the more I feel that in that land a man needs not shrink from uttering his deepest thoughts, inasmuch as he that understands them not will not therefore revile him. —"But you are not there yet. You are in the land in which the brother speaketh evil of that which he understandeth not." —True, friend; too true. But I only do as Dr Donne did in writing that poem in his sickness, when he thought he was near to the world of which we speak: I rehearse now, that I may find it easier then.

> "Since I am coming to that holy room,
>   Where, with the choir of saints for evermore,
>   I shall be made thy music, as I come,
>   I tune the instrument here at the door;
>   And what I must do then, think here before."

When Rogers had thanked God, he rose, took my hand, and said: —

"Mr Walton, you WILL preach now. I thank God for the good we shall all get from the trouble you have gone through."

"I ought to be the better for it," I answered.

"You WILL be the better for it," he returned. "I believe I've allus been the better for any trouble as ever I had to go through with. I couldn't quite say the same for every bit of good luck I had; leastways, I consider trouble the best luck a man can have. And I wish you a good night, sir. Thank God! again."

"But, Rogers, you don't mean it would be good for us to have bad luck always, do you? You shouldn't be pleased at what's come to me now, in that case."

"No, sir, sartinly not."

"How can you say, then, that bad luck is the best luck?"

"I mean the bad luck that comes to us-not the bad luck that doesn't come. But you're right, sir. Good luck or bad luck's both best when HE sends 'em, as He allus does. In fac', sir, there is no bad luck but what comes out o' the man hisself. The rest's all good."

But whether it was the consequence of a reaction from the mental strain I had suffered, or the depressing effect of Miss Oldcastle's illness coming so close upon the joy of winning her; or that I was more careless and less anxious to do my duty than I ought to have been —I greatly fear that Old Rogers must have been painfully disappointed in the sermons which I did preach for several of the following Sundays. He never even hinted at such a fact, but I felt it much myself. A man has often to be humbled through failure, especially after success. I do not clearly know how my failures worked upon me; but I think a man may sometimes get spiritual good without being conscious of the point of its arrival, or being able to trace the process by which it was wrought in him. I believe that my failures did work some humility in me, and a certain carelessness of outward success even in spiritual matters, so far as the success affected me, provided only the will of God was done in the dishonour of my weakness. And I think, but I am not sure, that soon after I approached this condition of mind, I began to preach better. But still I found for some time that however much the subject of my sermon interested me in my study or in the church or vestry on the Saturday evening; nay, even although my heart was full of fervour during the prayers and lessons; no sooner had I begun to speak than the glow died out of the sky of my thoughts; a dull clearness of the intellectual faculties took its place; and I was painfully aware that what I could speak without being moved myself was not the most likely utterance to move the feelings of those who only listened. Still a man may occasionally be used by the Spirit of God as the inglorious "trumpet of a prophecy" instead of being inspired with the life of the Word, and hence speaking out of a full heart in testimony of that which he hath known and seen.

I hardly remember when or how I came upon the plan, but now, as often as I find myself in such a condition, I turn away from any attempt to produce a sermon; and, taking up one of the sayings of our Lord which He himself has said "are spirit and are life," I labour simply to make the people see in it what I see in it; and when I find that thus my own heart is warmed, I am justified in the hope that the hearts of some at least of my hearers are thereby warmed likewise.

But no doubt the fact that the life of Miss Oldcastle seemed to tremble in the balance, had something to do with those results of which I may have already said too much. My design had been to go at once to London and make preparation for as early a wedding as she would consent to; but the very day after I brought her home, life and not marriage was the question. Dr Duncan looked very grave, and although he gave me all the encouragement he could, all his encouragement did not amount to much. There was such a lack of vitality about her! The treatment to which she had been for so long a time subjected had depressed her till life was nearly quenched from lack of hope. Nor did the sudden change seem able to restore the healthy action of what the old physicians called the animal spirits. Possibly the strong reaction paralysed their channels, and thus prevented her gladness from reaching her physical nature so as to operate on its health. Her whole complaint appeared in excessive weakness. Finding that she fainted after every little excitement, I left her for four weeks entirely to my sister and Dr Duncan, during which time she never saw me; and it was long before I could venture to stay in her room more than a minute or two. But as the summer approached she began to show signs of reviving life, and by the end of May was able to be wheeled into the garden in a chair.

During her aunt's illness, Judy came often to the vicarage. But Miss Oldcastle was unable to see her any more than myself without the painful consequence which I have mentioned. So the dear child always came to me in the study, and through her endless vivacity infected me with some of her hope. For she had no fears whatever about her aunt's recovery.

I had had some painful apprehensions as to the treatment Judy herself might meet with from her grandmother, and had been doubtful whether I ought not to have carried her off as well as her aunt; but the first time she came, which was the next day, she set my mind at rest on that subject.

"But does your grannie know where you are come?" I had asked her.

"So well, Mr Walton," sne replied, "that there was no occasion to tell her. Why shouldn't I rebel as well as Aunt Wynnie, I wonder?" she added, looking archness itself.

"How does she bear it?"

"Bear what, Mr Walton?"

"The loss of your aunt."

"You don't think grannie cares about that, do you! She's vexed enough at the loss of Captain Everard, —Do you know, I think he had too much wine yesterday, or he wouldn't have made quite such a fool of himself."

"I fear he hadn't had quite enough to give him courage, Judy. I daresay he was brave enough once, but a bad conscience soon destroys a man's courage."

"Why do you call it a bad conscience, Mr Walton? I should have thought that a bad conscience was one that would let a girl go on anyhow and say nothing about it to make her uncomfortable."

"You are quite right, Judy; that is the worst kind of conscience, certainly. But tell me, how does Mrs Oldcastle bear it?"

"You asked me that already."

Somehow Judy's words always seem more pert upon paper than they did upon her lips. Her naivete, the twinkling light in her eyes, and the smile flitting about her mouth, always modified greatly the expression of her words.

"—Grannie never says a word about you or auntie either."

"But you said she was vexed: how do you know that?"

"Because ever since the captain went away this morning, she won't speak a word to Sarah even."

"Are you not afraid of her locking you up some day or other?"

"Not a bit of it. Grannie won't touch me. And you shouldn't tempt me to run away from her like auntie. I won't. Grannie is a naughty old lady, and I don't believe anybody loves her but me-not Sarah, I'm certain. Therefore I can't leave her, and I won't leave her, Mr Walton, whatever you may say about her."

"Indeed, I don't want you to leave her, Judy."

And Judy did not leave her as long as she lived. And the old lady's love to that child was at least one redeeming point in her fierce character. No one can tell how mucn good it may have done her before she died-though but a few years passed before her soul was required of her. Before that time came, however, a quarrel took place between her and Sarah, which quarrel I incline to regard as a hopeful sign. And to this day Judy has never heard how her old grannie treated her mother. When she learns it now from these pages I think she will be glad that she did not know it before her death.

The old lady would see neither doctor nor parson; nor would she hear of sending for her daughter. The only sign of softening that she gave was that once she folded her granddaughter in her arms and wept long and bitterly. Perhaps the thought of her dying child came back upon her, along with the reflection that the only friend she had was the child of that marriage which she had persecuted to dissolution.

CHAPTER XXXIV
TOM'S STORY.

My reader will perceive that this part of my story is drawing to a close. It embraces but a brief period of my life, and I have plenty more behind not altogether unworthy of record. But the portions of any man's life most generally interesting are those in which, while the outward history is most stirring, it derives its chief significance from accompanying conflict within. It is not the rapid change of events, or the unusual concourse of circumstances that alone can interest the thoughtful mind; while, on the other hand, internal change and tumult can be ill set forth to the reader, save they be accompanied and in part, at least, occasioned by outward events capable of embodying and elucidating the things that are of themselves unseen. For man's life ought to be a whole; and not to mention the spiritual necessities of our nature-to leave the fact alone that a man is a mere thing of shreds and patches until his heart is united, as the Psalmist says, to fear the name of God-to leave these considerations aside, I say, no man's life is fit for representation as a work of art save in proportion as there has been a significant relation between his outer and inner life, a visible outcome of some sort of harmony between them. Therefore I chose the portion in which I had suffered most, and in which the outward occurrences of my own life had been most interesting, for the fullest representation; while I reserve for a more occasional and fragmentary record many things in the way of experience, thought, observation, and facts in the history both of myself and individuals of my flock, which admit of, and indeed require, a more individual treatment than would be altogether suitable to a continuous story. But before I close this part of my communications with those whom I count my friends, for till they assure me of the contrary I mean to flatter myself with considering my readers generally as such, I must gather up the ends of my thread, and dispose them in such a manner that they shall neither hang too loose, nor yet refuse length enough for what my friend Rogers would call splicing.

It was yet summer when Miss Oldcastle and I were married. It was to me a day awful in its gladness. She was now quite well, and no shadow hung upon her half-moon forehead. We went for a fortnight into Wales, and then returned to the vicarage and the duties of the parish, in which my wife was quite ready to assist me.

Perhaps it would help the wives of some clergymen out of some difficulties, and be their protection against some reproaches, if they would at once take the position with regard to the parishioners which Mrs Walton took, namely, that of their servant, but not in her own right-in her husband's. She saw, and told them so, that the best thing she could do for them was to help me, that she held no office whatever in the parish, and they must apply to me when anything went amiss. Had she not constantly refused to be a "judge or a divider," she would have been constantly troubled with quarrels too paltry to be referred to me, and which were the sooner forgotten that the litigants were not drawn on further and further into the desert of dispute by the mirage of a justice that could quench no thirst. Only when any such affair was brought before me, did she use her good offices to bring about a right feeling between the contending parties, generally next-door neighbours, and mostly women, who, being at home all day, found their rights clash in a manner that seldom happened with those that worked in the fields. Whatever her counsel could do, however, had full scope through me, who earnestly sought it. And whatever she gave the poor, she gave as a private person, out of her own pocket. She never administered the communion offering-that is, after finding out, as she soon did, that it was a source of endless dispute between some of the recipients, who regarded it as their common property, and were never satisfied with what they received. This is the case in many country parishes, I fear. As soon as I came to know it, I simply told the recipients that, although the communion offering belonged to them, yet the distribution of it rested entirely with me; and that I would distribute it neither according to their fancied merits nor the degree of friendship I felt for them, but according to the best judgment I could form as to their necessities; and if any of them thought these were underrated, they were quite at liberty to make a fresh representation of them to me; but that I, who knew more about their neighbours than it was likely they did, and was not prejudiced by the personal regards which they could hardly fail to be influenced by, was more likely than they were to arrive at an equitable distribution of the money-upon my principles if not on theirs. And at the same time I tried to show them that a very great part of the disputes in the world came from our having a very keen feeling of our own troubles, and a very dull feeling of our neighbour's; for if the case was reversed, and our neighbour's condition became ours, ten to one our judgment would be reversed likewise. And I think some of them got some sense out of what I said. But I ever found the great difficulty in my dealing with my people to be the preservation of the authority which was needful for service; for when the elder serve the younger-and in many cases it is not age that determines seniority-they must not forget that without which the service they offer will fail to be received as such by those to whom it is offered. At the same time they must ever take heed that their claim to authority be founded on the truth, and not on ecclesiastical or social position. Their standing in the church accredits their offer of service: the service itself can only be accredited by the Truth and the Lord of Truth, who is the servant of all.

But it cost both me and my wife some time and some suffering before we learned how to deport ourselves in these respects.

In the same manner she avoided the too near, because unprofitable, approaches of a portion of the richer part of the community. For from her probable position in time to come, rather than her position in time past, many of the fashionable people in the county began to call upon her-in no small degree to her annoyance, simply from the fact that she and they had so little in common. So, while she performed all towards them that etiquette demanded, she excused herself from the closer intimacy which some of them courted, on the ground of the many duties which naturally fell to the parson's wife in a country parish like ours; and I am sure that long before we had gained the footing we now have, we had begun to reap the benefits of this mode of regarding our duty in the parish as one, springing from the same source, and tending to the same end. The parson's wife who takes to herself authority in virtue of her position, and the parson's wife who disclaims all connexion with the professional work of her husband, are equally out of place in being parsons' wives. The one who refuses to serve denies her greatest privilege; the one who will be a mistress receives the greater condemnation. When the wife is one with her husband, and the husband is worthy, the position will soon reveal itself.

But there cannot be many clergymen's wives amongst my readers; and I may have occupied more space than reasonable with this "large discourse." I apologize, and, there is room to fear, go on to do the same again.

As I write I am seated in that little octagonal room overlooking the quarry, with its green lining of trees, and its deep central well. It is my study now. My wife is not yet too old to prefer the little room in which she thought and suffered so much, to every other, although the stair that leads to it is high and steep. Nor do I object to her preference because there is no ready way to reach it save through this: I see her the oftener. And although I do not like any one to look over my shoulder while I write-it disconcerts me somehow-yet the moment the sheet is finished and flung on the heap, it is her property, as the print, reader, is yours. I hear her step overhead now. She is opening her window. Now I hear her door close; and now her foot is on the stair.

"Come in, love. I have just finished another sheet. There it is. What shall I end the book with? What shall I tell the friends with whom I have been conversing so often and so long for the last thing ere for a little while I bid them good-bye?"

And Ethelwyn bends her smooth forehead-for she has a smooth forehead still, although the hair that crowns it is almost white-over the last few sheets; and while she reads, I will tell those who will read, one of the good things that come of being married. It is, that there is one face upon which the changes come without your seeing them; or rather, there is one face which you can still see the same through all the shadows which years have gathered and heaped upon it. No, stay; I have got a better way of putting it still: there is one face whose final beauty you can see the mere clearly as the bloom of youth departs, and the loveliness of wisdom and the beauty of holiness take its place; for in it you behold all that you loved before, veiled, it is true, but glowing with gathered brilliance under the veil ("Stop one moment, my dear") from which it will one day shine out like the moon from under a cloud, when a stream of the upper air floats it from off her face.

"Now, Ethelwyn, I am ready. What shall I write about next?"

"I don't think you have told them anywhere about Tom."

"No more I have. I meant to do so. But I am ashamed of it."

"The more reason to tell it."

"You are quite right. I will go on with it at once. But you must not stand there behind me. When I was a child, I could always confess best when I hid my face with my hands."

"Besides," said Ethelwyn, without seeming to hear what I said, "I do not want to have people saying that the vicar has made himself out so good that nobody can believe in him."

"That would be a great fault in my book, Ethelwyn. What does it come from in me? Let me see. I do not think I want to appear better than I am; but it sounds hypocritical to make merely general confessions, and it is indecorous to make particular ones. Besides, I doubt if it is good to write much about bad things even in the way of confession —-"

"Well, well, never mind justifying it," said Ethelwyn. "*I* don't want any justification. But here is a chance for you. The story will, I think, do good, and not harm. You had better tell it, I do think. So if you are inclined, I will go away at once, and let you go on without interruption. You will have it finished before dinner, and Tom is coming, and you can tell him what you have done."

So, reader, now my wife has left me, I will begin. It shall not be a long story.

As soon as my wife and I had settled down at home, and I had begun to arrange my work again, it came to my mind that for a long time I had been doing very little for Tom Weir. I could not blame myself much for this, and I was pretty sure neither he nor his father blamed me at all; but I now saw that it was time we should recommence something definite in the way of study. When he came to my house the next morning, and I proceeded to acquaint myself with what he had been doing, I found to my great pleasure that he had made very considerable progress both in Latin and Mathematics, and I resolved that I would now push him a little. I found this only brought out his mettle; and his progress, as it seemed to me, was extraordinary. Nor was this all. There were such growing signs of goodness in addition to the uprightness which had first led to our acquaintance, that although I carefully abstained from making the suggestion to him, I was more than pleased when I discovered, from some remark he made, that he would gladly give himself to the service of the Church. At the same time I felt compelled to be the more cautious in anything I said, from the fact that the prospect of the social elevation which would be involved in the change might be a temptation to him, as no doubt it has been to many a man of humble birth. However, as I continued to observe him closely, my conviction was deepened that he was rarely fitted for ministering to his fellows; and soon it came to speech between his father and me, when I found that Thomas, so far from being unfavourably inclined to the proposal, was prepared to spend the few savings of his careful life upon his education. To this, however, I could not listen, because there was his daughter Mary, who was very delicate, and his grandchild too, for whom he ought to make what little provision he could. I therefore took the matter in my own hands, and by means of a judicious combination of experience and what money I could spare, I managed, at less expense than most parents suppose to be unavoidable, to maintain my young friend at Oxford till such time as he gained a fellowship. I felt justified in doing so in part from the fact that some day or other Mrs Walton would inherit the Oldcastle property, as well as come into possession of certain moneys of her own, now in the trust of her mother and two gentlemen in London, which would be nearly sufficient to free the estate from incumbrance, although she could not touch it as long as her mother lived and chose to refuse her the use of it, at least without a law-suit, with which neither of us was inclined to have anything to do. But I did not lose a penny by the affair. For of the very first money Tom received after he had got his fellowship, he brought the half to me, and continued to do so until he had repaid me every shilling I had spent upon him. As soon as he was in deacon's orders, he came to assist me for a while as curate, and I found him a great help and comfort. He occupied the large room over his father's shop which had been his grandfather's: he had been dead for some years.

I was now engaged on a work which I had been contemplating for a long time, upon the development of the love of Nature as shown in the earlier literature of the Jews and Greeks, through that of the Romans, Italians, and other nations, with the Anglo-Saxon for a fresh starting-point, into its latest forms in Gray, Thomson, Cowper, Crabbe, Wordsworth, Keats, and Tennyson; and Tom supplied me with much of the time which I bestowed upon this object, and I was really grateful to him. But, in looking back, and trying to account to myself for the snare into which I fell, I see plainly enough that I thought too much of what I had done for Tom, and too little of the honour God had done me in allowing me to help Tom. I took the high-dais-throne over him, not consciously, I believe, but still with a contemptible condescension, not of manner but of heart, so delicately refined by the innate sophistry of my selfishness, that the better nature in me called it only fatherly friendship, and did not recognize it as that abominable thing so favoured of all those that especially worship themselves. But I abuse my fault instead of confessing it.

One evening, a gentle tap came to my door, and Tom entered. He looked pale and anxious, and there was an uncertainty about his motions which I could not understand.

"What is the matter, Tom?" I asked.

"I wanted to say something to you, sir," answered Tom.

"Say on," I returned, cheerily.

"It is not so easy to say, sir," rejoined Tom, with a faint smile. "Miss Walton, sir —"

"Well, what of her? There's nothing happened to her? She was here a few minutes ago-though, now I think of it —"

Here a suspicion of the truth flashed on me, and struck me dumb. I am now covered with shame to think how, when the thing approached myself on that side, it swept away for the moment all my fine theories about the equality of men in Christ their Head. How could Tom Weir, whose father was a joiner, who had been a lad in a London shop himself, dare to propose marrying my sister? Instead of thinking of what he really was, my regard rested upon this and that stage through which he had passed to reach his present condition. In fact, I regarded him rather as of my making than of God's.

Perhaps it might do something to modify the scorn of all classes for those beneath them, to consider that, by regarding others thus, they justify those above them in looking down upon them in their turn. In London shops, I am credibly informed, the young women who serve in the show-rooms, or behind the counters, are called LADIES, and talk of the girls who make up the articles for sale as PERSONS. To the learned professions, however, the distinction between the shopwomen and milliners is, from their superior height, unrecognizable; while doctors and lawyers are again, I doubt not, massed by countesses and other blue-blooded realities, with the literary lions who roar at soirees and kettle-drums, or even with chiropodists and violin-players! But I am growing scornful at scorn, and forget that I too have been scornful. Brothers, sisters, all good men and true women, let the Master seat us where He will. Until he says, "Come up higher," let us sit at the foot of the board, or stand behind, honoured in waiting upon His guests. All that kind of thing is worth nothing in the kingdom; and nothing will be remembered of us but the Master's judgment.

I have known a good churchwoman who would be sweet as a sister to the abject poor, but offensively condescending to a shopkeeper or a dissenter, exactly as if he was a Pariah, and she a Brahmin. I have known good people who were noble and generous towards their so-called inferiors and full of the rights of the race-until it touched their own family, and just no longer. Yea I, who had talked like this for years, at once, when Tom Weir wanted to marry my sister, lost my faith in the broad lines of human distinction judged according to appearances in which I did not even believe, and judged not righteous judgment.

"For," reasoned the world in me, "is it not too bad to drag your wife in for such an alliance? Has she not lowered herself enough already? Has she not married far below her accredited position in society? Will she not feel injured by your family if she see it capable of forming such a connexion?"

What answer I returned to Tom I hardly know. I remember that the poor fellow's face fell, and that he murmured something which I did not heed. And then I found myself walking in the garden under the great cedar, having stepped out of the window almost unconsciously, and left Tom standing there alone. It was very good of him ever to forgive me.

Wandering about in the garden, my wife saw me from her window, and met me as I turned a corner in the shrubbery.

And now I am going to have my revenge upon her in a way she does not expect, for making me tell the story: I will tell her share in it.

"What is the matter with you, Henry?" she asked.

"Oh, not much," I answered. "Only that Weir has been making me rather uncomfortable."

"What has he been doing?" she inquired, in some alarm. "It is not possible he has done anything wrong."

My wife trusted him as much as I did.

"No —o —o," I answered. "Not anything exactly wrong."

"It must be very nearly wrong, Henry, to make you look so miserable."

I began to feel ashamed and more uncomfortable.

"He has been falling in love with Martha," I said; "and when I put one thing to another, I fear he may have made her fall in love with him too." My wife laughed merrily.

"Whal a wicked curate!"

"Well, but you know it is not exactly agreeable."

"Why?"

"You know why well enough."

"At least, I am not going to take it for granted. Is he not a good man?"

"Yes."

"Is he not a well-educated man?"

"As well as myself-for his years."

"Is he not clever?"

"One of the cleverest fellows I ever met"

"Is he not a gentleman?"

"I have not a fault to find with his manners."

"Nor with his habits?" my wife went on.

"No."

"Nor with his ways of thinking?"

"No. —But, Ethelwyn, you know what I mean quite well. His family, you know."

"Well, is his father not a respectable man?"

"Oh, yes, certainly. Thoroughly respectable."

"He wouldn't borrow money of his tailor instead of paying for his clothes, would he?"

"Certainly not"

"And if he were to die to-day he would carry no debts to heaven with him?"

"I believe not."

"Does he bear false witness against his neighbour?"

"No. He scorns a lie as much as any man I ever knew."

"Which of the commandments is it in particular that he breaks, then?"

"None that I know of; excepting that no one can keep them yet that is only human. He tries to keep every one of them I do believe."

"Well, I think Tom very fortunate in having such a father. I wish my mother had been as good."

"That is all true, and yet —"

"And yet, suppose a young man you liked had had a fashionable father who had ruined half a score of trades-people by his extravagance-would you object to him because of his family?"

"Perhaps not."

"Then, with you, position outweighs honesty-in fathers, at least."

To this I was not ready with an answer, and my wife went on.

"It might be reasonable if you did though, from fear lest he should turn out like his father. — But do you know why I would not accept your offer of taking my name when I should succeed to the property?"

"You said you liked mine better," I answered.

"So I did. But I did not tell you that I was ashamed that my good husband should take a name which for centuries had been borne by hard-hearted, worldly minded people, who, to speak the truth of my ancestors to my husband, were neither gentle nor honest, nor high-minded."

"Still, Ethelwyn, you know there is something in it, though it is not so easy to say what. And you avoid that. I suppose Martha has been talking you over to her side."

"Harry," my wife said, with a shade of solemnity, "I am almost ashamed of you for the first time. And I will punish you by telling you the truth. Do you think I had nothing of that sort to get over when I began to find that I was thinking a little more about you than was quite convenient under the circumstances? Your manners, dear Harry, though irreproachable, just had not the tone that I had been accustomed to. There was a diffidence about you also that did not at first advance you in my regard."

"Yes, yes," I answered, a little piqued, "I dare say. I have no doubt you thought me a boor."

"Dear Harry!"

"I beg your pardon, wifie. I know you didn't. But it is quite bad enough to have brought you down to my level, without sinking you still lower."

"Now there you are wrong, Harry. And that is what I want to show you. I found that my love to you would not be satisfied with making an exception in your favour. I must see what force there really was in the notions I had been bred in."

"Ah!" I said. "I see. You looked for a principle in what you had thought was an exception."

"Yes," returned my wife; "and I soon found one. And the next step was to throw away all false judgment in regard to such things. And so I can see more clearly than you into the right of the matter. —Would you hesitate a moment between Tom Weir and the dissolute son of an earl, Harry?"

"You know I would not."

"Well, just carry out the considerations that suggests, and you will find that where there is everything personally noble, pure, simple, and good, the lowliness of a man's birth is but an added honour to him; for it shows that his nobility is altogether from within him, and therefore is his own. It cannot then have been put on him by education or imitation, as many men's manners are, who wear their good breeding like their fine clothes, or as the Pharisee his prayers, to be seen of men."

"But his sister?"

"Harry, Harry! You were preaching last Sunday about the way God thinks of things. And you said that was the only true way of thinking about them. Would the Mary that poured the ointment on Jesus's head have refused to marry a good man because he was the brother of that Mary who poured it on His feet? Have you thought what God would think of Tom for a husband to Martha?"

I did not answer, for conscience had begun to speak. When I lifted my eyes from the ground, thinking Ethelwyn stood beside me, she was gone. I felt as if she were dead, to punish me for my pride. But still I could not get over it, though I was ashamed to follow and find her. I went and got my hat instead, and strolled out.

What was it that drew me towards Thomas Weir's shop? I think it must have been incipient repentance —a feeling that I had wronged the man. But just as I turned the corner, and the smell of the wood reached me, the picture so often associated in my mind with such a scene of human labour, rose before me. I saw the Lord of Life bending over His bench, fashioning some lowly utensil for some housewife of Nazareth. And He would receive payment for it too; for He at least could see no disgrace in the order of things that His Father had appointed. It is the vulgar mind that looks down on the earning and worships the inheriting of money. How infinitely more poetic is the belief that our Lord did His work like any other honest man, than that straining after His glorification in the early centuries of the Church by the invention of fables even to the disgrace of his father! They say that Joseph was a bad carpenter, and our Lord had to work miracles to set the things right which he had made wrong! To such a class of mind as invented these fables do those belong who think they honour our Lord when they judge anything human too common or too unclean for Him to have done.

And the thought sprung up at once in my mind—"If I ever see our Lord face to face, how shall I feel if He says to me; 'Didst thou do well to murmur that thy sister espoused a certain man for that in his youth he had earned his bread as I earned mine? Where was then thy right to say unto me, Lord, Lord?'"

I hurried into the workshop.

"Has Tom told you about it?" I said.

"Yes, sir. And I told him to mind what he was about; for he was not a gentleman, and you was, sir."

"I hope I am. And Tom is as much a gentleman as I have any claim to be."

Thomas Weir held out his hand.

"Now, sir, I do believe you mean in my shop what you say in your pulpit; and there is ONE Christian in the world at least. —But what will your good lady say? She's higher-born than you-no offence, sir."

"Ah, Thomas, you shame me. I am not so good as you think me. It was my wife that brought me to reason about it."

"God bless her."

"Amen. I'm going to find Tom."

At the same moment Tom entered the shop, with a very melancholy face. He started when he saw me, and looked confused.

"Tom, my boy," I said, "I behaved very badly to you. I am sorry for it. Come back with me, and have a walk with my sister. I don't think she'll be sorry to see you."

His face brightened up at once, and we left the shop together. Evidently with a great effort Tom was the first to speak.

"I know, sir, how many difficulties my presumption must put you in."

"Not another word about it, Tom. You are blameless. I wish I were. If we only act as God would have us, other considerations may look after themselves-or, rather, He will look after them. The world will never be right till the mind of God is the measure of things, and the will of God the law of things. In the kingdom of Heaven nothing else is acknowledged. And till that kingdom come, the mind and will of God must, with those that look for that kingdom, over-ride every other way of thinking, feeling, and judging. I see it more plainly than ever I did. Take my sister, in God's name, Tom, and be good to her."

Tom went to find Martha, and I to find Ethelwyn.

"It is all right," I said, "even to the shame I feel at having needed your reproof."

"Don't think of that. God gives us all time to come to our right minds, you know," answered my wife.

"But how did you get on so far a-head of me, wifie?"

Ethelwyn laughed.

"Why," she said, "I only told you back again what you have been telling me for the last seven or eight years."

So to me the message had come first, but my wife had answered first with the deed.

And now I have had my revenge on her.

Next to her and my children, Tom has been my greatest comfort for many years. He is still my curate, and I do not think we shall part till death part us for a time. My sister is worth twice what she was before, though they have no children. We have many, and they have taught me much.

Thomas Weir is now too old to work any longer. He occupies his father's chair in the large room of the old house. The workshop I have had turned into a school-room, of the external condition of which his daughter takes good care, while a great part of her brother Tom's time is devoted to the children; for he and I agree that, where it can be done, the pastoral care ought to be at least equally divided between the sheep and the lambs. For the sooner the children are brought under right influences —I do not mean a great deal of religious speech, but the right influences of truth and honesty, and an evident regard to what God wants of us-not only are they the more easily wrought upon, but the sooner do they recognize those influences as right and good. And while Tom quite agrees with me that there must not be much talk about religion, he thinks that there must be just the more acting upon religion; and that if it be everywhere at hand in all things taught and done, it will be ready to show itself to every one who looks for it. And besides that action is more powerful than speech in the inculcation of religion, Tom says there is no such corrective of sectarianism of every kind as the repression of speech and the encouragement of action.

Besides being a great help to me and everybody else almost in Marshmallows, Tom has distinguished himself in the literary world j and when I read his books I am yet prouder of my brother-in-law. I am only afraid that Martha is not good enough for him. But she certainly improves, as I have said already.

Jane Rogers was married to young Brownrigg about a year after we were married. The old man is all but confined to the chimney-corner now, and Richard manages the farm, though not quite to his father's satisfaction, of course. But they are doing well notwithstanding. The old mill has been superseded by one of new and rare device, built by Richard; but the old cottage where his wife's parents lived has slowly mouldered back to the dust.

For the old people have been dead for many years.

Often in the summer days as I go to or come from the vestry, I sit down for a moment on the turf that covers my old friend, and think that every day is mouldering away this body of mine till it shall fall a heap of dust into its appointed place. But what is that to me? It is to me the drawing nigh of the fresh morning of life, when I shall be young and strong again, glad in the presence of the wise and beloved dead, and unspeakably glad in the presence of my God, which I have now but hope to possess far more hereafter.

I will not take a solemn leave of my friends iust yet. For I hope to hold a little more communion with them ere I go hence. I know that my mental faculty is growing weaker, but some power yet remains; and I say to myself, "Perhaps this is the final trial of your faith-to trust in God to take care of your intellect for you, and to believe, in weakness, the truths He revealed to you in strength. Remember that Truth depends not upon your seeing it, and believe as you saw when your sight was at its best. For then you saw that the Truth was beyond all you could see." Thus I try to prepare for dark days that may come, but which cannot come without God in them.

And meantime I hope to be able to communicate some more of the good things experience and thought have taught me, and it may be some more of the events that have befallen my friends and myself in our pilgrimage. So, kind readers, God be with you. That is the older and better form of GOOD-BYE.

THE SEABOARD PARISH

VOLUME I.

CHAPTER I
HOMILETIC.

Dear Friends,—I am beginning a new book like an old sermon; but, as you know, I have been so accustomed to preach all my life, that whatever I say or write will more or less take the shape of a sermon; and if you had not by this time learned at least to bear with my oddities, you would not have wanted any more of my teaching. And, indeed, I did not think you would want any more. I thought I had bidden you farewell. But I am seated once again at my writing-table, to write for you-with a strange feeling, however, that I am in the heart of some curious, rather awful acoustic contrivance, by means of which the words which I have a habit of whispering over to myself as I write them, are heard aloud by multitudes of people whom I cannot see or hear. I will favour the fancy, that, by a sense of your presence, I may speak the more truly, as man to man.

But let me, for a moment, suppose that I am your grandfather, and that you have all come to beg for a story; and that, therefore, as usually happens in such cases, I am sitting with a puzzled face, indicating a more puzzled mind. I know that there are a great many stories in the holes and corners of my brain; indeed, here is one, there is one, peeping out at me like a rabbit; but alas, like a rabbit, showing me almost at the same instant the tail-end of it, and vanishing with a contemptuous *thud* of its hind feet on the ground. For I must have suitable regard to the desires of my children. It is a fine thing to be able to give people what they want, if at the same time you can give them what you want. To give people what they want, would sometimes be to give them only dirt and poison. To give them what you want, might be to set before them something of which they could not eat a mouthful. What both you and I want, I am willing to think, is a dish of good wholesome venison. Now I suppose my children around me are neither young enough nor old enough to care about a fairy tale, go that will not do. What they want is, I believe, something that I know about-that has happened to myself. Well, I confess, that is the kind of thing I like best to hear anybody talk to me about. Let anyone tell me something that has happened to himself, especially if he will give me a peep into how his heart took it, as it sat in its own little room with the closed door, and that person will, so telling, absorb my attention: he has something true and genuine and valuable to communicate. They are mostly old people that can do so. Not that young people have nothing happen to them; but that only when they grow old, are they able to see things right, to disentangle confusions, and judge righteous judgment. Things which at the time appeared insignificant or wearisome, then give out the light that was in them, show their own truth, interest, and influence: they are far enough off to be seen. It is not when we are nearest to anything that we know best what it is. How I should like to write a story for old people! The young are always having stories written for them. Why should not the old people come in for a share? A story without a young person in it at all! Nobody under fifty admitted! It could hardly be a fairy tale, could it? Or a love story either? I am not so sure about that. The worst of it would be, however, that hardly a young person would read it. Now, we old people would not like that. We can read young people's books and enjoy them: they would not try to read old men's books or old women's books; they would be so sure of their being dry. My dear old brothers and sisters, we know better, do we not? We have nice old jokes, with no end of fun in them; only they cannot see the fun. We have strange tales, that we know to be true, and which look more and more marvellous every time we turn them over again; only somehow they do not belong to the ways of this year—I was going to say *week*,—and so the young people generally do not care to hear them. I have had one pale-faced boy, to be sure, who will sit at his mother's feet, and listen for hours to what took place before he was born. To him his mother's wedding-gown was as old as Eve's coat of skins. But then he was young enough not yet to have had a chance of losing the childhood common to the young and the old. Ah! I should like to write for you, old men, old women, to help you to read the past, to help you to look for the future. Now is your salvation nearer than when you believed; for, however your souls may be at peace, however your quietness and confidence may give you strength, in the decay of your earthly tabernacle, in the shortening of its cords, in the weakening of its stakes, in the rents through which you see the stars, you have yet your share in the cry of the creation after the sonship. But the one thing I should keep saying to you, my companions in old age, would be, "Friends, let us not grow old." Old age is but a mask; let us not call the mask the face. Is the acorn old, because its cup dries and drops it from its hold-because its skin has grown brown and cracks in the earth? Then only is a man growing old when he ceases to have sympathy with the young. That is a sign that his heart has begun to wither. And that is a dreadful kind of old age. The heart needs never be old. Indeed it should always be growing younger. Some of us feel younger, do we not, than when we were nine or ten? It is not necessary to be able to play at leapfrog to enjoy the game. There are young creatures whose turn it is, and perhaps whose duty it would be, to play at leap-frog if there was any necessity for putting the matter in that light; and for us, we have the privilege, or if we will not accept the privilege, then I say we have the duty, of enjoying their leap-frog. But if we must withdraw in a measure from sociable relations with our fellows, let it be as the wise creatures that creep aside and wrap themselves up and lay themselves by that their wings may grow and put on the lovely hues of their coming resurrection. Such a withdrawing is in the name of youth. And while it is pleasant-no one knows how pleasant except him who experiences it-to sit apart and see the drama of life going on around him, while his feelings are calm and free, his vision clear, and his judgment righteous, the old man must ever be ready, should the sweep of action catch him in its skirts, to get on his tottering old legs, and go with brave heart to do the work of a true man, none the less true that his hands tremble, and that he would gladly return to his chimney-corner. If he is never thus called out, let him examine himself, lest he should be falling into the number of those that say, "I go, sir," and go not; who are content with thinking beautiful things in an Atlantis, Oceana, Arcadia, or what it may be, but put not forth one of their fingers to work a salvation in the earth. Better than such is the man who, using just weights and a true balance, sells good flour, and never has a thought of his own.

I have been talking-to my reader is it? or to my supposed group of grandchildren? I remember-to my companions in old age. It is time I returned to the company who are hearing my whispers at the other side of the great thundering gallery. I take leave of my old friends with one word: We have yet a work to do, my friends; but a work we shall never do aright after ceasing to understand the new generation. We are not the men, neither shall wisdom die with us. The Lord hath not forsaken his people because the young ones do not think just as the old ones choose. The Lord has something fresh to tell them, and is getting them ready to receive his message. When we are out of sympathy with the young, then I think our work in this world is over. It might end more honourably.

Now, readers in general, I have had time to consider what to tell you about, and how to begin. My story will be rather about my family than myself now. I was as it were a little withdrawn, even by the time of which I am about to write. I had settled into a gray-haired, quite elderly, yet active man-young still, in fact, to what I am now. But even then, though my faith had grown stronger, life had grown sadder, and needed all my stronger faith; for the vanishing of beloved faces, and the trials of them that are dear, will make even those that look for a better country both for themselves and their friends, sad, though it will be with a preponderance of the first meaning of the word *sad*, which was *settled, thoughtful*.

I am again seated in the little octagonal room, which I have made my study because I like it best. It is rather a shame, for my books cover over every foot of the old oak panelling. But they make the room all the pleasanter to the eye, and after I am gone, there is the old oak, none the worse, for anyone who prefers it to books.

I intend to use as the central portion of my present narrative the history of a year during part of which I took charge of a friend's parish, while my brother-in-law, Thomas Weir, who was and is still my curate, took the entire charge of Marshmallows. What led to this will soon appear. I will try to be minute enough in my narrative to make my story interesting, although it will cost me suffering to recall some of the incidents I have to narrate.

CHAPTER II
CONSTANCE'S BIRTHDAY.

Was it from observation of nature in its association with human nature, or from artistic feeling alone, that Shakspere so often represents Nature's mood as in harmony with the mood of the principal actors in his drama? I know I have so often found Nature's mood in harmony with my own, even when she had nothing to do with forming mine, that in looking back I have wondered at the fact. There may, however, be some self-deception about it. At all events, on the morning of my Constance's eighteenth birthday, a lovely October day with a golden east, clouds of golden foliage about the ways, and an air that seemed filled with the ether of an *aurum potabile*, there came yet an occasional blast of wind, which, without being absolutely cold, smelt of winter, and made one draw one's shoulders together with the sense of an unfriendly presence. I do not think Constance felt it at all, however, as she stood on the steps in her riding-habit, waiting till the horses made their appearance. It had somehow grown into a custom with us that each of the children, as his or her birthday came round, should be king or queen for that day, and, subject to the veto of father and mother, should have everything his or her own way. Let me say for them, however, that in the matter of choosing the dinner, which of course was included in the royal prerogative, I came to see that it was almost invariably the favourite dishes of others of the family that were chosen, and not those especially agreeable to the royal palate. Members of families where children have not been taught from their earliest years that the great privilege of possession is the right to bestow, may regard this as an improbable assertion; but others will know that it might well enough be true, even if I did not say that so it was. But there was always the choice of some individual treat, which was determined solely by the preference of the individual in authority. Constance had chosen "a long ride with papa."

I suppose a parent may sometimes be right when he speaks with admiration of his own children. The probability of his being correct is to be determined by the amount of capacity he has for admiring other people's children. However this may be in my own case, I venture to assert that Constance did look very lovely that morning. She was fresh as the young day: we were early people-breakfast and prayers were over, and it was nine o'clock as she stood on the steps and I approached her from the lawn.

"O, papa! isn't it jolly?" she said merrily.

"Very jolly indeed, my dear," I answered, delighted to hear the word from the lips of my gentle daughter. She very seldom used a slang word, and when she did, she used it like a lady. Shall I tell you what she was like? Ah! you could not see her as I saw her that morning if I did. I will, however, try to give you a general idea, just in order that you and I should not be picturing to ourselves two very different persons while I speak of her.

She was rather little, and so slight that she looked tall. I have often observed that the impression of height is an affair of proportion, and has nothing to do with feet and inches. She was rather fair in complexion, with her mother's blue eyes, and her mother's long dark wavy hair. She was generally playful, and took greater liberties with me than any of the others; only with her liberties, as with her slang, she knew instinctively when, where, and how much. For on the borders of her playfulness there seemed ever to hang a fringe of thoughtfulness, as if she felt that the present moment owed all its sparkle and brilliance to the eternal sunlight. And the appearance was not in the least a deceptive one. The eternal was not far from her-none the farther that she enjoyed life like a bird, that her laugh was merry, that her heart was careless, and that her voice rang through the house —a sweet soprano voice-singing snatches of songs (now a street tune she had caught from a London organ, now an air from Handel or Mozart), or that she would sometimes tease her elder sister about her solemn and anxious looks; for Wynnie, the eldest, had to suffer for her grandmother's sins against her daughter, and came into the world with a troubled little heart, that was soon compelled to flee for refuge to the rock that was higher than she. Ah! my Constance! But God was good to you and to us in you.

"Where shall we go, Connie?" I said, and the same moment the sound of the horses' hoofs reached us.

"Would it be too far to go to Addicehead?" she returned.

"It is a long ride," I answered.

"Too much for the pony?"

"O dear, no-not at all. I was thinking of you, not of the pony."

"I'm quite as able to ride as the pony is to carry me, papa. And I want to get something for Wynnie. Do let us go."

"Very well, my dear," I said, and raised her to the saddle-if I may say *raised*, for no bird ever hopped more lightly from one twig to another than she sprung from the ground on her pony's back.

In a moment I was beside her, and away we rode.

The shadows were still long, the dew still pearly on the spiders' webs, as we trotted out of our own grounds into a lane that led away towards the high road. Our horses were fresh and the air was exciting; so we turned from the hard road into the first suitable field, and had a gallop to begin with. Constance was a good horse-woman, for she had been used to the saddle longer than she could remember. She was now riding a tall well-bred pony, with plenty of life-rather too much, I sometimes thought, when I was out with Wynnie; but I never thought so when I was with Constance. Another field or two sufficiently quieted both animals —I did not want to have all our time taken up with their frolics-and then we began to talk.

"You are getting quite a woman now, Connie, my dear," I said.

"Quite an old grannie, papa," she answered.

"Old enough to think about what's coming next," I said gravely.

"O, papa! And you are always telling us that we must not think about the morrow, or even the next hour. But, then, that's in the pulpit," she added, with a sly look up at me from under the drooping feather of her pretty hat.

"You know very well what I mean, you puss," I answered. "And I don't say one thing in the pulpit and another out of it."

She was at my horse's shoulder with a bound, as if Spry, her pony, had been of one mind and one piece with her. She was afraid she had offended me. She looked up into mine with as anxious a face as ever I saw upon Wynnie.

"O, thank you, papa!" she said when I smiled. "I thought I had been rude. I didn't mean it, indeed I didn't. But I do wish you would make it a little plainer to me. I do think about things sometimes, though you would hardly believe it."

"What do you want made plainer, my child?" I asked.

"When we're to think, and when we're not to think," she answered.

I remember all of this conversation because of what came so soon after.

"If the known duty of to-morrow depends on the work of to-day," I answered, "if it cannot be done right except you think about it and lay your plans for it, then that thought is to-day's business, not to-morrow's."

"Dear papa, some of your explanations are more difficult than the things themselves. May I be as impertinent as I like on my birthday?" she asked suddenly, again looking up in my face.

We were walking now, and she had a hold of my horse's mane, so as to keep her pony close up.

"Yes, my dear, as impertinent as you like-not an atom more, mind."

"Well, papa, I sometimes wish you wouldn't explain things so much. I seem to understand you all the time you are preaching, but when I try the text afterwards by myself, I can't make anything of it, and I've forgotten every word you said about it."

"Perhaps that is because you have no right to understand it."

"I thought all Protestants had a right to understand every word of the Bible," she returned.

"If they can," I rejoined. "But last Sunday, for instance, I did not expect anybody there to understand a certain bit of my sermon, except your mamma and Thomas Weir."

"How funny! What part of it was that?"

"O! I'm not going to tell you. You have no right to understand it. But most likely you thought you understood it perfectly, and it appeared to you, in consequence, very commonplace."

"In consequence of what?"

"In consequence of your thinking you understood it."

"O, papa dear! you're getting worse and worse. It's not often I ask you anything-and on my birthday too! It is really too bad of you to bewilder my poor little brains in this way."

"I will try to make you see what I mean, my pet. No talk about an idea that you never had in your head at all, can make you have that idea. If you had never seen a horse, no description even, not to say no amount of remark, would bring the figure of a horse before your mind. Much more is this the case with truths that belong to the convictions and feelings of the heart. Suppose a man had never in his life asked God for anything, or thanked God for anything, would his opinion as to what David meant in one of his worshipping psalms be worth much? The whole thing would be beyond him. If you have never known what it is to have care of any kind upon you, you cannot understand what our Lord means when he tells us to take no thought for the morrow."

"But indeed, papa, I am very full of care sometimes, though not perhaps about to-morrow precisely. But that does not matter, does it?"

"Certainly not. Tell me what you are full of care about, my child, and perhaps I can help you."

"You often say, papa, that half the misery in this world comes from idleness, and that you do not believe that in a world where God is at work every day, Sundays not excepted, it could have been intended that women any more than men should have nothing to do. Now what am I to do? What have I been sent into the world for? I don't see it; and I feel very useless and wrong sometimes."

"I do not think there is very much to complain of you in that respect, Connie. You, and your sister as well, help me very much in my parish. You take much off your mother's hands too. And you do a good deal for the poor. You teach your younger brothers and sister, and meantime you are learning yourselves."

"Yes, but that's not work."

"It is work. And it is the work that is given you to do at present. And you would do it much better if you were to look at it in that light. Not that I have anything to complain of."

"But I don't want to stop at home and lead an easy, comfortable life, when there are so many to help everywhere in the world."

"Is there anything better in doing something where God has not placed you, than in doing it where he has placed you?"

"No, papa. But my sisters are quite enough for all you have for us to do at home. Is nobody ever to go away to find the work meant for her? You won't think, dear papa, that I want to get away from home, will you?"

"No, my dear. I believe that you are really thinking about duty. And now comes the moment for considering the passage to which you began by referring: —What God may hereafter require of you, you must not give yourself the least trouble about. Everything he gives you to do, you must do as well as ever you can, and that is the best possible preparation for what he may want you to do next. If people would but do what they have to do, they would always find themselves ready for what came next. And I do not believe that those who follow this rule are ever left floundering on the sea-deserted sands of inaction, unable to find water enough to swim in."

"Thank you, dear papa. That's a little sermon all to myself, and I think I shall understand it even when I think about it afterwards. Now let's have a trot."

"There is one thing more I ought to speak about though, Connie. It is not your moral nature alone you ought to cultivate. You ought to make yourself as worth God's making as you possibly can. Now I am a little doubtful whether you keep up your studies at all."

She shrugged her pretty shoulders playfully, looking up in my face again.

"I don't like dry things, papa."

"Nobody does."

"Nobody!" she exclaimed. "How do the grammars and history-books come to be written then?"

In talking to me, somehow, the child always put on a more childish tone than when she talked to anyone else. I am certain there was no affection in it, though. Indeed, how could she be affected with her fault-finding old father?

"No. Those books are exceedingly interesting to the people that make them. Dry things are just things that you do not know enough about to care for them. And all you learn at school is next to nothing to what you have to learn."

"What must I do then?" she asked with a sigh. "Must I go all over my French Grammar again? O dear! I do hate it so!"

"If you will tell me something you like, Connie, instead of something you don't like, I may be able to give you advice. Is there nothing you are fond of?" I continued, finding that she remained silent.

"I don't know anything in particular-that is, I don't know anything in the way of school-work that I really liked. I don't mean that I didn't try to do what I had to do, for I did. There was just one thing I liked-the poetry we had to learn once a week. But I suppose gentlemen count that silly-don't they?"

"On the contrary, my dear, I would make that liking of yours the foundation of all your work. Besides, I think poetry the grandest thing God has given us-though perhaps you and I might not quite agree about what poetry was poetry enough to be counted an especial gift of God. Now, what poetry do you like best?"

"Mrs. Hemans's, I think, papa."

"Well, very well, to begin with. 'There is,' as Mr. Carlyle said to a friend of mine —'There is a thin vein of true poetry in Mrs. Hemans.' But it is time you had done with thin things, however good they may be. Most people never get beyond spoon-meat —in this world, at least, and they expect nothing else in the world to come. I must take you in hand myself, and see what I can do for you. It is wretched to see capable enough creatures, all for want of a little guidance, bursting with admiration of what owes its principal charm to novelty of form, gained at the cost of expression and sense. Not that that applies to Mrs. Hemans. She is simple enough, only diluted to a degree. But I hold that whatever mental food you take should be just a little too strong for you. That implies trouble, necessitates growth, and involves delight."

"I sha'n't mind how difficult it is if you help me, papa. But it is anything but satisfactory to go groping on without knowing what you are about."

I ought to have mentioned that Constance had been at school for two years, and had only been home a month that very day, in order to account for my knowing so little about her tastes and habits of mind. We went on talking a little more in the same way, and if I were writing for young people only, I should be tempted to go on a little farther with the account of what we said to each other; for it might help some of them to see that the thing they like best should, circumstances and conscience permitting, be made the centre from which they start to learn; that they should go on enlarging their knowledge all round from that one point at which God intended them to begin. But at length we fell into a silence, a very happy one on my part; for I was more than delighted to find that this one too of my children was following after the truth-wanting to do what was right, namely, to obey the word of the Lord, whether openly spoken to all, or to herself in the voice of her own conscience and the light of that understanding which is the candle of the Lord. I had often said to myself in past years, when I had found myself in the company of young ladies who announced their opinions-probably of no deeper origin than the prejudices of their nurses-as if these distinguished them from all the world besides; who were profound upon passion and ignorant of grace; who had not a notion whether a dress was beautiful, but only whether it was of the newest cut —I had often said to myself: "What shall I do if my daughters come to talk and think like that-if thinking it can be called?" but being confident that instruction for which the mind is not prepared only lies in a rotting heap, producing all kinds of mental evils correspondent to the results of successive loads of food which the system cannot assimilate, my hope had been to rouse wise questions in the minds of my children, in place of overwhelming their digestions with what could be of no instruction or edification without the foregoing appetite. Now my Constance had begun to ask me questions, and it made me very happy. We had thus come a long way nearer to each other; for however near the affection of human animals may bring them, there are abysses between soul and soul-the souls even of father and daughter-over which they must pass to meet. And I do not believe that any two human beings alive know yet what it is to love as love is in the glorious will of the Father of lights.

I linger on with my talk, for I shrink from what I must relate.

We were going at a gentle trot, silent, along a woodland path—a brown, soft, shady road, nearly five miles from home, our horses scattering about the withered leaves that lay thick upon it. A good deal of underwood and a few large trees had been lately cleared from the place. There were many piles of fagots about, and a great log lying here and there along the side of the path. One of these, when a tree, had been struck by lightning, and had stood till the frosts and rains had bared it of its bark. Now it lay white as a skeleton by the side of the path, and was, I think, the cause of what followed. All at once my daughter's pony sprang to the other side of the road, shying sideways; unsettled her so, I presume; then rearing and plunging, threw her from the saddle across one of the logs of which I have spoken. I was by her side in a moment. To my horror she lay motionless. Her eyes were closed, and when I took her up in my arms she did not open them. I laid her on the moss, and got some water and sprinkled her face. Then she revived a little; but seemed in much pain, and all at once went off into another faint. I was in terrible perplexity.

Presently a man who, having been cutting fagots at a little distance, had seen the pony careering through the wood, came up and asked what he could do to help me. I told him to take my horse, whose bridle I had thrown over the latch of a gate, and ride to Oldcastle Hall, and ask Mrs. Walton to come with the carriage as quickly as possible. "Tell her," I said, "that her daughter has had a fall from her pony, and is rather shaken. Ride as hard as you can go."

The man was off in a moment; and there I sat watching my poor child, for what seemed to be a dreadfully long time before the carriage arrived. She had come to herself quite, but complained of much pain in her back; and, to my distress, I found that she could not move herself enough to make the least change of her position. She evidently tried to keep up as well as she could; but her face expressed great suffering: it was dreadfully pale, and looked worn with a month's illness. All my fear was for her spine.

At length I caught sight of the carriage, coming through the wood as fast as the road would allow, with the woodman on the box, directing the coachman. It drew up, and my wife got out. She was as pale as Constance, but quiet and firm, her features composed almost to determination. I had never seen her look like that before. She asked no questions: there was time enough for that afterwards. She had brought plenty of cushions and pillows, and we did all we could to make an easy couch for the poor girl; but she moaned dreadfully as we lifted her into the carriage. We did our best to keep her from being shaken; but those few miles were the longest journey I ever made in my life.

When we reached home at length, we found that Ethel, or, as we commonly called her, using the other end of her name, Wynnie-for she was named after her mother-had got a room on the ground-floor, usually given to visitors, ready for her sister; and we were glad indeed not to have to carry her up the stairs. Before my wife left, she had sent the groom off to Addicehead for both physician and surgeon. A young man who had settled at Marshmallows as general practitioner a year or two before, was waiting for us when we arrived. He helped us to lay her upon a mattress in the position in which she felt the least pain. But why should I linger over the sorrowful detail? All agreed that the poor child's spine was seriously injured, and that probably years of suffering were before her. Everything was done that could be done; but she was not moved from that room for nine months, during which, though her pain certainly grew less by degrees, her want of power to move herself remained almost the same.

When I had left her at last a little composed, with her mother seated by her bedside, I called my other two daughters-Wynnie, the eldest, and Dorothy, the youngest, whom I found seated on the floor outside, one on each side of the door, weeping-into my study, and said to them: "My darlings, this is very sad; but you must remember that it is God's will; and as you would both try to bear it cheerfully if it had fallen to your lot to bear, you must try to be cheerful even when it is your sister's part to endure."

"O, papa! poor Connie!" cried Dora, and burst into fresh tears.

Wynnie said nothing, but knelt down by my knee, and laid her cheek upon it.

"Shall I tell you what Constance said to me just before I left the room?" I asked.

"Please do, papa."

"She whispered, 'You must try to bear it, all of you, as well as you can. I don't mind it very much, only for you.' So, you see, if you want to make her comfortable, you must not look gloomy and troubled. Sick people like to see cheerful faces about them; and I am sure Connie will not suffer nearly so much if she finds that she does not make the household gloomy."

This I had learned from being ill myself once or twice since my marriage. My wife never came near me with a gloomy face, and I had found that it was quite possible to be sympathetic with those of my flock who were ill without putting on a long face when I went to see them. Of course, I do not mean that I could, or that it was desirable that I should, look cheerful when any were in great pain or mental distress. But in ordinary conditions of illness a cheerful countenance is as a message of *all's well*, which may surely be carried into a sick chamber by the man who believes that the heart of a loving Father is at the centre of things, that he is light all about the darkness, and that he will not only bring good out of evil at last, but will be with the sufferer all the time, making endurance possible, and pain tolerable. There are a thousand alleviations that people do not often think of, coming from God himself. Would you not say, for instance, that time must pass very slowly in pain? But have you never observed, or has no one ever made the remark to you, how strangely fast, even in severe pain, the time passes after all?

"We will do all we can, will we not," I went on, "to make her as comfortable as possible? You, Dora, must attend to your little brothers, that your mother may not have too much to think about now that she will have Connie to nurse."

They could not say much, but they both kissed me, and went away leaving me to understand clearly enough that they had quite understood me. I then returned to the sick chamber, where I found that the poor child had fallen asleep.

My wife and I watched by her bedside on alternate nights, until the pain had so far subsided, and the fever was so far reduced, that we could allow Wynnie to take a share in the office. We could not think of giving her over to the care of any but one of ourselves during the night. Her chief suffering came from its being necessary that she should keep nearly one position on her back, because of her spine, while the external bruise and the swelling of the muscles were in consequence so painful, that it needed all that mechanical contrivance could do to render the position endurable. But these outward conditions were greatly ameliorated before many days were over.

This is a dreary beginning of my story, is it not? But sickness of all kinds is such a common thing in the world, that it is well sometimes to let our minds rest upon it, lest it should take us altogether at unawares, either in ourselves or our friends, when it comes. If it were not a good thing in the end, surely it would not be; and perhaps before I have done my readers will not be sorry that my tale began so gloomily. The sickness in Judaea eighteen hundred and thirty-five years ago, or thereabouts, has no small part in the story of him who came to put all things under our feet. Praise be to him for evermore!

It soon became evident to me that that room was like a new and more sacred heart to the house. At first it radiated gloom to the remotest corners; but soon rays of light began to appear mingling with the gloom. I could see that bits of news were carried from it to the servants in the kitchen, in the garden, in the stable, and over the way to the home-farm. Even in the village, and everywhere over the parish, I was received more kindly, and listened to more willingly, because of the trouble I and my family were in; while in the house, although we had never been anything else than a loving family, it was easy to discover that we all drew more closely together in consequence of our common anxiety. Previous to this, it had been no unusual thing to see Wynnie and Dora impatient with each other; for Dora was none the less a wild, somewhat lawless child, that she was a profoundly affectionate one. She rather resembled her cousin Judy, in fact-whom she called Aunt Judy, and with whom she was naturally a great favourite. Wynnie, on the other hand, was sedate, and rather severe-more severe, I must in justice say, with herself than with anyone else. I had sometimes wished, it is true, that her mother, in regard to the younger children, were more like her; but there I was wrong. For one of the great goods that come of having two parents, is that the one balances and rectifies the motions of the other. No one is good but God. No one holds the truth, or can hold it, in one and the same thought, but God. Our human life is often, at best, but an oscillation between the extremes which together make the truth; and it is not a bad thing in a family, that the pendulums of father and mother should differ in movement so far, that when the one is at one extremity of the swing, the other should be at the other, so that they meet only in the point of *indifference*, in the middle; that the predominant tendency of the one should not be the predominant tendency of the other. I was a very strict disciplinarian-too much so, perhaps, sometimes: Ethelwyn, on the other hand, was too much inclined, I thought, to excuse everything. I was law, she was grace. But grace often yielded to law, and law sometimes yielded to grace. Yet she represented the higher; for in the ultimate triumph of grace, in the glad performance of the command from love of what is commanded, the law is fulfilled: the law is a schoolmaster to bring us to Christ. I must say this for myself, however, that, although obedience was the one thing I enforced, believing it the one thing upon which all family economy primarily depends, yet my object always was to set my children free from my law as soon as possible; in a word, to help them to become, as soon as it might be, a law unto themselves. Then they would need no more of mine. Then I would go entirely over to the mother's higher side, and become to them, as much as in me lay, no longer law and truth, but grace and truth. But to return to my children-it was soon evident not only that Wynnie had grown more indulgent to Dora's vagaries, but that Dora was more submissive to Wynnie, while the younger children began to obey their eldest sister with a willing obedience, keeping down their effervescence within doors, and letting it off only out of doors, or in the out-houses.

When Constance began to recover a little, then the sacredness of that chamber began to show itself more powerfully, radiating on all sides a yet stronger influence of peace and goodwill. It was like a fountain of gentle light, quieting and bringing more or less into tune all that came within the circle of its sweetness. This brings me to speak again of my lovely child. For surely a father may speak thus of a child of God. He cannot regard his child as his even as a book he has written may be his. A man's child is his because God has said to him, "Take this child and nurse it for me." She is God's making; God's marvellous invention, to be tended and cared for, and ministered unto as one of his precious things; a young angel, let me say, who needs the air of this lower world to make her wings grow. And while he regards her thus, he will see all other children in the same light, and will not dare to set up his own against others of God's brood with the new-budding wings. The universal heart of truth will thus rectify, while it intensifies, the individual feeling towards one's own; and the man who is most free from poor partisanship in regard to his own family, will feel the most individual tenderness for the lovely human creatures whom God has given into his own especial care and responsibility. Show me the man who is tender, reverential, gracious towards the children of other men, and I will show you the man who will love and tend his own best, to whose heart his own will flee for their first refuge after God, when they catch sight of the cloud in the wind.

CHAPTER III
THE SICK CHAMBER.

In the course of a month there was a good deal more of light in the smile with which my darling greeted me when I entered her room in the morning. Her pain was greatly gone, but the power of moving her limbs had not yet even begun to show itself.

One day she received me with a still happier smile than I had yet seen upon her face, put out her thin white hand, took mine and kissed it, and said, "Papa," with a lingering on the last syllable.

"What is it, my pet?" I asked.

"I am so happy!"

"What makes you so happy?" I asked again.

"I don't know," she answered. "I haven't thought about it yet. But everything looks so pleasant round me. Is it nearly winter yet, papa? I've forgotten all about how the time has been going."

"It is almost winter, my dear. There is hardly a leaf left on the trees-just two or three disconsolate yellow ones that want to get away down to the rest. They go fluttering and fluttering and trying to break away, but they can't."

"That is just as I felt a little while ago. I wanted to die and get away, papa; for I thought I should never be well again, and I should be in everybody's way. —I am afraid I shall not get well, after all," she added, and the light clouded on her sweet face.

"Well, my darling, we are in God's hands. We shall never get tired of you, and you must not get tired of us. Would you get tired of nursing me, if I were ill?"

"O, papa!" And the tears began to gather in her eyes.

"Then you must think we are not able to love so well as you."

"I know what you mean. I did not think of it that way. I will never think so about it again. I was only thinking how useless I was."

"There you are quite mistaken, my dear. No living creature ever was useless. You've got plenty to do there."

"But what have I got to do? I don't feel able for anything," she said; and again the tears came in her eyes, as if I had been telling her to get up and she could not.

"A great deal of our work," I answered, "we do without knowing what it is. But I'll tell you what you have got to do: you have got to believe in God, and in everybody in this house."

"I do, I do. But that is easy to do," she returned.

"And do you think that the work God gives us to do is never easy? Jesus says his yoke is easy, his burden is light. People sometimes refuse to do God's work just because it is easy. This is, sometimes, because they cannot believe that easy work is his work; but there may be a very bad pride in it: it may be because they think that there is little or no honour to be got in that way; and therefore they despise it. Some again accept it with half a heart, and do it with half a hand. But, however easy any work may be, it cannot be well done without taking thought about it. And such people, instead of taking thought about their work, generally take thought about the morrow, in which no work can be done any more than in yesterday. The Holy Present! —I think I must make one more sermon about it-although you, Connie," I said, meaning it for a little joke, "do think that I have said too much about it already."

"Papa, papa! do forgive me. This is a judgment on me for talking to you as I did that dreadful morning. But I was so happy that I was impertinent."

"You silly darling!" I said. "A judgment! God be angry with you for that! Even if it had been anything wrong, which it was not, do you think God has no patience? No, Connie. I will tell you what seems to me much more likely. You wanted something to do; and so God gave you something to do."

"Lying in bed and doing nothing!"

"Yes. Just lying in bed, and doing his will."

245

"If I could but feel that I was doing his will!"

"When you do it, then you will feel you are doing it."

"I know you are coming to something, papa. Please make haste, for my back is getting so bad."

"I've tired you, my pet. It was very thoughtless of me. I will tell you the rest another time," I said, rising.

"No, no. It will make me much worse not to hear it all now."

"Well, I will tell you. Be still, my darling, I won't be long. In the time of the old sacrifices, when God so kindly told his ignorant children to do something for him in that way, poor people were told to bring, not a bullock or a sheep, for that was more than they could get, but a pair of turtledoves, or two young pigeons. But now, as Crashaw the poet says, 'Ourselves become our own best sacrifice.' God wanted to teach people to offer themselves. Now, you are poor, my pet, and you cannot offer yourself in great things done for your fellow-men, which was the way Jesus did. But you must remember that the two young pigeons of the poor were just as acceptable to God as the fat bullock of the rich. Therefore you must say to God something like this: —'O heavenly Father, I have nothing to offer thee but my patience. I will bear thy will, and so offer my will a burnt-offering unto thee. I will be as useless as thou pleasest.' Depend upon it, my darling, in the midst of all the science about the world and its ways, and all the ignorance of God and his greatness, the man or woman who can thus say, *Thy will be done*, with the true heart of giving up is nearer the secret of things than the geologist and theologian. And now, my darling, be quiet in God's name."

She held up her mouth to kiss me, but did not speak, and I left her, and sent Dora to sit with her.

In the evening, when I went into her room again, having been out in my parish all the morning, I began to unload my budget of small events. Indeed, we all came in like pelicans with stuffed pouches to empty them in her room, as if she had been the only young one we had, and we must cram her with news. Or, rather, she was like the queen of the commonwealth sending out her messages into all parts, and receiving messages in return. I might call her the brain of the house; but I have used similes enough for a while.

After I had done talking, she said—

"And you have been to the school too, papa?"

"Yes. I go to the school almost every day. I fancy in such a school as ours the young people get more good than they do in church. You know I had made a great change in the Sunday-school just before you came home."

"I heard of that, papa. You won't let any of the little ones go to school on the Sunday."

"No. It is too much for them. And having made this change, I feel the necessity of being in the school myself nearly every day, that I may do something direct for the little ones."

"And you'll have to take me up soon, as you promised, you know, papa-just before Sprite threw me."

"As soon as you like, my dear, after you are able to read again."

"O, you must begin before that, please. —You could spare time to read a little to me, couldn't you?" she said doubtfully, as if she feared she was asking too much.

"Certainly, my dear; and I will begin to think about it at once."

It was in part the result of this wish of my child's that it became the custom to gather in her room on Sunday evenings. She was quite unable for any kind of work such as she would have had me commence with her, but I used to take something to read to her every now and then, and always after our early tea on Sundays.

What a thing it is to have one to speak and think about and try to find out and understand, who is always and altogether and perfectly good! Such a centre that is for all our thoughts and words and actions and imaginations! It is indeed blessed to be human beings with Jesus Christ for the centre of humanity.

In the papers wherein I am about to record the chief events of the following years of my life, I shall give a short account of what passed at some of these assemblies in my child's room, in the hope that it may give my friends something, if not new, yet fresh to think about. For God has so made us that everyone who thinks at all thinks in a way that must be more or less fresh to everyone else who thinks, if he only have the gift of setting forth his thoughts so that we can see what they are.

I hope my readers will not be alarmed at this, and suppose that I am about to inflict long sermons upon them. I am not. I do hope, as I say, to teach them something; but those whom I succeed in so teaching will share in the delight it will give me to write about what I love most.

As far as I can remember, I will tell how this Sunday-evening class began. I was sitting by Constance's bed. The fire was burning brightly, and the twilight had deepened so nearly into night that it was reflected back from the window, for the curtains had not yet been drawn. There was no light in the room but that of the fire.

Now Constance was in the way of asking often what kind of day or night it was, for there never was a girl more a child of nature than she. Her heart seemed to respond at once to any and every mood of the world around her. To her the condition of air, earth, and sky was news, and news of poetic interest too. "What is it like?" she would often say, without any more definite shaping of the question. This same evening she said:

"What is it like, papa?"

"It is growing dark," I answered, "as you can see. It is a still evening, and what they call a black frost. The trees are standing as still as if they were carved out of stone, and would snap off everywhere if the wind were to blow. The ground is dark, and as hard as if it were of cast iron. A gloomy night rather, my dear. It looks as if there were something upon its mind that made it sullenly thoughtful; but the stars are coming out one after another overhead, and the sky will be all awake soon. A strange thing the life that goes on all night, is it not? The life of owlets, and mice, and beasts of prey, and bats, and stars," I said, with no very categorical arrangement, "and dreams, and flowers that don't go to sleep like the rest, but send out their scent all night long. Only those are gone now. There are no scents abroad, not even of the earth in such a frost as this."

"Don't you think it looks sometimes, papa, as if God turned his back on the world, or went farther away from it for a while?"

"Tell me a little more what you mean, Connie."

"Well, this night now, this dark, frozen, lifeless night, which you have been describing to me, isn't like God at all–is it?"

"No, it is not. I see what you mean now."

"It is just as if he had gone away and said, 'Now you shall see what you can do without me.'"

"Something like that. But do you know that English people–at least I think so–enjoy the changeful weather of their country much more upon the whole than those who have fine weather constantly? You see it is not enough to satisfy God's goodness that he should give us all things richly to enjoy, but he must make us able to enjoy them as richly as he gives them. He has to consider not only the gift, but the receiver of the gift. He has to make us able to take the gift and make it our own, as well as to give us the gift. In fact, it is not real giving, with the full, that is, the divine, meaning of giving, without it. He has to give us to the gift as well as give the gift to us. Now for this, a break, an interruption is good, is invaluable, for then we begin to think about the thing, and do something in the matter ourselves. The wonder of God's teaching is that, in great part, he makes us not merely learn, but teach ourselves, and that is far grander than if he only made our minds as he makes our bodies."

"I think I understand you, papa. For since I have been ill, you would wonder, if you could see into me, how even what you tell me about the world out of doors gives me more pleasure than I think I ever had when I could go about in it just as I liked."

"It wouldn't do that, though, you know, if you hadn't had the other first. The pleasure you have comes as much from your memory as from my news."

"I see that, papa."

"Now can you tell me anything in history that confirms what I have been saying?"

"I don't know anything about history, papa. The only thing that comes into my head is what you were saying yourself the other day about Milton's blindness."

"Ah, yes. I had not thought of that. Do you know, I do believe that God wanted a grand poem from that man, and therefore blinded him that he might be able to write it. But he had first trained him up to the point-given him thirty years in which he had not to provide the bread of a single day, only to learn and think; then set him to teach boys; then placed him at Cromwell's side, in the midst of the tumultuous movement of public affairs, into which the late student entered with all his heart and soul; and then last of all he cast the veil of a divine darkness over him, sent him into a chamber far more retired than that in which he laboured at Cambridge, and set him like the nightingale to sing darkling. The blackness about him was just the great canvas which God gave him to cover with forms of light and music. Deep wells of memory burst upwards from below; the windows of heaven were opened from above; from both rushed the deluge of song which flooded his soul, and which he has poured out in a great river to us."

"It was rather hard for poor Milton, though, wasn't it, papa?"

"Wait till he says so, my dear. We are sometimes too ready with our sympathy, and think things a great deal worse than those who have to undergo them. Who would not be glad to be struck with *such* blindness as Milton's?"

"Those that do not care about his poetry, papa," answered Constance, with a deprecatory smile.

"Well said, my Connie. And to such it never can come. But, if it please God, you will love Milton before you are about again. You can't love one you know nothing about."

"I have tried to read him a little."

"Yes, I daresay. You might as well talk of liking a man whose face you had never seen, because you did not approve of the back of his coat. But you and Milton together have led me away from a far grander instance of what we had been talking about. Are you tired, darling?"

"Not the least, papa. You don't mind what I said about Milton?"

"Not at all, my dear. I like your honesty. But I should mind very much if you thought, with your ignorance of Milton, that your judgment of him was more likely to be right than mine, with my knowledge of him."

"O, papa! I am only sorry that I am not capable of appreciating him."

"There you are wrong again. I think you are quite capable of appreciating him. But you cannot appreciate what you have never seen. You think of him as dry, and think you ought to be able to like dry things. Now he is not dry, and you ought not to be able to like dry things. You have a figure before you in your fancy, which is dry, and which you call Milton. But it is no more Milton than your dull-faced Dutch doll, which you called after her, was your merry Aunt Judy. But here comes your mamma; and I haven't said what I wanted to say yet."

"But surely, husband, you can say it all the same," said my wife. "I will go away if you can't."

"I can say it all the better, my love. Come and sit down here beside me. I was trying to show Connie —"

"You did show me, papa."

"Well, I was showing Connie that a gift has sometimes to be taken away again before we can know what it is worth, and so receive it right."

Ethelwyn sighed. She was always more open to the mournful than the glad. Her heart had been dreadfully wrung in her youth.

"And I was going on to give her the greatest instance of it in human history. As long as our Lord was with his disciples, they could not see him right: he was too near them. Too much light, too many words, too much revelation, blinds or stupefies. The Lord had been with them long enough. They loved him dearly, and yet often forgot his words almost as soon as he said them. He could not get it into them, for instance, that he had not come to be a king. Whatever he said, they shaped it over again after their own fancy; and their minds were so full of their own worldly notions of grandeur and command, that they could not receive into their souls the gift of God present before their eyes. Therefore he was taken away, that his Spirit, which was more himself than his bodily presence, might come into them-that they might receive the gift of God into their innermost being. After he had gone out of their sight, and they might look all around and down in the grave and up in the air, and not see him anywhere-when they thought they had lost him, he began to come to them again from the other side-from the inside. They found that the image of him which his presence with them had printed in light upon their souls, began to revive in the dark of his absence; and not that only, but that in looking at it without the overwhelming of his bodily presence, lines and forms and meanings began to dawn out of it which they had never seen before. And his words came back to them, no longer as they had received them, but as he meant them. The spirit of Christ filling their hearts and giving them new power, made them remember, by making them able to understand, all that he had said to them. They were then always saying to each other, 'You remember how;' whereas before, they had been always staring at each other with astonishment and something very near incredulity, while he spoke to them. So that after he had gone away, he was really nearer to them than he had been before. The meaning of anything is more than its visible presence. There is a soul in everything, and that soul is the meaning of it. The soul of the world and all its beauty has come nearer to you, my dear, just because you are separated from it for a time."

"Thank you, dear papa. I do like to get a little sermon all to myself now and then. That is another good of being ill."

"You don't mean me to have a share in it, then, Connie, do you?" said my wife, smiling at her daughter's pleasure.

"O, mamma! I should have thought you knew all papa had got to say by this time. I daresay he has given you a thousand sermons all to yourself."

"Then you suppose, Connie, that I came into the world with just a boxful of sermons, and after I had taken them all out there were no more. I should be sorry to think I should not have a good many new things to say by this time next year."

"Well, papa, I wish I could be sure of knowing more next year."

"Most people do learn, whether they will or not. But the kind of learning is very different in the two cases."

"But I want to ask you one question, papa: do you think that we should not know Jesus better now if he were to come and let us see him-as he came to the disciples so long, long ago? I wish it were not so long ago."

"As to the time, it makes no difference whether it was last year or two thousand years ago. The whole question is how much we understand, and understanding, obey him. And I do not think we should be any nearer that if he came amongst us bodily again. If we should, he would come. I believe we should be further off it."

"Do you think, then," said Connie, in an almost despairing tone, as if I were the prophet of great evil, "that we shall never, never, never see him?"

"That is *quite* another thing, my Connie. That is the heart of my hopes by day and my dreams by night. To behold the face of Jesus seems to me the one thing to be desired. I do not know that it is to be prayed for; but I think it will be given us as the great bounty of God, so soon as ever we are capable of it. That sight of the face of Jesus is, I think, what is meant by his glorious appearing, but it will come as a consequence of his spirit in us, not as a cause of that spirit in us. The pure in heart shall see God. The seeing of him will be the sign that we are like him, for only by being like him can we see him as he is. All the time that he was with them, the disciples never saw him as he was. You must understand a man before you can see and read his face aright; and as the disciples did not understand our Lord's heart, they could neither see nor read his face aright. But when we shall be fit to look that man in the face, God only knows."

"Then do you think, papa, that we, who have never seen him, could know him better than the disciples? I don't mean, of course, better than they knew him after he was taken away from them, but better than they knew him while he was still with them?"

"Certainly I do, my dear."

"O, papa! Is it possible? Why don't we all, then?"

"Because we won't take the trouble; that is the reason."

"O, what a grand thing to think! That would be worth living-worth being ill for. But how? how? Can't you help me? Mayn't one human being help another?"

"It is the highest duty one human being owes to another. But whoever wants to learn must pray, and think, and, above all, obey-that is simply, do what Jesus says."

There followed a little silence, and I could hear my child sobbing. And the tears stood in; my wife's eyes-tears of gladness to hear her daughter's sobs.

"I will try, papa," Constance said at last. "But you *will* help me?"

"That I will, my love. I will help you in the best way I know; by trying to tell you what I have heard and learned about him-heard and learned of the Father, I hope and trust. It is coming near to the time when he was born;—but I have spoken quite as long as you are able to bear to-night."

"No, no, papa. Do go on."

"No, my dear; no more to-night. That would be to offend against the very truth I have been trying to set forth to you. But next Sunday-you have plenty to think about till then—I will talk to you about the baby Jesus; and perhaps I may find something more to help you by that time, besides what I have got to say now."

"But," said my wife, "don't you think, Connie, this is too good to keep all to ourselves? Don't you think we ought to have Wynnie and Dora in?"

"Yes, yes, mamma. Do let us have them in. And Harry and Charlie too."

"I fear they are rather young yet," I said. "Perhaps it might do them harm."

"It would be all the better for us to have them anyhow," said Ethelwyn, smiling.

"How do you mean, my dear?"

"Because you will say things more simply if you have them by you. Besides, you always say such things to children as delight grown people, though they could never get them out of you."

It was a wife's speech, reader. Forgive me for writing it.

"Well," I said, "I don't mind them coming in, but I don't promise to say anything directly to them. And you must let them go away the moment they wish it."

"Certainly," answered my wife; and so the matter was arranged.

CHAPTER IV
A SUNDAY EVENING.

When I went in to see Constance the next Sunday morning before going to church, I knew by her face that she was expecting the evening. I took care to get into no conversation with her during the day, that she might be quite fresh. In the evening, when I went into her room again with my Bible in my hand, I found all our little company assembled. There was a glorious fire, for it was very cold, and the little ones were seated on the rug before it, one on each side of their mother; Wynnie sat by the further side of the bed, for she always avoided any place or thing she thought another might like; and Dora sat by the further chimney-corner, leaving the space between the fire and my chair open that I might see and share the glow.

"The wind is very high, papa," said Constance, as I seated myself beside her.

"Yes, my dear. It has been blowing all day, and since sundown it has blown harder. Do you like the wind, Connie?"

"I am afraid I do like it. When it roars like that in the chimneys, and shakes the windows with a great rush as if it *would* get into the house and tear us to pieces, and then goes moaning away into the woods and grumbles about in them till it grows savage again, and rushes up at us with fresh fury, I am afraid I delight in it. I feel so safe in the very jaws of danger."

"Why, you are quite poetic, Connie," said Wynnie.

"Don't laugh at me, Wynnie. Mind I'm an invalid, and I can't bear to be laughed at," returned Connie, half laughing herself, and a little more than a quarter crying.

Wynnie rose and kissed her, whispered something to her which made her laugh outright, and then sat down again.

"But tell me, Connie," I said, "why you are *afraid* you enjoy hearing the wind about the house."

"Because it must be so dreadful for those that are out in it."

"Perhaps not quite so bad as we think. You must not suppose that God has forgotten them, or cares less for them than for you because they are out in the wind."

"But if we thought like that, papa," said Wynnie, "shouldn't we come to feel that their sufferings were none of our business?"

"If our benevolence rests on the belief that God is less loving than we, it will come to a bad end somehow before long, Wynnie."

"Of course, I could not think that," she returned.

"Then your kindness would be such that you dared not, in God's name, think hopefully for those you could not help, lest you should, believing in his kindness, cease to help those whom you could help! Either God intended that there should be poverty and suffering, or he did not. If he did not intend it-for similar reasons to those for which he allows all sorts of evils-then there is nothing between but that we should sell everything that we have and give it away to the poor."

"Then why don't we?" said Wynnie, looking truth itself in my face.

"Because that is not God's way, and we should do no end of harm by so doing. We should make so many more of those who will not help themselves who will not be set free from themselves by rising above themselves. We are not to gratify our own benevolence at the expense of its object-not to save our own souls as we fancy, by putting other souls into more danger than God meant for them."

"It sounds hard doctrine from your lips, papa," said Wynnie.

"Many things will look hard in so many words, which yet will be found kindness itself when they are interpreted by a higher theory. If the one thing is to let people have everything they want, then of course everyone ought to be rich. I have no doubt such a man as we were reading of in the papers the other day, who saw his servant girl drown without making the least effort to save her, and then bemoaned the loss of her labour for the coming harvest, thinking himself ill-used in her death, would hug his own selfishness on hearing my words, and say, 'All right, parson! Every man for himself! I made my own money, and they may make theirs!' *You* know that is not exactly the way I should think or act with regard to my neighbour. But if it were only that I have seen such noble characters cast in the mould of poverty, I should be compelled to regard poverty as one of God's powers in the world for raising the children of the kingdom, and to believe that it was not because it could not be helped that our Lord said, 'The poor ye have always with you.' But what I wanted to say was, that there can be no reason why Connie should not enjoy what God has given her, although he has not thought fit to give as much to everybody; and above all, that we shall not help those right whom God gives us to help, if we do not believe that God is caring for every one of them as much as he is caring for every one of us. There was once a baby born in a stable, because his poor mother could get no room in a decent house. Where she lay I can hardly think. They must have made a bed of hay and straw for her in the stall, for we know the baby's cradle was the manger. Had God forsaken them? or would they not have been more *comfortable*, if that was the main thing, somewhere else? Ah! if the disciples, who were being born about the same time of fisher-fathers and cottage-mothers, to get ready for him to call and teach by the time he should be thirty years of age-if they had only been old enough, and had known that he was coming-would they not have got everything ready for him? They would have clubbed their little savings together, and worked day and night, and some rich women would have helped them, and they would have dressed the baby in fine linen, and got him the richest room their money would get, and they would have made the gold that the wise men brought into a crown for his little head, and would have burnt the frankincense before him. And so our little manger-baby would have been taken away from us. No more the stable-born Saviour-no more the poor Son of God born for us all, as strong, as noble, as loving, as worshipful, as beautiful as he was poor! And we should not have learned that God does not care for money; that if he does not give more of it it is not that it is scarce with him, or that he is unkind, but that he does not value it himself. And if he sent his own son to be not merely brought up in the house of the carpenter of a little village, but to be born in the stable of a village inn, we need not suppose because a man sleeps under a haystack and is put in prison for it next day, that God does not care for him."

"But why did Jesus come so poor, papa?"

"That he might be just a human baby. That he might not be distinguished by this or by that accident of birth; that he might have nothing but a mother's love to welcome him, and so belong to everybody; that from the first he might show that the kingdom of God and the favour of God lie not in these external things at all-that the poorest little one, born in the meanest dwelling, or in none at all, is as much God's own and God's care as if he came in a royal chamber with colour and shine all about him. Had Jesus come amongst the rich, riches would have been more worshipped than ever. See how so many that count themselves good Christians honour possession and family and social rank, and I doubt hardly get rid of them when they are all swept away from them. The furthest most of such reach is to count Jesus an exception, and therefore not despise him. See how, even in the services of the church, as they call them, they will accumulate gorgeousness and cost. Had I my way, though I will never seek to rouse men's thoughts about such external things, I would never have any vessel used in the eucharist but wooden platters and wooden cups."

"But are we not to serve him with our best?" said my wife.

"Yes, with our very hearts and souls, with our wills, with our absolute being. But all external things should be in harmony with the spirit of his revelation. And if God chose that his Son should visit the earth in homely fashion, in homely fashion likewise should be everything that enforces and commemorates that revelation. All church-forms should be on the other side from show and expense. Let the money go to build decent houses for God's poor, not to give them his holy bread and wine out of silver and gold and precious stones-stealing from the significance of the *content* by the meretricious grandeur of the *continent*. I would send all the church-plate to fight the devil with his own weapons in our overcrowded cities, and in our villages where the husbandmen are housed like swine, by giving them room to be clean and decent air from heaven to breathe. When the people find the clergy thus in earnest, they will follow them fast enough, and the money will come in like salt and oil upon the sacrifice. I would there were a few of our dignitaries that could think grandly about things, even as Jesus thought-even as God thought when he sent him. There are many of them willing to stand any amount of persecution about trifles: the same enthusiasm directed by high thoughts about the kingdom of heaven as within men and not around them, would redeem a vast region from that indifference which comes of judging the gospel of God by the church of Christ with its phylacteries and hems."

"There is one thing," said Wynnie, after a pause, "that I have often thought about-why it was necessary for Jesus to come as a baby: he could not do anything for so long."

"First, I would answer, Wynnie, that if you would tell me why it is necessary for all of us to come as babies, it would be less necessary for me to tell you why he came so: whatever was human must be his. But I would say next, Are you sure that he could not do anything for so long? Does a baby do nothing? Ask mamma there. Is it for nothing that the mother lifts up such heartfuls of thanks to God for the baby on her knee? Is it nothing that the baby opens such fountains of love in almost all the hearts around? Ah! you do not think how much every baby has to do with the saving of the world-the saving of it from selfishness, and folly, and greed. And for Jesus, was he not going to establish the reign of love in the earth? How could he do better than begin from babyhood? He had to lay hold of the heart of the world. How could he do better than begin with his mother's —the best one in it. Through his mother's love first, he grew into the world. It was first by the door of all the holy relations of the family that he entered the human world, laying hold of mother, father, brothers, sisters, all his friends; then by the door of labour, for he took his share of his father's work; then, when he was thirty years of age, by the door of teaching; by kind deeds, and sufferings, and through all by obedience unto the death. You must not think little of the grand thirty years wherein he got ready for the chief work to follow. You must not think that while he was thus preparing for his public ministrations, he was not all the time saving the world even by that which he was in the midst of it, ever laying hold of it more and more. These were things not so easy to tell. And you must remember that our records are very scanty. It is a small biography we have of a man who became-to say nothing more-the Man of the world-the Son of Man. No doubt it is enough, or God would have told us more; but surely we are not to suppose that there was nothing significant, nothing of saving power in that which we are not told. —Charlie, wouldn't you have liked to see the little baby Jesus?"

"Yes, that I would. I would have given him my white rabbit with the pink eyes."

"That is what the great painter Titian must have thought, Charlie; for he has painted him playing with a white rabbit, —not such a pretty one as yours."

"I would have carried him about all day," said Dora, "as little Henny Parsons does her baby-brother."

"Did he have any brother or sister to carry him about, papa?" asked Harry.

"No, my boy; for he was the eldest. But you may be pretty sure he carried about his brothers and sisters that came after him."

"Wouldn't he take care of them, just!" said Charlie.

"I wish I had been one of them," said Constance.

"You are one of them, my Connie. Now he is so great and so strong that he can carry father and mother and all of us in his bosom."

Then we sung a child's hymn in praise of the God of little children, and the little ones went to bed. Constance was tired now, and we left her with Wynnie. We too went early to bed.

About midnight my wife and I awoke together-at least neither knew which waked the other. The wind was still raving about the house, with lulls between its charges.

"There's a child crying!" said my wife, starting up.

I sat up too, and listened.

"There is some creature," I granted.

"It is an infant," insisted my wife. "It can't be either of the boys."

I was out of bed in a moment, and my wife the same instant. We hurried on some of our clothes, going to the windows and listening as we did so. We seemed to hear the wailing through the loudest of the wind, and in the lulls were sure of it. But it grew fainter as we listened. The night was pitch dark. I got a lantern, and hurried out. I went round the house till I came under our bed-room windows, and there listened. I heard it, but not so clearly as before. I set out as well as I could judge in the direction of the sound. I could find nothing. My lantern lighted only a few yards around me, and the wind was so strong that it blew through every chink, and threatened momently to blow it out. My wife was by my side before I knew she was coming.

"My dear!" I said, "it is not fit for you to be out."

"It is as fit for me as for a child, anyhow," she said. "Do listen."

It was certainly no time for expostulation. All the mother was awake in Ethelwyn's bosom. It would have been cruelty to make her go in, though she was indeed ill-fitted to encounter such a night-wind.

Another wail reached us. It seemed to come from a thicket at one corner of the lawn. We hurried thither. Again a cry, and we knew we were much nearer to it. Searching and searching we went.

"There it is!" Ethelwyn almost screamed, as the feeble light of the lantern fell on a dark bundle of something under a bush. She caught at it. It gave another pitiful wail-the poor baby of some tramp, rolled up in a dirty, ragged shawl, and tied round with a bit of string, as if it had been a parcel of clouts. She set off running with it to the house, and I followed, much fearing she would miss her way in the dark, and fall. I could hardly get up with her, so eager was she to save the child. She darted up to her own room, where the fire was not yet out.

"Run to the kitchen, Harry, and get some hot water. Take the two jugs there-you can empty them in the sink: you won't know where to find anything. There will be plenty in the boiler."

By the time I returned with the hot water, she had taken off the child's covering, and was sitting with it, wrapped in a blanket, before the fire. The little thing was cold as a stone, and now silent and motionless. We had found it just in time. Ethelwyn ordered me about as if I had been a nursemaid. I poured the hot water into a footbath.

"Some cold water, Harry. You would boil the child."

"You made me throw away the cold water," I said, laughing.

"There's some in the bottles," she returned. "Make haste."

I did try to make haste, but I could not be quick enough to satisfy Ethelwyn.

"The child will be dead," she cried, "before we get it in the water."

She had its rags off in a moment-there was very little to remove after the shawl. How white the little thing was, though dreadfully neglected! It was a girl-not more than a few weeks old, we agreed. Her little heart was still beating feebly; and as she was a well-made, apparently healthy infant, we had every hope of recovering her. And we were not disappointed. She began to move her little legs and arms with short, convulsive motions.

"Do you know where the dairy is, Harry?" asked my wife, with no great compliment to my bumps of locality, which I had always flattered myself were beyond the average in development.

"I think I do," I answered.

"Could you tell which was this night's milk, now?"

"There will be less cream on it," I answered.

"Bring a little of that and some more hot water. I've got some sugar here. I wish we had a bottle."

I executed her commands faithfully. By the time I returned the child was lying on her lap clean and dry—a fine baby I thought. Ethelwyn went on talking to her, and praising her as if she had not only been the finest specimen of mortality in the world, but her own child to boot. She got her to take a few spoonfuls of milk and water, and then the little thing fell fast asleep.

Ethelwyn's nursing days were not so far gone by that she did not know where her baby's clothes were. She gave me the child, and going to a wardrobe in the room brought out some night-things, and put them on. I could not understand in the least why the sleeping darling must be indued with little chemise, and flannel, and nightgown, and I do not know what all, requiring a world of nice care, and a hundred turnings to and fro, now on its little stomach, now on its back, now sitting up, now lying down, when it would have slept just as well, and I venture to think much more comfortably, if laid in blankets and well covered over. But I had never ventured to interfere with any of my own children, devoutly believing up to this moment, though in a dim unquestioning way, that there must be some hidden feminine wisdom in the whole process; and now that I had begun to question it, I found that my opportunity had long gone by, if I had ever had one. And after all there may be some reason for it, though I confess I do strongly suspect that all these matters are so wonderfully complicated in order that the girl left in the woman may have her heart's content of playing with her doll; just as the woman hid in the girl expends no end of lovely affection upon the dull stupidity of wooden cheeks and a body of sawdust. But it was a delight to my heart to see how Ethelwyn could not be satisfied without treating the foundling in precisely the same fashion as one of her own. And if this was a necessary preparation for what, should follow, I would be the very last to complain of it.

We went to bed again, and the forsaken child of some half-animal mother, now perhaps asleep in some filthy lodging for tramps, lay in my Ethelwyn's bosom. I loved her the more for it; though, I confess, it would have been very painful to me had she shown it possible for her to treat the baby otherwise, especially after what we had been talking about that same evening.

So we had another child in the house, and nobody knew anything about it but ourselves two. The household had never been disturbed by all the going and coming. After everything had been done for her, we had a good laugh over the whole matter, and then Ethelwyn fell a-crying.

"Pray for the poor thing, Harry," she sobbed, "before you come to bed."

I knelt down, and said:

"O Lord our Father, this is as much thy child and as certainly sent to us as if she had been born of us. Help us to keep the child for thee. Take thou care of thy own, and teach us what to do with her, and how to order our ways towards her."

Then I said to Ethelwyn,

"We will not say one word more about it tonight. You must try to go to sleep. I daresay the little thing will sleep till the morning, and I am sure I shall if she does. Good-night, my love. You are a true mother. Mind you go to sleep."

"I am half asleep already, Harry. Good-night," she returned.

I know nothing more about anything till I in the morning, except that I had a dream, which I have not made up my mind yet whether I shall tell or not. We slept soundly-God's baby and all.

CHAPTER V
MY DREAM.

I think I will tell the dream I had. I cannot well account for the beginning of it: the end will appear sufficiently explicable to those who are quite satisfied that they get rid of the mystery of a thing when they can associate it with something else with which they are familiar. Such do not care to see that the thing with which they associate it may be as mysterious as the other. For although use too often destroys marvel, it cannot destroy the marvellous. The origin of our thoughts is just as wonderful as the origin of our dreams.

In my dream I found myself in a pleasant field full of daisies and white clover. The sun was setting. The wind was going one way, and the shadows another. I felt rather tired, I neither knew nor thought why. With an old man's prudence, I would not sit down upon the grass, but looked about for a more suitable seat. Then I saw, for often in our dreams there is an immediate response to our wishes, a long, rather narrow stone lying a few yards from me. I wondered how it could have come there, for there were no mountains or rocks near: the field was part of a level country. Carelessly, I sat down upon it astride, and watched the setting of the sun. Somehow I fancied that his light was more sorrowful than the light of the setting sun should be, and I began to feel very heavy at the heart. No sooner had the last brilliant spark of his light vanished, than I felt the stone under me begin to move. With the inactivity of a dreamer, however, I did not care to rise, but wondered only what would come next. My seat, after several strange tumbling motions, seemed to rise into the air a little way, and then I found that I was astride of a gaunt, bony horse —a skeleton horse almost, only he had a gray skin on him. He began, apparently with pain, as if his joints were all but too stiff to move, to go forward in the direction in which he found himself. I kept my seat. Indeed, I never thought of dismounting. I was going on to meet what might come. Slowly, feebly, trembling at every step, the strange steed went, and as he went his joints seemed to become less stiff, and he went a little faster. All at once I found that the pleasant field had vanished, and that we were on the borders of a moor. Straight forward the horse carried me, and the moor grew very rough, and he went stumbling dreadfully, but always recovering himself. Every moment it seemed as if he would fall to rise no more, but as often he found fresh footing. At length the surface became a little smoother, and he began a horrible canter which lasted till he reached a low, broken wall, over which he half walked, half fell into what was plainly an ancient neglected churchyard. The mounds were low and covered with rank grass. In some parts, hollows had taken the place of mounds. Gravestones lay in every position except the level or the upright, and broken masses of monuments were scattered about. My horse bore me into the midst of it, and there, slow and stiff as he had risen, he lay down again. Once more I was astride of a long narrow stone. And now I found that it was an ancient gravestone which I knew well in a certain Sussex churchyard, the top of it carved into the rough resemblance of a human skeleton-that of a man, tradition said, who had been killed by a serpent that came out of a bottomless pool in the next field. How long I sat there I do not know; but at last I saw the faint gray light of morning begin to appear in front of me. The horse of death had carried me eastward. The dawn grew over the top of a hill that here rose against the horizon. But it was a wild dreary dawn —a blot of gray first, which then stretched into long lines of dreary yellow and gray, looking more like a blasted and withered sunset than a fresh sunrise. And well it suited that waste, wide, deserted churchyard, if churchyard I ought to call it where no church was to be seen-only a vast hideous square of graves. Before me I noticed especially one old grave, the flat stone of which had broken in two and sunk in the middle. While I sat with my eyes fixed on this stone, it began to move; the crack in the middle closed, then widened again as the two halves of the stone were lifted up, and flung outward, like the two halves of a folding door. From the grave rose a little child, smiling such perfect contentment as if he had just come from kissing his mother. His little arms had flung the stones apart, and as he stood on the edge of the grave next to me, they remained outspread from the action for a moment, as if blessing the sleeping people. Then he came towards me with the same smile, and took my hand. I rose, and he led me away over another broken wall towards the hill that lay before us. And as we went the sun came nearer, the pale yellow bars flushed into orange and rosy red, till at length the edges of the clouds were swept with an agony of golden light, which even my dreamy eyes could not endure, and I awoke weeping for joy.

This waking woke my wife, who said in some alarm:

"What is the matter, husband?"

So I told her my dream, and how in my sleep my gladness had overcome me.

"It was this little darling that set you dreaming so," she said, and turning, put the baby in my arms.

CHAPTER VI
THE NEW BABY.

I will not attempt to describe the astonishment of the members of our household, each in succession, as the news of the child spread. Charlie was heard shouting across the stable-yard to his brother:

"Harry, Harry! Mamma has got a new baby. Isn't it jolly?"

"Where did she get it?" cried Harry in return.

"In the parsley-bed, I suppose," answered Charlie, and was nearer right than usual, for the information on which his conclusion was founded had no doubt been imparted as belonging to the history of the human race.

But my reader can easily imagine the utter bewilderment of those of the family whose knowledge of human affairs would not allow of their curiosity being so easily satisfied as that of the boys. In them was exemplified that confusion of the intellectual being which is produced by the witness of incontestable truth to a thing incredible-in which case the probability always is, that the incredibility results from something in the mind of the hearer falsely associated with and disturbing the true perception of the thing to which witness is borne.

Nor was the astonishment confined to the family, for it spread over the parish that Mrs. Walton had got another baby. And so, indeed, she had. And seldom has baby met with a more hearty welcome than this baby met with from everyone of our family. They hugged it first, and then asked questions. And that, I say, is the right way of receiving every good gift of God. Ask what questions you will, but when you see that the gift is a good one, make sure that you take it. There is plenty of time for you to ask questions afterwards. Then the better you love the gift, the more ready you will be to ask, and the more fearless in asking.

The truth, however, soon became known. And then, strange to relate, we began to receive visits of condolence. O, that poor baby! how it was frowned upon, and how it had heads shaken over it, just because it was not Ethelwyn's baby! It could not help that, poor darling!

"Of course, you'll give information to the police," said, I am sorry to say, one of my brethren in the neighbourhood, who had the misfortune to be a magistrate as well.

"Why?" I asked.

"Why! That they may discover the parents, to be sure."

"Wouldn't it be as hard a matter to prove the parentage, as it would be easy to suspect it?" I asked. "And just think what it would be to give the baby to a woman who not only did not want her, but who was not her mother. But if her own mother came to claim her now, I don't say I would refuse her, but I should think twice about giving her up after she had once abandoned her for a whole night in the open air. In fact I don't want the parents."

"But you don't want the child."

"How do you know that?" I returned-rather rudely, I am afraid, for I am easily annoyed at anything that seems to me heartless-about children especially.

"O! of course, if you want to have an orphan asylum of your own, no one has a right to interfere. But you ought to consider other people."

"That is just what I thought I was doing," I answered; but he went on without heeding my reply—

"We shall all be having babies left at our doors, and some of us are not so fond of them as you are. Remember, you are your brother's keeper."

"And my sister's too," I answered. "And if the question lies between keeping a big, burly brother like you, and a tiny, wee sister like that, I venture to choose for myself."

"She ought to go to the workhouse," said the magistrate —a friendly, good-natured man enough in ordinary-and rising, he took his hat and departed.

This man had no children. So he was-or was not, so much to blame. Which? *I* say the latter.

Some of Ethelwyn's friends were no less positive about her duty in the affair. I happened to go into the drawing-room during the visit of one of them-Miss Bowdler.

"But, my dear Mrs. Walton," she was saying, "you'll be having all the tramps in England leaving their babies at your door."

"The better for the babies," interposed I, laughing.

"But you don't think of your wife, Mr. Walton."

"Don't I? I thought I did," I returned dryly.

"Depend upon it, you'll repent it."

"I hope I shall never repent of anything but what is bad."

"Ah! but, really! it's not a thing to be made game of."

"Certainly not. The baby shall be treated with all due respect in this house."

"What a provoking man you are! You know what I mean well enough."

"As well as I choose to know-certainly," I answered.

This lady was one of my oldest parishioners, and took liberties for which she had no other justification, except indeed an unhesitating belief in the superior rectitude of whatever came into her own head can be counted as one. When she was gone, my wife turned to me with a half-comic, half-anxious look, and said:

"But it would be rather alarming, Harry, if this were to get abroad, and we couldn't go out at the door in the morning without being in danger of stepping on a baby on the door-step."

"You might as well have said, when you were going to be married, 'If God should send me twenty children, whatever should I do?' He who sent us this one can surely prevent any more from coming than he wants to come. All that we have to think of is to do right-not the consequences of doing right. But leaving all that aside, you must not suppose that wandering mothers have not even the attachment of animals to their offspring. There are not so many that are willing to part with babies as all that would come to. If you believe that God sent this one, that is enough for the present. If he should send another, we should know by that that we had to take it in."

My wife said the baby was a beauty. I could see that she was a plump, well-to-do baby; and being by nature no particular lover of babies as babies-that is, feeling none of the inclination of mothers and nurses and elder sisters to eat them, or rather, perhaps, loving more for what I believed than what I saw-that was all I could pretend to discover. But even the aforementioned elderly parishioner was compelled to allow before three months were over that little Theodora-for we turned the name of my youngest daughter upside down for her—"was a proper child." To none, however, did she seem to bring so much delight as to our dear Constance. Oftener than not, when I went into her room, I found the sleepy, useless little thing lying beside her on the bed, and her staring at it with such loving eyes! How it began, I do not know, but it came at last to be called Connie's Dora, or Miss Connie's baby, all over the house, and nothing pleased Connie better. Not till she saw this did her old nurse take quite kindly to the infant; for she regarded her as an interloper, who had no right to the tenderness which was lavished upon her. But she had no sooner given in than the baby began to grow dear to her as well as to the rest. In fact, the house was ere long full of nurses. The staff included everyone but myself, who only occasionally, at the entreaty of some one or other of the younger ones, took her in my arms.

But before she was three months old, anxious thoughts began to intrude, all centering round the question in what manner the child was to be brought up. Certainly there was time enough to think of this, as Ethelwyn constantly reminded me; but what made me anxious was that I could not discover the principle that ought to guide me. Now no one can tell how soon a principle in such a case will begin, even unconsciously, to operate; and the danger was that the moment when it ought to begin to operate would be long past before the principle was discovered, except I did what I could now to find it out. I had again and again to remind myself that there was no cause for anxiety; for that I might certainly claim the enlightenment which all who want to do right are sure to receive; but still I continued uneasy just from feeling a vacancy where a principle ought to have been.

CHAPTER VII
ANOTHER SUNDAY EVENING.

During all this time Connie made no very perceptible progress-in the recovery of her bodily powers, I mean, for her heart and mind advanced remarkably. We held our Sunday-evening assemblies in her room pretty regularly, my occasional absence in the exercise of my duties alone interfering with them. In connection with one of these, I will show how I came at length to make up my mind as to what I would endeavour to keep before me as my object in the training of little Theodora, always remembering that my preparation might be used for a very different end from what I purposed. If my intention was right, the fact that it might be turned aside would not trouble me.

We had spoken a good deal together about the infancy and childhood of Jesus, about the shepherds, and the wise men, and the star in the east, and the children of Bethlehem. I encouraged the thoughts of all the children to rest and brood upon the fragments that are given us, and, believing that the imagination is one of the most powerful of all the faculties for aiding the growth of truth in the mind, I would ask them questions as to what they thought he might have said or done in ordinary family occurrences, thus giving a reality in their minds to this part of his history, and trying to rouse in them a habit of referring their conduct to the standard of his. If we do not thus employ our imagination on sacred things, his example can be of no use to us except in exactly corresponding circumstances-and when can such occur from one end to another of our lives? The very effort to think how he would have done, is a wonderful purifier of the conscience, and, even if the conclusion arrived at should not be correct from lack of sufficient knowledge of his character and principles, it will be better than any that can be arrived at without this inquiry. Besides, the asking of such questions gave me good opportunity, through the answers they returned, of seeing what their notions of Jesus and of duty were, and thus of discovering how to help the dawn of the light in their growing minds. Nor let anyone fear that such employment of the divine gift of imagination will lead to foolish vagaries and useless inventions; while the object is to discover the right way-the truth-there is little danger of that. Besides, there I was to help hereby in the actual training of their imaginations to truth and wisdom. To aid in this, I told them some of the stories that were circulated about him in the early centuries of the church, but which the church has rejected as of no authority; and I showed them how some of them could not be true, because they were so unlike those words and actions which we had the best of reasons for receiving as true; and how one or two of them might be true-though, considering the company in which we found them, we could say nothing for certain concerning them. And such wise things as those children said sometimes! It is marvellous how children can reach the heart of the truth at once. Their utterances are sometimes entirely concordant with the results arrived at through years of thought by the earnest mind-results which no mind would ever arrive at save by virtue of the child-like in it.

Well, then, upon this evening I read to them the story of the boy Jesus in the temple. Then I sought to make the story more real to them by dwelling a little on the growing fears of his parents as they went from group to group of their friends, tracing back the road towards Jerusalem and asking every fresh company they knew if they had seen their boy, till at length they were in great trouble when they could not find him even in Jerusalem. Then came the delight of his mother when she did find him at last, and his answer to what she said. Now, while I thus lingered over the simple story, my children had put many questions to me about Jesus being a boy, and not seeming to know things which, if he was God, he must have known, they thought. To some of these I had just to reply that I did not understand myself, and therefore could not teach them; to others, that I could explain them, but that they were not yet, some of them, old enough to receive and understand my explanation; while others I did my best to answer as simply as I could. But at this point we arrived at a question put by Wynnie, to answer which aright I considered of the greatest importance. Wynnie said:

"That is just one of the things about Jesus that have always troubled me, papa."

"What is, my dear?" I said; for although I thought I knew well enough what she meant, I wished her to set it forth in her own words, both for her own sake, and the sake of the others, who would probably understand the difficulty much better if she presented it herself.

"I mean that he spoke to his mother—"

"Why don't you say *mamma*, Wynnie?" said Charlie. "She was his own mamma, wasn't she, papa?"

"Yes, my dear; but don't you know that the shoemaker's children down in the village always call their mamma *mother*?"

"Yes; but they are shoemaker's children."

"Well, Jesus was one of that class of people. He was the son of a carpenter. He called his mamma, *mother*. But, Charlie, *mother* is the more beautiful word of the two, by a great deal, I think. *Lady* is a very pretty word; but *woman* is a very beautiful word. Just so with *mamma* and *mother*. *Mamma* is pretty, but *mother* is beautiful."

"Why don't we always say *mother* then?"

"Just because it is the most beautiful, and so we keep it for Sundays-that is, for the more solemn times of life. We don't want it to get common to us with too much use. We may think it as much as we like; thinking does not spoil it; but saying spoils many things, and especially beautiful words. Now we must let Wynnie finish what she was saying."

"I was saying, papa, that I can't help feeling as if—I know it can't be true-but I feel as if Jesus spoke unkindly to his mother when he said that to her."

I looked at the page and read the words, "How is it that ye sought me? wist ye not that I must be about my Father's business?" And I sat silent for a while.

"Why don't you speak, papa?" said Harry.

"I am sitting wondering at myself, Harry," I said. "Long after I was your age, Wynnie, I remember quite well that those words troubled me as they now trouble you. But when I read them over now, they seemed to me so lovely that I could hardly read them aloud. I can recall the fact that they troubled me, but the mode of the fact I scarcely can recall. I can hardly see now wherein lay the hurt or offence the words gave me. And why is that? Simply because I understand them now, and I did not understand them then. I took them as uttered with a tone of reproof; now I hear them as uttered with a tone of loving surprise. But really I cannot feel sure what it was that I did not like. And I am confident it is so with a great many things that we reject. We reject them simply because we do not understand them. Therefore, indeed, we cannot with truth be said to reject them at all. It is some false appearance that we reject. Some of the grandest things in the whole realm of truth look repellent to us, and we turn away from them, simply because we are not-to use a familiar phrase-we are not up to them. They appear to us, therefore, to be what they are not. Instruction sounds to the proud man like reproof; illumination comes on the vain man like scorn; the manifestation of a higher condition of motive and action than his own, falls on the self-esteeming like condemnation; but it is consciousness and conscience working together that produce this impression; the result is from the man himself, not from the higher source. From the truth comes the power, but the shape it assumes to the man is from the man himself."

"You are quite beyond me now, papa," said Wynnie.

"Well, my dear," I answered, "I will return to the words of the boy Jesus, instead of talking more about them; and when I have shown you what they mean, I think you will allow that that feeling you have about them is all and altogether an illusion."

"There is one thing first," said Connie, "that I want to understand. You said the words of Jesus rather indicated surprise. But how could he be surprised at anything? If he was God, he must have known everything."

"He tells us himself that he did not know everything. He says once that even *he* did not know one thing-only the Father knew it."

"But how could that be if he was God?"

"My dear, that is one of the things that it seems to me impossible I should understand. Certainly I think his trial as a man would not have been perfect had he known everything. He too had to live by faith in the Father. And remember that for the Divine Sonship on earth perfect knowledge was not necessary, only perfect confidence, absolute obedience, utter holiness. There is a great tendency in our sinful natures to put knowledge and power on a level with goodness. It was one of the lessons of our Lord's life that they are not so; that the one grand thing in humanity is faith in God; that the highest in God is his truth, his goodness, his rightness. But if Jesus was a real man, and no mere appearance of a man, is it any wonder that, with a heart full to the brim of the love of God, he should be for a moment surprised that his mother, whom he loved so dearly, the best human being he knew, should not have taken it as a matter of course that if he was not with her, he must be doing something his Father wanted him to do? For this is just what his answer means. To turn it into the ordinary speech of our day, it is just this: 'Why did you look for me? Didn't you know that I must of course be doing something my Father had given me to do?' Just think of the quiet sweetness of confidence in this. And think what a life his must have been up to that twelfth year of his, that such an expostulation with his mother was justified. It must have had reference to a good many things that had passed before then, which ought to have been sufficient to make Mary conclude that her missing boy must be about God's business somewhere. If her heart had been as full of God and God's business as his, she would not have been in the least uneasy about him. And here is the lesson of his whole life: it was all his Father's business. The boy's mind and hands were full of it. The man's mind and hands were full of it. And the risen conqueror was full of it still. For the Father's business is everything, and includes all work that is worth doing. We may say in a full grand sense, that there is nothing but the Father and his business."

"But we have so many things to do that are not his business," said Wynnie, with a sigh of oppression.

"Not one, my darling. If anything is not his business, you not only have not to do it, but you ought not to do it. Your words come from the want of spiritual sight. We cannot see the truth in common things-the will of God in little everyday affairs, and that is how they become so irksome to us. Show a beautiful picture, one full of quiet imagination and deep thought, to a common-minded man; he will pass it by with some slight remark, thinking it very ordinary and commonplace. That is because he is commonplace. Because our minds are so commonplace, have so little of the divine imagination in them, therefore we do not recognise the spiritual meaning and worth, we do not perceive the beautiful will of God, in the things required of us, though they are full of it. But if we do them we shall thus make acquaintance with them, and come to see what is in them. The roughest kernel amongst them has a tree of life in its heart."

"I wish he would tell me something to do," said Charlie. "Wouldn't I do it!"

I made no reply, but waited for an opportunity which I was pretty sure was at hand, while I carried the matter a little further.

"But look here, Wynnie; listen to this," I said, "'And he went down with them, and came to Nazareth, and was subject unto them.' Was that not doing his Father's business too? Was it not doing the business of his Father in heaven to honour his father and his mother, though he knew that his days would not be long in that land? Did not his whole teaching, his whole doing, rest on the relation of the Son to the Father and surely it was doing his Father's business then to obey his parents-to serve them, to be subject to them. It is true that the business God gives a man to do may be said to be the peculiar walk in life into which he is led, but that is only as distinguishing it from another man's peculiar business. God gives us all our business, and the business which is common to humanity is more peculiarly God's business than that which is one man's and not another's —because it lies nearer the root, and is essential. It does not matter whether a man is a farmer or a physician, but it greatly matters whether he is a good son, a good husband, and so on. O my children!" I said, "if the world could but be brought to believe-the world did I say? —if the best men in the world could only see, as God sees it, that service is in itself the noblest exercise of human powers, if they could see that God is the hardest worker of all, and that his nobility are those who do the most service, surely it would alter the whole aspect of the church. Menial offices, for instance, would soon cease to be talked of with that contempt which shows that there is no true recognition of the fact that the same principle runs through the highest duty and the lowest-that the lowest work which God gives a man to do must be in its nature noble, as certainly noble as the highest. This would destroy condescension, which is the rudeness, yes, impertinence, of the higher, as it would destroy insolence, which is the rudeness of the lower. He who recognised the dignity of his own lower office, would thereby recognise the superiority of the higher office, and would be the last either to envy or degrade it. He would see in it his own-only higher, only better, and revere it. But I am afraid I have wearied you, my children."

"O, no, papa!" said the elder ones, while the little ones gaped and said nothing.

"I know I am in danger of doing so when I come to speak upon this subject: it has such a hold of my heart and mind!—Now, Charlie, my boy, go to bed."

But Charlie was very comfortable before the fire, on the rug, and did not want to go. First one shoulder went up, and then the other, and the corners of his mouth went down, as if to keep the balance true. He did not move to go. I gave him a few moments to recover himself, but as the black frost still endured, I thought it was time to hold up a mirror to him. When he was a very little boy, he was much in the habit of getting out of temper, and then as now, he made a face that was hideous to behold; and to cure him of this, I used to make him carry a little mirror about his neck, that the means might be always at hand of showing himself to him: it was a sort of artificial conscience which, by enabling him to see the picture of his own condition, which the face always is, was not unfrequently operative in rousing his real conscience, and making him ashamed of himself. But now the mirror I wanted to hold up to him was a past mood, in the light of which the present would show what it was.

"Charlie," I said, "a little while ago you were wishing that God would give you something to do. And now when he does, you refuse at once, without even thinking about it."

"How do you know that God wants me to go to bed?" said Charlie, with something of surly impertinence, which I did not meet with reproof at once because there was some sense along with the impudence.

"I know that God wants you to do what I tell you, and to do it pleasantly. Do you think the boy Jesus would have put on such a face as that—I wish I had the little mirror to show it to you-when his mother told him it was time to go to bed?"

And now Charlie began to look ashamed. I left the truth to work in him, because I saw it was working. Had I not seen that, I should have compelled him to go at once, that he might learn the majesty of law. But now that his own better self, the self enlightened of the light that lighteneth every man that cometh into the world, was working, time might well be afforded it to work its perfect work. I went on talking to the others. In the space of not more than one minute, he rose and came to me, looking both good and ashamed, and held up his face to kiss me, saying, "Goodnight, papa." I bade him good-night, and kissed him more tenderly than usual, that he might know that it was all right between us. I required no formal apology, no begging of my pardon, as some parents think right. It seemed enough to me that his heart was turned. It is a terrible thing to run the risk of changing humility into humiliation. Humiliation is one of the proudest conditions in the human world. When he felt that it would be a relief to say more explicitly, "Father, I have sinned," then let him say it; but not till then. To compel manifestation is one surest way to check feeling.

My readers must not judge it silly to record a boy's unwillingness to go to bed. It is precisely the same kind of disobedience that some of them are guilty of themselves, and that in things not one whit more important than this, only those things happen to be *their* wish at the moment, and not Charlie's, and so gain their superiority.

CHAPTER VIII
THEODORA'S DOOM.

Try not to get weary, respected reader, of so much of what I am afraid most people will call tiresome preaching. But I know if you get anything practicable out of it, you will not be so soon tired of it. I promise you more story by and by. Only an old man, like an old horse, must be allowed to take very much his own way-go his own pace, I should have said. I am afraid there must be a little more of a similar sort in this chapter.

On the Monday morning I set out to visit one or two people whom the severity of the weather had kept from church on the Sunday. The last severe frost, as it turned out, of the season, was possessing the earth. The sun was low in the wintry sky, and what seemed a very cold mist up in the air hid him from the earth. I was walking along a path in a field close by a hedge. A tree had been cut down, and lay upon the grass. A short distance from it lay its own figure marked out in hoar-frost. There alone was there any hoar-frost on the field; the rest was all of the loveliest tenderest green. I will not say the figure was such an exact resemblance as a photograph would have been; still it was an indubitable likeness. It appeared to the hasty glance that not a branch not a knot of the upper side of the tree at least was left unrepresented in shining and glittering whiteness upon the green grass. It was very pretty, and, I confess, at first, very puzzling. I walked on, meditating on the phenomenon, till at length I found out its cause. The hoar-frost had been all over the field in the morning. The sun had been shining for a time, and had melted the frost away, except where he could only cast a shadow. As he rose and rose, the shadow of the tree had shortened and come nearer and nearer to its original, growing more and more like as it came nearer, while the frost kept disappearing as the shadow withdrew its protection. When the shadow extended only to a little way from the tree, the clouds came and covered the sun, and there were no more shadows, only one great one of the clouds. Then the frost shone out in the shape of the vanished shadow. It lay at a little distance from the tree, because the tree having been only partially lopped, some great stumps of boughs held it up from the ground, and thus, when the sun was low, his light had shone a little way through beneath, as well as over the trunk.

My reader needs not be afraid; I am not going to "moralise this spectacle with a thousand similes." I only tell it him as a very pretty phenomenon. But I confess I walked on moralising it. Any new thing in nature —I mean new in regard to my knowledge, of course-always made me happy; and I was full of the quiet pleasure it had given me and of the thoughts it had brought me, when, as I was getting over a stile, whom should I see in the next field, coming along the footpath, but the lady who had made herself so disagreeable about Theodora. The sight was rather a discord in my feeling at that moment; perhaps it would have been so at any moment. But I prepared myself to meet her in the strength of the good humour which nature had just bestowed upon me. For I fear the failing will go with me to the grave that I am very ready to be annoyed, even to the loss of my temper, at the urgings of ignoble prudence.

"Good-morning, Miss Bowdler," I said.

"Good-morning, Mr. Walton," she returned "I am afraid you thought me impertinent the other week; but you know by this time it is only my way."

"As such I take it," I answered with a smile.

She did not seem quite satisfied that I did not defend her from her own accusation; but as it was a just one, I could not do so. Therefore she went on to repeat the offence by way of justification.

"It was all for Mrs. Walton's sake. You ought to consider her, Mr. Walton. She has quite enough to do with that dear Connie, who is likely to be an invalid all her days-too much to take the trouble of a beggar's brat as well."

"Has Mrs. Walton been complaining to you about it, Miss Bowdler?" I asked.

"O dear, no!" she answered. "She is far too good to complain of anything. That's just why her friends must look after her a bit, Mr. Walton."

"Then I beg you won't speak disrespectfully of my little Theodora."

"O dear me! no. Not at all. I don't speak disrespectfully of her."

"Even amongst the class of which she comes, 'a beggar's brat' would be regarded as bad language."

"I beg your pardon, I'm sure, Mr. Walton! If you *will* take offence —"

"I do take offence. And you know there is One who has given especial warning against offending the little ones."

Miss Bowdler walked away in high displeasure-let me hope in conviction of sin as well. She did not appear in church for the next two Sundays. Then she came again. But she called very seldom at the Hall after this, and I believe my wife was not sorry.

Now whether it came in any way from what that lady had said as to my wife's trouble with Constance and Theodora together, I can hardly tell; but, before I had reached home, I had at last got a glimpse of something like the right way, as it appeared to me, of bringing up Theodora. When I went into the house, I looked for my wife to have a talk with her about it; but, indeed, it always necessary to find her every time I got home. I found her in Connie's room as I had expected. Now although we were never in the habit of making mysteries of things in which there was no mystery, and talked openly before our children, and the more openly the older they grew, yet there were times when we wanted to have our talks quite alone, especially when we had not made up our minds about something. So I asked Ethelwyn to walk out with me.

"I'm afraid I can't just this moment, husband," she answered. She was in the way of using that form of address, for she said it meant everything without saying it aloud. "I can't just this moment, for there is no one at liberty to stay with Connie."

"O, never mind me, mamma," said Connie cheerfully. "Theodora will take care of me," and she looked fondly at the child, who was lying by her side fast asleep.

"There!" I said. And both, looked up surprised, for neither knew what I meant. "I will tell you afterwards," I said, laughing. "Come along, Ethel."

"You can ring the bell, you know, Connie, if you should want anything, or your baby should wake up and be troublesome. You won't want me long, will you, husband?"

"I'm not sure about that. You must tell Susan to watch for the bell."

Susan was the old nurse.

Ethel put on her hooded cloak, and we went out together. I took her across to the field where I had seen the hoary shadow. The sun had not shone out, and I hoped it would be there to gladden her dear eyes as it had gladdened mine; but it was gone. The warmth of the sun, without his direct rays, had melted it away, as sacred influences will sometimes do with other shadows, without the mind knowing any more than the grass how the shadow departed. There, reader! I have got a bit of a moral in about it before you knew what I was doing. But I was sorry my wife could see it only through my eyes and words. Then I told her about Miss Bowdler, and what she had said. Ethel was very angry at her impertinence in speaking so to me. That was a wife's feeling, you know, and perhaps excusable in the first impression of the thing.

"She seems to think," she said, "that she was sent into the world to keep other people right instead of herself. I am very glad you set her down, as the maids say."

"O, I don't think there's much harm in her," I returned, which was easy generosity, seeing my wife was taking my part. "Indeed, I am not sure that we are not both considerably indebted to her; for it was after I met her that a thought came into my head as to how we ought to do with Theodora."

"Still troubling yourself about that, husband?"

"The longer the difficulty lasts, the more necessary is it that it should be met," I answered. "Our measures must begin sometime, and when, who can tell? We ought to have them in our heads, or they will never begin at all."

"Well, I confess they are rather of a general nature at present-belonging to humanity rather than the individual, as you would say-consisting chiefly in washing, dressing, feeding, and apostrophe, varied with lullabying. But our hearts are a better place for our measures than our heads, aren't they?"

"Certainly; I walk corrected. Only there's no fear about your heart. I'm not quite so sure about your head."

"Thank you, husband. But with you for a head it doesn't matter, does it?"

"I don't know that. People should always strengthen the weaker part, for no chain is stronger than its weakest link; no fortification stronger than its most assailable point. But, seriously, wife, I trust your head nearly, though not quite, as much as your heart. Now to go to business. There's one thing we have both made up our minds about-that there is to be no concealment with the child. God's fact must be known by her. It would be cruel to keep the truth from her, even if it were not sure to come upon her with a terrible shock some day. She must know from the first, by hearing it talked of-not by solemn and private communication-that she came out of the shrubbery. That's settled, is it not?"

"Certainly. I see that to be the right way," responded Ethelwyn.

"Now, are we bound to bring her up exactly as our own, or are we not?"

"We are bound to do as well for her as for our own."

"Assuredly. But if we brought her up just as our own, would that, the facts being as they are, be to do as well for her as for our own?"

"I doubt it; for other people would not choose to receive her as we have done."

"That is true. She would be continually reminded of her origin. Not that that in itself would be any evil; but as they would do it by excluding or neglecting her, or, still worse, by taking liberties with her, it would be a great pain. But keeping that out of view, would it be good for herself, knowing what she will know, to be thus brought up? Would it not be kinder to bring her up in a way that would make it easier for her to relieve the gratitude which I trust she will feel, not for our sakes —I hope we are above doing anything for the sake of the gratitude which will be given for it, and which is so often far beyond the worth of the thing done —"

> "Alas! the gratitude of men
> Hath oftener left me mourning,"

said Ethel.

"Ah! you understand that now, my Ethel!"

"Yes, thank you, I do."

"But we must wish for gratitude for others' sake, though we may be willing to go without it for our own. Indeed, gratitude is often just as painful as Wordsworth there represents it. It makes us so ashamed; makes us think how much more we *might* have done; how lovely a thing it is to give in return for such common gifts as ours; how needy the man or woman must be in whom a trifle awakes so much emotion."

"Yes; but we must not in justice think that it is merely that our little doing seems great to them: it is the kindness shown them therein, for which, often, they are more grateful than for the gift, though they can't show the difference in their thanks."

"And, indeed, are not aware of it themselves, though it is so. And yet, the same remarks hold good about the kindness as about the gift. But to return to Theodora. If we put her in a way of life that would be recognisant of whence she came, and how she had been brought thence, might it not be better for her? Would it not be building on the truth? Would she not be happier for it?"

"You are putting general propositions, while all the time you have something particular and definite in your own mind; and that is not fair to my place in the conference," said Ethel. "In fact, you think you are trying to approach me wisely, in order to persuade, I will not say *wheedle*, me into something. It's a good thing you have the harmlessness of the dove, Harry, for you've got the other thing."

"Well, then, I will be as plain as ever I can be, only premising that what you call the cunning of the serpent —"

"Wisdom, Harry, not cunning."

"Is only that I like to give my arguments before my proposition. But here it is-bare and defenceless, only-let me warn you-with a whole battery behind it: it is, to bring up little Theodora as a servant to Constance."

My wife laughed.

"Well," she said, "for one who says so much about not thinking of the morrow, you do look rather far forward."

"Not with any anxiety, however, if only I know that I am doing right."

"But just think: the child is about three months old."

"Well; Connie will be none the worse that she is being trained for her. I don't say that she is to commence her duties at once."

"But Connie may be at the head of a house of her own long before that."

"The training won't be lost to the child though. But I much fear, my love, that Connie will never be herself again. There is no sign of it. And Turner does not give much hope."

"O Harry, Harry, don't say so! I can't bear it. To think of the darling child lying like that all her life!"

"It is sad, indeed; but no such awful misfortune surely, Ethel. Haven't you seen, as well as I, that the growth of that child's nature since her accident has been marvellous? Ten times rather would I have her lying there such as she is, than have her well and strong and silly, with her bonnets inside instead of outside her head."

"Yes, but she needn't have been like that. Wynnie never will."

"Well, but God does all things not only well, but best, absolutely best. But just think what it would be in any circumstances to have a maid that had begun to wait upon her from the first days that she was able to toddle after something to fetch it for her."

"Won't it be like making a slave of her?"

"Won't it be like giving her a divine freedom from the first? The lack of service is the ruin of humanity."

"But we can't train her then like one of our own."

"Why not? Could we not give her all the love and all the teaching?"

"Because it would not be fair to give her the education of a lady, and then make a servant of her."

"You forget that the service would be part of her training from the first; and she would know no change of position in it. When we tell her that she was found in the shrubbery, we will add that we think God sent her to take care of Constance. I do not believe myself that you can have perfect service except from a lady. Do not forget the true notion of service as the essence of Christianity, yea, of divinity. It is not education that unfits for service: it is the want of it."

"Well, I know that the reading girls I have had, have, as a rule, served me worse than the rest."

"Would you have called one of those girls educated? Or even if they had been educated, as any of them might well have been, better than nine-tenths of the girls that go to boarding-schools, you must remember that they had never been taught service-the highest accomplishment of all. To that everything aids, when any true feeling of it is there. But for service of this high sort, the education must begin with the beginning of the dawn of will. How often have you wished that you had servants who would believe in you, and serve you with the same truth with which you regarded them! The servants born in a man's house in the old times were more like his children than his servants. Here is a chance for you, as it were of a servant born in your own house. Connie loves the child: the child will love Connie, and find her delight in serving her like a little cherub. Not one of the maids to whom you have referred had ever been taught to think service other than an unavoidable necessity, the end of life being to serve yourself, not to serve others; and hence most of them would escape from it by any marriage almost that they had a chance of making. I don't say all servants are like that; but I do think that most of them are. I know very well that most mistresses are as much to blame for this result as the servants are; but we are not talking about them. Servants nowadays despise work, and yet are forced to do it —a most degrading condition to be in. But they would not be in any better condition if delivered from the work. The lady who despises work is in as bad a condition as they are. The only way to set them free is to get them to regard service not only as their duty, but as therefore honourable, and besides and beyond this, in its own nature divine. In America, the very name of servant is repudiated as inconsistent with human dignity. There is *no* dignity but of service. How different the whole notion of training is now from what it was in the middle ages! Service was honourable then. No doubt we have made progress as a whole, but in some things we have degenerated sadly. The first thing taught then was how to serve. No man could rise to the honour of knighthood without service. A nobleman's son even had to wait on his father, or to go into the family of another nobleman, and wait upon him as a page, standing behind his chair at dinner. This was an honour. No notion of degradation was in it. It was a necessary step to higher honour. And what was the next higher honour? To be set free from service? No. To serve in the harder service of the field; to be a squire to some noble knight; to tend his horse, to clean his armour, to see that every rivet was sound, every buckle true, every strap strong; to ride behind him, and carry his spear, and if more than one attacked him, to rush to his aid. This service was the more honourable because it was harder, and was the next step to higher honour yet. And what was this higher honour? That of knighthood. Wherein did this knighthood consist? The very word means simply *service*. And for what was the knight thus waited upon by his squire? That he might be free to do as he pleased? No, but that he might be free to be the servant of all. By being a squire first, the servant of one, he learned to rise to the higher rank, that of servant of all. His horse was tended, this armour observed, his sword and spear and shield held to his hand, that he might have no trouble looking after himself, but might be free, strong, unwearied, to shoot like an arrow to the rescue of any and every one who needed his ready aid. There was a grand heart of Christianity in that old chivalry, notwithstanding all its abuses which must be no more laid to its charge than the burning of Jews and heretics to Christianity. It was the lack of it, not the presence of it that occasioned the abuses that coexisted with it. Train our Theodora as a holy child-servant, and there will be no need to restrain any impulse of wise affection from pouring itself forth upon her. My firm belief is that we should then love and honour her far more than if we made her just like one of our own."

"But what if she should turn out utterly unfit for it?"

"Ah! then would come an obstacle. But it will not come till that discovery is made."

"But if we should be going wrong all the time?"

"Now, there comes the kind of care that never troubles me, and which I so strongly object to. It won't hurt her anyhow. And we ought always to act upon the ideal; it is the only safe ground of action. When that which contradicts and resists, and would ruin our ideal, opposes us, then we must take measures; but not till then can we take measures, or know what measures it may be necessary to take. But the ideal itself is the only thing worth striving after. Remember what our Lord himself said: 'Be ye therefore perfect, even as your Father which is in heaven is perfect.'"

"Well, I will think about it, Harry. There is time enough."

"Plenty. No time only not to think about it. The more you think about it the better. If a thing be a good thing, the more you think about it the better it will look; for its real nature will go on coming out and showing itself. I cannot doubt that you will soon see how good it is."

We then went home. It was only two days after that my wife said to me —

"I am more than reconciled to your plan, husband. It seems to me delightful."

When we reentered Connie's room, we found that her baby had just waked, and she had managed to get one arm under her, and was trying to comfort her, for she was crying.

CHAPTER IX
A SPRING CHAPTER.

More especially now in my old age, I find myself "to a lingering motion bound." I would, if I might, tell a tale day by day, hour by hour, following the movement of the year in its sweet change of seasons. This may not be, but I will indulge myself now so far as to call this a spring chapter, and so pass to the summer, when my reader will see why I have called my story "The Seaboard Parish."

I was out one day amongst my people, and I found two precious things: one, a lovely little fact, the other a lovely little primrose. This was a pinched, dwarfish thing, for the spring was but a baby herself, and so could not mother more than a brave-hearted weakling. The frost lay all about it under the hedge, but its rough leaves kept it just warm enough, and hardly. Now, I should never have pulled the little darling; it would have seemed a kind of small sacrilege committed on the church of nature, seeing she had but this one; only with my sickly cub at home, I felt justified in ravening like a beast of prey. I even went so far in my greed as to dig up the little plant with my fingers, and bear it, leaves and all, with a lump of earth about it to keep it alive, home to my little woman—a present from the outside world which she loved so much. And as I went there dawned upon me the recollection of a little mirror in which, if I could find it, she would see it still more lovely than in a direct looking at itself. So I set myself to find it; for it lay in fragments in the drawers and cabinets of my memory. And before I got home I had found all the pieces and put them together; and then it was a lovely little sonnet which a friend of mine had written and allowed me to see many years before. I was in the way of writing verses myself; but I should have been proud to have written this one. I never could have done that. Yet, as far as I knew, it had never seen the light through the windows of print. It was with some difficulty that I got it all right; but I thought I had succeeded very nearly, if not absolutely, and I said it over and over, till I was sure I should not spoil its music or its meaning by halting in the delivery of it.

"Look here, my Connie, what I have brought you," I said.

She held out her two white, half-transparent hands, took it as if it had been a human baby and looked at it lovingly till the tears came in her eyes. She would have made a tender picture, as she then lay, with her two hands up, holding the little beauty before her eyes. Then I said what I have already written about the mirror, and repeated the sonnet to her. Here it is, and my readers will owe me gratitude for it. My friend had found the snowdrop in February, and in frost. Indeed he told me that there was a tolerable sprinkling of snow upon the ground:

> "I know not what among the grass thou art,
>   Thy nature, nor thy substance, fairest flower,
>   Nor what to other eyes thou hast of power
> To send thine image through them to the heart;
> But when I push the frosty leaves apart,
>   And see thee hiding in thy wintry bower,
>   Thou growest up within me from that hour,
> And through the snow I with the spring depart.
> I have no words. But fragrant is the breath,
>
>   Pale Beauty, of thy second life within.
> There is a wind that cometh for thy death,
>   But thou a life immortal dost begin,
> Where, in one soul, which is thy heaven, shall dwell
> Thy spirit, beautiful Unspeakable!"

"Will you say it again, papa?" said Connie; "I do not quite understand it."

"I will, my dear. But I will do something better as well. I will go and write it out for you, as soon as I have given you something else that I have brought."

"Thank you, papa. And please write it in your best Sunday hand, that I may read it quite easily."

I promised, and repeated the poem.

"I understand it a little better," she said; "but the meaning is just like the primrose itself, hidden up in its green leaves. When you give it me in writing, I will push them apart and find it. Now, tell me what else you have brought me."

I was greatly pleased with the resemblance the child saw between the plant and the sonnet; but I did not say anything in praise; I only expressed satisfaction. Before I began my story, Wynnie came in and sat down with us.

"I have been to see Miss Aylmer, this morning," I said. "She feels the loss of her mother very much, poor thing."

"How old was she, papa?" asked Connie.

"She was over ninety, my dear; but she had forgotten how much herself, and her daughter could not be sure about it. She was a peculiar old lady, you know. She once reproved me for inadvertently putting my hat on the tablecloth. 'Mr. Shafton,' she said, 'was one of the old school; he would never have done that. I don't know what the world is coming to.'"

My two girls laughed at the idea of their papa being reproved for bad manners.

"What did you say, papa?" they asked.

"I begged her pardon, and lifted it instantly. 'O, it's all right now, my dear,' she said, 'when you've taken it up again. But I like good manners, though I live in a cottage now.'"

"Had she seen better days, then?" asked Wynnie.

"She was a farmer's daughter, and a farmer's widow. I suppose the chief difference in her mode of life was that she lived in a cottage instead of a good-sized farmhouse."

"But what is the story you have to tell us?"

"I'm coming to that when you have done with your questions."

"We have done, papa."

"After talking awhile, during which she went bustling a little about the cottage, in order to hide her feelings, as I thought, for she has a good deal of her mother's sense of dignity about her,—but I want your mother to hear the story. Run and fetch her, Wynnie."

"O, do make haste, Wynnie," said Connie.

When Ethelwyn came, I went on.

"Miss Aylmer was bustling a little about the cottage, putting things to rights. All at once she gave a cry of surprise, and said, 'Here it is, at last!' She had taken up a stuff dress of her mother's, and was holding it in one hand, while with the other she drew from the pocket-what do you think?"

Various guesses were hazarded.

"No, no-nothing like it. I know you *could* never guess. Therefore it would not be fair to keep you trying. A great iron horseshoe. The old woman of ninety years had in the pocket of the dress that she was wearing at the very moment when she died, for her death was sudden, an iron horseshoe."

"What did it mean? Could her daughter explain it?"

"That she proceeded at once to do. 'Do you remember, sir,' she said, 'how that horseshoe used to hang on a nail over the chimneypiece?' 'I do remember having observed it there,' I answered; 'for once when I took notice of it, I said to your mother, laughing, "I hope you are not afraid of witches, Mrs. Aylmer?" And she looked a little offended, and assured me to the contrary.' 'Well,' her daughter went on, 'about three months ago, I missed it. My mother would not tell me anything about it. And here it is! I can hardly think she can have carried it about all that time without me finding it out, but I don't know. Here it is, anyhow. Perhaps when she felt death drawing nearer, she took it from somewhere where she had hidden it, and put it in her pocket. If I had found it in time, I would have put it in her coffin.' 'But why?' I asked. 'Do tell me the story about it, if you know it.' 'I know it quite well, for she told me all about it once. It is the shoe of a favourite mare of my father's—one he used to ride when he went courting my mother. My grandfather did not like to have a young man coming about the house, and so he came after the old folks were gone to bed. But he had a long way to come, and he rode that mare. She had to go over some stones to get to the stable, and my mother used to spread straw there, for it was under the window of my grandfather's room, that her shoes mightn't make a noise and wake him. And that's one of the shoes,' she said, holding it up to me. 'When the mare died, my mother begged my father for the one off her near forefoot, where she had so often stood and patted her neck when my father was mounted to ride home again.'"

"But it was very naughty of her, wasn't it," said Wynnie, "to do that without her father's knowledge?"

"I don't say it was right, my dear. But in looking at what is wrong, we ought to look for the beginning of the wrong; and possibly we might find that in this case farther back. If, for instance, a father isn't a father, we must not be too hard in blaming the child for not being a child. The father's part has to come first, and teach the child's part. Now, if I might guess from what I know of the old lady, in whom probably it was much softened, her father was very possibly a hard, unreasoning, and unreasonable man-such that it scarcely ever came into the daughter's head that she had anything else to do with regard to him than beware of the consequences of letting him know that she had a lover. The whole thing, I allow, was wrong; but I suspect the father was first to blame, and far more to blame than the daughter. And that is the more likely from the high character of the old dame, and the romantic way in which she clung to the memory of the courtship. A true heart only does not grow old. And I have, therefore, no doubt that the marriage was a happy one. Besides, I daresay it was very much the custom of the country where they were, and that makes some difference."

"Well, I'm sure, papa, you wouldn't like any of us to go and do like that," said Wynnie.

"Assuredly not, my dear," I answered, laughing. "Nor have I any fear of it. But shall I tell you what I think would be one of the chief things to trouble me if you did?"

"If you like, papa. But it sounds rather dreadful to hear such an *if*" said Wynnie.

"It would be to think how much I had failed of being such a father to you as I ought to be, and as I wished to be, if it should prove at all possible for you to do such a thing."

"It's too dreadful to talk about, papa," said Wynnie; and the subject was dropped.

She was a strange child, this Wynnie of ours. Whereas most people are in danger of thinking themselves in the right, or insisting that they are whether they think so or not, she was always thinking herself in the wrong. Nay more, she always expected to find herself in the wrong. If the perpetrator of any mischief was inquired after, she always looked into her own bosom to see whether she could not with justice aver that she was the doer of the deed. I believe she felt at that moment as if she had been deceiving me already, and deserved to be driven out of the house. This came of an over-sensitiveness, accompanied by a general dissatisfaction with herself, which was not upheld by a sufficient faith in the divine sympathy, or sufficient confidence of final purification. She never spared herself; and if she was a little severe on the younger ones sometimes, no one was yet more indulgent to them. She would eat all their hard crusts for them, always give them the best and take the worst for herself. If there was any part in the dish that she was helping that she thought nobody would like, she invariably assigned it to her own share. It looked like a determined self-mortification sometimes; but that was not it. She did not care for her own comfort enough to feel it any mortification; though I observed that when her mother or I helped her to anything nice, she ate it with as much relish as the youngest of the party. And her sweet smile was always ready to meet the least kindness that was offered her. Her obedience was perfect, and had been so for very many years, as far as we could see. Indeed, not since she was the merest child had there been any contest between us. Now, of course, there was no demand of obedience: she was simply the best earthly friend that her father and mother had. It often caused me some passing anxiety to think that her temperament, as well as her devotion to her home, might cause her great suffering some day; but when those thoughts came, I just gave her to God to take care of. Her mother sometimes said to her that she would make an excellent wife for a poor man. She would brighten up greatly at this, taking it for a compliment of the best sort. And she did not forget it, as the sequel will show. She would choose to sit with one candle lit when there were two on the table, wasting her eyes to save the candles. "Which will you have for dinner to-day, papa, roast beef or boiled?" she asked me once, when her mother was too unwell to attend to the housekeeping. And when I replied that I would have whichever she liked best —"The boiled beef lasts longest, I think," she said. Yet she was not only as liberal and kind as any to the poor, but she was, which is rarer, and perhaps more important for the final formation of a character, carefully just to everyone with whom she had any dealings. Her sense of law was very strong. Law with her was something absolute, and not to be questioned. In her childhood there was one lady to whom for years she showed a decided aversion, and we could not understand it, for it was the most inoffensive Miss Boulderstone. When she was nearly grown up, one of us happening to allude to the fact, she volunteered an explanation. Miss Boulderstone had happened to call one day when Wynnie, then between three and four was in disgrace —*in the corner*, in fact. Miss Boulderstone interceded for her; and this was the whole front of her offending.

"I *was* so angry!" she said. "'As if my papa did not know best when I ought to come out of the corner!' I said to myself. And I couldn't bear her for ever so long after that."

Miss Boulderstone, however, though not very interesting, was quite a favourite before she died. She left Wynnie-for she and her brother were the last of their race —a death's-head watch, which had been in the family she did not know how long. I think it is as old as Queen Elizabeth's time. I took it to London to a skilful man, and had it as well repaired as its age would admit of; and it has gone ever since, though not with the greatest accuracy; for what could be expected of an old death's-head, the most transitory thing in creation? Wynnie wears it to this day, and wouldn't part with it for the best watch in the world.

I tell the reader all this about my daughter that he may be the more able to understand what will follow in due time. He will think that as yet my story has been nothing but promises. Let him only hope that I will fulfil them, and I shall be content.

Mr. Boulderstone did not long outlive his sister. Though the old couple, for they were rather old before they died, if, indeed, they were not born old, which I strongly suspect, being the last of a decaying family that had not left the land on which they were born for a great many generations-though the old people had not, of what the French call sentiments, one between them, they were yet capable of a stronger and, I had almost said, more romantic attachment, than many couples who have married from love; for the lady's sole trouble in dying was what her brother *would* do without her; and from the day of her death, he grew more and more dull and seemingly stupid. Nothing gave him any pleasure but having Wynnie to dinner with him. I knew that it must be very dull for her, but she went often, and I never heard her complain of it, though she certainly did look fagged-not *bored*, observe, but fagged-showing that she had been exerting herself to meet the difficulties of the situation. When the good man died, we found that he had left all his money in my hands, in trust for the poor of the parish, to be applied in any way I thought best. This involved me in much perplexity, for nothing is more difficult than to make money useful to the poor. But I was very glad of it, notwithstanding.

My own means were not so large as my readers may think. The property my wife brought me was much encumbered. With the help of her private fortune, and the income of several years (not my income from the church, it may be as well to say), I succeeded in clearing off the encumbrances. But even then there remained much to be done, if I would be the good steward that was not to be ashamed at his Lord's coming. First of all there were many cottages to be built for the labourers on the estate. If the farmers would not, or could not, help, I must do it; for to provide decent dwellings for them, was clearly one of the divine conditions in the righteous tenure of property, whatever the human might be; for it was not for myself alone, or for myself chiefly, that this property was given to me; it was for those who lived upon it. Therefore I laid out what money I could, not only in getting all the land clearly in its right relation to its owner, but in doing the best I could for those attached to it who could not help themselves. And when I hint to my reader that I had some conscience in paying my curate, though, as they had no children, they did not require so much as I should otherwise have felt compelled to give them, he will easily see that as my family grew up I could not have so much to give away of my own as I should have liked. Therefore this trust of the good Mr. Boulderstone was the more acceptable to me.

One word more ere I finish this chapter.—I should not like my friends to think that I had got tired of our Christmas gatherings, because I have made no mention of one this year. It had been pretermitted for the first time, because of my daughter's illness. It was much easier to give them now than when I lived at the vicarage, for there was plenty of room in the old hall. But my curate, Mr. Weir, still held a similar gathering there every Easter.

Another one word more about him. Some may wonder why I have not mentioned him or my sister, especially in connection with Connie's accident. The fact was, that he had taken, or rather I had given him, a long holiday. Martha had had several disappointing illnesses, and her general health had suffered so much in consequence that there was even some fear of her lungs, and a winter in the south of France had been strongly recommended. Upon this I came in with more than a recommendation, and insisted that they should go. They had started in the beginning of October, and had not returned up to the time of which I am now about to write-somewhere in the beginning of the month of April. But my sister was now almost quite well, and I was not sorry to think that I should soon have a little more leisure for such small literary pursuits as I delighted in-to my own enrichment, and consequently to the good of my parishioners and friends.

CHAPTER X
AN IMPORTANT LETTER.

It was, then, in the beginning of April that I received one morning an epistle from an old college friend of mine, with whom I had renewed my acquaintance of late, through the pleasure which he was kind enough to say he had derived from reading a little book of mine upon the relation of the mind of St. Paul to the gospel story. His name was Shepherd —a good name for a clergyman. In his case both Christian name and patronymic might remind him well of his duty. David Shepherd ought to be a good clergyman.

As soon as I had read the letter, I went with it open in my hand to find my wife.

"Here is Shepherd," I said, "with a clerical sore-throat, and forced to give up his duty for a whole summer. He writes to ask me whether, as he understands I have a curate as good as myself-that is what the old fellow says-it might not suit me to take my family to his place for the summer. He assures me I should like it, and that it would do us all good. His house, he says, is large enough to hold us, and he knows I should not like to be without duty wherever I was. And so on Read the letter for yourself, and turn it over in your mind. Weir will come back so fresh and active that it will be no oppression to him to take the whole of the duty here. I will run and ask Turner whether it would be safe to move Connie, and whether the sea-air would be good for her."

"One would think you were only twenty, husband-you make up your mind so quickly, and are in such a hurry."

The fact was, a vision of the sea had rushed in upon me. It was many years since I had seen the sea, and the thought of looking on it once more, in its most glorious show, the Atlantic itself, with nothing between us and America, but the round of the ridgy water, had excited me so that my wife's reproof, if reproof it was, was quite necessary to bring me to my usually quiet and sober senses. I laughed, begged old grannie's pardon, and set off to see Turner notwithstanding, leaving her to read and ponder Shepherd's letter.

"What do you think, Turner?" I said, and told him the case. He looked rather grave.

"When would you think of going?" he asked.

"About the beginning of June."

"Nearly two months," he said, thoughtfully. "And Miss Connie was not the worse for getting on the sofa yesterday?"

"The better, I do think."

"Has she had any increase of pain since?"

"None, I quite believe; for I questioned her as to that."

He thought again. He was a careful man, although young.

"It is a long journey."

"She could make it by easy stages."

"It would certainly do her good to breathe the sea-air and have such a thorough change in every way-if only it could be managed without fatigue and suffering. I think, if you can get her up every day between this and that, we shall be justified in trying it at least. The sooner you get her out of doors the better too; but the weather is scarcely fit for that yet."

"A good deal will depend on how she is inclined, I suppose."

"Yes. But in her case you must not mind that too much. An invalid's instincts as to eating and drinking are more to be depended upon than those of a healthy person; but it is not so, I think with regard to anything involving effort. That she must sometimes be urged to. She must not judge that by inclination. I have had, in my short practice, two patients, who considered themselves *bedlars*, as you will find the common people in the part you are going to, call them-bedridden, that is. One of them I persuaded to make the attempt to rise, and although her sense of inability was anything but feigned, and she will be a sufferer to the end of her days, yet she goes about the house without much inconvenience, and I suspect is not only physically but morally the better for it. The other would not consent to try, and I believe lies there still."

"The will has more to do with most things than people generally suppose," I said. "Could you manage, now, do you think, supposing we resolve to make the experiment, to accompany us the first stage or two?"

"It is very likely I could. Only you must not depend upon me. I cannot tell beforehand. You yourself would teach me that I must not be a respecter of persons, you know."

I returned to my wife. She was in Connie's room.

"Well, my dear," I said, "what do you think of it?"

"Of what?" she asked.

"Why, of Shepherd's letter, of course," I answered.

"I've been ordering the dinner since, Harry."

"The dinner!" I returned with some show of contempt, for I knew my wife was only teasing me. "What's the dinner to the Atlantic?"

"What do you mean by the Atlantic, papa?" said Connie, from whose roguish eyes I could see that her mother had told her all about it, and that *she* was not disinclined to get up, if only she could.

"The Atlantic, my dear, is the name given to that portion of the waters of the globe which divides Europe from America. I will fetch you the Universal Gazetteer, if you would like to consult it on the subject."

"O papa!" laughed Connie; "you know what I mean."

"Yes; and you know what I mean too, you squirrel!"

"But do you really mean, papa," she said "that you will take me to the Atlantic?"

"If you will only oblige me by getting Well enough to go as soon as possible."

The poor child half rose on her elbow, but sank back again with a moan, which I took for a cry of pain. I was beside her in a moment.

"My darling! You have hurt yourself!"

"O no, papa. I felt for the moment as if I could get up if I liked. But I soon found that I hadn't any back or legs. O! what a plague I am to you!"

"On the contrary, you are the nicest plaything in the world, Connie. One always knows where to find you."

She half laughed and half cried, and the two halves made a very bewitching whole.

"But," I went on, "I mean to try whether my dolly won't bear moving. One thing is clear, I can't go without it. Do you think you could be got on the sofa to-day without hurting you?"

"I am sure I could, papa. I feel better today than I have felt yet. Mamma, do send for Susan, and get me up before dinner."

When I went in after a couple of hours or so, I found her lying on the conch, propped up with pillows. She lay looking out of the window on the lawn at the back of the house. A smile hovered about her bloodless lips, and the blue of her eyes, though very gray, looked sunny. Her white face showed the whiter because her dark brown hair was all about it. We had had to cut her hair, but it had grown to her neck again.

"I have been trying to count the daisies on the lawn," she said.

"What a sharp sight you must have, child!"

"I see them all as clear as if they were enamelled on that table before me."

I was not so anxious to get rid of the daisies as some people are. Neither did I keep the grass quite so close shaved.

"But," she went on, "I could not count them, for it gave me the fidgets in my feet."

"You don't say so!" I exclaimed.

She looked at me with some surprise, but concluding that I was only making a little of my mild fun at her expense, she laughed.

"Yes. Isn't it a wonderful fact?" she said.

"It is a fact, my dear, that I feel ready to go on my knees and thank God for. I may be wrong, but I take it as a sign that you are beginning to recover a little. But we mustn't make too much of it, lest I should be mistaken," I added, checking myself, for I feared exciting her too much.

But she lay very still; only the tears rose slowly and lay shimmering in her eyes. After about five minutes, during which we were both silent, —

"O papa!" she said, "to think of ever walking out with you again, and feeling the wind on my face! I can hardly believe it possible."

"It is so mild, I think you might have half that pleasure at once," I answered..

And I opened the window, let the spring air gently move her hair for one moment, and then shut it again. Connie breathed deep, and said after a little pause, —

"I had no idea how delightful it was. To think that I have been in the way of breathing that every moment for so many years and never thought about it!"

"It is not always just like that in this climate. But I ought not to have made that remark when I wanted to make this other: that I suspect we shall find some day that the loss of the human paradise consists chiefly in the closing of the human eyes; that at least far more of it than people think remains about us still, only we are so filled with foolish desires and evil cares, that we cannot see or hear, cannot even smell or taste the pleasant things round about us. We have need to pray in regard to the right receiving of the things of the senses even, 'Lord, open thou our hearts to understand thy word;' for each of these things is as certainly a word of God as Jesus is the Word of God. He has made nothing in vain. All is for our teaching. Shall I tell you what such a breath of fresh air makes me think of?"

"It comes to me," said Connie, "like forgiveness when I was a little girl and was naughty. I used to feel just like that."

"It is the same kind of thing I feel," I said —"as if life from the Spirit of God were coming into my soul: I think of the wind that bloweth where it listeth. Wind and spirit are the same word in the Greek; and the Latin word *spirit* comes even nearer to what we are saying, for it is the wind as *breathed*. And now, Connie, I will tell you-and you will see how I am growing able to talk to you like quite an old friend-what put me in such a delight with Mr. Shepherd's letter and so exposed me to be teased by mamma and you. As I read it, there rose up before me a vision of one sight of the sea which I had when I was a young man, long before I saw your mamma. I had gone out for a walk along some high downs. But I ought to tell you that I had been working rather hard at Cambridge, and the life seemed to be all gone out of me. Though my holidays had come, they did not feel quite like holidays-not as holidays used to feel when I was a boy. Even when walking along those downs with the scents of sixteen grasses or so in my brain, like a melody with the odour of the earth for the accompaniment upon which it floated, and with just enough of wind to stir them up and set them in motion, I could not feel at all. I remembered something of what I had used to feel in such places, but instead of believing in that, I doubted now whether it had not been all a trick that I played myself—a fancied pleasure only. I was walking along, then, with the sea behind me. It was a warm, cloudy day —I had had no sunshine since I came out. All at once I turned —I don't know why. There lay the gray sea, but not as I had seen it last, not all gray. It was dotted, spotted, and splashed all over with drops, pools, and lakes of light, of all shades of depth, from a light shimmer of tremulous gray, through a half light that turned the prevailing lead colour into translucent green that seemed to grow out of its depths-through this, I say, to brilliant light, deepening and deepening till my very soul was stung by the triumph of the intensity of its molten silver. There was no sun upon me. But there were breaks in the clouds over the sea, through which, the air being filled with vapour, I could see the long lines of the sun-rays descending on the waters like rain-so like a rain of light that the water seemed to plash up in light under their fall. I questioned the past no more; the present seized upon me, and I knew that the past was true, and that nature was more lovely, more awful in her loveliness than I could grasp. It was a lonely place: I fell on my knees, and worshipped the God that made the glory and my soul."

While I spoke Connie's tears had been flowing quietly.

"And mamma and I were making fun while you were seeing such things as those!" she said pitifully.

"You didn't hurt them one bit, my darling-neither mamma nor you. If I had been the least cross about it, as I should have been when I was as young as at the time of which I was thinking, that would have ruined the vision entirely. But your merriment only made me enjoy it more. And, my Connie, I hope you will see the Atlantic before long; and if one vision should come as brilliant as that, we shall be fortunate indeed, if we went all the way to the west to see that only."

"O papa! I dare hardly think of it-it is too delightful. But do you think we shall really go?"

"I do. Here comes your mamma—I am going to say to Shepherd, my dear, that I will take his parish in hand, and if I cannot, after all, go myself, will find some one, so that he need be in no anxiety from the uncertainty which must hang over our movements even till the experiment itself is made."

"Very well, husband. I am quite satisfied."

And as I watched Connie, I saw that hope and expectation did much to prepare her.

CHAPTER XI
CONNIE'S DREAM.

Mr. Turner, being a good mechanic as well as surgeon, proceeded to invent, and with his own hands in a great measure construct, a kind of litter, which, with a water-bed laid upon it, could be placed in our own carriage for Connie to lie upon, and from that lifted, without disturbing her, and placed in a similar manner in the railway carriage. He had laid Connie repeatedly upon it before he was satisfied that the arrangement of the springs, &c., was successful. But at length she declared that it was perfect, and that she would not mind being carried across the Arabian desert on a camel's back with that under her.

As the season advanced, she continued to improve. I shall never forget the first time she was carried out upon the lawn. If you can imagine an infant coming into the world capable of the observation and delight of a child of eight or ten, you will have some idea of how Connie received the new impressions of everything around her. They were almost too much for her at first, however. She who had been used to scamper about like a wild thing on a pony, found the delight of a breath of wind almost more than she could bear. After she was laid down she closed her eyes, and the smile that flickered about her mouth was of a sort that harmonised entirely with the two great tears that crept softly out from under her eyelids, and sank, rather than ran, down her cheeks. She lay so that she faced a rich tract of gently receding upland, plentifully wooded to the horizon's edge, and through the wood peeped the white and red houses of a little hamlet, with the square tower of its church just rising above the trees. A kind of frame was made to the whole picture by the nearer trees of our own woods, through an opening in which, evidently made or left for its sake, the distant prospect was visible. It was a morning in early summer, when the leaves were not quite full-grown but almost, and their green was shining and pure as the blue of the sky, when the air had no touch of bitterness or of lassitude, but was thoroughly warm, and yet filled the lungs with the reviving as of a draught of cold water. We had fastened the carriage umbrella to the sofa, so that it should shade her perfectly without obscuring her prospect; and behind this we all crept, leaving her to come to herself without being looked at, for emotion is a shy and sacred thing and should be tenderly hidden by those who are near. The bees kept very *beesy* all about us. To see one huge fellow, as big as three ordinary ones with pieces of red and yellow about him, as if he were the beadle of all bee-dom, and overgrown in consequence-to see him, I say, down in a little tuft of white clover, rolling about in it, hardly able to move for fatness, yet bumming away as if his business was to express the delight of the whole creation-was a sight! Then there were the butterflies, so light that they seemed to tumble up into the air, and get down again with difficulty. They bewildered me with their inscrutable variations of purpose. "If I could but see once, for an hour, into the mind of a butterfly," I thought, "it would be to me worth all the natural history I ever read. If I could but see why he changes his mind so often and so suddenly-what he saw about that flower to make him seek it-then why, on a nearer approach, he should decline further acquaintance with it, and go rocking away through the air, to do the same fifty times over again-it would give me an insight into all animal and vegetable life that ages of study could not bring me up to." I was thinking all this behind my daughter's umbrella, while a lark, whose body had melted quite away in the heavenly spaces, was scattering bright beads of ringing melody straight down upon our heads; while a cock was crowing like a clarion from the home-farm, as if in defiance of the golden glitter of his silent brother on the roof of the stable; while a little stream that scampered down the same slope as the lawn lay upon, from a well in the stable-yard, mingled its sweet undertone of contentment with the jubilation of the lark and the business-like hum of the bees; and while white clouds floated in the majesty of silence across the blue deeps of the heavens. The air was so full of life and reviving, that it seemed like the crude substance that God might take to make babies' souls of-only the very simile smells of materialism, and therefore I do not like it.

"Papa," said Connie at length, and I was beside her in a moment. Her face looked almost glorified with delight: there was a hush of that awe upon it which is perhaps one of the deepest kinds of delight. She put out her thin white hand, took hold of a button of my coat, drew me down towards her, and said in a whisper:

"Don't you think God is here, papa?"

"Yes, I do, my darling," I answered.

"Doesn't *he* enjoy this?"

"Yes, my dear. He wouldn't make us enjoy it if he did not enjoy it. It would be to deceive us to make us glad and blessed, while our Father did not care about it, or how it came to us. At least it would amount to making us no longer his children."

"I am so glad you think so. I do. And I shall enjoy it so much more now."

She could hardly finish her sentence, but burst out sobbing so that I was afraid she would hurt herself. I saw, however, that it was best to leave her to quiet herself, and motioned to the rest to keep back and let her recover as she could. The emotion passed off in a summer shower, and when I went round once more, her face was shining just like a wet landscape after the sun has come out and Nature has begun to make gentle game of her own past sorrows. In a little while, she was merry-merrier, notwithstanding her weakness, than I think I had ever seen her before.

"Look at that comical sparrow," she said. "Look how he cocks his head first on one side and then on the other. Does he want us to see him? Is he bumptious, or what?"

"I hardly know, my dear. I think sparrows are very like schoolboys; and I suspect that if we understood the one class thoroughly, we should understand the other. But I confess I do not yet understand either."

"Perhaps you will when Charlie and Harry are old enough to go to school," said Connie.

"It is my only chance of making any true acquaintance with the sparrows," I answered. "Look at them now," I exclaimed, as a little crowd of them suddenly appeared where only one had stood a moment before, and exploded in objurgation and general unintelligible excitement. After some obscure fluttering of wings and pecking, they all vanished except two, which walked about in a dignified manner, trying apparently to seem quite unconscious each of the other's presence.

"I think it was a political meeting of some sort," said Connie, laughing merrily.

"Well, they have this advantage over us," I answered, "that they get through their business whatever it may be, with considerably greater expedition than we get through ours."

A short silence followed, during which Connie lay contemplating everything.

"What do you think we girls are like, then, papa?" she asked at length. "Don't say you don't know, now."

"I ought to know something more about you than I do about schoolboys. And I think I do know a little about girls-not much though. They puzzle me a good deal sometimes. I know what a great-hearted woman is, Connie."

"You can't help doing that, papa," interrupted Connie, adding with her old roguishness, "You mustn't pass yourself off for very knowing for that. By the time Wynnie is quite grown up, your skill will be tried."

"I hope I shall understand her then, and you too, Connie."

A shadow, just like the shadow of one of those white clouds above us, passed over her face, and she said, trying to smile:

"I shall never grow up, papa. If I live, I shall only be a girl at best — a creature you can't understand."

"On the contrary, Connie, I think I understand you almost as well as mamma. But there isn't so much to understand yet, you know, as there will be."

Her merriment returned.

"Tell me what girls are like, then, or I shall sulk all day because you say there isn't so much in me as in mamma."

"Well, I think, if the boys are like sparrows, the girls are like swallows. Did you ever watch them before rain, Connie, skimming about over the lawn as if it were water, low towards its surface, but never alighting? You never see them grubbing after worms. Nothing less than things with wings like themselves will satisfy them. They will be obliged to the earth only for a little mud to build themselves nests with. For the rest, they live in the air, and on the creatures of the air. And then, when they fancy the air begins to be uncivil, sending little shoots of cold through their warm feathers, they vanish. They won't stand it. They're off to a warmer climate, and you never know till you find they're not there any more. There, Connie!"

"I don't know, papa, whether you are making game of us or not. If you are not, then I wish all you say were quite true of us. If you are then I think it is not quite like you to be satirical."

"I am no believer in satire, Connie. And I didn't mean any. The swallows are lovely creatures, and there would be no harm if the girls were a little steadier than the swallows. Further satire than that I am innocent of."

"I don't mind that much, papa. Only I'm steady enough, and no thanks to me for it," she added with a sigh.

"Connie," I said, "it's all for the sake of your wings that you're kept in your nest."

She did not stay out long this first day, for the life the air gave her soon tired her weak body. But the next morning she was brighter and better, and longing to get up and go out again. When she was once more laid on her couch on the lawn, in the midst of the world of light and busy-ness, in which the light was the busiest of all, she said to me:

"Papa, I had such a strange dream last night: shall I tell it you?"

"If you please, my dear. I am very fond of dreams that have any sense in them-or even of any that have good nonsense in them. I woke this morning, saying to myself, 'Dante, the poet, must have been a respectable man, for he was permitted by the council of Florence to carry the Nicene Creed and the Multiplication Table in his coat of arms.' Now tell me your dream."

Connie laughed. All the household tried to make Connie laugh, and generally succeeded. It was quite a triumph to Charlie or Harry, and was sure to be recounted with glee at the next meal, when he succeeded in making Connie laugh.

"Mine wasn't a dream to make me laugh. It was too dreadful at first, and too delightful afterwards. I suppose it was getting out for the first time yesterday that made me dream it. I thought I was lying quite still, without breathing even, with my hands straight down by my sides and my eyes closed. I did not choose to open them, for I knew that if I did I should see nothing but the inside of the lid of my coffin. I did not mind it much at first, for I was very quiet, and not uncomfortable. Everything was as silent as it should be, for I was ten feet and a half under the surface of the earth in the churchyard. Old Sogers was not far from me on one side, and that was a comfort; only there was a thick wall of earth between. But as the time went on, I began to get uncomfortable. I could not help thinking how long I should have to wait for the resurrection. Somehow I had forgotten all that you teach us about that. Perhaps it was a punishment-the dream-for forgetting it."

"Silly child! Your dream is far better than your reflections."

"Well, I'll go on with my dream. I lay a long time till I got very tired, and wanted to get up, O, so much! But still I lay, and although I tried, I could not move hand or foot. At last I burst out crying. I was ashamed of crying in my coffin, but I couldn't bear it any longer. I thought I was quite disgraced, for everybody was expected to be perfectly quiet and patient down there. But the moment I began to cry, I heard a sound. And when I listened it was the sound of spades and pickaxes. It went on and on, and came nearer and nearer. And then-it was so strange —I was dreadfully frightened at the idea of the light and the wind, and of the people seeing me in my coffin and my night-dress, and tried to persuade myself that it was somebody else they were digging for, or that they were only going to lay another coffin over mine. And I thought that if it was you, papa, I shouldn't mind how long I lay there, for I shouldn't feel a bit lonely, even though we could not speak a word to each other all the time. But the sounds came on, nearer and nearer, and at last a pickaxe struck, with a blow that jarred me all through, upon the lid of the coffin, right over my head.

"'Here she is, poor thing!' I heard a sweet voice say.

"'I'm so glad we've found her,' said another voice.

"'She couldn't bear it any longer,' said a third more pitiful voice than either of the others. 'I heard her first,' it went on. 'I was away up in Orion, when I thought I heard a woman crying that oughtn't to be crying. And I stopped and listened. And I heard her again. Then I knew that it was one of the buried ones, and that she had been buried long enough, and was ready for the resurrection. So as any business can wait except that, I flew here and there till I fell in with the rest of you.'

"I think, papa, that this must have been because of what you were saying the other evening about the mysticism of St. Paul; that while he defended with all his might the actual resurrection of Christ and the resurrection of those he came to save, he used it as meaning something more yet, as a symbol for our coming out of the death of sin into the life of truth. Isn't that right, papa?"

"Yes, my dear; I believe so. But I want to hear your dream first, and then your way of accounting for it."

"There isn't much more of it now."

"There must be the best of it."

"Yes; I allow that. Well, while they spoke-it was a wonderfully clear and connected dream: I never had one like it for that, or for anything else-they were clearing away the earth and stones from the top of my coffin. And I lay trembling and expecting to be looked at, like a thing in a box as I was, every moment. But they lifted me, coffin and all, out of the grave, for I felt the motion of it up. Then they set it down, and I heard them taking the lid off. But after the lid was off, it did not seem to make much difference to me. I could not open my eyes. I saw no light, and felt no wind blowing upon me. But I heard whispering about me. Then I felt warm, soft hands washing my face, and then I felt wafts of wind coming on my face, and thought they came from the waving of wings. And when they had washed my eyes, the air came upon them so sweet and cool! and I opened them, I thought, and here I was lying on this couch, with butterflies and bees flitting and buzzing about me, the brook singing somewhere near me, and a lark up in the sky. But there were no angels-only plenty of light and wind and living creatures. And I don't think I ever knew before what happiness meant. Wasn't it a resurrection, papa, to come out of the grave into such a world as this?"

"Indeed it was, my darling-and a very beautiful and true dream. There is no need for me to moralise it to you, for you have done so for yourself already. But not only do I think that the coming out of sin into goodness, out of unbelief into faith in God, is like your dream; but I do expect that no dream of such delight can come up to the sense of fresh life and being that we shall have when we get on the higher body after this one won't serve our purpose any longer, and is worn out and cast aside. The very ability of the mind, whether of itself, or by some inspiration of the Almighty, to dream such things, is a proof of our capacity for such things, a proof, I think, that for such things we were made. Here comes in the chance for faith in God-the confidence in his being and perfection that he would not have made us capable without meaning to fill that capacity. If he is able to make us capable, that is the harder half done already. The other he can easily do. And if he is love he will do it. You should thank God for that dream, Connie."

"I was afraid to do that, papa."

"That is as much as to fear that there is one place to which David might have fled, where God would not find him-the most terrible of all thoughts."

"Where do you mean, papa?"

"Dreamland, my dear. If it is right to thank God for a beautiful thought —I mean a thought of strength and grace giving you fresh life and hope-why should you be less bold to thank him when such thoughts arise in plainer shape-take such vivid forms to your mind that they seem to come through the doors of the eyes into the vestibule of the brain, and thence into the inner chambers of the soul?"

CHAPTER XII
THE JOURNEY.

For more than two months Charlie and Harry had been preparing for the journey. The moment they heard of the prospect of it, they began to prepare, accumulate, and pack stores both for the transit and the sojourn. First of all there was an extensive preparation of ginger-beer, consisting, as I was informed in confidence, of brown sugar, ground ginger, and cold water. This store was, however, as near as I can judge, exhausted and renewed about twelve times before the day of departure arrived; and when at last the auspicious morning dawned, they remembered with dismay that they had drunk the last drop two days before, and there was none in stock. Then there was a wonderful and more successful hoarding of marbles, of a variety so great that my memory refuses to bear the names of the different kinds, which, I think, must have greatly increased since the time when I too was a boy, when some marbles-one of real, white marble with red veins especially-produced in my mind something of the delight that a work of art produces now. These were carefully deposited in one of the many divisions of a huge old hair-trunk, which they had got their uncle Weir, who could use his father's tools with pleasure if not to profit, to fit up for them with a multiplicity of boxes, and cupboards, and drawers, and trays, and slides, that was quite bewildering. In this same box was stowed also a quantity of hair, the gleanings of all the horse-tails upon the premises. This was for making fishing-tackle, with a vague notion on the part of Harry that it was to be employed in catching whales and crocodiles. Then all their favourite books were stowed away in the same chest, in especial a packet of a dozen penny books, of which I think I could give a complete list now. For one afternoon as I searched about in the lumber-room after a set of old library steps, which I wanted to get repaired, I came upon the chest, and opening it, discovered my boys' hoard, and in it this packet of books. I sat down on the top of the chest and read them all through, from Jack the Giant-killer down to Hop o' my Thumb without rising, and this in the broad daylight, with the yellow sunshine nestling beside me on the rose-coloured silken seat, richly worked, of a large stately-looking chair with three golden legs. Yes I could tell you all those stories, not to say the names of them, over yet. Only I knew every one of them before; finding now that they had fared like good vintages, for if they had lost something in potency, they had gained much in flavour. Harry could not read these, and Charlie not very well, but they put confidence in them notwithstanding, in virtue of the red, blue, and yellow prints. Then there was a box of sawdust, the design of which I have not yet discovered; a huge ball of string; a rabbit's skin; a Noah's ark; an American clock, that refused to go for all the variety of treatment they gave it; a box of lead-soldiers, and twenty other things, amongst which was a huge gilt ball having an eagle of brass with outspread wings on the top of it.

Great was their consternation and dismay when they found that this magazine could not be taken in the post-chaise in which they were to follow us to the station. A good part of our luggage had been sent on before us, but the boys had intended the precious box to go with themselves. Knowing well, however, how little they would miss it, and with what shouts of south-sea discovery they would greet the forgotten treasure when they returned, I insisted on the lumbering article being left in peace. So that, as man goeth treasureless to his grave, whatever he may have accumulated before the fatal moment, they had to set off for the far country without chest or ginger-beer—not therefore altogether so desolate and unprovided for as they imagined. The abandoned treasure was forgotten the moment the few tears it had occasioned were wiped away.

It was the loveliest of mornings when we started upon our journey. The sun shone, the wind was quiet, and everything was glad. The swallows were twittering from the corbels they had added to the adornment of the dear old house.

"I'm sorry to leave the swallows behind," said Wynnie, as she stepped into the carriage after her mother. Connie, of course, was already there, eager and strong-hearted for the journey.

We set off. Connie was in delight with everything, especially with all forms of animal life and enjoyment that we saw on the road. She seemed to enter into the spirit of the cows feeding on the rich green grass of the meadows, of the donkeys eating by the roadside, of the horses we met bravely diligent at their day's work, as they trudged along the road with wagon or cart behind them. I sat by the coachman, but so that I could see her face by the slightest turning of my head. I knew by its expression that she gave a silent blessing to the little troop of a brown-faced gipsy family, which came out of a dingy tent to look at the passing carriage. A fleet of ducklings in a pool, paddling along under the convoy of the parent duck, next attracted her.

"Look; look. Isn't that delicious?" she cried.

"I don't think I should like it though," said Wynnie.

"What shouldn't you like, Wynnie?" asked her mother.

"To be in the water and not feel it wet. Those feathers!"

"They feel it with their legs and their webby toes," said Connie.

"Yes, that is some consolation," answered Wynnie.

"And if you were a duck, you would feel the good of your feathers in winter, when you got into your cold bath of a morning."

I give all this chat for the sake of showing how Connie's illness had not in the least withdrawn her from nature and her sympathies-had rather, as it were, made all the fibres of her being more delicate and sympathetic, so that the things around her could enter her soul even more easily than before, and what had seemed to shut her out had in reality brought her into closer contact with the movements of all vitality.

We had to pass through the village to reach the railway station. Everybody almost was out to bid us good-bye. I did not want, for Connie's sake chiefly, to have any scene, but recalling something I had forgotten to say to one of my people, I stopped the carriage to speak to him. The same instant there was a crowd of women about us. But Connie was the centre of all their regards. They hardly looked at her mother or sister. Had she been a martyr who had stood the test and received her aureole, she could hardly have been more regarded. The common use of the word martyr is a curious instance of how words get degraded. The sufferings involved in martyrdom, and not the pure will giving occasion to that suffering, is fixed upon by the common mind as the martyrdom. The witness-bearing is lost sight of, except we can suppose that "a martyr to the toothache" means a witness of the fact of the toothache and its tortures. But while *martyrdom* really means a bearing for the sake of the truth, yet there is a way in which any suffering, even that we have brought upon ourselves, may become martyrdom. When it is so borne that the sufferer therein bears witness to the presence and fatherhood of God, in quiet, hopeful submission to his will, in gentle endurance, and that effort after cheerfulness which is not seldom to be seen where the effort is hardest to make; more than all, perhaps, and rarest of all, when it is accepted as the just and merciful consequence of wrong-doing, and is endured humbly, and with righteous shame, as the cleansing of the Father's hand, indicating that repentance unto life which lifts the sinner out of his sins, and makes him such that the holiest men of old would talk to him with gladness and respect, then indeed it may be called a martyrdom. This latter could not be Connie's case, but the former was hers, and so far she might be called a martyr, even as the old women of the village designated her.

After we had again started, our ears were invaded with shouts from the post-chaise behind us, in which Charlie and Harry, their grief at the abandoned chest forgotten as if it had never been, were yelling in the exuberance of their gladness. Dora, more staid as became her years, was trying to act the matron with them in vain, and old nursie had enough to do with Miss Connie's baby to heed what the young gentlemen were about, so long as explosions of noise was all the mischief. Walter, the man-servant, who had been with us ten years, and was the main prop of the establishment, looking after everything and putting his hand to everything, with an indefinite charge ranging from the nursery to the wine-cellar, and from the corn-bin to the pig-trough, and who, as we could not possibly get on without him, sat on the box of the post-chaise beside the driver from the Griffin, rather connived, I fear, than otherwise at the noise of the youngsters.

"Good-bye, Marshmallows," they were shouting at the top of their voices, as if they had just been released from a prison, where they had spent a wretched childhood; and, as it could hardly offend anybody's ears on the open country road I allowed them to shout till they were tired, which condition fortunately arrived before we reached the station, so that there was no occasion for me to interfere. I always sought to give them as much liberty as could be afforded them.

At the station we found Weir waiting to see us off, with my sister, now in wonderful health. Turner was likewise there, and ready to accompany us a good part of the way. But beyond the valuable assistance he lent us in moving Connie, no occasion arose for the exercise of his professional skill. She bore the journey wonderfully, slept not unfrequently, and only at the end showed herself at length wearied. We stopped three times on the way: first at Salisbury, where the streams running through the streets delighted her. There we remained one whole day, but sent the children and servants, all but my wife's maid, on before us, under the charge of Walter. This left us more at our ease. At Exeter, we stopped only the night, for Connie found herself quite able to go on the next morning. Here Turner left us, and we missed him very much. Connie looked a little out of spirits after his departure, but soon recovered herself. The next night we spent at a small town on the borders of Devonshire, which was the limit of our railway travelling. Here we remained for another whole day, for the remnant of the journey across part of Devonshire and Cornwall to the shore must be posted, and was a good five hours' work. We started about eleven o'clock, full of spirits at the thought that we had all but accomplished the only part of the undertaking about which we had had any uneasiness. Connie was quite merry. The air was thoroughly warm. We had an open carriage with a hood. Wynnie sat opposite her mother, Dora and Eliza the maid in the rumble, and I by the coachman. The road being very hilly, we had four horses; and with four horses, sunshine, a gentle wind, hope and thankfulness, who would not be happy?

There is a strange delight in motion, which I am not sure that I altogether understand. The hope of the end as bringing fresh enjoyment has something to do with it, no doubt; the accompaniments of the motion, the change of scene, the mystery that lies beyond the next hill or the next turn in the road, the breath of the summer wind, the scent of the pine-trees especially, and of all the earth, the tinkling jangle of the harness as you pass the trees on the roadside, the life of the horses, the glitter and the shadow, the cottages and the roses and the rosy faces, the scent of burning wood or peat from the chimneys, these and a thousand other things combine to make such a journey delightful. But I believe it needs something more than this-something even closer to the human life-to account for the pleasure that motion gives us. I suspect it is its living symbolism; the hidden relations which it bears to the eternal soul in its aspirations and longings-ever following after, ever attaining, never satisfied. Do not misunderstand me, my reader. A man, you will allow, perhaps, may be content although he is not and cannot be happy: I feel inclined to turn all this the other way, saying that a man ought always to be happy, never to be content. You will see I do not say *contented*; I say *content*. Here comes in his faith: his life is hid with Christ in God, measureless, unbounded. All things are his, to become his by blessed lovely gradations of gift, as his being enlarges to receive; and if ever the shadow of his own necessary incompleteness falls upon the man, he has only to remember that in God's idea he is complete, only his life is hid from himself with Christ in God the Infinite. If anyone accuses me here of mysticism, I plead guilty with gladness: I only hope it may be of that true mysticism which, inasmuch as he makes constant use of it, St. Paul would understand at once. I leave it, however.

I think I must have been the very happiest of the party myself. No doubt I was younger much than I am now, but then I was quite middle-aged, with full confession thereof in gray hairs and wrinkles. Why should not a man be happy when he is growing old, so long as his faith strengthens the feeble knees which chiefly suffer in the process of going down the hill? True, the fever heat is over, and the oil burns more slowly in the lamp of life; but if there is less fervour, there is more pervading warmth; if less of fire, more of sunshine; there is less smoke and more light. Verily, youth is good, but old age is better-to the man who forsakes not his youth when his youth forsakes him. The sweet visitings of nature do not depend upon youth or romance, but upon that quiet spirit whose meekness inherits the earth. The smell of that field of beans gives me more delight now than ever it could have given me when I was a youth. And if I ask myself why I find it is simply because I have more faith now than I had then. It came to me then as an accident of nature —a passing pleasure flung to me only as the dogs' share of the crumbs. Now I believe that God *means* that odour of the bean-field; that when Jesus smelled such a scent about Jerusalem or in Galilee, he thought of his Father. And if God means it, it is mine, even if I should never smell it again. The music of the spheres is mine if old age should make me deaf as the adder. Am I mystical again, reader? Then I hope you are too, or will be before you have done with this same beautiful mystical life of ours. More and more nature becomes to me one of God's books of poetry-not his grandest-that is history-but his loveliest, perhaps.

And ought I not to have been happy when all who were with me were happy? I will not run the risk of wearying even my contemplative reader by describing to him the various reflexes of happiness that shone from the countenances behind me in the carriage, but I will try to hit each off in a word, or a single simile. My Ethelwyn's face was bright with the brightness of a pale silvery moon that has done her harvest work, and, a little weary, lifts herself again into the deeper heavens from stooping towards the earth. Wynnie's face was bright with the brightness of the morning star, ever growing pale and faint over the amber ocean that brightens at the sun's approach; for life looked to Wynnie severe in its light, and somewhat sad because severe. Connie's face was bright with the brightness of a lake in the rosy evening, the sound of the river flowing in and the sound of the river flowing forth just audible, but itself still, and content to be still and mirror the sunset. Dora's was bright with the brightness of a marigold that follows the sun without knowing it; and Eliza's was bright with the brightness of a half-blown cabbage rose, radiating good-humour. This last is not a good simile, but I cannot find a better. I confess failure, and go on.

After stopping once to bait, during which operation Connie begged to be carried into the parlour of the little inn that she might see the china figures that were certain to be on the chimney-piece, as indeed they were, where she drank a whole tumbler of new milk before we lifted her to carry her back, we came upon a wide high moorland country the roads through which were lined with gorse in full golden bloom, while patches of heather all about were showing their bells, though not yet in their autumnal outburst of purple fire. Here I began to be reminded of Scotland, in which I had travelled a good deal between the ages of twenty and five-and-twenty. The further I went the stronger I felt the resemblance. The look of the fields, the stone fences that divided them, the shape and colour and materials of the houses, the aspect of the people, the feeling of the air, and of the earth and sky generally, made me imagine myself in a milder and more favoured Scotland. The west wind was fresh, but had none of that sharp edge which one can so often detect in otherwise warm winds blowing under a hot sun. Though she had already travelled so many miles, Connie brightened up within a few minutes after we got on this moor; and we had not gone much farther before a shout from the rumble informed us that keen-eyed little Dora had discovered the Atlantic: a dip in the high coast revealed it blue and bright. We soon lost sight of it again, but in Connie's eyes it seemed to linger still. As often as I looked round, the blue of them seemed the reflection of the sea in their little convex mirrors. Ethelwyn's eyes, too, were full of it, and a flush on her generally pale cheek showed that she too expected the ocean. After a few miles along this breezy expanse, we began to descend towards the sea-level. Down the winding of a gradual slope, interrupted by steep descents, we approached this new chapter in our history. We came again upon a few trees here and there, all with their tops cut off in a plane inclined upwards away from the sea. For the sea-winds, like a sweeping scythe, bend the trees all away towards the land, and keep their tops mown with their sharp rushing, keen with salt spray off the crests of the broken waves. Then we passed through some ancient villages, with streets narrow, and steep and sharp-angled, that needed careful driving and the frequent pressure of the break upon the wheel. And now the sea shone upon us with nearer greeting, and we began to fancy we could hear its talk with the shore. At length we descended a sharp hill, reached the last level, drove over a bridge and down the line of the stream, saw the land vanish in the sea—a wide bay; then drove over another wooden drawbridge, and along the side of a canal in which lay half-a-dozen sloops and schooners. Then came a row of pretty cottages; then a gate, and an ascent, and ere we reached the rectory, we were aware of its proximity by loud shouts, and the sight of Charlie and Harry scampering along the top of a stone wall to meet us. This made their mother nervous, but she kept quiet, knowing that unrestrained anxiety is always in danger of bringing about the evil it fears. A moment after, we drew up at a long porch, leading through the segment of a circle to the door of the house. The journey was over. We got down in the little village of Kilkhaven, in the county of Cornwall.

CHAPTER XIII
WHAT WE DID WHEN WE ARRIVED.

We carried Connie in first of all, of course, and into the room which nurse had fixed upon for her-the best in the house, of course, again. She did seem tired now, and no wonder. She had a cup of tea at once, and in half an hour dinner was ready, of which we were all very glad. After dinner I went up to Connie's room. There I found her fast asleep on the sofa, and Wynnie as fast asleep on the floor beside her. The drive and the sea air had had the same effect on both of them. But pleased as I was to see Connie sleeping so sweetly, I was even more pleased to see Wynnie asleep on the floor. What a wonderful satisfaction it may give to a father and mother to see this or that child asleep! It is when her kittens are asleep that the cat creeps away to look after her own comforts. Our cat chose to have her kittens in my study once, and as I would not have her further disturbed than to give them another cushion to lie on in place of that which belonged to my sofa, I had many opportunities of watching them as I wrote, or prepared my sermons. But I must not talk about the cat and her kittens now. When parents see their children asleep, especially if they have been suffering in any way, they breathe more freely; a load is lifted off their minds; their responsibility seems over; the children have gone back to their Father, and he alone is looking after them for a while. Now, I had not been comfortable about Wynnie for some time, and especially during our journey, and still more especially during the last part of our journey. There was something amiss with her. She seemed constantly more or less dejected, as if she had something to think about that was too much for her, although, to tell the truth, I really believe now that she had not quite enough to think about. Some people can thrive tolerably without much thought: at least, they both live comfortably without it, and do not seem to be capable of effecting it if it were required of them; while for others a large amount of mental and spiritual operation is necessary for the health of both body and mind, and when the matter or occasion for so much is not afforded them, the consequence is analogous to what follows when a healthy physical system is not supplied with sufficient food: the oxygen, the source of life, begins to consume the life itself; it tears up the timbers of the house to burn against the cold. Or, to use a different simile, when the Moses-rod of circumstance does not strike the rock and make the waters flow, such a mind-one that must think to live-will go digging into itself, and is in danger of injuring the very fountain of thought, by drawing away its living water into ditches and stagnant pools. This was, I say, the case in part with my Wynnie, although I did not understand it at that moment. She did not look quite happy, did not always meet a smile with a smile, looked almost reprovingly upon the frolics of the little brother-imps, and though kindness itself when any real hurt or grief befell them, had reverted to her old, somewhat dictatorial manner, of which I have already spoken as interrupted by Connie's accident. To her mother and me she was service itself, only service without the smile which is as the flame of the sacrifice and makes it holy. So we were both a little uneasy about her, for we did not understand her. On the journey she had seemed almost annoyed at Connie's ecstasies, and said to Dora many times: "Do be quiet, Dora;" although there was not a single creature but ourselves within hearing, and poor Connie seemed only delighted with the child's explosions. So I was-but although I say *so*, I hardly know why I was pleased to see her thus, except it was from a vague belief in the anodyne of slumber. But this pleasure did not last long; for as I stood regarding my two treasures, even as if my eyes had made her uncomfortable, she suddenly opened hers, and started to her feet, with the words, "I beg your pardon, papa," looking almost guiltily round her, and putting up her hair hurriedly, as if she had committed an impropriety in being caught untidy. This was fresh sign of a condition of mind that was not healthy.

"My dear," I said, "what do you beg my pardon for? I was so pleased to see you asleep! and you look as if you thought I were going to scold you."

"O papa," she said, laying her head on my shoulder, "I am afraid I must be very naughty. I so often feel now as if I were doing something wrong, or rather as if you would think I was doing something wrong. I am sure there must be something wicked in me somewhere, though

I do not clearly know what it is. When I woke up now, I felt as if I had neglected something, and you had come to find fault with me. *Is* there anything, papa?"

"Nothing whatever, my child. But you cannot be well when you feel like that."

"I am perfectly well, so far as I know. I was so cross to Dora to-day! Why shouldn't I feel happy when everybody else is? I must be wicked, papa."

Here Connie woke up.

"There now! I've waked Connie," Wynnie resumed. "I'm always doing something I ought not to do. Please go to sleep again, Connie, and take that sin off my poor conscience."

"What nonsense is Wynnie talking about being wicked?" asked Connie.

"It isn't nonsense, Connie. You know I am."

"I know nothing of the sort, Wynnie. If it were me now! And yet I don't *feel* wicked."

"My dear children," I said, "we must all pray to God for his Spirit, and then we shall feel just as we ought to feel. It is not for anyone to say to himself how he ought to feel at any given moment; still less for one man to say to another how he ought to feel; that is in the former case to do as St. Paul says he had learned to give up doing-to judge our own selves, which ought to be left to God; in the latter case it is to do what our Lord has told us expressly we are not to do-to judge other people. You get your bonnet, Wynnie, and come out with me. I am going to explore a little of this desert island upon which we have been cast away. And you, Connie, just to please Wynnie, must try and go to sleep again."

Wynnie ran for her bonnet, a little afraid perhaps that I was going to talk seriously to her, but showing no reluctance anyhow to accompany me.

Now I wonder whether it will be better to tell what we saw, or only what we talked about, and give what we saw in the shape in which we reported it to Connie, when we came back into her room, bearing, like the spies who went to search the land, our bunch of grapes, that is, of sweet news of nature, to her who could not go to gather them for herself. It think it will be the best plan to take part of both plans.

When we left the door of the house, we went up the few steps of a stair leading on to the downs, against and amidst, and indeed *in*, the rocks, buttressing the sea-edge of which our new abode was built. A life for a big-winged angel seemed waiting us upon those downs. The wind still blew from the west, both warm and strong—I mean strength-giving—and the wind was the first thing we were aware of. The ground underfoot was green and soft and springy, and sprinkled all over with the bright flowers, chiefly yellow, that live amidst the short grasses of the downs, the shadows of whose unequal surface were now beginning to be thrown east, for the sun was going seawards. I stood up, stretched out my arms, threw back my shoulders and my head, and filled my chest with a draught of the delicious wind, feeling thereafter like a giant refreshed with wine. Wynnie stood apparently unmoved amidst the life-nectar, thoughtful, and turning her eyes hither and thither.

"That makes me feel young again," I said.

"I wish it would make me feel old then," said Wynnie.

"What do you mean, my child?"

"Because then I should have a chance of knowing what it is like to feel young," she answered rather enigmatically. I did not reply. We were walking up the brow which hid the sea from us. The smell of the down-turf was indescribable in its homely delicacy; and by the time we had reached the top, almost every sense was filled with its own delight. The top of the hill was the edge of the great shore-cliff; and the sun was hanging on the face of the mightier sky-cliff opposite, and the sea stretched for visible miles and miles along the shore on either hand, its wide blue mantle fringed with lovely white wherever it met the land, and scalloped into all fantastic curves, according to the whim of the nether fires which had formed its bed; and the rush of the waves, as they bore the rising tide up on the shore, was the one music fit for the whole. Ear and eye, touch and smell, were alike invaded with blessedness. I ought to have kept this to give my reader in Connie's room; but he shall share with her presently. The sense of space-of mighty room for life and growth-filled my soul, and I thanked God in my heart. The wind seemed to bear that growth into my soul, even as the wind of God first breathed into man's nostrils the breath of life, and the sun was the pledge of the fulfilment of every aspiration. I turned and looked at Wynnie. She stood pleased but listless amidst that which lifted me into the heaven of the Presence.

"Don't you enjoy all this grandeur, Wynnie?"

"I told you I was very wicked, papa."

"And I told you not to say so, Wynnie."

"You see I cannot enjoy it, papa. I wonder why it is."

"I suspect it is because you haven't room, Wynnie."

"I know you mean something more than I know, papa."

"I mean, my dear, that it is not because you are wicked, but because you do not know God well enough, and therefore your being, which can only live in him, is 'cabined, cribbed, confined, bound in.' It is only in him that the soul has room. In knowing him is life and its gladness. The secret of your own heart you can never know; but you can know Him who knows its secret. Look up, my darling; see the heavens and the earth. You do not feel them, and I do not call upon you to feel them. It would be both useless and absurd to do so. But just let them look at you for a moment, and then tell me whether it must not be a blessed life that creates such a glory as this All."

She stood silent for a moment, looked up at the sky, looked round on the earth, looked far across the sea to the setting sun, and then turned her eyes upon me. They were filled with tears, but whether from feeling, or sorrow that she could not feel, I would not inquire. I made haste to speak again.

"As this world of delight surrounds and enters your bodily frame, so does God surround your soul and live in it. To be at home with the awful source of your being, through the child-like faith which he not only permits, but requires, and is ever teaching you, or rather seeking to rouse up in you, is the only cure for such feelings as those that trouble you. Do not say it is too high for you. God made you in his own image, therefore capable of understanding him. For this final end he sent his Son, that the Father might with him come into you, and dwell with you. Till he does so, the temple of your soul is vacant; there is no light behind the veil, no cloudy pillar over it; and the priests, your thoughts, feelings, loves, and desires, moan, and are troubled-for where is the work of the priest when the God is not there? When He comes to you, no mystery, no unknown feeling, will any longer distress you. You will say, 'He knows, though I do not.' And you will be at the secret of the things he has made. You will feel what they are, and that which his will created in gladness you will receive in joy. One glimmer of the present God in this glory would send you home singing. But do not think I blame you, Wynnie, for feeling sad. I take it rather as the sign of a large life in you, that will not be satisfied with little things. I do not know when or how it may please God to give you the quiet of mind that you need; but I tell you that I believe it is to be had; and in the mean time, you must go on doing your work, trusting in God even for this. Tell him to look at your sorrow, ask him to come and set it right, making the joy go up in your heart by his presence. I do not know when this may be, I say, but you must have patience, and till he lays his hand on your head, you must be content to wash his feet with your tears. Only he will be better pleased if your faith keep you from weeping and from going about your duties mournful. Try to be brave and cheerful for the sake of Christ, and for the sake of your confidence in the beautiful teaching of God, whose course and scope you cannot yet understand. Trust, my daughter, and let that give you courage and strength."

Now the sky and the sea and the earth must have made me able to say these things to her; but I knew that, whatever the immediate occasion of her sadness, such was its only real cure. Other things might, in virtue of the will of God that was in them, give her occupation and interest enough for a time, but nothing would do finally, but God himself. Here I was sure I was safe; here I knew lay the hunger of humanity. Humanity may, like other vital forms, diseased systems, fix on this or that as the object not merely of its desire but of its need: it can never be stilled by less than the bread of life-the very presence in the innermost nature of the Father and the Son.

We walked on together. Wynnie made me no reply, but, weeping silently, clung to my arm. We walked a long way by the edge of the cliffs, beheld the sun go down, and then turned and went home. When we reached the house, Wynnie left me, saying only, "Thank you, papa. I think it is all true. I will try to be a better girl."

I went straight to Connie's room: she was lying as I saw her last, looking out of her window.

"Connie," I said, "Wynnie and I have had such a treat-such a sunset!"

"I've seen a little of the light of it on the waves in the bay there, but the high ground kept me from seeing the sunset itself. Did it set in the sea?"

"You do want the General Gazetteer, after all, Connie. Is that water the Atlantic, or is it not? And if it be, where on earth could the sun set but in it?"

"Of course, papa. What a goose I am! But don't make game of me —*please*. I am too deliciously happy to be made game of to-night."

"I won't make game of you, my darling. I will tell you about the sunset-the colours of it, at least. This must be one of the best places in the whole world to see sunsets."

"But you have had no tea, papa. I thought you would come and have your tea with me. But you were so long, that mamma would not let me wait any longer."

"O, never mind the tea, my dear. But Wynnie has had none. You've got a tea-caddy of your own, haven't you?"

"Yes, and a teapot; and there's the kettle on the hob-for I can't do without a little fire in the evenings."

"Then I'll make some tea for Wynnie and myself, and tell you at the same time about the sunset. I never saw such colours. I cannot tell you what it was like while the sun was yet going down, for the glory of it has burned the memory of it out of me. But after the sun was down, the sky remained thinking about him; and the thought of the sky was in delicate translucent green on the horizon, just the colour of the earth etherealised and glorified —a broad band; then came another broad band of pale rose-colour; and above that came the sky's own eternal blue, pale likewise, but so sure and changeless. I never saw the green and the blue divided and harmonised by the rose-colour before. It was a wonderful sight. If it is warm enough to-morrow, we will carry you out on the height, that you may see what the evening will bring."

"There is one thing about sunsets," returned Connie —"two things, that make me rather sad-about themselves, not about anything else. Shall I tell you them?"

"Do, my love. There are few things more precious to learn than the effects of Nature upon individual minds. And there is not a feeling of yours, my child, that is not of value to me."

"You are so kind, papa! I am so glad of my accident. I think I should never have known how good you are but for that. But my thoughts seem so little worth after you say so much about them."

"Let me be judge of that, my dear."

"Well, one thing is, that we shall never, never, never, see the same sunset again."

"That is true. But why should we? God does not care to do the same thing over again. When it is once done, it is done, and he goes on doing something new. For, to all eternity, he never will have done showing himself by new, fresh things. It would be a loss to do the same thing again."

"But that just brings me to my second trouble. The thing is lost. I forget it. Do what I can, I cannot remember sunsets. I try to fix them fast in my memory, that I may recall them when I want them; but just as they fade out of the sky, all into blue or gray, so they fade out of my mind and leave it as if they had never been there-except perhaps two or three. Now, though I did not see this one, yet, after you have talked about it, I shall never forget *it*."

"It is not, and never will be, as if they had never been. They have their influence, and leave that far deeper than your memory-in your very being, Connie. But I have more to say about it, although it is only an idea, hardly an assurance. Our brain is necessarily an imperfect instrument. For its right work, perhaps it is needful that it should forget in part. But there are grounds for believing that nothing is ever really forgotten. I think that, when we have a higher existence than we have now, when we are clothed with that spiritual body of which St. Paul speaks, you will be able to recall any sunset you have ever seen with an intensity proportioned to the degree of regard and attention you gave it when it was present to you. But here comes Wynnie to see how you are. —I've been making some tea for you, Wynnie, my love."

"O, thank you, papa—I shall be so glad of some tea!" said Wynnie, the paleness of whose face showed the red rims of her eyes the more plainly. She had had what girls call a good cry, and was clearly the better for it.

The same moment my wife came in. "Why didn't you send for me, Harry, to get your tea?" she said.

"I did not deserve any, seeing I had disregarded proper times and seasons. But I knew you must be busy."

"I have been superintending the arrangement of bedrooms, and the unpacking, and twenty different things," said Ethelwyn. "We shall be so comfortable! It is such a curious house! Have you had a nice walk?"

"Mamma, I never had such a walk in my life," returned Wynnie. "You would think the shore had been built for the sake of the show-just for a platform to see sunsets from. And the sea! Only the cliffs will be rather dangerous for the children."

"I have just been telling Connie about the sunset. She could see something of the colours on the water, but not much more."

"O, Connie, it will be so delightful to get you out here! Everything is so big! There is such room everywhere! But it must be awfully windy in winter," said Wynnie, whose nature was always a little prospective, if not apprehensive.

But I must not keep my reader longer upon mere family chat.

CHAPTER XIV
MORE ABOUT KILKHAVEN.

Our dining-room was one story below the level at which we had entered the parsonage; for, as I have said, the house was built into the face of the cliff, just where it sunk nearly to the level of the shores of the bay. While at dinner, on the evening of our arrival, I kept looking from the window, of course, and I saw before me, first a little bit of garden, mostly in turf, then a low stone wall; beyond, over the top of the wall, the blue water of the bay; then beyond the water, all alive with light and motion, the rocks and sand-hills of the opposite side of the little bay, not a quarter of a mile across. I could likewise see where the shore went sweeping out and away to the north, with rock after rock standing far into the water, as if gazing over the awful wild, where there was nothing to break the deathly waste between Cornwall and Newfoundland. But for the moment I did not regard the huge power lying outside so much as the merry blue bay between me and those rocks and sand-hills. If I moved my head a little to the right, I saw, over the top of the low wall already mentioned, and apparently quite close to it the slender yellow masts of a schooner, her mainsail hanging loose from the gaff, whose peak was lowered. We must, I thought, be on the very harbour-quay. When I went out for my walk with Wynnie, I had turned from the bay, and gone to the brow of the cliffs overhanging the open sea on our own side of it.

When I came down to breakfast in the same room next morning, I stared. The blue had changed to yellow. The life of the water was gone. Nothing met my eyes but a wide expanse of dead sand. You could walk straight across the bay to the hills opposite. From the look of the rocks, from the perpendicular cliffs on the coast, I had almost, without thinking, concluded that we were on the shore of a deep-water bay. It was high-water, or nearly so, then; and now, when I looked westward, it was over a long reach of sands, on the far border of which the white fringe of the waves was visible, as if there was their *hitherto*, and further towards us they could not come. Beyond the fringe lay the low hill of the Atlantic. To add to my confusion, when I looked to the right, that is, up the bay towards the land, there was no schooner there. I went out at the window, which opened from the room upon the little lawn, to look, and then saw in a moment how it was.

"Do you know, my dear," I said to my wife, "we are just at the mouth of that canal we saw as we came along? There are gates and a lock just outside there. The schooner that was under this window last night must have gone in with the tide. She is lying in the basin above now."

"O, yes, papa," Charlie and Harry broke in together. "We saw it go up this morning. We've been out ever so long. It was so funny," Charlie went on-everything was *funny* with Charlie —"to see it rise up like a Jack-in-the-box, and then slip into the quiet water through the other gates!"

And when I thought about the waves tumbling and breaking away out there, and the wide yellow sands between, it was wonderful-which was what Charlie meant by funny-to see the little vessel lying so many feet above it all, in a still plenty of repose, gathering strength, one might fancy to rush out again, when its time was come, into the turmoil beyond, and dash its way through the breasts of the billows.

After breakfast we had prayers, as usual, and after a visit to Connie, whom I found tired, but wonderfully well, I went out for a walk by myself, to explore the neighbourhood, find the church, and, in a word, do something to shake myself into my new garments. The day was glorious. I wandered along a green path, in the opposite direction from our walk the evening before, with a fir-wood on my right hand, and a belt of feathery tamarisks on my left, behind which lay gardens sloping steeply to a lower road, where stood a few pretty cottages. Turning a corner, I came suddenly in sight of the church, on the green down above me —a sheltered yet commanding situation; for, while the hill rose above it, protecting it from the east, it looked down the bay, and the Atlantic lay open before it. All the earth seemed to lie behind it, and all its gaze to be fixed on the symbol of the infinite. It stood as the church ought to stand, leading men up the mount of vision, to the verge of the eternal, to send them back with their hearts full of the strength that springs from hope, by which alone the true work of the world can be done. And when I saw it I rejoiced to think that once more I was favoured with a church that had a history. Of course it is a happy thing to see new churches built wherever there is need of such; but to the full idea of the building it is necessary that it should be one in which the hopes and fears, the cares and consolations, the loves and desires of our forefathers should have been roofed; where the hearts of those through whom our country has become that which it is-from whom not merely the life-blood of our bodies, but the life-blood of our spirits, has come down to us, whose existence and whose efforts have made it possible for us to be that which we are-have before us worshipped that Spirit from whose fountain the whole torrent of being flows, who ever pours fresh streams into the wearying waters of humanity, so ready to settle down into a stagnant repose. Therefore I would far rather, when I may, worship in an old church, whose very stones are a history of how men strove to realise the infinite, compelling even the powers of nature into the task-as I soon found on the very doorway of this church, where the ripples of the outspread ocean, and grotesque imaginations of the monsters of its deeps, fixed, as it might seem, for ever in stone, gave a distorted reflex, from the little mirror of the artist's mind, of that mighty water, so awful, so significant to the human eye, which yet lies in the hollow of the Father's palm, like the handful that the weary traveller lifts from the brook by the way. It is in virtue of the truth that went forth in such and such like attempts that we are able to hold our portion of the infinite reality which God only knows. They have founded our Church for us, and such a church as this will stand for the symbol of it; for here we too can worship the God of Abraham, of Isaac, and of Jacob-the God of Sidney, of Hooker, of Herbert. This church of Kilkhaven, old and worn, rose before me a history in stone-so beaten and swept about by the "wild west wind,"

> "For whose path the Atlantic's level powers
> Cleave themselves into chasms,"

and so streamed upon, and washed, and dissolved, by the waters lifted from the sea and borne against it on the upper tide of the wind, that you could almost fancy it one of those churches that have been buried for ages beneath the encroaching waters, lifted again, by some mighty revulsion of nature's heart, into the air of the sweet heavens, there to stand marked for ever with the tide-flows of the nether world-scooped, and hollowed, and worn like aeonian rocks that have slowly, but for ever, responded to the swirl and eddy of the wearing waters. So, from the most troublous of times, will the Church of our land arise, in virtue of what truth she holds, and in spite, if she rises at all, of the worldliness of those who, instead of seeking her service, have sought and gained the dignities which, if it be good that she have it in her power to bestow them, need the corrective of a sharply wholesome persecution which of late times she has not known. But God knows, and the fire will come in its course-first in the form of just indignation, it may be, against her professed servants, and then in the form of the furnace seven times heated, in which the true builders shall yet walk unhurt save as to their mortal part.

I looked about for some cottage where the sexton might be supposed to live, and spied a slated roof, nearly on a level with the road, at a little distance in front of me. I could at least inquire there. Before I reached it, however, an elderly woman came out and approached me. She was dressed in a white cap and a dark-coloured gown. On her face lay a certain repose which attracted me. She looked as if she had suffered but had consented to it, and therefore could smile. Her smile lay near the surface. A kind word was enough to draw it up from the well where it lay shimmering: you could always see the smile there, whether it was born or not. But even when she smiled, in the very glimmering of that moonbeam, you could see the deep, still, perhaps dark, waters under. O! if one could but understand what goes on in the souls that have no words, perhaps no inclination, to set it forth! What had she endured? How had she learned to have that smile always near? What had consoled her, and yet left her her grief-turned it, perhaps, into hope? Should I ever know?

She drew near me, as if she would have passed me, as she would have done, had I not spoken. I think she came towards me to give me the opportunity of speaking if I wished, but she would not address me.

"Good morning," I said. "Can you tell me where to find the sexton?"

"Well, sir," she answered, with a gleam of the smile brightening underneath her old skin, as it were, "I be all the sexton you be likely to find this mornin', sir. My husband, he be gone out to see one o' Squire Tregarva's hounds as was took ill last night. So if you want to see the old church, sir, you'll have to be content with an old woman to show you, sir."

"I shall be quite content, I assure you," I answered. "Will you go and get the key?"

"I have the key in my pocket, sir; for I thought that would be what you'd be after, sir. And by the time you come to my age, sir, you'll learn to think of your old bones, sir. I beg your pardon for making so free. For mayhap, says I to myself, he be the gentleman as be come to take Mr. Shepherd's duty for him. Be ye now, sir?"

All this was said in a slow sweet subdued tone, nearly of one pitch. You would have felt that she claimed the privilege of age with a kind of mournful gaiety, but was careful, and anxious even, not to presume upon it, and, therefore, gentle as a young girl.

"Yes," I answered. "My name is Walton I have come to take the place of my friend Mr. Shepherd; and, of course, I want to see the church."

"Well, she be a bee-utiful old church. Some things, I think, sir, grows more beautiful the older they grows. But it ain't us, sir."

"I'm not so sure of that," I said. "What do you mean?"

"Well, sir, there's my little grandson in the cottage there: he'll never be so beautiful again. Them children du be the loves. But we all grows uglier as we grows older. Churches don't seem to, sir."

"I'm not so sure about all that," I said again.

"They did say, sir, that I was a pretty girl once. I'm not much to look at now."

And she smiled with such a gracious amusement, that I felt at once that if there was any vanity left in this memory of her past loveliness, it was sweet as the memory of their old fragrance left in the withered leaves of the roses.

"But it du not matter, du it, sir? Beauty is only skin-deep."

"I don't believe that," I answered. "Beauty is as deep as the heart at least."

"Well to be sure, my old husband du say I be as handsome in his eyes as ever I be. But I beg your pardon, sir, for talkin' about myself. I believe it was the old church-she set us on to it."

"The old church didn't lead you into any harm then," I answered. "The beauty that is in the heart will shine out of the face again some day-be sure of that. And after all, there is just the same kind of beauty in a good old face that there is in an old church. You can't say the church is so trim and neat as it was the day that the first blast of the organ filled it as with, a living soul. The carving is not quite so sharp, the timbers are not quite so clean. There is a good deal of mould and worm-eating and cobwebs about the old place. Yet both you and I think it more beautiful now than it was then. Well, I believe it is, as nearly as possible, the same with an old face. It has got stained, and weather-beaten, and worn; but if the organ of truth has been playing on inside the temple of the Lord, which St. Paul says our bodies are, there is in the old face, though both form and complexion are gone, just the beauty of the music inside. The wrinkles and the brownness can't spoil it. A light shines through it all-that of the indwelling spirit. I wish we all grew old like the old churches."

She did not reply, but I thought I saw in her face that she understood my mysticism. We had been walking very slowly, had passed through the quaint lych-gate, and now the old woman had got the key in the lock of the door, whose archway was figured and fashioned as I have described above, with a dozen mouldings or more, most of them "carved so curiously."

CHAPTER XV
THE OLD CHURCH.

The awe that dwells in churches fell upon me as I crossed the threshold-an awe I never fail to feel-heightened in many cases, no doubt, by the sense of antiquity and of art, but an awe which I have felt all the same in crossing the threshold of an old Puritan conventicle, as the place where men worship and have worshipped the God of their fathers, although for art there was only the science of common bricklaying, and for beauty staring ugliness. To the involuntary fancy, the air of petition and of holy need seems to linger in the place, and the uncovered head acknowledges the sacred symbols of human inspiration and divine revealing. But this was no ordinary church into which I followed the gentlewoman who was my guide. As entering I turned my eyes eastward, a flush of subdued glory invaded them from the chancel, all the windows of which were of richly stained glass, and the roof of carved oak lavishly gilded. I had my thoughts about this chancel, and thence about chancels generally which may appear in another part of my story. Now I have to do only with the church, not with the cogitations to which it gave rise. But I will not trouble my reader with even what I could tell him of the blending and contradicting of styles and modes of architectural thought in the edifice. Age is to the work of contesting human hands a wonderful harmoniser of differences. As nature brings into harmony all fractures of her frame, and even positive intrusions upon her realm, clothes and discolours them, in the old sense of the word, so that at length there is no immediate shock at sight of that which in itself was crude, and is yet coarse, so the various architecture of this building had been gone over after the builders by the musical hand of Eld, with wonder of delicate transition and change of key, that one could almost fancy the music of its exquisite organ had been at work *informing* the building, half melting the sutures, wearing the sharpness, and blending the angles, until in some parts there was but the gentle flickering of the original conception left, all its self-assertion vanished under the file of the air and the gnawing of the worm. True, the hand of the restorer had been busy, but it had wrought lovingly and gently, and wherein it had erred, the same influences of nature, though as yet their effects were invisible, were already at work-of the many making one. I will not trouble my reader, I say, with any architectural description, which, possibly even more than a detailed description of natural beauty dissociated from human feeling, would only weary him, even if it were not unintelligible. When we are reading a poem, we do not first of all examine the construction and dwell on the rhymes and rhythms; all that comes after, if we find that the poem itself is so good that its parts are therefore worth examining, as being probably good in themselves, and elucidatory of the main work. There were carvings on the ends of the benches all along the aisle on both sides, well worth examination, and some of them even of description; but I shall not linger on these. A word only about the columns: they supported arches of different fashion on the opposite sides, but they were themselves similar in matter and construction, both remarkable. They were of coarse granite of the country, chiselled, but very far from smooth, not to say polished. Each pillar was a single stone with chamfered sides.

Walking softly through the ancient house, forgetting in the many thoughts that arose within me that I had a companion, I came at length into the tower, the basement of which was open, forming part of the body of the church. There hung many ropes through holes in a ceiling above, for bell-ringing was encouraged and indeed practised by my friend Shepherd. And as I regarded them, I thought within myself how delightful it would be if in these days as in those of Samuel, the word of God was precious; so that when it came to the minister of his people —a fresh vision of his glory, a discovery of his meaning-he might make haste to the church, and into the tower, lay hold of the rope that hung from the deepest-toned bell of all, and constrain it by the force of strong arms to utter its voice of call, "Come hither, come hear, my people, for God hath spoken;" and from the streets or the lanes would troop the eager folk; the plough be left in the furrow, the cream in the churn; and the crowding people bring faces into the church, all with one question upon them —"What hath the Lord spoken?" But now it would be answer sufficient to such a call to say, "But what will become of the butter?" or, "An hour's ploughing will be lost." And the clergy-how would they bring about such a time? They do not even believe that God has a word to his people through them. They think that his word is petrified for use in the Bible and Prayer-book; that the wise men of old heard so much of the word of God, and have so set it down, that there is no need for any more words of the Lord coming to the prophets of a land; therefore they look down upon the prophesying-that is, the preaching of the word-make light of it, the best of them, say these prayers are everything, or all but everything: *their* hearts are not set upon hearing what God the Lord will speak that they may speak it abroad to his people again. Therefore it is no wonder if the church bells are obedient only to the clock, are no longer subject to the spirit of the minister, and have nothing to do in telegraphing between heaven and earth. They make little of this part of their duty; and no wonder, if what is to be spoken must remain such as they speak. They put the Church for God, and the prayers which are the word of man to God, for the word of God to man. But when the prophets see no vision, how should they have any word to speak?

These thoughts were passing through my mind when my eye fell upon my guide. She was seated against the south wall of the tower, on a stool, I thought, or small table. While I was wandering about the church she had taken her stocking and wires out of her pocket, and was now knitting busily. How her needles did go! Her eyes never regarded them, however, but, fixed on the slabs that paved the tower at a yard or two from her feet, seemed to be gazing far out to sea, for they had an infinite objectless outlook. To try her, I took for the moment the position of an accuser.

"So you don't mind working in church?" I said.

When I spoke she instantly rose, her eyes turned as from the far sea-waves to my face, and light came out of them. With a smile she answered—

"The church knows me, sir."

"But what has that to do with it?"

"I don't think she minds it. We are told to be diligent in business, you know, sir."

"Yes, but it does not say in church and out of church. You could be diligent somewhere else, couldn't you?"

As soon as I said this, I began to fear she would think I meant it. But she only smiled and said, "It won't hurt she, sir; and my good man, who does all he can to keep her tidy, is out at toes and heels, and if I don't keep he warm he'll be laid up, and then the church won't be kep' nice, sir, till he's up again."

I was tempted to go on.

"But you could have sat down outside-there are some nice gravestones near-and waited till I came out."

"But what's the church for, sir? The sun's werry hot to-day, sir; and Mr. Shepherd, he say, sir, that the church is like the shadow of a great rock in a weary land. So, you see, if I was to sit out in the sun, instead of comin' in here to the cool o' the shadow, I wouldn't be takin' the church at her word. It does my heart good to sit in the old church, sir. There's a something do seem to come out o' the old walls and settle down like the cool o' the day upon my old heart that's nearly tired o' crying, and would fain keep its eyes dry for the rest o' the journey. My old man's stockin' won't hurt the church, sir, and, bein' a good deed as I suppose it is, it's none the worse for the place. I think, if He was to come by wi' the whip o' small cords, I wouldn't be afeared of his layin' it upo' my old back. Do you think he would, sir?"

Thus driven to speak as I thought, I made haste to reply, more delighted with the result of my experiment than I cared to let her know.

"Indeed I do not. I was only talking. It is but selfish, cheating, or ill-done work that the church's Master drives away. All our work ought to be done in the shadow of the church."

"I thought you be only having a talk about it, sir," she said, smiling her sweet old smile. "Nobody knows what this old church is to me."

Now the old woman had a good husband, apparently: the sorrows which had left their mark even upon her smile, must have come from her family, I thought.

"You have had a family?" I said, interrogatively.

"I've had thirteen," she answered. "Six bys and seven maidens."

"Why, you are rich!" I returned. "And where are they all?"

"Four maidens be lying in the churchyard, sir; two be married, and one be down in the mill, there."

"And your boys?"

"One of them be lyin' beside his sisters-drownded afore my eyes, sir. Three o' them be at sea, and two o' them in it, sir."

At sea! I thought. What a wide *where*! As vague to the imagination, almost, as *in the other world*. How a mother's thoughts must go roaming about the waste, like birds that have lost their nest, to find them!

As this thought kept me silent for a few moments, she resumed.

"It be no wonder, be it, sir? that I like to creep into the church with my knitting. Many's the stormy night, when my husband couldn't keep still, but would be out on the cliffs or on the breakwater, for no good in life, but just to hear the roar of the waves that he could only see by the white of them, with the balls o' foam flying in his face in the dark-many's the such a night that I have left the house after he was gone, with this blessed key in my hand, and crept into the old church here, and sat down where I'm sittin' now-leastways where I was sittin' when your reverence spoke to me-and hearkened to the wind howling about the place. The church windows never rattle, sir-like the cottage windows, as I suppose you know, sir. Somehow, I feel safe in the church."

"But if you had sons at sea," said I, again wishing to draw her out, "it would not be of much good to you to feel safe yourself, so long as they were in danger."

"O! yes, it be, sir. What's the good of feeling safe yourself but it let you know other people be safe too? It's when you don't feel safe yourself that you feel other people ben't safe."

"But," I said-and such confidence I had from what she had already uttered, that I was sure the experiment was not a cruel one —"some of your sons *were* drowned for all that you say about their safety."

"Well, sir," she answered, with a sigh, "I trust they're none the less safe for that. It would be a strange thing for an old woman like me, well-nigh threescore and ten, to suppose that safety lay in not being drownded. Why, they might ha' been cast on a desert island, and wasted to skin an' bone, and got home again wi' the loss of half the wits they set out with. Wouldn't that ha' been worse than being drownded right off? And that wouldn't ha' been the worst, either. The church she seem to tell me all the time, that for all the roaring outside, there be really no danger after all. What matter if they go to the bottom? What is the bottom of the sea, sir? You bein' a clergyman can tell that, sir. I shouldn't ha' known it if I hadn't had bys o' my own at sea, sir. But you can tell, sir, though you ain't got none there."

And though she was putting her parson to his catechism, the smile that returned on her face was as modest as if she had only been listening to his instruction. I had not long to look for my answer.

"The hollow of his hand," I said, and said no more.

"I thought you would know it, sir," she returned, with a little glow of triumph in her tone. "Well, then, that's just what the church tells me when I come in here in the stormy nights. I bring my knitting then too, sir, for I can knit in the dark as well as in the light almost; and when they come home, if they do come home, they're none the worse that I went to the old church to pray for them. There it goes roaring about them poor dears, all out there; and their old mother sitting still as a stone almost in the quiet old church, a caring for them. And then it do come across me, sir, that God be a sitting in his own house at home, hearing all the noise and all the roaring in which his children are tossed about in the world, watching it all, letting it drown some o' them and take them back to him, and keeping it from going too far with others of them that are not quite ready for that same. I have my thoughts, you see, sir, though I be an old woman; and not nice to look at."

I had come upon a genius. How nature laughs at our schools sometimes! Education, so-called, is a fine thing, and might be a better thing; but there is an education, that of life, which, when seconded by a pure will to learn, leaves the schools behind, even as the horse of the desert would leave behind the slow pomposity of the common-fed goose. For life is God's school, and they that will listen to the Master there will learn at God's speed. For one moment, I am ashamed to say, I was envious of Shepherd, and repined that, now old Rogers was gone, I had no such glorious old stained-glass window in my church to let in the eternal upon my light-thirsty soul. I must say for myself that the feeling lasted but for a moment, and that no sooner had the shadow of it passed and the true light shined after it, than I was heartily ashamed of it. Why should not Shepherd have the old woman as well as I? True, Shepherd was more of what would now be called a ritualist than I; true, I thought my doctrine simpler and therefore better than his; but was this any reason why I should have all the grand people to minister to in my parish! Recovering myself, I found her last words still in my ears.

"You are very nice to look at," I said. "You must not find fault with the work of God, because you would like better to be young and pretty than to be as you now are. Time and time's rents and furrows are all his making and his doing. God makes nothing ugly."

"Are you quite sure of that, sir?"

I paused. Such a question from such a woman "must give us pause." And, as I paused, the thought of certain animals flashed into my mind and I could not insist that God had never made anything ugly.

"No. I am not sure of it," I answered. For of all things my soul recoiled from, any professional pretence of knowing more than I did know seemed to me the most repugnant to the spirit and mind of the Master, whose servants we are, or but the servants of mere priestly delusion and self-seeking. "But if he does," I went on to say, "it must be that we may see what it is like, and therefore not like it."

Then, unwilling all at once to plunge with her into such an abyss as the question opened, I turned the conversation to an object on which my eyes had been for some time resting half-unconsciously. It was the sort of stool or bench on which my guide had been sitting. I now thought it was some kind of box or chest. It was curiously carved in old oak, very much like the ends of the benches and book-boards.

"What is that you were sitting on?" I asked. "A chest or what?"

"It be there when we come to this place, and that be nigh fifty years agone, sir. But what it be, you'll be better able to tell than I be, sir."

"Perhaps a chest for holding the communion-plate in old time," I said. "But how should it then come to be banished to the tower?"

"No, sir; it can't be that. It be some sort of ancient musical piano, I be thinking."

I stooped and saw that its lid was shaped like the cover of an organ. With some difficulty I opened it; and there, to be sure, was a row of huge keys, fit for the fingers of a Cyclops. I pressed upon them, one after another, but no sound followed. They were stiff to the touch; and once down, so they mostly remained until lifted again. I looked if there was any sign of a bellows, thinking it must have been some primitive kind of reed-instrument, like what we call a seraphine or harmonium now-a-days. But there was no hole through which there could have been any communication with or from a bellows, although there might have been a small one inside. There were, however, a dozen little round holes in the fixed part of the top, which might afford some clue to the mystery of its former life. I could not find any way of reaching the inside of it, so strongly was it put together; therefore I was left, I thought, to the efforts of my imagination alone for any hope of discovery with regard to the instrument, seeing further observation was impossible. But here I found that I was mistaken in two important conclusions, the latter of which depended on the former. The first of these was that it was an instrument: it was only one end of an instrument; therefore, secondly, there might be room for observation still. But I found this out by accident, which has had a share in most discoveries, and which, meaning a something that falls into our hands unlocked for, is so far an unobjectionable word even to the man who does not believe in chance. I had for the time given up the question as insoluble, and was gazing about the place, when, glancing up at the holes in the ceiling through which the bell-ropes went, I spied two or three thick wires hanging through the same ceiling close to the wall, and right over the box with the keys. The vague suspicion of a discovery dawned upon me.

"Have you got the key of the tower?" I asked.

"No, sir. But I'll run home for it at once," she answered. And rising, she went out in haste.

"Run!" thought I, looking after her. "It is a word of the will and the feeling, not of the body." But I was mistaken. The dear old creature had no sooner got outside of the church-yard, within which, I presume, she felt that she must be decorous, than she did run, and ran well too. I was on the point of starting after her at full speed, to prevent her from hurting herself, but reflecting that her own judgment ought to be as good as mine in such a case, I returned, and sitting down on her seat, awaited her reappearance, gazing at the ceiling. There I either saw or imagined I saw signs of openings corresponding in number and position with those in the lid under me. In about three minutes the old woman returned, panting but not distressed, with a great crooked old key in her hand. Why are all the keys of a church so crooked? I did not ask her that question, though. What I said to her, was —

"You shouldn't run like that. I am in no hurry."

"Be you not, sir? I thought, by the way you spoke, you be taken with a longing to get a-top o' the tower, and see all about you like. For you see, sir, fond as I be of the old church, I du feel sometimes as if she'd smother me; and then nothing will do but I must get at the top of the old tower. And then, what with the sun, if there be any sun, and what with the fresh air which there always be up there, sir, —it du always be fresh up there, sir," she repeated, "I come back down again blessing the old church for its tower."

As she spoke she was toiling up the winding staircase after me, where there was just room enough for my shoulders to get through by turning themselves a little across the lie of the steps. They were very high, but she kept up with me bravely, bearing out her statement that she was no stranger to them. As I ascended, however, I was not thinking of her, but of what she had said. Strange to tell, the significance of the towers or spires of our churches had never been clear to me before. True, I was quite awake to their significance, at least to that of the spires, as fingers pointing ever upwards to

> "regions mild of calm and serene air,
> Above the smoke and stir of this dim spot,
> Which men call Earth;"

but I had not thought of their symbolism as lifting one up above the church itself into a region where no church is wanted because the Lord God almighty and the Lamb are the temple of it.

Happy church indeed, if it destroys the need of itself by lifting men up into the eternal kingdom! Would that I and all her servants lived pervaded with the sense of this her high end, her one high calling! We need the church towers to remind us that the mephitic airs in the church below are from the churchyard at its feet, which so many take for the church, worshipping over the graves and believing in death-or at least in the material substance over which alone death hath power. Thus the church, even in her corruption, lifts us out of her corruption, sending us up her towers and her spires to admonish us that she too lives in the air of truth: that her form too must pass away, while the truth that is embodied in her lives beyond forms and customs and prejudices, shining as the stars for ever and ever. He whom the church does not lift up above the church is not worthy to be a doorkeeper therein.

Such thoughts passed through me, satisfied me, and left me peaceful, so that before I had reached the top, I was thanking the Lord-not for his church-tower, but for his sexton's wife.

The old woman was a jewel. If her husband was like her, which was too much to expect-if he believed in her, it would be enough, quite-then indeed the little child, who answered on being questioned thereanent, as the Scotch would say, that the three orders of ministers in the church were the parson, clerk, and sexton, might not be so far wrong in respect of this individual case. So in the ascent, and the thinking associated therewith, I forgot all about the special object for which I had requested the key of the tower, and led the way myself up to the summit, where stepping out of a little door, which being turned only heavenwards had no pretence for, or claim upon a curiously crooked key, but opened to the hand laid upon the latch, I thought of the words of the judicious Hooker, that "the assembling of the church to learn" was "the receiving of angels descended from above;" and in such a whimsical turn as our thoughts will often take when we are not heeding them, I wondered for a moment whether that was why the upper door was left on the latch, forgetting that that could not be of much use, if the door in the basement was kept locked with the crooked key. But the whole suggested something true about my own heart and that of my fellows, if not about the church: Revelation is not enough, the open trap-door is not enough, if the door of the heart is not open likewise.

As soon, however, as I stepped out upon the roof of the tower, I forgot again all that had thus passed through my mind, swift as a dream. For, filling the west, lay the ocean beneath, with a dark curtain of storm hanging in perpendicular lines over part of its horizon, and on the other side was the peaceful solid land, with its numberless shades of green, its heights and hollows, its farms and wooded vales-there was not much wood-its scattered villages and country dwellings, lighted and shadowed by the sun and the clouds. Beyond lay the blue heights of Dartmoor. And over all, bathing us as it passed, moved the wind, the life-bearing spirit of the whole, the servant of the sun. The old woman stood beside me, silently enjoying my enjoyment, with a still smile that seemed to say in kindly triumph, "Was I not right about the tower and the wind that dwells among its pinnacles?" I drank deep of the universal flood, the outspread peace, the glory of the sun, and the haunting shadow of the sea that lay beyond like the visual image of the eternal silence-as it looks to us-that rounds our little earthly life.

There were a good many trees in the church-yard, and as I looked down, the tops of them in their richest foliage hid all the graves directly below me, except a single flat stone looking up through an opening in the leaves, which seemed to have been just made for it to let it see the top of the tower. Upon the stone a child was seated playing with a few flowers she had gathered, not once looking up to the gilded vanes that rose from the four pinnacles at the corners of the tower. I turned to the eastern side, and looked over upon the church roof. It lay far below-looking very narrow and small, but long, with the four ridges of four steep roofs stretching away to the eastern end. It was in excellent repair, for the parish was almost all in one lord's possession, and he was proud of his church: between them he and Mr. Shepherd had made it beautiful to behold and strong to endure.

When I turned to look again, the little child was gone. Some butterfly fancy had seized her, and she was away. A little lamb was in her place, nibbling at the grass that grew on the side of the next mound. And when I looked seaward there was a sloop, like a white-winged sea-bird, rounding the end of a high projecting rock from the south, to bear up the little channel that led to the gates of the harbour canal. Out of the circling waters it had flown home, not from a long voyage, but hardly the less welcome therefore to those that waited and looked for her signal from the barrier rock.

Reentering by the angels' door to descend the narrow cork-screw stair, so dark and cool, I caught a glimpse, one turn down, by the feeble light that came through its chinks after it was shut behind us, of a tiny maiden-hair fern growing out of the wall. I stopped, and said to the old woman—

"I have a sick daughter at home, or I wouldn't rob your tower of this lovely little thing."

"Well, sir, what eyes you have! I never saw the thing before. Do take it home to miss. It'll do her good to see it. I be main sorry to hear you've got a sick maiden. She ben't a bedlar, be she, sir?"

I was busy with my knife getting out all the roots I could without hurting them, and before I had succeeded I had remembered Turner's using the word.

"Not quite that," I answered, "but she can't even sit up, and must be carried everywhere."

"Poor dear! Everyone has their troubles, sir. The sea's been mine."

She continued talking and asking kind questions about Connie as we went down the stair. Not till she opened a little door I had passed without observing it as we came up, was I reminded of my first object in ascending the tower. For this door revealed a number of bells hanging in silent power in the brown twilight of the place. I entered carefully, for there were only some planks laid upon the joists to keep one's feet from going through the ceiling. In a few moments I had satisfied myself that my conjecture about the keys below was correct. The small iron rods I had seen from beneath hung down from this place. There were more of them hanging shorter above, and there was yet enough of a further mechanism remaining to prove that those keys, by means of the looped and cranked rods, had been in connection with hammers, one of them indeed remaining also, which struck the bells, so that a tune could be played upon them as upon any other keyed instrument. This was the first contrivance of the kind I had ever seen, though I have heard of it in other churches since.

"If I could find a clever blacksmith in the neighbourhood, now," I said to myself, "I would get this all repaired, so that it should not interfere with the bell-ringing when the ringers were to be had, and yet Shepherd could play a psalm tune to his parish at large when he pleased." For Shepherd was a very fair musician, and gave a good deal of time to the organ. "It's a grand notion, to think of him sitting here in the gloom, with that great musical instrument towering above him, whence he sends forth the voice of gladness, almost of song to his people, while they are mowing the grass, binding the sheaves, or gazing abroad over the stormy ocean in doubt, anxiety, and fear. 'There's the parson at his bells,' they would say, and stop and listen; and some phrase might sink into their hearts, waking some memory, or giving birth to some hope or faint aspiration. I will see what can be done." Having come to this conclusion, I left the abode of the bells, descended to the church, bade my conductress good morning, saying I would visit her soon in her own house, and bore home to my child the spoil which, without kirk-rapine, I had torn from the wall of the sanctuary. By this time the stormy veil had lifted from the horizon, and the sun was shining in full power without one darkening cloud.

Ere I left the churchyard I would have a glance at the stone which ever seemed to lie gazing up at the tower. I soon found it, because it was the only one in that quarter from which I could see the top of the tower. It recorded the life and death of an aged pair who had been married fifty years, concluding with the couplet —

"A long time this may seem to be, But it did not seem long to we."

The whole story of a human life lay in that last verse. True, it was not good grammar; but they had got through fifty years of wedded life probably without any knowledge of grammar to harmonise or to shorten them, and I daresay, had they been acquainted with the lesson he had put into their dumb mouths, they would have been aware of no ground of quarrel with the poetic stone-cutter, who most likely had thrown the verses in when he made his claim for the stone and the cutting. Having learnt this one by heart, I went about looking for anything more in the shape of sepulchral flora that might interest or amuse my crippled darling; nor had I searched long before I found one, the sole but triumphant recommendation of which was the thorough "puzzle-headedness" of its construction. I quite reckoned on seeing Connie trying to make it out, looking as bewildered over its excellent grammar, as the poet of the other ought to have looked over his rhymes, ere he gave in to the use of the nominative after a preposition.

> "If you could view the heavenly shore,
> Where heart's content you hope to find,
> You would not murmur were you gone before,
> But grieve that you are left behind."

CHAPTER XVI
CONNIE'S WATCH-TOWER.

As I walked home, the rush of the rising tide was in my ears. To my fancy, the ocean, awaking from a swoon in which its life had ebbed to its heart, was sending that life abroad to its extremities, and waves breaking in white were the beats of its reviving pulse, the flashes of returning light. But so gentle was its motion, and so lovely its hue, that I could not help contrasting it with its reflex in the mind of her who took refuge from the tumult of its noises in the hollow of the old church. To her, let it look as blue as the sky, as peaceful and as moveless, it was a wild, reckless, false, devouring creature, a prey to its own moods, and to that of the blind winds which, careless of consequences, urged it to raving fury. Only, while the sea took this form to her imagination, she believed in that which held the sea, and knew that, when it pleased God to part his confining fingers, there would be no more sea.

When I reached home, I went straight to Connie's room. Now the house was one of a class to every individual of which, whatever be its style or shape, I instantly become attached almost as if it possessed a measure of the life which it has sheltered. This class of human dwellings consists of the houses that have *grown*. They have not been, built after a straight-up-and-down model of uninteresting convenience or money-loving pinchedness. They must have had some plan, good, bad, or indifferent, as the case may be, at first, I suppose; but that plan they have left far behind, having grown with the necessities or ambitions of succeeding possessors, until the fact that they have a history is as plainly written on their aspect as on that of any you or daughter of Adam. These are the houses which the fairies used to haunt, and if there is any truth in ghost-stories, the houses which ghosts will yet haunt; and hence perhaps the sense of soothing comfort which pervades us when we cross their thresholds. You do not know, the moment you have cast a glance about the hall, where the dining-room, drawing-room, and best bedroom are. You have got it all to find out, just as the character of a man; and thus had I to find out this house of my friend Shepherd. It had formerly been a kind of manor-house, though altogether unlike any other manor-house I ever saw; for after exercising all my constructive ingenuity reversed in pulling it to pieces in my mind, I came to the conclusion that the germ-cell of it was a cottage of the simplest sort which had grown by the addition of other cells, till it had reached the development in which we found it.

I have said that the dining-room was almost on the level of the shore. Certainly some of the flat stones that coped the low wall in front of it were thrown into the garden before the next winter by the waves. But Connie's room looked out on a little flower-garden almost on the downs, only sheltered a little by the rise of a short grassy slope above it. This, however, left the prospect, from her window down the bay and out to sea, almost open. To reach this room I had now to go up but one simple cottage stair; for the door of the house entered on the first floor, that is, as regards the building, midway between heaven and earth. It had a large bay-window; and in this window Connie was lying on her couch, with the lower sash wide open, through which the breeze entered, smelling of sea-weed tempered with sweet grasses and the wall-flowers and stocks that were in the little plot under it. I thought I could see an improvement in her already. Certainly she looked very happy.

"O, papa!" she said, "isn't it delightful?"

"What is, my dear?"

"O, everything. The wind, and the sky, and the sea, and the smell of the flowers. Do look at that sea-bird. His wings are like the barb of a terrible arrow. How he goes undulating, neck and body, up and down as he flies. I never felt before that a bird moves his wings. It always looked as if the wings flew with the bird. But I see the effort in him."

"An easy effort, though, I should certainly think."

"No doubt. But I see that he chooses and means to fly, and so does it. It makes one almost reconciled to the idea of wings. Do angels really have wings, papa?"

"It is generally so represented, I think, in the Bible. But whether it is meant as a natural fact about them, is more than I take upon me to decide. For one thing, I should have to examine whether in simple narrative they are ever represented with them, as, I think, in records of visions they are never represented without them. But wings are very beautiful things, and I do not exactly see why you should need reconciling to them."

Connie gave a little shrug of her shoulders.

"I don't like the notion of them growing out at my shoulder-blades. And however would you get on your clothes? If you put them over your wings, they would be of no use, and would, besides, make you hump-backed; and if you did not, everything would have to be buttoned round the roots of them. You could not do it yourself, and even on Wynnie I don't think I could bear to touch the things—I don't mean the feathers, but the skinny, folding-up bits of them."

I laughed at her fastidious fancy.

"You want to fly, I suppose?" I said.

"O, yes; I should like that."

"And you don't want to have wings?"

"Well, I shouldn't mind the wings exactly; but however would one be able to keep them nice?"

"There you go; starting from one thing to another, like a real bird already. When you can't answer one thing, off to another, and, from your new perch on the hawthorn, talk as if you were still on the topmost branch of the lilac!"

"O, yes, papa! That's what I've heard you say to mamma twenty times."

"And did I ever say to your mamma anything but the truth? or to you either, you puss?"

I had not yet discovered that when I used this epithet to my Connie, she always thought she had gone too far. She looked troubled. I hastened to relieve her.

"When women have wings," I said, "their logic will be good."

"How do you make that out, papa?" she asked, a little re-assured.

"Because then every shadow of feeling that turns your speech aside from the straight course will be recognised in that speech; the whole utterance will be instinct not only with the meaning of what you are thinking, but with the reflex of the forces in you that make the utterance take this or that shape; just as to a perfect palate, the source and course of a stream would be revealed in every draught of its water.

"I have just a glimmering of your meaning, papa. Would you like to have wings?"

"I should like to fly like a bird, to swim like a fish, to gallop like a horse, to creep like a serpent, but I suspect the good of all these is to be got without doing any of them."

"I know what you mean now, but I can't put it in words."

"I mean by a perfect sympathy with the creatures that do these things: what it may please God to give to ourselves, we can quite comfortably leave to him. A higher stratum of the same kind is the need we feel of knowing our fellow-creatures through and through, of walking into and out of their worlds as if we were, because we are, perfectly at home in them. —But I am talking what the people who do not understand such things lump all together as mysticism, which is their name for a kind of spiritual ash-pit, whither they consign dust and stones, never asking whether they may not be gold-dust and rubies, all in a heap. —You had better begin to think about getting out, Connie."

"Think about it, papa! I have been thinking about it ever since daylight."

"I will go and see what your mother is doing then, and if she is ready to go out with us."

In a few moments all was arranged. Without killing more than a snail or two, which we could not take time to beware of, Walter and I—finding that the window did not open down to the ground in French fashion, for which there were two good reasons, one the fierceness of the winds in winter, the other, the fact that the means of egress were elsewise provided-lifted the sofa, Connie and all, out over the window-sill, and then there was only a little door in the garden-wall to get her through before we found ourselves upon the down. I think the ascent of this hill was the first experience I had—a little to my humiliation, nothing to my sorrow-that I was descending another hill. I had to set down the precious burden rather oftener before we reached the brow of the cliffs than would have been necessary ten years before. But this was all right, and the newly-discovered weakness then was strength to the power which carries me about on my two legs now. It is all right still. I shall be stronger by and by.

We carried her high enough for her to see the brilliant waters lying many feet below her, with the sea-birds of which we had talked winging their undulating way between heaven and ocean. It is when first you have a chance of looking a bird in the face on the wing that you know what the marvel of flight is. There it hangs or rests, which you please, borne up, as far as eye or any of the senses can witness, by its own will alone. This Connie, quicker than I in her observation of nature, had already observed. Seated on the warm grass by her side, while neither talked, but both regarded the blue spaces, I saw one of those same barb-winged birds rest over my head, regarding me from above, as if doubtful whether I did not afford some claim to his theory of treasure-trove. I knew at once that what Connie had been saying to me just before was true.

She lay silent a long time. I too was silent. At length I spoke.

"Are you longing to be running about amongst the rocks, my Connie?"

"No, papa; not a bit. I don't know how it is, but I don't think I ever wished much for anything I knew I could not have. I am enjoying everything more than I can tell you. I wish Wynnie were as happy as I am."

"Why? Do you think she's not happy, my dear?"

"That doesn't want any thinking, papa. You can see that."

"I am afraid you're right, Connie. What do you think is the cause of it?"

"I think it is because she can't wait. She's always going out to meet things; and then when they're not there waiting for her, she thinks they're nowhere. But I always think her way is finer than mine. If everybody were like me, there wouldn't be much done in the world, would there, papa?"

"At all events, my dear, your way is wise for you, and I am glad you do not judge your sister."

"Judge Wynnie, papa! That would be cool impudence. She's worth ten of me. Don't you think, papa," she added, after a pause, "that if Mary had said the smallest word against Martha, as Martha did against Mary, Jesus would have had a word to say on Martha's side next?"

"Indeed I do, my dear. And I think that did not sit very long without asking Jesus if she mightn't go and help her sister. There is but one thing needful-that is, the will of God; and when people love that above everything, they soon come to see that to everything else there are two sides, and that only the will of God gives fair play, as we call it, to both of them."

Another silence followed. Then Connie spoke.

"Is it not strange, papa, that the only thine here that makes me want to get up to look, is nothing of all the grand things round about me? I am just lying like the convex mirror in the school-room at home, letting them all paint themselves in me."

"What is it then that makes you wish to get up and go and see?" I asked with real curiosity.

"Do you see down there-away across the bay-amongst the rocks at the other side, a man sitting sketching?"

I looked for some time before I could discover him.

"Your sight is good, Connie: I see the man, but I could not tell what he was doing."

"Don't you see him lifting his head every now and then for a moment, and then keeping it down for a longer while?"

"I cannot distinguish that. But then I am shortsighted rather, you know."

"I wonder how you see so many little things that nobody else seems to notice, then, papa."

"That is because I have trained myself to observe. The degree of power in the sight is of less consequence than the habit of seeing. But you have not yet told me what it is that makes you desirous of getting up."

"I want to look over his shoulder, and see what he is doing. Is it not strange that in the midst of all this plenty of beautifulness, I should want to rise to look at a few lines and scratches, or smears of colour, upon a bit of paper?"

"No, my dear; I don't think it is strange. There a new element of interest is introduced-the human. No doubt there is deep humanity in all this around us. No doubt all the world, in all its moods, is human, as those for whose abode and instruction it was made. No doubt, it would be void of both beauty and significance to our eyes, were it not that it is one crowd of pictures of the human mind, blended in one living fluctuating whole. But these meanings are there in solution as it were. The individual is a centre of crystallisation to this solution. Around him meanings gather, are separated from other meanings; and if he be an artist, by which I mean true painter, true poet, or true musician, as the case may be he so isolates and represents them, that we see them-not what nature shows to us, but what nature has shown, to him, determined by his nature and choice. With it is mingled therefore so much of his own individuality, manifested both in this choice and certain modifications determined by his way of working, that you have not only a representation of an aspect of nature, as far as that may be with limited powers and materials, but a revelation of the man's own mind and nature. Consequently there is a human interest in every true attempt to reproduce nature, an interest of individuality which does not belong to nature herself, who is for all and every man. You have just been saying that you were lying there like a convex mirror reflecting all nature around you. Every man is such a convex mirror; and his drawing, if he can make one, is an attempt to show what is in this little mirror of his, kindled there by the grand world outside. And the human mirrors being all differently formed, vary infinitely in what they would thus represent of the same scene. I have been greatly interested in looking alternately over the shoulders of two artists, both sketching in colour the same, absolutely the same scene, both trying to represent it with all the truth in their power. How different, notwithstanding, the two representations came out!"

"I think I understand you, papa. But look a little farther off. Don't you see over the top of another rock a lady's bonnet. I do believe that's Wynnie. I know she took her box of water-colours out with her this morning, just before you came home. Dora went with her."

"Can't you tell by her ribbons, Connie? You seem sharp-sighted enough to see her face if she would show it. I don't even see the bonnet. If I were like some people I know, I should feel justified in denying its presence, attributing the whole to your fancy, and refusing anything to superiority of vision."

"That wouldn't be like you, papa."

"I hope not; for I have no fancy for being shut up in my own blindness, when other people offer me their eyes to eke out the defects of my own with. But here comes mamma at last."

Connie's face brightened as if she had not seen her mother for a fortnight. My Ethelwyn always brought the home gladness that her name signified with her. She was a centre of radiating peace.

"Mamma, don't you think that's Wynnie's bonnet over that black rock there, just beyond where you see that man drawing?"

"You absurd child! How should I know Wynnie's bonnet at this distance?"

"Can't you see the little white feather you gave her out of your wardrobe just before we left? She put it in this morning before she went out."

"I think I do see something white. But I want you to look out there, towards what they call the Chapel Rock, at the other end of that long mound they call the breakwater. You will soon see a boat appear full of the coast-guard. I saw them going on board just as I left the house to come up to you. Their officer came down with his sword, and each of the men had a cutlass. I wonder what it can mean."

We looked. But before the boat made its appearance, Connie cried out —

"Look there! What a big boat that is rowing for the land, away northwards there!"

I turned my eyes in the direction she indicated, and saw a long boat with some half-dozen oars, full of men, rowing hard, apparently for some spot on the shore at a considerable distance to the north of our bay.

"Ah!" I said, "that boat has something to do with the coast-guard and their cutlasses. You'll see that, as soon as they get out of the bay, they will row in the same direction."

So it was. Our boat appeared presently from under the concealment of the heights on which we were, and made at full speed after the other boat.

"Surely they can't be smugglers," I said. "I thought all that was over and done with."

In the course of another twenty minutes, during which we watched their progress, both boats had disappeared behind the headland to the northward. Then, thinking Connie had had nearly enough of the sea air for her first experience of its influences, I went and fetched Walter, and we carried her back as we had brought her. She had not been in the shadow of her own room for five minutes before she was fast asleep.

It was now nearly time for our early dinner. We always dined early when we could, that we might eat along with our children. We were both convinced that the only way to make them behave like ladies and gentlemen was to have them always with us at meals. We had seen very unpleasant results in the children of those who allowed them to dine with no other supervision than the nursery afforded: they were a constant anxiety and occasional horror to those whom they visited-snatching like monkeys, and devouring like jackals, as selfishly as if they were mere animals.

"O! we've seen such a nice gentleman!" said Dora, becoming lively under the influence of her soup.

"Have you, Dora? Where?"

"Sitting on the rocks, taking a portrait of the sea."

"What makes you say he was a nice gentleman?"

"He had such beautiful boots!" answered Dora, at which there was a great laugh about the table.

"O! we must run and tell Connie that," said Harry. "It will make her laugh."

"What will you tell Connie, then, Harry?"

"O! what was it, Charlie? I've forgotten."

Another laugh followed at Harry's expense now, and we were all very merry, when Dora, who sat opposite to the window, called out, clapping her hands—

"There's Niceboots again! There's Niceboots again!"

The same moment the head of a young man appeared over the wall that separated the garden from the little beach that lay by the entrance of the canal. I saw at once that he must be more than ordinarily tall to show his face, for he was not close to the wall. It was a dark countenance, with a long beard, which few at that time wore, though now it is getting not uncommon, even in my own profession—a noble, handsome face, a little sad, with downbent eyes, which, released from their more immediate duty towards nature, had now bent themselves upon the earth.

"Counting the dewy pebbles, fixed in thought."

"I suppose he's contemplating his boots," said Wynnie, with apparent maliciousness.

"That's too bad of you, Wynnie," I said, and the child blushed.

"I didn't mean anything, papa. It was only following up Dora's wise discrimination," said Wynnie.

"He is a fine-looking fellow," said I, "and ought, with that face and head, to be able to paint good pictures."

"I should like to see what he has done," said Wynnie; "for, by the way we were sitting, I should think we were attempting the same thing."

"And what was that then, Wynnie?" I asked.

"A rock," she answered, "that you could not see from where you were sitting. I saw you on the top of the cliff."

"Connie said it was you, by your bonnet. She, too, was wishing she could look over the shoulder of the artist at work beside you."

"Not beside me. There were yards and yards of solid rock between us."

"Space, you see, in removing things from the beholder, seems always to bring them nearer to each other, and the most differing things are classed under one name by the man who knows nothing about them. But what sort of a rock was it you were trying to draw?"

"A strange-looking, conical rock, that stands alone in front of one of the ridges that project from the shore into the water. Three sea-birds, with long white wings, were flying about it, and the little waves of the rising tide were beating themselves against it and breaking in white plashes. So the rock stood between the blue and white below and the blue and white above; for, though there were no clouds, the birds gave the touches of white to the upper sea."

"Now, Dora," I said, "I don't know if you are old enough to understand me; but sometimes little people are long in understanding, just because the older people think they can't, and don't try them. —Do you see, Dora, why I want you to learn to draw? Look how Wynnie sees things. That is, in a great measure, because she draws things, and has, by that, learned to watch in order to find out. It is a great thing to have your eyes open."

Dora's eyes were large, and she opened them to their full width, as if she would take in the universe at their little doors. Whether that indicated that she did not in the least understand what I had been saying, or that she was in sympathy with it, I cannot tell.

"Now let us go up to Connie, and tell her about the rock and everything else you have seen since you went out. We are all her messengers sent out to discover things, and bring back news of them."

After a little talk with Connie, I retired to the study, which was on the same floor as her room completing, indeed, the whole of that part of the house, which, seen from without, looked like a separate building; for it had a roof of its own, and stood higher up the rock than the rest of the dwelling. Here I began to glance over the books. To have the run of another man's library, especially if it has all been gathered by himself, is like having a pass-key into the chambers of his thought. Only, one must be wary, when he opens them, what marks on the books he takes for those of the present owner. A mistake here would breed considerable confusion and falsehood in any judgment formed from the library. I found, however, one thing plain enough, that Shepherd had kept up that love for an older English literature, which had been one of the cords to draw us towards each other when we were students together. There had been one point on which we especially agreed-that a true knowledge of the present, in literature, as in everything else, could only be founded upon a knowledge of what had gone before; therefore, that any judgment, in regard to the literature of the present day, was of no value which was not guided and influenced by a real acquaintance with the best of what had gone before, being liable to be dazzled and misled by novelty of form and other qualities which, whatever might be the real worth of the substance, were, in themselves, purely ephemeral. I had taken down a last-century edition of the poems of the brothers Fletcher, and, having begun to read a lovely passage in "Christ's Victory and Triumph," had gone into what I can only call an intellectual rage, at the impudence of the editor, who had altered innumerable words and phrases to suit the degenerate taste of his own time, —when a knock came to the door, and Charlie entered, breathless with eagerness.

"There's the boat with the men with the swords in it, and another boat behind them, twice as big."

I hurried out upon the road, and there, close under our windows, were the two boats we had seen in the morning, landing their crews on the little beach. The second boat was full of weather-beaten men, in all kinds of attire, some in blue jerseys, some in red shirts, some in ragged coats. One man, who looked their superior, was dressed in blue from head to foot.

"What's the matter?" I asked the officer of the coast-guard, a sedate, thoughtful-looking man.

"Vessel foundered, sir," he answered. "Sprung a leak on Sunday morning. She was laden with iron, and in a heavy ground swell it shifted and knocked a hole in her. The poor fellows are worn out with the pump and rowing, upon little or nothing to eat."

They were trooping past us by this time, looking rather dismal, though not by any means abject.

"What are you going to do with them now?"

"They'll be taken in by the people. We'll get up a little subscription for them, but they all belong to the society the sailors have for sending the shipwrecked to their homes, or where they want to go."

"Well, here's something to help," I said.

"Thank you, sir. They'll be very glad of it."

"And if there's anything wanted that I can do for them, you must let me know."

"I will, sir. But I don't think there will be any occasion to trouble you. You are our new clergyman, I believe."

"Not exactly that. Only for a little while, till my friend Mr. Shepherd is able to come back to you."

"We don't want to lose Mr. Shepherd, sir. He's what they call high in these parts, but he's a great favourite with all the poor people, because you see he understands them as if he was of the same flesh and blood with themselves-as, for that matter, I suppose we all are."

"If we weren't there would be nothing to say at all. Will any of these men be at church to-morrow, do you suppose? I am afraid sailors are not much in the way of going to church?"

"I am afraid not. You see they are all anxious to get home. Most likely they'll be all travelling to-morrow. It's a pity. It would be a good chance for saying something to them that they might think of again. But I often think that, perhaps-it's only my own fancy, and I don't set it up for anything-that sailors won't be judged exactly like other people. They're so knocked about, you see, sir."

"Of course not. Nobody will be judged like any other body. To his own Master, who knows all about him, every man stands or falls. Depend upon it, God likes fair play, to use a homely phrase, far better than any sailor of them all. But that's not exactly the question. It seems to me the question is this: shall we, who know what a blessed thing life is because we know what God is like, who can trust in him with all our hearts because he is the Father of our Lord Jesus Christ, the friend of sinners, shall we not try all we can to let them, too, know the blessedness of trusting in their Father in heaven? If we could only get them to say the Lord's prayer, *meaning it*, think what that would be! Look here! This can't be called bribery, for they are in want of it, and it will show them I am friendly. Here's another sovereign. Give them my compliments, and say that if any of them happen to be in Kilkhaven tomorrow, I shall be quite pleased to welcome them to church. Tell them I will give them of my best there if they will come. Make the invitation merrily, you know. No long faces and solemn speech. I will give them the solemn speech when they come to church. But even there I hope God will keep the long face far from me. That is fittest for fear and suffering. And the house of God is the casket that holds the antidote against all fear and most suffering. But I am preaching my sermon on Saturday instead of Sunday, and keeping you from your ministration to the poor fellows. Good-bye."

"I will give them your message as near as I can," he said, and we shook hands and parted.

This was the first experience we had of the might and battle of the ocean. To our eyes it lay quiet as a baby asleep. On that Sunday morning there had been no commotion here. Yet now at last, on the Saturday morning, home come the conquered and spoiled of the sea. As if with a mock she takes all they have, and flings them on shore again, with her weeds, and her shells, and her sand. Before the winter was over we had learned-how much more of that awful power that surrounds the habitable earth! By slow degrees the sense of its might grew upon us, first by the vision of its many aspects and moods, and then by more awful things that followed; for there are few coasts upon which the sea rages so wildly as upon this, the whole force of the Atlantic breaking upon it. Even when there is no storm within perhaps hundreds of miles, when all is still as a church on the land, the storm that raves somewhere out upon the vast waste, will drive the waves in upon the shore with such fury that not even a lifeboat could make its way through their yawning hollows, and their fierce, shattered, and tumbling crests.

CHAPTER XVII
MY FIRST SERMON IN THE SEABOARD PARISH.

In the hope that some of the shipwrecked mariners might be present in the church the next day, I proceeded to consider my morning's sermon for the occasion. There was no difficulty in taking care at the same time that it should be suitable to the congregation, whether those sailors were there or not. I turned over in my mind several subjects. I thought, for instance, of showing them how this ocean that lay watchful and ready all about our island, all about the earth, was but a visible type or symbol of two other oceans, one very still, the other very awful and fierce; in fact, that three oceans surrounded us: one of the known world; one of the unseen world, that is, of death; one of the spirit-the devouring ocean of evil-and might I not have added yet another, encompassing and silencing all the rest-that of truth! The visible ocean seemed to make war upon the land, and the dwellers thereon. Restrained by the will of God and by him made subject more and more to the advancing knowledge of those who were created to rule over it, it was yet like a half-tamed beast ever ready to break loose and devour its masters. Of course this would have been but one aspect or appearance of it-for it was in truth all service; but this was the aspect I knew it must bear to those, seafaring themselves or not, to whom I had to speak. Then I thought I might show, that its power, like that of all things that man is ready to fear, had one barrier over which no commotion, no might of driving wind, could carry it, beyond which its loudest waves were dumb-the barrier of death. Hitherto and no further could its power reach. It could kill the body. It could dash in pieces the last little cock-boat to which the man clung, but thus it swept the man beyond its own region into the second sea of stillness, which we call death, out upon which the thoughts of those that are left behind can follow him only in great longings, vague conjectures, and mighty faith. Then I thought I could show them how, raving in fear, or lying still in calm deceit, there lay about the life of man a far more fearful ocean than that which threatened his body; for this would cast, could it but get a hold of him, both body and soul into hell-the sea of evil, of vice, of sin, of wrong-doing—they might call it by what name they pleased. This made war against the very essence of life, against God who is the truth, against love, against fairness, against fatherhood, motherhood, sisterhood, brotherhood, manhood, womanhood, against tenderness and grace and beauty, gathering into one pulp of festering death all that is noble, lovely, worshipful in the human nature made so divine that the one fearless man, the Lord Jesus Christ, shared it with us. This, I thought I might make them understand, was the only terrible sea, the only hopeless ocean from whose awful shore we must shrink and flee, the end of every voyage upon whose bosom was the bottom of its filthy waters, beyond the reach of all that is thought or spoken in the light, beyond life itself, but for the hand that reaches down from the upper ocean of truth, the hand of the Redeemer of men. I thought, I say, for a while, that I could make this, not definite, but very real to them. But I did not feel quite confident about it. Might they not in the symbolism forget the thing symbolised? And would not the symbol itself be ready to fade quite from their memory, or to return only in the vaguest shadow? And with the thought I perceived a far more excellent way. For the power of the truth lies of course in its revelation to the mind, and while for this there are a thousand means, none are so mighty as its embodiment in human beings and human life. There it is itself alive and active. And amongst these, what embodiment comes near to that in him who was perfect man in virtue of being at the root of the secret of humanity, in virtue of being the eternal Son of God? We are his sons in time: he is his Son in eternity, of whose sea time is but the broken sparkle. Therefore, I would talk to them about-but I will treat my reader now as if he were not my reader, but one of my congregation on that bright Sunday, my first in the Seaboard Parish, with the sea outside the church, flashing in the sunlight.

While I stood at the lectern, which was in front of the altar-screen, I could see little of my congregation, partly from my being on a level with them, partly from the necessity for keeping my eyes and thoughts upon that which I read. When, however, I rose from prayer in the pulpit; then I felt, as usual with me, that I was personally present for personal influence with my people, and then I saw, to my great pleasure, that one long bench nearly in the middle of the church was full of such sunburnt men as could not be mistaken for any but mariners, even if their torn and worn garments had not revealed that they must be the very men about whom we had been so much interested. Not only were they behaving with perfect decorum, but their rough faces wore an aspect of solemnity which I do not suppose was by any means their usual aspect.

I gave them no text. I had one myself, which was the necessary thing. They should have it by and by.

"Once upon a time," I said, "a man went up a mountain, and stayed there till it was dark, and stayed on. Now, a man who finds himself on a mountain as the sun is going down, especially if he is alone, makes haste to get down before it is dark. But this man went up when the sun was going down, and, as I say, continued there for a good long while after it was dark. You will want to know why. I will tell you. He wished to be alone. He hadn't a house of his own. He never had all the time he lived. He hadn't even a room of his own into which he could go, and bolt the door of it. True, he had kind friends, who gave him a bed: but they were all poor people, and their houses were small, and very likely they had large families, and he could not always find a quiet place to go into. And I dare say, if he had had a room, he would have been a little troubled with the children constantly coming to find him; for however much he loved them—and no man was ever so fond of children as he was—he needed to be left quiet sometimes. So, upon this occasion, he went up the mountain just to be quiet. He had been all day with a crowd of people, and he felt that it was time to be alone. For he had been talking with men all day, which tires and sometimes confuses a man's thoughts, and now he wanted to talk with God—for that makes a man strong, and puts all the confusion in order again, and lets a man know what he is about. So he went to the top of the hill. That was his secret chamber. It had no door; but that did not matter—no one could see him but God. There he stayed for hours—sometimes, I suppose, kneeling in his prayer to God; sometimes sitting, tired with his own thinking, on a stone; sometimes walking about, looking forward to what would come next—not anxious about it, but contemplating it. For just before he came up here, some of the people who had been with him wanted to make him a king; and this would not do—this was not what God wanted of him, and therefore he got rid of them, and came up here to talk to God. It was so quiet up here! The earth had almost vanished. He could see just the bare hilltop beneath him, a glimmer below, and the sky and the stars over his head. The people had all gone away to their own homes, and perhaps next day would hardly think about him at all, busy catching fish, or digging their gardens, or making things for their houses. But he knew that God would not forget him the next day any more than this day, and that God had sent him not to be the king that these people wanted him to be, but their servant. So, to make his heart strong, I say, he went up into the mountain alone to have a talk with his Father. How quiet it all was up here, I say, and how noisy it had been down there a little while ago! But God had been in the noise then as much as he was in the quiet now—the only difference being that he could not then be alone with him. I need not tell you who this man was—it was the king of men, the servant of men, the Lord Jesus Christ, the everlasting son of our Father in heaven.

"Now this mountain on which he was praying had a small lake at the foot of it—that is, about thirteen miles long, and five miles broad. Not wanting even his usual companions to be with him this evening—partly, I presume, because they were of the same mind as those who desired to take him by force and make him a king—he had sent them away in their boat, to go across this water to the other side, where were their homes and their families. Now, it was not pitch dark either on the mountain-top or on the water down below; yet I doubt if any other man than he would have been keen-eyed enough to discover that little boat down in the middle of the lake, much distressed by the west wind that blew right in their teeth. But he loved every man in it so much, that I think even as he was talking to his Father, his eyes would now and then go looking for and finding it—watching it on its way across to the other side. You must remember that it was a little boat; and there are often tremendous storms upon these small lakes with great mountains about them. For the wind will come all at once, rushing down through the clefts in as sudden a squall as ever overtook a sailor at sea. And then, you know, there is no sea-room. If the wind get the better of them, they are on the shore in a few minutes, whichever way the wind may blow. He saw them worn out at the oar, toiling in rowing, for the wind was contrary unto them. So the time for loneliness and prayer was over, and the time to go down out of his secret chamber and help his brethren was come. He did not need to turn and say good-bye to his Father, as if he dwelt on that mountain-top alone: his Father was down there on the lake as well. He went straight down. Could not his Father, if he too was down on the lake, help them without him? Yes. But he wanted him to do it, that they might see that he did it. Otherwise they would only have thought that the wind fell and the waves lay down, without supposing for a moment that their Master or his Father had had anything to do with it. They would have done just as people do now-a-days: they think that the help comes of itself, instead of by the will of him who determined from the first that men should be helped. So the Master went down the hill. When he reached the border of the lake, the wind being from the other side, he must have found the waves breaking furiously upon the rocks. But that made no difference to him. He looked out as he stood alone on the edge amidst the rushing wind and the noise of the water, out over the waves under the clear, starry sky, saw where the tiny boat was tossed about like a nutshell, and set out."

The mariners had been staring at me up to this point, leaning forward on their benches, for sailors are nearly as fond of a good yarn as they are of tobacco; and I heard afterwards that they had voted parson's yarn a good one. Now, however, I saw one of them, probably more ignorant than the others, cast a questioning glance at his neighbour. It was not returned, and he fell again into a listening attitude. He had no idea of what was coming. He probably thought parson had forgotten to say how Jesus had come by a boat.

"The companions of our Lord had not been willing to go away and leave him behind. Now, I dare say, they wished more than ever that he had been with them-not that they thought he could do anything with a storm, only that somehow they would have been less afraid with his face to look at. They had seen him cure men of dreadful diseases; they had seen him turn water into wine-some of them; they had seen him feed five thousand people the day before with five loaves and two small fishes; but had one of their number suggested that if he had been with them, they would have been safe from the storm, they would not have talked any nonsense about the laws of nature, not having learned that kind of nonsense, but they would have said that was quite a different thing-altogether too much to expect or believe: *nobody* could make the wind mind what it was about, or keep the water from drowning you if you fell into it and couldn't swim; or such-like.

"At length, when they were nearly worn out, taking feebler and feebler strokes, sometimes missing the water altogether, at other times burying their oars in it up to the handles-as they rose on the crest of a huge wave, one of them gave a cry, and they all stopped rowing and stared, leaning forward to peer through the darkness. And through the spray which the wind tore from the tops of the waves and scattered before it like dust, they saw, perhaps a hundred yards or so from the boat, something standing up from the surface of the water. It seemed to move towards them. It was a shape like a man. They all cried out with fear, as was natural, for they thought it must be a ghost."

How the faces of the sailors strained towards me at this part of the story! I was afraid one of them especially was on the point of getting up to speak, as we have heard of sailors doing in church. I went on.

"But then, over the noise of the wind and the waters came the voice they knew so well. It said, 'Be of good cheer: it is I. Be not afraid.' I should think, between wonder and gladness, they hardly knew for some moments where they were or what they were about. Peter was the first to recover himself apparently. In the first flush of his delight he felt strong and full of courage. 'Lord, if it be thou,' he said, 'bid me come unto thee on the water.' Jesus just said, 'Come;' and Peter unshipped his oar, and scrambled over the gunwale on to the sea. But when he let go his hold of the boat, and began to look about him, and saw how the wind was tearing the water, and how it tossed and raved between him and Jesus, he began to be afraid. And as soon as he began to be afraid he began to sink; but he had, notwithstanding his fear, just sense enough to do the one sensible thing; he cried out, 'Lord, save me.' And Jesus put out his hand, and took hold of him, and lifted him up out of the water, and said to him, 'O thou of little faith, wherefore didst thou doubt? And then they got into the boat, and the wind fell all at once, and altogether.

"Now, you will not think that Peter was a coward, will you? It wasn't that he hadn't courage, but that he hadn't enough of it. And why was it that he hadn't enough of it? Because he hadn't faith enough. Peter was always very easily impressed with the look of things. It wasn't at all likely that a man should be able to walk on the water; and yet Peter found himself standing on the water: you would have thought that when once he found himself standing on the water, he need not be afraid of the wind and the waves that lay between him and Jesus. But they looked so ugly that the fearfulness of them took hold of his heart, and his courage went. You would have thought that the greatest trial of his courage was over when he got out of the boat, and that there was comparatively little more ahead of him. Yet the sight of the waves and the blast of the boisterous wind were too much for him. I will tell you how I fancy it was; and I think there are several instances of the same kind of thing in Peter's life. When he got out of the boat, and found himself standing on the water, he began to think much of himself for being able to do so, and fancy himself better and greater than his companions, and an especial favourite of God above them. Now, there is nothing that kills faith sooner than pride. The two are directly against each other. The moment that Peter grew proud, and began to think about himself instead of about his Master, he began to lose his faith, and then he grew afraid, and then he began to sink-and that brought him to his senses. Then he forgot himself and remembered his Master, and then the hand of the Lord caught him, and the voice of the Lord gently rebuked him for the smallness of his faith, asking, 'Wherefore didst thou doubt?' I wonder if Peter was able to read his own heart sufficiently well to answer that *wherefore*. I do not think it likely at this period of his history. But God has immeasurable patience, and before he had done teaching Peter, even in this life, he had made him know quite well that pride and conceit were at the root of all his failures. Jesus did not point it out to him now. Faith was the only thing that would reveal that to him, as well as cure him of it; and was, therefore, the only thing he required of him in his rebuke. I suspect Peter was helped back into the boat by the eager hands of his companions already in a humbler state of mind than when he left it; but before his pride would be quite overcome, it would need that same voice of loving-kindness to call him Satan, and the voice of the cock to bring to his mind his loud boast, and his sneaking denial; nay, even the voice of one who had never seen the Lord till after his death, but was yet a readier disciple than he-the voice of St. Paul, to rebuke him because he dissembled, and was not downright honest. But at the last even he gained the crown of martyrdom, enduring all extremes, nailed to the cross like his Master, rather than deny his name. This should teach us to distrust ourselves, and yet have great hope for ourselves, and endless patience with other people. But to return to the story and what the story itself teaches us.

"If the disciples had known that Jesus saw them from the top of the mountain, and was watching them all the time, would they have been frightened at the storm, as I have little doubt they were, for they were only fresh-water fishermen, you know? Well, to answer my own question"—I went on in haste, for I saw one or two of the sailors with an audible answer hovering on their lips—"I don't know that, as they then were, it would have made so much difference to them; for none of them had risen much above the look of the things nearest them yet. But supposing you, who know something about him, were alone on the sea, and expecting your boat to be swamped every moment-if you found out all at once, that he was looking down at you from some lofty hilltop, and seeing all round about you in time and space too, would you be afraid? He might mean you to go to the bottom, you know. Would you mind going to the bottom with him looking at you? I do not think I should mind it myself. But I must take care lest I be boastful like Peter.

"Why should we be afraid of anything with him looking at us who is the Saviour of men? But we are afraid of him instead, because we do not believe that he is what he says he is-the Saviour of men. We do not believe what he offers us is salvation. We think it is slavery, and therefore continue slaves. Friends, I will speak to you who think you do believe in him. I am not going to say that you do not believe in him; but I hope I am going to make you say to yourselves that you too deserve to have those words of the Saviour spoken to you that were spoken to Peter, 'O ye of little faith!' Floating on the sea of your troubles, all kinds of fears and anxieties assailing you, is He not on the mountain-top? Sees he not the little boat of your fortunes tossed with the waves and the contrary wind? Assuredly he will come to you walking on the waters. It may not be in the way you wish, but if not, you will say at last, 'This is better.' It may be that he will come in a form that will make you cry out for fear in the weakness of your faith, as the disciples cried out-not believing any more than they did, that it can be he. But will not each of you arouse his courage that to you also he may say, as to the woman with the sick daughter whose confidence he so sorely tried, 'Great is thy faith'? Will you not rouse yourself, I say, that you may do him justice, and cast off the slavery of your own dread? O ye of little faith, wherefore will ye doubt? Do not think that the Lord sees and will not come. Down the mountain assuredly he will come, and you are now as safe in your troubles as the disciples were in theirs with Jesus looking on. They did not know it, but it was so: the Lord was watching them. And when you look back upon your past lives, cannot you see some instances of the same kind-when you felt and acted as if the Lord had forgotten you, and found afterwards that he had been watching you all the time?

"But the reason why you do not trust him more is that you obey him so little. If you would only, ask what God would have you to do, you would soon find your confidence growing. It is because you are proud, and envious, and greedy after gain, that you do not trust him more. Ah! trust him if it were only to get rid of these evil things, and be clean and beautiful in heart.

"O sailors with me on the ocean of life, will you, knowing that he is watching you from his mountain-top, do and say the things that hurt, and wrong, and disappoint him? Sailors on the waters that surround this globe, though there be no great mountain that overlooks the little lake on which you float, not the less does he behold you, and care for you, and watch over you. Will you do that which is unpleasing, distressful to him? Will you be irreverent, cruel, coarse? Will you say evil things, lie, and delight in vile stories and reports, with his eye on you, watching your ship on its watery ways, ever ready to come over the waves to help you? It is a fine thing, sailors, to fear nothing; but it would be far finer to fear nothing *because* he is above all, and over all, and in you all. For his sake and for his love, give up everything bad, and take him for your captain. He will be both captain and pilot to you, and steer you safe into the port of glory. Now to God the Father," &c.

This is very nearly the sermon I preached that first Sunday morning. I followed it up with a short enforcement in the afternoon.

END OF VOL. I.

VOLUME II.

CHAPTER I
ANOTHER SUNDAY EVENING.

In the evening we met in Connie's room, as usual, to have our talk. And this is what came out of it.

The window was open. The sun was in the west. We sat a little aside out of the course of his radiance, and let him look full into the room. Only Wynnie sat back in a dark corner, as if she would get out of his way. Below him the sea lay bluer than you could believe even when you saw it-blue with a delicate yet deep silky blue, the exquisiteness of which was thrown up by the brilliant white lines of its lapping on the high coast, to the northward. We had just sat down, when Dora broke out with—

"I saw Niceboots at church. He did stare at you, papa, as if he had never heard a sermon before."

"I daresay he never heard such a sermon before!" said Connie, with the perfect confidence of inexperience and partiality-not to say ignorance, seeing she had not heard the sermon herself.

Here Wynnie spoke from her dark corner, apparently forcing herself to speak, and thereby giving what seemed an unpleasant tone to what she said.

"Well, papa, I don't know what to think. You are always telling us to trust in Him; but how can we, if we are not good?"

"The first good thing you can do is to look up to him. That is the beginning of trust in him, and the most sensible thing that it is possible for us to do. That is faith."

"But it's no use sometimes."

"How do you know that?"

"Because you—I mean I—can't feel good, or care about it at all."

"But is that any ground for saying that it is no use-that he does not heed you? that he disregards the look cast up to him? that, till the heart goes with the will, he who made himself strong to be the helper of the weak, who pities most those who are most destitute-and who so destitute as those who do not love what they want to love-except, indeed, those who don't want to love? —that, till you are well on towards all right by earnestly seeking it, he won't help you? You are to judge him from yourself, are you? —forgetting that all the misery in you is just because you have not got his grand presence with you?"

I spoke so earnestly as to be somewhat incoherent in words. But my reader will understand. Wynnie was silent. Connie, as if partly to help her sister, followed on the same side.

"I don't know exactly how to say what I mean, papa, but I wish I could get this lovely afternoon, all full of sunshine and blue, into unity with all that you teach us about Jesus Christ. I wish this beautiful day came in with my thought of him, like the frame-gold and red and blue-that you have to that picture of him at home. Why doesn't it?"

"Just because you have not enough of faith in him, my dear. You do not know him well enough yet. You do not yet believe that he means you all gladness, heartily, honestly, thoroughly."

"And no suffering, papa?"

"I did not say that, my dear. There you are on your couch and can't move. But he does mean you such gladness, such a full sunny air and blue sea of blessedness that this suffering shall count for little in it; nay more, shall be taken in for part, and, like the rocks that interfere with the roll of the sea, flash out the white that glorifies and intensifies the whole-to pass away by and by, I trust, none the less. What a chance you have, my Connie, of believing in him, of offering upon his altar!"

"But," said my wife, "are not these feelings in a great measure dependent upon the state of one's health? I find it so different when the sunshine is inside me as well as outside me."

"Not a doubt of it, my dear. But that is only the more reason for rising above all that. From the way some people speak of physical difficulties—I don't mean you, wife-you would think that they were not merely the inevitable which they are, but the insurmountable which they are not. That they are physical and not spiritual is not only a great consolation, but a strong argument for overcoming them. For all that is physical is put, or is in the process of being put, under the feet of the spiritual. Do not mistake me. I do not say you can make yourself feel merry or happy when you are in a physical condition which is contrary to such mental condition. But you can withdraw from it-not all at once; but by practice and effort you can learn to withdraw from it, refusing to allow your judgments and actions to be ruled by it. You can climb up out of the fogs, and sit quiet in the sunlight on the hillside of faith. You cannot be merry down below in the fog, for there is the fog; but you can every now and then fly with the dove-wings of the soul up into the clear, to remind yourself that all this passes away, is but an accident, and that the sun shines always, although it may not at any given moment be shining on you. 'What does that matter?' you will learn to say. 'It is enough for me to know that the sun does shine, and that this is only a weary fog that is round about me for the moment. I shall come out into the light beyond presently.' This is faith-faith in God, who is the light, and is all in all. I believe that the most glorious instances of calmness in suffering are thus achieved; that the sufferers really do not suffer what one of us would if thrown into their physical condition without the refuge of their spiritual condition as well; for they have taken refuge in the inner chamber. Out of the spring of their life a power goes forth that quenches the flames of the furnace of their suffering, so far at least that it does not touch the deep life, cannot make them miserable, does not drive them from the possession of their soul in patience, which is the divine citadel of the suffering. Do you understand me, Connie?"

"I do, papa. I think perfectly."

"Still less, then, is the fact that the difficulty is physical to be used as an excuse for giving way to ill-temper, and, in fact, leaving ourselves to be tossed and shaken by every tremble of our nerves. That is as if a man should give himself into the hands and will and caprice of an organ-grinder, to work upon him, not with the music of the spheres, but with the wretched growling of the streets."

"But," said Wynnie, "I have heard you yourself, papa, make excuse for people's ill-temper on this very ground, that they were out of health. Indeed," she went on, half-crying, "I have heard you do so for myself, when you did not know that I was within hearing."

"Yes, my dear, most assuredly. It is no fiction, but a real difference that lies between excusing ourselves and excusing other people. No doubt the same excuse is just for ourselves that is just for other people. But we can do something to put ourselves right upon a higher principle, and therefore we should not waste our time in excusing, or even in condemning ourselves, but make haste up the hill. Where we cannot work-that is, in the life of another-we have time to make all the excuse we can. Nay more; it is only justice there. We are not bound to insist on our own rights, even of excuse; the wisest thing often is to forego them. But we are bound by heaven, earth, and hell to give them to other people. And, besides, what a comfort to ourselves to be able to say, 'It is true So-and-so was cross to-day. But it wasn't in the least that he wasn't friendly, or didn't like me; it was only that he had eaten something that hadn't agreed with him. I could see it in his eye. He had one of his headaches.' Thus, you see, justice to our neighbour, and comfort to ourselves, is one and the same thing. But it would be a sad thing to have to think that when we found ourselves in the same ungracious condition, from whatever cause, we had only to submit to it, saying, 'It is a law of nature,' as even those who talk most about laws will not do, when those laws come between them and their own comfort. They are ready enough then to call in the aid of higher laws, which, so far from being contradictory, overrule the lower to get things into something like habitable, endurable condition. It may be a law of nature; but what has the Law of the Spirit of Life to *propound anent* it? as the Scotch lawyers would say."

A little pause followed, during which I hope some of us were thinking. That Wynnie, at least, was, her next question made evident.

"What you say about a law of nature and a law of the Spirit makes me think again how that walking on the water has always been a puzzle to me."

"It could hardly be other, seeing that we cannot possibly understand it," I answered.

"But I find it so hard to believe. Can't you say something, papa, to help me to believe it?"

"I think if you admit what goes before, you will find there is nothing against reason in the story."

"Tell me, please, what you mean."

"If all things were made by Jesus, the Word of God, would it be reasonable that the water that he had created should be able to drown him?"

"It might drown his body."

"It would if he had not the power over it still, to prevent it from laying hold of him. But just think for a moment. God is a Spirit. Spirit is greater than matter. Spirit makes matter. Think what it was for a human body to have such a divine creative power dwelling in it as that which dwelt in the human form of Jesus! What power, and influence, and utter rule that spirit must have over the body in which it dwells! We cannot imagine how much; but if we have so much power over our bodies, how much more must the pure, divine Jesus, have had over his! I suspect this miracle was wrought, not through anything done to the water, but through the power of the spirit over the body of Jesus, which was all obedient thereto. I am not explaining the miracle, for that I cannot do. One day I think it will be plain common sense to us. But now I am only showing you what seems to me to bring us a step nearer to the essential region of the miracle, and so far make it easier to believe. If we look at the history of our Lord, we shall find that, true real human body as his was, it was yet used by his spirit after a fashion in which we cannot yet use our bodies. And this is only reasonable. Let me give you an instance. You remember how, on the Mount of Transfiguration, that body shone so that the light of it illuminated all his garments. You do not surely suppose that this shine was external-physical light, as we say, *merely?* No doubt it was physical light, for how else would their eyes have seen it? But where did it come from? What was its source? I think it was a natural outburst of glory from the mind of Jesus, filled with the perfect life of communion with his Father-the light of his divine blessedness taking form in physical radiance that permeated and glorified all that surrounded him. As the body is the expression of the soul, as the face of Jesus himself was the expression of the being, the thought, the love of Jesus in like manner this radiance was the natural expression of his gladness, even in the face of that of which they had been talking-Moses, Elias, and he-namely, the decease that he should accomplish at Jerusalem. Again, after his resurrection, he convinced the hands, as well as eyes, of doubting Thomas, that he was indeed there in the body; and yet that body could appear and disappear as the Lord willed. All this is full of marvel, I grant you; but probably far more intelligible to us in a further state of existence than some of the most simple facts with regard to our own bodies are to us now, only that we are so used to them that we never think how unintelligible they really are."

"But then about Peter, papa? What you have been saying will not apply to Peter's body, you know."

"I confess there is more difficulty there. But if you can suppose that such power were indwelling in Jesus, you cannot limit the sphere of its action. As he is the head of the body, his church, in all spiritual things, so I firmly believe, however little we can understand about it, is he in all natural things as well. Peter's faith in him brought even Peter's body within the sphere of the outgoing power of the Master. Do you suppose that because Peter ceased to be brave and trusting, therefore Jesus withdrew from him some sustaining power, and allowed him to sink? I do not believe it. I believe Peter's sinking followed naturally upon his loss of confidence. Thus he fell away from the life of the Master; was no longer, in that way I mean, connected with the Head, was instantly under the dominion of the natural law of gravitation, as we call it, and began to sink. Therefore the Lord must take other means to save him. He must draw nigh to him in a bodily manner. The pride of Peter had withdrawn him from the immediate spiritual influence of Christ, conquering his matter; and therefore the Lord must come over the stormy space between, come nearer to him in the body, and from his own height of safety above the sphere of the natural law, stretch out to him the arm of physical aid, lift him up, lead him to the boat. The whole salvation of the human race is figured in this story. It is all Christ, my love. —Does this help you to believe at all?"

"I think it does, papa. But it wants thinking over a good deal. I always find as I think, that lighter bits shine out here and there in a thing I have no hope of understanding altogether. That always helps me to believe that the rest might be understood too, if I were only clever enough."

"Simple enough, not clever enough, my dear."

"But there's one thing," said my wife, "that is more interesting to me than what you have been talking about. It is the other instances in the life of St. Peter in which you said he failed in a similar manner from pride or self-satisfaction."

"One, at least, seems to me very clear. You have often remarked to me, Ethel, how little praise servants can stand; how almost invariably after you have commended the diligence or skill of any of your household, as you felt bound to do, one of the first visible results was either a falling away in the performance by which she had gained the praise, or a more or less violent access, according to the nature of the individual, of self-conceit, soon breaking out in bad temper or impertinence. Now you will see precisely the same kind of thing in Peter."

Here I opened my New Testament, and read fragmentarily, '"But whom say ye that I am?... Thou art the Christ, the Son of the living God....Blessed art thou, Simon....My Father hath revealed that unto thee. I will give unto thee the keys of the kingdom of heaven....I must suffer many things, and be killed, and be raised again the third day....Be it far from thee, Lord. This shall not be unto thee....Get thee behind me, Satan. Thou art an offence unto me.' Just contemplate the change here in the words of our Lord. 'Blessed art thou.' 'Thou art an offence unto me.' Think what change has passed on Peter's mood before the second of these words could be addressed to him to whom the first had just been spoken. The Lord had praised him. Peter grew self-sufficient, even to the rebuking of him whose praise had so uplifted him. But it is ever so. A man will gain a great moral victory: glad first, then uplifted, he will fall before a paltry temptation. I have sometimes wondered, too, whether his denial of our Lord had anything to do with his satisfaction with himself for making that onslaught upon the high priest's servant. It was a brave thing and a faithful to draw a single sword against a multitude. In his fiery eagerness and inexperience, the blow, well meant to cleave Malchus's head, missed, and only cut off his ear; but Peter had herein justified his confident saying that he would not deny him. He was not one to deny his Lord who had been the first to confess him! Yet ere the cock had crowed, ere the morning had dawned, the vulgar grandeur of the palace of the high priest (for let it be art itself, it was vulgar grandeur beside that grandeur which it caused Peter to deny), and the accusing tone of a maid-servant, were enough to make him quail whom the crowd with lanterns, and torches, and weapons, had only roused to fight. True, he was excited then, and now he was cold in the middle of the night, with Jesus gone from his sight a prisoner, and for the faces of friends that had there surrounded him and strengthened him with their sympathy, now only the faces of those who were, or whom at least Peter thought to be on the other side, looking at him curiously, as a strange intruder into their domains. Alas, that the courage which led him to follow the Lord should have thus led him, not to deny him, but into the denial of him! Yet why should I say *alas?* If the denial of our Lord lay in his heart a possible thing, only prevented by his being kept in favourable circumstances for confessing him, it was a thousand times better that he should deny him, and thus know what a poor weak thing that heart of his was, trust it no more, and give it up to the Master to make it strong, and pure, and grand. For such an end the Lord was willing to bear all the pain of Peter's denial. O, the love of that Son of Man, who in the midst of all the wretched weaknesses of those who surrounded him, loved the best in them, and looked forward to his own victory for them that they might become all that they were meant to be-like him; that the lovely glimmerings of truth and love that were in them now-the breakings forth of the light that lighteneth every man-might grow into the perfect human day; loving them even the more that they were so helpless, so oppressed, so far from that ideal which was their life, and which all their dim desires were reaching after!"

Here I ceased, and a little overcome with the great picture in my soul to which I had been able only to give the poorest expression, rose, and retired to my own room. There I could only fall on my knees and pray that the Lord Christ, who had died for me, might have his own way with me-that it might be worth his while to have done what he did and what he was doing now for me. To my Elder Brother, my Lord, and my God, I gave myself yet again, confidently, because he cared to have me, and my very breath was his. I *would* be what he wanted, who knew all about it, and had done everything that I might be a son of God —a living glory of gladness.

CHAPTER II
NICEBOOTS.

The next morning the captain of the lost vessel called upon me early to thank me for himself and his men. He was a fine honest-looking burly fellow, dressed in blue from head to heel. He might have sat for a portrait of Chaucer's shipman, as far as his hue and the first look of him went. It was clear that "in many a tempest had his beard be shake," and certainly "the hote somer had made his hew all broun;" but farther the likeness would hardly go, for the "good fellow" which Chaucer applies with such irony to the shipman of his time, who would filch wine, and drown all the captives he made in a sea-fight, was clearly applicable in good earnest to this shipman. Still, I thought I had something to bring against him, and therefore before we parted I said to him —

"They tell me, captain, that your vessel was not seaworthy, and that you could not but have known that."

"She was my own craft, sir, and I judged her fit for several voyages more. If she had been A 1 she couldn't have been mine; and a man must do what he can for his family."

"But you were risking your life, you know."

"A few chances more or less don't much signify to a sailor, sir. There ain't nothing to be done without risk. You'll find an old tub go voyage after voyage, and she beyond bail, and a clipper fresh off the stocks go down in the harbour. It's all in the luck, sir, I assure you."

"Well, if it were your own life I should have nothing to say, seeing you have a family to look after; but what about the poor fellows who made the voyage with you? Did they know what kind of a vessel they were embarking in?"

"Wherever the captain's ready to go he'll always find men ready to follow him. Bless you, sir, they never asks no questions. If a sailor was always to be thinking of the chances, he'd never set his foot off shore."

"Still, I don't think it's right they shouldn't know."

"I daresay they knowed all about the old brig as well as I did myself. You gets to know all about a craft just as you do about her captain. She's got a character of her own, and she can't hide it long, any more than you can hide yours, sir, begging your pardon."

"I daresay that's all correct, but still I shouldn't like anyone to say to me, 'You ought to have told me, captain.' Therefore, you see, I'm telling you, captain, and now I'm clear. —Have a glass of wine before you go," I concluded, ringing the bell.

"Thank you, sir. I'll turn over what you've been saying, and anyhow I take it kind of you."

So we parted. I have never seen him since, and shall not, most likely, in this world. But he looked like a man that could understand why and wherefore I spoke as I did. And I had the advantage of having had a chance of doing something for him first of all. Let no man who wants to do anything for the soul of a man lose a chance of doing something for his body. He ought to be willing, and ready, which is more than willing, to do that whether or not; but there are those who need this reminder. Of many a soul Jesus laid hold by healing the suffering the body brought upon it. No one but himself can tell how much the nucleus of the church was composed of and by those who had received health from his hands, loving-kindness from the word of his mouth. My own opinion is that herein lay the very germ of the kernel of what is now the ancient, was then the infant church; that from them, next to the disciples themselves, went forth the chief power of life in love, for they too had seen the Lord, and in their own humble way could preach and teach concerning him. What memories of him theirs must have been!

Things went on very quietly, that is, as I mean now, from the view-point of a historian, without much to record bearing notably upon after events, for the greater part of the next week. I wandered about my parish, making acquaintance with different people in an outside sort of way, only now and then finding an opportunity of seeing into their souls except by conclusion. But I enjoyed endlessly the aspects of the country. It was not picturesque except in parts. There was little wood and there were no hills, only undulations, though many of them were steep enough even from a pedestrian's point of view. Neither, however, were there any plains except high moorland tracts. But the impression of the whole country was large, airy, sunshiny, and it was clasped in the arms of the infinite, awful, yet how bountiful sea-if one will look at the ocean in its world-wide, not to say its eternal aspects, and not out of the fears of a hidebound love of life! The sea and the sky, I must confess, dwarfed the earth, made it of small account beside them; but who could complain of such an influence? At least, not I. My children bathed in this sea every day, and gathered strength and knowledge from it. It was, as I have indicated, a dangerous coast to bathe upon. The sweep of the tides varied with the varying sands that were cast up. There was now in one place, now in another, a strong *undertow*, as they called it —a reflux, that is, of the inflowing waters, which was quite sufficient to carry those who could not swim out into the great deep, and rendered much exertion necessary, even in those who could, to regain the shore. But there was a fine strong Cornish woman to take charge of the ladies and the little boys, and she, watching the ways of the wild monster, knew the when and the where, and all about it.

Connie got out upon the downs every day. She improved in health certainly, and we thought a little even in her powers of motion. The weather continued superb. What rain there was fell at night, just enough for Nature to wash her face with and so look quite fresh in the morning. We contrived a dinner on the sands on the other side of the bay, for the Friday of this same week.

The morning rose gloriously. Harry and Charlie were turning the house upside down, to judge by their noise, long before I was in the humour to get up, for I had been reading late the night before. I never made much objection to mere noise, knowing that I could stop it the moment I pleased, and knowing, which was of more consequence, that so far from there being anything wrong in making a noise, the sea would make noise enough in our ears before we left Kilkhaven. The moment, however, that I heard a thread of whining or a burst of anger in the noise, I would interfere at once-treating these just as things that must be dismissed at once. Harry and Charlie were, I say, to use their own form of speech, making such a row that morning, however, that I was afraid of some injury to the house or furniture, which were not our own. So I opened my door and called out—

"Harry! Charlie! What on earth are you about?"

"Nothing, papa," answered Charlie. "Only it's so jolly!"

"What is jolly, my boy?" I asked.

"O, I don't know, papa! It's *so* jolly!"

"Is it the sunshine?" thought I; "and the wind? God's world all over? The God of gladness in the hearts of the lads? Is it that? No wonder, then, that they cannot tell yet what it is!"

I withdrew into my room; and so far from seeking to put an end to the noise —I knew Connie did not mind it-listened to it with a kind of reverence, as the outcome of a gladness which the God of joy had kindled in their hearts. Soon after, however, I heard certain dim growls of expostulation from Harry, and having, from experience, ground for believing that the elder was tyrannising over the younger, I stopped that and the noise together, sending Charlie to find out where the tide would be between one and two o'clock, and Harry to run to the top of the hill, and find out the direction of the wind. Before I was dressed, Charlie was knocking at my door with the news that it would be half-tide about one; and Harry speedily followed with the discovery that the wind was north-east by south-west, which of course determined that the sun would shine all day.

As the dinner-hour drew near, the servants went over, with Walter at their head, to choose a rock convenient for a table, under the shelter of the rocks on the sands across the bay. Thither, when Walter returned, we bore our Connie, carrying her litter close by the edge of the retreating tide, which sometimes broke in a ripple of music under her, wetting our feet with innocuous rush. The child's delight was extreme, as she thus skimmed the edge of the ocean, with the little ones gambolling about her, and her mamma and Wynnie walking quietly on the landward side, for she wished to have no one between her and the sea.

After scrambling with difficulty over some rocky ledges, and stopping at Connie's request, to let her look into a deep pool in the sand, which somehow or other retained the water after the rest had retreated, we set her down near the mouth of a cave, in the shadow of a rock. And there was our dinner nicely laid for us on a flat rock in front of the cave. The cliffs rose behind us, with curiously curved and variously angled strata. The sun in his full splendour threw dark shadows on the brilliant yellow sand, more and more of which appeared as the bright blue water withdrew itself, now rippling over it as if it meant to hide it all up again, now uncovering more as it withdrew for another rush. Before we had finished our dinner, the foremost wavelets appeared so far away over the plain of the sand, that it seemed a long walk to the edge that had been almost at our feet a little while ago. Between us and it lay a lovely desert of glittering sand.

When even Charlie and Harry had arrived at the conclusion that it was time to stop eating, we left the shadow and went out into the sun, carrying Connie and laying her down in the midst of "the ribbed sea-sand," which was very ribby to-day. On a shawl a little way off from her lay her baby, crowing and kicking with the same jollity that had possessed the boys ever since the morning. I wandered about with Wynnie on the sands, picking up amongst other things strange creatures in thin shells ending in vegetable-like tufts, if I remember rightly. My wife sat on the end of Connie's litter, and Dora and the boys, a little way off, were trying how far the full force of three wooden spades could, in digging a hole, keep ahead of the water which was ever tumbling in the sand from the sides of the same. Behind, the servants were busy washing the plates in a pool, and burying the fragments of the feast; for I made it a rule wherever we went that the fair face of nature was not to be defiled. I have always taken the part of excursionists in these latter days of running to and fro, against those who complain that the loveliest places are being destroyed by their inroads. But there is one most offensive, even disgusting habit amongst them-that of leaving bones, fragments of meat pies, and worse than all, pieces of greasy paper about the place, which I cannot excuse, or at least defend. Even the surface of Cumberland and Westmoreland lakes will be defiled with these floating abominations-not abominations at all if they are decently burned or buried when done with, but certainly abominations when left to be cast hither and thither in the wind, over the grass, or on the eddy and ripple of the pure water, for days after those who have thus left their shame behind them have returned to their shops or factories. I forgive them for trampling down the grass and the ferns. That cannot be helped, and in comparison of the good they get, is not to be considered at all. But why should they leave such a savage trail behind them as this, forgetting too that though they have done with the spot, there are others coming after them to whom these remnants must be an offence?

At length in our roaming, Wynnie and I approached a long low ridge of rock, rising towards the sea into which it ran. Crossing this, we came suddenly upon the painter whom Dora had called Niceboots, sitting with a small easel before him. We were right above him ere we knew. He had his back towards us, so that we saw at once what he was painting.

"O, papa!" cried Wynnie involuntarily, and the painter looked round.

"I beg your pardon," I said. "We came over from the other side, and did not see you before. I hope we have not disturbed you much."

"Not in the least," he answered courteously, and rose as he spoke.

I saw that the subject on his easel suggested that of which Wynnie had been making a sketch at the same time, on the day when Connie first lay on the top of the opposite cliff. But he was not even looking in the same direction now.

"Do you mind having your work seen before it is finished?"

"Not in the least, if the spectators will do me the favour to remember that most processes have to go through a seemingly chaotic stage," he answered.

I was struck with the mode and tone of the remark.

"Here is no common man," I said to myself, and responded to him in something of a similar style.

"I wish we could always keep that in mind with regard to human beings themselves, as well as their works," I said aloud.

The painter looked at me, and I looked at him.

"We speak each from the experience of his own profession, I presume," he said.

"But," I returned, glancing at the little picture in oils upon his easel, "your work here, though my knowledge of painting is next to nothing-perhaps I ought to say nothing at all-this picture must have long ago passed the chaotic stage."

"It is nearly as much finished as I care to make it," he returned. "I hardly count this work at all. I am chiefly amusing, or rather pleasing, my own fancy at present."

"Apparently," I remarked, "you had the conical rock outside the hay for your model, and now you are finishing it with your back turned towards it. How is that?"

"I will soon explain," he answered. "The moment I saw this rock, it reminded me of Dante's Purgatory."

"Ah, you are a reader of Dante?" I said. "In the original, I hope."

"Yes. A friend of mine, a brother painter, an Italian, set me going with that, and once going with Dante, nobody could well stop. I never knew what intensity *per se* was till I began to read Dante."

"That is quite my own feeling. Now, to return to your picture."

"Without departing at all from natural forms, I thought to make it suggest the Purgatorio to anyone who remembered the description given of the place *ab extra* by Ulysses, in the end of the twenty-sixth canto of the Inferno. Of course, that thing there is a mere rock, yet it has certain mountain forms about it. I have put it at a much greater distance, you see, and have sought to make it look a solitary mountain in the midst of a great water. You will discover even now that the circles of the Purgatory are suggested without any approach, I think, to artificial structure; and there are occasional hints at figures, which you cannot definitely detach from the rocks-which, by the way, you must remember, were in one part full of sculptures. I have kept the mountain near enough, however, to indicate the great expanse of wild flowers on the top, which Matilda was so busy gathering. I want to indicate too the wind up there in the terrestrial paradise, ever and always blowing one way. You remember, Mr. Walton?" —for the young man, getting animated, began to talk as if we had known each other for some time-and here he repeated the purport of Dante's words in English:

> "An air of sweetness, changeless in its flow,
> With no more strength than in a soft wind lies,
> Smote peacefully against me on the brow.
> By which the leaves all trembling, level-wise,
> Did every one bend thitherward to where
> The high mount throws its shadow at sunrise."

"I thought you said you did not use translations?"

"I thought it possible that-Miss Walton (?)" interrogatively this —"might not follow the Italian so easily, and I feared to seem pedantic."

"She won't lag far behind, I flatter myself," I returned. "Whose translation do you quote?"

He hesitated a moment; then said carelessly:

"I have cobbled a few passages after that fashion myself."

"It has the merit of being near the original at least," I returned; "and that seems to me one of the chief merits a translation can possess."

"Then," the painter resumed, rather hastily, as if to avoid any further remark upon his verses, "you see those white things in the air above?" Here he turned to Wynnie. "Miss Walton will remember —I think she was making a drawing of the rock at the same time I was-how the seagulls, or some such birds-only two or three of them-kept flitting about the top of it?"

"I remember quite well," answered Wynnie, with a look of appeal to me.

"Yes," I interposed; "my daughter, in describing what she had been attempting to draw, spoke especially of the birds over the rock. For she said the white lapping of the waves looked like spirits trying to get loose, and the white birds like foam that had broken its chains, and risen in triumph into the air."

Here Mr. Niceboots, for as yet I did not know what else to call him, looked at Wynnie almost with a start.

"How wonderfully that falls in with my fancy about the rock!" he said. "Purgatory indeed! with imprisoned souls lapping at its foot, and the free souls winging their way aloft in ether. Well, this world is a kind of purgatory anyhow-is it not, Mr. Walton?"

"Certainly it is. We are here tried as by fire, to see what our work is-whether wood, hay, and stubble, or gold and silver and precious stones."

"You see," resumed the painter, "if anybody only glanced at my little picture, he would take those for sea-birds; but if he looked into it, and began to suspect me, he would find out that they were Dante and Beatrice on their way to the sphere of the moon."

"In one respect at least, then, your picture has the merit of corresponding to fact; for what thing is there in the world, or what group of things, in which the natural man will not see merely the things of nature, but the spiritual man the things of the spirit?"

"I am no theologian," said the painter, turning away, I thought somewhat coldly.

But I could see that Wynnie was greatly interested in him. Perhaps she thought that here was some enlightenment of the riddle of the world for her, if she could but get at what he was thinking. She was used to my way of it: here might be something new.

"If I can be of any service to Miss Walton with her drawing, I shall be happy," he said, turning again towards me.

But his last gesture had made me a little distrustful of him, and I received his advances on this point with a coldness which I did not wish to make more marked than his own towards my last observation.

"You are very kind," I said; "but Miss Walton does not presume to be an artist."

I saw a slight shade pass over Wynnie's countenance. When I turned to Mr. Niceboots, a shade of a different sort was on his. Surely I had said something wrong to cast a gloom on two young faces. I made haste to make amends.

"We are just going to have some coffee," I said, "for my servants, I see, have managed to kindle a fire. Will you come and allow me to introduce you to Mrs. Walton?"

"With much pleasure," he answered, rising from the rock whereon, as he spoke about his picture, he had again seated himself. He was a fine-built, black-bearded, sunburnt fellow, with clear gray eyes notwithstanding, a rather Roman nose, and good features generally. But there was an air of suppression, if not of sadness, about him, however, did not in the least interfere with the manliness of his countenance, or of its expression.

"But," I said, "how am I to effect an introduction, seeing I do not yet know your name."

I had had to keep a sharp look-out on myself lest I should call him Mr. Niceboots. He smiled very graciously and replied,

"My name is Percivale-Charles Percivale."

"A descendant of Sir Percivale of King Arthur's Round Table?"

"I cannot count quite so far back," he answered, "as that-not quite to the Conquest," he added, with a slight deepening of his sunburnt hue. "I do come of a fighting race, but I cannot claim Sir Percivale."

We were now walking along the edge of the still retreating waves towards the group upon the sands, Mr. Percivale and I foremost, and Wynnie lingering behind.

"O, do look here papa!" she cried, from some little distance.

We turned and saw her gazing at something on the sand at her feet. Hastening back, we found it to be a little narrow line of foam-bubbles, which the water had left behind it on the sand, slowly breaking and passing out of sight. Why there should be foam-bubbles there then, and not always, I do not know. But there they were-and such colours! deep rose and grassy green and ultramarine blue; and, above all, one dark, yet brilliant and intensely-burnished, metallic gold. All of them were of a solid-looking burnished colour, like opaque body-colour laid on behind translucent crystal. Those little ocean bubbles were well worth turning to see; and so I said to Wynnie. But, as we gazed, they went on vanishing, one by one. Every moment a heavenly glory of hue burst, and was nowhere.

We walked away again towards the rest of our party.

"Don't you think those bubbles more beautiful than any precious stones you ever saw, papa?"

"Yes, my love, I think they are, except it be the opal. In the opal, God seems to have fixed the evanescent and made the vanishing eternal."

"And flowers are more beautiful things than jewels?' she said interrogatively.

"Many-perhaps most flowers are," I granted. "And did you ever see such curves and delicate textures anywhere else as in the clouds, papa?"

"I think not-in the cirrhous clouds at least-the frozen ones. But what are you putting me to my catechism for in this way, my child?"

"O, papa, I could go on a long time with that catechism; but I will end with one question more, which you will perhaps find a little harder to answer. Only I daresay you have had an answer ready for years lest one of us should ask you some day."

"No, my love. I never got an answer ready for anything lest one of my children should ask me. But it is not surprising either that children should be puzzled about the things that have puzzled their father, or that by the time they are able to put the questions, he should have found out some sort of an answer to most of them. Go on with your catechism, Wynnie. Now for your puzzle!"

"It's not a funny question, papa; it's a very serious one. I can't think why the unchanging God should have made all the most beautiful things wither and grow ugly, or burst and vanish, or die somehow and be no more. Mamma is not so beautiful as she once was, is she?"

"In one way, no; but in another and better way, much more so. But we will not talk about her kind of beauty just now; we will keep to the more material loveliness of which you have been speaking-though, in truth, no loveliness can be only material. Well, then, for my answer; it is, I think, because God loves the beauty so much that he makes all beautiful things vanish quickly."

"I do not understand you, papa."

"I daresay not, my dear. But I will explain to you a little, if Mr. Percivale will excuse me."

"On the contrary, I am greatly interested, both in the question and the answer."

"Well, then, Wynnie; everything has a soul and a body, or something like them. By the body we know the soul. But we are always ready to love the body instead of the soul. Therefore, God makes the body die continually, that we may learn to love the soul indeed. The world is full of beautiful things, but God has saved many men from loving the mere bodies of them, by making them poor; and more still by reminding them that if they be as rich as Croesus all their lives, they will be as poor as Diogenes-poorer, without even a tub-when this world, with all its pictures, scenery, books, and-alas for some Christians! —bibles even, shall have vanished away."

"Why do you say *alas*, papa-if they are Christians especially?"

"I say *alas* only from their point of view, not from mine. I mean such as are always talking and arguing from the Bible, and never giving themselves any trouble to do what it tells them. They insist on the anise and cummin, and forget the judgment, mercy, and faith. These worship the body of the truth, and forget the soul of it. If the flowers were not perishable, we should cease to contemplate their beauty, either blinded by the passion for hoarding the bodies of them, or dulled by the hebetude of commonplaceness that the constant presence of them would occasion. To compare great things with small, the flowers wither, the bubbles break, the clouds and sunsets pass, for the very same holy reason, in the degree of its application to them, for which the Lord withdrew from his disciples and ascended again to his Father-that the Comforter, the Spirit of Truth, the Soul of things, might come to them and abide with them, and so the Son return, and the Father be revealed. The flower is not its loveliness, and its loveliness we must love, else we shall only treat them as flower-greedy children, who gather and gather, and fill hands and baskets, from a mere desire of acquisition, excusable enough in them, but the same in kind, however harmless in mode, and degree, and object, as the avarice of the miser. Therefore God, that we may always have them, and ever learn to love their beauty, and yet more their truth, sends the beneficent winter that we may think about what we have lost, and welcome them when they come again with greater tenderness and love, with clearer eyes to see, and purer hearts to understand, the spirit that dwells in them. We cannot do without the 'winter of our discontent.' Shakspere surely saw that when he makes Titania say, in *A Midsummer Night's Dream*:

'The human mortals want their winter here' —

namely, to set things right; and none of those editors who would alter the line seem to have been capable of understanding its import."

"I think I understand you a little," answered Wynnie. Then, changing her tone, "I told you, papa, you would have an answer ready; didn't I?"

"Yes, my child; but with this difference —I found the answer to meet my own necessities, not yours."

"And so you had it ready for me when I wanted it."

"Just so. That is the only certainty you have in regard to what you give away. No one who has not tasted it and found it good has a right to offer any spiritual dish to his neighbour."

Mr. Percivale took no part in our conversation. The moment I had presented him to Mrs. Walton and Connie, and he had paid his respects by a somewhat stately old-world obeisance, he merged the salutation into a farewell, and, either forgetting my offer of coffee, or having changed his mind, withdrew, a little to my disappointment, for, notwithstanding his lack of response where some things he said would have led me to expect it, I had begun to feel much interested in him.

He was scarcely beyond hearing, when Dora came up to me from her digging, with an eager look on her sunny face.

"Hasn't he got nice boots, papa?"

"Indeed, my dear, I am unable to support you in that assertion, for I never saw his boots."

"I did, then," returned the child; "and I never saw such nice boots."

"I accept the statement willingly," I replied; and we heard no more of the boots, for his name was now substituted for his nickname. Nor did I see himself again for some days-not in fact till next Sunday-though why he should come to church at all was something of a puzzle to me, especially when I knew him better.

CHAPTER III
THE BLACKSMITH.

The next day I set out after breakfast to inquire about a blacksmith. It was not every or any blacksmith that would do. I must not fix on the first to do my work because he was the first. There was one in the village, I soon learned; but I found him an ordinary man, who, I have no doubt, could shoe a horse and avoid the quick, but from whom any greater delicacy of touch was not to be expected. Inquiring further, I heard of a young smith who had lately settled in a hamlet a couple of miles distant, but still within the parish. In the afternoon I set out to find him. To my surprise, he was a pale-faced, thoughtful-looking man, with a huge frame, which appeared worn rather than naturally thin, and large eyes that looked at the anvil as if it was the horizon of the world. He had got a horse-shoe in his tongs when I entered. Notwithstanding the fire that glowed on the hearth, and the sparks that flew like a nimbus in eruption from about his person, the place looked very dark to me entering from the glorious blaze of the almost noontide sun, and felt cool after the deep lane through which I had come, and which had seemed a very reservoir of sunbeams. I could see the smith by the glow of his horse-shoe; but all between me and the shoe was dark.

"Good-morning," I said. "It is a good thing to find a man by his work. I heard you half a mile off or so, and now I see you, but only by the glow of your work. It is a grand thing to work in fire."

He lifted his hammered hand to his forehead courteously, and as lightly as if the hammer had been the butt-end of a whip.

"I don't know if you would say the same if you had to work at it in weather like this," he answered.

"If I did not," I returned, "that would be the fault of my weakness, and would not affect the assertion I have just made, that it is a fine thing to work in fire."

"Well, you may be right," he rejoined with a sigh, as, throwing the horse-shoe he had been fashioning from the tongs on the ground, he next let the hammer drop beside the anvil, and leaning against it held his head for a moment between his hands, and regarded the floor. "It does not much matter to me," he went on, "if I only get through my work and have done with it. No man shall say I shirked what I'd got to do. And then when it's over there won't be a word to say agen me, or —"

He did not finish the sentence. And now I could see the sunlight lying in a somewhat dreary patch, if the word *dreary* can be truly used with respect to any manifestation of sunlight, on the dark clay floor.

"I hope you are not ill," I said.

He made no answer, but taking up his tongs caught with it from a beam one of a number of roughly-finished horse-shoes which hung there, and put it on the fire to be fashioned to a certain fit. While he turned it in the fire, and blew the bellows, I stood regarding him. "This man will do for my work," I said to myself; "though I should not wonder from the look of him if it was the last piece of work he ever did under the New Jerusalem." The smith's words broke in on my meditations.

"When I was a little boy," he said, "I once wanted to stay at home from school. I had, I believe, a little headache, but nothing worth minding. I told my mother that I had a headache, and she kept me, and I helped her at her spinning, which was what I liked best of anything. But in the afternoon the Methodist preacher came in to see my mother, and he asked me what was the matter with me, and my mother answered for me that I had a bad head, and he looked at me; and as my head was quite well by this time, I could not help feeling guilty. And he saw my look, I suppose, sir, for I can't account for what he said any other way; and he turned to me, and he said to me, solemn-like, 'Is your head bad enough to send you to the Lord Jesus to make you whole?' I could not speak a word, partly from bashfulness, I suppose, for I was but ten years old. So he followed it up, as they say: 'Then you ought to be at school,' says he. I said nothing, because I couldn't. But never since then have I given in as long as I could stand. And I can stand now, and lift my hammer, too," he said, as he took the horse-shoe from the forge, laid it on the anvil, and again made a nimbus of coruscating iron.

"You are just the man I want," I said. "I've got a job for you, down to Kilkhaven, as you say in these parts."

"What is it, sir? Something about the church? I should ha' thought the church was all spick and span by this time."

"I see you know who I am," I said.

"Of course I do," he answered. "I don't go to church myself, being brought up a Methodist; but anything that happens in the parish is known the next day all over it."

"You won't mind doing my job though you are a Methodist, will you?" I asked.

"Not I, sir. If I've read right, it's the fault of the Church that we don't pull all alongside. You turned us out, sir; we didn't go out of ourselves. At least, if all they say is true, which I can't be sure of, you know, in this world."

"You are quite right there though," I answered. "And in doing so, the Church had the worst of it-as all that judge and punish their neighbours have. But you have been the worse for it, too: all of which is to be laid to the charge of the Church. For there is not one clergyman I know-mind, I say, that I know-who would have made such a cruel speech to a boy as that the Methodist parson made to you."

"But it did me good, sir?"

"Are you sure of that? I am not. Are you sure, first of all, it did not make you proud? Are you sure it has not made you work beyond your strength —I don't mean your strength of arm, for clearly that is all that could be wished, but of your chest, your lungs? Is there not some danger of your leaving someone who is dependent on you too soon unprovided for? Is there not some danger of your having worked as if God were a hard master? —of your having worked fiercely, indignantly, as if he wronged you by not caring for you, not understanding you?"

He returned me no answer, but hammered momently on his anvil. Whether he felt what I meant, or was offended at my remark, I could not then tell. I thought it best to conclude the interview with business.

"I have a delicate little job that wants nice handling, and I fancy you are just the man to do it to my mind," I said.

"What is it, sir?" he asked, in a friendly manner enough.

"If you will excuse me, I would rather show it to you than talk about it," I returned.

"As you please, sir. When do you want me?"

"The first hour you can come."

"To-morrow morning?"

"If you feel inclined."

"For that matter, I'd rather go to bed."

"Come to me instead: it's light work."

"I will, sir-at ten o'clock."

"If you please."

And so it was arranged.

CHAPTER IV
THE LIFE-BOAT.

The next day rose glorious. Indeed, early as the sun rose, I saw him rise-saw him, from the down above the house, over the land to the east and north, ascend triumphant into his own light, which had prepared the way for him; while the clouds that hung over the sea glowed out with a faint flush, as anticipating the hour when the west should clasp the declining glory in a richer though less dazzling splendour, and shine out the bride of the bridegroom east, which behold each other from afar across the intervening world, and never mingle but in the sight of the eyes. The clear pure light of the morning made me long for the truth in my heart, which alone could make me pure and clear as the morning, tune me up to the concert-pitch of the nature around me. And the wind that blew from the sunrise made me hope in the God who had first breathed into my nostrils the breath of life, that he would at length so fill me with his breath, his wind, his spirit, that I should think only his thoughts and live his life, finding therein my own life, only glorified infinitely.

After breakfast and prayers, I would go to the church to await the arrival of my new acquaintance the smith. In order to obtain entrance, I had, however, to go to the cottage of the sexton. This was not my first visit there, so that I may now venture to take my reader with me. To reach the door, I had to cross a hollow by a bridge, built, for the sake of the road, over what had once been the course of a rivulet from the heights above. Now it was a kind of little glen, or what would in Scotland be called a den, I think, grown with grass and wild flowers and ferns, some of them, rare and fine. The roof of the cottage came down to the road, and, until you came quite near, you could not but wonder where the body that supported this head could be. But you soon saw that the ground fell suddenly away, leaving a bank against which the cottage was built. Crossing a garden of the smallest, the principal flowers of which were the stonecrop on its walls, by a flag-paved path, you entered the building, and, to your surprise, found yourself, not in a little cottage kitchen, as you expected, but in a waste-looking space, that seemed to have forgotten the use for which it had been built. There was a sort of loft along one side of it, and it was heaped with indescribable lumber-looking stuff with here and there a hint at possible machinery. The place had been a mill for grinding corn, and its wheel had been driven by the stream which had run for ages in the hollow of which I have already spoken. But when the canal came to be constructed, the stream had to be turned aside from its former course, and indeed was now employed upon occasion to feed the canal; so that the mill of necessity had fallen into disuse and decay. Crossing this floor, you entered another door, and turning sharp to the left, went down a few steps of a ladder-sort of stair, and after knocking your hat against a beam, emerged in the comfortable quaint little cottage kitchen you had expected earlier. A cheerful though small fire burns in the grate-for even here the hearth-fire has vanished from the records of cottage-life —and is pleasant here even in the height of summer, though it is counted needful only for cooking purposes. The ceiling, which consists only of the joists and the boards that floor the bedroom above, is so low, that necessity, if not politeness, would compel you to take off your already-bruised hat. Some of these joists, you will find, are made further useful by supporting each a shelf, before which hangs a little curtain of printed cotton, concealing the few stores and postponed eatables of the house-forming, in fact, both store-room and larder of the family. On the walls hang several coloured prints, and within a deep glazed frame the figure of a ship in full dress, carved in rather high relief in sycamore.

As I now entered, Mrs. Coombes rose from a high-backed settle near the fire, and bade me good-morning with a courtesy.

"What a lovely day it is, Mrs. Coombes! It is so bright over the sea," I said, going to the one little window which looked out on the great Atlantic, "that one almost expects a great merchant navy to come sailing into Kilkhaven-sunk to the water's edge with silks, and ivory, and spices, and apes, and peacocks, like the ships of Solomon that we read about-just as the sun gets up to the noonstead."

Before I record her answer, I turn to my reader, who in the spirit accompanies me, and have a little talk with him. I always make it a rule to speak freely with the less as with the more educated of my friends. I never *talk down* to them, except I be expressly explaining something to them. The law of the world is as the law of the family. Those children grow much the faster who hear all that is going on in the house. Reaching ever above themselves, they arrive at an understanding at fifteen, which, in the usual way of things, they would not reach before five-and-twenty or thirty; and this in a natural way, and without any necessary priggishness, except such as may belong to their parents. Therefore I always spoke to the poor and uneducated as to my own people,—freely, not much caring whether I should be quite understood or not; for I believed in influences not to be measured by the measure of the understanding.

But what was the old woman's answer? It was this:

"I know, sir. And when I was as young as you"—I was not so very young, my reader may well think—"I thought like that about the sea myself. Everything come from the sea. For my boy Willie he du bring me home the beautifullest parrot and the talkingest you ever see, and the red shawl all worked over with flowers: I'll show it to you some day, sir, when you have time. He made that ship you see in the frame there, sir, all with his own knife, out on a bit o' wood that he got at the Marishes, as they calls it, sir—a bit of an island somewheres in the great sea. But the parrot's gone dead like the rest of them, sir.—Where am I? and what am I talking about?" she added, looking down at her knitting as if she had dropped a stitch, or rather as if she had forgotten what she was making, and therefore what was to come next.

"You were telling me how you used to think of the sea—"

"When I was as young as you. I remember, sir. Well, that lasted a long time-lasted till my third boy fell asleep in the wide water; for it du call it falling asleep, don't it, sir?"

"The Bible certainly does," I answered.

"It's the Bible I be meaning, of course," she returned. "Well, after that, but I don't know what began it, only I did begin to think about the sea as something that took away things and didn't bring them no more. And somehow or other she never look so blue after that, and she give me the shivers. But now, sir, she always looks to me like one o' the shining ones that come to fetch the pilgrims. You've heard tell of the *Pilgrim's Progress*, I daresay, sir, among the poor people; for they du say it was written by a tinker, though there be a power o' good things in it that I think the gentlefolk would like if they knowed it."

"I do know the book-nearly as well as I know the Bible," I answered; "and the shining ones are very beautiful in it. I am glad you can think of the sea that way."

"It's looking in at the window all day as I go about the house," she answered, "and all night too when I'm asleep; and if I hadn't learned to think of it that way, it would have driven me mad, I du believe. I was forced to think that way about it, or not think at all. And that wouldn't be easy, with the sound of it in your ears the last thing at night and the first thing in the morning."

"The truth of things is indeed the only refuge from the look of things," I replied. "But now I want the key of the church, if you will trust me with it, for I have something to do there this morning; and the key of the tower as well, if you please."

With her old smile, ripened only by age, she reached the ponderous keys from the nail where they hung, and gave them into my hand. I left her in the shadow of her dwelling, and stepped forth into the sunlight. The first thing I observed was the blacksmith waiting for me at the church door.

Now that I saw him in the full light of day, and now that he wore his morning face upon which the blackness of labour had not yet gathered, I could see more plainly how far he was from well. There was a flush on his thin cheek by which the less used exercise of walking revealed his inward weakness, and the light in his eyes had something of the far-country in them—"the light that never was on sea or shore." But his speech was cheerful, for he had been walking in the light of this world, and that had done something to make the light within him shine a little more freely.

"How do you find yourself to-day?" I asked.

"Quite well, sir, I thank you," he answered. "A day like this does a man good. But," he added, and his countenance fell, "the heart knoweth its own bitterness."

"It may know it too much," I returned, "just because it refuses to let a stranger intermeddle therewith."

He made no reply. I turned the key in the great lock, and the iron-studded oak opened and let us into the solemn gloom.

It did not require many minutes to make the man understand what I wanted of him.

"We must begin at the bells and work down," he said.

So we went up into the tower, where, with the help of a candle I fetched for him from the cottage, he made a good many minute measurements; found that carpenter's work was necessary for the adjustment of the hammers and cranks and the leading of the rods, undertook the management of the whole, and in the course of an hour and a half went home to do what had to be done before any fixing could be commenced, assuring me that he had no doubt of bringing the job to a satisfactory conclusion, although the force of the blow on the bell would doubtless have to be regulated afterwards by repeated trials.

"In a fortnight, I hope you will be able to play a tune to the parish, sir," he added, as he took his leave.

I resolved, if possible, to know more of the man, and find out his trouble, if haply I might be able to give him any comfort, for I was all but certain that there was a deeper cause for his gloom than the state of his health.

When he was gone I stood with the key of the church in my hand, and looked about me. Nature at least was in glorious health-sunshine in her eyes, light fantastic cloud-images passing through her brain, her breath coming and going in soft breezes perfumed with the scents of meadows and wild flowers, and her green robe shining in the motions of her gladness. I turned to lock the church door, though in my heart I greatly disapproved of locking the doors of churches, and only did so now because it was not my church, and I had no business to force my opinions upon other customs. But when I turned I received a kind of questioning shock. There was the fallen world, as men call it, shining in glory and gladness, because God was there; here was the way into the lost Paradise, yea, the door into an infinitely higher Eden than that ever had or ever could have been, iron-clamped and riveted, gloomy and low-browed like the entrance to a sepulchre, and surrounded with the grim heads of grotesque monsters of the deep. What did it mean? Here was contrast enough to require harmonising, or if that might not be, then accounting for. Perhaps it was enough to say that although God made both the kingdom of nature and the kingdom of grace, yet the symbol of the latter was the work of man, and might not altogether correspond to God's idea of the matter. I turned away thoughtful, and went through the churchyard with my eye on the graves.

As I left the churchyard, still looking to the earth, the sound of voices reached my ear. I looked up. There, down below me, at the foot of the high bank on which I stood, lay a gorgeous shining thing upon the bosom of the canal, full of men, and surrounded by men, women, and children, delighting in its beauty. I had never seen such a thing before, but I knew at once, as by instinct, which of course it could not have been, that it was the life-boat. But in its gorgeous colours, red and white and green, it looked more like the galley that bore Cleopatra to Actium. Nor, floating so light on the top of the water, and broad in the beam withal, curved upward and ornamented at stern and stem, did it look at all like a creature formed to battle with the fierce elements. A pleasure-boat for floating between river banks it seemed, drawn by swans mayhap, and regarded in its course by fair eyes from green terrace-walks, or oriel windows of ancient houses on verdant lawns. Ten men sat on the thwarts, and one in the stern by the yet useless rudder, while men and boys drew the showy thing by a rope downward to the lock-gates. The men in the boat, wore blue jerseys, but you could see little of the colour for strange unshapely things that they wore above them, like an armour cut out of a row of organ pipes. They were their cork-jackets; for every man had to be made into a life-boat himself. I descended the bank, and stood on the edge of the canal as it drew near. Then I saw that every oar was loosely but firmly fastened to the rowlock, so that it could be dropped and caught again in a moment; and that the gay sides of the unwieldy-looking creature were festooned with ropes from the gunwale, for the men to lay hold of when she capsized, for the earlier custom of fastening the men to their seats had been quite given up, because their weight under the water might prevent the boat from righting itself again, and the men could not come to the surface. Now they had a better chance in their freedom, though why they should not be loosely attached to the boat, I do not quite see.

They towed the shining thing through the upper gate of the lock, and slowly she sank from my sight, and for some moments was no more to be seen, for I had remained standing where first she passed me. All at once there she was beyond the covert of the lock-head, abroad and free, fleeting from the strokes of ten swift oars over the still waters of the bay towards the waves that roared further out where the ground-swell was broken by the rise of the sandy coast. There was no vessel in danger now, as the talk of the spectators informed me; it was only for exercise and show that they went out. It seemed all child's play for a time; but when they got among the broken waves, then it looked quite another thing. The motion of the waters laid hold upon her, and soon tossed her fearfully, now revealing the whole of her capacity on the near side of one of their slopes, now hiding her whole bulk in one of their hollows beyond. She, careless as a child in the troubles of the world, floated about amongst them with what appeared too much buoyancy for the promise of a safe return. Again and again she was driven from her course towards the low rocks on the other side of the bay, and again and again, returned to disport herself, like a sea-animal, as it seemed, upon the backs of the wild, rolling, and bursting billows.

"Can she go no further?" I asked of the captain of the coastguard, whom I found standing by my side.

"Not without some danger," he answered.

"What, then, must it be in a storm!" I remarked.

"Then of course," he returned, "they must take their chance. But there is no good in running risks for nothing. That swell is quite enough for exercise."

"But is it enough to accustom them to face the danger that will come?" I asked.

"With danger comes courage," said the old sailor.

"Were you ever afraid?"

"No, sir. I don't think I ever was afraid. Yes, I believe I was once for one moment, no more, when I fell from the maintop-gallant yard, and felt myself falling. But it was soon over, for I only fell into the maintop. I was expecting the smash on deck when I was brought up there. But," he resumed, "I don't care much about the life-boat. My rockets are worth a good deal more, as you may see, sir, before the winter is over; for seldom does a winter pass without at least two or three wrecks close by here on this coast. The full force of the Atlantic breaks here, sir. I *have* seen a life-boat —not that one —*she's* done nothing yet-pitched stern over stem; not capsized, you know, sir, in the ordinary way, but struck by a wave behind while she was just hanging in the balance on the knife-edge of a wave, and flung a somerset, as I say, stern over stem, and four of her men lost."

While we spoke I saw on the pier-head the tall figure of the painter looking earnestly at the boat. I thought he was regarding it chiefly from an artistic point of view, but I became aware before long that that would not have been consistent with the character of Charles Percivale. He had been, I learned afterwards, a crack oarsman at Oxford, and had belonged to the University boat, so that he had some almost class-sympathy with the doings of the crew.

In a little while the boat sped swiftly back, entered the lock, was lifted above the level of the storm-heaved ocean, and floated up the smooth canal calmly as if she had never known what trouble was. Away up to the pretty little Tudor-fashioned house in which she lay-one could almost fancy dreaming of storms to come-she went, as softly as if moved only by her "own sweet will," in the calm consolation for her imprisonment of having tried her strength, and found therein good hope of success for the time when she should rush to the rescue of men from that to which, as a monster that begets monsters, she a watching Perseis, lay ready to offer battle. The poor little boat lying in her little house watching the ocean, was something signified in my eyes, and not less so after what came in the course of changing seasons and gathered storms.

All this time I had the keys in my hand, and now went back to the cottage to restore them to their place upon the wall. When I entered there was a young woman of a sweet interesting countenance talking to Mrs. Coombes. Now as it happened, I had never yet seen the daughter who lived with her, and thought this was she.

"I've found your daughter at last then?" I said, approaching them.

"Not yet, sir. She goes out to work, and her hands be pretty full at present. But this be almost my daughter, sir," she added. "This is my next daughter, Mary Trehern, from the south. She's got a place near by, to be near her mother that is to be, that's me."

Mary was hanging her head and blushing, as the old woman spoke.

"I understand," I said. "And when are you going to get your new mother, Mary? Soon I hope."

But she gave me no reply-only hung her head lower and blushed deeper.

Mrs. Coombes spoke for her.

"She's shy, you see, sir. But if she was to speak her mind, she would ask you whether you wouldn't marry her and Willie when he comes home from his next voyage."

Mary's hands were trembling now, and she turned half away.

"With all my heart," I said.

The girl tried to turn towards me, but could not. I looked at her face a little more closely. Through all its tremor, there was a look of constancy that greatly pleased me. I tried to make her speak.

"When do you expect Willie home?" I said.

She made a little gasp and murmur, but no articulate words came.

"Don't be frightened, Mary," said her mother, as I found she always called her. "The gentleman won't be sharp with you."

She lifted a pair of soft brown eyes with one glance and a smile, and then sank them again.

"He'll be home in about a month, we think," answered the mother. "She's a good ship he's aboard of, and makes good voyages."

"It is time to think about the bans, then," I said.

"If you please, sir," said the mother.

"Just come to me about it, and I will attend to it-when you think proper."

I thought I could hear a murmured "Thank you, sir," from the girl, but I could not be certain that she spoke. I shook hands with them, and went for a stroll on the other side of the bay.

CHAPTER V
MR. PERCIVALE.

When I reached home I found that Connie was already on her watch-tower. For while I was away, they had carried her out that she might see the life-boat. I followed her, and found the whole family about her couch, and with them Mr. Percivale, who was showing her some sketches that he had made in the neighbourhood. Connie knew nothing of drawing; but she seemed to me always to catch the feeling of a thing. Her remarks therefore were generally worth listening to, and Mr. Percivale was evidently interested in them. Wynnie stood behind Connie, looking over her shoulder at the drawing in her hand.

"How do you get that shade of green?" I heard her ask as I came up.

And then Mr. Percivale proceeded to tell her; from which beginning they went on to other things, till Mr. Percivale said —

"But it is hardly fair, Miss Walton; to criticise my work while you keep your own under cover."

"I wasn't criticising, Mr. Percivale; was I, Connie?"

"I didn't hear her make a single remark, Mr. Percivale," said Connie, taking her sister's side.

To my surprise they were talking away with the young man as if they had known him for years, and my wife was seated at the foot of the couch, apparently taking no exception to the suddenness of the intimacy. I am afraid, when I think of it, that a good many springs would be missing from the world's history if they might not flow till the papas gave their wise consideration to everything about the course they were to take.

"I think, though," added Connie, "it is only fair that Mr. Percivale *should* see your work, Wynnie."

"Then I will fetch my portfolio, if Mr. Percivale will promise to remember that I have no opinion of it. At the same time, if I could do what I wanted to do, I think I should not be ashamed of showing my drawings even to him."

And now I was surprised to find how like grown women my daughters could talk. To me they always spoke like the children they were; but when I heard them now it seemed as if they had started all at once into ladies experienced in the ways of society. There they were chatting lightly, airily, and yet decidedly, a slight tone of badinage interwoven, with a young man of grace and dignity, whom they had only seen once before, and who had advanced no farther, with Connie at least, than a stately bow. They had, however, been a whole hour together before I arrived, and their mother had been with them all the while, which gives great courage to good girls, while, I am told, it shuts the mouths of those who are sly. But then it must be remembered that there are as great differences in mothers as in girls. And besides, I believe wise girls have an instinct about men that all the experience of other men cannot overtake. But yet again, there are many girls foolish enough to mistake a mere impulse for instinct, and vanity for insight.

As Wynnie spoke, she turned and went back to the house to fetch some of her work. Now, had she been going a message for me, she would have gone like the wind; but on this occasion she stepped along in a stately manner, far from devoid of grace, but equally free from frolic or eagerness. And I could not help noting as well that Mr. Percivale's eyes followed her. What I felt or fancied is of no consequence to anybody. I do not think, even if I were writing an autobiography, I should be forced to tell *all* about myself. But an autobiography is further from my fancy, however much I may have trenched upon its limits, than any other form of literature with which I am acquainted.

She was not long in returning, however, though she came back with the same dignified motion.

"There is nothing really worth either showing or concealing," she said to Mr. Percivale, as she handed him the portfolio, to help himself, as it were. She then turned away, as if a little feeling of shyness had come over her, and began to look for something to do about Connie. I could see that, although she had hitherto been almost indifferent about the merit of her drawings, she had a new-born wish that they might not appear altogether contemptible in the eyes of Mr.

Percivale. And I saw, too, that Connie's wide eyes were taking in everything. It was wonderful how Connie's deprivations had made her keen in observing. Now she hastened to her sister's rescue even from such a slight inconvenience as the shadow of embarrassment in which she found herself-perhaps from having seen some unusual expression in my face, of which I was unconscious, though conscious enough of what might have occasioned such.

"Give me your hand, Wynnie," said Connie, "and help me to move one inch further on my side.—I may move just that much on my side, mayn't I, papa?"

"I think you had better not, my dear, if you can do without it," I answered; for the doctor's injunctions had been strong.

"Very well, papa; but I feel as if it would do me good."

"Mr. Turner will be here next week, you know; and you must try to stick to his rules till he comes to see you. Perhaps he will let you relax a little."

Connie smiled very sweetly and lay still, while Wynnie stood holding her hand.

Meantime Mr. Percivale, having received the drawings, had walked away with them towards what they called the storm tower—a little building standing square to the points of the compass, from little windows, in which the coastguard could see with their telescopes along the coast on both sides and far out to sea. This tower stood on the very edge of the cliff, but behind it there was a steep descent, to reach which apparently he went round the tower and disappeared. He evidently wanted to make a leisurely examination of the drawings-somewhat formidable for Wynnie, I thought. At the same time, it impressed me favourably with regard to the young man that he was not inclined to pay a set of stupid and untrue compliments the instant the portfolio was opened, but, on the contrary, in order to speak what was real about them, would take the trouble to make himself in some adequate measure acquainted with them. I therefore, to Wynnie's relief, I fear, strolled after him, seeing no harm in taking a peep at his person, while he was taking a peep at my daughter's mind. I went round the tower to the other side, and there saw him at a little distance below me, but further out on a great rock that overhung the sea, connected with the cliff by a long narrow isthmus, a few yards lower than the cliff itself, only just broad enough to admit of a footpath along its top, and on one side going sheer down with a smooth hard rock-face to the sands below. The other side was less steep, and had some grass upon it. But the path was too narrow, and the precipice too steep, for me to trust my head with the business of guiding my feet along it. So I stood and saw him from the mainland-saw his head at least bent over the drawings; saw how slowly he turned from one to the other; saw how, after having gone over them once, he turned to the beginning and went over them again, even more slowly than before; saw how he turned the third time to the first. Then, getting tired, I went back to the group on the down; caught sight of Charlie and Harry turning heels over head down the slope toward the house; found that my wife had gone home-in fact, that only Connie and Wynnie were left. The sun had disappeared under a cloud, and the sea had turned a little slaty; the yellow flowers in the short down-grass no longer caught the eye with their gold, and the wind that bent their tops had just the suspicion of an edge in it. And Wynnie's face looked a little cloudy too, I thought, and I feared that it was my fault. I fancied there was just a tinge of beseeching in Connie's eye, as I looked at her, thinking there might be danger for her in the sunlessness of the wind. But I do not know that all this, even the clouding of the sun, may not have come out of my own mind, the result of my not being quite satisfied with myself because of the mood I had been in. My feeling had altered considerably in the mean time.

"Run, Wynnie, and ask Mr. Percivale, with my compliments, to come and lunch with us," I said-more to let her see I was not displeased, however I might have looked, than for any other reason. She went-sedately as before.

Almost as soon as she was gone, I saw that I had put her in a difficulty. For I had discovered, very soon after coming into these parts, that her head was no more steady than my own on high places, for she up had never been used to such in our own level country, except, indeed, on the stair that led down to the old quarry and the well, where, I can remember now, she always laid her hand on the balustrade with some degree of tremor, although she had been in the way of going up and down from childhood. But if she could not cross that narrow and really dangerous isthmus, still less could she call to a man she had never seen but once, across the intervening chasm. I therefore set off after her, leaving Connie lying there in loneliness, between the sea and the sky. But when I got to the other side of the little tower, instead of finding her standing hesitating on the brink of action, there she was on the rock beyond. Mr. Percivale had risen, and was evidently giving an answer to my invitation; at least, the next moment she turned to come back, and he followed. I stood trembling almost to see her cross the knife-back of that ledge. If I had not been almost fascinated, I should have turned and left them to come together, lest the evil fancy should cross her mind that I was watching them, for it was one thing to watch him with her drawings, and quite another to watch him with herself. But I stood and stared as she crossed. In the middle of the path, however-up to which point she had been walking with perfect steadiness and composure-she lifted her eyes-by what influence I cannot tell-saw me, looked as if she saw ghost, half lifted her arms, swayed as if she would fall, and, indeed, was falling over the precipice when Percivale, who was close behind her caught her in his arms, almost too late for both of them. So nearly down was she already, that her weight bent him over the rocky side, till it seemed as if he must yield, or his body snap. For he bent from the waist, and looked as if his feet only kept a hold on the ground. It was all over in a moment, but in that moment it made a sun-picture on my brain, which returns, ever and again, with such vivid agony that I cannot hope to get rid of it till I get rid of the brain itself in which lies the impress. In another moment they were at my side-she with a wan, terrified smile, he in a ruddy alarm. I was unable to speak, and could only, with trembling steps, lead the way from the dreadful spot. I reproached myself afterwards for my want of faith in God; but I had not had time to correct myself yet. Without a word on their side either, they followed me. Before we reached Connie, I recovered myself sufficiently to say, "Not a word to Connie," and they understood me. I told Wynnie to run to the house, and send Walter to help me to carry Connie home. She went, and, until Walter came, I talked to Mr. Percivale as if nothing had happened. And what made me feel yet more friendly towards him was, that he did not do as some young men wishing to ingratiate themselves would have done: he did not offer to help me to carry Connie home. I saw that the offer rose in his mind, and that he repressed it. He understood that I must consider such a permission as a privilege not to be accorded to the acquaintance of a day; that I must know him better before I could allow the weight of my child to rest on his strength. I was even grateful to him for this knowledge of human nature. But he responded cordially to my invitation to lunch with us, and walked by my side as Walter and I bore the precious burden home.

During our meal, he made himself quite agreeable; talked well on the topics of the day, not altogether as a man who had made up his mind, but not the less, rather the more, as a man who had thought about them, and one who did not find it so easy to come to a conclusion as most people do-or possibly as not feeling the necessity of coming to a conclusion, and therefore preferring to allow the conclusion to grow instead of constructing one for immediate use. This I rather liked than otherwise. His behaviour, I need hardly say, after what I have told of him already, was entirely that of a gentleman; and his education was good. But what I did not like was, that as often as the conversation made a bend in the direction of religious matters, he was sure to bend it away in some other direction as soon as ever he laid his next hold upon it. This, however, might have various reasons to account for it, and I would wait.

After lunch, as we rose from the table, he took Wynnie's portfolio from the side-table where he had laid it, and with no more than a bow and thanks returned it to her. She, I thought, looked a little disappointed, though she said as lightly as she could:

"I am afraid you have not found anything worthy of criticism in my poor attempts, Mr. Percivale?"

"On the contrary, I shall be most happy to tell you what I think of them if you would like to hear the impression they have made upon me," he replied, holding out his hand to take the portfolio again.

"I shall be greatly obliged to you," she said, returning it, "for I have had no one to help me since I left school, except a book called *Modern Painters*, which I think has the most beautiful things in it I ever read, but which I lay down every now and then with a kind of despair, as if I never could do anything worth doing. How long the next volume is in coming! Do you know the author, Mr. Percivale?"

"I wish I did. He has given me much help. I do not say I can agree with everything he writes; but when I do not, I have such a respect for him that I always feel as if he must be right whether he seems to me to be right or not. And if he is severe, it is with the severity of love that will speak only the truth."

This last speech fell on my ear like the tone of a church bell. "That will do, my friend," thought I. But I said nothing to interrupt.

By this time he had laid the portfolio open on the side-table, and placed a chair in front of it for my daughter. Then seating himself by her side, but without the least approach to familiarity, he began to talk to her about her drawings, praising, in general, the feeling, but finding fault with the want of nicety in the execution-at least so it appeared to me from what I could understand of the conversation.

"But," said my daughter, "it seems to me that if you get the feeling right, that is the main thing."

"No doubt," returned Mr. Percivale; "so much the main thing that any imperfection or coarseness or untruth which interferes with it becomes of the greatest consequence."

"But can it really interfere with the feeling?"

"Perhaps not with most people, simply because most people observe so badly that their recollections of nature are all blurred and blotted and indistinct, and therefore the imperfections we are speaking of do not affect them. But with the more cultivated it is otherwise. It is for them you ought to work, for you do not thereby lose the others. Besides, the feeling is always intensified by the finish, for that belongs to the feeling too, and must, I should think, have some influence even where it is not noted."

"But is it not a hopeless thing to attempt the finish of nature?"

"Not at all; to the degree, that is, in which you can represent anything else of nature. But in this drawing now you have no representative of, nothing to hint at or recall the feeling of the exquisiteness of nature's finish. Why should you not at least have drawn a true horizon-line there? Has the absolute truth of the meeting of sea and sky nothing to do with the feeling which such a landscape produces? I should have thought you would have learned that, if anything, from Mr. Ruskin."

Mr. Percivale spoke earnestly. Wynnie, either from disappointment or despair, probably from a mixture of both, apparently fancied that, or rather felt as if, he was scolding her, and got cross. This was anything but dignified, especially with a stranger, and one who was doing his best to help her. And yet, somehow, I must with shame confess I was not altogether sorry to see it. In fact, my reader, I must just uncover my sin, and say that I felt a little jealous of Mr. Percivale. The negative reason was that I had not yet learned to love him. The only cure for jealousy is love. But I was ashamed too of Wynnie's behaving so childishly. Her face flushed, the tears came in her eyes, and she rose, saying, with a little choke in her voice —

"I see it's no use trying. I won't intrude any more into things I am incapable of. I am much obliged to you, Mr. Percivale, for showing me how presumptuous I have been."

The painter rose as she rose, looking greatly concerned. But he did not attempt to answer her. Indeed she gave him no time. He could only spring after her to open the door for her. A more than respectful bow as she left the room was his only adieu. But when he turned his face again towards me, it expressed even a degree of consternation.

"I fear," he said, approaching me with an almost military step, much at variance with the shadow upon his countenance, "I fear I have been rude to Miss Walton, but nothing was farther —"

"You mistake entirely, Mr. Percivale. I heard all you were saying, and you were not in the least rude. On the contrary, I consider you were very kind to take the trouble with her you did. Allow me to make the apology for my daughter which I am sure she will wish made when she recovers from the disappointment of finding more obstacles in the way of her favourite pursuit than she had previously supposed. She is only too ready to lose heart, and she paid too little attention to your approbation and too much-in proportion, I mean-to your-criticism. She felt discouraged and lost her temper, but more with herself and her poor attempts, I venture to assure you, than with your remarks upon them. She is too much given to despising her own efforts."

"But I must have been to blame if I caused any such feeling with regard to those drawings, for I assure you they contain great promise."

"I am glad you think so. That I should myself be of the same opinion can be of no consequence."

"Miss Walton at least sees what ought to be represented. All she needs is greater severity in the quality of representation. And that would have grown without any remark from onlookers. Only a friendly criticism is sometimes a great help. It opens the eyes a little sooner than they would have opened of themselves. And time," he added, with a half sigh and with an appeal in his tone, as if he would justify himself to my conscience, "is half the battle in this world. It is over so soon."

"No sooner than it ought to be," I rejoined.

"So it may appear to you," he returned; "for you, I presume to conjecture, have worked hard and done much. I may or may not have worked hard-sometimes I think I have, sometimes I think I have not-but I certainly have done little. Here I am nearly thirty, and have made no mark on the world yet."

"I don't know that that is of so much consequence," I said. "I have never hoped for more than to rub out a few of the marks already made."

"Perhaps you are right," he returned. "Every man has something he can do, and more, I suppose, that he can't do. But I have no right to turn a visit into a visitation. Will you please tell Miss Walton that I am very sorry I presumed on the privileges of a drawing-master, and gave her pain. It was so far from my intention that it will be a lesson to me for the future."

With these words he took his leave, and I could not help being greatly pleased both with them and with his bearing. He was clearly anything but a common man.

CHAPTER VI
THE SHADOW OP DEATH.

When Wynnie appeared at dinner she looked ashamed of herself, and her face betrayed that she had been crying. But I said nothing, for I had confidence that all she needed was time to come to herself, that the voice that speaks louder than any thunder might make its stillness heard. And when I came home from my walk the next morning I found Mr. Percivale once more in the group about Connie, and evidently on the best possible terms with all. The same afternoon Wynnie went out sketching with Dora. I had no doubt that she had made some sort of apology to Mr. Percivale; but I did not make the slightest attempt to discover what had passed between them, for though it is of all things desirable that children should be quite open with their parents, I was most anxious to lay upon them no burden of obligation. For such burden lies against the door of utterance, and makes it the more difficult to open. It paralyses the speech of the soul. What I desired was that they should trust me so that faith should overcome all difficulty that might lie in the way of their being open with me. That end is not to be gained by any urging of admonition. Against such, growing years at least, if nothing else, will bring a strong reaction. Nor even, if so gained would the gain be at all of the right sort. The openness would not be faith. Besides, a parent must respect the spiritual person of his child, and approach it with reverence, for that too looks the Father in the face, and has an audience with him into which no earthly parent can enter even if he dared to desire it. Therefore I trusted my child. And when I saw that she looked at me a little shyly when we next met, I only sought to show her the more tenderness and confidence, telling her all about my plans with the bells, and my talks with the smith and Mrs. Coombes. She listened with just such interest as I had always been accustomed to see in her, asking such questions, and making such remarks as I might have expected, but I still felt that there was the thread of a little uneasiness through the web of our intercourse,—such a thread of a false colour as one may sometimes find wandering through the labour of the loom, and seek with pains to draw from the woven stuff. But it was for Wynnie to take it out, not for me. And she did not leave it long. For as she bade me good-night in my study, she said suddenly, yet with hesitating openness,

"Papa, I told Mr. Percivale that I was sorry I had behaved so badly about the drawings."

"You did right, my child," I replied. At the same moment a pang of anxiety passed through me lest under the influence of her repentance she should have said anything more than becoming. But I banished the doubt instantly as faithlessness in the womanly instincts of my child. For we men are always so ready and anxious to keep women right, like the wretched creature, Laertes, in *Hamlet*, who reads his sister such a lesson on her maidenly duties, but declines almost with contempt to listen to a word from her as to any co-relative obligation on his side!

And here I may remark in regard to one of the vexed questions of the day-the rights of women-that what women demand it is not for men to withhold. It is not their business to lay the law for women. That women must lay down for themselves. I confess that, although I must herein seem to many of my readers old-fashioned and conservative, I should not like to see any woman I cared much for either in parliament or in an anatomical class-room; but on the other hand I feel that women must be left free to settle that matter. If it is not good, good women will find it out and recoil from it. If it is good then God give them good speed. One thing they *have* a right to —a far wider and more valuable education than they have been in the way of receiving. When the mothers are well taught the generations will grow in knowledge at a fourfold rate. But still the teaching of life is better than all the schools, and common sense than all learning. This common sense is a rare gift, scantier in none than in those who lay claim to it on the ground of following commonplace, worldly, and prudential maxims. But I must return to my Wynnie.

"And what did Mr. Percivale say?" I resumed, for she was silent.

"He took the blame all on himself, papa."

"Like a gentleman," I said.

"But I could not leave it so, you know, papa, because that was not the truth."

"Well?"

"I told him that I had lost my temper from disappointment; that I had thought I did not care for my drawings because I was so far from satisfied with them, but when he made me feel that they were worth nothing, then I found from the vexation I felt that I had cared for them. But I do think, papa, I was more ashamed of having shown them, and vexed with myself, than cross with him. But I was very silly."

"Well, and what did he say?"

"He began to praise them then. But you know I could not take much of that, for what could he do?"

"You might give him credit for a little honesty, at least."

"Yes; but things may be true in a way, you know, and not mean much."

"He seems to have succeeded in reconciling you to the prosecution of your efforts, however; for I saw you go out with your sketching apparatus this afternoon."

"Yes," she answered shyly. "He was so kind that somehow I got heart to try again. He's very nice, isn't he?"

My answer was not quite ready.

"Don't you like him, papa?"

"Well—I like him-yes. But we must not be in haste with our judgments, you know. I have had very little opportunity of seeing into him. There is much in him that I like, but—"

"But what? please, papa."

"To tell the truth then, Wynnie, for I can speak my mind to you, my child, there is a certain shyness of approaching the subject of religion; so that I have my fears lest he should belong to any of these new schools of a fragmentary philosophy which acknowledge no source of truth but the testimony of the senses and the deductions made therefrom by the intellect."

"But is not that a hasty conclusion, papa?"

"That is a hasty question, my dear. I have come to no conclusion. I was only speaking confidentially about my fears."

"Perhaps, papa, it's only that he's not sure enough, and is afraid of appearing to profess more than he believes. I'm sure, if that's it, I have the greatest sympathy with him."

I looked at her, and saw the tears gathering fast in her eyes.

"Pray to God on the chance of his hearing you, my darling, and go to sleep," I said. "I will not think hardly of you because you cannot be so sure as I am. How could you be? You have not had my experience. Perhaps you are right about Mr. Percivale too. But it would be an awkward thing to get intimate with him, you know, and then find out that we did not like him after all. You couldn't like a man much, could you, who did not believe in anything greater than himself, anything marvellous, grand, beyond our understanding-who thought that he had come out of the dirt and was going back to the dirt?"

"I could, papa, if he tried to do his duty notwithstanding-for I'm sure I couldn't. I should cry myself to death."

"You are right, my child. I should honour him too. But I should be very sorry for him. For he would be so disappointed in himself."

I do not know whether this was the best answer to make, but I had little time to think.

"But you don't know that he's like that."

"I do not, my dear. And more, I will not associate the idea with him till I know for certain. We will leave it to ignorant old ladies who lay claim to an instinct for theology to jump at conclusions, and reserve ours-as even such a man as we have been supposing might well teach us-till we have sufficient facts from which to draw them. Now go to bed, my child."

"Good-night then, dear papa," she said, and left me with a kiss.

I was not altogether comfortable after this conversation. I had tried to be fair to the young man both in word and thought, but I could not relish the idea of my daughter falling in love with him, which looked likely enough, before I knew more about him, and found that *more* good and hope-giving. There was but one rational thing left to do, and that was to cast my care on him that careth for us–on the Father who loved my child more than even I could love her–and loved the young man too, and regarded my anxiety, and would take its cause upon himself. After I had lifted up my heart to him I was at ease, read a canto of Dante's *Paradise*, and then went to bed. The prematurity of a conversation with my wife, in which I found that she was very favourably impressed with Mr. Percivale, must be pardoned to the forecasting hearts of fathers and mothers.

As I went out for my walk the next morning, I caught sight of the sexton, with whom as yet I had had but little communication, busily trimming some of the newer graves in the churchyard. I turned in through the nearer gate, which was fashioned like a lych-gate, with seats on the sides and a stone table in the centre, but had no roof. The one on the other side of the church was roofed, but probably they had found that here no roof could resist the sea-blasts in winter. The top of the wall where the roof should have rested, was simply covered with flat slates to protect it from the rain.

"Good-morning, Coombes," I said.

He turned up a wizened, humorous old face, the very type of a gravedigger's, and with one hand leaning on the edge of the green mound, upon which he had been cropping with a pair of shears the too long and too thin grass, touched his cap with the other, and bade me a cheerful good-morning in return.

"You're making things tidy," I said.

"It take time to make them all comfortable, you see, sir," he returned, taking up his shears again and clipping away at the top and sides of the mound.

"You mean the dead, Coombes?"

"Yes, sir; to be sure, sir."

"You don't think it makes much difference to their comfort, do you, whether the grass is one length or another upon their graves?"

"Well no, sir. I don't suppose it makes *much* difference to them. But it look more comfortable, you know. And I like things to look comfortable. Don't you, sir?"

"To be sure I do, Coombes. And you are quite right. The resting-place of the body, although the person it belonged to be far away, should be respected."

"That's what I think, though I don't get no credit for it. I du believe the people hereabouts thinks me only a single hair better than a Jack Ketch. But I'm sure I du my best to make the poor things comfortable."

He seemed unable to rid his mind of the idea that the comfort of the departed was dependent upon his ministrations.

"The trouble I have with them sometimes! There's now this same one as lies here, old Jonathan Giles. He have the gout so bad! and just as I come within a couple o' inches o' the right depth, out come the edge of a great stone in the near corner at the foot of the bed. Thinks I, he'll never lie comfortable with that same under his gouty toe. But the trouble I had to get out that stone! I du assure you, sir, it took me nigh half the day. —But this be one of the nicest places to lie in all up and down the coast —a nice gravelly soil, you see, sir; dry, and warm, and comfortable. Them poor things as comes out of the sea must quite enjoy the change, sir."

There was something grotesque in the man's persistence in regarding the objects of his interest from this point of view. It was a curious way for the humanity that was in him to find expression; but I did not like to let him go on thus. It was so much opposed to all that I believed and felt about the change from this world to the next!

"But, Coombes," I said, "why will you go on talking as if it made an atom of difference to the dead bodies where they were buried? They care no more about it than your old coat would care where it was thrown after you had done with it."

He turned and regarded his coat where it hung beside him on the headstone of the same grave at which he was working, shook his head with a smile that seemed to hint a doubt whether the said old coat would be altogether so indifferent to its treatment when, it was past use as I had implied. Then he turned again to his work, and after a moment's silence began to approach me from another side. I confess he had the better of me before I was aware of what he was about.

"The church of Boscastle stands high on the cliff. You've been to Boscastle, sir?"

I told him I had not yet, but hoped to go before the summer was over.

"Ah, you should see Boscastle, sir. It's a wonderful place. That's where I was born, sir. When I was a by that church was haunted, sir. It's a damp place, and the wind in it awful. I du believe it stand higher than any church in the country, and have got more wind in it of a stormy night than any church whatsomever. Well, they said it was haunted; and sure enough every now and then there was a knocking heard down below. And this always took place of a stormy night, as if there was some poor thing down in the low wouts (*vaults*), and he wasn't comfortable and wanted to get out. Well, one night it was so plain and so fearful it was that the sexton he went and took the blacksmith and a ship's carpenter down to the harbour, and they go up together, and they hearken all over the floor, and they open one of the old family wouts that belongs to the Penhaligans, and they go down with a light. Now the wind it was a-blowing all as usual, only worse than common. And there to be sure what do they see but the wout half-full of sea-water, and nows and thens a great spout coming in through a hole in the rock; for it was high-water and a wind off the sea, as I tell you. And there was a coffin afloat on the water, and every time the spout come through, it set it knocking agen the side o' the wout, and that was the ghost."

"What a horrible idea!" I said, with a half-shudder at the unrest of the dead.

The old man uttered a queer long-drawn sound,—neither a chuckle, a crow, nor a laugh, but a mixture of all three,—and turned himself yet again to the work which, as he approached the end of his narration, he had suspended, that he might make his story *tell*, I suppose, by looking me in the face. And as he turned he said, "I thought you would like to be comfortable then as well as other people, sir."

I could not help laughing to see how the cunning old fellow had caught me. I have not yet been able to find out how much of truth there was in his story. From the twinkle of his eye I cannot help suspecting that if he did not invent the tale, he embellished it, at least, in order to produce the effect which he certainly did produce. Humour was clearly his predominant disposition, the reflex of which was to be seen, after a mild lunar fashion, on the countenance of his wife. Neither could I help thinking with pleasure, as I turned away, how the merry little old man would enjoy telling his companions how he had posed the new parson. Very welcome was he to his laugh for my part. Yet I gladly left the churchyard, with its sunshine above and its darkness below. Indeed I had to look up to the glittering vanes on the four pinnacles of the church-tower, dwelling aloft in the clean sunny air, to get the feeling of the dark vault, and the floating coffin, and the knocking heard in the windy church, out of my brain. But the thing that did free me was the reflection with what supreme disregard the disincarcerated spirit would look upon any possible vicissitudes of its abandoned vault. For in proportion as the body of man's revelation ceases to be in harmony with the spirit that dwells therein, it becomes a vault, a prison, from which it must be freedom to escape at length. The house we like best would be a prison of awful sort if doors and windows were built up. Man's abode, as age begins to draw nigh, fares thus. Age is in fact the mason that builds up the doors and the windows, and death is the angel that breaks the prison-house and lets the captives free. Thus I got something out of the sexton's horrible story.

But before the week was over, death came near indeed-in far other fashion than any funereal tale could have brought it.

One day, after lunch, I had retired to my study, and was dozing in my chair, for the day was hot, when I was waked by Charlie rushing into the room with the cry, "Papa, papa, there's a man drowning."

I started up, and hurried down to the drawing-room, which looked out over the bay. I could see nothing but people running about on the edge of the quiet waves. No sign of human being was on-the water. But the one boat belonging to the pilot was coming out from the shelter of the lock of the canal where it usually lay, and my friend of the coastguard was running down from the tower on the cliff with ropes in his hand. He would not stop the boat even for the moment it would need to take him on board, but threw them in and urged to haste. I stood at the window and watched. Every now and then I fancied I saw something white heaved up on the swell of a wave, and as often was satisfied that I had but fancied it. The boat seemed to be floating about lazily, if not idly. The eagerness to help made it appear as if nothing was going on. Could it, after all, have been a false alarm? Was there, after all, no insensible form swinging about in the sweep of those waves, with life gradually oozing away? Long, long as it seemed to me, I watched, and still the boat kept moving from place to place, so far out that I could see nothing distinctly of the motions of its crew. At length I saw something. Yes; a long white thing rose from the water slowly, and was drawn into the boat. It rowed swiftly to the shore. There was but one place fit to land upon, —a little patch of sand, nearly covered at high-water, but now lying yellow in the sun, under the window at which I stood, and immediately under our garden-wall. Thither the boat shot along; and there my friend of the coastguard, earnest and sad, was waiting to use, though without hope, every appliance so well known to him from the frequent occurrence of such necessity in the course of his watchful duties along miles and miles of stormy coast.

I will not linger over the sad details of vain endeavour. The honoured head of a family, he had departed and left a good name behind him. But even in the midst of my poor attentions to the quiet, speechless, pale-faced wife, who sat at the head of the corpse, I could not help feeling anxious about the effect on my Connie. It was impossible to keep the matter concealed from her. The undoubted concern on the faces of the two boys was enough to reveal that something serious and painful had occurred; while my wife and Wynnie, and indeed the whole household, were busy in attending to every remotest suggestion of aid that reached them from the little crowd gathered about the body. At length it was concluded, on the verdict of the medical man who had been sent for, that all further effort was useless. The body was borne away, and I led the poor lady to her lodging, and remained there with her till I found that, as she lay on the sofa, the sleep that so often dogs the steps of sorrow had at length thrown its veil over her consciousness, and put her for the time to rest. There is a gentle consolation in the firmness of the grasp of the inevitable, known but to those who are led through the valley of the shadow. I left her with her son and daughter, and returned to my own family. They too were of course in the skirts of the cloud. Had they only heard of the occurrence, it would have had little effect; but death had appeared to them. Everyone but Connie had seen the dead lying there; and before the day was over, I wished that she too had seen the dead. For I found from what she said at intervals, and from the shudder that now and then passed through her, that her imagination was at work, showing but the horrors that belong to death; for the enfolding peace that accompanies it can be known but by sight of the dead. When I spoke to her, she seemed, and I suppose for the time felt tolerably quiet and comfortable; but I could see that the words she had heard fall in the going and coming, and the communications of Charlie and Harry to each other, had made as it were an excoriation on her fancy, to which her consciousness was ever returning. And now I became more grateful than I had yet been for the gift of that gipsy-child. For I felt no anxiety about Connie so long as she was with her. The presence even of her mother could not relieve her, for she and Wynnie were both clouded with the same awe, and its reflex in Connie was distorted by her fancy. But the sweet ignorance of the baby, which rightly considered is more than a type or symbol of faith, operated most healingly; for she appeared in her sweet merry ways-no baby was ever more filled with the mere gladness of life than Connie's baby-to the mood in which they all were, like a little sunny window in a cathedral crypt, telling of a whole universe of sunshine and motion beyond those oppressed pillars and low-groined arches. And why should not the baby know best? I believe the babies do know best. I therefore favoured her having the child more than I might otherwise have thought good for her, being anxious to get the dreary, unhealthy impression healed as soon as possible, lest it should, in the delicate physical condition in which she was, turn to a sore.

But my wife suffered for a time nearly as much as Connie. As long as she was going about the house or attending to the wants of her family, she was free; but no sooner did she lay her head on the pillow than in rushed the cry of the sea, fierce, unkind, craving like a wild beast. Again and again she spoke of it to me, for it came to her mingled with the voice of the tempter, saying, "*Cruel chance,*" over and over again. For although the two words contradict each other when put together thus, each in its turn would assert itself.

A great part of the doubt in the world comes from the fact that there are in it so many more of the impressible as compared with the originating minds. Where the openness to impression is balanced by the power of production, the painful questions of the world are speedily met by their answers; where such is not the case, there are often long periods of suffering till the child-answer of truth is brought to the birth. Hence the need for every impressible mind to be, by reading or speech, held in living association with an original mind able to combat those suggestions of doubt and even unbelief, which the look of things must often occasion—a look which comes from our inability to gain other than fragmentary visions of the work that the Father worketh hitherto. When the kingdom of heaven is at hand, one sign thereof will be that all clergymen will be more or less of the latter sort, and mere receptive goodness, no more than education and moral character, will be considered sufficient reason for a man's occupying the high position of an instructor of his fellows. But even now this possession of original power is not by any means to be limited to those who make public show of the same. In many a humble parish priest it shows itself at the bedside of the suffering, or in the admonition of the closet, although as yet there are many of the clergy who, so far from being able to console wisely, are incapable of understanding the condition of those that need consolation.

"It is all a fancy, my dear," I said to her. "There is nothing more terrible in this than in any other death. On the contrary, I can hardly imagine a less fearful one. A big wave falls on the man's head and stuns him, and without further suffering he floats gently out on the sea of the unknown."

"But it is so terrible for those left behind!"

"Had you seen the face of his widow, so gentle, so loving, so resigned in its pallor, you would not have thought it so *terrible.*"

But though she always seemed satisfied, and no doubt felt nearly so, after any conversation of the sort, yet every night she would call out once and again, "O, that sea, out there!" I was very glad indeed when Mr. Turner, who had arranged to spend a short holiday with us, arrived.

He was concerned at the news I gave him of the shock both Connie and her mother had received, and counselled an immediate change, that time might, in the absence of surrounding associations, obliterate something of the impression that had been made. The consequence was, that we resolved to remove our household, for a short time, to some place not too far off to permit of my attending to my duties at Kilkhaven, but out of the sight and sound of the sea. It was Thursday when Mr. Turner arrived, and he spent the next two days in inquiring and looking about for a suitable spot to which we might repair as early in the week as possible.

On the Saturday the blacksmith was busy in the church-tower, and I went in to see how he was getting on.

"You had a sad business here the last week, sir," he said, after we had done talking about the repairs.

"A very sad business indeed," I answered.

"It was a warning to us all," he said.

"We may well take it so," I returned. "But it seems to me that we are too ready to think of such remarkable things only by themselves, instead of being roused by them to regard everything, common and uncommon, as ordered by the same care and wisdom."

"One of our local preachers made a grand use of it."

I made no reply. He resumed.

"They tell me you took no notice of it last Sunday, sir."

"I made no immediate allusion to it, certainly. But I preached under the influence of it. And I thought it better that those who could reflect on the matter should be thus led to think for themselves than that they should be subjected to the reception of my thoughts and feelings about it; for in the main it is life and not death that we have to preach."

"I don't quite understand you, sir. But then you don't care much for preaching in your church."

"I confess," I answered, "that there has been much indifference on that point. I could, however, mention to you many and grand exceptions. Still there is, even in some of the best in the church, a great amount of disbelief in the efficacy of preaching. And I allow that a great deal of what is called preaching, partakes of its nature only in the remotest degree. But, while I hold a strong opinion of its value-that is, where it is genuine —I venture just to suggest that the nature of the preaching to which the body you belong to has resorted, has had something to do, by way of a reaction, in driving the church to the other extreme."

"How do you mean that, sir?"

"You try to work upon people's feelings without reference to their judgment. Anyone who can preach what you call rousing sermons is considered a grand preacher amongst you, and there is a great danger of his being led thereby to talk more nonsense than sense. And then when the excitement goes off, there is no seed left in the soil to grow in peace, and they are always craving after more excitement."

"Well, there is the preacher to rouse them up again."

"And the consequence is that they continue like children-the good ones, I mean-and have hardly a chance of making a calm, deliberate choice of that which is good; while those who have been only excited and nothing more, are hardened and seared by the recurrence of such feeling as is neither aroused by truth nor followed by action."

"You daren't talk like that if you knew the kind of people in this country that the Methodists, as you call them, have got a hold of. They tell me it was like hell itself down in those mines before Wesley come among them."

"I should be a fool or a bigot to doubt that the Wesleyans have done incalculable good in the country. And that not alone to the people who never went to church. The whole Church of England is under obligations to Methodism such as no words can overstate."

"I wonder you can say such things against them, then."

"Now there you show the evil of thinking too much about the party you belong to. It makes a man touchy; and then he fancies when another is merely, it may be, analysing a difference, or insisting strongly on some great truth, that he is talking against his party."

"But you said, sir, that our clergy don't care about moving our judgments, only our feelings. Now I know preachers amongst us of whom that would be anything but true."

"Of course there must be. But there is what I say-your party-feeling makes you touchy. A man can't always be saying in the press of utterance, '*Of course there are exceptions.*' That is understood. I confess I do not know much about your clergy, for I have not had the opportunity. But I do know this, that some of the best and most liberal people I have ever known have belonged to your community."

"They do gather a deal of money for good purposes."

"Yes. But that was not what I meant by *liberal*. It is far easier to give money than to be generous in judgment. I meant by *liberal*, able to see the good and true in people that differ from you-glad to be roused to the reception of truth in God's name from whatever quarter it may come, and not readily finding offence where a remark may have chanced to be too sweeping or unguarded. But I see that I ought to be more careful, for I have made you, who certainly are not one of the quarrelsome people I have been speaking of, misunderstand me."

"I beg your pardon, sir. I was hasty. But I do think I am more ready to lose my temper since —"

Here he stopped. A fit of coughing came on, and, to my concern, was followed by what I saw plainly could be the result only of a rupture in the lungs. I insisted on his dropping his work and coming home with me, where I made him rest the remainder of the day and all Sunday, sending word to his mother that I could not let him go home. When we left on the Monday morning, we took him with us in the carriage hired for the journey, and set him down at his mother's, apparently no worse than usual.

CHAPTER VII
AT THE FARM.

Leaving the younger members of the family at home with the servants, we set out for a farm-house, some twenty miles off, which Turner had discovered for us. Connie had stood the journey down so well, and was now so much stronger, that we had no anxiety about her so far as regarded the travelling. Through deep lanes with many cottages, and here and there a very ugly little chapel, over steep hills, up which Turner and Wynnie and I walked, and along sterile moors we drove, stopping at roadside inns, and often besides to raise Connie and let her look about upon the extended prospect, so that it was drawing towards evening before we arrived at our destination. On the way Turner had warned us that we were not to expect a beautiful country, although the place was within reach of much that was remarkable. Therefore we were not surprised when we drew up at the door of a bare-looking, shelterless house, with scarcely a tree in sight, and a stretch of undulating fields on every side.

"A dreary place in winter, Turner," I said, after we had seen Connie comfortably deposited in the nice white-curtained parlour, smelling of dried roses even in the height of the fresh ones, and had strolled out while our tea-dinner was being got ready for us.

"Not a doubt of it; but just the place I wanted for Miss Connie," he replied. "We are high above the sea, and the air is very bracing, and not, at this season, too cold. A month later I should not on any account have brought her here."

"I think even now there is a certain freshness in the wind that calls up a kind of will in the nerves to meet it."

"That is precisely what I wanted for you all. You observe there is no rasp in its touch, however. There are regions in this island of ours where even in the hottest day in summer you would frequently discover a certain unfriendly edge in the air, that would set you wondering whether the seasons had not changed since you were a boy, and used to lie on the grass half the idle day."

"I often do wonder whether it may not be so, but I always come to the conclusion that even this is but an example of the involuntary tendency of the mind of man towards the ideal. He forgets all that comes between and divides the hints of perfection scattered here and there along the scope of his experience. I especially remember one summer day in my childhood, which has coloured all my ideas of summer and bliss and fulfilment of content. It is made up of only mossy grass, and the scent of the earth and wild flowers, and hot sun, and perfect sky-deep and blue, and traversed by blinding white clouds. I could not have been more than five or six, I think, from the kind of dress I wore, the very pearl buttons of which, encircled on their face with a ring of half-spherical hollows, have their undeniable relation in my memory to the heavens and the earth, to the march of the glorious clouds, and the tender scent of the rooted flowers; and, indeed, when I think of it, must, by the delight they gave me, have opened my mind the more to the enjoyment of the eternal paradise around me. What a thing it is to please a child!"

"I know what you mean perfectly," answered Turner. "It is as I get older that I understand what Wordsworth says about childhood. It is indeed a mercy that we were not born grown men, with what we consider our wits about us. They are blinding things those wits we gather. I fancy that the single thread by which God sometimes keeps hold of a man is such an impression of his childhood as that of which you have been speaking."

"I do not doubt it; for conscience is so near in all those memories to which you refer. The whole surrounding of them is so at variance with sin! A sense of purity, not in himself, for the child is not feeling that he is pure, is all about him; and when afterwards the condition returns upon him,—returns when he is conscious of so much that is evil and so much that is unsatisfied in him,—it brings with it a longing after the high clear air of moral well-being."

"Do you think, then, that it is only by association that nature thus impresses us? that she has no power of meaning these things?"

"Not at all. No doubt there is something in the recollection of the associations of childhood to strengthen the power of nature upon us; but the power is in nature herself, else it would be but a poor weak thing to what it is. There *is* purity and state in that sky. There *is* a peace now in this wide still earth-not so very beautiful, you own-and in that overhanging blue, which my heart cries out that it needs and cannot be well till it gains-gains in the truth, gains in God, who is the power of truth, the living and causing truth. There is indeed a rest that remaineth, a rest pictured out even here this night, to rouse my dull heart to desire it and follow after it, a rest that consists in thinking the thoughts of Him who is the Peace because the Unity, in being filled with that spirit which now pictures itself forth in this repose of the heavens and the earth."

"True," said Turner, after a pause. "I must think more about such things. The science the present day is going wild about will not give us that rest."

"No; but that rest will do much to give you that science. A man with this repose in his heart will do more by far, other capabilities being equal, to find out the laws that govern things. For all law is living rest."

"What you have been saying," resumed Turner, after another pause, "reminds me much of one of Wordsworth's poems. I do not mean the famous ode."

"You mean the 'Ninth Evening Voluntary,' I know-one of his finest and truest and deepest poems. It begins, 'Had this effulgence disappeared.'"

"Yes, that is the one I mean. I shall read it again when I go home. But you don't agree with Wordsworth, do you, about our having had an existence previous to this?"

He gave a little laugh as he asked the question.

"Not in the least. But an opinion held by such men as Plato, Origen, and Wordsworth, is not to be laughed at, Mr. Turner. It cannot be in its nature absurd. I might have mentioned Shelley as holding it, too, had his opinion been worth anything."

"Then you don't think much of Shelley?"

"I think his *feeling* most valuable; his *opinion* nearly worthless."

"Well, perhaps I had no business to laugh, at it; but—"

"Do not suppose for a moment that I even lean to it. I dislike it. It would make me unhappy to think there was the least of sound argument for it. But I respect the men who have held it, and know there must be *something* good in it, else they could not have held it."

"Are you able then to sympathise with that ode of Wordsworth's? Does it not depend for all its worth on the admission of this theory?"

"Not in the least. Is it necessary to admit that we must have had a conscious life before this life to find meaning in the words, —

> 'But trailing clouds of glory do we come
> From God who is our home'?

Is not all the good in us his image? Imperfect and sinful as we are, is not all the foundation of our being his image? Is not the sin all ours, and the life in us all God's? We cannot be the creatures of God without partaking of his nature. Every motion of our conscience, every admiration of what is pure and noble, is a sign and a result of this. Is not every self-accusation a proof of the presence of his spirit? That comes not of ourselves-that is not without him. These are the clouds of glory we come trailing from him. All feelings of beauty and peace and loveliness and right and goodness, we trail with us from our home. God is the only home of the human soul. To interpret in this manner what Wordsworth says, will enable us to enter into perfect sympathy with all that grandest of his poems. I do not say this is what he meant; but I think it includes what he meant by being greater and wider than what he meant. Nor am I guilty of presumption in saying so, for surely the idea that we are born of God is a greater idea than that we have lived with him a life before this life. But Wordsworth is not the first among our religious poets to give us at least what is valuable in the notion. I came upon a volume amongst my friend Shepherd's books, with which I had made no acquaintance before-Henry Vaughan's poems. I brought it with me, for it has finer lines, I almost think, than any in George

Herbert, though not so fine poems by any means as his best. When we go into the house I will read one of them to you."

"Thank you," said Turner. "I wish I could have such talk once a week. The shades of the prison-house, you know, Mr. Walton, are always trying to close about us, and shut out the vision of the glories we have come from, as Wordsworth says."

"A man," I answered, "who ministers to the miserable necessities of his fellows has even more need than another to believe in the light and the gladness-else a poor Job's comforter will he be. *I* don't want to be treated like a musical snuff-box."

The doctor laughed.

"No man can *prove*," he said, "that there is not a being inside the snuff-box, existing in virtue of the harmony of its parts, comfortable when they go well, sick when they go badly, and dying when it is dismembered, or even when it stops."

"No," I answered. "No man can prove it. But no man can convince a human being of it. And just as little can anyone convince me that my conscience, making me do sometimes what I *don't* like, comes from a harmonious action of the particles of my brain. But it is time we went in, for by the law of things in general, I being ready for my dinner, my dinner ought to be ready for me."

"A law with more exceptions than instances, I fear," said Turner.

"I doubt that," I answered. "The readiness is everything, and that we constantly blunder in. But we had better see whether we are really ready for it, by trying whether it is ready for us."

Connie went to bed early, as indeed we all did, and she was rather better than worse the next morning. My wife, for the first time for many nights, said nothing about the crying of the sea. The following day Turner and I set out to explore the neighbourhood. The rest remained quietly at home.

It was, as I have said, a high bare country. The fields lay side by side, parted from each other chiefly, as so often in Scotland, by stone walls; and these stones being of a laminated nature, the walls were not unfrequently built by laying thin plates on their edges, which gave a neatness to them not found in other parts of the country as far as I am aware. In the middle of the fields came here and there patches of yet unreclaimed moorland.

Now in a region like this, beauty must be looked for below the surface. There is a probability of finding hollows of repose, sunken spots of loveliness, hidden away altogether from the general aspect of sternness, or perhaps sterility, that meets the eye in glancing over the outspread landscape; just as in the natures of stern men you may expect to find, if opportunity should be afforded you, sunny spots of tender verdure, kept ever green by that very sternness which is turned towards the common gaze-thus existent because they are below the surface, and not laid bare to the sweep of the cold winds that roam the world. How often have not men started with amaze at the discovery of some feminine sweetness, some grace of protection in the man whom they had judged cold and hard and rugged, inaccessible to the more genial influences of humanity! It may be that such men are only fighting against the wind, and keep their hearts open to the sun.

I knew this; and when Turner and I set out that morning to explore, I expected to light upon some instance of it-some mine or other in which nature had hidden away rare jewels; but I was not prepared to find such as I did find. With our hearts full of a glad secret we returned home, but we said nothing about it, in order that Ethelwyn and Wynnie might enjoy the discovery even as we had enjoyed it.

There was another grand fact with regard to the neighbourhood about which we judged it better to be silent for a few days, that the inland influences might be free to work. We were considerably nearer the ocean than my wife and daughters supposed, for we had made a great round in order to arrive from the land-side. We were, however, out of the sound of its waves, which broke all along the shore, in this part, at the foot of tremendous cliffs. What cliffs they were we shall soon find.

CHAPTER VIII
THE KEEVE.

"Now, my dear! now, Wynnie!" I said, after prayers the next morning, "you must come out for a walk as soon as ever you can get your bonnets on."

"But we can't leave Connie, papa," objected Wynnie.

"O, yes, you can, quite well. There's nursie to look after her. What do you say, Connie?"

For, for some time now, Connie had been able to get up so early, that it was no unusual thing to have prayers in her room.

"I am entirely independent of help from my family," returned Connie grandiloquently. "I am a woman of independent means," she added. "If you say another word, I will rise and leave the room."

And she made a movement as if she would actually do as she had said. Seized with an involuntary terror, I rushed towards her, and the impertinent girl burst out laughing in my face-threw herself back on her pillows, and laughed delightedly.

"Take care, papa," she said. "I carry a terrible club for rebellious people." Then, her mood changing, she added, as if to suppress the tears gathering in her eyes, "I am the queen-of luxury and self-will—and I won't have anybody come near me till dinner-time. I mean to enjoy myself."

So the matter was settled, and we went out for our walk. Ethelwyn was not such a good walker as she had been; but even if she had retained the strength of her youth, we should not have got on much the better for it-so often did she and Wynnie stop to grub ferns out of the chinks and roots of the stone-walls. Now, I admire ferns as much as anybody-that is, not, I fear, so much as my wife and daughter, but quite enough notwithstanding-but I do not quite enjoy being pulled up like a fern at every turn.

"Now, my dear, what is the use of stopping to torture that harmless vegetable?" I say, but say in vain. "It is much more beautiful where it is than it will be anywhere where you can put it. Besides, you know they never come to anything with you. They *always* die."

Thereupon my wife reminds me of this fern and that fern, gathered in such and such places, and now in such and such corners of the garden or the greenhouse, or under glass-shades in this or that room, of the very existence of which I am ignorant, whether from original inattention, or merely from forgetfulness, I do not know. Certainly, out of their own place I do not care much for them.

At length, partly by the inducement I held out to them of a much greater variety of ferns where we were bound, I succeeded in getting them over the two miles in little more than two hours. After passing from the lanes into the fields, our way led downwards till we reached a very steep large slope, with a delightful southern exposure, and covered with the sweetest down-grasses. It was just the place to lie in, as on the edge of the earth, and look abroad upon the universe of air and floating worlds.

"Let us have a rest here, Ethel," I said. "I am sure this is much more delightful than uprooting ferns. What an awful thing to think that here we are on this great round tumbling ball of a world, held by the feet, and lifting up the head into infinite space-without choice or wish of our own-compelled to think and to be, whether we will or not! Just God must know it to be very good, or he would not have taken it in his hands to make individual lives without a possible will of theirs. He must be our Father, or we are wretched creatures-the slaves of a fatal necessity! Did it ever strike you, Turner, that each one of us stands on the apex of the world? With a sphere, you know, it must be so. And thus is typified, as it seems to me, that each one of us must look up for himself to find God, and then look abroad to find his fellows."

"I think I know what you mean," was all Turner's reply.

"No doubt," I resumed, "the apprehension of this truth has, in otherwise ill-ordered minds, given rise to all sorts of fierce and grotesque fanaticism. But the minds which have thus conceived the truth, would have been immeasurably worse without it; nay, this truth affords at last the only possible door out of the miseries of their own chaos, whether inherited or the result of their own misconduct."

"What's that in the grass?" cried Wynnie, in a tone of alarm.

I looked where she indicated, and saw a slow-worm, or blind-worm, lying basking in the sun. I rose and went towards it.

"Here's your stick," said Turner.

"What for?" I asked. "Why should I kill it? It is perfectly harmless, and, to my mind, beautiful."

I took it in my hands, and brought it to my wife. She gave an involuntary shudder as it came near her.

"I assure you it is harmless," I said, "though it has a forked tongue." And I opened its mouth as I spoke. "I do not think the serpent form is essentially ugly."

"It makes me feel ugly," said Wynnie.

"I allow I do not quite understand the mystery of it," I said. "But you never saw lovelier ornamentation than these silvery scales, with all the neatness of what you ladies call a set pattern, and none of the stiffness, for there are not two of them the same in form. And you never saw lovelier curves than this little patient creature, which does not even try to get away from me, makes with the queer long thin body of him."

"I wonder how it can look after its tail, it is so far off," said Wynnie.

"It does though-better than you ladies look after your long dresses. I wonder whether it is descended from creatures that once had feet, and did not make a good use of them. Perhaps they had wings even, and would not use them at all, and so lost them. Its ancestors may have had poison-fangs; it is innocent enough. But it is a terrible thing to be all feet, is it not? There is an awful significance in the condemnation of the serpent —'On thy belly shalt thou go, and eat dust.' But it is better to talk of beautiful things. *My* soul at least has dropped from its world apex. Let us go on. Come, wife. Come, Turner."

They did not seem willing to rise. But the glen drew me. I rose, and my wife followed my example with the help of my hand. She returned to the subject, however, as we descended the slope.

"Is it possible that in the course of ever so many ages wings and feet should be both lost?" she said.

"The most presumptuous thing in the world is to pronounce on the possible and the impossible. I do not know what is possible and what is impossible. I can only tell a little of what is true and what is untrue. But I do say this, that between the condition of many decent members of society and that for the sake of which God made them, there is a gulf quite as vast as that between a serpent and a bird. I get peeps now and then into the condition of my own heart, which, for the moment, make it seem impossible that I should ever rise into a true state of nature-that is, into the simplicity of God's will concerning me. The only hope for ourselves and for others lies in him-in the power the creating spirit has over the spirits he has made."

By this time the descent on the grass was getting too steep and slippery to admit of our continuing to advance in that direction. We turned, therefore, down the valley in the direction of the sea. It was but a narrow cleft, and narrowed much towards a deeper cleft, in which we now saw the tops of trees, and from which we heard the rush of water. Nor had we gone far in this direction before we came upon a gate in a stone wall, which led into what seemed a neglected garden. We entered, and found a path turning and winding, among small trees, and luxuriant ferns, and great stones, and fragments of ruins down towards the bottom of the chasm. The noise of falling water increased as we went on, and at length, after some scrambling and several sharp turns, we found ourselves with a nearly precipitous wall on each side, clothed with shrubs and ivy, and creeping things of the vegetable world. Up this cleft there was no advance. The head of it was a precipice down which shot the stream from the vale above, pouring out of a deep slit it had itself cut in the rock as with a knife. Halfway down, it tumbled into a great basin of hollowed stone, and flowing from a chasm in its side, which left part of the lip of the basin standing like the arch of a vanished bridge, it fell into a black pool below, whence it crept as if half-stunned or weary down the gentle decline of the ravine. It was a perfect little picture. I, for my part, had never seen such a picturesque fall. It was a little gem of nature, complete in effect. The ladies were full of pleasure. Wynnie, forgetting her usual reserve, broke out in frantic exclamations of delight.

We stood for a while regarding the ceaseless pour of the water down the precipice, here shot slanting in a little trough of the rock, full of force and purpose, here falling in great curls of green and gray, with an expression of absolute helplessness and conscious perdition, as if sheer to the centre, but rejoicing the next moment to find itself brought up boiling and bubbling in the basin, to issue in the gathered hope of experience. Then we turned down the stream a little way, crossed it by a plank, and stood again to regard it from the opposite side. Small as the whole affair was-not more than about a hundred and fifty feet in height-it was so full of variety that I saw it was all my memory could do, if it carried away anything like a correct picture of its aspect. I was contemplating it fixedly, when a little stifled cry from Wynnie made me start and look round. Her face was flushed, yet she was trying to look unconcerned.

"I thought we were quite alone, papa," she said; "but I see a gentleman sketching."

I looked whither she indicated. A little way down, the bed of the ravine widened considerably, and was no doubt filled with water in rainy weather. Now it was swampy-full of reeds and willow bushes. But on the opposite side of the stream, with a little canal from it going all around it, lay a great flat rectangular stone, not more than a foot above the level of the water, and upon a camp-stool in the centre of this stone sat a gentleman sketching. I had no doubt that Wynnie had recognised him at once. And I was annoyed, and indeed angry, to think that Mr. Percivale had followed us here. But while I regarded him, he looked up, rose very quietly, and, with his pencil in his hand, came towards us. With no nearer approach to familiarity than a bow, and no expression of either much pleasure or any surprise, he said —

"I have seen your party for some time, Mr. Walton-since you crossed the stream; but I would not break in upon your enjoyment with the surprise which my presence here must cause you."

I suppose I answered with a bow of some sort; for I could not say with truth that I was glad to see him. He resumed, doubtless penetrating my suspicion —

"I have been here almost a week. I certainly had no expectation of the pleasure of seeing you."

This he said lightly, though no doubt with the object of clearing himself. And I was, if not reassured, yet disarmed, by his statement; for I could not believe, from what I knew of him, that he would be guilty of such a white lie as many a gentleman would have thought justifiable on the occasion. Still, I suppose he found me a little stiff, for presently he said —

"If you will excuse me, I will return to my work."

Then I felt as if I must say something, for I had shown him no courtesy during the interview.

"It must be a great pleasure to carry away such talismans with you-capable of bringing the place back to your mental vision at any moment."

"To tell the truth," he answered, "I am a little ashamed of being found sketching here. Such bits of scenery are not of my favourite studies. But it is a change."

"It is very beautiful here," I said, in a tone of contravention.

"It is very pretty," he answered —"very lovely, if you will-not very beautiful, I think. I would keep that word for things of larger regard. Beauty requires width, and here is none. I had almost said this place was fanciful-the work of imagination in her play-hours, not in her large serious moods. It affects me like the face of a woman only pretty, about which boys and guardsmen will rave-to me not very interesting, save for its single lines."

"Why, then, do you sketch the place?"

"A very fair question," he returned, with a smile. "Just because it is soothing from the very absence of beauty. I would far rather, however, if I were only following my taste, take the barest bit of the moor above, with a streak of the cold sky over it. That gives room."

"You would like to put a skylark in it, wouldn't you?"

"That I would if I knew how. I see you know what I mean. But the mere romantic I never had much taste for; though if you saw the kind of pictures I try to paint, you would not wonder that I take sketches of places like this, while in my heart of hearts I do not care much for them. They are so different, and just *therefore* they are good for me. I am not working now; I am only playing."

"With a view to working better afterwards, I have no doubt," I answered.

"You are right there, I hope," was his quiet reply, as he turned and walked back to the island.

He had not made a step towards joining us. He had only taken his hat off to the ladies. He was gaining ground upon me rapidly.

"Have you quarrelled with our new friend, Harry?" said my wife, as I came up to her.

She was sitting on a stone. Turner and Wynnie were farther off towards the foot of the fall.

"Not in the least," I answered, slightly outraged —I did not at first know why-by the question. "He is only gone to his work, which is a duty belonging both to the first and second tables of the law."

"I hope you have asked him to come home to our early dinner, then," she rejoined.

"I have not. That remains for you to do. Come, I will take you to him."

Ethelwyn rose at once, put her hand in mine, and with a little help soon reached the table-rock. When Percivale saw that she was really on a visit to him on his island-perch, he rose, and when she came near enough, held out his hand. It was but a step, and she was beside him in a moment. After the usual greetings, which on her part, although very quiet, like every motion and word of hers, were yet indubitably cordial and kind, she said, "When you get back to London, Mr. Percivale, might I ask you to allow some friends of mine to call at your studio, and see your paintings?"

"With all my heart," answered Percivale. "I must warn you, however, that I have not much they will care to see. They will perhaps go away less happy than they entered. Not many people care to see my pictures twice."

"I would not send you anyone I thought unworthy of the honour," answered my wife.

Percivale bowed-one of his stately, old-world bows, which I greatly liked.

"Any friend of yours-that is guarantee sufficient," he answered.

There was this peculiarity about any compliment that Percivale paid, that you had not a doubt of its being genuine.

"Will you come and take an early dinner with us?" said my wife. "My invalid daughter will be very pleased to see you."

"I will with pleasure," he answered, but in a tone of some hesitation, as he glanced from Ethelwyn to me.

"My wife speaks for us all," I said. "It will give us all pleasure."

"I am only afraid it will break in upon your morning's work," remarked Ethelwyn.

"O, that is not of the least consequence," he rejoined. "In fact, as I have just been saying to Mr. Walton, I am not working at all at present. This is pure recreation."

As he spoke he turned towards his easel, and began hastily to bundle up his things.

"We're not quite ready to go yet," said my wife, loath to leave the lovely spot. "What a curious flat stone this is!" she added.

"It is," said Percivale. "The man to whom the place belongs, a worthy yeoman of the old school, says that this wider part of the channel must have been the fish-pond, and that the portly monks stood on this stone and fished in the pond."

"Then was there a monastery here?" I asked.

"Certainly. The ruins of the chapel, one of the smallest, are on the top, just above the fall-rather a fearful place to look down from. I wonder you did not observe them as you came. They say it had a silver bell in the days of its glory, which now lies in a deep hole under the basin, half-way between the top and bottom of the fall. But the old man says that nothing will make him look, or let anyone else lift the huge stone; for he is much better pleased to believe that it may be there, than he would be to know it was not there; for certainly, if it were found, it would not be left there long."

As he spoke Percivale had continued packing his gear. He now led our party up to the chapel, and thence down a few yards to the edge of the chasm, where the water fell headlong. I turned away with that fear of high places which is one of my many weaknesses; and when I turned again towards the spot, there was Wynnie on the very edge, looking over into the flash and tumult of the water below, but with a nervous grasp of the hand of Percivale, who stood a little farther back.

In going home, the painter led us by an easier way out of the valley, left his little easel and other things at a cottage, and then walked on in front between my wife and daughter, while Turner and I followed. He seemed quite at his ease with them, and plenty of talk and laughter rose on the way. I, however, was chiefly occupied with finding out Turner's impression of Connie's condition.

"She is certainly better," he said. "I wonder you do not see it as plainly as I do. The pain is nearly gone from her spine, and she can move herself a good deal more, I am certain, than she could when she left. She asked me yesterday if she might not turn upon one side. 'Do you think you could?' I asked. —'I think so,' she answered. 'At any rate, I have often a great inclination to try; only papa said I had better wait till you came.' I do think she might be allowed a little more change of posture now."

"Then you have really some hope of her final recovery?"

"I have *hope* most certainly. But what is hope in me, you must not allow to become certainty in you. I am nearly sure, though, that she can never be other than an invalid; that is, if I am to judge by what I know of such cases."

"I am thankful for the hope," I answered. "You need not be afraid of my turning upon you, should the hope never pass into sight. I should do so only if I found that you had been treating me irrationally-inspiring me with hope which you knew to be false. The element of uncertainty is essential to hope, and for all true hope, even as hope, man has to be unspeakably thankful."

CHAPTER IX
THE WALK TO CHURCH.

I was glad to be able to arrange with a young clergyman who was on a visit to Kilkhaven, that he should take my duty for me the next Sunday, for that was the only one Turner could spend with us. He and I and Wynnie walked together two miles to church. It was a lovely morning, with just a tint of autumn in the air. But even that tint, though all else was of the summer, brought a shadow, I could see, on Wynnie's face.

"You said you would show me a poem of-Vaughan, I think you said, was the name of the writer. I am too ignorant of our older literature," said Turner.

"I have only just made acquaintance with him," I answered. "But I think I can repeat the poem. You shall judge whether it is not like Wordsworth's Ode.

> 'Happy those early days, when I
> Shined in my angel infancy;
> Before I understood the place
> Appointed for my second race,
> Or taught my soul to fancy ought
> But a white, celestial thought;
> When yet I had not walked above
> A mile or two from my first love,
> And looking back, at that short space,
> Could see a glimpse of his bright face;
> When on some gilded cloud or flower
> My gazing soul would dwell an hour,
> And in those weaker glories spy
> Some shadows of eternity;
> Before I taught my tongue to wound
> My conscience with a sinful sound,
> But felt through all this fleshly dress
> Bright shoots of everlastingness.
> O how I long to travel back — —'"

But here I broke down, for I could not remember the rest with even approximate accuracy.

"When did this Vaughan live?" asked Turner.

"He was born, I find, in 1621 —five years, that is, after Shakspere's death, and when Milton was about thirteen years old. He lived to the age of seventy-three, but seems to have been little known. In politics he was on the Cavalier side. By the way, he was a medical man, like you, Turner-an M.D. We'll have a glance at the little book when we go back. Don't let me forget to show it you. A good many of your profession have distinguished themselves in literature, and as profound believers too."

"I should have thought the profession had been chiefly remarkable for such as believe only in the evidence of the senses."

"As if having searched into the innermost recesses of the body, and not having found a soul, they considered themselves justified in declaring there was none."

"Just so."

"Well, that is true of the commonplace amongst them, I do believe. You will find the exceptions have been men of fine minds and characters-not such as he of whom Chaucer says,

> 'His study was but little on the Bible;'

for if you look at the rest of the description of the man, you will find that he was in alliance with his apothecary for their mutual advantage, that he was a money-loving man, and that some of Chaucer's keenest irony is spent on him in an off-hand, quiet manner. Compare the tone in which he writes of the doctor of physic, with the profound reverence wherewith he bows himself before the poor country-parson."

Here Wynnie spoke, though with some tremor in her voice.

"I never know, papa, what people mean by talking about childhood in that way. I never seem to have been a bit younger and more innocent than I am."

"Don't you remember a time, Wynnie, when the things about you-the sky and the earth, say-seemed to you much grander than they seem now? You are old enough to have lost something."

She thought for a little while before she answered.

"My dreams were, I know. I cannot say so of anything else."

I in my turn had to be silent, for I did not see the true answer, though I was sure there was one somewhere, if I could only find it. All I could reply, however, even after I had meditated a good while, was-and perhaps, after all, it was the best thing I could have said:

"Then you must make a good use of your dreams, my child."

"Why, papa?"

"Because they are the only memorials of childhood you have left."

"How am I to make a good use of them? I don't know what to do with my silly old dreams."

But she gave a sigh as she spoke that testified her silly old dreams had a charm for her still.

"If your dreams, my child, have ever testified to you of a condition of things beyond that which you see around you, if they have been to you the hints of a wonder and glory beyond what visits you now, you must not call them silly, for they are just what the scents of Paradise borne on the air were to Adam and Eve as they delved and spun, reminding them that they must aspire yet again through labour into that childhood of obedience which is the only paradise of humanity-into that oneness with the will of the Father, which our race, our individual selves, need just as much as if we had personally fallen with Adam, and from which we fall every time we are disobedient to the voice of the Father within our souls-to the conscience which is his making and his witness. If you have had no childhood, my Wynnie, yet permit your old father to say that everything I see in you indicates more strongly in you than in most people that it is this childhood after which you are blindly longing, without which you find that life is hardly to be endured. Thank God for your dreams, my child. In him you will find that the essence of those dreams is fulfilled. We are saved by hope, Turner. Never man hoped too much, or repented that he had hoped. The plague is that we don't hope in God half enough. The very fact that hope is strength, and strength the outcome, the body of life, shows that hope is at one with life, with the very essence of what says 'I am' —yea, of what doubts and says 'Am I?' and therefore is reasonable to creatures who cannot even doubt save in that they live."

By this time, for I have, of course, only given the outlines, or rather salient points, of our conversation, we had reached the church, where, if I found the sermon neither healing nor inspiring, I found the prayers full of hope and consolation. They at least are safe beyond human caprice, conceit, or incapacity. Upon them, too, the man who is distressed at the thought of how little of the needful food he had been able to provide for his people, may fall back for comfort, in the thought that there at least was what ought to have done them good, what it was well worth their while to go to church for. But I did think they were too long for any individual Christian soul, to sympathise with from beginning to end, that is, to respond to, like organ-tube to the fingered key, in every touch of the utterance of the general Christian soul. For my reader must remember that it is one thing to read prayers and another to respond; and that I had had very few opportunities of being in the position of the latter duty. I had had suspicions before, and now they were confirmed-that the present crowding of services was most inexpedient. And as I pondered on the matter, instead of trying to go on praying after I had already uttered my soul, which is but a heathenish attempt after much speaking, I thought how our Lord had given us such a short prayer to pray, and I began to wonder when or how the services came to be so heaped the one on the back of the other as they now were. No doubt many people defended them; no doubt many people could sit them out; but how many people could pray from beginning to end of them I On this point we had some talk as we went home. Wynnie was opposed to any change of the present use on the ground that we should only have the longer sermons.

"Still," I said, "I do not think even that so great an evil. A sensitive conscience will not reproach itself so much for not listening to the whole of a sermon, as for kneeling in prayer and not praying. I think myself, however, that after the prayers are over, everyone should be at liberty to go out and leave the sermon unheard, if he pleases. I think the result would be in the end a good one both for parson and people. It would break through the deadness of this custom, this use and wont. Many a young mind is turned for life against the influences of church-going—one of the most sacred influences when *pure*, that is, un-mingled with non-essentials—just by the feeling that he *must* do so and so, that he must go through a certain round of duty. It is a willing service that the Lord wants; no forced devotions are either acceptable to him, or other than injurious to the worshipper, if such he can be called."

After an early dinner, I said to Turner—"Come out with me, and we will read that poem of Vaughan's in which I broke down today."

"O, papa!" said Connie, in a tone of injury, from the sofa.

"What is it, my dear?" I asked.

"Wouldn't it be as good for us as for Mr. Turner?"

"Quite, my dear. Well, I will keep it for the evening, and meantime Mr. Turner and I will go and see if we can find out anything about the change in the church-service."

For I had thrown into my bag as I left the rectory a copy of *The Clergyman's Vade Mecum*—a treatise occupied with the externals of the churchman's relations-in which I soon came upon the following passage:

"So then it appears that the common practice of reading all three together, is an innovation, and if an ancient or infirm clergyman do read them at two or three several times, he is more strictly conformable; however, this is much better than to omit any part of the liturgy, or to read all three offices into one, as is now commonly done, without any pause or distinction."

"On the part of the clergyman, you see, Turner," I said, when I had finished reading the whole passage to him. "There is no care taken of the delicate women of the congregation, but only of the ancient or infirm clergyman. And the logic, to say the least, is rather queer: is it only in virtue of his antiquity and infirmity that he is to be upheld in being more strictly conformable? The writer's honesty has its heels trodden upon by the fear of giving offence. Nevertheless there should perhaps be a certain slowness to admit change, even back to a more ancient form."

"I don't know that I can quite agree with you there," said Turner. "If the form is better, no one should hesitate to advocate the change. If it is worse, then slowness is not sufficient-utter obstinacy is the right condition."

"You are right, Turner. For the right must be the rule, and where *the right* is beyond our understanding or our reach, then *the better*, as indeed not only right compared with the other, but the sole ascent towards the right."

In the evening I took Henry Vaughan's poems into the common sitting-room, and to Connie's great delight read the whole of the lovely, though unequal little poem, called "The Retreat," in recalling which I had failed in the morning. She was especially delighted with the "white celestial thought," and the "bright shoots of everlastingness." Then I gave a few lines from another yet more unequal poem, worthy in themselves of the best of the other. I quote the first strophe entire:

CHILDHOOD.
"I cannot reach it; and my striving eye

Dazzles at it, as at eternity.
Were now that chronicle alive,

Those white designs which children drive,
And the thoughts of each harmless hour,
With their content too in my power,
Quickly would I make my path even,
And by mere playing go to heaven.

And yet the practice worldlings call
Business and weighty action all,
Checking the poor child for his play,
But gravely cast themselves away.

An age of mysteries! which he
Must live twice that would God's face see;
Which angels guard, and with it play,
Angels! which foul men drive away.
How do I study now, and scan
Thee more than ere I studied man,
And only see through a long night
Thy edges and thy bordering light I
O for thy centre and midday!
For sure that is the *narrow way!*"

"For of such is the kingdom of heaven." said my wife softly, as I closed the book.

"May I have the book, papa?" said Connie, holding out her thin white cloud of a hand to take it.

"Certainly, my child. And if Wynnie would read it with you, she will feel more of the truth of what Mr. Percivale was saying to her about finish. Here are the finest, grandest thoughts, set forth sometimes with such carelessness, at least such lack of neatness, that, instead of their falling on the mind with all their power of loveliness, they are like a beautiful face disfigured with patches, and, what is worse, they put the mind out of the right, quiet, unquestioning, open mood, which is the only fit one for the reception of such true things as are embodied in the poems. But they are too beautiful after all to be more than a little spoiled by such a lack of the finish with which Art ends off all her labours. A gentleman, however, thinks it of no little importance to have his nails nice as well as his face and his shirt."

CHAPTER X
THE OLD CASTLE.

The place Turner had chosen suited us all so well, that after attending to my duties on the two following Sundays at Kilkhaven, I returned on the Monday or Tuesday to the farmhouse. But Turner left us in the middle of the second week, for he could not be longer absent from his charge at home, and we missed him much. It was some days before Connie was quite as cheerful again as usual. I do not mean that she was in the least gloomy-that she never was; she was only a little less merry. But whether it was that Turner had opened our eyes, or that she had visibly improved since he allowed her to make a little change in her posture-certainly she appeared to us to have made considerable progress, and every now and then we were discovering some little proof of the fact. One evening, while we were still at the farm, she startled us by calling out suddenly, —

"Papa, papa! I moved my big toe! I did indeed."

We were all about her in a moment. But I saw that she was excited, and fearing a reaction I sought to calm her.

"But, my dear," I said, as quietly as I could, "you are probably still aware that you are possessed of two big toes: which of them are we to congratulate on this first stride in the march of improvement?"

She broke out in the merriest laugh. A pause followed in which her face wore a puzzled expression. Then she said all at once, "Papa, it is very odd, but I can't tell which of them," and burst into tears. I was afraid that I had done more harm than good.

"It is not of the slightest consequence, my child," I said. "You have had so little communication with the twins of late, that it is no wonder you should not be able to tell the one from the other."

She smiled again through her sobs, but was silent, with shining face, for the rest of the evening. Our hopes took a fresh start, but we heard no more from her of her power over her big toe. As often as I inquired she said she was afraid she had made a mistake, for she had not had another hint of its existence. Still I thought it could not have been a fancy, and I would cleave to my belief in the good sign.

Percivale called to see us several times, but always appeared anxious not to intrude more of his society upon us than might be agreeable. He grew in my regard, however; and at length I asked him if he would assist me in another surprise which I meditated for my companions, and this time for Connie as well, and which I hoped would prevent the painful influences of the sight of the sea from returning upon them when they went back to Kilkhaven: they must see the sea from a quite different shore first. In a word I would take them to Tintagel, of the near position of which they were not aware, although in some of our walks we had seen the ocean in the distance. An early day was fixed for carrying out our project, and I proceeded to get everything ready. The only difficulty was to find a carriage in the neighbourhood suitable for receiving Connie's litter. In this, however, I at length succeeded, and on the morning of a glorious day of blue and gold, we set out for the little village of Trevenna, now far better known than at the time of which I write. Connie had been out every day since she came, now in one part of the fields, now in another, enjoying the expanse of earth and sky, but she had had no drive, and consequently had seen no variety of scenery. Therefore, believing she was now thoroughly able to bear it, I quite reckoned of the good she would get from the inevitable excitement. We resolved, however, after finding how much she enjoyed the few miles' drive, that we would not demand more, of her strength that day, and therefore put up at the little inn, where, after ordering dinner, Percivale and I left the ladies, and sallied forth to reconnoitre.

We walked through the village and down the valley beyond, sloping steeply between hills towards the sea, the opening closed at the end by the blue of the ocean below and the more ethereal blue of the sky above. But when we reached the mouth of the valley we found that we were not yet on the shore, for a precipice lay between us and the little beach below. On the left a great peninsula of rock stood out into the sea, upon which rose the ruins of the keep of Tintagel, while behind on the mainland stood the ruins of the castle itself, connected with the other only by a narrow isthmus. We had read that this peninsula had once been an island, and that the two parts of the castle were formerly connected by a drawbridge. Looking up at the great gap which now divided the two portions, it seemed at first impossible to believe that they had ever been thus united; but a little reflection cleared up the mystery.

The fact was that the isthmus, of half the height of the two parts connected by it, had been formed entirely by the fall of portions of the rock and soil on each side into the narrow dividing space, through which the waters of the Atlantic had been wont to sweep. And now the fragments of walls stood on the very verge of the precipice, and showed that large portions of the castle itself had fallen into the gulf between. We turned to the left along the edge of the rock, and so by a narrow path reached and crossed to the other side of the isthmus. We then found that the path led to the foot of the rock, formerly island, of the keep, and thence in a zigzag up the face of it to the top. We followed it, and after a great climb reached a door in a modern battlement. Entering, we found ourselves amidst grass, and ruins haggard with age. We turned and surveyed the path by which we had come. It was steep and somewhat difficult. But the outlook was glorious. It was indeed one of God's mounts of vision upon which we stood. The thought, "O that Connie could see this!" was swelling in my heart, when Percivale broke the silence-not with any remark on the glory around us, but with the commonplace question—

"You haven't got your man with you, I think, Mr. Walton?"

"No," I answered; "we thought it better to leave him to look after the boys."

He was silent for a few minutes, while I gazed in delight.

"Don't you think," he said, "it would be possible to bring Miss Constance up here?"

I almost started at the idea, and had not replied before he resumed:

"It would be something for her to recur to with delight all the rest of her life."

"It would indeed. But it is impossible."

"I do not think so-if you would allow me the honour to assist you. I think we could do it perfectly between us."

I was again silent for a while. Looking down on the way we had come, it seemed an almost dreadful undertaking. Percivale spoke again.

"As we shall come here to-morrow, we need not explore the place now. Shall we go down at once and observe the whole path, with a view to the practicability of carrying her up?"

"There can be no objection to that," I answered, as a little hope, and courage with it, began to dawn in my heart. "But you must allow it does not look very practicable."

"Perhaps it would seem more so to you, if you had come up with the idea in your head all the way, as I did. Any path seems more difficult in looking back than at the time when the difficulties themselves have to be met and overcome."

"Yes, but then you must remember that we have to take the way back whether we will or no, if we once take the way forward."

"True; and now I will go down with the descent in my head as well as under my feet."

"Well, there can be no harm in reconnoitring it at least. Let us go."

"You know we can rest almost as often as we please," said Percivale, and turned to lead the way.

It certainly was steep, and required care even in our own descent; but for a man who had climbed mountains, as I had done in my youth, it could hardly be called difficult even in middle age. By the time we had got again into the valley road I was all but convinced of the practicability of the proposal. I was a little vexed, however, I must confess, that a stranger should have thought of giving such a pleasure to Connie, when the bare wish that she might have enjoyed it had alone arisen in my mind. I comforted myself with the reflection that this was one of the ways in which we were to be weaned from the world and knit the faster to our fellows. For even the middle-aged, in the decay of their daring, must look for the fresh thought and the fresh impulse to the youth which follows at their heels in the march of life. Their part is to *will* the relation and the obligation, and so, by love to and faith in the young, keep themselves in the line along which the electric current flows, till at length they too shall once more be young and daring in the strength of the Lord. A man must always seek to rise above his moods and feelings, to let them move within him, but not allow them to storm or gloom around him. By the time we reached home we had agreed to make the attempt, and to judge by the path to the foot of the rock, which was difficult in parts, whether we should be likely to succeed, without danger, in attempting the rest of the way and the following descent. As soon as we had arrived at this conclusion, I felt so happy in the prospect that I grew quite merry, especially after we had further agreed that, both for the sake of her nerves and for the sake of the lordly surprise, we should bind Connie's eyes so that she should see nothing till we had placed her in a certain position, concerning the preferableness of which we were not of two minds.

"What mischief have you two been about?" said my wife, as we entered our room in the inn, where the cloth was already laid for dinner. "You look just like two schoolboys that have been laying some plot, and can hardly hold their tongues about it."

"We have been enjoying our little walk amazingly," I answered. "So much so, that we mean to set out for another the moment dinner is over."

"I hope you will take Wynnie with you then."

"Or you, my love," I returned.

"No; I will stay with Connie."

"Very well. You, and Connie too, shall go out to-morrow, for we have found a place we want to take you to. And, indeed, I believe it was our anticipation of the pleasure you and she would have in the view that made us so merry when you accused us of plotting mischief."

My wife replied only with a loving look, and dinner appearing at this moment, we sat down a happy party.

When that was over-and a very good dinner it was, just what I like, homely in material but admirable in cooking-Wynnie and Percivale and I set out again. For as Percivale and I came back in the morning we had seen the church standing far aloft and aloof on the other side of the little valley, and we wanted to go to it. It was rather a steep climb, and Wynnie accepted Percivale's offered arm. I led the way, therefore, and left them to follow-not so far in the rear, however, but that I could take a share in the conversation. It was some little time before any arose, and it was Wynnie who led the way into it.

"What kind of things do you like best to paint, Mr. Percivale?" she asked.

He hesitated for several seconds, which between a question and an answer look so long, that most people would call them minutes.

"I would rather you should see some of my pictures —I should prefer that to answering your question," he said, at length.

"But I have seen some of your pictures," she returned.

"Pardon me. Indeed you have not, Miss Walton."

"At least I have seen some of your sketches and studies."

"Some of my sketches-none of my studies."

"But you make use of your sketches for your pictures, do you not?"

"Never of such as you have seen. They are only a slight antidote to my pictures."

"I cannot understand you."

"I do not wonder at that. But I would rather, I repeat, say nothing about my pictures till you see some of them."

"But how am I to have that pleasure, then?"

"You go to London sometimes, do you not?"

"Very rarely. More rarely still when the Royal Academy is open."

"That does not matter much. My pictures are seldom to be found there."

"Do you not care to send them there?"

"I send one, at least, every year. But they are rarely accepted."

"Why?"

This was a very improper question, I thought; but if Wynnie had thought so she would not have put it. He hesitated a little before he replied—

"It is hardly for me to say why," he answered; "but I cannot wonder much at it, considering the subjects I choose. —But I daresay," he added, in a lighter tone, "after all, that has little to do with it, and there is something about the things themselves that precludes a favourable judgment. I avoid thinking about it. A man ought to try to look at his own work as if it were none of his, but not as with the eyes of other people. That is an impossibility, and the attempt a bewilderment. It is with his own eyes he must look, with his own judgment he must judge. The only effort is to get it set far away enough from him to be able to use his own eyes and his own judgment upon it."

"I think I see what you mean. A man has but his own eyes and his own judgment. To look with those of other people is but a fancy."

"Quite so. You understand me quite."

He said no more in explanation of his rejection by the Academy. Till we reached the church, nothing more of significance passed between them.

What a waste, bare churchyard that was! It had two or three lych-gates, but they had no roofs. They were just small enclosures, with the low stone tables, to rest the living from the weight of the dead, while the clergyman, as the keeper of heaven's wardrobe, came forth to receive the garment they restored-to be laid aside as having ended its work, as having been worn done in the winds, and rains, and labours of the world. Not a tree stood in that churchyard. Hank grass was the sole covering of the soil heaved up with the dead beneath. What blasts from the awful space of the sea must rush athwart the undefended garden! The ancient church stood in the midst, with its low, strong, square tower, and its long, narrow nave, the ridge bowed with age, like the back of a horse worn out in the service of man, and its little homely chancel, like a small cottage that had leaned up against its end for shelter from the western blasts. It was locked, and we could not enter. But of all world-worn, sad-looking churches, that one-sad, even in the sunset-was the dreariest I had ever beheld. Surely, it needed the gospel of the resurrection fervently preached therein, to keep it from sinking to the dust with dismay and weariness. Such a soul alone could keep it from vanishing utterly of dismal old age. Near it was one huge mound of grass-grown rubbish, looking like the grave where some former church of the dead had been buried, when it could stand erect no longer before the onsets of Atlantic winds. I walked round and round it, gathering its architecture, and peeping in at every window I could reach. Suddenly I was aware that I was alone. Returning to the other side, I found that Percivale was seated on the churchyard wall, next the sea-it would have been less dismal had it stood immediately on the cliffs, but they were at some little distance beyond bare downs and rough stone walls; he was sketching the place, and Wynnie stood beside him, looking over his shoulder. I did not interrupt him, but walked among the graves, reading the poor memorials of the dead, and wondering how many of the words of laudation that were inscribed on their tombs were spoken of them while they were yet alive. Yet, surely, in the lives of those to whom they applied the least, there had been moments when the true nature, the nature God had given them, broke forth in faith and tenderness, and would have justified the words inscribed on their gravestones! I was yet wandering and reading, and stumbling over the mounds, when my companions joined me, and, without a word, we walked out of the churchyard. We were nearly home before one of us spoke.

"That church is oppressive," said Percivale. "It looks like a great sepulchre, a place built only for the dead-the church of the dead."

"It is only that it partakes with the living," I returned; "suffers with them the buffetings of life, outlasts them, but shows, like the shield of the Red-Cross Knight, the 'old dints of deep wounds.'"

"Still, is it not a dreary place to choose for a church to stand in?"

"The church must stand everywhere. There is no region into which it must not, ought not to enter. If it refuses any earthly spot, it is shrinking from its calling. Here this one stands for the sea as for the land, high-uplifted, looking out over the waters as a sign of the haven from all storms, the rest in God. And down beneath in its storehouse lie the bodies of men-you saw the grave of some of them on the other side-flung ashore from the gulfing sea. It may be a weakness, but one would rather have the bones of his friend laid in the still Sabbath of the churchyard earth, than sweeping and swaying about as Milton imagines the bones of his friend Edward King, in that wonderful 'Lycidas.'" Then I told them the conversation I had had with the sexton at Kilkhaven. "But," I went on, "these fancies are only the ghostly mists that hang about the eastern hills before the sun rises. We shall look down on all that with a smile by and by; for the Lord tells us that if we believe in him we shall never die."

By this time we were back once more at the inn. We gave Connie a description of what we had seen.

"What a brave old church!" said Connie.

The next day I awoke very early, full of the anticipated attempt. I got up at once, found the weather most promising, and proceeded first of all to have a look at Connie's litter, and see that it was quite sound. Satisfied of this, I rejoiced in the contemplation of its lightness and strength.

After breakfast I went to Connie's room, and told her that Mr. Percivale and I had devised a treat for her. Her face shone at once.

"But we want to do it our own way."

"Of course, papa," she answered.

"Will you let us tie your eyes up?"

"Yes; and my ears and my hands too. It would be no good tying my feet, when I don't know one big toe from the other."

And she laughed merrily.

"We'll try to keep up the talk all the way, so that you sha'n't weary of the journey."

"You're going to carry me somewhere with my eyes tied up. O! how jolly! And then I shall see something all at once! Jolly! jolly!—Getting tired!" she repeated. "Even the wind on my face would be pleasure enough for half a day. I sha'n't get tired so soon as you will-you dear, kind papa! I am afraid I shall be dreadfully heavy. But I sha'n't jerk your arms much. I will lie so still!"

"And you won't mind letting Mr. Percivale help me to carry you?"

"No. Why should I, if he doesn't mind it? He looks strong enough; and I am sure he is nice, and won't think me heavier than I am."

"Very well, then. I will send mamma and Wynnie to dress you at once; and we shall set out as soon as you are ready."

She clapped her hands with delight, then caught me round the neck and gave me one of my own kisses as she called the best she had, and began to call as loud as she could on her mamma and Wynnie to come and dress her.

It was indeed a glorious morning. The wind came in little wafts, like veins of cool white silver amid the great, warm, yellow gold of the sunshine. The sea lay before us a mound of blue closing up the end of the valley, as if overpowered into quietness by the lordliness of the sun overhead; and the hills between which we went lay like great sheep, with green wool, basking in the blissful heat. The gleam from the waters came up the pass; the grand castle crowned the left-hand steep, seeming to warm its old bones, like the ruins of some awful megatherium in the lighted air; one white sail sped like a glad thought across the spandrel of the sea; the shadows of the rocks lay over our path, like transient, cool, benignant deaths, through which we had to pass again and again to yet higher glory beyond; and one lark was somewhere in whose little breast the whole world was reflected as in the convex mirror of a dewdrop, where it swelled so that he could not hold it, but let it out again through his throat, metamorphosed into music, which he poured forth over all as the libation on the outspread altar of worship.

And of all this we talked to Connie as we went; and every now and then she would clap her hands gently in the fulness of her delight, although she beheld the splendour only as with her ears, or from the kisses of the wind on her cheeks. But she seemed, since her accident, to have approached that condition which Milton represents Samson as longing for in his blindness, wherein the sight should be

> "through all parts diffused,
> That she might look at will through every pore."

I had, however, arranged with the rest of the company, that the moment we reached the cliff over the shore, and turned to the left to cross the isthmus, the conversation should no longer be about the things around us; and especially I warned my wife and Wynnie that no exclamation of surprise or delight should break from them before Connie's eyes were uncovered. I had said nothing to either of them about the difficulties of the way, that, seeing us take them as ordinary things, they might take them so too, and not be uneasy.

We never stopped till we reached the foot of the peninsula, *née* island, upon which the keep of Tintagel stands. There we set Connie down, to take breath and ease our arms before we began the arduous way.

"Now, now!" said Connie eagerly, lifting her hands in the belief that we were on the point of undoing the bandage from her eyes.

"No, no, my love, not yet," I said, and she lay still again, only she looked more eager than before.

"I am afraid I have tired out you and Mr. Percivale, papa," she said.

Percivale laughed so amusedly, that she rejoined roguishly —

"O yes! I know every gentleman is a Hercules-at least, he chooses to be considered one! But, notwithstanding my firm faith in the fact, I have a little womanly conscience left that is hard to hoodwink."

There was a speech for my wee Connie to make! The best answer and the best revenge was to lift her and go on. This we did, trying as well as we might to prevent the difference of level between us from tilting the litter too much for her comfort.

"Where *are* you going, papa?" she said once, but without a sign of fear in her voice, as a little slip I made lowered my end of the litter suddenly. "You must be going up a steep place. Don't hurt yourself, dear papa."

We had changed our positions, and were now carrying her, head foremost, up the hill. Percivale led, and I followed. Now I could see every change on her lovely face, and it made me strong to endure; for I did find it hard work, I confess, to get to the top. It lay like a little sunny pool, on which all the cloudy thoughts that moved in some unseen heaven cast exquisitely delicate changes of light and shade as they floated over it. Percivale strode on as if he bore a feather behind him. I did wish we were at the top, for my arms began to feel like iron-cables, stiff and stark-only I was afraid of my fingers giving way. My heart was beating uncomfortably too. But Percivale, I felt almost inclined to quarrel with him before it was over, he strode on so unconcernedly, turning every corner of the zigzag where I expected him to propose a halt, and striding on again, as if there could be no pretence for any change of procedure. But I held out, strengthened by the play on my daughter's face, delicate as the play on an opal-one that inclines more to the milk than the fire.

When at length we turned in through the gothic door in the battlemented wall, and set our lovely burden down upon the grass —

"Percivale," I said, forgetting the proprieties in the affected humour of being angry with him, so glad was I that we had her at length on the mount of glory, "why did you go on walking like a castle, and pay no heed to me?"

"You didn't speak, did you, Mr. Walton," he returned, with just a shadow of solicitude in the question.

"No. Of course not," I rejoined.

"O, then," he returned, in a tone of relief, "how could I? You were my captain: how could I give in so long as you were holding on?"

I am afraid the *Percivale*, without the *Mister*, came again and again after this, though I pulled myself up for it as often as I caught myself.

"Now, papa!" said Connie from the grass.

"Not yet, my dear. Wait till your mamma and Wynnie come. Let us go and meet them, Mr. Percivale."

"O yes, do, papa. Leave me alone here without knowing where I am or what kind of a place I am in. I should like to know how it feels. I have never been alone in all my life."

"Very well, my dear," I said; and Percivale and I left her alone in the ruins.

We found Ethelwyn toiling up with Wynnie helping her all she could.

"Dear Harry," she said, "how could you think of bringing Connie up such an awful place? I wonder you dared to do it."

"It's done you see, wife," I answered, "thanks to Mr. Percivale, who has nearly torn the breath out of me. But now we must get you up, and you will say that to see Connie's delight, not to mention your own, is quite wages for the labour."

"Isn't she afraid to find herself so high up?"

"She knows nothing about it yet."

"You do not mean you have left the child there with her eyes tied up."

"To be sure. We could not uncover them before you came. It would spoil half the pleasure."

"Do let us make haste then. It is surely dangerous to leave her so."

"Not in the least; but she must be getting tired of the darkness. Take my arm now."

"Don't you think Mrs. Walton had better take my arm," said Percivale, "and then you can put your hand on her back, and help her a little that way."

We tried the plan, found it a good one, and soon reached the top. The moment our eyes fell upon Connie, we could see that she had found the place neither fearful nor lonely. The sweetest ghost of a smile hovered on her pale face, which shone in the shadow of the old gateway of the keep, with light from within her own sunny soul. She lay in such still expectation, that you would have thought she had just fallen asleep after receiving an answer to a prayer, reminding me of a little-known sonnet of Wordsworth's, in which he describes as the type of Death —

> "the face of one
> Sleeping alone within a mossy cave
> With her face up to heaven; that seemed to have
> Pleasing remembrance of a thought foregone;
> A lovely beauty in a summer grave."

[Footnote: *Miscellaneous Sonnets*, part i.28.]

But she heard our steps, and her face awoke.

"Is mamma come?"

"Yes, my darling. I am here," said her mother. "How do you feel?"

"Perfectly well, mamma, thank you. Now, papa!"

"One moment more, my love. Now, Percivale."

We carried her to the spot we had agreed upon, and while we held her a little inclined that she might see the better, her mother undid the bandage from her head.

"Hold your hands over her eyes, a little way from them," I said to her as she untied the handkerchief, "that the light may reach them by degrees, and not blind her."

Ethelwyn did so for a few moments, then removed them. Still for a moment or two more, it was plain from her look of utter bewilderment, that all was a confused mass of light and colour. Then she gave a little cry, and to my astonishment, almost fear, half rose to a sitting posture. One moment more and she laid herself gently back, and wept and sobbed.

And now I may admit my reader to a share, though at best but a dim reflex in my poor words, of the glory that made her weep.

Through the gothic-arched door in the battlemented wall, which stood on the very edge of the precipitous descent, so that nothing of the descent was seen, and the door was as a framework to the picture, Connie saw a great gulf at her feet, full to the brim of a splendour of light and colour. Before her rose the great ruins of rock and castle, the ruin of rock with castle; rough stone below, clear green happy grass above, even to the verge of the abrupt and awful precipice; over it the summer sky so clear that it must have been clarified by sorrow and thought; at the foot of the rocks, hundreds of feet below, the blue waters breaking in white upon the dark gray sands; all full of the gladness of the sun overflowing in speechless delight, and reflected in fresh gladness from stone and water and flower, like new springs of light rippling forth from the earth itself to swell the universal tide of glory-all this seen through the narrow gothic archway of a door in a wall-up-down-on either hand. But the main marvel was the look sheer below into the abyss full of light and air and colour, its sides lined with rock and grass, and its bottom lined with blue ripples and sand. Was it any wonder that my Connie should cry aloud when the vision dawned upon her, and then weep to ease a heart ready to burst with delight? "O Lord God," I said, almost involuntarily, "thou art very rich. Thou art the one poet, the one maker. We worship thee. Make but our souls as full of glory in thy sight as this chasm is to our eyes glorious with the forms which thou hast cloven and carved out of nothingness, and we shall be worthy to worship thee, O Lord, our God." For I was carried beyond myself with delight, and with sympathy with Connie's delight and with the calm worship of gladness in my wife's countenance. But when my eye fell on Wynnie, I saw a trouble mingled with her admiration, a self-accusation, I think, that she did not and could not enjoy it more; and when I turned from her, there were the eyes of Percivale fixed on me in wonderment; and for the moment I felt as David must have felt when, in his dance of undignified delight that he had got the ark home again, he saw the contemptuous eyes of Michal fixed on him from the window. But I could not leave it so. I said to him-coldly I daresay:

"Excuse me, Mr. Percivale; I forgot for the moment that I was not amongst my own family." Percivale took his hat off.

"Forgive my seeming rudeness, Mr. Walton. I was half-envying and half-wondering. You would not be surprised at my unconscious behaviour if you had seen as much of the wrong side of the stuff as I have seen in London."

I had some idea of what he meant; but this was no time to enter upon a discussion. I could only say —

"My heart was full, Mr. Percivale, and I let it overflow."

"Let me at least share in its overflow," he rejoined, and nothing more passed on the subject.

For the next ten minutes we stood in absolute silence. We had set Connie down on the grass again, but propped up so that she could see through the doorway. And she lay in still ecstasy. But there was more to be seen ere we descended. There was the rest of the little islet with its crop of down-grass, on which the horses of all the knights of King Arthur's round table might have fed for a week-yes, for a fortnight, without, by any means, encountering the short commons of war. There were the ruins of the castle so built of plates of the laminated stone of the rocks on which they stood, and so woven in or more properly incorporated with the outstanding rocks themselves, that in some parts I found it impossible to tell which was building and which was rock-the walls themselves seeming like a growth out of the island itself, so perfectly were they in harmony with, and in kind the same as, the natural ground upon which and of which they had been constructed. And this would seem to me to be the perfection of architecture. The work of man's hands should be so in harmony with the place where it stands that it must look as if it had grown out of the soil. But the walls were in some parts so thin that one wondered how they could have stood so long. They must have been built before the time of any formidable artillery-enough only for defence from arrows. But then the island was nowhere commanded, and its own steep cliffs would be more easily defended than any erections upon it. Clearly the intention was that no enemy should thereon find rest for the sole of his foot; for if he was able to land, farewell to the notion of any further defence. Then there was outside the walls the little chapel-such a tiny chapel! of which little more than the foundation remained, with the ruins of the altar still standing, and outside the chancel, nestling by its wall, a coffin hollowed in the rock; then the churchyard a little way off full of graves, which, I presume, would have vanished long ago were it not that the very graves were founded on the rock. There still stood old worn-out headstones of thin slate, but no memorials were left. Then there was the fragment of arched passage underground laid open to the air in the centre of the islet; and last, and grandest of all, the awful edges of the rock, broken by time, and carved by the winds and the waters into grotesque shapes and threatening forms. Over all the surface of the islet we carried Connie, and from three sides of this sea-fortress she looked abroad over "the Atlantic's level powers." It blew a gentle ethereal breeze on the top; but had there been such a wind as I have since stood against on that fearful citadel of nature, I should have been in terror lest we should all be blown, into the deep. Over the edge she peeped at the strange fantastic needle-rock, and round the corner she peeped to see Wynnie and her mother seated in what they call Arthur's chair —a canopied hollow wrought in the plated rock by the mightiest of all solvents-air and water; till at length it was time that we should take our leave of the few sheep that fed over the place, and issuing by the gothic door, wind away down the dangerous path to the safe ground below.

"I think we had better tie up your eyes again, Connie?" I said.

"Why?" she asked, in wonderment. "There's nothing higher yet, is there?"

"No, my love. If there were, you would hardly be able for it to-day, I should think. It is only to keep you from being frightened at the precipice as you go down."

"But I sha'n't be frightened, papa."

"How do you know that?"

"Because you are going to carry me."

"But what if I should slip? I might, you know."

"I don't mind. I sha'n't mind being tumbled over the precipice, if you do it. I sha'n't be to blame, and I'm sure you won't, papa." Then she drew my head down and whispered in my ear, "If I get as much more by being killed, as I have got by having my poor back hurt, I'm sure it will be well worth it."

I tried to smile a reply, for I could not speak one. We took her just as she was, and with some tremor on my part, but not a single slip, we bore her down the winding path, her face showing all the time that, instead of being afraid, she was in a state of ecstatic delight. My wife, I could see, was nervous, however; and she breathed a sigh of relief when we were once more at the foot.

"Well, I'm glad that's over," she said.

"So am I," I returned, as we set down the litter.

"Poor papa! I've pulled his arms to pieces! and Mr. Percivale's too!"

Percivale answered first by taking up a huge piece of stone. Then turning towards her, he said, "Look here, Miss Connie;" and flung it far out from the isthmus on which we were resting. We heard it strike on a rock below, and then fall in a shower of fragments. "My arms are all right, you see," he said.

Meantime, Wynnie had scrambled down to the shore, where we had not yet been. In a few minutes, we still lingering, she came running back to us out of breath with the news:

"Papa! Mr. Percivale! there's such a grand cave down there! It goes right through under the island."

Connie looked so eager, that Percivale and I glanced at each other, and without a word, lifted her, and followed Wynnie. It was a little way that we had to carry her down, but it was very broken, and insomuch more difficult than the other. At length we stood in the cavern. What a contrast to the vision overhead! —nothing to be seen but the cool, dark vault of the cave, long and winding, with the fresh seaweed lying on its pebbly floor, and its walls wet with the last tide, for every tide rolled through in rising and falling-the waters on the opposite sides of the islet greeting through this cave; the blue shimmer of the rising sea, and the forms of huge outlying rocks, looking in at the further end, where the roof rose like a grand cathedral arch; and the green gleam of veins rich with copper, dashing and streaking the darkness in gloomy little chapels, where the floor of heaped-up pebbles rose and rose within till it met the descending roof. It was like a going-down from Paradise into the grave-but a cool, friendly, brown-lighted grave, which even in its darkest recesses bore some witness to the wind of God outside, in the occasional ripple of shadowed light, from the play of the sun on the waves, that, fleeted and reflected, wandered across its jagged roof. But we dared not keep Connie long in the damp coolness; and I have given my reader quite enough of description for one hour's reading. He can scarcely be equal to more.

My invalids had now beheld the sea in such a different aspect, that I no longer feared to go back to Kilkhaven. Thither we went three days after, and at my invitation, Percivale took Turner's place in the carriage.

CHAPTER XI
JOE AND HIS TROUBLE.

How bright the yellow shores of Kilkhaven looked after the dark sands of Tintagel! But how low and tame its highest cliffs after the mighty rampart of rocks which there face the sea like a cordon of fierce guardians! It was pleasant to settle down again in what had begun to look like home, and was indeed made such by the boisterous welcome of Dora and the boys. Connie's baby crowed aloud, and stretched forth her chubby arms at sight of her. The wind blew gently around us, full both of the freshness of the clean waters and the scents of the down-grasses, to welcome us back. And the dread vision of the shore had now receded so far into the past, that it was no longer able to hurt.

We had called at the blacksmith's house on our way home, and found that he was so far better as to be working at his forge again. His mother said he was used to such attacks, and soon got over them. I, however, feared that they indicated an approaching break-down.

"Indeed, sir," she said, "Joe might be well enough if he liked. It's all his own fault."

"What do you mean?" I asked. "I cannot believe that your son is in any way guilty of his own illness."

"He's a well-behaved lad, my Joe," she answered; "but he hasn't learned what I had to learn long ago."

"What is that?" I asked.

"To make up his mind, and stick to it. To do one thing or the other."

She was a woman with a long upper lip and a judicial face, and as she spoke, her lip grew longer and longer; and when she closed her mouth in mark of her own resolution, that lip seemed to occupy two-thirds of all her face under the nose.

"And what is it he won't do?"

"I don't mind whether he does it or not, if he would only make-up-his-mind-and-stick-to-it."

"What is it you want him to do, then?"

"I don't want him to do it, I'm sure. It's no good to me-and wouldn't be much to him, that I'll be bound. Howsomever, he must please himself."

I thought it not very wonderful that he looked gloomy, if there was no more sunshine for him at home than his mother's face indicated. Few things can make a man so strong and able for his work as a sun indoors, whose rays are smiles, ever ready to shine upon him when he opens the door,—the face of wife or mother or sister. Now his mother's face certainly was not sunny. No doubt it must have shone upon him when he was a baby. God has made that provision for babies, who need sunshine so much that a mother's face cannot help being sunny to them: why should the sunshine depart as the child grows older?

"Well, I suppose I must not ask. But I fear your son is very far from well. Such attacks do not often occur without serious mischief somewhere. And if there is anything troubling him, he is less likely to get over it."

"If he would let somebody make up his mind for him, and then stick to it —"

"O, but that is impossible, you know. A man must make up his own mind."

"That's just what he won't do."

All the time she looked naughty, only after a self-righteous fashion. It was evident that whatever was the cause of it, she was not in sympathy with her son, and therefore could not help him out of any difficulty he might be in. I made no further attempt to learn from her the cause of her son's discomfort, clearly a deeper cause than his illness. In passing his workshop, we stopped for a moment, and I made an arrangement to meet him at the church the next day.

I was there before him, and found that he had done a good deal since we left. Little remained except to get the keys put to rights, and the rods attached to the cranks in the box. To-day he was to bring a carpenter, a cousin of his own, with him.

They soon arrived, and a small consultation followed. The cousin was a bright-eyed, cheruby-cheeked little man, with a ready smile and white teeth: I thought he might help me to understand what was amiss in Joseph's affairs. But I would not make the attempt except openly. I therefore said half in a jocular fashion, as with gloomy, self-withdrawn countenance the smith was fitting one loop into another in two of his iron rods, —

"I wish we could get this cousin of yours to look a little more cheerful. You would think he had quarrelled with the sunshine."

The carpenter showed his white teeth between his rosy lips.

"Well, sir, if you'll excuse me, you see my cousin Joe is not like the rest of us. He's a religious man, is Joe."

"But I don't see how that should make him miserable. It hasn't made me miserable. I hope I'm a religious man myself. It makes me happy every day of my life."

"Ah, well," returned the carpenter, in a thoughtful tone, as he worked away gently to get the inside out of the oak-chest without hurting it, "I don't say it's the religion, for I don't know; but perhaps it's the way he takes it up. He don't look after hisself enough; he's always thinking about other people, you see, sir; and it seems to me, sir, that if you don't look after yourself, why, who is to look after you? That's common sense, *I* think."

It was a curious contrast-the merry friendly face, which shone good-fellowship to all mankind, accusing the sombre, pale, sad, severe, even somewhat bitter countenance beside him, of thinking too much about other people, and too little about himself. Of course it might be correct in a way. There is all the difference between a comfortable, healthy inclination, and a pained, conscientious principle. It was a smile very unlike his cousin's with which Joe heard his remarks on himself.

"But," I said, "you will allow, at least, that if everybody would take Joe's way of it, there would then be no occasion for taking care of yourself."

"I don't see why, sir."

"Why, because everybody would take care of everybody else."

"Not so well, I doubt, sir."

"Yes, and a great deal better."

"At any rate, that's a long way off; and mean time, *who's* to take care of the odd man like Joe there, that don't look after hisself?"

"Why, God, of course."

"Well, there's just where I'm out. I don't know nothing about that branch, sir."

I saw a grateful light mount up in Joe's gloomy eyes as I spoke thus upon his side of the question. He said nothing, however; and his cousin volunteering no further information, I did not push any advantage I might have gained.

At noon I made them leave their work, and come home with me to have their dinner; they hoped to finish the job before dusk. Harry Cobb and I dropped behind, and Joe Harper walked on in front, apparently sunk in meditation.

Scarcely were we out of the churchyard, and on the road leading to the rectory, when I saw the sexton's daughter meeting us. She had almost come up to Joe before he saw her, for his gaze was bent on the ground, and he started. They shook hands in what seemed to me an odd, constrained, yet familiar fashion, and then stood as if they wanted to talk, but without speaking. Harry and I passed, both with a nod of recognition to the young woman, but neither of us had the ill-manners to look behind. I glanced at Harry, and he answered me with a queer look. When we reached the turning that would hide them from our view, I looked back almost involuntarily, and there they were still standing. But before we reached the door of the rectory, Joe got up with us.

There was something remarkable in the appearance of Agnes Coombes, the sexton's daughter. She was about six-and-twenty, I should imagine, the youngest of the family, with a sallow, rather sickly complexion, somewhat sorrowful eyes, a smile rare and sweet, a fine figure, tall and slender, and a graceful gait. I now saw, I thought, a good hair's-breadth further into the smith's affairs. Beyond the hair's-breadth, however, all was dark. But I saw likewise that the well of truth, whence I might draw the whole business, must be the girl's mother.

After the men had had their dinner and rested a while, they went back to the church, and I went to the sexton's cottage. I found the old man seated at the window, with his pot of beer on the sill, and an empty plate beside it.

"Come in, sir," he said, rising, as I put my head in at the door. "The mis'ess ben't in, but she'll be here in a few minutes."

"O, it's of no consequence," I said. "Are they all well?"

"All comfortable, sir. It be fine dry weather for them, this, sir. It be in winter it be worst for them."

"But it's a snug enough shelter you've got here. It seems such, anyhow; though, to be sure, it is the blasts of winter that find out the weak places both in house and body."

"It ben't the wind touch *them*" he said; "they be safe enough from the wind. It be the wet, sir. There ben't much snow in these parts; but when it du come, that be very bad for them, poor things!"

Could it be that he was harping on the old theme again?

"But at least this cottage keeps out the wet," I said. "If not, we must have it seen to."

"This cottage du well enough, sir. It'll last my time, anyhow."

"Then why are you pitying your family for having to live in it?"

"Bless your heart, sir! It's not them. They du well enough. It's my people out yonder. You've got the souls to look after, and I've got the bodies. That's what it be, sir. To be sure!"

The last exclamation was uttered in a tone of impatient surprise at my stupidity in giving all my thoughts and sympathies to the living, and none to the dead. I pursued the subject no further, but as I lay in bed that night, it began to dawn upon me as a lovable kind of hallucination in which the man indulged. He too had an office in the Church of God, and he would magnify that office. He could not bear that there should be no further outcome of his labour; that the burying of the dead out of sight should be "the be-all and the end-all." He was God's vicar, the gardener in God's Acre, as the Germans call the churchyard. When all others had forsaken the dead, he remained their friend, caring for what little comfort yet remained possible to them. Hence in all changes of air and sky above, he attributed to them some knowledge of the same, and some share in their consequences even down in the darkness of the tomb. It was his way of keeping up the relation between the living and the dead. Finding I made him no reply, he took up the word again.

"You've got your part, sir, and I've got mine. You up into the pulpit, and I down into the grave. But it'll be all the same by and by."

"I hope it will," I answered. "But when you do go down into your own grave, you'll know a good deal less about it than you do now. You'll find you've got other things to think about. But here comes your wife. She'll talk about the living rather than the dead."

"That's natural, sir. She brought 'em to life, and I buried 'em-at least, best part of 'em. If only I had the other two safe down with the rest!"

I remembered what the old woman had told me-that she had two boys *in* the sea; and I knew therefore what he meant. He regarded his drowned boys as still tossed about in the weary wet cold ocean, and would have gladly laid them to rest in the warm dry churchyard.

He wiped a tear from the corner of his eye with the back of his hand, and saying, "Well, I must be off to my gardening," left me with his wife. I saw then that, humorist as the old man might be, his humour, like that of all true humorists, lay close about the wells of weeping.

"The old man seems a little out of sorts," I said to his wife.

"Well, sir," she answered, with her usual gentleness, a gentleness which obedient suffering had perfected, "this be the day he buried our Nancy, this day two years; and to-day Agnes be come home from her work poorly; and the two things together they've upset him a bit."

"I met Agnes coming this way. Where is she?"

"I believe she be in the churchyard, sir. I've been to the doctor about her."

"I hope it's nothing serious."

"I hope not, sir; but you see-four on 'em, sir!"

"Well, she's in God's hands, you know."

"That she be, sir."

"I want to ask you about something, Mrs. Coombes."

"What be that, sir? If I can tell, I will, you may be sure, sir."

"I want to know what's the matter with Joe Harper, the blacksmith."

"They du say it be a consumption, sir."

"But what has he got on his mind?"

"He's got nothing on his mind, sir. He be as good a by as ever stepped, I assure you, sir."

"But I am sure there is something or other on his mind. He's not so happy as he should be. He's not the man, it seems to me, to be unhappy because he's ill. A man like him would not be miserable because he was going to die. It might make him look sad sometimes, but not gloomy as he looks."

"Well, sir, I believe you be right, and perhaps I know summat. But it's part guessing.—I believe my Agnes and Joe Harper are as fond upon one another as any two in the county."

"Are they not going to be married then?"

"There be the pint, sir. I don't believe Joe ever said a word o' the sort to Aggy. She never could ha' kep it from me, sir."

"Why doesn't he then?"

"That's the pint again, sir. All as knows him says it's because he be in such bad health, and he thinks he oughtn't to go marrying with one foot in the grave. He never said so to me; but I think very likely that be it."

"For that matter, Mrs. Coombes, we've all got one foot in the grave, I think."

"That be very true, sir."

"And what does your daughter think?"

"I believe she thinks the same. And so they go on talking to each other, quiet-like, like old married folks, not like lovers at all, sir. But I can't help fancying it have something to do with my Aggy's pale face."

"And something to do with Joe's pale face too, Mrs. Coombes," I said. "Thank you. You've told me more than I expected. It explains everything. I must have it out with Joe now."

"O deary me! sir, don't go and tell him I said anything, as if I wanted him to marry my daughter."

"Don't you be afraid. I'll take good care of that. And don't fancy I'm fond of meddling with other people's affairs. But this is a case in which I ought to do something. Joe's a fine fellow."

"That he be, sir. I couldn't wish a better for a son-in-law."

I put on my hat.

"You won't get me into no trouble with Joe, will ye, sir!"

"Indeed I will not, Mrs. Coombes. I should be doing a great deal more harm than good if I said a word to make him doubt you."

I went straight to the church. There were the two men working away in the shadowy tower, and there was Agnes standing beside, knitting like her mother, so quiet, so solemn even, that it did indeed look as if she were a long-married wife, hovering about her husband at his work. Harry was saying something to her as I went in, but when they saw me they were silent, and Agnes gently withdrew.

"Do you think you will get through to-night?" I asked.

"Sure of it, sir," answered Harry.

"You shouldn't be sure of anything, Harry. We are told in the New Testament that we ought to say *If the Lord will*," said Joe.

"Now, Joe, you're too hard upon Harry," I said. "You don't think that the Bible means to pull a man up every step like that, till he's afraid to speak a word. It was about a long journey and a year's residence that the Apostle James was speaking."

"No doubt, sir. But the principle's the same. Harry can no more be sure of finishing his work before it be dark, than those people could be of going their long journey."

"That is perfectly true. But you are taking the letter for the spirit, and that, I suspect, in more ways than one. The religion does not lie in not being sure about anything, but in a loving desire that the will of God in the matter, whatever it be, may be done. And if Harry has not learned yet to care about the will of God, what is the good of coming down upon him that way, as if that would teach him in the least. When he loves God, then, and not till then, will he care about his will. Nor does the religion lie in saying, *if the Lord will*, every time anything is to be done. It is a most dangerous thing to use sacred words often. It makes them so common to our ear that at length, when used most solemnly, they have not half the effect they ought to have, and that is a serious loss. What the Apostle means is, that we should always be in the mood of looking up to God and having regard to his will, not always writing D.V. for instance, as so many do—most irreverently, I think—using a Latin contraction for the beautiful words, just as if they were a charm, or as if God would take offence if they did not make the salvo of acknowledgment. It seems to me quite heathenish. Our hearts ought ever to be in the spirit of those words; our lips ought to utter them rarely. Besides, there are some things a man might be pretty sure the Lord wills."

"It sounds fine, sir; but I'm not sure that I understand what you mean to say. It sounds to me like a darkening of wisdom."

I saw that I had irritated him, and so had in some measure lost ground. But Harry struck in —

"How *can* you say that now, Joe? *I* know what the parson means well enough, and everybody knows I ain't got half the brains you've got."

"The reason is, Harry, that he's got something in his head that stands in the way."

"And there's nothing in my head *to* stand in the way!" returned Harry, laughing.

This made me laugh too, and even Joe could not help a sympathetic grin. By this time it was getting dark.

"I'm afraid, Harry, after all, you won't get through to-night."

"I begin to think so too, sir. And there's Joe saying, 'I told you so,' over and over to himself, though he won't say it out like a man."

Joe answered only with another grin.

"I tell you what it is, Harry," I said —"you must come again on Monday. And on your way home, just look in and tell Joe's mother that I have kept him over to-morrow. The change will do him good."

"No, sir, that can't he. I haven't got a clean shirt."

"You can have a shirt of mine," I said. "But I'm afraid you'll want your Sunday clothes."

"I'll bring them for you, Joe—before you're up," interposed Harry. "And then you can go to church with Aggy Coombes, you know."

Here was just what I wanted.

"Hold your tongue, Harry," said Joe angrily. "You're talking of what you don't know anything about."

"Well, Joe, I ben't a fool, if I ben't so religious as you be. You ben't a bad fellow, though you be a Methodist, and I ben't a fool, though I be Harry Cobb."

"What do you mean, Harry? Do hold your tongue."

"Well, I'll tell you what I mean first, and then I'll hold my tongue. I mean this—that nobody with two eyes, or one eye, for that matter, in his head, could help seeing the eyes you and Aggy make at each other, and why you don't port your helm and board her —I won't say it's more than I know, but I du say it to be more than I think be fair to the young woman."

"Hold your tongue, Harry."

"I said I would when I'd answered you as to what I meaned. So no more at present; but I'll be over with your clothes afore you're up in the morning."

As Harry spoke he was busy gathering his tools.

"They won't be in the way, will they, sir?" he said, as he heaped them together in the furthest corner of the tower.

"Not in the least," I returned. "If I had my way, all the tools used in building the church should be carved on the posts and pillars of it, to indicate the sacredness of labour, and the worship of God that lies, not in building the church merely, but in every honest trade honestly pursued for the good of mankind and the need of the workman. For a necessity of God is laid upon every workman as well as on St. Paul. Only St. Paul saw it, and every workman doesn't, Harry."

"Thank you, sir. I like that way of it. I almost think I could be a little bit religious after your way of it, sir."

"Almost, Harry!" growled Joe-not unkindly.

"Now, you hold your tongue, Joe," I said. "Leave Harry to me. You may take him, if you like, after I've done with him."

Laughing merrily, but making no other reply than a hearty good-night, Harry strode away out of the church, and Joe and I went home together.

When he had had his tea, I asked him to go out with me for a walk.

The sun was shining aslant upon the downs from over the sea. We rose out of the shadowy hollow to the sunlit brow. I was a little in advance of Joe. Happening to turn, I saw the light full on his head and face, while the rest of his body had not yet emerged from the shadow.

"Stop, Joe," I said. "I want to see you so for a moment."

He stood —a little surprised.

"You look just like a man rising from the dead, Joe," I said.

"I don't know what you mean, sir," he returned.

"I will describe yourself to you. Your head and face are full of sunlight, the rest of your body is still buried in the shadow. Look; I will stand where you are now; and you come here. You will soon see what I mean."

We changed places. Joe stared for a moment. Then his face brightened.

"I see what you mean, sir," he said. "I fancy you don't mean the resurrection of the body, but the resurrection of righteousness."

"I do, Joe. Did it ever strike you that the whole history of the Christian life is a series of such resurrections? Every time a man bethinks himself that he is not walking in the light, that he has been forgetting himself, and must repent, that he has been asleep and must awake, that he has been letting his garments trail, and must gird up the loins of his mind-every time this takes place, there is a resurrection in the world. Yes, Joe; and every time that a man finds that his heart is troubled, that he is not rejoicing in God, a resurrection must follow—a resurrection out of the night of troubled thoughts into the gladness of the truth. For the truth is, and ever was, and ever must be, gladness, however much the souls on which it shines may be obscured by the clouds of sorrow, troubled by the thunders of fear, or shot through with the lightnings of pain. Now, Joe, will you let me tell you what you are like—I do not know your thoughts; I am only judging from your words and looks?"

"You may if you like, sir," answered Joe, a little sulkily. But I was not to be repelled.

I stood up in the sunlight, so that my eyes caught only about half the sun's disc. Then I bent my face towards the earth.

"What part of me is the light shining on now, Joe?"

"Just the top of your head," answered he.

"There, then," I returned, "that is just what you are like —a man with the light on his head, but not on his face. And why not on your face? Because you hold your head down."

"Isn't it possible, sir, that a man might lose the light on his face, as you put it, by doing his duty?"

"That is a difficult question," I replied. "I must think before I answer it."

"I mean," added Joe —"mightn't his duty be a painful one?"

"Yes. But I think that would rather etherealise than destroy the light. Behind the sorrow would spring a yet greater light from the very duty itself. I have expressed myself badly, but you will see what I mean. —To be frank with you, Joe, I do not see that light in your face. Therefore I think something must be wrong with you. Remember a good man is not necessarily in the right. St. Peter was a good man, yet our Lord called him Satan-and meant it of course, for he never said what he did not mean."

"How can I be wrong when all my trouble comes from doing my duty-nothing else, as far as I know?"

"Then," I replied, a sudden light breaking in on my mind, "I doubt whether what you suppose to be your duty can be your duty. If it were, I do not think it would make you so miserable. At least —I may be wrong, but I venture to think so."

"What is a man to go by, then? If he thinks a thing is his duty, is he not to do it?"

"Most assuredly-until he knows better. But it is of the greatest consequence whether the supposed duty be the will of God or the invention of one's own fancy or mistaken judgment. A real duty is always something right in itself. The duty a man makes his for the time, by supposing it to be a duty, may be something quite wrong in itself. The duty of a Hindoo widow is to burn herself on the body of her husband. But that duty lasts no longer than till she sees that, not being the will of God, it is not her duty. A real duty, on the other hand, is a necessity of the human nature, without seeing and doing which a man can never attain to the truth and blessedness of his own being. It was the duty of the early hermits to encourage the growth of vermin upon their bodies, for they supposed that was pleasing to God; but they could not fare so well as if they had seen the truth that the will of God was cleanliness. And there may be far more serious things done by Christian people against the will of God, in the fancy of doing their duty, than such a trifle as swarming with worms. In a word, thinking a thing is your duty makes it your duty only till you know better. And the prime duty of every man is to seek and find, that he may do, the will of God."

"But do you think, sir, that a man is likely to be doing what he ought not, if he is doing what he don't like?"

"Not so likely, I allow. But there may be ambition in it. A man must not want to be better than the right. That is the delusion of the anchorite —a delusion in which the man forgets the rights of others for the sake of his own sanctity."

"It might be for the sake of another person, and not for the person's own sake at all."

"It might be; but except it were the will of God for that other person, it would be doing him or her a real injury."

We were coming gradually towards what I wanted to make the point in question. I wished him to tell me all about it himself, however, for I knew that while advice given on request is generally disregarded, to offer advice unasked is worthy only of a fool.

"But how are you to know the will of God in every case?" asked Joe.

"By looking at the general laws of life, and obeying them-except there be anything special in a particular case to bring it under a higher law."

"Ah! but that be just what there is here."

"Well, my dear fellow, that may be; but the special conduct may not be right for the special case for all that. The speciality of the case may not be even sufficient to take it from under the ordinary rule. But it is of no use talking generals. Let us come to particulars. If you can trust me, tell me all about it, and we may be able to let some light in. I am sure there is darkness somewhere."

"I will turn it over in my mind, sir; and if I can bring myself to talk about it, I will. I would rather tell you than anyone else."

I said no more. We watched a glorious sunset-there never was a grander place for sunsets-and went home.

CHAPTER XII
A SMALL ADVENTURE.

The next morning Harry came with the clothes. But Joe did not go to church. Neither did Agnes make her appearance that morning. They were both present at the evening service, however.

When we came out of church, it was cloudy and dark, and the wind was blowing cold from the sea. The sky was covered with one cloud, but the waves tossing themselves against the rocks, flashed whiteness out of the general gloom. As the tide rose the wind increased. It was a night of surly temper-hard and gloomy. Not a star cracked the blue above-there was no blue; and the wind was *gurly*; I once heard that word in Scotland, and never forgot it.

After one of our usual gatherings in Connie's room, which were much shorter here because of the evening service in summer, I withdrew till supper should be ready.

Now I have always had, as I think I have incidentally stated before, a certain peculiar pleasure in the surly aspects of nature. When I was a young man this took form in opposition and defiance; since I had begun to grow old the form had changed into a sense of safety. I welcomed such aspects, partly at least, because they roused my faith to look through and beyond the small region of human conditions in which alone the storm can be and blow, and thus induced a feeling like that of the child who lies in his warm crib and listens to the howling of one of these same storms outside the strong-built house which yet trembles at its fiercer onsets: the house is not in danger; or, if it be, that is his father's business, not his. Hence it came that, after supper, I put on my great-coat and travelling-cap, and went out into the ill-tempered night-speaking of it in its human symbolism.

I meant to have a stroll down to the breakwater, of which I have yet said little, but which was a favourite resort, both of myself and my children. At the further end of it, always covered at high water, was an outlying cluster of low rocks, in the heart of which the lord of the manor, a noble-hearted Christian gentleman of the old school, had constructed a bath of graduated depth-an open-air swimming-pool —the only really safe place for men who were swimmers to bathe in. Thither I was in the habit of taking my two little men every morning, and bathing with them, that I might develop the fish that was in them; for, as George Herbert says:

> "Man is everything,
> And more: he is a tree, yet bears no fruit;
> A beast, yet is, or should be, more;"

and he might have gone on to say that he is, or should be, a fish as well.

It will seem strange to any reader who can recall the position of my Connie's room, that the nearest way to the breakwater should be through that room; but so it was. I mention the fact because I want my readers to understand a certain peculiarity of the room. By the side of the window which looked out upon the breakwater was a narrow door, apparently of a closet or cupboard, which communicated, however, with a narrow, curving, wood-built passage, leading into a little wooden hut, the walls of which were by no means impervious to the wind, for they were formed of outside-planks, with the bark still upon them. From this hut one or two little windows looked seaward, and a door led out on the bit of sward in which lay the flower-bed under Connie's window. From this spot again a door in the low wall and thick hedge led out on the downs, where a path wound along the cliffs that formed the side of the bay, till, descending under the storm-tower, it brought you to the root of the breakwater.

This mole stretched its long strong low back to a rock a good way out, breaking the force of the waves, and rendering the channel of a small river, that here flowed into the sea across the sands from the mouth of the canal, a refuge from the Atlantic. But it was a roadway often hard to reach. In fair weather even, the wind falling as the vessel rounded the point of the breakwater into the calm of the projecting headlands, the under-current would sometimes dash her helpless on the rocks. During all this heavenly summer there had been no thought or fear of any such disaster. The present night was a hint of what weather would yet come.

When I went into Connie's room, I found her lying in bed a very picture of peace. But my entrance destroyed the picture.

"Papa," she said, "why have you got your coat on? Surely you are not going out to-night. The wind is blowing dreadfully."

"Not very dreadfully, Connie. It blew much worse the night we found your baby."

"But it is very dark."

"I allow that; but there is a glimmer from the sea. I am only going on the breakwater for a few minutes. You know I like a stormy night quite as much as a fine one."

"I shall be miserable till you come home, papa."

"Nonsense, Connie. You don't think your father hasn't sense to take care of himself! Or rather, Connie, for I grant that is poor ground of comfort, you don't think I can go anywhere without my Father to take care of me?"

"But there is no occasion-is there, papa?"

"Do you think I should be better pleased with my boys if they shrunk from everything involving the least possibility of danger because there was no occasion for it? That is just the way to make cowards. And I am certain God would not like his children to indulge in such moods of self-preservation as that. He might well be ashamed of them. The fearful are far more likely to meet with accidents than the courageous. But really, Connie, I am almost ashamed of talking so. It is all your fault. There is positively no ground for apprehension, and I hope you won't spoil my walk by the thought that my foolish little girl is frightened."

"I will be good-indeed I will, papa," she said, holding up her mouth to kiss me.

I left her room, and went through the wooden passage into the bark hut. The wind roared about it, shook it, and pawed it, and sung and whistled in the chinks of the planks. I went out and shut the door. That moment the wind seized upon me, and I had to fight with it. When I got on the path leading along the edge of the downs, I felt something lighter than any feather fly in my face. When I put up my hand, I found my cheek wet. Again and again I was thus assailed, but when I got to the breakwater I found what it was. They were flakes of foam, bubbles worked up into little masses of adhering thousands, which the wind blew off the waters and across the downs, carrying some of them miles inland. When I reached the breakwater, and looked along its ridge through the darkness of the night, I was bewildered to see a whiteness lying here and there in a great patch upon its top. They were but accumulations of these foam-flakes, like soap-suds, lying so thick that I expected to have to wade through them, only they vanished at the touch of my feet. Till then I had almost believed it was snow I saw. On the edge of the waves, in quieter spots, they lay like yeast, foaming and working. Now and then a little rush of water from a higher wave swept over the top of the broad breakwater, as with head bowed sideways against the wind, I struggled along towards the rock at its end; but I said to myself, "The tide is falling fast, and salt water hurts nobody," and struggled on over the huge rough stones of the mighty heap, outside which the waves were white with wrath, inside which they had fallen asleep, only heaving with the memory of their late unrest. I reached the tall rock at length, climbed the rude stair leading up to the flagstaff, and looked abroad, if looking it could be called, into the thick dark. But the wind blew so strong on the top that I was glad to descend. Between me and the basin where yesterday morning I had bathed in still water and sunshine with my boys, rolled the deathly waves. I wandered on the rough narrow space yet uncovered, stumbling over the stones and the rocky points between which they lay, stood here and there half-meditating, and at length, finding a sheltered nook in a mass of rock, sat with the wind howling and the waves bursting around me. There I fell into a sort of brown study-almost a half-sleep.

But I had not sat long before I came broad awake, for I heard voices, low and earnest. One I recognised as Joe's voice. The other was a woman's. I could not tell what they said for some time, and therefore felt no immediate necessity for disclosing my proximity, but sat debating with myself whether I should speak to them or not. At length, in a lull of the wind, I heard the woman say—I could fancy with a sigh—

"I'm sure you'll du what is right, Joe. Don't 'e think o' me, Joe."

"It's just of you that I du think, Aggy. You know it ben't for my sake. Surely you know that?"

There was no answer for a moment. I was still doubting what I had best do-go away quietly or let them know I was there-when she spoke again. There was a momentary lull now in the noises of both wind and water, and I heard what she said well enough.

"It ben't for me to contradict you, Joe. But I don't think you be going to die. You be no worse than last year. Be you now, Joe?"

It flashed across me how once before, a stormy night and darkness had brought me close to a soul in agony. Then I was in agony myself; now the world was all fair and hopeful around me-the portals of the world beyond ever opening wider as I approached them, and letting out more of their glory to gladden the path to their threshold. But here were two souls straying in a mist which faith might roll away, and leave them walking in the light. The moment was come. I must speak.

"Joe!" I called out.

"Who's there?" he cried; and I heard him start to his feet.

"Only Mr. Walton. Where are you?"

"We can't be very far off," he answered, not in a tone of any pleasure at finding me so nigh.

I rose, and peering about through the darkness, found that they were a little higher up on the same rock by which I was sheltered.

"You mustn't think," I said, "that I have been eavesdropping. I had no idea anyone was near me till I heard your voices, and I did not hear a word till just the last sentence or two."

"I saw someone go up the Castle-rock," said Joe; "but I thought he was gone away again. It will be a lesson to me."

"I'm no tell-tale, Joe," I returned, as I scrambled up the rock. "You will have no cause to regret that I happened to overhear a little. I am sure, Joe, you will never say anything you need be ashamed of. But what I heard was sufficient to let me into the secret of your trouble. Will you let me talk to Joe, Agnes? I've been young myself, and, to tell the truth, I don't think I'm old yet."

"I am sure, sir," she answered, "you won't be hard on Joe and me. I don't suppose there be anything wrong in liking each other, though we can't be-married."

She spoke in a low tone, and her voice trembled very much; yet there was a certain womanly composure in her utterance. "I'm sure it's very bold of me to talk so," she added, "but Joe will tell you all about it."

I was close beside them now, and fancied I saw through the dusk the motion of her hand stealing into his.

"Well, Joe, this is just what I wanted," I said. "A woman can be braver than a big smith sometimes. Agnes has done her part. Now you do yours, and tell me all about it."

No response followed my adjuration. I must help him.

"I think I know how the matter lies, Joe. You think you are not going to live long, and that therefore you ought not to marry. Am I right?"

"Not far off it, sir," he answered.

"Now, Joe," I said, "can't we talk as friends about this matter? I have no right to intrude into your affairs-none in the least-except what friendship gives me. If you say I am not to talk about it, I shall be silent. To force advice upon you would be as impertinent as useless."

"It's all the same, I'm afraid, sir. My mind has been made up for a long time. What right have I to bring other people into trouble? But I take it kind of you, sir, though I mayn't look over-pleased. Agnes wants to hear your way of it. I'm agreeable."

This was not very encouraging. Still I thought it sufficient ground for proceeding.

"I suppose you will allow that the root of all Christian behaviour is the will of God?"

"Surely, sir."

"Is it not the will of God, then, that when a man and woman love each other, they should marry?"

"Certainly, sir-where there be no reasons against it."

"Of course. And you judge you see reason for not doing so, else you would?"

"I do see that a man should not bring a woman into trouble for the sake of being comfortable himself for the rest of a few weary days."

Agnes was sobbing gently behind her handkerchief. I knew how gladly she would be Joe's wife, if only to nurse him through his last illness.

"Not except it would make her comfortable too, I grant you, Joe. But listen to me. In the first place, you don't know, and you are not required to know, when you are going to die. In fact, you have nothing to do with it. Many a life has been injured by the constant expectation of death. It is life we have to do with, not death. The best preparation for the night is to work while the day lasts, diligently. The best preparation for death is life. Besides, I have known delicate people who have outlived all their strong relations, and been left alone in the earth-because they had possibly taken too much care of themselves. But marriage is God's will, and death is God's will, and you have no business to set the one over against, as antagonistic to, the other. For anything you know, the gladness and the peace of marriage may be the very means intended for your restoration to health and strength. I suspect your desire to marry, fighting against the fancy that you ought not to marry, has a good deal to do with the state of health in which you now find yourself. A man would get over many things if he were happy, that he cannot get over when he is miserable."

"But it's for Aggy. You forget that."

"I do not forget it. What right have you to seek for her another kind of welfare than you would have yourself? Are you to treat her as if she were worldly when you are not-to provide for her a comfort which yourself you would despise? Why should you not marry because you have to die soon? —if you *are* thus doomed, which to me is by no means clear. Why not have what happiness you may for the rest of your sojourn? If you find at the end of twenty years that here you are after all, you will be rather sorry you did not do as I say."

"And if I find myself dying at the end of six months'?"

"You will thank God for those six months. The whole thing, my dear fellow, is a want of faith in God. I do not doubt you think you are doing right, but, I repeat, the whole thing comes from want of faith in God. You will take things into your own hands, and order them after a preventive and self-protective fashion, lest God should have ordained the worst for you, which worst, after all, would be best met by doing his will without inquiry into the future; and which worst is no evil. Death is no more an evil than marriage is."

"But you don't see it as I do," persisted the blacksmith.

"Of course I don't. I think you see it as it is not."

He remained silent for a little. A shower of spray fell upon us. He started.

"What a wave!" he cried. "That spray came over the top of the rock. We shall have to run for it."

I fancied that he only wanted to avoid further conversation.

"There's no hurry," I said. "It was high water an hour and a half ago."

"You don't know this coast, sir," returned he, "or you wouldn't talk like that."

As he spoke he rose, and going from under the shelter of the rock, looked along.

"For God's sake, Aggy!" he cried in terror, "come at once. Every other wave be rushing across the breakwater as if it was on the level."

So saying, he hurried back, caught her by the hand, and began to draw her along.

"Hadn't we better stay where we are?" I suggested.

"If you can stand the night in the cold. But Aggy here is delicate; and I don't care about being out all night. It's not the tide, sir; it's a ground swell-from a storm somewhere out at sea. That never asks no questions about tide or no tide."

"Come along, then," I said. "But just wait one minute more. It is better to be ready for the worst."

For I remembered that the day before I had seen a crowbar lying among the stones, and I thought it might be useful. In a moment or two I had found it, and returning, gave it to Joe. Then I took the girl's disengaged hand. She thanked me in a voice perfectly calm and firm. Joe took the bar in haste, and drew Agnes towards the breakwater.

Any real thought of danger had not yet crossed my mind. But when I looked along the outstretched back of the mole, and saw a dim sheet of white sweep across it, I felt that there was ground for his anxiety, and prepared myself for a struggle.

"Do you know what to do with the crowbar, Joe?" I said, grasping my own stout oak-stick more firmly.

"Perfectly," answered Joe. "To stick between the stones and hold on. We must watch our time between the waves."

"You take the command, then, Joe," I returned. "You see better than I do, and you know the ways of that raging wild beast there better than I do. I will obey orders-one of which, no doubt, will be, not for wind or sea to lose hold of Agnes-eh, Joe?"

Joe gave a grim enough laugh in reply, and we started, he carrying his crowbar in his right hand towards the advancing sea, and I my oak-stick in my left towards the still water within.

"Quick march!" said Joe, and away we went out on the breakwater.

Now the back of the breakwater was very rugged, for it was formed of huge stones, with wide gaps between, where the waters had washed out the cement, and worn their edges. But what impeded our progress secured our safety.

"Halt!" cried Joe, when we were yet but a few yards beyond the shelter of the rocks. "There's a topper coming."

We halted at the word of command, as a huge wave, with combing crest, rushed against the far out-sloping base of the mole, and flung its heavy top right over the middle of the mass, a score or two of yards in front of us.

"Now for it!" cried Joe. "Run!"

We did run. In my mind there was just sense enough of danger to add to the pleasure of the excitement. I did not know how much danger there was. Over the rough worn stones we sped stumbling.

"Halt!" cried the smith once more, and we did halt; but this time, as it turned out, in the middle front of the coming danger.

"God be with us!" I exclaimed, when the huge billow showed itself through the night, rushing towards the mole. The smith stuck his crowbar between two great stones. To this he held on with one hand, and threw the other arm round Agnes's waist. I, too, had got my oak firmly fixed, held on with one hand, and threw the other arm round Agnes. It took but a moment.

"Now then!" cried Joe. "Here she comes! Hold on, sir. Hold on, Aggy!"

But when I saw the height of the water, as it rushed on us up the sloping side of the mound, I cried out in my turn, "Down, Joe! Down on your face, and let it over us easy! Down Agnes!"

They obeyed. We threw ourselves across the breakwater, with our heads to the coming foe, and I grasped my stick close to the stones with all the power of a hand that was then strong. Over us burst the mighty wave, floating us up from the stones where we lay. But we held on, the wave passed, and we sprung gasping to our feet.

"Now, now!" cried Joe and I together, and, heavy as we were, with the water pouring from us, we flew across the remainder of the heap, and arrived, panting and safe, at the other end, ere one wave more had swept the surface. The moment we were in safety we turned and looked back over the danger we had traversed. It was to see a huge billow sweep the breakwater from end to end. We looked at each other for a moment without speaking.

"I believe, sir," said Joe at length, with slow and solemn speech, "if you hadn't taken the command at that moment we should all have been lost."

"It seems likely enough, when I look back on it. For one thing, I was not sure that my stick would stand, so I thought I had better grasp it low down."

"We were awfully near death," said Joe.

"Nearer than you thought, Joe; and yet we escaped it. Things don't go all as we fancy, you see. Faith is as essential to manhood as foresight-believe me, Joe. It is very absurd to trust God for the future, and not trust him for the present. The man who is not anxious is the man most likely to do the right thing. He is cool and collected and ready. Our Lord therefore told his disciples that when they should be brought before kings and rulers, they were to take no thought what answer they should make, for it would be given them when the time came."

We were climbing the steep path up to the downs. Neither of my companions spoke.

"You have escaped one death together," I said at length: "dare another."

Still neither of them returned an answer. When we came near the parsonage, I said, "Now, Joe, you must go in and get to bed at once. I will take Agnes home. You can trust me not to say anything against you?"

Joe laughed rather hoarsely, and replied: "As you please, sir. Good night, Aggie. Mind you get to bed as fast as you can."

When I returned from giving Agnes over to her parents, I made haste to change my clothes, and put on my warm dressing-gown. I may as well mention at once, that not one of us was the worse for our ducking. I then went up to Connie's room.

"Here I am, you see, Connie, quite safe."

"I've been lying listening to every blast of wind since you went out, papa. But all I could do was to trust in God."

"Do you call that *all*, Connie? Believe me, there is more power in that than any human being knows the tenth part of yet. It is indeed *all*."

I said no more then. I told my wife about it that night, but we were well into another month before I told Connie.

When I left her, I went to Joe's room to see how he was, and found him having some gruel. I sat down on the edge of his bed, and said,

"Well, Joe, this is better than under water. I hope you won't be the worse for it."

"I don't much care what comes of me, sir. It will be all over soon."

"But you ought to care what comes of you, Joe. I will tell you why. You are an instrument out of which ought to come praise to God, and, therefore, you ought to care for the instrument."

"That way, yes, sir, I ought."

"And you have no business to be like some children who say, 'Mamma won't give me so and so,' instead of asking her to give it them."

"I see what you mean, sir. But really you put me out before the young woman. I couldn't say before her what I meant. Suppose, you know, sir, there was to come a family. It might be, you know."

"Of course. What else would you have?"

"But if I was to die, where would she be then?"

"In God's hands; just as she is now."

"But I ought to take care that she is not left with a burden like that to provide for."

"O, Joe! how little you know a woman's heart! It would just be the greatest comfort she could have for losing you-that's all. Many a woman has married a man she did not care enough for, just that she might have a child of her own to let out her heart upon. I don't say that is right, you know. Such love cannot be perfect. A woman ought to love her child because it is her husband's more than because it is her own, and because it is God's more than either's. I saw in the papers the other day, that a woman was brought before the Recorder of London for stealing a baby, when the judge himself said that there was no imaginable motive for her action but a motherly passion to possess the child. It is the need of a child that makes so many women take to poor miserable, broken-nosed lap-dogs; for they are self-indulgent, and cannot face the troubles and dangers of adopting a child. They would if they might get one of a good family, or from a respectable home; but they dare not take an orphan out of the dirt, lest it should spoil their silken chairs. But that has nothing to do with our argument. What I mean is this, that if Agnes really loves you, as no one can look in her face and doubt, she will be far happier if you leave her a child-yes, she will be happier if you only leave her your name for hers-than if you died without calling her your wife."

I took Joe's basin from him, and he lay down. He turned his face to the wall. I waited a moment, but finding him silent, bade him good-night, and left the room.

A month after, I married them.

CHAPTER XIII
THE HARVEST.

It was some time before we got the bells to work to our mind, but at last we succeeded. The worst of it was to get the cranks, which at first required strong pressure on the keys, to work easily enough. But neither Joe nor his cousin spared any pains to perfect the attempt, and, as I say, at length we succeeded. I took Wynnie down to the instrument and made her try whether she could not do something, and she succeeded in making the old tower discourse loudly and eloquently.

By this time the thanksgiving for the harvest was at hand: on the morning of that first of all would I summon the folk to their prayers with the sound of the full peal. And I wrote a little hymn of praise to the God of the harvest, modelling it to one of the oldest tunes in that part of the country, and I had it printed on slips of paper and laid plentifully on the benches. What with the calling of the bells, like voices in the highway, and the solemn meditation of the organ within to bear aloft the thoughts of those who heard, and came to the prayer and thanksgiving in common, and the message which God had given me to utter to them, I hoped that we should indeed keep holiday.

Wynnie summoned the parish with the hundredth psalm pealed from aloft, dropping from the airy regions of the tower on village and hamlet and cottage, calling aloud-for who could dissociate the words from the music, though the words are in the Scotch psalms? —written none the less by an Englishman, however English wits may amuse themselves with laughing at their quaintness-calling aloud,

> "All people that on earth do dwell
> Sing to the Lord with cheerful voice;
> Him serve with mirth, his praise forth tell—
> Come ye before him and rejoice."

Then we sang the psalm before the communion service, making bold in the name of the Lord to serve him with *mirth* as in the old version, and not with the *fear* with which some editor, weak in faith, has presumed to alter the line. Then before the sermon we sang the hymn I had prepared —a proceeding justifiable by many an example in the history of the church while she was not only able to number singers amongst her clergy, but those singers were capable of influencing the whole heart and judgment of the nation with their songs. Ethelwyn played the organ. The song I had prepared was this:

> "We praise the Life of All;
> From buried seeds so small
> Who makes the ordered ranks of autumn stand;
> Who stores the corn
> In rick and barn
> To feed the winter of the land.
> We praise the Life of Light!
>
> Who from the brooding night
> Draws out the morning holy, calm, and grand;
> Veils up the moon,
> Sends out the sun,
> To glad the face of all the land.
> We praise the Life of Work,
>
> Who from sleep's lonely dark

> Leads forth his children to arise and stand,
> Then go their way,
> The live-long day,
> To trust and labour in the land.
> We praise the Life of Good,
>
> Who breaks sin's lazy mood,
> Toilsomely ploughing up the fruitless sand.
> The furrowed waste
> They leave, and haste
> Home, home, to till their Father's land.
> We praise the Life of Life,
>
> Who in this soil of strife
> Casts us at birth, like seed from sower's hand;
> To die and so
> Like corn to grow
> A golden harvest in his land."

After we had sung this hymn, the meaning of which is far better than the versification, I preached from the words of St. Paul, "If by any means I might attain unto the resurrection of the dead. Not as though I had already attained, either were already perfect." And this is something like what I said to them:

"The world, my friends, is full of resurrections, and it is not always of the same resurrection that St. Paul speaks. Every night that folds us up in darkness is a death; and those of you that have been out early and have seen the first of the dawn, will know it-the day rises out of the night like a being that has burst its tomb and escaped into life. That you may feel that the sunrise is a resurrection-the word resurrection just means a rising again —I will read you a little description of it from a sermon by a great writer and great preacher called Jeremy Taylor. Listen. 'But as when the sun approaching towards the gates of the morning, he first opens a little eye of heaven and sends away the spirits of darkness, and gives light to a cock, and calls up the lark to matins, and by and by gilds the fringes of a cloud, and peeps over the eastern hills, thrusting out his golden horns like those which decked the brows of Moses, when he was forced to wear a veil, because himself had seen the face of God; and still, while a man tells the story, the sun gets up higher, till he shows a fair face and a full light, and then he shines one whole day, under a cloud often, and sometimes weeping great and little showers, and sets quickly; so is a man's reason and his life.' Is not this a resurrection of the day out of the night? Or hear how Milton makes his Adam and Eve praise God in the morning, —

> 'Ye mists and exhalations that now rise
> From hill or streaming lake, dusky or gray,
> Till the sun paint your fleecy skirts with gold,
> In honour to the world's great Author rise,
> Whether to deck with clouds the uncoloured sky,
> Or wet the thirsty earth with falling showers,
> Rising or falling still advance his praise.'

But it is yet more of a resurrection to you. Think of your own condition through the night and in the morning. You die, as it were, every night. The death of darkness comes down over the earth; but a deeper death, the death of sleep, descends on you. A power overshadows you; your eyelids close, you cannot keep them open if you would; your limbs lie moveless; the day is gone;

your whole life is gone; you have forgotten everything; an evil man might come and do with your goods as he pleased; you are helpless. But the God of the Resurrection is awake all the time, watching his sleeping men and women, even as a mother who watches her sleeping baby, only with larger eyes and more full of love than hers; and so, you know not how, all at once you know that you are what you are; that there is a world that wants you outside of you, and a God that wants you inside of you; you rise from the death of sleep, not by your own power, for you knew nothing about it; God put his hand over your eyes, and you were dead; he lifted his hand and breathed light on you and you rose from the dead, thanked the God who raised you up, and went forth to do your work. From darkness to light; from blindness to seeing; from knowing nothing to looking abroad on the mighty world; from helpless submission to willing obedience,—is not this a resurrection indeed? That St. Paul saw it to be such may be shown from his using the two things with the same meaning when he says, 'Awake, thou that sleepest, and arise from the dead, and Christ shall give thee light.' No doubt he meant a great deal more. No man who understands what he is speaking about can well mean only one thing at a time.

"But to return to the resurrections we see around us in nature. Look at the death that falls upon the world in winter. And look how it revives when the sun draws near enough in the spring to wile the life in it once more out of its grave. See how the pale, meek snowdrops come up with their bowed heads, as if full of the memory of the fierce winds they encountered last spring, and yet ready in the strength of their weakness to encounter them again. Up comes the crocus, bringing its gold safe from the dark of its colourless grave into the light of its parent gold. Primroses, and anemones, and blue-bells, and a thousand other children of the spring, hear the resurrection-trumpet of the wind from the west and south, obey, and leave their graves behind to breathe the air of the sweet heavens. Up and up they come till the year is glorious with the rose and the lily, till the trees are not only clothed upon with new garments of loveliest green, but the fruit-tree bringeth forth its fruit, and the little children of men are made glad with apples, and cherries, and hazel-nuts. The earth laughs out in green and gold. The sky shares in the grand resurrection. The garments of its mourning, wherewith it made men sad, its clouds of snow and hail and stormy vapours, are swept away, have sunk indeed to the earth, and are now humbly feeding the roots of the flowers whose dead stalks they beat upon all the winter long. Instead, the sky has put on the garments of praise. Her blue, coloured after the sapphire-floor on which stands the throne of him who is the Resurrection and the Life, is dashed and glorified with the pure white of sailing clouds, and at morning and evening prayer, puts on colours in which the human heart drowns itself with delight-green and gold and purple and rose. Even the icebergs floating about in the lonely summer seas of the north are flashing all the glories of the rainbow. But, indeed, is not this whole world itself a monument of the Resurrection? The earth was without form and void. The wind of God moved on the face of the waters, and up arose this fair world. Darkness was on the face of the deep: God said, 'Let there be light,' and there was light.

"In the animal world as well, you behold the goings of the Resurrection. Plainest of all, look at the story of the butterfly-so plain that the pagan Greeks called it and the soul by one name-Psyche. Psyche meant with them a butterfly or the soul, either. Look how the creeping thing, ugly to our eyes, so that we can hardly handle it without a shudder, finding itself growing sick with age, straightway falls a spinning and weaving at its own shroud, coffin, and grave, all in one-to prepare, in fact, for its resurrection; for it is for the sake of the resurrection that death exists. Patiently it spins its strength, but not its life, away, folds itself up decently, that its body may rest in quiet till the new body is formed within it; and at length when the appointed hour has arrived, out of the body of this crawling thing breaks forth the winged splendour of the butterfly-not the same body—a new one built out of the ruins of the old-even as St. Paul tells us that it is not the same body *we* have in the resurrection, but a nobler body like ourselves, with all the imperfect and evil thing taken away. No more creeping for the butterfly; wings of splendour now. Neither yet has it lost the feet wherewith to alight on all that is lovely and sweet. Think of it-up from the toilsome journey over the low ground, exposed to the foot of every passer-by, destroying the lovely leaves upon which it fed, and the fruit which they should shelter, up to the path at will through the air, and a gathering of food which hurts not the source of it, a food which is but as a tribute from the loveliness of the flowers to the yet higher loveliness of the flower-angel: is not this a resurrection? Its children too shall pass through the same process, to wing the air of a summer noon, and rejoice in the ethereal and the pure.

"To return yet again from the human thoughts suggested by the symbol of the butterfly"—

Here let me pause for a moment-and there was a corresponding pause, though but momentary, in the sermon as I spoke it-to mention a curious, and to me at the moment an interesting fact. At this point of my address, I caught sight of a white butterfly, a belated one, flitting about the church. Absorbed for a moment, my eye wandered after it. It was near the bench where my own people sat, and, for one flash of thought, I longed that the butterfly would alight on my Wynnie, for I was more anxious about her resurrection at the time than about anything else. But the butterfly would not. And then I told myself that God would, and that the butterfly was only the symbol of a grand truth, and of no private interpretation, to make which of it was both selfishness and superstition. But all this passed in a flash, and I resumed my discourse.

—"I come now naturally to speak of what we commonly call the Resurrection. Some say: 'How can the same dust be raised again, when it may be scattered to the winds of heaven?' It is a question I hardly care to answer. The mere difficulty can in reason stand for nothing with God; but the apparent worthlessness of the supposition renders the question uninteresting to me. What is of import is, that I should stand clothed upon, with a body which is *my* body because it serves my ends, justifies my consciousness of identity by being, in all that was good in it, like that which I had before, while now it is tenfold capable of expressing the thoughts and feelings that move within me. How can I care whether the atoms that form a certain inch of bone should be the same as those which formed that bone when I died? All my life-time I never felt or thought of the existence of such a bone! On the other hand, I object to having the same worn muscles, the same shrivelled skin with which I may happen to die. Why give me the same body as that? Why not rather my youthful body, which was strong, and facile, and capable? The matter in the muscle of my arm at death would not serve to make half the muscle I had when young. But I thank God that St. Paul says it will *not* be the same body. That body dies-up springs another body. I suspect myself that those are right who say that this body being the seed, the moment it dies in the soil of this world, that moment is the resurrection of the new body. The life in it rises out of it in a new body. This is not after it is put in the mere earth; for it is dead then, and the germ of life gone out of it. If a seed rots, no new body comes of it. The seed dies into a new life, and so does man. Dying and rotting are two very different things. —But I am not sure by any means. As I say, the whole question is rather uninteresting to me. What do I care about my old clothes after I have done with them? What is it to me to know what becomes of an old coat or an old pulpit gown? I have no such clinging to the flesh. It seems to me that people believe their bodies to be themselves, and are therefore very anxious about them-and no wonder then. Enough for me that I shall have eyes to see my friends, a face that they shall know me by, and a mouth to praise God withal. I leave the matter with one remark, that I am well content to rise as Jesus rose, however that was. For me the will of God is so good that I would rather have his will done than my own choice given me.

"But I now come to the last, because infinitely the most important part of my subject-the resurrection for the sake of which all the other resurrections exist-the resurrection unto Life. This is the one of which St. Paul speaks in my text. This is the one I am most anxious-indeed, the only one I am anxious to set forth, and impress upon you.

"Think, then, of all the deaths you know; the death of the night, when the sun is gone, when friend says not a word to friend, but both lie drowned and parted in the sea of sleep; the death of the year, when winter lies heavy on the graves of the children of summer, when the leafless trees moan in the blasts from the ocean, when the beasts even look dull and oppressed, when the children go about shivering with cold, when the poor and improvident are miserable with suffering or think of such a death of disease as befalls us at times, when the man who says,

'Would God it were morning!' changes but his word, and not his tune, when the morning comes, crying, 'Would God it were evening!' when what life is left is known to us only by suffering, and hope is amongst the things that were once and are no more-think of all these, think of them all together, and you will have but the dimmest, faintest picture of the death from which the resurrection of which I have now to speak, is the rising. I shrink from the attempt, knowing how weak words are to set forth *the* death, set forth *the* resurrection. Were I to sit down to yonder organ, and crash out the most horrible dissonances that ever took shape in sound, I should give you but a weak figure of this death; were I capable of drawing from many a row of pipes an exhalation of dulcet symphonies and voices sweet, such as Milton himself could have invaded our ears withal, I could give you but a faint figure of this resurrection. Nevertheless, I must try what I can do in my own way.

"If into the face of the dead body, lying on the bed, waiting for its burial, the soul of the man should begin to dawn again, drawing near from afar to look out once more at those eyes, to smile once again through those lips, the change on that face would be indeed great and wondrous, but nothing for marvel or greatness to that which passes on the countenance, the very outward bodily face of the man who wakes from his sleep, arises from the dead and receives light from Christ. Too often indeed, the reposeful look on the face of the dead body would be troubled, would vanish away at the revisiting of the restless ghost; but when a man's own right true mind, which God made in him, is restored to him again, and he wakes from the death of sin, then comes the repose without the death. It may take long for the new spirit to complete the visible change, but it begins at once, and will be perfected. The bloated look of self-indulgence passes away like the leprosy of Naaman, the cheek grows pure, the lips return to the smile of hope instead of the grin of greed, and the eyes that made innocence shrink and shudder with their yellow leer grow childlike and sweet and faithful. The mammon-eyes, hitherto fixed on the earth, are lifted to meet their kind; the lips that mumbled over figures and sums of gold learn to say words of grace and tenderness. The truculent, repellent, self-satisfied face begins to look thoughtful and doubtful, as if searching for some treasure of whose whereabouts it had no certain sign. The face anxious, wrinkled, peering, troubled, on whose lines you read the dread of hunger, poverty, and nakedness, thaws into a smile; the eyes reflect in courage the light of the Father's care, the back grows erect under its burden with the assurance that the hairs of its head are all numbered. But the face can with all its changes set but dimly forth the rising from the dead which passes within. The heart, which cared but for itself, becomes aware of surrounding thousands like itself, in the love and care of which it feels a dawning blessedness undreamt of before. From selfishness to love-is not this a rising from the dead? The man whose ambition declares that his way in the world would be to subject everything to his desires, to bring every human care, affection, power, and aspiration to his feet-such a world it would be, and such a king it would have, if individual ambition might work its will! if a man's opinion of himself could be made out in the world, degrading, compelling, oppressing, doing everything for his own glory! —and such a glory! —but a pang of light strikes this man to the heart; an arrow of truth, feathered with suffering and loss and dismay, finds out-the open joint in his armour, I was going to say-no, finds out the joint in the coffin where his heart lies festering in a death so dead that itself calls it life. He trembles, he awakes, he rises from the dead. No more he seeks the slavery of all: where can he find whom to serve? how can he become if but a threshold in the temple of Christ, where all serve all, and no man thinks first of himself? He to whom the mass of his fellows, as he massed them, was common and unclean, bows before every human sign of the presence of the making God. The sun, which was to him but a candle with which to search after his own ends, wealth, power, place, praise-the world, which was but the cavern where he thus searched-are now full of the mystery of loveliness, full of the truth of which sun and wind and land and sea are symbols and signs. From a withered old age of unbelief, the dim eyes of which refuse the glory of things a passage to the heart, he is raised up a child full of admiration, wonder, and gladness. Everything is glorious to him; he can believe, and therefore he sees. It is from the grave into the sunshine, from the night into the morning, from death into life. To come out of the ugly into the beautiful; out of the mean and selfish into the noble and loving; out of the paltry into the great; out of the false into the true; out of the filthy into the clean; out of the commonplace into the glorious; out of the corruption of disease into the fine vigour and gracious movements of health; in a word, out of evil into good-is not this a resurrection indeed —*the* resurrection of all, the resurrection of Life? God grant that with St. Paul we may attain to this resurrection of the dead.

"This rising from the dead is often a long and a painful process. Even after he had preached the gospel to the Gentiles, and suffered much for the sake of his Master, Paul sees the resurrection of the dead towering grandly before him, not yet climbed, not yet attained unto — a mountainous splendour and marvel, still shining aloft in the air of existence, still, thank God, to be attained, but ever growing in height and beauty as, forgetting those things that are behind, he presses towards the mark, if by any means he may attain to the resurrection of the dead. Every blessed moment in which a man bethinks himself that he has been forgetting his high calling, and sends up to the Father a prayer for aid; every time a man resolves that what he has been doing he will do no more; every time that the love of God, or the feeling of the truth, rouses a man to look first up at the light, then down at the skirts of his own garments-that moment a divine resurrection is wrought in the earth. Yea, every time that a man passes from resentment to forgiveness, from cruelty to compassion, from hardness to tenderness, from indifference to carefulness, from selfishness to honesty, from honesty to generosity, from generosity to love, —a resurrection, the bursting of a fresh bud of life out of the grave of evil, gladdens the eye of the Father watching his children. Awake, then, thou that sleepest, and arise from the dead, and Christ will give thee light. As the harvest rises from the wintry earth, so rise thou up from the trials of this world a full ear in the harvest of Him who sowed thee in the soil that thou mightest rise above it. As the summer rises from the winter, so rise thou from the cares of eating and drinking and clothing into the fearless sunshine of confidence in the Father. As the morning rises out of the night, so rise thou from the darkness of ignorance to do the will of God in the daylight; and as a man feels that he is himself when he wakes from the troubled and grotesque visions of the night into the glory of the sunrise, even so wilt thou feel that then first thou knowest what thy life, the gladness of thy being, is. As from painful tossing in disease, rise into the health of well-being. As from the awful embrace of thy own dead body, burst forth in thy spiritual body. Arise thou, responsive to the indwelling will of the Father, even as thy body will respond to thy indwelling soul.

'White wings are crossing;
Glad waves are tossing;
The earth flames out in crimson and green:
Spring is appearing,

Summer is nearing—
Where hast thou been?
Down in some cavern,

Death's sleepy tavern,
Housing, carousing with spectres of night?
The trumpet is pealing
Sunshine and healing —
Spring to the light.'"

With this quotation from a friend's poem, I closed my sermon, oppressed with a sense of failure; for ever the marvel of simple awaking, the mere type of the resurrection eluded all my efforts to fix it in words. I had to comfort myself with the thought that God is so strong that he can work even with our failures.

END OF VOL. II.

VOLUME III.

CHAPTER I
A WALK WITH MY WIFE.

The autumn was creeping up on the earth, with winter holding by its skirts behind; but before I loose my hold of the garments of summer, I must write a chapter about a walk and a talk I had one night with my wife. It had rained a good deal during the day, but as the sun went down the air began to clear, and when the moon shone out, near the full, she walked the heavens, not "like one that hath been led astray," but as "queen and huntress, chaste and fair."

"What a lovely night it is!" said Ethelwyn, who had come into my study-where I always sat with unblinded windows, that the night and her creatures might look in upon me-and had stood gazing out for a moment.

"Shall we go for a little turn?" I said.

"I should like it very much," she answered. "I will go and put on my bonnet at once."

In a minute or two she looked in again, all ready. I rose, laid aside my Plato, and went with her. We turned our steps along the edge of the down, and descended upon the breakwater, where we seated ourselves upon the same spot where in the darkness I had heard the voices of Joe and Agnes. What a different night it was from that! The sea lay as quiet as if it could not move for the moonlight that lay upon it. The glory over it was so mighty in its peacefulness, that the wild element beneath was afraid to toss itself even with the motions of its natural unrest. The moon was like the face of a saint before which the stormy people has grown dumb. The rocks stood up solid and dark in the universal aether, and the pulse of the ocean throbbed against them with a lapping gush, soft as the voice of a passionate child soothed into shame of its vanished petulance. But the sky was the glory. Although no breath moved below, there was a gentle wind abroad in the upper regions. The air was full of masses of cloud, the vanishing fragments of the one great vapour which had been pouring down in rain the most of the day. These masses were all setting with one steady motion eastward into the abysses of space; now obscuring the fair moon, now solemnly sweeping away from before her. As they departed, out shone her marvellous radiance, as calm as ever. It was plain that she knew nothing of what we called her covering, her obscuration, the dimming of her glory. She had been busy all the time weaving her lovely opaline damask on the other side of the mass in which we said she was swallowed up.

"Have you ever noticed, wifie," I said, "how the eyes of our minds-almost our bodily eyes-are opened sometimes to the cubicalness of nature, as it were?"

"I don't know, Harry, for I don't understand your question," she answered.

"Well, it was a stupid way of expressing what I meant. No human being could have understood it from that. I will make you understand in a moment, though. Sometimes-perhaps generally-we see the sky as a flat dome, spangled with star-points, and painted blue. *Now* I see it as an awful depth of blue air, depth within depth; and the clouds before me are not passing away to the left, but sinking away from the front of me into the marvellous unknown regions, which, let philosophers say what they will about time and space,—and I daresay they are right,—are yet very awful to me. Thank God, my dear," I said, catching hold of her arm, as the terror of mere space grew upon me, "for himself. He is deeper than space, deeper than time; he is the heart of all the cube of history."

"I understand you now, husband," said my wife.

"I knew you would," I answered.

"But," she said again, "is it not something the same with the things inside us? I can't put it in words as you do. Do you understand me now?"

"I am not sure that I do. You must try again."

"You understand me well enough, only you like to make me blunder where you can talk," said my wife, putting her hand in mine. "But I will try. Sometimes, after thinking about something for a long time, you come to a conclusion about it, and you think you have settled it plain and clear to yourself, for ever and a day. You hang it upon your wall, like a picture, and are satisfied for a fortnight. But some day, when you happen to cast a look at it, you find that instead of hanging flat on the wall, your picture has gone through it-opens out into some region you don't know where-shows you far-receding distances of air and sea-in short, where you thought one question was settled for ever, a hundred are opened up for the present hour."

"Bravo, wife!" I cried in true delight. "I do indeed understand you now. You have said it better than I could ever have done. That's the plague of you women! You have been taught for centuries and centuries that there is little or nothing to be expected of you, and so you won't try. Therefore we men know no more than you do whether it is in you or not. And when you do try, instead of trying to think, you want to be in Parliament all at once."

"Do you apply that remark to me, sir?" demanded Ethelwyn.

"You must submit to bear the sins of your kind upon occasion," I answered.

"I am content to do that, so long as yours will help mine," she replied.

"Then I may go on?" I said, with interrogation.

"Till sunrise if you like. We were talking of the cubicalness —I believe you called it-of nature."

"And you capped it with the cubicalness of thought. And quite right too. There are people, as a dear friend of mine used to say, who are so accustomed to regard everything in the *flat*, as dogma cut and-not *always* dried my moral olfactories aver-that if you prove to them the very thing they believe, but after another mode than that they have been accustomed to, they are offended, and count you a heretic. There is no help for it. Even St. Paul's chief opposition came from the Judaizing Christians of his time, who did not believe that God *could* love the Gentiles, and therefore regarded him as a teacher of falsehood. We must not be fierce with them. Who knows what wickedness of their ancestors goes to account for their stupidity? For that there are stupid people, and that they are, in very consequence of their stupidity, conceited, who can deny? The worst of it is, that no man who is conceited can be convinced of the fact."

"Don't say that, Harry. That is to deny conversion."

"You are right, Ethelwyn. The moment a man is convinced of his folly, he ceases to be a fool. The moment a man is convinced of his conceit, he ceases to be conceited. But there *must* be a final judgment, and the true man will welcome it, even if he is to appear a convicted fool. A man's business is to see first that he is not acting the part of a fool, and next, to help any honest people who care about the matter to take heed likewise that they be not offering to pull the mote out of their brother's eye. But there are even societies established and supported by good people for the express purpose of pulling out motes. —'The Mote-Pulling Society!' —That ought to take with a certain part of the public."

"Come, come, Harry. You are absurd. Such people don't come near you."

"They can't touch me. No. But they come near good people whom I know, brandishing the long pins with which they pull the motes out, and threatening them with judgment before their time. They are but pins, to be sure-not daggers."

"But you have wandered, Harry, into the narrowest underground, musty ways, and have forgotten all about 'the cubicalness of nature.'"

"You are right, my love, as you generally are," I answered, laughing. "Look at that great antlered elk, or moose-fit quarry for Diana of the silver bow. Look how it glides solemnly away into the unpastured depths of the aerial deserts. Look again at that reclining giant, half raised upon his arm, with his face turned towards the wilderness. What eyes they must be under those huge brows! On what message to the nations is he borne as by the slow sweep of ages, on towards his mysterious goal?"

"Stop, stop, Harry," said my wife. "It makes me unhappy to hear grand words clothing only cloudy fancies. Such words ought to be used about the truth, and the truth only."

"If I could carry it no further, my dear, then it would indeed be a degrading of words. But there never was a vagary that uplifted the soul, or made the grand words flow from the gates of speech, that had not its counterpart in truth itself. Man can imagine nothing, even in the clouds of the air, that God has not done, or is not doing. Even as that cloudy giant yields, and is 'shepherded by the slow unwilling wind,' so is each of us borne onward to an unseen destiny—a glorious one if we will but yield to the Spirit of God that bloweth where it listeth-with a grand listing-coming whence we know not, and going whither we know not. The very clouds of the air are hung up as dim pictures of the thoughts and history of man."

"I do not mind how long you talk like that, husband, even if you take the clouds for your text. But it did make me miserable to think that what you were saying had no more basis than the fantastic forms which the clouds assume. I see I was wrong, though."

"The clouds themselves, in such a solemn stately march as this, used to make me sad for the very same reason. I used to think, What is it all for? They are but vapours blown by the wind. They come nowhence, and they go nowhither. But now I see them and all things as ever moving symbols of the motions of man's spirit and destiny."

A pause followed, during which we sat and watched the marvellous depth of the heavens, deep as I do not think I ever saw them before or since, covered with a stately procession of ever-appearing and ever-vanishing forms-great sculpturesque blocks of a shattered storm-the icebergs of the upper sea. These were not far off against a blue background, but floating near us in the heart of a blue-black space, gloriously lighted by a golden rather than silvery moon. At length my wife spoke.

"I hope Mr. Percivale is out to-night," she said. "How he must be enjoying it if he is!"

"I wonder the young man is not returning to his professional labours," I said. "Few artists can afford such long holidays as he is taking."

"He is laying in stock, though, I suppose," answered my wife.

"I doubt that, my dear. He said not, on one occasion, you may remember."

"Yes, I remember. But still he must paint better the more familiar he gets with the things God cares to fashion."

"Doubtless. But I am afraid the work of God he is chiefly studying at present is our Wynnie."

"Well, is she not a worthy object of his study?" returned Ethelwyn, looking up in my face with an arch expression.

"Doubtless again, Ethel; but I hope she is not studying him quite so much in her turn. I have seen her eyes following him about."

My wife made no answer for a moment. Then she said,

"Don't you like him, Harry?"

"Yes. I like him very much."

"Then why should you not like Wynnie to like him?"

"I should like to be surer of his principles, for one thing."

"I should like to be surer of Wynnie's."

I was silent. Ethelwyn resumed.

"Don't you think they might do each other good?"

Still I could not reply.

"They both love the truth, I am sure; only they don't perhaps know what it is yet. I think if they were to fall in love with each other, it would very likely make them both more desirous of finding it still."

"Perhaps," I said at last. "But you are talking about awfully serious things, Ethelwyn."

"Yes, as serious as life," she answered.

"You make me very anxious," I said. "The young man has not, I fear, any means of gaining a livelihood for more than himself."

"Why should he before he wanted it? I like to see a man who can be content with an art and a living by it."

"I hope I have not been to blame in allowing them to see so much of each other," I said, hardly heeding my wife's words.

"It came about quite naturally," she rejoined. "If you had opposed their meeting, you would have been interfering just as if you had been Providence. And you would have only made them think more about each other."

"He hasn't said anything-has he?" I asked in positive alarm.

"O dear no. It may be all my fancy. I am only looking a little ahead. I confess I should like him for a son-in-law. I approve of him," she added, with a sweet laugh.

"Well," I said, "I suppose sons-in-law are possible, however disagreeable, results of having daughters."

I tried to laugh, but hardly succeeded.

"Harry," said my wife, "I don't like you in such a mood. It is not like you at all. It is unworthy of you."

"How can I help being anxious when you speak of such dreadful things as the possibility of having to give away my daughter, my precious wonder that came to me through you, out of the infinite-the tender little darling!"

" 'Out of the heart of God,' you used to say, Henry. Yes, and with a destiny he had ordained. It is strange to me how you forget your best and noblest teaching sometimes. You are always telling us to trust in God. Surely it is a poor creed that will only allow us to trust in God for ourselves —a very selfish creed. There must be something wrong there. I should say that the man who can only trust God for himself is not half a Christian. Either he is so selfish that that satisfies him, or he has such a poor notion of God that he cannot trust him with what most concerns him. The former is not your case, Harry: is the latter, then? —You see I must take my turn at the preaching sometimes. Mayn't I, dearest?"

She took my hand in both of hers. The truth arose in my heart. I never loved my wife more than at that moment. And now I could not speak for other reasons. I saw that I had been faithless to my God, and the moment I could command my speech, I hastened to confess it.

"You are right, my dear," I said, "quite right. I have been wicked, for I have been denying my God. I have been putting my providence in the place of his-trying, like an anxious fool, to count the hairs on Wynnie's head, instead of being content that the grand loving Father should count them. My love, let us pray for Wynnie; for what is prayer but giving her to God and his holy, blessed will?"

We sat hand in hand. Neither spoke aloud for some minutes, but we spoke in our hearts to God, talking to him about Wynnie. Then we rose together, and walked homeward, still in silence. But my heart and hand clung to my wife as to the angel whom God had sent to deliver me out of the prison of my faithlessness. And as we went, lo! the sky was glorious again. It had faded from my sight, had grown flat as a dogma, uninteresting as "a foul and pestilent congregation of vapours;" the moon had been but a round thing with the sun shining upon it, and the stars were only minding their own business. But now the solemn march towards an unseen, unimagined goal had again begun. Wynnie's life was hid with Christ in God. Away strode the cloudy pageant with its banners blowing in the wind, which blew where it grandly listed, marching as to a solemn triumphal music that drew them from afar towards the gates of pearl by which the morning walks out of the New Jerusalem to gladden the nations of the earth. Solitary stars, with all their sparkles drawn in, shone, quiet as human eyes, in the deep solemn clefts of dark blue air. They looked restrained and still, as if they knew all about it-all about the secret of this midnight march. For the moon-she saw the sun, and therefore made the earth glad.

"You have been a moon to me this night, my wife," I said. "You were looking full at the truth, while I was dark. I saw its light in your face, and believed, and turned my soul to the sun. And now I am both ashamed and glad. God keep me from sinning so again."

"My dear husband, it was only a mood —a passing mood," said Ethelwyn, seeking to comfort me.

"It was a mood, and thank God it is now past; but it was a wicked one. It was a mood in which the Lord might have called me a devil, as he did St. Peter. Such moods have to be grappled with and fought the moment they appear. They must not have their way for a single thought even."

"But we can't help it always, can we, husband?"

"We can't help it out and out, because our wills are not yet free with the freedom God is giving us as fast as we will let him. When we are able to will thoroughly, then we shall do what we will. At least, I think we shall. But there is a mystery in it God only understands. All we know is, that we can struggle and pray. But a mood is an awful oppression sometimes when you least believe in it and most wish to get rid of it. It is like a headache in the soul."

"What do the people do that don't believe in God?" said Ethelwyn.

The same moment Wynnie, who had seen us pass the window, opened the door of the bark-house for us, and we passed into Connie's chamber and found her lying in the moonlight, gazing at the same heavens as her father and mother had been revelling in.

CHAPTER II
OUR LAST SHORE-DINNER.

The next day was very lovely. I think it is the last of the kind of which I shall have occasion to write in my narrative of the Seaboard Parish. I wonder if my readers are tired of so much about the common things of Nature. I reason about it something in this way: We are so easily affected by the smallest things that are of the unpleasant kind, that we ought to train ourselves to the influence of those that are of an opposite nature. The unpleasant ones are like the thorns which make themselves felt as we scramble-for we often do scramble in a very undignified manner-through the thickets of life; and, feeling the thorns, we grumble, and are blind to all but the thorns. The flowers, and the lovely leaves, and the red berries, and the clusters of filberts, and the birds'-nests do not force themselves upon our attention as the thorns do, and the thorns make us forget to look for them. But a scratch would be forgotten-and that in mental hurts is often equivalent to a cure, for a forgotten scratch on the mind or heart will never fester-if we but allowed our being a moment's repose upon any of the quiet, waiting, unobtrusive beauties that lie around the half-trodden way, offering their gentle healing. And when I think how, not unfrequently, otherwise noble characters are anything but admirable when under the influence of trifling irritations, the very paltriness of which seems what the mind, which would at once rouse itself to a noble endurance of any mighty evil, is unable to endure, I would gladly help so with sweet antidotes to defeat the fly in the ointment of the apothecary that the whole pot shall send forth a pure savour. We ought for this to cultivate the friendships of little things. Beauty is one of the surest antidotes to vexation. Often when life looked dreary about me, from some real or fancied injustice or indignity, has a thought of truth been flashed into my mind from a flower, a shape of frost, or even a lingering shadow-not to mention such glories as angel-winged clouds, rainbows, stars, and sunrises. Therefore I hope that in my loving delay over such aspects of Nature as impressed themselves upon me in this most memorable part of my history I shall not prove wearisome to my reader, for therein I should utterly contravene my hope and intent in the recording of them.

This day there was to be an unusually low tide, and we had reckoned on enlarging our acquaintance with the bed of the ocean-of knowing a few yards more of the millions of miles lapt in the mystery of waters. It was to be low water about two o'clock, and we resolved to dine upon the sands. But all the morning the children were out playing on the threshold of old Neptune's palace; for in his quieter mood he will, like a fierce mastiff, let children do with him what they will. I gave myself a whole holiday-sometimes the most precious part of my life both for myself and those for whom I labour-and wandered about on the shore, now passing the children, and assailed with a volley of cries and entreaties to look at this one's castle and that one's ditch, now leaving them behind, with what in its ungraduated flatness might well enough personate an endless desert of sand between, over the expanse of which I could imagine them disappearing on a far horizon, whence however a faint occasional cry of excitement and pleasure would reach my ears. The sea was so calm, and the shore so gently sloping, that you could hardly tell where the sand ceased and the sea began-the water sloped to such a thin pellicle, thinner than any knife-edge, upon the shining brown sand, and you saw the sand underneath the water to such a distance out. Yet this depth, which would not drown a red spider, was the ocean. In my mind I followed that bed of shining sand, bared of its hiding waters, out and out, till I was lost in an awful wilderness of chasms, precipices, and mountain-peaks, in whose caverns the sea-serpent may dwell, with his breath of pestilence; the kraken, with "his skaly rind," may there be sleeping

> "His ancient dreamless, uninvaded sleep,"

while

"faintest sunlights flee
About his shadowy sides,"

as he lies

"Battening upon huge seaworms in his sleep."

There may lie all the horrors that Schiller's diver encountered-the frightful Molch, and that worst of all, to which he gives no name, which came creeping with a hundred knots at once; but here are only the gracious rainbow-woven shells, an evanescent jelly or two, and the queer baby-crabs that crawl out from the holes of the bordering rocks. What awful gradations of gentleness lead from such as these down to those cabins where wallow the inventions of Nature's infancy, when, like a child of untutored imagination, she drew on the slate of her fancy creations in which flitting shadows of beauty serve only to heighten the shuddering, gruesome horror. The sweet sun and air, the hand of man, and the growth of the ages, have all but swept such from the upper plains of the earth. What hunter's bow has twanged, what adventurer's rifle has cracked in those leagues of mountain-waste, vaster than all the upper world can show, where the beasts of the ocean "graze the sea-weed, their pasture"! Diana of the silver bow herself, when she descends into the interlunar caves of hell, sends no such monsters fleeing from her spells. Yet if such there be, such horrors too must lie in the undiscovered caves of man's nature, of which all this outer world is but a typical analysis. By equally slow gradations may the inner eye descend from the truth of a Cordelia to the falsehood of an Iago. As these golden sands slope from the sunlight into the wallowing abyss of darkness, even so from the love of the child to his holy mother slopes the inclined plane of humanity to the hell of the sensualist. "But with one difference in the moral world," I said aloud, as I paced up and down on the shimmering margin, "that everywhere in the scale the eye of the all-seeing Father can detect the first quiver of the eyelid that would raise itself heavenward, responsive to his waking spirit." I lifted my eyes in the relief of the thought, and saw how the sun of the autumn hung above the waters oppressed with a mist of his own glory; far away to the left a man who had been clambering on a low rock, inaccessible save in such a tide, gathering mussels, threw himself into the sea and swam ashore; above his head the storm-tower stood in the stormless air; the sea glittered and shone, and the long-winged birds knew not which to choose, the balmy air or the cool deep, now flitting like arrow-heads through the one, now alighting eagerly upon the other, to forsake it anew for the thinner element. I thanked God for his glory.

"O, papa, it's so jolly-so jolly!" shouted the children as I passed them again.

"What is it that's so jolly, Charlie?" I asked.

"My castle," screeched Harry in reply; "only it's tumbled down. The water *would* keep coming in underneath."

"I tried to stop it with a newspaper," cried Charlie, "but it wouldn't. So we were forced to let it be, and down it went into the ditch."

"We blew it up rather than surrender," said Dora. "We did; only Harry always forgets, and says it was the water did it."

I drew near the rock that held the bath. I had never approached it from this side before. It was high above my head, and a stream of water was flowing from it. I scrambled up, undressed, and plunged into its dark hollow, where I felt like one of the sea-beasts of which I had been dreaming, down in the caves of the unvisited ocean. But the sun was over my head, and the air with an edge of the winter was about me. I dressed quickly, descended on the other side of the rock, and wandered again on the sands to seaward of the breakwater, which lay above, looking dry and weary, and worn with years of contest with the waves, which had at length withdrawn defeated to their own country, and left it as if to victory and a useless age of peace. How different was the scene when a raving mountain of water filled all the hollow where I now wandered, and rushed over the top of that mole now so high above me; and I had to cling to its stones to keep me from being carried off like a bit of floating sea-weed! This was the loveliest and strangest part of the shore. Several long low ridges of rock, of whose existence I scarcely knew, worn to a level with the sand, hollowed and channelled with the terrible run of the tide across them, and looking like the old and outworn cheek-teeth of some awful beast of prey, stretched out seawards. Here and there amongst them rose a well-known rock, but now so changed in look by being lifted all the height between the base on the waters, and the second base in the sand, that I wondered at each, walking round and viewing it on all sides. It seemed almost a fresh growth out of the garden of the shore, with uncouth hollows around its fungus root, and a forsaken air about its brows as it stood in the dry sand and looked seaward. But what made the chief delight of the spot, closed in by rocks from the open sands, was the multitude of fairy rivers that flowed across it to the sea. The gladness these streams gave me I cannot communicate. The tide had filled thousands of hollows in the breakwater, hundreds of cracked basins in the rocks, huge sponges of sand; from all of which-from cranny and crack, and oozing sponge-the water flowed in restricted haste back, back to the sea, tumbling in tiny cataracts down the faces of the rocks, bubbling from their roots as from wells, gathering in tanks of sand, and overflowing in broad shallow streams, curving and sweeping in their sandy channels, just like, the great rivers of a continent; —here spreading into smooth silent lakes and reaches, here babbling along in ripples and waves innumerable-flowing, flowing, to lose their small beings in the same ocean that met on the other side the waters of the Mississippi, the Orinoco, the Amazon. All their channels were of golden sand, and the golden sunlight was above and through and in them all: gold and gold met, with the waters between. And what gave an added life to their motion was, that all the ripples made shadows on the clear yellow below them. The eye could not see the rippling on the surface; but the sun saw it, and drew it in multitudinous shadowy motion upon the sand, with the play of a thousand fancies of gold burnished and dead, of sunlight and yellow, trembling, melting, curving, blending, vanishing ever, ever renewed. It was as if all the water-marks upon a web of golden silk had been set in wildest yet most graceful curvilinear motion by the breath of a hundred playful zephyrs. My eye could not be filled with seeing. I stood in speechless delight for a while, gazing at the "endless ending" which was "the humour of the game," and thinking how in all God's works the laws of beauty are wrought out in evanishment, in birth and death. There, there is no hoarding, but an ever-fresh creating, an eternal flow of life from the heart of the All-beautiful. Hence even the heart of man cannot hoard. His brain or his hand may gather into its box and hoard; but the moment the thing has passed into the box, the heart has lost it and is hungry again. If man would *have*, it is the giver he must have; the eternal, the original, the ever-outpouring is alone within his reach; the everlasting *creation* is his heritage. Therefore all that he makes must be free to come and go through the heart of his child; he can enjoy it only as it passes, can enjoy only its life, its soul, its vision, its meaning, not itself. To hoard rubies and sapphires is as useless and hopeless for the heart, as if I were to attempt to hoard this marvel of sand and water and sunlight in the same iron chest with the musty deeds of my wife's inheritance.

"Father," I murmured half aloud, "thou alone art, and I am because thou art. Thy will shall be mine."

I know that I must have spoken aloud, because I remember the start of consciousness and discomposure occasioned by the voice of Percivale greeting me.

"I beg your pardon," he added; "I did not mean to startle you, Mr. Walton. I thought you were only looking at Nature's childplay-not thinking."

"I know few things *more* fit to set one thinking than what you have very well called Nature's childplay," I returned. "Is Nature very heartless now, do you think, to go on with this kind of thing at our feet, when away up yonder lies the awful London, with so many sores festering in her heart?"

"You must answer your own question, Mr. Walton. You know I cannot. I confess I feel the difficulty deeply. I will go further, and confess that the discrepancy makes me doubt many things I would gladly believe. I know *you* are able to distinguish between a glad unbelief and a sorrowful doubt."

"Else were I unworthy of the humblest place in the kingdom-unworthy to be a doorkeeper in the house of my God," I answered, and recoiled from the sound of my own words; for they seemed to imply that I believed myself worthy of the position I occupied. I hastened to correct them: "But do not mistake my thoughts," I said; "I do not dream of worthiness in the way of honour-only of fitness for the work to be done. For that I think God has fitted me in some measure. The doorkeeper's office may be given him, not because he has done some great deed worthy of the honour, but because he can sweep the porch and scour the threshold, and will, in the main, try to keep them clean. That is all the worthiness I dare to claim, even to hope that I possess."

"No one who knows you can mistake your words, except wilfully," returned Percivale courteously.

"Thank you," I said. "Now I will just ask you, in reference to the contrast between human life and nature, how you will go back to your work in London, after seeing all this child's and other play of Nature? Suppose you had had nothing here but rain and high winds and sea-fogs, would you have been better fitted for doing something to comfort those who know nothing of such influences than you will be now? One of the most important qualifications of a sick-nurse is a ready smile. A long-faced nurse in a sickroom is a visible embodiment and presence of the disease against which the eager life of the patient is fighting in agony. Such ought to be banished, with their black dresses and their mourning-shop looks, from every sick-chamber, and permitted to minister only to the dead, who do not mind looks. With what a power of life and hope does a woman-young or old I do not care-with a face of the morning, a dress like the spring, a bunch of wild flowers in her hand, with the dew upon them, and perhaps in her eyes too (I don't object to that-that is sympathy, not the worship of darkness), —with what a message from nature and life does she, looking death in the face with a smile, dawn upon the vision of the invalid! She brings a little health, a little strength to fight, a little hope to endure, actually lapt in the folds of her gracious garments; for the soul itself can do more than any medicine, if it be fed with the truth of life."

"But are you not —I beg your pardon for interposing on your eloquence with dull objection," said Percivale —"are you not begging all the question? *Is* life such an affair of sunshine and gladness?"

"If life is not, then I confess all this show of nature is worse than vanity-it is a vile mockery. Life is gladness; it is the death in it that makes the misery. We call life-in-death life, and hence the mistake. If gladness were not at the root, whence its opposite sorrow, against which we arise, from which we recoil, with which we fight? We recognise it as death-the contrary of life. There could be no sorrow but for a recognition of primordial bliss. This in us that fights must be life. It is of the nature of light, not of darkness; darkness is nothing until the light comes. This very childplay, as you call it, of Nature, is her assertion of the secret that life is the deepest, that life shall conquer death. Those who believe this must bear the good news to them that sit in darkness and the shadow of death. Our Lord has conquered death-yea, the moral death that he called the world; and now, having sown the seed of light, the harvest is springing in human hearts, is springing in this dance of radiance, and will grow and grow until the hearts of the children of the kingdom shall frolic in the sunlight of the Father's presence. Nature has God at her heart; she is but the garment of the Invisible. God wears his singing robes in a day like this, and says to his children, 'Be not afraid: your brothers and sisters up there in London are in my hands; go and help them. I am with you. Bear to them the message of joy. Tell them to be of good cheer: I have overcome the world. Tell them to endure hunger, and not sin; to endure passion, and not yield; to admire, and not desire. Sorrow and pain are serving my ends; for by them will I slay sin; and save my children.'"

"I wish I could believe as you do, Mr. Walton."

"I wish you could. But God will teach you, if you are willing to be taught."

"I desire the truth, Mr. Walton."

"God bless you! God is blessing you," I said.

"Amen," returned Percivale devoutly; and we strolled away together in silence towards the cliffs.

The recession of the tide allowed us to get far enough away from the face of the rocks to see the general effect. With the lisping of the inch-deep wavelets at our heels we stood and regarded the worn yet defiant, the wasted and jagged yet reposeful face of the guardians of the shore.

"Who could imagine, in weather like this, and with this baby of a tide lying behind us, low at our feet, and shallow as the water a schoolboy pours upon his slate to wash it withal, that those grand cliffs before us bear on their front the scars and dints of centuries, of chiliads of stubborn resistance, of passionate contest with this same creature that is at this moment unable to rock the cradle of an infant? Look behind you, at your feet, Mr. Percivale; look before you at the chasms, rents, caves, and hollows of those rocks."

"I wish you were a painter, Mr. Walton," he said.

"I wish I were," I returned. "At least I know I should rejoice in it, if it had been given me to be one. But why do you say so now?"

"Because you have always some individual predominating idea, which would give interpretation to Nature while it gave harmony, reality, and individuality to your representation of her."

"I know what you mean," I answered; "but I have no gift whatever in that direction. I have no idea of drawing, or of producing the effects of light and shade; though I think I have a little notion of colour-perhaps about as much as the little London boy, who stopped a friend of mine once to ask the way to the field where the buttercups grew, had of nature."

"I wish I could ask your opinion of some of my pictures."

"That I should never presume to give. I could only tell you what they made me feel, or perhaps only think. Some day I may have the pleasure of looking at them."

"May I offer you my address?" he said, and took a card from his pocket-book. "It is a poor place, but if you should happen to think of me when you are next in London, I shall be honoured by your paying me a visit."

"I shall be most happy," I returned, taking his card. —"Did it ever occur to you, in reference to the subject we were upon a few minutes ago, how little you can do without shadow in making a picture?"

"Little indeed," answered Percivale. "In fact, it would be no picture at all."

"I doubt if the world would fare better without its shadows."

"But it would be a poor satisfaction, with regard to the nature of God, to be told that he allowed evil for artistic purposes."

"It would indeed, if you regard the world as a picture. But if you think of his art as expended, not upon the making of a history or a drama, but upon the making of an individual, a being, a character, then I think a great part of the difficulty concerning the existence of evil which oppresses you will vanish. So long as a creature has not sinned, sin is possible to him. Does it seem inconsistent with the character of God that in order that sin should become impossible he should allow sin to come? that, in order that his creatures should choose the good and refuse the evil, in order that they might become such, with their whole nature infinitely enlarged, as to turn from sin with a perfect repugnance of the will, he should allow them to fall? that, in order that, from being sweet childish children, they should become noble, child-like men and women, he should let them try to walk alone? Why should he not allow the possible in order that it should become impossible? for possible it would ever have been, even in the midst of all the blessedness, until it had been, and had been thus destroyed. Thus sin is slain, uprooted. And the war must ever exist, it seems to me, where there is creation still going on. How could I be content to guard my children so that they should never have temptation, knowing that in all probability they would fail if at any moment it should cross their path? Would the deepest communion of father and child ever be possible between us? Evil would ever seem to be in the child, so long as it was possible it should be there developed. And if this can be said for the existence of moral evil, the existence of all other evil becomes a comparative trifle; nay, a positive good, for by this the other is combated."

"I think I understand you," returned Percivale. "I will think over what you have said. These are very difficult questions."

"Very. I don't think argument is of much use about them, except as it may help to quiet a man's uneasiness a little, and so give his mind peace to think about duty. For about the doing of duty there can be no question, once it is seen. And the doing of duty is the shortest-in very fact, the only way into the light."

As we spoke, we had turned from the cliffs, and wandered back across the salt streams to the sands beyond. From the direction of the house came a little procession of servants, with Walter at their head, bearing the preparations for our dinner-over the gates of the lock, down the sides of the embankment of the canal, and across the sands, in the direction of the children, who were still playing merrily.

"Will you join our early dinner, which is to be out of doors, as you see, somewhere hereabout on the sands?" I said.

"I shall be delighted," he answered, "if you will let me be of some use first. I presume you mean to bring your invalid out."

"Yes; and you shall help me to carry her, if you will."

"That is what I hoped," said Percivale; and we went together towards the parsonage.

As we approached, I saw Wynnie sitting at the drawing-room window; but when we entered the room, she was gone. My wife was there, however.

"Where is Wynnie?" I asked.

"She saw you coming," she answered, "and went to get Connie ready; for I guessed Mr. Percivale had come to help you to carry her out."

But I could not help doubting there might be more than that in Wynnie's disappearance. "What if she should have fallen in love with him," I thought, "and he should never say a word on the subject? That would be dreadful for us all."

They had been repeatedly but not very much together of late, and I was compelled to allow to myself that if they did fall in love with each other it would be very natural on both sides, for there was evidently a great mental resemblance between them, so that they could not help sympathising with each other's peculiarities. And anyone could see what a fine couple they would make.

Wynnie was much taller than Connie-almost the height of her mother. She had a very fair skin, and brown hair, a broad forehead, a wise, thoughtful, often troubled face, a mouth that seldom smiled, but on which a smile seemed always asleep, and round soft cheeks that dimpled like water when she did smile. I have described Percivale before. Why should not two such walk together along the path to the gates of the light? And yet I could not help some anxiety. I did not know anything of his history. I had no testimony concerning him from anyone that knew him. His past life was a blank to me; his means of livelihood probably insufficient-certainly, I judged, precarious; and his position in society-but there I checked myself: I had had enough of that kind of thing already. I would not willingly offend in that worldliness again. The God of the whole earth could not choose that I should look at such works of his hands after that fashion. And I was his servant-not Mammon's or Belial's.

All this passed through my mind in about three turns of the winnowing-fan of thought. Mr. Percivale had begun talking to my wife, who took no pains to conceal that his presence was pleasant to her, and I went upstairs, almost unconsciously, to Connie's room.

When I opened the door, forgetting to announce my approach as I ought to have done, I saw Wynnie leaning over Connie, and Connie's arm round her waist. Wynnie started back, and Connie gave a little cry, for the jerk thus occasioned had hurt her. Wynnie had turned her head away, but turned it again at Connie's cry, and I saw a tear on her face.

"My darlings, I beg your pardon," I said. "It was very stupid of me not to knock at the door."

Connie looked up at me with large resting eyes, and said —

"It's nothing, papa, Wynnie is in one of her gloomy moods, and didn't want you to see her crying. She gave me a little pull, that was all. It didn't hurt me much, only I'm such a goose! I'm in terror before the pain comes. Look at me," she added, seeing, doubtless, some perturbation on my countenance, "I'm all right now." And she smiled in my face perfectly.

I turned to Wynnie, put my arm about her, kissed her cheek, and left the room. I looked round at the door, and saw that Connie was following me with her eyes, but Wynnie's were hidden in her handkerchief.

I went back to the drawing-room, and in a few minutes Walter came to announce that dinner was about to be served. The same moment Wynnie came to say that Connie was ready. She did not lift her eyes, or approach to give Percivale any greeting, but went again as soon as she had given her message. I saw that he looked first concerned and then thoughtful.

"Come, Mr. Percivale," I said; and he followed me up to Connie's room.

Wynnie was not there; but Connie lay, looking lovely, all ready for going. We lifted her, and carried her by the window out on the down, for the easiest way, though the longest, was by the path to the breakwater, along its broad back and down from the end of it upon the sands. Before we reached the breakwater, I found that Wynnie was following behind us. We stopped in the middle of it, and set Connie down, as if I wanted to take breath. But I had thought of something to say to her, which I wanted Wynnie to hear without its being addressed to her.

"Do you see, Connie," I said, "how far off the water is?"

"Yes, papa; it is a long way off. I wish I could get up and run down to it."

"You can hardly believe that all between, all those rocks, and all that sand, will be covered before sunset."

"I know it will be. But it doesn't *look* likely, does it, papa!"

"Not the least likely, my dear. Do you remember that stormy night when I came through your room to go out for a walk in the dark?"

"Remember it, papa? I cannot forget it. Every time I hear the wind blowing when I wake in the night I fancy you are out in it, and have to wake myself up' quite to get rid of the thought."

"Well, Connie, look down into the great hollow there, with rocks and sand at the bottom of it, stretching far away."

"Yes, papa."

"Now look over the side of your litter. You see those holes all about between the stones?"

"Yes, papa."

"Well, one of those little holes saved my life that night, when the great gulf there was full of huge mounds of roaring water, which rushed across this breakwater with force enough to sweep a whole cavalry regiment off its back."

"Papa!" exclaimed Connie, turning pale.

Then first I told her all the story. And Wynnie listened behind.

"Then I *was* right in being frightened, papa!" cried Connie, bursting into tears; for since her accident she could not well command her feelings.

"You were right in trusting in God, Connie."

"But you might have been drowned, papa!" she sobbed.

"Nobody has a right to say that anything might have been other than what has been. Before a thing has happened we can say might or might not; but that has to do only with our ignorance. Of course I am not speaking of things wherein we ought to exercise will and choice. That is *our* department. But this does not look like that now, does it? Think what a change—from the dark night and the roaring water to this fulness of sunlight and the bare sands, with the water lisping on their edge away there in the distance. Now, I want you to think that in life troubles will come which look as if they would never pass away; the night and the storm look as if they would last for ever; but the calm and the morning cannot be stayed; the storm in its very nature is transient. The effort of Nature, as that of the human heart, ever is to return to its repose, for God is Peace."

"But if you will excuse me, Mr. Walton," said Percivale, "you can hardly expect experience to be of use to any but those who have had it. It seems to me that its influences cannot be imparted."

"That depends on the amount of faith in those to whom its results are offered. Of course, as experience, it can have no weight with another; for it is no longer experience. One remove, and it ceases. But faith in the person who has experienced can draw over or derive-to use an old Italian word-some of its benefits to him who has the faith. Experience may thus, in a sense, be accumulated, and we may go on to fresh experience of our own. At least I can hope that the experience of a father may take the form of hope in the minds of his daughters. Hope never hurt anyone, never yet interfered with duty; nay, always strengthens to the performance of duty, gives courage, and clears the judgment. St. Paul says we are saved by hope. Hope is the most rational thing in the universe. Even the ancient poets, who believed it was delusive, yet regarded it as an antidote given by the mercy of the gods against some, at least, of the ills of life."

"But they counted it delusive. A wise man cannot consent to be deluded."

"Assuredly not. The sorest truth rather than a false hope! But what is a false hope? Only one that ought not to be fulfilled. The old poets could give themselves little room for hope, and less for its fulfilment; for what were the gods in whom they believed—I cannot say in whom they trusted? Gods who did the best their own poverty of being was capable of doing for men when they gave them the *illusion* of hope. But I see they are waiting for us below. One thing I repeat-the waves that foamed across the spot where we now stand are gone away, have sunk and vanished."

"But they will come again, papa," faltered Wynnie.

"And God will come with them, my love," I said, as we lifted the litter.

In a few minutes more we were all seated on the sand around a table-cloth spread upon it. I shall never forgot the peace and the light outside and in, as far as I was concerned at least, and I hope the others too, that afternoon. The tide had turned, and the waves were creeping up over the level, soundless almost as thought; but it would be time to go home long before they had reached us. The sun was in the western half of the sky, and now and then a breath of wind came from the sea, with a slight saw-edge in it, but not enough to hurt. Connie could stand much more in that way now. And when I saw how she could move herself on her couch, and thought how much she had improved since first she was laid upon it, hope for her kept fluttering joyously in my heart. I could not help fancying even that I saw her move her legs a little; but I could not be in the least sure; and she, if she did move them, was clearly unconscious of it. Charles and Harry were every now and then starting up from their dinner and running off with a shout, to return with apparently increased appetite for the rest of it; and neither their mother nor I cared to interfere with the indecorum. Dora alone took it upon her to rebuke them. Wynnie was very silent, but looked more cheerful. Connie seemed full of quiet bliss. My wife's face was a picture of heavenly repose. The old nurse was walking about with the baby, occasionally with one hand helping the other servants to wait upon us. They, too, seemed to have a share in the gladness of the hour, and, like Ariel, did their spiriting gently.

"This is the will of God," I said, after the things were removed, and we had sat for a few moments in silence.

"What is the will of God, husband?" asked Ethelwyn.

"Why, this, my love," I answered; "this living air, and wind, and sea, and light, and land all about us; this consenting, consorting harmony of Nature, that mirrors a like peace in our souls. The perfection of such visions, the gathering of them all in one was, is, I should say, in the face of Christ Jesus. You will say that face was troubled sometimes. Yes, but with a trouble that broke not the music, but deepened the harmony. When he wept at the grave of Lazarus, you do not think it was for Lazarus himself, or for his own loss of him, that he wept? That could not be, seeing he had the power to call him back when he would. The grief was for the poor troubled hearts left behind, to whom it was so dreadful because they had not faith enough in his Father, the God of life and love, who was looking after it all, full of tenderness and grace, with whom Lazarus was present and blessed. It was the aching, loving heart of humanity for which he wept, that needed God so awfully, and could not yet trust in him. Their brother was only hidden in the skirts of their Father's garment, but they could not believe that: they said he was dead-lost-away-all gone, as the children say. And it was so sad to think of a whole world full of the grief of death, that he could not bear it without the human tears to help his heart, as they help ours. It was for our dark sorrows that he wept. But the peace could be no less plain on the face that saw God. Did you ever think of that wonderful saying: 'Again a little while, and ye shall see me, because I go to the Father'? The heart of man would have joined the 'because I go to the Father' with the former result-the not seeing of him. The heart of man is not able, without more and more light, to understand that all vision is in the light of the Father. Because Jesus went to the Father, therefore the disciples saw him tenfold more. His body no longer in their eyes, his very being, his very self was in their hearts-not in their affections only-in their spirits, their heavenly consciousness."

As I said this, a certain hymn, for which I had and have an especial affection, came into my mind, and, without prologue or introduction, I repeated it:

"If I Him but have,
  If he be but mine,
    If my heart, hence to the grave,
    Ne'er forgets his love divine —
Know I nought of sadness,
Feel I nought but worship, love, and gladness.
If I Him but have,

  Glad with all I part;
    Follow on my pilgrim staff
  My Lord only, with true heart;
Leave them, nothing saying,
On broad, bright, and crowded highways straying.
If I Him but have,

  Glad I fall asleep;
    Aye the flood that his heart gave
    Strength within my heart shall keep,
And with soft compelling
Make it tender, through and through it swelling.
If I Him but have,

  Mine the world I hail!
    Glad as cherub smiling grave,
    Holding back the virgin's veil.
Sunk and lost in seeing,
Earthly fears have died from all my being.
Where I have but Him

  Is my Fatherland;
    And all gifts and graces come
    Heritage into my hand:
Brothers long deplored
I in his disciples find restored."

"What a lovely hymn, papa!" exclaimed Connie. She could always speak more easily than either her mother or sister. "Who wrote it?"

"Friedrich von Hardenberg, known, where he is known, as Novalis."

"But he must have written it in German. Did you translate it?"

"Yes. You will find, I think, that I have kept form, thought, and feeling, however I may have failed in making an English poem of it."

"O, you dear papa, it is lovely! Is it long since you did it?"

"Years before you were born, Connie."

"To think of you having lived so long, and being one of us!" she returned. "Was he a Roman Catholic, papa?"

"No, he was a Moravian. At least, his parents were. I don't think he belonged to any section of the church in particular."

"But oughtn't he, papa?"

"Certainly not, my dear, except he saw good reason for it. But what is the use of asking such questions, after a hymn like that?"

"O, I didn't think anything bad, papa, I assure you. It was only that I wanted to know more about him."

The tears were in her eyes, and I was sorry I had treated as significant what was really not so. But the constant tendency to consider Christianity as associated of necessity with this or that form of it, instead of as simply obedience to Christ, had grown more and more repulsive to me as I had grown myself, for it always seemed like an insult to my brethren in Christ; hence the least hint of it in my children I was too ready to be down upon like a most unchristian ogre. I took her hand in mine, and she was comforted, for she saw in my face that I was sorry, and yet she could see that there was reason at the root of my haste.

"But," said Wynnie, who, I thought afterwards, must have strengthened herself to speak from the instinctive desire to show Percivale how far she was from being out of sympathy with what he might suppose formed a barrier between him and me —"But," she said, "the lovely feeling in that poem seems to me, as in all the rest of such poems, to belong only to the New Testament, and have nothing to do with this world round about us. These things look as if they were only for drawing and painting and being glad in, not as if they had relations with all those awful and solemn things. As soon as I try to get the two together, I lose both of them."

"That is because the human mind must begin with one thing and grow to the rest. At first, Christianity seemed to men to have only to do with their conscience. That was the first relation, of course. But even with art it was regarded as having no relation except for the presentment of its history. Afterwards, men forgot the conscience almost in trying to make Christianity comprehensible to the understanding. Now, I trust, we are beginning to see that Christianity is everything or nothing. Either the whole is a lovely fable setting forth the loftiest longing of the human soul after the vision of the divine, or it is such a fact as is the heart not only of theology so called, but of history, politics, science, and art. The treasures of the Godhead must be hidden in him, and therefore by him only can be revealed. This will interpret all things, or it has not yet been. Teachers of men have not taught this, because they have not seen it. If we do not find him in nature, we may conclude either that we do not understand the expression of nature, or have mistaken ideas or poor feelings about him. It is one great business in our life to find the interpretation which will render this harmony visible. Till we find it, we have not seen him to be all in all. Recognising a discord when they touched the notes of nature and society, the hermits forsook the instrument altogether, and contented themselves with a partial symphony-lofty, narrow, and weak. Their example, more or less, has been followed by almost all Christians. Exclusion is so much the easier way of getting harmony in the orchestra than study, insight, and interpretation, that most have adopted it. It is for us, and all who have hope in the infinite God, to widen its basis as we may, to search and find the true tone and right idea, place, and combination of instruments, until to our enraptured ear they all, with one voice of multiform yet harmonious utterance, declare the glory of God and of his Christ."

"A grand idea," said Percivale.

"Therefore likely to be a true one," I returned. "People find it hard to believe grand things; but why? If there be a God, is it not likely everything is grand, save where the reflection of his great thoughts is shaken, broken, distorted by the watery mirrors of our unbelieving and troubled souls? Things ought to be grand, simple, and noble. The ages of eternity will go on showing that such they are and ever have been. God will yet be victorious over our wretched unbeliefs."

I was sitting facing the sea, but with my eyes fixed on the sand, boring holes in it with my stick, for I could talk better when I did not look my familiar faces in the face. I did not feel thus in the pulpit; there I sought the faces of my flock, to assist me in speaking to their needs. As I drew to the close of my last monologue, a colder and stronger blast from the sea blew in my face. I lifted my head, and saw that the tide had crept up a long way, and was coming in fast. A luminous fog had sunk down over the western horizon, and almost hidden the sun, had obscured the half of the sea, and destroyed all our hopes of a sunset. A certain veil as of the commonplace, like that which so often settles down over the spirit of man after a season of vision and glory and gladness, had dropped over the face of Nature. The wind came in little bitter gusts across the dull waters. It was time to lift Connie and take her home.

This was the last time we ate together on the open shore.

CHAPTER III
A PASTORAL VISIT.

The next morning rose neither "cherchef't in a comely cloud" nor "roab'd in flames and amber light," but covered all in a rainy mist, which the wind mingled with salt spray torn from the tops of the waves. Every now and then the wind blew a blastful of larger drops against the window of my study with an angry clatter and clash, as if daring me to go out and meet its ire. The earth was very dreary, for there were no shadows anywhere. The sun was hustled away by the crowding vapours; and earth, sea, and sky were possessed by a gray spirit that threatened wrath. The breakfast-bell rang, and I went down, expecting to find my Wynnie, who was always down first to make the tea, standing at the window with a sad face, giving fit response to the aspect of nature without, her soul talking with the gray spirit. I did find her at the window, looking out upon the restless tossing of the waters, but with no despondent answer to the trouble of nature. On the contrary, her cheek, though neither rosy nor radiant, looked luminous, and her eyes were flashing out upon the ebb-tide which was sinking away into the troubled ocean beyond. Does my girl-reader expect me to tell her next that something had happened? that Percivale had said something to her? or that, at least, he had just passed the window, and given her a look which she might interpret as she pleased? I must disappoint her. It was nothing of the sort. I knew the heart and feeling of my child. It was only that kind nature was in sympathy with her mood. The girl was always more peaceful in storm than in sunshine. I remembered that now. A movement of life instantly began in her when the obligation of gladness had departed with the light. Her own being arose to provide for its own needs. She could smile now when nature required from her no smile in response to hers. And I could not help saying to myself, "She must marry a poor man some day; she is a creature of the north, and not of the south; the hot sun of prosperity would wither her up. Give her a bleak hill-side, and a glint or two of sunshine between the hailstorms, and she will live and grow; give her poverty and love, and life will be interesting to her as a romance; give her money and position, and she will grow dull and haughty. She will believe in nothing that poet can sing or architect build. She will, like Cassius, scorn her spirit for being moved to smile at anything."

I had stood regarding her for a moment. She turned and saw me, and came forward with her usual morning greeting.

"I beg your pardon, papa: I thought it was Walter."

"I am glad to see a smile on your face, my love."

"Don't think me very disagreeable, papa. I know I am a trouble to you. But I am a trouble to myself first. I fear I have a discontented mind and a complaining temper. But I do try, and I will try hard to overcome it."

"It will not get the better of you, so long as you do the duty of the moment. But I think, as I told you before, that you are not very well, and that your indisposition is going to do you good by making you think about some things you are ready to think about, but which you might have banished if you had been in good health and spirits. You are feeling as you never felt before, that you need a presence in your soul of which at least you haven't enough yet. But I preached quite enough to you yesterday, and I won't go on the same way to-day again. Only I wanted to comfort you. Come and give me my breakfast."

"You do comfort me, papa," she answered, approaching the table. "I know I don't show what I feel as I ought, but you do comfort me much. Don't you like a day like this, papa?"

"I do, my dear. I always did. And I think you take after me in that, as you do in a good many things besides. That is how I understand you so well."

"Do I really take after you, papa? Are you sure that you understand me so well?" she asked, brightening up.

"I know I do," I returned, replying to her last question.

"Better than I do myself?" she asked with an arch smile.

"Considerably, if I mistake not," I answered.

"How delightful! To think that I am understood even when I don't understand myself!"

"But even if I am wrong, you are yet understood. The blessedness of life is that we can hide nothing from God. If we could hide anything from God, that hidden thing would by and by turn into a terrible disease. It is the sight of God that keeps and makes things clean. But as we are both, by mutual confession, fond of this kind of weather, what do you say to going out with me? I have to visit a sick woman."

"You don't mean Mrs. Coombes, papa?"

"No, my dear. I did not hear she was ill."

"O, I daresay it is nothing much. Only old nursey said yesterday she was in bed with a bad cold, or something of that sort."

"We'll call and inquire as we pass,—that is, if you are inclined to go with me."

"How can you put an *if* to that, papa?"

"I have just had a message from that cottage that stands all alone on the corner of Mr. Barton's farm-over the cliff, you know-that the woman is ill, and would like to see me. So the sooner we start the better."

"I shall have done my breakfast in five minutes, papa. O, here's mamma! —Mamma, I'm going out for a walk in the rain with papa. You won't mind, will you?"

"I don't think it will do you any harm, my dear. That's all I mind, you know. It was only once or twice when you were not well that I objected to it. I quite agree with your papa, that only lazy people are *glad* to stay in-doors when it rains."

"And it does blow so delightfully!" said Wynnie, as she left the room to put on her long cloak and her bonnet.

We called at the sexton's cottage, and found him sitting gloomily by the low window, looking seaward.

"I hope your wife is not *very* poorly, Coombes," I said.

"No, sir. She be very comfortable in bed. Bed's not a bad place to be in in such weather," he answered, turning again a dreary look towards the Atlantic. "Poor things!"

"What a passion for comfort you have, Coombes! How does that come about, do you think?"

"I suppose I was made so, sir."

"To be sure you were. God made you so."

"Surely, sir. Who else?"

"Then I suppose he likes making people comfortable if he makes people like to be comfortable."

"It du look likely enough, sir."

"Then when he takes it out of your hands, you mustn't think he doesn't look after the people you would make comfortable if you could."

"I must mind my work, you know, sir."

"Yes, surely. And you mustn't want to take his out of his hands, and go grumbling as if you would do it so much better if he would only let you get *your* hand to it."

"I daresay you be right, sir," he said. "I must just go and have a look about, though. Here's Agnes. She'll tell you about mother."

He took his spade from the corner, and went out. He often brought his tools into the cottage. He had carved the handle of his spade all over with the names of the people he had buried.

"Tell your mother, Agnes, that I will call in the evening and see her, if she would like to see me. We are going now to see Mrs. Stokes. She is very poorly, I hear."

"Let us go through the churchyard, papa," said Wynnie, "and see what the old man is doing."

"Very well, my dear. It is only a few steps round."

"Why do you humour the sexton's foolish fancy so much, papa? It is such nonsense! You taught us it was, surely, in your sermon about the resurrection?"

"Most certainly, my dear. But it would be of no use to try to get it out of his head by any argument. He has a kind of craze in that direction. To get people's hearts right is of much more importance than convincing their judgments. Right judgment will follow. All such fixed ideas should be encountered from the deepest grounds of truth, and not from the outsides of their relations. Coombes has to be taught that God cares for the dead more than he does, and *therefore* it is unreasonable for him to be anxious about them."

When we reached the churchyard we found the old man kneeling on a grave before its head-stone. It was a very old one, with a death's-head and cross-bones carved upon the top of it in very high relief. With his pocket-knife he was removing the lumps of green moss out of the hollows of the eyes of the carven skull. We did not interrupt him, but walked past with a nod.

"You saw what he was doing, Wynnie? That reminds me of almost the only thing in Dante's grand poem that troubles me. I cannot think of it without a renewal of my concern, though I have no doubt he is as sorry now as I am that ever he could have written it. When, in the *Inferno,* he reaches the lowest region of torture, which is a solid lake of ice, he finds the lost plunged in it to various depths, some, if I remember rightly, entirely submerged, and visible only through the ice, transparent as crystal, like the insects found in amber. One man with his head only above the ice, appeals to him as condemned to the same punishment to take pity on him, and remove the lumps of frozen tears from his eyes, that he may weep a little before they freeze again and stop the relief once more. Dante says to him, 'Tell me who you are, and if I do not assist you, I deserve to lie at the bottom of the ice myself.' The man tells him who he is, and explains to him one awful mystery of these regions. Then he says, 'Now stretch forth thy hand, and open my eyes.' 'And,' says Dante, I did not open them for him; and rudeness to him was courtesy.'"

"But he promised, you said."

"He did; and yet he did not do it. Pity and truth had abandoned him together. One would think little of it comparatively, were it not that Dante is so full of tenderness and grand religion. It is very awful, and may teach us many things."

"But what made you think of that now?"

"Merely what Coombes was about. The visual image was all. He was scooping the green moss out of the eyes of the death's-head on the gravestone."

By this time we were on the top of the downs, and the wind was buffeting us, and every other minute assailing us with a blast of rain. Wynnie drew her cloak closer about her, bent her head towards the blast, and struggled on bravely by my side. No one who wants to enjoy a walk in the rain must carry an umbrella; it is pure folly. When we came to one of the stone fences, we cowered down by its side for a few moments to recover our breath, and then struggled on again. Anything like conversation was out of the question. At length we dropped into a hollow, which gave us a little repose. Down below the sea was dashing into the mouth of the glen, or coomb, as they call it there. On the opposite side of the hollow, the little house to which we were going stood up against the gray sky.

"I begin to doubt whether I ought to have brought you, Wynnie. It was thoughtless of me; I don't mean for your sake, but because your presence may be embarrassing in a small house; for probably the poor woman may prefer seeing me alone."

"I will go back, papa. I sha'n't mind it a bit."

"No; you had better come on. I shall not be long with her, I daresay. We may find some place that you can wait in. Are you wet?"

"Only my cloak. I am as dry as a tortoise inside."

"Come along, then. We shall soon be there."

When we reached the house I found that Wynnie would not be in the way. I left her seated by the kitchen-fire, and was shown into the room where Mrs. Stokes lay. I cannot say I perceived. But I guessed somehow, the moment I saw her that there was something upon her mind. She was a hard-featured woman, with a cold, troubled black eye that rolled restlessly about. She lay on her back, moving her head from side to side. When I entered she only looked at me, and turned her eyes away towards the wall. I approached the bedside, and seated myself by it. I always do so at once; for the patient feels more at rest than if you stand tall up before her. I laid my hand on hers.

"Are you very ill, Mrs. Stokes?" I said.

"Yes, very," she answered with a groan. "It be come to the last with me."

"I hope not, indeed, Mrs. Stokes. It's not come to the last with us, so long as we have a Father in heaven."

"Ah! but it be with me. He can't take any notice of the like of me."

"But indeed he does, whether you think it or not. He takes notice of every thought we think, and every deed we do, and every sin we commit."

I said the last words with emphasis, for I suspected something more than usual upon her conscience. She gave another groan, but made no reply. I therefore went on.

"Our Father in heaven is not like some fathers on earth, who, so long as their children don't bother them, let them do anything they like. He will not have them do what is wrong. He loves them too much for that."

"He won't look at me," she said half murmuring, half sighing it out, so that I could hardly, hear what she said.

"It is because he *is* looking at you that you are feeling uncomfortable," I answered. "He wants you to confess your sins. I don't mean to me, but to himself; though if you would like to tell me anything, and I can help you, I shall be *very* glad. You know Jesus Christ came to save us from our sins; and that's why we call him our Saviour. But he can't save us from our sins if we won't confess that we have any."

"I'm sure I never said but what I be a great sinner, as well as other people."

"You don't suppose that's confessing your sins?" I said. "I once knew a woman of very bad character, who allowed to me she was a great sinner; but when I said, 'Yes, you have done so and so,' she would not allow one of those deeds to be worthy of being reckoned amongst her sins. When I asked her what great sins she had been guilty of, then, seeing these counted for nothing, I could get no more out of her than that she was a great sinner, like other people, as you have just been saying."

"I hope you don't be thinking I ha' done anything of that sort," she said with wakening energy. "No man or woman dare say I've done anything to be ashamed of."

"Then you've committed no sins?" I returned. "But why did you send for me? You must have something to say to me."

"I never did send for you. It must ha' been my husband."

"Ah, then I'm afraid I've no business here!" I returned, rising. "I thought you had sent for me."

She returned no answer. I hoped that by retiring I should set her thinking, and make her more willing to listen the next time I came. I think clergymen may do much harm by insisting when people are in a bad mood, as if they had everything to do, and the Spirit of God nothing at all. I bade her good-day, hoped she would be better soon, and returned to Wynnie.

As we walked home together, I said:

"Wynnie, I was right. It would not have done at all to take you into the sick-room. Mrs. Stokes had not sent for me herself, and rather resented my appearance. But I think she will send for me before many days are over."

CHAPTER IV
THE ART OF NATURE.

We had a week of hazy weather after this. I spent it chiefly in my study and in Connie's room. A world of mist hung over the sea; it refused to hold any communion with mortals. As if ill-tempered or unhappy, it folded itself in its mantle and lay still.

What was it thinking about? All Nature is so full of meaning, that we cannot help fancying sometimes that she knows her own meanings. She is busy with every human mood in turn—sometimes with ten of them at once—picturing our own inner world before us, that we may see, understand, develop, reform it.

I was turning over some such thought in my mind one morning, when Dora knocked at the door, saying that Mr. Percivale had called, and that mamma was busy, and would I mind if she brought him up to the study.

"Not in the least, my dear," I answered; "I shall be very glad to see him."

"Not much of weather for your sacred craft, Percivale," I said as he entered. "I suppose, if you were asked to make a sketch to-day, it would be much the same as if a stupid woman were to ask you to take her portrait?"

"Not quite so bad as that," said Percivale.

"Surely the human face is more than nature."

"Nature is never stupid."

"The woman might be pretty."

"Nature is full of beauty in her worst moods; while the prettier such a woman, the more stupid she would look, and the more irksome you would feel the task; for you could not help making claims upon her which you would never think of making upon Nature."

"I daresay you are right. Such stupidity has a good deal to do with moral causes. You do not ever feel that Nature is to blame."

"Nature is never ugly. She may be dull, sorrowful, troubled; she may be lost in tears and pallor, but she cannot be ugly. It is only when you rise into animal nature that you find ugliness."

"True in the main only; for no lines of absolute division can be drawn in nature. I have seen ugly flowers."

"I grant it; but they are exceptional; and none of them are without beauty."

"Surely not. The ugliest soul even is not without some beauty. But I grant you that the higher you rise the more is ugliness possible, just because the greater beauty is possible. There is no ugliness to equal in its repulsiveness the ugliness of a beautiful face."

A pause followed.

"I presume," I said, "you are thinking of returning to London now, there seems so little to be gained by remaining here. When this weather begins to show itself I could wish myself in my own parish; but I am sure the change, even through the winter, will be good for my daughter."

"I must be going soon," he answered; "but it would be too bad to take offence at the old lady's first touch of temper. I mean to wait and see whether we shall not have a little bit of St. Martin's summer, as Shakspere calls it; after which, hail London, queen of smoke and—"

"And what?" I asked, seeing he hesitated.

"'And soap,' I was fancying you would say; for you never will allow the worst of things, Mr. Walton."

"No, surely I will not. For one thing, the worst has never been seen by anybody yet. We have no experience to justify it."

We were chatting in this loose manner when Walter came to the door to tell me that a messenger had come from Mrs. Stokes.

I went down to see him, and found her husband.

"My wife be very bad, sir," he said. "I wish you could come and see her."

"Does she want to see me?" I asked.

"She's been more uncomfortable than ever since you was there last," he said.

"But," I repeated, "has she said she would like to see me?"

"I can't say it, sir," answered the man.

"Then it is you who want me to see her?"

"Yes, sir; but I be sure she do want to see you. I know her way, you see, sir. She never would say she wanted anything in her life; she would always leave you to find it out: so I got sharp at that, sir."

"And then would she allow she had wanted it when you got it her?"

"No, never, sir. She be peculiar-my wife; she always be."

"Does she know that you have come to ask me now?"

"No, sir."

"Have you courage to tell her?"

The man hesitated.

"If you haven't courage to tell her," I resumed, "I have nothing more to say. I can't go; or, rather, I will not go."

"I will tell her, sir."

"Then you will tell her that I refused to come until she sent for me herself."

"Ben't that rather hard on a dying woman, sir?"

"I have my reasons. Except she send for me herself, the moment I go she will take refuge in the fact that she did not send for me. I know your wife's peculiarity too, Mr. Stokes."

"Well, I *will* tell her, sir. It's time to speak my own mind."

"I think so. It was time long ago. When she sends for me, if it be in the middle of the night, I shall be with her at once."

He left me and I returned to Percivale.

"I was just thinking before you came," I said, "about the relation of Nature to our inner world. You know I am quite ignorant of your art, but I often think about the truths that lie at the root of it."

"I am greatly obliged to you," he said, "for talking about these things. I assure you it is of more service to me than any professional talk. I always think the professions should not herd together so much as they do; they want to be shone upon from other quarters."

"I believe we have all to help each other, Percivale. The sun himself could give us no light that would be of any service to us but for the reflective power of the airy particles through which he shines. But anything I know I have found out merely by foraging for my own necessities."

"That is just what makes the result valuable," he replied. "Tell me what you were thinking."

"I was thinking," I answered, "how everyone likes to see his own thoughts set outside of him, that he may contemplate them *objectively,* as the philosophers call it. He likes to see the other side of them, as it were."

"Yes, that is, of course, true; else, I suppose, there would be no art at all."

"Surely. But that is not the aspect in which I was considering the question. Those who can so set them forth are artists; and however they may fail of effecting such a representation of their ideas as will satisfy themselves, they yet experience satisfaction in the measure in which they have succeeded. But there are many more men who cannot yet utter their ideas in any form. Mind, I do expect that, if they will only be good, they shall have this power some day; for I do think that many things we call differences in kind, may in God's grand scale prove to be only differences in degree. And indeed the artist-by artist, I mean, of course, architect, musician, painter, poet, sculptor-in many things requires it just as much as the most helpless and dumb of his brethren, seeing in proportion to the things that he can do, he is aware of the things he cannot do, the thoughts he cannot express. Hence arises the enthusiasm with which people hail the work of an artist; they rejoice, namely, in seeing their own thoughts, or feelings, or something like them, expressed; and hence it comes that of those who have money, some hang their walls with pictures of their own choice, others —"

"I beg your pardon," said Percivale, interrupting; "but most people, I fear, hang their walls with pictures of other people's choice, for they don't buy them at all till the artist has got a name."

"That is true. And yet there is a shadow of choice even there; for they won't at least buy what they dislike. And again the growth in popularity may be only what first attracted their attention-not determined their choice."

"But there are others who only buy them for their value in the market."

"'Of such is not the talk,' as the Germans would say. In as far as your description applies, such are only tradesmen, and have no claim to be considered now."

"Then I beg your pardon for interrupting. I am punished more than I deserve, if you have lost your thread."

"I don't think I have. Let me see. Yes. I was saying that people hang their walls with pictures of their choice; or provide music, &c., of their choice. Let me keep to the pictures: their choice, consciously or unconsciously, is determined by some expression that these pictures give to what is in themselves-the buyers, I mean. They like to see their own feelings outside of themselves."

"Is there not another possible motive-that the pictures teach them something?"

"That, I venture to think, shows a higher moral condition than the other, but still partakes of the other; for it is only what is in us already that makes us able to lay hold of a lesson. It is there in the germ, else nothing from without would wake it up."

"I do not quite see what all this has to do with Nature and her influences."

"One step more, and I shall arrive at it. You will admit that the pictures and objects of art of all kinds, with which a man adorns the house he has chosen or built to live in, have thenceforward not a little to do with the education of his tastes and feelings. Even when he is not aware of it, they are working upon him,—for good, if he has chosen what is good, which alone shall be our supposition."

"Certainly; that is clear."

"Now I come to it. God, knowing our needs, built our house for our needs-not as one man may build for another, but as no man can build for himself. For our comfort, education, training, he has put into form for us all the otherwise hidden thoughts and feelings of our heart. Even when he speaks of the hidden things of the Spirit of God, he uses the forms or pictures of Nature. The world is, as it were, the human, unseen world turned inside out, that we may see it. On the walls of the house that he has built for us, God has hung up the pictures-ever-living, ever-changing pictures-of all that passes in our souls. Form and colour and motion are there,—ever-modelling, ever-renewing, never wearying. Without this living portraiture from within, we should have no word to utter that should represent a single act of the inner world. Metaphysics could have no existence, not to speak of poetry, not to speak of the commonest language of affection. But all is done in such spiritual suggestion, portrait and definition are so avoided, the whole is in such fluent evanescence, that the producing mind is only aided, never overwhelmed. It never amounts to representation. It affords but the material which the thinking, feeling soul can use, interpret, and apply for its own purposes of speech. It is, as it were, the forms of thought cast into a lovely chaos by the inferior laws of matter, thence to be withdrawn by what we call the creative genius that God has given to men, and moulded, and modelled, and arranged, and built up to its own shapes and its own purposes."

"Then I presume you would say that no mere transcript, if I may use the word, of nature is the worthy work of an artist."

"It is an impossibility to make a mere transcript. No man can help seeing nature as he is himself, for she has all in her; but if he sees no meaning in especial that he wants to give, his portrait of her will represent only her dead face, not her living impassioned countenance."

"Then artists ought to interpret nature?"

"Indubitably; but that will only be to interpret themselves-something of humanity that is theirs, whether they have discovered it already or not. If to this they can add some teaching for humanity, then indeed they may claim to belong to the higher order of art, however imperfect they may be in their powers of representing-however lowly, therefore, their position may be in that order."

CHAPTER V
THE SORE SPOT.

We went on talking for some time. Indeed we talked so long that the dinner-hour was approaching, when one of the maids came with the message that Mr. Stokes had called again, wishing to see me. I could not help smiling inwardly at the news. I went down at once, and found him smiling too.

"My wife do send me for you this time, sir," he said. "Between you and me, I cannot help thinking she have something on her mind she wants to tell you, sir."

"Why shouldn't she tell you, Mr. Stokes? That would be most natural. And then, if you wanted any help about it, why, of course, here I am."

"She don't think well enough of my judgment for that, sir; and I daresay she be quite right. She always do make me give in before she have done talking. But she have been a right good wife to me, sir."

"Perhaps she would have been a better if you hadn't given in quite so much. It is very wrong to give in when you think you are right."

"But I never be sure of it when she talk to me awhile."

"Ah, then I have nothing to say except that you ought to have been surer—*sometimes*; I don't say *always*."

"But she do want you very bad now, sir. I don't think she'll behave to you as she did before. Do come, sir."

"Of course I will-instantly."

I returned to the study, and asked Percivale if he would like to go with me. He looked, I thought, as if he would rather not. I saw that it was hardly kind to ask him.

"Well, perhaps it is better not," I said; "for I do not know how long I may have to be with the poor woman. You had better wait here and take my place at the dinner-table. I promise not to depose you if I should return before the meal is over."

He thanked me very heartily. I showed him into the drawing-room, told my wife where I was going, and not to wait dinner for me—I would take my chance-and joined Mr. Stokes.

"You have no idea, then," I said, after we had gone about half-way, "what makes your wife so uneasy?"

"No, I haven't," he answered; "except it be," he resumed, "that she was too hard, as I thought, upon our Mary, when she wanted to marry beneath her, as wife thought."

"How beneath her? Who was it she wanted to marry?"

"She did marry him, sir. She has a bit of her mother's temper, you see, and she would take her own way."

"Ah, there's a lesson to mothers, is it not? If they want to have their own way, they mustn't give their own temper to their daughters."

"But how are they to help it, sir?"

"Ah, how indeed? But what is your daughter's husband?"

"A labourer, sir. He works on a farm out by Carpstone."

"But you have worked on Mr. Barton's farm for many years, if I don't mistake?"

"I have, sir; but I am a sort of a foreman now, you see."

"But you weren't so always; and your son-in-law, whether he work his way up or not, is, I presume, much where you were when you married Mrs. Stokes?"

"True as you say, sir; and it's not me that has anything to say about it. I never gave the man a nay. But you see, my wife, she always do be wanting to get her head up in the world; and since she took to the shopkeeping—"

"The shopkeeping!" I said, with some surprise; "I didn't know that."

"Well, you see, sir, it's only for a quarter or so of the year. You know it's a favourite walk for the folks as comes here for the bathing-past our house, to see the great cave down below; and my wife, she got a bit of a sign put up, and put a few ginger-beer bottles in the window, and —"

"A bad place for the ginger-beer," I said.

"They were only empty ones, with corks and strings, you know, sir. My wife, she know better than put the ginger-beer its own self in the sun. But I do think she carry her head higher after that; and a farm-labourer, as they call them, was none good enough for her daughter."

"And hasn't she been kind to her since she married, then?"

"She's never done her no harm, sir."

"But she hasn't gone to see her very often, or asked her to come and see you very often, I suppose?"

"There's ne'er a one o' them crossed the door of the other," he answered, with some evident feeling of his own in the matter.

"Ah; but you don't approve of that yourself, Stokes?"

"Approve of it? No, sir. I be a farm-labourer once myself; and so I do want to see my own daughter now and then. But she take after her mother, she do. I don't know which of the two it is as does it, but there's no coming and going between Carpstone and this."

We were approaching the house. I told Stokes he had better let her know I was there; for that, if she had changed her mind, it was not too late for me to go home again without disturbing her. He came back saying she was still very anxious to see me.

"Well, Mrs. Stokes, how do you feel to-day?" I asked, by way of opening the conversation. "I don't think you look much worse."

"I he much worse, sir. You don't know what I suffer, or you wouldn't make so little of it. I be very bad."

"I know you are very ill, but I hope you are not too ill to tell me why you are so anxious to see me. You have got something to tell me, I suppose."

With pale and death-like countenance, she appeared to be fighting more with herself than with the disease which yet had nearly overcome her. The drops stood upon her forehead, and she did not speak. Wishing to help her, if I might, I said —

"Was it about your daughter you wanted to speak to me?"

"No," she muttered. "I have nothing to say about my daughter. She was my own. I could do as I pleased with her."

I thought with myself, we must have a word about that by and by, but meantime she must relieve her heart of the one thing whose pressure she feels.

"Then," I said, "you want to tell me about something that was not your own?"

"Who said I ever took what was not my own?" she returned fiercely. "Did Stokes dare to say I took anything that wasn't my own?"

"No one has said anything of the sort. Only I cannot help thinking, from your own words and from your own behaviour, that that must be the cause of your misery."

"It is very hard that the parson should think such things," she muttered again.

"My poor woman," I said, "you sent for me because you had something to confess to me. I want to help you if I can. But you are too proud to confess it yet, I see. There is no use in my staying here. It only does you harm. So I will bid you good-morning. If you cannot confess to me, confess to God."

"God knows it, I suppose, without that."

"Yes. But that does not make it less necessary for you to confess it. How is he to forgive you, if you won't allow that you have done wrong?"

"It be not so easy that as you think. How would you like to say you had took something that wasn't your own?"

"Well, I shouldn't like it, certainly; but if I had it to do, I think I should make haste and do it, and so get rid of it."

"But that's the worst of it; I can't get rid of it."

"But," I said, laying my hand on hers, and trying to speak as kindly as I could, although her whole behaviour would have been exceedingly repulsive but for her evidently great suffering, "you have now all but confessed taking something that did not belong to you. Why don't you summon courage and tell me all about it? I want to help you out of the trouble as easily as ever I can; but I can't if you don't tell me what you've got that isn't yours."

"I haven't got anything," she muttered.

"You had something, then, whatever may have become of it now."

She was again silent.

"What did you do with it?"

"Nothing."

I rose and took up my hat. She stretched out her hand, as if to lay hold of me, with a cry.

"Stop, stop. I'll tell you all about it. I lost it again. That's the worst of it. I got no good of it."

"What was it?"

"A sovereign," she said, with a groan. "And now I'm a thief, I suppose."

"No more a thief than you were before. Rather less, I hope. But do you think it would have been any better for you if you hadn't lost it, and had got some good of it, as you say?"

She was silent yet again.

"If you hadn't lost it you would most likely have been a great deal worse for it than you are—a more wicked woman altogether."

"I'm not a wicked woman."

"It is wicked to steal, is it not?"

"I didn't steal it."

"How did you come by it, then?"

"I found it."

"Did you try to find out the owner?"

"No. I knew whose it was."

"Then it was very wicked not to return it. And I say again, that if you had not lost the sovereign you would have been most likely a more wicked woman than you are."

"It was very hard to lose it. I could have given it back. And then I wouldn't have lost my character as I have done this day."

"Yes, you could; but I doubt if you would."

"I would."

"Now, if you had it, you are sure you would give it back?"

"Yes, that I would," she said, looking me so full in the face that I was sure she meant it.

"How would you give it back? Would you get your husband to take it?"

"No; I wouldn't trust him."

"With the story, you mean I You do not wish to imply that he would not restore it?"

"I don't mean that. He would do what I told him."

"How would you return it, then?"

"I should make a parcel of it, and send it."

"Without saying anything about it?"

"Yes. Where's the good? The man would have his own."

"No, he would not. He has a right to your confession, for you have wronged him. That would never do."

"You are too hard upon me," she said, beginning to weep angrily.

"Do you want to get the weight of this sin off your mind?" I said.

"Of course I do. I am going to die. O dear! O dear!"

"Then that is just what I want to help you in. You must confess, or the weight of it will stick there."

"But, if I confess, I shall be expected to pay it back?"

"Of course. That is only reasonable."

"But I haven't got it, I tell you. I have lost it."

"Have you not a sovereign in your possession?"

"No, not one."

"Can't you ask your husband to let you have one?"

"There! I knew it was no use. I knew you would only make matters worse. I do wish I had never seen that wicked money."

"You ought not to abuse the money; it was not wicked. You ought to wish that you had returned it. But that is no use; the thing is to return it now. Has your husband got a sovereign?"

"No. He may ha' got one since I be laid up. But I never can tell him about it; and I should be main sorry to spend one of his hard earning in that way, poor man."

"Well, I'll tell him, and we'll manage it somehow."

I thought for a few moments she would break out in opposition; but she hid her face with the sheet instead, and burst into a great weeping.

I took this as a permission to do as I had said, and went to the room-door and called her husband. He came, looking scared. His wife did not look up, but lay weeping. I hoped much for her and him too from this humiliation before him, for I had little doubt she needed it.

"Your wife, poor woman," I said, "is in great distress because —I do not know when or how— she picked up a sovereign that did not belong to her, and, instead of returning, put it away somewhere and lost it. This is what is making her so miserable."

"Deary me!" said Stokes, in the tone with which he would have spoken to a sick child; and going up to his wife, he sought to draw down the sheet from her face, apparently that he might kiss her; but she kept tight hold of it, and he could not. "Deary me!" he went on; "we'll soon put that all to rights. When was it, Jane, that you found it?"

"When we wanted so to have a pig of our own; and I thought I could soon return it," she sobbed from under the sheet.

"Deary me! Ten years ago! Where did you find it, old woman?"

"I saw Squire Tresham drop it, as he paid me for some ginger-beer he got for some ladies that was with him. I do believe I should ha' given it back at the time; but he made faces at the ginger-beer, and said it was very nasty; and I thought, well, I would punish him for it."

"You see it was your temper that made a thief of you, then," I said.

"My old man won't be so hard on me as you, sir. I wish I had told him first."

"I would wish that too," I said, "were it not that I am afraid you might have persuaded him to be silent about it, and so have made him miserable and wicked too. But now, Stokes, what is to be done? This money must be paid. Have you got it?"

The poor man looked blank.

"She will never be at ease till this money is paid," I insisted.

"Well, sir, I ain't got it, but I'll borrow it of someone; I'll go to master, and ask him."

"No, my good fellow, that won't do. Your master would want to know what you were going to do with it, perhaps; and we mustn't let more people know about it than just ourselves and Squire Tresham. There is no occasion for that. I'll tell you what: I'll give you the money, and you must take it; or, if you like, I will take it to the squire, and tell him all about it. Do you authorise me to do this, Mrs. Stokes?"

"Please, sir. It's very kind of you. I will work hard to pay you again, if it please God to spare me. I am very sorry I was so cross-tempered to you, sir; but I couldn't bear the disgrace of it."

She said all this from under the bed-clothes.

"Well, I'll go," I said; "and as soon as I've had my dinner I'll get a horse and ride over to Squire Tresham's. I'll come back to-night and tell you about it. And now I hope you will be able to thank God for forgiving you this sin; but you must not hide and cover it up, but confess it clean out to him, you know."

She made me no answer, but went on sobbing.

I hastened home, and as I entered sent Walter to ask the loan of a horse which a gentleman, a neighbour, had placed at my disposal.

When I went into the dining-room, I found that they had not sat down to dinner. I expostulated: it was against the rule of the house, when my return was uncertain.

"But, my love," said my wife, "why should you not let us please ourselves sometimes? Dinner is so much nicer when you are with us."

"I am very glad you think so," I answered. "But there are the children: it is not good for growing creatures to be kept waiting for their meals."

"You see there are no children; they have had their dinner."

"Always in the right, wife; but there's Mr. Percivale."

"I never dine till seven o'clock, to save daylight," he said.

"Then I am beaten on all points. Let us dine."

During dinner I could scarcely help observing how Percivale's eyes followed Wynnie, or, rather, every now and then settled down upon her face. That she was aware, almost conscious of this, I could not doubt. One glance at her satisfied me of that. But certain words of the apostle kept coming again and again into my mind; for they were winged words those, and even when they did not enter they fluttered their wings at my window: "Whatsoever is not of faith is sin." And I kept reminding myself that I must heave the load of sin off me, as I had been urging poor Mrs. Stokes to do; for God was ever seeking to lift it, only he could not without my help, for that would be to do me more harm than good by taking the one thing in which I was like him away from me-my action. Therefore I must have faith in him, and not be afraid; for surely all fear is sin, and one of the most oppressive sins from which the Lord came to save us.

Before dinner was over the horse was at the door. I mounted, and set out for Squire Tresham's.

I found him a rough but kind-hearted elderly man. When I told him the story of the poor woman's misery, he was quite concerned at her suffering. When I produced the sovereign he would not receive it at first, but requested me to take it back to her and say she must keep it by way of an apology for his rudeness about her ginger-beer; for I took care to tell him the whole story, thinking it might be a lesson to him too. But I begged him to take it; for it would, I thought, not only relieve her mind more thoroughly, but help to keep her from coming to think lightly of the affair afterwards. Of course I could not tell him that I had advanced the money, for that would have quite prevented him from receiving it. I then got on my horse again, and rode straight to the cottage.

"Well, Mrs. Stokes," I said, "it's all over now. That's one good thing done. How do you feel yourself now?"

"I feel better now, sir. I hope God will forgive me."

"God does forgive you. But there are more things you need forgiveness for. It is not enough to get rid of one sin. We must get rid of all our sins, you know. They're not nice things, are they, to keep in our hearts? It is just like shutting up nasty corrupting things, dead carcasses, under lock and key, in our most secret drawers, as if they were precious jewels."

"I wish I could be good, like some people, but I wasn't made so. There's my husband now. I do believe he never do anything wrong in his life. But then, you see, he would let a child take him in."

"And far better too. Infinitely better to be taken in. Indeed there is no harm in being taken in; but there is awful harm in taking in."

She did not reply, and I went on:

"I think you would feel a good deal better yet, if you would send for your daughter and her husband now, and make it up with them, especially seeing you are so ill."

"I will, sir. I will directly. I'm tired of having my own way. But I was made so."

"You weren't made to continue so, at all events. God gives us the necessary strength to resist what is bad in us. He is making at you now; only you must give in, else he cannot get on with the making of you. I think very likely he made you ill now, just that you might bethink yourself, and feel that you had done wrong."

"I have been feeling that for many a year."

"That made it the more needful to make you ill; for you had been feeling your duty, and yet not doing it; and that was worst of all. You know Jesus came to lift the weight of our sins, our very sins themselves, off our hearts, by forgiving them and helping us to cast them away from us. Everything that makes you uncomfortable must have sin in it somewhere, and he came to save you from it. Send for your daughter and her husband, and when you have done that you will think of something else to set right that's wrong."

"But there would be no end to that way of it, sir."

"Certainly not, till everything was put right."

"But a body might have nothing else to do, that way."

"Well, that's the very first thing that has to be done. It is our business in this world. We were not sent here to have our own way and try to enjoy ourselves."

"That is hard on a poor woman that has to work for her bread."

"To work for your bread is not to take your own way, for it is God's way. But you have wanted many things your own way. Now, if you would just take his way, you would find that he would take care you should enjoy your life."

"I'm sure I haven't had much enjoyment in mine."

"That was just because you would not trust him with his own business, but must take it into your hands. If you will but do his will, he will take care that you have a life to be very glad of and very thankful for. And the longer you live, the more blessed you will find it. But I must leave you now, for I have talked to you long enough. You must try and get a sleep. I will come and see you again to-morrow, if you like."

"Please do, sir; I shall be very grateful."

As I rode home I thought, if the lifting of one sin off the human heart was like a resurrection, what would it be when every sin was lifted from every heart! Every sin, then, discovered in one's own soul must be a pledge of renewed bliss in its removing. And when the thought came again of what St. Paul had said somewhere, "whatsoever is not of faith is sin," I thought what a weight of sin had to be lifted from the earth, and how blessed it might be. But what could I do for it? I could just begin with myself, and pray God for that inward light which is his Spirit, that so I might see him in everything and rejoice in everything as his gift, and then all things would be holy, for whatsoever is of faith must be the opposite of sin; and that was my part towards heaving the weight of sin, which, like myriads of gravestones, was pressing the life out of us men, off the whole world. Faith in God is life and righteousness-the faith that trusts so that it will obey-none other. Lord, lift the people thou hast made into holy obedience and thanksgiving, that they may be glad in this thy world.

CHAPTER VI
THE GATHERING STORM.

The weather cleared up again the next day, and for a fortnight it was lovely. In this region we saw less of the sadness of the dying year than in our own parish, for there being so few trees in the vicinity of the ocean, the autumn had nowhere to hang out her mourning flags. But there, indeed, so mild is the air, and so equable the temperature all the winter through, compared with the inland counties, that the bitterness of the season is almost unknown. This, however, is no guarantee against furious storms of wind and rain.

Not long after the occurrence last recorded, Turner paid us another visit. I confess I was a little surprised at his being able to get away so soon again; for of all men a country surgeon can least easily find time for a holiday; but he had managed it, and I had no doubt, from what I knew of him, had made thorough provision for his cure in his absence.

He brought us good news from home. Everything was going on well. Weir was working as hard as usual; and everybody agreed that I could not have got a man to take my place better.

He said he found Connie much improved; and, from my own observations, I was sure he was right. She was now able to turn a good way from one side to the other, and finding her health so steady besides, Turner encouraged her in making gentle and frequent use of her strength, impressing it upon her, however, that everything depended on avoiding everything like a jerk or twist of any sort. I was with them when he said this. She looked up at him with a happy smile.

"I will do all I can, Mr. Turner," she said, "to get out of people's way as soon as possible."

Perhaps she saw something in our faces that made her add—

"I know you don't mind the bother I am; but I do. I want to help, and not be helped-more than other people-as soon as possible. I will therefore be as gentle as mamma and as brave as papa, and see if we don't get well, Mr. Turner. I mean to have a ride on old Spry next summer.—I do," she added, nodding her pretty head up from the pillow, when she saw the glance the doctor and I exchanged. "Look here," she went on, poking the eider-down quilt up with her foot.

"Magnificent!" said Turner; "but mind, you must do nothing out of bravado. That won't do at all."

"I have done," said Connie, putting on a face of mock submission.

That day we carried her out for a few minutes, but hardly laid her down, for we were afraid of the damp from the earth. A few feet nearer or farther from the soil will make a difference. It was the last time for many weeks. Anyone interested in my Connie need not be alarmed: it was only because of the weather, not because of her health.

One day I was walking home from a visit I had been paying to Mrs. Stokes. She was much better, in a fair way to recover indeed, and her mental health was improved as well. Her manner to me was certainly very different, and the tone of her voice, when she spoke to her husband especially, was changed: a certain roughness in it was much modified, and I had good hopes that she had begun to climb up instead of sliding down the hill of difficulty, as she had been doing hitherto.

It was a cold and gusty afternoon. The sky eastward and overhead was tolerably clear when I set out from home; but when I left the cottage to return, I could see that some change was at hand. Shaggy vapours of light gray were blowing rapidly across the sky from the west. A wind was blowing fiercely up there, although the gusts down below came from the east. The clouds it swept along with it were formless, with loose fringes-disreputable, troubled, hasty clouds they were, looking like mischief. They reminded me of Shelley's "Ode to the West Wind," in which he compares the "loose clouds" to hair, and calls them "the locks of the approaching storm." Away to the west, a great thick curtain of fog, of a luminous yellow, covered all the sea-horizon, extending north and south as far as the eye could reach. It looked ominous. A surly secret seemed to lie in its bosom. Now and then I could discern the dim ghost of a vessel through it, as tacking for north or south it came near enough to the edge of the fog to show itself for a few moments, ere it retreated again into its bosom. There was exhaustion, it seemed to me, in the air, notwithstanding the coolness of the wind, and I was glad when I found myself comfortably seated by the drawing-room fire, and saw Wynnie bestirring herself to make the tea.

"It looks stormy, I think, Wynnie," I said.

Her eye lightened, as she looked out to sea from the window.

"You seem to like the idea of it," I added.

"You told me I was like you, papa; and you look as if you liked the idea of it too."

"*Per se*, certainly, a storm is pleasant to me. I should not like a world without storms any more than I should like that Frenchman's idea of the perfection of the earth, when all was to be smooth as a trim-shaven lawn, rocks and mountains banished, and the sea breaking on the shore only in wavelets of ginger-beer or lemonade, I forget which. But the older you grow, the more sides of a thing will present themselves to your contemplation. The storm may be grand and exciting in itself, but you cannot help thinking of the people that are in it. Think for a moment of the multitude of vessels, great and small, which are gathered within the skirts of that angry vapour out there. I fear the toils of the storm are around them. Look at the barometer in the hall, my dear, and tell me what it says."

She went and returned.

"It was not very low, papa-only at rain; but the moment I touched it, the hand dropped an inch."

"Yes, I thought so. All things look stormy. It may not be very bad here, however."

"That doesn't make much difference though, does it, papa?"

"No further than that being creatures in time and space, we must think of things from our own standpoint."

"But I remember very well how, when we were children, you would not let nurse teach us Dr. Watts's hymns for children, because you said they tended to encourage selfishness."

"Yes; I remember it very well. Some of them make the contrast between the misery of others and our own comforts so immediately the apparent-mind, I only say apparent-ground of thankfulness, that they are not fit for teaching. I do think that if you could put Dr. Watts to the question, he would abjure any such intention, saying that only he meant to heighten the sense of our obligation. But it does tend to selfishness and, what is worse, self-righteousness, and is very dangerous therefore. What right have I to thank God that I am not as other men are in anything? I have to thank God for the good things he has given to me; but how dare I suppose that he is not doing the same for other people in proportion to their capacity? I don't like to appear to condemn Dr. Watts's hymns. Certainly he has written the very worst hymns I know; but he has likewise written the best-for public worship, I mean."

"Well, but, papa, I have heard you say that any simple feeling that comes of itself cannot be wrong in itself. If I feel a delight in the idea of a storm, I cannot help it coming."

"I never said you could, my dear. I only said that as we get older, other things we did not feel at first come to show themselves more to us, and impress us more."

Thus my child and I went on, like two pendulums crossing each other in their swing, trying to reach the same dead beat of mutual intelligence.

"But," said Wynnie, "you say everybody is in God's hands as well as we."

"Yes, surely, my dear; as much out in yon stormy haze as here beside the fire."

"Then we ought not to be miserable about them, even if there comes a storm, ought we?"

"No, surely. And, besides, I think if we could help any of them, the very persons that enjoyed the storm the most would be the busiest to rescue them from it. At least, I fancy so. But isn't the tea ready?"

"Yes, papa. I'll just go and tell mamma."

When she returned with her mother, and the children had joined us, Wynnie resumed the talk.

"I know what I am going to say is absurd, papa, and yet I don't see my way out of it-logically, I suppose you would call it. What is the use of taking any trouble about them if they are in God's hands? Why should we try to take them out of God's hands?"

"Ah, Wynnie! at least you do not seek to hide your bad logic, or whatever you call it. Take them out of God's hands! If you could do that, it would be perdition indeed. God's hands is the only safe place in the universe; and the universe is in his hands. Are we not in God's hands on the shore because we say they are in his hands who go down to the sea in ships? If we draw them on shore, surely they are not out of God's hands."

"I see—I see. But God could save them without us."

"Yes; but what would become of us then? God is so good to us, that we must work our little salvation in the earth with him. Just as a father lets his little child help him a little, that the child may learn to be and to do, so God puts it in our hearts to save this life to our fellows, because we would instinctively save it to ourselves, if we could. He requires us to do our best."

"But God may not mean to save them."

"He may mean them to be drowned-we do not know. But we know that we must try our little salvation, for it will never interfere with God's great and good and perfect will. Ours will be foiled if he sees that best."

"But people always say, when anyone escapes unhurt from an accident, 'by the mercy of God.' They don't say it is by the mercy of God when he is drowned."

"But *people* cannot be expected, ought not, to say what they do not feel. Their own first sensation of deliverance from impending death would break out in a 'thank God,' and therefore they say it is God's mercy when another is saved. If they go farther, and refuse to consider it God's mercy when a man is drowned, that is just the sin of the world-the want of faith. But the man who creeps out of the drowning, choking billows into the glory of the new heavens and the new earth-do you think his thanksgiving for the mercy of God which has delivered him is less than that of the man who creeps, exhausted and worn, out of the waves on to the dreary, surf-beaten shore? In nothing do we show less faith than the way in which we think and speak about death. 'O Death, where is thy sting? O Grave, where is thy victory?' says the apostle. 'Here, here, here,' cry the Christian people, 'everywhere. It is an awful sting, a fearful victory. But God keeps it away from us many a time when we ask him-to let it pierce us to the heart, at last, to be sure; but that can't be helped.' I mean this is how they feel in their hearts who do not believe that God is as merciful when he sends death as when he sends life; who, Christian people as they are, yet look upon death as an evil thing which cannot be avoided, and would, if they might live always, be content to live always. Death or Life-each is God's; for he is not the God of the dead, but of the living: there are no dead, for all live to him."

"But don't you think we naturally shrink from death, Harry?" said my wife.

"There can be no doubt about that, my dear."

"Then, if it be natural, God must have meant that it should be so."

"Doubtless, to begin with, but not to continue or end with. A child's sole desire is for food-the very best possible to begin with. But how would it be if the child should reach, say, two years of age, and refuse to share this same food with his little brother? Or what comes of the man who never so far rises above the desire for food that *nothing* could make him forget his dinner-hour? Just so the life of Christians should be strong enough to overcome the fear of death. We ought to love and believe him so much, that when he says we shall not die, we should at least believe that death must be something very different from what it looks to us to be-so different, that what we mean by the word does not apply to the reality at all; and so Jesus cannot use the word, because it would seem to us that he meant what we mean by it, which he, seeing it all round, cannot mean."

"That does seem quite reasonable," said Ethelwyn.

Turner had taken no part in the conversation. He, too, had just come in from a walk over the hills. He was now standing looking out at the sea.

"She looks uneasy, does she not?" I said.

"You mean the Atlantic?" he returned, looking round. "Yes, I think so. I am glad she is not a patient of mine. I fear she is going to be very feverish, probably delirious before morning. She won't sleep much, and will talk rather loud when the tide comes in."

"Disease has often an ebb and flow like the tide, has it not?"

"Often. Some diseases are like a plant that has its time to grow and blossom, then dies; others, as you say, ebb and flow again and again before they vanish."

"It seems to me, however, that the ebb and flow does not belong to the disease, but to Nature, which works through the disease. It seems to me that my life has its tides, just like the ocean, only a little more regularly. It is high water with me always in the morning and the evening; in the afternoon life is at its lowest; and I believe it is lowest again while we sleep, and hence it comes that to work the brain at night has such an injurious effect on the system. But this is perhaps all a fancy."

"There may be some truth in it. But I was just thinking when you spoke to me what a happy thing it is that the tide does not vary by an even six hours, but has the odd minutes; whence we see endless changes in the relation of the water to the times of the day. And then the spring-tides and the neap-tides! What a provision there is in the world for change!"

"Yes. Change is one of the forms that infinitude takes for the use of us human immortals. But come and have some tea, Turner. You will not care to go out again. What shall we do this evening? Shall we all go to Connie's room and have some Shakspere?"

"I could wish nothing better. What play shall we have?"

"Let us have the *Midsummer Night's Dream,*" said Ethelwyn.

"You like to go by contraries, apparently, Ethel. But you're quite right. It is in the winter of the year that art must give us its summer. I suspect that most of the poetry about spring and summer is written in the winter. It is generally when we do not possess that we lay full value upon what we lack."

"There is one reason," said Wynnie with a roguish look, "why I like that play."

"I should think there might be more than one, Wynnie."

"But one reason is enough for a woman at once; isn't it, papa?"

"I'm not sure of that. But what is your reason?"

"That the fairies are not allowed to play any tricks with the women. *They* are true throughout."

"I might choose to say that was because they were not tried."

"And I might venture to answer that Shakspere-being true to nature always, as you say, papa-knew very well how absurd it would be to represent a woman's feelings as under the influence of the juice of a paltry flower."

"Capital, Wynnie!" said her mother; and Turner and I chimed in with our approbation.

"Shall I tell you what I like best in the play?" said Turner. "It is the common sense of Theseus in accounting for all the bewilderments of the night."

"But," said Ethelwyn, "he was wrong after all. What is the use of common sense if it leads you wrong? The common sense of Theseus simply amounted to this, that he would only believe his own eyes."

"I think Mrs. Walton is right, Turner," I said. "For my part, I have more admired the open-mindedness of Hippolyta, who would yield more weight to the consistency of the various testimony than could be altogether counterbalanced by the negation of her own experience. Now I will tell you what I most admire in the play: it is the reconciling power of the poet. He brings together such marvellous contrasts, without a single shock or jar to your feeling of the artistic harmony of the conjunction. Think for a moment-the ordinary commonplace courtiers; the lovers, men and women in the condition of all conditions in which fairy-powers might get a hold of them; the quarrelling king and queen of Fairyland, with their courtiers, Blossom, Cobweb, and the rest, and the court-jester, Puck; the ignorant, clownish artisans, rehearsing their play, —fairies and clowns, lovers and courtiers, are all mingled in one exquisite harmony, clothed with a night of early summer, rounded in by the wedding of the king and queen. But I have talked enough about it. Let us get our books."

As we sat in Connie's room, delighting ourselves with the reflex of the poet's fancy, the sound of the rising tide kept mingling with the fairy-talk and the foolish rehearsal. "Musk roses," said Titania; and the first of the blast, going round by south to west, rattled the window. "Good hay, sweet hay, hath no fellow," said Bottom; and the roar of the waters was in our ears. "So doth the woodbine the sweet honeysuckle Gently entwist," said Titania; and the blast poured the rain in a spout against the window. "Slow in pursuit, but matched in mouth like bells," said Theseus; and the wind whistled shrill through the chinks of the bark-house opening from the room. We drew the curtains closer, made up the fire higher, and read on. It was time for supper ere we had done; and when we left Connie to have hers and go to sleep, it was with the hope that, through all the rising storm, she would dream of breeze-haunted summer woods.

CHAPTER VII
THE GATHERED STORM.

I woke in the middle of the night and the darkness to hear the wind howling. It was wide awake now, and up with intent. It seized the house, and shook it furiously; and the rain kept pouring, only I could not hear it save in the *rallentondo* passages of the wind; but through all the wind I could hear the roaring of the big waves on the shore. I did not wake my wife; but I got up, put on my dressing-gown, and went softly to Connie's room, to see whether she was awake; for I feared, if she were, she would be frightened. Wynnie always slept in a little bed in the same room. I opened the door very gently, and peeped in. The fire was burning, for Wynnie was an admirable stoker, and could generally keep the fire in all night. I crept to the bedside: there was just light enough to see that Connie was fast asleep, and that her dreams were not of storms. It was a marvel how well the child always slept. But, as I turned to leave the room, Wynnie's voice called me in a whisper. Approaching her bed, I saw her wide eyes, like the eyes of the darkness, for I could scarcely see anything of her face.

"Awake, darling?" I said.

"Yes, papa. I have been awake a long time; but isn't Connie sleeping delightfully? She does sleep so well! Sleep is surely very good for her."

"It is the best thing for us all, next to God's spirit, I sometimes think, my dear. But are you frightened by the storm? Is that what keeps you awake?"

"I don't think that is what keeps me awake; but sometimes the house shakes so that I do feel a little nervous. I don't know how it is. I never felt afraid of anything natural before."

"What our Lord said about not being afraid of anything that could only hurt the body applies here, and in all the terrors of the night. Think about him, dear."

"I do try, papa. Don't you stop; you will get cold. It is a dreadful storm, is it not? Suppose there should be people drowning out there now!"

"There may be, my love. People are dying almost every other moment, I suppose, on the face of the earth. Drowning is only an easy way of dying. Mind, they are all in God's hands."

"Yes, papa. I will turn round and shut my eyes, and fancy that his hand is over them, making them dark with his care."

"And it will not be fancy, my darling, if you do. You remember those odd but no less devout lines of George Herbert? Just after he says, so beautifully, 'And now with darkness closest weary eyes,' he adds:

> Thus in thy ebony box
> Thou dost enclose us, till the day
> Put our amendment in our way,
> And give new wheels to our disordered clocks."

"He is very fond of boxes, by the way. So go to sleep, dear. You are a good clock of God's making; but you want new wheels, according to our beloved brother George Herbert. Therefore sleep. Good-night."

This was tiresome talk-was it-in the middle of the night, reader? Well, but my child did not think so, I know.

Dark, dank, weeping, the morning dawned. All dreary was the earth and sky. The wind was still hunting the clouds across the heavens. It lulled a little while we sat at breakfast, but soon the storm was up again, and the wind raved. I went out. The wind caught me as if with invisible human hands, and shook me. I fought with it, and made my way into the village. The streets were deserted. I peeped up the inn-yard as I passed: not a man or horse was to be seen. The little shops looked as if nobody had crossed their thresholds for a week. Not a door was open. One child came out of the baker's with a big loaf in her apron. The wind threatened to blow the hair off her head, if not herself first into the canal. I took her by the hand and led her, or rather, let her lead me home, while I kept her from being carried away by the wind. Having landed her safely inside her mother's door, I went on, climbed the heights above the village, and looked abroad over the Atlantic. What a waste of aimless tossing to and fro! Gray mist above, full of falling rain; gray, wrathful waters underneath, foaming and bursting as billow broke upon billow. The tide was ebbing now, but almost every other wave swept the breakwater. They burst on the rocks at the end of it, and rushed in shattered spouts and clouds of spray far into the air over their heads. "Will the time ever come," I thought, "when man shall be able to store up even this force for his own ends? Who can tell?" The solitary form of a man stood at some distance gazing, as I was gazing, out on the ocean. I walked towards him, thinking with myself who it could be that loved Nature so well that he did not shrink from her even in her most uncompanionable moods. I suspected, and soon found I was right; it was Percivale.

"What a clashing of water-drops!" I said, thinking of a line somewhere in Coleridge's Remorse. "They are but water-drops, after all, that make this great noise upon the rocks; only there is a great many of them."

"Yes," said Percivale. "But look out yonder. You see a single sail, close-reefed—that is all I can see-away in the mist there? As soon as you think of the human struggle with the elements, as soon as you know that hearts are in the midst of it, it is a clashing of water-drops no more. It is an awful power, with which the will and all that it rules have to fight for the mastery, or at least for freedom."

"Surely you are right. It is the presence of thought, feeling, effort that gives the majesty to everything. It is even a dim attribution of human feelings to this tormented, passionate sea that gives it much of its awe; although, as we were saying the other day, it is only *a picture* of the troubled mind. But as I have now seen how matters are with the elements, and have had a good pluvial bath as well, I think I will go home and change my clothes."

"I have hardly had enough of it yet," returned Percivale. "I shall have a stroll along the heights here, and when the tide has fallen a little way from the foot of the cliffs I shall go down on the sands and watch awhile there."

"Well, you're a younger man than I am; but I've seen the day, as Lear says. What an odd tendency we old men have to boast of the past: we would be judged by the past, not by the present. We always speak of the strength that is withered and gone, as if we had some claim upon it still. But I am not going to talk in this storm. I am always talking."

"I will go with you as far as the village, and then I will turn and take my way along the downs for a mile or two; I don't mind being wet."

"I didn't once."

"Don't you think," resumed Percivale, "that in some sense the old man-not that I can allow *you* that dignity yet, Mr. Walton-has a right to regard the past as his own?"

"That would be scanned," I answered, as we walked towards the village. "Surely the results of the past are the man's own. Any action of the man's, upon which the life in him reposes, remains his. But suppose a man had done a good deed once, and instead of making that a foundation upon which to build more good, grew so vain of it that he became incapable of doing anything more of the same sort, you could not say that the action belonged to him still. Therein he has severed his connection with the past. Again, what has never in any deep sense been a man's own, cannot surely continue to be his afterwards. Thus the things that a man has merely possessed once, the very people who most admired him for their sakes when he had them, give him no credit for after he has lost them. Riches that have taken to themselves wings leave with the poor man only a surpassing poverty. Strength, likewise, which can so little depend on any exercise of the will in man, passes from him with the years. It was not his all the time; it was but lent him, and had nothing to do with his inward force. A bodily feeble man may put forth a mighty life-strength in effort, and show nothing to the eyes of his neighbour; while the strong man gains endless admiration for what he could hardly help. But the effort of the one remains, for it was his own; the strength of the other passes from him, for it was never his own. So with beauty, which the commonest woman acknowledges never to have been hers in seeking to restore it by deception. So, likewise, in a great measure with intellect."

"But if you take away intellect as well, what do you leave a man that can in any way be called his own?"

"Certainly his intellect is not his own. One thing only is his own-to will the truth. This, too, is as much God's gift as everything else: I ought to say is more God's gift than anything else, for he gives it to be the man's own more than anything else can be. And when he wills the truth, he has God himself. Man *can* possess God: all other things follow as necessary results. What poor creatures we should have been if God had not made us to do something-to look heavenwards-to lift up the hands that hang down, and strengthen the feeble knees! Something like this was in the mind of the prophet Jeremiah when he said, 'Thus saith the Lord, Let not the wise man glory in his wisdom, neither let the mighty man glory in his might, let not the rich man glory in his riches; but let him that glorieth glory in this, that he understandeth and knoweth me, that I am the Lord which exercise loving-kindness, judgment, and righteousness in the earth: for in these things I delight, saith the Lord.' My own conviction is, that a vague sense of a far higher life in ourselves than we yet know anything about is at the root of all our false efforts to be able to think something of ourselves. We cannot commend ourselves, and therefore we set about priding ourselves. We have little or no strength of mind, faculty of operation, or worth of will, and therefore we talk of our strength of body, worship the riches we have, or have not, it is all one, and boast of our paltry intellectual successes. The man most ambitious of being considered a universal genius must at last confess himself a conceited dabbler, and be ready to part with all he knows for one glimpse more of that understanding of God which the wise men of old held to be essential to every man, but which the growing luminaries of the present day will not allow to be even possible for any man."

We had reached the brow of the heights, and here we parted. A fierce blast of wind rushed at me, and I hastened down the hill. How dreary the streets did look! —how much more dreary than the stormy down! I saw no living creature as I returned but a terribly draggled dog, a cat that seemed to have a bad conscience, and a lovely little girl-face, which, forgetful of its own rights, would flatten the tip of the nose belonging to it against a window-pane. Every rain-pool was a mimic sea, and had a mimic storm within its own narrow bounds. The water went hurrying down the kennels like a long brown snake anxious to get to its hole and hide from the tormenting wind, and every now and then the rain came in full rout before the conquering blast.

When I got home, I peeped in at Connie's door the first thing, and saw that she was raised a little more than usual; that is, the end of the conch against which she leaned was at a more acute angle. She was sitting staring, rather than gazing, out at the wild tumult which she could see over the shoulder of the down on which her window immediately looked. Her face was paler and keener than usual.

"Why, Connie, who set you up so straight?"

"Mr. Turner, papa. I wanted to see out, and he raised me himself. He says I am so much better, I may have it in the seventh notch as often as I like."

"But you look too tired for it. Hadn't you better lie down again?"

"It's only the storm, papa."

"The more reason you should not see it if it tires you so."

"It does not tire me, papa. Only I keep constantly wondering what is going to come out of it. It looks so as if something must follow."

"You didn't hear me come into your room last night, Connie. The storm was raging then as loud as it is now, but you were out of its reach-fast asleep. Now it is too much for you. You must lie down."

"Very well, papa."

I lowered the support, and when I returned from changing my wet garments she was already looking much better.

After dinner I went to my study, but when evening began to fall I went out again. I wanted to see how our next neighbours, the sexton and his wife, were faring. The wind had already increased in violence. It threatened to blow a hurricane. The tide was again rising, and was coming in with great rapidity. The old mill shook to the foundation as I passed through it to reach the lower part where they lived. When I peeped in from the bottom of the stair, I saw no one; but, hearing the steps of someone overhead, I called out.

Agnes's voice made answer, as she descended an inner stair which led to the bedrooms above —

"Mother's gone to church, sir."

"Gone to church!" I said, a vague pang darting through me as I thought whether I had forgotten any service; but the next moment I recalled what the old woman had herself told me of her preference for the church during a storm.

"O yes, Agnes, I remember!" I said; "your mother thinks the weather bad enough to take to the church, does she? How do you come to be here now? Where is your husband?"

"He'll be here in an hour or so, sir. He don't mind the wet. You see, we don't like the old people to be left alone when it blows what the sailors call 'great guns.'"

"And what becomes of his mother then?"

"There don't be any sea out there, sir. Leastways," she added with a quiet smile, and stopped.

"You mean, I suppose, Agnes, that there is never any perturbation of the elements out there?"

She laughed; for she understood me well enough. The temper of Joe's mother was proverbial.

"But really, sir," she said, "she don't mind the weather a bit; and though we don't live in the same cottage with her, for Joe wouldn't hear of that, we see her far oftener than we see my mother, you know."

"I'm sure it's quite fair, Agnes. Is Joe very sorry that he married you, now?"

She hung her head, and blushed so deeply through all her sallow complexion, that I was sorry I had teased her, and said so. This brought a reply.

"I don't think he be, sir. I do think he gets better. He's been working very hard the last week or two, and he says it agrees with him."

"And how are you?"

"Quite well, thank you, sir."

I had never seen her look half so well. Life was evidently a very different thing to both of them now. I left her, and took my way to the church.

When I reached the churchyard, there, in the middle of the rain and the gathering darkness, was the old man busy with the duties of his calling. A certain headstone stood right under a drip from the roof of the southern transept; and this drip had caused the mould at the foot of the stone, on the side next the wall, to sink, so that there was a considerable crack between the stone and the soil. The old man had cut some sod from another part of the churchyard, and was now standing, with the rain pouring on him from the roof, beating this sod down in the crack. He was sheltered from the wind by the church, but he was as wet as he could be. I may mention that he never appeared in the least disconcerted when I came upon him in the discharge of his functions: he was so content with his own feeling in the matter, that no difference of opinion could disturb him.

"This will never do, Coombes," I said. "You will get your death of cold. You must be as full of water as a sponge. Old man, there's rheumatism in the world!"

"It be only my work, sir. But I believe I ha' done now for a night. I think he'll be a bit more comfortable now. The very wind could get at him through that hole."

"Do go home, then," I said, "and change your clothes. Is your wife in the church?"

"She be, sir. This door, sir-this door," he added, as he saw me going round to the usual entrance. "You'll find her in there."

I lifted the great latch and entered. I could not see her at first, for it was much darker inside the church. It felt very quiet in there somehow, although the place was full of the noise of winds and waters. Mrs. Coombes was not sitting on the bell-keys, where I looked for her first, for the wind blew down the tower in many currents and draughts-how it did roar up there-as if the louvres had been a windsail to catch the wind and send it down to ventilate the church!—she was sitting at the foot of the chancel-rail, with her stocking as usual.

The sight of her sweet old face, lighted up by a moonlike smile as I drew near her, in the middle of the ancient dusk filled with sounds, but only sounds of tempest, gave me a sense of one dwelling in the secret place of the Most High, such as I shall never forget. It was no time to say much, however.

"How long do you mean to stay here, Mrs. Coombes?" I asked. "Not all night?"

"No, not all night, surely, sir. But I hadn't thought o' going yet for a bit."

"Why there's Coombes out there, wet to the skin; and I'm afraid he'll go on pottering at the churchyard bed-clothes till he gets his bones as full of rheumatism as they can hold."

"Deary me! I didn't know as my old man was there. He tould me he had them all comforble for the winter a week ago. But to be sure there's always some mendin' to do."

I heard the voice of Joe outside, and the next moment he came into the church. After speaking to me, he turned to Mrs. Coombes.

"You be comin' home with me, mother. This will never do. Father's as wet as a mop. I ha' brought something for your supper, and Aggy's a-cookin' of it; and we're going to be comfortable over the fire, and have a chapter or two of the New Testament to keep down the noise of the sea. There! Come along."

The old woman drew her cloak over her head, put her knitting carefully in her pocket, and stood aside for me to lead the way.

"No, no," I said; "I'm the shepherd and you're the sheep, so I'll drive you before me-at least, you and Coombes. Joe here will be offended if I take on me to say I am *his* shepherd."

"Nay, nay, don't say that, sir. You've been a good shepherd to me when I was a very sulky sheep. But if you'll please to go, sir, I'll lock the door behind; for you know in them parts the shepherd goes first and the sheep follow the shepherd. And I'll follow like a good sheep," he added, laughing.

"You're right, Joe," I said, and took the lead without more ado.

I was struck by his saying *them parts*, which seemed to indicate a habit of pondering on the places as well as circumstances of the gospel-story. The sexton joined us at the door, and we all walked to his cottage, Joe taking care of his mother-in-law and I taking what care I could of Coombes by carrying his tools for him. But as we went I feared I had done ill in that, for the wind blew so fiercely that I thought the thin feeble little man would have got on better if he had been more heavily weighted against it. But I made him take a hold of my arm, and so we got in. The old man took his tools from me and set them down in the mill, for the roof of which I felt some anxiety as we passed through, so full of wind was the whole space. But when we opened the inner door the welcome of a glowing fire burst up the stair as if that had been a well of warmth and light below. I went down with them. Coombes departed to change his clothes, and the rest of us stood round the fire, where Agnes was busy cooking something like white puddings for their supper.

"Did you hear, sir," said Joe, "that the coastguard is off to the Goose-pot? There's a vessel ashore there, they say. I met them on the road with the rocket-cart."

"How far off is that, Joe?"

"Some five or six miles, I suppose, along the coast nor'ards."

"What sort of a vessel is she?"

"That I don't know. Some say she be a schooner, others a brigantine. The coast-guard didn't know themselves."

"Poor things!" said Mrs. Coombes. "If any of them comes ashore, they'll be sadly knocked to pieces on the rocks in a night like this."

She had caught a little infection of her husband's mode of thought.

"It's not likely to clear up before morning, I fear; is it, Joe?"

"I don't think so, sir. There's no likelihood."

"Will you condescend to sit down and take a share with us, sir?" said the old woman.

"There would be no condescension in that, Mrs. Coombes. I will another time with all my heart; but in such a night I ought to be at home with my own people. They will be more uneasy if I am away."

"Of coorse, of coorse, sir."

"So I'll bid you good-night. I wish this storm were well over."

I buttoned my great-coat, pulled my hat down on my head, and set out. It was getting on for high water. The night was growing very dark. There would be a moon some time, but the clouds were so dense she could not do much while they came between. The roaring of the waves on the shore was terrible; all I could see of them now was the whiteness of their breaking, but they filled the earth and the air with their furious noises. The wind roared from the sea; two oceans were breaking on the land, only to the one had been set a hitherto-to the other none. Ere the night was far gone, however, I had begun to doubt whether the ocean itself had not broken its bars.

I found the whole household full of the storm. The children kept pressing their faces to the windows, trying to pierce, as by force of will, through the darkness, and discover what the wild thing out there was doing. They could see nothing: all was one mass of blackness and dismay, with a soul in it of ceaseless roaring. I ran up to Connie's room, and found that she was left alone. She looked restless, pale, and frightened. The house quivered, and still the wind howled and whistled through the adjoining bark-hut.

"Connie, darling, have they left you alone?" I said.

"Only for a few minutes, papa. I don't mind it."

"Don't be frightened at the storm, my dear. He who could walk on the sea of Galilee, and still the storm of that little pool, can rule the Atlantic just as well. Jeremiah says he 'divideth the sea when the waves thereof roar.'"

The same moment Dora came running into the room.

"Papa," she cried, "the spray—such a lot of it—came dashing on the windows in the dining-room. Will it break them?"

"I hope not, my dear. Just stay with Connie while I run down."

"O, papa! I do want to see."

"What do you want to see, Dora?"

"The storm, papa."

"It is as black as pitch. You can't see anything."

"O, but I want to—to—be beside it."

"Well, you sha'n't stay with Connie, if you are not willing. Go along. Ask Wynnie to come here."

The child was so possessed by the commotion without that she did not seem even to see my rebuke, not to say feel it. She ran off, and Wynnie presently came. I left her with Connie, put on a long waterproof cloak, and went down to the dining-room. A door led from it immediately on to the little green in front of the house, between it and the sea. The dining-room was dark, for they had put out the lights that they might see better from the windows. The children and some of the servants were there looking out. I opened the door cautiously. It needed the strength of two of the women to shut it behind me. The moment I opened it a great sheet of spray rushed over me. I went down the little grassy slope. The rain had ceased, and it was not quite so dark as I had expected. I could see the gleaming whiteness all before me. The next moment a wave rolled over the low wall in front of me, breaking on it and wrapping me round in a sheet of water. Something hurt me sharply on the leg; and I found, on searching, that one of the large flat stones that lay for coping on the top of the wall was on the grass beside me. If it had struck me straight, it must have broken my leg.

There came a little lull in the wind, and just as I turned to go into the house again, I thought I heard a gun. I stood and listened, but heard nothing more, and fancied I must have been mistaken. I returned and tapped at the door; but I had to knock loudly before they heard me within. When I went up to the drawing-room, I found that Percivale had joined our party. He and Turner were talking together at one of the windows.

"Did you hear a gun?" I asked them.

"No. Was there one?"

"I'm not sure. I half-fancied I heard one, but no other followed. There will be a good many fired to-night, though, along this awful coast."

"I suppose they keep the life-boat always ready," said Turner.

"No life-boat even, I fear, would live in such a sea," I said, remembering what the officer of the coast-guard had told me.

"They would try, though, I suppose," said Turner.

"I do not know," said Percivale. "I don't know the people. But I have seen a life-boat out in as bad a night-whether in as bad a sea, I cannot tell: that depends on the coast, I suppose."

We went on chatting for some time, wondering how the coast-guard had fared with the vessel ashore at the Goose-pot. Wynnie joined us.

"How is Connie, now, my dear?"

"Very restless and excited, papa. I came down to say, that if Mr. Turner didn't mind, I wish he would go up and see her."

"Of course-instantly," said Turner, and moved to follow Winnie.

But the same moment, as if it had been beside us in the room, so clear, so shrill was it, we heard Connie's voice shrieking, "Papa, papa! There's a great ship ashore down there. Come, come!"

Turner and I rushed from the room in fear and dismay. "How? What? Where could the voice come from?" was the unformed movement of our thoughts. But the moment we left the drawing-room the thing was clear, though not the less marvellous and alarming. We forgot all about the ship, and thought only of our Connie. So much does the near hide the greater that is afar! Connie kept on calling, and her voice guided our eyes.

A little stair led immediately from this floor up to the bark-hut, so that it might be reached without passing through the bedroom. The door at the top of it was open. The door that led from Connie's room into the bark-hut was likewise open, and light shone through it into the place-enough to show a figure standing by the furthest window with face pressed against the glass. And from this figure came the cry, "Papa, papa! Quick, quick! The waves will knock her to pieces!"

In very truth it was Connie standing there.

CHAPTER VIII
THE SHIPWRECK.

Things that happen altogether have to be told one after the other. Turner and I both rushed at the narrow stair. There was not room for more than one upon it. I was first, but stumbled on the lowest step and fell. Turner put his foot on my back, jumped over me, sprang up the stair, and when I reached the top of it after him, he was meeting me with Connie in his arms, carrying her back to her room. But the girl kept crying—"Papa, papa, the ship, the ship!"

My duty woke in me. Turner could attend to Connie far better than I could. I made one spring to the window. The moon was not to be seen, but the clouds were thinner, and light enough was soaking through them to show a wave-tormented mass some little way out in the bay; and in that one moment in which I stood looking, a shriek pierced the howling of the wind, cutting through it like a knife. I rushed bare-headed from the house. When or how the resolve was born in me I do not know, but I flew straight to the sexton's, snatched the key from the wall, crying only "ship ashore!" and rushed to the church.

I remember my hand trembled so that I could hardly get the key into the lock. I made myself quieter, opened the door, and feeling my way to the tower, knelt before the keys of the bell-hammers, opened the chest, and struck them wildly, fiercely. An awful jangling, out of tune and harsh, burst into monstrous being in the storm-vexed air. Music itself was untuned, corrupted, and returning to chaos. I struck and struck at the keys. I knew nothing of their normal use. Noise, outcry, *reveillé* was all I meant.

In a few minutes I heard voices and footsteps. From some parts of the village, out of sight of the shore, men and women gathered to the summons. Through the door of the church, which I had left open, came voices in hurried question. "Ship ashore!" was all I could answer, for what was to be done I was helpless to think.

I wondered that so few appeared at the cry of the bells. After those first nobody came for what seemed a long time. I believe, however, I was beating the alarum for only a few minutes altogether, though when I look back upon the time in the dark church, it looks like half-an-hour at least. But indeed I feel so confused about all the doings of that night that in attempting to describe them in order, I feel as if I were walking in a dream. Still, from comparing mine with the recollected impressions of others, I think I am able to give a tolerably correct result. Most of the incidents seem burnt into my memory so that nothing could destroy the depth of the impression; but the order in which they took place is none the less doubtful.

A hand was laid on my shoulder.

"Who is there?" I said; for it was far too dark to know anyone.

"Percivale. What is to be done? The coastguard is away. Nobody seems to know about anything. It is of no use to go on ringing more. Everybody is out, even to the maid-servants. Come down to the shore, and you will see."

"But is there not the life-boat?"

"Nobody seems to know anything about it, except 'it's no manner of use to go trying of that with such a sea on.'"

"But there must be someone in command of it," I said.

"Yes," returned Percivale; "but there doesn't seem to be one of the crew amongst the crowd. All the sailor-like fellows are going about with their hands in their pockets."

"Let us make haste, then," I said; "perhaps we can find out. Are you sure the coastguard have nothing to do with the life-boat?"

"I believe not. They have enough to do with their rockets."

"I remember now that Roxton told me he had far more confidence in his rockets than in anything a life-boat could do, upon this coast at least."

While we spoke we came to the bank of the canal. This we had to cross, in order to reach that part of the shore opposite which the wreck lay. To my surprise the canal itself was in a storm, heaving and tossing and dashing over its banks.

"Percivale," I exclaimed, "the gates are gone; the sea has torn them away."

"Yes, I suppose so. Would God I could get half-a-dozen men to help me. I have been doing what I could; but I have no influence amongst them."

"What do you mean?" I asked. "What could you do if you had a thousand men at your command?"

He made me no answer for a few moments, during which we were hurrying on for the bridge over the canal. Then he said:

"They regard me only as a meddling stranger, I suppose; for I have been able to get no useful answer. They are all excited; but nobody is doing anything."

"They must know about it a great deal better than we," I returned; "and we must take care not to do them the injustice of supposing they are not ready to do all that can be done."

Percivale was silent yet again.

The record of our conversation looks as quiet on the paper as if we had been talking in a curtained room; but all the time the ocean was raving in my very ear, and the awful tragedy was going on in the dark behind us. The wind was almost as loud as ever, but the rain had quite ceased, and when we reached the bridge the moon shone out white, as if aghast at what she had at length succeeded in pushing the clouds aside that she might see. Awe and helplessness oppressed us. Having crossed the canal, we turned to the shore. There was little of it left; for the waves had rushed up almost to the village. The sand and the roads, every garden wall, every window that looked seaward was crowded with gazers. But it was a wonderfully quiet crowd, or seemed so at least; for the noise of the wind and the waves filled the whole vault, and what was spoken was heard only in the ear to which it was spoken. When we came amongst them we heard only a murmur as of more articulated confusion. One turn, and we saw the centre of strife and anxiety-the heart of the storm that filled heaven and earth, upon which all the blasts and the billows broke and raved.

Out there in the moonlight lay a mass of something whose place was discernible by the flashing of the waves as they burst over it. She was far above low-water mark-lay nearer the village by a furlong than the spot where we had taken our last dinner on the shore. It was strange to think that yesterday the spot lay bare to human feet, where now so many men and women were isolated in a howling waste of angry waters; for the cry of women came plainly to our ears, and we were helpless to save them. It was terrible to have to do nothing. Percivale went about hurriedly, talking to this one and that one, as if he still thought something might be done. He turned to me.

"Do try, Mr. Walton, and find out for me where the captain of the life-boat is."

I turned to a sailor-like man who stood at my elbow and asked him.

"It's no use, I assure you, sir," he answered; "no boat could live in such a sea. It would be throwing away the men's lives."

"Do you know where the captain lives?" Percivale asked.

"If I did, I tell you it is of no use."

"Are you the captain yourself?" returned Percivale.

"What is that to you?" he answered, surly now. "I know my own business."

The same moment several of the crowd nearest the edge of the water made a simultaneous rush into the surf, and laid hold of something, which, as they returned drawing it to the shore, I saw to be a human form. It was the body of a woman-alive or dead I could not tell. I could just see the long hair hanging from the head, which itself hung backward helplessly as they bore her up the bank. I saw, too, a white face, and I can recall no more.

"Run, Percivale," I said, "and fetch Turner. She may not be dead yet."

"I can't," answered Percivale. "You had better go yourself, Mr. Walton."

He spoke hurriedly. I saw he must have some reason for answering me so abruptly. He was talking to a young fellow whom I recognised as one of the most dissolute in the village; and just as I turned to go they walked away together.

I sped home as fast as I could. It was easier to get along now that the moon shone. I found that Turner had given Connie a composing draught, and that he had good hopes she would at least be nothing the worse for the marvellous result of her excitement. She was asleep exhausted, and her mother was watching by her side. It, seemed strange that she could sleep; but Turner said it was the safest reaction, partly, however, occasioned by what he had given her. In her sleep she kept on talking about the ship.

We hurried back to see if anything could be done for the woman. As we went up the side of the canal we perceived a dark body meeting us. The clouds had again obscured, though not quite hidden the moon, and we could not at first make out what it was. When we came nearer it showed itself a body of men hauling something along. Yes, it was the life-boat, afloat on the troubled waves of the canal, each man seated in his own place, his hands quiet upon his oar, his cork-jacket braced about him, his feet out before him, ready to pull the moment they should pass beyond the broken gates of the lock out on the awful tossing of the waves. They sat very silent, and the men on the path towed them swiftly along. The moon uncovered her face for a moment, and shone upon the faces of two of the rowers.

"Percivale! Joe!" I cried.

"All right, sir!" said Joe.

"Does your wife know of it, Joe?" I almost gasped.

"To be sure," answered Joe. "It's the first chance I've had of returning thanks for her. Please God, I shall see her again to-night."

"That's good, Joe. Trust in God, my men, whether you sink or swim."

"Ay, ay, sir!" they answered as one man.

"This is your doing, Percivale," I said, turning and walking alongside of the boat for a little way.

"It's more Jim Allen's," said Percivale. "If I hadn't got a hold of him I couldn't have done anything."

"God bless you, Jim Allen!" I said. "You'll be a better man after this, I think."

"Donnow, sir," returned Jim cheerily. "It's harder work than pulling an oar."

The captain himself was on board. Percivale having persuaded Jim Allen, the two had gone about in the crowd seeking proselytes. In a wonderfully short space they had found almost all the crew, each fresh one picking up another or more; till at length the captain, protesting against the folly of it, gave in, and once having yielded, was, like a true Englishman, as much in earnest as any of them. The places of two who were missing were supplied by Percivale and Joe, the latter of whom would listen to no remonstrance.

"I've nothing to lose," Percivale had said. "You have a young wife, Joe."

"I've everything to win," Joe had returned. "The only thing that makes me feel a bit faint-hearted over it, is that I'm afraid it's not my duty that drives me to it, but the praise of men, leastways of a woman. What would Aggy think of me if I was to let them drown out there and go to my bed and sleep? I must go."

"Very well, Joe," returned Percivale, "I daresay you are right. You can row, of course?"

"I can row hard, and do as I'm told," said Joe.

"All right," said Percivale; "come along."

This I heard afterwards. We were now hurrying against the wind towards the mouth of the canal, some twenty men hauling on the tow-rope. The critical moment would be in the clearing of the gates, I thought, some parts of which might remain swinging; but they encountered no difficulty there, as I heard afterwards. For I remembered that this was not my post, and turned again to follow the doctor.

"God bless you, my men!" I said, and left them.

They gave a great hurrah, and sped on to meet their fate. I found Turner in the little public-house, whither they had carried the body. The woman was quite dead.

"I fear it is an emigrant vessel," he said.

"Why do you think so?" I asked, in some consternation.

"Come and look at the body," he said.

It was that of a woman about twenty, tall, and finely formed. The face was very handsome, but it did not need the evidence of the hands to prove that she was one of our sisters who have to labour for their bread.

"What should such a girl be doing on board ship but going out to America or Australia-to her lover, perhaps," said Turner. "You see she has a locket on her neck; I hope nobody will dare to take it off. Some of these people are not far derived from those who thought a wreck a Godsend."

A sound of many feet was at the door just as we turned to leave the house. They were bringing another body-that of an elderly woman-dead, quite dead. Turner had ceased examining her, and we were going out together, when, through all the tumult of the wind and waves, a fierce hiss, vindictive, wrathful, tore the air over our heads. Far up, seawards, something like a fiery snake shot from the high ground on the right side of the bay, over the vessel, and into the water beyond it.

"Thank God! that's the coastguard," I cried.

We rushed through the village, and up on the heights, where they had planted their apparatus. A little crowd surrounded them. How dismal the sea looked in the struggling moonlight! I felt as if I were wandering in the mazes of an evil dream. But when I approached the cliff, and saw down below the great mass, of the vessel's hulk, with the waves breaking every moment upon her side, I felt the reality awful indeed. Now and then there would come a kind of lull in the wild sequence of rolling waters, and then I fancied for a moment that I saw how she rocked on the bottom. Her masts had all gone by the board, and a perfect chaos of cordage floated and swung in the waves that broke over her. But her bowsprit remained entire, and shot out into the foamy dark, crowded with human beings. The first rocket had missed. They were preparing to fire another. Roxton stood with his telescope in his hand, ready to watch the result.

"This is a terrible job, sir," he said when I approached him; "I doubt if we shall save one of them."

"There's the life-boat!" I cried, as a dark spot appeared on the waters approaching the vessel from the other side.

"The life-boat!" he returned with contempt. "You don't mean to say they've got *her* out! She'll only add to the mischief. We'll have to save her too."

She was still some way from the vessel, and in comparatively smooth water. But between her and the hull the sea raved in madness; the billows rode over each other, in pursuit, as it seemed, of some invisible prey. Another hiss, as of concentrated hatred, and the second rocket was shooting its parabola through the dusky air. Roxton raised his telescope to his eye the same moment.

"Over her starn!" he cried. "There's a fellow getting down from the cat-head to run aft. — Stop, stop!" he shouted involuntarily. "There's an awful wave on your quarter."

His voice was swallowed in the roaring of the storm. I fancied I could distinguish a dark something shoot from the bows towards the stern. But the huge wave fell upon the wreck. The same moment Roxton exclaimed-so coolly as to amaze me, forgetting how men must come to regard familiar things without discomposure —

"He's gone! I said so. The next'll have better luck, I hope."

That man came ashore alive, though.

All were forward of the foremast. The bowsprit, when I looked through Roxton's telescope, was shapeless as with a swarm of bees. Now and then a single shriek rose upon the wild air. But now my attention was fixed on the life-boat. She had got into the wildest of the broken water; at one moment she was down in a huge cleft, the next balanced like a beam on the knife-edge of a wave, tossed about hither and thither, as if the waves delighted in mocking the rudder; but hitherto she had shipped no water. I am here drawing upon the information I have since received; but I did see how a huge wave, following close upon the back of that on which she floated, rushed, towered up over her, toppled, and fell upon the life-boat with tons of water: the moon was shining brightly enough to show this with tolerable distinctness. The boat vanished. The next moment, there she was, floating helplessly about, like a living thing stunned by the blow of the falling wave. The struggle was over. As far as I could see, every man was in his place; but the boat drifted away before the storm shore-wards, and the men let her drift. Were they all killed as they sat? I thought of my Wynnie, and turned to Roxton.

"That wave has done for them," he said. "I told you it was no use. There they go."

"But what is the matter?" I asked. "The men are sitting every man in his place."

"I think so," he answered. "Two were swept overboard, but they caught the ropes and got in again. But don't you see they have no oars?"

That wave had broken every one of them off at the rowlocks, and now they were as helpless as a sponge.

I turned and ran. Before I reached the brow of the hill another rocket was fired and fell wide shorewards, partly because the wind blew with fresh fury at the very moment. I heard Roxton say—"She's breaking up. It's no use. That last did for her;" but I hurried off for the other side of the bay, to see what became of the life-boat. I heard a great cry from the vessel as I reached the brow of the hill, and turned for a parting glance. The dark mass had vanished, and the waves were rushing at will over the space. When I got to the shore the crowd was less. Many were running, like myself, towards the other side, anxious about the life-boat. I hastened after them; for Percivale and Joe filled my heart.

They led the way to the little beach in front of the parsonage. It would be well for the crew if they were driven ashore there, for it was the only spot where they could escape being dashed on rocks.

There was a crowd before the garden-wall, a bustle, and great confusion of speech. The people, men and women, boys and girls, were all gathered about the crew of the life-boat,—which already lay, as if it knew of nothing but repose, on the grass within.

"Percivale!" I cried, making my way through the crowd.

There was no answer.

"Joe Harper!" I cried again, searching with eager eyes amongst the crew, to whom everybody was talking.

Still there was no answer; and from the disjointed phrases I heard, I could gather nothing. All at once I saw Wynnie looking over the wall, despair in her face, her wide eyes searching wildly through the crowd. I could not look at her till I knew the worst. The captain was talking to old Coombes. I went up to him. As soon as he saw me, he gave me his attention.

"Where is Mr. Percivale?" I asked, with all the calmness I could assume.

He took me by the arm, and drew me out of the crowd, nearer to the waves, and a little nearer to the mouth of the canal. The tide had fallen considerably, else there would not have been standing-room, narrow as it was, which the people now occupied. He pointed in the direction of the Castle-rock.

"If you mean the stranger gentleman—"

"And Joe Harper, the blacksmith," I interposed.

"They're there, sir."

"You don't mean those two-just those two-are drowned?" I said.

"No, sir; I don't say that; but God knows they have little chance."

I could not help thinking that God might know they were not in the smallest danger. But I only begged him to tell me where they were.

"Do you see that schooner there, just between you and the Castle-rock?"

"No," I answered; "I can see nothing. Stay. I fancy I can. But I am always ready to fancy I see a thing when I am told it is there. I can't say I see it."

"I can, though. The gentleman you mean, and Joe Harper too, are, I believe, on board of that schooner."

"Is she aground?"

"O dear no, sir. She's a light craft, and can swim there well enough. If she'd been aground, she'd ha' been ashore in pieces hours ago. But whether she'll ride it out, God only knows, as I said afore."

"How ever did they get aboard of her? I never saw her from the heights opposite."

"You were all taken up by the ship ashore, you see, sir. And she don't make much show in this light. But there she is, and they're aboard of her. And this is how it was."

He went on to give me his part of the story; but I will now give the whole of it myself, as I have gathered and pieced it together.

Two men had been swept overboard, as Roxton said—one of them was Percivale—but they had both got on board again, to drift, oarless, with the rest—now in a windless valley—now aloft on a tempest-swept hill of water—away towards a goal they knew not, neither had chosen, and which yet they could by no means avoid.

A little out of the full force of the current, and not far from the channel of the small stream, which, when the tide was out, flowed across the sands nearly from the canal gates to the Castle-rock, lay a little schooner, belonging to a neighbouring port, Boscastle, I think, which, caught in the storm, had been driven into the bay when it was almost dark, some considerable time before the great ship. The master, however, knew the ground well. The current carried him a little out of the wind, and would have thrown him upon the rocks next, but he managed to drop anchor just in time, and the cable held; and there the little schooner hung in the skirts of the storm, with the jagged teeth of the rocks within an arrow flight. In the excitement of the great wreck, no one had observed the danger of the little coasting bird. If the cable held till the tide went down, and the anchor did not drag, she would be safe; if not, she must be dashed to pieces.

In the schooner were two men and a boy: two men had been washed overboard an hour or so before they reached the bay. When they had dropped their anchor, they lay down exhausted on the deck. Indeed they were so worn out that they had been unable to drop their sheet anchor, and were holding on only by their best bower. Had they not been a good deal out of the wind, this would have been useless. Even if it held she was in danger of having her bottom stove in by bumping against the sands as the tide went out. But that they had not to think of yet. The moment they lay down they fell fast asleep in the middle of the storm. While they slept it increased in violence.

Suddenly one of them awoke, and thought he saw a vision of angels. For over his head faces looked down upon him from the air—that is, from the top of a great wave. The same moment he heard a voice, two of the angels dropped on the deck beside him, and the rest vanished. Those angels were Percivale and Joe. And angels they were, for they came just in time, as all angels do—never a moment too soon or a moment too late: the schooner *was* dragging her anchor. This was soon plain even to the less experienced eyes of the said angels.

But it did not take them many minutes now to drop their strongest anchor, and they were soon riding in perfect safety for some time to come.

One of the two men was the son of old Coombes, the sexton, who was engaged to marry the girl I have spoken of in the end of the fourth chapter in the second volume.

Percivale's account of the matter, as far as he was concerned, was, that as they drifted helplessly along, he suddenly saw from the top of a huge wave the little vessel below him. They were, in fact, almost upon the rigging. The wave on which they rode swept the quarter-deck of the schooner.

Percivale says the captain of the lifeboat called out "Aboard!" The captain said he remembered nothing of the sort. If he did, he must have meant it for the men on the schooner to get on board the lifeboat. Percivale, however, who had a most chivalrous (ought I not to say Christian?) notion of obedience, fancying the captain meant them to board the schooner, sprang at her fore-shrouds. Thereupon the wave sweeping them along the schooner's side, Joe sprang at the main-shrouds, and they dropped on the deck together.

But although my reader is at ease about their fate, we who were in the affair were anything but easy at the time corresponding to this point of the narrative. It was a terrible night we passed through.

When I returned, which was almost instantly, for I could do nothing by staring out in the direction of the schooner, I found that the crowd was nearly gone. One little group alone remained behind, the centre of which was a woman. Wynnie had disappeared. The woman who remained behind was Agnes Harper.

The moon shone out clear as I approached the group; indeed, the clouds were breaking-up and drifting away off the heavens. The storm had raved out its business, and was departing into the past.

"Agnes," I said.

"Yes, sir," she answered, and looked up as if waiting for a command. There was no colour in her cheeks or in her lips-at least it seemed so in the moonlight-only in her eyes. But she was perfectly calm. She was leaning against the low wall, with her hands clasped, but hanging quietly down before her.

"The storm is breaking-up, Agnes," I said.

"Yes, sir," she answered in the same still tone. Then, after just a moment's pause, she spoke out of her heart.

"Joe's at his duty, sir?"

I have given the utterance a point of interrogation; whether she meant that point I am not quite sure.

"Indubitably," I returned. "I have such faith in Joe, that I should be sure of that in any case. At all events, he's not taking care of his own life. And if one is to go wrong, I would ten thousand times rather err on that side. But I am sure Joe has been doing right, and nothing else."

"Then there's nothing to be said, sir, is there?" she returned, with a sigh that sounded as of relief.

I presume some of the surrounding condolers had been giving her Job's comfort by blaming her husband.

"Do you remember, Agnes, what the Lord said to his mother when she reproached him with having left her and his father?"

"I can't remember anything at this moment, sir," was her touching answer.

"Then I will tell you. He said, 'Why did you look for me? Didn't you know that I must be about something my Father had given me to do?' Now, Joe was and is about his Father's business, and you must not be anxious about him. There could be no better reason for not being anxious."

Agnes was a very quiet woman. When without a word she took my hand and kissed it, I felt what a depth there was in the feeling she could not utter. I did not withdraw my hand, for I knew that would be to rebuke her love for Joe.

"Will you come in and wait?" I said indefinitely.

"No, thank you, sir. I must go to my mother. God will look after Joe, won't he, sir?"

"As sure as there is a God, Agnes," I said; and she went away without another word.

I put my hand on the top of the wall and jumped over. I started back with terror, for I had almost alighted on the body of a woman lying there. The first insane suggestion was that it had been cast ashore; but the next moment I knew that it was my own Wynnie.

She had not even fainted. She was lying with her handkerchief stuffed into her mouth to keep her from screaming. When I uttered her name she rose, and, without looking at me, walked away towards the house. I followed. She went straight to her own room and shut the door. I went to find her mother. She was with Connie, who was now awake, lying pale and frightened. I told Ethelwyn that Percivale and Joe were on board the little schooner, which was holding on by her anchor, that Wynnie was in terror about Percivale, that I had found her lying on the wet grass, and that she must get her into a warm bath and to bed. We went together to her room.

She was standing in the middle of the floor, with her hands pressed against her temples.

"Wynnie," I said, "our friends are not drowned. I think you will see them quite safe in the morning. Pray to God for them."

She did not hear a word.

"Leave her with me," said Ethelwyn, proceeding to undress her; "and tell nurse to bring up the large bath. There is plenty of hot water in the boiler. I gave orders to that effect, not knowing what might happen."

Wynnie shuddered as her mother said this; but I waited no longer, for when Ethelwyn spoke everyone felt her authority. I obeyed her, and then went to Connie's room.

"Do you mind being left alone a little while?" I asked her.

"No, papa; only-are they all drowned?" she said with a shudder.

"I hope not, my dear; but be sure of the mercy of God, whatever you fear. You must rest in him, my love; for he is life, and will conquer death both in the soul and in the body."

"I was not thinking of myself, papa."

"I know that, my dear. But God is thinking of you and every creature that he has made. And for our sakes you must be quiet in heart, that you may get better, and be able to help us."

"I will try, papa," she said; and, turning slowly on her side, she lay quite still.

Dora and the boys were all fast asleep, for it was very late. I cannot, however, say what hour it was.

Telling nurse to be on the watch because Connie was alone, I went again to the beach. I called first, however, to inquire after Agnes. I found her quite composed, sitting with her parents by the fire, none of them doing anything, scarcely speaking, only listening intently to the sounds of the storm now beginning to die away.

I next went to the place where I had left Turner. Five bodies lay there, and he was busy with a sixth. The surgeon of the place was with him, and they quite expected to recover this man.

I then went down to the sands. An officer of the revenue was taking charge of all that came ashore-chests, and bales, and everything. For a week the sea went on casting out the fragments of that which she had destroyed. I have heard that, for years after, the shifting of the sands would now and then discover things buried that night by the waves.

All the next day the bodies kept coming ashore, some peaceful as in sleep, others broken and mutilated. Many were cast upon other parts of the coast. Some four or five only, all men, were recovered. It was strange to me how I got used to it. The first horror over, the cry that yet another body had come awoke only a gentle pity-no more dismay or shuddering. But, finding I could be of no use, I did not wait longer than just till the morning began to dawn with a pale ghastly light over the seething raging sea; for the sea raged on, although the wind had gone down. There were many strong men about, with two surgeons and all the coastguard, who were well accustomed to similar though not such extensive destruction. The houses along the shore were at the disposal of any who wanted aid; the Parsonage was at some distance; and I confess that when I thought of the state of my daughters, as well as remembered former influences upon my wife, I was very glad to think there was no necessity for carrying thither any of those whom the waves cast on the shore.

When I reached home, and found Wynnie quieter and Connie again asleep, I walked out along our own downs till I came whence I could see the little schooner still safe at anchor. From her position I concluded-correctly as I found afterwards-that they had let out her cable far enough to allow her to reach the bed of the little stream, where the tide would leave her more gently. She was clearly out of all danger now; and if Percivale and Joe had got safe on board of her, we might confidently expect to see them before many hours were passed. I went home with the good news.

For a few moments I doubted whether I should tell Wynnie, for I could not know with any certainty that Percivale was in the schooner. But presently I recalled former conclusions to the effect that we have no right to modify God's facts for fear of what may be to come. A little hope founded on a present appearance, even if that hope should never be realised, may be the very means of enabling a soul to bear the weight of a sorrow past the point at which it would otherwise break down. I would therefore tell Wynnie, and let her share my expectation of deliverance.

I think she had been half-asleep, for when I entered her room she started up in a sitting posture, looking wild, and putting her hands to her head.

"I have brought you good news, Wynnie," I said. "I have been out on the downs, and there is light enough now to see that the little schooner is quite safe."

"What schooner?" she asked listlessly, and lay down again, her eyes still staring, awfully unappeased.

"Why the schooner they say Percivale got on board."

"He isn't drowned then!" she cried with a choking voice, and put her hands to her face and burst into tears and sobs.

"Wynnie," I said, "look what your faithlessness brings upon you. Everybody but you has known all night that Percivale and Joe Harper are probably quite safe. They may be ashore in a couple of hours."

"But you don't know it. He may be drowned yet."

"Of course there is room for doubt, but none for despair. See what a poor helpless creature hopelessness makes you."

"But how can I help it, papa?" she asked piteously. "I am made so."

But as she spoke the dawn was clear upon the height of her forehead.

"You are not made yet, as I am always telling you; and God has ordained that you shall have a hand in your own making. You have to consent, to desire that what you know for a fault shall be set right by his loving will and spirit."

"I don't know God, papa."

"Ah, my dear, that is where it all lies. You do not know him, or you would never be without hope."

"But what am I to do to know him!" she asked, rising on her elbow.

The saving power of hope was already working in her. She was once more turning her face towards the Life.

"Read as you have never read before about Christ Jesus, my love. Read with the express object of finding out what God is like, that you may know him and may trust him. And now give yourself to him, and he will give you sleep."

"What are we to do," I said to my wife, "if Percivale continue silent? For even if he be in love with her, I doubt if he will speak."

"We must leave all that, Harry," she answered.

She was turning on myself the counsel I had been giving Wynnie. It is strange how easily we can tell our brother what he ought to do, and yet, when the case comes to be our own, do precisely as we had rebuked him for doing. I lay down and fell fast asleep.

CHAPTER IX
THE FUNERAL.

It was a lovely morning when I woke once more. The sun was flashing back from the sea, which was still tossing, but no longer furiously, only as if it wanted to turn itself every way to flash the sunlight about. The madness of the night was over and gone; the light was abroad, and the world was rejoicing. When I reached the drawing-room, which afforded the best outlook over the shore, there was the schooner lying dry on the sands, her two cables and anchors stretching out yards behind her; but half way between the two sides of the bay rose a mass of something shapeless, drifted over with sand. It was all that remained together of the great ship that had the day before swept over the waters like a live thing with wings-of all the works of man's hands the nearest to the shape and sign of life. The wind had ceased altogether, only now and then a little breeze arose which murmured "I am very sorry," and lay down again. And I knew that in the houses on the shore dead men and women were lying.

I went down to the dining-room. The three children were busy at their breakfast, but neither wife, daughter, nor visitor had yet appeared. I made a hurried meal, and was just rising to go and inquire further into the events of the night, when the door opened, and in walked Percivale, looking very solemn, but in perfect health and well-being. I grasped his hand warmly.

"Thank God," I said, "that you are returned to us, Percivale."

"I doubt if that is much to give thanks for," he said.

"We are the judges of that," I rejoined. "Tell me all about it."

While he was narrating the events I have already communicated, Wynnie entered. She started, turned pale and then very red, and for a moment hesitated in the doorway.

"Here is another to rejoice at your safety, Percivale," I said.

Thereupon he stepped forward to meet her, and she gave him her hand with an emotion so evident that I felt a little distressed-why, I could not easily have told, for she looked most charming in the act,—more lovely than I had ever seen her. Her beauty was unconsciously praising God, and her heart would soon praise him too. But Percivale was a modest man, and I think attributed her emotion to the fact that he had been in danger in the way of duty,—a fact sufficient to move the heart of any good woman.

She sat down and began to busy herself with the teapot. Her hand trembled. I requested Percivale to begin his story once more; and he evidently enjoyed recounting to her the adventures of the night.

I asked him to sit down and have a second breakfast while I went into the village, whereto he seemed nothing loth.

As I crossed the floor of the old mill to see how Joe was, the head of the sexton appeared emerging from it. He looked full of weighty solemn business. Bidding me good-morning, he turned to the corner where his tools lay, and proceeded to shoulder spade and pickaxe.

"Ah, Coombes! you'll want them," I said.

"A good many o' my people be come all at once, you see, sir," he returned. "I shall have enough ado to make 'em all comfortable like."

"But you must get help, you know; you can never make them all comfortable yourself alone."

"We'll see what I can do," he returned. "I ben't a bit willin' to let no one do my work for me, I do assure you, sir."

"How many are there wanting your services?" I asked.

"There be fifteen of them now, and there be more, I don't doubt, on the way."

"But you won't think of making separate graves for them all," I said. "They died together: let them lie together."

The old man set down his tools, and looked me in the face with indignation. The face was so honest and old, that, without feeling I had deserved it, I yet felt the rebuke.

"How would you like, sir," he said, at length, "to be put in the same bed with a lot of people you didn't know nothing about?"

I knew the old man's way, and that any argument which denied the premiss of his peculiar fancy was worse than thrown away upon him. I therefore ventured no farther than to say that I had heard death was a leveller.

"That be very true; and, mayhap, they mightn't think of it after they'd been down awhile-six weeks, mayhap, or so. But anyhow, it can't be comfortable for 'em, poor things. One on 'em be a baby: I daresay he'd rather lie with his mother. The doctor he say one o' the women be a mother. I don't know," he went on reflectively, "whether she be the baby's own mother, but I daresay neither o' them 'll mind it if I take it for granted, and lay 'em down together. So that's one bed less."

One thing was clear, that the old man could not dig fourteen graves within the needful time. But I would not interfere with his office in the church, having no reason to doubt that he would perform its duties to perfection. He shouldered his tools again and walked out. I descended the stair, thinking to see Joe; but there was no one there but the old woman.

"Where are Joe and Agnes?" I asked.

"You see, sir, Joe had promised a little job of work to be ready to-day, and so he couldn't stop. He did say Agnes needn't go with him; but she thought she couldn't part with him so soon, you see, sir."

"She had received him from the dead-raised to life again," I said; "it was most natural. But what a fine fellow Joe is; nothing will make him neglect his work!"

"I tried to get him to stop, sir, saying he had done quite enough last night for all next day; but he told me it was his business to get the tire put on Farmer Wheatstone's cart-wheel to-day just as much as it was his business to go in the life-boat yesterday. So he would go, and Aggy wouldn't stay behind."

"Fine fellow, Joe!" I said, and took my leave.

As I drew near the village, I heard the sound of hammering and sawing, and apparently everything at once in the way of joinery; they were making the coffins in the joiners' shops, of which there were two in the place.

I do not like coffins. They seem to me relics of barbarism. If I had my way, I would have the old thing decently wound in a fair linen cloth, and so laid in the bosom of the earth, whence it was taken. I would have it vanish, not merely from the world of vision, but from the world of form, as soon as may be. The embrace of the fine life-hoarding, life-giving mould, seems to me comforting, in the vague, foolish fancy that will sometimes emerge from the froth of reverie —I mean, of subdued consciousness remaining in the outworn frame. But the coffin is altogether and vilely repellent. Of this, however, enough, I hate even the shadow of sentiment, though some of my readers, who may not yet have learned to distinguish between sentiment and feeling, may wonder how I dare to utter such a barbarism.

I went to the house of the county magistrate hard by, for I thought something might have to be done in which I had a share. I found that he had sent a notice of the loss of the vessel to the Liverpool papers, requesting those who might wish to identify or claim any of the bodies to appear within four days at Kilkhaven.

This threw the last upon Saturday, and before the end of the week it was clear that they must not remain above ground over Sunday. I therefore arranged that they should be buried late on the Saturday night.

On the Friday morning, a young woman and an old man, unknown to each other, arrived by the coach from Barnstaple. They had come to see the last of their friends in this world; to look, if they might, at the shadow left behind by the departing soul. For as the shadow of any object remains a moment upon the magic curtain of the eye after the object itself has gone, so the shadow of the soul, namely, the body, lingers a moment upon the earth after the object itself has gone to the "high countries." It was well to see with what a sober sorrow the dignified little old man bore his grief. It was as if he felt that the loss of his son was only for a moment. But the young woman had taken on the hue of the corpse she came to seek. Her eyes were sunken as if with the weight of the light she cared not for, and her cheeks had already pined away as if to be ready for the grave. A being thus emptied of its glory seized and possessed my thoughts. She never even told us whom she came seeking, and after one involuntary question, which simply received no answer, I was very careful not even to approach another. I do not think the form she sought was there; and she may have gone home with the lingering hope to cast the gray aurora of a doubtful dawn over her coming days, that, after all, that one had escaped.

On the Friday afternoon, with the approbation of the magistrate, I had all the bodies removed to the church. Some in their coffins, others on stretchers, they were laid in front of the communion-rail. In the evening these two went to see them. I took care to be present. The old man soon found his son. I was at his elbow as he walked between the rows of the dead. He turned to me and said quietly—

"That's him, sir. He was a good lad. God rest his soul. He's with his mother; and if I'm sorry, she's glad."

With that he smiled, or tried to smile. I could only lay my hand on his arm, to let him know that I understood him, and was with him. He walked out of the church, sat down, upon a stone, and stared at the mould of a new-made grave in front of him. What was passing behind those eyes God only knew-certainly the man himself did not know. Our lightest thoughts are of more awful significance than the most serious of us can imagine.

For the young woman, I thought she left the church with a little light in her eyes; but she had said nothing. Alas! that the body was not there could no more justify her than Milton in letting her

"frail thoughts dally with false surmise."

With him, too, she might well add—

"Ay me! whilst thee the shores and sounding seas Wash far away."

But God had them in his teaching, and all I could do was to ask them to be my guests till the funeral and the following Sunday were over. To this they kindly consented, and I took them to my wife, who received them like herself, and had in a few minutes made them at home with her, to which no doubt their sorrow tended, for that brings out the relations of humanity and destroys its distinctions.

The next morning a Scotchman of a very decided type, originally from Aberdeen, but resident in Liverpool, appeared, seeking the form of his daughter. I had arranged that whoever came should be brought to me first. I went with him to the church. He was a tall, gaunt, bony man, with long arms and huge hands, a rugged granite-like face, and a slow ponderous utterance, which I had some difficulty in understanding. He treated the object of his visit with a certain hardness, and at the same time lightness, which also I had some difficulty in understanding.

"You want to see the —" I said, and hesitated.

"Ow ay-the boadies," he answered. "She winna be there, I daursay, but I wad jist like to see; for I wadna like her to be beeried gin sae be 'at she was there, wi'oot biddin' her good-bye like."

When we reached the church, I opened the door and entered. An awe fell upon me fresh and new. The beautiful church had become a tomb: solemn, grand, ancient, it rose as a memorial of the dead who lay in peace before her altar-rail, as if they had fled thither for sanctuary from a sea of troubles. And I thought with myself, Will the time ever come when the churches shall stand as the tombs of holy things that have passed away, when Christ shall have rendered up the kingdom to his Father, and no man shall need to teach his neighbour or his brother, saying, "Know the Lord"? The thought passed through my mind and vanished, as I led my companion up to the dead. He glanced at one and another, and passed on. He had looked at ten or twelve ere he stopped, gazing on the face of the beautiful form which had first come ashore. He stooped and stroked the white cheeks, taking the head in his great rough hands, and smoothed the brown hair tenderly, saying, as if he had quite forgotten that she was dead—

"Eh, Maggie! hoo cam *ye* here, lass?"

Then, as if for the first time the reality had grown comprehensible, he put his hands before his face, and burst into tears. His huge frame was shaken with sobs for one long minute, while I stood looking on with awe and reverence. He ceased suddenly, pulled a blue cotton handkerchief with yellow spots on it—I see it now-from his pocket, rubbed his face with it as if drying it with a towel, put it back, turned, and said, without looking at me, "I'll awa' hame."

"Wouldn't you like a piece of her hair?" I asked.

"Gin ye please," he answered gently, as if his daughter's form had been mine now, and her hair were mine to give.

By the vestry door sat Mrs. Coombes, watching the dead, with her sweet solemn smile, and her constant ministration of knitting.

"Have you got a pair of scissors there, Mrs. Coombes?" I asked.

"Yes, to be sure, sir," she answered, rising, and lifting a huge pair by the string suspending them from her waist.

"Cut off a nice piece of this beautiful hair," I said.

She lifted the lovely head, chose, and cut off a long piece, and handed it respectfully to the father.

He took it without a word, sat down on the step before the communion-rail, and began to smooth out the wonderful sleave of dusky gold. It was, indeed, beautiful hair. As he drew it out, I thought it must be a yard long. He passed his big fingers through and through it, but tenderly, as if it had been still growing on the live lovely head, stopping every moment to pick out the bits of sea-weed and shells, and shake out the sand that had been wrought into its mass. He sat thus for nearly half-an-hour, and we stood looking on with something closely akin to awe. At length he folded it up, drew from his pocket an old black leather book, laid it carefully in the innermost pocket, and rose. I led the way from the church, and he followed me.

Outside the church, he laid his hand on my arm, and said, groping with his other hand in his trousers-pocket—

"She'll hae putten ye to some expense-for the coffin an' sic like."

"We'll talk about that afterwards," I answered. "Come home with me now, and have some refreshment."

"Na, I thank ye. I hae putten ye to eneuch o' tribble already. I'll jist awa' hame."

"We are going to lay them down this evening. You won't go before the funeral. Indeed, I think you can't get away till Monday morning. My wife and I will be glad of your company till then."

"I'm no company for gentle-fowk, sir."

"Come and show me in which of these graves you would like to have her laid," I said.

He yielded and followed me.

Coombes had not dug many spadefuls before he saw what had been plain enough-that ten such men as he could not dig the graves in time. But there was plenty of help to be had from the village and the neighbouring farms. Most of them were now ready, but a good many men were still at work. The brown hillocks lay all about the church-yard—the mole-heaps of burrowing Death.

The stranger looked around him. His face grew critical. He stepped a little hither and thither. At length he turned to me and said—

"I wadna like to be greedy; but gin ye wad lat her lie next the kirk there—i' that neuk, I wad tak' it kindly. And syne gin ever it cam' aboot that I cam' here again, I wad ken whaur she was. Could ye get a sma' bit heidstane putten up? I wad leave the siller wi' ye to pay for't."

"To be sure I can. What will you have put on the stone?"

"Ow jist-let me see-Maggie Jamieson-nae Marget, but jist Maggie. She was aye Maggie at home. Maggie Jamieson, frae her father. It's the last thing I can gie her. Maybe ye micht put a verse o' Scripter aneath't, ye ken."

"What verse would you like?"

He thought for a little.

"Isna there a text that says, 'The deid shall hear his voice'?"

"Yes: 'The dead shall hear the voice of the Son of God.'"

"Ay. That's it. Weel, jist put that on. —They canna do better than hear his voice," he added, with a strange mixture of Scotch ratiocination.

I led the way home, and he accompanied me without further objection or apology. After dinner, I proposed that we should go upon the downs, for the day was warm and bright. We sat on the grass. I felt that I could not talk to them as from myself. I knew nothing of the possible gulfs of sorrow in their hearts. To me their forms seemed each like a hill in whose unseen bosom lay a cavern of dripping waters, perhaps with a subterranean torrent of anguish raving through its hollows and tumbling down hidden precipices, whose voice God only heard, and God only could still. This daughter *might*, though from her face I did not think it, have gone away against her father's will. That son *might* have been a ne'er-do-well at home-how could I tell? The woman *might* be looking for the lover that had forsaken her —I could not divine. I would speak no words of my own. The Son of God had spoken words of comfort to his mourning friends, when he was the present God and they were the forefront of humanity; I would read some of the words he spoke. From them the human nature in each would draw what comfort it could. I took my New Testament from my pocket, and said, without any preamble,

"When our Lord was going to die, he knew that his friends loved him enough to be very wretched about it. He knew that they would be overwhelmed for a time with trouble. He knew, too, that they could not believe the glad end of it all, to which end he looked, across the awful death that awaited him —a death to which that of our friends in the wreck was ease itself. I will just read to you what he said."

I read from the fourteenth to the seventeenth chapter of St. John's Gospel. I knew there were worlds of meaning in the words into which I could hardly hope any of them would enter. But I knew likewise that the best things are just those from which the humble will draw the truth they are capable of seeing. Therefore I read as for myself, and left it to them to hear for themselves. Nor did I add any word of comment, fearful of darkening counsel by words without knowledge. For the Bible is awfully set against what is not wise.

When I had finished, I closed the book, rose from the grass, and walked towards the brow of the shore. They rose likewise and followed me. I talked of slight things; the tone was all that communicated between us. But little of any sort was said. The sea lay still before us, knowing nothing of the sorrow it had caused.

We wandered a little way along the cliff. The burial-service was at seven o'clock.

"I have an invalid to visit out in this direction," I said; "would you mind walking with me? I shall not stay more than five minutes, and we shall get back just in time for tea."

They assented kindly. I walked first with one, then with another; heard a little of the story of each; was able to say a few words of sympathy, and point, as it were, a few times towards the hills whence cometh our aid. I may just mention here, that since our return to Marshmallows I have had two of them, the young woman and the Scotchman, to visit us there.

The bell began to toll, and we went to church. My companions placed themselves near the dead. I went into the vestry till the appointed hour. I thought as I put on my surplice how, in all religions but the Christian, the dead body was a pollution to the temple. Here the church received it, as a holy thing, for a last embrace ere it went to the earth.

As the dead were already in the church, the usual form could not be carried out. I therefore stood by the communion-table, and there began to read, "I am the resurrection and the life, saith the Lord: he that believeth in me, though he were dead, yet shall he live: and whosoever liveth and believeth in me shall never die."

I advanced, as I read, till I came outside the rails and stood before the dead. There I read the Psalm, "Lord, thou hast been our refuge," and the glorious lesson, "Now is Christ risen from the dead, and become the first-fruits of them that slept." Then the men of the neighbourhood came forward, and in long solemn procession bore the bodies out of the church, each to its grave. At the church-door I stood and read, "Man that is born of a woman;" then went from one to another of the graves, and read over each, as the earth fell on the coffin-lid, "Forasmuch as it hath pleased Almighty God, of his great mercy." Then again, I went back to the church-door and read, "I heard a voice from heaven;" and so to the end of the service.

Leaving the men to fill up the graves, I hastened to lay aside my canonicals, that I might join my guests; but my wife and daughter had already prevailed on them to leave the churchyard.

A word now concerning my own family. Turner insisted on Connie's remaining in bed for two or three days. She looked worse in face-pale and worn; but it was clear, from the way she moved in bed, that the fresh power called forth by the shock had not vanished with the moment. Wynnie was quieter almost than ever; but there was a constant *secret* light, if I may use the paradox, in her eyes. Percivale was at the house every day, always ready to make himself useful. My wife bore up wonderfully. As yet the much greater catastrophe had come far short of the impression made by the less. When quieter hours should come, however, I could not help fearing that the place would be dreadfully painful to all but the younger ones, who, of course, had the usual child-gift of forgetting. The servants-even Walter-looked thin and anxious.

That Saturday night I found myself, as I had once or twice found myself before, entirely unprepared to preach. I did not feel anxious, because I did not feel that I was to blame: I had been so much occupied. I had again and again turned my thoughts thitherward, but nothing recommended itself to me so that I could say "I must take that;" nothing said plainly, "This is what you have to speak of."

As often as I had sought to find fitting matter for my sermon, my mind had turned to death and the grave; but I shrunk from every suggestion, or rather nothing had come to me that interested myself enough to justify me in giving it to my people. And I always took it as my sole justification, in speaking of anything to the flock of Christ, that I cared heartily in my own soul for that thing. Without this consciousness I was dumb. And I do think, highly as I value prophecy, that a clergyman ought to be at liberty upon occasion to say, "My friends, I cannot preach to-day." What a riddance it would be for the Church, I do not say if every priest were to speak sense, but only if every priest were to abstain from speaking of that in which, at the moment, he feels little or no interest!

I went to bed, which is often the very best thing a man can do; for sleep will bring him from God that which no effort of his own will can compass. I have read somewhere —I will verify it by present search-that Luther's translation, of the verse in the psalm, "So he giveth to his beloved sleep," is, "He giveth his beloved sleeping," or while asleep. Yes, so it is, literally, in English, "It is in vain that ye rise early, and then sit long, and eat your bread with care, for to his friends he gives it sleeping." This was my experience in the present instance; for the thought of which I was first conscious when I awoke was, "Why should I talk about death? Every man's heart is now full of death. We have enough of that-even the sum that God has sent us on the wings of the tempest. What I have to do, as the minister of the new covenant, is to speak of life." It flashed in on my mind: "Death is over and gone. The resurrection comes next. I will speak of the raising of Lazarus."

The same moment I knew that I was ready to speak. Shall I or shall I not give my reader the substance of what I said? I wish I knew how many of them would like it, and how many would not. I do not want to bore them with sermons, especially seeing I have always said that no sermons ought to be printed; for in print they are but what the old alchymists would have called a *caput mortuum*, or death's head, namely, a lifeless lump of residuum at the bottom of the crucible; for they have no longer the living human utterance which gives all the power on the minds of the hearers. But I have not, either in this or in my preceding narrative, attempted to give a sermon as I preached it. I have only sought to present the substance of it in a form fitter for being read, somewhat cleared of the unavoidable, let me say necessary-yes, I will say *valuable*—repetitions and enforcements by which the various considerations are pressed upon the minds of the hearers. These are entirely wearisome in print-useless too, for the reader may ponder over every phrase till he finds out the purport of it-if indeed there be such readers nowadays.

I rose, went down to the bath in the rocks, had a joyous physical ablution, and a swim up and down the narrow cleft, from which I emerged as if myself newly born or raised anew, and then wandered about on the downs full of hope and thankfulness, seeking all I could to plant deep in my mind the long-rooted truths of resurrection, that they might be not only ready to blossom in the warmth of the spring-tides to come, but able to send out some leaves and promissory buds even in the wintry time of the soul, when the fogs of pain steam up from the frozen clay soil of the body, and make the monarch-will totter dizzily upon his throne, to comfort the eyes of the bewildered king, reminding him that the King of kings hath conquered Death and the Grave. There is no perfect faith that cannot laugh at winters and graveyards, and all the whole array of defiant appearances. The fresh breeze of the morning visited me. "O God," I said in my heart, "would that when the dark day comes, in which I can feel nothing, I may be able to front it with the memory of this day's strength, and so help myself to trust in the Father! I would call to mind the days of old, with David the king."

When I returned to the house, I found that one of the sailors, who had been cast ashore with his leg broken, wished to see me. I obeyed, and found him very pale and worn.

"I think I am going, sir," he said; "and I wanted to see you before I die."

"Trust in Christ, and do not be afraid," I returned.

"I prayed to him to save me when I was hanging to the rigging, and if I wasn't afraid then, I'm not going to be afraid now, dying quietly in my bed. But just look here, sir."

He took from under his pillow something wrapped up in paper, unfolded the envelope, and showed a lump of something—I could not at first tell what. He put it in my hand, and then I saw that it was part of a bible, with nearly the upper half of it worn or cut away, and the rest partly in a state of pulp.

"That's the bible my mother gave me when I left home first," he said. "I don't know how I came to put it in my pocket, but I think the rope that cut through that when I was lashed to the shrouds would a'most have cut through my ribs if it hadn't been for it."

"Very likely," I returned. "The body of the Bible has saved your bodily life: may the spirit of it save your spiritual life."

"I think I know what you mean, sir," he panted out. "My mother was a good woman, and I know she prayed to God for me."

"Would you like us to pray for you in church to-day?"

"If you please, sir; me and Bob Fox. He's nearly as bad as I am."

"We won't forget you," I said. "I will come in after church and see how you are."

I knelt and offered the prayers for the sick, and then took my leave. I did not think the poor fellow was going to die.

I may as well mention here, that he has been in my service ever since. We took him with us to Marshmallows, where he works in the garden and stables, and is very useful. We have to look after him though, for his health continues delicate.

CHAPTER X
THE SERMON.

When I stood up to preach, I gave them no text; but, with the eleventh chapter of the Gospel of St. John open before me, to keep me correct, I proceeded to tell the story in the words God gave me; for who can dare to say that he makes his own commonest speech?

"When Jesus Christ, the Son of God, and therefore our elder brother, was going about on the earth, eating and drinking with his brothers and sisters, there was one family he loved especially—a family of two sisters and a brother; for, although he loves everybody as much as they can be loved, there are some who can be loved more than others. Only God is always trying to make us such that we can be loved more and more. There are several stories—O, such lovely stories!—about that family and Jesus; and we have to do with one of them now.

"They lived near the capital of the country, Jerusalem, in a village they called Bethany; and it must have been a great relief to our Lord, when he was worn out with the obstinacy and pride of the great men of the city, to go out to the quiet little town and into the refuge of Lazarus's house, where everyone was more glad at the sound of his feet than at any news that could come to them.

"They had at this time behaved so ill to him in Jerusalem-taking up stones to stone him even, though they dared not quite do it, mad with anger as they were-and all because he told them the truth-that he had gone away to the other side of the great river that divided the country, and taught the people in that quiet place. While he was there his friend Lazarus was taken ill; and the two sisters, Martha and Mary, sent a messenger to him, to say to him, 'Lord, your friend is very ill.' Only they said it more beautifully than that: 'Lord, behold, he whom thou lovest is sick.' You know, when anyone is ill, we always want the person whom he loves most to come to him. This is very wonderful. In the worst things that can come to us the first thought is of love. People, like the Scribes and Pharisees, might say, 'What good can that do him?' And we may not in the least suppose that the person we want knows any secret that can cure his pain; yet love is the first thing we think of. And here we are more right than we know; for, at the long last, love will cure everything: which truth, indeed, this story will set forth to us. No doubt the heart of Lazarus, ill as he was, longed after his friend; and, very likely, even the sight of Jesus might have given him such strength that the life in him could have driven out the death which had already got one foot across the threshold. But the sisters expected more than this: they believed that Jesus, whom they knew to have driven disease and death out of so many hearts, had only to come and touch him-nay, only to speak a word, to look at him, and their brother was saved. Do you think they presumed in thus expecting? The fact was, they did not believe enough; they had not yet learned to believe that he could cure him all the same whether he came to them or not, because he was always with them. We cannot understand this; but our understanding is never a measure of what is true.

"Whether Jesus knew exactly all that was going to take place I cannot tell. Some people may feel certain upon points that I dare not feel certain upon. One thing I am sure of: that he did not always know everything beforehand, for he said so himself. It is infinitely more valuable to us, because more beautiful and godlike in him, that he should trust his Father than that he should foresee everything. At all events he knew that his Father did not want him to go to his friends yet. So he sent them a message to the effect that there was a particular reason for this sickness-that the end of it was not the death of Lazarus, but the glory of God. This, I think, he told them by the same messenger they sent to him; and then, instead of going to them, he remained where he was.

"But O, my friends, what shall I say about this wonderful message? Think of being sick for the glory of God! of being shipwrecked for the glory of God! of being drowned for the glory of God! How can the sickness, the fear, the broken-heartedness of his creatures be for the glory of God? What kind of a God can that be? Why just a God so perfectly, absolutely good, that the things that look least like it are only the means of clearing our eyes to let us see how good he is. For he is so good that he is not satisfied with *being* good. He loves his children, so that except he can make them good like himself, make them blessed by seeing how good he is, and desiring the same goodness in themselves, he is not satisfied. He is not like a fine proud benefactor, who is content with doing that which will satisfy his sense of his own glory, but like a mother who puts her arm round her child, and whose heart is sore till she can make her child see the love which is her glory. The glorification of the Son of God is the glorification of the human race; for the glory of God is the glory of man, and that glory is love. Welcome sickness, welcome sorrow, welcome death, revealing that glory!

"The next two verses sound very strangely together, and yet they almost seem typical of all the perplexities of God's dealings. The old painters and poets represented Faith as a beautiful woman, holding in her hand a cup of wine and water, with a serpent coiled up within. High-hearted Faith! she scruples not to drink of the life-giving wine and water; she is not repelled by the upcoiled serpent. The serpent she takes but for the type of the eternal wisdom that looks repellent because it is not understood. The wine is good, the water is good; and if the hand of the supreme Fate put that cup in her hand, the serpent itself must be good too, —harmless, at least, to hurt the truth of the water and the wine. But let us read the verses.

"'Now Jesus loved Martha, and her sister, and Lazarus. When he had heard therefore that he was sick, he abode two days still in the same place where he was.'

"Strange! his friend was sick: he abode two days where he was! But remember what we have already heard. The glory of God was infinitely more for the final cure of a dying Lazarus, who, give him all the life he could have, would yet, without that glory, be in death, than the mere presence of the Son of God. I say *mere* presence, for, compared with the glory of God, the very presence of his Son, so dissociated, is nothing. He abode where he was that the glory of God, the final cure of humanity, the love that triumphs over death, might shine out and redeem the hearts of men, so that death could not touch them.

"After the two days, the hour had arrived. He said to his disciples, 'Let us go back to Judæa.' They expostulated, because of the danger, saying, 'Master, the Jews of late sought to stone thee; and goest thou thither again?' The answer which he gave them I am not sure whether I can thoroughly understand; but I think, in fact I know, it must bear on the same region of life-the will of God. I think what he means by walking in the day is simply doing the will of God. That was the sole, the all-embracing light in which Jesus ever walked. I think he means that now he saw plainly what the Father wanted him to do. If he did not see that the Father wanted him to go back to Judæa, and yet went, that would be to go stumblingly, to walk in the darkness. There are twelve hours in the day-one time to act —a time of light and the clear call of duty; there is a night when a man, not seeing where or hearing how, must be content to rest. Something not inharmonious with this, I think, he must have intended; but I do not see the whole thought clearly enough to be sure that I am right. I do think, further, that it points at a clearer condition of human vision and conviction than I am good enough to understand; though I hope one day to rise into this upper stratum of light.

"Whether his scholars had heard anything of Lazarus yet, I do not know. It looks a little as if Jesus had not told them the message he had had from the sisters. But he told them now that he was asleep, and that he was going to wake him. You would think they might have understood this. The idea of going so many miles to wake a man might have surely suggested death. But the disciples were sorely perplexed with many of his words. Sometimes they looked far away for the meaning when the meaning lay in their very hearts; sometimes they looked into their hands for it when it was lost in the grandeur of the ages. But he meant them to see into all that he said by and by, although they could not see into it now. When they understood him better, then they would understand what he said better. And to understand him better they must be more like him; and to make them more like him he must go away and give them his spirit-awful mystery which no man but himself can understand.

"Now he had to tell them plainly that Lazarus was dead. They had not thought of death as a sleep. I suppose this was altogether a new and Christian idea. Do not suppose that it applied more to Lazarus than to other dead people. He was none the less dead that Jesus meant to take a weary two days' journey to his sepulchre and wake him. If death is not a sleep, Jesus did not speak the truth when he said Lazarus slept. You may say it was a figure; but a figure that is not like the thing it figures is simply a lie.

"They set out to go back to Judæa. Here we have a glimpse of the faith of Thomas, the doubter. For a doubter is not without faith. The very fact that he doubts, shows that he has some faith. When I find anyone hard upon doubters, I always doubt the *quality* of his faith. It is of little use to have a great cable, if the hemp is so poor that it breaks like the painter of a boat. I have known people whose power of believing chiefly consisted in their incapacity for seeing difficulties. Of what fine sort a faith must be that is founded in stupidity, or far worse, in indifference to the truth and the mere desire to get out of hell! That is not a grand belief in the Son of God, the radiation of the Father. Thomas's want of faith was shown in the grumbling, self-pitying way in which he said, 'Let us also go that we may die with him.' His Master had said that he was going to wake him. Thomas said, 'that we may die with him.' You may say, 'He did not understand him.' True, it may be, but his unbelief was the cause of his not understanding him. I suppose Thomas meant this as a reproach to Jesus for putting them all in danger by going back to Judæa; if not, it was only a poor piece of sentimentality. So much for Thomas's unbelief. But he had good and true faith notwithstanding; for *he went with his Master.*

"By the time they reached the neighbourhood of Bethany, Lazarus had been dead four days. Someone ran to the house and told the sisters that Jesus was coming. Martha, as soon as she heard it, rose and went to meet him. It might be interesting at another time to compare the difference of the behaviour of the two sisters upon this occasion with the difference of their behaviour upon another occasion, likewise recorded; but with the man dead in his sepulchre, and the hope dead in these two hearts, we have no inclination to enter upon fine distinctions of character. Death and grief bring out the great family likenesses in the living as well as in the dead.

"When Martha came to Jesus, she showed her true though imperfect faith by almost attributing her brother's death to Jesus' absence. But even in the moment, looking in the face of the Master, a fresh hope, a new budding of faith, began in her soul. She thought—'What if, after all, he were to bring him to life again!' O, trusting heart, how thou leavest the dull-plodding intellect behind thee! While the conceited intellect is reasoning upon the impossibility of the thing, the expectant faith beholds it accomplished. Jesus, responding instantly to her faith, granting her half-born prayer, says, 'Thy brother shall rise again;' not meaning the general truth recognised, or at least assented to by all but the Sadducees, concerning the final resurrection of the dead, but meaning, 'Be it unto thee as thou wilt. I will raise him again.' For there is no steering for a fine effect in the words of Jesus. But these words are too good for Martha to take them as he meant them. Her faith is not quite equal to the belief that he actually will do it. The thing she could hope for afar off she could hardly believe when it came to her very door. 'O, yes,' she said, her mood falling again to the level of the commonplace, 'of course, at the last day.' Then the Lord turns away her thoughts from the dogmas of her faith to himself, the Life, saying, 'I am the resurrection and the life: he that believeth in me, though he were dead, yet shall he live. And whosoever liveth and believeth in me, shall never die. Believest thou this?' Martha, without understanding what he said more than in a very poor part, answered in words which preserved her honesty entire, and yet included all he asked, and a thousandfold more than she could yet believe: 'Yea, Lord; I believe that thou art the Christ, the Son of God, which should come into the world.'

"I dare not pretend to have more than a grand glimmering of the truth of Jesus' words 'shall never die;' but I am pretty sure that when Martha came to die, she found that there was indeed no such thing as she had meant when she used the ghastly word *death*, and said with her first new breath, 'Verily, Lord, I am not dead.'

"But look how this declaration of her confidence in the Christ operated upon herself. She instantly thought of her sister; the hope that the Lord would do something swelled within her, and, leaving Jesus, she went to find Mary. Whoever has had a true word with the elder brother, straightway will look around him to find his brother, his sister. The family feeling blossoms: he wants his friend to share the glory withal. Martha wants Mary to go to Jesus too.

"Mary heard her, forgot her visitors, rose, and went. They thought she went to the grave: she went to meet its conqueror. But when she came to him, the woman who had chosen the good part praised of Jesus, had but the same words to embody her hope and her grief that her careful and troubled sister had uttered a few minutes before. How often during those four days had not the self-same words passed between them! 'Ah, if he had been here, our brother had not died!' She said so to himself now, and wept, and her friends who had followed her wept likewise. A moment more, and the Master groaned; yet a moment, and he too wept. 'Sorrow is catching;' but this was not the mere infection of sorrow. It went deeper than mere sympathy; for he groaned in his spirit and was troubled. What made him weep? It was when he saw them weeping that he wept. But why should he weep, when he knew how soon their weeping would be turned into rejoicing? It was not for their weeping, so soon to be over, that he wept, but for the human heart everywhere swollen with tears, yea, with griefs that can find no such relief as tears; for these, and for all his brothers and sisters tormented with pain for lack of faith in his Father in heaven, Jesus wept. He saw the blessed well-being of Lazarus on the one side, and on the other the streaming eyes from whose sight he had vanished. The veil between was so thin! yet the sight of those eyes could not pierce it: their hearts must go on weeping-without cause, for his Father was so good. I think it was the helplessness he felt in the impossibility of at once sweeping away the phantasm death from their imagination that drew the tears from the eyes of Jesus. Certainly it was not for Lazarus; it could hardly be for these his friends-save as they represented the humanity which he would help, but could not help even as he was about to help them.

"The Jews saw herein proof that he loved Lazarus; but they little thought it was for them and their people, and for the Gentiles whom they despised, that his tears were now flowing-that the love which pressed the fountains of his weeping was love for every human heart, from Adam on through the ages.

"Some of them went a little farther, nearly as far as the sisters, saying, 'Could he not have kept the man from dying?' But it was such a poor thing, after all, that they thought he might have done. They regarded merely this unexpected illness, this early death; for I daresay Lazarus was not much older than Jesus. They did not think that, after all, Lazarus must die some time; that the beloved could be saved, at best, only for a little while. Jesus seems to have heard the remark, for he again groaned in himself.

"Meantime they were drawing near the place where he was buried. It was a hollow in the face of a rock, with a stone laid against it. I suppose the bodies were laid on something like shelves inside the rock, as they are in many sepulchres. They were not put into coffins, but wound round and round with linen.

"When they came before the door of death, Jesus said to them, 'Take away the stone.' The nature of Martha's reply-the realism of it, as they would say now-a-days-would seem to indicate that her dawning faith had sunk again below the horizon, that in the presence of the insignia of death, her faith yielded, even as the faith of Peter failed him when he saw around him the grandeur of the high-priest, and his Master bound and helpless. Jesus answered —O, what an answer! —To meet the corruption and the stink which filled her poor human fancy, 'the glory of God' came from his lips: human fear; horror speaking from the lips of a woman in the very jaws of the devouring death; and the 'said I not unto thee?' from the mouth of him who was so soon to pass worn and bloodless through such a door! 'He stinketh,' said Martha. 'The glory of God,' said Jesus. 'Said I not unto thee, that, if thou wouldest believe, thou shouldest see the glory of God?'

"Before the open throat of the sepulchre Jesus began to speak to his Father aloud. He had prayed to him in his heart before, most likely while he groaned in his spirit. Now he thanked him that he had comforted him, and given him Lazarus as a first-fruit from the dead. But he will be true to the listening people as well as to his ever-hearing Father; therefore he tells why he said the word of thanks aloud—a thing not usual with him, for his Father was always hearing, him. Having spoken it for the people, he would say that it was for the people.

"The end of it all was that they might believe that God had sent him—a far grander gift than having the dearest brought back from the grave; for he is the life of men.

"'Lazarus, come forth!'

"And Lazarus came forth, creeping helplessly with inch-long steps of his linen-bound limbs. 'Ha, ha! brother, sister!' cries the human heart. The Lord of Life hath taken the prey from the spoiler; he hath emptied the grave. Here comes the dead man, welcome as never was child from the womb-new-born, and in him all the human race new-born from the grave! 'Loose him and let him go,' and the work is done. The sorrow is over, and the joy is come. Home, home, Martha, Mary, with your Lazarus! He too will go with you, the Lord of the Living. Home and get the feast ready, Martha! Prepare the food for him who comes hungry from the grave, for him who has called him thence. Home, Mary, to help Martha! What a household will yours be! What wondrous speech will pass between the dead come to life and the living come to die!

"But what pang is this that makes Lazarus draw hurried breath, and turns Martha's cheek so pale? Ah, at the little window of the heart the pale eyes of the defeated Horror look in. What! is he there still! Ah, yes, he will come for Martha, come for Mary, come yet again for Lazarus-yea, come for the Lord of Life himself, and carry all away. But look at the Lord: he knows all about it, and he smiles. Does Martha think of the words he spoke, 'He that liveth and believeth in me shall never die'? Perhaps she does, and, like the moon before the sun, her face returns the smile of her Lord.

"This, my friends, is a fancy in form, but it embodies a dear truth. What is it to you and me that he raised Lazarus? We are not called upon to believe that he will raise from the tomb that joy of our hearts which lies buried there beyond our sight. Stop! Are we not? We are called upon to believe this; else the whole story were for us a poor mockery. What is it to us that the Lord raised Lazarus? —Is it nothing to know that our Brother is Lord over the grave? Will the harvest be behind the first-fruits? If he tells us he cannot, for good reasons, raise up our vanished love to-day, or to-morrow, or for all the years of our life to come, shall we not mingle the smile of faithful thanks with the sorrow of present loss, and walk diligently waiting? That he called forth Lazarus showed that he was in his keeping, that he is Lord of the living, and that all live to him, that he has a hold of them, and can draw them forth when he will. If this is not true, then the raising of Lazarus is false; I do not mean merely false in fact, but false in meaning. If we believe in him, then in his name, both for ourselves and for our friends, we must deny death and believe in life. Lord Christ, fill our hearts with thy Life!"

CHAPTER XI
CHANGED PLANS.

In a day or two Connie was permitted to rise and take to her couch once more. It seemed strange that she should look so much worse, and yet be so much stronger. The growth of her power of motion was wonderful. As they carried her, she begged to be allowed to put her feet to the ground. Turner yielded, though without quite ceasing to support her. He was satisfied, however, that she could have stood upright for a moment at least. He would not, of course, risk it, and made haste to lay her down.

The time of his departure was coming near, and he seemed more anxious the nearer it came; for Connie continued worn-looking and pale; and her smile, though ever ready to greet me when I entered, had lost much of its light. I noticed, too, that she had the curtain of her window constantly so arranged as to shut out the sea. I said something to her about it once. Her reply was:

"Papa, I can't bear it. I know it is very silly; but I think I can make you understand how it is: I was so fond of the sea when I came down; it seemed to lie close to my window, with a friendly smile ready for me every morning when I looked out. I daresay it is all from want of faith, but I can't help it: it looks so far away now, like a friend that had failed me, that I would rather not see it."

I saw that the struggling life within her was grievously oppressed, that the things which surrounded her were no longer helpful. Her life had been driven as to its innermost cave; and now, when it had been enticed to venture forth and look abroad, a sudden pall had descended upon nature. I could not help thinking that the good of our visit to Kilkhaven had come, and that evil, from which I hoped we might yet escape, was following. I left her, and sought Turner.

"It strikes me, Turner," I said, "that the sooner we get out of this the better for Connie."

"I am quite of your opinion. I think the very prospect of leaving the place would do something to restore her. If she is so uncomfortable now, think what it will be in the many winter nights at hand."

"Do you think it would be safe to move her?"

"Far safer than to let her remain. At the worst, she is now far better than when she came. Try her. Hint at the possibility of going home, and see how she will take it."

"Well, I sha'n't like to be left alone; but if she goes they must all go, except, perhaps, I might keep Wynnie. But I don't know how her mother would get on without her."

"I don't see why you should stay behind. Mr. Weir would be as glad to come as you would be to go; and it can make no difference to Mr. Shepherd."

It seemed a very sensible suggestion. I thought a moment. Certainly it was a desirable thing for both my sister and her husband. They had no such reasons as we had for disliking the place; and it would enable her to avoid the severity of yet another winter. I said as much to Turner, and went back to Connie's room.

The light of a lovely sunset was lying outside her window. She was sitting so that she could not see it. I would find out her feeling in the matter without any preamble.

"Would you like to go back to Marshmallows, Connie?" I asked.

Her countenance flashed into light.

"O, dear papa, do let us go," she said; "that would be delightful."

"Well, I think we can manage it, if you will only get a little stronger for the journey. The weather is not so good to travel in as when we came down."

"No; but I am ever so much better, you know, than I was then."

The poor girl was already stronger from the mere prospect of going home again. She moved restlessly on her couch, half mechanically put her hand to the curtain, pulled it aside, looked out, faced the sun and the sea, and did not draw back. My mind was made up. I left her, and went to find Ethelwyn. She heartily approved of the proposal for Connie's sake, and said that it would be scarcely less agreeable to herself. I could see a certain troubled look above her eyes, however.

"You are thinking of Wynnie," I said.

"Yes. It is hard to make one sad for the sake of the rest."

"True. But it is one of the world's recognised necessities."

"No doubt."

"Besides, you don't suppose Percivale can stay here the whole winter. They must part some time."

"Of course. Only they did not expect it so soon."

But here my wife was mistaken.

I went to my study to write to Weir. I had hardly finished my letter when Walter came to say that Mr. Percivale wished to see me. I told him to show him in.

"I am just writing home to say that I want my curate to change places with me here, which I know he will be glad enough to do. I see Connie had better go home."

"You will all go, then, I presume?" returned Percivale.

"Yes, yes; of course."

"Then I need not so much regret that I can stay no longer. I came to tell you that I must leave to-morrow."

"Ah! Going to London?"

"Yes. I don't know how to thank you for all your kindness. You have made my summer something like a summer; very different, indeed, from what it would otherwise have been."

"We have had our share of advantage, and that a large one. We are all glad to have made your acquaintance, Mr. Percivale."

He made no answer.

"We shall be passing through London within a week or ten days in all probability. Perhaps you will allow us the pleasure of looking at some of your pictures then?"

His face flushed. What did the flush mean? It was not one of mere pleasure. There was confusion and perplexity in it. But he answered at once:

"I will show you them with pleasure. I fear, however, you will not care for them."

Would this fear account for his embarrassment? I hardly thought it would; but I could not for a moment imagine, with his fine form and countenance before me, that he had any serious reason for shrinking from a visit.

He began to search for a card.

"O, I have your address. I shall be sure to pay you a visit. But you will dine with us to-day, of course?" I said.

"I shall have much pleasure," he answered; and took his leave.

I finished my letter to Weir, and went out for a walk.

I remember particularly the thoughts that moved in me and made that walk memorable. Indeed, I think I remember all outside events chiefly by virtue of the inward conditions with which they were associated. Mere outside things I am very ready to forget. Moods of my own mind do not so readily pass away; and with the memory of some of them every outward circumstance returns; for a man's life is where the kingdom of heaven is-within him. There are people who, if you ask the story of their lives, have nothing to tell you but the course of the outward events that have constituted, as it were, the clothes of their history. But I know, at the same time, that some of the most important crises in my own history (by which word *history* I mean my growth towards the right conditions of existence) have been beyond the grasp and interpretation of my intellect. They have passed, as it were, without my consciousness being awake enough to lay hold of their phenomena. The wind had been blowing; I had heard the sound of it, but knew not whence it came nor whither it went; only, when it was gone, I found myself more responsible, more eager than before.

I remember this walk from the thoughts I had about the great change hanging over us all. I had now arrived at the prime of middle life; and that change which so many would escape if they could, but which will let no man pass, had begun to show itself a real fact upon the horizon of the future. Death looks so far away to the young, that while they acknowledge it unavoidable, the path stretches on in such vanishing perspective before them, that they see no necessity for thinking about the end of it yet; and far would I be from saying they ought to think of it. Life is the true object of a man's care: there is no occasion to make himself think about death. But when the vision of the inevitable draws nigh, when it appears plainly on the horizon, though but as a cloud the size of a man's hand, then it is equally foolish to meet it by refusing to meet it, to answer the questions that will arise by declining to think about them. Indeed, it is a question of life then, and not of death. We want to keep fast hold of our life, and, in the strength of that, to look the threatening death in the face. But to my walk that morning.

I wandered on the downs till I came to the place where a solitary rock stands on the top of a cliff looking seaward, in the suggested shape of a monk praying. On the base on which he knelt I seated myself, and looked out over the Atlantic. How faded the ocean appeared! It seemed as if all the sunny dyes of the summer had been diluted and washed with the fogs of the coming winter, when I thought of the splendour it wore when first from these downs I gazed on the outspread infinitude of space and colour.

"What," I said to myself at length, "has she done since then? Where is her work visible? She has riven, and battered, and destroyed, and her destruction too has passed away. So worketh Time and its powers! The exultation of my youth is gone; my head is gray; my wife is growing old; our children are pushing us from our stools; we are yielding to the new generation; the glory for us hath departed; our life lies weary before us like that sea; and the night cometh when we can no longer work."

Something like this was passing vaguely through my mind. I sat in a mournful stupor, with a half-consciousness that my mood was false, and that I ought to rouse myself and shake it off. There is such a thing as a state of moral dreaming, which closely resembles the intellectual dreaming in sleep. I went on in this false dreamful mood, pitying myself like a child tender over his hurt and nursing his own cowardice, till, all at once, "a little pipling wind" blew on my cheek. The morning was very still: what roused that little wind I cannot tell; but what that little wind roused I will try to tell. With that breath on my cheek, something within me began to stir. It grew, and grew, until the memory of a certain glorious sunset of red and green and gold and blue, which I had beheld from these same heights, dawned within me. I knew that the glory of my youth had not departed, that the very power of recalling with delight that which I had once felt in seeing, was proof enough of that; I knew that I could believe in God all the night long, even if the night were long. And the next moment I thought how I had been reviling in my fancy God's servant, the sea. To how many vessels had she not opened a bounteous highway through the waters, with labour, and food, and help, and ministration, glad breezes and swelling sails, healthful struggle, cleansing fear and sorrow, yea, and friendly death! Because she had been commissioned to carry this one or that one, this hundred or that thousand of his own creatures from one world to another, was I to revile the servant of a grand and gracious Master? It was blameless in Connie to feel the late trouble so deeply that she could not be glad: she had not had the experience of life, yea, of God, that I had had; she must be helped from without. But for me, it was shameful that I, who knew the heart of my Master, to whom at least he had so often shown his truth, should ever be doleful and oppressed. Yet even me he had now helped from within. The glory of existence as the child of the Infinite had again dawned upon me. The first hour of the evening of my life had indeed arrived; the shadows had begun to grow long-so long that I had begun to mark their length; this last little portion of my history had vanished, leaving its few gray ashes behind in the crucible of my life; and the final evening must come, when all my life would lie behind me, and all the memory of it return, with its mornings of gold and red, with its evenings of purple and green; with its dashes of storm, and its foggy glooms; with its white-winged aspirations, its dull-red passions, its creeping envies in brown and black and earthy yellow. But from all the accusations of my conscience, I would turn me to the Lord, for he was called Jesus because he should save his people from their sins. Then I thought what a grand gift it would be to give his people the power hereafter to fight the consequences of their sins. Anyhow, I would trust the Father, who loved me with a perfect love, to lead the soul he had made, had compelled to be, through the gates of the death-birth, into the light of life beyond. I would cast on him the care, humbly challenge him with the responsibility he had himself undertaken, praying only for perfect confidence in him, absolute submission to his will.

I rose from my seat beside the praying monk, and walked on. The thought of seeing my own people again filled me with gladness. I would leave those I had here learned to love with regret; but I trusted I had taught them something, and they had taught me much; therefore there could be no end to our relation to each other-it could not be broken, for it was *in the Lord*, which alone can give security to any tie. I should not, therefore, sorrow as if I were to see their faces no more.

I now took my farewell of that sea and those cliffs. I should see them often ere we went, but I should not feel so near them again. Even this parting said that I must "sit loose to the world" —an old Puritan phrase, I suppose; that I could gather up only its uses, treasure its best things, and must let all the rest go; that those things I called mine-earth, sky, and sea, home, books, the treasured gifts of friends-had all to leave me, belong to others, and help to educate them. I should not need them. I should have my people, my souls, my beloved faces tenfold more, and could well afford to part with these. Why should I mind this chain passing to my eldest boy, when it was only his mother's hair, and I should have his mother still?

So my thoughts went on thinking themselves, until at length I yielded passively to their flow.

I found Wynnie looking very grave when I went into the drawing-room. Her mother was there, too, and Mr. Percivale. It seemed rather a moody party. They wakened up a little, however, after I entered, and before dinner was over we were all chatting together merrily.

"How is Connie?" I asked Ethelwyn.

"Wonderfully better already," she answered.

"I think everybody seems better," I said. "The very idea of home seems reviving to us all."

Wynnie darted a quick glance at me, caught my eyes, which was more than she had intended, and blushed; sought refuge in a bewildered glance at Percivale, caught his eye in turn, and blushed yet deeper. He plunged instantly into conversation, not without a certain involuntary sparkle in his eye.

"Did you go to see Mrs. Stokes this morning?" he asked.

"No," I answered. "She does not want much visiting now; she is going about her work, apparently in good health. Her husband says she is not like the same woman; and I hope he means that in more senses than one, though I do not choose to ask him any questions about his wife."

I did my best to keep up the conversation, but every now and then after this it fell like a wind that would not blow. I withdrew to my study. Percivale and Wynnie went out for a walk. The next morning he left by the coach-early. Turner went with him.

Wynnie did not seem very much dejected. I thought that perhaps the prospect of meeting him again in London kept her up.

CHAPTER XII
THE STUDIO.

I will not linger over our preparations or our leave-takings. The most ponderous of the former were those of the two boys, who, as they had wanted to bring down a chest as big as a cornbin, full of lumber, now wanted to take home two or three boxes filled with pebbles, great oystershells, and sea-weed.

Weir, as I had expected, was quite pleased to make the exchange. An early day had been fixed for his arrival; for I thought it might be of service to him to be introduced to the field of his labours. Before he came, I had gone about among the people, explaining to them some of my reasons for leaving them sooner than I had intended, and telling them a little about my successor, that he might not appear among them quite as a stranger. He was much gratified with their reception of him, and had no fear of not finding himself quite at home with them. I promised, if I could comfortably manage it, to pay them a short visit the following summer, and as the weather was now getting quite cold, hastened our preparations for departure.

I could have wished that Turner had been with us on the journey, but he had been absent from his cure to the full extent that his conscience would permit, and I had not urged him. He would be there to receive us, and we had got so used to the management of Connie, that we did not feel much anxiety about the travelling. We resolved, if she seemed strong enough as we went along, to go right through to London, making a few days there the only break in the transit.

It was a bright, cold morning when we started. But Connie could now bear the air so well, that we set out with the carriage open, nor had we occasion to close it. The first part of our railway journey was very pleasant. But when we drew near London, we entered a thick fog, and before we arrived, a small dense November rain was falling. Connie looked a little dispirited, partly from weariness, but no doubt from the change in the weather.

"Not very cheerful, this, Connie, my dear," I said.

"No, papa," she answered; "but we are going home, you know."

Going home. It set me thinking-as I had often been set thinking before, always with fresh discovery and a new colour on the dawning sky of hope. I lay back in the carriage and thought how the November fog this evening in London, was the valley of the shadow of death we had to go through on the way *home*. A shadow like this would fall upon me; the world would grow dark and life grow weary; but I should know it was the last of the way home.

Then I began to question myself wherein the idea of this home consisted. I knew that my soul had ever yet felt the discomfort of strangeness, more or less, in the midst of its greatest blessedness. I knew that as the thought of water to the thirsty *soul*, for it is the soul far more than the body that thirsts even for the material water, such is the thought of home to the wanderer in a strange country. As the weary soul pines for sleep, and every heart for the cure of its own bitterness, so my heart and soul had often pined for their home. Did I know, I asked myself, where or what that home was? It could consist in no change of place or of circumstance; no mere absence of care; no accumulation of repose; no blessed communion even with those whom my soul loved; in the midst of it all I should be longing for a homelier home-one into which I might enter with a sense of infinitely more absolute peace, than a conscious child could know in the arms, upon the bosom of his mother. In the closest contact of human soul with human soul, when all the atmosphere of thought was rosy with love, again and yet again on the far horizon would the dun, lurid flame of unrest shoot for a moment through the enchanted air, and Psyche would know that not yet had she reached her home. As I thought this I lifted my eyes, and saw those of my wife and Connie fixed on mine, as if they were reproaching me for saying in my soul that I could not be quite at home with them. Then I said in my heart, "Come home with me, beloved-there is but one home for us all. When we find-in proportion as each of us finds-that home, shall we be gardens of delight to each other-little chambers of rest-galleries of pictures-wells of water."

Again, what was this home? God himself. His thoughts, his will, his love, his judgment, are man's home. To think his thoughts, to choose his will, to love his loves, to judge his judgments, and thus to know that he is in us, with us, is to be at home. And to pass through the valley of the shadow of death is the way home, but only thus, that as all changes have hitherto led us nearer to this home, the knowledge of God, so this greatest of all outward changes-for it is but an outward change-will surely usher us into a region where there will be fresh possibilities of drawing nigh in heart, soul, and mind to the Father of us. It is the father, the mother, that make for the child his home. Indeed, I doubt if the home-idea is complete to the parents of a family themselves, when they remember that their fathers and mothers have vanished.

At this point something rose in me seeking utterance.

"Won't it be delightful, wife," I began, "to see our fathers and mothers such a long way back in heaven?"

But Ethelwyn's face gave so little response, that I felt at once how dreadful a thing it was not to have had a good father or mother. I do not know what would have become of me but for a good father. I wonder how anybody ever can be good that has not had a good father. How dreadful not to be a good father or good mother! Every father who is not good, every mother who is not good, just makes it as impossible to believe in God as it can be made. But he is our one good Father, and does not leave us, even should our fathers and mothers have thus forsaken us, and left him without a witness.

Here the evil odour of brick-burning invaded my nostrils, and I knew that London was about us. A few moments after, we reached the station, where a carriage was waiting to take us to our hotel.

Dreary was the change from the stillness and sunshine of Kilkhaven to the fog and noise of London; but Connie slept better that night than she had slept for a good many nights before.

After breakfast the next morning, I said to Wynnie,

"I am going to see Mr. Percivale's studio, my dear: have you any objection to going with me?"

"No, papa," she answered, blushing. "I have never seen an artist's studio in my life."

"Come along, then. Get your bonnet at once. It rains, but we shall take a cab, and it won't matter."

She ran off, and was ready in a few minutes. We gave the driver directions, and set off. It was a long drive. At length he stopped at the door of a very common-looking house, in a very dreary-looking street, in which no man could possibly identify his own door except by the number. I knocked. A woman who looked at once dirty and cross, the former probably the cause of the latter, opened the door, gave a bare assent to my question whether Mr. Percivale was at home, withdrew to her den with the words "second-floor," and left us to find our own way up the two flights of stairs. This, however, involved no great difficulty. We knocked at the door of the front room. A well-known voice cried, "Come in," and we entered.

Percivale, in a short velvet coat, with his palette on his thumb, advanced to meet us cordially. His face wore a slight flush, which I attributed solely to pleasure, and nothing to any awkwardness in receiving us in such a poor place as he occupied. I cast my eyes round the room. Any romantic notions Wynnie might have indulged concerning the marvels of a studio, must have paled considerably at the first glance around Percivale's room-plainly the abode if not of poverty, then of self-denial, although I suspected both. A common room, with no carpet save a square in front of the fireplace; no curtains except a piece of something like drugget nailed flat across all the lower half of the window to make the light fall from upwards; two or three horsehair chairs, nearly worn out; a table in a corner, littered with books and papers; a horrible lay-figure, at the present moment dressed apparently for a scarecrow; a large easel, on which stood a half-finished oil-painting—these constituted almost the whole furniture of the room. With his pocket-handkerchief Percivale dusted one chair for Wynnie and another for me. Then standing before us, he said:

"This is a very shabby place to receive you in, Miss Walton, but it is all I have got."

"A man's life consisteth not in the abundance of the things he possesses," I ventured to say.

"Thank you," said Percivale. "I hope not. It is well for me it should not."

"It is well for the richest man in England that it should not," I returned. "If it were not so, the man who could eat most would be the most blessed."

"There are people, even of my acquaintance, however, who seem to think it does."

"No doubt; but happily their thinking so will not make it so even for themselves."

"Have you been very busy since you left us, Mr. Percivale?" asked Wynnie.

"Tolerably," he answered. "But I have not much to show for it. That on the easel is all. I hardly like to let you look at it, though."

"Why?" asked Wynnie.

"First, because the subject is painful. Next, because it is so unfinished that none but a painter could do it justice."

"But why should you paint subjects you would not like people to look at?"

"I very much want people to look at them."

"Why not us, then?" said Wynnie.

"Because you do not need to be pained."

"Are you sure it is good for you to pain anybody?" I said.

"Good is done by pain-is it not?" he asked.

"Undoubtedly. But whether *we* are wise enough to know when and where and how much, is the question."

"Of course I do not make the pain my object."

"If it comes only as a necessary accompaniment, that may alter the matter greatly," I said. "But still I am not sure that anything in which the pain predominates can be useful in the best way."

"Perhaps not," he returned. —"Will you look at the daub?"

"With much pleasure," I replied, and we rose and stood before the easel. Percivale made no remark, but left us to find out what the picture meant. Nor had I long to look before I understood it-in a measure at least.

It represented a garret-room in a wretchedly ruinous condition. The plaster had come away in several places, and through between the laths in one spot hung the tail of a great rat. In a dark corner lay a man dying. A woman sat by his side, with her eyes fixed, not on his face, though she held his hand in hers, but on the open door, where in the gloom you could just see the struggles of two undertaker's men to get the coffin past the turn of the landing towards the door. Through the window there was one peep of the blue sky, whence a ray of sunlight fell on the one scarlet blossom of a geranium in a broken pot on the window-sill outside.

"I do not wonder you did not like to show it," I said. "How can you bear to paint such a dreadful picture?"

"It is a true one. It only represents a fact."

"All facts have not a right to be represented."

"Surely you would not get rid of painful things by huddling them out of sight?"

"No; nor yet by gloating upon them."

"You will believe me that it gives me anything but pleasure to paint such pictures-as far as the subject goes," he said with some discomposure.

"Of course. I know you well enough by this time to know that. But no one could hang it on his wall who would not either gloat on suffering or grow callous to it. Whence, then, would come the good I cannot doubt you propose to yourself as your object in painting the picture? If it had come into my possession, I would —"

"Put it in the fire," suggested Percivale with a strange smile.

"No. Still less would I sell it. I would hang it up with a curtain before it, and only look at it now and then, when I thought my heart was in danger of growing hardened to the sufferings of my fellow-men, and forgetting that they need the Saviour."

"I could not wish it a better fate. That would answer my end."

"Would it, now? Is it not rather those who care little or nothing about such matters that you would like to influence? Would you be content with one solitary person like me? And, remember, I wouldn't buy it. I would rather not have it. I could hardly bear to know it was in my house. I am certain you cannot do people good by showing them *only* the painful. Make it as painful as you will, but put some hope into it-something to show that action is worth taking in the affair. From mere suffering people will turn away, and you cannot blame them. Every show of it, without hinting at some door of escape, only urges them to forget it all. Why should they be pained if it can do no good?"

"For the sake of sympathy, I should say," answered Percivale.

"They would rejoin, 'It is only a picture. Come along.' No; give people hope, if you would have them act at all, in anything."

"I was almost hoping you would read the picture rather differently. You see there is a bit of blue sky up there, and a bit of sunshiny scarlet in the window."

He looked at me curiously as he spoke.

"I can read it so for myself, and have metamorphosed its meaning so. But you only put in the sky and the scarlet to heighten the perplexity, and make the other look more terrible."

"Now I know that as an artist I have succeeded, however I may have failed otherwise. I did so mean it; but knowing you would dislike the picture, I almost hoped in my cowardice, as I said, that you would read your own meaning into it."

Wynnie had not said a word. As I turned away from the picture, I saw that she was looking quite distressed, but whether by the picture or the freedom with which I had remarked upon it, I do not know. My eyes falling on a little sketch in sepia, I began to examine it, in the hope of finding something more pleasant to say. I perceived in a moment, however, that it was nearly the same thought, only treated in a gentler and more poetic mode. A girl lay dying on her bed. A youth held her hand. A torrent of summer sunshine fell through the window, and made a lake of glory upon the floor. I turned away.

"You like that better, don't you, papa?" said Wynnie tremulously.

"It is beautiful, certainly," I answered. "And if it were only one, I should enjoy it-as a mood. But coming after the other, it seems but the same thing more weakly embodied."

I confess I was a little vexed; for I had got much interested in Percivale, for his own sake as well as for my daughter's, and I had expected better things from him. But I saw that I had gone too far.

"I beg your pardon, Mr. Percivale," I said.

"I fear I have been too free in my remarks. I know, likewise, that I am a clergyman, and not a painter, and therefore incapable of giving the praise which I have little doubt your art at least deserves."

"I trust that honesty cannot offend me, however much and justly it may pain me."

"But now I have said my worst, I should much like to see what else you have at hand to show me."

"Unfortunately I have too much at hand. Let me see."

He strode to the other end of the room, where several pictures were leaning against the wall, with their faces turned towards it. From these he chose one, but, before showing it, fitted it into an empty frame that stood beside. He then brought it forward and set it on the easel. I will describe it, and then my reader will understand the admiration which broke from me after I had regarded it for a time.

A dark hill rose against the evening sky, which shone through a few thin pines on its top. Along a road on the hill-side four squires bore a dying knight—a man past the middle age. One behind carried his helm, and another led his horse, whose fine head only appeared in the picture. The head and countenance of the knight were very noble, telling of many a battle, and ever for the right. The last had doubtless been gained, for one might read victory as well as peace in the dying look. The party had just reached the edge of a steep descent, from which you saw the valley beneath, with the last of the harvest just being reaped, while the shocks stood all about in the fields, under the place of the sunset. The sun had been down for some little time. There was no gold left in the sky, only a little dull saffron, but plenty of that lovely liquid green of the autumn sky, divided with a few streaks of pale rose. The depth of the sky overhead, which you could not see for the arrangement of the picture, was mirrored lovelily in a piece of water that lay in the centre of the valley.

"My dear fellow," I cried, "why did you not show me this first, and save me from saying so many unkind things? Here is a picture to my own heart; it is glorious. Look here, Wynnie," I went on; "you see it is evening; the sun's work is done, and he has set in glory, leaving his good name behind him in a lovely harmony of colour. The old knight's work is done too; his day has set in the storm of battle, and he is lying lapt in the coming peace. They are bearing him home to his couch and his grave. Look at their faces in the dusky light. They are all mourning for and honouring the life that is ebbing away. But he is gathered to his fathers like a shock of corn fully ripe; and so the harvest stands golden in the valley beneath. The picture would not be complete, however, if it did not tell us of the deep heaven overhead, the symbol of that heaven whither he who has done his work is bound. What a lovely idea to represent it by means of the water, the heaven embodying itself in the earth, as it were, that we may see it! And observe how that dusky hill-side, and those tall slender mournful-looking pines, with that sorrowful sky between, lead the eye and point the heart upward towards that heaven. It is indeed a grand picture, full of feeling—a picture and a parable."

[Footnote: This is a description, from memory only, of a picture painted by Arthur Hughes.]

I looked at the girl. Her eyes were full of tears, either called forth by the picture itself or by the pleasure of finding Percivale's work appreciated by me, who had spoken so hardly of the others.

"I cannot tell you how glad I am that you like it," she said.

"Like it!" I returned; "I am simply delighted with it, more than I can express-so much delighted that if I could have this alongside of it, I should not mind hanging that other-that hopeless garret-on the most public wall I have."

"Then," said Wynnie bravely, though in a tremulous voice, "you confess-don't you, papa? — that you were *too* hard on Mr. Percivale at first?"

"Not too hard on his picture, my dear; and that was all he had yet given me to judge by. No man should paint a picture like that. You are not bound to disseminate hopelessness; for where there is no hope there can be no sense of duty."

"But surely, papa, Mr. Percivale has *some* sense of duty," said Wynnie in an almost angry tone.

"Assuredly my love. Therefore I argue that he has some hope, and therefore, again, that he has no right to publish such a picture."

At the word *publish* Percivale smiled. But Wynnie went on with her defence:

"But you see, papa, that Mr. Percivale does not paint such pictures only. Look at the other."

"Yes, my dear. But pictures are not like poems, lying side by side in the same book, so that the one can counteract the other. The one of these might go to the stormy Hebrides, and the other to the Vale of Avalon; but even then I should be strongly inclined to criticise the poem, whatever position it stood in, that had *nothing*—positively nothing-of the aurora in it."

Here let me interrupt the course of our conversation to illustrate it by a remark on a poem which has appeared within the last twelvemonth from the pen of the greatest living poet, and one who, if I may dare to judge, will continue the greatest for many, many years to come. It is only a little song, "I stood on a tower in the wet." I have found few men who, whether from the influence of those prints which are always on the outlook for something to ridicule, or from some other cause, did not laugh at the poem. I thought and think it a lovely poem, although I am not quite sure of the transposition of words in the last two lines. But I do not *approve* of the poem, just because there is no hope in it. It lacks that touch or hint of *red* which is as essential, I think, to every poem as to every picture-the life-blood—the one pure colour. In his hopeful moods, let a man put on his singing robes, and chant aloud the words of gladness-or of grief, I care not which-to his fellows; in his hours of hopelessness, let him utter his thoughts only to his inarticulate violin, or in the evanescent sounds of any his other stringed instrument; let him commune with his own heart on his bed, and be still; let him speak to God face to face if he may-only he cannot do that and continue hopeless; but let him not sing aloud in such a mood into the hearts of his fellows, for he cannot do them much good thereby. If it were a fact that there is no hope, it would not be a *truth*. No doubt, if it were a fact, it ought to be known; but who will dare be confident that there is no hope? Therefore, I say, let the hopeless moods, at least, if not the hopeless men, be silent.

"He could refuse to let the one go without the other," said Wynnie.

"Now you are talking like a child, Wynnie, as indeed all partisans do at the best. He might sell them together, but the owner would part them. —If you will allow me, I will come and see both the pictures again to-morrow."

Percivale assured me of welcome, and we parted, I declining to look at any more pictures that day, but not till we had arranged that he should dine with us in the evening.

CHAPTER XIII
HOME AGAIN.

I will not detain my readers with the record of the few days we spent in London. In writing the account of it, as in the experience of the time itself, I feel that I am near home, and grow the more anxious to reach it. Ah! I am growing a little anxious after another home, too; for the house of my tabernacle is falling to ruins about me. What a word *home* is! To think that God has made the world so that you have only to be born in a certain place, and live long enough in it to get at the secret of it, and henceforth that place is to you a *home* with all the wonderful meaning in the word. Thus the whole earth is a home to the race; for every spot of it shares in the feeling: some one of the family loves it as *his* home. How rich the earth seems when we so regard it-crowded with the loves of home! Yet I am now getting ready to go home —to leave this world of homes and go home. When I reach that home, shall I even then seek yet to go home? Even then, I believe, I shall seek a yet warmer, deeper, truer home in the deeper knowledge of God-in the truer love of my fellow-man. Eternity will be, my heart and my faith tell me, a travelling homeward, but in jubilation and confidence and the vision of the beloved.

When we had laid Connie once more in her own room, at least the room which since her illness had come to be called hers, I went up to my study. The familiar faces of my books welcomed me. I threw myself in my reading-chair, and gazed around me with pleasure. I felt it so homely here. All my old friends-whom somehow I hoped to see some day-present there in the spirit ready to talk with me any moment when I was in the mood, making no claim upon my attention when I was not! I felt as if I should like, when the hour should come, to die in that chair, and pass into the society of the witnesses in the presence of the tokens they had left behind them.

I heard shouts on the stair, and in rushed the two boys.

"Papa, papa!" they were crying together.

"What is the matter?"

"We've found the big chest just where we left it."

"Well, did you expect it would have taken itself off?"

"But there's everything in it just as we left it."

"Were you afraid, then, that the moment you left it it would turn itself upside down, and empty itself of all its contents on the floor?"

They laughed, but apparently with no very keen appreciation of the attempt at a joke.

"Well, papa, I did not think anything about it; but-but-but-there everything is as we left it."

With this triumphant answer they turned and hurried, a little abashed, out of the room; but not many moments elapsed before the sounds that arose from them were sufficiently reassuring as to the state of their spirits. When they were gone, I forgot my books in the attempt to penetrate and understand the condition of my boys' thoughts; and I soon came to see that they were right and I was wrong. It was the movement of that undeveloped something in us which makes it possible for us in everything to give thanks. It was the wonder of the discovery of the existence of law. There was nothing that they could understand, *à priori*, to necessitate the remaining of the things where they had left them. No doubt there was a reason in the nature of God, why all things should hold together, whence springs the law of gravitation, as we call it; but as far as the boys could understand of this, all things might as well have been arranged for flying asunder, so that no one could expect to find anything where he had left it. I began to see yet further into the truth that in everything we must give thanks, and whatever is not of faith is sin. Even the laws of nature reveal the character of God, not merely as regards their ends, but as regards their kind, being of necessity fashioned after ideal facts of his own being and will.

I rose and went down to see if everybody was getting settled, and how the place looked. I found Ethel already going about the house as if she had never left it, and as if we all had just returned from a long absence and she had to show us home-hospitality. Wynnie had vanished; but I found her by and by in the favourite haunt of her mother before her marriage-beside the little pond called the Bishop's Basin, of which I do not think I have ever told my readers the legend. But why should I mention it, for I cannot tell it now? The frost lay thick in the hollow when I went down there to find her; the branches, lately clothed with leaves, stood bare and icy around her. Ethelwyn and I had almost forgotten that there was anything out of the common in connection with the house. The horror of this mysterious spot had laid hold upon Wynnie. I resolved that that night I would, in her mother's presence, tell her all the legend of the place, and the whole story of how I won her mother. I did so; and I think it made her trust us more. But now I left her there, and went to Connie. She lay in her bed; for her mother had got her thither at once, a perfect picture of blessed comfort. There was no occasion to be uneasy about her. I was so pleased to be at home again with such good hopes, that I could not rest, but went wandering everywhere-into places even which I had not entered for ten years at least, and found fresh interest in everything; for this was home, and here I was.

Now I fancy my readers, looking forward to the end, and seeing what a small amount of print is left, blaming me; some, that I have roused curiosity without satisfying it; others, that I have kept them so long over a dull book and a lame conclusion. But out of a life one cannot always cut complete portions, and serve them up in nice shapes. I am well aware that I have not told them the *fate*, as some of them would call it, of either of my daughters. This I cannot develop now, even as far as it is known to me; but, if it is any satisfaction to them to know this much-and it will be all that some of them mean by *fate*, I fear—I may as well tell them now that Wynnie has been Mrs. Percivale for many years, with a history well worth recounting; and that Connie has had a quiet, happy life for nearly as long, as Mrs. Turner. She has never got strong, but has very tolerable health. Her husband watches her with the utmost care and devotion. My Ethelwyn is still with me. Harry is gone home. Charlie is a barrister of the Middle Temple. And Dora—I must not forget Dora-well, I will say nothing about her *fate*, for good reasons-it is not quite determined yet. Meantime she puts up with the society of her old father and mother, and is something else than unhappy, I fully believe.

"And Connie's baby?" asks some one out of ten thousand readers. I have no time to tell you about her now; but as you know her so little, it cannot be such a trial to remain, for a time at least, unenlightened with regard to her *fate*.

The only other part of my history which could contain anything like incident enough to make it interesting in print, is a period I spent in London some few years after the time of which I have now been writing. But I am getting too old to regard the commencement of another history with composure. The labour of thinking into sequences, even the bodily labour of writing, grows more and more severe. I fancy I can think correctly still; but the effort necessary to express myself with corresponding correctness becomes, in prospect, at least, sometimes almost appalling. I must therefore take leave of my patient reader-for surely every one who has followed me through all that I have here written, well deserves the epithet-as if the probability that I shall write no more were a certainty, bidding him farewell with one word: *"Friend, hope thou in God,"* and for a parting gift offering him a new, and, I think, a true rendering of the first verse of the eleventh chapter of the Epistle to the Hebrews:

"Now faith is the essence of hopes, the trying of things unseen."

Good-bye.

THE END.

THE VICAR'S DAUGHTER

CHAPTER I
INTRODUCTORY.

I think that is the way my father would begin. My name is Ethelwyn Percivale, and used to be Ethelwyn Walton. I always put the Walton in between when I write to my father; for I think it is quite enough to have to leave father and mother behind for a husband, without leaving their name behind you also. I am fond of lumber-rooms, and in some houses consider them far the most interesting spots; but I don't choose that my old name should lie about in the one at home.

I am much afraid of writing nonsense; but my father tells me that to see things in print is a great help to recognizing whether they are nonsense or not. And he tells me, too, that his friend the publisher, who, —but I will speak of him presently, —his friend the publisher is not like any other publisher he ever met with before; for he never grumbles at any alterations writers choose to make, —at least he never says any thing, although it costs a great deal to shift the types again after they are once set up. The other part of my excuse for attempting to write lies simply in telling how it came about.

Ten days ago, my father came up from Marshmallows to pay us a visit. He is with us now, but we don't see much of him all day; for he is generally out with a friend of his in the east end, the parson of one of the poorest parishes in London, —who thanks God that he wasn't the nephew of any bishop to be put into a good living, for he learns more about the ways of God from having to do with plain, yes, vulgar human nature, than the thickness of the varnish would ever have permitted him to discover in what are called the higher orders of society. Yet I must say, that, amongst those I have recognized as nearest, the sacred communism of the early church —a phrase of my father's —are two or three people of rank and wealth, whose names are written in heaven, and need not be set down in my poor story.

A few days ago, then, my father, coming home to dinner, brought with him the publisher of the two books called, "The Annals of a Quiet Neighborhood," and "The Seaboard Parish." The first of these had lain by him for some years before my father could publish it; and then he remodelled it a little for the magazine in which it came out, a portion at a time. The second was written at the request of Mr. S., who wanted something more of the same sort; and now, after some years, he had begun again to represent to my father, at intervals, the necessity for another story to complete the *trilogy*, as he called it: insisting, when my father objected the difficulties of growing years and failing judgment, that indeed he owed it to him; for he had left him in the lurch, as it were, with an incomplete story, not to say an uncompleted series. My father still objected, and Mr. S. still urged, until, at length, my father said-this I learned afterwards, of course —"What would you say if I found you a substitute?" "That depends on who the substitute might be, Mr. Walton," said Mr. S. The result of their talk was that my father brought him home to dinner that day; and hence it comes, that, with some real fear and much metaphorical trembling, I am now writing this. I wonder if anybody will ever read it. This my first chapter shall be composed of a little of the talk that passed at our dinner-table that day. Mr. Blackstone was the only other stranger present; and he certainly was not much of a stranger.

"Do you keep a diary, Mrs. Percivale?" asked Mr. S., with a twinkle in his eye, as if he expected an indignant repudiation.

"I would rather keep a rag and bottle shop," I answered: at which Mr. Blackstone burst into one of his splendid roars of laughter; for if ever a man could laugh like a Christian who believed the world was in a fair way after all, that man was Mr. Blackstone; and even my husband, who seldom laughs at any thing I say with more than his eyes, was infected by it, and laughed heartily.

"That's rather a strong assertion, my love," said my father. "Pray, what do you mean by it?"

"I mean, papa," I answered, "that it would be a more profitable employment to keep the one than the other."

"I suppose you think," said Mr. Blackstone, "that the lady who keeps a diary is in the same danger as the old woman who prided herself in keeping a strict account of her personal expenses.

And it always was correct; for when she could not get it to balance at the end of the week, she brought it right by putting down the deficit as *charity*."

"That's just what I mean," I said.

"But," resumed Mr. S., "I did not mean a diary of your feelings, but of the events of the day and hour."

"Which are never in themselves worth putting down," I said. "All that is worth remembering will find for itself some convenient cranny to go to sleep in till it is wanted, without being made a poor mummy of in a diary."

"If you have such a memory, I grant that is better, even for my purpose, much better," said Mr. S.

"For your purpose!" I repeated, in surprise. "I beg your pardon; but what designs can you have upon my memory?"

"Well, I suppose I had better be as straightforward as I know you would like me to be, Mrs. Percivale. I want you to make up the sum your father owes me. He owed me three books; he has paid me two. I want the third from you."

I laughed; for the very notion of writing a book seemed preposterous.

"I want you, under feigned names of course," he went on, "as are all the names in your father's two books, to give me the further history of the family, and in particular your own experiences in London. I am confident the history of your married life must contain a number of incidents which, without the least danger of indiscretion, might be communicated to the public to the great advantage of all who read them."

"You forget," I said, hardly believing him to be in earnest, "that I should be exposing my story to you and Mr. Blackstone at least. If I were to make the absurd attempt, —I mean absurd as regards my ability, —I should be always thinking of you two as my public, and whether it would be right for me to say this and say that; which you may see at once would render it impossible for me to write at all."

"I think I can suggest a way out of that difficulty, Wynnie," said my father. "You must write freely, all you feel inclined to write, and then let your husband see it. You may be content to let all pass that he passes."

"You don't say you really mean it, papa! The thing is perfectly impossible. I never wrote a book in my life, and"—

"No more did I, my dear, before I began my first."

"But you grew up to it by degrees, papa!"

"I have no doubt that will make it the easier for you, when you try. I am so far, at least, a Darwinian as to believe that."

"But, really, Mr. S. ought to have more sense —I beg your pardon, Mr. S.; but it is perfectly absurd to suppose me capable of finishing any thing my father has begun. I assure you I don't feel flattered by your proposal. I have got a man of more consequence for a father than that would imply."

All this time my tall husband sat silent at the foot of the table, as if he had nothing on earth to do with the affair, instead of coming to my assistance, when, as I thought, I really needed it, especially seeing my own father was of the combination against me; for what can be more miserable than to be taken for wiser or better or cleverer than you know perfectly well you are. I looked down the table, straight and sharp at him, thinking to rouse him by the most powerful of silent appeals; and when he opened his mouth very solemnly, staring at me in return down all the length of the table, I thought I had succeeded. But I was not a little surprised, when I heard him say,—

"I think, Wynnie, as your father and Mr. S. appear to wish it, you might at least try."

This almost overcame me, and I was very near,—never mind what. I bit my lips, and tried to smile, but felt as if all my friends had forsaken me, and were about to turn me out to beg my bread. How on earth could I write a book without making a fool of myself?

"You know, Mrs. Percivale," said Mr. S., "you needn't be afraid about the composition, and the spelling, and all that. We can easily set those to rights at the office."

He couldn't have done any thing better to send the lump out of my throat; for this made me angry.

"I am not in the least anxious about the spelling," I answered; "and for the rest, pray what is to become of me, if what you print should happen to be praised by somebody who likes my husband or my father, and therefore wants to say a good word for me? That's what a good deal of reviewing comes to, I understand. Am I to receive in silence what doesn't belong to me, or am I to send a letter to the papers to say that the whole thing was patched and polished at the printing-office, and that I have no right to more than perhaps a fourth part of the commendation? How would that do?"

"But you forget it is not to have your name to it," he said; "and so it won't matter a bit. There will be nothing dishonest about it."

"You forget, that, although nobody knows my real name, everybody will know that I am the daughter of that Mr. Walton who would have thrown his pen in the fire if you had meddled with any thing he wrote. They would be praising *me*, if they praised at all. The name is nothing. Of all things, to have praise you don't deserve, and not to be able to reject it, is the most miserable! It is as bad as painting one's face."

"Hardly a case in point," said Mr. Blackstone. "For the artificial complexion would be your own work, and the other would not."

"If you come to discuss that question," said my father, "we must all confess we have had in our day to pocket a good many more praises than we had a right to. I agree with you, however, my child, that we must not connive at any thing of the sort. So I will propose this clause in the bargain between you and Mr. S.; namely, that, if he finds any fault with your work, he shall send it back to yourself to be set right, and, if you cannot do so to his mind, you shall be off the bargain."

"But papa,—Percivale,—both of you know well enough that nothing ever happened to me worth telling."

"I am sorry your life has been so very uninteresting, wife," said my husband grimly; for his fun is always so like earnest!

"You know well enough what I mean, husband. It does *not* follow that what has been interesting enough to you and me will be interesting to people who know nothing at all about us to begin with."

"It depends on how it is told," said Mr. S.

"Then, I beg leave to say, that I never had an original thought in my life; and that, if I were to attempt to tell my history, the result would be as silly a narrative as ever one old woman told another by the workhouse fire."

"And I only wish I could hear the one old woman tell her story to the other," said my father.

"Ah! but that's because you see ever so much more in it than shows. You always see through the words and the things to something lying behind them," I said.

"Well, if you told the story rightly, other people would see such things behind it too."

"Not enough of people to make it worth while for Mr. S. to print it," I said.

"He's not going to print it except he thinks it worth his while; and you may safely leave that to him," said my husband.

"And so I'm to write a book as big as 'The Annals;' and, after I've been slaving at it for half a century or so, I'm to be told it won't do, and all my labor must go for nothing? I must say the proposal is rather a cool one to make,—to the mother of a family."

"Not at all; that's not it, I mean," said Mr. S.; "if you will write a dozen pages or so, I shall be able to judge by those well enough,—at least, I will take all the responsibility on myself after that."

"There's a fair offer!" said my husband. "It seems to me, Wynnie, that all that is wanted of you is to tell your tale so that other people can recognize the human heart in it,—the heart that is like their own, and be able to feel as if they were themselves going through the things you recount."

"You describe the work of a genius, and coolly ask me to do it. Besides, I don't want to be set thinking about my heart, and all that," I said peevishly.

"Now, don't be raising objections where none exist," he returned.

"If you mean I am pretending to object, I have only to say that I feel all one great objection to the whole affair, and that I won't touch it."

They were all silent; and I felt as if I had behaved ungraciously. Then first I felt as if I might *have* to do it, after all. But I couldn't see my way in the least.

"Now, what is there," I asked, "in all my life that is worth setting down,—I mean, as I should be able to set it down?"

"What do you ladies talk about now in your morning calls?" suggested Mr. Blackstone, with a humorous glance from his deep black eyes.

"Nothing worth writing about, as I am sure *you* will readily believe, Mr. Blackstone," I answered.

"How comes it to be interesting, then?"

"But it isn't. They-we-only talk about the weather and our children and servants, and that sort of thing."

"*Well!*" said Mr. S., "and I wish I could get any thing sensible about the weather and children and servants, and that sort of thing, for my magazine. I have a weakness in the direction of the sensible."

"But there never is any thing sensible said about any of them,—not that I know of."

"Now, Wynnie, I am sure you are wrong," said my father. "There is your friend, Mrs. Cromwell: I am certain she, sometimes at least, must say what is worth hearing about such matters."

"Well, but she's an exception. Besides, she hasn't any children."

"Then," said my husband, "there's Lady Bernard"—

"Ah! but she was like no one else. Besides, she is almost a public character, and any thing said about her would betray my original."

"It would be no matter. She is beyond caring for that now; and not one of her friends could object to any thing you who loved her so much would say about her."

The mention of this lady seemed to put some strength into me. I felt as if I did know something worth telling, and I was silent in my turn.

"Certainly," Mr. S. resumed, "whatever is worth talking about is worth writing about, — though not perhaps in the way it is talked about. Besides, Mrs. Percivale, my clients want to know more about your sisters, and little Theodora, or Dorothea, or-what was her name in the book?"

The end of it was, that I agreed to try to the extent of a dozen pages or so.

CHAPTER II
I TRY.

I hope no one will think I try to write like my father; for that would be to go against what he always made a great point of, —that nobody whatever should imitate any other person whatever, but in modesty and humility allow the seed that God had sown in her to grow. He said all imitation tended to dwarf and distort the plant, if it even allowed the seed to germinate at all. So, if I do write like him, it will be because I cannot help it.

I will just look how "The Seaboard Parish" ends, and perhaps that will put into my head how I ought to begin. I see my father does mention that I had then been Mrs. Percivale for many years. Not so very many though, —five or six, if I remember rightly, and that is three or four years ago. Yes; I nave been married nine years. I may as well say a word as to how it came about; and, if Percivale doesn't like it, the remedy lies in his pen. I shall be far more thankful to have any thing struck out on suspicion than remain on sufferance.

After our return home from Kilkhaven, my father and mother had a good many talks about me and Percivale, and sometimes they took different sides. I will give a shadow of one of these conversations. I think ladies can write fully as natural talk as gentlemen can, though the bits between mayn't be so good.

Mother. —I am afraid, my dear husband [This was my mother's most solemn mode of addressing my father], "they are too like each other to make a suitable match."

Father. —I am sorry to learn you consider me so very unlike yourself, Ethelwyn. I had hoped there was a very strong resemblance indeed, and that the match had not proved altogether unsuitable.

Mother. —Just think, though, what would have become of me by this time, if you had been half as unbelieving a creature as I was. Indeed, I fear sometimes I am not much better now.

Father. —I think I am, then; and I know you've done me nothing but good with your unbelief. It was just because I was of the same sort precisely that I was able to understand and help you. My circumstances and education and superior years —

Mother. —Now, don't plume yourself on that, Harry; for you know everybody says you look much the younger of the two.

Father. —I had no idea that everybody was so rude. I repeat, that my more years, as well as my severer education, had, no doubt, helped me a little further on before I came to know you; but it was only in virtue of the doubt in me that I was able to understand and appreciate the doubt in you.

Mother. —But then you had at least begun to leave it behind before I knew you, and so had grown able to help me. And Mr. Percivale does not seem, by all I can make out, a bit nearer believing in any thing than poor Wynnie herself.

Father. —At least, he doesn't fancy he believes when he does not, as so many do, and consider themselves superior persons in consequence. I don't know that it would have done you any great harm, Miss Ethelwyn, to have made my acquaintance when I was in the worst of my doubts concerning the truth of things. Allow me to tell you that I was nearer making shipwreck of my faith at a certain period than I ever was before or have been since.

Mother. —What period was that?

Father. —Just the little while when I had lost all hope of ever marrying you, —unbeliever as you counted yourself.

Mother. —You don't mean to say you would have ceased to believe in God, if he hadn't given you your own way?

Father. —No, my dear. I firmly believe, that, had I never married you, I should have come in the end to say, "*Thy will be done*," and to believe that it must be all right, however hard to bear. But, oh, what a terrible thing it would have been, and what a frightful valley of the shadow of death I should have had to go through first!

[I know my mother *said* nothing more just then, but let my father have it all his own way for a while.]

Father. —You see, this Percivale is an honest man. I don't exactly know how he has been brought up; and it is quite possible he may have had such evil instruction in Christianity that he attributes to it doctrines which, if I supposed they actually belonged to it, would make me reject it at once as ungodlike and bad. I have found this the case sometimes. I remember once being astonished to hear a certain noble-minded lady utter some indignant words against what I considered a very weighty doctrine of Christianity; but, listening, I soon found that what she supposed the doctrine to contain was something considered vastly unchristian. This may be the case with Percivale, though I never heard him say a word of the kind. I think his difficulty comes mainly from seeing so much suffering in the world, that he cannot imagine the presence and rule of a good God, and therefore lies with religion rather than with Christianity as yet. I am all but certain, the only thing that will ever make him able to believe in a God at all is meditation on the Christian idea of God,—I mean the idea of God *in* Christ reconciling the world to himself,—not that pagan corruption of Christ in God reconciling him to the world. He will then see that suffering is not either wrath or neglect, but pure-hearted love and tenderness. But we must give him time, wife; as God has borne with us, we must believe that he bears with others, and so learn to wait in hopeful patience until they, too, see as we see.

And as to trusting our Wynnie with Percivale, he seems to be as good as she is. I should for my part have more apprehension in giving her to one who would be called a thoroughly religious man; for not only would the unfitness be greater, but such a man would be more likely to confirm her in doubt, if the phrase be permissible. She wants what some would call homoeopathic treatment. And how should they be able to love one another, if they are not fit to be married to each other? The fitness, seems inherent to the fact.

Mother. —But many a two love each other who would have loved each other a good deal more if they hadn't been married.

Father. —Then it was most desirable they should find out that what they thought a grand affection was not worthy of the name. But I don't think there is much fear of that between those two.

Mother. —I don't, however, see how that man is to do her any good, when *you* have tried to make her happy for so long, and all in vain.

Father. —I don't know that it has been all in vain. But it is quite possible she does not understand me. She fancies, I dare say, that I believe every thing without any trouble, and therefore cannot enter into her difficulties.

Mother. —But you have told her many and many a time that you do.

Father. —Yes: and I hope I was right; but the same things look so different to different people that the same words won't describe them to both; and it may seem to her that I am talking of something not at all like what she is feeling or thinking of. But when she sees the troubled face of Percivale, she knows that he is suffering; and sympathy being thus established between them, the least word of the one will do more to help the other than oceans of argument. Love is the one great instructor. And each will try to be good, and to find out for the sake of the other.

Mother. —I don't like her going from home for the help that lay at her very door.

Father. —You know, my dear, you like the Dean's preaching much better than mine.

Mother. —Now, that is unkind of you!

Father. —And why? [My father went on, taking no heed of my mother's expostulation.] Because, in the first place, it *is* better; because, in the second, it comes in a newer form to you, for you have got used to all my modes; in the third place, it has more force from the fact that it is not subject to the doubt of personal preference; and lastly, because he has a large, comprehensive way of asserting things, which pleases you better than my more dubitant mode of submitting them,—all very sound and good reasons: but still, why be so vexed with Wynnie?

[My mother was now, however, so vexed with my father for saying she preferred the Dean's preaching to his,—although I doubt very much whether it wasn't true,—that she actually walked out of the octagon room where they were, and left him to meditate on his unkindness. Vexed with herself the next moment, she returned as if nothing had happened. I am only telling what my mother told me; for to her grown daughters she is blessedly trusting.]

Mother. —Then if you will have them married, husband, will you say how on earth you expect them to live? He just makes both ends meet now: I suppose he doesn't make things out worse than they are; and that is his own account of the state of his affairs.

Father. —Ah, yes! that *is* —a secondary consideration, my dear. But I have hardly begun to think about it yet. There will be a difficulty there, I can easily imagine; for he is far too independent to let us do any thing for him.

Mother. —And you can't do much, if they would. Really, they oughtn't to marry yet.

Father. —Really, we must leave it to themselves. I don't think you and I need trouble our heads about it. When Percivale considers himself prepared to marry, and Wynnie thinks he is right, you may be sure they see their way to a livelihood without running in hopeless debt to their tradespeople.

Mother. —Oh, yes! I dare say: in some poky little lodging or other!

Father. —For my part, Ethelwyn, I think it better to build castles in the air than huts in the smoke. But seriously, a little poverty and a little struggling would be a most healthy and healing thing for Wynnie. It hasn't done Percivale much good yet, I confess; for he is far too indifferent to his own comforts to mind it: but it will be quite another thing when he has a young wife and perhaps children depending upon him. Then his poverty may begin to hurt him, and so do him some good.

* * * * *

It may seem odd that my father and mother should now be taking such opposite sides to those they took when the question of our engagement was first started, as represented by my father in "The Seaboard Parish." But it will seem inconsistent to none of the family; for it was no unusual thing for them to take opposite sides to those they had previously advocated,—each happening at the time, possibly enlightened by the foregone arguments of the other, to be impressed with the correlate truth, as my father calls the other side of a thing. Besides, engagement and marriage are two different things; and although my mother was the first to recognize the good of our being engaged, when it came to marriage she got frightened, I think. Any how, I have her authority for saying that something like this passed between her and my father on the subject.

Discussion between them differed in this from what I have generally heard between married people, that it was always founded on a tacit understanding of certain unmentioned principles; and no doubt sometimes, if a stranger had been present, he would have been bewildered as to the very meaning of what they were saying. But we girls generally understood: and I fancy we learned more from their differences than from their agreements; for of course it was the differences that brought out their minds most, and chiefly led us to think that we might understand. In our house there were very few of those mysteries which in some houses seem so to abound; and I think the openness with which every question, for whose concealment there was no special reason, was discussed, did more than even any direct instruction we received to develop what thinking faculty might be in us. Nor was there much reason to dread that my small brothers might repeat any thing. I remember hearing Harry say to Charley once, they being then eight and nine years old, "That is mamma's opinion, Charley, not yours; and you know we must not repeat what we hear."

They soon came to be of one mind about Mr. Percivale and me: for indeed the only *real* ground for doubt that had ever existed was, whether I was good enough for him; and for my part, I knew then and know now, that I was and am dreadfully inferior to him. And notwithstanding the tremendous work women are now making about their rights (and, in as far as they are their rights, I hope to goodness they may get them, if it were only that certain who make me feel ashamed of myself because I, too, am a woman, might perhaps then drop out of the public regard),—notwithstanding this, I venture the sweeping assertion, that every woman is not as good as every man, and that it is not necessary to the dignity of a wife that she should assert even equality with her husband. Let him assert her equality or superiority if he will; but, were it a fact, it would be a poor one for her to assert, seeing her glory is in her husband. To seek the chief place is especially unfitting the marriage-feast. Whether I be a Christian or not,—and I have good reason to doubt it every day of my life,—at least I see that in the New Jerusalem one essential of citizenship consists in knowing how to set the good in others over against the evil in ourselves.

There, now, my father might have said that! and no doubt has said so twenty times in my hearing. It is, however, only since I was married that I have come to see it for myself; and, now that I do see it, I have a right to say it.

So we were married at last. My mother believes it was my father's good advice to Percivale concerning the sort of pictures he painted, that brought it about. For certainly soon after we were engaged, he began to have what his artist friends called a run of luck: he sold one picture after another in a very extraordinary and hopeful manner. But Percivale says it was his love for me-indeed he does-which enabled him to see not only much deeper into things, but also to see much better the bloom that hangs about every thing, and so to paint much better pictures than before. He felt, he said, that he had a hold now where before he had only a sight. However this may be, he had got on so well for a while that he wrote at last, that, if I was willing to share his poverty, it would not, he thought, be absolute starvation; and I was, of course, perfectly content. I can't put in words-indeed I dare not, for fear of writing what would be, if not unladylike, at least uncharitable-my contempt for those women who, loving a man, hesitate to run every risk with him. Of course, if they cannot trust him, it is a different thing. I am not going to say any thing about that; for I should be out of my depth,—not in the least understanding how a woman can love a man to whom she cannot look up. I believe there are who can; I see some men married whom I don't believe any woman ever did or ever could respect; all I say is, I don't understand it.

My father and mother made no objection, and were evidently at last quite agreed that it would be the best thing for both of us; and so, I say, we were married.

I ought to just mention, that, before the day arrived, my mother went up to London at Percivale's request, to help him in getting together the few things absolutely needful for the barest commencement of housekeeping. For the rest, it had been arranged that we should furnish by degrees, buying as we saw what we liked, and could afford it. The greater part of modern fashions in furniture, having both been accustomed to the stateliness of a more artistic period, we detested for their ugliness, and chiefly, therefore, we desired to look about us at our leisure.

My mother came back more satisfied with the little house he had taken than I had expected. It was not so easy to get one to suit us; for of course he required a large room to paint in, with a good north light. He had however succeeded better than he had hoped.

"You will find things very different from what you have been used to, Wynnie," said my mother.

"Of course, mamma; I know that," I answered. "I hope I am prepared to meet it. If I don't like it, I shall have no one to blame but myself; and I don't see what right people have to expect what they have been used to."

"There is just this advantage," said my father, "in having been used to nice things, that it ought to be easier to keep from sinking into the sordid, however straitened the new circumstances may be, compared with the old."

On the evening before the wedding, my father took me into the octagon room, and there knelt down with me and my mother, and prayed for me in such a wonderful way that I was perfectly astonished and overcome. I had never known him to do any thing of the kind before. He was not favorable to extempore prayer in public, or even in the family, and indeed had often seemed willing to omit prayers for what I could not always count sufficient reason: he had a horror at their getting to be a matter of course, and a form; for then, he said, they ceased to be worship at all, and were a mere pagan rite, better far left alone. I remember also he said, that those, however good they might be, who urged attention to the forms of religion, such as going to church and saying prayers, were, however innocently, just the prophets of Pharisaism; that what men had to be stirred up to was to lay hold upon God, and then they would not fail to find out what religious forms they ought to cherish. "The spirit first, and then the flesh," he would say. To put the latter before the former was a falsehood, and therefore a frightful danger, being at the root of all declensions in the Church, and making ever-recurring earthquakes and persecutions and repentances and reformations needful. I find what my father used to say coming back so often now that I hear so little of it,—especially as he talks much less, accusing himself of having always talked too much,—and I understand it so much better now, that I shall be always in danger of interrupting my narrative to say something that he said. But when I commence the next chapter, I shall get on faster, I hope. My story is like a vessel I saw once being launched: it would stick on the stocks, instead of sliding away into the expectant waters.

CHAPTER III
MY WEDDING.

I confess the first thing I did when I knew myself the next morning was to have a good cry. To leave the place where I had been born was like forsaking the laws and order of the Nature I knew, for some other Nature it might be, but not known to me as such. How, for instance, could one who has been used to our bright white sun, and our pale modest moon, with our soft twilights, and far, mysterious skies of night, be willing to fall in with the order of things in a planet, such as I have read of somewhere, with three or four suns, one red and another green and another yellow? Only perhaps I've taken it all up wrong, and I do like looking at a landscape for a minute or so through a colored glass; and if it be so, of course it all blends, and all we want is harmony. What I mean is, that I found it a great wrench to leave the dear old place, and of course loved it more than I had ever loved it. But I would get all my crying about that over beforehand. It would be bad enough afterwards to have to part with my father and mother and Connie, and the rest of them. Only it wasn't like leaving them. You can't leave hearts as you do rooms. You can't leave thoughts as you do books. Those you love only come nearer to you when you go away from them. The same rules don't hold with *thinks* and *things*, as my eldest boy distinguished them the other day.

But somehow I couldn't get up and dress. I seemed to have got very fond of my own bed, and the queer old crows, as I had called them from babyhood, on the chintz curtains, and the Chinese paper on the walk with the strangest birds and creeping things on it. It Was a lovely spring morning, and the sun was shining gloriously. I knew that the rain of the last night must be glittering on the grass and the young leaves; and I heard the birds singing as if they knew far more than mere human beings, and believed a great deal more than they knew. Nobody will persuade me that the birds don't mean it; that they sing from any thing else than gladness of heart. And if they don't think about cats and guns, why should they? Even when they fall on the ground, it is not without our Father. How horridly dull and stupid it seems to say that "without your Father" means without *his knowing it*. The Father's mere *knowledge* of a thing-if that could be, which my father says can't —is not the Father. The Father's tenderness and care and love of it all the time, that is the not falling without him. When the cat kills the bird, as I have seen happen so often in our poor little London garden, God yet saves his bird from his cat. There is nothing so bad as it looks to our half-sight, our blinding perceptions. My father used to say we are all walking in a spiritual twilight, and are all more or less affected with twilight blindness, as some people are physically. Percivale, for one, who is as brave as any wife could wish, is far more timid than I am in crossing a London street in the twilight; he can't see what is coming, and fancies he sees what is not coming. But then he has faith in me, and never starts when I am leading him.

Well, the birds were singing, and Dora and the boys were making a great chatter, like a whole colony of sparrows, under my window. Still I felt as if I had twenty questions to settle before I could get up comfortably, and so lay on and on till the breakfast-bell rang: and I was not more than half dressed when my mother came to see why I was late; for I had not been late forever so long before.

She comforted me as nobody but a mother can comfort. Oh, I do hope I shall be to my children what my mother has been to me! It would be such a blessed thing to be a well of water whence they may be sure of drawing comfort. And all she said to me has come true.

Of course, my father gave me away, and Mr. Weir married us.

It had been before agreed that we should have no wedding journey. We all liked the old-fashioned plan of the bride going straight from her father's house to her husband's. The other way seemed a poor invention, just for the sake of something different. So after the wedding, we spent the time as we should have done any other day, wandering about in groups, or sitting and reading, only that we were all more smartly dressed; until it was time for an early dinner, after which we drove to the station, accompanied only by my father and mother. After they left us, or rather we left them, my husband did not speak to me for nearly an hour: I knew why, and was very grateful. He would not show his new face in the midst of my old loves and their sorrows, but would give me time to re-arrange the grouping so as myself to bring him in when all was ready for him. I know that was what he was thinking, or feeling rather; and I understood him perfectly. At last, when I had got things a little tidier inside me, and had got my eyes to stop, I held out my hand to him, and then-knew that I was his wife.

This is all I have got to tell, though I have plenty more to keep, till we get to London. There, instead of my father's nice carriage, we got into a jolting, lumbering, horrid cab, with my five boxes and Percivale's little portmanteau on the top of it, and drove away to Camden Town. It *was* to a part of it near the Regent's Park; and so our letters were always, according to the divisions of the post-office, addressed to Regent's Park, but for all practical intents we were in Camden Town. It was indeed a change from a fine old house in the country; but the street wasn't much uglier than Belgrave Square, or any other of those heaps of uglinesses, called squares, in the West End; and, after what I had been told to expect, I was surprised at the prettiness of the little house, when I stepped out of the cab and looked about me. It was stuck on like a swallow's nest to the end of a great row of commonplace houses, nearly a quarter of a mile in length, but itself was not the work of one of those wretched builders who care no more for beauty in what they build than a scavenger in the heap of mud he scrapes from the street. It had been built by a painter for himself, in the Tudor style; and though Percivale says the idea is not very well carried out, I like it much.

I found it a little dreary when I entered though, —from its emptiness. The only sitting-room at all prepared had just a table and two or three old-fashioned chairs in it; not even a carpet on the floor. The bedroom and dressing-room were also as scantily furnished as they well could be.

"Don't be dismayed, my darling," said my husband.

"Look here," —showing me a bunch of notes, —"we shall go out to-morrow and buy all we want, —as far as this will go, —and then wait for the rest. It will be such a pleasure to buy the things with you, and see them come home, and have you appoint their places. You and Sarah will make the carpets; won't you? And I will put them down, and we shall be like birds building their nest."

"We have only to line it; the nest is built already."

"Well, neither do the birds build the tree. I wonder if they ever sit in their old summer nests in the winter nights."

"I am afraid not," I answered; "but I'm ashamed to say I can't tell."

"It is the only pretty house I know in all London," he went on, "with a studio at the back of it. I have had my eye on it for a long time, but there seemed no sign of a migratory disposition in the bird who had occupied it for three years past. All at once he spread his wings and flew. I count myself very fortunate."

"So do I. But now you must let me see your study," I said. "I hope I may sit in it when you've got nobody there."

"As much as ever you like, my love," he answered. "Only I don't want to make all my women like you, as I've been doing for the last two years. You must get me out of that somehow."

"Easily. I shall be so cross and disagreeable that you will get tired of me, and find no more difficulty in keeping me out of your pictures."

But he got me out of his pictures without that; for when he had me always before him he didn't want to be always producing me.

He led me into the little hall, —made lovely by a cast of an unfinished Madonna of Michael Angelo's let into the wall, —and then to the back of it, where he opened a small cloth-covered door, when there yawned before me, below me, and above me, a great wide lofty room. Down into it led an almost perpendicular stair.

"So you keep a little private precipice here," I said.

"No, my dear," he returned; "you mistake. It is a Jacob's ladder, —or will be in one moment more."

He gave me his hand, and led me down.

"This is quite a banqueting-hall, Percivale!" I cried, looking round me.

"It shall be, the first time I get a thousand pounds for a picture," he returned.

"How grand you talk!" I said, looking up at him with some wonder; for big words rarely came out of his mouth.

"Well," he answered merrily, "I had two hundred and seventy-five for the last."

"That's a long way off a thousand," I returned, with a silly sigh.

"Quite right; and, therefore, this study is a long way off a banqueting-hall."

There was literally nothing inside the seventeen feet cube except one chair, one easel, a horrible thing like a huge doll, with no end of joints, called a lay figure, but Percivale called it his bishop; a number of pictures leaning their faces against the walls in attitudes of grief that their beauty was despised and no man would buy them; a few casts of legs and arms and faces, half a dozen murderous-looking weapons, and a couple of yards square of the most exquisite tapestry I ever saw.

"Do you like being read to when you are at work?" I asked him.

"Sometimes, —at certain kinds of work, but not by any means always," he answered. "Will you shut your eyes for one minute," he went on, "and, whatever I do, not open them till I tell you?"

"You mustn't hurt me, then, or I may open them without being able to help it, you know," I said, closing my eyes tight.

"Hurt you!" he repeated, with a tone I would not put on paper if I could, and the same moment I found myself in his arms, carried like a baby, for Percivale is one of the strongest of men.

It was only for a few yards, however. He laid me down somewhere, and told me to open my eyes.

I could scarcely believe them when I did. I was lying on a couch in a room, —small, indeed, but beyond exception the loveliest I had ever seen. At first I was only aware of an exquisite harmony of color, and could not have told of what it was composed. The place was lighted by a soft lamp that hung in the middle; and when my eyes went up to see where it was fastened, I found the ceiling marvellous in deep blue, with a suspicion of green, just like some of the shades of a peacock's feathers, with a multitude of gold and red stars upon it. What the walls were I could not for some time tell, they were so covered with pictures and sketches; against one was a lovely little set of book-shelves filled with books, and on a little carved table stood a vase of white hot-house flowers, with one red camellia. One picture had a curtain of green silk before it, and by its side hung the wounded knight whom his friends were carrying home to die.

"O my Percivale!" I cried, and could say no more.

"Do you like it?" he asked quietly, but with shining eyes.

"Like it?" I repeated. "Shall I like Paradise when I get there? But what a lot of money it must have cost you!"

"Not much," he answered; "not more than thirty pounds or so. Every spot of paint there is from my own brush."

"O Percivale!"

I must make a conversation of it to tell it at all; but what I really did say I know no more than the man in the moon.

"The carpet was the only expensive thing. That must be as thick as I could get it; for the floor is of stone, and must not come near your pretty feet. Guess what the place was before."

"I should say, the flower of a prickly-pear cactus, full of sunlight from behind, which a fairy took the fancy to swell into a room."

"It was a shed, in which the sculptor who occupied the place before me used to keep his wet clay and blocks of marble."

"Seeing is hardly believing," I said. "Is it to be my room? I know you mean it for my room, where I can ask you to come when I please, and where I can hide when any one comes you don't want me to see."

"That is just what I meant it for, my Ethelwyn,—and to let you know what I *would* do for you if I could."

"I hate the place, Percivale," I said. "What right has it to come poking in between you and me, telling me what I know and have known-for, well, I won't say how long-far better than even you can tell me?"

He looked a little troubled.

"Ah, my dear!" I said, "let my foolish words breathe and die."

I wonder sometimes to think how seldom I am in that room now. But there it is; and somehow I seem to know it all the time I am busy elsewhere.

He made me shut my eyes again, and carried me into the study.

"Now," he said, "find your way to your own room."

I looked about me, but could see no sign of door. He took up a tall stretcher with a canvas on it, and revealed the door, at the same time showing a likeness of myself,—at the top of the Jacob's ladder, as he called it, with me foot on the first step, and the other half way to the second. The light came from the window on my left, which he had turned into a western window, in order to get certain effects from a supposed sunset. I was represented in a white dress, tinged with the rose of the west; and he had managed, attributing the phenomenon to the inequalities of the glass in the window, to suggest one rosy wing behind me, with just the shoulder-roof of another visible.

"There!" he said. "It is not finished yet, but that is how I saw you one evening as I was sitting here all alone in the twilight."

"But you didn't really see me like that!" I said.

"I hardly know," he answered. "I had been forgetting every thing else in dreaming about you, and-how it was I cannot tell, but either in the body or out of the body there I saw you, standing just so at the top of the stair, smiling to me as much as to say, 'Have patience. My foot is on the first step. I'm coming.' I turned at once to my easel, and before the twilight was gone had sketched the vision. To-morrow, you must sit to me for an hour or so; for I will do nothing else till I have finished it, and sent it off to your father and mother."

I may just add that I hear it is considered a very fine painting. It hangs in the great dining-room at home. I wish I were as good as he has made it look.

The next morning, after I had given him the sitting he wanted, we set out on our furniture hunt; when, having keen enough eyes, I caught sight of this and of that and of twenty different things in the brokers' shops. We did not agree about the merits of everything by which one or the other was attracted; but an objection by the one always turned the other, a little at least, and we bought nothing we were not agreed about. Yet that evening the hall was piled with things sent home to line our nest. Percivale, as I have said, had saved up some money for the purpose, and I had a hundred pounds my father had given me before we started, which, never having had more than ten of my own at a time, I was eager enough to spend. So we found plenty to do for the fortnight during which time my mother had promised to say nothing to her friends in London of our arrival. Percivale also keeping out of the way of his friends, everybody thought we were on the Continent, or somewhere else, and left us to ourselves. And as he had sent in his pictures to the Academy, he was able to take a rest, which rest consisted in working hard at all sorts of upholstery, not to mention painters' and carpenters' work; so that we soon got the little house made into a very warm and very pretty nest. I may mention that Percivale was particularly pleased with a cabinet I bought for him on the sly, to stand in his study, and hold his paints and brushes and sketches; for there were all sorts of drawers in it, and some that it took us a good deal of trouble to find out, though he was clever enough to suspect them from the first, when I hadn't a thought of such a thing; and I have often fancied since that that cabinet was just like himself, for I have been going on finding out things in him that I had no idea were there when I married him. I had no idea that he was a poet, for instance. I wonder to this day why he never showed me any of his verses before we were married. He writes better poetry than my father,—at least my father says so. Indeed, I soon came to feel very ignorant and stupid beside him; he could tell me so many things, and especially in art (for he had thought about all kinds of it), making me understand that there is no end to it, any more than to the Nature which sets it going, and that the more we see into Nature, and try to represent it, the more ignorant and helpless we find ourselves, until at length I began to wonder whether God might not have made the world so rich and full just to teach his children humility. For a while I felt quite stunned. He very much wanted me to draw; but I thought it was no use trying, and, indeed, had no heart for it. I spoke to my father about it. He said it was indeed of no use, if my object was to be able to think much of myself, for no one could ever succeed in that in the long run; but if my object was to reap the delight of the truth, it was worth while to spend hours and hours on trying to draw a single tree-leaf, or paint the wing of a moth.

CHAPTER IV
JUDY'S VISIT.

The very first morning after the expiry of the fortnight, when I was in the kitchen with Sarah, giving her instructions about a certain dish as if I had made it twenty times, whereas I had only just learned how from a shilling cookery-book, there came a double knock at the door. I guessed who it must be.

"Run, Sarah," I said, "and show Mrs. Morley into the drawing-room."

When I entered, there she was,—Mrs. Morley, *alias* Cousin Judy.

"Well, little cozzie!" she cried, as she kissed me three or four times, "I'm glad to see you gone the way of womankind,—wooed and married and a'! Fate, child! inscrutable fate!" and she kissed me again.

She always calls me little coz, though I am a head taller than herself. She is as good as ever, quite as brusque, and at the first word apparently more overbearing. But she is as ready to listen to reason as ever was woman of my acquaintance; and I think the form of her speech is but a somewhat distorted reflex of her perfect honesty. After a little trifling talk, which is sure to come first when people are more than ordinarily glad to meet, I asked after her children. I forget how many there were of them, but they were then pretty far into the plural number.

"Growing like ill weeds," she said; "as anxious as ever their grandfathers and mothers were to get their heads up and do mischief. For my part I wish I was Jove,—to start them full grown at once. Or why shouldn't they be made like Eve out of their father's ribs? It would be a great comfort to their mother."

My father had always been much pleased with the results of Judy's training, as contrasted with those of his sister's. The little ones of my aunt Martha's family were always wanting something, and always looking care-worn like their mother, while she was always reading them lectures on their duty, and never making them mind what she said. She would represent the self-same thing to them over and over, until not merely all force, but all sense as well, seemed to have forsaken it. Her notion of duty was to tell them yet again the duty which they had been told at least a thousand times already, without the slightest result. They were dull children, wearisome and uninteresting. On the other hand, the little Morleys were full of life and eagerness. The fault in them was that they wouldn't take petting; and what's the good of a child that won't be petted? They lacked that something which makes a woman feel motherly.

"When did you arrive, cozzie?" she asked.

"A fortnight ago yesterday."

"Ah, you sly thing! What have you been doing with yourself all the time?"

"Furnishing."

"What! you came into an empty house?"

"Not quite that, but nearly."

"It is very odd I should never have seen your husband. We have crossed each other twenty times."

"Not so *very* odd, seeing he has been my husband only a fortnight."

"What is he like?"

"Like nothing but himself."

"Is he tall?"

"Yes."

"Is he stout?"

"No."

"An Adonis?"

"No."

"A Hercules?"

"No."

"Very clever, I believe."

"Not at all."

For my father had taught me to look down on that word.

"Why did you marry him then?"

"I didn't. He married me."

"What did you marry him for then?"

"For love."

"What did you love him for?"

"Because he was a philosopher."

"That's the oddest reason I ever heard for marrying a man."

"I said for loving him, Judy."

Her bright eyes were twinkling with fun.

"Come, cozzie," she said, "give me a proper reason for falling in love with this husband of yours."

"Well, I'll tell you, then," I said; "only you mustn't tell any other body; he's got such a big shaggy head, just like a lion's."

"And such a huge big foot,—just like a bear's?"

"Yes, and such great huge hands! Why, the two of them go quite round my waist! And such big eyes, that they look right through me; and such a big heart, that if he saw me doing any thing wrong, he would kill me, and bury me in it."

"Well, I must say, it is the most extraordinary description of a husband I ever heard. It sounds to me very like an ogre."

"Yes; I admit the description is rather ogrish. But then he's poor, and that makes up for a good deal."

I was in the humor for talking nonsense, and of course expected of all people that Judy would understand my fun.

"How does that make up for any thing?"

"Because if he is a poor man, he isn't a rich man, and therefore not so likely to be a stupid."

"How do you make that out?"

"Because, first of all, the rich man doesn't know what to do with his money, whereas my ogre knows what to do without it. Then the rich man wonders in the morning which waistcoat he shall put on, while my ogre has but one, besides his Sunday one. Then supposing the rich man has slept well, and has done a fair stroke or two of business, he wants nothing but a well-dressed wife, a well-dressed dinner, a few glasses of his favorite wine, and the evening paper, well-diluted with a sleep in his easy chair, to be perfectly satisfied that this world is the best of all possible worlds. Now my ogre, on the other hand"—

I was going on to point out how frightfully different from all this my ogre was,—how he would devour a half-cooked chop, and drink a pint of ale from the public-house, &c., &c., when she interrupted me, saying with an odd expression of voice,—

"You are satirical, cozzie. He's not the worst sort of man you've just described. A woman might be very happy with him. If it weren't such early days, I should doubt if you were as comfortable as you would have people think; for how else should you be so ill-natured?"

It flashed upon me, that, without the least intention, I had been giving a very fair portrait of Mr. Morley. I felt my face grow as red as fire.

"I had no intention of being satirical, Judy," I replied.

"I was only describing a man the very opposite of my husband."

"You don't know mine yet," she said. "You may think"—

She actually broke down and cried. I had never in my life seen her cry, and I was miserable at what I had done. Here was a nice beginning of social relations in my married life!

I knelt down, put my arms round her, and looked up in her face.

"Dear Judy," I said, "you mistake me quite. I never thought of Mr. Morley when I said that. How should I have dared to say such things if I had? He is a most kind, good man, and papa and every one is glad when he comes to see us. I dare say he does like to sleep well,—I know Percivale does; and I don't doubt he likes to get on with what he's at: Percivale does, for he's ever so much better company when he has got on with his picture; and I know he likes to see me well dressed,—at least I haven't tried him with any thing else yet, for I have plenty of clothes for a while; and then for the dinner, which I believe was one of the points in the description I gave, I wish Percivale cared a little more for his, for then it would be easier to do something for him. As to the newspaper, there I fear I must give him up, for I have never yet seen him with one in his hand. He's *so* stupid about some things!"

"Oh, you've found that out! have you? Men *are* stupid; there's no doubt of that. But you don't know my Walter yet."

I looked up, and, behold, Percivale was in the room! His face wore such a curious expression that. I could hardly help laughing. And no wonder: for here was I on my knees, clasping my first visitor, and to all appearance pouring out the woes of my wedded life in her lap,—woes so deep that they drew tears from her as she listened. All this flashed upon me as I started to my feet: but I could give no explanation; I could only make haste to introduce my husband to my cousin Judy.

He behaved, of course, as if he had heard nothing. But I fancy Judy caught a glimpse of the awkward position, for she plunged into the affair at once.

"Here is my cousin, Mr. Percivale, has been abusing my husband to my face, calling him rich and stupid, and I don't know what all. I confess he is so stupid as to be very fond of me, but that's all I know against him."

And her handkerchief went once more to her eyes.

"Dear Judy!" I expostulated, "you know I didn't say one word about him."

"Of course I do, you silly coz!" she cried, and burst out laughing. "But I won't forgive you except you make amends by dining with us to-morrow."

Thus for the time she carried it off; but I believe, and have since had good reason for believing, that she had really mistaken me at first, and been much annoyed.

She and Percivale got on very well. He showed her the portrait he was still working at,—even accepted one or two trifling hints as to the likeness, and they parted the best friends in the world. Glad as I had been to see her, how I longed to see the last of her! The moment she was gone, I threw myself into his arms, and told him how it came about. He laughed heartily.

"I *was* a little puzzled," he said, "to hear you informing a lady I had never seen that I was so very stupid."

"But I wasn't telling a story, either, for you know you are ve-e-e-ry stupid, Percivale. You don't know a leg from a shoulder of mutton, and you can't carve a bit. How ever you can draw as you do, is a marvel to me, when you know nothing about the shapes of things. It was very wrong to say it, even for the sake of covering poor Mrs. Morley's husband; but it was quite true you know."

"Perfectly true, my love," he said, with something else where I've only put commas; "and I mean to remain so, in order that you may always have something to fall back upon when you get yourself into a scrape by forgetting that other people have husbands as well as you."

CHAPTER V
"GOOD SOCIETY."

We had agreed, rather against the inclination of both of us, to dine the next evening with the Morleys. We should have preferred our own society, but we could not refuse.

"They will be talking to me about my pictures," said my husband, "and that is just what I hate. People that know nothing of art, that can't distinguish purple from black, will yet parade their ignorance, and expect me to be pleased."

"Mr. Morley is a well-bred man, Percivale," I said.

"That's the worst of it,—they do it for good manners; I know the kind of people perfectly. I hate to have my pictures praised. It is as bad as talking to one's face about the nose upon it."

I wonder if all ladies keep their husbands waiting. I did that night, I know, and, I am afraid, a good many times after,—not, however, since Percivale told me very seriously that being late for dinner was the only fault of mine the blame of which he would not take on his own shoulders. The fact on this occasion was, that I could not get my hair right. It was the first time I missed what I had been used to, and longed for the deft fingers of my mother's maid to help me. When I told him the cause, he said he would do my hair for me next time, if I would teach him how. But I have managed very well since without either him or a lady's-maid.

When we reached Bolivar Square, we found the company waiting; and, as if for a rebuke to us, the butler announced dinner the moment we entered. I was seated between Mr. Morley and a friend of his who took me down, Mr. Baddeley, a portly gentleman, with an expanse of snowy shirt from which flashed three diamond studs. A huge gold chain reposed upon his front, and on his finger shone a brilliant of great size. Every thing about him seemed to say, "Look how real I am! No shoddy about me!" His hands were plump and white, and looked as if they did not know what dust was. His talk sounded very rich, and yet there was no pretence in it. His wife looked less of a lady than he of a gentleman, for she betrayed conscious importance. I found afterwards that he was the only son of a railway contractor, who had himself handled the spade, but at last died enormously rich. He spoke blandly, but with a certain quiet authority which I disliked.

"Are you fond of the opera, Mrs. Percivale?" he asked me in order to make talk.

"I have never been to the opera," I answered.

"Never been to the opera? Ain't you fond of music?"

"Did you ever know a lady that wasn't?"

"Then you must go to the opera."

"But it is just because I fancy myself fond of music that I don't think I should like the opera."

"You can't hear such music anywhere else."

"But the antics of the singers, pretending to be in such furies of passion, yet modulating every note with the cunning of a carver in ivory, seems to me so preposterous! For surely song springs from a brooding over past feeling,—I do not mean lost feeling; never from present emotion."

"Ah! you would change your mind after having once been. I should strongly advise you to go, if only for once. You ought now, really."

"An artist's wife must do without such expensive amusements,—except her husband's pictures be very popular indeed. I might as well cry for the moon. The cost of a box at the opera for a single night would keep my little household for a fortnight."

"Ah, well! but you should see 'The Barber,'" he said.

"Perhaps if I could hear without seeing, I should like it better," I answered.

He fell silent, busying himself with his fish, and when he spoke again turned to the lady on his left. I went on with my dinner. I knew that our host had heard what I said, for I saw him turn rather hastily to his butler.

Mr. Morley is a man difficult to describe, stiff in the back, and long and loose in the neck, reminding me of those toy-birds that bob head and tail up and down alternately. When he agrees with any thing you say, down comes his head with a rectangular nod; when he does not agree with you, he is so silent and motionless that he leaves you in doubt whether he has heard a word of what you have been saying. His face is hard, and was to me then inscrutable, while what he said always seemed to have little or nothing to do with what he was thinking; and I had not then learned whether he had a heart or not. His features were well formed, but they and his head and face too small for his body. He seldom smiled except when in doubt. He had, I understood, been very successful in business, and always looked full of schemes.

"Have you been to the Academy yet?" he asked.

"No; this is only the first day of it."

"Are your husband's pictures well hung?"

"As high as Haman," I answered; "skied, in fact. That is the right word, I believe."

"I would advise you to avoid slang, my dear cousin,—*professional* slang especially; and to remember that in London there are no professions after six o clock."

"Indeed!" I returned. "As we came along in the carriage,—cabbage, I mean,—I saw no end of shops open."

"I mean in society,—at dinner,—amongst friends, you know."

"My dear Mr. Morley, you have just done asking me about my husband's pictures; and, if you will listen a moment, you will hear that lady next my husband talking to him about Leslie and Turner, and I don't know who more,—all in the trade."

"Hush! hush! I beg," he almost whispered, looking agonized. "That's Mrs. Baddeley. Her husband, next to you, is a great picture-buyer. That's why I asked him to meet you."

"I thought there were no professions in London after six o'clock."

"I am afraid I have not made my meaning quite clear to you."

"Not quite. Yet I think I understand you."

"We'll have a talk about it another time."

"With pleasure."

It irritated me rather that he should talk to me, a married woman, as to a little girl who did not know how to behave herself; but his patronage of my husband displeased me far more, and I was on the point of committing the terrible blunder of asking Mr. Baddeley if he had any poor relations; but I checked myself in time, and prayed to know whether he was a member of Parliament. He answered that he was not in the house at present, and asked in return why I had wished to know. I answered that I wanted a bill brought in for the punishment of fraudulent milkmen; for I couldn't get a decent pennyworth of milk in all Camden Town. He laughed, and said it would be a very desirable measure, only too great an interference with the liberty of the subject. I told him that kind of liberty was just what law in general owed its existence to, and was there on purpose to interfere with; but he did not seem to see it.

The fact is, I was very silly. Proud of being the wife of an artist, I resented the social injustice which I thought gave artists no place but one of sufferance. Proud also of being poor for Percivale's sake, I made a show of my poverty before people whom I supposed, rightly enough in many cases, to be proud of their riches. But I knew nothing of what poverty really meant, and was as yet only playing at being poor; cherishing a foolish, though unacknowledged notion of protecting my husband's poverty with the ægis of my position as the daughter of a man of consequence in his county. I was thus wronging the dignity of my husband's position, and complimenting wealth by making so much of its absence. Poverty or wealth ought to have been in my eyes such a trifle that I never thought of publishing whether I was rich or poor. I ought to have taken my position without wasting a thought on what it might appear in the eyes of those about me, meeting them on the mere level of humanity, and leaving them to settle with themselves how they were to think of me, and where they were to place me. I suspect also, now that I think of it, that I looked down upon my cousin Judy because she had a mere man of business for her husband; forgetting that our Lord had found a collector of conquered taxes,—a man, I presume, with little enough of the artistic about him,—one of the fittest in his nation to bear the message of his redemption to the hearts of his countrymen. It is his loves and his hopes, not his visions and intentions, by which a man is to be judged. My father had taught me all this; but I did not understand it then, nor until years after I had left him.

"Is Mrs. Percivale a lady of fortune?" asked Mr. Baddeley of my cousin Judy when we were gone, for we were the first to leave.

"Certainly not. Why do you ask?" she returned.

"Because, from her talk, I thought she must be," he answered.

Cousin Judy told me this the next day, and I could see she thought I had been bragging of my family. So I recounted all the conversation I had had with him, as nearly as I could recollect, and set down the question to an impertinent irony. But I have since changed my mind: I now judge that he could not believe any poor person would joke about poverty. I never found one of those people who go about begging for charities believe me when I told him the simple truth that I could not afford to subscribe. None but a rich person, they seem to think, would dare such an excuse, and that only in the just expectation that its very assertion must render it incredible.

CHAPTER VI
A REFUGE FROM THE HEAT.

There was a little garden, one side enclosed by the house, another by the studio, and the remaining two by walls, evidently built for the nightly convenience of promenading cats. There was one pear-tree in the grass-plot which occupied the centre, and a few small fruit-trees, which, I may now safely say, never bore any thing, upon the walls. But the last occupant had cared for his garden; and, when I came to the cottage, it was, although you would hardly believe it now that my garden is inside the house, a pretty little spot,—only, if you stop thinking about a garden, it begins at once to go to the bad. Used although I had been to great wide lawns and park and gardens and wilderness, the tiny enclosure soon became to me the type of the boundless universe. The streets roared about me with ugly omnibuses and uglier cabs, fine carriages, huge earth-shaking drays, and, worse far, with the cries of all the tribe, of costermongers,—one especially offensive which soon began to haunt me. I almost hated the man who sent it forth to fill the summer air with disgust. He always But his hollowed hand to his jaw, as if it were loose and he had to hold it in its place, before he uttered his hideous howl, which would send me hurrying up the stairs to bury my head under all the pillows of my bed until, coming back across the wilderness of streets and lanes like the cry of a jackal growing fainter and fainter upon the wind, it should pass, and die away in the distance. Suburban London, I say, was roaring about me, and I was confined to a few square yards of grass and gravel-walk and flower-plot; but above was the depth of the sky, and thence at night the hosts of heaven looked in upon me with the same calm assured glance with which they shone upon southern forests, swarming with great butterflies and creatures that go flaming through the tropic darkness; and there the moon would come, and cast her lovely shadows; and there was room enough to feel alone and to try to pray. And what was strange, the room seemed greater, though the loneliness was gone, when my husband walked up and down in it with me. True, the greater part of the walk seemed to be the turnings, for they always came just when you wanted to go on and on; but, even with the scope of the world for your walk, you must turn and come back some time. At first, when he was smoking his great brown meerschaum, he and I would walk in opposite directions, passing each other in the middle, and so make the space double the size, for he had all the garden to himself, and I had it all to myself; and so I had his garden and mine too. That is how by degrees I got able to bear the smoke of tobacco, for I had never been used to it, and found it a small trial at first; but now I have got actually to like it, and greet a stray whiff from the study like a message from my husband. I fancy I could tell the smoke of that old black and red meerschaum from the smoke of any other pipe in creation.

"You *must* cure him of that bad habit," said cousin Judy to me once.

It made me angry. What right had she to call any thing my husband did a bad habit? and to expect me to agree with her was ten times worse. I am saving my money now to buy him a grand new pipe; and I may just mention here, that once I spent ninepence out of my last shilling to get him a packet of Bristol bird's-eye, for he was on the point of giving up smoking altogether because of-well, because of what will appear by and by.

England is getting dreadfully crowded with mean, ugly houses. If they were those of the poor and struggling, and not of the rich and comfortable, one might be consoled. But rich barbarism, in the shape of ugliness, is again pushing us to the sea. There, however, its "control stops;" and since I lived in London the sea has grown more precious to me than it was even in those lovely days at Kilkhaven,—merely because no one can build upon it. Ocean and sky remain as God made them. He must love space for us, though it be needless for himself; seeing that in all the magnificent notions of creation afforded us by astronomers,—shoal upon shoal of suns, each the centre of complicated and infinitely varied systems,—the spaces between are yet more overwhelming in their vast inconceivableness. I thank God for the room he thus gives us, and hence can endure to see the fair face of his England disfigured by the mud-pies of his children.

There was in the garden a little summer-house, of which I was fond, chiefly because, knowing my passion for the flower, Percivale had surrounded it with a multitude of sweet peas, which, as they grew, he had trained over the trellis-work of its sides. Through them filtered the sweet airs of the summer as through an Æolian harp of unheard harmonies. To sit there in a warm evening, when the moth-airs just woke and gave two or three wafts of their wings and ceased, was like sitting in the midst of a small gospel.

The summer had come on, and the days were very hot,—so hot and changeless, with their unclouded skies and their glowing centre, that they seemed to grow stupid with their own heat. It was as if-like a hen brooding over her chickens-the day, brooding over its coming harvests, grew dull and sleepy, living only in what was to come. Notwithstanding the feelings I have just recorded, I began to long for a wider horizon, whence some wind might come and blow upon me, and wake me up, not merely to live, but to know that I lived.

One afternoon I left my little summer-seat, where I had been sitting at work, and went through the house, and down the precipice, into my husband's study.

"It is so hot," I said, "I will try my little grotto: it may be cooler."

He opened the door for me, and, with his palette on his thumb, and a brush in his hand, sat down for a moment beside me.

"This heat is too much for you, darling," he said.

"I do feel it. I wish I could get from the garden into my nest without going up through the house and down the Jacob's ladder," I said. "It is so hot! I never felt heat like it before."

He sat silent for a while, and then said,—

"I've been thinking I must get you into the country for a few weeks. It would do you no end of good."

"I suppose the wind does blow somewhere," I returned. "But"—

"You don't want to leave me?" he said.

"I don't. And I know with that ugly portrait on hand you can't go with me."

"He happened to be painting the portrait of a plain red-faced lady, in a delicate lace cap,—a very unfit subject for art,—much needing to be made over again first, it seemed to me. Only there she was, with a right to have her portrait painted if she wished it; and there was Percivale, with time on his hands, and room in his pockets, and the faith that whatever God had thought worth making could not be unworthy of representation. Hence he had willingly undertaken a likeness of her, to be finished within a certain time, and was now working at it as conscientiously as if it had been the portrait of a lovely young duchess or peasant-girl. I was only afraid he would make it too like to please the lady herself. His time was now getting short, and he could not leave home before fulfilling his engagement.

"But," he returned, "why shouldn't you go to the Hall for a week or two without me? I will take you down, and come and fetch you."

"I'm so stupid you want to get rid of me!" I said.

I did not in the least believe it, and yet was on the edge of crying, which is not a habit with me.

"You know better than that, my Wynnie," he answered gravely. "You want your mother to comfort you. And there must be some air in the country. So tell Sarah to put up your things, and I'll take you down to-morrow morning. When I get this portrait done, I will come and stay a few days, if they will have me, and then take you home."

The thought of seeing my mother and my father, and the old place, came over me with a rush. I felt all at once as if I had been absent for years instead of weeks. I cried in earnest now,—with delight though,—and there is no shame in that. So it was all arranged; and next afternoon I was lying on a couch in the yellow drawing-room, with my mother seated beside me, and Connie in an easy-chair by the open window, through which came every now and then such a sweet wave of air as bathed me with hope, and seemed to wash all the noises, even the loose-jawed man's hateful howl, from my brain.

Yet, glad as I was to be once more at home, I felt, when Percivale left me the next morning to return by a third-class train to his ugly portrait,—for the lady was to sit to him that same afternoon,—that the idea of home was already leaving Oldcastle Hall, and flitting back to the suburban cottage haunted by the bawling voice of the costermonger.

But I soon felt better: for here there was plenty of shadow, and in the hottest days my father could always tell where any wind would be stirring; for he knew every out and in of the place like his own pockets, as Dora said, who took a little after cousin Judy in her way. It will give a notion of his tenderness if I set down just one tiniest instance of his attention to me. The forenoon was oppressive. I was sitting under a tree, trying to read when he came up to me. There was a wooden gate, with open bars near. He went and set it wide, saying,—

"There, my love! You will fancy yourself cooler if I leave the gate open."

Will my reader laugh at me for mentioning such a trifle? I think not, for it went deep to my heart, and I seemed to know God better for it ever after. A father is a great and marvellous truth, and one you can never get at the depth of, try how you may.

Then my mother! She was, if possible, yet more to me than my father. I could tell her any thing and every thing without fear, while I confess to a little dread of my father still. He is too like my own conscience to allow of my being quite confident with him. But Connie is just as comfortable with him as I am with my mother. If in my childhood I was ever tempted to conceal any thing from her, the very thought of it made me miserable until I had told her. And now she would watch me with her gentle, dove-like eyes, and seemed to know at once, without being told, what was the matter with me. She never asked me what I should like, but went and brought something; and, if she saw that I didn't care for it, wouldn't press me, or offer any thing instead, but chat for a minute or two, carry it away, and return with something else. My heart was like to break at times with the swelling of the love that was in it. My eldest child, my Ethelwyn,—for my husband would have her called the same name as me, only I insisted it should be after my mother and not after me,—has her very eyes, and for years has been trying to mother me over again to the best of her sweet ability.

CHAPTER VII
CONNIE.

It is high time, though, that I dropped writing about myself for a while. I don't find my self so interesting as it used to be.

The worst of some kinds especially of small illnesses is, that they make you think a great deal too much about yourself. Connie's, which was a great and terrible one, never made her do so. She was always forgetting herself in her interest about others. I think I was made more selfish to begin with; and yet I have a hope that a too-much-thinking about yourself may not *always* be pure selfishness. It may be something else wrong in you that makes you uncomfortable, and keeps drawing your eyes towards the aching place. I will hope so till I get rid of the whole business, and then I shall not care much how it came or what it was.

Connie was now a thin, pale, delicate-looking—not handsome, but lovely girl. Her eyes, some people said, were too big for her face; but that seemed to me no more to the discredit of her beauty than it would have been a reproach to say that her soul was too big for her body. She had been early ripened by the hot sun of suffering, and the self-restraint which pain had taught her. Patience had mossed her over and made her warm and soft and sweet. She never looked for attention, but accepted all that was offered with a smile which seemed to say, "It is more than I need, but you are so good I mustn't spoil it." She was not confined to her sofa now, though she needed to lie down often, but could walk about pretty well, only you must give her time. You could always make her merry by saying she walked like an old woman; and it was the only way we could get rid of the sadness of seeing it. We betook ourselves to her to laugh *her* sadness away from us.

Once, as I lay on a couch on the lawn, she came towards me carrying a bunch of grapes from the greenhouse,—a great bunch, each individual grape ready to burst with the sunlight it had bottled up in its swollen purple skin.

"They are too heavy for you, old lady," I cried.

"Yes; I *am* an old lady," she answered. "Think what good use of my time I have made compared with you! I have got ever so far before you: I've nearly forgotten how to walk!"

The tears gathered in my eyes as she left me with the bunch; for how could one help being sad to think of the time when she used to bound like a fawn over the grass, her slender figure borne like a feather on its own slight yet firm muscles, which used to knot so much harder than any of ours. She turned to say something, and, perceiving my emotion, came slowly back.

"Dear Wynnie," she said, "you wouldn't have me back with my old foolishness, would you? Believe me, life is ten times more precious than it was before. I feel and enjoy and love so much more! I don't know how often I thank God for what befell me."

I could only smile an answer, unable to speak, not now from pity, but from shame of my own petulant restlessness and impatient helplessness.

I believe she had a special affection for poor Sprite, the pony which threw her,—special, I mean, since the accident,—regarding him as in some sense the angel which had driven her out of paradise into a better world. If ever he got loose, and Connie was anywhere about, he was sure to find her: he was an omnivorous animal, and she had always something he would eat when his favorite apples were unattainable. More than once she had been roused from her sleep on the lawn by the lips and the breath of Sprite upon her face; but, although one painful sign of her weakness was, that she started at the least noise or sudden discovery of a presence, she never started at the most unexpected intrusion of Sprite, any more than at the voice of my father or mother. Need I say there was one more whose voice or presence never startled her?

The relation between them was lovely to see. Turner was a fine, healthy, broad-shouldered fellow, of bold carriage and frank manners, above the middle height, with rather large features, keen black eyes, and great personal strength. Yet to such a man, poor little wan-faced, big-eyed Connie assumed imperious airs, mostly, but perhaps not entirely, for the fun of it; while he looked only enchanted every time she honored him with a little tyranny.

"There! I'm tired," she would say, holding out her arms like a baby. "Carry me in."

And the great strong man would stoop with a worshipping look in his eyes, and, taking her carefully, would carry her in as lightly and gently and steadily as if she had been but the baby whose manners she had for the moment assumed. This began, of course, when she was unable to walk; but it did not stop then, for she would occasionally tell him to carry her after she was quite capable of crawling at least. They had now been engaged for some months; and before me, as a newly-married woman, they did not mind talking a little.

One day she was lying on a rug on the lawn, with him on the grass beside her, leaning on his elbow, and looking down into her sky-like eyes. She lifted her hand, and stroked his mustache with a forefinger, while he kept as still as a statue, or one who fears to scare the bird that is picking up the crumbs at his feet.

"Poor, poor man!" she said; and from the tone I knew the tears had begun to gather in those eyes.

"Why do you pity me, Connie?" he asked.

"Because you will have such a wretched little creature for a wife some day,—or perhaps never,—which would be best after all."

He answered cheerily.

"If you will kindly allow me my choice, I prefer just *such* a wretched little creature to any one else in the world."

"And why, pray? Give a good reason, and I will forgive your bad taste."

"Because she won't be able to hurt me much when she beats me."

"A better reason, or she will."

"Because I can punish her if she isn't good by taking her up in my arms, and carrying her about until she gives in."

"A better reason, or I shall be naughty directly."

"Because I shall always know where to find her."

"Ah, yes! she must leave *you* to find *her*. But that's a silly reason. If you don't give me a better, I'll get up and walk into the house."

"Because there won't be any waste of me. Will that do?"

"What do you mean?" she asked, with mock imperiousness.

"I mean that I shall be able to lay not only my heart but my brute strength at her feet. I shall be allowed to be her beast of burden, to carry her whither she would; and so with my body her to worship more than most husbands have a chance of worshipping their wives."

"There! take me, take me!" she said, stretching up her arms to him. "How good you are! I don't deserve such a great man one bit. But I *will* love him. Take me directly; for there's Wynnie listening to every word we say to each other, and laughing at us. She can laugh without looking like it."

The fact is, I was crying, and the creature knew it. Turner brought her to me, and held her down for me to kiss; then carried her in to her mother.

I believe the county people round considered our family far gone on the inclined plane of degeneracy. First my mother, the heiress, had married a clergyman of no high family; then they had given their eldest daughter to a poor artist, something of the same standing as-well, I will be rude to no order of humanity, and therefore avoid comparisons; and now it was generally known that Connie was engaged to a country practitioner, a man who made up his own prescriptions. We talked and laughed over certain remarks of the kind that reached us, and compared our two with the gentlemen about us,—in no way to the advantage of any of the latter, you may be sure. It was silly work; but we were only two loving girls, with the best possible reasons for being proud of the men who had honored us with their love.

CHAPTER VIII
CONNIE'S BABY.

It is time I told my readers something about the little Theodora. She was now nearly four years old I think,—a dark-skinned, lithe-limbed, wild little creature, very pretty,—at least most people said so, while others insisted that she had a common look. I admit she was not like a lady's child-only one has seen ladies' children look common enough; neither did she look like the child of working people-though amongst such, again, one sees sometimes a child the oldest family in England might be proud of. The fact is, she had a certain tinge of the savage about her, specially manifest in a certain furtive look of her black eyes, with which she seemed now and then to be measuring you, and her prospects in relation to you. I have seen the child of cultivated parents sit and stare at a stranger from her stool in the most persistent manner, never withdrawing her eyes, as if she would pierce to his soul, and understand by very force of insight whether he was or was not one to be honored with her confidence; and I have often seen the side-long glance of sly merriment, or loving shyness, or small coquetry; but I have never, in any other child, seen *that* look of self-protective speculation; and it used to make me uneasy, for of course, like every one else in the house, I loved the child. She was a wayward, often unmanageable creature, but affectionate,—sometimes after an insane, or, at least, very ape-like fashion. Every now and then she would take an unaccountable preference for some one of the family or household, at one time for the old housekeeper, at another for the stable-boy, at another for one of us; in which fits of partiality she would always turn a blind and deaf side upon every one else, actually seeming to imagine she showed the strength of her love to the one by the paraded exclusion of the others. I cannot tell how much of this was natural to her, and how much the result of the foolish and injurious jealousy of the servants. I say *servants*, because I know such an influencing was all but impossible in the family itself. If my father heard any one utter such a phrase as "Don't you love me best?"—or, "better than" such a one? or, "Ain't I your favorite?"—well, you all know my father, and know him really, for he never wrote a word he did not believe-but you would have been astonished, I venture to think, and perhaps at first bewildered as well, by the look of indignation flashed from his eyes. He was not the gentle, all-excusing man some readers, I know, fancy him from his writings. He was gentle even to tenderness when he had time to think a moment, and in any quiet judgment he always took as much the side of the offender as was possible with any likelihood of justice; but in the first moments of contact with what he thought bad in principle, and that in the smallest trifle, he would speak words that made even those who were not included in the condemnation tremble with sympathetic fear. "There, Harry, you take it-quick, or Charley will have it," said the nurse one day, little thinking who overheard her. "Woman!" cried a voice of wrath from the corridor, "do you know what you are doing? Would you make him twofold more the child of hell than yourself?" An hour after, she was sent for to the study; and when she came out her eyes were very red. My father was unusually silent at dinner; and, after the younger ones were gone, he turned to my mother, and said, "Ethel, I spoke the truth. All *that* is of the Devil,—horribly bad; and yet I am more to blame in my condemnation of them than she for the words themselves. The thought of so polluting the mind of a child makes me fierce, and the wrath of man worketh not the righteousness of God. The old Adam is only too glad to get a word in, if even in behalf of his supplanting successor." Then he rose, and, taking my mother by the arm, walked away with her. I confess I honored him for his self-condemnation the most. I must add that the offending nurse had been ten years in the family, and ought to have known better.

But to return to Theodora. She was subject to attacks of the most furious passion, especially when any thing occurred to thwart the indulgence of the ephemeral partiality I have just described. Then, wherever she was, she would throw herself down at once,—on the floor, on the walk or lawn, or, as happened on one occasion, in the water,—and kick and scream. At such times she cared nothing even for my father, of whom generally she stood in considerable awe,—a feeling he rather encouraged. "She has plenty of people about her to represent the gospel," he said once. "I will keep the department of the law, without which she will never appreciate the gospel. My part will, I trust, vanish in due time, and the law turn out to have been, after all, only the imperfect gospel, just as the leaf is the imperfect flower. But the gospel is no gospel till it gets into the heart, and it sometimes wants a torpedo to blow the gates of that open." For no torpedo or Krupp gun, however, did Theodora care at such times; and, after repeated experience of the inefficacy of coaxing, my father gave orders, that, when a fit occurred, every one, without exception, should not merely leave her alone, but go out of sight, and if possible out of hearing,—at least out of her hearing-that she might know she had driven her friends far from her, and be brought to a sense of loneliness and need. I am pretty sure that if she had been one of us, that is, one of his own, he would have taken sharper measures with her; but he said we must never attempt to treat other people's children as our own, for they are not our own. We did not love them enough, he said, to make severity safe either for them or for us.

The plan worked so far well, that after a time, varied in length according to causes inscrutable, she would always re-appear smiling; but, as to any conscience of wrong, she seemed to have no more than Nature herself, who looks out with *her* smiling face after hours of thunder, lightning, and rain; and, although this treatment brought her out of them sooner, the fits themselves came quite as frequently as before.

But she had another habit, more alarming, and more troublesome as well: she would not unfrequently vanish, and have to be long sought, for in such case she never reappeared of herself. What made it so alarming was that there were dangerous places about our house; but she would generally be found seated, perfectly quiet, in some out-of-the-way nook where she had never been before, playing, not with any of her toys, but with something she had picked up and appropriated, finding in it some shadowy amusement which no one understood but herself.

She was very fond of bright colors, especially in dress; and, if she found a brilliant or gorgeous fragment of any substance, would be sure to hide it away in some hole or corner, perhaps known only to herself. Her love of approbation was strong, and her affection demonstrative; but she had not yet learned to speak the truth. In a word, she must, we thought, have come of wild parentage, so many of her ways were like those of a forest animal.

In our design of training her for a maid to Connie, we seemed already likely enough to be frustrated; at all events, there was nothing to encourage the attempt, seeing she had some sort of aversion to Connie, amounting almost to dread. We could rarely persuade her to go near her. Perhaps it was a dislike to her helplessness,—some vague impression that her lying all day on the sofa indicated an unnatural condition of being, with which she could have no sympathy. Those of us who had the highest spirits, the greatest exuberance of animal life, were evidently those whose society was most attractive to her. Connie tried all she could to conquer her dislike, and entice the wayward thing to her heart; but nothing would do. Sometimes she would seem to soften for a moment; but all at once, with a wriggle and a backward spasm in the arms of the person who carried her, she would manifest such a fresh access of repulsion, that, for fear of an outburst of fierce and objurgatory wailing which might upset poor Connie altogether, she would be borne off hurriedly,—sometimes, I confess, rather ungently as well. I have seen Connie cry because of the child's treatment of her.

You could not interest her so much in any story, but that if the buzzing of a fly, the flutter of a bird, reached eye or ear, away she would dart on the instant, leaving the discomfited narrator in lonely disgrace. External nature, and almost nothing else, had free access to her mind: at the suddenest sight or sound, she was alive on the instant. She was a most amusing and sometimes almost bewitching little companion; but the delight in her would be not unfrequently quenched by some altogether unforeseen outbreak of heartless petulance or turbulent rebellion. Indeed, her resistance to authority grew as she grew older, and occasioned my father and mother, and indeed all of us, no little anxiety. Even Charley and Harry would stand with open mouths, contemplating aghast the unheard-of atrocity of resistance to the will of the unquestioned authorities. It was what they could not understand, being to them an impossibility. Such resistance was almost always accompanied by storm and tempest; and the treatment which carried away the latter, generally carried away the former with it; after the passion had come and gone, she would obey. Had it been otherwise, —had she been sullen and obstinate as well, —I do not know what would have come of it, or how we could have got on at all. Miss Bowdler, I am afraid, would have had a very satisfactory crow over papa. I have seen him sit for minutes in silent contemplation of the little puzzle, trying, no doubt, to fit her into his theories, or, as my mother said, to find her a three-legged stool and a corner somewhere in the kingdom of heaven; and we were certain something or other would come out of that pondering, though whether the same night or a twelvemonth after, no one could tell. I believe the main result of his thinking was, that he did less and less with her.

"Why do you take so little notice of the child?" my mother said to him one evening. "It is all your doing that she is here, you know. You mustn't cast her off now."

"Cast her off!" exclaimed my father: "what *do* you mean, Ethel?"

"You never speak to her now."

"Oh, yes I do, sometimes!"

"Why only sometimes?"

"Because —I believe because I am a little afraid of her. I don't know how to attack the small enemy. She seems to be bomb-proof, and generally impregnable."

"But you mustn't therefore make *her* afraid of *you*."

"I don't know that. I suspect it is my only chance with her. She wants a little of Mount Sinai, in order that she may know where the manna comes from. But indeed I am laying myself out only to catch the little soul. I am but watching and pondering how to reach her. I am biding my time to come in with my small stone for the building up of this temple of the Holy Ghost."

At that very moment-in the last fold of the twilight, with the moon rising above the wooded brow of Gorman Slope-the nurse came through the darkening air, her figure hardly distinguishable from the dusk, saying, —

"Please, ma'am, have you seen Miss Theodora?"

"I don't want you to call her *Miss*," said my father.

"I beg your pardon, sir," said the nurse; "I forgot."

"I have not seen her for an hour or more," said my mother.

"I declare," said my father, "I'll get a retriever pup, and train him to find Theodora. He will be capable in a few months, and she will be foolish for years."

Upon this occasion the truant was found in the apple-loft, sitting in a corner upon a heap of straw, quite in the dark. She was discovered only by the munching of her little teeth; for she had found some wizened apples, and was busy devouring them. But my father actually did what he had said: a favorite spaniel had pups a few days after, and he took one of them in hand. In an incredibly short space of time, the long-drawn nose of Wagtail, as the children had named him, in which, doubtless, was gathered the experience of many thoughtful generations, had learned to track Theodora to whatever retreat she might have chosen; and very amusing it was to watch the course of the proceedings. Some one would come running to my father with the news that Theo was in hiding. Then my father would give a peculiar whistle, and Wagtail, who (I must say *who*) very seldom failed to respond, would come bounding to his side. It was necessary that my father should *lay him on* (is that the phrase?); for he would heed no directions from any one else. It was not necessary to follow him, however, which would have involved a tortuous and fatiguing pursuit; but in a little while a joyous barking would be heard, always kept up until the ready pursuers were guided by the sound to the place. There Theo was certain to be found, hugging the animal, without the least notion of the traitorous character of his blandishments: it was long before she began to discover that there was danger in that dog's nose. Thus Wagtail became a very important member of the family, —a bond of union, in fact, between its parts. Theo's disappearances, however, became less and less frequent, —not that she made fewer attempts to abscond, but that, every one knowing how likely she was to vanish, whoever she was with had come to feel the necessity of keeping both eyes upon her.

CHAPTER IX
THE FOUNDLING RE-FOUND.

One evening, during this my first visit to my home, we had gone to take tea with the widow of an old servant, who lived in a cottage on the outskirts of the home farm,—Connie and I in the pony carriage, and my father and mother on foot. It was quite dark when we returned, for the moon was late. Connie and I got home first, though we had a good round to make, and the path across the fields was but a third of the distance; for my father and mother were lovers, and sure to be late when left out by themselves. When we arrived, there was no one to take the pony; and when I rung the bell, no one answered. I could not leave Connie in the carriage to go and look; so we waited and waited till we were getting very tired, and glad indeed we were to hear the voices of my father and mother as they came through the shrubbery. My mother went to the rear to make inquiry, and came back with the news that Theo was missing, and that they had been searching for her in vain for nearly an hour. My father instantly called Wagtail, and sent him after her. We then got Connie in, and laid her on the sofa, where I kept her company while the rest went in different directions, listening from what quarter would come the welcome voice of the dog. This was so long delayed, however, that my father began to get alarmed. At last he whistled very loud; and in a little while Wagtail came creeping to his feet, with his tail between his legs,—no wag left in it,—clearly ashamed of himself. My father was now thoroughly frightened, and began questioning the household as to the latest knowledge of the child. It then occurred to one of the servants to mention that a strange-looking woman had been seen about the place in the morning,—a tall, dark woman, with a gypsy look. She had come begging; but my father's orders were so strict concerning such cases, that nothing had been given her, and she had gone away in anger. As soon as he heard this, my father ordered his horse, and told two of the men to get ready to accompany him. In the mean time, he came to us in the little drawing-room, trying to look calm, but evidently in much perturbation. He said he had little doubt the woman had taken her.

"Could it be her mother?" said my mother.

"Who can tell?" returned my father. "It is the less likely that the deed seems to have been prompted by revenge."

"If she be a gypsy's child,"—said my mother.

"The gypsies," interrupted my father, "have always been more given to taking other people's children than forsaking their own. But one of them might have had reason for being ashamed of her child, and, dreading the severity of her family, might have abandoned it, with the intention of repossessing herself of it, and passing it off as the child of gentlefolks she had picked up. I don't know their habits and ways sufficiently; but, from what I have heard, that seems possible. However, it is not so easy as it might have been once to succeed in such an attempt. If we should fail in finding her to-night, the police all over the country can be apprised of the fact in a few hours, and the thief can hardly escape."

"But if she *should* be the mother?" suggested my mother.

"She will have to *prove* that."

"And then?"

"What then?" returned my father, and began pacing up and down the room, stopping now and then to listen for the horses' hoofs.

"Would you give her up?" persisted my mother.

Still my father made no reply. He was evidently much agitated,—more, I fancied, by my mother's question than by the present trouble. He left the room, and presently his whistle for Wagtail pierced the still air. A moment more, and we heard them all ride out of the paved yard. I had never known him leave my mother without an answer before.

We who were left behind were in evil plight. There was not a dry eye amongst the women, I am certain; while Harry was in floods of tears, and Charley was howling. We could not send them to bed in such a state; so we kept them with us in the drawing-room, where they soon fell

497

fast asleep, one in an easy-chair, the other on a sheepskin mat. Connie lay quite still, and my mother talked so sweetly and gently that she soon made me quiet too. But I was haunted with the idea somehow,—I think I must have been wandering a little, for I was not well,—that it was a child of my own that was lost out in the dark night, and that I could not anyhow reach her. I cannot explain the odd kind of feeling it was,—as if a dream had wandered out of the region of sleep, and half-possessed my waking brain. Every now and then my mother's voice would bring me back to my senses, and I would understand it all perfectly; but in a few moments I would be involved once more in a mazy search after my child. Perhaps, however, as it was by that time late, sleep had, if such a thing be possible, invaded a part of my brain, leaving another part able to receive the impressions of the external about me. I can recall some of the things my mother said,—one in particular.

"It is more absurd," she said, "to trust God by halves, than it is not to believe in him at all. Your papa taught me that before one of you was born."

When my mother said any thing in the way of teaching us, which was not often, she would generally add, "Your papa taught me that," as if she would take refuge from the assumption of teaching even her own girls. But we set a good deal of such assertion down to her modesty, and the evidently inextricable blending of the thought of my father with every movement of her mental life.

"I remember quite well," she went on, "how he made that truth dawn upon me one night as we sat together beside the old mill. Ah, you don't remember the old mill! it was pulled down while Wynnie was a mere baby."

"No, mamma; I remember it perfectly," I said.

"Do you really?—Well, we were sitting beside the mill one Sunday evening after service; for we always had a walk before going home from church. You would hardly think it now; but after preaching he was then always depressed, and the more eloquently he had spoken, the more he felt as if he had made an utter failure. At first I thought it came only from fatigue, and wanted him to go home and rest; but he would say he liked Nature to come before supper, for Nature restored him by telling him that it was not of the slightest consequence if he had failed, whereas his supper only made him feel that he would do better next time. Well, that night, you will easily believe he startled me when he said, after sitting for some time silent, 'Ethel, if that yellow-hammer were to drop down dead now, and God not care, God would not be God any longer.' Doubtless I showed myself something between puzzled and shocked, for he proceeded with some haste to explain to me how what he had said was true. 'Whatever belongs to God is essential to God,' he said. 'He is one pure, clean essence of being, to use our poor words to describe the indescribable. Nothing hangs about him that does not belong to him,—that he could part with and be nothing the worse. Still less is there any thing he could part with and be the worse. Whatever belongs to him is of his own kind, is part of himself, so to speak. Therefore there is nothing indifferent to his character to be found in him; and therefore when our Lord says not a sparrow falls to the ground without our Father, that, being a fact with regard to God, must be an essential fact,—one, namely, without which he could be no God.' I understood him, I thought; but many a time since, when a fresh light has broken in upon me, I have thought I understood him then only for the first time. I told him so once; and he said he thought that would be the way forever with all truth,—we should never get to the bottom of any truth, because it was a vital portion of the all of truth, which is God."

I had never heard so much philosophy from my mother before. I believe she was led into it by her fear of the effect our anxiety about the child might have upon us: with what had quieted her heart in the old time she sought now to quiet ours, helping us to trust in the great love that never ceases to watch. And she did make us quiet. But the time glided so slowly past that it seemed immovable.

When twelve struck, we heard in the stillness every clock in the house, and it seemed as if they would never have done. My mother left the room, and came back with three shawls, with which, having first laid Harry on the rug, she covered the boys and Dora, who also was by this time fast asleep, curled up at Connie's feet.

Still the time went on; and there was no sound of horses or any thing to break the silence, except the faint murmur which now and then the trees will make in the quietest night, as if they were dreaming, and talked in their sleep; for the motion does not seem to pass beyond them, but to swell up and die again in the heart of them. This and the occasional cry of an owl was all that broke the silent flow of the undivided moments,—glacier-like flowing none can tell how. We seldom spoke, and at length the house within seemed possessed by the silence from without; but we were all ear,—one hungry ear, whose famine was silence,—listening intently.

We were not so far from the high road, but that on a night like this the penetrating sound of a horse's hoofs might reach us. Hence, when my mother, who was keener of hearing than any of her daughters, at length started up, saying, "I hear them! They're coming!" the doubt remained whether it might not be the sound of some night-traveller hurrying along that high road that she had heard. But when *we* also heard the sound of horses, we knew they must belong to our company; for, except the riders were within the gates, their noises could not have come nearer to the house. My mother hurried down to the hall. I would have staid with Connie; but she begged me to go too, and come back as soon as I knew the result; so I followed my mother. As I descended the stairs, notwithstanding my anxiety, I could not help seeing what a picture lay before me, for I had learned already to regard things from the picturesque point of view,—the dim light of the low-burning lamp on the forward-bent heads of the listening, anxious group of women, my mother at the open door with the housekeeper and her maid, and the men-servants visible through the door in the moonlight beyond.

The first news that reached me was my father's shout the moment he rounded the sweep that brought him in sight of the house.

"All right! Here she is!" he cried.

And, ere I could reach the stair to run up to Connie, Wagtail was jumping upon me and barking furiously. He rushed up before me with the scramble of twenty feet, licked Connie's face all over in spite of her efforts at self-defence, then rushed at Dora and the boys one after the other, and woke them all up. He was satisfied enough with himself now; his tail was doing the wagging of forty; there was no tucking of it away now,—no drooping of the head in mute confession of conscious worthlessness; he was a dog self-satisfied because his master was well pleased with him.

But here I am talking about the dog, and forgetting what was going on below.

My father cantered up to the door, followed by the two men. My mother hurried to meet him, and then only saw the little lost lamb asleep in his bosom. He gave her up, and my mother ran in with her; while he dismounted, and walked merrily but wearily up the stair after her. The first thing he did was to quiet the dog; the next to sit down beside Connie; the third to say, "Thank God!" and the next, "God bless Wagtail!" My mother was already undressing the little darling, and her maid was gone to fetch her night things. Tumbled hither and thither, she did not wake, but was carried off stone-sleeping to her crib.

Then my father,—for whom some supper, of which he was in great need, had been brought,—as soon as he had had a glass of wine and a mouthful or two of cold chicken, began to tell us the whole story.

CHAPTER X
WAGTAIL COMES TO HONOR.

As they rode out of the gate, one of the men, a trustworthy man, who cared for his horses like his children, and knew all their individualities as few men know those of their children, rode up along side of my father, and told him that there was an encampment of gypsies on the moor about five miles away, just over Gorman Slope, remarking, that if the woman had taken the child, and belonged to them, she would certainly carry her thither. My father thought, in the absence of other indication, they ought to follow the suggestion, and told Burton to guide them to the place as rapidly as possible. After half an hour's sharp riding, they came in view of the camp,—or rather of a rising ground behind which it lay in the hollow. The other servant was an old man, who had been whipper-in to a baronet in the next county, and knew as much of the ways of wild animals as Burton did of those of his horses; it was his turn now to address my father, who had halted for a moment to think what ought to be done next.

"She can't well have got here before us, sir, with that child to carry. But it's wonderful what the likes of her can do. I think I had better have a peep over the brow first. She may be there already, or she may not; but, if we find out, we shall know better what to do."

"I'll go with you," said my father.

"No, sir; excuse me; that won't do. You can't creep like a sarpent. I can. They'll never know I'm a stalking of them. No more you couldn't show fight if need was, you know, sir."

"How did you find that out, Sim?" asked my father, a little amused, notwithstanding the weight at his heart.

"Why, sir, they do say a clergyman mustn't show fight."

"Who told you that, Sim?" he persisted.

"Well, I can't say, sir. Only it wouldn't be respectable; would it, sir?"

"There's nothing respectable but what's right, Sim; and what's right always *is* respectable, though it mayn't *look* so one bit."

"Suppose you was to get a black eye, sir?"

"Did you ever hear of the martyrs, Sim?"

"Yes, sir. I've heerd you talk on 'em in the pulpit, sir."

"Well, they didn't get black eyes only,—they got black all over, you know,—burnt black; and what for, do you think, now?"

"Don't know, sir, except it was for doing right."

"That's just it. Was it any disgrace to them?"

"No, sure, sir."

"Well, if I were to get a black eye for the sake of the child, would that be any disgrace to me, Sim?"

"None that I knows on, sir. Only it'd *look* bad."

"Yes, no doubt. People might think I had got into a row at the Griffin. And yet I shouldn't be ashamed of it. I should count my black eye the more respectable of the two. I should also regard the evil judgment much as another black eye, and wait till they both came round again. Lead on, Sim."

They left their horses with Burton, and went toward the camp. But when they reached the slope behind which it lay, much to Sim's discomfiture, my father, instead of lying down at the foot of it, as he expected, and creeping up the side of it, after the doom of the serpent, walked right up over the brow, and straight into the camp, followed by Wagtail. There was nothing going on,—neither tinkering nor cooking; all seemed asleep; but presently out of two or three of the tents, the dingy squalor of which no moonshine could silver over, came three or four men, half undressed, who demanded of my father, in no gentle tones, what he wanted there.

"I'll tell you all about it," he answered. "I'm the parson of this parish, and therefore you're my own people, you see."

"We don't go to *your* church, parson," said one of them.

"I don't care; you're my own people, for all that, and I want your help."

"Well, what's the matter? Who's cow's dead?" said the same man.

"This evening," returned my father, "one of my children is missing; and a woman who might be one of your clan, —mind, I say *might be*; I don't know, and I mean no offence, —but such a woman was seen about the place. All I want is the child, and if I don't find her, I shall have to raise the county. I should be very sorry to disturb you; but I am afraid, in that case, whether the woman be one of you or not, the place will be too hot for you. I'm no enemy to honest gypsies; but you know there is a set of tramps that call themselves gypsies, who are nothing of the sort, —only thieves. Tell me what I had better do to find my child. You know all about such things."

The men turned to each other, and began talking in undertones, and in a language of which what my father heard he could not understand. At length the spokesman of the party addressed him again.

"We'll give you our word, sir, if that will satisfy you," he said, more respectfully than he had spoken before, "to send the child home directly if any one should bring her to our camp. That's all we can say."

My father saw that his best chance lay in accepting the offer.

"Thank you," he said. "Perhaps I may have an opportunity of serving you some day."

They in their turn thanked him politely enough, and my father and Sim left the camp.

Upon this side the moor was skirted by a plantation which had been gradually creeping up the hill from the more sheltered hollow. It was here bordered by a deep trench, the bottom of which was full of young firs. Through the plantation there was a succession of green rides, by which the outskirts of my father's property could be reached. But, the moon being now up, my father resolved to cross the trench, and halt for a time, watching the moor from the shelter of the firs, on the chance of the woman's making her appearance; for, if she belonged to the camp, she would most probably approach it from the plantation, and might be overtaken before she could cross the moor to reach it.

They had lain ensconced in the firs for about half an hour, when suddenly, without any warning, Wagtail rushed into the underwood and vanished. They listened with all their ears, and in a few moments heard his joyous bark, followed instantly, however, by a howl of pain; and, before they had got many yards in pursuit, he came cowering to my father's feet, who, patting his side, found it bleeding. He bound his handkerchief round him, and, fastening the lash of Sim's whip to his collar that he might not go too fast for them, told him to find Theodora. Instantly he pulled away through the brushwood, giving a little yelp now and then as the stiff remnant of some broken twig or stem hurt his wounded side.

Before we reached the spot for which he was making, however, my father heard a rustling, nearer to the outskirts of the wood, and the same moment Wagtail turned, and tugged fiercely in that direction. The figure of a woman rose up against the sky, and began to run for the open space beyond. Wagtail and my father pursued at speed; my father crying out, that, if she did not stop, he would loose the dog on her. She paid no heed, but ran on.

"Mount and head her, Sim. Mount, Burton. Ride over every thing," cried my father, as he slipped Wagtail, who shot through the underwood like a bird, just as she reached the trench, and in an instant had her by the gown. My father saw something gleam in the moonlight, and again a howl broke from Wagtail, who was evidently once more wounded. But he held on. And now the horsemen, having crossed the trench, were approaching her in front, and my father was hard upon her behind. She gave a peculiar cry, half a shriek, and half a howl, clasped the child to her bosom, and stood rooted like a tree, evidently in the hope that her friends, hearing her signal, would come to her rescue. But it was too late. My father rushed upon her the instant she cried out. The dog was holding her by the poor ragged skirt, and the horses were reined snorting on the bank above her. She heaved up the child over her head, but whether in appeal to Heaven, or about to dash her to the earth in the rage of frustration, she was not allowed time to show; for my father caught both her uplifted arms with his, so that she could not lower them, and Burton, having flung himself from his horse and come behind her, easily took Theodora from them, for from their position they were almost powerless. Then my father called off Wagtail; and the poor creature sunk down in the bottom of the trench amongst the young firs without a sound, and there lay. My father went up to her; but she only stared at him with big blank black eyes, and yet such a lost look on her young, handsome, yet gaunt face, as almost convinced him she was the mother of the child. But, whatever might be her rights, she could not be allowed to recover possession, without those who had saved and tended the child having a word in the matter of her fate.

As he was thinking what he could say to her, Sim's voice reached his ear.

"They're coming over the brow, sir,—five or six from the camp. We'd better be off."

"The child is safe," he said, as he turned to leave her.

"From *me*," she rejoined, in a pitiful tone; and this ambiguous utterance was all that fell from her.

My father mounted hurriedly, took the child from Burton, and rode away, followed by the two men and Wagtail. Through the green rides they galloped in the moonlight, and were soon beyond all danger of pursuit. When they slackened pace, my father instructed Sim to find out all he could about the gypsies,—if possible to learn their names and to what tribe or community they belonged. Sim promised to do what was in his power, but said he did not expect much success.

The children had listened to the story wide awake. Wagtail was lying at my father's feet, licking his wounds, which were not very serious, and had stopped bleeding.

"It is all your doing, Wagtail," said Harry, patting the dog.

"I think he deserves to be called *Mr.* Wagtail," said Charley.

And from that day he was no more called bare Wagtail, but Mr. Wagtail, much to the amusement of visitors, who, hearing the name gravely uttered, as it soon came to be, saw the owner of it approach on all fours, with a tireless pendulum in his rear.

CHAPTER XI
A STUPID CHAPTER.

Before proceeding with my own story, I must mention that my father took every means in his power to find out something about the woman and the gang of gypsies to which she appeared to belong. I believe he had no definite end in view further than the desire to be able at some future time to enter into such relations with her, for her own and her daughter's sake, —if, indeed, Theodora were her daughter, —as might be possible. But, the very next day, he found that they had already vanished from the place; and all the inquiries he set on foot, by means of friends and through the country constabulary, were of no avail. I believe he was dissatisfied with himself in what had occurred, thinking he ought to have laid himself out at the time to discover whether she was indeed the mother, and, in that case, to do for her what he could. Probably, had he done so, he would only have heaped difficulty upon difficulty; but, as it was, if he was saved from trouble, he was not delivered from uneasiness. Clearly, however, the child must not be exposed to the danger of the repetition of the attempt; and the whole household was now so fully alive to the necessity of not losing sight of her for a moment, that her danger was far less than it had been at any time before.

I continued at the Hall for six weeks, during which my husband came several times to see me; and, at the close of that period, took me back with him to my dear little home. The rooms, all but the study, looked very small after those I had left; but I felt, notwithstanding, that the place was my home. I was at first a little ashamed of the feeling; for why should I be anywhere more at home than in the house of such parents as mine? But I presume there is a certain amount of the queenly element in every woman, so that she cannot feel perfectly at ease without something to govern, however small and however troublesome her queendom may be. At my father's, I had every ministration possible, and all comforts in profusion; but I had no responsibilities, and no rule; so that sometimes I could not help feeling as if I was idle, although I knew I was not to blame. Besides, I could not be at all sure that my big bear was properly attended to; and the knowledge that he was the most independent of comforts of all the men I had ever come into any relation with, made me only feel the more anxious that he should not be left to his own neglect. For although my father, for instance, was ready to part with any thing, even to a favorite volume, if the good reason of another's need showed itself, he was not at all indifferent in his own person to being comfortable. One with his intense power of enjoying the gentleness of the universe could not be so. Hence it was always easy to make him a little present; whereas I have still to rack my brains for weeks before my bear's birthday comes round, to think of something that will in itself have a chance of giving him pleasure. Of course, it would be comparatively easy if I had plenty of money to spare, and hadn't "to muddle it all away" in paying butchers and bakers, and such like people.

So home I went, to be queen again. Friends came to see me, but I returned few of their calls. I liked best to sit in my bedroom. I would have preferred sitting in my wonderful little room off the study, and I tried that first; but, the same morning, somebody called on Percivale, and straightway I felt myself a prisoner. The moment I heard the strange voice through the door, I wanted to get out, and could not, of course. Such a risk I would not run again. And when Percivale asked me, the next day, if I would not go down with him, I told him I could not bear the feeling of confinement it gave me.

"I did mean," he said, "to have had a door made into the garden for you, and I consulted an architect friend on the subject; but he soon satisfied me it would make the room much too cold for you, and so I was compelled to give up the thought."

"You dear!" I said. That was all; but it was enough for Percivale, who never bothered me, as I have heard of husbands doing, for demonstrations either of gratitude or affection. Such must be of the mole-eyed sort, who can only read large print. So I betook myself to my chamber, and there sat and worked; for I did a good deal of needle-work now, although I had never been fond of it as a girl. The constant recurrence of similar motions of the fingers, one stitch just the same as another in countless repetition, varied only by the bother when the thread grew short and would slip out of the eye of the needle, and yet not short enough to be exchanged with still more bother for one too long, had been so wearisome to me in former days, that I spent half my pocket-money in getting the needle-work done for me which my mother and sister did for themselves. For this my father praised me, and my mother tried to scold me, and couldn't. But now it was all so different! Instead of toiling at plain stitching and hemming and sewing, I seemed to be working a bit of lovely tapestry all the time,—so many thoughts and so many pictures went weaving themselves into the work; while every little bit finished appeared so much of the labor of the universe actually done,—accomplished, ended: for the first time in my life, I began to feel myself of consequence enough to be taken care of. I remember once laying down the little-what I was working at-but I am growing too communicative and important.

My father used often to say that the commonest things in the world were the loveliest,—sky and water and grass and such; now I found that the commonest feelings of humanity-for what feelings could be commoner than those which now made me blessed amongst women?—are those that are fullest of the divine. Surely this looks as if there were a God of the whole earth,—as if the world existed in the very foundations of its history and continuance by the immediate thought of a causing thought. For simply because the life of the world was moving on towards its unseen goal, and I knew it and had a helpless share in it, I felt as if God was with me. I do not say I always felt like this,—far from it: there were times when life itself seemed vanishing in an abyss of nothingness, when all my consciousness consisted in this, that I knew I was *not*, and when I could not believe that I should ever be restored to the well-being of existence. The worst of it was, that, in such moods, it seemed as if I had hitherto been deluding myself with rainbow fancies as often as I had been aware of blessedness, as there was, in fact, no wine of life apart from its effervescence. But when one day I told Percivale-not while I was thus oppressed, for then I could not speak; but in a happier moment whose happiness I mistrusted-something of what I felt, he said one thing which has comforted me ever since in such circumstances:—

"Don't grumble at the poverty, darling, by which another is made rich."

I confess I did not see all at once what he meant; but I did after thinking over it for a while. And if I have learned any valuable lesson in my life, it is this, that no one's feelings are a measure of eternal facts.

The winter passed slowly away,—fog, rain, frost, snow, thaw, succeeding one another in all the seeming disorder of the season. A good many things happened, I believe; but I don't remember any of them. My mother wrote, offering me Dora for a companion; but somehow I preferred being without her. One great comfort was good news about Connie, who was getting on famously. But even this moved me so little that I began to think I was turning into a crab, utterly incased in the shell of my own selfishness. The thought made me cry. The fact that I could cry consoled me, for how could I be heartless so long as I could cry? But then came the thought it was for myself, my own hard-heartedness I was crying,—not certainly for joy that Connie was getting better. "At least, however," I said to myself, "I am not content to be selfish. I am a little troubled that I am not good." And then I tried to look up, and get my needlework, which always did me good, by helping me to reflect. It is, I can't help thinking, a great pity that needlework is going so much out of fashion; for it tends more to make a woman-one who thinks, that is-acquainted with herself than all the sermons she is ever likely to hear.

My father came to see me several times, and was all himself to me; but I could not feel quite comfortable with him,—I don't in the least know why. I am afraid, much afraid, it indicates something very wrong in me somewhere. But he seemed to understand me; and always, the moment he left me, the tide of confidence began to flow afresh in the ocean that lay about the little island of my troubles. Then I knew he was my own father,—something that even my husband could not be, and would not wish to be to me.

In the month of March, my mother came to see me; and that was all pleasure. My father did not always see when I was not able to listen to him, though he was most considerate when he did; but my mother-why, to be with her was like being with one's own—*mother*, I was actually going to write. There is nothing better than that when a woman is in such trouble, except it be-what my father knows more about than I do: I wish I did know *all* about it.

She brought with her a young woman to take the place of cook, or rather general servant, in our little household. She had been kitchen-maid in a small family of my mother's acquaintance, and had a good character for honesty and plain cooking. Percivale's more experienced ear soon discovered that she was Irish. This fact had not been represented to my mother; for the girl had been in England from childhood, and her mistress seemed either not to have known it, or not to have thought of mentioning it. Certainly, my mother was far too just to have allowed it to influence her choice, notwithstanding the prejudices against Irish women in English families, — prejudices not without a general foundation in reason. For my part, I should have been perfectly satisfied with my mother's choice, even if I had not been so indifferent at the time to all that was going on in the lower regions of the house. But while my mother was there, I knew well enough that nothing could go wrong; and my housekeeping mind had never been so much at ease since we were married. It was very delightful not to be accountable; and, for the present, I felt exonerated from all responsibilities.

CHAPTER XII
AN INTRODUCTION.

I woke one morning, after a sound sleep, —not so sound, however, but that I had been dreaming, and that, when I awoke, I could recall my dream. It was a very odd one. I thought I was a hen, strutting about amongst ricks of corn, picking here and scratching there, followed by a whole brood of chickens, toward which I felt exceedingly benevolent and attentive. Suddenly I heard the scream of a hawk in the air above me, and instantly gave the proper cry to fetch the little creatures under my wings. They came scurrying to me as fast as their legs could carry them, —all but one, which wouldn't mind my cry, although I kept repeating it again and again. Meantime the hawk kept screaming; and I felt as if I didn't care for any of those that were safe under my wings, but only for the solitary creature that kept pecking away as if nothing was the matter. About it I grew so terribly anxious, that at length I woke with a cry of misery and terror.

The moment I opened my eyes, there was my mother standing beside me. The room was so dark that I thought for a moment what a fog there must be; but the next, I forgot every thing at hearing a little cry, which I verily believe, in my stupid dream, I had taken for the voice of the hawk; whereas it was the cry of my first and only chicken, which I had not yet seen, but which my mother now held in her grandmotherly arms, ready to hand her to me. I dared not speak; for I felt very weak, and was afraid of crying from delight. I looked in my mother's face; and she folded back the clothes, and laid the baby down beside me, with its little head resting on my arm.

"Draw back the curtain a little bit, mother dear," I whispered, "and let me see what it is like."

I believe I said *it*, for I was not quite a mother yet. My mother did as I requested; a ray of clear spring light fell upon the face of the little white thing by my side, —for white she was, though most babies are red, —and if I dared not speak before, I could not now. My mother went away again, and sat down by the fireside, leaving me with my baby. Never shall I forget the unutterable content of that hour. It was not gladness, nor was it thankfulness, that filled my heart, but a certain absolute contentment, —just on the point, but for my want of strength, of blossoming into unspeakable gladness and thankfulness. Somehow, too, there was mingled with it a sense of dignity, as if I had vindicated for myself a right to a part in the creation; for was I not proved at least a link in the marvellous chain of existence, in carrying on the designs of the great Maker? Not that the thought was there, —only the feeling, which afterwards found the thought, in order to account for its own being. Besides, the state of perfect repose after what had passed was in itself bliss; the very sense of weakness was delightful, for I had earned the right to be weak, to rest as much as I pleased, to be important, and to be congratulated.

Somehow I had got through. The trouble lay behind me; and here, for the sake of any one who will read my poor words, I record the conviction, that, in one way or other, special individual help is given to every creature to endure to the end. I think I have heard my father say, and hitherto it has been my own experience, that always when suffering, whether mental or bodily, approached the point where further endurance appeared impossible, the pulse of it began to ebb, and a lull ensued. I do not venture to found any general assertion upon this: I only state it as a fact of my own experience. He who does not allow any man to be tempted above that he is able to bear, doubtless acts in the same way in all kinds of trials.

I was listening to the gentle talk about me in the darkened room-not listening, indeed, only aware that loving words were spoken. Whether I was dozing, I do not know; but something touched my lips. I did not start. I had been dreadfully given to starting for a long time, —so much so that I was quite ashamed sometimes, for I would even cry out, —I who had always been so sharp on feminine affectations before; but now it seemed as if nothing could startle me. I only opened my eyes; and there was my great big huge bear looking down on me, with something in his eyes I had never seen there before. But even his presence could not ripple the waters of my deep rest. I gave him half a smile, —I knew it was but half a smile, but I thought it would do, —closed my eyes, and sunk again, not into sleep, but into that same blessed repose.

I remember wondering if I should feel any thing like that for the first hour or two after I was dead. May there not one day be such a repose for all, —only the heavenly counterpart, coming of perfect activity instead of weary success?

This was all but the beginning of endlessly varied pleasures. I dare say the mothers would let me go on for a good while in this direction, —perhaps even some of the fathers could stand a little more of it; but I must remember, that, if anybody reads this at all, it will have multitudes of readers in whom the chord which could alone respond to such experiences hangs loose over the sounding-board of their being.

By slow degrees the daylight, the light of work, that is, began to penetrate me, or rather to rise in my being from its own hidden sun. First I began to wash and dress my baby myself. One who has not tried that kind of amusement cannot know what endless pleasure it affords. I do not doubt that to the paternal spectator it appears monotonous, unproductive, unprogressive; but then he, looking upon it from the outside, and regarding the process with a speculative compassion, and not with sympathy, so cannot know the communion into which it brings you with the baby. I remember well enough what my father has written about it in "The Seaboard Parish;" but he is all wrong—I mean him to confess that before this is printed. If things were done as he proposes, the tenderness of mothers would be far less developed, and the moral training of children would be postponed to an indefinite period. There, papa! that's something in your own style!

Next I began to order the dinners; and the very day on which I first ordered the dinner, I took my place at the head of the table. A happier little party-well, of course, I saw it all through the rose-mists of my motherhood, but I am nevertheless bold to assert that my husband was happy, and that my mother was happy; and if there was one more guest at the table concerning whom I am not prepared to assert that he was happy, I can confidently affirm that he was merry and gracious and talkative, originating three parts of the laughter of the evening. To watch him with the baby was a pleasure even to the heart of a mother, anxious as she must be when any one, especially a gentleman, more especially a bachelor, and most especially a young bachelor, takes her precious little wax-doll in his arms, and pretends to know all about the management of such. It was he indeed who introduced her to the dining-room; for, leaving the table during dessert, he returned bearing her in his arms, to my astonishment, and even mild maternal indignation at the liberty. Resuming his seat, and pouring out for his charge, as he pretended, a glass of old port, he said in the soberest voice:—

"Charles Percivale, with all the solemnity suitable to the occasion, I, the old moon, with the new moon in my arms, propose the health of Miss Percivale on her first visit to this boring bullet of a world. By the way, what a mercy it is that she carries her atmosphere with her!"

Here I, stupidly thinking he reflected on the atmosphere of baby, rose to take her from him with suppressed indignation; for why should a man, who assumes a baby unbidden, be so very much nicer than a woman who accepts her as given, and makes the best of it? But he declined giving her up.

"I'm not pinching her," he said.

"No; but I am afraid you find her disagreeable."

"On the contrary, she is the nicest of little ladies; for she lets you talk all the nonsense you like, and never takes the least offence."

I sat down again directly.

"I propose her health," he repeated, "coupled with that of her mother, to whom I, for one, am more obliged than I can explain, for at length convincing me that I belong no more to the youth of my country, but am an uncle with a homuncle in his arms."

"Wifie, your health! Baby, yours too!" said my husband; and the ladies drank the toast in silence.

It is time I explained who this fourth-or should I say fifth? —person in our family party was. He was the younger brother of my Percivale, by name Roger, —still more unsuccessful than he; of similar trustworthiness, but less equanimity; for he was subject to sudden elevations and depressions of the inner barometer. I shall have more to tell about him by and by. Meantime it is enough to mention that my daughter-how grand I thought it when I first said *my daughter*! — now began her acquaintance with him. Before long he was her chief favorite next to her mother and —I am sorry I cannot conscientiously add *father*; for, at a certain early period of her history, the child showed a decided preference for her uncle over her father.

But it is time I put a stop to this ooze of maternal memories. Having thus introduced my baby and her Uncle Roger, I close the chapter.

CHAPTER XIII
MY FIRST DINNER-PARTY. A NEGATIVED PROPOSAL.

It may well be believed that we had not yet seen much company in our little house. To parties my husband had a great dislike; evening parties he eschewed utterly, and never accepted an invitation to dinner, except it were to the house of a friend, or to that of one of my few relatives in London, whom, for my sake, he would not displease. There were not many, even among his artist-acquaintances, whom he cared to visit; and, altogether, I fear he passed for an unsociable man. I am certain he would have sold more pictures if he had accepted what invitations came in his way. But to hint at such a thing would, I knew, crystallize his dislike into a resolve.

One day, after I had got quite strong again, as I was sitting by him in the study, with my baby on my knee, I proposed that we should ask some friends to dinner. Instead of objecting to the procedure upon general principles, which I confess I had half anticipated, he only asked me whom I thought of inviting. When I mentioned the Morleys, he made no reply, but went on with his painting as if he had not heard me; whence I knew, of course, that the proposal was disagreeable to him.

"You see, we have been twice to dine with them," I said.

"Well, don't you think that enough for a while?"

"I'm talking of asking them here now."

"Couldn't you go and see your cousin some morning instead?"

"It's not that I want to see my cousin particularly. I want to ask them to dinner."

"Oh!" he said, as if he couldn't in the least make out what I was after, "I thought people asked people because they desired their company."

"But, you see, we owe them a dinner."

"Owe them a dinner! Did you borrow one, then?"

"Percivale, why will you pretend to be so stupid?"

"Perhaps I'm only pretending to be the other thing."

"Do you consider yourself under no obligation to people who ask you to dinner?"

"None in the least-if I accept the invitation. That is the natural acknowledgment of their kindness. Surely my company is worth my dinner. It is far more trouble to me to put on black clothes and a white choker and go to their house, than it is for them to ask me, or, in a house like theirs, to have the necessary preparations made for receiving me in a manner befitting their dignity. I do violence to my own feelings in going: is not that enough? You know how much I prefer a chop with my wife alone to the grandest dinner the grandest of her grand relations could give me."

"Now, don't you make game of my grand relations. I'm not sure that you haven't far grander relations yourself, only you say so little about them, they might all have been transported for housebreaking. Tell me honestly, don't you think it natural, if a friend asks you to dinner, that you should ask him again?"

"Yes, if it would give him any pleasure. But just imagine your Cousin Morley dining at our table. Do you think he would enjoy it?"

"Of course we must have somebody in to help Jemima."

"And somebody to wait, I suppose?"

"Yes, of course, Percivale."

"And what Thackeray calls cold balls handed about?"

"Well, I wouldn't have them cold."

"But they would be."

I was by this time so nearly crying, that I said nothing here.

"My love," he resumed, "I object to the whole thing. It's all false together. I have not the least disinclination to asking a few friends who would enjoy being received in the same style as your father or my brother; namely, to one of our better dinners, and perhaps something better to drink than I can afford every day; but just think with what uneasy compassion Mr.

Morley would regard our poor ambitions, even if you had an occasional cook and an undertaker's man. And what would he do without his glass of dry sherry after his soup, and his hock and champagne later, not to mention his fine claret or tawny port afterwards? I don't know how to get these things good enough for him without laying in a stock; and, that you know, would be as absurd as it is impossible."

"Oh, you gentlemen always think so much of the wine!"

"Believe me, it is as necessary to Mr. Morley's comfort as the dainties you would provide him with. Indeed, it would be a cruelty to ask him. He would not, could not, enjoy it."

"If he didn't like it, he needn't come again," I said, cross with the objections of which I could not but see the justice.

"Well, I must say you have an odd notion of hospitality," said my bear. "You may be certain," he resumed, after a moment's pause, "that a man so well aware of his own importance will take it far more as a compliment that you do not presume to invite him to your house, but are content to enjoy his society when he asks you to his."

"I don't choose to take such an inferior position," I said.

"You can't help it, my dear," he returned. "Socially considered, you *are* his inferior. You cannot give dinners he would regard with any thing better than a friendly contempt, combined with a certain mild indignation at your having presumed to ask *him*, used to such different ways. It is far more graceful to accept the small fact, and let him have his whim, which is not a subversive one or at all dangerous to the community, being of a sort easy to cure. Ha! ha! ha!"

"May I ask what you are laughing at?" I said with severity.

"I was only fancying how such a man must feel,—if what your blessed father believes be true,—when he is stripped all at once of every possible source of consequence,—stripped of position, funds, house, including cellar, clothes, body, including stomach" —

"There, there! don't be vulgar. It is not like you, Percivale."

"My love, there is far greater vulgarity in refusing to acknowledge the inevitable, either in society or in physiology. Just ask my brother his experience in regard of the word to which you object."

"I will leave that to you."

"Don't be vexed with me, my wife," he said.

"I don't like not to be allowed to pay my debts."

"Back to the starting-point, like a hunted hare! A woman's way," he said merrily, hoping to make me laugh; for he could not doubt I should see the absurdity of my position with a moment's reflection. But I was out of temper, and chose to pounce upon the liberty taken with my sex, and regard it as an insult. Without a word I rose, pressed my baby to my bosom as if her mother had been left a widow, and swept away. Percivale started to his feet. I did not see, but I knew he gazed after me for a moment; then I heard him sit down to his painting as if nothing had happened, but, I knew, with a sharp pain inside his great chest. For me, I found the precipice, or Jacob's ladder, I had to climb, very subversive of my dignity; for when a woman has to hold a baby in one arm, and with the hand of the other lift the front of her skirt in order to walk up an almost perpendicular staircase, it is quite impossible for her to *sweep* any more.

When I reached the top, I don't know how it was, but the picture he had made of me, with the sunset-shine coming through the window, flashed upon my memory. All dignity forgotten, I bolted through the door at the top, flung my baby into the arms of her nurse, turned, almost tumbled headlong down the precipice, and altogether tumbled down at my husband's chair. I couldn't speak; I could only lay my head on his knees.

"Darling," he said, "you shall ask the great Pan Jan with his button atop, if you like. I'll do my best for him."

Between crying and laughing, I nearly did what I have never really done yet,—I nearly *went off*. There! I am sure that phrase is quite as objectionable as the word I wrote a little while ago; and there it shall stand, as a penance for having called any word my husband used *vulgar*.

"I was very naughty, Percivale," I said. "I will give a dinner-party, and it shall be such as you shall enjoy, and I won't ask Mr. Morley."

"Thank you, my love," he said; "and the next time Mr. Morley asks us I will go without a grumble, and make myself as agreeable as I can."

* * * * *

It may have seemed, to some of my readers, occasion for surprise that the mistress of a household should have got so far in the construction of a book without saying a word about her own or other people's servants in general. Such occasion shall no longer be afforded them; for now I am going to say several things about one of mine, and thereby introduce a few results of much experience and some thought. I do not pretend to have made a single discovery, but only to have achieved what I count a certain measure of success; which, however, I owe largely to my own poverty, and the stupidity of my cook.

I have had a good many servants since, but Jemima seems a fixture. How this has come about, it would be impossible to say in ever so many words. Over and over I have felt, and may feel again before the day is ended, a profound sympathy with Sindbad the sailor, when the Old Man of the Sea was on his back, and the hope of ever getting him off it had not yet begun to dawn. She has by turns every fault under the sun, —I say *fault* only; will struggle with one for a day, and succumb to it for a month; while the smallest amount of praise is sufficient to render her incapable of deserving a word of commendation for a week. She is intensely stupid, with a remarkable genius-yes, genius-for cooking. My father says that all stupidity is caused, or at least maintained, by conceit. I cannot quite accompany him to his conclusions; but I have seen plainly enough that the stupidest people are the most conceited, which in some degree favors them. It was long an impossibility to make her see, or at least own, that she was to blame for any thing. If the dish she had last time cooked to perfection made its appearance the next time uneatable, she would lay it all to the *silly* oven, which was too hot or too cold; or the silly pepper-pot, the top of which fell off as she was using it. She had no sense of the value of proportion, —would insist, for instance, that she had made the cake precisely as she had been told, but suddenly betray that she had not weighed the flour, which *could* be of no consequence, seeing she had weighed every thing else.

"Please, 'm, could you eat your dinner now? for it's all ready," she came saying an hour before dinner-time, the very first day after my mother left. Even now her desire to be punctual is chiefly evidenced by absurd precipitancy, to the danger of doing every thing either to a pulp or a cinder. Yet here she is, and here she is likely to remain, so far as I see, till death, or some other catastrophe, us do part. The reason of it is, that, with all her faults-and they are innumerable-she has some heart; yes, after deducting all that can be laid to the account of a certain cunning perception that she is well off, she has yet a good deal of genuine attachment left; and after setting down the half of her possessions to the blarney which is the natural weapon of the weak-witted Celt, there seems yet left in her of the vanishing clan instinct enough to render her a jealous partisan of her master and mistress.

Those who care only for being well-served will of course feel contemptuous towards any one who would put up with such a woman for a single moment after she could find another; but both I and my husband have a strong preference for living in a family, rather than in a hotel. I know many houses in which the master and mistress are far more like the lodgers, on sufferance of their own servants. I have seen a worthy lady go about wringing her hands because she could not get her orders attended to in the emergency of a slight accident, not daring to go down to her own kitchen, as her love prompted, and expedite the ministration. I am at least mistress in my own house; my servants are, if not yet so much members of the family as I could wish, gradually becoming more so; there is a circulation of common life through the household, rendering us an organization, although as yet perhaps a low one; I am sure of being obeyed, and there are no underhand out-of-door connections. When I go to the houses of my rich relations, and hear what they say concerning their servants, I feel as if they were living over a mine, which might any day be sprung, and blow them into a state of utter helplessness; and I return to my house blessed in the knowledge that my little kingdom is my own, and that, although it is not free from internal upheavings and stormy commotions, these are such as to be within the control and restraint of the general family influences; while the blunders of the cook seem such trifles beside the evil customs established in most kitchens of which I know any thing, that they are turned even into sources of congratulation as securing her services for ourselves. More than once my husband has insisted on raising her wages, on the ground of the endless good he gets in his painting from the merriment her oddities afford him, —namely, the clear insight, which, he asserts, is the invariable consequence. I must in honesty say, however, that I have seen him something else than merry with her behavior, many a time.

But I find the things I have to say so crowd upon me, that I must either proceed to arrange them under heads, —which would immediately deprive them of any right to a place in my story, —or keep them till they are naturally swept from the bank of my material by the slow wearing of the current of my narrative. I prefer the latter, because I think my readers will.

What with one thing and another, this thing to be done and that thing to be avoided, there was nothing more said about the dinner-party, until my father came to see us in the month of July. I was to have paid them a visit before then; but things had come in the way of that also, and now my father was commissioned by my mother to arrange for my going the next month.

As soon as I had shown my father to his little room, I ran down to Percivale.

"Papa is come," I said.

"I am delighted to hear it," he answered, laying down his palette and brushes. "Where is he?"

"Gone up stairs," I answered. "I wouldn't disturb you till he came down again."

He answered with that world-wide English phrase, so suggestive of a hopeful disposition, "All right!" And with all its grumbling, and the *tristesse* which the French consider its chief characteristic, I think my father is right, who says, that, more than any other nation, England has been, is, and will be, saved by hope. Resuming his implements, my husband added, —

"I haven't quite finished my pipe, —I will go on till he comes down."

Although he laid it on his pipe, I knew well enough it was just that little bit of paint he wanted to finish, and not the residue of tobacco in the black and red bowl.

"And now we'll have our dinner party," I said.

I do believe, that, for all the nonsense I had talked about returning invitations, the real thing at my heart even then was an impulse towards hospitable entertainment, and the desire to see my husband merry with his friends, under-shall I say it? —the protecting wing of his wife. For, as mother of the family, the wife has to mother her husband also; to consider him as her first-born, and look out for what will not only give him pleasure but be good for him. And I may just add here, that for a long time my bear has fully given in to this.

"And who are you going to ask?" he said. "Mr. and Mrs. Morley to begin with, and"—

"No, no," I answered. "We are going to have a jolly evening of it, with nobody present who will make you either anxious or annoyed. Mr. Blackstone," —he wasn't married then, —"Miss Clare, I think, —and"—

"What do you ask her for?"

"I won't if you don't like her, but"—

"I haven't had a chance of liking or disliking her yet."

"That is partly why I want to ask her, —I am so sure you would like her if you knew her."

"Where did you tell me you had met her?"

"At Cousin Judy's. I must have one lady to keep me in countenance with so many gentlemen, you know. I have another reason for asking her, which I would rather you should find out than I tell you. Do you mind?"

"Not in the least, if you don't think she will spoil the fun."

"I am sure she won't. Then there's your brother Roger."

"Of course. Who more?"

"I think that will do. There will be six of us then, —quite a large enough party for our little dining-room."

"Why shouldn't we dine here? It wouldn't be so hot, and we should have more room."

I liked the idea. The night before, Percivale arranged every thing, so that not only his paintings, of which he had far too many, and which were huddled about the room, but all his *properties* as well, should be accessory to a picturesque effect. And when the table was covered with the glass and plate, —of which latter my mother had taken care I should not be destitute, —and adorned with the flowers which Roger brought me from Covent Garden, assisted by a few of our own, I thought the bird's-eye view from the top of Jacob's ladder a very pretty one indeed.

Resolved that Percivale should have no cause of complaint as regarded the simplicity of my arrangements, I gave orders that our little Ethel, who at that time of the evening was always asleep, should be laid on the couch in my room off the study, with the door ajar, so that Sarah, who was now her nurse, might wait with an easy mind. The dinner was brought in by the outer door of the study, to avoid the awkwardness and possible disaster of the private precipice.

The principal dish, a small sirloin of beef, was at the foot of the table, and a couple of boiled fowls, as I thought, before me. But when the covers were removed, to my surprise I found they were roasted.

"What have you got there, Percivale?" I asked. "Isn't it sirloin?"

"I'm not an adept in such matters," he replied. "I should say it was."

My father gave a glance at the joint. Something seemed to be wrong. I rose and went to my husband's side. Powers of cuisine! Jemima had roasted the fowls, and boiled the sirloin. My exclamation was the signal for an outbreak of laughter, led by my father. I was trembling in the balance between mortification on my own account and sympathy with the evident amusement of my father and Mr. Blackstone. But the thought that Mr. Morley might have been and was not of the party came with such a pang and such a relief, that it settled the point, and I burst out laughing.

"I dare say it's all right," said Roger. "Why shouldn't a sirloin be boiled as well as roasted? I venture to assert that it is all a whim, and we are on the verge of a new discovery to swell the number of those which already owe their being to blunders."

"Let us all try a slice, then," said Mr. Blackstone, "and compare results."

This was agreed to; and a solemn silence followed, during which each sought acquaintance with the new dish.

"I am sorry to say," remarked my father, speaking first, "that Roger is all wrong, and we have only made the discovery that custom is right. It is plain enough why sirloin is always roasted."

"I yield myself convinced," said Roger.

"And I am certain," said Mr. Blackstone, "that if the loin set before the king, whoever he was, had been boiled, he would never have knighted it."

Thanks to the loin, the last possible touch of constraint had vanished, and the party grew a very merry one. The apple-pudding which followed was declared perfect, and eaten up. Percivale produced some good wine from somewhere, which evidently added to the enjoyment of the gentlemen, my father included, who likes a good glass of wine as well as anybody. But a tiny little whimper called me away, and Miss Clare accompanied me; the gentlemen insisting that we should return as soon as possible, and bring the homuncle, as Roger called the baby, with us.

When we returned, the two clergymen were in close conversation, and the other two gentlemen were chiefly listening. My father was saying, —

"My dear sir, I don't see how any man can do his duty as a clergyman who doesn't visit his parishioners."

"In London it is simply impossible," returned Mr. Blackstone. "In the country you are welcome wherever you go; any visit I might pay would most likely be regarded either as an intrusion, or as giving the right to pecuniary aid, of which evils the latter is the worse. There are portions of every London parish which clergymen and their coadjutors have so degraded by the practical teaching of beggary, that they have blocked up every door to a healthy spiritual relation between them and pastor possible."

"Would you not give alms at all, then?"

"One thing, at least, I have made up my mind upon, —that alms from any but the hand of personal friendship tend to evil, and will, in the long run, increase misery."

"What, then, do you suppose the proper relation between a London clergyman and his parishioners?"

"One, I am afraid, which does not at present exist, —one which it is his first business perhaps to bring about. I confess I regard with a repulsion amounting to horror the idea of walking into a poor man's house, except either I have business with him, or desire his personal acquaintance."

"But if our office" —

"Makes it my business to serve-not to assume authority over them especially to the degree of forcing service upon them. I will not say how far intimacy may not justify you in immediate assault upon a man's conscience; but I shrink from any plan that seems to take it for granted that the poor are more wicked than the rich. Why don't we send missionaries to Belgravia? The outside of the cup and platter may sometimes be dirtier than the inside."

"Your missionary could hardly force his way through the servants to the boudoir or drawing-room."

"And the poor have no servants to defend them."

I have recorded this much of the conversation chiefly for the sake of introducing Miss Clare, who now spoke.

"Don't you think, sir," she asked, addressing my father, "that the help one can give to another must always depend on the measure in which one is free one's self?"

My father was silent-thinking. We were all silent. I said to myself, "There, papa! that is something after your own heart." With marked deference and solemnity he answered at length, —

"I have little doubt you are right, Miss Clare. That puts the question upon its own eternal foundation. The mode used must be of infinitely less importance than the person who uses it."

As he spoke, he looked at her with a far more attentive regard than hitherto. Indeed, the eyes of all the company seemed to be scanning the small woman; but she bore the scrutiny well, if indeed she was not unconscious of it; and my husband began to find out one of my reasons for asking her, which was simply that he might see her face. At this moment it was in one of its higher phases. It was, at its best, a grand face, —at its worst, a suffering face; a little too large, perhaps, for the small body which it crowned with a flame of soul; but while you saw her face you never thought of the rest of her; and her attire seemed to court an escape from all observation.

"But," my father went on, looking at Mr. Blackstone, "I am anxious from the clergyman's point of view, to know what my friend here thinks he must try to do in his very difficult position."

"I think the best thing I could do," returned Mr. Blackstone, laughing, "would be to go to school to Miss Clare."

"I shouldn't wonder," my father responded.

"But, in the mean time, I should prefer the chaplaincy of a suburban cemetery."

"Certainly your charge would be a less troublesome one. Your congregation would be quiet enough, at least," said Roger.

"'Then are they glad because they be quiet,'" said my father, as if unconsciously uttering his own reflections. But he was a little cunning, and would say things like that when, fearful of irreverence, he wanted to turn the current of the conversation.

"But, surely," said Miss Clare, "a more active congregation would be quite as desirable."

She had one fault-no, defect: she was slow to enter into the humor of a thing. It seemed almost as if the first aspect of any bit of fun presented to her was that of something wrong. A moment's reflection, however, almost always ended in a sunny laugh, partly at her own stupidity, as she called it.

"You mistake my meaning," said Mr. Blackstone. "My chief, almost sole, attraction to the regions of the grave is the sexton, and not the placidity of the inhabitants; though perhaps Miss

Clare might value that more highly if she had more experience of how noisy human nature can be."

Miss Clare gave a little smile, which after-knowledge enabled me to interpret as meaning, "Perhaps I do know a trifle about it;" but she said nothing.

"My first inquiry," he went on, "before accepting such an appointment, would be as to the character and mental habits of the sexton. If I found him a man capable of regarding human nature from a stand-point of his own, I should close with the offer at once. If, on the contrary, he was a common-place man, who made faultless responses, and cherished the friendship of the undertaker, I should decline. In fact, I should regard the sexton as my proposed master; and whether I should accept the place or not would depend altogether on whether I liked him or not. Think what revelations of human nature a real man in such a position could give me: 'Hand me the shovel. You stop a bit,—you're out of breath. Sit down on that stone there, and light your pipe; here's some tobacco. Now tell me the rest of the story. How did the old fellow get on after he had buried his termagant wife?' That's how I should treat him; and I should get, in return, such a succession of peeps into human life and intent and aspirations, as, in the course of a few years, would send me to the next vicarage that turned up a sadder and wiser man, Mr. Walton."

"I don't doubt it," said my father; but whether in sympathy with Mr. Blackstone, or in latent disapproval of a tone judged unbecoming to a clergyman, I cannot tell. Sometimes, I confess, I could not help suspecting the source of the deficiency in humor which he often complained of in me; but I always came to the conclusion that what seemed such a deficiency in him was only occasioned by the presence of a deeper feeling.

Miss Clare was the first to leave.

"What a lovely countenance that is!" said my husband, the moment she was out of hearing.

"She is a very remarkable woman," said my father.

"I suspect she knows a good deal more than most of us," said Mr. Blackstone. "Did you see how her face lighted up always before she said any thing? You can never come nearer to seeing a thought than in her face just before she speaks."

"What is she?" asked Roger.

"Can't you see what she is?" returned his brother. "She's a saint,—Saint Clare."

"If you had been a Scotchman, now," said Roger "that fine name would have sunk to *Sinkler* in your mouth."

"Not a more vulgar corruption, however, than is common in the mouths of English lords and ladies, when they turn *St. John* into *Singen*, reminding one of nothing but the French for an ape," said my father.

"But what does she do?" persisted Roger.

"Why should you think she does any thing?" I asked.

"She looks as if she had to earn her own living."

"She does. She teaches music."

"Why didn't you ask her to play?"

"Because this is the first time she has been to the house."

"Does she go to church, do you suppose?"

"I have no doubt of it; but why do you ask?"

"Because she looks as if she didn't want it. I never saw such an angelic expression upon a countenance."

"You must take me to call upon her," said my father.

"I will with pleasure," I answered.

I found, however, that this was easier promised than performed; for I had asked her by word of mouth at Cousin Judy's, and had not the slightest idea where she lived. Of course I applied to Judy; but she had mislaid her address, and, promising to ask her for it, forgot more than once. My father had to return home without seeing her again.

CHAPTER XIV
A PICTURE.

Things went on very quietly for some time. Of course I was fully occupied, as well I might be, with a life to tend and cultivate which must blossom at length into the human flowers of love and obedience and faith. The smallest service I did the wonderful thing that lay in my lap seemed a something in itself so well worth doing, that it was worth living to do it. As I gazed on the new creation, so far beyond my understanding, yet so dependent upon me while asserting an absolute and divine right to all I did for her, I marvelled that God should intrust me with such a charge, that he did not keep the lovely creature in his own arms, and refuse her to any others. Then I would bethink myself that in giving her into mine, he had not sent her out of his own; for I, too, was a child in his arms, holding and tending my live doll, until it should grow something like me, only ever so much better. Was she not given to me that she might learn what I had begun to learn, namely, that a willing childhood was the flower of life? How can any mother sit with her child on her lap and not know that there is a God over all,—know it by the rising of her own heart in prayer to him? But so few have had parents like mine! If my mother felt thus when I lay in her arms, it was no wonder I should feel thus when my child lay in mine.

Before I had children of my own, I did not care about children, and therefore did not understand them; but I had read somewhere,—and it clung to me although I did not understand it,—that it was in laying hold of the heart of his mother that Jesus laid his first hold on the world to redeem it; and now at length I began to understand it. What a divine way of saving us it was,—to let her bear him, carry him in her bosom, wash him and dress him and nurse him and sing him to sleep,—offer him the adoration of mother's love, misunderstand him, chide him, forgive him even for fancied wrong! Such a love might well save a world in which were mothers enough. It was as if he had said, "Ye shall no more offer vain sacrifices to one who needs them not, and cannot use them. I will need them, so require them at your hands. I will hunger and thirst and be naked and cold, and ye shall minister to me. Sacrifice shall be no more a symbol, but a real giving unto God; and when I return to the Father, inasmuch as ye do it to one of the least of these, ye do it unto me." So all the world is henceforth the temple of God; its worship is ministration; the commonest service is divine service.

I feared at first that the new strange love I felt in my heart came only of the fact that the child was Percivale's and mine; but I soon found it had a far deeper source,—that it sprung from the very humanity of the infant woman, yea, from her relation in virtue of that humanity to the Father of all. The fountain *appeared* in my heart: it arose from an infinite store in the unseen.

Soon, however, came jealousy of my love for my baby. I feared lest it should make me-nay, was making me-neglect my husband. The fear first arose in me one morning as I sat with her half dressed on my knees. I was dawdling over her in my fondness, as I used to dawdle over the dressing of my doll, when suddenly I became aware that never once since her arrival had I sat with my husband in his study. A pang of dismay shot through me. "Is this to be a wife?" I said to myself,—"to play with a live love like a dead doll, and forget her husband!" I caught up a blanket from the cradle,—I am not going to throw away that good old word for the ugly outlandish name they give it now, reminding one only of a helmet,—I caught up a blanket from the cradle, I say, wrapped it round the treasure, which was shooting its arms and legs in every direction like a polypus feeling after its food,—and rushed down stairs, and down the precipice into the study. Percivale started up in terror, thinking something fearful had happened, and I was bringing him all that was left of the child.

"What-what-what's the matter?" he gasped.

I could not while he was thus frightened explain to him what had driven me to him in such alarming haste.

"I've brought you the baby to kiss," I said, unfolding the blanket, and holding up the sprawling little goddess towards the face that towered above me.

"Was it dying for a kiss then?" he said, taking her, blanket and all, from my arms.

The end of the blanket swept across his easel, and smeared the face of the baby in a picture of the *Three Kings*, at which he was working.

"O Percivale!" I cried, "you've smeared your baby!"

"But this is a real live baby; she may smear any thing she likes."

"Except her own face and hands, please, then, Percivale."

"Or her blessed frock," said Percivale. "She hasn't got one, though. Why hasn't the little angel got her feathers on yet?"

"I was in such a hurry to bring her."

"To be kissed?"

"No, not exactly. It wasn't her I was in a hurry to bring; it was myself."

"Ah! you wanted to be kissed, did you?"

"No, sir. I didn't want to be kissed; but I did so want to kiss you, Percivale."

"Isn't it all the same, though, darling?" he said. "It seems so to me."

"Sometimes, Percivale, you are so very stupid! It's not the same at all. There's a world of difference between the two; and you ought to know it, or be told it, if you don't."

"I shall think it over as soon as you leave me," he said.

"But I'm not going to leave you for a long time. I haven't seen you paint for weeks and weeks,—not since this little troublesome thing came poking in between us."

"But she's not dressed yet."

"That doesn't signify. She's well wrapped up, and quite warm."

He put me a chair where I could see his picture without catching the shine of the paint. I took the baby from him, and he went on with his work.

"You don't think I am going to sacrifice all my privileges to this little tyrant, do you?" I said.

"It would be rather hard for me, at least," he rejoined.

"You did think I was neglecting you, then, Percivale?"

"Not for a moment."

"Then you didn't miss me?"

"I did, very much."

"And you didn't grumble?"

"No."

"Do I disturb you?" I asked, after a little pause. "Can you paint just as well when I am here as when you are alone?"

"Better. I feel warmer to my work somehow."

I was satisfied, and held my peace. When I am best pleased I don't want to talk. But Percivale, perhaps not having found this out yet, looked anxiously in my face; and, as at the moment my eyes were fixed on his picture, I thought he wanted to find out whether I liked the design.

"I see it now!" I cried. "I could not make out where the Magi were."

He had taken for the scene of his picture an old farm kitchen, or yeoman's hall, with its rich brown rafters, its fire on the hearth, and its red brick floor. A tub half full of bright water, stood on one side; and the mother was bending over her baby, which, undressed for the bath, she was holding out for the admiration of the Magi. Immediately behind the mother stood, in the garb of a shepherd, my father, leaning on the ordinary shepherd's crook; my mother, like a peasant-woman in her Sunday-best, with a white handkerchief crossed upon her bosom, stood beside him, and both were gazing with a chastened yet profound pleasure on the lovely child.

In front stood two boys and a girl,—between the ages of five and nine,—gazing each with a peculiar wondering delight on the baby. The youngest boy, with a great spotted wooden horse in his hand, was approaching to embrace the infant in such fashion as made the toy look dangerous, and the left hand of the mother was lifted with a motion of warning and defence. The little girl, the next youngest, had, in her absorption, dropped her gaudily dressed doll at her feet, and stood sucking her thumb, her big blue eyes wide with contemplation. The eldest boy had brought his white rabbit to give the baby, but had forgotten all about it, so full was his heart of his new brother. An expression of mingled love and wonder and perplexity had already begun to dawn upon the face, but it was as yet far from finished. He stood behind the other two peeping over their heads.

"Were you thinking of that Titian in the Louvre, with the white rabbit in it?" I asked Percivale.

"I did not think of it until after I had put in the rabbit," he replied. "And it shall remain; for it suits my purpose, and Titian would not claim all the white rabbits because of that one."

"Did you think of the black lamb in it, then, when you laid that black pussy on the hearth?" I asked.

"Black lamb?" he returned.

"Yes," I insisted; "a black lamb, in the dark background-such a very black lamb, and in such a dark background, that it seems you never discovered it."

"Are you sure?" he persisted.

"Absolutely certain," I replied. "I pointed it out to papa in the picture itself in the Louvre; he had not observed it before either."

"I am very glad to know there is such a thing there. I need not answer your question, you see. It is odd enough I should have put in the black puss. Upon some grounds I might argue that my puss is better than Titian's lamb."

"What grounds? tell me."

"If the painter wanted a contrast, a lamb, be he as black as ever paint could make him, must still be a more Christian animal than a cat as white as snow. Under what pretence could a cat be used for a Christian symbol?"

"What do you make of her playfulness?"

"I should count that a virtue, were it not for the fatal objection that it is always exercised at the expense of other creatures."

"A ball of string, or a reel, or a bit of paper, is enough for an uncorrupted kitten."

"But you must not forget that it serves only in virtue of the creature's imagination representing it as alive. If you do not make it move, she will herself set it in motion as the initiative of the game. If she cannot do that, she will take no notice of it."

"Yes, I see. I give in."

All this time he had been painting diligently. He could now combine talking and painting far better than he used. But a knock came to the study door; and, remembering baby's unpresentable condition, I huddled her up, climbed the stair again, and finished the fledging of my little angel in a very happy frame of mind.

CHAPTER XV
RUMORS.

Hardly was it completed, when Cousin Judy called, and I went down to see her, carrying my baby with me. As I went, something put me in mind that I must ask her for Miss Clare's address. Lest I should again forget, as soon as she had kissed and admired the baby, I said, —
"Have you found out yet where Miss Clare lives, Judy?"
"I don't choose to find out," she answered. "I am sorry to say I have had to give her up. It is a disappointment, I confess."
"What do you mean?" I said. "I thought you considered her a very good teacher."
"I have no fault to find with her on that score. She was always punctual, and I must allow both played well and taught the children delightfully. But I have heard such questionable things about her!—very strange things indeed!"
"What are they?"
"I can't say I've been able to fix on more than one thing directly against her character, but"—
"Against her character!" I exclaimed.
"Yes, indeed. She lives by herself in lodgings, and the house is not at all a respectable one."
"But have you made no further inquiry?"
"I consider that quite enough. I had already met more than one person, however, who seemed to think it very odd that I should have her to teach music in my family."
"Did they give any reason for thinking her unfit?"
"I did not choose to ask them. One was Miss Clarke-you know her. She smiled in her usual supercilious manner, but in her case I believe it was only because Miss Clare looks so dowdy. But nobody knows any thing about her except what I've just told you."
"And who told you that?"
"Mrs. Jeffreson."
"But you once told me that she was a great gossip."
"Else she wouldn't have heard it. But that doesn't make it untrue. In fact, she convinced me of its truth, for she knows the place she lives in, and assured me it was at great risk of infection to the children that I allowed her to enter the house; and so, of course, I felt compelled to let her know that I didn't require her services any longer."
"There must be some mistake, surely!" I said.
"Oh, no! not the least, I am sorry to say."
"How did she take it?"
"Very sweetly indeed. She didn't even ask me why, which was just as well, seeing I should have found it awkward to tell her. But I suppose she knew too many grounds herself to dare the question."
I was dreadfully sorry, but I could not say much more then. I ventured only to express my conviction that there could not be any charge to bring against Miss Clare herself; for that one who looked and spoke as she did could have nothing to be ashamed of. Judy, however, insisted that what she had heard was reason enough for at least ending the engagement; indeed, that no one was fit for such a situation of whom such things could be said, whether they were true or not.
When she left me, I gave baby to her nurse, and went straight to the study, peeping in to see if Percivale was alone.
He caught sight of me, and called to me to come down.
"It's only Roger," he said.
I was always pleased to see Roger. He was a strange creature, —one of those gifted men who are capable of any thing, if not of every thing, and yet carry nothing within sight of proficiency. He whistled like a starling, and accompanied his whistling on the piano; but never played. He could copy a drawing to a hair's-breadth, but never drew. He could engrave well on wood; but although he had often been employed in that way, he had always got tired of it after a few

weeks. He was forever wanting to do something other than what he was at; and the moment he got tired of a thing, he would work at it no longer; for he had never learned to *make* himself. He would come every day to the study for a week to paint in backgrounds, or make a duplicate; and then, perhaps, we wouldn't see him for a fortnight. At other times he would work, say for a month, modelling, or carving marble, for a sculptor friend, from whom he might have had constant employment if he had pleased. He had given lessons in various branches, for he was an excellent scholar, and had the finest ear for verse, as well as the keenest appreciation of the loveliness of poetry, that I have ever known. He had stuck to this longer than to any thing else, strange to say; for one would have thought it the least attractive of employments to one of his volatile disposition. For some time indeed he had supported himself comfortably in this way; for through friends of his family he had had good introductions, and, although he wasted a good deal of money in buying nick-nacks that promised to be useful and seldom were, he had no objectionable habits except inordinate smoking. But it happened that a pupil—a girl of imaginative disposition, I presume-fell so much in love with him that she betrayed her feelings to her countess-mother, and the lessons were of course put an end to. I suspect he did not escape heart-whole himself; for he immediately dropped all his other lessons, and took to writing poetry for a new magazine, which proved of ephemeral constitution, and vanished after a few months of hectic existence.

It was remarkable that with such instability his moral nature should continue uncorrupted; but this I believe he owed chiefly to his love and admiration of his brother. For my part, I could not help liking him much. There was a half-plaintive playfulness about him, alternated with gloom, and occasionally with wild merriment, which made him interesting even when one felt most inclined to quarrel with him. The worst of him was that he considered himself a generally misunderstood, if not ill-used man, who could not only distinguish himself, but render valuable service to society, if only society would do him the justice to give him a chance. Were it only, however, for his love to my baby, I could not but be ready to take up his defence. When I mentioned what I had just heard about Miss Clare, Percivale looked both astonished and troubled; but before he could speak, Roger, with the air of a man of the world whom experience enabled to come at once to a decision, said,—

"Depend upon it, Wynnie, there is falsehood there somewhere. You will always be nearer the truth if you believe nothing, than if you believe the half of what you hear."

"That's very much what papa says," I answered. "He affirms that he never searched into an injurious report in his own parish without finding it so nearly false as to deprive it of all right to go about."

"Besides," said Roger, "look at that face! How I should like to model it. She's a good woman that, depend upon it."

I was delighted with his enthusiasm.

"I wish you would ask her again, as soon as you can," said Percivale, who always tended to embody his conclusions in acts rather than in words. "Your cousin Judy is a jolly good creature, but from your father's description of her as a girl, she must have grown a good deal more worldly since her marriage. Respectability is an awful snare."

"Yes," said Roger; "one ought to be very thankful to be a Bohemian, and have nothing expected of him, for respectability is a most fruitful mother of stupidity and injustice."

I could not help thinking that *he* might, however, have a little more and be none the worse.

"I should be very glad to do as you desire, husband," I said, "but how can I? I haven't learned where she lives. It was asking Judy for her address once more that brought it all out. I certainly didn't insist, as I might have done, notwithstanding what she told me; but, if she didn't remember it before, you may be sure she could not have given it me then."

"It's very odd," said Roger, stroking his long mustache, the sole ornament of the kind he wore. "It's very odd," he repeated thoughtfully, and then paused again.

"What's so very odd, Roger?" asked Percivale.

"The other evening," answered Roger, after yet a short pause, "happening to be in Tottenham Court Road, I walked for some distance behind a young woman carrying a brown beer-jug in her hand-for I sometimes amuse myself in the street by walking persistently behind some one, devising the unseen face in my mind, until the recognition of the same step following causes the person to look round at me, and give me the opportunity of comparing the two —I mean the one I had devised and the real one. When the young woman at length turned her head, it was only my astonishment that kept me from addressing her as Miss Clare. My surprise, however, gave me time to see how absurd it would have been. Presently she turned down a yard and disappeared."

"Don't tell my cousin Judy," I said. "She would believe it *was* Miss Clare."

"There isn't much danger," he returned. "Even if I knew your cousin, I should not be likely to mention such an incident in her hearing."

"Could it have been she?" said Percivale thoughtfully.

"Absurd!" said Roger. "Miss Clare is a lady, wherever she may live."

"I don't know," said his brother thoughtfully; "who can tell? It mightn't have been beer she was carrying."

"I didn't say it was beer," returned Roger. "I only said it was a beer-jug, —one of those brown, squat, stone jugs, —the best for beer that I know, after all, —brown, you know, with a dash of gray."

"Brown jug or not, I wish I could get a few sittings from her. She would make a lovely St. Cecilia," said my husband.

"Brown jug and all?" asked Roger.

"If only she were a little taller," I objected.

"And had an aureole," said my husband. "But I might succeed in omitting the jug as well as in adding the aureole and another half-foot of stature, if only I could get that lovely countenance on the canvas, —so full of life and yet of repose."

"Don't you think it a little hard?" I ventured to say.

"I think so," said Roger.

"I don't," said my husband. "I know what in it looks like hardness; but I think it comes of the repression of feeling."

"You have studied her well for your opportunities," I said.

"I have; and I am sure, whatever Mrs. Morley may say, that, if there be any truth at all in those reports, there is some satisfactory explanation of whatever has given rise to them. I wish we knew anybody else that knew her. Do try to find some one that does, Wynnie."

"I don't know how to set about it," I said. "I should be only too glad."

"I will try," said Roger. "Does she sing?"

"I have heard Judy say she sang divinely; but the only occasion on which I met her-at their house, that time you couldn't go, Percivale-she was never asked to sing."

"I suspect," remarked Roger, "it will turn out to be only that she's something of a Bohemian, like ourselves."

"Thank you, Roger; but for my part, I don't consider myself a Bohemian at all," I said.

"I am afraid you must rank with your husband, wifie," said *mine*, as the wives of the working people of London often call their husbands.

"Then you do count yourself a Bohemian: pray, what significance do you attach to the epithet?" I asked.

"I don't know, except it signifies our resemblance to the gypsies," he answered.

"I don't understand you quite."

"I believe the gypsies used to be considered Bohemians," interposed Roger, "though they are doubtless of Indian origin. Their usages being quite different from those amongst which they live, the name Bohemian came to be applied to painters, musicians, and such like generally, to whom, save by courtesy, no position has yet been accorded by society-so called."

"But why have they not yet vindicated for themselves a social position," I asked, "and that a high one?"

"Because they are generally poor, I suppose," he answered; "and society is generally stupid."

"May it not be because they are so often, like the gypsies, lawless in their behavior, as well as peculiar in their habits?" I suggested.

"I understand you perfectly, Mrs. Percivale," rejoined Roger with mock offence. "But how would that apply to Charlie?"

"Not so well as to you, I confess," I answered. "But there is ground for it with him too."

"I have thought it all over many a time," said Percivale; "and I suppose it comes in part from inability to understand the worth of our calling, and in part from the difficulty of knowing where to put us."

"I suspect," I said, "one thing is that so many of them are content to be received as merely painters, or whatever they may be by profession. Many, you have told me, for instance, accept invitations which do not include their wives."

"They often go to parties, of course, where there are no ladies," said Roger.

"That is not what I mean," I replied. "They go to dinner-parties where there are ladies, and evening parties, too, without their wives."

"Whoever does that," said Percivale, "has at least no right to complain that he is regarded as a Bohemian; for in accepting such invitations, he accepts insult, and himself insults his wife."

Nothing irritated my bear so much as to be asked to dinner without me. He would not even offer the shadow of a reason for declining the invitation. "For," he would say, "if I give the real reason, namely, that I do not choose to go where my wife is excluded, they will set it down to her jealous ambition of entering a sphere beyond her reach; I will not give a false reason, and indeed have no objection to their seeing that I am offended; therefore, I assign none. If they have any chivalry in them, they may find out my reason readily enough."

I don't think I ever displeased him so much as once when I entreated him to accept an invitation to dine with the Earl of H——. The fact was, I had been fancying it my duty to persuade him to get over his offence at the omission of my name, for the sake of the advantage it would be to him in his profession. I laid it before him as gently and coaxingly as I could, representing how expenses increased, and how the children would be requiring education by and by,—reminding him that the reputation of more than one of the most popular painters had been brought about in some measure by their social qualities and the friendships they made.

"Is it likely your children will be ladies and gentlemen," he said, "if you prevail on their father to play the part of a sneaking parasite?"

I was frightened. He had never spoken to me in such a tone, but I saw too well how deeply he was hurt to take offence at his roughness. I could only beg him to forgive me, and promise never to say such a word again, assuring him that I believed as strongly as himself that the best heritage of children was their father's honor.

Free from any such clogs as the possession of a wife encumbers a husband withal, Roger could of course accept what invitations his connection with an old and honorable family procured him. One evening he came in late from a dinner at Lady Bernard's.

"Whom do you think I took down to dinner?" he asked, almost before he was seated.

"Lady Bernard?" I said, flying high.

"Her dowager aunt?" said Percivale.

"No, no; Miss Clare."

"Miss Clare!" we both repeated, with mingled question and exclamation.

"Yes, Miss Clare, incredible as it may appear," he answered.

"Did you ask her if it was she you saw carrying the jug of beer in Tottenham Court Road?" said Percivale.

"Did you ask her address?" I said. "That is a question more worthy of an answer."

"Yes, I did. I believe I did. I think I did."

"What is it, then?"

"Upon my word, I haven't the slightest idea."

"So, Mr. Roger! You have had a perfect opportunity, and have let it slip! You are a man to be trusted indeed!"

"I don't know how it could have been. I distinctly remember approaching the subject more than once or twice; and now first I discover that I never asked the question. Or if I did, I am certain I got no answer."

"Bewitched!"

"Yes, I suppose so."

"Or," suggested Percivale, "she did not choose to tell you; saw the question coming, and led you away from it; never let you ask it."

"I have heard that ladies can keep one from saying what they don't want to hear. But she sha'n't escape me so a second time."

"Indeed, you don't deserve another chance," I said. "You're not half so clever as I took you to be, Roger."

"When I think of it, though, it wasn't a question so easy to ask, or one you would like to be overheard asking."

"Clearly bewitched," I said. "But for that I forgive you. Did she sing?"

"No. I don't suppose any one there ever thought of asking such a dingy-feathered bird to sing."

"You had some music?"

"Oh, yes! Pretty good, and very bad. Miss Clare's forehead was crossed by no end of flickering shadows as she listened."

"It wasn't for want of interest in her you forgot to find out where she lived! You had better take care, Master Roger."

"Take care of what?"

"Why, you don't know her address."

"What has that to do with taking care?"

"That you won't know where to find your heart if you should happen to want it."

"Oh! I am past that kind of thing long ago. You've made an uncle of me."

And so on, with a good deal more nonsense, but no news of Miss Clare's retreat.

I had before this remarked to my husband that it was odd she had never called since dining with us; but he made little of it, saying that people who gained their own livelihood ought to be excused from attending to rules which had their origin with another class; and I had thought no more about it, save in disappointment that she had not given me that opportunity of improving my acquaintance with her.

CHAPTER XVI
A DISCOVERY.

One Saturday night, my husband happening to be out, an event of rare occurrence, Roger called; and as there were some things I had not been able to get during the day, I asked him to go with me to Tottenham Court Road. It was not far from the region where we lived, and I did a great part of my small shopping there. The early closing had, if I remember rightly, begun to show itself; anyhow, several of the shops were shut, and we walked a long way down the street, looking for some place likely to supply what I required.

"It was just here I came up with the girl and the brown jug," said Roger, as we reached the large dissenting chapel.

"That adventure seems to have taken a great hold of you, Roger," I said.

"She *was* so like Miss Clare!" he returned. "I can't get the one face clear of the other. When I met her at Lady Bernard's, the first thing I thought of was the brown jug."

"Were you as much pleased with her conversation as at our house?" I asked.

"Even more," he answered. "I found her ideas of art so wide, as well as just and accurate, that I was puzzled to think where she had had opportunity of developing them. I questioned her about it, and found she was in the habit of going, as often as she could spare time, to the National Gallery, where her custom was, she said, not to pass from picture to picture, but keep to one until it formed itself in her mind,—that is the expression she used, explaining herself to mean, until she seemed to know what the painter had set himself to do, and why this was and that was which she could not at first understand. Clearly, without ever having taken a pencil in her hand, she has educated herself to a keen perception of what is demanded of a true picture. Of course the root of it lies in her musical development.—There," he cried suddenly, as we came opposite a paved passage, "that is the place I saw her go down."

"Then you do think the girl with the beer-jug was Miss Clare, after all?"

"Not in the least. I told you I could not separate them in my mind."

"Well, I must say, it seems odd. A girl like that and Miss Clare! Why, as often as you speak of the one, you seem to think of the other."

"In fact," he returned, "I am, as I say, unable to dissociate them. But if you had seen the girl, you would not wonder. The likeness was absolutely complete."

"I believe you do consider them one and the same; and I am more than half inclined to think so myself, remembering what Judy said."

"Isn't it possible some one who knows Miss Clare may have seen this girl, and been misled by the likeness?"

"But where, then, does Miss Clare live? Nobody seems to know."

"You have never asked any one but Mrs. Morley."

"You have yourself, however, given me reason to think she avoids the subject. If she did live anywhere hereabout, she would have some cause to avoid it."

I had stopped to look down the passage.

"Suppose," said Roger, "some one were to come past now and see Mrs. Percivale, the wife of the celebrated painter, standing in Tottenham Court Road beside the swing-door of a corner public-house, talking to a young man."

"Yes; it might have given occasion for scandal," I said. "To avoid it, let us go down the court and see what it is like."

"It's not a fit place for you to go into."

"If it were in my father's parish, I should have known everybody in it."

"You haven't the slightest idea what you are saying."

"Come, anyhow, and let us see what the place is like," I insisted.

Without another word he gave me his arm, and down the court we went, past the flaring gin-shop, and into the gloom beyond. It was one of those places of which, while the general effect remains vivid in one's mind, the salient points are so few that it is difficult to say much by way of description. The houses had once been occupied by people in better circumstances than its present inhabitants; and indeed they looked all decent enough until, turning two right angles, we came upon another sort. They were still as large, and had plenty of windows; but, in the light of a single lamp at the corner, they looked very dirty and wretched and dreary. A little shop, with dried herrings and bull's-eyes in the window, was lighted by a tallow candle set in a ginger-beer bottle, with a card of "Kinahan's LL Whiskey" for a reflector.

"They can't have many customers to the extent of a bottle," said Roger. "But no doubt they have some privileges from the public-house at the corner for hanging up the card."

The houses had sunk areas, just wide enough for a stair, and the basements seemed full of tenants. There was a little wind blowing, so that the atmosphere was tolerable, notwithstanding a few stray leaves of cabbage, suggestive of others in a more objectionable condition not far off.

A confused noise of loud voices, calling and scolding, hitherto drowned by the tumult of the street, now reached our ears. The place took one turn more, and then the origin of it became apparent. At the farther end of the passage was another lamp, the light of which shone upon a group of men and women, in altercation, which had not yet come to blows. It might, including children, have numbered twenty, of which some seemed drunk, and all more or less excited. Roger turned to go back the moment he caught sight of them; but I felt inclined, I hardly knew why, to linger a little. Should any danger offer, it would be easy to gain the open thoroughfare.

"It's not at all a fit place for a lady," he said.

"Certainly not," I answered; "it hardly seems a fit place for human beings. These are human beings, though. Let us go through it."

He still hesitated; but as I went on, he could but follow me. I wanted to see what the attracting centre of the little crowd was; and that it must be occupied with some affair of more than ordinary interest, I judged from the fact that a good many superterrestrial spectators looked down from the windows at various elevations upon the disputants, whose voices now and then lulled for a moment only to break out in fresh objurgation and dispute.

Drawing a little nearer, a slight parting of the crowd revealed its core to us. It was a little woman, without bonnet or shawl, whose back was towards us. She turned from side to side, now talking to one, and now to another of the surrounding circle. At first I thought she was setting forth her grievances, in the hope of sympathy, or perhaps of justice; but I soon perceived that her motions were too calm for that. Sometimes the crowd would speak altogether, sometimes keep silent for a full minute while she went on talking. When she turned her face towards us, Roger and I turned ours, and stared at each other. The face was disfigured by a swollen eye, evidently from a blow; but clearly enough, if it was not Miss Clare, it was the young woman of the beer-jug. Neither of us spoke, but turned once more to watch the result of what seemed to have at length settled down into an almost amicable conference. After a few more grumbles and protestations, the group began to break up into twos and threes. These the young woman seemed to set herself to break up again. Here, however, an ill-looking fellow like a costermonger, with a broken nose, came up to us, and with a strong Irish accent and offensive manner, but still with a touch of Irish breeding, requested to know what our business was. Roger asked if the place wasn't a thoroughfare.

"Not for the likes o' you," he answered, "as comes pryin' after the likes of us. We manage our own affairs down here —*we* do. You'd better be off, my lady."

I have my doubts what sort of reply Roger might have returned if he had been alone, but he certainly spoke in a very conciliatory manner, which, however, the man did not seem to appreciate, for he called it blarney; but the young woman, catching sight of our little group, and supposing, I presume, that it also required dispersion, approached us. She had come within a yard of us, when suddenly her face brightened, and she exclaimed, in a tone of surprise, —

"Mrs. Percivale! You here?"

It was indeed Miss Clare. Without the least embarrassment, she held out her hand to me, but I am afraid I did not take it very cordially. Roger, however, behaved to her as if they stood in a drawing-room, and this brought me to a sense of propriety.

"I don't look very respectable, I fear," she said, putting her hand over her eye. "The fact is, I have had a blow, and it will look worse to-morrow. Were you coming to find me?"

I forget what lame answer either of us gave.

"Will you come in?" she said.

On the spur of the moment, I declined. For all my fine talk to Roger, I shrunk from the idea of entering one of those houses. I can only say, in excuse, that my whole mind was in a condition of bewilderment.

"Can I do any thing for you, then?" she asked, in a tone slightly marked with disappointment, I thought.

"Thank you, no," I answered, hardly knowing what my words were.

"Then good-night," she said, and, nodding kindly, turned, and entered one of the houses.

We also turned in silence, and walked out of the court.

"Why didn't you go with her?" said Roger, as soon as we were in the street.

"I'm sorry I didn't if you wanted to go, Roger; but"—

"I think you might have gone, seeing I was with you," he said.

"I don't think it would have been at all a proper thing to do, without knowing more about her," I answered, a little hurt. "You can't tell what sort of a place it may be."

"It's a good place, wherever she is, or I am much mistaken," he returned.

"You may be much mistaken, Roger."

"True. I have been mistaken more than once in my life. I am not mistaken this time, though."

"I presume you would have gone if I hadn't been with you?"

"Certainly, if she had asked me, which is not very likely."

"And you lay the disappointment of missing a glimpse into the sweet privacy of such a home to my charge?"

It was a spiteful speech; and Roger's silence made me feel it was, which, with the rather patronizing opinion I had of Roger, I found not a little galling. So I, too, kept silence, and nothing beyond a platitude had passed between us when I found myself at my own door, my shopping utterly forgotten, and something acid on my mind.

"Don't you mean to come in?" I said, for he held out his hand at the top of the stairs to bid me good-night. "My husband will be home soon, if he has not come already. You needn't be bored with my company-you can sit in the study."

"I think I had better not," he answered.

"I am very sorry, Roger, if I was rude to you," I said; "but how could you wish me to be hand-and-glove with a woman who visits people who she is well aware would not think of inviting her if they had a notion of her surroundings. That can't be right, I am certain. I protest I feel just as if I had been reading an ill-invented story,—an unnatural fiction. I cannot get these things together in my mind at all, do what I will."

"There must be some way of accounting for it," said Roger.

"No doubt," I returned; "but who knows what that way may be?"

"You may be wrong in supposing that the people at whose houses she visits know nothing about her habits."

"Is it at all likely they do, Roger? Do you think it is? I know at least that my cousin dispensed with her services as soon as she came to the knowledge of certain facts concerning these very points."

"Excuse me-certain rumors-very uncertain facts."

When you are cross, the slightest play upon words is an offence. I knocked at the door in dudgeon, then turned and said,—

"My cousin Judy, Mr. Roger"—

But here I paused, for I had nothing ready. Anger makes some people cleverer for the moment, but when I am angry I am always stupid. Roger finished the sentence for me.

—"Your cousin Judy is, you must allow, a very conventional woman," he said.

"She is very good-natured, anyhow. And what do you say to Lady Bernard?"

"She hasn't repudiated Miss Clare's acquaintance, so far as I know."

"But, answer me, —do you believe Lady Bernard would invite her to meet her friends if she knew all?"

"Depend upon it, Lady Bernard knows what she is about. People of her rank can afford to be unconventional."

This irritated me yet more, for it implied that I was influenced by the conventionality which both he and my husband despised; and Sarah opening the door that instant, I stepped in, without even saying good-night to him. Before she closed it, however, I heard my husband's voice, and ran out again to welcome him.

He and Roger had already met in the little front garden. They did not shake hands-they never did-they always met as if they had parted only an hour ago.

"What were you and my wife quarrelling about, Rodge?" I heard Percivale ask, and paused on the middle of the stair to hear his answer.

"How do you know we were quarrelling?" returned Roger gloomily.

"I heard you from the very end of the street," said my husband.

"That's not so far," said Roger; for indeed one house, with, I confess, a good space of garden on each side of it, and the end of another house, finished the street. But notwithstanding the shortness of the distance it stung me to the quick. Here had I been regarding, not even with contempt, only with disgust, the quarrel in which Miss Clare was mixed up; and half an hour after, my own voice was heard in dispute with my husband's brother from the end of the street in which we lived! I felt humiliated, and did not rush down the remaining half of the steps to implore my husband's protection against Roger's crossness.

"Too far to hear a wife and a brother, though," returned Percivale jocosely.

"Go on," said Roger; "pray go on. *Let dogs delight* comes next. I beg Mrs. Percivale's pardon. I will amend the quotation: 'Let dogs delight to worry'"—

"Cats," I exclaimed; and rushing down the steps, I kissed Roger before I kissed my husband. "I meant —I mean —I was going to say *lambs*."

"Now, Roger, don't add to your vices flattery and"—

"And fibbing," he subjoined.

"I didn't say so."

"You only meant it."

"Don't begin again," interposed Percivale: "Come in, and refer the cause in dispute to me."

We did go in, and we did refer the matter to him. By the time we had between us told him the facts of the case, however, the point in dispute between us appeared to have grown hazy, the fact being that neither of us cared to say any thing more about it. Percivale insisted that there was no question before the court. At length Roger, turning from me to his brother, said, —

"It's not worth mentioning, Charley; but what led to our irreconcilable quarrel was this: I thought Wynnie might have accepted Miss Clare's invitation to walk in and pay her a visit; and Wynnie thought me, I suppose, too ready to sacrifice her dignity to the pleasure of seeing a little more of the object of our altercation. There!"

My husband turned to me and said, —

"Mrs. Percivale, do you accept this as a correct representation of your difference?"

"Well," I answered, hesitating—"yes, on the whole. All I object to is the word *dignity*."

"I retract it," cried Roger, "and accept any substitute you prefer."

"Let it stand," I returned. "It will do as well as a better. I only wish to say that it was not exactly my dignity"—

"No, no; your sense of propriety," said my husband; and then sat silent for a minute or two, pondering like a judge. At length he spoke: —

"Wife," he said, "you might have gone with your brother, I think; but I quite understand your disinclination. At the same time, a more generous judgment of Miss Clare might have prevented any difference of feeling in the matter."

"But," I said, greatly inclined to cry, "I only postponed my judgment concerning her."

And I only postponed my crying, for I was very much ashamed of myself.

CHAPTER XVII
MISS CLARE.

Of course my husband and I talked a good deal more about what I ought to have done; and I saw clearly enough that I ought to have run any risk there might be in accepting her invitation. I had been foolishly taking more care of myself than was necessary. I told him I would write to Roger, and ask him when he could take me there again.

"I will tell you a better plan," he said. "I will go with you myself. And that will get rid of half the awkwardness there would be if you went with Roger, after having with him refused to go in."

"But would that be fair to Roger? She would think I didn't like going with him, and I would go with Roger anywhere. It was I who did not want to go. He did."

"My plan, however, will pave the way for a full explanation-or confession rather, I suppose it will turn out to be. I know you are burning to make it, with your mania for confessing your faults."

I knew he did not like me the worse for that *mania*, though.

"The next time," he added, "you can go with Roger, always supposing you should feel inclined to continue the acquaintance, and then you will be able to set him right in her eyes."

The plan seemed unobjectionable. But just then Percivale was very busy; and I being almost as much occupied with my baby as he was with his, day after day and week after week passed, during which our duty to Miss Clare was, I will not say either forgotten or neglected, but unfulfilled.

One afternoon I was surprised by a visit from my father. He not unfrequently surprised us.

"Why didn't you let us know, papa?" I said. "A surprise is very nice; but an expectation is much nicer, and lasts so much longer."

"I might have disappointed you."

"Even if you had, I should have already enjoyed the expectation. That would be safe."

"There's a good deal to be said in excuse of surprises," he rejoined; "but in the present case, I have a special one to offer. I was taken with a sudden desire to see you. It was very foolish no doubt, and you are quite right in wishing I weren't here, only going to come to-morrow."

"Don't be so cruel, papa. Scarcely a day passes in which *I* do not long to see *you*. My baby makes me think more about my home than ever."

"Then she's a very healthy baby, if one may judge by her influences. But you know, if I had had to give you warning, I could not have been here before to-morrow; and surely you will acknowledge, that, however nice expectation may be, presence is better."

"Yes, papa. We will make a compromise, if you please. Every time you think of coming to me, you must either come at once, or let me know you are coming. Do you agree to that?"

"I agree," he said.

So I have the pleasure of a constant expectation. Any day he may walk in unheralded; or by any post I may receive a letter with the news that he is coming at such a time.

As we sat at dinner that evening, he asked if we had lately seen Miss Clare.

"I've seen her only once, and Percivale not at all, since you were here last, papa," I answered.

"How's that?" he asked again, a little surprised. "Haven't you got her address yet? I want very much to know more of her."

"So do we. I haven't got her address, but I know where she lives."

"What do you mean, Wynnie? Has she taken to dark sayings of late, Percivale?"

I told him the whole story of my adventure with Roger, and the reports Judy had prejudiced my judgment withal. He heard me through in silence, for it was a rule with him never to interrupt a narrator. He used to say, "You will generally get at more, and in a better fashion, if you let any narrative take its own devious course, without the interruption of requested explanations. By the time it is over, you will find the questions you wanted to ask mostly vanished."

"Describe the place to me, Wynnie," he said, when I had ended. "I must go and see her. I have a suspicion, amounting almost to a conviction, that she is one whose acquaintance ought to be cultivated at any cost. There is some grand explanation of all this contradictory strangeness."

"I don't think I could describe the place to you so that you would find it. But if Percivale wouldn't mind my going with you instead of with him, I should be only too happy to accompany you. May I, Percivale?"

"Certainly. It will do just as well to go with your father as with me. I only stipulate, that, if you are both satisfied, you take Roger with you next time."

"Of course I will."

"Then we'll go to-morrow morning," said my father.

"I don't think she is likely to be at home in the morning," I said. "She goes out giving lessons, you know; and the probability is, that at that time we should not find her."

"Then why not to-night?" he rejoined.

"Why not, if you wish it?"

"I do wish it, then."

"If you knew the place, though, I think you would prefer going a little earlier than we can to-night."

"Ah, well! we will go to-morrow evening. We could dine early, couldn't we?"

So it was arranged. My father went about some business in the morning. We dined early, and set out about six o'clock.

My father was getting an old man, and if any protection had been required, he could not have been half so active as Roger; and yet I felt twice as safe with him. I am satisfied that the deepest sense of safety, even in respect of physical dangers, can spring only from moral causes; neither do you half so much fear evil happening to you, as fear evil happening which ought not to happen to you. I believe what made me so courageous was the undeveloped fore-feeling, that, if any evil should overtake me in my father's company, I should not care; it would be all right then, anyhow. The repose was in my father himself, and neither in his strength nor his wisdom. The former might fail, the latter might mistake; but so long as I was with him in what I did, no harm worth counting harm could come to me,—only such as I should neither lament nor feel. Scarcely a shadow of danger, however, showed itself.

It was a cold evening in the middle of November. The light, which had been scanty enough all day, had vanished in a thin penetrating fog. Round every lamp in the street was a colored halo; the gay shops gleamed like jewel-caverns of Aladdin hollowed out of the darkness; and the people that hurried or sauntered along looked inscrutable. Where could they live? Had they anybody to love them? Were their hearts quiet under their dingy cloaks and shabby coats?

"Yes," returned my father, to whom I had said something to this effect, "what would not one give for a peep into the mysteries of all these worlds that go crowding past us. If we could but see through the opaque husk of them, some would glitter and glow like diamond mines; others perhaps would look mere earthy holes; some of them forsaken quarries, with a great pool of stagnant water in the bottom; some like vast coal-pits of gloom, into which you dared not carry a lighted lamp for fear of explosion. Some would be mere lumber-rooms; others ill-arranged libraries, without a poets' corner anywhere. But what a wealth of creation they show, and what infinite room for hope it affords!"

"But don't you think, papa, there may be something of worth lying even in the earth-pit, or at the bottom of the stagnant water in the forsaken quarry?"

"Indeed I do; though I *have* met more than one in my lifetime concerning whom I felt compelled to say that it wanted keener eyes than mine to discover the hidden jewel. But then there *are* keener eyes than mine, for there are more loving eyes. Myself I have been able to see good very clearly where some could see none; and shall I doubt that God can see good where my mole-eyes can see none? Be sure of this, that, as he is keen-eyed for the evil in his creatures to destroy it, he would, if it were possible, be yet keener-eyed for the good to nourish and cherish it. If men would only side with the good that is in them, —will that the seed should grow and bring forth fruit!"

CHAPTER XVIII
MISS CLARE'S HOME.

We had now arrived at the passage. The gin-shop was flaring through the fog. A man in a fustian jacket came out of it, and walked slowly down before us, with the clay of the brick-field clinging to him as high as the leather straps with which his trousers were confined, garter-wise, under the knee. The place was quiet. We and the brickmaker seemed the only people in it. When we turned the last corner, he was walking in at the very door where Miss Clare had disappeared. When I told my father that was the house, he called after the man, who came out again, and, standing on the pavement, waited until we came up.

"Does Miss Clare live in this house?" my father asked.

"She do," answered the man curtly.

"First floor?"

"No. Nor yet the second, nor the third. She live nearer heaven than 'ere another in the house 'cep' myself. I live in the attic, and so do she."

"There is a way of living nearer to heaven than that," said my father, laying his hand, "with a right old man's grace," on his shoulder.

"I dunno, 'cep' you was to go up in a belloon," said the man, with a twinkle in his eye, which my father took to mean that he understood him better than he chose to acknowledge; but he did not pursue the figure.

He was a rough, lumpish young man, with good but dull features-only his blue eye was clear. He looked my father full in the face, and I thought I saw a dim smile about his mouth.

"You know her, then, I suppose?"

"Everybody in the house knows *her*. There ain't many the likes o' her as lives wi' the likes of us. You go right up to the top. I don't know if she's in, but a'most any one'll be able to tell you. I ain't been home yet."

My father thanked him, and we entered the house, and began to ascend. The stair was very much worn and rather dirty, and some of the banisters were broken away, but the walls were tolerably clean. Half-way up we met a little girl with tangled hair and tattered garments, carrying a bottle.

"Do you know, my dear," said my father to her, "whether Miss Clare is at home?"

"I dunno," she answered. "I dunno who you mean. I been mindin' the baby. He ain't well. Mother says his head's bad. She's a-going up to tell grannie, and see if she can't do suthin' for him. You better ast mother. —Mother!" she called out —"here's a lady an' a gen'lem'."

"You go about yer business, and be back direckly," cried a gruff voice from somewhere above.

"That's mother," said the child, and ran down the stair.

When we reached the second floor, there stood a big fat woman on the landing, with her face red, and her hair looking like that of a doll ill stuck on. She did not speak, but stood waiting to see what we wanted.

"I'm told Miss Clare lives here," said my father. "Can you tell me, my good woman, whether she's at home?"

"I'm neither good woman nor bad woman," she returned in an insolent tone.

"I beg your pardon," said my father; "but you see I didn't know your name."

"An' ye don't know it yet. You've no call to know my name. I'll ha' nothing to do wi' the likes o' you as goes about takin' poor folks's childer from 'em. There's my poor Glory's been an' took atwixt you an' grannie, and shet up in a formatory as you calls it; an' I should like to know what right you've got to go about that way arter poor girls as has mothers to help."

"I assure you I had nothing to do with it," said my father. "I'm a country clergyman myself, and have no duty in London."

"Well, that's where they've took her-down in the country. I make no doubt but you've had your finger in that pie. You don't come here to call upon us for the pleasure o' makin' our acquaintance-ha! ha! ha! —You're allus arter somethin' troublesome. I'd adwise you, sir and miss, to let well alone. Sleepin' dogs won't bite; but you'd better let 'em lie-and that I tell you."

"Believe me," said my father quite quietly, "I haven't the least knowledge of your daughter. The country's a bigger place than you seem to think,—far bigger than London itself. All I wanted to trouble you about was to tell us whether Miss Clare was at home or not."

"I don't know no one o' that name. If it's grannie you mean, she's at home, I know-though it's not much reason I've got to care whether she's at home or not."

"It's a young-woman, I mean," said my father.

"'Tain't a young lady, then? —Well, I don't care what you call her. I dare say it'll be all one, come judgment. You'd better go up till you can't go no further, an' knocks yer head agin the tiles, and then you may feel about for a door, and knock at that, and see if the party as opens it is the party you wants."

So saying, she turned in at a door behind her, and shut it. But we could hear her still growling and grumbling.

"It's very odd," said my father, with a bewildered smile. "I think we'd better do as she says, and go up till we knock our heads against the tiles."

We climbed two stairs more, —the last very steep, and so dark that when we reached the top we found it necessary to follow the woman's directions literally, and feel about for a door. But we had not to feel long or far, for there was one close to the top of the stair. My father knocked. There was no reply; but we heard the sound of a chair, and presently some one opened it. The only light being behind her, I could not see her face, but the size and shape were those of Miss Clare.

She did not leave us in doubt, however; for, without a moment's hesitation, she held out her hand to me, saying, "This *is* kind of you, Mrs. Percivale;" then to my father, saying, "I'm very glad to see you, Mr. Walton. Will you walk in?"

We followed her into the room. It was not very small, for it occupied nearly the breadth of the house. On one side the roof sloped so nearly to the floor that there was not height enough to stand erect in. On the other side the sloping part was partitioned off, evidently for a bedroom. But what a change it was from the lower part of the house! By the light of a single mould candle, I saw that the floor was as clean as old boards could be made, and I wondered whether she scrubbed them herself. I know now that she did. The two dormer windows were hung with white dimity curtains. Back in the angle of the roof, between the windows, stood an old bureau. There was little more than room between the top of it and the ceiling for a little plaster statuette with bound hands and a strangely crowned head. A few books on hanging shelves were on the opposite side by the door to the other room; and the walls, which were whitewashed, were a good deal covered with-whether engravings or etchings or lithographs I could not then see-none of them framed, only mounted on card-board. There was a fire cheerfully burning in the gable, and opposite to that stood a tall old-fashioned cabinet piano, in faded red silk. It was open; and on the music-rest lay Handel's "Verdi Prati," —for I managed to glance at it as we left. A few wooden chairs, and one very old-fashioned easy-chair, covered with striped chintz, from which not glaze only but color almost had disappeared, with an oblong table of deal, completed the furniture of the room. She made my father sit down in the easy-chair, placed me one in front of the fire, and took another at the corner opposite my father. A moment of silence followed, which I, having a guilty conscience, felt awkward. But my father never allowed awkwardness to accumulate.

"I had hoped to have been able to call upon you long ago, Miss Clare, but there was some difficulty in finding out where you lived."

"You are no longer surprised at that difficulty, I presume," she returned with a smile.

"But," said my father, "if you will allow an old man to speak freely" —

"Say what you please, Mr. Walton. I promise to answer *any* question *you* think proper to ask me."

"My dear Miss Clare, I had not the slightest intention of catechising you, though, of course, I shall be grateful for what confidence you please to put in me. What I meant to say might indeed have taken the form of a question, but as such could have been intended only for you to answer to yourself,—whether, namely, it was wise to place yourself at such a disadvantage as living in this quarter must be to you."

"If you were acquainted with my history, you would perhaps hesitate, Mr. Walton, before you said I *placed myself* at such disadvantage."

Here a thought struck me.

"I fancy, papa, it is not for her own sake Miss Clare lives here."

"I hope not," she interposed.

"I believe," I went on, "she has a grandmother, who probably has grown accustomed to the place, and is unwilling to leave it."

She looked puzzled for a moment, then burst into a merry laugh.

"I see," she exclaimed. "How stupid I am! You have heard some of the people in the house talk about *grannie*: that's me! I am known in the house as grannie, and have been for a good many years now—I can hardly, without thinking, tell for how many."

Again she laughed heartily, and my father and I shared her merriment.

"How many grandchildren have you then, pray, Miss Clare?"

"Let me see."

She thought for a minute.

"I could easily tell you if it were only the people in this house I had to reckon up. They are about five and thirty; but unfortunately the name has been caught up in the neighboring houses, and I am very sorry that in consequence I cannot with certainty say how many grandchildren I have. I think I know them all, however; and I fancy that is more than many an English grandmother, with children in America, India, and Australia, can say for herself."

Certainly she was not older than I was; and while hearing her merry laugh, and seeing her young face overflowed with smiles, which appeared to come sparkling out of her eyes as out of two well-springs, one could not help feeling puzzled how, even in the farthest-off jest, she could have got the name of grannie. But I could at the same time, recall expressions of her countenance which would much better agree with the name than that which now shone from it.

"Would you like to hear," she said, when our merriment had a little subsided, "how I have so easily arrived at the honorable name of grannie,—at least all I know about it?"

"I should be delighted," said my father.

"You don't know what you are pledging yourself to when you say so," she rejoined, again laughing. "You will have to hear the whole of my story from the beginning."

"Again I say I shall be delighted," returned my father, confident that her history could be the source of nothing but pleasure to him.

CHAPTER XIX
HER STORY.

Thereupon Miss Clare began. I do not pretend to give her very words, but I must tell her story as if she were telling it herself. I shall be as true as I can to the facts, and hope to catch something of the tone of the narrator as I go on.

"My mother died when I was very young, and I was left alone with my father, for I was his only child. He was a studious and thoughtful man. It *may* be the partiality of a daughter, I know, but I am not necessarily wrong in believing that diffidence in his own powers alone prevented him from distinguishing himself. As it was, he supported himself and me by literary work of, I presume, a secondary order. He would spend all his mornings for many weeks in the library of the British Museum,—reading and making notes; after which he would sit writing at home for as long or longer. I should have found it very dull during the former of these times, had he not early discovered that I had some capacity for music, and provided for me what I now know to have been the best instruction to be had. His feeling alone had guided him right, for he was without musical knowledge. I believe he could not have found me a better teacher in all Europe. Her character was lovely, and her music the natural outcome of its harmony. But I must not forget it is about myself I have to tell you. I went to her, then, almost every day for a time-but how long that was, I can only guess. It must have been several years, I think, else I could not have attained what proficiency I had when my sorrow came upon me.

"What my father wrote I cannot tell. How gladly would I now read the shortest sentence I knew to be his! He never told me for what journals he wrote, or even for what publishers. I fancy it was work in which his brain was more interested than his heart, and which he was always hoping to exchange for something more to his mind. After his death I could discover scarcely a scrap of his writings, and not a hint to guide me to what he had written.

"I believe we went on living from hand to mouth, my father never getting so far ahead of the wolf as to be able to pause and choose his way. But I was very happy, and would have been no whit less happy if he had explained our circumstances, for that would have conveyed to me no hint of danger. Neither has any of the suffering I have had-at least any keen enough to be worth dwelling upon-sprung from personal privation, although I am not unacquainted with hunger and cold.

"My happiest time was when my father asked me to play to him while he wrote, and I sat down to my old cabinet Broadwood,—the one you see there is as like it as I could find,— and played any thing and every thing I liked,—for somehow I never forgot what I had once learned,—while my father sat, as he said, like a mere extension of the instrument, operated upon, rather than listening, as he wrote. What I then *thought*, I cannot tell. I don't believe I thought at all. I only *musicated*, as a little pupil of mine once said to me, when, having found her sitting with her hands on her lap before the piano, I asked her what she was doing: 'I am only musicating,' she answered. But the enjoyment was none the less that there was no conscious thought in it.

"Other branches he taught me himself, and I believe I got on very fairly for my age. We lived then in the neighborhood of the Museum, where I was well known to all the people of the place, for I used often to go there, and would linger about looking at things, sometimes for hours before my father came to me but he always came at the very minute he had said, and always found me at the appointed spot. I gained a great deal by thus haunting the Museum —a great deal more than I supposed at the time. One gain was, that I knew perfectly where in the place any given sort of thing was to be found, if it were there at all: I had unconsciously learned something of classification.

"One afternoon I was waiting as usual, but my father did not come at the time appointed. I waited on and on till it grew dark, and the hour for closing arrived, by which time I was in great uneasiness; but I was forced to go home without him. I must hasten over this part of my history, for even yet I can scarcely bear to speak of it. I found that while I was waiting, he had been seized with some kind of fit in the reading-room, and had been carried home, and that I was alone in the world. The landlady, for we only rented rooms in the house, was very kind to me, at least until she found that my father had left no money. He had then been only reading for a long time; and, when I looked back, I could see that he must have been short of money for some weeks at least. A few bills coming in, all our little effects-for the furniture was our own-were sold, without bringing sufficient to pay them. The things went for less than half their value, in consequence, I believe, of that well-known conspiracy of the brokers which they call *knocking out*. I was especially miserable at losing my father's books, which, although in ignorance, I greatly valued, —more miserable even, I honestly think, than at seeing my loved piano carried off.

"When the sale was over, and every thing removed, I sat down on the floor, amidst the dust and bits of paper and straw and cord, without a single idea in my head as to what was to become of me, or what I was to do next. I didn't cry, —that I am sure of; but I doubt if in all London there was a more wretched child than myself just then. The twilight was darkening down, —the twilight of a November afternoon. Of course there was no fire in the grate, and I had eaten nothing that day; for although the landlady had offered me some dinner, and I had tried to please her by taking some, I found I could not swallow, and had to leave it. While I sat thus on the floor, I heard her come into the room, and some one with her; but I did not look round, and they, not seeing me, and thinking, I suppose, that I was in one of the other rooms, went on talking about me. All I afterwards remembered of their conversation was some severe reflections on my father, and the announcement of the decree that I must go to the workhouse. Though I knew nothing definite as to the import of this doom, it filled me with horror. The moment they left me alone, to look for me, as I supposed, I got up, and, walking as softly as I could, glided down the stairs, and, unbonneted and unwrapped, ran from the house, half-blind with terror.

"I had not gone farther, I fancy, than a few yards, when I ran up against some one, who laid hold of me, and asked me gruffly what I meant by it. I knew the voice: it was that of an old Irishwoman who did all the little charing we wanted, —for I kept the rooms tidy, and the landlady cooked for us. As soon as she saw who it was, her tone changed; and then first I broke out in sobs, and told her I was running away because they were going to send me to the workhouse. She burst into a torrent of Irish indignation, and assured me that such should never be my fate while she lived. I must go back to the house with her, she said, and get my things; and then I should go home with her, until something better should turn up. I told her I would go with her anywhere, except into that house again; and she did not insist, but afterwards went by herself and got my little wardrobe. In the mean time she led me away to a large house in a square, of which she took the key from her pocket to open the door. It looked to me such a huge place!—the largest house I had ever been in; but it was rather desolate, for, except in one little room below, where she had scarcely more than a bed and a chair, a slip of carpet and a frying-pan, there was not an article of furniture in the whole place. She had been put there when the last tenant left, to take care of the place, until another tenant should appear to turn her out. She had her houseroom and a trifle a week besides for her services, beyond which she depended entirely on what she could make by charing. When she had no house to live in on the same terms, she took a room somewhere.

"Here I lived for several months, and was able to be of use; for as Mrs. Conan was bound to be there at certain times to show any one over the house who brought an order from the agent, and this necessarily took up a good part of her working time; and as, moreover, I could open the door and walk about the place as well as another, she willingly left me in charge as often as she had a job elsewhere.

"On such occasions, however, I found it very dreary indeed, for few people called, and she would not unfrequently be absent the whole day. If I had had my piano, I should have cared little; but I had not a single book, except one-and what do you think that was? An odd volume of the Newgate Calendar. I need hardly say that it had not the effect on me which it is said to have on some of its students: it moved me, indeed, to the profoundest sympathy, not with the crimes of the malefactors, only with the malefactors themselves, and their mental condition after the deed was actually done. But it was with the fascination of a hopeless horror, making me feel almost as if I had committed every crime as I perused its tale, that I regarded them. They were to me like living crimes. It was not until long afterwards that I was able to understand that a man's actions are not the man, but may be separated from him; that his character even is not the man, but may be changed while he yet holds the same individuality,—is the man who was blind though he now sees; whence it comes, that, the deeds continuing his, all stain of them may yet be washed out of him. I did not, I say, understand all this until afterwards; but I believe, odd as it may seem, that volume of the Newgate Calendar threw down the first deposit of soil, from which afterwards sprung what grew to be almost a passion in me, for getting the people about me clean,—a passion which might have done as much harm as good, if its companion, patience, had not been sent me to guide and restrain it. In a word, I came at length to understand, in some measure, the last prayer of our Lord for those that crucified him, and the ground on which he begged from his Father their forgiveness,—that they knew not what they did. If the Newgate Calendar was indeed the beginning of this course of education, I need not regret having lost my piano, and having that volume for a while as my only aid to reflection.

"My father had never talked much to me about religion; but when he did, it was with such evident awe in his spirit, and reverence in his demeanor, as had more effect on me, I am certain, from the very paucity of the words in which his meaning found utterance. Another thing which had still more influence upon me was, that, waking one night after I had been asleep for some time, I saw him on his knees by my bedside. I did not move or speak, for fear of disturbing him; and, indeed, such an awe came over me, that it would have required a considerable effort of the will for any bodily movement whatever. When he lifted his head, I caught a glimpse of a pale, tearful face; and it is no wonder that the virtue of the sight should never have passed away.

"On Sundays we went to church in the morning, and in the afternoon, in fine weather, went out for a walk; or, if it were raining or cold, I played to him till he fell asleep on the sofa. Then in the evening, after tea, we had more music, some poetry, which we read alternately, and a chapter of the New Testament, which he always read to me. I mention this, to show you that I did not come all unprepared to the study of the Newgate Calendar. Still, I cannot think, that, under any circumstances, it could have done an innocent child harm. Even familiarity with vice is not necessarily pollution. There cannot be many women of my age as familiar with it in every shape as I am; and I do not find that I grow to regard it with one atom less of absolute abhorrence, although I neither shudder at the mention of it, nor turn with disgust from the person in whom it dwells. But the consolations of religion were not yet consciously mine. I had not yet begun to think of God in any relation to myself.

"The house was in an old square, built, I believe, in the reign of Queen Anne, which, although many of the houses were occupied by well-to-do people, had fallen far from its first high estate. No one would believe, to look at it from the outside, what a great place it was. The whole of the space behind it, corresponding to the small gardens of the other houses, was occupied by a large music-room, under which was a low-pitched room of equal extent, while all under that were cellars, connected with the sunk story in front by a long vaulted passage, corresponding to a wooden gallery above, which formed a communication between the drawing-room floor and the music-room. Most girls of my age, knowing these vast empty spaces about them, would have been terrified at being left alone there, even in mid-day. But I was, I suppose, too miserable to be frightened. Even the horrible facts of the Newgate Calendar did not thus affect me, not even when Mrs. Conan was later than usual, and the night came down, and I had to sit, perhaps for hours, in the dark,—for she would not allow me to have a candle for fear of fire. But you will not wonder that I used to cry a good deal, although I did my best to hide the traces of it, because I knew it would annoy my kind old friend. She showed me a great deal of rough tenderness, which would not have been rough had not the natural grace of her Irish nature been injured by the contact of many years with the dull coarseness of the uneducated Saxon. You may be sure I learned to love her dearly. She shared every thing with me in the way of eating, and would have shared also the tumbler of gin and water with which she generally ended the day, but something, I don't know what, I believe a simple physical dislike, made me refuse that altogether.

"One evening I have particular cause to remember, both for itself, and because of something that followed many years after. I was in the drawing-room on the first floor, a double room with folding doors and a small cabinet behind communicating with a back stair; for the stairs were double all through the house, adding much to the *eeriness* of the place as I look back upon it in my memory. I fear, in describing the place so minutely, I may have been rousing false expectations of an adventure; but I have a reason for being rather minute, though it will not appear until afterwards. I had been looking out of the window all the afternoon upon the silent square, for, as it was no thoroughfare, it was only enlivened by the passing and returning now and then of a tradesman's cart; and, as it was winter, there were no children playing in the garden. It was a rainy afternoon. A gray cloud of fog and soot hung from the whole sky. About a score of yellow leaves yet quivered on the trees, and the statue of Queen Anne stood bleak and disconsolate among the bare branches. I am afraid I am getting long-winded, but somehow that afternoon seems burned into me in enamel. I gazed drearily without interest. I brooded over the past; I never, at this time, so far as I remember, dreamed of looking forward. I had no hope. It never occurred to me that things might grow better. I was dull and wretched. I may just say here in passing, that I think this experience is in a great measure what has enabled me to understand the peculiar misery of the poor in our large towns, —they have no hope, no impulse to look forward, nothing to expect; they live but in the present, and the dreariness of that soon shapes the whole atmosphere of their spirits to its own likeness. Perhaps the first thing one who would help them has to do is to aid the birth of some small vital hope in them; that is better than a thousand gifts, especially those of the ordinary kind, which mostly do harm, tending to keep them what they are, —a prey to present and importunate wants.

"It began to grow dark; and, tired of standing, I sat down upon the floor, for there was nothing to sit upon besides. There I still sat, long after it was quite dark. All at once a surge of self-pity arose in my heart. I burst out wailing and sobbing, and cried aloud, 'God has forgotten me altogether!' The fact was, I had had no dinner that day, for Mrs. Conan had expected to return long before; and the piece of bread she had given me, which was all that was in the house, I had eaten many hours ago. But I was not thinking of my dinner, though the want of it may have had to do with this burst of misery. What I was really thinking of was, —that I could do nothing for anybody. My little ambition had always been to be useful. I knew I was of some use to my father; for I kept the rooms tidy for him, and dusted his pet books-oh, so carefully! for they were like household gods to me. I had also played to him, and I knew he enjoyed that: he said so, many times. And I had begun, though not long before he left me, to think how I should be able to help him better by and by. For I saw that he worked very hard, —so hard that it made him silent; and I knew that my music-mistress made her livelihood, partly at least, by giving lessons; and I thought that I might, by and by, be able to give lessons too, and then papa would not require to work so hard, for I too should bring home money to pay for what we wanted. But now I was of use to nobody, I said, and not likely to become of any. I could not even help poor Mrs. Conan, except by doing what a child might do just as well as I, for I did not earn a penny of our living; I only gave the poor old thing time to work harder, that I might eat up her earnings! What added to the misery was, that I had always thought of myself as a lady; for was not papa a gentleman, let him be ever so poor? Shillings and sovereigns in his pocket could not determine whether a man was a gentleman or not! And if he was a gentleman, his daughter must be a lady. But how could I be a lady if I was content to be a burden to a poor charwoman, instead of earning my own living, and something besides with which to help her? For I had the notion —*how* it came I cannot tell, though I know well enough *whence* it came-that position depended on how much a person was able to help other people; and here I was, useless, worse than useless to anybody! Why did not God remember me, if it was only for my father's sake? He was worth something, if I was not! And I would be worth something, if only I had a chance! —'I am of no use,' I cried, 'and God has forgotten me altogether!' And I went on weeping and moaning in my great misery, until I fell fast asleep on the floor.

"I have no theory about dreams and visions; and I don't know what you, Mr. Walton, may think as to whether these ended with the first ages of the church; but surely if one falls fast asleep without an idea in one's head, and a whole dismal world of misery in one's heart, and wakes up quiet and refreshed, without the misery, and with an idea, there can be no great fanaticism in thinking that the change may have come from somewhere near where the miracles lie, —in fact, that God may have had something-might I not say every thing? —to do with it. For my part, if I were to learn that he had no hand in this experience of mine, I couldn't help losing all interest in it, and wishing that I had died of the misery which it dispelled. Certainly, if it had a physical source, it wasn't that I was more comfortable, for I was hungrier than ever, and, you may well fancy, cold enough, having slept on the bare floor without any thing to cover me on Christmas Eve-for Christmas Eve it was. No doubt my sleep had done me good, but I suspect the sleep came to quiet my mind for the reception of the new idea.

"The way Mrs. Conan kept Christmas Day, as she told me in the morning, was, to comfort her old bones in bed until the afternoon, and then to have a good tea with a chop; after which she said she would have me read the Newgate Calendar to her. So, as soon as I had washed up the few breakfast things, I asked, if, while she lay in bed, I might not go out for a little while to look for work. She laughed at the notion of my being able to do any thing, but did not object to my trying. So I dressed myself as neatly as I could, and set out.

"There were two narrow streets full of small shops, in which those of furniture-brokers predominated, leading from the two lower corners of the square down into Oxford Street; and in a shop in one of these, I was not sure which, I had seen an old piano standing, and a girl of about my own age watching. I found the shop at last, although it was shut up; for I knew the name, and knocked at the door. It was opened by a stout matron, with a not unfriendly expression, who asked me what I wanted. I told her I wanted work. She seemed amused at the idea, —for I was very small for my age then as well as now, —but, apparently willing to have a chat with me, asked what I could do. I told her I could teach her daughter music. She asked me what made me come to her, and I told her. Then she asked me how much I should charge. I told her that some ladies had a guinea a lesson; at which she laughed so heartily, that I had to wait until the first transports of her amusement were over before I could finish by saying, that for my part I should be glad to give an hour's lesson for threepence, only, if she pleased, I should prefer it in silver. But how was she to know, she asked, that I could teach her properly. I told her I would let her hear me play; whereupon she led me into the shop, through a back room in which her husband sat smoking a long pipe, with a tankard at his elbow. Having taken down a shutter, she managed with some difficulty to clear me a passage through a crowd of furniture to the instrument, and with a struggle I squeezed through and reached it; but at the first chord I struck, I gave a cry of dismay. In some alarm she asked what was the matter, calling me *child* very kindly. I told her it was so dreadfully out of tune I couldn't play upon it at all; but, if she would get it tuned, I should not be long in showing her that I could do what I professed. She told me she could not afford to have it tuned; and if I could not teach Bertha on it as it was, she couldn't help it. This, however, I assured her, was utterly impossible; upon which, with some show of offence, she reached over a chest of drawers, and shut down the cover. I believe she doubted whether I could play at all, and had not been merely amusing myself at her expense. Nothing was left but to thank her, bid her good-morning, and walk out of the house, dreadfully disappointed.

"Unwilling to go home at once, I wandered about the neighborhood, through street after street, until I found myself in another square, with a number of business-signs in it, —one of them that of a piano-forte firm, at sight of which, a thought came into my head. The next morning I went in, and requested to see the master. The man to whom I spoke stared, no doubt; but he went, and returning after a little while, during which my heart beat very fast, invited me to walk into the counting-house. Mr. Perkins was amused with the story of my attempt to procure teaching, and its frustration. If I had asked him for money, to which I do not believe hunger itself could have driven me, he would probably have got rid of me quickly enough,—and small blame to him, as Mrs. Conan would have said; but to my request that he would spare a man to tune Mrs. Lampeter's piano, he replied at once that he would, provided I could satisfy him as to my efficiency. Thereupon he asked me a few questions about music, of which some I could answer and some I could not. Next he took me into the shop, set me a stool in front of a grand piano, and told me to play. I could not help trembling a good deal, but I tried my best. In a few moments, however, the tears were dropping on the keys; and, when he asked me what was the matter, I told him it was months since I had touched a piano. The answer did not, however, satisfy him; he asked very kindly how that was, and I had to tell him my whole story. Then he not only promised to have the piano tuned for me at once, but told me that I might go and practise there as often as I pleased, so long as I was a good girl, and did not take up with bad company. Imagine my delight! Then he sent for a tuner, and I suppose told him a little about me, for the man spoke very kindly to me as we went to the broker's.

"Mr. Perkins has been a good friend to me ever since.

"For six months I continued to give Bertha Lampeter lessons. They were broken off only when she went to a dressmaker to learn her business. But her mother had by that time introduced me to several families of her acquaintance, amongst whom I found five or six pupils on the same terms. By this teaching, if I earned little, I learned much; and every day almost I practised at the music-shop.

"When the house was let, Mrs. Conan took a room in the neighborhood, that I might keep up my connection, she said. Then first I was introduced to scenes and experiences with which I am now familiar. Mrs. Percivale might well recoil if I were to tell her half the wretchedness, wickedness, and vulgarity I have seen, and often had to encounter. For two years or so we changed about, at one time in an empty house, at another in a hired room, sometimes better, sometimes worse off, as regarded our neighbors, until, Mrs. Conan having come to the conclusion that it would be better for her to confine herself to charing, we at last settled down here, where I have now lived for many years.

"You may be inclined to ask why I had not kept up my acquaintance with my music-mistress. I believe the shock of losing my father, and the misery that followed, made me feel as if my former world had vanished; at all events, I never thought of going to her until Mr. Perkins one day, after listening to something I was playing, asked me who had taught me; and this brought her back to my mind so vividly that I resolved to go and see her. She welcomed me with more than kindness,—with tenderness,—and told me I had caused her much uneasiness by not letting her know what had become of me. She looked quite aghast when she learned in what sort of place and with whom I lived; but I told her Mrs. Conan had saved me from the workhouse, and was as much of a mother to me as it was possible for her to be, that we loved each other, and that it would be very wrong of me to leave her now, especially that she was not so well as she had been; and I believe she then saw the thing as I saw it. She made me play to her, was pleased,—indeed surprised, until I told her how I had been supporting myself,—and insisted on my resuming my studies with her, which I was only too glad to do. I now, of course, got on much faster; and she expressed satisfaction with my progress, but continued manifestly uneasy at the kind of thing I had to encounter, and become of necessity more and more familiar with.

"When Mrs. Conan fell ill, I had indeed hard work of it. Unlike most of her class, she had laid by a trifle of money; but as soon as she ceased to add to it, it began to dwindle, and was very soon gone. Do what I could for a while, if it had not been for the kindness of the neighbors, I should sometimes have been in want of bread; and when I hear hard things said of the poor, I often think that surely improvidence is not so bad as selfishness. But, of course, there are all sorts amongst them, just as there are all sorts in every class. When I went out to teach, now one, now another of the women in the house would take charge of my friend; and when I came home, except her guardian happened to have got tipsy, I never found she had been neglected. Miss Harper said I must raise my terms; but I told her that would be the loss of my pupils. Then she said she must see what could be done for me, only no one she knew was likely to employ a child like me, if I were able to teach ever so well. One morning, however, within a week, a note came from Lady Bernard, asking me to go and see her.

"I went, and found —a mother. You do not know her, I think? But you must one day. Good people like you must come together. I will not attempt to describe her. She awed me at first, and I could hardly speak to her,—I was not much more than thirteen then; but with the awe came a certain confidence which was far better than ease. The immediate result was, that she engaged me to go and play for an hour, five days a week, at a certain hospital for sick children in the neighborhood, which she partly supported. For she had a strong belief that there was in music a great healing power. Her theory was, that all healing energy operates first on the mind, and from it passes to the body, and that medicines render aid only by removing certain physical obstacles to the healing force. She believes that when music operating on the mind has procured the peace of harmony, the peace in its turn operates outward, reducing the vital powers also into the harmonious action of health. *How much* there may be in it, I cannot tell; but I do think that good has been and is the result of my playing to those children; for I go still, though not quite so often, and it is music to me to watch my music thrown back in light from some of those sweet, pale, suffering faces. She was too wise to pay me much for it at first. She inquired, before making me the offer, how much I was already earning, asked me upon how much I could support Mrs. Conan and myself comfortably, and then made the sum of my weekly earnings up to that amount. At the same time, however, she sent many things to warm and feed the old woman, so that my mind was set at ease about her. She got a good deal better for a while, but continued to suffer so much from rheumatism, that she was quite unfit to go out charing any more; and I would not hear of her again exposing herself to the damps and draughts of empty houses, so long as I was able to provide for her,—of which ability you may be sure I was not a little proud at first.

"I have been talking for a long time, and yet may seem to have said nothing to account for your finding me where she left me; but I will try to come to the point as quickly as possible.

"Before she was entirely laid up, we had removed to this place,—a rough shelter, but far less so than some of the houses in which we had been. I remember one in which I used to dart up and down like a hunted hare at one time; at another to steal along from stair to stair like a well-meaning ghost afraid of frightening people; my mode of procedure depending in part on the time of day, and which of the inhabitants I had reason to dread meeting. It was a good while before the inmates of this house and I began to know each other. The landlord had turned out the former tenant of this garret after she had been long enough in the house for all the rest to know her; and, notwithstanding she had been no great favorite, they all took her part against the landlord; and fancying, perhaps because we kept more to ourselves, that we were his *protégées*, and that he had turned out Muggy Moll, as they called her, to make room for us, regarded us from the first with disapprobation. The little girls would make grimaces at me, and the bigger girls would pull my hair, slap my face, and even occasionally push me down stairs, while the boys made themselves far more terrible in my eyes. But some remark happening to be dropped one day, which led the landlord to disclaim all previous knowledge of us, things began to grow better. And this is not by any means one of the worst parts of London. I could take Mr. Walton to houses in the East End, where the manners are indescribable. We are all earning our bread here. Some have an occasional attack of drunkenness, and idle about; but they are sick of it again after a while. I remember asking a woman once if her husband would be present at a little entertainment to which Lady Bernard had invited them: she answered that he would be there if he was drunk, but if he was sober he couldn't spare the time.

"Very soon they began to ask me after Mrs. Conan; and one day I invited one of them, who seemed a decent though not very tidy woman, to walk up and see her; for I was anxious she should have a visitor now and then when I was out, as she complained a good deal of the loneliness. The woman consented, and ever after was very kind to her. But my main stay and comfort was an old woman who then occupied the room opposite to this. She was such a good creature! Nearly blind, she yet kept her room the very pink of neatness. I never saw a speck of dust on that chest of drawers, which was hers then, and which she valued far more than many a rich man values the house of his ancestors,—not only because it had been her mother's, but because it bore testimony to the respectability of her family. Her floor and her little muslin window-curtain, her bed and every thing about her, were as clean as lady could desire. She objected to move into a better room below, which the landlord kindly offered her,—for she was a favorite from having been his tenant a long time and never having given him any trouble in collecting her rent,—on the ground that there were two windows in it, and therefore too much light for her bits of furniture. They would, she said, look nothing in that room. She was very pleased when I asked her to pay a visit to Mrs. Conan; and as she belonged to a far higher intellectual grade than my protectress, and as she had a strong practical sense of religion, chiefly manifested in a willing acceptance of the decrees of Providence, I think she did us both good. I wish I could draw you a picture of her coming in at that door, with her all but sightless eyes, the broad borders of her white cap waving, and her hands stretched out before her; for she was more apprehensive than if she had been quite blind, because she could see things without knowing what, or even in what position they were. The most remarkable thing to me was the calmness with which she looked forward to her approaching death, although without the expectation which so many good people seem to have in connection with their departure. I talked to her about it more than once,—not with any presumption of teaching her, for I felt she was far before me, but just to find out how she felt and what she believed. Her answer amounted to this, that she had never known beforehand what lay round the next corner, or what was going to happen to her, for if Providence had meant her to know, it could not be by going to fortune-tellers, as some of the neighbors did; but that she always found things turn out right and good for her, and she did not doubt she would find it so when she came to the last turn.

"By degrees I knew everybody in the house, and of course I was ready to do what I could to help any of them. I had much to lift me into a higher region of mental comfort than was open to them; for I had music, and Lady Bernard lent me books.

"Of course also I kept my rooms as clean and tidy as I could; and indeed, if I had been more carelessly inclined in that way, the sight of the blind woman's would have been a constant reminder to me. By degrees also I was able to get a few more articles of furniture for it, and a bit of carpet to put down before the fire. I whitewashed the walls myself, and after a while began to whitewash the walls of the landing as well, and all down the stair, which was not of much use to the eye, for there is no light. Before long some of the other tenants began to whitewash their rooms also, and contrive to keep things a little tidier. Others declared they had no opinion of such uppish notions; they weren't for the likes of them. These were generally such as would rejoice in wearing finery picked up at the rag-shop; but even some of them began by degrees to cultivate a small measure of order. Soon this one and that began to apply to me for help in various difficulties that arose. But they didn't begin to call me grannie for a long time after this. They used then to call the blind woman grannie, and the name got associated with the top of the house; and I came to be associated with it because I also lived there and we were friends. After her death, it was used from habit, at first with a feeling of mistake, seeing its immediate owner was gone; but by degrees it settled down upon me, and I came to be called grannie by everybody in the house. Even Mrs. Conan would not unfrequently address me, and speak of me too, as grannie, at first with a laugh, but soon as a matter of course.

"I got by and by a few pupils amongst tradespeople of a class rather superior to that in which I had begun to teach, and from whom I could ask and obtain double my former fee; so that things grew, with fluctuations, gradually better. Lady Bernard continued a true friend to me-but she never was other than that to any. Some of her friends ventured on the experiment whether I could teach their children; and it is no wonder if they were satisfied, seeing I had myself such a teacher.

"Having come once or twice to see Mrs. Conan, she discovered that we were gaining a little influence over the people in the house; and it occurred to her, as she told me afterwards, that the virtue of music might be tried there with a *moral* end in view. Hence it came that I was beyond measure astonished and delighted one evening by the arrival of a piano,—not that one, for it got more worn than I liked, and I was able afterwards to exchange it for a better. I found it an invaluable aid in the endeavor to work out my glowing desire of getting the people about me into a better condition. First I asked some of the children to come and listen while I played. Everybody knows how fond the least educated children are of music; and I feel assured of its elevating power. Whatever the street-organs may be to poets and mathematicians, they are certainly a godsend to the children of our courts and alleys. The music takes possession of them at once, and sets them moving to it with rhythmical grace. I should have been very sorry to make it a condition with those I invited, that they should sit still: to take from them their personal share in it would have been to destroy half the charm of the thing. A far higher development is needful before music can be enjoyed in silence and motionlessness. The only condition I made was, that they should come with clean hands and faces, and with tidy hair. Considerable indignation was at first manifested on the part of those parents whose children I refused to admit because they had neglected the condition. This necessity, however, did not often occur; and the anger passed away, while the condition gathered weight. After a while, guided by what some of the children let fall; I began to invite the mothers to join them; and at length it came to be understood that, every Saturday evening, whoever chose to make herself tidy would be welcome, to an hour or two of my music. Some of the husbands next began to come, but there were never so many of them present. I may just add, that although the manners of some of my audience would be very shocking to cultivated people, and I understand perfectly how they must be so, I am very rarely annoyed on such occasions.

"I must now glance at another point in my history, one on which I cannot dwell. Never since my father's death had I attended public worship. Nothing had drawn me thither; and I hardly know what induced me one evening to step into a chapel of which I knew nothing. There was not even Sunday to account for it. I believe, however, it had to do with this, that all day I had been feeling tired. I think people are often ready to suppose that their bodily condition is the cause of their spiritual discomfort, when it may be only the occasion upon which some inward lack reveals itself. That the spiritual nature should be incapable of meeting and sustaining the body in its troubles is of itself sufficient to show that it is not in a satisfactory condition. For a long time the struggle for mere existence had almost absorbed my energies; but things had been easier for some time, and a re-action had at length come. It was not that I could lay any thing definite to my own charge; I only felt empty all through; I felt that something was not right with me, that something was required of me which I was not rendering. I could not, however, have told you what it was. Possibly the feeling had been for some time growing; but that day, so far as I can tell, I was first aware of it; and I presume it was the dim cause of my turning at the sound of a few singing voices, and entering that chapel. I found about a dozen people present. Something in the air of the place, meagre and waste as it looked, yet induced me to remain. An address followed from a pale-faced, weak-looking man of middle age, who had no gift of person, voice, or utterance, to recommend what he said. But there dwelt a more powerful enforcement in him than any of those,—that of earnestness. I went again, and again; and slowly, I cannot well explain how, the sense of life and its majesty grew upon me. Mr. Walton will, I trust, understand me when I say, that to one hungering for bread, it is of little consequence in what sort of platter it is handed him. This was a dissenting chapel,—of what order, it was long before I knew,—and my predilection was for the Church-services, those to which my father had accustomed me; but any comparison of the two to the prejudice of either, I should still-although a communicant of the Church of England-regard with absolute indifference.

"It will be sufficient for my present purpose to allude to the one practical thought which was the main fruit I gathered from this good man,—the fruit by which I know that he was good. [Footnote: Something like this is the interpretation of the word: "By their fruits ye shall know them" given by Mr. Maurice, —an interpretation which opens much. —G.M.D.] It was this, —that if all the labor of God, as my teacher said, was to bring sons into glory, lifting them out of the abyss of evil bondage up to the rock of his pure freedom, the only worthy end of life must be to work in the same direction, —to be a fellow-worker with God. Might I not, then, do something such, in my small way, and lose no jot of my labor? I thought. The urging, the hope, grew in me. But I was not left to feel blindly after some new and unknown method of labor. My teacher taught me that the way for *me* to help others was not to tell them their duty, but myself to learn of Him who bore our griefs and carried our sorrows. As I learned of him, I should be able to help them. I have never had any theory but just to be their friend, —to do for them the best I can. When I feel I may, I tell them what has done me good, but I never urge any belief of mine upon their acceptance.

"It will now seem no more wonderful to you than to me, that I should remain where I am. I simply have no choice. I was sixteen when Mrs. Conan died. Then my friends, amongst whom Lady Bernard and Miss Harper have ever been first, expected me to remove to lodgings in another neighborhood. Indeed, Lady Bernard came to see me, and said she knew precisely the place for me. When I told her I should remain where I was, she was silent, and soon left me?—I thought offended. I wrote to her at once, explaining why I chose my part here; saying that I would not hastily alter any thing that had been appointed me; that I loved the people; that they called me grannie; that they came to me with their troubles; that there were few changes in the house now; that the sick looked to me for help, and the children for teaching; that they seemed to be steadily rising in the moral scale; that I knew some of them were trying hard to be good; and I put it to her whether, if I were to leave them, in order merely, as servants say, to better myself, I should not be forsaking my post, almost my family; for I knew it would not be to better either myself or my friends: if I was at all necessary to them, I knew they were yet more necessary to me.

"I have a burning desire to help in the making of the world clean, —if it be only by sweeping one little room in it. I want to lead some poor stray sheep home-not home to the church, Mr. Walton —I would not be supposed to curry favor with you. I never think of what they call the church. I only care to lead them home to the bosom of God, where alone man is true man.

"I could talk to you till night about what Lady Bernard has been to me since, and what she has done for me and my grandchildren; but I have said enough to explain how it is that I am in such a questionable position. I fear I have been guilty of much egotism, and have shown my personal feelings with too little reserve. But I cast myself on your mercy."

CHAPTER XX
A REMARKABLE FACT.

A silence followed. I need hardly say we had listened intently. During the story my father had scarcely interrupted the narrator. I had not spoken a word. She had throughout maintained a certain matter-of-fact, almost cold style, no doubt because she was herself the subject of her story; but we could read between the lines, imagine much she did not say, and supply color when she gave only outline; and it moved us both deeply. My father sat perfectly composed, betraying his emotion in silence alone. For myself, I had a great lump in my throat, but in part from the shame which mingled with my admiration. The silence had not lasted more than a few seconds, when I yielded to a struggling impulse, rose, and kneeling before her, put my hands on her knees, said, "Forgive me," and could say no more. She put her hand on my shoulder, whispered. "My dear Mrs. Percivale!" bent down her face, and kissed me on the forehead.

"How could you help being shy of me?" she said. "Perhaps I ought to have come to you and explained it all; but I shrink from self-justification, —at least before a fit opportunity makes it comparatively easy."

"That is the way to give it all its force," remarked my father.

"I suppose it may be," she returned. "But I hate talking about myself: it is an unpleasant subject."

"Most people do not find it such," said my father. "I could not honestly say that I do not enjoy talking of my own experiences of life."

"But there are differences, you see," she rejoined. "My history looks to me such a matter of course, such a something I could not help, or have avoided if I would, that the telling of it is unpleasant, because it implies an importance which does not belong to it."

"St. Paul says something of the same sort, —that a necessity of preaching the gospel was laid upon him," remarked my father; but it seemed to make no impression on Miss Clare, for she went on as if she had not heard him.

"You see, Mr. Walton, it is not in the least as if, living in comfort, I had taken notice of the misery of the poor for the want of such sympathy and help as I could give them, and had therefore gone to live amongst them that I might so help them: it is quite different from that. If I had done so, I might be in danger of magnifying not merely my office but myself. On the contrary, I have been trained to it in such slow and necessitous ways, that it would be a far greater trial to me to forsake my work than it has ever been to continue it."

My father said no more, but I knew he had his own thoughts. I remained kneeling, and felt for the first time as if I understood what had led to saint-worship.

"Won't you sit, Mrs. Percivale?" she said, as if merely expostulating with me for not making myself comfortable.

"Have you forgiven me?" I asked.

"How can I say I have, when I never had any thing to forgive?"

"Well, then, I must go unforgiven, for I cannot forgive myself," I said.

"O Mrs. Percivale! if you think how the world is flooded with forgiveness, you will just dip in your cup, and take what you want."

I felt that I was making too much even of my own shame, rose humbled, and took my former seat.

Narration being over, and my father's theory now permitting him to ask questions, he did so plentifully, bringing out many lights, and elucidating several obscurities. The story grew upon me, until the work to which Miss Clare had given herself seemed more like that of the Son of God than any other I knew. For she was not helping her friends from afar, but as one of themselves, —nor with money, but with herself; she was not condescending to them, but finding her highest life in companionship with them. It seemed at least more like what his life must have been before he was thirty, than any thing else I could think of. I held my peace however; for I felt that to hint at such a thought would have greatly shocked and pained her.

No doubt the narrative I have given is plainer and more coherent for the questions my father put; but it loses much from the omission of one or two parts which she gave dramatically, with evident enjoyment of the fun that was in them. I have also omitted all the interruptions which came from her not unfrequent reference to my father on points that came up. At length I ventured to remind her of something she seemed to have forgotten.

"When you were telling us, Miss Clare," I said, "of the help that came to you that dreary afternoon in the empty house, I think you mentioned that something which happened afterwards made it still more remarkable." "Oh, yes!" she answered: "I forgot about that. I did not carry my history far enough to be reminded of it again.

"Somewhere about five years ago, Lady Bernard, having several schemes on foot for helping such people as I was interested in, asked me if it would not be nice to give an entertainment to my friends, and as many of the neighbors as I pleased, to the number of about a hundred. She wanted to put the thing entirely in my hands, and it should be my entertainment, she claiming only the privilege of defraying expenses. I told her I should be delighted to convey *her* invitation, but that the entertainment must not pretend to be mine; which, besides that it would be a falsehood, and therefore not to be thought of, would perplex my friends, and drive them to the conclusion either that it was not mine, or that I lived amongst them under false appearances. She confessed the force of my arguments, and let me have it my own way.

"She had bought a large house to be a home for young women out of employment, and in it she proposed the entertainment should be given: there were a good many nice young women inmates at the time, who, she said, would be all willing to help us to wait upon our guests. The idea was carried out, and the thing succeeded admirably. We had music and games, the latter such as the children were mostly acquainted with, only producing more merriment and conducted with more propriety than were usual in the court or the streets. I may just remark, in passing, that, had these been children of the poorest sort, we should have had to teach them; for one of the saddest things is that such, in London at least, do not know how to play. We had tea and coffee and biscuits in the lower rooms, for any who pleased; and they were to have a solid supper afterwards. With none of the arrangements, however, had I any thing to do; for my business was to be with them, and help them to enjoy themselves. All went on capitally; the parents entering into the merriment of their children, and helping to keep it up.

"In one of the games, I was seated on the floor with a handkerchief tied over my eyes, waiting, I believe, for some gentle trick to be played upon me, that I might guess at the name of the person who played it. There was a delay-of only a few seconds-long enough, however, for a sudden return of that dreary November afternoon in which I sat on the floor too miserable even to think that I was cold and hungry. Strange to say, it was not the picture of it that came back to me first, but the sound of my own voice calling aloud in the ringing echo of the desolate rooms that I was of no use to anybody, and that God had forgotten me utterly. With the recollection, a doubtful expectation arose which moved me to a scarce controllable degree. I jumped to my feet, and tore the bandage from my eyes.

"Several times during the evening I had had the odd yet well-known feeling of the same thing having happened before; but I was too busy entertaining my friends to try to account for it: perhaps what followed may suggest the theory, that in not a few of such cases the indistinct remembrance of the previous occurrence of some portion of the circumstances may cast the hue of memory over the whole. As-my eyes blinded with the light and straining to recover themselves—I stared about the room, the presentiment grew almost conviction that it was the very room in which I had so sat in desolation and despair. Unable to restrain myself, I hurried into the back room: there was the cabinet beyond! In a few moments more I was absolutely satisfied that this was indeed the house in which I had first found refuge. For a time I could take no further share in what was going on, but sat down in a corner, and cried for joy. Some one went for Lady Bernard, who was superintending the arrangements for supper in the music-room behind. She came in alarm. I told her there was nothing the matter but a little too much happiness, and, if she would come into the cabinet, I would tell her all about it. She did so, and a few words made her a hearty sharer in my pleasure. She insisted that I should tell the company all about it; 'for' she said, 'you do not know how much it may help some poor creature to trust in God.' I promised I would, if I found I could command myself sufficiently. She left me alone for a little while, and after that I was able to join in the games again.

"At supper I found myself quite composed, and, at Lady Bernard's request, stood up, and gave them all a little sketch of grannie's history, of which sketch what had happened that evening was made the central point. Many of the simpler hearts about me received it, without question, as a divine arrangement for my comfort and encouragement, —at least, thus I interpreted their looks to each other, and the remarks that reached my ear; but presently a man stood up, —one who thought more than the rest of them, perhaps because he was blind, —a man at once conceited, honest, and sceptical; and silence having been made for him, —'Ladies and gentlemen,' he began, as if he had been addressing a public meeting, 'you've all heard what grannie has said. It's very kind of her to give us so much of her history. It's a very remarkable one, *I* think, and she deserves to have it. As to what upset her this very night as is, —and I must say for her, I've knowed her now for six years, and I never knowed *her* upset afore, —and as to what upset her, all I can say is, it may or may not ha' been what phylosophers call a coincydence; but at the same time, if it wasn't a coincydence, and if the Almighty had a hand in it, it were no more than you might expect. He would look at it in this light, you see, that maybe she was wrong to fancy herself so down on her luck as all that, but she was a good soul, notwithstandin,' and he would let her know he hadn't forgotten her. And so he set her down in that room there, —wi' her eyes like them here o' mine, as never was no manner o' use to me, —for a minute, jest to put her in mind o' what had been, and what she had said there, an' how it was all so different now. In my opinion, it were no wonder as she broke down, God bless her! I beg leave to propose her health.' So they drank my health in lemonade and ginger-beer; for we were afraid to give some of them stronger drink than that, and therefore had none. Then we had more music and singing; and a clergyman, who knew how to be neighbor to them that had fallen among thieves, read a short chapter and a collect or two, and said a few words to them. Then grannie and her children went home together, all happy, but grannie the happiest of them all."

"Strange and beautiful!" said my father. "But," he added, after a pause, "you must have met with many strange and beautiful things in such a life as yours; for it seems to me that such a life is open to the entrance of all simple wonders. Conventionality and routine and arbitrary law banish their very approach."

"I believe," said Miss Clare, "that every life has its own private experience of the strange and beautiful. But I have sometimes thought that perhaps God took pains to bar out such things of the sort as we should be no better for. The reason why Lazarus was not allowed to visit the brothers of Dives was, that the repentance he would have urged would not have followed, and they would have been only the worse in consequence."

"Admirably said," remarked my father.

Before we took our leave, I had engaged Miss Clare to dine with us while my father was in town.

CHAPTER XXI
LADY BERNARD.

When she came we had no other guest, and so had plenty of talk with her. Before dinner I showed her my husband's pictures; and she was especially pleased with that which hung in the little room off the study, which I called my boudoir,—a very ugly word, by the way, which I am trying to give up,—with a curtain before it. My father has described it in "The Seaboard Parish:" a pauper lies dead, and they are bringing in his coffin. She said it was no wonder it had not been sold, notwithstanding its excellence and force; and asked if I would allow her to bring Lady Bernard to see it. After dinner Percivale had a long talk with her, and succeeded in persuading her to sit to him; not, however, before I had joined my entreaties with his, and my father had insisted that her face was not her own, but belonged to all her kind.

The very next morning she came with Lady Bernard. The latter said she knew my husband well by reputation, and had, before our marriage, asked him to her house, but had not been fortunate enough to possess sufficient attraction. Percivale was much taken with her, notwithstanding a certain coldness, almost sternness of manner, which was considerably repellent,—but only for the first few moments, for, when her eyes lighted up, the whole thing vanished. She was much pleased with some of his pictures, criticising freely, and with evident understanding. The immediate result was, that she bought both the pauper picture and that of the dying knight.

"But I am sorry to deprive your lovely room of such treasures, Mrs. Percivale," she said, with a kind smile.

"Of course I shall miss them," I returned; "but the thought that you have them will console me. Besides, it is good to have a change; and there are only too many lying in the study, from which he will let me choose to supply their place."

"Will you let me come and see which you have chosen?" she asked.

"With the greatest pleasure," I answered.

"And will you come and see me? Do you think you could persuade your husband to bring you to dine with me?"

I told her I could promise the one with more than pleasure, and had little doubt of being able to do the other, now that my husband had seen her.

A reference to my husband's dislike to fashionable society followed, and I had occasion to mention his feeling about being asked without me. Of the latter, Lady Bernard expressed the warmest approval; and of the former, said that it would have no force in respect of her parties, for they were not at all fashionable.

This was the commencement of a friendship for which we have much cause to thank God. Nor did we forget that it came through Miss Clare.

I confess I felt glorious over my cousin Judy; but I would bide my time. Now that I am wiser, and I hope a little better, I see that I was rather spiteful; but I thought then I was only jealous for my new and beautiful friend. Perhaps, having wronged her myself, I was the more ready to take vengeance on her wrongs from the hands of another; which was just the opposite feeling to that I ought to have had.

In the mean time, our intimacy with Miss Clare grew. She interested me in many of her schemes for helping the poor; some of which were for providing them with work in hard times, but more for giving them an interest in life itself, without which, she said, no one would begin to inquire into its relations and duties. One of her positive convictions was, that you ought not to give them any thing they *ought* to provide for themselves, such as food or clothing or shelter. In such circumstances as rendered it impossible for them to do so, the *ought* was in abeyance. But she heartily approved of making them an occasional present of something they could not be expected to procure for themselves,—flowers, for instance. "You would not imagine," I have heard her say, "how they delight in flowers. All the finer instincts of their being are drawn to the surface at the sight of them. I am sure they prize and enjoy them far more, not merely than most people with gardens and greenhouses do, but far more even than they would if they were deprived of them. A gift of that sort can only do them good. But I would rather give a workman a gold watch than a leg of mutton. By a present you mean a compliment; and none feel more grateful for such an acknowledgment of your human relation to them, than those who look up to you as their superior."

Once, when she was talking thus, I ventured to object, for the sake of hearing her further.

"But," I said, "sometimes the most precious thing you can give a man is just that compassion which you seem to think destroys the value of a gift."

"When compassion itself is precious to a man," she answered, "it must be because he loves you, and believes you love him. When that is the case, you may give him any thing you like, and it will do neither you nor him harm. But the man of independent feeling, except he be thus your friend, will not unlikely resent your compassion, while the beggar will accept it chiefly as a pledge for something more to be got from you; and so it will tend to keep him in beggary."

"Would you never, then, give money, or any of the necessaries of life, except in extreme, and, on the part of the receiver, unavoidable necessity?" I asked.

"I would not," she answered; "but in the case where a man *cannot* help himself, the very suffering makes a way for the love which is more than compassion to manifest itself. In every other case, the true way is to provide them with work, which is itself a good thing, besides what they gain by it. If a man will not work, neither should he eat. It must be work with an object in it, however: it must not be mere labor, such as digging a hole and filling it up again, of which I have heard. No man could help resentment at being set to such work. You ought to let him feel that he is giving something of value to you for the money you give to him. But I have known a whole district so corrupted and degraded by clerical alms-giving, that one of the former recipients of it declared, as spokesman for the rest; that threepence given was far more acceptable than five shillings earned."

A good part of the little time I could spare from my own family was now spent with Miss Clare in her work, through which it was chiefly that we became by degrees intimate with Lady Bernard. If ever there was a woman who lived this outer life for the sake of others, it was she. Her inner life was, as it were, sufficient for herself, and found its natural outward expression in blessing others. She was like a fountain of living water that could find no vent but into the lives of her fellows. She had suffered more than falls to the ordinary lot of women, in those who were related to her most nearly, and for many years had looked for no personal blessing from without. She said to me once, that she could not think of any thing that could happen to herself to make her very happy now, except a loved grandson, who was leading a strange, wild life, were to turn out a Harry the Fifth, —a consummation which, however devoutly wished, was not granted her; for the young man died shortly after. I believe no one, not even Miss Clare, knew half the munificent things she did, or what an immense proportion of her large income she spent upon other people. But, as she said herself, no one understood the worth of money better; and no one liked better to have the worth of it: therefore she always administered her charity with some view to the value of the probable return, —with some regard, that is, to the amount of good likely to result to others from the aid given to one. She always took into consideration whether the good was likely to be propagated, or to die with the receiver. She confessed to frequent mistakes; but such, she said, was the principle upon which she sought to regulate that part of her stewardship.

I wish I could give a photograph of her. She was slight, and appeared taller than she was, being rather stately than graceful, with a commanding forehead and still blue eyes. She gave at first the impression of coldness, with a touch of haughtiness. But this was, I think, chiefly the result of her inherited physique; for the moment her individuality appeared, when her being, that is, came into contact with that of another, all this impression vanished in the light that flashed into her eyes, and the smile that illumined her face. Never did woman of rank step more triumphantly over the barriers which the cumulated custom of ages has built between the classes of society. She laid great stress on good manners, little on what is called good birth; although to the latter, in its deep and true sense, she attributed the greatest *à priori* value, as the ground of obligation in the possessor, and of expectation on the part of others. But I shall have an opportunity of showing more of what she thought on this subject presently; for I bethink me that it occupied a great part of our conversation at a certain little gathering, of which I am now going to give an account.

CHAPTER XXII
MY SECOND DINNER-PARTY.

For I judged that I might now give another little dinner: I thought, that, as Percivale had been doing so well lately, he might afford, with his knowing brother's help, to provide, for his part of the entertainment, what might be good enough to offer even to Mr. Morley; and I now knew Lady Bernard sufficiently well to know also that she would willingly accept an invitation from me, and would be pleased to meet Miss Clare, or, indeed, would more likely bring her with her.

I proposed the dinner, and Percivale consented to it. My main object being the glorification of Miss Clare, who had more engagements of one kind and another than anybody I knew, I first invited her, asking her to fix her own day, at some considerable remove. Next I invited Mr. and Mrs. Morley, and next Lady Bernard, who went out very little. Then I invited Mr. Blackstone, and last of all Roger-though I was almost as much interested in his meeting Miss Clare as in any thing else connected with the gathering. For he had been absent from London for some time on a visit to an artist friend at the Hague, and had never seen Miss Clare since the evening on which he and I quarrelled-or rather, to be honest, I quarrelled with him. All accepted, and I looked forward to the day with some triumph.

I had better calm the dread of my wifely reader by at once assuring her that I shall not harrow her feelings with any account of culinary blunders. The moon was in the beginning of her second quarter, and my cook's brain tolerably undisturbed. Lady Bernard offered me her cook for the occasion; but I convinced her that my wisdom would be to decline the offer, seeing such external influence would probably tend to disintegration. I went over with her every item of every dish and every sauce many times,—without any resulting sense of security, I confess; but I had found, that, odd as it may seem, she always did better the more she had to do. I believe that her love of approbation, excited by the difficulty before her, in its turn excited her intellect, which then arose to meet the necessities of the case.

Roger arrived first, then Mr. Blackstone; Lady Bernard brought Miss Clare; and Mr. and Mrs. Morley came last. There were several introductions to be gone through,—a ceremony in which Percivale, being awkward, would give me no assistance; whence I failed to observe how the presence of Miss Clare affected Mr. and Mrs. Morley; but my husband told me that Judy turned red, and that Mr. Morley bowed to her with studied politeness. I took care that Mr. Blackstone should take her down to dinner, which was served in the study as before.

The conversation was broken and desultory at first, as is generally the case at a dinner-party — and perhaps ought to be; but one after another began to listen to what was passing between Lady Bernard and my husband at the foot of the table, until by degrees every one became interested, and took a greater or less part in the discussion. The first of it I heard was as next follows.

"Then you do believe," my husband was saying, "in the importance of what some of the Devonshire people call *havage?*"

"Allow me to ask what they mean by the word," Lady Bernard returned.

"Birth, descent,—the people you come of," he answered.

"Of course I believe that descent involves very important considerations."

"No one," interposed Mr. Morley, "can have a better right than your ladyship to believe that."

"One cannot nave a better right than another to believe a fact, Mr. Morley," she answered with a smile. "It is but a fact that you start better or worse according to the position of your starting-point."

"Undeniably," said Mr. Morley. "And for all that is feared from the growth of levelling notions in this country, it will be many generations before a profound respect for birth is eradicated from the feelings of the English people."

He drew in his chin with a jerk, and devoted himself again to his plate, with the air of a "Dixi." He was not permitted to eat in peace, however.

"If you allow," said Mr. Blackstone, "that the feeling can wear out, and is wearing out, it matters little how long it may take to prove itself of a false, because corruptible nature. No growth of notions will blot love, honesty, kindness, out of the human heart."

"Then," said Lady Bernard archly, "am I to understand, Mr. Blackstone, that you don't believe it of the least importance to come of decent people?"

"Your ladyship puts it well," said Mr. Morley, laughing mildly, "and with authority. The longer the descent"—

"The more doubtful," interrupted Lady Bernard, laughing. "One can hardly have come of decent people all through, you know. Let us only hope, without inquiring too closely, that their number preponderates in our own individual cases."

Mr. Morley stared for a moment, and then tried to laugh, but unable to determine whereabout he was in respect of the question, betook himself to his glass of sherry.

Mr. Blackstone considered it the best policy in general not to explain any remark he had made, but to say the right thing better next time instead. I suppose he believed, with another friend of mine, that "when explanations become necessary, they become impossible," a paradox well worth the consideration of those who write letters to newspapers. But Lady Bernard understood him well enough, and was only unwinding the clew of her idea.

"On the contrary, it must be a most serious fact," he rejoined, "to any one who like myself believes that the sins of the fathers are visited on the children."

"Mr. Blackstone," objected Roger, "I can't imagine you believing such a manifest injustice."

"It has been believed in all ages by the best of people," he returned.

"To whom possibly the injustice of it never suggested itself. For my part, I must either disbelieve that, or disbelieve in a God."

"But, my dear fellow, don't you see it is a fact? Don't you see children born with the sins of their parents nestling in their very bodies? You see on which horn of your own dilemma you would impale yourself."

"Wouldn't you rather not believe in a God than believe in an unjust one?"

"An unjust god," said Mr. Blackstone, with the honest evasion of one who will not answer an awful question hastily, "must be a false god, that is, no god. Therefore I presume there is some higher truth involved in every fact that appears unjust, the perception of which would nullify the appearance."

"I see none in the present case," said Roger.

"I will go farther than assert the mere opposite," returned Mr. Blackstone. "I will assert that it is an honor to us to have the sins of our fathers laid upon us. For thus it is given into our power to put a stop to them, so that they shall descend no farther. If I thought my father had committed any sins for which I might suffer, I should be unspeakably glad to suffer for them, and so have the privilege of taking a share in his burden, and some of the weight of it off his mind. You see the whole idea is that of a family, in which we are so grandly bound together, that we must suffer with and for each other. Destroy this consequence, and you destroy the lovely idea itself, with all its thousand fold results of loveliness."

"You anticipate what I was going to say, Mr. Blackstone," said Lady Bernard. "I would differ from you only in one thing. The chain of descent is linked after such a complicated pattern, that the non-conducting condition of one link, or of many links even, cannot break the transmission of qualities. I may inherit from my great-great-grandfather or mother, or some one ever so much farther back. That which was active wrong in some one or other of my ancestors, may appear in me as an impulse to that same wrong, which of course I have to overcome; and if I succeed, then it is so far checked. But it may have passed, or may yet pass, to others of his descendants, who have, or will have, to do the same-for who knows how many generations to come? —before it shall cease. Married people, you see, Mrs. Percivale, have an awful responsibility in regard of the future of the world. You cannot tell to how many millions you may transmit your failures or your victories."

"If I understand you right, Lady Bernard," said Roger, "it is the personal character of your ancestors, and not their social position, you regard as of importance."

"It was of their personal character alone I was thinking. But of course I do not pretend to believe that there are not many valuable gifts more likely to show themselves in what is called a long descent; for doubtless a continuity of education does much to develop the race."

"But if it is personal character you chiefly regard, we may say we are all equally far descended," I remarked; "for we have each had about the same number of ancestors with a character of some sort or other, whose faults and virtues have to do with ours, and for both of which we are, according to Mr. Blackstone, in a most real and important sense accountable."

"Certainly," returned Lady Bernard; "and it is impossible to say in whose descent the good or the bad may predominate. I cannot tell, for instance, how much of the property I inherit has been honestly come by, or is the spoil of rapacity and injustice."

"You are doing the best you can to atone for such a possible fact, then, by its redistribution," said my husband.

"I confess," she answered, "the doubt has had some share in determining my feeling with regard to the management of my property. I have no right to throw up my stewardship, for that was none of my seeking, and I do not know any one who has a better claim to it; but I count it only a stewardship. I am not at liberty to throw my orchard open, for that would result not only in its destruction, but in a renewal of the fight of centuries ago for its possession; but I will try to distribute my apples properly. That is, I have not the same right to give away foolishly that I have to keep wisely."

"Then," resumed Roger, who had evidently been pondering what Lady Bernard had previously said, "you would consider what is called kleptomania as the impulse to steal transmitted by a thief-ancestor?"

"Nothing seems to me more likely. I know a nobleman whose servant has to search his pockets for spoons or forks every night as soon as he is in bed."

"I should find it very hard to define the difference between that and stealing," said Miss Clare, now first taking a part in the conversation. "I have sometimes wondered whether kleptomania was not merely the fashionable name for stealing."

"The distinction is a difficult one, and no doubt the word is occasionally misapplied. But I think there is a difference. The nobleman to whom I referred makes no objection to being thus deprived of his booty; which, for one thing, appears to show that the temptation is intermittent, and partakes at least of the character of a disease."

"But are there not diseases which are only so much the worse diseases that they are not intermittent?" said Miss Clare. "Is it not hard that the privileges of kleptomania should be confined to the rich? You never hear the word applied to a poor child, even if his father was, habit and repute, a thief. Surely, when hunger and cold aggravate the attacks of inherited temptation, they cannot at the same time aggravate the culpability of yielding to them?"

"On the contrary," said Roger, "one would naturally suppose they added immeasurable excuse."

"Only," said Mr. Blackstone, "there comes in our ignorance, and consequent inability to judge. The very fact of the presence of motives of a most powerful kind renders it impossible to be certain of the presence of the disease; whereas other motives being apparently absent, we presume disease as the readiest way of accounting for the propensity; I do not therefore think it is the only way. I believe there are cases in which it comes of pure greed, and is of the same kind as any other injustice the capability of exercising which is more generally distributed. Why should a thief be unknown in a class, a proportion of the members of which is capable of wrong, chicanery, oppression, indeed any form of absolute selfishness?"

"At all events," said Lady Bernard, "so long as we do our best to help them to grow better, we cannot make too much allowance for such as have not only been born with evil impulses, but have had every animal necessity to urge them in the same direction; while, on the other hand, they have not had one of those restraining influences which a good home and education would have afforded. Such must, so far as development goes, be but a little above the beasts."

"You open a very difficult question," said Mr. Morley: "What are we to do with them? Supposing they *are* wild beasts, we can't shoot them; though that would, no doubt, be the readiest way to put an end to the breed."

"Even that would not suffice," said Lady Bernard. "There would always be a deposit from the higher classes sufficient to keep up the breed. But, Mr. Morley, I did not say *wild* beasts: I only said *beasts*. There is a great difference between a tiger and a sheep-dog."

"There is nearly as much between a Seven-Dialsrough and a sheep-dog."

"In moral attainment, I grant you," said Mr. Blackstone; "but in moral capacity, no. Besides, you must remember, both what a descent the sheep-dog has, and what pains have been taken with his individual education, as well as that of his ancestors."

"Granted all that," said Mr. Morley, "there the fact remains. For my part, I confess I don't see what is to be done. The class to which you refer goes on increasing. There's this garrotting now. I spent a winter at Algiers lately, and found even the suburbs of that city immeasurably safer than any part of London is now, to judge from the police-reports. Yet I am accused of inhumanity and selfishness if I decline to write a check for every shabby fellow who calls upon me pretending to be a clergyman, and to represent this or that charity in the East End!"

"Things are bad enough in the West End, within a few hundred yards of Portland Place, for instance," murmured Miss Clare.

"It seems to me highly unreasonable," Mr. Morley went on. "Why should I spend my money to perpetuate such a condition of things?"

"That would in all likelihood be the tendency of your subscription," said Mr. Blackstone.

"Then why should I?" repeated Mr. Morley with a smile of triumph.

"But," said Miss Clare, in an apologetic tone, "it seems to me you make a mistake in regarding the poor as if their poverty were the only distinction by which they could be classified. The poor are not *all* thieves and garroters, nor even all unthankful and unholy. There are just as strong and as delicate distinctions too, in that stratum of social existence as in the upper strata. I should imagine Mr. Morley knows a few, belonging to the same social grade with himself, with whom, however, he would be sorry to be on any terms of intimacy."

"Not a few," responded Mr. Morley with a righteous frown.

"Then I, who know the poor as well at least as you can know the rich, having lived amongst them almost from childhood, assert that I am acquainted with not a few, who, in all the essentials of human life and character, would be an honor to any circle."

"I should be sorry to seem to imply that there may not be very worthy people amongst them, Miss Clare; but it is not such who draw our attention to the class."

"Not such who force themselves upon your attention certainly," said Miss Clare; "but the existence of such may be an additional reason for bestowing some attention on the class to which they belong. Is there not such a mighty fact as the body of Christ? Is there no connection between the head and the feet?"

"I had not the slightest purpose of disputing the matter with you, Miss Clare," said Mr. Morley—I thought rudely, for who would use the word *disputing* at a dinner-table? "On the contrary, being a practical man, I want to know what is to be done. It is doubtless a great misfortune to the community that there should be such sinks in our cities; but who is to blame for it?—that is the question."

"Every man who says, Am I my brother's keeper? Why, just consider, Mr. Morley: suppose in a family there were one less gifted than the others, and that in consequence they all withdrew from him, and took no interest in his affairs: what would become of him? Must he not sink?"

"Difference of rank is a divine appointment,—you must allow that. If there were not a variety of grades, the social machine would soon come to a stand-still."

"A strong argument for taking care of the smallest wheel, for all the parts are interdependent. That there should be different classes is undoubtedly a divine intention, and not to be turned aside. But suppose the less-gifted boy is fit for some manual labor; suppose he takes to carpentering, and works well, and keeps the house tidy, and every thing in good repair, while his brothers pursue their studies and prepare for professions beyond his reach: is the inferior boy degraded by doing the best he can? Is there any reason in the nature of things why he should sink? But he will most likely sink, sooner or later, if his brothers take no interest in his work, and treat him as a being of nature inferior to their own."

"I beg your pardon," said Mr. Morley, "but is he not on the very supposition inferior to them?"

"Intellectually, yes; morally, no; for he is doing his work, possibly better than they, and therefore taking a higher place in the eternal scale. But granting all kinds of inferiority, his *nature* remains the same with their own; and the question is, whether they treat him as one to be helped up, or one to be kept down; as one unworthy of sympathy, or one to be honored for filling his part: in a word, as one belonging to them, or one whom they put up with only because his work is necessary to them."

"What do you mean by being 'helped up'?" asked Mr. Morley.

"I do not mean helped out of his trade, but helped to make the best of it, and of the intellect that finds its development in that way."

"Very good. But yet I don't see how you apply your supposition."

"For an instance of application, then: How many respectable people know or care a jot about their servants, except as creatures necessary to their comfort?"

"Well, Miss Clare," said Judy, addressing her for the first time, "if you had had the half to do with servants I have had, you would alter your opinion of them."

"I have expressed no opinion," returned Miss Clare. "I have only said that masters and mistresses know and care next to nothing about them."

"They are a very ungrateful class, do what you will for them."

"I am afraid they are at present growing more and more corrupt as a class," rejoined Miss Clare; "but gratitude is a high virtue, therefore in any case I don't see how you could look for much of it from the common sort of them. And yet while some mistresses do not get so much of it as they deserve, I fear most mistresses expect far more of it than they have any right to."

"You *can't* get them to speak the truth."

"That I am afraid is a fact."

"I have never known one on whose word I could depend," insisted Judy.

"My father says he *has* known one," I interjected.

"A sad confirmation of Mrs. Morley," said Miss Clare. "But for my part I know very few persons in any rank on whose representation of things I could absolutely depend. Truth is the highest virtue, and seldom grows wild. It is difficult to speak the truth, and those who have tried it longest best know how difficult it is. Servants need to be taught that as well as everybody else."

"There is nothing they resent so much as being taught," said Judy.

"Perhaps: they are very far from docile; and I believe it is of little use to attempt giving them direct lessons."

"How, then, are you to teach them?"

"By making it very plain to them, but without calling their attention to it, that *you* speak the truth. In the course of a few years they may come to tell a lie or two the less for that."

"Not a very hopeful prospect," said Judy.

"Not a very rapid improvement," said her husband.

"I look for no rapid improvement, so early in a history as the supposition implies," said Miss Clare.

"But would you not tell them how wicked it is?" I asked.

"They know already that it is wicked to tell lies; but they do not feel that *they* are wicked in making the assertions they do. The less said about the abstract truth, and the more shown of practical truth, the better for those whom any one would teach to forsake lying. So, at least, it appears to me. I despair of teaching others, except by learning myself."

"If you do no more than that, you will hardly produce an appreciable effect in a lifetime."

"Why should it be appreciated?" rejoined Miss Clare.

"I should have said, on the contrary," interposed Mr. Blackstone, addressing Mr. Morley, "if you do less-for more you cannot do-you will produce no effect whatever."

"We have no right to make it a condition of our obedience, that we shall see its reflex in the obedience of others," said Miss Clare. "We have to pull out the beam, not the mote."

"Are you not, then, to pull the mote out of your brother's eye?" said Judy.

"In no case and on no pretence, *until* you have pulled the beam out of your own eye," said Mr. Blackstone; "which I fancy will make the duty of finding fault with one's neighbor a rare one; for who will venture to say he has qualified himself for the task?"

It was no wonder that a silence followed upon this; for the talk had got to be very serious for a dinner-table. Lady Bernard was the first to speak. It was easier to take up the dropped thread of the conversation than to begin a new reel.

"It cannot be denied," she said, "whoever may be to blame for it, that the separation between the rich and the poor has either been greatly widened of late, or, which involves the same practical necessity, we have become more aware of the breadth and depth of a gulf which, however it may distinguish their circumstances, ought not to divide them from each other. Certainly the rich withdraw themselves from the poor. Instead, for instance, of helping them to bear their burdens, they leave the still struggling poor of whole parishes to sink into hopeless want, under the weight of those who have already sunk beyond recovery. I am not sure that to shoot them would not involve less injustice. At all events, he that hates his brother is a murderer."

"But there is no question of hating here," objected Mr. Morley.

"I am not certain that absolute indifference to one's neighbor is not as bad. It came pretty nearly to the same thing in the case of the priest and the Levite, who passed by on the other side," said Mr. Blackstone.

"Still," said Mr. Morley, in all the self-importance of one who prided himself on the practical, "I do not see that Miss Clare has proposed any remedy for the state of things concerning the evil of which we are all agreed. What is to be *done*? What can *I* do now? Come, Miss Clare."

Miss Clare was silent.

"Marion, my child," said Lady Bernard, turning to her, "will you answer Mr. Morley?"

"Not, certainly, as to what *he* can do: that question I dare not undertake to answer. I can only speak of what principles I may seem to have discovered. But until a man begins to behave to those with whom he comes into personal contact as partakers of the same nature, to recognize, for instance, between himself and his trades-people a bond superior to that of supply and demand, I cannot imagine how he is to do any thing towards the drawing together of the edges of the gaping wound in the social body."

"But," persisted Mr. Morley, who, I began to think, showed some real desire to come at a practical conclusion, "suppose a man finds himself incapable of that sort of thing-for it seems to me to want some rare qualification or other to be able to converse with an uneducated person"—

"There are many such, especially amongst those who follow handicrafts," interposed Mr. Blackstone, "who think a great deal more than most of the so-called educated. There is a truer education to be got in the pursuit of a handicraft than in the life of a mere scholar. But I beg your pardon, Mr. Morley."

"Suppose," resumed Mr. Morley, accepting the apology without disclaimer,—"Suppose I find I can do nothing of that sort; is there nothing of any sort I can do?"

"Nothing of the best sort, I firmly believe," answered Miss Clare; "for the genuine recognition of the human relationship can alone give value to whatever else you may do, and indeed can alone guide you to what ought to be done. I had a rather painful illustration of this the other day. A gentleman of wealth and position offered me the use of his grounds for some of my poor friends, whom I wanted to take out for a half-holiday. In the neighborhood of London, that is a great boon. But unfortunately, whether from his mistake or mine, I was left with the impression that he would provide some little entertainment for them; I am certain that at least milk was mentioned. It was a lovely day; every thing looked beautiful; and although they were in no great spirits, poor things, no doubt the shade and the grass and the green trees wrought some good in them. Unhappily, two of the men had got drunk on the way; and, fearful of giving offence, I had to take them back to the station.—for their poor helpless wives could only cry,—and send them home by train. I should have done better to risk the offence, and take them into the grounds, where they might soon have slept it off under a tree. I had some distance to go, and some difficulty in getting them along; and when I got back I found things in an unhappy condition, for nothing had been given them to eat or drink,—indeed, no attention, had been paid them whatever. There was company at dinner in the house, and I could not find any one with authority. I hurried into the neighboring village, and bought the contents of two bakers' shops, with which I returned in time to give each a piece of bread before the company came out to *look at* them. A gayly-dressed group, they stood by themselves languidly regarding the equally languid but rather indignant groups of ill-clad and hungry men and women upon the lawn. They made no attempt to mingle with them, or arrive at a notion of what was moving in any of their minds. The nearest approach to communion I saw was a poke or two given to a child with the point of a parasol. Were my poor friends likely to return to their dingy homes with any great feeling of regard for the givers of such cold welcome?"

"But that was an exceptional case," said Mr. Morley.

"Chiefly in this," returned Miss Clare, "that it was a case at all-that they were thus presented with a little more room on the face of the earth for a few hours."

"But you think the fresh air may have done them good?"

"Yes; but we were speaking, I thought, of what might serve towards the filling up of the gulf between the classes."

"Well, will not all kindness shown to the poor by persons in a superior station tend in that direction?"

"I maintain that you can do nothing for them in the way of kindness that shall not result in more harm than good, except you do it from and with genuine charity of soul; with some of that love, in short, which is the heart of religion. Except what is done for them is so done as to draw out their trust and affection, and so raise them consciously in the human scale, it can only tend either to hurt their feelings and generate indignation, or to encourage fawning and beggary. But"—

"I am entirely of your mind," said Mr. Blackstone. "But do go on."

"I was going to add," said Miss Clare, "that while no other charity than this can touch the sore, a good deal might yet be effected by bare justice. It seems to me high time that we dropped talking about charity, and took up the cry of justice. There, now, is a ground on which a man of your influence, Mr. Morley, might do much."

"I don't know what you mean, Miss Clare. So long as I pay the market value for the labor I employ, I do not see how more can be demanded of me-as a right, that is."

"We will not enter on that question, Marion, if you please," said Lady Bernard.

Miss Clare nodded, and went on.

"Is it just in the nation," she said, "to abandon those who can do nothing to help themselves, to be preyed upon by bad landlords, railway-companies, and dishonest trades-people with their false weights, balances, and measures, and adulterations to boot,—from all of whom their more wealthy brethren are comparatively safe? Does not a nation exist for the protection of its parts? Have these no claims on the nation? Would you call it just in a family to abandon its less gifted to any moral or physical spoiler who might be bred within it? To say a citizen must take care of himself *may* be just where he *can* take care of himself, but cannot be just where that is impossible. A thousand causes, originating mainly in the neglect of their neighbors, have combined to sink the poor into a state of moral paralysis: are we to say the paralyzed may be run over in our streets with impunity? *Must* they take care of themselves? Have we not to awake them to the very sense that life is worth caring for? I cannot but feel that the bond between such a neglected class, and any nation in which it is to be found, is very little stronger than, if indeed as strong as, that between slaves and their masters. Who could preach to them their duty to the nation, except on grounds which such a nation acknowledges only with the lips?"

"You have to prove, Miss Clare," said Mr. Morley, in a tone that seemed intended to imply that he was not in the least affected by mistimed eloquence, "that the relation is that of a family."

"I believe," she returned, "that it is closer than the mere human relation of the parts of any family. But, at all events, until we *are* their friends it is worse than useless to pretend to be such, and until they feel that we are their friends it is worse than useless to talk to them about God and religion. They will none of it from our lips."

"Will they from any lips? Are they not already too far sunk towards the brutes to be capable of receiving any such rousing influence?" suggested Mr. Blackstone with a smile, evidently wishing to draw Miss Clare out yet further.

"You turn me aside, Mr. Blackstone. I wanted to urge Mr. Morley to go into parliament as spiritual member for the poor of our large towns. Besides, I know you don't think as your question would imply. As far as my experience guides me, I am bound to believe that there is a spot of soil in every heart sufficient for the growth of a gospel seed. And I believe, moreover, that not only is he a fellow-worker with God who sows that seed, but that he also is one who opens a way for that seed to enter the soil. If such preparation were not necessary, the Saviour would have come the moment Adam and Eve fell, and would have required no Baptist to precede him."

A good deal followed which I would gladly record, enabled as I now am to assist my memory by a more thorough acquaintance with the views of Miss Clare. But I fear I have already given too much conversation at once.

CHAPTER XXIII
THE END OF THE EVENING.

What specially delighted me during the evening, was the marked attention, and the serious look in the eyes, with which Roger listened. It was not often that he did look serious. He preferred, if possible, to get a joke out of a thing; but when he did enter into an argument, he was always fair. Although prone to take the side of objection to any religious remark, he yet never said any thing against religion itself. But his principles, and indeed his nature, seemed as yet in a state of solution,—uncrystallized, as my father would say. Mr. Morley, on the other hand, seemed an insoluble mass, incapable of receiving impressions from other minds. Any suggestion of his own mind, as to a course of action or a mode of thinking, had a good chance of being without question regarded as reasonable and right: he was more than ordinarily prejudiced in his own favor. The day after they thus met at our house, Miss Clare had a letter from him, in which he took the high hand with her, rebuking her solemnly for her presumption in saying, as he represented it, that no good could be done except after the fashion she laid down, and assuring her that she would thus alienate the most valuable assistance from any scheme she might cherish for the amelioration of the condition of the lower classes. It ended with the offer of a yearly subscription of five pounds to any project of the wisdom of which she would take the trouble to convince him. She replied, thanking him both, for his advice and his offer, but saying that, as she had no scheme on foot requiring such assistance, she could not at present accept the latter; should, however, any thing show itself for which that sort of help was desirable, she would take the liberty of reminding him of it.

When the ladies rose, Judy took me aside, and said,—
"What does it all mean, Wynnie?"
"Just what you hear," I answered.
"You asked us, to have a triumph over me, you naughty thing!"
"Well-partly-if I am to be honest; but far more to make you do justice to Miss Clare. You being my cousin, she had a right to that at my hands."
"Does Lady Bernard know as much about her as she seems?"
"She knows every thing about her, and visits her, too, in her very questionable abode. You see, Judy, a report may be a fact, and yet be untrue."
"I'm not going to be lectured by a chit like you. But I should like to have a little talk with Miss Clare."
"I will make you an opportunity."

I did so, and could not help overhearing a very pretty apology; to which Miss Clare replied, that she feared she only was to blame, inasmuch as she ought to have explained the peculiarity of her circumstances before accepting the engagement. At the time, it had not appeared to her necessary, she said; but now she would make a point of explaining before she accepted any fresh duty of the kind, for she saw it would be fairer to both parties. It was no wonder such an answer should entirely disarm cousin Judy, who forthwith begged she would, if she had no objection, resume her lessons with the children at the commencement of the next quarter.

"But I understand from Mrs. Percivale," objected Miss Clare, "that the office is filled to your thorough satisfaction."
"Yes; the lady I have is an excellent teacher; but the engagement was only for a quarter."
"If you have no other reason for parting with her, I could not think of stepping into her place. It would be a great disappointment to her, and my want of openness with you would be the cause of it. If you should part with her for any other reason, I should be very glad to serve you again."

Judy tried to argue with her, but Miss Clare was immovable.
"Will you let me come and see you, then?" said Judy.
"With all my heart," she answered. "You had better come with Mrs. Percivale, though, for it would not be easy for you to find the place."

We went up to the drawing-room to tea, passing through the study, and taking the gentlemen with us. Miss Clare played to us, and sang several songs,—the last a ballad of Schiller's, "The Pilgrim," setting forth the constant striving of the soul after something of which it never lays hold. The last verse of it I managed to remember. It was this:—

> Thither, ah! no footpath bendeth;
> Ah! the heaven above, so clear,
> Never, earth to touch, descendeth;
> And the There is never Here!"

"That is a beautiful song, and beautifully sung," said Mr. Blackstone; "but I am a little surprised at your choosing to sing it, for you cannot call it a Christian song."

"Don't you find St. Paul saying something very like it again and again?" Miss Clare returned with a smile, as if she perfectly knew what he objected to. "You find him striving, journeying, pressing on, reaching out to lay hold, but never having attained,—ever conscious of failure."

"That is true; but there is this huge difference,—that St. Paul expects to attain,—is confident of one day attaining; while Schiller, in that lyric at least, seems—I only say seems-hopeless of any satisfaction: *Das Dort ist niemals Hier.*"

"It may have been only a mood," said Miss Clare. "St. Paul had his moods also, from which he had to rouse himself to fresh faith and hope and effort."

"But St. Paul writes only in his hopeful moods. Such alone he counts worthy of sharing with his fellows. If there is no hope, why, upon any theory, take the trouble to say so? It is pure weakness to desire sympathy in hopelessness. Hope alone justifies as well as excites either utterance or effort."

"I admit all you say, Mr. Blackstone; and yet I think such a poem invaluable; for is not Schiller therein the mouth of the whole creation groaning and travailling and inarticulately crying out for the sonship?"

"Unconsciously, then. He does not know what he wants."

"*Apparently*, not. Neither does the creation. Neither do we. We do know it is oneness with God we want; but of what that means we have only vague, though glowing hints."

I saw Mr. Morley scratch his left ear like a young calf, only more impatiently.

"But," Miss Clare went on, "is it not invaluable as the confession of one of the noblest of spirits, that he had found neither repose nor sense of attainment?"

"But," said Roger, "did you ever know any one of those you call Christians who professed to have reached satisfaction; or, if so, whose life would justify you in believing him?"

"I have never known a satisfied Christian, I confess," answered Miss Clare. "Indeed, I should take satisfaction as a poor voucher for Christianity. But I have known several contented Christians. I might, in respect of one or two of them, use a stronger word,—certainly not *satisfied*. I believe there is a grand, essential unsatisfaction,—I do not mean dissatisfaction,—which adds the delight of expectation to the peace of attainment; and that, I presume, is the very consciousness of heaven. But where faith may not have produced even contentment, it will yet sustain hope: which, if we may judge from the ballad, no mere aspiration can. We must believe in a living ideal, before we can have a tireless heart; an ideal which draws our poor vague ideal to itself, to fill it full and make it alive."

I should have been amazed to hear Miss Clare talk like this, had I not often heard my father say that aspiration and obedience were the two mightiest forces for development. Her own needs and her own deeds had been her tutors; and the light by which she had read their lessons was the candle of the Lord within her.

When my husband would have put her into Lady Bernard's carriage, as they were leaving, she said she should prefer walking home; and, as Lady Bernard did not press her to the contrary, Percivale could not remonstrate. "I am sorry I cannot walk with you, Miss Clare," he said. "*I must not leave my duties, but*"—

"There's not the slightest occasion," she interrupted. "I know every yard of the way. Good-night."

The carriage drove off in one direction, and Miss Clare tripped lightly along in the other. Percivale darted into the house, and told Roger, who snatched up his hat, and bounded after her. Already she was out of sight; but he, following light-footed, overtook her in the crescent. It was, however, only after persistent entreaty that he prevailed on her to allow him to accompany her.

"You do not know, Mr. Roger," she said pleasantly, "what you may be exposing yourself to, in going with me. I may have to do something you wouldn't like to have a share in."

"I shall be only too glad to have the humblest share in any thing you draw me into," said Roger.

As it fell out, they had not gone far before they came upon a little crowd, chiefly of boys, who ought to have been in bed long before, gathered about a man and woman. The man was forcing his company on a woman who was evidently annoyed that she could not get rid of him.

"Is he your husband?" asked Miss Clare, making her way through the crowd.

"No, miss," the woman answered. "I never saw him afore. I'm only just come in from the country."

She looked more angry than frightened. Roger said her black eyes flashed dangerously, and she felt about the bosom of her dress-for a knife, he was certain.

"You leave her alone," he said to the man, getting between him and her.

"Mind your own business," returned the man, in a voice that showed he was drunk.

For a moment Roger was undecided what to do; for he feared involving Miss Clare in a *row*, as he called it. But when the fellow, pushing suddenly past him, laid his hand on Miss Clare, and shoved her away, he gave him a blow that sent him staggering into the street; whereupon, to his astonishment, Miss Clare, leaving the woman, followed the man, and as soon as he had recovered his equilibrium, laid her hand on his arm and spoke to him, but in a voice so low and gentle that Roger, who had followed her, could not hear a word she said. For a moment or two the man seemed to try to listen, but his condition was too much for him; and, turning from her, he began again to follow the woman, who was now walking wearily away. Roger again interposed.

"Don't strike him, Mr. Roger," cried Miss Clare: "he's too drunk for that. But keep him back if you can, while I take the woman away. If I see a policeman, I will send him."

The man heard her last words, and they roused him to fury. He rushed at Roger, who, implicitly obedient, only dodged to let him pass, and again confronted him, engaging his attention until help arrived. He was, however, by this time so fierce and violent, that Roger felt bound to assist the policeman.

As soon as the man was locked up, he went to Lime Court. The moon was shining, and the narrow passage lay bright beneath her. Along the street, people were going and coming, though it was past midnight, but the court was very still. He walked into it as far as the spot where we had together seen Miss Clare. The door at which she had entered was open; but he knew nothing of the house or its people, and feared to compromise her by making inquiries. He walked several times up and down, somewhat anxious, but gradually persuading himself that in all probability no further annoyance had befallen her; until at last he felt able to leave the place.

He came back to our house, where, finding his brother at his final pipe in the study, he told him all about their adventure.

CHAPTER XXIV
MY FIRST TERROR.

One of the main discomforts in writing a book is, that there are so many ways in which every thing, as it comes up, might be told, and you can't tell which is the best. You believe there must be a *best* way; but you might spend your life in trying to satisfy yourself which was that best way, and, when you came to the close of it, find you had done nothing,—hadn't even found out the way. I have always to remind myself that something, even if it be far from the best thing, is better than nothing. Perhaps the only way to arrive at the best way is to make plenty of blunders, and find them out.

This morning I had been sitting a long time with my pen in my hand, thinking what this chapter ought to be about,—that is, what part of my own history, or of that of my neighbors interwoven therewith, I ought to take up next,—when my third child, my little Cecilia, aged five, came into the room, and said,—

"Mamma, there's a poor man at the door, and Jemima won't give him any thing."

"Quite right, my dear. We must give what we can to people we know. We are sure then that it is not wasted."

"But he's so *very* poor, mamma!"

"How do you know that?"

"Poor man! he has *only* three children. I heard him tell Jemima. He was *so* sorry! And *I'm* very sorry, too."

"But don't you know you mustn't go to the door when any one is talking to Jemima?" I said.

"Yes, mamma. I didn't go to the door: I stood in the hall and peeped."

"But you mustn't even stand in the hall," I said. "Mind that."

This was, perhaps, rather an oppressive reading of a proper enough rule; but I had a very special reason for it, involving an important event in my story, which occurred about two years after what I have last set down.

One morning Percivale took a holiday in order to give me one, and we went to spend it at Richmond. It was the anniversary of our marriage; and as we wanted to enjoy it thoroughly, and, precious as children are, *every* pleasure is not enhanced by their company, we left ours at home,—Ethel and her brother Roger (named after Percivale's father), who was now nearly a year old, and wanted a good deal of attention. It was a lovely day, with just a sufficient number of passing clouds to glorify-that is, to do justice to-the sunshine, and a gentle breeze, which itself seemed to be taking a holiday, for it blew only just when you wanted it, and then only enough to make you think of that wind which, blowing where it lists, always blows where it is wanted. We took the train to Hammersmith; for my husband, having consulted the tide-table, and found that the river would be propitious, wished to row me from there to Richmond. How gay the river-side looked, with its fine broad landing stage, and the numberless boats ready to push off on the swift water, which kept growing and growing on the shingly shore! Percivale, however, would hire his boat at a certain builder's shed, that I might see it. That shed alone would have been worth coming to see-such a picture of loveliest gloom-as if it had been the cave where the twilight abode its time! You could not tell whether to call it light or shade,—that diffused presence of a soft elusive brown; but is what we call shade any thing but subdued light? All about, above, and below, lay the graceful creatures of the water, moveless and dead here on the shore, but there-launched into their own elemental world, and blown upon by the living wind-endowed at once with life and motion and quick response.

Not having been used to boats, I felt nervous as we got into the long, sharp-nosed, hollow fish which Percivale made them shoot out on the rising tide; but the slight fear vanished almost the moment we were afloat, when, ignorant as I was of the art of rowing, I could not help seeing how perfectly Percivale was at home in it. The oars in his hands were like knitting-needles in mine, so deftly, so swimmingly, so variously, did he wield them. Only once my fear returned, when he stood up in the swaying thing—a mere length without breadth-to pull off his coat and waistcoat; but he stood steady, sat down gently, took his oars quietly, and the same instant we were shooting so fast through the rising tide that it seemed as if *we* were pulling the water up to Richmond.

"Wouldn't you like to steer?" said my husband. "It would amuse you."

"I should like to learn," I said,—"not that I want to be amused; I am too happy to care for amusement."

"Take those two cords behind you, then, one in each hand, sitting between them. That will do. Now, if you want me to go to your right, pull your right-hand cord; if you want me to go to your left, pull your left-hand one."

I made an experiment or two, and found the predicted consequences follow: I ran him aground, first on one bank, then on the other. But when I did so a third time,—

"Come! come!" he said: "this won't do, Mrs. Percivale. You're not trying your best. There is such a thing as gradation in steering as well as in painting, or music, or any thing else that is worth doing."

"I pull the right line, don't I?" I said; for I was now in a mood to tease him.

"Yes-to a wrong result," he answered. "You must feel your rudder, as you would the mouth of your horse with the bit, and not do any thing violent, except in urgent necessity."

I answered by turning the head of the boat right towards the nearer bank.

"I see!" he said, with a twinkle in his eyes. "I have put a dangerous power into your hands. But never mind. The queen may decree as she likes; but the sinews of war, you know"—

I thought he meant that if I went on with my arbitrary behavior, he would drop his oars; and for a little while I behaved better. Soon, however, the spirit of mischief prompting me, I began my tricks again: to my surprise I found that I had no more command over the boat than over the huge barge, which, with its great red-brown sail, was slowly ascending in front of us; I couldn't turn its head an inch in the direction I wanted.

"What does it mean, Percivale?" I cried, pulling with all my might, and leaning forward that I might pull the harder.

"What does what mean?" he returned coolly.

"That I can't move the boat."

"Oh! It means that I have resumed the reins of government."

"But how? I can't understand it."

"And I am wiser than to make you too wise. Education is *not* a panacea for moral evils. I quote your father, my dear."

And he pulled away as if nothing were the matter.

"Please, I like steering," I said remonstratingly. "And I like rowing."

"I don't see why the two shouldn't go together."

"Nor I. They ought. But not only does the steering depend on the rowing, but the rower can steer himself."

"I will be a good girl, and steer properly."

"Very well; steer away."

He looked shorewards as he spoke; and then first I became aware that he had been watching my hands all the time. The boat now obeyed my lightest touch.

How merrily the water rippled in the sun and the wind! while so responsive were our feelings to the play of light and shade around us, that more than once when a cloud crossed us, I saw its shadow turn almost into sadness on the countenance of my companion,—to vanish the next moment when the one sun above and the thousand mimic suns below shone out in universal laughter. When a steamer came in sight, or announced its approach by the far-heard sound of its beating paddles, it brought with it a few moments of almost awful responsibility; but I found that the presence of danger and duty together, instead of making me feel flurried, composed my nerves, and enabled me to concentrate my whole attention on getting the head of the boat as nearly as possible at right angles with the waves from the paddles; for Percivale had told me that if one of any size struck us on the side, it would most probably capsize us. But the way to give pleasure to my readers can hardly be to let myself grow garrulous in the memory of an ancient pleasure of my own. I will say nothing more of the delights of that day. They were such a contrast to its close, that twelve months at least elapsed before I was able to look back upon them without a shudder; for I could not rid myself of the foolish feeling that our enjoyment had been somehow to blame for what was happening at home while we were thus revelling in blessed carelessness.

When we reached our little nest, rather late in the evening, I found to my annoyance that the front door was open. It had been a fault of which I thought I had cured the cook,—to leave it thus when she ran out to fetch any thing. Percivale went down to the study; and I walked into the drawing-room, about to ring the bell in anger. There, to my surprise and farther annoyance, I found Sarah, seated on the sofa with her head in her hands, and little Roger wide awake on the floor.

"What *does* this mean?" I cried. "The front door open! Master Roger still up! and you seated in the drawing-room!"

"O ma'am!" she almost shrieked, starting up the moment I spoke, and, by the time I had put my angry interrogation, just able to gasp out—"Have you found her, ma'am?"

"Found whom?" I returned in alarm, both at the question and at the face of the girl; for through the dusk I now saw that it was very pale, and that her eyes were red with crying.

"Miss Ethel," she answered in a cry choked with a sob; and dropping again on the sofa, she hid her face once more between her hands.

I rushed to the study-door, and called Percivale; then returned to question the girl. I wonder now that I did nothing outrageous; but fear kept down folly, and made me unnaturally calm.

"Sarah," I said, as quietly as I could, while I trembled all over, "tell me what has happened. Where is the child?"

"Indeed it's not my fault, ma'am. I was busy with Master Roger, and Miss Ethel was down stairs with Jemima."

"Where is she?" I repeated sternly.

"I don't know no more than the man in the moon, ma'am."

"Where's Jemima?"

"Run out to look for her?"

"How long have you missed her?"

"An hour. Or perhaps two hours. I don't know, my head's in such a whirl. I can't remember when I saw her last. O ma'am! What *shall* I do?"

Percivale had come up, and was standing beside me. When I looked round, he was as pale as death; and at the sight of his face, I nearly dropped on the floor. But he caught hold of me, and said, in a voice so dreadfully still that it frightened me more than any thing,—

"Come, my love; do not give way, for we must go to the police at once." Then, turning to Sarah, "Have you searched the house and garden?" he asked.

"Yes, sir; every hole and corner. We've looked under every bed, and into every cupboard and chest,—the coal-cellar, the boxroom,—everywhere."

"The bathroom?" I cried.

"Oh, yes, ma'am! the bathroom, and everywhere."

"Have there been any tramps about the house since we left?" Percivale asked.

"Not that I know of; but the nursery window looks into the garden, you know, sir. Jemima didn't mention it."

"Come then, my dear," said my husband.

He compelled me to swallow a glass of wine, and led me away, almost unconscious of my bodily movements, to the nearest cab-stand. I wondered afterwards, when I recalled the calm gaze with which he glanced along the line, and chose the horse whose appearance promised the best speed. In a few minutes we were telling the inspector at the police-station in Albany Street what had happened. He took a sheet of paper, and asking one question after another about her age, appearance, and dress, wrote down our answers. He then called a man, to whom he gave the paper, with some words of direction.

"The men are now going on their beats for the night," he said, turning again to us. "They will all hear the description of the child, and some of them have orders to search."

"Thank you," said my husband. "Which station had we better go to next?"

"The news will be at the farthest before you can reach the nearest," he answered. "We shall telegraph to the suburbs first."

"Then what more is there we can do?" asked Percivale.

"Nothing," said the inspector, —"except you find out whether any of the neighbors saw her, and when and where. It would be something to know in what direction she was going. Have you any ground for suspicion? Have you ever discharged a servant? Were any tramps seen about the place?"

"I know, who it is!" I cried. "It's the woman that took Theodora! It's Theodora's mother! I know it is!"

Percivale explained what I meant.

"That's what people get, you see, when they take on themselves other people's business," returned the inspector. "That child ought to have been sent to the workhouse."

He laid his head on his hand for a moment.

"It seems likely enough," he added. Then after another pause —"I have your address. The child shall be brought back to you the moment she's found. We can't mistake her after your description."

"Where are you going now?" I said to my husband, as we left the station to re-enter the cab.

"I don't know," he answered, "except we go home and question all the shops in the neighborhood."

"Let us go to Miss Clare first," I said.

"By all means," he answered.

We were soon at the entrance of Lime Court.

When we turned the corner in the middle of it, we heard the sound of a piano.

"She's at home!" I cried, with a feeble throb of satisfaction. The fear that she might be out had for the last few moments been uppermost.

We entered the house, and ascended the stairs in haste. Not a creature did we meet, except a wicked-looking cat. The top of her head was black, her forehead and face white; and the black and white were shaped so as to look like hair parted over a white forehead, which gave her green eyes a frightfully human look as she crouched in the corner of a window-sill in the light of a gas-lamp outside. But before we reached the top of the first stair we heard the sounds of dancing, as well as of music. In a moment after, with our load of gnawing fear and helpless eagerness, we stood in the midst of a merry assembly of men, women, and children, who filled Miss Clare's room to overflowing. It was Saturday night, and they were gathered according to custom for their weekly music.

They made a way for us; and Miss Clare left the piano, and came to meet us with a smile on her beautiful face. But, when she saw our faces, hers fell.

"What *is* the matter, Mrs. Percivale?" she asked in alarm.

I sunk on the chair from which she had risen.

"We've lost Ethel," said my husband quietly.

"What do you mean? You don't"—

"No, no: she's gone; she's stolen. We don't know where she is," he answered with faltering voice. "We've just been to the police."

Miss Clare turned white; but, instead of making any remark, she called out to some of her friends whose good manners were making them leave the room, —

"Don't go, please; we want you." Then turning to me, she asked, "May I do as I think best?"

"Yes, certainly," answered my husband.

"My friend, Mrs. Percivale," she said, addressing the whole assembly, "has lost her little girl."

A murmur of dismay and sympathy arose.

"What can we do to find her?" she went on.

They fell to talking among themselves. The next instant, two men came up to us, making their way from the neighborhood of the door. The one was a keen-faced, elderly man, with iron-gray whiskers and clean-shaved chin; the other was my first acquaintance in the neighborhood, the young bricklayer. The elder addressed my husband, while the other listened without speaking.

"Tell us what she's like, sir, and how she was dressed-though that ain't much use. She'll be all different by this time."

The words shot a keener pang to my heart than it had yet felt. My darling stripped of her nice clothes, and covered with dirty, perhaps infected garments. But it was no time to give way to feeling.

My husband repeated to the men the description he had given the police, loud enough for the whole room to hear; and the women in particular, Miss Clare told me afterwards, caught it up with remarkable accuracy. They would not have done so, she said, but that their feelings were touched.

"Tell them also, please, Mr. Percivale, about the child Mrs. Percivale's father and mother found and brought up. That may have something to do with this."

My husband told them all the story; adding that the mother of the child might have found out who we were, and taken ours as a pledge for the recovery of her own.

Here one of the women spoke.

"That dark woman you took in one night-two years ago, miss-she say something. I was astin' of her in the mornin' what her trouble was, for that trouble *she* had on *her* mind was plain to see, and she come over something, half-way like, about losin' of a child; but whether it were dead, or strayed, or stolen, or what, I couldn't tell; and no more, I believe, she wanted me to."

Here another woman spoke.

"I'm 'most sure I saw her-the same woman-two days ago, and no furrer off than Gower Street," she said. "You're too good by half, miss," she went on, "to the likes of sich. They ain't none of them respectable."

"Perhaps you'll see some good come out of it before long," said Miss Clare in reply.

The words sounded like a rebuke, for all this time I had hardly sent a thought upwards for help. The image of my child had so filled my heart, that there was no room left for the thought of duty, or even of God.

Miss Clare went on, still addressing the company, and her words had a tone of authority.

"I will tell you what you must do," she said. "You must, every one of you, run and tell everybody you know, and tell every one to tell everybody else. You mustn't stop to talk it over with each other, or let those you tell it to stop to talk to you about it; for it is of the greatest consequence no time should be lost in making it as quickly and as widely known as possible. Go, please."

In a few moments the room was empty of all but ourselves. The rush on the stairs was tremendous for a single minute, and then all was still. Even the children had rushed out to tell what other children they could find.

"What must we do next?" said my husband.

Miss Clare thought for a moment.

"I would go and tell Mr. Blackstone," she said. "It is a long way from here, but whoever has taken the child would not be likely to linger in the neighborhood. It is best to try every thing."

"Right," said my husband. "Come, Wynnie."

"Wouldn't it be better to leave Mrs. Percivale with me?" said Miss Clare. "It is dreadfully fatiguing to go driving over the stones."

It was very kind of her; but if she had been a mother she would not have thought of parting me from my husband; neither would she have fancied that I could remain inactive so long as it was possible even to imagine I was doing something; but when I told her how I felt, she saw at once that it would be better for me to go.

We set off instantly, and drove to Mr. Blackstone's. What a long way it was! Down Oxford Street and Holborn we rattled and jolted, and then through many narrow ways in which I had never been, emerging at length in a broad road, with many poor and a few fine old houses in it; then again plunging into still more shabby regions of small houses, which, alas! were new, and yet wretched! At length, near an open space, where yet not a blade of grass could grow for the trampling of many feet, and for the smoke from tall chimneys, close by a gasometer of awful size, we found the parsonage, and Mr. Blackstone in his study. The moment he heard our story he went to the door and called his servant. "Run, Jabez," he said, "and tell the sexton to ring the church-bell. I will come to him directly I hear it."

I may just mention that Jabez and his wife, who formed the whole of Mr. Blackstone's household, did not belong to his congregation, but were members of a small community in the neighborhood, calling themselves Peculiar Baptists.

About ten minutes passed, during which little was said: Mr. Blackstone never seemed to have any mode of expressing his feelings except action, and where that was impossible they took hardly any recognizable shape. When the first boom of the big bell filled the little study in which we sat, I gave a cry, and jumped up from my chair: it sounded in my ears like the knell of my lost baby, for at the moment I was thinking of her as once when a baby she lay for dead in my arms. Mr. Blackstone got up and left the room, and my husband rose and would have followed him; but, saying he would be back in a few minutes, he shut the door and left us. It was half an hour, a dreadful half-hour, before he returned; for to sit doing nothing, not even being carried somewhere to do something, was frightful.

"I've told them all about it," he said. "I couldn't do better than follow Miss Clare's example. But my impression is, that, if the woman you suspect be the culprit, she would make her way out to the open as quickly as possible. Such people are most at home on the commons: they are of a less gregarious nature than the wild animals of the town. What shall you do next?"

"That is just what I want to know," answered my husband.

He never asked advice except when he did not know what to do; and never except from one whose advice he meant to follow.

"Well," returned Mr. Blackstone, "I should put an advertisement into every one of the morning papers."

"But the offices will all be closed," said Percivale.

"Yes, the publishing, but not the printing offices."

"How am I to find out where they are?"

"I know one or two of them, and the people there will tell us the rest."

"Then you mean to go with us?"

"Of course I do,—that is, if you will have me. You don't think I would leave you to go alone? Have you had any supper?"

"No. Would you like something, my dear?" said Percivale turning to me.

"I couldn't swallow a mouthful," I said.

"Nor I either," said Percivale.

"Then I'll just take a hunch of bread with me," said Mr. Blackstone, "for I am hungry. I've had nothing since one o'clock."

We neither asked him not to go, nor offered to wait till he had had his supper. Before we reached Printing-House Square he had eaten half a loaf.

"Are you sure," said my husband, as we were starting, "that they will take an advertisement at the printing-office?"

"I think they will. The circumstances are pressing. They will see that we are honest people, and will make a push to help us. But for any thing I know it may be quite *en règle*."

"We must pay, though," said Percivale, putting his hand in his pocket, and taking out his purse. "There! Just as I feared! No money!—Two-three shillings-and sixpence!"

Mr. Blackstone stopped the cab.

"I've not got as much," he said. "But it's of no consequence. I'll run and write a check."

"But where can you change it? The little shops about here won't be able."

"There's the Blue Posts."

"Let me take it, then. You won't be seen going into a public-house?" said Percivale.

"Pooh! pooh!" said Mr. Blackstone. "Do you think my character won't stand that much? Besides, they wouldn't change it for you. But when I think of it, I used the last check in my book in the beginning of the week. Never mind; they will lend me five pounds."

We drove to the Blue Posts. He got out, and returned in one minute with five sovereigns.

"What will people say to your borrowing five pounds at a public-house?" said Percivale.

"If they say what is right, it won't hurt me."

"But if they say what is wrong?"

"That they can do any time, and that won't hurt me, either."

"But what will the landlord himself think?"

"I have no doubt he feels grateful to me for being so friendly. You can't oblige a man more than by asking a *light* favor of him."

"Do you think it well in your position to be obliged to a man in his?" asked Percivale.

"I do. I am glad of the chance. It will bring me into friendly relations with him."

"Do you wish, then, to be in friendly relations with him?"

"Indubitably. In what other relations do you suppose a clergyman ought to be with one of his parishioners?"

"You didn't invite *him* into your parish, I presume."

"No; and he didn't invite me. The thing was settled in higher quarters. There we are, anyhow; and I have done quite a stroke of business in borrowing that money of him."

Mr. Blackstone laughed, and the laugh sounded frightfully harsh in my ears.

"A man" —my husband went on, who was surprised that a clergyman should be so liberal— "a man who sells drink! —in whose house so many of your parishioners will to-morrow night get too drunk to be in church the next morning!"

"I wish having been drunk were what *would* keep them from being in church. Drunk or sober, it would be all the same. Few of them care to go. They are turning out better, however, than when first I came. As for the publican, who knows what chance of doing him a good turn it may put in my way?"

"You don't expect to persuade him to shut up shop?"

"No: he must persuade himself to that."

"What good, then, can you expect to do him?"

"Who knows? I say. You can't tell what good may or may not come out of it, any more than you can tell which of your efforts, or which of your helpers, may this night be the means of restoring your child."

"What do you expect the man to say about it?"

"I shall provide him with something to say. I don't want him to attribute it to some foolish charity. He might. In the New Testament, publicans are acknowledged to have hearts."

"Yes; but the word has a very different meaning in the New Testament."

"The feeling religious people bear towards them, however, comes very near to that with which society regarded the publicans of old."

"They are far more hurtful to society than those tax-gatherers."

"They may be. I dare say they are. Perhaps they are worse than the sinners with whom their namesakes of the New Testament are always coupled."

I will not follow the conversation further. I will only give the close of it. Percivale told me afterwards that he had gone on talking in the hope of diverting my thoughts a little.

"What, then, do you mean to tell him?" asked Percivale.

"The truth, the whole truth, and nothing but the truth," said Mr. Blackstone. "I shall go in to-morrow morning, just at the time when there will probably be far too many people at the bar, —a little after noon. I shall return him his five sovereigns, ask for a glass of ale, and tell him the whole story, —how my friend, the celebrated painter, came with his wife, —and the rest of it, adding, I trust, that the child is all right, and at the moment probably going out for a walk with her mother, who won't let her out of her sight for a moment."

He laughed again, and again I thought him heartless; but I understand him better now. I wondered, too, that Percivale *could* go on talking, and yet I found that their talk did make the time go a little quicker. At length we reached the printing-office of "The Times,"—near Blackfriars' Bridge, I think.

After some delay, we saw an overseer, who, curt enough at first, became friendly when he heard our case. If he had not had children of his own, we might perhaps have fared worse. He took down the description and address, and promised that the advertisement should appear in the morning's paper in the best place he could now find for it.

Before we left, we received minute directions as to the whereabouts of the next nearest office. We spent the greater part of the night in driving from one printing-office to another. Mr. Blackstone declared he would not leave us until we had found her.

"You have to preach twice to-morrow," said Percivale: it was then three o'clock.

"I shall preach all the better," he returned. "Yes: I feel as if I should give them *one* good sermon to-morrow."

"The man talks as if the child were found already!" I thought, with indignation. "It's a pity he hasn't a child of his own! he would be more sympathetic." At the same time, if I had been honest, I should have confessed to myself that his confidence and hope helped to keep me up.

At last, having been to the printing-office of every daily paper in London, we were on our dreary way home.

Oh, how dreary it was! —and the more dreary that the cool, sweet light of a spring dawn was growing in every street, no smoke having yet begun to pour from the multitudinous chimneys to sully its purity! From misery and want of sleep, my soul and body both felt like a gray foggy night. Every now and then the thought of my child came with a fresh pang, —not that she was one moment absent from me, but that a new thought about her would dart a new sting into the ever-burning throb of the wound. If you had asked me the one blessed thing in the world, I should have said *sleep* —with my husband and children beside me. But I dreaded sleep now, both for its visions and for the frightful waking. Now and then I would start violently, thinking I heard my Ethel cry; but from the cab-window no child was ever to be seen, down all the lonely street. Then I would sink into a succession of efforts to picture to myself her little face, —white with terror and misery, and smeared with the dirt of the pitiful hands that rubbed the streaming eyes. They might have beaten her! she might have cried herself to sleep in some wretched hovel; or, worse, in some fever-stricken and crowded lodging-house, with horrible sights about her and horrible voices in her ears! Or she might at that moment be dragged wearily along a country-road, farther and farther from her mother! I could have shrieked, and torn my hair. What if I should never see her again? She might be murdered, and I never know it! O my darling! my darling!

At the thought a groan escaped me. A hand was laid on my arm. That I knew was my husband's. But a voice was in my ear, and that was Mr. Blackstone's.

"Do you think God loves the child less than you do? Or do you think he is less able to take care of her than you are? When the disciples thought themselves sinking, Jesus rebuked them for being afraid. Be still, and you will see the hand of God in this. Good you cannot foresee will come out of it."

I could not answer him, but I felt both rebuked and grateful.

All at once I thought of Roger. What would he say when he found that his pet was gone, and we had never told him?

"Roger!" I said to my husband. "We've never told him!"

"Let us go now," he returned.

We were at the moment close to North Crescent. After a few thundering raps at the door, the landlady came down. Percivale rushed up, and in a few minutes returned with Roger. They got into the cab. A great talk followed; but I heard hardly any thing, or rather I heeded nothing. I only recollect that Roger was very indignant with his brother for having been out all night without him to help.

"I never thought of you, Roger," said Percivale.

"So much the worse!" said Roger.

"No," said Mr. Blackstone. "A thousand things make us forget. I dare say your brother all but forgot God in the first misery of his loss. To have thought of you, and not to have told you, would have been another thing."

A few minutes after, we stopped at our desolate house, and the cabman was dismissed with one of the sovereigns from the Blue Posts. I wondered afterwards what manner of man or woman had changed it there. A dim light was burning in the drawing-room. Percivale took his pass-key, and opened the door. I hurried in, and went straight to my own room; for I longed to be alone that I might weep-nor weep only. I fell on my knees by the bedside, buried my face, and sobbed, and tried to pray. But I could not collect my thoughts; and, overwhelmed by a fresh access of despair, I started again to my feet.

Could I believe my eyes? What was that in the bed? Trembling as with an ague, —in terror lest the vision should by vanishing prove itself a vision, —I stooped towards it. I heard a breathing! It was the fair hair and the rosy face of my darling-fast asleep-without one trace of suffering on her angelic loveliness! I remember no more for a while. They tell me I gave a great cry, and fell on the floor. When I came to myself I was lying on the bed. My husband was bending over me, and Roger and Mr. Blackstone were both in the room. I could not speak, but my husband understood my questioning gaze.

"Yes, yes, my love," he said quietly: "she's all right-safe and sound, thank God!"

And I did thank God.

Mr. Blackstone came to the bedside, with a look and a smile that seemed to my conscience to say, "I told you so." I held out my hand to him, but could only weep. Then I remembered how we had vexed Roger, and called him.

"Dear Roger," I said, "forgive me, and go and tell Miss Clare."

I had some reason to think this the best amends I could make him.

"I will go at once," he said. "She will be anxious."

"And I will go to my sermon," said Mr. Blackstone, with the same quiet smile.

They shook hands with me, and went away. And my husband and I rejoiced over our first-born.

CHAPTER XXV
ITS SEQUEL.

My darling was recovered neither through Miss Clare's injunctions nor Mr. Blackstone's bell-ringing. A woman was walking steadily westward, carrying the child asleep in her arms, when a policeman stopped her at Turnham Green. She betrayed no fear, only annoyance, and offered no resistance, only begged he would not wake the child, or take her from her. He brought them in a cab to the police-station, whence the child was sent home. As soon as she arrived, Sarah gave her a warm bath, and put her to bed; but she scarcely opened her eyes.

Jemima had run about the streets till midnight, and then fallen asleep on the doorstep, where the policeman found her when he brought the child. For a week she went about like one dazed; and the blunders she made were marvellous. She ordered a brace of cod from the poulterer, and a pound of anchovies at the crockery shop. One day at dinner, we could not think how the chops were so pulpy, and we got so many bits of bone in our mouth: she had powerfully beaten them, as if they had been steaks. She sent up melted butter for bread-sauce, and stuffed a hare with sausages.

After breakfast, Percivale walked to the police-station, to thank the inspector, pay what expenses had been incurred, and see the woman. I was not well enough to go with him. My Marion is a white-faced thing, and her eyes look much too big for her small face. I suggested that he should take Miss Clare. As it was early, he was fortunate enough to find her at home, and she accompanied him willingly, and at once recognized the woman as the one she had befriended.

He told the magistrate he did not wish to punish her, but that there were certain circumstances which made him desirous of detaining her until a gentleman, who, he believed, could identify her, should arrive. The magistrate therefore remanded her.

The next day but one my father came. When he saw her, he had little doubt she was the same that had carried off Theo; but he could not be absolutely certain, because he had seen her only by moonlight. He told the magistrate the whole story, saying, that, if she should prove the mother of the child, he was most anxious to try what he could do for her. The magistrate expressed grave doubts whether he would find it possible to befriend her to any effectual degree. My father said he would try, if he could but be certain she was the mother.

"If she stole the child merely to compel the restitution of her own," he said. "I cannot regard her conduct with any abhorrence. But, if she is not the mother of the child, I must leave her to the severity of the law."

"I once discharged a woman," said the magistrate, "who had committed the same offence, for I was satisfied she had done so purely from the desire to possess the child."

"But might not a thief say he was influenced merely by the desire to add another sovereign to his hoard?"

"The greed of the one is a natural affection; that of the other a vice."

"But the injury to the loser is far greater in the one case than in the other."

"To set that off, however, the child is more easily discovered. Besides, the false appetite grows with indulgence; whereas one child would still the natural one."

"Then you would allow her to go on stealing child after child, until she succeeded in keeping one," said my father, laughing.

"I dismissed her with the warning, that, if ever she did so again, this would be brought up against her, and she would have the severest punishment the law could inflict. It may be right to pass a first offence, and wrong to pass a second. I tried to make her measure the injury done to the mother, by her own sorrow at losing the child; and I think not without effect. At all events, it was some years ago, and I have not heard of her again."

Now came in the benefit of the kindness Miss Clare had shown the woman. I doubt if any one else could have got the truth from her. Even she found it difficult; for to tell her that if she was Theo's mother she should not be punished, might be only to tempt her to lie. All Miss

Clare could do was to assure her of the kindness of every one concerned, and to urge her to disclose her reasons for doing such a grievous wrong as steal another woman's child.

"They stole my child," she blurted out at last, when the cruelty of the action was pressed upon her.

"Oh, no!" said Miss Clare: "you left her to die in the cold."

"No, no!" she cried. "I wanted somebody to hear her, and take her in. I wasn't far off, and was just going to take her again, when I saw a light, and heard them searching for her. Oh, dear! Oh, dear!"

"Then how can you say they stole her? You would have had no child at all, but for them. She was nearly dead when they found her. And in return you go and steal their grandchild!"

"They took her from me afterwards. They wouldn't let me have my own flesh and blood. I wanted to let them know what it was to have *their* child taken from them."

"How could they tell she was your child, when you stole her away like a thief? It might, for any thing they knew, be some other woman stealing her, as you stole theirs the other day? What would have become of you if it had been so?"

To this reasoning she made no answer.

"I want my child; I want my child," she moaned. Then breaking out —"I shall kill myself if I don't get my child!" she cried. "Oh, lady, you don't know what it is to have a child and not have her! I shall kill myself if they don't give me her back. They can't say I did their child any harm. I was as good to her as if she had been my own."

"They know that quite well, and don't want to punish you. Would you like to see your child?"

She clasped her hands above her head, fell on her knees at Miss Clare's feet, and looked up in her face without uttering a word.

"I will speak to Mr. Walton," said Miss Clare; and left her.

The next morning she was discharged, at the request of my husband, who brought her home with him.

Sympathy with the mother-passion in her bosom had melted away all my resentment. She was a fine young woman, of about five and twenty, though her weather-browned complexion made her look at first much older. With the help of the servants, I persuaded her to have a bath, during which they removed her clothes, and substituted others. She objected to putting them on; seemed half-frightened at them, as if they might involve some shape of bondage, and begged to have her own again. At last Jemima, who, although so sparingly provided with brains, is not without genius, prevailed upon her, insisting that her little girl would turn away from her if she wasn't well dressed, for she had been used to see ladies about her. With a deep sigh, she yielded; begging, however, to have her old garments restored to her.

She had brought with her a small bundle, tied up in a cotton handkerchief; and from it she now took a scarf of red silk, and twisted it up with her black hair in a fashion I had never seen before. In this head-dress she had almost a brilliant look; while her carriage had a certain dignity hard of association with poverty-not inconsistent, however, with what I have since learned about the gypsies. My husband admired her even more than I did, and made a very good sketch of her. Her eyes were large and dark-unquestionably fine; and if there was not much of the light of thought in them, they had a certain wildness which in a measure made up for the want. She had rather a Spanish than an Eastern look, I thought, with an air of defiance that prevented me from feeling at ease with her; but in the presence of Miss Clare she seemed humbler, and answered her questions more readily than ours. If Ethel was in the room, her eyes would be constantly wandering after her, with a wistful, troubled, eager look. Surely, the mother-passion must have infinite relations and destinies.

As I was unable to leave home, my father persuaded Miss Clare to accompany him and help him to take charge of her. I confess it was a relief to me when she left the house; for though I wanted to be as kind to her as I could, I felt considerable discomfort in her presence.

When Miss Clare returned, the next day but one, I found she had got from her the main points of her history, fully justifying previous conjectures of my father's, founded on what he knew of the character and customs of the gypsies.

She belonged to one of the principal gypsy families in this country. The fact that they had no settled habitation, but lived in tents, like Abraham and Isaac, had nothing to do with poverty. The silver buttons on her father's coat, were, she said, worth nearly twenty pounds; and when a friend of any distinction came to tea with them, they spread a table-cloth of fine linen on the grass, and set out upon it the best of china, and a tea-service of hall-marked silver. She said her friends-as much as any gentleman in the land-scorned stealing; and affirmed that no real gypsy would "risk his neck for his belly," except he were driven by hunger. All her family could read, she said, and carried a big Bible about with them.

One summer they were encamped for several months in the neighborhood of Edinburgh, making horn-spoons and baskets, and some of them working in tin. There they were visited by a clergyman, who talked and read the Bible to them, and prayed with them. But all their visitors ware not of the same sort with him. One of them was a young fellow of loose character, a clerk in the city, who, attracted by her appearance, prevailed upon her to meet him often. She was not then eighteen. Any aberration from the paths of modesty is exceedingly rare among the gypsies, and regarded with severity; and her father, hearing of this, gave her a terrible punishment with the whip he used in driving his horses. In terror of what would follow when the worst came to be known, she ran away; and, soon forsaken by her so-called lover, wandered about, a common vagrant, until her baby was born-under the stars, on a summer night, in a field of long grass.

For some time she wandered up and down, longing to join some tribe of her own people, but dreading unspeakably the disgrace of her motherhood. At length, having found a home for her child, she associated herself with a gang of gypsies of inferior character, amongst whom she had many hardships to endure. Things, however, bettered a little after one of their number was hanged for stabbing a cousin, and her position improved. It was not, however, any intention of carrying off her child to share her present lot, but the urgings of mere mother-hunger for a sight of her, that drove her to the Hall. When she had succeeded in enticing her out of sight of the house, however, the longing to possess her grew fierce; and braving all consequences, or rather, I presume, unable to weigh them, she did carry her away. Foiled in this attempt, and seeing that her chances of future success in any similar one were diminished by it, she sought some other plan. Learning that one of the family was married, and had removed to London, she succeeded, through gypsy acquaintances who lodged occasionally near Tottenham Court Road, in finding out where we lived, and carried off Ethel with the vague intent, as we had rightly conjectured, of using her as a means for the recovery of her own child.

Theodora was now about seven years of age-almost as wild as ever. Although tolerably obedient, she was not nearly so much so as the other children had been at her age; partly, perhaps, because my father could not bring himself to use that severity to the child of other people with which he had judged it proper to treat his own.

Miss Clare was present, with my father and the rest of the family, when the mother and daughter met. They were all more than curious to see how the child would behave, and whether there would be any signs of an instinct that drew her to her parent. In this, however, they were disappointed.

It was a fine warm forenoon when she came running on to the lawn where they were assembled,—the gypsy mother with them.

"There she is!" said my father to the woman. "Make the best of yourself you can."

Miss Clare said the poor creature turned very pale, but her eyes glowed with such a fire!

With the cunning of her race, she knew better than bound forward and catch up the child in her arms. She walked away from the rest, and stood watching the little damsel, romping merrily with Mr. Wagtail. They thought she recognized the dog, and was afraid of him. She had put on a few silver ornaments which she had either kept or managed to procure, notwithstanding her poverty; for both the men and women of her race manifest in a strong degree that love for barbaric adornment which, as well as their other peculiarities, points to an Eastern origin. The glittering of these in the sun, and the glow of her red scarf in her dark hair, along with the strangeness of her whole appearance, attracted the child, and she approached to look at her nearer. Then the mother took from her pocket a large gilded ball, which had probably been one of the ornaments on the top of a clock, and rolled it gleaming golden along the grass. Theo and Mr. Wagtail bounded after it with a shriek and a bark. Having examined it for a moment, the child threw it again along the lawn; and this time the mother, lithe as a leopard and fleet as a savage, joined in the chase, caught it first, and again sent it spinning away, farther from the assembled group. Once more all three followed in swift pursuit; but this time the mother took care to allow the child to seize the treasure. After the sport had continued a little while, what seemed a general consultation, of mother, child, and dog, took place over the bauble; and presently they saw that Theo was eating something.

"I trust," said my mother, "she won't hurt the child with any nasty stuff."

"She will not do so wittingly," said my father, "you may be sure. Anyhow, we must not interfere."

In a few minutes more the mother approached them with a subdued look of triumph, and her eyes overflowing with light, carrying the child in her arms. Theo was playing with some foreign coins which adorned her hair, and with a string of coral and silver beads round her neck.

For the rest of the day they were left to do much as they pleased; only every one kept good watch.

But in the joy of recovering her child, the mother seemed herself to have gained a new and childlike spirit. The more than willingness with which she hastened to do what, even in respect of her child, was requested of her, as if she fully acknowledged the right of authority in those who had been her best friends, was charming. Whether this would last when the novelty of the new experience had worn off, whether jealousy would not then come in for its share in the ordering of her conduct, remained to be shown; but in the mean time the good in her was uppermost.

She was allowed to spend a whole fortnight in making friends with her daughter, before a word was spoken about the future; the design of my father being through the child to win the mother. Certain people considered him not eager enough to convert the wicked: whatever apparent indifference he showed in that direction arose from his utter belief in the guiding of God, and his dread of outrunning his designs. He would *follow* the operations of the Spirit.

"Your forced hot-house fruits," he would say, "are often finer to look at than those which have waited for God's wind and weather; but what are they worth in respect of all for the sake of which fruit exists?"

Until an opportunity, then, was thrown in his way, he would hold back; but when it was clear to him that he had to minister, then was he thoughtful, watchful, instant, unswerving. You might have seen him during this time, as the letters of Connie informed me, often standing for minutes together watching the mother and daughter, and pondering in his heart concerning them.

Every advantage being thus afforded her, not without the stirring of some natural pangs in those who had hitherto mothered the child, the fortnight had not passed, before, to all appearance, the unknown mother was with the child the greatest favorite of all. And it was my father's expectation, for he was a profound believer in blood, that the natural and generic instincts of the child would be developed together; in other words, that as she grew in what was common to humanity, she would grow likewise in what belonged to her individual origin. This was not an altogether comforting expectation to those of us who neither had so much faith as he, nor saw so hopefully the good that lay in every evil.

One twilight, he overheard the following talk between them. When they came near where he sat, Theodora, carried by her mother, and pulling at her neck with her arms, was saying, "Tell me; tell me; tell me," in the tone of one who would compel an answer to a question repeatedly asked in vain.

"What do you want me to tell you?" said her mother. "You know well enough. Tell me your name."

In reply, she uttered a few words my father did not comprehend, and took to be Zingaree. The child shook her petulantly and with violence, crying,—

"That's nonsense. I don't know what you say, and I don't know what to call you."

My father had desired the household, if possible, to give no name to the woman in the child's hearing.

"Call me mam, if you like."

"But you're not a lady, and I won't say ma'am to you," said Theo, rude as a child will sometimes be when least she intends offence.

Her mother set her down, and gave a deep sigh. Was it only that the child's restlessness and roughness tired her? My father thought otherwise.

"Tell me; tell me," the child persisted, beating her with her little clenched fist. "Take me up again, and tell me, or I will make you."

My father thought it time to interfere. He stepped forward. The mother started with a little cry, and caught up the child.

"Theo," said my father, "I cannot allow you to be rude, especially to one who loves you more than any one else loves you."

The woman set her down again, dropped on her knees, and caught and kissed his hand.

The child stared; but she stood in awe of my father,—perhaps the more that she had none for any one else,—and, when her mother lifted her once more, was carried away in silence.

The difficulty was got over by the child's being told to call her mother *Nurse*.

My father was now sufficiently satisfied with immediate results to carry out the remainder of his contingent plan, of which my mother heartily approved. The gardener and his wife being elderly people, and having no family, therefore not requiring the whole of their cottage, which was within a short distance of the house, could spare a room, which my mother got arranged for the gypsy; and there she was housed, with free access to her child, and the understanding that when Theo liked to sleep with her, she was at liberty to do so.

She was always ready to make herself useful; but it was little she could do for some time, and it was with difficulty that she settled to any occupation at all continuous.

Before long it became evident that her old habits were working in her and making her restless. She was pining after the liberty of her old wandering life, with sun and wind, space and change, all about her. It was spring; and the reviving life of nature was rousing in her the longing for motion and room and variety engendered by the roving centuries which had passed since first her ancestors were driven from their homes in far Hindostan. But my father had foreseen the probability, and had already thought over what could be done for her if the wandering passion should revive too powerfully. He reasoned that there was nothing bad in such an impulse,—one doubtless, which would have been felt in all its force by Abraham himself, had he quitted his tents and gone to dwell in a city,—however much its indulgence might place her at a disadvantage in the midst of a settled social order. He saw, too, that any attempt to coerce it would probably result in entire frustration; that the passion for old forms of freedom would gather tenfold vigor in consequence. It would be far better to favor its indulgence, in the hope that the love of her child would, like an elastic but infrangible cord, gradually tame her down to a more settled life.

He proposed, therefore, that she should, as a matter of duty, go and visit her parents, and let them know of her welfare. She looked alarmed.

"Your father will show you no unkindness, I am certain, after the lapse of so many years," he added. "Think it over, and tell me to-morrow how you feel about it. You shall go by train to Edinburgh, and once there you will soon be able to find them. Of course you couldn't take the child with you; but she will be safe with us till you come back."

The result was that she went; and having found her people, and spent a fortnight with them, returned in less than a month. The rest of the year she remained quietly at home, stilling her desires by frequent and long rambles with her child, in which Mr. Wagtail always accompanied them. My father thought it better to run the risk of her escaping, than force the thought of it upon her by appearing not to trust her. But it came out that she had a suspicion that the dog was there to prevent, or at least expose, any such imprudence. The following spring she went on a second visit to her friends, but was back within a week, and the next year did not go at all.

Meantime my father did what he could to teach her, presenting every truth as something it was necessary she should teach her child. With this duty, he said, he always baited the hook with which he fished for her; "or, to take a figure from the old hawking days, her eyas is the lure with which I would reclaim the haggard hawk."

What will be the final result, who dares prophesy? At my old home she still resides; grateful, and in some measure useful, idolizing, but not altogether spoiling her child, who understands the relation between them, and now calls her mother.

Dora teaches Theo, and the mother comes in for what share she inclines to appropriate. She does not take much to reading, but she is fond of listening; and is a regular and devout attendant at public worship. Above all, they have sufficing proof that her conscience is awake, and that she gives some heed to what it says.

Mr. Blackstone was right when he told me that good I was unable to foresee would result from the loss which then drowned me in despair.

CHAPTER XXVI
TROUBLES.

In the beginning of the following year, the lady who filled Miss Clare's place was married, and Miss Clare resumed the teaching of Judy's children. She was now so handsomely paid for her lessons, that she had reduced the number of her engagements very much, and had more time to give to the plans in which she labored with Lady Bernard. The latter would willingly have settled such an annuity upon her as would have enabled her to devote all her time to this object; but Miss Clare felt that the earning of her bread was one of the natural ties that bound her in the bundle of social life; and that in what she did of a spiritual kind, she must be untrammelled by money-relations. If she could not do both,—provide for herself and assist others,—it would be a different thing, she said; for then it would be clear that Providence intended her to receive the hire of the laborer for the necessity laid upon her. But what influenced her chiefly was the dread of having anything she did for her friends attributed to professional motives, instead of the recognition of eternal relations. Besides, as she said, it would both lessen the means at Lady Bernard's disposal, and cause herself to feel bound to spend all her energies in that one direction; in which case she would be deprived of the recreative influences of change and more polished society. In her labor, she would yet feel her freedom, and would not serve even Lady Bernard for money, except she saw clearly that such was the will of the one Master. In thus refusing her offer, she but rose in her friend's estimation.

In the spring, great trouble fell upon the Morleys. One of the children was taken with scarlet-fever; and then another and another was seized in such rapid succession-until five of them were lying ill together-that there was no time to think of removing them. Cousin Judy would accept no assistance in nursing them, beyond that of her own maids, until her strength gave way, and she took the infection herself in the form of diphtheria; when she was compelled to take to her bed, in such agony at the thought of handing her children over to hired nurses, that there was great ground for fearing her strength would yield.

She lay moaning, with her eyes shut, when a hand was laid on hers, and Miss Clare's voice was in her ear. She had come to give her usual lesson to one of the girls who had as yet escaped the infection: for, while she took every precaution, she never turned aside from her work for any dread of consequences; and when she heard that Mrs. Morley had been taken ill, she walked straight to her room.

"Go away!" said Judy. "Do you want to die too?"

"Dear Mrs. Morley," said Miss Clare, "I will just run home, and make a few arrangements, and then come back and nurse you."

"Never mind me," said Judy. "The children! the children! What *shall* I do?"

"I am quite able to look after you all-if you will allow me to bring a young woman to help me."

"You are an angel!" said poor Judy. "But there is no occasion to bring any one with you. My servants are quite competent."

"I must have every thing in my own hands," said Miss Clare; "and therefore must have some one who will do exactly as I tell her. This girl has been with me now for some time, and I can depend upon her. Servants always look down upon governesses."

"Do whatever you like, you blessed creature," said Judy. "If any one of my servants behaves improperly to you, or neglects your orders, she shall go as soon as I am up again."

"I would rather give them as little opportunity as I can of running the risk. If I may bring this friend of my own, I shall soon have the house under hospital regulations. But I have been talking too much. I might almost have returned by this time. It is a bad beginning if I have hurt you already by saying more than was necessary."

She had hardly left the room before Judy had fallen asleep, so much was she relieved by the offer of her services. Ere she awoke, Marion was in a cab on her way back to Bolivar Square, with her friend and two carpet-bags. Within an hour, she had intrenched herself in a spare bedroom, had lighted a fire, got encumbering finery out of the way, arranged all the medicines on a chest of drawers, and set the clock on the mantle-piece going; made the round of the patients, who were all in adjoining rooms, and the round of the house, to see that the disinfectants were fresh and active, added to their number, and then gone to await the arrival of the medical attendant in Mrs. Morley's room.

"Dr. Brand might have been a little more gracious," said Judy; "but I thought it better not to interrupt him by explaining that you were not the professional nurse he took you for."

"Indeed, there was no occasion," answered Miss Clare. "I should have told him so myself, had it not been that I did a nurse's regular work in St. George's Hospital for two months, and have been there for a week or so, several times since, so that I believe I have earned the right to be spoken to as such. Anyhow, I understood every word he said."

Meeting Mr. Morley in the hall, the doctor advised him not to go near his wife, diphtheria being so infectious; but comforted him with the assurance that the nurse appeared an intelligent young person, who would attend to all his directions; adding, —

"I could have wished she had been older; but there is a great deal of illness about, and experienced nurses are scarce."

Miss Clare was a week in the house before Mr. Morley saw her, or knew she was there. One evening she ran down to the dining-room, where he sat over his lonely glass of Madeira, to get some brandy, and went straight to the sideboard. As she turned to leave the room, he recognized her, and said, in some astonishment, —

"You need not trouble yourself, Miss Clare. The nurse can get what she wants from Hawkins. Indeed, I don't see" —

"Excuse me, Mr. Morley. If you wish to speak to me, I will return in a few minutes; but I have a good deal to attend to just at this moment."

She left the room; and, as he had said nothing in reply, did not return.

Two days after, about the same hour, whether suspecting the fact, or for some other reason, he requested the butler to send the nurse to him.

"The nurse from the nursery, sir; or the young person as teaches the young ladies the piano?" asked Hawkins.

"I mean the sick-nurse," said his master.

In a few minutes Miss Clare entered the dining-room, and approached Mr. Morley.

"How do you do, Miss Clare?" he said stiffly; for to any one in his employment he was gracious only now and then. "Allow me to say that I doubt the propriety of your being here so much. You cannot fail to carry the infection. I think your lessons had better be postponed until *all* your pupils are able to benefit by them. I have just sent for the nurse; and, —if you please" —

"Yes. Hawkins told me you wanted me," said Miss Clare.

"I did not want you. He must have mistaken."

"I am the nurse, Mr. Morley."

"Then I *must* say it is not with my approval," he returned, rising from his chair in anger. "I was given to understand that a properly-qualified person was in charge of my wife and family. This is no ordinary case, where a little coddling is all that is wanted."

"I am perfectly qualified, Mr. Morley."

He walked up and down the room several times.

"I must speak to Mrs. Morley about this." he said.

"I entreat you will not disturb her. She is not so well this afternoon."

"How *is* this, Miss Clare? Pray explain to me how it is that you come to be taking a part in the affairs of the family so very different from that for which Mrs. Morley-which-was arranged between Mrs. Morley and yourself."

"It is but an illustration of the law of supply and demand," answered Marion. "A nurse was wanted; Mrs. Morley had strong objections to a hired nurse, and I was very glad to be able to set her mind at rest."

"It was very obliging in you, no doubt," he returned, forcing the admission; "but-but" —

"Let us leave it for the present, if you please; for while I am nurse, I must mind my business. Dr. Brand expresses himself quite satisfied with me, so far as we have gone; and it is better for the children, not to mention Mrs. Morley, to have some one about them they are used to."

She left the room without waiting further parley.

Dr. Brand, however, not only set Mr. Morley's mind at rest as to her efficiency, but when a terrible time of anxiety was at length over, during which one after another, and especially Judy herself, had been in great danger, assured him that, but for the vigilance and intelligence of Miss Clare, joined to a certain soothing influence which she exercised over every one of her patients, he did not believe he could have brought Mrs. Morley through. Then, indeed, he changed his tone to her, in a measure, still addressing her as from a height of superiority.

They had recovered so far that they were to set out the next morning for Hastings, when he thus addressed her, having sent for her once more to the dining-room: —

"I hope you will accompany them, Miss Clare," he said. "By this time you must be in no small need of a change yourself."

"The best change for me will be Lime Court," she answered, laughing.

"Now, pray don't drive your goodness to the verge of absurdity," he said pleasantly.

"Indeed, I am anxious about my friends there," she returned. "I fear they have not been getting on quite so well without me. A Bible-woman and a Roman Catholic have been quarrelling dreadfully, I hear."

Mr. Morley compressed his lips. It *was* annoying to be so much indebted to one who, from whatever motives, called such people her friends.

"Oblige me, then," he said loftily, taking an envelope from the mantle-piece, and handing it to her, "by opening that at your leisure."

"I will open it now, if you please," she returned.

It contained a bank-note for a hundred pounds. Mr. Morley, though a hard man, was not by any means stingy. She replaced it in the envelope, and laid it again on the chimney-piece.

"You owe me nothing, Mr. Morley," she said.

"Owe you nothing! I owe you more than I can ever repay."

"Then don't try it, please. You are *very* generous; but indeed I could not accept it."

"You must oblige me. You *might* take it from *me*," he added, almost pathetically, as if the bond was so close that money was nothing between them.

"You are the last-one of the last I *could* take money from, Mr. Morley."

"Why?"

"Because you think so much of it, and yet would look down on me the more if I accepted it."

He bit his lip, rubbed his forehead with his hand, threw back his head, and turned away from her.

"I should be very sorry to offend you," she said; "and, believe me, there is hardly any thing I value less than money. I have enough, and could have plenty more if I liked. I would rather have your friendship than all the money you possess. But that cannot be, so long as" —

She stopped: she was on the point of going too far, she thought.

"So long as what?" he returned sternly.

"So long as you are a worshipper of Mammon," she answered; and left the room.

She burst out crying when she came to this point. She had narrated the whole with the air of one making a confession.

"I am afraid it was very wrong," she said; "and if so, then it was very rude as well. But something seemed to force it out of me. Just think: there was a generous heart, clogged up with self-importance and wealth! To me, as he stood there on the hearth-rug, he was a most pitiable object-with an impervious wall betwixt him and the kingdom of heaven! He seemed like a man in a terrible dream, from which I *must* awake him by calling aloud in his ear-except that, alas! the dream was not terrible to him, only to me! If he had been one of my poor friends, guilty of some plain fault, I should have told him so without compunction; and why not, being what he was? There he stood, —a man of estimable qualities, of beneficence, if not bounty;

no miser, nor consciously unjust; yet a man whose heart the moth and rust were eating into a sponge!—who went to church every Sunday, and had many friends, not one of whom, not even his own wife, would tell him that he was a Mammon-worshipper, and losing his life. It may have been useless, it may have been wrong; but I felt driven to it by bare human pity for the misery I saw before me."

"It looks to me as if you had the message given you to give him," I said.

"But-though I don't know it-what if I was annoyed with him for offering me that wretched hundred pounds,—in doing which he was acting up to the light that was in him?"

I could not help thinking of the light which is darkness, but I did not say so. Strange tableau, in this our would-be grand nineteenth century,—a young and poor woman prophet-like rebuking a wealthy London merchant on his own hearth-rug, as a worshipper of Mammon! I think she was right; not because he was wrong, but because, as I firmly believe, she did it from no personal motives whatever, although in her modesty she doubted herself. I believe it was from pure regard for the man and for the truth, urging her to an irrepressible utterance. If so, should we not say that she spoke by the Spirit? Only I shudder to think what utterance might, with an equal outward show, be attributed to the same Spirit. Well, to his own master every one standeth or falleth; whether an old prophet who, with a lie in his right hand, entraps an honorable guest, or a young prophet who, with repentance in his heart, walks calmly into the jaws of the waiting lion. [Footnote: See the Sermons of the Rev. Henry Whitehead, vicar of St. John's, Limehouse; as remarkable for the profundity of their insight us for the noble severity of their literary modelling. —G.M.D.]

And no one can tell what effects the words may have had upon him. I do not believe he ever mentioned the circumstance to his wife. At all events, there was no change in her manner to Miss Clare. Indeed, I could not help fancying that a little halo of quiet reverence now encircled the love in every look she cast upon her.

She firmly believed that Marion had saved her life, and that of more than one of her children. Nothing, she said, could equal the quietness and tenderness and tirelessness of her nursing. She was never flurried, never impatient, and never frightened. Even when the tears would be flowing down her face, the light never left her eyes nor the music her voice; and when they were all getting better, and she had the nursery piano brought out on the landing in the middle of the sick-rooms, and there played and sung to them, it was, she said, like the voice of an angel, come fresh to the earth, with the same old news of peace and good-will. When the children-this I had from the friend she brought with her-were tossing in the fever, and talking of strange and frightful things they saw, one word from her would quiet them; and her gentle, firm command was always sufficient to make the most fastidious and rebellious take his medicine.

She came out of it very pale, and a good deal worn. But the day they set off for Hastings, she returned to Lime Court. The next day she resumed her lessons, and soon recovered her usual appearance. A change of work, she always said, was the best restorative. But before a month was over I succeeded in persuading her to accept my mother's invitation to spend a week at the Hall; and from this visit she returned quite invigorated. Connie, whom she went to see,—for by this time she was married to Mr. Turner,—was especially delighted with her delight in the simplicities of nature. Born and bred in the closest town-environment, she had yet a sensitiveness to all that made the country so dear to us who were born in it, which Connie said surpassed ours, and gave her special satisfaction as proving that my oft recurring dread lest such feelings might but be the result of childish associations was groundless, and that they were essential to the human nature, and so felt by God himself. Driving along in the pony-carriage,—for Connie is not able to walk much, although she is well enough to enjoy life thoroughly,—Marion would remark upon ten things in a morning, that my sister had never observed. The various effects of light and shade, and the variety of feeling they caused, especially interested her. She would spy out a lurking sunbeam, as another would find a hidden flower. It seemed as if not a glitter in its nest of gloom could escape her. She would leave the carriage, and make a long round through the fields or woods, and, when they met at the appointed spot, would have her hands full not of flowers only, but of leaves and grasses and weedy things, showing the deepest interest in such lowly forms as few would notice except from a scientific knowledge, of which she had none: it was the thing itself-its look and its home-that drew her attention. I cannot help thinking that this insight was profoundly one with her interest in the corresponding regions of human life and circumstance.

CHAPTER XXVII
MISS CLARE AMONGST HER FRIENDS.

I must give an instance of the way in which Marion—I am tired of calling her *Miss Clare*, and about this time I began to drop it-exercised her influence over her friends. I trust the episode, in a story so fragmentary as mine, made up of pieces only of a quiet and ordinary life, will not seem unsuitable. How I wish I could give it you as she told it to me! so graphic was her narrative, and so true to the forms of speech amongst the London poor. I must do what I can, well assured it must come far short of the original representation.

One evening, as she was walking up to her attic, she heard a noise in one of the rooms, followed by a sound of weeping. It was occupied by a journeyman house-painter and his wife, who had been married several years, but whose only child had died about six months before, since which loss things had not been going on so well between them. Some natures cannot bear sorrow: it makes them irritable, and, instead of drawing them closer to their own, tends to isolate them. When she entered, she found the woman crying, and the man in a lurid sulk.

"What *is* the matter?" she asked, no doubt in her usual cheerful tone.

"I little thought it would come to this when I married him," sobbed the woman, while the man remained motionless and speechless on his chair, with his legs stretched out at full length before him.

"Would you mind telling me about it? There may be some mistake, you know."

"There ain't no mistake in *that*," said the woman, removing the apron she had been holding to her eyes, and turning a cheek towards Marion, upon which the marks of an open-handed blow were visible enough. "I didn't marry him to be knocked about like that."

"She calls that knocking about, do she?" growled the husband. "What did she go for to throw her cotton gownd in my teeth for, as if it was my blame she warn't in silks and satins?"

After a good deal of questioning on her part, and confused and recriminative statement on theirs, Marion made out the following as the facts of the case: —

For the first time since they were married, the wife had had an invitation to spend the evening with some female friends. The party had taken place the night before; and although she had returned in ill-humor, it had not broken out until just as Marion entered the house. The cause was this: none of the guests were in a station much superior to her own, yet she found herself the only one who had not a silk dress: hers was a print, and shabby. Now, when she was married, she had a silk dress, of which she said her husband had been proud enough when they were walking together. But when she saw the last of it, she saw the last of its sort, for never another had he given her to her back; and she didn't marry him to come down in the world-that she didn't!

"Of course not," said Marion. "You married him because you loved him, and thought him the finest fellow you knew."

"And so he was then, grannie. But just look at him now!"

The man moved uneasily, but without bending his outstretched legs. The fact was, that since the death of the child he had so far taken to drink that he was not unfrequently the worse for it; which had been a rare occurrence before.

"It ain't my fault," he said, "when work ain't a-goin,' if I don't dress her like a duchess. I'm as proud to see my wife rigged out as e'er a man on 'em; and that *she* know! and when she cast the contrairy up to me, I'm blowed if I could keep my hands off on her. She ain't the woman I took her for, miss. She 'ave a temper!"

"I don't doubt it," said Marion. "Temper is a troublesome thing with all of us, and makes us do things we're sorry for afterwards. *You*'re sorry for striking her-ain't you, now?"

There was no response. Around the sullen heart silence closed again. Doubtless he would have given much to obliterate the fact, but he would not confess that he had been wrong. We are so stupid, that confession seems to us to fix the wrong upon us, instead of throwing it, as it does, into the depths of the eternal sea.

"I may have my temper," said the woman, a little mollified at finding, as she thought, that Miss Clare took her part; "but here am I, slaving from morning to night to make both ends meet, and goin' out every job I can get a-washin' or a-charin', and never 'avin' a bit of fun from year's end to year's end, and him off to his club, as he calls it!—an' it's a club he's like to blow out my brains with some night, when he comes home in a drunken fit; for it's worse *and* worse he'll get, miss, like the rest on 'em, till no woman could be proud, as once I was, to call him hers. And when I do go out to tea for once in a way, to be jeered at by them as is no better nor no worse 'n myself, acause I ain't got a husband as cares enough for me to dress me decent!—that do stick i' my gizzard. I do dearly love to have neighbors think my husband care a bit about me, let-a-be 'at he don't, one hair; and when he send me out like that"—

Here she broke down afresh.

"Why didn't ye stop at home then? I didn't tell ye to go," he said fiercely, calling her a coarse name.

"Richard," said Marion, "such words are not fit for *me* to hear, still less for your own wife."

"Oh! never mind me: I'm used to sich," said the woman spitefully.

"It's a lie," roared the man: "I never named sich a word to ye afore. It do make me mad to hear ye. I drink the clothes off your back, do I? If I bed the money, ye might go in velvet and lace for aught I cared!"

"*She* would care little to go in gold and diamonds, if *you* didn't care to see her in them," said Marion.

At this the woman burst into fresh tears, and the man put on a face of contempt,—the worst sign, Marion said, she had yet seen in him, not excepting the blow; for to despise is worse than to strike.

I can't help stopping my story here to put in a reflection that forces itself upon me. Many a man would regard with disgust the idea of striking his wife, who will yet cherish against her an aversion which is infinitely worse. The working-man who strikes his wife, but is sorry for it, and tries to make amends by being more tender after it, a result which many a woman will consider cheap at the price of a blow endured,—is an immeasurably superior husband to the gentleman who shows his wife the most absolute politeness, but uses that very politeness as a breastwork to fortify himself in his disregard and contempt.

Marion saw that while the tides ran thus high, nothing could be done; certainly, at least, in the way of argument. Whether the man had been drinking she could not tell, but suspected that must have a share in the evil of his mood. She went up to him, laid her hand on his shoulder, and said,—

"You're out of sorts, Richard. Come and have a cup of tea, and I will sing to you."

"I don't want no tea."

"You're fond of the piano, though. And you like to hear me sing, don't you?"

"Well, I do," he muttered, as if the admission were forced from him.

"Come with me, then."

He dragged himself up from his chair, and was about to follow her.

"You ain't going to take him from me, grannie, after he's been and struck me?" interposed his wife, in a tone half pathetic, half injured.

"Come after us in a few minutes," said Marion, in a low voice, and led the way from the room.

Quiet as a lamb Richard followed her up stairs. She made him sit in the easy-chair, and began with a low, plaintive song, which she followed with other songs and music of a similar character. He neither heard nor saw his wife enter, and both sat for about twenty minutes without a word spoken. Then Marion made a pause, and the wife rose and approached her husband. He was fast asleep.

"Don't wake him," said Marion; "let him have his sleep out. You go down and get the place tidy, and a nice bit of supper for him-if you can."

"Oh, yes! he brought me home his week's wages this very night."

"The whole?"

"Yes, grannie."

"Then weren't you too hard upon him? Just think: he had been trying to behave himself, and had got the better of the public-house for once, and come home fancying you'd be so pleased to see him; and you" —

"He'd been drinking," interrupted Eliza. "Only he said as how it was but a pot of beer he'd won in a wager from a mate of his."

"Well, if, after that beginning, he yet brought you home his money, he ought to have had another kind of reception. To think of the wife of a poor man making such a fuss about a silk dress! Why, Eliza, I never had a silk dress in my life; and I don't think I ever shall."

"Laws, grannie! who'd ha' thought that now!"

"You see I have other uses for my money than buying things for show."

"That you do, grannie! But you see," she added, somewhat inconsequently, "we ain't got no child, and Dick he take it ill of me, and don't care to save his money; so he never takes me out nowheres, and I do be so tired o' stopping indoors, every day and all day long, that it turns me sour, I do believe. I didn't use to be cross-grained, miss. But, laws! I feels now as if I'd let him knock me about ever so, if only he wouldn't say as how it was nothing to him if I was dressed ever so fine."

"You run and get his supper."

Eliza went; and Marion, sitting down again to her instrument, improvised for an hour. Next to her New Testament, this was her greatest comfort. She sung and prayed both in one then, and nobody but God heard any thing but the piano. Nor did it impede the flow of her best thoughts, that in a chair beside her slumbered a weary man, the waves of whose evil passions she had stilled, and the sting of whose disappointments she had soothed, with the sweet airs and concords of her own spirit. Who could say what tender influences might not be stealing over him, borne on the fair sounds? for even the formless and the void was roused into life and joy by the wind that roamed over the face of its deep. No humanity jarred with hers. In the presence of the most degraded, she felt God there. A face, even if besotted, *was* a face, only in virtue of being in the image of God. That a man was a man at all, must be because he was God's. And this man was far indeed from being of the worst. With him beside her, she could pray with most of the good of having the door of her closet shut, and some of the good of the gathering together as well. Thus was love, as ever, the assimilator of the foreign, the harmonizer of the unlike; the builder of the temple in the desert, and of the chamber in the market-place.

As she sat and discoursed with herself, she perceived that the woman was as certainly suffering from *ennui* as any fine lady in Mayfair.

"Have you ever been to the National Gallery, Richard?" she asked, without turning her head, the moment she heard him move.

"No, grannie," he answered with a yawn. "Don'a' most know what sort of a place it be now. Waxwork, ain't it?"

"No. It's a great place full of pictures, many of them hundreds of years old. They're taken care of by the Government, just for people to go and look at. Wouldn't you like to go and see them some day?"

"Donno as I should much."

"If I were to go with you, now, and explain some of them to you? I want you to take your wife and me out for a holiday. You can't think, you who go out to your work every day, how tiresome it is to be in the house from morning to night, especially at this time of the year, when the sun's shining, and the very sparrows trying to sing!"

"She may go out when she please, grannie. I ain't no tyrant."

"But she doesn't care to go without you. You wouldn't have her like one of those slatternly women you see standing at the corners, with their fists in their sides and their elbows sticking out, ready to talk to anybody that comes in the way."

"*My* wife was never none o' sich, grannie. I knows her as well's e'er a one, though she do 'ave a temper of her own."

At this moment Eliza appeared in the door-way, saying, —

"Will ye come to yer supper, Dick? I ha' got a slice o' ham an' a hot tater for ye. Come along."

"Well, I don't know as I mind-jest to please *you*, Liza. I believe I ha' been asleep in grannie's cheer there, her a playin' an' a singin', I make no doubt, like a werry nightingerl, bless her, an' me a snorin' all to myself, like a runaway locomotive! Won't *you* come and have a slice o' the 'am, an' a tater, grannie? The more you ate, the less we'd grudge it."

"I'm sure o' that," chimed in Eliza. "Do now, grannie; please do."

"I will, with pleasure," said Marion; and they went down together.

Eliza had got the table set out nicely, with a foaming jug of porter beside the ham and potatoes. Before they had finished, Marion had persuaded Richard to take his wife and her to the National Gallery, the next day but one, which, fortunately for her purpose, was Whit Monday, a day whereon Richard, who was from the north always took a holiday.

At the National Gallery, the house-painter, in virtue of his craft, claimed the exercise of criticism; and his remarks were amusing enough. He had more than once painted a sign-board for a country inn, which fact formed a bridge between the covering of square yards with color and the painting of pictures; and he naturally used the vantage-ground thus gained to enhance his importance with his wife and Miss Clare. He was rather a clever fellow too, though as little educated in any other direction than that of his calling as might well be.

All the woman seemed to care about in the pictures was this or that something which reminded her, often remotely enough I dare say, of her former life in the country. Towards the close of their visit, they approached a picture-one of Hobbima's, I think-which at once riveted her attention.

"Look, look, Dick!" she cried. "There's just such a cart as my father used to drive to the town in. Farmer White always sent *him* when the mistress wanted any thing and he didn't care to go hisself. And, O Dick! there's the very moral of the cottage we lived in! Ain't it a love, now?"

"Nice enough," Dick replied. "But it warn't there I seed you, Liza. It wur at the big house where you was housemaid, you know. That'll be it, I suppose, —away there like, over the trees."

They turned and looked at each other, and Marion turned away. When she looked again, they were once more gazing at the picture, but close together, and hand in hand, like two children.

As they went home in the omnibus, the two averred they had never spent a happier holiday in their lives; and from that day to this no sign of their quarrelling has come to Marion's knowledge. They are not only her regular attendants on Saturday evenings, but on Sunday evenings as well, when she holds a sort of conversation-sermon with her friends.

CHAPTER XXVIII
MR. MORLEY.

As soon as my cousin Judy returned from Hastings, I called to see her, and found them all restored, except Amy, a child of between eight and nine. There was nothing very definite the matter with her, but she was white and thin, and looked wistful; the blue of her eyes had grown pale, and her fair locks had nearly lost the curl which had so well suited her rosy cheeks. She had been her father's pride for her looks, and her mother's for her sayings,—at once odd and simple. Judy that morning reminded me how, one night, when she was about three years old, some time after she had gone to bed, she had called her nurse, and insisted on her mother's coming. Judy went, prepared to find her feverish; for there had been jam-making that day, and she feared she had been having more than the portion which on such an occasion fell to her share. When she reached the nursery, Amy begged to be taken up that she might say her prayers over again. Her mother objected; but the child insisting, in that pretty, petulant way which so pleased her father, she yielded, thinking she must have omitted some clause in her prayers, and be therefore troubled in her conscience. Amy accordingly knelt by the bedside in her night-gown, and, having gone over all her petitions from beginning to end, paused a moment before the final word, and inserted the following special and peculiar request: "And, p'ease God, give me some more jam to-morrow-day, for ever and ever. Amen."

I remember my father being quite troubled when he heard that the child had been rebuked for offering what was probably her very first genuine prayer. The rebuke, however, had little effect on the equanimity of the petitioner, for she was fast asleep a moment after it.

"There is one thing that puzzles and annoys me," said Judy. "I can't think what it means. My husband tells me that Miss Clare was so rude to him, the day before we left for Hastings, that he would rather not be aware of it any time she is in the house. Those were his very words. 'I will not interfere with your doing as you think proper,' he said, 'seeing you consider yourself under such obligation to her; and I should be sorry to deprive her of the advantage of giving lessons in a house like this; but I wish you to be careful that the girls do not copy her manners. She has not by any means escaped the influence of the company she keeps.' I was utterly astonished, you may well think; but I could get no further explanation from him. He only said that when I wished to have her society of an evening, I must let him know, because he would then dine at his club. Not knowing the grounds of his offence, there was little other argument I could use than the reiteration of my certainty that he must have misunderstood her. 'Not in the least,' he said. 'I have no doubt she is to you every thing amiable; but she has taken some unaccountable aversion to me, and loses no opportunity of showing it. And I *don't* think I deserve it.' I told him I was so sure he did not deserve it, that I must believe there was some mistake. But he only shook his head and raised his newspaper. You must help me, little coz."

"How am I to help you, Judy dear?" I returned. "I can't interfere between husband and wife, you know. If I dared such a thing, he would quarrel with me too-and rightly."

"No, no," she returned, laughing: "I don't want your intercession. I only want you to find out from Miss Clare whether she knows how she has so mortally offended my husband. I believe she knows nothing about it. She *has* a rather abrupt manner sometimes, you know; but then my husband is not so silly as to have taken such deep offence at that. Help me, now-there's a dear!"

I promised I would, and hence came the story I have already given. But Marion was so distressed at the result of her words, and so anxious that Judy should not be hurt, that she begged me, if I could manage it without a breach of verity, to avoid disclosing the matter; especially seeing Mr. Morley himself judged it too heinous to impart to his wife.

How to manage it I could not think. But at length we arranged it between us. I told Judy that Marion confessed to having said something which had offended Mr. Morley; that she was very sorry, and hoped she need not say that such had not been her intention, but that, as Mr. Morley evidently preferred what had passed between them to remain unmentioned, to disclose it would be merely to swell the mischief. It would be better for them all, she requested me to say, that she should give up her lessons for the present; and therefore she hoped Mrs. Morley would excuse her. When I gave the message, Judy cried, and said nothing. When the children heard that Marion was not coming for a while, Amy cried, the other girls looked very grave, and the boys protested.

I have already mentioned that the fault I most disliked in those children was their incapacity for being petted. Something of it still remains; but of late I have remarked a considerable improvement in this respect. They have not only grown in kindness, but in the gift of receiving kindness. I cannot but attribute this, in chief measure, to their illness and the lovely nursing of Marion. They do not yet go to their mother for petting, and from myself will only endure it; but they are eager after such crumbs as Marion, by no means lavish of it, will vouchsafe them.

Judy insisted that I should let Mr. Morley hear Marion's message.

"But the message is not to Mr. Morley," I said. "Marion would never have thought of sending one to him."

"But if I ask you to repeat it in his hearing, you will not refuse?"

To this I consented; but I fear she was disappointed in the result. Her husband only smiled sarcastically, drew in his chin, and showed himself a little more cheerful than usual.

One morning, about two months after, as I was sitting in the drawing-room, with my baby on the floor beside me, I was surprised to see Judy's brougham pull up at the little gate-for it was early. When she got out, I perceived at once that something was amiss, and ran to open the door. Her eyes were red, and her cheeks ashy. The moment we reached the drawing-room, she sunk on the couch and burst into tears.

"Judy!" I cried, "what *is* the matter? Is Amy worse?"

"No, no, cozzy dear; but we are ruined. We haven't a penny in the world. The children will be beggars."

And there were the gay little horses champing their bits at the door, and the coachman sitting in all his glory, erect and impassive!

I did my best to quiet her, urging no questions. With difficulty I got her to swallow a glass of wine, after which, with many interruptions and fresh outbursts of misery, she managed to let me understand that her husband had been speculating, and had failed. I could hardly believe myself awake. Mr. Morley was the last man I should have thought capable either of speculating, or of failing in it if he did.

Knowing nothing about business, I shall not attempt to explain the particulars. Coincident failures amongst his correspondents had contributed to his fall. Judy said he had not been like himself for months; but it was only the night before that he had told her they must give up their house in Bolivar Square, and take a small one in the suburbs. For any thing he could see, he said, he must look out for a situation.

"Still you may be happier than ever, Judy. I can tell you that happiness does not depend on riches," I said, though I could not help crying with her.

"It's a different thing though, after you've been used to them," she answered. "But the question is of bread for my children, not of putting down my carriage."

She rose hurriedly.

"Where are you going? Is there any thing I can do for you?" I asked.

"Nothing," she answered. "I left my husband at Mr. Baddeley's. He is as rich as Croesus, and could write him a check that would float him."

"He's too rich to be generous, I'm afraid," I said.

"What do you mean by that?" she asked.

"If he be so generous, how does it come that he is so rich?"

"Why, his father made the money."

"Then he most likely takes after his father. Percivale says he does not believe a huge fortune was ever made of nothing, without such pinching of one's self and such scraping of others, or else such speculation, as is essentially dishonorable."

"He stands high," murmured Judy hopelessly.

"Whether what is dishonorable be also disreputable depends on how many there are of his own sort in the society in which he moves."

"Now, coz, you know nothing to his discredit, and he's our last hope."

"I will say no more," I answered. "I hope I may be quite wrong. Only I should expect nothing of *him*."

When she reached Mr. Baddeley's her husband was gone. Having driven to his counting-house, and been shown into his private room, she found him there with his head between his hands. The great man had declined doing any thing for him, and had even rebuked him for his imprudence, without wasting a thought on the fact that every penny he himself possessed was the result of the boldest speculation on the part of his father. A very few days only would elapse before the falling due of certain bills must at once disclose the state of his affairs.

As soon as she had left me, Percivale not being at home, I put on my bonnet, and went to find Marion. I must tell *her* every thing that caused me either joy or sorrow; and besides, she had all the right that love could give to know of Judy's distress. I knew all her engagements, and therefore where to find her; and sent in my card, with the pencilled intimation that I would wait the close of her lesson. In a few minutes she came out and got into the cab. At once I told her my sad news.

"Could you take me to Cambridge Square to my next engagement?" she said.

I was considerably surprised at the cool way in which she received the communication, but of course I gave the necessary directions.

"Is there any thing to be done?" she asked, after a pause.

"I know of nothing," I answered.

Again she sat silent for a few minutes.

"One can't move without knowing all the circumstances and particulars," she said at length. "And how to get at them? He wouldn't make a confidante of *me*," she said, smiling sadly.

"Ah! you little think what vast sums are concerned in such a failure as his!" I remarked, astounded that one with her knowledge of the world should talk as she did.

"It will be best," she said, after still another pause, "to go to Mr. Blackstone. He has a wonderful acquaintance with business for a clergyman, and knows many of the city people."

"What could any clergyman do in such a case?" I returned. "For Mr. Blackstone, Mr. Morley would not accept even consolation at his hands."

"The time for that is not come yet," said Marion. "We must try to help him some other way first. We will, if we can, make friends with him by means of the very Mammon that has all but ruined him."

She spoke of the great merchant just as she might of Richard, or any of the bricklayers or mechanics, whose spiritual condition she pondered that she might aid it.

"But what could Mr. Blackstone do?" I insisted.

"All I should want of him would be to find out for me what Mr. Morley's liabilities are, and how much would serve to tide him over the bar of his present difficulties. I suspect he has few friends who would risk any thing for him. I understand he is no favorite in the city; and, if friendship do not come in, he must be stranded. You believe him an honorable man,—do you not?" she asked abruptly.

"It never entered my head to doubt it," I replied.

The moment we reached Cambridge Square she jumped out, ran up the steps, and knocked at the door. I waited, wondering if she was going to leave me thus without a farewell. When the door was opened, she merely gave a message to the man, and the same instant was again in the cab by my side.

"Now I am free!" she said, and told the man to drive to Mile End.

"I fear I can't go with you so far, Marion," I said. "I must go home—I have so much to see to, and you can do quite as well without me. I don't know what you intend, but *please* don't let any thing come out. I can trust *you*, but"—

"If you can trust me, I can trust Mr. Blackstone. He is the most cautious man in the world. Shall I get out, and take another cab?"

"No. You can drop me at Tottenham Court Road, and I will go home by omnibus. But you must let me pay the cab."

"No, no; I am richer than you: I have no children. What fun it is to spend money for Mr. Morley, and lay him under an obligation he will never know!" she said, laughing.

The result of her endeavors was, that Mr. Blackstone, by a circuitous succession of introductions, reached Mr. Morley's confidential clerk, whom he was able so far to satisfy concerning his object in desiring the information, that he made him a full disclosure of the condition of affairs, and stated what sum would be sufficient to carry them over their difficulties; though, he added, the greatest care, and every possible reduction of expenditure for some years, would be indispensable to their complete restoration.

Mr. Blackstone carried his discoveries to Miss Clare and she to Lady Bernard.

"My dear Marion," said Lady Bernard, "this is a serious matter you suggest. The man may be honest, and yet it may be of no use trying to help him. I don't want to bolster him up for a few months in order to see my money go after his. That's not what I've got to do with it. No doubt I could lose as much as you mention, without being crippled by it, for I hope it's no disgrace in me to be rich, as it's none in you to be poor; but I hate waste, and I will *not* be guilty of it. If Mr. Morley will convince me and any friend or man of business to whom I may refer the matter, that there is good probability of his recovering himself by means of it, then, and not till then, I shall feel justified in risking the amount. For, as you say, it would prevent much misery to many besides that good-hearted creature, Mrs. Morley, and her children. It is worth doing if it can be done-not worth trying if it can't."

"Shall I write for you, and ask him to come and see you?"

"No, my dear. If I do a kindness, I must do it humbly. It is a great liberty to take with a man to offer him a kindness. I must go to him. I could not use the same freedom with a man in misfortune as with one in prosperity. I would have such a one feel that his money or his poverty made no difference to me; and Mr. Morley wants that lesson, if any man does. Besides, after all, I may not be able to do it for him, and he would have good reason to be hurt if I had made him dance attendance on me."

The same evening Lady Bernard's shabby one-horse-brougham stopped at Mr. Morley's door. She asked to see Mrs. Morley, and through her had an interview with her husband. Without circumlocution, she told him that if he would lay his affairs before her and a certain accountant she named, to use their judgment regarding them in the hope of finding it possible to serve him, they would wait upon him for that purpose at any time and place he pleased. Mr. Morley expressed his obligation,—not very warmly, she said,—repudiating, however, the slightest objection to her ladyship's knowing now what all the world must know the next day but one.

Early the following morning Lady Bernard and the accountant met Mr. Morley at his place in the city, and by three o'clock in the afternoon fifteen thousand pounds were handed in to his account at his banker's.

The carriage was put down, the butler, one of the footmen, and the lady's maid, were dismissed, and household arrangements fitted to a different scale.

One consequence of this chastisement, as of the preceding, was, that the whole family drew yet more closely and lovingly together; and I must say for Judy, that, after a few weeks of what she called poverty, her spirits seemed in no degree the worse for the trial.

At Marion's earnest entreaty no one told either Mr. or Mrs. Morley of the share she had had in saving his credit and social position. For some time she suffered from doubt as to whether she had had any right to interpose in the matter, and might not have injured Mr. Morley by depriving him of the discipline of poverty; but she reasoned with herself, that, had it been necessary for him, her efforts would have been frustrated; and reminded herself, that, although his commercial credit had escaped, it must still be a considerable trial to him to live in reduced style.

But that it was not all the trial needful for him, was soon apparent; for his favorite Amy began to pine more rapidly, and Judy saw, that, except some change speedily took place, they could not have her with them long. The father, however, refused to admit the idea that she was in danger. I suppose he felt as if, were he once to allow the possibility of losing her, from that moment there would be no stay between her and the grave: it would be a giving of her over to death. But whatever Dr. Brand suggested was eagerly followed. When the chills of autumn drew near, her mother took her to Ventnor; but little change followed, and before the new year she was gone. It was the first death, beyond that of an infant, they had had in their family, and took place at a time when the pressure of business obligations rendered it impossible for her father to be out of London: he could only go to lay her in the earth, and bring back his wife. Judy had never seen him weep before. Certainly I never saw such a change in a man. He was literally bowed with grief, as if he bore a material burden on his back. The best feelings of his nature, unimpeded by any jar to his self-importance or his prejudices, had been able to spend themselves on the lovely little creature; and I do not believe any other suffering than the loss of such a child could have brought into play that in him which was purely human.

He was at home one morning, ill for the first time in his life, when Marion called on Judy. While she waited in the drawing-room, he entered. He turned the moment he saw her, but had not taken two steps towards the door, when he turned again, and approached her. She went to meet him. He held out his hand.

"She was very fond of you, Miss Clare," he said. "She was talking about you the very last time I saw her. Let by-gones be by-gones between us."

"I was very rough and rude to you, Mr. Morley, and I am very sorry," said Marion.

"But you spoke the truth," he rejoined. "I thought I was above being spoken to like a sinner, but I don't know now why not."

He sat down on a couch, and leaned his head on his hand. Marion took a chair near him, but could not speak.

"It is very hard," he murmured at length.

"Whom the Lord loveth he chasteneth," said Marion.

"That may be true in some cases, but I have no right to believe it applies to me. He loved the child, I would fain believe; for I dare not think of her either as having ceased to be, or as alone in the world to which she has gone. You do think, Miss Clare, do you not, that we shall know our friends in another world?"

"I believe," answered Marion, "that God sent you that child for the express purpose of enticing you back to himself; and, if I believe any thing at all, I believe that the gifts of God are without repentance."

Whether or not he understood her she could not tell, for at this point Judy came in. Seeing them together she would have withdrawn again; but her husband called her, with more tenderness in his voice than Marion could have imagined belonging to it.

"Come, my dear. Miss Clare and I were talking about our little angel. I didn't think ever to speak of her again, but I fear I am growing foolish. All the strength is out of me; and I feel so tired,—so weary of every thing!"

She sat down beside him, and took his hand. Marion crept away to the children. An hour after, Judy found her in the nursery, with the youngest on her knee, and the rest all about her. She was telling them that we were sent into this world to learn to be good, and then go back to God from whom we came, like little Amy.

"When I go out to-mowwwow," said one little fellow, about four years old, "I'll look up into the sky vewy hard, wight up; and then I shall see Amy, and God saying to her, 'Hushaby, poo' Amy! You bette' now, Amy?' Sha'n't I, Mawion?"

She had taught them to call her Marion.

"No, my pet: you might look and look, all day long, and every day, and never see God or Amy."

"Then they *ain't* there!" he exclaimed indignantly.

"God is there, anyhow," she answered; "only you can't see him that way."

"I don't care about seeing God," said the next elder: "it's Amy I want to see. Do tell me, Marion, how we are to see Amy. It's too bad if we're never to see her again; and I don't think it's fair."

"I will tell you the only way I know. When Jesus was in the world, he told us that all who had clean hearts should see God. That's how Jesus himself saw God."

"It's Amy, I tell you, Marion-it's not God I want to see," insisted the one who had last spoken.

"Well, my dear, but how can you see Amy if you can't even see God? If Amy be in God's arms, the first thing, in order to find her, is to find God. To be good is the only way to get near to anybody. When you're naughty, Willie, you can't get near your mamma, can you?"

"Yes, I can. I can get close up to her."

"Is that near enough? Would you be quite content with that? Even when she turns away her face and won't look at you?"

The little caviller was silent.

"Did you ever see God, Marion?" asked one of the girls.

She thought for a moment before giving an answer. "No," she said. "I've seen things just after he had done them; and I think I've heard him speak to me; but I've never seen him yet."

"Then you're not good, Marion," said the free-thinker of the group.

"No: that's just it. But I hope to be good some day, and then I *shall* see him."

"How do you grow good, Marion?" asked the girl.

"God is always trying to make me good," she answered; "and I try not to interfere with him."

"But sometimes you forget, don't you?"

"Yes, I do."

"And what do you do then?"

"Then I'm sorry and unhappy, and begin to try again."

"And God don't mind much, does he?"

"He minds very much until I mind; but after that he forgets it all, —takes all my naughtiness and throws it behind his back, and won't look at it."

"That's very good of God," said the reasoner, but with such a self-satisfied air in his approval, that Marion thought it time to stop.

She came straight to me, and told me, with a face perfectly radiant, of the alteration in Mr. Morley's behavior to her, and, what was of much more consequence, the evident change that had begun to be wrought in him.

I am not prepared to say that he has, as yet, shown a very shining light, but that some change has passed is evident in the whole man of him. I think the eternal wind must now be able to get in through some chink or other which the loss of his child has left behind. And, if the change were not going on, surely he would ere now have returned to his wallowing in the mire of Mammon; for his former fortune is, I understand, all but restored to him.

I fancy his growth in goodness might be known and measured by his progress in appreciating Marion. He still regards her as extreme in her notions; but it is curious to see how, as they gradually sink into his understanding, he comes to adopt them as, and even to mistake them for, his own.

CHAPTER XXIX
A STRANGE TEXT.

For some time after the events last related, things went on pretty smoothly with us for several years. Indeed, although I must confess that what I said in my haste, when Mr. S. wanted me to write this book, namely, that nothing had ever happened to me worth telling, was by no means correct, and that I have found out my mistake in the process of writing it; yet, on the other hand, it must be granted that my story could never have reached the mere bulk required if I had not largely drawn upon the history of my friends to supplement my own. And it needs no prophetic gift to foresee that it will be the same to the end of the book. The lives of these friends, however, have had so much to do with all that is most precious to me in our own life, that, if I were to leave out only all that did not immediately touch upon the latter, the book, whatever it might appear to others, could not possibly then appear to myself any thing like a real representation of my actual life and experiences. The drawing might be correct,—but the color?

What with my children, and the increase of social duty resulting from the growth of acquaintance,—occasioned in part by my success in persuading Percivale to mingle a little more with his fellow-painters,—my heart and mind and hands were all pretty fully occupied; but I still managed to see Marion two or three times a week, and to spend about so many hours with her, sometimes alone, sometimes with her friends as well. Her society did much to keep my heart open, and to prevent it from becoming selfishly absorbed in its cares for husband and children. For love which is *only* concentrating its force, that is, which is not at the same time widening its circle, is itself doomed, and for its objects ruinous, be those objects ever so sacred. God himself could never be content that his children should love him only; nor has he allowed the few to succeed who have tried after it: perhaps their divinest success has been their most mortifying failure. Indeed, for exclusive love sharp suffering is often sent as the needful cure,—needful to break the stony crust, which, in the name of love for one's own, gathers about the divinely glowing core; a crust which, promising to cherish by keeping in the heat, would yet gradually thicken until all was crust; for truly, in things of the heart and spirit, as the warmth ceases to spread, the molten mass within ceases to glow, until at length, but for the divine care and discipline, there would be no love left for even spouse or child, only for self,—which is eternal death.

For some time I had seen a considerable change in Roger. It reached even to his dress. Hitherto, when got up for dinner, he was what I was astonished to hear my eldest boy, the other day, call "a howling swell;" but at other times he did not even escape remark,—not for the oddity merely, but the slovenliness of his attire. He had worn, for more years than I dare guess, a brown coat, of some rich-looking stuff, whose long pile was stuck together in many places with spots and dabs of paint, so that he looked like our long-haired Bedlington terrier Fido, towards the end of the week in muddy weather. This was now discarded; so far at least, as to be hung up in his brother's study, to be at hand when he did any thing for him there, and replaced by a more civilized garment of tweed, of which he actually showed himself a little careful: while, if his necktie *was* red, it was of a very deep and rich red, and he had seldom worn one at all before; and his brigand-looking felt hat was exchanged for one of half the altitude, which he did not crush on his head with quite as many indentations as its surface could hold. He also began to go to church with us sometimes.

But there was a greater and more significant change than any of these. We found that he was sticking more steadily to work. I can hardly say *his* work; for he was Jack-of-all-trades, as I have already indicated. He had a small income, left him by an old maiden aunt with whom he had been a favorite, which had hitherto seemed to do him nothing but harm, enabling him to alternate fits of comparative diligence with fits of positive idleness. I have said also, I believe, that, although he could do nothing thoroughly, application alone was wanted to enable him to distinguish himself in more than one thing. His forte was engraving on wood; and my husband said, that, if he could do so well with so little practice as he had had, he must be capable of becoming an admirable engraver. To our delight, then, we discovered, all at once, that he had been working steadily for three months for the Messrs. D——, whose place was not far from our house. He had said nothing about it to his brother, probably from having good reason to fear that he would regard it only as a *spurt*. Having now, however, executed a block which greatly pleased himself, he had brought a proof impression to show Percivale; who, more pleased with it than even Roger himself, gave him a hearty congratulation, and told him it would be a shame if he did not bring his execution in that art to perfection; from which, judging by the present specimen, he said it could not be far off. The words brought into Roger's face an expression of modest gratification which it rejoiced me to behold: he accepted Percivale's approbation more like a son than a brother, with a humid glow in his eyes and hardly a word on his lips. It seemed to me that the child in his heart had begun to throw off the swaddling clothes which foolish manhood had wrapped around it, and the germ of his being was about to assert itself. I have seldom indeed seen Percivale look so pleased.

"Do me a dozen as good as that," he said, "and I'll have the proofs framed in silver gilt."

It *has* been done; but the proofs had to wait longer for the frame than Percivale for the proofs.

But he need have held out no such bribe of brotherly love, for there was another love already at work in himself more than sufficing to the affair. But I check myself: who shall say what love is sufficing for this or for that? Who, with the most enduring and most passionate love his heart can hold, will venture to say that he could have done without the love of a brother? Who will say that he could have done without the love of the dog whose bones have lain mouldering in his garden for twenty years? It is enough to say that there was a more engrossing, a more marvellous love at work.

Roger always, however, took a half-holiday on Saturdays, and now generally came to us. On one of these occasions I said to him,—

"Wouldn't you like to come and hear Marion play to her friends this evening, Roger?"

"Nothing would give me greater pleasure," he answered; and we went.

It was delightful. In my opinion Marion is a real artist. I do not claim for her the higher art of origination, though I could claim for her a much higher faculty than the artistic itself. I suspect, for instance, that Moses was a greater man than the writer of the Book of Job, notwithstanding that the poet moves me so much more than the divine politician. Marion combined in a wonderful way the critical faculty with the artistic; which two, however much of the one may be found without the other, are mutually essential to the perfection of each. While she uttered from herself, she heard with her audience; while she played and sung with her own fingers and mouth, she at the same time listened with their ears, knowing what they must feel, as well as what she meant to utter. And hence it was, I think, that she came into such vital contact with them, even through her piano.

As we returned home, Roger said, after some remark of mine of a cognate sort,—

"Does she never try to teach them any thing, Ethel?"

"She is constantly teaching them, whether she tries or not," I answered. "If you can make any one believe that there is something somewhere to be trusted, is not that the best lesson you can give him? That can be taught only by being such that people cannot but trust you."

"I didn't need to be told that," he answered. "What I want to know is, whether or not she ever teaches them by word of mouth,—an ordinary and inferior mode, if you will."

"If you had ever heard her, you would not call hers an ordinary or inferior mode," I returned. "Her teaching is the outcome of her life, the blossom of her being, and therefore has the whole force of her living truth to back it."

"Have I offended you, Ethel?" he asked.

Then I saw, that, in my eagerness to glorify my friend, I had made myself unpleasant to Roger,—a fault of which I had been dimly conscious before now. Marion would never have fallen into that error. She always made her friends feel that she was *with* them, side by side with them, and turning her face in the same direction, before she attempted to lead them farther.

I assured him that he had not offended me, but that I had been foolishly backing him from the front, as I once heard an Irishman say, —some of whose bulls were very good milch cows.

"She teaches them every Sunday evening," I added.

"Have you ever heard her?"

"More than once. And I never heard any thing like it."

"Could you take me with you some time?" he asked, in an assumed tone of ordinary interest, out of which, however, he could not keep a slight tremble.

"I don't know. I don't quite see why I shouldn't. And yet"—

"Men do go," urged Roger, as if it were a mere half-indifferent suggestion.

"Oh, yes! you would have plenty to keep you in countenance!" I returned, —"men enough- and worth teaching, too-some of them at least!"

"Then, I don't see why she should object to me for another."

"I don't know that she would. You are not exactly of the sort, you know-that"—

"I don't see the difference. I see no essential difference, at least. The main thing is, that I am in want of teaching, as much as any of them. And, if she stands on circumstances, I am a working-man as much as any of them-perhaps more than most of them. Few of them work after midnight, I should think, as I do, not unfrequently."

"Still, all admitted, I should hardly like"—

"I didn't mean you were to take me without asking her," he said: "I should never have dreamed of that."

"And if I were to ask her, I am certain she would refuse. But," I added, thinking over the matter a little, "I will take you without asking her. Come with me to-morrow night. I don't think she will have the heart to send you away."

"I will," he answered, with more gladness in his voice than he intended, I think, to manifest itself.

We arranged that he should call for me at a certain hour.

I told Percivale, and he pretended to grumble that I was taking Roger instead of him.

"It was Roger, and not you, that made the request," I returned. "I can't say I see why you should go because Roger asked. A woman's logic is not equal to that."

"I didn't mean he wasn't to go. But why shouldn't I be done good to as well as he?"

"If you really want to go," I said, "I don't see why you shouldn't. It's ever so much better than going to any church I know of-except one. But we must be prudent. I can't take more than one the first time. We must get the thin edge of the wedge in first."

"And you count Roger the thin edge?"

"Yes."

"I'll tell him so."

"Do. The thin edge, mind, without which the thicker the rest is the more useless! Tell him that if you like. But, seriously, I quite expect to take you there, too, the Sunday after."

Roger and I went. Intending to be a little late, we found when we readied the house, that, as we had wished, the class was already begun. In going up the stairs, we saw very few of the grown inhabitants, but in several of the rooms, of which the doors stood open, elder girls taking care of the younger children; in one, a boy nursing the baby with as much interest as any girl could have shown. We lingered on the way, wishing to give Marion time to get so thoroughly into her work that she could take no notice of our intrusion. When we reached the last stair we could at length hear her voice, of which the first words we could distinguish, as we still ascended, were, —

"I will now read to you the chapter of which I spoke."

The door being open, we could hear well enough, although she was sitting where we could not see her. We would not show ourselves until the reading was ended: so much, at least, we might overhear without offence.

Before she had read many words, Roger and I began to cast strange looks on each other. For this was the chapter she read: —

"And Joseph, wheresoever he went in the city, took the Lord Jesus with him, where he was sent for to work, to make gates, or milk-pails, or sieves, or boxes; the Lord Jesus was with him wheresoever he went. And as often as Joseph had any thing in his work to make longer or shorter, or wider or narrower, the Lord Jesus would stretch his hand towards it. And presently it became as Joseph would have it. So that he had no need to finish any thing with his own hands, for he was not very skilful at his carpenter's trade.

"On a certain time the king of Jerusalem sent for him, and said, I would have thee make me a throne of the same dimensions with that place in which I commonly sit. Joseph obeyed, and forthwith began the work, and continued two years in the king's palace before he finished. And when he came to fix it in its place, he found it wanted two spans on each side of the appointed measure. Which, when the king saw, he was very angry with Joseph; and Joseph, afraid of the king's anger, went to bed without his supper, taking not any thing to eat. Then the Lord Jesus asked him what he was afraid of. Joseph replied, Because I have lost my labor in the work which I have been about these two years. Jesus said to him, Fear not, neither be cast down; do thou lay hold on one side of the throne, and I will the other, and we will bring it to its just dimensions. And when Joseph had done as the Lord Jesus said, and each of them had with strength drawn his side, the throne obeyed, and was brought to the proper dimensions of the place; which miracle when they who stood by saw, they were astonished, and praised God. The throne was made of the same wood which was in being in Solomon's time, namely, wood adorned with various shapes and figures."

Her voice ceased, and a pause followed.

"We must go in now," I whispered.

"She'll be going to say something now; just wait till she's started," said Roger.

"Now, what do you think of it?" asked Marion in a meditative tone.

We crept within the scope of her vision, and stood. A voice, which I knew, was at the moment replying to her question.

"*I* don't think it's much of a chapter, that, grannie."

The speaker was the keen-faced, elderly man, with iron-gray whiskers, who had come forward to talk to Percivale on that miserable evening when we were out searching for little Ethel. He sat near where we stood by the door, between two respectable looking women, who had been listening to the chapter as devoutly as if it had been of the true gospel.

"Sure, grannie, that ain't out o' the Bible?" said another voice, from somewhere farther off.

"We'll talk about that presently," answered Marion.

"I want to hear what Mr. Jarvis has to say to it: he's a carpenter himself, you see,—a joiner, that is, you know."

All the faces in the room were now turned towards Jarvis.

"Tell me why you don't think much of it, Mr. Jarvis," said Marion.

"'Tain't a bit likely," he answered.

"What isn't likely?"

"Why, not one single thing in the whole kit of it. And first and foremost, 'tain't a bit likely the old man 'ud ha' been sich a duffer."

"Why not? There must have been stupid people then as well as now."

"Not *his* father." said Jarvis decidedly.

"He wasn't but his step-father, like, you know, Mr. Jarvis," remarked the woman beside him in a low voice.

"Well, he'd never ha' been *hers*, then. *She* wouldn't ha' had a word to say to *him*."

"I have seen a good-and wise woman too-with a dull husband," said Marion.

"You know you don't believe a word of it yourself, grannie," said still another voice.

"Besides," she went on without heeding the interruption, "in those times, I suspect, such things were mostly managed by the parents, and the woman herself had little to do with them."

A murmur of subdued indignation arose,—chiefly of female voices.

"Well, *they* wouldn't then," said Jarvis.

"He might have been rich," suggested Marion.

"I'll go bail *he* never made the money then," said Jarvis. "An old idget! I don't believe sich a feller 'ud ha' been *let* marry a woman like her—I *don't*."

"You mean you don't think God would have let him?"

"Well, that's what I *do* mean, grannie. The thing couldn't ha' been, nohow."

"I agree with you quite. And now I want to hear more of what in the story you don't consider likely."

"Well, it ain't likely sich a workman 'ud ha' stood so high i' the trade that the king of Jerusalem would ha' sent for *him* of all the tradesmen in the town to make his new throne for him. No more it ain't likely-and let him be as big a duffer as ever was, to be a jiner at all-that he'd ha' been two year at work on that there throne-an' a carvin' of it in figures too!—and never found out it was four spans too narrer for the place it had to stand in. Do ye 'appen to know now, grannie, how much is a span?"

"I don't know. Do you know, Mrs. Percivale?"

The sudden reference took me very much by surprise; but I had not forgotten, happily, the answer I received to the same question, when anxious to realize the monstrous height of Goliath.

"I remember my father telling me," I replied, "that it was as much as you could stretch between your thumb and little finger."

"There!" cried Jarvis triumphantly, parting the extreme members of his right hand against the back of the woman in front of him—"that would be seven or eight inches! Four times that? Two foot and a half at least! Think of that!"

"I admit the force of both your objections," said Marion. "And now, to turn to a more important part of the story, what do you think of the way in which according to it he got his father out of his evil plight?"

I saw plainly enough that she was quietly advancing towards some point in her view,—guiding the talk thitherward, steadily, without haste or effort.

Before Jarvis had time to make any reply, the blind man, mentioned in a former chapter, struck in, with the tone of one who had been watching his opportunity.

"*I* make more o' that pint than the t'other," he said. "A man as is a duffer may well make a mull of a thing; but a man as knows what he's up to can't. I don't make much o' them miracles, you know, grannie-that is, I don't know, and what I don't know, I won't say as I knows; but what I'm sure of is this here one thing,—that man or boy as *could* work a miracle, you know, grannie, wouldn't work no miracle as there wasn't no good working of."

"It was to help his father," suggested Marion.

Here Jarvis broke in almost with scorn.

"To help him to pass for a clever fellow, when he was as great a duffer as ever broke bread!"

"I'm quite o' your opinion, Mr. Jarvis," said the blind man. "It 'ud ha' been more like him to tell his father what a duffer he was, and send him home to learn his trade."

"He couldn't do that, you know," said Marion gently. "He *couldn't* use such words to his father, if he were ever so stupid."

"His step-father, grannie," suggested the woman who had corrected Jarvis on the same point. She spoke very modestly, but was clearly bent on holding forth what light she had.

"Certainly, Mrs. Renton; but you know he couldn't be rude to any one,—leaving his own mother's husband out of the question."

"True for you, grannie," returned the woman.

"I think, though," said Jarvis, "for as hard as he'd ha' found it, it would ha' been more like him to set to work and teach his father, than to scamp up his mulls."

"Certainly," acquiesced Marion. "To hide any man's faults, and leave him not only stupid, but, in all probability, obstinate and self-satisfied, would not be like *him*. Suppose our Lord had had such a father: what do you think he would have done?"

"He'd ha' done all he could to make a man of him," answered Jarvis.

"Wouldn't he have set about making him comfortable then, in spite of his blunders?" said Marion.

A significant silence followed this question.

"Well, *no*; not first thing, I don't think," returned Jarvis at length. "He'd ha' got him o' some good first, and gone in to make him comfortable arter."

"Then I suppose you would rather be of some good and uncomfortable, than of no good and comfortable?" said Marion.

"I hope so, grannie," answered Jarvis; and "*I* would;" "Yes;" "That I would," came from several voices in the little crowd, showing what an influence Marion must have already had upon them.

"Then," she said, —and I saw by the light which rose in her eyes that she was now coming to the point, —"Then, surely it must be worth our while to bear discomfort in order to grow of some good! Mr. Jarvis has truly said, that, if Jesus had had such a father, he would have made him of some good before he made him comfortable: that is just the way your Father in heaven is acting with you. Not many of you would say you are of much good yet; but you would like to be better. And yet, —put it to yourselves, —do you not grumble at every thing that comes to you that you don't like, and call it bad luck, and worse-yes, even when you know it comes of your own fault, and nobody else's? You think if you had only this or that to make you comfortable, you would be content; and you call it very hard that So-and-so should be getting on well, and saving money, and you down on your luck, as you say. Some of you even grumble that your neighbors' children should be healthy when yours are pining. You would allow that you are not of much good yet; but you forget that to make you comfortable as you are would be the same as to pull out Joseph's misfitted thrones and doors, and make his misshapen buckets over again for him. That you think so absurd that you can't believe the story a bit; but you would be helped out of all *your* troubles, even those you bring on yourselves, not thinking what the certain consequence would be, namely, that you would grow of less and less value, until you were of no good, either to God or man. If you think about it, you will see that I am right. When, for instance, are you most willing to do right? When are you most ready to hear about good things? When are you most inclined to pray to God? When you have plenty of money in your pockets, or when you are in want? when you have had a good dinner, or when you have not enough to get one? when you are in jolly health, or when the life seems ebbing out of you in misery and pain? No matter that you may have brought it on yourselves; it is no less God's way of bringing you back to him, for he decrees that suffering shall follow sin: it is just then you most need it; and, if it drives you to God, that is its end, and there will be an end of it. The prodigal was himself to blame for the want that made him a beggar at the swine's trough; yet that want was the greatest blessing God could give to him, for it drove him home to his father.

"But some of you will say you are no prodigals; nor is it your fault that you find yourselves in such difficulties that life seems hard to you. It would be very wrong in me to set myself up as your judge, and to tell you that it *was* your fault. If it is, God will let you know it. But if it be not your fault, it does not follow that you need the less to be driven back to God. It is not only in punishment of our sins that we are made to suffer: God's runaway children must be brought back to their home and their blessedness, —back to their Father in heaven. It is not always a sign that God is displeased with us when he makes us suffer. 'Whom the Lord loveth he chasteneth, and scourgeth every son whom he receiveth. If ye endure chastening, God dealeth with you as with sons.' But instead of talking more about it, I must take it to myself; and learn not to grumble when *my* plans fail."

"That's what *you* never goes and does, grannie," growled a voice from somewhere.

I learned afterwards it was that of a young tailor, who was constantly quarrelling with his mother.

"I think I have given up grumbling at my circumstances," she rejoined; "but then I have nothing to grumble at in them. I haven't known hunger or cold for a great many years now. But I do feel discontented at times when I see some of you not getting better so fast as I should like. I ought to have patience, remembering how patient God is with my conceit and stupidity, and not expect too much of you. Still, it can't be wrong to wish that you tried a good deal more to do what he wants of you. Why should his children not be his friends? If you would but give yourselves up to him, you would find his yoke so easy, his burden so light! But you do it half only, and some of you not at all.

"Now, however, that we have got a lesson from a false gospel, we may as well get one from the true."

As she spoke, she turned to her New Testament which lay beside her. But Jarvis interrupted her.

"Where did you get that stuff you was a readin' of to us, grannie?" he asked.

"The chapter I read to you," she answered, "is part of a pretended gospel, called, 'The First Gospel of the Infancy of Jesus Christ.' I can't tell you who wrote it, or how it came to be written. All I can say is, that, very early in the history of the church, there were people who indulged themselves in inventing things about Jesus, and seemed to have had no idea of the importance of keeping to facts, or, in other words, of speaking and writing only the truth. All they seemed to have cared about was the gratifying of their own feelings of love and veneration; and so they made up tales about him, in his honor as they supposed, no doubt, just as if he had been a false god of the Greeks or Romans. It is long before some people learn to speak the truth, even after they know it is wicked to lie. Perhaps, however, they did not expect their stories to be received as facts, intending them only as a sort of recognized fiction about him,—amazing presumption at the best."

"Did anybody, then, ever believe the likes of that, grannie?" asked Jarvis.

"Yes: what I read to you seems to have been believed within a hundred years after the death of the apostles. There are several such writings, with a great deal of nonsense in them, which were generally accepted by Christian people for many hundreds of years."

"I can't imagine how anybody could go inwentuating such things!" said the blind man.

"It is hard for us to imagine. They could not have seen how their inventions would, in later times, be judged any thing but honoring to him in whose honor they wrote them. Nothing, be it ever so well invented, can be so good as the bare truth. Perhaps, however, no one in particular invented some of them, but the stories grew, just as a report often does amongst yourselves. Although everybody fancies he or she is only telling just what was told to him or her, yet, by degrees, the pin's-point of a fact is covered over with lies upon lies, almost everybody adding something, until the report has grown to be a mighty falsehood. Why, you had such a story yourselves, not so very long ago, about one of your best friends! One comfort is, such a story is sure not to be consistent with itself; it is sure to show its own falsehood to any one who is good enough to doubt it, and who will look into it, and examine it well. You don't, for instance, want any other proof than the things themselves to show you that what I have just read to you can't be true."

"But then it puzzles me to think how anybody could believe them," said the blind man.

"Many of the early Christians were so childishly simple that they would believe almost any thing that was told them. In a time when such nonsense could be written, it is no great wonder there should be many who could believe it."

"Then, what was their faith worth," said the blind man, "if they believed false and true all the same?"

"Worth no end to them," answered Marion with eagerness; "for all the false things they might believe about him could not destroy the true ones, or prevent them from believing in Jesus himself, and bettering their ways for his sake. And as they grew better and better, by doing what he told them, they would gradually come to disbelieve this and that foolish or bad thing."

"But wouldn't that make them stop believing in him altogether?"

"On the contrary, it would make them hold the firmer to all that they saw to be true about him. There are many people, I presume, in other countries, who believe those stories still; but all the Christians I know have cast aside every one of those writings, and keep only to those we call the Gospels. To throw away what is not true, because it is not true, will always help the heart to be truer; will make it the more anxious to cleave to what it sees must be true. Jesus remonstrated with the Jews that they would not of themselves judge what was right; and the man who lets God teach him is made abler to judge what is right a thousand-fold."

"Then don't you think it likely this much is true, grannie," —said Jarvis, probably interested in the question, in part at least, from the fact that he was himself a carpenter, —"that he worked with his father, and helped him in his trade?"

"I do, indeed," answered Marion. "I believe that is the one germ of truth in the whole story. It is possible even that some incidents of that part of his life may have been handed down a little way, at length losing all their shape, however, and turning into the kind of thing I read to you. Not to mention that they called him the carpenter, is it likely he who came down for the express purpose of being a true man would see his father toiling to feed him and his mother and his brothers and sisters, and go idling about, instead of putting to his hand to help him? Would that have been like him?"

"Certainly not," said Mr. Jarvis.

But a doubtful murmur came from the blind man, which speedily took shape in the following remark: —

"I can't help thinkin', grannie, of one time-you read it to us not long ago-when he laid down in the boat and went fast asleep, takin' no more heed o' them a slavin' o' theirselves to death at their oars, than if they'd been all comfortable like hisself; that wasn't much like takin' of his share-was it now?"

"John Evans," returned Marion with severity, "it is quite right to put any number of questions, and express any number of doubts you honestly feel; but you have no right to make remarks you would not make if you were anxious to be as fair to another as you would have another be to you. Have you considered that he had been working hard all day long, and was, in fact, worn out? You don't think what hard work it is, and how exhausting, to speak for hours to great multitudes, and in the open air too, where your voice has no help to make it heard. And that's not all; for he had most likely been healing many as well; and I believe every time the power went out of him to cure, he suffered in the relief he gave; it left him weakened, —with so much the less of strength to support his labors, —so that, even in his very body, he took our iniquities and bare our infirmities. Would you, then, blame a weary man, whose perfect faith in God rendered it impossible for him to fear any thing, that he lay down to rest in God's name, and left his friends to do their part for the redemption of the world in rowing him to the other side of the lake, —a thing they were doing every other day of their lives? You ought to consider before you make such remarks, Mr. Evans. And you forget also that the moment they called him, he rose to help them."

"And find fault with them," interposed Evans, rather viciously I thought.

"Yes; for they were to blame for their own trouble, and ought to send it away."

"What! To blame for the storm? How could they send that away?"

"Was it the storm that troubled them then? It was their own fear of it. The storm could not have troubled them if they had had faith in their Father in heaven."

"They had good cause to be afraid of it, anyhow."

"He judged they had not, for he was not afraid himself. You judge they had, because you would have been afraid."

"He could help himself, you see."

"And they couldn't trust either him or his Father, notwithstanding all he had done to manifest himself and his Father to them. Therefore he saw that the storm about them was not the thing that most required rebuke."

"I never pretended to much o' the sort," growled Evans. "Quite the contrairy."

"And why? Because, like an honest man, you wouldn't pretend to what you hadn't got. But, if you carried your honesty far enough, you would have taken pains to understand our Lord first. Like his other judges, you condemn him beforehand. You will not call that honesty?"

"I don't see what right you've got to badger me like this before a congregation o' people," said the blind man, rising in indignation. "If I ain't got my heyesight, I ha' got my feelin's."

"And do you think *he* has no feelings, Mr. Evans? You have spoken evil of *him*: I have spoken but the truth of *you*!"

"Come, come, grannie," said the blind man, quailing a little; "don't talk squash. I'm a livin' man afore the heyes o' this here company, an' he ain't nowheres. Bless you, *he* don't mind!"

"He minds so much," returned Marion, in a subdued voice, which seemed to tremble with coming tears, "that he will never rest until you think fairly of him. And he is here now; for he said, 'I am with you alway, to the end of the world;' and he has heard every word you have been saying against him. He isn't angry like me; but your words may well make him feel sad-for your sake, John Evans-that you should be so unfair."

She leaned her forehead on her hand, and was silent. A subdued murmur arose. The blind man, having stood irresolute for a moment, began to make for the door, saying, —

"I think I'd better go. I ain't wanted here."

"If you *are* an honest man, Mr. Evans," returned Marion, rising, "you will sit down and hear the case out."

With a waving, fin-like motion of both his hands, Evans sank into his seat, and spoke no word.

After but a moment's silence, she resumed as if there had been no interruption.

"That he should sleep, then, during the storm was a very different thing from declining to assist his father in his workshop; just as the rebuking of the sea was a very different thing from hiding up his father's bad work in miracles. Had that father been in danger, he might perhaps have aided him as he did the disciples. But" —

"Why do you say *perhaps*, grannie?" interrupted a bright-eyed boy who sat on the hob of the empty grate. "Wouldn't he help his father as soon as his disciples?"

"Certainly, if it was good for his father; certainly not, if it was not good for him: therefore I say *perhaps*. But now," she went on, turning to the joiner, "Mr. Jarvis, will you tell me whether you think the work of the carpenter's son would have been in any way distinguishable from that of another man?"

"Well, I don't know, grannie. He wouldn't want to be putting of a private mark upon it. He wouldn't want to be showing of it off-would he? He'd use his tools like another man, anyhow."

"All that we may be certain of. He came to us a man, to live a man's life, and do a man's work. But just think a moment. I will put the question again: Do you suppose you would have been able to distinguish his work from that of any other man?"

A silence followed. Jarvis was thinking. He and the blind man were of the few that can think. At last his face brightened.

"Well, grannie," he said, "I think it would be very difficult in any thing easy, but very easy in any thing difficult."

He laughed, —for he had not perceived the paradox before uttering it.

"Explain yourself, if you please, Mr. Jarvis. I am not sure that I understand you," said Marion.

"I mean, that, in an easy job, which any fair workman could do well enough, it would not be easy to tell his work. But, where the job was difficult, it would be so much better done, that it would not be difficult to see the better hand in it."

"I understand you, then, to indicate, that the chief distinction would lie in the quality of the work; that whatever he did, he would do in such a thorough manner, that over the whole of what he turned out, as you would say, the perfection of the work would be a striking characteristic. Is that it?"

"That is what I do mean, grannie."

"And that is just the conclusion I had come to myself."

"*I* should like to say just one word to it, grannie, so be you won't cut up crusty," said the blind man.

"If you are fair, I sha'n't be crusty, Mr. Evans. At least, I hope not," said Marion.

"Well, it's this: Mr. Jarvis he say as how the jiner-work done by Jesus Christ would be better done than e'er another man's,—tip-top fashion,—and there would lie the differ. Now, it do seem to me as I've got no call to come to that 'ere conclusion. You been tellin' on us, grannie, I donno how long now, as how Jesus Christ was the Son of God, and that he come to do the works of God,—down here like, afore our faces, that we might see God at work, by way of. Now, I ha' nothin' to say agin that: it may be, or it mayn't be—I can't tell. But if that be the way on it, then I don't see how Mr. Jarvis can be right; the two don't curryspond,—not by no means. For the works o' God-there ain't one on'em as I can see downright well managed-tip-top jiner's work, as I may say; leastways,—Now stop a bit, grannie; don't trip a man up, and then say as he fell over his own dog,—leastways, I don't say about the moon an' the stars an' that; I dessay the sun he do get up the werry moment he's called of a mornin', an' the moon when she ought to for her night-work,—I ain't no 'stronomer strawnry, and I ain't heerd no complaints about *them*; but I do say as how, down here, we ha' got most uncommon bad weather more'n at times; and the walnuts they turns out, every now an' then, full o' mere dirt; an' the oranges awful. There 'ain't been a good crop o' hay, they tells me, for many's the year. An' i' furren parts, what wi' earthquakes an' wolcanies an' lions an' tigers, an' savages as eats their wisiters, an' chimley-pots blowin' about, an' ships goin' down, an' fathers o' families choked an' drownded an' burnt i' coal-pits by the hundred,—it do seem to me that if his jinerin' hadn't been tip-top, it would ha' been but like the rest on it. There, grannie! Mind, I mean no offence; an' I don't doubt you ha' got somethink i' your weskit pocket as 'll turn it all topsy-turvy in a moment. Anyhow, I won't purtend to nothink, and that's how it look to me."

"I admit," said Marion, "that the objection is a reasonable one. But why do you put it, Mr. Evans, in such a triumphant way, as if you were rejoiced to think it admitted of no answer, and believed the world would be ever so much better off if the storms and the tigers had it all their own way, and there were no God to look after things?"

"Now, you ain't fair to *me*, grannie. Not avin' of my heyesight like the rest on ye, I may be a bit fond of a harguyment; but I tries to hit fair, and when I hears what ain't logic, I can no more help comin' down upon it than I can help breathin' the air o' heaven. And why shouldn't I? There ain't no law agin a harguyment. An' more an' over, it do seem to me as how you and Mr. Jarvis is wrong i' *it is* harguyment."

"If I was too sharp upon you, Mr. Evans, and I may have been," said Marion, "I beg your pardon."

"It's granted, grannie."

"I don't mean, you know, that I give in to what you say,—not one bit."

"I didn't expect it of you. I'm a-waitin' here for you to knock me down."

"I don't think a mere victory is worth the breath spent upon it," said Marion. "But we should all be glad to get or give more light upon any subject, if it be by losing ever so many arguments. Allow me just to put a question or two to Mr. Jarvis, because he's a joiner himself-and that's a great comfort to me to-night: What would you say, Mr. Jarvis, of a master who planed the timber he used for scaffolding, and tied the crosspieces with ropes of silk?"

"I should say he was a fool, grannie,—not only for losin' of his money and his labor, but for weakenin' of his scaffoldin',—summat like the old throne-maker i' that chapter, I should say."

"What's the object of a scaffold, Mr. Jarvis?"

"To get at something else by means of,—say build a house."

"Then, so long as the house was going up all right, the probability is there wouldn't be much amiss with the scaffold?"

"Certainly, provided it stood till it was taken down."

"And now, Mr. Evans," she said next, turning to the blind man, "I am going to take the liberty of putting a question or two to you."

"All right, grannie. Fire away."

"Will you tell me, then, what the object of this world is?"

"Well, most people makes it their object to get money, and make theirselves comfortable."

"But you don't think that is what the world was made for?"

"Oh! as to that, how should I know, grannie? And not knowin', I won't say."

"If you saw a scaffold," said Marion, turning again to Jarvis, "would you be in danger of mistaking it for a permanent erection?"

"Nobody wouldn't be such a fool," he answered. "The look of it would tell you that."

"You wouldn't complain, then, if it should be a little out of the square, and if there should be no windows in it?"

Jarvis only laughed.

"Mr. Evans," Marion went on, turning again to the blind man, "do you think the design of this world was to make men comfortable?"

"If it was, it don't seem to ha' succeeded," answered Evans.

"And you complain of that-don't you?"

"Well, yes, rather,"—said the blind man, adding, no doubt, as he recalled the former part of the evening's talk,—"for harguyment, ye know, grannie."

"You think, perhaps, that God, having gone so far to make this world a pleasant and comfortable place to live in, might have gone farther and made it quite pleasant and comfortable for everybody?"

"Whoever could make it at all could ha' done that, grannie."

"Then, as he hasn't done it, the probability is he didn't mean to do it?"

"Of course. That's what I complain of."

"Then he meant to do something else?"

"It looks like it."

"The whole affair has an unfinished look, you think?"

"I just do."

"What if it were not meant to stand, then? What if it were meant only for a temporary assistance in carrying out something finished and lasting, and of unspeakably more importance? Suppose God were building a palace for you, and had set up a scaffold, upon which he wanted you to help him; would it be reasonable in you to complain that you didn't find the scaffold at all a comfortable place to live in?—that it was draughty and cold? This World is that scaffold; and if you were busy carrying stones and mortar for the palace, you would be glad of all the cold to cool the glow of your labor."

"I'm sure I work hard enough when I get a job as my heyesight will enable me to do," said Evans, missing the spirit of her figure.

"Yes: I believe you do. But what will all the labor of a workman who does not fall in with the design of the builder come to? You may say you don't understand the design: will you say also that you are under no obligation to put so much faith in the builder, who is said to be your God and Father, as to do the thing he tells you? Instead of working away at the palace, like men, will you go on tacking bits of matting and old carpet about the corners of the scaffold to keep the wind off, while that same wind keeps tearing them away and scattering them? You keep trying to live in a scaffold, which not all you could do to all eternity would make a house of. You see what I mean, Mr. Evans?"

"Well, not ezackly," replied the blind man.

"I mean that God wants to build you a house whereof the walls shall be *goodness*: you want a house whereof the walls shall be *comfort*. But God knows that such walls cannot be built,— that that kind of stone crumbles away in the foolish workman's hands. He would make you comfortable; but neither is that his first object, nor can it be gained without the first, which is to make you good. He loves you so much that he would infinitely rather have you good and uncomfortable, for then he could take you to his heart as his own children, than comfortable and not good, for then he could not come near you, or give you any thing he counted worth having for himself or worth giving to you."

"So," said Jarvis, "you've just brought us round, grannie, to the same thing as before."

"I believe so," returned Marion. "It comes to this, that when God would build a palace for himself to dwell in with his children, he does not want his scaffold so constructed that they shall be able to make a house of it for themselves, and live like apes instead of angels."

"But if God can do any thing he please," said Evans, "he might as well *make* us good, and there would be an end of it."

"That is just what he is doing," returned Marion. "Perhaps, by giving them perfect health, and every thing they wanted, with absolute good temper, and making them very fond of each other besides, God might have provided himself a people he would have had no difficulty in governing, and amongst whom, in consequence, there would have been no crime and no struggle or suffering. But I have known a dog with more goodness than that would come to. We cannot be good without having consented to be made good. God shows us the good and the bad; urges us to be good; wakes good thoughts and desires in us; helps our spirit with his Spirit, our thought with his thought: but we must yield; we must turn to him; we must consent, yes, try to be made good. If we could grow good without trying, it would be a poor goodness: *we* should not be good, after all; at best, we should only be not bad. God wants us to choose to be good, and so be partakers of his holiness; he would have us lay hold of him. He who has given his Son to suffer for us will make us suffer too, bitterly if needful, that we may bethink ourselves, and turn to him. He would make us as good as good can be, that is, perfectly good; and therefore will rouse us to take the needful hand in the work ourselves, —rouse us by discomforts innumerable.

"You see, then, it is not inconsistent with the apparent imperfections of the creation around us, that Jesus should have done the best possible carpenter's work; for those very imperfections are actually through their imperfection the means of carrying out the higher creation God has in view, and at which he is working all the time.

"Now let me read you what King David thought upon this question."

She read the hundred and seventh Psalm. Then they had some singing, in which the children took a delightful part. I have seldom heard children sing pleasantly. In Sunday schools I have always found their voices painfully harsh. But Marion made her children restrain their voices, and sing softly; which had, she said, an excellent moral effect on themselves, all squalling and screeching, whether in art or morals, being ruinous to either.

Toward the close of the singing, Roger and I slipped out. We had all but tacitly agreed it would be best to make no apology, but just vanish, and come again with Percivale the following Sunday.

The greater part of the way home we walked in silence.

"What did you think of that, Roger?" I asked at length.

"Quite Socratic as to method," he answered, and said no more.

I sent a full report of the evening to my father, who was delighted with it, although, of course, much was lost in the reporting of the mere words, not to mention the absence of her sweet face and shining eyes, of her quiet, earnest, musical voice. My father kept the letter, and that is how I am able to give the present report.

CHAPTER XXX
ABOUT SERVANTS.

I went to call on Lady Bernard the next day: for there was one subject on which I could better talk with her than with Marion; and that subject was Marion herself. In the course of our conversation, I said that I had had more than usual need of such a lesson as she gave us the night before,—I had been, and indeed still was, so vexed with my nurse.

"What is the matter?" asked Lady Bernard.

"She has given me warning," I answered.

"She has been with you some time-has she not?"

"Ever since we were married."

"What reason does she give?"

"Oh! she wants *to better herself*, of course," I replied,—in such a tone, that Lady Bernard rejoined,—

"And why should she not better herself?"

"But she has such a false notion of bettering herself. I am confident what she wants will do any thing but better her, if she gets it."

"What is her notion, then? Are you sure you have got at the real one?"

"I believe I have *now*. When I asked her first, she said she was very comfortable, and condescended to inform me that she had nothing against either me or her master, but thought it was time she was having more wages; for a friend of hers, who had left home a year after herself, was having two more pounds than she had."

"It is very natural, and certainly not wrong, that she should wish for more wages."

"I told her she need not have taken such a round-about way of asking for an advance, and said I would raise her wages with pleasure. But, instead of receiving the announcement with any sign of satisfaction, she seemed put out by it; and, after some considerable amount of incoherence, blurted out that the place was dull, and she wanted a change. At length, however, I got at her real reason, which was simply ambition: she wanted to rise in the world,—to get a place where men-servants were kept,—a more fashionable place, in fact."

"A very mistaken ambition certainly," said Lady Bernard, "but one which would be counted natural enough in any other line of life. Had she given you ground for imagining higher aims in her?"

"She had been so long with us, that I thought she must have some regard for us."

"She has probably a good deal more than she is aware of. But change is as needful to some minds, for their education, as an even tenor of life is to others. Probably she has got all the good she is capable of receiving from you, and there may be some one ready to take her place for whom you will be able to do more. However inconvenient it may be for you to change, the more young people pass through your house the better."

"If it were really for her good, I hope I shouldn't mind."

"You cannot tell what may be needful to cause the seed you have sown to germinate. It may be necessary for her to pass to another class in the school of life, before she can realize what she learned in yours."

I was silent, for I was beginning to feel ashamed; and Lady Bernard went on,—

"When I hear mistresses lamenting, over some favorite servant, as marrying certain misery in exchange for a comfortable home, with plenty to eat and drink and wear, I always think of the other side to it, namely, how, through the instincts of his own implanting, God is urging her to a path in which, by passing through the fires and waters of suffering, she may be stung to the life of a true humanity. And such suffering is far more ready to work its perfect work on a girl who has passed through a family like yours."

"I wouldn't say a word to keep her if she were going to be married," I said; "but you will allow there is good reason to fear she will be no better for such a change as she desires."

"You have good reason to fear, my child," said Lady Bernard, smiling so as to take all sting out of the reproof, "that you have too little faith in the God who cares for your maid as for you. It is not indeed likely that she will have such help as yours where she goes next; but the loss of it may throw her back on herself, and bring out her individuality, which is her conscience. Still, I am far from wondering at your fear for her, —knowing well what dangers she may fall into. Shall I tell you what first began to open my eyes to the evils of a large establishment? Wishing to get rid of part of the weight of my affairs, and at the same time to assist a relative who was in want of employment, I committed to him, along with larger matters, the oversight of my household expenses, and found that he saved me the whole of his salary. This will be easily understood from a single fact. Soon after his appointment, he called on a tradesman to pay him his bill. The man, taking him for a new butler, offered him the same discount he had been in the habit of giving his supposed predecessor, namely, twenty-five per cent, —a discount, I need not say, never intended to reach my knowledge, any more than my purse. The fact was patent: I had been living in a hotel, of which I not only paid the rent, but paid the landlord for cheating me. With such a head to an establishment, you may judge what the members may become."

"I remember an amusing experience my brother-in-law, Roger Percivale, once had of your household," I said.

"I also remember it perfectly," she returned. "That was how I came to know him. But I knew something of his family long before. I remember his grandfather, a great buyer of pictures and marbles."

Lady Bernard here gave me the story from her point of view; but Roger's narrative being of necessity the more complete, I tell the tale as he told it me.

At the time of the occurrence, he was assisting Mr. F., the well-known sculptor, and had taken a share in both the modelling and the carving of a bust of Lady Bernard's father. When it was finished, and Mr. F. was about to take it home, he asked Roger to accompany him, and help him to get it safe into the house and properly placed.

Roger and the butler between them carried it to the drawing-room, where were Lady Bernard and a company of her friends, whom she had invited to meet Mr. F, at lunch, and see the bust. There being no pedestal yet ready, Mr. F. made choice of a certain small table for it to stand upon, and then accompanied her ladyship and her other guests to the dining-room, leaving Roger to uncover the bust, place it in the proper light, and do whatever more might be necessary to its proper effect on the company when they should return. As she left the room, Lady Bernard told Roger to ring for a servant to clear the table for him, and render what other assistance he might want. He did so. A lackey answered the bell, and Roger requested him to remove the things from the table. The man left the room, and did not return. Roger therefore cleared and moved the table himself, and with difficulty got the bust upon it. Finding then several stains upon the pure half transparency of the marble, he rang the bell for a basin of water and a sponge. Another man appeared, looked into the room, and went away. He rang once more, and yet another servant came. This last condescended to hear him; and, informing him that he could get what he wanted in the scullery, vanished in his turn. By this time Roger confesses to have been rather in a rage; but what could he do? Least of all allow Mr. F.'s work, and the likeness of her ladyship's father, to make its debut with a spot on its nose; therefore, seeing he could not otherwise procure what was necessary, he set out in quest of the unknown appurtenances of the kitchen.

It is unpleasant to find one's self astray, even in a moderately sized house; and Roger did not at all relish wandering about the huge place, with no finger-posts to keep him in its business-thoroughfares, not to speak of directing him to the remotest recesses of a house "full," as Chaucer says, "of crenkles." At last, however, he found himself at the door of the servants' hall. Two men were lying on their backs on benches, with their knees above their heads in the air; a third was engaged in emptying a pewter pot, between his draughts tossing *facetiæ* across its mouth to a damsel who was removing the remains of some private luncheon; and a fourth sat in one of the windows reading "Bell's Life." Roger took it all in at a glance, while to one of the giants supine, or rather to a perpendicular pair of white stockings, he preferred his request for a basin and a sponge. Once more he was informed that he would find what he wanted in the scullery. There was no time to waste on unavailing demands, therefore he only begged further to be directed how to find it. The fellow, without raising his head or lowering his knees, jabbered out such instructions as, from the rapidity with which he delivered them, were, if not unintelligible, at all events incomprehensible; and Roger had to set out again on the quest, only not quite so bewildered as before. He found a certain long passage mentioned, however, and happily, before he arrived at the end of it, met a maid, who with the utmost civility gave him full instructions to find the place. The scullery-maid was equally civil; and Roger returned with basin and sponge to the drawing-room, where he speedily removed the too troublesome stains from the face of the marble.

When the company re-entered, Mr. F. saw at once, from the expression and bearing of Roger, that something had happened to discompose him, and asked him what was amiss. Roger having briefly informed him, Mr. F. at once recounted the facts to Lady Bernard, who immediately requested a full statement from Roger himself, and heard the whole story.

She walked straight to the bell, and ordered up every one of her domestics, from the butler to the scullery-maid.

Without one hasty word, or one bodily sign of the anger she was in, except the flashing of her eyes, she told them she could not have had a suspicion that such insolence was possible in her house; that they had disgraced her in her own eyes, as having gathered such people about her; that she would not add to Mr. Percivale's annoyance by asking him to point out the guilty persons, but that they might assure themselves she would henceforth keep both eyes and ears open, and if the slightest thing of the sort happened again, she would most assuredly dismiss every one of them at a moment's warning. She then turned to Roger and said,—

"Mr. Percivale, I beg your pardon for the insults you have received from my servants."

"I did think," she said, as she finished telling me the story, "to dismiss them all on the spot, but was deterred by the fear of injustice. The next morning, however, four or five of them gave my housekeeper warning: I gave orders that they should leave the house at once, and from that day I set about reducing my establishment. My principal objects were two: first, that my servants might have more work; and second, that I might be able to know something of every one of them; for one thing I saw, that, until I ruled my own house well, I had no right to go trying to do good out of doors. I think I do know a little of the nature and character of every soul under my roof now; and I am more and more confident that nothing of real and lasting benefit can be done for a class except through personal influence upon the individual persons who compose it-such influence, I mean, as at the very least sets for Christianity."

CHAPTER XXXI
ABOUT PERCIVALE.

I should like much, before in my narrative approaching a certain hard season we had to encounter, to say a few words concerning my husband, if I only knew how. I find women differ much, both in the degree and manner in which their feelings will permit them to talk about their husbands. I have known women set a whole community against their husbands by the way in which they trumpeted their praises; and I have known one woman set everybody against herself by the way in which she published her husband's faults. I find it difficult to believe either sort. To praise one's husband is so like praising one's self, that to me it seems immodest, and subject to the same suspicion as self-laudation; while to blame one's husband, even justly and openly, seems to me to border upon treachery itself. How, then, am I to discharge a sort of half duty my father has laid upon me by what he has said in "The Seaboard Parish," concerning my husband's opinions? My father is one of the few really large-minded men I have yet known; but I am not certain that he has done Percivale justice. At the same time, if he has not, Percivale himself is partly to blame, inasmuch as he never took pains to show my father what he was; for, had he done so, my father of all men would have understood him. On the other hand, this fault, if such it was, could have sprung only from my husband's modesty, and his horror of possibly producing an impression on my father's mind more favorable than correct. It is all right now, however.

Still, my difficulty remains as to how I am to write about him. I must encourage myself with the consideration that none but our own friends, with whom, whether they understood us or not, we are safe, will know to whom the veiled narrative points.

But some acute reader may say, —

"You describe your husband's picture: he will be known by that."

In this matter I have been cunning—I hope not deceitful, inasmuch as I now reveal my cunning. Instead of describing any real picture of his, I have always substituted one he has only talked about. The picture actually associated with the facts related is not the picture I have described.

Although my husband left the impression on my father's mind, lasting for a long time, that he had some definite repugnance to Christianity itself, I had been soon satisfied, perhaps from his being more open with me, that certain unworthy representations of Christianity, coming to him with authority, had cast discredit upon the whole idea of it. In the first year or two of our married life, we had many talks on the subject; and I was astonished to find what things he imagined to be acknowledged essentials of Christianity, which have no place whatever in the New Testament; and I think it was in proportion as he came to see his own misconceptions, that, although there was little or no outward difference to be perceived in him, I could more and more clearly distinguish an under-current of thought and feeling setting towards the faith which Christianity preaches. He said little or nothing, even when I attempted to draw him out on the matter; for he was almost morbidly careful not to seem to know any thing he did not know, or to appear what he was not. The most I could get out of him was-but I had better give a little talk I had with him on one occasion. It was some time before we began to go to Marion's on a Sunday evening, and I had asked him to go with me to a certain, little chapel in the neighborhood.

"What!" he said merrily, "the daughter of a clergyman be seen going to a conventicle?"

"If I did it, I would be seen doing it," I answered.

"Don't you know that the man is no conciliatory, or even mild dissenter, but a decided enemy to Church and State and all that?" pursued Percivale.

"I don't care," I returned. "I know nothing about it. What I know is, that he's a poet and a prophet both in one. He stirs up my heart within me, and makes me long to be good. He is no orator, and yet breaks into bursts of eloquence such as none of the studied orators, to whom you profess so great an aversion, could ever reach."

"You may well be right there. It is against nature for a speaker to be eloquent throughout his discourse, and the false will of course quench the true. I don't mind going if you wish it. I suppose he believes what he says, at least."

"Not a doubt of it. He could not speak as he does from less than a thorough belief."

"Do you mean to say, Wynnie, that he is *sure* of every thing,—I don't want to urge an unreasonable question,—but is he *sure* that the story of the New Testament is, in the main, actual fact? I should be very sorry to trouble your faith, but"—

"My father says," I interrupted, "that a true faith is like the Pool of Bethesda: it is when troubled that it shows its healing power."

"That depends on where the trouble comes from, perhaps," said Percivale.

"Anyhow," I answered, "it is only that which cannot be shaken that shall remain."

"Well, I will tell you what seems to me a very common-sense difficulty. How is any one to be *sure* of the things recorded? I cannot imagine a man of our time absolutely certain of them. If you tell me I have testimony, I answer, that the testimony itself requires testimony. I never even saw the people who bear it; have just as good reason to doubt their existence, as that of him concerning whom they bear it; have positively no means of verifying it, and indeed, have so little confidence in all that is called evidence, knowing how it can be twisted, that I should distrust any conclusion I might seem about to come to on the one side or the other. It does appear to me, that, if the thing were of God, he would have taken care that it should be possible for an honest man to place a hearty confidence in its record."

He had never talked to me so openly, and I took it as a sign that he had been thinking more of these things than hitherto. I felt it a serious matter to have to answer such words, for how could I have any better assurance of that external kind than Percivale himself? That I was in the same intellectual position, however, enabled me the better to understand him. For a short time I was silent, while he regarded me with a look of concern,—fearful, I fancied, lest he should have involved me in his own perplexity.

"Isn't it possible, Percivale," I said, "that God may not care so much for beginning at that end?"

"I don't quite understand you, Wynnie," he returned.

"A man might believe every fact recorded concerning our Lord, and yet not have the faith in him that God wishes him to have."

"Yes, certainly. But will you say the converse of that is true?"

"Explain, please."

"Will you say a man may have the faith God cares for without the faith you say he does not care for?"

"I didn't say that God does not care about our having assurance of the facts; for surely, if every thing depends on those facts, much will depend on the degree of our assurance concerning them. I only expressed a doubt whether, in the present age, he cares that we should have that assurance first. Perhaps he means it to be the result of the higher kind of faith which rests in the will."

"I don't, at the moment, see how the higher faith, as you call it, can precede the lower."

"It seems to me possible enough. For what is the test of discipleship the Lord lays down? Is it not obedience? 'If ye love me, keep my commandments.' 'If a man love me, he will keep my commandments.' 'I never knew you: depart from me, ye workers of iniquity.' Suppose a man feels in himself that he must have some saviour or perish; suppose he feels drawn, by conscience, by admiration, by early memories, to the form of Jesus, dimly seen through the mists of ages; suppose he cannot be sure there ever was such a man, but reads about him, and ponders over the words attributed to him, until he feels they are the right thing, whether *he* said them or not, and that if he could but be sure there were such a being, he would believe in him with heart and soul; suppose also that he comes upon the words, 'If any man is willing to do the will of the Father, he shall know whether I speak of myself or he sent me;' suppose all these things, might not the man then say to himself, 'I cannot tell whether all this is true, but I know nothing that seems half so good, and I will try to do the will of the Father in the hope of the promised knowledge'? Do you think God would, or would not, count that to the man for faith?"

I had no more to say, and a silence followed. After a pause of some duration, Percivale said, —
"I will go with you, my dear;" and that was all his answer.

When we came out of the little chapel, —the same into which Marion had stepped on that evening so memorable to her, —we walked homeward in silence, and reached our own door ere a word was spoken. But, when I went to take off my things, Percivale followed me into the room and said, —

"Whether that man is *certain* of the facts or not, I cannot tell yet; but I am perfectly satisfied he believes in the manner of which you were speaking, —that of obedience, Wynnie. He must believe with his heart and will and life."

"If so, he can well afford to wait for what light God will give him on things that belong to the intellect and judgment."

"I would rather think," he returned, "that purity of life must re-act on the judgment, so as to make it likewise clear, and enable it to recognize the true force of the evidence at command."

"That is how my father came to believe," I said.

"He seems to me to rest his conviction more upon external proof."

"That is only because it is easier to talk about. He told me once that he was never able to estimate the force and weight of the external arguments until after he had believed for the very love of the eternal truth he saw in the story. His heart, he said, had been the guide of his intellect."

"That is just what I would fain believe. But, O Wynnie! the pity of it if that story should not be true, after all!"

"Ah, my love!" I cried, "that very word makes me surer than ever that it cannot but be true. Let us go on putting it to the hardest test; let us try it until it crumbles in our hands, —try it by the touchstone of action founded on its requirements."

"There may be no other way," said Percivale, after a thoughtful pause, "of becoming capable of recognizing the truth. It may be beyond the grasp of all but the mind that has thus yielded to it. There may be no contact for it with any but such a mind. Such a conviction, then, could neither be forestalled nor communicated. Its very existence must remain doubtful until it asserts itself. I see that."

CHAPTER XXXII
MY SECOND TERROR.

"Please, ma'am, is Master Fido to carry Master Zohrab about by the back o' the neck?" said Jemima, in indignant appeal, one afternoon late in November, bursting into the study where I sat with my husband.

Fido was our Bedlington terrier, which, having been reared by Newcastle colliers, and taught to draw a badger,—whatever that may mean,—I am hazy about it,—had a passion for burrowing after any thing buried. Swept away by the current of the said passion, he had with his strong forepaws unearthed poor Zohrab, which, being a tortoise, had ensconced himself, as he thought, for the winter, in the earth at the foot of a lilac-tree; but now, much to his jeopardy, from the cold and the shock of the surprise more than from the teeth of his friend, was being borne about the garden in triumph, though whether exactly as Jemima described may be questionable. Her indignation at the inroad of the dog upon the personal rights of the tortoise had possibly not lessened her general indifference to accuracy.

Alarmed at the danger to the poor animal, of a kind from which his natural defences were powerless to protect him, Percivale threw down his palette and brushes, and ran to the door.

"Do put on your coat and hat, Percivale!" I cried; but he was gone.

Cold as it was, he had been sitting in the light blouse he had worn at his work all the summer. The stove had got red-hot, and the room was like an oven, while outside a dank fog filled the air. I hurried after him with his coat, and found him pursuing Fido about the garden, the brute declining to obey his call, or to drop the tortoise. Percivale was equally deaf to my call, and not until he had beaten the dog did he return with the rescued tortoise in his hands. The consequences were serious,—first the death of Zohrab, and next a terrible illness to my husband. He had caught cold: it settled on his lungs, and passed into bronchitis.

It was a terrible time to me; for I had no doubt, for some days, that he was dying. The measures taken seemed thoroughly futile.

It is an awful moment when first Death looks in at the door. The positive recognition of his presence is so different from any vividest imagination of it! For the moment I believed nothing,—felt only the coming blackness of absolute loss. I cared neither for my children, nor for my father or mother. Nothing appeared of any worth more. I had conscience enough left to try to pray, but no prayer would rise from the frozen depths of my spirit. I could only move about in mechanical and hopeless ministration to one whom it seemed of no use to go on loving any more; for what was nature but a soulless machine, the constant clank of whose motion sounded only, "Dust to dust; dust to dust," forevermore? But I was roused from this horror-stricken mood by a look from my husband, who, catching a glimpse of my despair, motioned me to him with a smile as of sunshine upon snow, and whispered in my ear,—

"I'm afraid you haven't much more faith than myself, after all, Wynnie."

It stung me into life,—not for the sake of my professions, not even for the honor of our heavenly Father, but by waking in me the awful thought of my beloved passing through the shadow of death with no one beside him to help or comfort him, in absolute loneliness and uncertainty. The thought was unendurable. For a moment I wished he might die suddenly, and so escape the vacuous despair of a conscious lingering betwixt life and the something or the nothing beyond it.

"But I cannot go with you!" I cried; and, forgetting all my duty as a nurse, I wept in agony.

"Perhaps another will, my Wynnie,—one who knows the way," he whispered; for he could not speak aloud, and closed his eyes.

It was as if an arrow of light had slain the Python coiled about my heart. If *he* believed, *I* could believe also; if *he* could encounter the vague dark, *I* could endure the cheerless light. I was myself again, and, with one word of endearment, left the bedside to do what had to be done.

At length a faint hope began to glimmer in the depths of my cavernous fear. It was long ere it swelled into confidence; but, although I was then in somewhat feeble health, my strength never gave way. For a whole week I did not once undress, and for weeks I was half-awake all the time I slept. The softest whisper would rouse me thoroughly; and it was only when Marion took my place that I could sleep at all.

I am afraid I neglected my poor children dreadfully. I seemed for the time to have no responsibility, and even, I am ashamed to say, little care for them. But then I knew that they were well attended to: friends were very kind-especially Judy-in taking them out; and Marion's daily visits were like those of a mother. Indeed, she was able to mother any thing human except a baby, to whom she felt no attraction,—any more than to the inferior animals, for which she had little regard beyond a negative one: she would hurt no creature that was not hurtful; but she had scarcely an atom of kindness for dog or cat, or any thing that is petted of woman. It is the only defect I am aware of in her character.

My husband slowly recovered, but it was months before he was able to do any thing he would call work. But, even in labor, success is not only to the strong. Working a little at the short best time of the day with him, he managed, long before his full recovery, to paint a small picture which better critics than I have thought worthy of Angelico, I will attempt to describe it.

Through the lighted windows of a great hall, the spectator catches broken glimpses of a festive company. At the head of the table, pouring out the red wine, he sees one like unto the Son of man, upon whom the eyes of all are turned. At the other end of the hall, seated high in a gallery, with rapt looks and quaint yet homely angelican instruments, he sees the orchestra pouring out their souls through their strings and trumpets. The hall is filled with a jewelly glow, as of light suppressed by color, the radiating centre of which is the red wine on the table; while mingled wings, of all gorgeous splendors, hovering in the dim height, are suffused and harmonized by the molten ruby tint that pervades the whole.

Outside, in the drizzly darkness, stands a lonely man. He stoops listening, with one ear laid almost against the door. His half-upturned face catches a ray of the light reflected from a muddy pool in the road. It discloses features wan and wasted with sorrow and sickness, but glorified with the joy of the music. He is like one who has been four days dead, to whose body the music has recalled the soul. Down by his knee he holds a violin, fashioned like those of the orchestra within; which, as he listens, he is tuning to their pitch.

To readers acquainted with a poem of Dr. Donne's,—"Hymn to God, my God, in my sickness,"—this description of mine will at once suggest the origin of the picture. I had read some verses of it to him in his convalescence; and, having heard them once, he requested them often again. The first stanza runs thus:—

> "Since I am coming to that holy room
> Where with the choir of saints forevermore
> I shall be made thy musique, as I come,
> I tune the instrument here at the door;
> And what I must do then, think here before."

The painting is almost the only one he has yet refused to let me see before it was finished; but, when it was, he hung it up in my own little room off the study, and I became thoroughly acquainted with it. I think I love it more than any thing else he has done. I got him, without telling him why, to put a touch or two to the listening figure, which made it really like himself.

During this period of recovery, I often came upon him reading his Greek New Testament, which he would shove aside when I entered. At length, one morning, I said to him,—

"Are you ashamed of the New Testament, Percivale? One would think it was a bad book from the way you try to hide it."

"No, my love," he said: "it is only that I am jealous of appearing to do that from suffering and weakness only, which I did not do when I was strong and well. But sickness has opened my eyes a good deal I think; and I am sure of this much, that, whatever truth there is here, I want it all the same whether I am feeling the want or not. I had no idea what there was in this book."

"Would you mind telling me," I said, "what made you take to reading it?"

"I will try. When I thought I was dying, a black cloud seemed to fall over every thing. It was not so much that I was afraid to die, —although I did dread the final conflict, —as that I felt so forsaken and lonely. It was of little use saying to myself that I mustn't be a coward, and that it was the part of a man to meet his fate, whatever it might be, with composure; for I saw nothing worth being brave about: the heart had melted out of me; there was nothing to give me joy, nothing for my life to rest up on, no sense of love at the heart of things. Didn't you feel something the same that terrible day?"

"I did," I answered. "I hope I never believed in Death all the time; and yet for one fearful moment the skeleton seemed to swell and grow till he blotted out the sun and the stars, and was himself all in all, while the life beyond was too shadowy to show behind him. And so Death was victorious, until the thought of your loneliness in the dark valley broke the spell; and for your sake I hoped in God again."

"And I thought with myself, —Would God set his children down in the dark, and leave them to cry aloud in anguish at the terrors of the night? Would he not make the very darkness light about them? Or, if they must pass through such tortures, would he not at least let them know that he was with them? How, then, can there be a God? Then arose in my mind all at once the old story, how, in the person of his Son, God himself had passed through the darkness now gathering about me; had gone down to the grave, and had conquered death by dying. If this was true, this was to be a God indeed. Well might he call on us to endure, who had himself borne the far heavier share. If there were an Eternal Life who would perfect my life, I could be brave; I could endure what he chose to lay upon me; I could go whither he led."

"And were you able to think all that when you were so ill, my love?" I said.

"Something like it, —practically very like it," he answered. "It kept growing in my mind, —coming and going, and gathering clearer shape. I thought with myself, that, if there was a God, he certainly knew that I would give myself to him if I could; that, if I knew Jesus to be verily and really his Son, however it might seem strange to believe in him and hard to obey him, I would try to do so; and then a verse about the smoking flax and the bruised reed came into my head, and a great hope arose in me. I do not know if it was what the good people would call faith; but I had no time and no heart to think about words: I wanted God and his Christ. A fresh spring of life seemed to burst up in my heart; all the world grew bright again: I seemed to love you and the children twice as much as before; a calmness came down upon my spirit which seemed to me like nothing but the presence of God; and, although I dare say you did not then perceive a change, I am certain that the same moment I began to recover."

CHAPTER XXXIII
THE CLOUDS AFTER THE RAIN.

But the clouds returned after the rain. It will be easily understood how the little money we had in hand should have rapidly vanished during Percivale's illness. While he was making nothing, the expenses of the family went on as usual; and not that only, but many little delicacies had to be got for him, and the doctor was yet to pay. Even up to the time when he had been taken ill, we had been doing little better than living from hand to mouth; for as often as we thought income was about to get a few yards ahead in the race with expense, something invariably happened to disappoint us.

I am not sorry that I have no *special* faculty for saving; for I have never known any, in whom such was well developed, who would not do things they ought to be ashamed of. The savings of such people seem to me to come quite as much off other people as off themselves; and, especially in regard of small sums, they are in danger of being first mean, and then dishonest. Certainly, whoever makes saving *the* end of her life, must soon grow mean, and will probably grow dishonest. But I have never succeeded in drawing the line betwixt meanness and dishonesty: what is mean, so far as I can see, slides by indistinguishable gradations into what is plainly dishonest. And what is more, the savings are commonly made at the cost of the defenceless. It is better far to live in constant difficulties than to keep out of them by such vile means as must, besides, poison the whole nature, and make one's judgments, both of God and her neighbors, mean as her own conduct. It is nothing to say that you must be just before you are generous, for that is the very point I am insisting on; namely, that one must be just to others before she is generous to herself. It will never do to make your two ends meet by pulling the other ends from the hands of those who are likewise puzzled to make them meet.

But I must now put myself at the bar, and cry *Peccavi*; for I was often wrong on the other side, sometimes getting things for the house before it was quite clear I could afford them, and sometimes buying the best when an inferior thing would have been more suitable, if not to my ideas, yet to my purse. It is, however, far more difficult for one with an uncertain income to learn to save, or even to be prudent, than for one who knows how much exactly every quarter will bring.

My husband, while he left the whole management of money matters to me, would yet spend occasionally without consulting me. In fact, he had no notion of money, and what it would or would not do. I never knew a man spend less upon himself; but he would be extravagant for me, and I dared hardly utter a foolish liking lest he should straightway turn it into a cause of shame by attempting to gratify it. He had, besides, a weakness for over-paying people, of which neither Marion nor I could honestly approve, however much we might admire the disposition whence it proceeded.

Now that I have confessed, I shall be more easy in my mind; for, in regard of the troubles that followed, I cannot be sure that I was free of blame. One word more in self-excuse, and I have done: however imperative, it is none the less hard to cultivate two opposing virtues at one and the same time.

While my husband was ill, not a picture had been disposed of; and even after he was able to work a little, I could not encourage visitors: he was not able for the fatigue, and in fact shrunk, with an irritability I had never perceived a sign of before, from seeing any one. To my growing dismay, I saw my little stock-which was bodily in my hand, for we had no banking account-rapidly approaching its final evanishment.

Some may think, that, with parents in the position of mine, a temporary difficulty need have caused me no anxiety: I must, therefore, mention one or two facts with regard to both my husband and my parents.

In the first place, although he had as complete a confidence in him as I had, both in regard to what he said and what he seemed, my husband could not feel towards my father as I felt. He had married me as a poor man, who yet could keep a wife; and I knew it would be a bitter humiliation to him to ask my father for money, on the ground that he had given his daughter. I should have felt nothing of the kind; for I should have known that my father would do him as well as me perfect justice in the matter, and would consider any money spent upon us as used to a divine purpose. For he regarded the necessaries of life as noble, its comforts as honorable, its luxuries as permissible,—thus reversing altogether the usual judgment of rich men, who in general like nothing worse than to leave their hoards to those of their relatives who will degrade them to the purchase of mere bread and cheese, blankets and clothes and coals. But I had no right to go against my husband's feeling. So long as the children had their bread and milk, I would endure with him. I am confident I could have starved as well as he, and should have enjoyed letting him see it.

But there were reasons because of which even I, in my fullest freedom, could not have asked help from my father just at this time. I am ashamed to tell the fact, but I must: before the end of his second year at Oxford, just over, the elder of my two brothers had, without any vice I firmly believe, beyond that of thoughtlessness and folly, got himself so deeply mired in debt, both to tradespeople and money-lenders, that my father had to pay two thousand pounds for him. Indeed, as I was well assured, although he never told me so, he had to borrow part of the money on a fresh mortgage in order to clear him. Some lawyer, I believe, told him that he was not bound to pay: but my father said, that, although such creditors deserved no protection of the law, he was not bound to give them a lesson in honesty at the expense of weakening the bond between himself and his son, for whose misdeeds he acknowledged a large share of responsibility; while, on the other hand, he was bound to give his son the lesson of the suffering brought on his family by his selfishness; and therefore would pay the money-if not gladly, yet willingly. How the poor boy got through the shame and misery of it, I can hardly imagine; but this I can say for him, that it was purely of himself that he accepted a situation in Ceylon, instead of returning to Oxford. Thither he was now on his way, with the intention of saving all he could in order to repay his father; and if at length he succeeds in doing so, he will doubtless make a fairer start the second time, because of the discipline, than if he had gone out with the money in his pocket.

It was natural, then, that in such circumstances a daughter should shrink from adding her troubles to those caused by a son. I ought to add, that my father had of late been laying out a good deal in building cottages for the laborers on his farms, and that the land was not yet entirely freed from the mortgages my mother had inherited with it.

Percivale continued so weak, that for some time I could not bring myself to say a word to him about money. But to keep them as low as possible did not prevent the household debts from accumulating, and the servants' wages were on the point of coming due. I had been careful to keep the milkman paid; and for the rest of the tradesmen, I consoled myself with the certainty, that, if the worst came to the worst, there was plenty of furniture in the house to pay every one of them. Still, of all burdens, next to sin, that of debt, I think, must be heaviest.

I tried to keep cheerful; but at length, one night, during our supper of bread and cheese, which I could not bear to see my poor, pale-faced husband eating, I broke down.

"What *is* the matter, my darling?" asked Percivale.

I took a half-crown from my pocket, and held it out on the palm of my hand.

"That's all I've got, Percivale," I said.

"Oh! that all-is it?" he returned lightly.

"Yes,—isn't that enough?" I said with some indignation.

"Certainly-for to-night," he answered, "seeing the shops are shut. But is that all that's troubling you?" he went on.

"It seems to me quite enough," I said again; "and if you had the housekeeping to do, and the bills to pay, you would think a solitary half-crown quite enough to make you miserable."

"Never mind-so long as it's a good one," he said. "I'll get you more to-morrow."

"How can you do that?" I asked.

"Easily," he answered. "You'll see. Don't you trouble your dear heart about it for a moment."

I felt relieved, and asked him no more questions.

The next morning, when I went into the study to speak to him, he was not there; and I guessed that he had gone to town to get the money, for he had not been out before since his illness, at least without me. But I hoped of all things he was not going to borrow it of a money-lender, of which I had a great and justifiable horror, having heard from himself how a friend of his had in such a case fared. I would have sold three-fourths of the things in the house rather. But as I turned to leave the study, anxious both about himself and his proceedings, I thought something was different, and soon discovered that a certain favorite picture was missing from the wall: it was clear he had gone either to sell it or raise money upon it.

By our usual early dinner-hour, he returned, and put into my hands, with a look of forced cheerfulness, two five-pound notes.

"Is that all you got for that picture?" I said.

"That is all Mr. —— would advance me upon it," he answered. "I thought he had made enough by me to have risked a little more than that; but picture-dealers—Well, never mind. That is enough to give time for twenty things to happen."

And no doubt twenty things did happen, but none of them of the sort he meant. The ten pounds sank through my purse like water through gravel. I paid a number of small bills at once, for they pressed the more heavily upon me that I knew the money was wanted; and by the end of another fortnight we were as badly off as before, with an additional trouble, which in the circumstances was any thing but slight.

In conjunction with more than ordinary endowments of stupidity and self-conceit, Jemima was possessed of a furious temper, which showed itself occasionally in outbursts of unendurable rudeness. She had been again and again on the point of leaving me, now she, now I, giving warning; but, ere the day arrived, her better nature had always got the upper hand,—she had broken down and given in. These outbursts had generally followed a season of better behavior than usual, and were all but certain if I ventured the least commendation; for she could stand any thing better than praise. At the least subsequent rebuke, self would break out in rage, vulgarity, and rudeness. On this occasion, however, I cannot tell whence it was that one of these cyclones arose in our small atmosphere; but it was Jemima, you may well believe, who gave warning, for it was out of my power to pay her wages; and there was no sign of her yielding.

My reader may be inclined to ask in what stead the religion I had learned of my father now stood me. I will endeavor to be honest in my answer.

Every now and then I tried to pray to God to deliver us; but I was far indeed from praying always, and still farther from not fainting. A whole day would sometimes pass under a weight of care that amounted often to misery; and not until its close would I bethink me that I had been all the weary hours without God. Even when more hopeful, I would keep looking and looking for the impossibility of something to happen of itself, instead of looking for some good and perfect gift to come down from the Father of lights; and, when I awoke to the fact, the fog would yet lie so deep on my soul, that I could not be sorry for my idolatry and want of faith. It was, indeed, a miserable time. There was, besides, one definite thought that always choked my prayers: I could not say in my conscience that I had been sufficiently careful either in my management or my expenditure. "If," I thought, "I could be certain that I had done my best, I should be able to trust in God for all that lies beyond my power; but now he may mean to punish me for my carelessness." Then why should I not endure it calmly and without complaint? Alas! it was not I alone that thus would be punished, but my children and my husband as well. Nor could I avoid coming on my poor father at last, who, of course, would interfere to prevent a sale; and the thought was, from the circumstances I have mentioned, very bitter to me. Sometimes, however, in more faithful moods, I would reason with myself that God would not be hard upon me, even if I had not been so saving as I ought. My father had taken his son's debts on himself, and would not allow him to be disgraced more than could be helped; and, if an earthly parent would act thus for his child, would our Father in heaven be less tender with us? Still, for very love's sake, it might be necessary to lay some disgrace upon me, for of late I had been thinking far too little of the best things. The cares more than the duties of life had been filling my mind. If it brought me nearer to God, I must then say it had been good for me to be afflicted; but while my soul was thus oppressed, how could my feelings have any scope? Let come what would, however, I must try and bear it,—even disgrace, if it was *his* will. Better people than I had been thus disgraced, and it might be my turn next. Meantime, it had not come to that, and I must not let the cares of to-morrow burden to-day.

Every day, almost, as it seems in looking back, a train of thought something like this would pass through my mind. But things went on, and grew no better. With gathering rapidity, we went sliding, to all appearance, down the inclined plane of disgrace.

Percivale at length asked Roger if he had any money by him to lend him a little; and he gave him at once all he had, amounting to six pounds,—a wonderful amount for Roger to have accumulated; with the help of which we got on to the end of Jemima's month. The next step I had in view was to take my little valuables to the pawnbroker's,—amongst them a watch, whose face was encircled with a row of good-sized diamonds. It had belonged to my great-grandmother, and my mother had given it me when I was married.

We had had a piece of boiled neck of mutton for dinner, of which we, that is my husband and I, had partaken sparingly, in order that there might be enough for the servants. Percivale had gone out; and I was sitting in the drawing-room, lost in any thing but a blessed reverie, with all the children chattering amongst themselves beside me, when Jemima entered, looking subdued.

"If you please, ma'am, this is my day," she said.

"Have you got a place, then, Jemima?" I asked; for I had been so much occupied with my own affairs that I had thought little of the future of the poor girl to whom I could have given but a lukewarm recommendation for any thing prized amongst housekeepers.

"No, ma'am. Please, ma'am, mayn't I stop?"

"No, Jemima. I am very sorry, but I can't afford to keep you. I shall have to do all the work myself when you are gone."

I thought to pay her wages out of the proceeds of my jewels, but was willing to delay the step as long as possible; rather, I believe, from repugnance to enter the pawn-shop, than from disinclination to part with the trinkets. But, as soon as I had spoken, Jemima burst into an Irish wail, mingled with sobs and tears, crying between the convulsions of all three,—

I thought there was something wrong, mis'ess. You and master looked so scared-like. Please, mis'ess, don't send me away."

"I never wanted to send you away, Jemima. You wanted to go yourself."

"No, ma'am; *that* I didn't. I only wanted you to ask me to stop. Wirra! wirra! It's myself is sorry I was so rude. It's not me; it's my temper, mis'ess. I do believe I was born with a devil inside me."

I could not help laughing, partly from amusement, partly from relief.

"But you see I can't ask you to stop," I said. "I've got no money,—not even enough to pay you to-day; so I can't keep you."

"I don't want no money, ma'am. Let me stop, and I'll cook for yez, and wash and scrub for yez, to the end o' my days. An' I'll eat no more than'll keep the life in me. I *must* eat something, or the smell o' the meat would turn me sick, ye see, ma'am; and then I shouldn't be no good to yez. Please 'm, I ha' got fifteen pounds in the savings bank: I'll give ye all that, if ye'll let me stop wid ye."

When I confess that I burst out crying, my reader will be kind enough to take into consideration that I hadn't had much to eat for some time; that I was therefore weak in body as well as in mind; and that this was the first gleam of sunshine I had had for many weeks.

"Thank you very much, Jemima," I said, as soon as I could speak. "I won't take your money, for then you would be as poor as I am. But, if you would like to stop with us, you shall; and I won't pay you till I'm able."

The poor girl was profuse in her thanks, and left the room sobbing in her apron.

It was a gloomy, drizzly, dreary afternoon. The children were hard to amuse, and I was glad when their bedtime arrived. It was getting late before Percivale returned. He looked pale, and I found afterwards that he had walked home. He had got wet, and had to change some of his clothes. When we went in to supper, there was the neck of mutton on the table, almost as we had left it. This led me, before asking him any questions, to relate what had passed with Jemima; at which news he laughed merrily, and was evidently a good deal relieved. Then I asked him where he had been.

"To the city," he answered.

"Have you sold another picture?" I asked, with an inward tribulation, half hope, half fear; for, much as we wanted the money, I could ill bear the thought of his pictures going for the price of mere pot-boilers.

"No," he replied: "the last is stopping the way. Mr. —— has been advertising it as a bargain for a hundred and fifty. But he hasn't sold it yet, and can't, he says, risk ten pounds on another. What's to come of it, I don't know," he added. "But meantime it's a comfort that Jemima can wait a bit for *her* money."

As we sat at supper, I thought I saw a look on Percivale's face which I had never seen there before. All at once, while I was wondering what it might mean, after a long pause, during which we had been both looking into the fire, he said, —

"Wynnie, I'm going to paint a better picture than I've ever painted yet. I can, and I will."

"But how are we to live in the mean time?" I said.

His face fell, and I saw with shame what a Job's comforter I was. Instead of sympathizing with his ardor, I had quenched it. What if my foolish remark had ruined a great picture! Anyhow, it had wounded a great heart, which had turned to labor as its plainest duty, and would thereby have been strengthened to endure and to hope. It was too cruel of me. I knelt by his knee, and told him I was both ashamed and sorry I had been so faithless and unkind. He made little of it, said I might well ask the question, and even tried to be merry over it; but I could see well enough that I had let a gust of the foggy night into his soul, and was thoroughly vexed with myself. We went to bed gloomy, but slept well, and awoke more cheerful.

CHAPTER XXXIV
THE SUNSHINE.

As we were dressing, it came into my mind that I had forgotten to give him a black-bordered letter which had arrived the night before. I commonly opened his letters; but I had not opened this one, for it looked like a business letter, and I feared it might be a demand for the rent of the house, which was over due. Indeed, at this time I dreaded opening any letter the writing on which I did not recognize.

"Here is a letter, Percivale," I said. "I'm sorry I forgot to give it you last night."

"Who is it from?" he asked, talking through his towel from his dressing-room.

"I don't know. I didn't open it. It looks like something disagreeable."

"Open it now, then, and see."

"I can't just at this moment," I answered; for I had my back hair half twisted in my hands. "There it is on the chimney-piece."

He came in, took it, and opened it, while I went on with my toilet. Suddenly his arms were round me, and I felt his cheek on mine.

"Read that," he said, putting the letter into my hand.

It was from a lawyer in Shrewsbury, informing him that his god-mother, with whom he had been a great favorite when a boy, was dead, and had left him three hundred pounds.

It was like a reprieve to one about to be executed. I could only weep and thank God, once more believing in my Father in heaven. But it was a humbling thought, that, if he had not thus helped me, I might have ceased to believe in him. I saw plainly, that, let me talk to Percivale as I might, my own faith was but a wretched thing. It is all very well to have noble theories about God; but where is the good of them except we actually trust in him as a real, present, living, loving being, who counts us of more value than many sparrows, and will not let one of them fall to the ground without him?

"I thought, Wynnie, if there was such a God as you believed in, and with you to pray to him, we shouldn't be long without a hearing," said my husband.

There was more faith in his heart all the time, though he could not profess the belief I thought I had, than there ever was in mine.

But our troubles weren't nearly over yet. Percivale wrote, acknowledging the letter, and requesting to know when it would be convenient to let him have the money, as he was in immediate want of it. The reply was, that the trustees were not bound to pay the legacies for a year, but that possibly they might stretch a point in his favor if he applied to them. Percivale did so, but received a very curt answer, with little encouragement to expect any thing but the extreme of legal delay. He received the money, however, about four months after; lightened, to the great disappointment of my ignorance, of thirty pounds legacy-duty.

In the mean time, although our minds were much relieved, and Percivale was working away at his new picture with great energy and courage, the immediate pressure of circumstances was nearly as painful as ever. It was a comfort, however, to know that we might borrow on the security of the legacy; but, greatly grudging the loss of the interest which that would involve, I would have persuaded Percivale to ask a loan of Lady Bernard. He objected: on what ground do you think? That it would be disagreeable to Lady Bernard to be repaid the sum she had lent us! He would have finally consented, however, I have little doubt, had the absolute necessity for borrowing arrived.

About a week or ten days after the blessed news, he had a note from Mr. ——, whom he had authorized to part with the picture for thirty guineas. How much this was under its value, it is not easy to say, seeing the money-value of pictures is dependent on so many things: but, if the fairy godmother's executors had paid her legacy at once, that picture would not have been sold for less than five times the amount; and I may mention that the last time it changed hands it fetched five hundred and seventy pounds.

Mr. —— wrote that he had an offer of five and twenty for it, desiring to know whether he might sell it for that sum. Percivale at once gave his consent, and the next day received a check for eleven pounds, odd shillings; the difference being the borrowed amount upon it, its interest, the commission charged on the sale, and the price of a small picture-frame.

The next day, Percivale had a visitor at the studio,—no less a person than Mr. Baddeley, with his shirt-front in full blossom, and his diamond wallowing in light on his fifth finger,—I cannot call it his little finger, for his hands were as huge as they were soft and white,—hands descended of generations of laborious ones, but which had never themselves done any work beyond paddling in money.

He greeted Percivale with a jolly condescension, and told him, that, having seen and rather liked a picture of his the other day, he had come to inquire whether he had one that would do for a pendant to it; as he should like to have it, provided he did not want a fancy price for it.

Percivale felt as if he were setting out his children for sale, as he invited him to look about the room, and turned round a few from against the wall. The great man flitted hither and thither, spying at one after another through the cylinder of his curved hand, Percivale going on with his painting as if no one were there.

"How much do you want for this sketch?" asked Mr. Baddeley, at length, pointing to one of the most highly finished paintings in the room.

"I put three hundred on it at the Academy Exhibition," answered Percivale. "My friends thought it too little; but as it has been on my hands a long time now, and pictures don't rise in price in the keeping of the painter, I shouldn't mind taking two for it."

"Two tens, I suppose you mean," said Mr. Baddeley.

"I gave him a look," said Percivale, as he described the interview to me; and I knew as well as if I had seen it what kind of a phenomenon that look must have been.

"Come, now," Mr. Baddeley went on, perhaps misinterpreting the look, for it was such as a man of his property was not in the habit of receiving, "you mustn't think I'm made of money, or that I'm a green hand in the market. I know what your pictures fetch; and I'm a pretty sharp man of business, I believe. What do you really mean to say and stick to? Ready money, you know."

"Three hundred," said Percivale coolly.

"Why, Mr. Percivale!" cried Mr. Baddeley, drawing himself up, as my husband said, with the air of one who knew a trick worth two of that, "I paid Mr. —— fifty pounds, neither more nor less, for a picture of yours yesterday—a picture, allow me to say, worth"—

He turned again to the one in question with a critical air, as if about to estimate to a fraction its value as compared with the other.

"Worth three of that, some people think," said Percivale.

"The price of this, then, joking aside, is—?"

"Three hundred pounds," answered Percivale,—I know well how quietly.

"I understood you wished to sell it," said Mr. Baddeley, beginning, for all his good nature, to look offended, as well he might.

"I do wish to sell it. I happen to be in want of money."

"Then I'll be liberal, and offer you the same I paid for the other. I'll send you a check this afternoon for fifty-with pleasure."

"You cannot have that picture under three hundred."

"Why!" said the rich man, puzzled, "you offered it for two hundred, not five minutes ago."

"Yes; and you pretended to think I meant two tens."

"Offended you, I fear."

"At all events, betrayed so much ignorance of painting, that I would rather not have a picture of mine in your house."

"You're the first man ever presumed to tell me I was ignorant of painting," said Mr. Baddeley, now thoroughly indignant.

"You have heard the truth, then, for the first time," said Percivale, and resumed his work.

Mr. Baddeley walked out of the study.

I am not sure that he was so very ignorant. He had been in the way of buying popular pictures for some time, paying thousands for certain of them. I suspect he had eye enough to see that my husband's would probably rise in value, and, with the true huckster spirit, was ambitious of boasting how little he had given compared with what they were really worth.

Percivale in this case was doubtless rude. He had an insuperable aversion to men of Mr. Baddeley's class,—men who could have no position but for their money, and who yet presumed upon it, as if it were gifts and graces, genius and learning, judgment and art, all in one. He was in the habit of saying that the plutocracy, as he called it, ought to be put down,—that is, negatively and honestly,—by showing them no more respect than you really entertained for them. Besides, although he had no great favors for Cousin Judy's husband, he yet bore Mr. Baddeley a grudge for the way in which he had treated one with whom, while things went well with him, he had been ready enough to exchange hospitalities.

Before long, through Lady Bernard, he sold a picture at a fair price; and soon after, seeing in a shop-window the one Mr. —— had sold to Mr. Baddeley, marked ten pounds, went in and bought it. Within the year he sold it for a hundred and fifty.

By working day and night almost, he finished his new picture in time for the Academy; and, as he had himself predicted, it proved, at least in the opinion of all his artist friends, the best that he had ever painted. It was bought at once for three hundred pounds; and never since then have we been in want of money.

CHAPTER XXXV
WHAT LADY BERNARD THOUGHT OF IT.

My reader may wonder, that, in my record of these troubles, I have never mentioned Marion. The fact is, I could not bring myself to tell her of them; partly because she was in some trouble herself, from strangers who had taken rooms in the house, and made mischief between her and her grandchildren; and partly because I knew she would insist on going to Lady Bernard; and, although I should not have minded it myself, I knew that nothing but seeing the children hungry would have driven my husband to consent to it.

One evening, after it was all over, I told Lady Bernard the story. She allowed me to finish it without saying a word. When I had ended, she still sat silent for a few moments; then, laying her hand on my arm, said, —

My dear child, you were very wrong, as well as very unkind. Why did you not let me know?"

"Because my husband would never have allowed me," I answered.

"Then I must have a talk with your husband," she said.

"I wish you would," I replied; "for I can't help thinking Percivale too severe about such things."

The very next day she called, and did have a talk with him in the study to the following effect: —

"I have come to quarrel with you, Mr. Percivale," said Lady Bernard.

"I'm sorry to hear it," he returned. "You're the last person I should like to quarrel with, for it would imply some unpardonable fault in me."

"It does imply a fault-and a great one," she rejoined; "though I trust not an unpardonable one. That depends on whether you can repent of it."

She spoke with such a serious air, that Percivale grew uneasy, and began to wonder what he could possibly have done to offend her. I had told him nothing of our conversation, wishing her to have her own way with him.

When she saw him troubled, she smiled.

"Is it not a fault, Mr. Percivale, to prevent one from obeying the divine law of bearing another's burden?"

"But," said Percivale, "I read as well, that every man shall bear his own burden."

"Ah!" returned Lady Bernard; "but I learn from Mr. Conybeare that two different Greek words are there used, which we translate only by the English *burden*. I cannot tell you what they are: I can only tell you the practical result. We are to bear one another's burdens of pain or grief or misfortune or doubt, —whatever weighs one down is to be borne by another; but the man who is tempted to exalt himself over his neighbor is taught to remember that he has his own load of disgrace to bear and answer for. It is just a weaker form of the lesson of the mote and the beam. You cannot get out at that door, Mr. Percivale. I beg you will read the passage in your Greek Testament, and see if you have not misapplied it. You *ought* to have let me bear your burden."

"Well, you see, my dear Lady Bernard," returned Percivale, at a loss to reply to such a vigorous assault, "I knew how it would be. You would have come here and bought pictures you didn't want; and I, knowing all the time you did it only to give me the money, should have had to talk to you as if I were taken in by it; and I really could *not* stand it."

"There you are altogether wrong. Besides depriving me of the opportunity of fulfilling a duty, and of the pleasure and the honor of helping you to bear your burden, you have deprived me of the opportunity of indulging a positive passion for pictures. I am constantly compelled to restrain it lest I should spend too much of the money given me for the common good on my own private tastes; but here was a chance for me! I might have had some of your lovely pictures in my drawing-room now-with a good conscience and a happy heart-if you had only been friendly. It was too bad of you, Mr. Percivale! I am not pretending in the least when I assert that I am really and thoroughly disappointed."

"I haven't a word to say for myself," returned Percivale.

"You couldn't have said a better," rejoined Lady Bernard; "but I hope you will never have to say it again."

"That I shall not. If ever I find myself in any difficulty worth speaking of, I will let you know at once."

"Thank you. Then we are friends again. And now I do think I am entitled to a picture, —at least, I think it will be pardonable if I yield to the *very* strong temptation I am under at this moment to buy one. Let me see: what have you in the slave-market, as your wife calls it?"

She bought "The Street Musician," as Percivale had named the picture taken from Dr. Donne. I was more miserable than I ought to have been when I found he had parted with it, but it was a great consolation to think it was to Lady Bernard's it had gone. She was the only one, except my mother or Miss Clare, I could have borne to think of as having become its possessor.

He had asked her what I thought a very low price for it; and I judge that Lady Bernard thought the same, but, after what had passed between them, would not venture to expostulate. With such a man as my husband, I fancy, she thought it best to let well alone. Anyhow, one day soon after this, her servant brought him a little box, containing a fine brilliant.

"The good lady's kindness is long-sighted," said my husband, as he placed it on his finger. "I shall be hard up, though, before I part with this. Wynnie, I've actually got a finer diamond than Mr. Baddeley! It *is* a beauty, if ever there was one!"

My husband, with all his carelessness of dress and adornment, has almost a passion for stones. It is delightful to hear him talk about them. But he had never possessed a single gem before Lady Bernard made him this present. I believe he is child enough to be happier for it all his life.

CHAPTER XXXVI
RETROSPECTIVE.

Suddenly I become aware that I am drawing nigh the close of my monthly labors for a long year. Yet the year seems to have passed more rapidly because of this addition to my anxieties. Not that I haven't enjoyed the labor while I have been actually engaged in it, but the prospect of the next month's work would often come in to damp the pleasure of the present; making me fancy, as the close of each chapter drew near, that I should not have material for another left in my head. I heard a friend once remark that it is not the cares of to-day, but the cares of to-morrow, that weigh a man down. For the day we have the corresponding strength given, for the morrow we are told to trust; it is not ours yet.

When I get my money for my work, I mean to give my husband a long holiday. I half think of taking him to Italy,—for of course I can do what I like with my own, whether husband or money,—and so have a hand in making him a still better painter. Incapable of imitation, the sight of any real work is always of great service to him, widening his sense of art, enlarging his idea of what can be done, rousing what part of his being is most in sympathy with it,—a part possibly as yet only half awake; in a word, leading him another step towards that simplicity which is at the root of all diversity, being so simple that it needs all diversity to set it forth.

How impossible it seemed to me that I should ever write a book! Well or ill done, it is almost finished, for the next month is the twelfth. I must look back upon what I have written, to see what loose ends I may have left, and whether any allusion has not been followed up with a needful explanation; for this way of writing by portions-the only way in which I could have been persuaded to attempt the work, however-is unfavorable to artistic unity; an unnecessary remark, seeing that to such unity my work makes no pretensions. It is but a collection of portions detached from an uneventful, ordinary, and perhaps in part *therefore* very blessed life. Hence, perhaps, it was specially fitted for this mode of publication. At all events, I can cast upon it none of the blame of what failure I may have to confess.

A biography cannot be constructed with the art of a novel, for this reason: that a novel is constructed on the artist's scale, with swift-returning curves; a biography on the divine scale, whose circles are so large that they shoot beyond this world, sometimes even before we are able to detect in them the curve by which they will at length round themselves back towards completion. Hence, every life must look more or less fragmentary, and more or less out of drawing perhaps; not to mention the questionable effects in color and tone where the model himself will insist on taking palette and brushes, and laying childish, if not passionate, conceited, ambitious, or even spiteful hands to the work.

I do not find that I have greatly blundered, or omitted much that I ought to have mentioned. One odd thing is, that, in the opening conversation in which they urge me to the attempt, I have not mentioned Marion. I do not mean that she was present, but that surely some one must have suggested her and her history as affording endless material for my record. A thing apparently but not really strange is, that I have never said a word about the Mrs. Cromwell mentioned in the same conversation. The fact is, that I have but just arrived at the part of my story where she first comes in. She died about three months ago; and I can therefore with the more freedom narrate in the next chapter what I have known of her.

I find also that I have, in the fourth chapter, by some odd cerebro-mechanical freak, substituted the name of my Aunt *Martha* for that of my Aunt Millicent, another sister of my father, whom he has not, I believe, had occasion to mention in either of his preceding books. My Aunt Martha is Mrs. Weir, and has no children; my Aunt Millicent is Mrs. Parsons, married to a hard-working attorney, and has twelve children, now mostly grown up.

I find also, in the thirteenth chapter, an unexplained allusion. There my husband says, "Just ask my brother his experience in regard of the word to which you object." The word was *stomach*, at the use of which I had in my ill-temper taken umbrage: however disagreeable a word in itself, surely a husband might, if need be, use it without offence. It will be proof enough that my objection arose from pure ill-temper when I state that I have since asked Roger to what Percivale referred. His reply was, that, having been requested by a certain person who had a school for young ladies-probably she called it a college-to give her pupils a few lectures on physiology, he could not go far in the course without finding it necessary to make a not unfrequent use of the word, explaining the functions of the organ to which the name belonged, as resembling those of a mill. After the lecture was over, the school-mistress took him aside, and said she really could not allow her young ladies to be made familiar with such words. Roger averred that the word was absolutely necessary to the subject upon which she had desired his lectures; and that he did not know how any instruction in physiology could be given without the free use of it. "No doubt," she returned, "you must recognize the existence of the organ in question; but, as the name of it is offensive to ears polite, could you not substitute another? You have just said that its operations resemble those of a mill: could you not, as often as you require to speak of it, refer to it in the future as *the mill?*" Roger, with great difficulty repressing his laughter, consented; but in his next lecture made far more frequent reference to *the mill* than was necessary, using the word every time —I know exactly how-with a certain absurd solemnity that must have been irresistible. The girls went into fits of laughter at the first utterance of it, and seemed, he said, during the whole lecture, intent only on the new term, at every recurrence of which their laughter burst out afresh. Doubtless their school-mistress had herself prepared them to fall into Roger's trap. The same night he received a note from her, enclosing his fee for the lectures given, and informing him that the rest of the course would not be required. Roger sent back the money, saying that to accept part payment would be to renounce his claim for the whole; and that, besides, he had already received an amount of amusement quite sufficient to reward him for his labor. I told him I thought he had been rather cruel; but he said such a woman wanted a lesson. He said also, that to see the sort of women who sometimes had the responsibility of training girls must make the angels weep; none but a heartless mortal like himself could laugh where conventionality and insincerity were taught in every hint as to posture and speech. It was bad enough, he said, to shape yourself into your own ideal; but to have to fashion yourself after the ideal of one whose sole object in teaching was to make money, was something wretched indeed.

I find, besides, that several intentions I had when I started have fallen out of the scheme. Somehow, the subjects would not well come in, or I felt that I was in danger of injuring the persons in the attempt to set forth their opinions.

CHAPTER XXXVII
MRS. CROMWELL COMES.

The moment the legacy was paid, our liabilities being already nearly discharged, my husband took us all to Hastings. I had never before been to any other seacoast town where the land was worthy of the sea, except Kilkhaven. Assuredly, there is no place within easy reach of London to be once mentioned with Hastings. Of course we kept clear of the more fashionable and commonplace St. Leonard's End, where yet the sea is the same, — a sea such that, not even off Cornwall, have I seen so many varieties of ocean-aspect. The immediate shore, with its earthy cliffs, is vastly inferior to the magnificent rock about Tintagel; but there is no outlook on the sea that I know more satisfying than that from the heights of Hastings, especially the East Hill; from the west side of which also you may, when weary of the ocean, look straight down on the ancient port, with its old houses, and fine, multiform red roofs, through the gauze of blue smoke which at eve of a summer day fills the narrow valley, softening the rough goings-on of life into harmony with the gentleness of sea and shore, field and sky. No doubt the suburbs are as unsightly as mere boxes of brick and lime can be, with an ugliness mean because pretentious, an altogether modern ugliness; but even this cannot touch the essential beauty of the place.

On the brow of this East Hill, just where it begins to sink towards Ecclesbourne Glen, stands a small, old, rickety house in the midst of the sweet grass of the downs. This house my husband was fortunate in finding to let, and took for three months. I am not, however, going to give any history of how we spent them; my sole reason for mentioning Hastings at all being that there I made the acquaintance of Mrs. Cromwell. It was on this wise.

One bright day, about noon, —almost all the days of those months were gorgeous with sunlight, —a rather fashionable maid ran up our little garden, begging for some water for her mistress. Sending her on with the water, I followed myself with a glass of sherry.

The door in our garden-hedge opened immediately on a green hollow in the hill, sloping towards the glen. As I stepped from the little gate on to the grass, I saw, to my surprise, that a white fog was blowing in from the sea. The heights on the opposite side of the glen, partially obscured thereby, looked more majestic than was their wont, and were mottled with patches of duller and brighter color as the drifts of the fog were heaped or parted here and there. Far down, at the foot of the cliffs, the waves of the rising tide, driven shore-wards with the added force of a south-west breeze, caught and threw back what sunlight reached them, and thinned with their shine the fog between. It was all so strange and fine, and had come on so suddenly, —for when I had looked out a few minutes before, sea and sky were purely resplendent, —that I stood a moment or two and gazed, almost forgetting why I was there.

When I bethought myself and looked about me, I saw, in the sheltered hollow before me, a lady seated in a curiously-shaped chair; so constructed, in fact, as to form upon occasion a kind of litter. It was plain she was an invalid, from her paleness, and the tension of the skin on her face, revealing the outline of the bones beneath. Her features were finely formed, but rather small, and her forehead low; a Greek-like face, with large, pale-blue eyes, that reminded me of little Amy Morley's. She smiled very sweetly when she saw me, and shook her head at the wine.

"I only wanted a little water," she said. "This fog seems to stifle me."

"It has come on very suddenly," I said. "Perhaps it is the cold of it that affects your breathing. You don't seem very strong, and any sudden change of temperature" —

"I am not one of the most vigorous of mortals," she answered, with a sad smile; "but the day seemed of such indubitable character, that, after my husband had brought me here in the carriage, he sent it home, and left me with my maid, while he went for a long walk across the downs. When he sees the change in the weather, though, he will turn directly."

"It won't do to wait him here," I said. "We must get you in at once. Would it be wrong to press you to take a little of this wine, just to counteract a chill?"

"I daren't touch any thing but water," she replied, "It would make me feverish at once."

"Run and tell the cook," I said to the maid, "that I want her here. You and she could carry your mistress in, could you not? I will help you."

"There's no occasion for that, ma'am: she's as light as a feather," was the whispered answer.

"I am quite ashamed of giving you so much trouble," said the lady, either hearing or guessing at our words. "My husband will be very grateful to you."

"It is only an act of common humanity," I said.

But, as I spoke, I fancied her fair brow clouded a little, as if she was not accustomed to common humanity, and the word sounded harsh in her ear. The cloud, however, passed so quickly that I doubted, until I knew her better, whether it had really been there.

The two maids were now ready; and, Jemima instructed by the other, they lifted her with the utmost ease, and bore her gently towards the house. The garden-gate was just wide enough to let the chair through, and in a minute more she was upon the sofa. Then a fit of coughing came on which shook her dreadfully. When it had passed she lay quiet, with closed eyes, and a smile hovering about her sweet, thin-lipped mouth. By and by she opened them, and looked at me with a pitiful expression.

"I fear you are far from well," I said.

"I'm dying," she returned quietly.

"I hope not," was all I could answer.

"Why should you hope not?" she returned. "I am in no strait betwixt two. I desire to depart. For me to die will be all gain."

"But your friends?" I ventured to suggest, feeling my way, and not quite relishing either the form or tone of her utterance.

"I have none but my husband."

"Then your husband?" I persisted.

"Ah!" she said mournfully, "he will miss me, no doubt, for a while. But it *must* be a weight off him, for I have been a sufferer so long!"

At this moment I heard a heavy, hasty step in the passage; the next, the room door opened, and in came, in hot haste, wiping his red face, a burly man, clumsy and active, with an umbrella in his hand, followed by a great, lumbering Newfoundland dog.

"Down, Polyphemus!" he said to the dog, which crept under a chair; while he, taking no notice of my presence, hurried up to his wife.

"My love! my little dove!" he said eagerly: "did you think I had forsaken you to the cruel elements?"

"No, Alcibiades," she answered, with a sweet little drawl; "but you do not observe that I am not the only lady in the room." Then, turning to me, "This is my husband, Mr. Cromwell," she said. "I cannot tell him *your* name."

"I am Mrs. Percivale," I returned, almost mechanically, for the gentleman's two names had run together and were sounding in my head: *Alcibiades Cromwell*! How could such a conjunction have taken place without the intervention of Charles Dickens?

"I beg your pardon, ma'am," said Mr. Cromwell, bowing. "Permit my anxiety about my poor wife to cover my rudeness. I had climbed the other side of the glen before I saw the fog; and it is no such easy matter to get up and down these hills of yours. I am greatly obliged to you for your hospitality. You have doubtless saved her life; for she is a frail flower, shrinking from the least breath of cold."

The lady closed her eyes again, and the gentleman took her hand, and felt her pulse. He seemed about twice her age,—she not thirty; he well past fifty, the top of his head bald, and his gray hair sticking out fiercely over his good-natured red cheeks. He laid her hand gently down, put his hat on the table and his umbrella in a corner, wiped his face again, drew a chair near the sofa, and took his place by her side. I thought it better to leave them.

When I re-entered after a while, I saw from the windows, which looked sea-ward, that the wind had risen, and was driving thin drifts no longer, but great, thick, white masses of sea-fog landwards. It was the storm-wind of that coast, the south-west, which dashes the pebbles over the Parade, and the heavy spray against the houses. Mr. Alcibiades Cromwell was sitting as I had left him, silent, by the side of his wife, whose blue-veined eyelids had apparently never been lifted from her large eyes.

"Is there any thing I could offer Mrs. Cromwell?" I said. "Could she not eat something?"

"It is very little she can take," he answered; "but you are very kind. If you could let her have a little beef-tea? She generally has a spoonful or two about this time of the day."

"I am sorry we have none," I said; "and it would be far too long for her to wait. I have a nice chicken, though, ready for cooking: if she could take a little chicken-broth, that would be ready in a very little while."

"Thank you a thousand times, ma'am," he said heartily; "nothing could be better. She might even be induced to eat a mouthful of the chicken. But I am afraid your extreme kindness prevents me from being so thoroughly ashamed as I ought to be at putting you to so much trouble for perfect strangers."

"It is but a pleasure to be of service to any one in want of it," I said.

Mrs. Cromwell opened her eyes and smiled gratefully. I left the room to give orders about the chicken, indeed, to superintend the preparation of it myself; for Jemima could not be altogether trusted in such a delicate affair as cooking for an invalid.

When I returned, having set the simple operation going, Mr. Cromwell had a little hymn-book of mine he had found on the table open in his hand, and his wife was saying to him, —

"That is lovely! Thank you, husband. How can it be I never saw it before? I am quite astonished."

"She little knows what multitudes of hymns there are!" I thought with myself, —my father having made a collection, whence I had some idea of the extent of that department of religious literature.

"This is a hymn-book we are not acquainted with," said Mr. Cromwell, addressing me.

"It is not much known," I answered. "It was compiled by a friend of my father's for his own schools."

"And this," he went on, "is a very beautiful hymn. You may trust my wife's judgment, Mrs. Percivale. She lives upon hymns."

He read the first line to show which he meant. I had long thought, and still think, it the most beautiful hymn I know. It was taken from the German, only much improved in the taking, and given to my father to do what he pleased with; and my father had given it to another friend for his collection. Before that, however, while still in manuscript, it had fallen into the hands of a certain clergyman, by whom it had been published without leave asked, or apology made: a rudeness of which neither my father nor the author would have complained, for it was a pleasure to think it might thus reach many to whom it would be helpful; but they both felt aggrieved and indignant that he had taken the dishonest liberty of altering certain lines of it to suit his own opinions. As I am anxious to give it all the publicity I can, from pure delight in it, and love to all who are capable of the same delight, I shall here communicate it, in the full confidence of thus establishing a claim on the gratitude of my readers.

> O Lord, how happy is the time
> When in thy love I rest!
> When from my weariness I climb
> Even to thy tender breast!
> The night of sorrow endeth there:
> Thou art brighter than the sun;
> And in thy pardon and thy care
> The heaven of heaven is won.

Let the world call herself my foe,
  Or let the world allure.
I care not for the world: I go
  To this dear Friend and sure.
And when life's fiercest storms are sent
  Upon life's wildest sea,
My little bark is confident,
  Because it holds by thee.

When the law threatens endless death
  Upon the awful hill,
Straightway from her consuming breath
  My soul goes higher still, —
Goeth to Jesus, wounded, slain,
  And maketh him her home,
Whence she will not go out again,
  And where death cannot come.

I do not fear the wilderness
  Where thou hast been before;
Nay, rather will I daily press
  After thee, near thee, more.
Thou art my food; on thee I lean;
  Thou makest my heart sing;
And to thy heavenly pastures green
  All thy dear flock dost bring.

And if the gate that opens there
  Be dark to other men,
It is not dark to those who share
  The heart of Jesus then.
That is not losing much of life
  Which is not losing thee,
Who art as present in the strife
  As in the victory.

Therefore how happy is the time
  When in thy love I rest!
When from my weariness I climb
  Even to thy tender breast!
The night of sorrow endeth there:
  Thou are brighter than the sun;
And in thy pardon and thy care
  The heaven of heaven is won.

In telling them a few of the facts connected with the hymn, I presume I had manifested my admiration of it with some degree of fervor.

"Ah!" said Mrs. Cromwell, opening her eyes very wide, and letting the rising tears fill them: "Ah, Mrs. Percivale! you are-you must be one of us!"

"You must tell me first who you are," I said.

She held out her hand; I gave her mine: she drew me towards her, and whispered almost in my ear-though why or whence the affectation of secrecy I can only imagine-the name of a certain small and exclusive sect. I will not indicate it, lest I should be supposed to attribute to it either the peculiar faults or virtues of my new acquaintance.

"No," I answered, speaking with the calmness of self-compulsion, for I confess I felt repelled: "I am not one of you, except in as far as we all belong to the church of Christ."

I have thought since how much better it would have been to say, "Yes: for we all belong to the church of Christ."

She gave a little sigh of disappointment, closed her eyes for a moment, opened them again with a smile, and said with a pleading tone, —

"But you do believe in personal religion?"

"I don't see," I returned, "how religion can be any thing but personal."

Again she closed her eyes, in a way that made me think how convenient bad health must be, conferring not only the privilege of passing into retirement at any desirable moment, but of doing so in such a ready and easy manner as the mere dropping of the eyelids.

I rose to leave the room once more. Mr. Cromwell, who had made way for me to sit beside his wife, stood looking out of the window, against which came sweeping the great volumes of mist. I glanced out also. Not only was the sea invisible, but even the brow of the cliffs. When he turned towards me, as I passed him, I saw that his face had lost much of its rubicund hue, and looked troubled and anxious.

"There is nothing for it," I said to myself, "but keep them all night," and so gave directions to have a bedroom prepared for them. I did not much like it, I confess; for I was not much interested in either of them, while of the sect to which she belonged I knew enough already to be aware that it was of the narrowest and most sectarian in Christendom. It was a pity she had sought to claim me by a would-be closer bond than that of the body of Christ. Still I knew I should be myself a sectary if I therefore excluded her from my best sympathies. At the same time I did feel some curiosity concerning the oddly-yoked couple, and wondered whether the lady was really so ill as she would appear. I doubted whether she might not be using her illness both as an excuse for self-indulgence, and as a means of keeping her husband's interest in her on the stretch. I did not like the wearing of her religion on her sleeve, nor the mellifluous drawl in which she spoke.

When the chicken-broth was ready, she partook daintily; but before she ended had made a very good meal, including a wing and a bit of the breast; after which she fell asleep.

"There seems little chance of the weather clearing," said Mr. Cromwell in a whisper, as I approached the window where he once more stood.

"You must make up your mind to remain here for the night," I said.

"My dear madam, I couldn't think of it," he returned, —I thought from unwillingness to incommode a strange household. "An invalid like her, sweet lamb!" he went on, "requires so many little comforts and peculiar contrivances to entice the repose she so greatly needs, that-that-in short, I must get her home."

"Where do you live?" I asked, not sorry to find his intention of going so fixed.

"We have a house in Warrior Square," he answered. "We live in London, but have been here all the past winter. I doubt if she improves, though. I doubt—I doubt."

He said the last words in a yet lower and more mournful whisper; then, with a shake of his head, turned and gazed again through the window.

A peculiar little cough from the sofa made us both look round. Mrs. Cromwell was awake, and searching for her handkerchief. Her husband understood her movements, and hurried to her assistance. When she took the handkerchief from her mouth, there was a red spot upon it. Mr. Cromwell's face turned the color of lead; but his wife looked up at him, and smiled; a sweet, consciously pathetic smile.

"He has sent for me," she said. "The messenger has come."

Her husband made no answer. His eyes seemed starting from his head.

"Who is your medical man?" I asked him.

He told me, and I sent off my housemaid to fetch him. It was a long hour before he arrived; during which, as often as I peeped in, I saw him sitting silent, and holding her hand, until the last time, when I found him reading a hymn to her. She was apparently once more asleep. Nothing could be more favorable to her recovery than such quietness of both body and mind.

When the doctor came, and had listened to Mr. Cromwell's statement, he proceeded to examine her chest with much care. That over, he averred in her hearing that he found nothing serious; but told her husband apart that there was considerable mischief, and assured me afterwards that her lungs were all but gone, and that she could not live beyond a month or two. She had better be removed to her own house, he said, as speedily as possible.

"But it would be cruelty to send her out a day like this," I returned.

"Yes, yes: I did not mean that," he said. "But to-morrow, perhaps. You'll see what the weather is like. Is Mrs. Cromwell an old friend?"

"I never saw her until to-day," I replied.

"Ah!" he remarked, and said no more.

We got her to bed as soon as possible. I may just mention that I never saw any thing to equal the *point-devise* of her underclothing. There was not a stitch of cotton about her, using the word *stitch* in its metaphorical sense. But, indeed, I doubt whether her garments were not all made with linen thread. Even her horse-hair petticoat was quilted with rose-colored silk inside.

"Surely she has no children!" I said to myself; and was right, as my mother-readers will not be surprised to learn.

It was a week before she got up again, and a month before she was carried down the hill; during which time her husband sat up with her, or slept on a sofa in the room beside her, every night. During the day I took a share in the nursing, which was by no means oppressive, for she did not suffer much, and required little. Her chief demand was for hymns, the only annoyance connected with which worth mentioning was, that she often wished me to admire with her such as I could only half like, and occasionally such as were thoroughly distasteful to me. Her husband had brought her own collection from Warrior Square, volumes of hymns in manuscript, copied by her own hand, many of them strange to me, none of those I read altogether devoid of literary merit, and some of them lovely both in feeling and form. But all, even the best, which to me were unobjectionable, belonged to one class, — a class breathing a certain tone difficult to describe; one, however, which I find characteristic of all the Roman Catholic hymns I have read. I will not indicate any of her selection; neither, lest I should be supposed to object to this or that one answering to the general description, and yet worthy of all respect, or even sympathy, will I go further with a specification of their sort than to say that what pleased me in them was their full utterance of personal devotion to the Saviour, and that what displeased me was a sort of sentimental regard of self in the matter, —an implied special, and thus partially exclusive predilection or preference of the Saviour for the individual supposed to be making use of them; a certain fundamental want of humility therefore, although the forms of speech in which they were cast might be laboriously humble. They also not unfrequently manifested a great leaning to the forms of earthly show as representative of the glories of that kingdom which the Lord says is *within us*.

Likewise the manner in which Mrs. Cromwell talked reminded me much of the way in which a nun would represent her individual relation to Christ. I can best show what I mean by giving a conversation I had with her one day when she was recovering, which she did with wonderful rapidity up to a certain point. I confess I shrink a little from reproducing it, because of the sacred name which, as it seemed to me, was far too often upon her lips, and too easily uttered. But then, she was made so different from me!

The fine weather had returned in all its summer glory, and she was lying on a couch in her own room near the window, whence she could gaze on the expanse of sea below, this morning streaked with the most delicate gradations of distance, sweep beyond sweep, line and band and ribbon of softly, often but slightly varied hue, leading the eyes on and on into the infinite. There may have been some atmospheric illusion ending off the show, for the last reaches mingled so with the air that you saw no horizon line, only a great breadth of border; no spot which could you appropriate with certainty either to sea or sky; while here and there was a vessel, to all appearance, pursuing its path in the sky, and not upon the sea. It was, as some of my readers will not require to be told, a still, gray forenoon, with a film of cloud over all the heavens, and many horizontal strata of deeper but varying density near the horizon.

Mrs. Cromwell had lain for some time with her large eyes fixed on the farthest confusion of sea and sky.

"I have been sending out my soul," she said at length, "to travel all across those distances, step by step, on to the gates of pearl. Who knows but that may be the path I must travel to meet the Bridegroom?"

"The way is wide," I said: "what if you should miss him?"

I spoke almost involuntarily. The style of her talk was very distasteful to me; and I had just been thinking of what I had once heard my father say, that at no time were people in more danger of being theatrical than when upon their death-beds.

"No," she returned, with a smile of gentle superiority; "no: that cannot be. Is he not waiting for me? Has he not chosen me, and called me for his own? Is not my Jesus mine? I shall *not* miss him. He waits to give me my new name, and clothe me in the garments of righteousness."

As she spoke, she clasped her thin hands, and looked upwards with a radiant expression. Far as it was from me to hint, even in my own soul, that the Saviour was not hers, tenfold more hers than she was able to think, I could not at the same time but doubt whether her heart and soul and mind were as close to him as her words would indicate she thought they were. She could not be wrong in trusting him; but could she be right in her notion of the measure to which her union with him had been perfected? I could not help thinking that a little fear, soon to pass into reverence, might be to her a salutary thing. The fear, I thought, would heighten and deepen the love, and purify it from that self which haunted her whole consciousness, and of which she had not yet sickened, as one day she certainly must.

"My lamp is burning," she said; "I feel it burning. I love my Lord. It would be false to say otherwise."

"Are you sure you have oil enough in your vessel as well as in your lamp?" I said.

"Ah, you are one of the doubting!" she returned kindly. "Don't you know that sweet hymn about feeding our lamps from the olive-trees of Gethsemane? The idea is taken from the lamp the prophet Zechariah saw in his vision, into which two olive-branches, through two golden pipes, emptied the golden oil out of themselves. If we are thus one with the olive-tree, the oil cannot fail us. It is not as if we had to fill our lamps from a cruse of our own. This is the cruse that cannot fail."

"True, true," I said; "but ought we not to examine our own selves whether we are in the faith?"

"Let those examine that doubt," she replied; and I could not but yield in my heart that she had had the best of the argument.

For I knew that the confidence in Christ which prevents us from thinking of ourselves, and makes us eager to obey his word, leaving all the care of our feelings to him, is a true and healthy faith. Hence I could not answer her, although I doubted whether her peace came from such confidence,—doubted for several reasons: one, that, so far from not thinking of herself, she seemed full of herself; another, that she seemed to find no difficulty with herself in any way; and, surely, she was too young for all struggle to be over! I perceived no reference to the will of God in regard of any thing she had to do, only in regard of what she had to suffer, and especially in regard of that smallest of matters, when she was to go. Here I checked myself, for what could she *do* in such a state of health? But then she never spoke as if she had any anxiety about the welfare of other people. That, however, might be from her absolute contentment in the will of God. But why did she always look to the Saviour through a mist of hymns, and never go straight back to the genuine old good news, or to the mighty thoughts and exhortations with which the first preachers of that news followed them up and unfolded the grandeur of their goodness? After all, was I not judging her? On the other hand, ought I not to care for her state? Should I not be inhuman, that is, unchristian, if I did not?

In the end I saw clearly enough, that, except it was revealed to me what I ought to say, I had no right to say any thing; and that to be uneasy about her was to distrust Him whose it was to teach her, and who would perfect that which he had certainly begun in her. For her heart, however poor and faulty and flimsy its faith might be, was yet certainly drawn towards the object of faith. I, therefore, said nothing more in the direction of opening her eyes to what I considered her condition: that view of it might, after all, be but a phantasm of my own projection. What was plainly my duty was to serve her as one of those the least of whom the Saviour sets forth as representing himself. I would do it to her as unto him.

My children were out the greater part of every day, and Dora was with me, so that I had more leisure than I had had for a long time. I therefore set myself to wait upon her as a kind of lady's maid in things spiritual. Her own maid, understanding her ways, was sufficient for things temporal. I resolved to try to help her after her own fashion, and not after mine; for, however strange the nourishment she preferred might seem, it must at least be of the *kind* she could best assimilate. My care should be to give her her gruel as good as I might, and her beef-tea strong, with chicken-broth instead of barley-water and delusive jelly. But much opportunity of ministration was not afforded me; for her husband, whose business in life she seemed to regard as the care of her, —for which, in truth, she was gently and lovingly grateful, —and who not merely accepted her view of the matter, but, I was pretty sure, had had a large share in originating it, was even more constant in his attentions than she found altogether agreeable, to judge by the way in which she would insist on his going out for a second walk, when it was clear, that, besides his desire to be with her, he was not inclined to walk any more.

I could set myself, however, as I have indicated, to find fitting pabulum for her, and that of her chosen sort. This was possible for me in virtue of my father's collection of hymns, and the aid he could give me. I therefore sent him a detailed description of what seemed to me her condition, and what I thought I might do for her. It was a week before he gave me an answer; but it arrived a thorough one, in the shape of a box of books, each bristling with paper marks, many of them inscribed with some fact concerning, or criticism upon, the hymn indicated. He wrote that he quite agreed with my notion of the right mode of serving her; for any other would be as if a besieging party were to batter a postern by means of boats instead of walking over a lowered drawbridge, and under a raised portcullis.

Having taken a survey of the hymns my father thus pointed out to me, and arranged them according to their degrees of approximation to the weakest of those in Mrs. Cromwell's collection, I judged that in all of them there was something she must appreciate, although the main drift of several would be entirely beyond her apprehension. Even these, however, it would be well to try upon her.

Accordingly, the next time she asked me to read from her collection, I made the request that she would listen to some which I believed she did not know, but would, I thought, like. She consented with eagerness, was astonished to find she knew none of them, expressed much approbation of some, and showed herself delighted with others.

That she must have had some literary faculty seems evident from the genuine pleasure she took in simple, quaint, sometimes even odd hymns of her own peculiar kind. But the very best of another sort she could not appreciate. For instance, the following, by John Mason, in my father's opinion one of the best hymn-writers, had no attraction for her: —

"Thou wast, O God, and thou was blest
   Before the world begun;
Of thine eternity possest
   Before time's glass did run.
Thou needest none thy praise to sing,
   As if thy joy could fade:
Couldst thou have needed any thing,
   Thou couldst have nothing made.

"Great and good God, it pleaseth thee
   Thy Godhead to declare;
And what thy goodness did decree,
   Thy greatness did prepare:
Thou spak'st, and heaven and earth appeared,
   And answered to thy call;
As if their Maker's voice they Heard,
   Which is the creature's All.

"Thou spak'st the word, most mighty Lord;
   Thy word went forth with speed:
Thy will, O Lord, it was thy word;
   Thy word it was thy deed.
Thou brought'st forth Adam from the ground,
   And Eve out of his side:
Thy blessing made the earth abound
   With these two multiplied.

"Those three great leaves, heaven, sea, and land,
   Thy name in figures show;
Brutes feel the bounty of thy hand,
   But I my Maker know.
Should not I here thy servant be,
   Whose creatures serve me here?
My Lord, whom should I fear but thee,
   Who am thy creatures' fear?

"To whom, Lord, should I sing but thee,
   The Maker of my tongue?
Lo! other lords would seize on me,
   But I to thee belong.
As waters haste unto their sea,
   And earth unto its earth,
So let my soul return to thee,
   From whom it had its birth.

> "But, ah! I'm fallen in the night,
>   And cannot come to thee:
> Yet speak the word, '*Let there be light;*'
>   It shall enlighten me.
> And let thy word, most mighty Lord,
>   Thy fallen creature raise:
> Oh! make me o'er again, and I
>   Shall sing my Maker's praise."

This and others, I say, she could not relish; but my endeavors were crowned with success in so far that she accepted better specimens of the sort she liked than any she had; and I think they must have had a good influence upon her.

She seemed to have no fear of death, contemplating the change she believed at hand, not with equanimity merely, but with expectation. She even wrote hymns about it, —sweet, pretty, and weak, always with herself and the love of her Saviour for *her*, in the foreground. She had not learned that the love which lays hold of that which is human in the individual, that is, which is common to the whole race, must be an infinitely deeper, tenderer, and more precious thing to the individual than any affection manifesting itself in the preference of one over another.

For the sake of revealing her modes of thought, I will give one more specimen of my conversations with her, ere I pass on. It took place the evening before her departure for her own house. Her husband had gone to make some final preparations, of which there had been many. For one who expected to be unclothed that she might be clothed upon, she certainly made a tolerable to-do about the garment she was so soon to lay aside; especially seeing she often spoke of it as an ill-fitting garment-never with peevishness or complaint, only, as it seemed to me, with far more interest than it was worth. She had even, as afterwards appeared, given her husband-good, honest, dog-like man-full instructions as to the ceremonial of its interment. Perhaps I should have been considerably less bewildered with her conduct had I suspected that she was not half so near death as she chose to think, and that she had as yet suffered little.

That evening, the stars just beginning to glimmer through the warm flush that lingered from the sunset, we sat together in the drawing-room looking out on the sea. My patient appearing, from the light in her eyes, about to go off into one of her ecstatic moods, I hastened to forestall it, if I might, with whatever came uppermost; for I felt my inability to sympathize with her in these more of a pain than my reader will, perhaps, readily imagine.

"It seems like turning you out to let you go to-morrow, Mrs. Cromwell," I said; "but, you see, our three months are up two days after, and I cannot help it."

"You have been very kind," she said, half abstractedly. "And you are really much better. Who would have thought three weeks ago to see you so well to-day?"

"Ah! you congratulate me, do you?" she rejoined, turning her big eyes full upon me; "congratulate me that I am doomed to be still a captive in the prison of this vile body? Is it kind? Is it well?"

"At least, you must remember, if you are *doomed*, who dooms you."

"'Oh that I had the wings of a dove!'" she cried, avoiding my remark, of which I doubt if she saw the drift. "Think, dear Mrs. Percivale: the society of saints and angels! —all brightness and harmony and peace! Is it not worth forsaking this world to inherit a kingdom like that? Wouldn't *you* like to go? Don't *you* wish to fly away and be at rest?"

She spoke as if expostulating and reasoning with one she would persuade to some kind of holy emigration.

"Not until I am sent for," I answered.

"I *am* sent for," she returned.

> "'The wave may be cold, and the tide may be strong;
>   But, hark! on the shore the angels' glad song!'

"Do you know that sweet hymn, Mrs. Percivale? There I shall be able to love him aright, to serve him aright!

> "'Here all my labor is so poor!
> Here all my love so faint!
> But when I reach the heavenly door,
> I cease the weary plaint.'"

I couldn't help wishing she would cease it a little sooner.

"But suppose," I ventured to say, "it were the will of God that you should live many years yet."

"That cannot be. And why should you wish it for me? Is it not better to depart and be with him? What pleasure could it be to a weak, worn creature like me to go on living in this isle of banishment?"

"But suppose you were to recover your health: would it not be delightful to *do* something for his sake? If you would think of how much there is to be done in the world, perhaps you would wish less to die and leave it."

"Do not tempt me," she returned reproachfully.

And then she quoted a passage the application of which to her own case appeared to me so irreverent, that I confess I felt like Abraham with the idolater; so far at least as to wish her out of the house, for I could bear with her, I thought, no longer.

She did leave it the next day, and I breathed more freely than since she had entered it.

My husband came down to fetch me the following day; and a walk with him along the cliffs in the gathering twilight, during which I recounted the affectations of my late visitor, completely wiped the cobwebs from my mental windows, and enabled me to come to the conclusion that Mrs. Cromwell was but a spoiled child, who would, somehow or other, be brought to her senses before all was over. I was ashamed of my impatience with her, and believed if I could have learned her history, of which she had told me nothing, it would have explained the rare phenomenon of one apparently able to look death in the face with so little of the really spiritual to support her, for she seemed to me to know Christ only after the flesh. But had she indeed ever looked death in the face?

CHAPTER XXXVIII
MRS. CROMWELL GOES.

I heard nothing more of her for about a year. A note or two passed between us, and then all communication ceased. This, I am happy to think, was not immediately my fault: not that it mattered much, for we were not then fitted for much communion; we had too little in common to commune.

"Did you not both believe in one Lord?" I fancy a reader objecting. "How, then, can you say you had too little in common to be able to commune?"

I said the same to myself, and tried the question in many ways. The fact remained, that we could not commune, that is, with any heartiness; and, although I may have done her wrong, it was, I thought, to be accounted for something in this way. The Saviour of whom she spoke so often, and evidently thought so much, was in a great measure a being of her own fancy; so much so, that she manifested no desire to find out what the Christ was who had spent three and thirty years in making a revelation of himself to the world. The knowledge she had about him was not even at second-hand, but at many removes. She did not study his words or his actions to learn his thoughts or his meanings; but lived in a kind of dreamland of her own, which could be interesting only to the dreamer. Now, if we are to come to God through Christ, it must surely be by knowing Christ; it must be through the knowledge of Christ that the Spirit of the Father mainly works in the members of his body; and it seemed to me she did not take the trouble to "know him and the power of his resurrection." Therefore we had scarcely enough of common ground, as I say, to meet upon. I could not help contrasting her religion with that of Marion Clare.

At length I had a note from her, begging me to go and see her at her house at Richmond, and apologizing for her not coming to me, on the score of her health. I felt it my duty to go, but sadly grudged the loss of time it seemed, for I expected neither pleasure nor profit from the visit. Percivale went with me, and left me at the door to have a row on the river, and call for me at a certain hour.

The house and grounds were luxurious and lovely both, two often dissociated qualities. She could have nothing to desire of this world's gifts, I thought. But the moment she entered the room into which I had been shown, I was shocked at the change I saw in her. Almost to my horror, she was in a widow's cap; and disease and coming death were plain on every feature. Such was the contrast, that the face in my memory appeared that of health.

"My dear Mrs. Cromwell!" I gasped out.

"You see," she said, and sitting down, on a straight-backed chair, looked at me with lustreless eyes.

Death had been hovering about her windows before, but had entered at last; not to take the sickly young woman longing to die, but the hale man, who would have clung to the last edge of life.

"He is taken, and I am left," she said abruptly, after a long pause.

Her drawl had vanished: pain and grief had made her simple. "Then," I thought with myself, "she did love him!" But I could say nothing. She took my silence for the sympathy it was, and smiled a heart-rending smile, so different from that little sad smile she used to have; really pathetic now, and with hardly a glimmer in it of the old self-pity. I rose, put my arms about her, and kissed her on the forehead; she laid her head on my shoulder, and wept.

"Whom the Lord loveth he chasteneth," I faltered out, for her sorrow filled me with a respect that was new.

"Yes," she returned, as gently as hopelessly; "and whom he does not love as well."

"You have no ground for saying so," I answered. "The apostle does not."

"My lamp is gone out," she said; "gone out in darkness, utter darkness. You warned me, and I did not heed the warning. I thought I knew better, but I was full of self-conceit. And now I am wandering where there is no way and no light. My iniquities have found me out."

I did not say what I thought I saw plain enough, —that her lamp was just beginning to burn. Neither did I try to persuade her that her iniquities were small.

"But the Bridegroom," I said, "is not yet come. There is time to go and get some oil."

"Where am I to get it?" she returned, in a tone of despair.

"From the Bridegroom himself," I said.

"No," she answered. "I have talked and talked and talked, and you know he says he abhors talkers. I am one of those to whom he will say 'I know you not.'"

"And you will answer him that you have eaten and drunk in his presence, and cast out devils, and —?"

"No, no: I will say he is right; that it is all my own fault; that I thought I was something when I was nothing, but that I know better now."

A dreadful fit of coughing interrupted her. As soon as it was over, I said, —

"And what will the Lord say to you, do you think, when you have said so to him?"

"Depart from me," she answered in a hollow, forced voice.

"No," I returned. "He will say, 'I know you well. You have told me the truth. Come in.'"

"*Do* you think so?" she cried. "You never used to think well of me."

"Those who were turned away," I said, avoiding her last words, "were trying to make themselves out better than they were: they trusted, not in the love of Christ, but in what they thought their worth and social standing. Perhaps, if their deeds had been as good as they thought them, they would have known better than to trust in them. If they had told him the truth; if they had said, 'Lord, we are workers of iniquity; Lord, we used to be hypocrites, but we speak the truth now: forgive us,' —do you think he would then have turned them away? No, surely. If your lamp has gone out, make haste and tell him how careless you have been; tell him all, and pray him for oil and light; and see whether your lamp will not straightway glimmer, —glimmer first and then glow."

"Ah, Mrs. Percivale!" she cried: "I would *do* something for His sake now if I might, but I cannot. If I had but resisted the disease in me for the sake of serving him, I might have been able now: but my chance is over; I cannot now; I have too much pain. And death looks such a different thing now! I used to think of it only as a kind of going to sleep, easy though sad-sad, I mean, in the eyes of mourning friends. But, alas! I have no friends, now that my husband is gone. I never dreamed of him going first. He loved me: indeed he did, though you will hardly believe it; but I always took it as a matter of course. I never saw how beautiful and unselfish he was till he was gone. I have been selfish and stupid and dull, and my sins have found me out. A great darkness has fallen upon me; and although weary of life, instead of longing for death, I shrink from it with horror. My cough will not let me sleep: there is nothing but weariness in my body, and despair in my heart. Oh how black and dreary the nights are! I think of the time in your house as of an earthly paradise. But where is the heavenly paradise I used to dream of then?" "Would it content you," I asked, "to be able to dream of it again?"

"No, no. I want something very different now. Those fancies look so uninteresting and stupid now! All I want now is to hear God say, 'I forgive you.' And my husband —I must have troubled him sorely. You don't know how good he was, Mrs. Percivale. *He* made no pretences like silly me. Do you know," she went on, lowering her voice, and speaking with something like horror in its tone, "Do you know, I cannot *bear* hymns!"

As she said it, she looked up in my face half-terrified with the anticipation of the horror she expected to see manifested there. I could not help smiling. The case was not one for argument of any kind: I thought for a moment, then merely repeated the verse, —

> "When the law threatens endless death,
> Upon the awful hill,
> Straightway, from her consuming breath,
> My soul goes higher still, —
> Goeth to Jesus, wounded, slain,
> And maketh him her home,

> Whence she will not go out again,
> And where Death cannot come."

"Ah! that is good," she said: "if only I could get to him! But I cannot get to him. He is so far off! He seems to be-nowhere."

I think she was going to say *nobody*, but changed the word.

"If you felt for a moment how helpless and wretched I feel, especially in the early morning," she went on; "how there seems nothing to look for, and no help to be had, —you would pity rather than blame me, though I know I deserve blame. I feel as if all the heart and soul and strength and mind, with which we are told to love God, had gone out of me; or, rather, as if I had never had any. I doubt if I ever had. I tried very hard for a long time to get a sight of Jesus, to feel myself in his presence; but it was of no use, and I have quite given it up now."

I made her lie on the sofa, and sat down beside her.

"Do you think," I said, "that any one, before he came, could have imagined such a visitor to the world as Jesus Christ?"

"I suppose not," she answered listlessly.

"Then, no more can you come near him now by trying to imagine him. You cannot represent to yourself the reality, the Being who can comfort you. In other words, you cannot take him into your heart. He only knows himself, and he only can reveal himself to you. And not until he does so, can you find any certainty or any peace."

"But he doesn't —he won't reveal himself to me."

"Suppose you had forgotten what some friend of your childhood was like-say, if it were possible, your own mother; suppose you could not recall a feature of her face, or the color of her eyes; and suppose, that, while you were very miserable about it, you remembered all at once that you had a portrait of her in an old desk you had not opened for years: what would you do?"

"Go and get it," she answered like a child at the Sunday school.

"Then why shouldn't you do so now? You have such a portrait of Jesus, far truer and more complete than any other kind of portrait can be, —the portrait his own deeds and words give us of him."

"I see what you mean; but that is all about long ago, and I want him now. That is in a book, and I want him in my heart."

"How are you to get him into your heart? How could you have him there, except by knowing him? But perhaps you think you do know him?"

"I am certain I do not know him; at least, as I want to know him," she said.

"No doubt," I went on, "he can speak to your heart without the record, and, I think, is speaking to you now in this very want of him you feel. But how could he show himself to you otherwise than by helping you to understand the revelation of himself which it cost him such labor to afford? If the story were millions of years old, so long as it was true, it would be all the same as if it had been ended only yesterday; for, being what he represented himself, he never can change. To know what he was then, is to know what he is now."

"But, if I knew him so, that wouldn't be to have him with me."

"No; but in that knowledge he might come to you. It is by the door of that knowledge that his Spirit, which is himself, comes into the soul. You would at least be more able to pray to him: you would know what kind of a being you had to cry to. *You* would thus come nearer to him; and no one ever drew nigh to him to whom he did not also draw nigh. If you would but read the story as if you had never read it before, as if you were reading the history of a man you heard of for the first time"—

"Surely you're not a Unitarian, Mrs. Percivale!" she said, half lifting her head, and looking at me with a dim terror in her pale eyes.

"God forbid!" I answered. "But I would that many who think they know better believed in him half as much as many Unitarians do. It is only by understanding and believing in that humanity of his, which in such pain and labor manifested his Godhead, that we can come to know it,—know that Godhead, I mean, in virtue of which alone he was a true and perfect man; that Godhead which alone can satisfy with peace and hope the poorest human soul, for it also is the offspring of God."

I ceased, and for some moments she sat silent. Then she said feebly,—

"There's a Bible somewhere in the room."

I found it, and read the story of the woman who came behind him in terror, and touched the hem of his garment. I could hardly read it for the emotion it caused in myself; and when I ceased I saw her weeping silently.

A servant entered with the message that Mr. Percivale had called for me.

"I cannot see him to-day," she sobbed.

"Of course not," I replied. "I must leave you now; but I will come again,—come often if you like."

"You are as kind as ever!" she returned, with a fresh burst of tears. "Will you come and be with me when-when—?"

She could not finish for sobs.

"I will," I said, knowing well what she meant.

This is how I imagined the change to have come about: what had seemed her faith had been, in a great measure, but her hope and imagination, occupying themselves with the forms of the religion towards which all that was highest in her nature dimly urged. The two characteristics of amicability and selfishness, not unfrequently combined, rendered it easy for her to deceive herself, or rather conspired to prevent her from undeceiving herself, as to the quality and worth of her religion. For, if she had been other than amiable, the misery following the outbreaks of temper which would have been of certain occurrence in the state of her health, would have made her aware in some degree of her moral condition; and, if her thoughts had not been centred upon herself, she would, in her care for others, have learned her own helplessness; and the devotion of her good husband, not then accepted merely as a natural homage to her worth, would have shown itself as a love beyond her deserts, and would have roused the longing to be worthy of it. She saw now that he must have imagined her far better than she was: but she had not meant to deceive him; she had but followed the impulses of a bright, shallow nature.

But that last epithet bids me pause, and remember that my father has taught me, and that I have found the lesson true, that there is no such thing as a shallow nature: every nature is infinitely deep, for the works of God are everlasting. Also, there is no nature that is not shallow to what it must become. I suspect every nature must have the subsoil ploughing of sorrow, before it can recognize either its present poverty or its possible wealth.

When her husband died, suddenly, of apoplexy, she was stunned for a time, gradually awaking to a miserable sense of unprotected loneliness, so much the more painful for her weakly condition, and the overcare to which she had been accustomed. She was an only child, and had become an orphan within a year or two after her early marriage. Left thus without shelter, like a delicate plant whose house of glass has been shattered, she speedily recognized her true condition. With no one to heed her whims, and no one capable of sympathizing with the genuine misery which supervened, her disease gathered strength rapidly, her lamp went out, and she saw no light beyond; for the smoke of that lamp had dimmed the windows at which the stars would have looked in. When life became dreary, her fancies, despoiled of the halo they had cast on the fogs of selfish comfort, ceased to interest her; and the future grew a vague darkness, an uncertainty teeming with questions to which she had no answer. Henceforth she was conscious of life only as a weakness, as the want of a deeper life to hold it up. Existence had become a during faint, and self hateful. She saw that she was poor and miserable and blind and naked,—that she had never had faith fit to support her.

But out of this darkness dawned at least a twilight, so gradual, so slow, that I cannot tell when or how the darkness began to melt. She became aware of a deeper and simpler need than hitherto she had known,—the need of life in herself, the life of the Son of God. I went to see her often. At the time when I began this history, I was going every other day, —sometimes oftener, for her end seemed to be drawing nigh. Her weakness had greatly increased: she could but just walk across the room, and was constantly restless. She had no great continuous pain, but oft-returning sharp fits of it. She looked genuinely sad, and her spirits never recovered themselves. She seldom looked out of the window; the daylight seemed to distress her: flowers were the only links between her and the outer world, —wild ones, for the scent of greenhouse-flowers, and even that of most garden ones, she could not bear. She had been very fond of music, but could no longer endure her piano: every note seemed struck on a nerve. But she was generally quiet in her mind, and often peaceful. The more her body decayed about her, the more her spirit seemed to come alive. It was the calm of a gray evening, not so lovely as a golden sunset or a silvery moonlight, but more sweet than either. She talked little of her feelings, but evidently longed after the words of our Lord. As she listened to some of them, I could see the eyes which had now grown dim with suffering, gleam with the light of holy longing and humble adoration.

For some time she often referred to her coming departure, and confessed that she "feared death; not so much what might be on the other side, as the dark way itself, —the struggle, the torture, the fainting; but by degrees her allusions to it became rarer, and at length ceased almost entirely. Once I said to her, —

"Are you afraid of death still, Eleanor?"

"No-not much," she replied, after a brief pause. "He may do with me whatever He likes."

Knowing so well what Marion could do to comfort and support, and therefore desirous of bringing them together, I took her one day with me. But certain that the thought of seeing a stranger would render my poor Eleanor uneasy, and that what discomposure a sudden introduction might cause would speedily vanish in Marion's presence, I did not tell her what I was going to do. Nor in this did I mistake. Before we left, it was plain that Marion had a far more soothing influence upon her than I had myself. She looked eagerly for her next visit, and my mind was now more at peace concerning her.

One evening, after listening to some stories from Marion about her friends, Mrs. Cromwell said, —

"Ah, Miss Clare! to think I might have done something for *Him* by doing it for *them!* Alas! I have led a useless life, and am dying out of this world without having borne any fruit! Ah, me, me!"

"You are doing a good deal for him now," said Marion, "and hard work too!" she added; "harder far than mine."

"I am only dying," she returned-so sadly!

"You are enduring chastisement," said Marion. "The Lord gives one one thing to do, and another another. We have no right to wish for other work than he gives us. It is rebellious and unchildlike, whatever it may seem. Neither have we any right to wish to be better in *our* way: we must wish to be better in *his*."

"But I *should* like to do something for *him*; bearing is only for myself. Surely I may wish that?"

"No: you may not. Bearing is not only for yourself. You are quite wrong in thinking you do nothing for him in enduring," returned Marion, with that abrupt decision of hers which seemed to some like rudeness. "What is the will of God? Is it not your sanctification? And why did he make the Captain of our salvation perfect through suffering? Was it not that he might in like manner bring many sons into glory? Then, if you are enduring, you are working with God, —for the perfection through suffering of one more: you are working for God in yourself, that the will of God may be done in you; that he may have his very own way with you. It is the only work he requires of you now: do it not only willingly, then, but contentedly. To make people good is all his labor: be good, and you are a fellow-worker with God in the highest region of labor. He does not want you for other people —*yet*."

At the emphasis Marion laid on the last word, Mrs. Cromwell glanced sharply up. A light broke over her face: she had understood, and with a smile was silent.

One evening, when we were both with her, it had grown very sultry and breathless.

"Isn't it very close, dear Mrs. Percivale?" she said.

I rose to get a fan; and Marion, leaving the window as if moved by a sudden resolve, went and opened the piano. Mrs. Cromwell made a hasty motion, as if she must prevent her. But, such was my faith in my friend's soul as well as heart, in her divine taste as well as her human faculty, that I ventured to lay my hand on Mrs. Cromwell's. It was enough for sweetness like hers: she yielded instantly, and lay still, evidently nerving herself to suffer. But the first movement stole so "soft and soullike" on her ear, trembling as it were on the border-land between sound and silence, that she missed the pain she expected, and found only the pleasure she looked not for. Marion's hands made the instrument sigh and sing, not merely as with a human voice, but as with a human soul. Her own voice next evolved itself from the dim uncertainty, in sweet proportions and delicate modulations, stealing its way into the heart, to set first one chord, then another, vibrating, until the whole soul was filled with responses. If I add that her articulation was as nearly perfect as the act of singing will permit, my reader may well believe that a song of hers would do what a song might.

Where she got the song she then sung, she always avoids telling me. I had told her all I knew and understood concerning Mrs. Cromwell, and have my suspicions. This is the song: —

"I fancy I hear a whisper
As of leaves in a gentle air:
Is it wrong, I wonder, to fancy
It may be the tree up there? —
The tree that heals the nations,
Growing amidst the street,
And dropping, for who will gather,
Its apples at their feet?

"I fancy I hear a rushing
As of waters down a slope:
Is it wrong, I wonder, to fancy
It may be the river of hope?
The river of crystal waters
That flows from the very throne,
And runs through the street of the city
With a softly jubilant tone?

"I fancy a twilight round me,
And a wandering of the breeze,
With a hush in that high city,
And a going in the trees.
But I know there will be no night there, —
No coming and going day;
For the holy face of the Father
Will be perfect light alway.

"I could do without the darkness,
   And better without the sun;
But, oh, I should like a twilight
   After the day was done!
Would he lay his hand on his forehead,
   On his hair as white as wool,
And shine one hour through his fingers,
   Till the shadow had made me cool?

"But the thought is very foolish:
   If that face I did but see,
All else would be all forgotten, —
   River and twilight and tree;
I should seek, I should care, for nothing,
   Beholding his countenance;
And fear only to lose one glimmer
   By one single sideway glance.

"'Tis but again a foolish fancy
   To picture the countenance so.
Which is shining in all our spirits,
   Making them white as snow.
Come to me, shine in me, Master,
   And I care not for river or tree, —
Care for no sorrow or crying,
   If only thou shine in me.

"I would lie on my bed for ages,
   Looking out on the dusty street,
Where whisper nor leaves nor waters,
   Nor any thing cool and sweet;
At my heart this ghastly fainting,
   And this burning in my blood, —
If only I knew thou wast with me, —
   Wast with me and making me good."

When she rose from the piano, Mrs. Cromwell stretched out her hand for hers, and held it some time, unable to speak. Then she said, —
   "That has done me good, I hope. I will try to be more patient, for I think He *is* teaching me."
   She died, at length, in my arms. I cannot linger over that last time. She suffered a good deal, but dying people are generally patient. She went without a struggle. The last words I heard her utter were, "Yes, Lord;" after which she breathed but once. A half-smile came over her face, which froze upon it, and remained, until the coffin-lid covered it. But I shall see it, I trust, a whole smile some day.

CHAPTER XXXIX
ANCESTRAL WISDOM.

I did think of having a chapter about children before finishing my book; but this is not going to be the kind of chapter I thought of. Like most mothers, I suppose, I think myself an authority on the subject; and, which is to me more assuring than any judgment of my own, my father says that I have been in a measure successful in bringing mine up, —only they're not brought up very far yet. Hence arose the temptation to lay down a few practical rules I had proved and found answer. But, as soon as I began to contemplate the writing of them down, I began to imagine So-and-so and So-and-so attempting to carry them out, and saw what a dreadful muddle they would make of it, and what mischief would thence lie at my door. Only one thing can be worse than the attempt to carry out rules whose principles are not understood; and that is the neglect of those which are understood, and seen to be right. Suppose, for instance, I were to say that corporal punishment was wholesome, involving less suffering than most other punishments, more effectual in the result, and leaving no sting or sense of unkindness; whereas mental punishment, considered by many to be more refined, and therefore less degrading, was often cruel to a sensitive child, and deadening to a stubborn one: suppose I said this, and a woman like my Aunt Millicent were to take it up: *her* whippings would have no more effect than if her rod were made of butterflies' feathers; they would be a mockery to her children, and bring law into contempt; while if a certain father I know were to be convinced by my arguments, he would fill his children with terror of him now, and with hatred afterwards. Of the last-mentioned result of severity, I know at least one instance. At present, the father to whom I refer disapproves of whipping even a man who has been dancing on his wife with hob-nailed shoes, because it would tend to brutalize him. But he taunts and stings, and confines in solitude for lengthened periods, high-spirited boys, and that for faults which I should consider very venial.

Then, again, if I were to lay down the rule that we must be as tender of the feelings of our children as if they were angel-babies who had to learn, alas! to understand our rough ways, how would that be taken by a certain French couple I know, who, not appearing until after the dinner to which they had accepted an invitation was over, gave as the reason, that it had been quite out of their power; for darling Désirée, their only child, had declared they shouldn't go, and that she would cry if they did; nay, went so far as to insist on their going to bed, which they were, however reluctant, compelled to do. They had actually undressed, and pretended to retire for the night; but, as soon as she was safely asleep, rose and joined their friends, calm in the consciousness of abundant excuse.

The marvel to me is that so many children turn out so well.

After all, I think there can be no harm in mentioning a few general principles laid down by my father. They are such as to commend themselves most to the most practical.

And first for a few negative ones.

1. Never *give in* to disobedience; and never threaten what you are not prepared to carry out.

2. Never lose your temper. I do not say *never be angry*. Anger is sometimes indispensable, especially where there has been any thing mean, dishonest, or cruel. But anger is very different from loss of temper. [Footnote: My Aunt Millicent is always saying, "I am grieeeved with you." But the announcement begets no sign of responsive grief on the face of the stolid child before her. She never whipped a child in her life. If she had, and it had but roused some positive anger in the child, instead of that undertone of complaint which is always oozing out of every one of them, I think It would have been a gain. But the poor lady is one of the whiny-piny people, and must be in preparation for a development of which I have no prevision. The only stroke of originality I thought I knew of her was this; to the register of her children's births, baptisms, and confirmations, entered on a grandly-ornamented fly-leaf of the family Bible, she has subjoined the record of every disease each has had, with the year, month, and day (and in one case the hour), when each distemper made its appearance. After most of the main entries, you may read, "*Cut his* (or her) *first tooth*" —at such a date. But, alas for the originality! she

has just told me that her maternal grandmother did the same. How strange that she and my father should have had the same father! If they had had the same mother, too, I should have been utterly bewildered.]

3. Of all things, never sneer at them; and be careful, even, how you rally them.

4. Do not try to work on their feelings. Feelings are far too delicate things to be used for tools. It is like taking the mainspring out of your watch, and notching it for a saw. It may be a wonderful saw, but how fares your watch? Especially avoid doing so in connection with religious things, for so you will assuredly deaden them to all that is finest. Let your feelings, not your efforts on theirs, affect them with a sympathy the more powerful that it is not forced upon them; and, in order to do this, avoid being too English in the hiding of your feelings. A man's own family has a right to share in his *good* feelings.

5. Never show that you doubt, except you are able to convict. To doubt an honest child is to do what you can to make a liar of him; and to believe a liar, if he is not altogether shameless, is to shame him.

The common-minded masters in schools, who, unlike the ideal Arnold, are in the habit of *disbelieving* boys, have a large share in making the liars they so often are. Certainly the vileness of a lie is not the same in one who knows that whatever he says will be regarded with suspicion; and the master, who does not know an honest boy after he has been some time in his class, gives good reason for doubting whether he be himself an honest man, and incapable of the lying he is ready to attribute to all alike.

This last is my own remark, not my father's. I have an honest boy at school, and I know how he fares. I say honest; for though, as a mother, I can hardly expect to be believed, I have ground for believing that he would rather die than lie. I know *I* would rather he died than lied.

6. Instil no religious doctrine apart from its duty. If it have no duty as its necessary embodiment, the doctrine may well be regarded as doubtful.

7. Do not be hard on mere quarrelling, which, like a storm in nature, is often helpful in clearing the moral atmosphere. Stop it by a judgment between the parties. But be severe as to the *kind* of quarrelling, and the temper shown in it. Especially give no quarter to any unfairness arising from greed or spite. Use your strongest language with regard to that.

Now for a few of my father's positive rules:

1. Always let them come to you, and always hear what they have to say. If they bring a complaint, always examine into it, and dispense pure justice, and nothing but justice.

2. Cultivate a love of *giving* fair-play. Every one, of course, likes to *receive* fair-play; but no one ought to be left to imagine, therefore, that he *loves fair-play*.

3. Teach from the very first, from the infancy capable of sucking a sugar-plum, to share with neighbors. Never refuse the offering a child brings you, except you have a good reason,—and *give* it. And never *pretend* to partake: that involves hideous possibilities in its effects on the child.

The necessity of giving a reason for refusing a kindness has no relation to what is supposed by some to be the necessity of giving a reason with every command. There is no such necessity. Of course there ought to be a reason in every command. That it *may* be desirable, sometimes, to explain it, is all my father would allow.

4. Allow a great deal of noise,—as much as is fairly endurable; but, the moment they seem getting beyond their own control, stop the noise at once. Also put a stop at once to all fretting and grumbling.

5. Favor the development of each in the direction of his own bent. Help him to develop himself, but do not *push* development. To do so is most dangerous.

6. Mind the moral nature, and it will take care of the intellectual. In other words, the best thing for the intellect is the cultivation of the conscience, not in casuistry, but in conduct. It may take longer to arrive; but the end will be the highest possible health, vigor, and ratio of progress.

7. Discourage emulation, and insist on duty,—not often, but strongly.

Having written these out, chiefly from notes I had made of a long talk with my father, I gave them to Percivale to read.

"Rather-ponderous, don't you think, for weaving into a narrative?" was his remark.

"My narrative is full of things far from light," I returned. "I didn't say they were heavy, you know. That is quite another thing."

"I am afraid you mean generally uninteresting. But there are parents who might make them useful, and the rest of my readers could skip them."

"I only mean that a narrative, be it ever so serious, must not intrench on the moral essay or sermon."

"It is much too late, I fear, to tell me that. But, please, remember I am not giving the precepts as of my own discovery, though I *have* sought to verify them by practice, but as what they are,—my father's."

He did not seem to see the bearing of the argument.

"I want my book to be useful," I said. "As a mother, I want to share the help I have had myself with other mothers."

"I am only speaking from the point of art," he returned.

"And that's a point I have never thought of; any farther, at least, than writing as good English as I might."

"Do you mean to say you have never thought of the shape of the book your monthly papers would make?"

"Yes. I don't think I have. Scarcely at all, I believe."

"Then you ought."

"But I know nothing about that kind of thing. I haven't an idea in my head concerning the art of book-making. And it is too late, so far at least as this book is concerned, to begin to study it now."

"I wonder how my pictures would get on in that way."

"You can see how my book has got on. Well or ill, there it all but is. I had to do with facts, and not with art."

"But even a biography, in the ordering of its parts, in the arrangement of its light and shade, and in the harmony of the"—

"It's too late, I tell you, husband. The book is all but done. Besides, one who would write a biography after the fashion of a picture would probably, even without attributing a single virtue that was not present, or suppressing a single fault that was, yet produce a false book. The principle I have followed has been to try from the first to put as much value, that is, as much truth, as I could, into my story. Perhaps, instead of those maxims of my father's for the education of children, you would have preferred such specimens of your own children's sermons as you made me read to you for the twentieth time yesterday?"

Instead of smiling with his own quiet kind smile, as he worked on at his picture of St. Athanasius with "no friend but God and Death," he burst into a merry laugh, and said, —

"A capital idea! If you give those, word for word, I shall yield the precepts."

"Are you out of your five wits, husband?" I exclaimed. "Would you have everybody take me for the latest incarnation of the oldest insanity in the world,—that of maternity? But I am really an idiot, for you could never have meant it!"

"I do most soberly and distinctly mean it. They would amuse your readers very much, and, without offending those who may prefer your father's maxims to your children's sermons, would incline those who might otherwise vote the former a bore, to regard them with the clemency resulting from amusement."

"But I desire no such exercise of clemency. The precepts are admirable; and those need not take them who do not like them."

"So the others can skip the sermons; but I am sure they will give a few mothers, at least, a little amusement. They will prove besides, that you follow your own rule of putting a very small quantity of sage into the stuffing of your goslings; as also that you have succeeded in making them capable of manifesting what nonsense is indigenous in them. I think them very funny; that may be paternal prejudice: *you* think them very silly as well; that may be maternal solicitude. I suspect, that, the more of a philosopher any one of your readers is, the more suggestive will he find these genuine utterances of an age at which the means of expression so much exceed the matter to be expressed."

The idea began to look not altogether so absurd as at first; and a little more argument sufficed to make me resolve to put the absurdities themselves to the test of passing leisurely through my brain while I copied them out, possibly for the press.

The result is, that I am going to risk printing them, determined, should I find afterwards that I have made a blunder, to throw the whole blame upon my husband.

What still makes me shrink the most is the recollection of how often I have condemned, as too silly to repeat, things which reporting mothers evidently regarded as proofs of a stupendous intellect. But the folly of these constitutes the chief part of their merit; and I do not see how I can be mistaken for supposing them clever, except it be in regard of a glimmer of purpose now and then, and the occasional manifestation of the cunning of the stump orator, with his subterfuges to conceal his embarrassment when he finds his oil failing him, and his lamp burning low.

CHAPTER XL
CHILD NONSENSE.

One word of introductory explanation.

During my husband's illness, Marion came often, but, until he began to recover, would generally spend with the children the whole of the time she had to spare, not even permitting me to know that she was in the house. It was a great thing for them; for, although they were well enough cared for, they were necessarily left to themselves a good deal more than hitherto. Hence, perhaps, it came that they betook themselves to an amusement not uncommon with children, of which I had as yet seen nothing amongst them.

One evening, when my husband had made a little progress towards recovery, Marion came to sit with me in his room for an hour.

"I've brought you something I want to read to you," she said, "if you think Mr. Percivale can bear it."

I told her I believed he could, and she proceeded to explain what it was.

"One morning, when I went into the nursery, I found the children playing at church, or rather at preaching; for, except a few minutes of singing, the preaching occupied the whole time. There were two clergymen, Ernest and Charles, alternately incumbent and curate. The chief duty of the curate for the time being was to lend his aid to the rescue of his incumbent from any difficulty in which the extemporaneous character of his discourse might land him."

I interrupt Marion to mention that the respective ages of Ernest and Charles were then eight and six.

"The pulpit," she continued, "was on the top of the cupboard under the cuckoo-clock, and consisted of a chair and a cushion. There were prayer-books in abundance; of which neither of them, I am happy to say, made other than a pretended use for reference. Charles, indeed, who was preaching when I entered, *can't* read; but both have far too much reverence to use sacred words in their games, as the sermons themselves will instance. I took down almost every word they said, frequent embarrassments and interruptions enabling me to do so. Ernest was acting as clerk, and occasionally prompted the speaker when his eloquence failed him, or reproved members of the congregation, which consisted of the two nurses and the other children, who were inattentive. Charles spoke with a good deal of *unction*, and had quite a professional air when he looked down on the big open book, referred to one or other of the smaller ones at his side, or directed looks of reprehension at this or that hearer. You would have thought he had cultivated the imitation of popular preachers, whereas he tells me he has been to church only three times. I am sorry I cannot give the opening remarks, for I lost them by being late; but what I did hear was this."

She then read from her paper as follows, and lent it me afterwards. I merely copy it.

"Once" (*Charles was proceeding when Marion entered*), "there lived an aged man, and another who was a *very* aged man; and the very aged man was going to die, and every one but the aged man thought the other, the *very* aged man, wouldn't die. I do this to *explain* it to you. He, the man who was *really* going to die, was —I will look in the dictionary" (*He looks in the book, and gives out with much confidence*), "was two thousand and eighty-eight years old. Well, the other man was-well, then, the other man 'at knew he was going to die, was about four thousand and two; not nearly so old, you see." (*Here Charles whispers with Ernest, and then announces very loud*), —"This is out of St. James. The *very* aged man had a wife and no children; and the other had no wife, but a *great many* children. The fact was —this was how it was-the wife *died*, and so *he* had the children. Well, the man I spoke of first, well, he died in the middle of the night." (*A look as much as to say, "There! what do you think of that?"*); "an' nobody but the aged man knew he was going to die. Well, in the morning, when his wife got up, she spoke to him, and he was dead!" (*A pause.*) "Perfectly, sure enough —dead!" (*Then, with a change of voice and manner*), "He wasn't really dead, because you know" (*abruptly and nervously*) —"Shut the door! —you know where he went, because in the morning next day" (*He pauses and looks round.*

Ernest, out of a book, prompts —"The angels take him away"), "came the angels to take him away, up to where you know." (*All solemn. He resumes quickly, with a change of manner*), "They, all the rest, died of grief. Now, you must expect, as they all died of grief, that lots of angels must have come to take *them* away. Freddy *will* go when the sermon isn't over! That *is* such a bother!"

At this point Marion paused in her reading, and resumed the narrative form.

"Freddy, however, was too much for them; so Ernest betook himself to the organ, which was a chest of drawers, the drawers doing duty as stops, while Freddy went up to the pulpit to say 'Good-by,' and shake hands, for which he was mildly reproved by both his brothers."

My husband and I were so much amused, that Marion said she had another sermon, also preached by Charles, on the same day, after a short interval; and at our request she read it. Here it is.

"Once upon a time —a long while ago, in a little-Ready now? —Well, there lived in a rather big house, with *quite* clean windows: it was in winter, so nobody noticed them, but they were quite *white*, they were so clean. There lived some angels in the house: it was in the air, nobody knew why, but it did. No: I don't think it did —I dunno, but there lived in it lots of children-two hundred and thirty-two —and they-Oh! I'm gettin' distracted! It is too bad!" (*Quiet is restored.*) "Their mother and father had died, but they were very rich. Now, you see what a heap of children, —two hundred and thirty-two! and yet it seemed like *one* to them, they were so rich. *That* was it! it seemed like *one* to them because they were so rich. Now, the children knew what to get, and I'll explain to you now *why* they knew; and *this* is how they knew. The angels came down on the earth, and told them their mother had sent messages to them; and their mother and father —*Don't* talk! I'm gettin' extracted!" (*Puts his hand to his head in a frenzied manner.*) "Now, my brother" (*This severely to a still inattentive member*), "I'll tell you what the angels told them-what to get. What-how-now I will tell you how, —yes, *how* they knew what they were to eat. Well, the fact was, that-Freddy's just towards my face, and he's laughing! I'm going to explain. The mother and father had the wings on, and so, of course-Ernest, I want you!" (*They whisper.*) —"they were he and she angels, and they told them what to have. Well, one thing was-shall I tell you what it was? Look at two hundred and two in another book-one thing was a leg of mutton. Of course, as the mother and father were angels, they had to fly up again. Now I'm going to explain how they got it done. They had four servants and one cook, so that would be five. Well, this cook did them. The eldest girl was sixteen, and her name was Snowdrop, because she had snowy arms and cheeks, and was a very nice girl. The eldest boy was seventeen, and his name was John. He always told the cook what they'd have-no, the girl did that. And the boy was now grown up. So they would be mother and father." (*Signs of dissent among the audience.*) "*Of course*, when they were so old, they would be mother and father, and master of the servants. And they were very happy, *but* —they didn't quite like it. And-and" —(*with a great burst*) "*you* wouldn't like it if *your* mother were to die! And I'll end it next Sunday. Let us sing."

"The congregation then sung 'Curly Locks,'" said Marion, "and dispersed; Ernest complaining that Charley gave them such large qualities of numbers, and there weren't so many in the whole of his book. After a brief interval the sermon was resumed."

"Text is No. 66. I've a good congregation! I got to where the children did not like it without their mother and father. Well, you must remember this was a long while ago, so what I'm going to speak about *could* be possible. Well, their house was on the top of a high and steep hill; and at the bottom, a little from the hill, was a knight's house. There were three knights living in it. Next to it was stables with three horses in it. Sometimes they went up to this house, and wondered what was in it. They never knew, but saw the angels come. The knights were out all day, and only came home for meals. And they wondered what *on earth* the angels were doin', goin' in the house. They found out *what* —what, and the question was —I'll explain what it was. Ernest, come here." (*Ernest remarks to the audience,* "I'm curate," *and to Charles,* "Well, but, Charles, you're going to explain, you know;" *and Charles resumes.*) "The fact was, that this was-if you'd like to explain it more to yourselves, you'd better look in your books, No. 1828.

Before, the angels didn't speak loud, so the knights couldn't hear; *now* they spoke louder, so that the knights could visit them, 'cause they knew their names. They hadn't many visitors, but they had the knights in there, and that's all."

I am still very much afraid that all this nonsense will hardly be interesting, even to parents. But I may as well suffer for a sheep as a lamb; and, as I had an opportunity of hearing two such sermons myself not long after, I shall give them, trusting they will occupy far less space in print than they do in my foolish heart.

It was Ernest who was in the pulpit and just commencing his discourse when I entered the nursery, and sat down with the congregation. Sheltered by a clothes-horse, apparently set up for a screen, I took out my pencil, and reported on a fly-leaf of the book I had been reading: —

"My brother was goin' to preach about the wicked: I will preach about the good. Twenty-sixth day. In the time of Elizabeth there was a very old house. It was so old that it was pulled down, and a quite new one was built instead. Some people who lived in it did not like it so much now as they did when it was old. I take their part, you know, and think they were quite right in preferring the old one to the ugly, bare, new one. They left it-sold it-and got into another old house instead."

Here, I am sorry to say, his curate interjected the scornful remark, —

"He's not lookin' in the book a bit!"

But the preacher went on, without heeding the attack on his orthodoxy.

"This other old house was still more uncomfortable: it was very draughty; the gutters were always leaking; and they wished themselves back in the new house. So, you see, if you wish for a better thing, you don't get it so good after all."

"Ernest, that *is* about the bad, after all!" cried Charles.

"Well, it's *silly*," remarked Freddy severely.

"But I wrote it myself," pleaded the preacher from the pulpit; and, in consideration of the fact, he was allowed to go on.

"I was reading about them being always uncomfortable. At last they decided to go back to their own house, which they had sold. They had to pay so much to get it back, that they had hardly any money left; and then they got so unhappy, and the husband whipped his wife, and took to drinking. That's a lesson." (*Here the preacher's voice became very plaintive*), "that's a lesson to show you shouldn't try to get the better thing, for it turns out worse, and then you get sadder, and every thing."

He paused, evidently too mournful to proceed. Freddy again remarked that it was *silly*; but Charles interposed a word for the preacher.

"It's a good *lesson*, I think. A good *lesson*, I say," he repeated, as if he would not be supposed to consider it much of a sermon.

But here the preacher recovered himself and summed up.

"See how it comes: wanting to get every thing, you come to the bad and drinking. And I think I'll leave off here. Let us sing."

The song was "Little Robin Redbreast;" during which Charles remarked to Freddy, apparently by way of pressing home the lesson upon his younger brother, —

"Fancy! floggin' his wife!"

Then he got into the pulpit himself, and commenced an oration.

"Chapter eighty-eight. *The wicked*. —Well, the time when the story was, was about Herod. There were some wicked people wanderin' about there, and they-not *killed* them, you know, but-went to the judge. We shall see what they did to them. I tell you this to make you understand. Now the story begins-but I must think a little. Ernest, let's sing 'Since first I saw your face.'

"When the wicked man was taken then to the good judge-there were *some* good people: when I said I was going to preach about the wicked, I did not mean that there were no good, only a good lot of wicked. There were pleacemans about here, and they put him in prison for a few days, and then the judge could see about what he is to do with him. At the end of the few days, the judge asked him if he would stay in prison for life or be hanged."

Here arose some inquiries among the congregation as to what the wicked, of whom the prisoner was one, had done that was wrong; to which Charles replied, —

"Oh! they murdered and killed; they stealed, and they were very wicked altogether. Well," he went on, resuming his discourse, "the morning came, and the judge said, 'Get the ropes and my throne, and order the people *not* to come to see the hangin'.' For the man was decided to be hanged. Now, the people *would* come. They were the wicked, and they would *persist* in comin'. They were the wicked; and, if that was the *fact*, the judge must do something to them.

"Chapter eighty-nine. *The hangin'*. —We'll have some singin' while I think."

"Yankee Doodle" was accordingly sung with much enthusiasm and solemnity. Then Charles resumed.

"Well, they had to put the other people, who persisted in coming, in prison, till the man who murdered people was hanged. I think my brother will go on."

He descended, and gave place to Ernest, who began with vigor.

"We were reading about Herod, weren't we? Then the wicked people *would* come, and had to be put to death. They were on the man's side; and they all called out that he hadn't had his wish before he died, as they did in those days. So of course he wished for his life, and of course the judge wouldn't let him have *that* wish; and so he wished to speak to his friends, and they let him. And the nasty wicked people took him away, and he was never seen in that country any more. And that's enough to-day, I think. Let us sing 'Lord Lovel he stood at his castle-gate, a combing his milk-white steed.'"

At the conclusion of this mournful ballad, the congregation was allowed to disperse. But, before they had gone far, they were recalled by the offer of a more secular entertainment from Charles, who re-ascended the pulpit, and delivered himself as follows: —

"Well, the play is called-not a proverb or a charade it isn't —it's a play called 'The Birds and the Babies.' Well!

"Once there was a little cottage, and lots of little babies in it. Nobody knew who the babies were. They were so happy! Now, I can't explain it to you how they came together: they had no father and mother, but they were brothers and sisters. They never *grew*, and they didn't like it. Now, *you* wouldn't like *not* to *grow*, would you? They had a little garden, and saw a great many birds in the trees. They *were* happy, but didn't *feel* happy-that's a funny thing now! The wicked fairies made them unhappy, and the good fairies made them happy; they gave them lots of toys. But then, how they got their living!

"Chapter second, called 'The Babies at Play.' —The fairies told them what to get —*that was it!* —and so they got their living Very nicely. And now I must explain what they played with. First was a house. *A house*. Another, dolls. They were very happy, and felt as if they had a mother and father; but they hadn't, and *couldn't* make it out. *Couldn't* —*make-it-out!*

"They had little pumps and trees. Then they had babies' rattles. *Babies' rattles*. —Oh! I've said hardly any thing about the birds, have I? an' it's called '*The Birds and the Babies!*' They had lots of little pretty robins and canaries hanging round the ceiling, and —*shall* I say?" —

Every one listened expectant during the pause that followed.

" —*And-lived-happy-ever-after.*"

The puzzle in it all is chiefly what my husband hinted at, —why and how both the desire and the means of utterance should so long precede the possession of any thing ripe for utterance. I suspect the answer must lie pretty deep in some metaphysical gulf or other.

At the same time, the struggle to speak where there is so little to utter can hardly fail to suggest the thought of some efforts of a more pretentious and imposing character.

But more than enough!

CHAPTER XLI
"DOUBLE, DOUBLE, TOIL AND TROUBLE."

I had for a day or two fancied that Marion was looking less bright than usual, as if some little shadow had fallen upon the morning of her life. I say *morning*, because, although Marion must now have been seven or eight and twenty, her life had always seemed to me lighted by a cool, clear, dewy morning sun, over whose face it now seemed as if some film of noonday cloud had begun to gather. Unwilling at once to assert the ultimate privilege of friendship, I asked her if any thing was amiss with her friends. She answered that all was going on well, at least so far that she had no special anxiety about any of them. Encouraged by a half-conscious and more than half-sad smile, I ventured a little farther.

"I am afraid there is something troubling you," I said.

"There is," she replied, "something troubling me a good deal; but I hope it will pass away soon."

The sigh which followed, however, was deep though gentle, and seemed to indicate a fear that the trouble might not pass away so very soon.

"I am not to ask you any questions, I suppose," I returned.

"Better not at present," she answered. "I am not quite sure that"—

She paused several moments before finishing her sentence, then added,—

"—that I am at liberty to tell you about it."

"Then don't say another word," I rejoined. "Only when I can be of service to you, you *will* let me, won't you?"

The tears rose to her eyes.

"I'm afraid it may be some fault of mine," she said. "I don't know. I can't tell. I don't understand such things."

She sighed again, and held her peace.

It was enigmatical enough. One thing only was clear, that at present I was not wanted. So I, too, held my peace, and in a few minutes Marion went, with a more affectionate leave-taking than usual, for her friendship was far less demonstrative than that of most women.

I pondered, but it was not of much use. Of course the first thing that suggested itself was, Could my angel be in love? and with some mortal mere? The very idea was a shock, simply from its strangeness. Of course, being a woman, she *might* be in love; but the two ideas, Marion and *love*, refused to coalesce. And again, was it likely that such as she, her mind occupied with so many other absorbing interests, would fall in love unprovoked, unsolicited? That, indeed, was not likely. Then if, solicited, she but returned love for love, why was she sad? The new experience might, it is true, cause such commotion in a mind like hers as to trouble her greatly. She would not know what to do with it, nor where to accommodate her new inmate so as to keep him from meddling with affairs he had no right to meddle with: it was easy enough to fancy him troublesome in a house like hers. But surely of all women *she* might be able to meet her own liabilities. And if this were all, why should she have said she hoped it would soon pass? That might, however, mean only that she hoped soon to get her guest brought amenable to her existing household economy.

There was yet a conjecture, however, which seemed to suit the case better. If Marion knew little of what is commonly called love, that is, "the attraction of correlative unlikeness," as I once heard it defined by a metaphysical friend of my father's, there was no one who knew more of the tenderness of compassion than she; and was it not possible some one might be wanting to marry her to whom she could not give herself away? This conjecture was at least ample enough to cover the facts in my possession-which were scanty indeed, in number hardly dual. But who was there to dare offer love to my saint? Roger? Pooh! pooh! Mr. Blackstone? Ah! I had seen him once lately looking at her with an expression of more than ordinary admiration. But what man that knew any thing of her could help looking at her with such an admiration? If it was Mr. Blackstone-why, *he* might dare-yes, why should he not dare to love her?—especially if he couldn't help it, as, of course, he couldn't. Was he not one whose love, simply because he was a *true* man from the heart to the hands, would honor any woman, even Saint Clare-as she must be when the church has learned to do its business without the pope? Only he mustn't blame me, if, after all, I should think he offered less than he sought; or her, if, entertaining no question of worth whatever, she should yet refuse to listen to him as, truly, there was more than a possibility she might.

If it were Mr. Blackstone, certainly I knew no man who could understand her better, or whose modes of thinking and working would more thoroughly fall in with her own. True, he was peculiar; that is, he had kept the angles of his individuality, for all the grinding of the social mill; his manners were too abrupt, and drove at the heart of things too directly, seldom suggesting a *by-your-leave* to those whose prejudices he overturned: true, also, that his person, though dignified, was somewhat ungainly, —with an ungainliness, however, which I could well imagine a wife learning absolutely to love; but, on the whole, the thing was reasonable. Only, what would become of her friends? There, I could hardly doubt, there lay the difficulty! Ay, *there* was the rub!

Let no one think, when I say we went to Mr. Blackstone's church the next Sunday, that it had any thing to do with these speculations. We often went on the first Sunday of the month.

"What's the matter with Blackstone?" said my husband as we came home.

"What do *you* think is the matter with him?" I returned.

"I don't know. He wasn't himself."

"I thought he was more than himself," I rejoined; "for I never heard even *him* read the litany with such fervor."

"In some of the petitions," said Percivale, "it amounted to a suppressed agony of supplication. I am certain he is in trouble."

I told him my suspicions.

"Likely-very likely," he answered, and became thoughtful.

"But you don't think she refused him?" he said at length.

"If he ever asked her," I returned, "I fear she did; for she is plainly in trouble too."

"She'll never stick to it," he said.

"You mustn't judge Marion by ordinary standards," I replied. "You must remember she has not only found her vocation, but for many years proved it. I never knew her turned aside from what she had made up her mind to. I can hardly imagine her forsaking her friends to keep house for any man, even if she loved him with all her heart. She is dedicated as irrevocably as any nun, and will, with St. Paul, cling to the right of self-denial."

"Yet what great difficulty would there be in combining the two sets of duties, especially with such a man as Blackstone? Of all the men I know, he comes the nearest to her in his devotion to the well-being of humanity, especially of the poor. Did you ever know a man with such a plentiful lack of condescension? His feeling of human equality amounts almost to a fault; for surely he ought sometimes to speak as knowing better than they to whom he speaks. He forgets that too many will but use his humility for mortar to build withal the Shinar-tower of their own superiority."

"That may be; yet it remains impossible for him to assume any thing. He is the same all through, and —I had almost said-worthy of Saint Clare. Well, they must settle it for themselves. We can do nothing."

"We can do nothing," he assented; and, although we repeatedly reverted to the subject on the long way home, we carried no conclusions to a different result.

Towards evening of the same Sunday, Roger came to accompany us, as I thought, to Marion's gathering, but, as it turned out, only to tell me he couldn't go. I expressed my regret, and asked him why. He gave me no answer, and his lip trembled. A sudden conviction seized me. I laid my hand on his arm, but could only say, "Dear Roger!" He turned his head aside, and, sitting down on the sofa, laid his forehead on his hand.

"I'm so sorry!" I said.

"She has told you, then?" he murmured.

"No one has told me any thing."

He was silent. I sat down beside him. It was all I could do. After a moment he rose, saying, —

"There's no good whining about it, only she might have made a man of me. But she's quite right. It's a comfort to think I'm so unworthy of her. That's all the consolation left me, but there's more in that than you would think till you try it."

He attempted to laugh, but made a miserable failure of it, then rose and caught up his hat to go. I rose also.

"Roger," I said, "I can't go, and leave you miserable. We'll go somewhere else, —anywhere you please, only you mustn't leave us."

"I don't want to go somewhere else. I don't know the place," he added, with a feeble attempt at his usual gayety.

"Stop at home, then, and tell me all about it. It will do you good to talk. You shall have your pipe, and you shall tell me just as much as you like, and keep the rest to yourself."

If you want to get hold of a man's deepest confidence, tell him to smoke in your drawing-room. I don't know how it is, but there seems no trouble in which a man can't smoke. One who scorns extraneous comfort of every other sort, will yet, in the profoundest sorrow, take kindly to his pipe. This is more wonderful than any thing I know about our kind. But I fear the sewing-machines will drive many women to tobacco.

I ran to Percivale, gave him a hint of how it was, and demanded his pipe and tobacco-pouch directly, telling him he must content himself with a cigar.

Thus armed with the calumet, as Paddy might say, I returned to Roger, who took it without a word of thanks, and began to fill it mechanically, but not therefore the less carefully. I sat down, laid my hands in my lap, and looked at him without a word. When the pipe was filled I rose and got him a light, for which also he made me no acknowledgment. The revenge of putting it in print is sweet. Having whiffed a good many whiffs in silence, he took at length his pipe from his mouth, and, as he pressed the burning tobacco with a forefinger, said, —

"I've made a fool of myself, Wynnie."

"Not more than a gentleman had a right to do, I will pledge myself," I returned.

"She *has* told you, then?" he said once more, looking rather disappointed than annoyed.

"No one has mentioned your name to me, Roger. I only guessed it from what Marion said when I questioned her about her sad looks."

"Her sad looks?"

"Yes."

"What did she say?" he asked eagerly.

"She only confessed she had had something to trouble her, and said she hoped it would be over soon."

"I dare say!" returned Roger dryly, looking gratified, however, for a moment.

My reader may wonder that I should compromise Marion, even so far as to confess that she was troubled; but I could not bear that Roger should think she had been telling his story to me. Every generous woman feels that she owes the man she refuses at least silence; and a man may well reckon upon that much favor. Of all failures, why should this be known to the world?

The relief of finding she had not betrayed him helped him, I think, to open his mind: *he* was under no obligation to silence.

"You see, Wynnie," he said, with pauses, and puffs at his pipe, "I don't mean I'm a fool for falling in love with Marion. Not to have fallen in love with her would have argued me a beast. Being a man, it was impossible for me to help it, after what she's been to me. But I was worse than a fool to open my mouth on the subject to an angel like her. Only there again, I couldn't, that is, I hadn't the strength to help it. I beg, however, you won't think me such a downright idiot as to fancy myself worthy of her. In that case, I should have deserved as much scorn as she gave me kindness. If you ask me how it was, then, that I dared to speak to her on the subject, I can only answer that I yielded to the impulse common to all kinds of love to make itself known. If you love God, you are not content with his knowing it even, but you must tell him as if he didn't know it. You may think from this cool talk of mine that I am very philosophical about it; but there are lulls in every storm, and I am in one of those lulls, else I shouldn't be sitting here with you."

"Dear Roger!" I said, "I am very sorry for your disappointment. Somehow, I can't be sorry you should have loved"—

"*Have loved!*" he murmured.

"*Should love* Marion, then," I went on. "That can do you nothing but good, and in itself must raise you above yourself. And how could I blame you, that, loving her, you wanted her to know it? But come, now, if you can trust me, tell me all about it, and especially what she said to you. I dare not give you any hope, for I am not in her confidence in this matter; and it is well that I am not, for then I might not be able to talk to you about it with any freedom. To confess the real truth, I do not see much likelihood, knowing her as I do, that she will recall her decision."

"It could hardly be called a decision," said Roger. "You would not have thought, from the way she took it, there was any thing to decide about. No more there was; and I thought I knew it, only I couldn't be quiet. To think you know a thing, and to know it, are two very different matters, however. But I don't repent having spoken my mind: if I am humbled, I am not humiliated. If she *had* listened to me, I fear I should have been ruined by pride. I should never have judged myself justly after it. I wasn't humble, though I thought I was. I'm a poor creature, Ethelwyn."

"Not too poor a creature to be dearly loved, Roger. But go on and tell me all about it. As your friend and sister, I am anxious to hear the whole."

Notwithstanding what I had said, I was not moved by sympathetic curiosity alone, but also by the vague desire of rendering some help beyond comfort. What he had now said, greatly heightened my opinion of him, and thereby, in my thoughts of the two, lessened the distance between him and Marion. At all events, by hearing the whole, I should learn how better to comfort him.

And he did tell me the whole, which, along with what I learned afterwards from Marion, I will set down as nearly as I can, throwing it into the form of direct narration. I will not pledge myself for the accuracy of every trifling particular which that form may render it necessary to introduce; neither, I am sure, having thus explained, will my reader demand it of me.

CHAPTER XLII
ROGER AND MARION.

During an all but sleepless night, Roger had made up his mind to go and see Marion: not, certainly, for the first time, for he had again and again ventured to call upon her; but hitherto he had always had some pretext sufficient to veil his deeper reason, and, happily or unhappily, sufficient also to prevent her, in her more than ordinary simplicity with regard to such matters, from suspecting one under it.

She was at home, and received him with her usual kindness. Feeling that he must not let an awkward silence intervene, lest she should become suspicious of his object, and thus the chance be lost of interesting, and possibly moving her before she saw his drift, he spoke at once.

"I want to tell you something, Miss Clare," he said as lightly as he could.

"Well?" she returned, with the sweet smile which graced her every approach to communication.

"Did my sister-in-law ever tell you what an idle fellow I used to be?"

"Certainly not. I never heard her say a word of you that wasn't kind."

"That I am sure of. But there would have been no unkindness in saying that; for an idle fellow I was, and the idler because I was conceited enough to believe I could do any thing. I actually thought at one time I could play the violin. I actually made an impertinent attempt in your presence one evening, years and years ago, I wonder if you remember it."

"I do; but I don't know why you should call it impertinent."

"Anyhow, I caught a look on your face that cured me of that conceit. I have never touched the creature since,—a Cremona too!"

"I am very sorry, indeed I am. I don't remember-Do you think you could have played a false note?"

"Nothing more likely."

"Then, I dare say I made an ugly face. One can't always help it, you know, when something unexpected happens. Do forgive me."

"Forgive *you*, you angel!" cried Roger, but instantly checked himself, afraid of reaching his mark before he had gathered sufficient momentum to pierce it. "I thought you would see what a good thing it was for me. I wanted to thank you for it."

"It's such a pity you didn't go on, though. Progress is the real cure for an overestimate of ourselves."

"The fact is, I was beginning to see what small praise there is in doing many things ill and nothing well. I wish you would take my Cremona. I could teach you the A B C of it well enough. How you would make it talk! That *would* be something to live for, to hear *you* play the violin! Ladies do, nowadays, you know."

"I have no time, Mr. Roger. I should have been delighted to be your pupil; but I am sorry to say it is out of the question."

"Of course it is. Only I wish-well, never mind, I only wanted to tell you something. I was leading a life then that wasn't worth leading; for where's the good of being just what happens, — one time full of right feeling and impulse, and the next a prey to all wrong judgments and falsehoods? It was you made me see it. I've been trying to get put right for a long time now. I'm afraid of seeming to talk goody, but you will know what I mean. You and your Sunday evenings have waked me up to know what I am, and what I ought to be. I am a little better. I work hard now. I used to work only by fits and starts. Ask Wynnie."

"Dear Mr. Roger, I don't need to ask Wynnie about any thing you tell me. I can take your word for it just as well as hers. I am very glad if I have been of any use to you. It is a great honor to me."

"But the worst of it is, I couldn't be content without letting you know, and making myself miserable."

"I don't understand you, I think. Surely there can be no harm in letting me know what makes me very happy! How it should make you miserable, I can't imagine."

"Because I can't stop there. I'm driven to say what will offend you, if it doesn't make you hate me-no, not that; for you don't know how to hate. But you must think me the most conceited and presumptuous fellow you ever knew. I'm not that, though; I'm not that; it's not me; I can't help it; I can't help loving you-dreadfully-and it's such impudence! To think of you and me in one thought! And yet I can't help it. O Miss Clare! don't drive me away from you."

He fell on his knees as he spoke, and laid his head on her lap, sobbing like a child who had offended his mother. He almost cried again as he told me this. Marion half started to her feet in confusion, almost in terror, for she had never seen such emotion in a man; but the divine compassion of her nature conquered: she sat down again, took his head in her hands, and began stroking his hair as if she were indeed a mother seeking to soothe and comfort her troubled child. She was the first to speak again, for Roger could not command himself.

"I'm very sorry, Roger," she said. "I must be to blame somehow."

"To blame!" he cried, lifting up his head. "*You* to blame for my folly! But it's not folly," he added impetuously: "it would be downright stupidity not to love you with all my soul."

"Hush! hush!" said Marion, in whose ears his language sounded irreverent. "You *couldn't* love me with all your soul if you would. God only *can* be loved with all the power of the human soul."

"If I love him at all, Marion, it is you who have taught me. Do not drive me from you-lest-lest—I should cease to love him, and fall back into my old dreary ways."

"It's a poor love to offer God,—love for the sake of another," she said very solemnly.

"But if it's all one has got?"

"Then it won't do, Roger. I wish you loved me for God's sake instead. Then all would be right. That would be a grand love for me to have."

"Don't drive me from you, Marion," he pleaded. It was all he could say.

"I will not drive you from me. Why should I?"

"Then I may come and see you again?"

"Yes: when you please."

"You *don't* mean I may come as often as I like?"

"Yes-when I have time to see you."

"Then," cried Roger, starting to his feet with clasped hands, " —perhaps-is it possible? —you will-you will let me love you? O my God!"

"Roger," said Marion, pale as death, and rising also; for, alas! the sunshine of her kindness had caused hopes to blossom whose buds she had taken only for leaves, "I thought you understood me! You spoke as if you understood perfectly that that could never be which I must suppose you to mean. Of course it cannot. I am not my own to keep or to give away. I belong to this people,—my friends. To take personal and private duties upon me, would be to abandon them; and how dare I? You don't know what it would result in, or you would not dream of it. Were I to do such a thing, I should hate and despise and condemn myself with utter reprobation. And then what a prize you would have got, my poor Roger!"

But even these were such precious words to hear from her lips! He fell again on his knees before her as she stood, caught her hands, and, hiding his face in them, poured forth the following words in a torrent,—

"Marion, do not think me so selfish as not to have thought about that. It should be only the better for them all. I can earn quite enough for you and me too, and so you would have the more time to give to them. I should never have dreamed of asking you to leave them. There are things in which a dog may help a man, doing what the man can't do: there may be things in which a man might help an angel."

Deeply moved by the unselfishness of his love, Marion could not help a pressure of her hands against the face which had sought refuge within them. Roger fell to kissing them wildly.

But Marion was a woman; and women, I think, though I may be only judging by myself and my husband, look forward and round about, more than men do: they would need at all events;

therefore Marion saw other things. A man-reader may say, that, if she loved him, she would not have thus looked about her; and that, if she did not love him, there was no occasion for her thus to fly in the face of the future. I can only answer that it is allowed on all hands women are not amenable to logic: look about her Marion did, and saw, that, as a married woman, she might be compelled to forsake her friends more or less; for there might arise other and paramount claims on her self-devotion. In a word, if she were to have children, she would have no choice in respect to whose welfare should constitute the main business of her life; and it even became a question whether she would have a right to place them in circumstances so unfavorable for growth and education. Therefore, to marry might be tantamount to forsaking her friends.

But where was the need of any such mental parley? Of course, she couldn't marry Roger. How could she marry a man she couldn't look up to? And look up to him she certainly did not, and could not.

"No, Roger," she said, this last thought large in her mind; and, as she spoke, she withdrew her hands, "it mustn't be. It is out of the question: I can't look up to you," she added, as simply as a child.

"I should think not," he burst out. "That *would* be a fine thing! If you looked up to a fellow like me, I think it would almost cure me of looking up to you; and what I want is to look up to you every day and all day long: only I can do that whether you let me or not."

"But I don't choose to have a—a—friend to whom I can't look up."

"Then I shall never be even a friend," he returned sadly. "But I would have tried hard to be less unworthy of you."

At this precise moment, Marion caught sight of a pair of great round blue eyes, wide open under a shock of red hair, about three feet from the floor, staring as if they had not winked for the last ten minutes. The child looked so comical, that Marion, reading perhaps in her looks the reflex of her own position, could not help laughing. Roger started up in dismay, but, beholding the apparition, laughed also.

"Please, grannie," said the urchin, "mother's took bad, and want's ye."

"Run and tell your mother I shall be with her directly," answered Marion; and the child departed.

"You told me I might come again," pleaded Roger.

"Better not. I didn't know what it would mean to you when I said it."

"Let it mean what you meant by it, only let me come."

"But I see now it can't mean that. No: I will write to you. At all events, you must go now, for I can't stop with you when Mrs. Foote"—

"Don't make me wretched, Marion. If you can't love me, don't kill me. Don't say I'm not to come and see you. I *will* come on Sundays, anyhow."

The next day came the following letter:—

> Dear Mr. Roger,—I am very sorry, both for your sake and my own, that I did not speak more plainly yesterday. I was so distressed for you, and my heart was so friendly towards you, that I could hardly think of any thing at first but how to comfort you; and I fear I allowed you, after all, to go away with the idea that what you wished was not altogether impossible. But indeed it is. If even I loved you in the way you love me, I should yet make every thing yield to the duties I have undertaken. In listening to you, I should be undermining the whole of my past labors; and the very idea of becoming less of a friend to my friends is horrible to me.
>
> But much as I esteem you, and much pleasure as your society gives me, the idea you brought before me yesterday was absolutely startling; and I think I have only to remind you, as I have just done, of the peculiarities of my position, to convince you that it could never become a familiar one to me. All that friendship can do or yield, you may ever claim of me; and I thank God if I have been of the smallest service to

you: but I should be quite unworthy of that honor, were I for any reason to admit even the thought of abandoning the work which has been growing up around me for so many years, and is so peculiarly mine that it could be transferred to no one else. Believe me yours most truly,

MARION CLARE

CHAPTER XLIII
A LITTLE MORE ABOUT ROGER, AND ABOUT MR. BLACKSTONE.

After telling me the greater part of what I have just written, Roger handed me this letter to read, as we sat together that same Sunday evening.

"It seems final, Roger?" I said with an interrogation, as I returned it to him.

"Of course it is," he replied. "How could any honest man urge his suit after that, —after she says that to grant it would be to destroy the whole of her previous life, and ruin her self-respect? But I'm not so miserable as you may think me, Wynnie," he went on; "for don't you see? though I couldn't quite bring myself to go to-night, I don't feel cut off from her. She's not likely, if I know her, to listen to anybody else so long as the same reasons hold for which she wouldn't give me a chance of persuading her. She can't help me loving her, and I'm sure she'll let me help her when I've the luck to find a chance. You may be sure I shall keep a sharp lookout. If I can be her servant, that will be something; yes, much. Though she won't give herself to me-and quite right, too! —why should she? —God bless her! —she can't prevent me from giving myself to her. So long as I may love her, and see her as often as I don't doubt I may, and things continue as they are, I sha'n't be down-hearted. I'll have another pipe, I think." Here he half-started, and hurriedly pulled out his watch, "I declare, there's time yet!" he cried, and sprung to his feet. "Let's go and hear what she's got to say to-night."

"Don't you think you had better not? Won't you put her out?" I suggested.

"If I understand her at all," he said, "she will be more put out by my absence; for she will fear I am wretched, caring only for myself, and not for what she taught me. You may come or stay—*I'm* off. You've done me so much good, Wynnie!" he added, looking back in the doorway. "Thank you a thousand times. There's no comforter like a sister!"

"And a pipe," I said; at which he laughed, and was gone.

When Percivale and I reached Lime Court, having followed as quickly as we could, there was Roger sitting in the midst, as intent on her words as if she had been, an old prophet, and Marion speaking with all the composure which naturally belonged to her.

When she shook hands with him after the service, a slight flush washed the white of her face with a delicate warmth, —nothing more. I said to myself, however, as we went home, and afterwards to my husband, that his case was not a desperate one.

"But what's to become of Blackstone?" said Percivale.

I will tell my reader how afterwards he seemed to me to have fared; but I have no information concerning his supposed connection with this part of my story. I cannot even be sure that he ever was in love with Marion. Troubled he certainly was, at this time; and Marion continued so for a while, —more troubled, I think, than the necessity she felt upon her with regard to Roger will quite account for. If, however, she had to make two men miserable in one week, that might well cover the case.

Before the week was over, my husband received a note from Mr. Blackstone, informing him that he was just about to start for a few weeks on the Continent. When he returned I was satisfied from his appearance that a notable change had passed upon him: a certain indescribable serenity seemed to have taken possession of his whole being; every look and tone indicated a mind that knew more than tongue could utter, —a heart that had had glimpses into a region of content. I thought of the words, "He that dwelleth in the secret place of the Most High," and my heart was at rest about him. He had fared, I thought, as the child who has had a hurt, but is taken up in his mother's arms and comforted. What hurt would not such comforting outweigh to the child? And who but he that has had the worst hurt man can receive, and the best comfort God can give, can tell what either is?

I was present the first time he met Marion after his return. She was a little embarrassed: he showed a tender dignity, a respect as if from above, like what one might fancy the embodiment of the love of a wise angel for such a woman. The thought of comparing the two had never before occurred to me; but now for the moment I felt as if Mr. Blackstone were a step above Marion. Plainly, I had no occasion to be troubled about either of them.

On the supposition that Marion had refused him, I argued with myself that it could not have been on the ground that she was unable to look up to him. And, notwithstanding what she had said to Roger, I was satisfied that any one she felt she could help to be a nobler creature; must have a greatly better chance of rousing all the woman in her; than one whom she must regard as needing no aid from her. All her life had been spent in serving and sheltering human beings whose condition she regarded with hopeful compassion: could she now help adding Roger to her number of such? and if she once looked upon him thus tenderly, was it not at least very possible, that, in some softer mood, a feeling hitherto unknown to her might surprise her consciousness with its presence, —floating to the surface of her sea from its strange depths, and leaning towards him with the outstretched arms of embrace?

But I dared not think what might become of Roger should his divine resolves fail, —should the frequent society of Marion prove insufficient for the solace and quiet of his heart. I had heard how men will seek to drown sorrow in the ruin of the sorrowing power, —will slay themselves that they may cause their hurt to cease, and I trembled for my husband's brother. But the days went on, and I saw no sign of failure or change. He was steady at his work, and came to see us as constantly as before; never missed a chance of meeting Marion: and at every treat she gave her friends, whether at the house of which I have already spoken, or at Lady Bernard's country-place in the neighborhood of London, whether she took them on the river, or had some one to lecture or read to them, Roger was always at hand for service and help. Still, I was uneasy; for might there not come a collapse, especially if some new event were to destroy the hope which he still cherished, and which I feared was his main support? Would his religion then prove of a quality and power sufficient to keep him from drifting away with the receding tide of his hopes and imaginations? In this anxiety perhaps I regarded too exclusively the faith of Roger, and thought too little about the faith of God. However this may be, I could not rest, but thought and thought, until at last I made up my mind to go and tell Lady Bernard all about it.

CHAPTER XLIV
THE DEA EX.

"And you think Marion likes him?" asked Lady Bernard, when she had in silence heard my story.

"I am sure she *likes* him. But you know he is so far inferior to her,—in every way."

"How do you know that? Questions are involved there which no one but God can determine. You must remember that both are growing. What matter if any two are unequal at a given moment, seeing their relative positions may be reversed twenty times in a thousand years? Besides, I doubt very much if any one who brought his favors with him would have the least chance with Marion. Poverty, to turn into wealth, is the one irresistible attraction for her; and, however duty may compel her to act, my impression is that she will not escape *loving* Roger."

I need not say I was gratified to find Lady Bernard's conclusion from Marion's character run parallel with my own.

"But what can come of it?" I said.

"Why, marriage, I hope."

"But Marion would as soon think of falling down and worshipping Baal and Ashtoreth as of forsaking her grandchildren."

"Doubtless. But there would be no occasion for that. Where two things are both of God, it is not likely they will be found mutually obstructive."

"Roger does declare himself quite ready to go and live amongst her friends, and do his best to help her."

"That is all as it should be, so far as he-as both of them are concerned; but there are contingencies; and the question naturally arises, How would that do in regard of their children?"

"If I could imagine Marion consenting." I said, "I know what she would answer to that question. She would say, Why should her children be better off than the children about them? She would say that the children must share the life and work of their parents."

"And I think she would be right, though the obvious rejoinder would be, 'You may waive your own social privileges, and sacrifice yourselves to the good of others; but have you a right to sacrifice your children, and heap disadvantages on their future?'"

"Now give us the answer on the other side, seeing you think Marion would be right after all."

"Marion's answer would, I think, be, that their children would be God's children; and he couldn't desire better for them than to be born in lowly conditions, and trained from the first to give themselves to the service of their fellows, seeing that in so far their history would resemble that of his own Son, our Saviour. In sacrificing their earthly future, as men would call it, their parents would but be furthering their eternal good."

"That would be enough in regard of such objections. But there would be a previous one on Marion's own part. How would her new position affect her ministrations?"

"There can be no doubt, I think," Lady Bernard replied, "that what her friends would lose thereby—I mean, what amount of her personal ministrations would be turned aside from them by the necessities of her new position-would be far more than made up to them by the presence among them of a whole well-ordered and growing family, instead of a single woman only. But all this jet leaves something for her more personal friends to consider,—as regards their duty in the matter. It naturally sets them on the track of finding out what could be done to secure for the children of such parents the possession of early advantages as little lower than those their parents had as may be; for the breed of good people ought, as much as possible, to be kept up. I will turn the thing over in my mind, and let you know what comes of it."

The result of Lady Bernard's cogitations is, in so far, to be seen in the rapid rise of a block of houses at no great distance from London, on the North-western Railway, planned under the instructions of Marion Clare. The design of them is to provide accommodation for all Marion's friends, with room to add largely to their number. Lady Bernard has also secured ground sufficient for great extension of the present building, should it prove desirable. Each family is to have the same amount of accommodation it has now, only far better, at the same rent it pays now, with the privilege of taking an additional room or rooms at a much lower rate. Marion has undertaken to collect the rents, and believes that she will thus in time gain an additional hold of the people for their good, although the plan may at first expose her to misunderstanding. From thorough calculation she is satisfied she can pay Lady Bernard five per cent for her money, lay out all that is necessary for keeping the property in thorough repair, and accumulate a fund besides to be spent on building more houses, should her expectations of these be answered. The removal of so many will also make a little room for the accommodation of the multitudes constantly driven from their homes by the wickedness of those, who, either for the sake of railways or fine streets, pull down crowded houses, and drive into other courts and alleys their poor inhabitants, to double the wretchedness already there from overcrowding.

In the centre of the building is a house for herself, where she will have her own private advantage in the inclusion of large space primarily for the entertainment of her friends. I believe Lady Bernard intends to give her a hint that a married couple would, in her opinion, be far more useful in such a position than a single woman. But although I rejoice in the prospect of greater happiness for two dear friends, I must in honesty say that I doubt this.

If the scheme should answer, what a strange reversion it will be to something like a right reading of the feudal system!

Of course it will be objected, that, should it succeed ever so well, it will all go to pieces at Marion's death. To this the answer lies in the hope that her influence may extend laterally, as well as downwards; moving others to be what she has been; and, in the conviction that such a work as hers can never be lost, for the world can never be the same as if she had not lived; while in any case there will be more room for her brothers and sisters who are now being crowded out of the world by the stronger and richer. It would be sufficient answer, however, that the work is worth doing for its own sake and its immediate result. Surely it will receive a *well-done* from the Judge of us all; and while his idea of right remains above hers, high as the heavens are above the earth, his approbation will be all that either Lady Bernard or Marion will seek.

If but a small proportion of those who love the right and have means to spare would, like Lady Bernard, use their wealth to make up to the poor for the wrongs they receive at the hands of the rich, —let me say, to defend the Saviour in their persons from the tyranny of Mammon, how many of the poor might they not lead with them into the joy of their Lord!

Should the plan succeed, I say once more, I intend to urge on Marion the duty of writing a history of its rise and progress from the first of her own attempts. Then there would at least remain a book for all future reformers and philanthropists to study, and her influence might renew itself in other ages after she was gone.

I have no more to say about myself or my people. We live in hope of the glory of God.

Here I was going to write, THE END; but was arrested by the following conversation between two of my children, —Ernest, eight, and Freddy, five years of age.

Ernest. —I'd do it for mamma, of course.

Freddy. —Wouldn't you do it for Harry?

Ernest. —No: Harry's nobody.

Freddy. —Yes, he is somebody.

Ernest. —You're nobody; I'm nobody; we are all nobody, compared to mamma.

Freddy. (*stolidly*). —Yes, I am somebody.

Ernest. —You're nothing; I'm nothing; we are all nothing in mamma's presence.

Freddy. —But, Ernest, *every thing* is something; so I must be something.

Ernest. —Yes, Freddy, but you're *no thing*; so you're nothing. You're nothing to mamma.

Freddy. —*But I'm mamma's.*

www.ingramcontent.com/pod-product-compliance
Lightning Source LLC
LaVergne TN
LVHW020103181224
799359LV00031B/335